PENGUIN BOOKS

STRANGERS AND BROTHERS

VOLUME THREE

C. P. Snow was born in Leicester in 1905 and educated at a secondary school. He started his career as a professional scientist, though writing was always his ultimate aim. He won a research scholarship to Cambridge, worked on molecular physics, and became a Fellow of his college in 1930. He continued his academic life in Cambridge until the beginning of the war, by which time he had already begun the 'Lewis Eliot' sequence of novels, the general title of which is *Strangers and Brothers*. The eleven books in the sequence are, in their correct order, which is not that of publication: *George Passant* (1940) – once known by the series title – *Time of Hope* (1949), *The Conscience of the Rich* (1958), *The Light and the Dark* (1947), *The Masters* (1951), *The New Men* (1954), *Homecomings* (1958), *The Affair* (1960), *Corridors of Power* (1964), *The Sleep of Reason* (1968), and *Last Things* (1970). His other novels include *The Search* (1934; revised 1938), *The Malcontents* (1972), *In Their Wisdom* (1974) and *A Coat of Varnish* (1979). He also wrote a collection of biographical portraits, *Variety of Men* (1967), a critical biography, *Trollope* (1975) and *The Realists* (1978).

In the war C. P. Snow became a civil servant, and because of his human and scientific knowledge was engaged in selecting scientific personnel. He had further experience of these problems after the war, both in industry and as a Civil Service commissioner, for which he received a knighthood in 1957. His Rede Lecture on *The Two Cultures and the Scientific Revolution* (1950), his Godkin Lectures on *Science and Government* (1960), his address to the A.A.A.S., *The Moral Un-Neutrality of Science*, and his Fulton Lecture, *The State of Siege* (1968), have been widely discussed and published in one volume, *Public Affairs* (1971). He received a barony in 1964, and was made Parliamentary Secretary to the Ministry of Technology. In 1950 he married Pamela Hansford Johnson.

C. P. Snow died on 1 July 1980.

Penguin also publish two other omnibus editions in the *Strangers and Brothers* sequence: Volume One containing *Time of Hope, George Passant, The Conscience of the Rich* and *The Light and the Dark* and Volume Two containing *The Masters, The New Men, Homecomings* and *The Affair*.

To Her
Who After The First Volume Was Part Of It
This Work
With Gratitude And Love

C. P. SNOW

STRANGERS
AND
BROTHERS

Volume Three

Corridors of Power (1955–59)
The Sleep of Reason (1963–64)
Last Things (1964–68)

PENGUIN BOOKS

Penguin Books Ltd, Harmondsworth, Middlesex, England
Penguin Books, 40 West 23rd Street, New York, New York 10010, U.S.A.
Penguin Books Australia Ltd, Ringwood, Victoria, Australia
Penguin Books Canada Ltd, 2801 John Street, Markham, Ontario, Canada L3R 1B4
Penguin Books (N.Z.) Ltd, 182–190 Wairau Road, Auckland 10, New Zealand

Corridors of Power first published by Macmillan 1964
Published in Penguin Books 1966
Copyright © Philip A. Snow and Edmund A. Williams-Ashman, 1964

The Sleep of Reason first published by Macmillan 1968
Published in Penguin Books 1970
Copyright © the Estate of C. P. Snow, 1968

Last Things first published by Macmillan 1970
Published in Penguin Books 1972
Copyright © the Estate of C. P Snow, 1970

Published by Macmillan as *Strangers and Brothers*, Volume 3, 1972
Published in Penguin Books 1984
Reprinted 1984

Revised text © the Estate of C. P. Snow, 1972
All rights reserved

Reproduced, printed and bound in Great Britain by
Hazell Watson & Viney Limited,
Member of the BPCC Group,
Aylesbury, Bucks

CONTENTS

Corridors of Power

Corridors of Power

1955 – 59

CONTENTS

PART ONE. THE FIRST THING

PART TWO. 'IN THE PALM OF MY HAND'

PART THREE. PRIVACY

5

Contents

THE FIRST THING

CHAPTER I

A LONDON DINNER PARTY

I STOPPED the taxi at the corner of Lord North Street. My wife and I had the habit of being obsessively punctual, and that night we had, as usual, overdone it. There was a quarter of an hour to kill, so we dawdled down to the river. It was a pleasant evening, I said, conciliating the moment. The air was warm against the cheek, the trees in the Embankment garden stood bulky, leaves filling out although it was only March, against the incandescent skyline. The light above Big Ben shone beneath the cloudcap: the House was sitting.

We walked a few yards further, in the direction of Whitehall. Across Parliament Square, in the Treasury building, another light was shining. A room lit up on the third storey, someone working late.

There was nothing special about the evening, either for my wife or me. We had dined with the Quaifes several times before. Roger Quaife was a youngish Conservative member who was beginning to be talked about. I had met him through one of my official jobs, and thought him an interesting man. It was the kind of friendly acquaintanceship, no more than that, which we all picked up, officials, politicians of both parties: not meeting often, but enough to make us feel at home in what they sometimes called 'this part of London'.

Prompt to the last stroke of eight, we were back in Lord North Street. A maid took us upstairs to the drawing-room, bright with chandeliers, drink-trays, the dinner-shirts of the two men already standing there, the necklace of Caro Quaife glittering as she took our hands.

'I expect you know everyone, don't you?' she said. 'Of course you do!'

She was tall and pretty, in her middle thirties, just beginning, though she was still elegant, to thicken a little through the waist. Her voice was warm, full, and often disconcertingly loud. She gave out a sense of natural and exuberant happiness – as though it were within the power of everyone round her to be as happy as she was.

Other people had followed us up. They all knew one another, establishing Caro's principle of mutual intimacy: Christian names flew about, so that, when the principle broke down, I didn't know whom I was being introduced to. There was, in fact, only one man whom Margaret and I had met as often as the Quaifes. That was Monty Cave, who, according to the political talent spotters, was another coming star. He had a plump face, lemur-like eyes, a quiet, subtle, modulated voice.

As for the others, there appeared to be three couples, all the men Tory back-benchers, none of them older than forty, with wives to match, young, strapping matrons such as one saw in the Kensington streets at four in the afternoon, collecting their children from fashionable pre-preparatory schools. There was also an elderly woman called Mrs Henneker.

As we sat down and drank, Roger Quaife not yet present, they were all talking politics, but politics which any outsider – even one as near to it as I was – needed a glossary to follow. This was House of Commons gossip, as esoteric as theatre-gossip, as continuously enthralling to them as theatre-gossip was to actors. Who was in favour, who wasn't. Who was going to finish up the debate next week. How Archie pulled a fast one with that question.

There was going to be an election soon, we all knew: this was the spring of 1955. They were swapping promises to speak for one another: one was bragging how two senior Ministers were 'in the bag' to speak for him. Roger was safe, someone said, he'd give a hand. What had the P.M. got in mind for Roger 'when we come back'? Monty Cave asked Caro. She shook her head, but she was pleased, and I thought she was touching wood.

The other men spoke of Roger as though he were the only one of them whose success was coming soon, or as though he were different from themselves. The gossip went on. The euphoria grew. Then the maid came in and announced, 'Lady Caroline, Dr Rubin is here.'

It was not that Roger Quaife had a title – but his wife was the daughter of an earl, one of a rich aristocratic family who in the nineteenth century had been Whig grandees.

I looked round, as Caro stood up with cries of welcome. I was taken aback. Yes, it was the David Rubin I knew well, the American physicist. He came in, very quiet and guarded, pearl cuff-links in his sleeves, his dinner jacket newer and more exquisite than any man's there. He was, so my scientific friends said, one of the most distinguished of scientists: but, unlike the rest of them, he was also something of a dandy.

Caro Quaife took him to my wife's side. By this time the drawing-room was filling up, and Caro threw a cushion on the floor and sat by me. 'You must be used to women sitting at your feet, mustn't you?' she said. She couldn't understand, she went on, why Roger, the old devil, was so late. She spoke of him with the cheerfulness, the lack of anxiety, of a happy marriage. When she spoke to me directly, it was in a manner at once high-spirited, deferential and aggressive, eager to be impressed, used to speaking out and not thinking twice.

'Hungry,' said Mrs Henneker, in a trumpeting tone.

She had a fleshy, bulbous nose and eyes which stared out, a fine bright blue, with a disconcerting fixity.

'Sorry. Have another drink,' said Caro, without any sign of caring. In fact, it was not yet half past eight, but it seemed late for a dinner-party in the fifties.

The conversation had switched. One of the members' wives had started talking about a friend of theirs who was having 'woman trouble'. Just for once, they had got away from the House of Commons. This friend was a banker: he had 'got it badly': his wife was worried.

'What's the woman like?' Caro gave a loud, crowing chuckle.

I observed David Rubin's sad face show signs of animation. He preferred this topic to the previous one.

'Oh, madly glamorous.'

'In that case,' cried Caro, 'I don't believe Elsa' (the wife) 'has much to worry about. It isn't the glamorous ones you ought to watch out for when the old man's showing signs of absent-mindedness. It's that little quiet grey mouse in the corner, who nobody's ever noticed. If *she's* got her claws into him, then the best thing is to call it a day and wonder how you're going to explain it to the children.'

The other wives were laughing with her. She was not a beauty, I thought, she was too hearty for that. Just then her eyes lit up, and she scrambled off her cushion.

'Here he is!' she said. 'And about time too!'

As Roger walked through the room from an inner door, he looked clumsy, a little comic, quite unselfconscious. He was a big man, heavy and strong: but neither his face nor his body seemed all of a piece. His head was smallish, for a man of his bulk, and well shaped, his eyes grey and bright, pulled down a little at the outer corners. His nose was flattened at the bridge, his lower lip receded. It was not a handsome face, but it was pleasant. His colleagues in the room, except for Cave, were neat, organised, officer-like; by their side he was shambling and unco-ordinated. When I first met him, he had brought back my impression of Pierre

Bezukhov in *War and Peace*. Yet his manner, quite unlike Pierre's, was briskly competent.

'I'm so sorry,' he said to his wife, 'someone caught me on the 'phone—'

It was, it appeared, one of his constituents. He said it simply, as if it were a matter of tactics that she would understand.

He had considerable physical presence, though it was the opposite of an actor's presence. He shook hands with Rubin and me. All he did and said was easy and direct.

For a moment he and his fellow members had edged away, and on the periphery of the group Mrs Henneker laid a substantial, ringed hand on my arm.

'Office,' she said.

I found her conversation hard to cope with.

'What?' I replied.

'That young man is going to get office.' By which she meant that he would be made a Minister if his party were returned again.

'Will he?' I said.

She asked, 'Are you an idiot?'

She asked it with a dense, confident twinkle, as though I should love her for being rude.

'I shouldn't have thought so,' I said.

'I meant it in the Greek sense, Sir Leonard,' she said, and then from a heavy aside, discovered from Caro that my name was Lewis Eliot. 'Yes, I meant it in the Greek sense,' she said, quite unabashed. 'Not interested in politics, y'know.'

She was so proud of her scrap of learning. I wondered how often she had trotted it out, knowing as much Greek as she did Eskimo. There was something childlike about her self-satisfaction. She was sure that she was a privileged soul. She was sure that no one could think otherwise.

'I am rather interested in politics,' I said.

'I don't believe it,' said Mrs Henneker triumphantly.

I tried to hush her, for I wanted to listen to Roger. His tone was different from that of his friends. I could not place his accent. But it was nothing like that of Eton and the Brigade; any of the others would have known, and Mrs Henneker might have said, that he did not come 'out of the top drawer'. In fact, his father had been a design engineer, solid provincial middle class. He wasn't young, despite Mrs Henneker's adjective. He was only five years younger than I was, which made him forty-four.

He had interested me from the beginning, though I couldn't have said why. Listening to him that evening, as we sat round the dinner-table downstairs, I was disappointed. Yes, his mind was crisper than the others', he was a good deal heavier-weight. But he too, just like the others, was talking about the chessboard of Parliament, the moves of their private game, as though nothing else existed under heaven. I thought that, with David Rubin present, they were all being impolite. I became impatient. These people's politics were not my politics. They didn't know the world they were living in, much less the world that was going to come. I looked at Margaret, who had the eager, specially attentive look she always wore when she was bored, and wished that the evening were over.

All of a sudden, I wasn't impatient any longer. The women had just gone back upstairs, and we were standing in the candlelight. 'Come and sit by me,' Roger said to Rubin, and snapped his fingers, not obtrusively, as if giving himself a signal of some kind. He put me on his other side. As he was pouring brandy into Rubin's glass, he said, 'I'm afraid we've been boring you stiff. You see, this election is rather on our minds.' He looked up and broke into a wide, sarcastic grin. 'But then, if you've been attending carefully, you may have gathered that.'

For the first time that evening, David Rubin began to take a part. 'Mr Quaife, I'd like to ask you something,' he said. 'What, according to present thinking, is the result of this election going to be? Or is that asking you to stick your neck out?'

'It's fair enough,' said Roger. 'I'll give you the limits. On one side, the worst that can happen to us' (he meant the Conservative party) 'is a stalemate. It can't be worse than that. At the other end, if we're lucky we might have a minor landslide.'

Rubin nodded. One of the members said: 'I'm betting on a hundred majority.'

'I'd judge a good deal less,' said Roger.

He was speaking like a real professional, I thought. But it was just afterwards that my attention sharpened. My neighbour's cigar smoke was spiralling round the candle-flame: it might have been any well-to-do London party, the men alone for another quarter of an hour. Then Roger, relaxed and solid in his chair, turned half-right to David Rubin and said: 'Now I'd like to ask you something, if I may.'

'Surely,' said Rubin.

'If there are things you mustn't say, then I hope you won't feel embarrassed. First, I'd like to ask you – how much does what we're doing about nuclear weapons make sense?'

Rubin's face was more sombre, worn and sensitive than those round him. He was no older than some of the other men; but among the fresh ruddy English skins his stood out dry, pallid, already lined, with great sepia pouches, like bruises, under his eyes. He seemed a finer-nerved, more delicate species of animal.

'I don't know that I'm following you,' he said. 'Do you mean what the U.K. is doing about your weapons? Or what we're doing? Or do you mean the whole world?'

'They all enter, don't they?' Everyone was looking at Roger as he asked the matter-of-fact question. 'Anyway, would you start on the local position, that is, ours? We have a certain uncomfortable interest in it, you know. Would you tell us whether what this country's doing makes sense?'

Rubin did not, in any case, find it easy to be as direct as Roger. He was an adviser to his own government; further, and more inhibiting, he was hyper-cautious about giving pain. So he did a lot of fencing. Was Roger talking about the bombs themselves, or the methods of delivery? He invoked me to help him out – as an official, I had heard these topics argued between the Americans and ourselves for years.

There were other considerations beside the scientific ones, beside military ones, said Rubin, back on his last line of defence, why the U.K. might want their own weapon.

'It's our job to worry about that, isn't it?' said Roger gently. 'Tell us – look, you know this as well as anyone in the world – how significant, just in the crudest practical terms, are our weapons going to be?'

'Well, if you must have it,' Rubin answered, flexing his shoulders, 'anything you can do doesn't count two per cent.'

'I say, Professor Rubin,' came a bass voice, 'you're kicking us downstairs pretty fast, aren't you?'

Rubin said: 'I wish I could tell you something different.' His interlocutor was Mrs Henneker's son-in-law, a man called Tom Wyndham. He confronted Rubin with a cheerful stare, full of the assurance of someone brought up in a ruling class, an assurance which did not exactly ignore changes in power, but shrugged them off. Rubin gave an apologetic smile. He was the most polite of men. He had been born in Brooklyn, his parents still spoke English as a foreign language. But he had his own kind of assurance: it did not surprise him to be told that he was the favourite for that year's Nobel physics prize.

'No,' said Monty Cave, 'Roger asked you to tell us.' He gave a sharp grin. 'He usually gets what he asks for.'

Roger smiled, as though they were friends as well as allies. For five years, since they entered the House, they had been leading their group of back-benchers.

'Now, David, if I may call you so,' he said, 'do you mind if I go one step further. About the United States – does your policy about the weapons make sense?'

'I hope so.'

'Doesn't it depend upon the assumption that you're going to have technical superiority for ever? Don't some of our scientists think you're underestimating the Russians? Is that so, Lewis?'

I was thinking to myself, Roger had been well briefed; for Francis Getliffe, Walter Luke and their colleagues had been pressing just that view.

'We don't know,' said Rubin.

He was not at his most detached. And yet, I saw that he had respect for Roger as an intelligent man. He was a good judge of intelligence and, courteous though he was, respect did not come easily to him.

'Well then,' said Roger, 'let us assume, as I should have thought for safety's sake we ought to, that the West – which means you – and the Soviet Union may get into a nuclear arms race on something like equal terms. Then how long have we got to do anything reasonable?'

'Not as long as I should like.'

'How many years?'

'Perhaps ten.'

There was a pause. The others, who had been listening soberly, did not want to argue. Roger said: 'Does that suggest an idea to anyone?'

He said it with a sarcastic twist, dismissively. He was pushing his chair back, signalling that we were going back to the drawing-room.

Just as he was holding open the door, bells began to ring in the passage, up the stairs, in the room we were leaving. It was something like being on board ship, with the bells ringing for lifeboat-drill. Immediately Roger, who a minute before had seemed dignified – more than that, formidable – took on a sheepish smile. 'Division bell,' he explained to David Rubin, still wearing the smile, ashamed, curiously boyish, and at the same time gratified, which comes on men when they are taking part in a collective private ritual. 'We shan't be long!' The members ran out of the house, like schoolboys frightened of being late, while David and I went upstairs alone.

'They've gone off, have they? Time something broke you up.' Caro greeted us robustly. 'Whose reputations have you been doing in? Men ought to have—' With lively hand, she exemplified cats' whiskers sprouting.

I shook my head, and said that we had been talking about David's expert subject, and the future. Margaret looked at me. But the division bell had quite smashed the mood. I no longer felt any eschatological sense, or even any responsibility. Instead, in the bright drawing-room, all seemed serene, anti-climactic and slightly comic.

They had just started on what was becoming more and more a sacramental subject in such a drawing-room – schools for the children, or more exactly, how to get them in. One young wife, proud both of maternity and her educational acumen, with a son born three months before, announced that within an hour of his birth he had been 'put down' not only for Eton, but for his first boarding-school – 'And we'd have put him down for Balliol too,' she went on, 'only they won't let you do that, nowadays.'

What had Caro arranged for her children? What was Margaret doing for ours? Across the room I watched David Rubin listening, with his beautiful, careful, considerate courtesy, to plans for buying places thirteen years ahead for children he had never seen, in a system which in his heart he thought fantastic. He just let it slip once that, though he was only forty-one, his eldest son was a sophomore at Harvard. Otherwise he listened, grave and attentive, and I felt a desire to give some instruction to Mrs Henneker, who was sitting beside me. I told her that American manners were the best in the world.

'What's that?' she cried.

'Russian manners are very good,' I added, as an afterthought. 'Ours are some of the worst.'

It was pleasing to have startled Mrs Henneker. It was true, I said, getting immersed in comparative sociology, that English lower-class manners were rather good, appreciably better than American; but once you approached and passed the mid-point of society, theirs got steadily better and ours got steadily worse. American professional or upper-class manners were out of comparison better. I proceeded to speculate as to why this should be.

I had a feeling that Mrs Henneker did not find this speculation profitable.

The men came pelting up the stairs, Roger in the rear. The division was over, the majority up to par. From then on, the party did not get going again and it was not later than half-past eleven when Margaret and I took David Rubin away. The taxi throbbed along the Embankment towards Chelsea, where he was staying. He and Margaret were talking about the evening, but as I gazed out of the window I did not join in much. I let myself drift into a kind of daydream.

When we had said good-night to David, Margaret took my hand.

'What are you thinking about?' she said.

I couldn't tell her. I was just staring out at the comfortable, familiar town. The Chelsea back-streets, which I used to know, the lights of Fulham Road: Kensington squares: the stretch of Queen's Gate up towards the park. All higgledy-piggledy, leafy, not pretty, nearer the ground than the other capital cities. I was not exactly remembering, although much had happened to me there; but I had a sense, not sharp, of joys hidden about the place, of love, of marriage, of miseries and elations, of coming out into the night air. The talk after dinner had not come back to my mind; it was one of many; we were used to them. And yet, I felt vulnerable, as if soft with tenderness towards the town itself, although in cold blood I should not have said that I liked it overmuch.

The dark road across the park, the sheen of the Serpentine, the livid lamps of Bayswater Road – I was full of the kind of emotion which one cannot hide from oneself, and yet which is so unrespectable that one wants to deny it, as when a foreigner says a few words in praise of one's country, and, after a lifetime's training in detachment, one finds oneself on the edge of tears.

CHAPTER II

THE OLD HERO

THE election went according to plan, or rather, according to the plan of Roger's friends. Their party came back with a majority of sixty; as prophesied by Mrs Henneker at that dinner-party in Lord North Street, Roger duly got office.

As soon as the appointment was announced, my civil service acquaintances started speculating. The rumour went around Whitehall that he was an ambitious man. It was not a malicious rumour; it was curiously impersonal, curiously certain, carried by people who had never met him, building up his official personality for good and all.

One summer afternoon, not long after the election, as I sat in his office with my chief, Sir Hector Rose – St James's Park lay green beneath his windows and the sunlight edged across the desk – I was being politely cross-questioned. I had worked under him for sixteen years. We trusted each other as colleagues, and yet we were not much easier in each other's company than we had been at the beginning. No, I did not know Roger Quaife well, I said – which, at the time, was true. I had a feeling, without much to support it, that he wasn't a simple character.

Rose was not impressed by psychological guesses. He was occupied with something more businesslike. He assumed that Quaife was, as they said, ambitious. Rose did not find that a matter for condemnation. But this job which Quaife had taken had been the end of other ambitious men. That was a genuine point. If he had had any choice, there must be something wrong with his judgment.

'Which, of course, my dear Lewis,' said Hector Rose, 'suggests rather strongly that he wasn't given any choice. In which case, some of our masters may conceivably not wish him all the good in the world. Fortunately, it's not for us to enquire into these remarkable and no doubt well-intentioned calculations. He's said to be a good chap. Which will be at least a temporary relief, so far as this department is concerned.'

The appointment had more than a conversational interest for Hector Rose. Since the war, what in our jargon we called 'the co-ordination of defence' had been split up. The greater part had gone to a new Ministry. It was this Ministry of which Roger had just been appointed Parliamentary Secretary. In the process, Rose had lost a slice of his responsibilities and powers. Very unfairly, I could not help admitting. When I first met him, he had been the youngest Permanent Secretary in the service. Now he was only three years from retirement, having been in the same rank, and at the same job, longer than any of his colleagues. They had given him the Grand Cross of the Bath, the sort of decoration he and his friends prized, but which no one else noticed. He still worked with the precision of a computer. Sometimes his politeness, so elaborate, which used to be as tireless as his competence, showed thin at the edges now. He continued to look strong, heavy-shouldered, thick; but his youthfulness, which had lasted into middle age, had vanished quite. His hair had whitened, there was a heavy line across his forehead. How deeply was he disappointed? To me, at least, he did not give so much as a hint. In his relations with the new super-department, of which he might reasonably have expected to be the permanent head, he did his duty, and a good deal more than his duty.

The new department was the civil servants' despair. It was true what Rose had said: it had become a good place to send an enemy to. Not that the civil servants had any quarrel with the Government about general policy. Rose and his colleagues were conservatives almost to a man, and they had been as pleased about the election results as the Quaifes' circle themselves.

The point was, the new department, like anything connected with modern war, spent money, but did not, in administrative terms, have anything to show for it. Rose and the other administrators had a feeling, the most disagreeable they could imagine, that things were slipping out of their control. No Minister had been any good. The present incumbent, Roger's boss, Lord Gilbey, was the worst of any. Civil servants were used to Ministers who had to be persuaded or bullied into decisions. But they were at a loss when they came against one who, with extreme cordiality, would neither make a decision nor leave it to them.

I had seen something of this imbroglio at first hand. At some points, the business of our department interweaved with theirs, and often Rose needed an emissary. It had to be an emissary of some authority, and he cast me for the job. There were bits of the work that, because I had been doing them so long, I knew better than anyone else. I also had a faint moral advantage. I was, through my books, financially independent now. I had made it clear that I wanted to get out of Whitehall and, perversely, this increased my usefulness. Or if not my usefulness, at least the attention they paid to me, rather like the superstitious veneration with which healthy people listen to someone known to be not long for this earth.

Thus I was frequently in and out of their offices, which were only a few hundred yards away from ours, at the corner of the park. Like everyone else, I had become attached to Lord Gilbey. I was no better than anyone else, and in some ways worse, at getting him to make up his mind. A few days after that talk with Rose, I was making another attempt, in conjunction with Gilbey's own Permanent Secretary, to do just that.

The Permanent Secretary was an old colleague of mine, Douglas Osbaldiston, who was being talked of now just as Rose had been, nearly twenty years before. He was the newest bright star, the man about whom they said, as they used to say about Rose, that he would be head of the civil service before he finished.

On the surface, he was very different from Rose, simple, unpretentious, straightforward where Rose was oblique, humbly born while Rose was the son of an Archdeacon, and yet as cultivated as an old-fashioned civil servant, and exuding the old-fashioned amateur air. He was no more an amateur than Rose, and at least as clever. Once, when he had been working under Rose, I had thought he would not be tough enough for the top jobs. I could not have been more wrong.

He had studied Rose's career with forethought, and was determined not to duplicate it. He wanted to get out of his present job as soon as he had cleaned it up a little – 'This is a hiding to nothing,' he said simply – and back to the Treasury.

He was long, thin, fresh-faced, still with the relics of an undergraduate air. He was quick-witted, unpompous, the easiest man to do business with. He was also affectionate, and he and I became friends as I could never have been with Hector Rose.

That morning, as we waited to go in to Gilbey, it did not take us five minutes to settle our tactics. First – we were both over-simplifying – there was a putative missile on which millions had been spent, and which had to be stopped: we had to persuade 'the Old Hero', as the civil servants called Lord Gilbey, to sign a cabinet paper. Second, a new kind of delivery system for warheads was just being talked about. Osbaldiston, who trusted my nose for danger, agreed that, if we didn't 'look at it' now, we should be under pressure. 'If we can get the O.H.', said Osbaldiston, 'to let the new boy take it over—' By the new boy he meant Roger Quaife.

I asked Osbaldiston what he thought of him. Osbaldiston said that he was shaping better than anyone they had had there; which, since with Gilbey in the Lords Quaife would have to handle the department's business in the Commons, was a consolation.

We set off down the corridor, empty except for a messenger, high and dark with the waste of space, the lavish clamminess, of nineteenth-century Whitehall. Two doors along, a rubric stood out from the tenebrous gloom: Parliamentary Secretary, Mr Roger Quaife. Osbaldiston jabbed his finger at it, harking back to our conversation about Roger, and remarked: 'One piece of luck, he doesn't get here too early in the morning.'

At the end of the corridor, the windows of Lord Gilbey's room, like those of Hector Rose's at the other corner of the building, gave on to St James's Park. In the murky light, the white-panelled walls gleamed spectrally, and Lord Gilbey stood between his desk and the window, surveying with equable disapproval the slashing rain, the lowering clouds, the seething summer trees.

'It's a brute,' he said, as though at last reaching a considered judgment on the weather. 'It's a brute.'

His face was pleasant, small-featured, open with that particular openness which doesn't tell one much. His figure was beautifully trim for a man in his sixties. He was affable and had no side. And yet our proposal, which had seemed modest enough in Osbaldiston's room, began to take on an aura of mysterious difficulty.

'Minister,' said Osbaldiston, 'I really think it's time we got a cabinet decision on the A——.' He gave the code-name of the missile.

'On the A——?' Gilbey repeated thoughtfully, in the manner of one hearing a new, original and probably unsound idea.

'We've got as much agreement as we shall ever get.'

'We oughtn't to rush things, you know,' Gilbey said reprovingly. 'Do you think we ought to rush things?'

'We got to a conclusion on paper eighteen months ago.'

'Paper, my dear chap? I'm a great believer in taking people with you, on this kind of thing.'

'Minister,' said Osbaldiston, 'that is precisely what we've been trying to do.'

'Do you think we ought to weary in well-doing? Do you really, Sir Douglas?'

The 'Sir Douglas' was a sign of gentle reproof. Normally Gilbey would have called Osbaldiston by his Christian name alone. I caught a side-glance from my colleague, as from one who was being beaten over the head with very soft pillows. Once more he was discovering that the Old Hero was not only affable, but obstinate and vain. Osbaldiston knew only too well that immediately he was away from the office, Gilbey was likely to be 'got at' by business tycoons like Lord Lufkin, to whom the stopping of this project meant the loss of millions, or old service friends, who believed that any weapon was better than none.

That was true; the latter being an argument to Osbaldiston for not having a soldier in this job at all. It was not even that Gilbey had been a soldier so eminent that his juniors could not nobble him now. When they called him the Old Hero, it was not a gibe; he had been an abnormally brave fighting officer in both wars, and had commanded a division in the second. That had been his ceiling. If he had been even reasonably capable, the military in the clubs used to say, he couldn't have helped but go right to the top, since it was hard for a man to be better connected. His peerage had come by birth, not as a military reward. So far as there were aristocrats in England, he was one.

'Minister,' said Osbaldiston, 'if you think it's wise to prove just how much agreement there is, we could easily run together an inter-departmental meeting, at your level. Or at mine. Or Ministers and officials together.'

'Do you know,' Gilbey said, 'I'm not a great believer in meetings or committees. They don't seem to result in action, don't you know.'

For once, Douglas Osbaldiston was at a loss. Then he said, 'There's another method. You and the three service Ministers could go and talk it over with the Prime Minister. We could brief you very quickly.'

(And I had no doubt Osbaldiston was thinking, we could also see to it that the Prime Minister was briefed.)

'No, I think that would be worrying him too much. These people have a lot on their plate, you know. No, I don't think I should like to do that.'

Gilbey gave a sweet, kind, obscurely triumphant smile and said: 'I tell you what I will do.'

'Minister?'

'I'll have another good look at the papers! You let me have them over the weekend, there's a good chap. And you might let me have a précis on one sheet of paper.'

Then he broke off, with an air of innocent satisfaction.

'What do you think of this suit I'm wearing?'

It was an extraordinary question. No one, whatever accusation he was bringing against me or Douglas Osbaldiston, could possibly think of us as dressy men: which, in a gentlemanly way, Lord Gilbey was. He sounded innocent, but, though he might not be capable of making decisions, he was entirely capable of pushing them out of sight.

It looked very nice, I said, with a total lack of interest.

'You'll never guess where I had it made.'

No, we found that beyond us.

'As a matter of fact, I had it made at ——.' Gilbey gave the name, not of a fashionable tailor, but of a large London departmental store. 'It doesn't sound very smart, but it's *all right*.'

Inconsiderately, we had to bring him back to the point. This was my turn. I didn't know whether any news had reached him, but there was 'a kite being flown' for a new delivery system: from what we knew of Brodzinski, he wasn't going to stop flying that kite just through lack of encouragement. Wouldn't it be prudent – Rose and Osbaldiston both agreed with this – to deal with the problem before it got talked about, to bring in Getliffe, Luke and the Barford scientists straight away? It probably wasn't pressing enough for the Minister himself, I said, but it might save trouble if Quaife, say, could start some informal talks.

'I think that's a very good idea,' said Osbaldiston, who did not miss a cue.

'Quaife? You mean my new Parliamentary Secretary?' Lord Gilbey replied, with a bright, open look. 'He's going to be a great help to me. This job is altogether too much for one man, you've both seen enough of it to know that. Of course, my colleagues are politicians, so is Quaife, and I'm a simple soldier, and perhaps some of them would find the job easier than I do, don't you know. Quaife is going to be a great help. There's just one fly in the ointment about your suggestion, Lewis. Is it fair on the chap to ask him to take this on before he's got his nose inside the office? I'm a great believer in working a man in gently—'

Amiably, Lord Gilbey went in for some passive resistance. He might find his job too much for one man, but nevertheless he liked it. He might be a simple soldier, but he had considerable talent for survival; quite as well as the next man, he could imagine the prospect of bright young men knocking at the door. On this point, however, we had a card to play. My department would be willing to arrange these first discussions, I said. If Luke and the other scientists took the view we expected, then the business need never come into Gilbey's office at all.

Gilbey didn't like the idea of delegating a piece of work within his own department: but he liked the idea of the work totally escaping his department even less. Finally, in a sweet, good-natured fashion, he gave us a hedging consent. He said: 'Yes, perhaps that is, what we should do.' Without a blink, Osbaldiston took a note and said that he would minute it to the Parliamentary Secretary.

'We mustn't overburden the poor chap,' said Gilbey, still hankering after a retreat. But he knew when he was beaten, and in a crisp tone, suggesting an efficiency expert addressing the woolly-minded, he said:

'Well, that's as far as we can go. I call it a good morning's work.'

As we knew, he had a cabinet at twelve. One might have thought that he would have shied from the approach of cabinet meetings, feeling them above his weight. Not a bit of it. He loved them. As he was preparing himself for the occasion, he took on a special look, a special manner. As a rule, leaving Osbaldiston or me, or the secretaries in the room outside, he would say: 'So long,' sounding, as he often did, as though transported back before the first war when he was a smart young officer in the Household Cavalry. But, leaving to go to a cabinet meeting, he would not have thought of saying, 'So long.' He inclined his head very gravely, without a word. He walked to the door, slow and erect, face solemn and pious, exactly as though he were going up the aisle in church.

CHAPTER III

A SPEECH IN THE COMMONS

AFTER we had by-passed Lord Gilbey, I began to see Roger at work. He was ready to listen to any of us. He did not show much of his own mind. There were things about him, one above all, which I needed to know: not just for curiosity's sake, though that was sharpening, but for the sake of my own actions.

In the middle of July, Roger was making his first ministerial speech. I did not need reminding, having drafted enough of them, how much speeches mattered – to parliamentary bosses, to any kind of tycoon. Draft after draft: the search for the supreme, the impossible, the more than Flaubertian perfection: the scrutiny for any phrase that said more than it ought to say, so that each speech at the end was bound, by the law of official inexplicitness, to be more porridge-like than when it started out in its first draft. I had always hated writing drafts for other people, and nowadays got out of it. To Hector Rose, to Douglas Osbaldiston, it was part of the job, which they took with their usual patience, their usual lack of egotism: when a minister crossed out their sharp, clear English and went in for literary composition of his own, they gave a wintry smile and let it stand.

Osbaldiston told me that, on the present occasion, Roger was doing most of his own writing. Further, it was Roger who was taking over the final draft of Gilbey's speech. They were each to make statements for the department on the same day, Gilbey in the Lords, Roger in the Commons.

When the day came, I went to listen to Roger. I met Osbaldiston in Palace Yard: half an hour before he had gone through the experience, in the line of duty, of hearing Lord Gilbey. 'If anyone can make head or tail of that,' he reported, with professional irritation, 'he damned well ought to be an authority on *l'explication du texte*.'

As we were on our way to our customary listening-point, his phlegm, usually impregnable as that of any of his colleagues, was showing signs of wear.

In the central lobby, I smelled scent near by me, and, glancing round, saw Caro Quaife. Her eyes were full and bright: she did not pretend to hide her nervousness. 'I'd better sit somewhere out of the way,' she said. 'Otherwise I'm going to fidget you.'

I said that he would be all right. Instead of going to the civil servants' box, we walked up with her to the Strangers' Gallery. 'This sort of speech is hell,' said Caro. 'I mean, when there's nothing to say.'

I could not argue with that. She knew the position as well as I did, and the House of Commons much better.

We sat in the front row of the gallery, deserted except for a party of Indians. We looked down on the chamber, half full of members, on the sea-green benches, the green carpet, hazy in the submarine light filtering through from the summer evening.

'I've got the needle,' said Caro. 'This is a bit too raw.'

Within two or three minutes of his getting to his feet, she must have been reassured. Down there, speaking from the despatch box, he looked a great hulk of a man. From a distance, his heavy shoulders seemed even more massive than they were. I had not heard him speak before, and I realised that he was effective quite out of the ordinary. Effective very much in a style of our time, I was thinking. He didn't go in for anything that used to be called oratory. Nearly everyone in that chamber, and men like Osbaldiston and me, felt more comfortable with him because he didn't. His manner was conversational; he had a typescript in front of him, but he did not glance at it. No metaphors, except in sarcasm. As Caro had realised, he had 'nothing to say' – but he didn't make the mistake of pretending he had. There was no policy settled: the decisions were complex: there weren't any easy solutions. He sounded competent, master of the details of the job. He also sounded quite uncomplacent, and listening to him, I believed it was that tone which went straight home.

So far as I could judge Commons receptions, his was a warm one, not only from his own side. Certainly Caro was in no doubt. Gazing down with an expression that was loving, gratified and knowledgeable, she said,

'Now I call *that* a bit of all right.'

On my other side, Osbaldiston, still preoccupied with professional values, was reflecting: 'I must say, it does make us look a bit more respectable, anyway.'

In the lobby, where we went to meet him, he was being congratulated. Members whom he scarcely knew, hounds of success, were trying to catch his eye. Shining with sweat and well-being, he nevertheless wanted our opinion too. 'Satisfactory?' he asked Osbaldiston and me, with a vigilant look. It was not until he had had enough praise that he switched to another topic. Now he was ready to think about some of the scientists' troubles, he said. He and Caro were going out to dinner. Could we come round to Lord North Street after eleven, and start straightaway?

Later that night, I sat in the Quaifes' drawing-room, waiting for them. I was sitting there alone, since Osbaldiston, who lived out in the suburbs, had left me to it. They were not late home: they ran up the stairs brimming with excitement: but it was a long time before Roger and I got down to business.

They were excited because they had been dining with the editor of *The Times*, and had been given a glimpse of next day's (Friday morning's) paper.

I was amused. This was real privilege, I said. In London at that time, one could not buy the earliest editions until the small hours. The other notices they would not see before the morning. Still, Roger was prepared to concede, *The Times* was the most important. They couldn't have done him better. His had been the speech they examined, while Lord Gilbey, his boss, received a few indifferent lines.

He saw me watching him. I asked, what did Gilbey's speech look like on paper? Roger shrugged, said he had been too close to it. He didn't know how it would read in the House of Lords *Hansard*.

Caro, radiant, gave us more drink, and took a stiff one herself. She was as excited as he was, but much more confident. She could trust her judgment about success much more easily than he could. He was still thinking of next morning's papers. That evening in the House, he had sounded grown-up, unusually speculative, responsible. It was arguable, unless one believed that we were wholly at the mercy of blind and faceless fortune, that his decisions might turn out to be important. More than most men, that was the feeling he gave one. Yet, in the bright drawing-room in Lord North Street, all he was thinking of, without any deviation or let-up, was what the *Telegraph*, the *Guardian*, the popular press, would say next day. Caro sat stroking the side of her glass, proud, full of certainties. She could have written the headlines herself.

Of the people I knew, I often thought, it was only the politicians and the artists who lived nakedly in public. The great administrative bosses, the Roses and Osbaldistons, scarcely ever heard a public word about themselves, certainly not a hostile one. As for the industrial tycoons like Paul Lufkin, as soon as they got near the top, they would have felt the virtues outraged if they had heard so much as a whisper of personal criticism. Those lives were out of comparison more shielded. It was the politicians and artists who had to get used to being talked about in public, rather as though they were patients in a hospital visited daily by troops of medical students, who didn't hate them, but who saw no reason to lower their voices. Of course, the politicians and artists had asked for it, or rather, some part of their temperament had. Yet, though they might have asked for it, they didn't like it. Their skins did not thicken, even if they became world figures. I was sure that Roger's never would.

I wished that I were as sure of what, in his job, he intended to do. That night, at last, we were talking business. He was as familiar with 'the papers' (which meant a drawer-full of files, memoranda marked 'Top Secret' and even one or two books, as I was. He had mastered both the proposals of the Brodzinski group, and what Getliffe and the others argued in reply. All Roger said was intelligent and precise – but he would not give me an opinion of his own.

I did not get any further that night. We went on in the same fashion, sniffing at each other like dogs, in the weeks before the summer recess. He must have guessed where I stood, I thought – even though guardedness was catching, and soon one didn't put out one's feelers as far.

Intermittently, during the summer, on holiday with the family, I wondered about him. It was possible that he was testing me. It was possible that he had not yet made up his mind.

As a rule I should have waited. This time I had to know. It was often naïf to be too suspicious, much more naïf than to believe too easily. It often led to crasser action. But there were occasions – and this was one – where you needed to trust.

In September, arriving back in London, I thought it would do no harm if I tried to spend an evening with him alone. Then, my first morning in Whitehall, I felt the old, the familiar sensation of having put one's shoulder hard against a door already on the latch. A telephone call came through before I had glanced at my in-tray. I heard a familiar, rich, off-beat voice. Roger was asking me whether I had any time free in the next few days, and whether we might spend a bachelor evening at his club.

CHAPTER IV

SOMETHING IN THE OPEN

AT the Carlton, Roger and I had our dinner at a corner table. Although he waved now and then to passers-by, he was concentrating on his meal. He was enjoying himself, we were sharing a bottle of wine and he ordered another. When I had been with him before, he had not cared what he ate or drank, or whether he did so at all. Now he was behaving like a gold-miner coming into town. It struck me that he had the irregular habits, the mixture of rapacity and self-denial, which I had seen before in people who set themselves big tasks.

Through the dinner, I was being cautious. He wanted something out of me: I wanted to find out something about him. But I could afford to let it ride. So we talked about books, where he uttered strong opinions, and about common acquaintances, where he was more interested and would not utter any opinion whatever. Rose, Osbaldiston, Luke, Getliffe, a couple of top Ministers: we discussed them all. He produced detail after detail, but would not admit that he liked one more than another. I taunted him by saying that this neutrality didn't suit his style. He was putting on the neutrality of men of action, who except under extreme provocation never admitted that one man was preferable to another.

Roger gave a boisterous laugh, a laugh so unrestrained that I saw other people glancing towards our table.

It was a point to me. Without any introduction, preparation or lead-in, Roger leaned across the table and suddenly said: 'Lewis, I want your help.'

I was taken by surprise. I looked, not at him, but at the people round about us, at an old man with a crimson face who was chewing with exaggerated slowness, at a serious youth impressed by his first glimpse of a London club.

I said, 'What for?'

'I thought you had just been blaming *me* for being neutral.'

'What am I being neutral about?' I asked.

'I can play that game as long as you can. Is it going to get us anywhere?'

Roger had seized the initiative and held it. He was speaking easily, with inexplicable intimacy, with something like anger.

A few drops of wine had spilled upon the table. He flicked them together with his forefinger, then made a cross with them, as if to emphasise an end to something.

'You've got some insight, haven't you? You're supposed to be a man of good will, aren't you? I believe you want some of the things I do. The trouble with you, you like to sit above the battle. I don't know that I've got much use for that. You're prepared to get your hands a bit dirty, but not very dirty. I'm not sure that that's as creditable as you would like to think. I must say, I sometimes lose my respect for people who know as much as you do, and still don't come and fight it out.'

He gave a comradely, savage grin, then broke out: 'Anyway, just to begin with, don't you think you might treat me as a moral equal?'

This was my second surprise – so sharp, it seemed I hadn't heard right and simultaneously knew that I had. We looked at each other, and then away, as one does when words have burrowed to a new level, when they have started to mean something. There was a pause, but I was not premeditating. I said: 'What do you want? What do you really want?'

Roger laughed, not loudly this time. 'You must have learned a *little* from your observations, mustn't you?'

His body was heaved back in his chair, relaxed, but his eyes were bright, half with malice, half with empathy, making me take part.

'Of course,' he said, 'I want everything that politics can give me. Somehow you never seem to have wanted that. If you'd been slightly different,

I've sometimes thought you could have done. But I don't think you were humble enough.'

He went on: 'Look, a politician lives in the present, you know. If he's got any sense, he can't think of leaving any memorial behind him. So you oughtn't to begrudge him the rewards he wants. One of them is – just possessing the power, that's the first thing. Being able to say yes or no. The power usually isn't very much, as power goes, but of course one wants it. And one waits a long time before one gets a smell of it. I was thinking about politics, I was working at politics, I was dreaming of a career nowhere else, from the time I was twenty. I was forty before I even got into the House. Do you wonder that some politicians are content when they manage to get a bit of power?'

He said: 'I'm not, you know.'

Once more intimate and simple, he said he thought he could have done other things. He believed he could have had a success at the Bar, or made money in business. He said in passing that money didn't matter much, since Caro was so rich. He went on: 'If I were content, it would all be nice and easy. I happen to be pretty comfortably placed. It isn't a matter of being liked. I doubt if they like me all that much. Being liked doesn't count so much in politics as outsiders think. Being taken for granted, becoming part of the furniture, counts for a great deal more. I've only got to sit on my backside, and I should become part of the furniture. If I played the game according to the rules, nothing could stop me getting a decent, safe Ministry in five years or so.' He gave a smile at once sarcastic, matey, calm. 'The trouble is, that isn't good enough.'

He said, as though it were straightforward: 'The first thing is to get the power. The next – is to do something with it.'

There was a silence. Then, heaving himself up, he suggested that we might have a change of scene. We went into the drawing-room, where he ordered brandy. For a moment or so he sat in silence, as though uncertain. Then he snapped his fingers and looked at me, with a glimmer of amusement. 'Why do you imagine I'm in this present job at all? I suppose you thought I wasn't given any choice?'

I said that I had heard speculations.

'Oh no,' he replied. 'I asked for it.'

He had been warned against it, he said, by all who believed in him: encouraged into it by some who didn't. It was of course a risk, he added, that a politician at his stage ought not to take. He looked at me, and said, without emphasis:

'I believe I can do something. I don't guarantee it, but there is a chance.

27

For a few years the situation is comparatively fluid. After that, I confess I don't see much hope.'

It was quiet in the drawing-room, only four other people there beside ourselves, and they were far away across the room. It was, as usual, rather dark, or gave the impression of darkness. There was no sense of time there, of the hurrying clock, or the inevitability of morning.

For some time we went over arguments which we both knew well. They were the arguments over which for months we had been fencing, not declaring ourselves. Yet, as he had known and I had suspected, we disagreed little. They were the arguments which had been implicit in his interrogation of David Rubin, that evening in the spring: when, so it seemed now, Roger was already preparing himself.

Neither of us needed to make a coherent case. Knowing the details of the debate so intimately, we used a kind of shorthand, which at that time would have been understood by a good many of our acquaintances, in particular by Francis Getliffe and most of the scientists. To put it at its simplest, we believed that most people in power, certainly in our own country, certainly in the West, had misjudged the meaning of nuclear arms. Yet we had got on to an escalator, and it would take abnormal daring to get off. There were two points of action, Roger and I both knew. One was in our own, English, hands. It was not realistic for us to try indefinitely to possess our own weapons. Could we slide out and manage to prevent the spread? The second point, about which I myself felt much more strongly, was not in our control. We might have an influence. If the nuclear arms race between the United States and the Soviet Union went on too long – how long was too long? none of us could guess – then I could see only one end.

'It mustn't happen,' said Roger. Neither of us smiled. It was an occasion when only a platitude gave one support. Roger went on speaking with energy, calculation and warmth. It had to be solved. There were enough forces to be used, by determined and skilful men. He sounded impersonal, immersed. He wasn't thinking about me; both his psychological attention and his vanity had dropped away. He was utterly sure that he could be of some use.

After a time, when the concentration had slackened, I said: 'All this is fine, but isn't it curious, coming from your side?'

He knew as well as I did that I was no conservative.

'It has to come from my side. It's the only chance. Look, we both agree that we haven't much time. In our kind of society – and I mean America too – the only things that can possibly get done are going to be done by

28

people like me. I don't care what you call me. Liberal conservative. Bourgeois capitalist. We're the only people who can get a political decision through. And the only decisions we can get through will come from people like me.

'Remember,' said Roger, 'these are going to be real decisions. There won't be many of them, but they're only too real. People like you, sitting outside, can influence them a bit, but you can't make them. Your scientists can't make them. Civil servants can't make them. So far as that goes, as a junior Minister, I can't make them. To make the real decisions, one's got to have the real power.'

'Are you going to get it?' I asked.

'If I don't,' said Roger, 'this discussion has been remarkably academic.'

In the last moment before we got ready to go, he was preoccupied, but not with decisions to come. He was thinking how soon he could manage to sit in Gilbey's chair. He mentioned the name, but he was being careful not to involve me. He was sensitive, perhaps in this case over-sensitive, to what he could ask his supporters. It sometimes made him seem, as now, more cagey, evasive, tricky than he was at heart.

He was, however, happy with the evening's talk. He foresaw that, when he had the power, he would be plunged in a network of what we called 'closed' politics, the politics of the civil servants, the scientists, the industrialists, before he got any scrap of his policy through. He thought I could be useful to him there. After this evening, he believed that he could rely on me.

When we had said good-night in St James's Street, and I made my way up that moderate incline (with a vestigial memory of how, when I was younger and had spent nights at Pratt's, it had sometimes seemed uncomfortably steep) I was thinking that he did not find his own personality easy to handle. It was not neat or sharp, any more than his face was. Like a lot of subtle men, he must often have been plunging into clever moves, and taken in no one but himself. Nevertheless, when he spoke about what he wanted to do, he had not been clever at all. He knew, and took it for granted that I knew, that in their deep concerns men aren't clever enough to dissimulate. Neither of us had been dissimulating that night.

CHAPTER V

THE SCIENTISTS

WITHIN two days of that dinner at the Carlton, Roger asked me to make some arrangements. He wanted us to have lunch with Francis Getliffe and Walter Luke – 'in a private room', he specified. After lunch, we would all pay a visit to Brodzinski. As I stood with Francis and Luke in the room at the Hyde Park Hotel, looking down at the Row and the bronzing trees, I was puzzled, and the others more so. There was nothing specially mysterious about the private room, if we were to discuss secret projects: but Roger met them both regularly on one of the defence committees. Why should he make an occasion of it now? Neither of them had any inclination to spend time with Brodzinski, nor saw any value in it.

As we waited for Roger, Francis was vexed. He was getting more impatient, more unwilling to waste time, as he grew older. At this time he was fifty-two, and already an elder statesman of science. He had thought more effectively about military-scientific strategy than anyone had, and it was his views which had influenced us most. But now he had to force himself to produce them. He had found a new field of research, and was working as obsessively as when he was a young man. It was a physical strain to be torn away from it, to be dragged up from Cambridge for that lunch. He stood by the window, his face sculptured, his fingers nervous, as he spun the stem of a glass.

By his side, Walter Luke looked seamed, confident, grizzled, low-slung, more prosaic. Yet the scientists said that he had been unlucky: he had a scientific imagination as powerful as Francis's, or more so: in a peaceful world, he might have done fundamental work. As it was, he had been busy on what he called 'hardware' since 1939: he was still not forty-four, but he had been head of the Atomic Energy establishment for years. He was not as vexed as Francis, but was swearing like the dockyard hand his father used to be.

When Roger arrived, he was friendly, businesslike, but did not exert his personal arts on either of them. As we ate, he was asking them questions about Brodzinski's project – as though refreshing his memory, or making certain they had not changed their minds, for in fact he had heard their opinions times before and knew them off by heart.

'I go on saying,' said Walter Luke, 'I believe technically it might be on. At least, there's a fifty-fifty chance it might be on. Brod's no fool, he's got a touch of the real stuff. And if we had these bloody things, we could call

ourselves independent in nuclear weapons, which we're not now except
for guff, and which we're probably never going to be. The whole point is,
we keep coming back to it – what price are you willing to pay for that?'

'What price are you?'

'Not this.'

Luke bristled with energy. From his manner, no one would have
guessed that he hadn't enjoyed coming down on this side. He had a simple,
integral patriotism. He had shared the scientists' moral concern, but if
his country could have kept the highest military power, he would have
made any sacrifice. His tough mind, though, told him it was impossible,
and he put the regret behind him. 'We just can't play in this league. If we
spent everything we've got, that is, everything we now spend on defence,
and I mean *everything*, we might bring this off – and what the bloody hell
have we bought at the end of it? The priceless thought that we could take
out Moscow and New York simultaneously. The only thing that scares me
is that too many people never grow up.'

Roger turned to Francis Getliffe.

'You know what I think, Parliamentary Secretary,' said Francis with
stiff courtesy. 'This business of Brodzinski's is a nonsense. And so are the
views of more important people.'

Francis, who did not often go in for public controversy, had not long
before screwed himself up to write a pamphlet. In it he had said that there
was no military rationale behind the nuclear policy. This analysis had got
him into trouble, mostly in America, but also in England. In some right-
thinking circles, it had seemed not only preposterous, but also heretical,
and something like wicked.

As we drove through the autumnal streets to the Imperial College, I
was still not sure why Roger was playing it this way. What was he aiming
at? Was he reckoning that Brodzinski, that lover of English flummery,
would be softened by the attentions, the paraphernalia?

If so, sitting in Brodzinski's room, gazing out at the lonely-looking
Colcutt tower, the pale green dome making the aesthetic protest in the
solitude of sky, I thought that Roger had reckoned wrong. It was true
that Brodzinski loved English flummery, with a passion that made Roger's
more conservative friends look like austere revolutionaries. He had been
a refugee from Poland in the late thirties. During the war he had made a
name, working in one of the Admiralty scientific departments. Afterwards he had spent some years at Barford, had quarrelled with Luke and
others, and recently taken a professorship. It was true that he had immersed himself, with fanatical devotion, in what he thought of as English

life. He knew all the English snobberies, and loved them so much that they seemed to him morally right. He had dedicated himself to the politics of the English ultra-right. He addressed Francis Getliffe and Walter Luke, with extreme relish, as Sir Francis and Sir Walter. Despite all that, or perhaps because of it, he was unyielding about his idea, and instead of listening to Quaife's persuasions, he was determined to make Quaife listen to him.

He was a tallish man, very thick in the chest and thighs, and his muscles filled his clothes. His voice boomed against the walls of his office. He had beautiful pure transparent eyes, in a flat Slavic face; his fair hair, now mingled with grey, was the colour of dust. He was always on the look-out for enemies, and yet he was vulnerable to help, appealing for it, certain that anyone, not already an enemy, given intelligence and willingness, would be convinced that he was right.

He explained the project over again. 'I must inform you, Parliamentary Secretary' (he was as familiar with English official etiquette as any of us), 'that there is nothing technically novel here! There is nothing that we do not know. Sir Walter will tell you that I am not over-stating my case.'

'With reservations,' said Luke.

'With what reservations?' Brodzinski burst out, brilliant with suspicion. 'What reservations, Sir Walter? Tell me that, now?'

'Come off it, Brod,' Luke was beginning, ready to settle down to a good harsh scientific argument. But Roger would not let it start. He was treating Brodzinski with a mixture of deference and flattery – or perhaps not pure flattery, but an extreme empathy. Just as Brodzinski felt a brilliance of suspicion when Walter Luke spoke, so with Roger he felt a brilliance of reassurance. Here was someone who knew what he had to fight against, who knew his urgencies.

'But, Parliamentary Secretary, when do we get something done?' he cried. 'Even if we start now, *tonight*, it will take us till 1962 or '63 before we have the weapons—'

'And they won't have any strategic meaning,' said Francis, irritated at the way the conversation was going.

'Sir Francis, Sir Francis, I believe there is meaning in having weapons in your hands, if the country is going to survive. I suppose you mean, I hope you mean, that America will have their own armaments, much greater than ours, and I hope they will. The more the better, and good luck to them. But I shall not sleep happy until we can stand beside them—'

'I mean something more serious—' Francis interrupted. But once more Roger stopped the argument.

Brodzinski burst out:

'Parliamentary Secretary, when can we get some action?'

After a pause, Roger replied, carefully, considerately:

'You know, I mustn't raise false hopes—'

Brodzinski raised his head. 'I know what you're going to say. And I agree with it. You are going to say that this will cost a thousand million pounds. Some say we cannot afford to do it. *I* say, we cannot afford not to do it.'

Roger smiled at him. 'Yes, I was going to raise that point. But also I was going to say that there are many people to convince. I am only a junior Minister, Professor. Let me say something to you in confidence that I really oughtn't to. Within these four walls, I think it will be necessary to convince my own Minister. Without him behind it, no government could even begin to listen—'

Brodzinski was nodding. He did not need explanations about the English political machine. He was nodding, passionately thoughtful. As for Luke and Francis, they were looking stupefied. They knew, or thought they knew, what Roger wanted as a policy. They had just heard him, not exactly state the opposite, but leave Brodzinski thinking that he had.

Soon Roger was saying goodbye, inviting Brodzinski to visit him in Whitehall, repeating that they would keep in touch. Brodzinski clung to his hand, looking at him with beautiful candid eyes, the colour of seawater. Brodzinski's goodbyes to Walter and Francis were cold, and when they were back in the car they themselves spoke coldly to Roger. They were, in their different fashions, straightforward and honourable men, and they were shocked.

Roger, apparently at ease, invited them to tea before the car had moved a hundred yards. Utterly aware of the chill, utterly ignoring it as he spoke, he said that, when he was a young man, he used to go to a café not far away: was it still there? Stiffly, Francis said that he ought to get back to Cambridge. No, said Roger, come and have tea. Again they refused. 'I want to talk to you,' said Roger – not with official authority, but his own. In a sullen silence, we sat at a table in the café window, the December mists thick in the street outside. It was one of those anonymous places, neither a rackety one for the young nor a tearoom for the elderly: the atmosphere was something between that of a respectable pull-up for carmen and a coffee-room for white-collar workers.

Roger said: 'You disapproved of what I've just done.'

'I'm afraid I did,' Francis replied.

'I think you're wrong,' said Roger.

Francis said curtly that he had given Brodzinski too much encouragement. Walter Luke, more violent, asked if he didn't realise that the man was a mad Pole, whose only uncertainty was whether he hated Russians as Russians more than Russians as communists, and who would cheerfully die himself along with the entire population of the United States and Great Britain, so long as there wasn't a Russian left alive. If that was the sort of lunacy we were going to get mixed up in, he, Luke, for one, hadn't bargained on it.

Roger said that he knew all that. But Walter was wrong on just one point. Brodzinski was not mad. He had a touch of paranoia. But a touch of paranoia was a very useful part of one's equipment. On far more people than not, it had a hypnotic effect.

'I wish I had it,' Roger added, with a grim smile. 'If I had, I shouldn't have to spend time telling you I am not deserting. No, your colleague Brodzinski is a man of power. Don't deceive yourselves about that. My bet is that his power is likely to influence quite a number of people before we're through. He's going to require very careful handling. You see, he's got one great advantage. What he wants, what he's saying, is very simple and it's what a lot of people want to hear. What you want – and what I want quite as much as you do, if I may say so – is very difficult and not in the least what a lot of people want to hear. That's why we're going to need all the luck in the world if we're going to get away with it. If you think it's going to be easy and painless, then my advice to you is to cut all your connections with Government as fast as you possibly can. It's going to be hell, and we may easily lose. As for me, I'm committed. But I'm taking bigger risks than any of you, and you'll let me do it in my own way.'

Yes, I thought then, and in cooler blood afterwards, he was taking risks. Just as he had done, talking to me at the Carlton Club. He was taking risks in speaking in that tone to Francis and Luke. And yet, he knew they were both, in spite of Luke's raucous tongue, men trained to discretion. He also knew, what was more significant, that they were 'committed' in the sense he had used the word. For years before Hiroshima, they had foreseen the technological dangers. They could be relied upon as allies.

Luke was still grumbling. Why had Roger taken them there? What did he think he had achieved?

Roger explained that he wanted to shower Brodzinski with attentions: he wouldn't be satisfied, but it might for the time being keep him quiet.

That reply satisfied Walter Luke. It would not have satisfied me.

It was part of Roger's technique (like that, it had sometimes occurred to me, of a distinctly less effective friend of mine, Tom Orbell) to seem more spontaneous than he was. Or rather, it was part of his nature which he had developed into a technique. His spontaneity was genuine, it gave him some of his bite: but he could govern it. He had not given Luke and Francis the slightest indication of what, I was now certain, was his strongest reason for buttering up Brodzinski.

The reason was simple. Roger was set on easing Lord Gilbey out and getting the job himself. He wanted Brodzinski to do the opposite of keeping quiet, to shout his discontent. I had seen too many examples of this process not to recognise it now.

Roger was less hypocritical than most men. He would have made the same moves without excuse. Yet, I was coming to believe that, as he had just said, he was committed. Old Thomas Bevill used to lecture me, in his Polonius-like fashion, on the forces driving the great politicians he had known. He rolled out his Victorian phrases: one force, Bevill used to say, was a consciousness of powers. Another, and a rarer one, was a consciousness of purpose. For men seeking excuses for themselves, that was the best of all.

Neither Francis nor Luke realised what Roger was up to. Yet, if they had, they would not have minded much. It seemed strange, but they would have minded less than I did. For I had an affection for Lord Gilbey. Sometimes my affections ran away with me. They had done so years before, I now believed, in a struggle on a pettier scale, when I had been voting for a Master of my college. They had made me forget function, or justice, or even the end to be served. Now I was getting older, I could realise those mistakes in the past, mistakes which a man like Francis, high principled as he was, would never have made. For him, this issue would be simple. Lord Gilbey never ought to have been in this job in the first place: the sooner he was removed the better. Roger had to be rough. Gilbey would cling like a mollusc, in distinguished incompetence. If Roger was not prepared to be rough, then he was no good to us.

Francis and Luke would be right. Yet they might not know that Roger was a more deeply forested character than they were. I believed in his purpose, but it would have comforted me to know why he had it. Perhaps, I thought once or twice that autumn, it would have comforted him too.

CHAPTER VI

A WEEKEND IN THE COUNTRY

DURING the winter, the gossip began to swirl out from the clubs and the Whitehall corridors that Lord Gilbey was 'getting past it'. At the same time, Roger's name crept into the political columns in the Sunday papers, as the first junior Minister in the new government to be talked about for promotion. It looked as though he were handling the press, or rather, the political link-men who added to their incomes (or simply to their influence) through leaking secret information to the press, with skill and nerve. About whether these link-men really existed, administrators like Hector Rose went on speculating, as though they were some species still in doubt, like the yeti, or the plesiosaur in Loch Ness. Rose, with his rigid propriety, could not easily believe in them. My guess was that Roger not only believed in them, but knew them. If so, he got himself liked, but never let out that he had a policy already formed, much less what it was. In fact, the political commentators, while agreeing that he was coming to the front, gave diametrically different reasons why he should do so.

Early in February, Roger told me that he was spending the weekend at Basset, Diana Skidmore's house in Hampshire. It was not a coincidence that Margaret and I had just received the same invitation. Diana had an intelligence network of her own, and this meant that the connection between Roger and me was already spotted. So far as Roger went, it meant more. Diana was a good judge of how people's stock was standing, whatever their profession was: upon stock prices within the government, her judgment was something like infallible. Since Diana had a marked preference for those on the rise, the frequency of a man's invitation to Basset bore a high correlation to his political progress.

People said that about her, and it was true. But, hearing it before one met her, one felt one had been misled. Driving down the Southampton road, the wiper skirling on the windscreen, the wind battering behind us, Margaret and I were saying that we should be glad to see her. The road was dark, the rain was pelting, we lost our way.

'I like her really,' said Margaret, 'she's so relaxing.'

I questioned this.

'One hasn't got to compete, because one can't. *You* wouldn't know. But I should never buy a special frock to go to Basset.'

I said it would be nice to get there, in any garments whatsoever. When at last we saw the lights of the Basset lodge, we felt as travellers might have done in a lonelier and less domesticated age, getting a glimpse of light over the empty fields.

It was a feeling that seemed a little fatuous once we had driven up from the lodge through the dark and tossing parkland and stood in the great hall of Basset itself. The façade of the house was eighteenth century, but this enormous hall was as warm as a New York apartment, smelling of flowers, flowers spread out in banks, flowers dominating the great warm space as though this were a wedding-breakfast. It was a welcome, not only of luxury, but of extreme comfort.

We went across the hall, over to the guest-list. The order of precedence had an eloquence of its own. Mr Reginald Collingwood got the star suite: Collingwood was a senior Cabinet Minister. The Viscount and Viscountess Bridgewater got the next best. That designation marked the transformation of an old acquaintance of mine, Horace Timberlake, not a great territorial magnate but an industrial boss, who had become one of the worthies of the Tory Party. We came third, presumably because we had been there a good many times. Then Mr Roger Quaife and Lady Caroline Quaife. Then Mr Montagu Cave. He had become a junior Minister at the same time as Roger. We noticed that, as had happened before, he was alone, without his wife. There were rumours that she was enjoying herself with other men. Then Mrs Henneker. I made a displeased noise and Margaret grinned. Finally Mr Robinson, by himself and unexplained.

Diana's brisk, commanding voice rang out from a passageway. She came into the hall, kissed us, led us into one of her sitting-rooms, brilliant, hung with Sisleys and Pissarros. She remembered what we drank, gave orders to the butler without asking us, said, 'Is that right?' – knowing that it was right – and looked at us with bold, sharp, appraising eyes.

She was a woman in her early fifties, but she had worn well. She was slender, but wiry, not delicate. She had never been beautiful, so I had heard, perhaps not even pretty, and it was possible that her looks, which in middle age suggested that she had once been lovely, were now at their best. She had a dashing, faintly monkey-like attractiveness, the air of a woman who had always known that she was attractive to men. As she herself was fond of saying, 'Once a beauty, always a beauty', by which she didn't mean that the flesh was permanent, but that the confidence which underlay it was. Her great charm, in fact, was the charm of confidence. She was not conceited, though she liked showing off. She knew, she was too worldly not to know, that some men were frightened away. But for many she had an appeal, and she had not doubted it since she was a child.

She was wearing a sunblaze of diamonds on her left shoulder. I looked a little apologetically at my wife, who had put on my latest present, a peridot brooch. Margaret's taste did not run to ostentation but, face to face with Diana, she would not have minded a little more.

The curious thing was that the two of them came from the same sort of family. Diana's father was a doctor and her relatives, like Margaret's, were academics, barristers, the upper stratum of professional people. Some of them even penetrated into the high Bloomsbury into which Margaret had been born. Nevertheless, despite her family, Diana had taken it for granted, from her childhood, that she belonged to the smartest of smart worlds. Taking it for granted, she duly got there, with remarkable speed. Before she was twenty-one, she had married Chauncey Skidmore, and one of the bigger American fortunes. Seeing her in middle age, one couldn't help thinking that it was she, not the Skidmores, not her friends in the international circuit, who had been made for just that world.

It seemed like the triumph of an adventuress: but it didn't seem so to her, and it didn't seem so when one was close to her. She was self-willed and strong-willed; she was unusually shrewd: but she had the brilliance and yes, the sweetness, of one who had enjoyed everything that happened to her. When she married Chauncey Skidmore, she loved him utterly. She had been widowed for over a year, and she still mourned him.

At dinner that night, there were – although the Quaifes were not arriving till the next day – eighteen at table. Diana had a habit of commanding extra guests from people to whom she let houses on the estate, or from masters at Winchester close by. I looked up at the ceiling, painted by some eighteenth-century Venetian now forgotten. The chatter had gone up several decibels, so that one could hear only in lulls the rain slashing against the windows at one's back. Confidentially, the butler filled my glass; the four footmen were going round soft-footed. For an instant it seemed to me bizarre that all this was still going on. It was, however, fair to say that it did not seem bizarre to others present. A spirited conversation was proceeding about what, when Diana's son inherited the house, would need doing to the structure: or whether she ought to start on it, bit by bit. In her ringing voice, Diana turned to Collingwood on her right: 'Reggie, what do you think I ought to do?' Collingwood did not usually utter unless spoken to. He replied: 'I should leave it for him to worry about.'

That seemed to show the elements of realism. It occurred to me that, a quarter of a century before, I had sat in rich houses, when I first heard Basset-like political gossip, listening to the younger Marches all assuming that before we were middle aged, such houses would exist no more.

Well, that hadn't happened. Now Diana's friends were talking as though it never would happen. Perhaps they had some excuse.

I was watching Collingwood. I had met him before, but only in a group. He struck me as the most puzzling of political figures – puzzling, because politics seemed the last career for him to choose.

He was a handsome man, lucky both in his bone-structure and his colouring. His skin tone was fresh and glowing, and he had eyes like blue quartz, as full of colour, as opaque. For his chosen career, however, he had what one might have thought a handicap; for he found speech, either in public or private, abnormally difficult. As a public speaker he was not only diffident and dull, but gave the impression that, just because he disliked doing it so much, he was going to persevere. In private he was not in the least diffident, but still the words would not come. He could not, or did not care to, make any kind of conversation. It seemed a singular piece of negative equipment for a politician.

And yet, he had deliberately made the choice. He was a well-to-do country gentleman who had gone into merchant banking and made a success of it. But he had broken off that career; it was politics that he could not resist; if it meant making speeches, well then, it meant making speeches.

He carried weight inside the cabinet, and even more inside his party, far more than colleagues of his who seemed to have ten times his natural gifts. That was why, that night at dinner, I was anxious when I heard, or thought I heard, a reply of his to Diana, which sounded like dubiety about the Quaifes. I could not be sure; at such a table, listening to one's partner, who in my case turned out, with an absence of surprise on my part, to be Mrs Henneker, one needed a kind of directional hearing-sense to pick up the gossip flowing by. If Roger had Collingwood against him, it was serious for us all – but I was captured again by Mrs Henneker, who was thinking of writing a life of her dead husband, who had been a Rear-Admiral, monstrously treated, so she explained to me, by the Board of Admiralty.

Across the table, Cave, who was a gourmet, was eating without pleasure; but, since for him quantity could be made to turn into quality, he was also eating like a glutton, or a hungry child.

Once more, maddeningly, a whiff of disapproval from the top of the table. A person whose name I could not catch was in trouble. I caught a remark from Lord Bridgewater, plethoric, pineapple-headed: 'He's letting us down, you know what I mean.' To which Collingwood replied, 'It won't do.' And a little later, mixed with a clarification about the Rear-Admiral, I heard Collingwood again: 'He's got to be stopped.' I had no idea who the man was. I had no idea, either, what kind of trouble he was in – except that I should have been prepared to bet that it wasn't sexual. If it had been, Diana would have been flashing signals of amusement, and the others would not have been so condemnatory and grave. Whatever they said in public, in private they were as sexually tolerant as people could be. They could not forgive public scandals, and sometimes they made special rules. In private, though, and within their own circle, or any circle which touched theirs, no one cared what anyone 'did'. Divorces – there had been several round this table, including Margaret's. A nephew of Diana's had been run in while picking up a guardsman in Hyde Park: 'That chap had hard luck,' I heard them say.

Nevertheless, there was constraint in the air. Margaret and I, when we were alone, told each other that we were puzzled.

Next morning, in mackintosh and wellingtons, I went for a walk in the rain with Monty Cave. Until we turned back to the house, he was pre-occupied – preoccupied, so it seemed, with sadness. I wished I knew him well enough to ask. Suddenly he burst out, in darts of flashing, malicious high spirits: wasn't Diana showing strange signs of taste in modern music? wasn't Mr Robinson a connoisseur? wasn't she capable of assimilating any man's tastes? And then: why did people have absurd pet-names? Sammikins – Bobbity – how would I like to be Lewikins? 'Or perhaps,' said Cave, with a fat man's sparkle, 'that's what your friends do call you.'

He wasn't restful; his mood changed too fast for that, until we talked politics. Then he was lucid, imaginative, unexpectedly humane. For the first time, I could understand how he was making his reputation.

Back in the house, I felt the constraint tightened again, as soon as the Quaifes arrived. I caught Margaret's eye: in the midst of the party we couldn't talk. Yet soon I realised that, whatever the reason, it was not that which had worried me most: for just before lunch, I found Caro and Diana drinking whisky, and agreeing that Gilbey must be got rid of.

'You're in on this, Lewis!' cried Diana. 'Old Bushy' (Gilbey) 'has never been the slightest bit of good to us, has he?'

I sat down. 'I don't think this is his line,' I said.

'Don't be pie-faced,' said Diana. 'He's a nice, smart cavalry officer, and he'd have married an actress if they'd let him, but that's his limit and you know it.'

'He'd never have married an actress, he's the biggest snob of the lot of them,' said Caro.

'Do you think the priests would have got to work?' said Diana. Gilbey's family was Catholic, and to these two he seemed to have lived in the backwoods. There was much hooting hilarity, which did not disguise the truth that Diana and Caro understood each other and meant business.

'The point is,' said Diana, 'he's no good. And we can't afford him.'

She glanced at Caro with appraising eyes, at a pretty woman twenty years younger than herself, at a pretty woman as tough as herself, at an ally.

'I can tell you this,' Diana added sharply, 'Reggie Collingwood is certain that we can't afford him.'

It ought to have been good news. After an instant, Caro frowned.

'I'm afraid I haven't any special use for Reggie,' she said.

'Listen,' said Diana, 'you have got to be careful. And Roger, of course. but *you* have got to be very careful.'

If I had not been there, she would have said more. A few minutes later we went in to lunch.

As for me, until after dinner on the Sunday night, I remained half-mystified. The hours seeped away, punctuated by meals, I might have been on an ocean crossing, wondering why I hadn't taken an aircraft. The rain beat down, the windows streamed, the horizon was a couple of fields away; it was, in fact, singularly like being on a ship in gloomy, but not rough, weather.

I did not get a word with Roger alone. Even with Margaret, I managed to speak only in our own rooms. She was having more than her share of the philosophy of Lord Bridgewater, while in the great drawing-room of Basset, in various subsidiary drawing-rooms, in the library, I found myself occupied with Mrs Henneker.

She was nothing like so brassy as I had previously known her. When she discovered me alone in the library on Saturday afternoon, she still looked dense, but her confidence had oozed away. The curious thing was, she was outfaced. Through the misted window, we watched Diana and Caro stepping it out along the drive in mackintoshes and hoods, taking their exercise in the drenching rain.

'The rich think they can buy anything,' said Mrs Henneker heavily. The *mana* of Diana's wealth was too much for her, just as it might have been for my relatives or my old friends or others really poor. There was a certain irony, I thought. Mrs Henneker herself must have been worth a hundred thousand pounds or so.

Mrs Henneker did not listen to any repartee of mine. But she had a use for me. Perhaps under the provocation of the Basset opulence, her purpose had crystallised. She was going to write that biography of her husband, and I could be of minor assistance.

'Of course,' she said, 'I've never done any writing, I've never had the time. But my friends always tell me that I write the most amusing letters. Of course, I should want a bit of help with the technique. I think the best thing would be for me to send you the first chapters when I've finished them. Then we can really get down to work.'

She had obsessive energy, and she was methodical. On the Sunday morning, while most of the house-party, Roger among them, went to church, cars squelching on the muddy gravel, she brought me a synopsis of her husband's life. After the drawn-out luncheon, Diana's neighbours staying until after tea, Mrs Henneker got hold of me again, and told me with triumph that she had already written the first two paragraphs, which she would like me to read.

When at last I got up to my dressing-room, light was streaming in from our bedroom and Margaret called out. I'd better hurry, she said. I replied that I had been with Mrs Henneker: she found my experience funnier than I did. As I pulled off my coat, she called out again: 'Caro's brother seems to have stirred up the dovecotes.'

She had been hearing about it after tea. At last I understood one of Cave's obliquities the morning before. For Caro's brother was called, not only by his family but by acquaintances, 'Sammikins'. He was also Lord Houghton, a Tory M.P., young and heterodox. Recently, Margaret and I recalled, he had published a short book on Anglo-Indian relations. Neither of us had read it, but the newspapers had splashed it about. From the reviews, it seemed to be anti-Churchill, pro-Nehru, and passionately pro-Gandhi. It sounded a curious book for a Tory M.P. to write. That was part of his offence. 'He's not exactly their favourite character, should you say?' said Margaret. She was frowning at herself, and her dress, in the glass. She was not quite so uncompetitive, these days, as she would have had me think.

I could guess what Diana had said to Caro. At dinner the topic was not mentioned, and I began to hope that we were, for the time being, safely through. The conversation had the half-intimacy, the fatigue, the diminuendo, of the close of a long weekend. Since there was no host, the men did not stay long round the dining-table, and in the drawing-room afterwards we sat round in a semi-circle, Diana, impresario-like, placing herself between Collingwood and Roger, encouraging them to talk across her.

Suddenly Lord Bridgewater, open-faced, open-eyed, cleared his throat. We knew what was coming. He hadn't been born in this society, but he had taken its colour. At home he was an amiable man, but he had a liking for unpleasant jobs. He spoke across the width of the room to Caro. 'I hope we shan't hear any more of Sammikins, you know what I mean.' For once, almost for the first time, I saw Caro put out. She flushed. She had to control herself: she hated doing so. It was in her nature not only not to give a damn, but to say that she didn't. After a pause, she replied, a little feebly: 'Horace, I'm sorry, but I'm not my brother's keeper.' Sammikins was a couple of years younger than she was, and listening, I was sure that she loved him.

'Some people,' said Collingwood, 'would say that he could do with one.'

'They'd better say that to him,' said Caro, 'that's all.'

'He's not doing any good to the Party,' said Lord Bridgewater, 'he's not doing any good at all.'

Collingwood looked at Caro. His eyes brightened in women's company, but his manner did not change and he said straight at her:

'It's got to be stopped.'

'What do you mean?'

'I mean, that if Sammikins won't stop it himself, we shall have to stop him.'

In Collingwood's difficult, senatorial tone, the nickname sounded more than ever ridiculous. Caro was still just keeping her temper.

'I don't think,' she replied, 'that any of you have the slightest idea what he's like.'

'That doesn't enter,' said Collingwood. 'I mean, that if he writes anything like this again, or makes any more speeches on the same lines, we can't have anything more to do with him.'

On the other side of Diana, I saw Roger's frowning face. He was gazing at his wife. She, dark with shame, was shaking her head as though telling him to keep quiet. Up to now, she knew – better than anyone there – that he had not made a false move, or one not calculated, since he entered the Government. This wasn't the time to let go.

Caro gave Collingwood a social smile.

'You mean,' she said, 'you're ready to take the whip away?'

'Certainly.'

'That wouldn't matter much, for him.'

I believed that, for an instant, she was talking professional politics in the sense Collingwood would understand. Her brother, as heir to his father's title, could not reckon on a serious political career.

'That's not all,' said Collingwood. 'No one likes – being right out of things.'

There was a pause. Caro thought successively of replies to make, discarded them all.

'I utterly disagree with nearly everything you've said.' It was Roger's voice, not quietened, addressed to the room as well as to Collingwood. He must have been enraged by the choice he had to make: now he had made it, he sounded spontaneous and free.

Like Caro, I had been afraid of this. Now that it had happened, I felt excited, upset, and at the same time relieved.

'I don't know how you can.' Collingwood looked lofty and cold.

'I assure you that I do. I have the advantage, of course, of knowing the man very well. I don't think many of you have that advantage, have you?' Roger asked the question with a flick, his glance moving towards his wife. 'I can tell you, if a few of us had his spirit and his idealism, then we should be doing a lot better than we are.'

Caro had flushed right up to her hair-line. She was anxious for Roger, she knew he was being unwise: but she was proud of him, proud because he had put her first. She had not known what to expect, had tried to persuade herself that she hoped for his silence. But he had not been silent: and she was filled with joy. I saw Margaret flash her an exhilarated glance, then flash me a worried one.

'Aren't you forgetting judgment, Quaife?' asked Lord Bridgewater.

Roger swept on. 'No, I'm not forgetting judgment. But we're too inclined to talk about judgment when we mean the ability to agree with everyone. That's death. Let's have a look at what this man has really done. He's stated a case – pretty roughly, that I'll grant you: he hasn't taken the meaning out of everything he said, which is another gift we tend to over-value. In one or two places he's overstated his case. That I accept, and it's a fault you're always going to find in sincere and passionate men. But still, the major points in his book are substantially true. What is more, everyone in this room, and almost everyone competent to express an opinion, knows they are substantially true.'

'I can't agree,' said Collingwood.

'You know it. You may disagree with the attitudes, but you know the points are true. That's why you're all so angry. These things are true. The sin this man has committed is to say them. It's quite all right for people like us to know these things. But it's quite wrong for anyone to say them – outside our charmed circle. Aren't we all coming to take that for granted more and more? Isn't it becoming much more desirable to observe the etiquette rather than tell the truth? I don't know whether it frightens you, but it certainly frightens me. Politics is too serious a business to be played like a private game at a private party. In the next ten years, it's going to be more serious than anything we've ever imagined. That's why we need every man who's got the spine enough to say what he really thinks. That's why we need this man you're all so bitter about. That's why – ' he finished, in a conversational tone, speaking to Collingwood – 'if there is any question of his being pushed out, I shouldn't be able to sit quietly by.'

'I'm sure you wouldn't,' Collingwood replied, in his own awkward kind of conversational tone. He was quite composed. There was no sign of what effect Roger had made on him, or whether he had made any effect at all. 'I'm sure you wouldn't.'

CHAPTER VII

ANOTHER HOME

THE next night, Monday, Margaret and I were due to dine at the Osbaldistons'. As our taxi drew up, we could not help reflecting that it was something of a change from Basset; for the Osbaldistons lived in a house, detached, but only just detached, on the west side of Clapham Common. It might have been one of the houses I had visited as a boy, feeling that I was going up in the world, in the provincial town where I was born, the houses of minor professional men, schoolmasters, accountants, dentists.

We went up the path between two rows of privets; the front door had a panel of coloured glass, leaded, in an acanthus design, and the passage light shone pinkly through.

Inside the house, I was thinking that there was no need for Douglas Osbaldiston to live like that. The decoration and furnishing had not been changed from the fashion of the early twenties: beige wallpaper with a satin stripe and a discreet floral dado: some indifferent romantic landscapes, water-colours in wooden frames, gate-legged tables, a sideboard of fumed oak with green handles. At the top of the civil service, he could have done much better for himself. But, just as some men of Douglas's origins or mine set themselves up as country gentlemen, Douglas did the reverse. It was done out of deliberate unpretentiousness, but, as with the bogus country gentlemen, it was becoming a little of an act. When, over dinner, we told him that we had been at Basset for the weekend, he whistled cheerfully, in excellent imitation of a clerk reading the gossip columns and dreaming of social altitudes inaccessible to him. Yet Douglas knew – for he was the most clear-headed of operators – that just as he suspected that places like Basset still had too much effect on government decisions, so Diana Skidmore and her friends had an identical, and perhaps a stronger, suspicion about his colleagues and himself. Neither side was sure where the real power rested. In the great rich house, among the Christian names of the eminent, there were glances backwards, from the knowledgeable, in the direction of suburban villas such as this.

In the tiny dining-room, we were having an excellent dinner, cooked by Mary Osbaldiston: clear soup, a steak-and-kidney pie, lemon soufflé. It was much better than anything to be found at Basset. When I praised the meal, she flushed with gratification. She was a fine-featured woman, intelligent and undecorated as Douglas himself; she had no style and much sweetness. Margaret and I were fond of her, Margaret especially so, both of us knowing that they had a deprivation we had been spared. They had longed for children, and had had none.

Douglas had the pertinacity and precision of a top administrator; he wanted to know exactly why and how I had come to know Diana Skidmore. He was not in the least envious of my extra-official life; he was not asking entirely through inquisitiveness, but through needing another piece of information about how the world ticks.

He listened, with the direct concentration of a detective. Anything about business, anything that might affect Ministers, was a concern of his. In particular, when I told him about Roger's outburst, he regarded that as very much a concern of his.

'I must say,' said Douglas, 'I thought he was a cooler customer.'

His face has ceased to look like a scholar's.

'Why in God's name did he choose this time of all times to blow his top? Lord love me, we don't have much luck in our masters—'

I was saying that I thought we had been lucky in Roger, but Douglas went on:

'I suppose he did it out of chivalry. Chivalry can be an expensive luxury. Not only for him, but for the rest of us.'

His wife said that we didn't know the relations of Caro Quaife and her brother. Perhaps that was the secret.

'No,' said Douglas. 'I don't see how that could be much excuse. It was an irresponsible thing to do. I can't imagine indulging in that sort of chivalry if anything hung on it—' He grinned at his wife. It sounded bleak, but it was said with trust. Douglas knew precisely what he wanted; he was tough and, in his fashion, ruthless; he was going to the top of his own tree, and his off-hand air wasn't enough disguise; but his affections were strong, and he was a passionate man, not a cold one.

'Mind you, Lewis,' said Douglas, 'if this man Quaife gets away with this performance, he's in a very strong position. The best way to arrive is to arrive with no one to thank for it. He must know that as well as we do.'

Douglas had his full share of a man of action's optimism. The optimism which makes a gulf between men of action and purely reflective men, which makes a man insensitive to defeat until it has really happened. He was telling us that he himself had some news on the brighter side: he would cheer us up with it after we had all moved together into the 'front room'.

As soon as I heard that phrase, I was amused. To talk about the 'front room' as his mother or mine might have done, was going a bit too far in the direction of modesty, even for Douglas. This house, though small, was not as small as that, and the so-called 'front room' was in fact a study. On the desk lay a black official briefcase. Round the walls, in bookshelves which ran up to the ceiling, was packed one of the most curious collections of nineteenth- and twentieth-century novels that I had seen. Douglas allowed himself something between a luxury and an affectation. He liked to read novels in much the state in which they had first been read. So in the shelves one could find most of the classical English, Russian, American and French novels in editions and bindings not more than a few years away from their original publication.

We sat within sight and smell of those volumes, while Douglas told us the hopeful news. He was not exaggerating. The news was as promising as he had said, and more unexpected. It was – that several influences, apparently independently, were lobbying against Gilbey and for Roger. They were influences which 'had the ear' of senior Ministers, who would be bound at least to listen. The first was the aircraft industry, or that part of it represented by my old boss, Lord Lufkin, who had extended his empire since the war. The second was a group of vociferous Air Marshals. The third, more heterogeneous, consisted of scientists. Lufkin had been to see the Chancellor: a couple of Air Marshals had lunched with the Prime Minister, the scientists had been talking 'at Ministerial level'.

'It's one of the slickest campaigns I've ever seen,' said Douglas.

'Who sparked it off?'

'You won't believe it, but some of the lines seem to go back to a chap of no consequence at all.'

'Who?'

'The man Brodzinski.'

Douglas added,

'Of course, if it hadn't been him, it would have been someone else.'

Like most high-class administrators, Douglas did not believe much in personal flukes. 'But I must say, he seems to have a pretty good eye for the people who cut ice in our part of London.'

We were each working out the chances. Personality for personality, Gilbey's backers were powerful, and had the social pull: but in the long run, big business, with the military and the scientists, usually won.

'Unless he did himself in irretrievably with your very smart friends,' said Douglas with an amiable jeer, 'I bet Quaife is in the job within twelve months.'

He passed the decanter round again. Then he asked: 'Tell me, Lewis, if he does get there, have you any idea what he's going to try to do?'

I hesitated. He suspected, or had guessed, that I was in Roger's confidence. In return, I had guessed that he was not. I knew for sure that some of the forces propelling Roger into power were just the forces that, once there, he would have to fight. Douglas had said earlier that the best way to arrive was to arrive with no one to thank for it. Had he now a shrewd idea that Roger might not arrive so free?

Mary Osbaldiston had taken out a piece of needlework, a tray-cloth, or something of the kind: she was working daisies round the edge of it, with finical care. Margaret, who could not sew a stitch, remarked on it, and asked her something about the pattern: but she was not missing a word of the conversation, and her gaze flickered up in my direction.

'Look, there are some peculiar features about the situation,' Douglas pressed on. 'It isn't only Brodzinski and the wild men who are clamouring for Quaife, you know. There's your old chum, Francis Getliffe and his friends. Now whatever sleight of hand Quaife goes in for, and I fancy he's pretty good at that, he's not going to please both gangs. Tell me, do you know what he's really going to do?'

I nearly came out into the open. I had one clear and conscious reason for not doing so. I knew that Douglas, like nearly all his colleagues, was deeply conservative. He was too clever not to see the arguments for Roger's policy, but he would not like them. Yet that was not the reason which kept me quiet. There was another, so worn into me that I did not notice it was there. I had lived too long in affairs; I had been in too many situations like this, where discretion was probably the right, and certainly the easiest, course. Sometimes in the past I had got into trouble, and that had happened when I followed my impulse and blasted discretion away.

So that night it was not exactly nature, but discipline, which led to say something noncommittal. Douglas gazed at me, his face for an instant more youthful. Then he smiled, and passed the decanter over.

We made something of a night of it. In the taxi going home, Margaret, holding my hand against her cheek, said:

'You made a mistake, you know.' She went on to say that he was a man one could trust completely. She did not say, but she meant, that we all four liked each other, and that it was a mistake to deny affection. I was angry with her. I had a sharp sense of injustice, the sense of injustice which is specially sharp when one knows one is in the wrong.

CHAPTER VIII

KNIGHT ON A TOMBSTONE

IN March, three weeks after the Basset and Clapham combination, there was more news, which none of us could have allowed for. One morning at the office, Douglas Osbaldiston rang me up: Gilbey had been taken ill during the night, and they were not certain that he would live.

The story ran round Whitehall all that morning, and reached the clubs at lunch-time. It was announced in the evening papers. Everyone that I met assumed from the start, just as I did myself, that Gilbey was going to die. A friend of mine was busy adding a hundred words about Gilbey's political achievements to an account of his career.

As usual, at the prospect of a death, everyone else was a little more alive. There was a tang of excitement in the air. As usual, also, the professional conversations were already beginning: Douglas was invited to have a drink with a Cabinet Minister, Rose spent the afternoon with our own Minister, talking about a scheme for redistributing the work between the two departments. I had seen the same in a smaller world twenty years before, when I was living in my college. How many deaths mattered, really mattered, mattered like an illness of one's own, to any individual man? We pretended they did, out of a kind of biological team-spirit; in some ways, it was a valuable hypocrisy. But the real number was smaller than we dared admit.

As I heard men talking about Gilbey during the next day or two, I could not help recalling once more what Thomas Bevill, that cunning, simple old man, used to tell me was the first rule of politics: *Always be on the spot. Never go away. Never be too proud to be present.* Perhaps, after all that was only the second rule, and the first was: *Keep alive.*

Another person seemed to have a similar thought that week. That other person was Lord Gilbey. Four days after the first news, I received a telephone call from his private secretary. The rumours of the illness, came a chanting Etonian voice, were very much exaggerated. It was utter nonsense to suggest that he was dying. All that had happened was a 'minor cardiac incident'. Lord Gilbey was extremely bored, and would welcome visitors: he very much hoped that I would call upon him at the London Clinic some afternoon the following week.

A similar message, I discovered, had been sent to politicians, senior officers, Douglas Osbaldiston and Hector Rose. Rose commented: 'Well, we may have to agree that the noble Lord is not precisely a nonpareil as a departmental Minister, but we can't reasonably refuse him marks for spirit, can we?'

When I visited him at the clinic, no one could have refused him marks, though it was a spirit we were not used to. He was lying flat, absolutely immobile – the sight recalled another invalid I used to visit, my first wife's father – like the effigy of a knight on a tomb, a knight who had not gone on crusade, for his legs were thrust straight out. The bed was so high that, as I sat by its side, my face was on a level with his, and he could have whispered. He did not whisper: he enunciated, quietly, but in something like his usual modulated and faintly histrionic tone.

'This is very civil of you,' he said. 'When I'm safely out of here, we must meet somewhere pleasanter. You must let me give you dinner at the In and Out.' I said I should like it.

'I ought to be out of here in about a month. It will be another two months, though' – he added in a minatory manner, as though I had been indulging in over-optimism – 'before I'm back in the saddle again.' I replied with something banal, that that wouldn't be very long.

'I never thought I was going to die.' He did not move at all: his cheeks were beautifully shaven, his hair was beautifully trimmed. Looking at the ceiling as he asked a question, he permitted himself one change of expression: his eyes opened into incredulous circles, as he said: 'Do you know, people have sat here in this very room and asked me if I was afraid of death?'

There was the slightest emphasis on the pronoun. He went on: 'I've been close to death too often to be frightened of it now.'

It sounded ham. It was ham. He began talking about his life. He had lost most of his closest friends, his brother officers, 'on the battlefield' in the first war. Every year he had been given since, he had counted as a bonus, he said. He had seen more of the battlefield in the second war than most men of his own age. Several times he thought his hour had come. Had he enjoyed the war? I asked. Yes, of course he had enjoyed it. More than anything in life.

I asked him, after all this, what virtues did he really admire?

'That's very simple. There's only one virtue for me, when it comes down to the last things.'

'What is it, then?'

'Physical courage. I can forgive anything in a man who has it. I can never respect a man without it.'

This seemed to me at the time, and even more later, the oddest conversation I had ever had with a brave man. I had met others who took their courage as a matter of course, and who were consoling to anyone who did not come up to their standard. Not so Lord Gilbey. He was the only soldier I knew who could refer, with poetic enthusiasm, to *the battlefield*.

It occurred to me that all his life Lord Gilbey had been in search of glory. Glory in the old pre-Christian sense, glory such as the Mycenaeans and Norsemen fought for. Put him in with a shipload of Vikings, and he would have endured what they did, and boasted as much. True, he was Catholic-born: he did his religious duties, and that morning, so he had told me, he had been visited by his 'confessor'. But it was not salvation that he prayed for, it was glory.

Looking at him prostrate, so handsome, so unlined, I wondered if that was why this attack had knocked him out. It must have been – one didn't need to be a doctor to see it – graver than we had officially been told. Was it the kind of attack that comes to men who have been taught to suppress their own anxieties? No one could be less introspective; but even he must have known that he had made a mess of his political job, which needed, by a curious irony, a variety of courage which he did not begin to possess. He must certainly have known that he was being criticised, conspired against, threatened with being (in his own idiom) kicked upstairs. He had shown no sign of it. He had sat among the colleagues who thought least of him, and remained charming, vain, armoured. Probably he didn't let himself think what their opinion of him was, or what they intended. Was this the price he paid?

Next afternoon, I went to see Roger in the House. I sat in the civil servants' box, within touching distance of the government benches, while he answered a question. It was a question put down by one of the members whom Lufkin used for these purposes, to embarrass Gilbey. 'Was the Minister aware that no decision had yet been announced on—' There followed a list of aircraft projects. Roger would, in any case, have had to answer in the Commons, but with Gilbey ill, he was in acting charge of the department. The questioner pointedly, and I suspected under instructions, demonstrated that he was not making difficulties for Roger himself. When Roger gave a dead-pan, stonewalling reply, neither the member nor any of the aircraft spokesmen followed with a supplementary. There were one or two half-smiles of understanding. After question-time Roger took me along to his room. It struck me that, although I often called on him now, he almost never took me to the tea-room or the bar. I had heard it mentioned that he spent too little time in casual mateyness among crowds of members, that he was either too arrogant or too shy. It seemed strange, when he was so easy with anyone in private.

The room was cramped, unlike his stately office in the Ministry across Whitehall. Beyond the window, mock gothic, the afternoon sky was sulphurous.

I asked him if he had visited Gilbey yet. Yes, of course, he said, twice.

'What do you think?' I said.

'Don't you think he's probably lucky to be alive?'

I said yes. Then I told him what I had thought in the clinic the day before, that it might be a psychosomatic illness. Or was I psychologising too much?

'You mean, if I hadn't put on the pressure, and we'd all said he was wonderful, he might still be on his feet? You may very well be right.'

'I meant a bit more than that,' I said. 'Presuming the old man gets better and comes back to the job: then what?'

I did not need to go further. I meant, a man in Gilbey's condition oughtn't to have to live among the in-fighting. If he did, there was a finite danger that he wouldn't live at all.

Roger had missed nothing. His eyes met mine in recognition. He was smoking a cigarette, and he did not answer for a time.

'No,' he said at last, 'I'm not going to take any more responsibility than I'm bound to. This isn't very real.'

'Isn't it?'

'He's out,' said Roger, 'whatever I do now. He'll never come back.'

'Is that settled?'

'I'm sure it is,' he said. He broke off, and then asked:

'Do you want an answer to the question you're really asking?'

I said, 'Leave it.'

'I'm prepared to answer,' he said. 'I should go on regardless.'

He had been speaking without smoothness, as though he were dredging up the words. Then he said, in a brisk tone: 'But this isn't real. He's out.'

He went on, with a sarcastic smile, 'I'm sure he's out. I'm not so sure I'm in.'

'What are the chances?'

Roger answered, with matter-of-fact precision: 'Slightly better than evens. Perhaps 6–4 on.'

'Did you do yourself harm', I put in, 'at Basset? That last night?'

'I may have done.' He went on, with a baffled frown, like a short-sighted child screwing up his eyes: 'The trouble was, I couldn't do anything else.'

A couple of days later, I arrived at the London Clinic immediately after lunch. Gilbey might not have moved a millimetre in seventy-two hours. Eyes staring at the ceiling, hair shining, face unblemished. He spoke of Roger, who had visited him that morning. Affably, with friendly condescension, Gilbey told me, what I knew myself, that Roger had had a distinguished record in the last war.

'You wouldn't think it to look at him,' said Gilbey, harking back to our previous conversation. 'But he's *all right*. He's quite *all right*.'

Gilbey proceeded to talk, enjoying himself, about his own campaigns. Within a few minutes, however, he received a reminder of mortality. His secretary busily entered the quiet, the marmoreally composed sickroom, Gilbey static except for his lips, me unmoving beside him, the trees motionless in the garden outside.

'Sir,' said the secretary. He was an elegant young man with a Brigade tie.

'Green?'

'I have a telegram for you, sir.'

'Read it, my dear chap, read it.'

Since Gilbey's eyes did not alter their upward gaze, he did not know that the telegram was still unopened. We heard the rip of paper.

'Read it, my dear chap.'

Green coughed. 'It comes from an address in S.W.10 – I think that's Fulham, sir.' He gave the signatory's name. 'Someone called Porson.'

'Please read it.'

Momentarily, I caught a glance from Green's eyes, pale, strained, hare-like. He read: 'All the trumpets will sound for you on the other side.'

Just for a second, Gilbey's mouth pursed, then tightened. Very soon, the modulated voice said to the ceiling: 'How nice!'

In a voice even more careful, unemphatic, clipped and trim, he added: 'How *very* nice!'

CHAPTER IX

TWO KINDS OF ALIENATION

As soon as I could, after the telegram had been read, I said goodbye to Gilbey. I indicated to Green that I wanted a word with him outside. Nurses were passing by, the corridor was busy, it was not until we reached the waiting-room that I could let my temper go.

In the panelled room, with its copies of the *Tatler*, the *Field*, *Punch* on the console table, I said: 'Give me that telegram.'

As I glanced at it – the words shining out as though innocent of trouble – I said: 'You bloody fool!'

'What?' said Green.

'Why in God's name don't you read telegrams before you bring them in? Why hadn't you got the wit to invent something, when you saw what you'd got in front of you?'

I looked at the telegram again. Porson. It might be. In this lunacy, anything was possible. An old acquaintance of mine. For the sake of action, for the sake of doing anything. I rushed out of the room, out of the clinic, shouted for a taxi, gave the address, just off the Fulham Road.

The taxi chugged through the afternoon traffic, south-west across London. I was so angry that I did not know why I was going there. I had lost touch with my own feelings. Guilt, concern, personal fates, public ends – I hadn't the patience to think of any of them. Nothing except pushing the taxi on.

At last, after the driver had made false shots, trying squares, places, mews, we drove up a street of tall terraced houses, shabby, unpainted. In front of one, I looked at the slips of cardboard by the bells. The other names were handwritten, but against the top-floor bell was a soiled visiting card: Mr R. Porson, Barrister-at-Law.

Empty milk bottles stood on the steps. Inside the door, which was on the latch, letters and newspapers lay in the unlit hall. I climbed upstairs. On the second landing, the door of a bathroom opened, the only one, it seemed, in the house. I went up to the top floor and knocked. A thick, strident voice answered, and I entered. Yes, it was the man I used to know – years older, more than half drunk. He greeted me noisily, but I cut him short by giving him the telegram.

'Did you send this?'

He nodded.

'Why?'

'I wanted to cheer him up.'

In the attic flat, which had a skylight and a high window, Porson peered at me. 'What's the matter, old boy? You look a bit white. I insist on prescribing for you. What you need is a good stiff drink.'

'Why did you send this?'

'The poor chap hasn't got long to go. It's been all over the papers,' said Porson. 'I've got a great respect for him. We don't breed men like him nowadays. He's a bit different from all these young pansies. So I wanted him to know that some of us were thinking about him. I wasn't prepared to let him go out without anyone saying goodbye.'

Fiercely he cried out: 'Well, is there anything the matter with that?'

He lurched back into his chair. He said:

'I don't mind telling you, I don't run to telegrams unless I have to. Four bob. But I thought it was the least I could do.'

'What in Heaven's name', I shouted, 'do you imagine it was like for him—'

He was too drunk to understand. I was shouting for my own benefit alone. In time I gave it up. There was nothing to do. I accepted his drink.

'Well,' he said, examining me with a critical, patronising air, 'from all I hear, you haven't done so badly, young man. I've always insisted you'd have done better, though, if you had listened to me more in the old days.'

'What about you?' I asked.

'I've got a great many talents. You know that as well as anybody. Somehow they haven't done as much for me as they should. There's still plenty of time to pull something off. Do you realise,' he said in a threatening tone, 'that I'm only sixty-two?'

He had gone many steps down into poverty since I last saw him before the war. This tiny room, furnished with a divan bed, a table, one easy chair and one hard one, showed still the almost pernickety, aunt-like tidiness that I remembered, but it must have been the cheapest he could find. Even then, the rent must have come out of his bit of capital. So far as I knew, he had done no work for years. On the mantelpiece he kept a picture of Ann March, his symbol of unrequited love, his *princesse lointaine*. There were also photographs of two young men. In himself he looked broken-down, his face puce, flecked with broken veins. The tic down his left cheek convulsed it more than ever. Yet at some moments he appeared, and this was a resemblance to George Passant – in his expression, not only in his spirit – much younger than he was, instead of older: as though unhappiness, discontent, frustration, failure, drink, had been a preservative which made time stand still, as it could not for luckier and stabler men. All his old hatreds came boiling out, just as fresh as they had always been – the Jews, the Reds, the Pansies. He was particularly violent about the pansies, much more so than in the past. I couldn't pretend that Lord Gilbey was any of those things, could I? 'He's a man after my own heart, I insist on that,' he cried belligerently. 'Do you understand why I had to send a personal message? Because if you don't now, my boy, you never will.'

The outburst died down. He seemed glad to have me there; he took it without surprise, as though I had seen him the day before and had just called in again. In a tone both gentle and defiant he said: 'You may not believe it, but I'm very comfortable here.'

He went on: 'There are a lot of young people round this neighbourhood. I like the young. I don't care what anyone says against them, I like the young. And it's very good for them to have an older man with plenty of experience to come to for advice.'

He was impatient for me to meet them. But we had to wait until the pub opened, he said. He was restless, he stumped over to the whisky bottle several times, he kept looking at his watch. As the afternoon light edged through the high window, he got to his feet and gazed out.

'Anyway,' he said loudly, 'you can't deny that I've got a nice view.'

Porson's acquaintances came to the pub at the corner of his street, where he installed us both at the crack of opening-time. They were mostly young, not many over thirty. Some of them were living on very little; one or two might have some money from home. There were painters there, there were one or two writers and schoolteachers. They were friendly, and gave Porson what he wanted. They made him a bit of a figure. They treated me amiably, as though I were someone of their age, and I liked them. It might have been a sentimentality, the consequence of my abortive anger and this resurrection of the past in Porson, an old acquaintance become not more respectable, but considerably less so. It might have been a sentimentality, but I was speculating whether there was a higher proportion of kind faces there than in the places I nowadays spent my time. It might have been a sentimentality, and probably was. But theirs was a life which, if one has ever lived it or been close to it, never quite relinquishes its last finger-hold upon one. I could think of contemporaries of mine, middle-aged persons with a public face, who dreamed a little more often than one would think likely of escaping back to places such as this.

Some of the people in that pub seemed to live in a present which to them was ideal. They could go on, as though the future would always be like this. It was a slap-happy March evening. They kept standing Porson drinks. I was enjoying myself: and yet, at the same time, I was both softened and shadowed. I knew well enough what anyone of political insight would say, whether they were Marxists, or irregulars like Roger Quaife, or hard anti-communists from the *Partisan Review*. They would agree about the condition, though they fought about the end. They would say that there was no protest in this pub. Not that these people shared Porson's fits of crazed reaction. They had good will, but except for one or two picked causes, they could not feel it mattered. Nearly everyone there would have joined in a demonstration against hanging. Otherwise, they shrugged their shoulders, lived their lives, and behaved as though they were immortal.

Was this their version of the Basset house-party, which also talked as though there would never be a change again?

They would have had no use for Roger Quaife. To them, he would be part of an apparatus with which they had no connection, from which they were alienated, as completely as if it were the governing class of San Domingo. So was he alienated from them. How could he reach them? How could he, or any politician, find a way through?

They were not going to worry about Roger Quaife, or the scientists, or the civil servants, or anybody else who had to take a decision. They did not thank anybody for worrying about them. Yes, there were unhappy people in the pub, now it was filling up. A schoolmaster with an anxiety-ridden face, who lived alone: a girl sitting at the bar, staring with schizoid stillness at a glass of beer. For them, there were friends here prepared to worry. Even for old Porson, drunken, boastful, violent, a little mad.

I should have liked to stay. But somehow, the fact that they were so un-anxious, so island-like, had the reverse effect on me. In the noisy and youthful pub, they were rooting up a half-memory, buried somewhere in my mind. Yes! It was another evening, another part of London, Roger questioning David Rubin, the uninflected replies.

This was not the place for me. I finished my drink, said goodbye to Porson, who 'insisted' on inviting me there another time. I pushed through the crowd, affable, cordial and happy, and went out into the street, lights from the shops doubled in the moist pavements of the Fulham Road.

CHAPTER X

NEWS IN SOUTH STREET

By the early summer, gossip was bubbling and bursting. Gilbey had left the clinic and gone home. One political columnist was prophesying that he would soon be back. Elsewhere, rumours appeared that he had already accepted a government post abroad. As for his successor, names were being mentioned, Roger's usually among them, but not prominently, except in one Sunday paper.

Nearer the point of action, we were mystified. Some of the rumours we knew to be nonsense, but not all. Men like Douglas Osbaldiston and Hector Rose, or even Roger himself, were not sure where they came from. Diana Skidmore and Caro's relatives, people who made an occupation out of being in the know, could pick up nothing, or at least what they did pick up was useless. It was one of those occasions, commoner than one might think, when the 'insiders' were reading their newspapers for enlightenment as inquisitively as anyone else.

Of us all, Roger put on the most impassive front. He did his job in the office without any fuss; he answered questions in the House: he made a couple of speeches. In all this, he was behaving like a competent stand-in. As I watched him, through those weeks, I realised that he had one singular natural advantage, besides his self-control. He had the knack of appearing more relaxed, far less formidable, than he really was. One night, after a debate which Douglas and I were attending, a young member took us all to Pratt's. In the tiny parlour, round the kitchen fire, there were several hard, able faces, but Roger's was not among them. He sat there, drinking pints of beer, a heavy, clumsy man, looking amiable, idealistic, clever, simple, rather like an impressive innocent among card-sharpers. Among hard-featured faces, his stood out, full of enjoyment, full of feeling, revealing neither ambition nor strain.

One afternoon in June, I received another summons from Lord Gilbey. This time I was asked to call, so my personal assistant said, at his 'private residence'. What for? No, the invitation had come, not from Green, but from some humbler person, who was unwilling to say. Had anyone else been asked? My p.a. missed nothing. She had already rung up Hector Rose's office, and Douglas's. Each had been summoned also: Rose was busy at a meeting, Douglas was already on his way.

It was a short distance to Gilbey's, for he had a flat, one of the last in private occupation, in Carlton House Terrace. It was a short distance, but it took some time. Cars were inching, bonnet to tail, along the Mall, cars with crosses on the windscreens, on their way to a Palace garden party. It must have been a Thursday.

The flat, when I finally got there, was at the top of the building. A smart young woman came to greet me. I enquired, 'Mr Green?'

Mr Green was no longer working for Lord Gilbey.

Lady Gilbey was out for tea, but Lord Gilbey would like to see me at once. He and Douglas were standing by the drawing-room window, from which one looked, in the gusty, sparkling sunshine, right across St James's Park, across the glitter of the lake, to the towers and turrets of our offices, away above the solid summer trees. Below the roofs of cars, hurrying now the Mall was thinning, flashed their semaphores in the sun. It was a pleasant London vista: but Lord Gilbey was regarding it without enthusiasm. He welcomed me gracefully, but he did not smile.

He moved to a chair. As he walked, and as he sat down, he seemed to be deliberating how each muscle worked. That must have been the result of his illness, automatic now. Otherwise he had forgotten it, he was pre-occupied with chagrin and etiquette.

'Sir Hector Rose isn't able to join us, I hear,' he said, with distant courtesy. 'I should be grateful if you would give him my regrets. I wanted to speak to some of you people who have been giving me advice. I've already spoken to some of my colleagues.' He gazed at us, immaculate, fresh-faced, sad. 'I'd rather you heard it from me first,' he went on. 'I don't suppose you'll believe it, but this morning, just before luncheon, I had a letter from the Prime Minister.'

Suddenly he broke out: 'He ought to have come himself. He *ought* to have!'

He lifted a hand carefully, as though not exerting himself too jerkily, and pointed out of the window in the direction of Downing Street.

'It's not very far,' he said. 'It's not *very* far.'

Another aspect of etiquette struck him, and he went on:

'I must say it was a very decent letter. Yes. It was a decent letter, I have to give him that.'

Neither of us knew when to begin condoling. It was some while before Gilbey got to the bare facts. At last he said:

'The long and the short of it is, they're getting rid of me.'

He turned his gaze, absently, from Douglas to me: 'Do you know, I really can't believe it.' He was having fugues, as we have all done, under the impact of bad news, in which the bad news hadn't happened and in which he was still planning his return to the department. I knew well enough what such fugues were like. Then the truth broke through again.

'They haven't even told me who my successor is going to be. They ought to have asked my advice. They ought to have.'

He looked at us: 'Who is it going to be?'

Douglas said none of us knew.

'If I believed what I saw in the papers,' said Gilbey, outrage too much for him, 'they're thinking of replacing a man like me' – very slowly he raised his right hand just above the height of his shoulder – 'by a man like Grigson.' This time his left hand descended carefully, palm outwards, below his knee.

He got on to a more cheerful topic. 'They' (after his first complaint he could not bring himself to refer to the Prime Minister in the singular, or by name) had offered him a 'step-up' in the peerage. 'It's civil of them, I suppose.'

It was the only step-up the Gilbeys had had since they were ennobled in the eighteenth century, when one of them, a Lancashire squire, had married the daughter of a wealthy slave-trader. 'Rascals. Awful rascals,' said Lord Gilbey, with the obscure satisfaction that came over him as he meditated on his origins. When anyone else meditated so, he did not feel the same satisfaction. I had heard him comment on a scholarly work which traced the connection of some English aristocratic families with the African slave-trade – 'I should have thought,' he had said in pain, 'that that kind of thing is rather *unnecessary*.'

Gilbey was dwelling on the consequences of the step-up. Place in ceremonies, change in the robes? 'I don't suppose I shall see another coronation, but you never know. I'm a great believer in being prepared.'

Gilbey was lonely, and we stayed for another half-hour. When at last we left, he said that he proposed to attend the Lords more regularly, not less. 'They can do with an eye on them, you know.' His tone was simple and embittered.

Out in the open, crossing the path beside the park, Douglas, black hat pulled down, gave a grin of surreptitious kindness. Then he said: 'That's that.'

Ministers came, Ministers went. On his side, Douglas wouldn't have expected his Minister to mourn for him if he were moved to a dim job, or rejoice if he clambered back to the Treasury.

'Now perhaps,' he said, 'we can get down to serious business.'

He did not speculate on who would get Gilbey's job. He might have been holding off, in case I knew more than I actually did. Whereas in fact, the moment I regained my own office, I rang up Roger and was asked to go round at once. He was in his Whitehall room, not across the way. When I got there, I looked at the clock. It was just after half past four.

'Yes,' said Roger, sitting loose and heavy behind his desk, 'I know all about it.'

'Have you heard anything?'

'Not yet.' He added evenly: 'Unless I hear tonight, of course, it's all gone wrong.'

I did not know whether that was true, or whether he was placating fate by getting ready for the worst.

'I didn't go to the House this afternoon. I thought that was asking a bit much.'

He gave a sarcastic grin, but I thought he was playing the same trick.

He would not mention his plans, or the future, or any shape or aspect of politics at all. We talked on, neither of us interested, finding it hard to spin out the time, with the clock ticking. A man from his private office came in with a file. 'Tomorrow,' said Roger roughly. As a rule he was polite with his subordinates.

Through the open window came the chimes of Big Ben. Half past five.

'This is getting a bit rough,' said Roger.

I asked if he wouldn't have a drink. He shook his head without speaking.

At nineteen minutes to six – I could not help but watch the clock – the telephone buzzed. 'You answer it,' said Roger. For an instant his nerve had frayed.

I heard an excited voice from his own office. The call was from Number 10. Soon I was speaking to the Prime Minister's principal private secretary, and passed the telephone to Roger.

'Yes,' said Roger, 'I can come along. I'll be with you at six.'

He looked at me without expression.

'This looks like it,' he remarked. 'I don't know, there may be a catch in it yet.'

I took a taxi home, with the whole afternoon's story, except for the dénouement, ready to tell Margaret. But she was dressed ready to go out, and laughing at me because my news was stale. Diana Skidmore had been tracking the day's events and had rung Margaret up, asking us round for drinks at her house in South Street.

Park Lane was full of party frocks, morning suits, grey top hats, those who had stuck out the royal garden party to an end and were now humbly walking to buses and tubes. One or two top hats and frocks turned, a little less humbly, into South Street, and into Diana's house.

It was, by the standards of Basset, small, the rooms high but narrow;

yet, because it was more crowded with valuable objects, gave an even greater sense of opulence, opulence compressed, each of its elements within arm's reach. At Basset, one could walk by a bank of flowers between one precious acquisition and the next: space itself gave some effect of simplicity, of open air. But here in South Street, despite Diana's efforts, the effect was not unlike that of an auctioneer's saleroom or a display of wedding-presents.

When Margaret and I arrived, Diana, with an air of concentrated sincerity, was explaining to a guest what an extremely small house it was. She was giving her explanation with a depth of architectural expertness which I didn't know she possessed: which she hadn't possessed until a month or two before. It sounded as though she had passed from the influence of her musician towards the influence of an architect, and got delight out of showing it off – just as a young girl, first in love, gets delight out of mentioning the man's name.

It was very foolish, I felt sometimes in the presence of Diana, to imagine that worldly people were cynical. Born worldlings, like herself, were not in the least cynical. They were worldlings just because they weren't, just because they loved the world.

Seeing Margaret and me, Diana slid her guest on to another group, and became her managing self, all nonsense swept away. Yes, she had found out that Roger was with the Prime Minister. He and Caro had been invited to come when they could, and if they felt like it.

'No one in politics here,' said Diana briskly. 'Is that right?'

She wasn't going to expose them, if the prize had been snatched away at the end.

We mingled among the party, most of them rich and leisured. Probably the majority had not so much as heard of Roger Quaife. Margaret and I were sharing the same thought, as we caught each other's eye: he ought to be here by now. I noticed that Diana, who did not easily get worried, had taken an extra drink.

Then they came, Caro on one side of Roger, and on the other her brother Sammikins, all of them tall, Roger inches taller than the other man, and stones heavier. We had only to look at Caro to know the answer. She was glowing with pleasure, with disrespectful pleasure, that she wanted to cast over us all. They each took a glass of champagne on their way towards us.

'That's all right,' Roger said. It sounded unconcerned, in the midst of kisses and handshakes. It sounded ludicrously tight-lipped. A stranger might have thought he looked the same as he had looked a couple of hours before. Yet, beneath a social smile, reserved, almost timid, his eyes were lit up, the lines round his mouth had settled – as though triumph were suffusing him and it was a luxury not to let it out. Beneath the timid smile, he gave an impression both savage and youthful. He was a man, I was thinking, who was not too opaque to suffer his sorrows or relish his victories.

'The old boy hasn't done too badly, has he?' said Caro to Margaret. Sammikins was trumpeting with laughter.

At close quarters he looked like an athlete, light on his feet with animal spirits. He had eyes like Caro's, large, innocent and daring. He had her air, even more highly developed, of not giving a damn. He showed more open delight at Roger's appointment than anyone there. Talking to me, he was enumerating in a resounding voice all the persons whom it would most displease.

Joining our group, Diana was avid for action. 'Look,' she said to Roger, 'I want to give you a real party. We can clear the decks here and lay it on for later tonight. Or have it tomorrow. Which would you like?'

Sammikins would have liked either. So would Caro, but she was looking at Roger.

Slowly he shook his head. He smiled diffidently at Diana, thanked her, and then said: 'I don't think it's the right time.'

She returned his smile, as though she had a soft spot for him, not just a political hostess's. With a rasp, she asked: 'Why isn't it the right time?'

'There have been thousands of Cabinet Ministers before me. Most of them didn't deserve a party.'

'Oh, rubbish. You're you. And I want to give a party for *you*.'

He said: 'Wait till I've done something.'

'Do you mean that?' cried Diana.

'I'd much rather you waited.'

She did not press him any further. Somehow she, and the rest of us, partly understood, or thought we did. What he said might have been priggish. It was not that, so much as superstitious. Just as he had been placating fate in his own office, so, in a different fashion, the job in his hands, he was doing now. It was the superstitiousness of a man in spiritual training, who had set himself a task, who could not afford to let himself be softened, who was going to feel he had wasted his life unless he brought it off.

PART TWO

'IN THE PALM OF MY HAND'

CHAPTER XI

INTRODUCTION OF AN OUTSIDER

ONCE or twice during the next few months, I found myself wondering whether Roger and his associates would qualify for a word in the history books. If so, what would the professionals make of them? I did not envy the historians the job. Of course there would be documents. There would be only too many documents. A good many of them I wrote myself. There were memoranda, minutes of meetings, official files, 'appreciations', notes of verbal discussions. None of these was faked.

And yet they gave no idea, in many respects were actually misleading, of what had really been done, and, even more, of what had really been intended. That was true of any documentary record of events that I had seen. I supposed that a few historians might make a strong guess as to what Roger was like. But how was a historian going to reach the motives of people who were just names on the file, Douglas Osbaldiston, Hector Rose, the scientists, the back-bench M.P.s? There would be no evidence left. But those were the men who were taking part in the decisions and we had to be aware of their motives every day of our lives.

There was, however, another insight which we didn't possess, and which might come easily to people looking back on us. In personal terms we knew, at least partially, what we were up to. Did we know in social terms? What kind of social forces were pushing together men as different as Roger, Francis Getliffe, Walter Luke, and the rest of us? What kind of social forces could a politician like Roger draw upon? In our particular society, were there any? Those were questions we might ask, and occasionally did: but it was in the nature of things that we shouldn't have any way of judging the answers, while to a future observer they would stand out, plain as platitudes.

One peaceful summer afternoon, soon after he had taken office, Roger had called some of the scientists into his room. Once, when he was off-guard, I had heard him say at Pratt's that he had only to open his door to find *four knights* wanting something from him. There they all were, but there were more than four, and this time he wanted something from them. He was setting up a committee for his own guidance, he said. He was just asking them for a forecast about nuclear armaments to cover the next ten years. He wanted conclusions as brutal as they could manage to make them. They could work as invisibly as they liked. If they wanted Lewis Eliot as convener or adviser at any time, they could have him. But above all, they had got to take the gloves off. He was asking them for naked opinions, and he was asking for them by October.

Deliberately – it was part of his touch with men like these – he had let the blarney dissolve away. He had spoken as harshly as any of them. He looked round the table, where the faces stood out, moulded in the diffused sunlight. On his right, Walter Luke, who had just become the chief scientist of Roger's department, tough, cube-headed, prematurely grey. Then Francis: then Sir Laurence Astill, smooth-faced, contented with himself: then Eric Pearson, scientific adviser to my own department, youthful and cocky, like a bright American undergraduate: three more, drawn in from the universities, like Francis and Astill, and so back to me.

Walter Luke grinned. He said: 'Well, as H.M.G. pays me my keep, I've got to play, haven't I? There's no need to ask me. It's what these chaps say that counts.' He pointed a stiff, strong arm at Astill and the others. As his reputation for scientific management grew, his manners had become more off-hand.

'Sir Francis,' said Roger, 'you'll come in?'

Francis hesitated. He said: 'Minister, of course it's an honour to be asked—'

'It's not an honour,' said Roger, 'it's an intolerable job. But you can bring more to it than most men.'

'I should really rather like to be excused—'

'I don't think I can let you. You've had more experience than any of us.'

'Minister, believe me, everyone here knows all that I know—'

'I can't accept that,' said Roger.

Francis hesitated again; courteously, but with a frown, he said: 'There doesn't seem any way out, Minister. I'll try to do what I can.'

It sounded like the familiar minuet, as though no one would have been more disappointed than Francis if he had been taken at his word. But that was the opposite of the truth. Other men, wanting flattery or a job, talked about their consciences. Francis was one of the few whom conscience drove. He was a radical through conscience, not through rebellion. He had always had to force himself into personal struggles. He would have liked to think that for him they were all over.

Just over eighteen months before, he had puzzled his friends at our old college. They assumed that he would be a candidate for the Mastership, and they believed that they could get him elected. At the last moment, he had refused to stand. The reason he gave was that he wanted all his time for his research, that he was having the best ideas of his life. I believed that was part of the truth, but not all. His skin was becoming paper-thin as he grew older. He had wanted the Mastership, but he knew he had enemies in the college. I fancied that he could not face being talked about, the gossip and the malice.

Incidentally, instead of electing my old friend Arthur Brown, the college astonished everyone outside, and a good few inside also. They had managed to choose G. S. Clark, and the college was becoming more factious than anyone could remember.

All Francis now wanted for himself was to live in Cambridge, to spend long days in his laboratory, to watch, with worried, disapproving love, how his second and favourite daughter was getting on with an American research student. He flinched away from more struggles. That afternoon, as he said yes, he felt nothing but trapped.

Sir Laurence Astill was speaking firmly: 'If in your judgment, Minister, you feel that I have a contribution to make, then I shall consider myself obliged to accept.'

'That's very good of you,' said Roger.

'Though how you expect us to fit in these various kinds of service and look after our departments at the same time—' Sir Laurence had not finished. 'Some time I'd like a word with you, on the position of the senior university scientist in general.'

'Any time,' said Roger.

Sir Laurence nodded his head with satisfaction. He liked being in the company of Ministers: talk with Ministers was big stuff. Just as Francis was sated with the high political world, Astill was insatiable.

The others, without fuss, agreed to serve. Then Roger came to what, in his mind and mine, was the point of the meeting. What he was going to suggest, we had agreed between ourselves. I was as much behind it as he was; later on, I had to remind myself of that. 'Now that we've got a committee together, and a quite exceptionally strong one,' said Roger, blandishment coming into his tone for the first time that afternoon, 'I should like to know what you'd all feel if I added another member.'

'Minister?' said Astill acquiescently.

'I'm bringing it up to you, because the man I'm thinking of does present some problems. That is, I know he doesn't see eye to eye with most of us. He might easily make you waste a certain amount of time. But I have a strongish feeling that it might be worth it.'

He paused and went on: 'I was thinking of Michael Brodzinski.'

Faces were impassive, the shut faces of committee men. After an interval, Astill took the lead. 'I think I can probably speak for our colleagues, Minister. Certainly I should have no objection to working with Dr Brodzinski.'

Astill liked agreeing with a Minister. This wasn't time-serving, it wasn't even self-seeking: it was just that Astill believed that Ministers were likely to be right. 'I dare say we shall have our points of difference. But no one has ever doubted that he is a man of great scientific quality. He will have his own contribution to make.'

Someone said, in a low voice – was it Pearson? – 'If you can't beat them, join them. But this is the other way round.'

The other academics said that they could get on with Brodzinski. Francis was looking at his watch, as though anxious to be back in Cambridge. He said: 'Minister, I agree with the rest. I'm inclined to think that he'd be more dangerous outside than in.'

'I'm afraid that doesn't quite represent my attitude,' said Astill.

'Still,' Roger said, 'you're quite happy about it, Astill?'

'I'm not. I think you're all wrong,' Walter Luke burst out. 'As bloody wrong as you can be. I thought so when I first heard this idea, and I think so now.'

Everyone looked at him. I said quietly, 'I've told you, we can watch him—'

'Look here,' said Walter, 'you're all used to reasonable ways of doing business, aren't you?'

No one replied.

'You're all used to taking people along with you, aren't you?'

Again, silence.

'So am I, God help me. Sometimes it works, I grant you that. But do you think it's going to work in anything as critical as this?'

Someone said we had to try it.

'You're wiser old bastards than I am,' said Walter, 'but I can't see any good coming out of it.'

The whole table was stirring with impatience. Walter's outburst had evoked the group-sense of a meeting. Francis, Astill, everyone there, wanted him to stop. Technical insight they all gave him credit for; but not psychological insight. He gave himself no credit for it, either. Battered-looking he might be, but he still often thought of himself as younger than he was. That strain of juvenility, of deliberate juvenility – for he was proud of this, and in his heart despised the 'wise old bastards' – took away the authority with which he might have spoken that afternoon.

Roger was regarding him with hard eyes.

'Would you take the responsibility, if I gave you your head and left Brodzinski outside?'

'I suppose so,' Walter said.

Roger said: 'You needn't worry. I'm going to overrule you.'

A week later, at the same place, at the same time, Michael Brodzinski was making his first appearance on the committee. The others were standing round, before the meeting, when a secretary came to tell me that Brodzinski had arrived. I went out to welcome him, and, before we had shaken hands, just from the joyful recognition on his face, I was certain that he had received some account of the first discussion, that he knew I was partly responsible for getting him there, and so gave me his trust.

I led him into Roger's room. Approaching the knot of scientists, who were still standing, Brodzinski looked a powerful hulk. He was much the most heavily muscled of them, more so than Walter, who was a strong man.

Once more I was certain that he had heard precisely how he had been discussed. 'Good afternoon, Sir Laurence,' he said to Astill, with great politeness and qualified trust. To Francis Getliffe the politeness was still great, the trust more qualified. To Walter the politeness became extreme, the politeness of an enemy.

Roger called out a greeting. It was a hearty, banal bit of cordiality, something like how grateful Roger was to have his help. At once Brodzinski left Walter, and listened as though he were receiving a citation. With his splendid, passionate, luminous eyes, he was looking at Roger as more than a supporter, as something like a saviour.

CHAPTER XII

AN EVEN BET

TWICE that month, I was invited out by Caro's brother. It seemed a little taxing, but on the second occasion, when my wife was staying with her sister, I said yes. It seemed more taxing still, face to face with Sammikins –

a name I found increasingly unsuitable for this loud-voiced, untameable man – in one of the military clubs.

He had given me dinner, and a good one. Then, sitting in the library, under the oil-paintings of generals of the Crimean war, the Mutiny, fierce-looking generals of the late-Victorian peace, we had gone on to the port. I was lying back relaxed in my chair. Opposite me, Sammikins sat straight up, wild and active as a hare. He was trying to persuade me to bet.

It might have been because he couldn't resist it. Earlier that evening he had been inviting me to a race-meeting. Like his sister, he owned race-horses, and he thought it was unnatural, he thought I was holding something back, when I professed boredom in the presence of those romantic animals. But if I wouldn't bet on horses, surely I would on something else? He kept making suggestions, with manic loud-voiced glee. It might have been just the addiction. Or it might have been that he was provoked by anyone like me. Here was I, years older, my manner restrained by the side of his (which didn't differentiate me too sharply from most of the human race). Did he want to prove that we weren't all that unlike?

I took him on. I said that, if we were going to bet, he had one advantage; he was, at any rate potentially, richer than I was. I also had an advantage: I understood the nature of odds, and I doubted if he did. If I were ready to bet, it was going to be on something which gave us each precisely an even chance.

'Done,' he said.

Finally we settled that Sammikins should order more glasses of port, and afterwards not touch the bell again. Then, for the period of the next half-hour, we would mark down the number of times the waiter's bell was rung. He would bet on an odd number, I on even. How much? he said.

'Ten pounds,' I replied.

Sammikins put his watch on the table between us. We agreed on the starting and finishing time, and watched the second hand go round. As it came up to the figure twelve, Sammikins cried: 'They're off!'

On a sheet of club writing-paper, I kept the score. There were only half a dozen men in the library, one of whom kept sniffing in an irritated fashion at Sammikins's barks of laughter. The only likely source of orders appeared to be a party of three senior officers. Immediately after the start, they rang for the waiter, and I heard them asking for large whiskies all round. With decent luck, I was reckoning, they ought to manage another.

Watching them with bold, excited eyes, Sammikins, who knew two of them, discussed their characters. I was embarrassed in case his voice should carry. Like his sister's, his judgments were simple and direct. He had much more insight than staider men. He told stories about those two in the last war. He liked talking about the military life. Why hadn't he stayed in the army? I asked him. Yes, he had loved it, he said. With his fierce, restless look, he added that he couldn't have stood being a peace-time officer. It occurred to me that, in different times, he might have been happy as a soldier of fortune.

No, he couldn't have stood being a peace-time officer, he said: any more than he could stand the thought of keeping up the estate when his father died.

'I suppose,' said Sammikins, with a laugh loud even for him, 'that I shall have to dodder about in the Lords. How would you like that? Eh?'

He meant, that he would detest it. He was speaking, as usual, the naked truth. Though it didn't seem to fit him, he had all his family's passion, which Caro shared, for politics. No one could possibly have less of a political temperament than Sammikins: yet he loved it all. He loved the House of Commons, it didn't matter how many enemies he made there. He was talking about his party's leaders, with the same devastating simplicity with which he had talked about the generals, but with his eyes popping with excitement. He didn't think any better of the politicians, but they entranced him more.

One of the generals pressed the button by the fireplace, and the waiter came in. Sixteen minutes had passed. They ordered another round. I made a stroke on the writing-paper and smiled.

'Soaking,' said Sammikins, who was not a specially abstemious man, with disapproval.

No movement from anyone else in the room. The man whom Sammikins's laugh made wretched, was reading a leather-bound volume, another was writing a letter, another gazing critically at a glossy magazine.

'They want stirring up,' said Sammikins, in a reproving tone. But he was surveying the room with a gambler's euphoria. He began speaking of the last appointment of a junior Minister – who was Roger's Parliamentary Secretary, occupying the job which Roger had filled under Gilbey.

'He's no good,' said Sammikins. The man's name was Leverett-Smith. He was spoken of as a safe appointment, which to Sammikins meant that there was no merit in it.

'He's rich,' I said.

'No, he's pretty well-off, that's all.'

It occurred to me that Sammikins did not have an indifference which, in my provincial youth, we should have expected of him. Romantically, we used to talk about the aristocratic contempt for money. Sammikins was rough on ordinary bourgeois affluence: but he had no contempt at all for money, when, as with Diana Skidmore, there was enough of it.

'He's no good,' cried Sammikins. 'He's just a boring little lawyer on the make. He doesn't want to do anything, blast him, he doesn't even want the power, he's just pushing on, simply to puff himself up.'

I suspected that Leverett-Smith had been put in as a counterweight to Roger, who scarcely knew him and had been consulted only in form. I said that such men, who didn't threaten anyone and who were in politics for the sake of the charade (for I believed Sammikins was right there), often went a long way.

'So do clothes-moths,' said Sammikins, 'that's what he is – a damned industrious clothes-moth. We've got too many of them, and they'll do us in.'

Sammikins, who had a store of unlikely information, most of which turned out to be accurate, had two addenda on Leverett-Smith. A, that he and his wife were only keeping together for social reasons, B. that she had been a protégée of Lord ——, who happened to be a *voyeur*. Then, with an insistence that I didn't understand, he returned to talking of government appointments, as though he had appointments on the brain. At that moment, when twenty-seven minutes had gone, I saw with surprise and chagrin one of the generals get up with long, creaking movements of the legs, and go to the bell.

'Put down one more, Lewis,' cried Sammikins, with a cracking laugh, 'three! That's an odd number, you know.'

The waiter was very quick. The general called for three pints of bitter, in tankards.

'That's a very good idea.' Sammikins gave another violent laugh. He looked at the watch. Twenty-nine minutes had passed, the second hand was going round.

'Well,' he said, staring at me, bold and triumphant.

I heard a sniff from close by. With a glance of hate towards Sammikins, the man who had been registering protest about his noisiness, soberly put a marker into his book, closed it, and went towards the bell.

'Twenty seconds to spare,' I said. 'My game, I think.'

Sammikins swore. Like any gambler I had ever known, he expected to make money out of it. It didn't seem an addiction so much as a process of interior logic. Both he and Caro lost hundreds a year on their horses, but they always thought of them as a business which would pull round. However, he had to write me out a cheque, while his enemy and bane, in a gravelly voice, still with a hostile glare at Sammikins, ordered a glass of tonic water.

Without any preamble, his cheque passed over to me, Sammikins said:

'The trouble with Roger is, he can't make up his mind.'

For an instant I was at a loss, as though I had suddenly got mixed up in a different conversation.

'That's why I've been chasing you,' he said, so directly, so arrogantly, so innocently, that it didn't seem either flattering or unflattering: it just sounded like, and was, the bare truth.

'That's what I wanted to talk to you about.'

By now I was ready for anything, but not for what he actually said. Noisily he asked me: 'Roger hasn't picked his P.P.S. yet, has he?'

It was a question to which I had not given a thought. I assumed that Roger would choose one of a dozen young back-benchers, glad to get their first touch of recognition.

'Or has he, and we haven't heard?' Sammikins insisted.

I said I had not heard the matter so much as mentioned.

'I want the job,' said Sammikins.

I found myself curiously embarrassed. I didn't want to meet his eyes, as though I had done something shady. Didn't he realise that he was a public figure? Didn't he realise that he would be a political liability? A good many people admired his devil-may-care, but not the party bosses or other solid men. No politician in his senses would want him as an ally, much less as a colleague, least of all Roger, who had to avoid all rows except the big ones.

I thought that I had better try to speak openly myself.

'He's taken one big risk for you already,' I said.

I was reminding him of the time Roger had defended him in Collingwood's face.

Yes, he knew all about that. 'He's a good chap,' said Sammikins. 'He's a damned clever chap, but I tell you, I wish he could make up his mind.'

'Has Caro told you anything?'

'What the hell can she tell me? I expect she's doing her best.' He took it for granted that she was persuading Roger on his behalf, working for him as she had done all their lives. I wondered whether she was. She must know that she would be doing her husband harm.

'She knows what I want. Of course she's doing her best,' he said with trust, with dismissive trust. It was a younger brother's feeling – with all the responsibility and most of the love on the sister's side.

'I want the job,' said Sammikins, speaking like a man who is saying his last word.

It was not his last word, however. In his restless fashion, he arranged for us to go round to Lord North Street for a night-cap, shamelessly hoping that his presence would act like blackmail. As he drove me in his Jaguar – it was getting late, Piccadilly was dark and empty under the trees, even after a vinous night he was a beautiful driver – he repeated his last word. Yes, he wanted the job. Listening to him as he went on talking, I was puzzled that he wanted it so much. True, he might be tired of doing nothing. True, his entire family assumed that political jobs were theirs by right, without any nonsense about qualifications. They were not intellectuals, he had scarcely heard intellectual conversation in his life, but since he was a child he had breathed day by day politics in the air, he had heard the familiar, authoritative gossip about who's in, who's out, who's going to get this or that. But it still seemed strange: here was the humblest of ambitions, and all his energies were fixed on it.

In Caro's drawing-room, he did not get a yes or no, or even an acknowledgment of suspense. Caro knew why he was there; she was protective, but gave nothing away. Roger also knew why he was there. He was friendly and paternal, himself having a kind of tenderness for Sammikins. Roger was skilled in keeping off the point, and even Sammikins was over-awed enough not to force it. Watching the three of them – Caro looked flushed and pretty, but subdued, and was drinking more than usual – I thought I could guess what had happened. I believed she had, in fact, mentioned Sammikins's hopes to Roger, full of the sneaking shame with which one tries to pull off something for a child one loves, and knows to be unsuited. I didn't think that she had pressed Roger: and I didn't think that he had told her that the idea was mad.

All the time, Roger was certain of what he was going to do. He did it within a week of Sammikins's – blackmail? appeal? It looked prosaic. Roger appointed Mrs Henneker's son-in-law, Tom Wyndham, who at the dinner-party when Roger was interrogating David Rubin had protested about the American scientists 'kicking us downstairs'. It was a commonplace choice: it was also a cool one.

Roger knew, as bleakly as anyone, that Tom Wyndham was a stupid man. That didn't matter. Roger was securing his base. He had calculated the forces against him – the Air Staff, the aircraft industry, the extreme right of his own party, some of the forces which had helped him into power, as Douglas Osbaldiston, another cool analyst, had pointed out in his own 'front room'.

Roger was making sure of his own forces, and one of them was the Admiralty. It was good tactics, he had decided, to get 'channels', private 'channels', to them from the start. That was where Wyndham came in. He had been a naval officer himself, his mother-in-law would have her uses. It was worth while making sure of your potential friends, said Roger. As a rule you couldn't win over your enemies, but you could lose your friends.

The more I saw of him, the sharper-edged he seemed. Now that he was making his first decisions, in private he threw off some of the tricks and covers of his personality, as though they had been an overcoat. When I saw him so, I thought we had a chance.

One morning, though, he did not seem sharp-edged at all. He was wearing a morning-coat, grey waistcoat, striped trousers. He was absent-mindedly nervous. I had watched him when he was anxious, but in nothing like this state. I asked him what was the matter. When I heard the answer, I thought he was joking. He was going to the Palace that morning – to have an audience with the Queen, and to be sworn into the Privy Council.

I had seen dignitaries, industrialists, academics, waiting in the queue at a Palace investiture, with their hands shaking, as though, when they entered into the Presence, they expected some sinister courtier to put out a foot and trip them up. It seemed absurd that Roger should feel as frightened in the shadow of *mana*. It was easy to feel with him as a detached modern soul – while in fact he concealed a romantic, or better, a superstitious, yearning for an older world. It was not for show, nor for propriety's sake, that he was a church-goer. When I asked him why he was a Tory, he had given me a rationalisation, and a good one; but he had left an obstinate part of his nature out of it. It was not an accident, perhaps, that he married into a family with an historic name: or at least, when he first met Caro, her name had its own magic for him.

He was fond of laughing off those who were in politics simply for the sake of the charm of government, of the charm of being in the inner circle. Sammikins's 'charade', the charmed circle – people who were lured by it, said Roger, were useless, and he was right. But, for him, there may have been another charm, deeper, subtler, less rational than that.

I felt relieved when he came back from the Palace, looking jaunty again, and produced brisk plans about how we might seduce Lord Lufkin away from the rest of the aircraft industry.

CHAPTER XIII

IN HONOUR OF LORD LUFKIN

THAT summer, Roger judged that we were doing a little better than we had calculated. As carefully as a competent intelligence officer, he was keeping track of his enemies. Not that they were enemies yet, in any personal sense: so far he had fewer of them than most politicians. The 'enemies' he watched were those who, just because of what they wanted, or because of the forces behind them, could not help trying to stop him.

About those, he was as realistic as a man could be. Yet, like most realistic men, he detested having the hard truth brought to him by another. I had to tell him, early in the scientists' series of meetings, that Brodzinski was not budging by an inch. It was news we had both feared, but for an afternoon Roger regarded me as though I were an enemy myself.

Soon he was in action again. Before the House rose in July, he had talked to the party's defence committee, which meant fifty back-bench members, some of whom he knew were already disquieted. Right from the beginning, he had made his calculation. He could live with disquiet on the extreme right, in the long run it would boil over: but if he lost the solid centre of his own party, then he was finished. So he talked – in what language I didn't know, though I could guess – to the respectable county members, the 'Knights of the Shire'. According to Wyndham, who was moved to unusual lyricism, the meeting went 'like a dream'.

During August, Roger asked Osbaldiston to convene a group of top civil servants, to get some administrative machinery ready in time for the scientists' report. Since this was an inter-departmental group, and Rose was the senior member, it met in his room. A vase of chrysanthemums on the desk, as usual, the window open on to the park, as usual, and as usual Rose welcoming us with a courtesy so exaggerated that it sounded faintly jeering.

'My dear Douglas, how extremely good of you to spare the time! My dear Lewis, how very good of you to come!' Since my office, since I moved up the hierarchy, was now about ten yards away, and since the summons was official, it was not in fact a benevolent exertion on my part.

As we sat round the table, Rose's opposite numbers in the service departments, Douglas, a Second Secretary from the Treasury, and me, Rose was just perceptibly tart. He didn't mean this to be a long meeting. He was irritated at having to hold it at all. He did not indulge his mood.

He merely said: 'I take it that we've all seen Lewis Eliot's memorandum on the scientists' first few meetings, haven't we? I believe they've been instructed to report to your Minister by October, Douglas, or have I got that wrong?'

'Quite right,' said Douglas.

'In that case, I'm obliged to confess that, in the meantime, even this distinguished gathering can only hope to produce a marginal result,' said Rose. 'We don't know what they're going to say. Nor, unless I seriously misjudge our scientific colleagues, do they. All that we can be reasonably certain about, is that they can be relied upon to say several different and probably contradictory things.'

There were grins. Rose was not alone in that room in having a generalised dislike of scientists.

'No, Hector, we can go a bit further than that,' said Douglas, neither piqued nor overborne. 'My master isn't asking you to do anything quite useless.'

'My dear Douglas, I should be the last person to suggest that your admirable department, or your admirable Minister, could ever ask anyone such a thing.'

Rose found it hard to forget that Douglas had once been a junior civil servant, working under him.

'Right,' said Douglas. 'I agree we shan't actually receive the report until October, but—'

'By the way,' Rose broke in, getting down to business, 'I take it there are remote chances we shall get the report by then?'

'We ought to,' I said.

'But before it comes along, we've got a pretty shrewd idea what it's going to say, in general terms. This paper' – Douglas tapped it – 'gives us enough. Some of the scientists are producing arguments at one extreme, and some at the other. There's this chap Brodzinski, and you ought to know that he's got some backers, who's trying to push us into investing a very sizeable fraction of our defence budget, and an even higher fraction of our total scientific manpower, in this pet scheme of his. I ought to say, and Lewis will correct me if I'm wrong, that none of the scientists, even those who think he's a national danger, have ever suggested this scheme is airy-fairy.'

They had studied the first estimates of the cost. Several would have liked to believe in the scheme. They had, though, to shake their heads. The Air Ministry man said his department wished for an opportunity of 'another look at it', and Rose said:

'Of course, my dear Edgar, of course. But I'm afraid we should all be mildly surprised if your ingenious friends can really persuade us that we can afford the unaffordable.'

'That's our view,' said Douglas. 'It's just not on.'

Someone, who was taking notes of the meeting, wrote a few words. Nothing more formal was said, and there was no formal decision. From that moment, however, it would have been innocent to think that Brodzinski's scheme stood a good chance.

Douglas said, 'The other extreme view – and this isn't such an easy one – is that the country hasn't got the resources, and won't have within foreseeable time, to have any genuine kind of independent weapon at all. That is, we shan't be able to make do without borrowing from the Americans: and the scientists think the balance of advantage is for us to be honest and say so, and slide out of the nuclear weapons business as soon as we conveniently can. As I said, this is the other extreme. But I ought to say that it seems to be held by chaps who are usually level-headed, like Francis Getliffe and our scientific adviser, Walter Luke.'

'No,' said Rose, 'this isn't such an easy one. They know as well as we do that this isn't just a scientific decision. It's an economic decision, and, I should have thought, even more a political one.'

Rose was speaking carefully. He knew precisely what Douglas was aiming at. Rose had not yet declared himself, but he was inclined to think that Douglas was right. Not that he liked him. Douglas was tipped to have the final professional success denied to himself, and he was envious. But liking mattered less than one might have thought, in these alliances.

Douglas, tilting back his chair like an undergraduate, speaking with his casual, lethal relevance, was arguing that the Luke–Getliffe view also wasn't really 'on'. Furthermore, it might be attractive to the public, and we ought to be prepared to 'damp it down'. It might be a practicable policy ten or fifteen years ahead, but it wasn't a practicable policy now. The scientists thought it was easy to find absolute solutions; there weren't any. None of the great world pundits, no one in the world – for once Douglas showed a trace of irritation – knew the right way, or whether there was a way at all.

Rose began to speak, massive, precise, qualified. I was thinking that until Brodzinski had been disposed of, Douglas had spoken like a correct departmental chief, representing his Minister's view. But what he had just said was nowhere near his Minister's view, and Douglas must have known it. I was sure that he did not feel either irregular or conspiratorial. This wasn't intrigue, it was almost the reverse. It was part of a process, not entirely conscious, often mysterious to those taking part in it and sometimes to them above all, which had no name, but which might be labelled the formation, or crystallisation, of 'official' opinion. This official opinion was expected to filter back to the politicians, so that out of the to-ing and fro-ing a decision would emerge. Who had the power? It was the question that had struck me, moving between Basset and Clapham Common. Perhaps it was a question without meaning – either way, the slick answers were all wrong.

I wanted to play for time. The longer it took for official opinion to crystallise, the better. But I was in an awkward position. Officially, I was junior to these heads of departments; further, I had to take care that I didn't speak as though I knew Roger's mind.

The talk went on. Someone had just said, 'We mustn't try to run before we can walk.' Douglas cocked an eyebrow at me, as he heard that well-judged remark – as though indicating that, though we might be on opposite sides, our literary comradeship was not impaired.

I thought this was my best time.

'I wonder if I could say something, Hector?' I put in. 'Just as a private person?'

Hector Rose was irritated. Although he had behaved to me honourably and even generously, we had never got on, our natures gritted on each other: but he had known me a long time, in this kind of situation he knew me very well, and he could guess that I was going to break the harmony. He wanted me to be quiet. He said: 'My dear Lewis. Anything you have to tell us, in any of your various capacities, we shall all be delighted to hear. Please instruct us, my dear Lewis.'

'I just wanted to raise a question, that's all.' I was as used to his techniques as he to mine.

'I'm sure that would be equally illuminating,' said Rose.

I asked my question: but I asked it in several different ways. Wasn't Douglas pre-judging the issue when he talked about Getliffe's view as the 'other extreme'? Wasn't this view, in fact, deliberately conceived as a means of taking one first step? Did they assume that no first step could ever be taken? Were they all accepting that the entire process had got out of conscious control?

Osbaldiston spoke first. 'I don't think it's possible, you know, to look too far ahead.'

'We're all grateful to you, Lewis,' said Rose, 'for a most interesting piece of exegesis. We're very, very grateful. But I suggest, with great respect, that we have to deal with immediate situations. The problem really is, isn't it, what our masters can actually perform in the course of the present Parliament? The point at issue is how much, in that time, they can alter their present defence policy, or whether they can alter it at all. We do appreciate, believe me, your taking the trouble to give us – what shall I call it? – a more uninhibited point of view. Thank you very, very, very much.'

I didn't mind. I had taken none of them with me, but I didn't expect to. I had done what I intended, that is, warn them that others were thinking flat contrary to them, that official opinion might not be altogether homogeneous. They knew now, since they were far from fools, that those other opinions must have reached Roger, and that I had intended most of all.

Other people were trying to nobble the civil servants, I thought, a night or two later, when Margaret and I were sitting in the stalls at Covent Garden. I looked at the lower right-hand box and there saw, in white tie, white waistcoat, Hector Rose. That was surprising, for Rose was tone-deaf and hated music. I didn't care for it myself, but had gone to please Margaret: and, as she had pointed out to me, opera at least had the benefit of words. It was even more surprising to see Rose as a guest of honour, with one of the most forceful of aircraft manufacturers on his right, the aircraft manufacturer's wife on his left, and two pretty daughters behind him.

It was absurd to suppose that Rose could be bought by dinner and a ticket to the opera. It was absurd to suppose that Rose could be bought by any money under heaven: it would be like trying to slip Robespierre a five-pound note. And yet, though he could not have wanted to, he had accepted this invitation. I remembered the instructions he used to give me during the war: that a civil servant ought not to be too finicky about accepting hospitality, but should take it if he felt it natural to do so, and if not, not. I wondered how natural Hector Rose felt in the box at Covent Garden.

It was equally absurd to suppose that, when Roger made a countermove, Lord Lufkin could be bought by a dinner, even by a lavish dinner in his honour. Lord Lufkin was financially capable of paying for his own dinners, even lavish ones. Yet he too, who disliked being entertained, accepted the invitation. He was one of the hardest and most austere of men, as I had known since the time, years before, when I worked for him. He would be about as easy to bribe as Rose himself. I had never heard a bribe, in the crude sense, so much as hinted at, anywhere near these people, much less offered. In my own life, I had been offered exactly one bribe, flat, across the table – but that had happened when I was a don at

Cambridge. Nothing of the sort was thinkable with the Roses and the Lufkins, although enormous contracts flowed from Rose and Osbaldiston towards Lufkin, and enormous influence flowed back. If Roger got his policy through, one enormous contract would cease to flow to Lufkin. That was a reason why Roger invented a pretext for fêting him – and the pretext was, rather improbably, the occasion of his sixty-first birthday.

The point was, Lufkin came. A crowd was waiting for him in the pent-house of the Dorchester. In the hot flowery room, door opened to the corridor so that men could watch for Lufkin himself, stood Hector Rose, Douglas, Walter Luke, Laurence Astill, Monty Cave, Leverett-Smith (the new Parliamentary Secretary), Tom Wyndham, M.P.s, civil servants, scientists, the whole of Roger's entourage, businessmen, even some of Lufkin's competitors. At last he was seen, sighted like the first sail of the Armada, turning out of the main passage, walking along the soundless corridor, flanked by two of his own staff and two hotel servants, like so many security men.

He had got lost on the penthouse floor, he said, as Roger greeted him. Lufkin spoke as though his getting lost was much to his credit, but even more to everyone else's discredit. He stood there, drinking tomato-juice, surrounded by people absorbing the radiations of power. There was one man whom I had seen absorbing such radiations before; he loved them for their own sake, he was an executive, something like a sales manager, of a rival organisation. Bald, rosy-cheeked, faintly Pickwickian, he stayed happy in the presence of the great man, smiling when the great man spoke. I remembered that his name was Hood.

When we moved into the dining-room, Lufkin sat on Roger's right, neat-headed, skull-faced, appearing younger than most of the company, although he was the oldest man present. He was also the most successful man present, in the terms of that world. He was a nonconformist minister's son who had made a big fortune. But it wasn't his money which made him so important to Roger: it was partly the concentration of industrial power he had in his hands, partly because he was the most unusual of tycoons. He had taken a peerage from a Labour government, but he was so power-ful, so indifferent, that his fellow tycoons had by now to forgive him even that. Able, technically far-sighted, bleak, he sat by Roger's side, like one who is above the necessity to talk. If I knew him, there would be only one subject on which he would discover the necessity to talk: he would not be above probing the Minister's intention about the contract. When he knew, which would not be tonight, that the contract might be cancelled, he would then discover the necessity to talk about which alternative contract the Minister was proposing to give him in exchange. I was certain that Roger was prepared for these bargains months ahead. With Lufkin placated, the other tycoons in the industry would have lost their hardest voice. This was one of the oldest tactics of all.

Lufkin's birthday party, the great table, the flowers, the glass, the miscellaneous crowd – looked a singular festivity. Lufkin himself, who was spare and ascetic, ate almost nothing – the caviare passed him, the *pâté* passed him. He allowed himself two strong whiskies, which he drank along with his fish, and let the rest of the meal go by. Meanwhile, as I heard, sitting opposite them, Roger was getting to work with flattery.

To an outsider, it would have sounded gross, the flattery squeezed out like toothpaste. My own fear was, not that Roger was overdoing it, but that he was not doing it enough. Lufkin was one of the ablest men, and certainly one of the most effective, that I had known. He was tough, shrewd, curiously imaginative, and for his own purposes a first-rate judge of men. But none of that, none of it at all, conflicted with a vanity so over-whelming that no one quite believed it. In days past, when he had paid me as a legal consultant, I used to hear his own staff chanting his praises like so many cherubim; yet even they, he felt, missed important points in his character and achievements. I remembered hearing spinster aunts of mine telling me in my childhood that great men never cared for flattery. Well, Lufkin would have been a shock to my aunts. It would have been even more of a shock for them to discover that among my most gifted acquaintances, he liked flattery more than the others – but not all that much more.

Lufkin showed no pleasure as he listened to the eulogies. Occasionally he corrected Roger on points of fact – such as when Roger suggested that, in stretching his interests from the chemical industry to aircraft, he had taken a risk. Lufkin commented: 'It wasn't a risk if you knew what you were doing.'

'It must have taken nerve as well as judgment,' said Roger.

'That's as maybe,' Lufkin replied. Perhaps from the set of his small, handsome head, one might have told that he was not displeased.

Once or twice they were exchanging serious questions. 'Don't touch it. You'll be throwing good money after bad,' said Lufkin, as though he couldn't be wrong. Roger knew, as I did, that he was not often wrong.

I could not guess how they were feeling about each other. I hoped that Lufkin, whose vanity did not fog his cold eye for ability, could scarcely miss Roger's. I was encouraged when, after Roger had proposed the guest of honour's health, Lufkin got up to reply. He began to tell the story of his life. I had heard it a good many times, and it was always a sign of favour.

He was a very bad speaker, following a very good one. He had no sense of an audience, while Roger's tone had been just right. None of that worried Lufkin. He stood, erect and bony as a young man, as confident of his oratory as Winston Churchill in one of his less diffident moods. He began by a few bleak words about governments in general, and Ministers in particular. He would have been a richer man, he informed us, if he had never listened to any Minister. Then, with his characteristic gift of getting the moral edge both ways, he added that money had never mattered to him. He just wanted to do his duty, and he was glad Roger Quaife had understood him.

There was nothing oblique or hypocritical about Lufkin. Like a supreme man of action, he believed in what he said and the obvious goodness of his intention. He proceeded to illustrate this by his own story. It was always the same. It bore a curious family resemblance to *Mein Kampf.* It consisted of about six highly abstract anecdotes, most of which had happened, so far as they had a historical origin at all, before he was twenty. One consisted of the young Lufkin being taken by the family doctor – it was not clear why – to see a factory working at half-strength. 'I decided there and then that when I had factories of my own, they were going to be full. Or they weren't going to be open at all. Period.' Another, which I specially liked, told of a slightly older Lufkin being warned by some anonymous wiseacre – 'Lufkin, you'll *fail*, because you won't remember that the best is the enemy of the good.' Lufkin's skull-face looked impassive, and he added ominously: 'Well, I had to make that chap an allowance in his old age.' The story of Lufkin's life always ended in his early twenties. It did so now, which meant that he had reached a date when many of the dinner-party were scarcely born. That did not concern him. Abruptly he sat down, with a grim smile of satisfaction, and folded his arms on his chest.

There was great sycophantic applause, Hood clapping his hands higher than the hands of the rest, his face radiant, as if he had been swept away by the performance of a world-famous soprano, and thought a standing ovation would be in order. Roger patted Lufkin on the back. Yet, I was becoming pretty sure, neither of them underrated the other. Roger had seen too much of powerful men to be put off by the grotesque aspect of Lufkin. It looked as though they might reach a working agreement, and if so, Roger had scored his first tactical success.

CHAPTER XIV

HUMILIATION AMONG FRIENDS

A week after Lufkin's birthday, I was standing in a crowded drawing-room at the American Ambassador's house, deafened by the party's surge and swell. Margaret and I had been exchanging a word or two with the wife of J. C. Smith, Collingwood's nephew. I had not met her before. She was a short, slender woman, dark, attractive in a muted way, not very talkative. I wondered incuriously why I hadn't seen her husband's name in *Hansard* for so long. She passed away from us. Someone else called out to Margaret, and in the huddle I found myself against David Rubin.

Soon I was shaking my fingers to restore the circulation while he looked at me with sombre-eyed *Schadenfreude*. I had asked for whisky with plenty of ice, and had got it: the glass was so thin that my hand had become numbed with cold. Just then, one of the embassy counsellors came towards Rubin, looking for him, not drifting in the party's stream. Although he knew me well, his manner was constrained. After a few cordialities, he apologised and took Rubin aside.

For an instant I was left alone in the ruck of the party. Over the heads of the people near I could see the flaxen hair of Arthur Plimpton, the young American who was going round with Francis Getliffe's daughter. I caught his eye and beckoned him: but before he could make his way through the crowd, Rubin and the diplomat were back.

'Lewis had better hear this,' said Rubin.

'It'll be all over town in an hour or so, anyway,' said the diplomat.

'What is it?'

'I don't know whether you're in the picture already,' he replied, 'but your people and the French are going into Suez.'

He pronounced the name in the American manner, with the accent on the second syllable.

I was not occupied with phonetic niceties. I cursed. Both of them were used to me as a man with an equable public face. Suddenly they had seen me lose my temper and were uncomfortable.

'Didn't you expect it?'

From the summer onwards I had heard forecasts and thought they were irresponsible. 'Good God Almighty,' I said, 'don't you think I believed that we had the faintest residue of sense? Do you think any sane man would have taken it seriously?'

'I'm afraid you have to now,' said the diplomat.

Just then Arthur Plimpton joined us. He greeted the other two, then looked at me and asked straight out: 'Is there anything wrong, sir?'

'Yes, Arthur, there is. We've gone off our blasted heads.'

He was a great favourite of mine. He was a craggily handsome young man of twenty-three. When he got older, the cheekbones would protrude and the bright blue eyes sink in: he already looked harder than an Englishman of the same age. He was capable, arrogant and had a pleasant touch of cheek. He was also considerate, though at that moment the most he could think of doing was reach me another drink.

Within half an hour, he and David Rubin had drawn my wife and me away from the party and had established us in a pub in St John's Wood. They were surprised, I realised as I became cooler, that we were so much outraged. But they were both kind and tactful men. They wanted to see us happier. For a time they kept off the evening's news but, finding that made us more preoccupied, Arthur, the younger and more direct, plunged in. He asked what was worrying us most.

Margaret burst out, 'What isn't?'

Just for a second, Arthur smiled.

Her eyes were bright, she had flushed down her neck. Then he realised that she was more violent, more intransigent, than I was.

'They've learned nothing and they're no good,' she said. 'I've never liked playing along behind them, and I wish we never had!'

'All I hope,' said David Rubin, with a sad, sardonic smile, 'is that if you must do something immoral, you manage to make it work.'

'How can we bring it off?' I cried. 'What century do you think we're living in? Do you think we can hold the Middle East with a couple of brigade groups?'

'I don't know how this'll go over in our country,' said Arthur.

'How will it?' I said angrily.

Rubin twitched his shoulders.

I said: 'Countries, when their power is slipping away, are always liable to do idiotic things. So are social classes. You may find yourselves in the same position some day.'

'Not yet,' said Arthur, with confidence.

'No, not yet,' said David Rubin.

Margaret and I were humiliated, and the others went on trying to cheer us up. When I had glimmers of detachment, which was not often that night, I thought that their attitudes were diametrically opposite to what one might expect. David Rubin was a man of deep and complex sophistication. His grandparents had been born in Poland, he had no English genes in him at all. Yet it was he who loved England more uncritically, which was strange, for he was one of the most critical of men. He did not like being patronised by English pundits, but he still had a love affair with England, just a little like that of Brodzinski, who was a scientific enemy of his. He loved the pretty, picture-book England – far more than Margaret and I could have loved it. And at first sight surprisingly, far more so than Arthur Plimpton, who was as Anglo-Saxon as we were, who had the run of Basset and Diana Skidmore's smart friends, who knew the privileged in our country as well as his own, and who had no special respect for any of them.

If Arthur had been an English boy, I should, when I first met him a couple of years before, have been able to place him within five minutes. As it was, it was apparent that he was well off. But it had taken Diana to enlighten me that that was putting it mildly. Diana did not show enthusiasm for the idea that he might marry Penelope Getliffe. Diana considered that marriage with the daughter of a scientist, however eminent, would be a come-down. She was laying plans for something more suitable.

Despite, or perhaps because of, all this, Arthur was not over-impressed by England. On that night of Suez, he was full of idealism, genuine idealism, damning the British Government. I distinctly recalled that when he spoke of capitalist enterprises, particularly of methods of adding to his own fortune, he showed an anti-idealism which would have made Commodore Vanderbilt look unduly fastidious. Yet that night, he talked with great hope and purity.

It heartened Margaret, whose nature was purer than mine. Myself, I was discouraged. I was remembering the outbursts of idealism that I had listened to, from young men as good as this one, back in my own group in the provincial town, when our hopes had been more revolutionary than Arthur could have believed, but still as pure as his. I fell silent, half-hearing the argument, Arthur and Margaret on one side, David Rubin on the other, Rubin becoming more and more elaborate and Byzantine. I was signalling to Margaret to come away. If I stayed there, I should just become more despondent, and more drunk.

There was one glint of original sin, as Arthur saw Margaret and me getting ready to go. He might have been talking with extreme purity; but he was not above using his charm on Margaret, persuading her to invite Penelope to stay at our flat, and, as it were coincidentally, him too. I supposed he was trying to get her out of the atmosphere of the Cambridge house. But I was feeling corrupt that night, and it occurred to me that, like most of the very rich people I had known, he was trying to save money.

CHAPTER XV

SELF-DEFENCE

ON the Sunday afternoon, Margaret and I walked down, under the smoky, blue-hazed autumn sky, to Trafalgar Square. We could not get nearer than the bottom of the Haymarket. Margaret was taken back, high-coloured, to the 'demos' of her teens. For her, more than for me, the past might be regained; she could not help hoping to recapture the spirit of it, just as she hoped that places we had visited together in the past might always hold a spark of their old magic. She was not as possessed by time lost as I was, yet I believed she could more easily possess herself of it. The speeches of protest boomed out. We were part of a crowd, we were all together. It was a long time since I had been part of a crowd, and, that day, I felt as Margaret did.

During the next few days, wherever I went, in the offices, clubs and dinner-parties, tempers were more bitter than they had been in this part of the London world since Munich. As at the time of Munich, one began to refuse invitations to houses where the quarrel would spring up. This time, however, the divide took a different line. Hector Rose and his colleagues, the top administrators, had most of them been devoted Municheers. Now, conservative as they were, disposed by temperament and training to be at one with Government, they couldn't take it. Rose astonished me when he talked.

'I don't like committing my own future actions, my dear Lewis, which in any case will shortly be of interest to no one but myself – but I confess that I don't see how I'm going to hypnotise myself into voting Conservative again.'

He was irked because for once he had known less than usual about the final decision: but also, he was shocked. 'I don't mind these people' – he meant the politicians, and for once did not use the mock-obsequious 'our masters' – 'failing to achieve an adequate level of intelligence. After all, I've been trying to make them understand the difference between a precise and an imprecise statement for nearly forty years. But I do mind, perhaps I mind rather excessively, when they fail to show the judgment of so many cockatoos.' Bitterly, Rose considered the parallel, and appeared to find it close enough.

He was sitting in his room behind the bowl of flowers. He said: 'Tell me, Lewis, you are rather close to Roger Quaife, is that true? Closer, that is, than one might expect a civil servant, even a somewhat irregular civil servant, to be to a politician, even a somewhat irregular politician?'

'That's more or less true.'

'He must have been in it, you know. Or did you hear?'

'Nothing at all,' I said.

'The rumour is that he put up some sort of opposition in cabinet. I should be mildly curious to know. I have seen a good many Ministers who were remarkably bold outside, but who somehow were not quite so immovable when they got round the cabinet table.'

There was a new rasp in Rose's tone. He went on: 'It might conceivably do a trivial amount of good, if you dropped the word to Quaife that a number of comparatively sensible and responsible persons have the feeling that they suddenly find themselves doing their sensible and responsible work in a lunatic asylum. It can't do any harm, if you communicate that impression. I should be very, very grateful to you.'

Even for Rose, it took an effort of discipline that afternoon to return to his duties, to his 'sensible and responsible work'.

Meanwhile, Tom Wyndham and his friends of the back benches were happy. 'I feel I can hold my head up at last,' said one of them. I did not see Diana Skidmore during those days, but I heard about her: the whole of the Basset circle was solid for Suez. Just as the officials seemed slumped in their chairs, the politicians became brilliant with euphoria. Sammikins, for once not odd man out, exuded more euphoria than any of them. In his case, there was a special reason. He happened, alone among his right-wing group, to be pro-Zionist. Whether this was just a whim, I didn't know, but he had applied for a commission in the Israeli Army, and he was riotously happy at the prospect of getting in one more bout of fighting before he grew too old.

In the clubs, the journalists and political commentators carried the rumours along. We were all at the pitch of credulity or suspiciousness – because in crises these states are the same, just as they are in extreme jealousy – when anything seemed as probable as anything else. Some supporters of the Government were restive, we heard. I had a conversation myself with Cave and a couple of his friends, who were speaking the same bitter language as the officials, the professional men. 'This is the last charge of Eton and the Brigade of Guards,' said one young Conservative. How could we stop it? How many members of the cabinet had been against it? Was —— going to resign? Above all, what had Roger done?

One morning, during a respite from cabinet meetings, Roger sent for me to give some instructions about the scientists' committee. He did not volunteer a word about Suez. I thought that, just then, it would do no good to press it. Soon a secretary came in: Mr Cave had called. Would the Minister see him?

On the instant, as soon as the name was mentioned, Roger's equable manner broke. 'Am I never going to get a minute's peace? Good God alive, why don't some of you protect me a bit?'

He relapsed into sullenness, saying he was too busy, too pestered, she must make some excuse. The girl waited. She knew, as well as Roger did, that Cave was the most talented of Roger's party supporters. She knew he ought not to be turned away. At last Roger, with a maximum of ill-grace, said he supposed she had better send him in.

I made to go out, but Roger, frowning, shook his head. When Cave entered, his head was thrown back from his slack, heavy body, eyes flickering under the thick arches of brow. Roger had made himself seem matey again. It was Cave who came to the point.

'We can't grumble about things being dull, can we?'

There were a few remarks, affable, half-malicious, to which Roger did not need to reply. All of a sudden, Cave ceased being devious.

'Is there really any bit of sanity in this affair?' he said.

'What am I expected to say to that?'

'I'm speaking for some of your friends, you know,' said Cave. 'Is there anything which you know and we don't, that would alter our opinion?'

'I shouldn't think so, should you?'

'No, Roger,' said Cave, who, having thrown away side-digs or any kind of malice, was speaking with authority. 'I was asking you seriously. Is there anything we don't know?'

Roger replied, for a second friendly and easy:

'Nothing that would make you change your minds.'

'Well, then; you must know what we think. This is stupid. It's wrong. On the lowest level, it won't work.'

'This isn't exactly an original opinion, is it?'

Neither Cave nor I knew then, though I was able to check the date later, that on the night before the cabinet had heard of the veto from Washington.

'I'm quite sure it's your own. But how much have you been able to put it across?'

'You don't expect me to tell you what's happened in cabinet, do you?'

'You have been known to drop a hint, you know.' Cave, his chin sunk down, had spoken with a touch of edge.

At that remark, Roger's temper, which I had not seen him lose before, except as a tactic, broke loose. His face went white: his voice became both thick and strangulated. He cried: 'I'll tell you one thing. I've not lost my senses. I don't believe this is the greatest stroke of English policy since 1688. How in hell can you imagine that I don't see what you see?' His anger was ugly and harsh. He did not relish the voice of conscience, perhaps most of all, when it came from a man as clever, as much a rival, as Monty Cave: but that wasn't all. That was only the trigger.

'I'll tell you another thing,' Roger shouted. 'You're wondering what I said in cabinet. I'll tell you. I said absolutely nothing.'

Cave stared at him, not put off by violence, for he was not an emotional coward, but astonished. In a moment he said, steadily:

'I think you should have done.'

'Do you? Then it's time you learned something about the world you're living in.' He rounded on me. 'You pretend to know what politics is like! It's time you learned something, too. I tell you, I said absolutely nothing. I'm sick and tired of having to explain myself every step of the way. *This* is the politics you all talk about. Nothing I could have said would make the slightest difference. Once these people had got the bit between their teeth, there was no doubt what was going to happen. Yes, I let it go on round me. Yes, I acquiesced in something much more indefensible than you've begun to guess. And you expect me to explain, do you? Nothing I could have said would have made the faintest difference. No, it would have made one difference. It would have meant that one newcomer would have lost whatever bit of credit he possessed. I've taken risks. You've both seen me take an unjustified risk.'

He was referring to his defence of Sammikins. He was speaking with extreme rancour, as though denouncing the folly, and worse, of somebody else. 'If I were any good at what I'm trying to do, I never ought to allow myself to take risks for the sake of feeling handsome. I only ought to take one risk. I've got a fifty per cent chance of doing what I set out to do.'

He snapped his fingers, less unobtrusively than usual. 'If I can't do what we believe in, then I reckon no one is going to do it. For that, I'll make a great many sacrifices you two would be too genteel to make. I'll sacrifice all the useless protests. I'll let you think I'm a trimmer and a time-server. I'll do anything. But I'm not prepared for you two to come and teach me when I have to be noble. It doesn't matter whether I look noble or contemptible, so long as I bring this off. I'm fighting on one front. That's going to be hard enough. Nothing that any of you say is going to make me start fighting on two fronts, or any number of fronts, or whatever you think I ought to fight on.' There was a pause.

'I don't find it as easy as you do,' said Monty Cave. 'Isn't it slightly too easy to find reasons for doing nothing, when it turns out to be advantageous to oneself?'

Roger's temper had subsided as suddenly as it had blown up.

'If I were going to fall over backwards to get into trouble, whenever there are decent reasons for keeping out of harm's way, then I shouldn't be any use to you, or in this job.'

For a man of action – which he was, as much so as Lord Lufkin – Roger was unusually in touch with his own experience. But as he made that reply, I thought he was speaking like other men of action, other politicians that I had known. They had the gift, common to college politicians like my old friend Arthur Brown, or national performers like Roger, of switching off self-distrust, of knowing when not to be too nice about themselves. It was not a romantic gift: but it was one, as more delicate souls like Francis Getliffe found to their disadvantage, the lack of which not only added to the pain of life, but cost one half the game.

CHAPTER XVI

PRETEXT FOR A CONVERSATION

THE days of Suez were over. Monty Cave, with two other junior Minsters, had resigned from the Government. There were still dinner-parties from which it was advisable to excuse ourselves. But I could not excuse myself from Gilbey's speech in the House of Lords.

It was not an occasion made for drama. There were perhaps forty men lolling on the red benches, under the elaboration of stained glass, the gold and scarlet round the throne, the chamber more flashy than the Commons, the colours hotter. If Roger had not asked me, I should not have thought of listening. The Government spokesman was uttering generalities, at the tranquillising length which Douglas Osbaldiston judged suitable, about the defence programme after Suez. The Opposition was expressing concern. One very old peer muttered mysteriously about the use of the camel. A young peer talked about bases. Then Gilbey rose, from the back of the Government benches. He was looking ill, iller than he really was, I thought. It occurred to me that he was doing his best to emulate the elder Pitt. But I hadn't realised what he was capable of.

Speaking to an official brief, he was fumbling, incompetent and had embarrassed us for years. On his own, he was eloquent, and as uninhibited as an actor of his own generation playing Sydney Carton.

'I should have liked to speak before your lordships in the uniform which has been the greatest pride and privilege of my life,' he told them in his light, resonant, reedy tenor. 'But a man should not wear uniform who is not well enough to fight.' Slowly he put his hand on his heart. 'In recent days, my lords, I have wished devoutly that I was well enough to fight. When the Prime Minister, God bless him, decided with a justice and righteousness that are as unchallengeable as any in our history, that we had to intervene by force of arms to keep the peace, and our own inalienable rights in Suez, I looked the world in the face as I have not been able to do these last ten years. For a few days, true Englishmen were able to look the whole world in the face. Is this *the last time* that true Englishmen will have that privilege, my lords?'

As usual with Lord Gilbey, it was ham. As usual with his kind of ham, it was perfectly sincere.

But Gilbey, despite his sincerity, was not so simple as he seemed. This speech began as a threnody for his own England: but it turned into an opportunity for revenge on those who had kicked him out. He was not clever, but he had some cunning. He had worked out that the enemies of Suez within the Government had been his own enemies. As the rumours that Roger was anti-Suez went round the clubs, Gilbey had decided that these were the forces, this man the intriguer, who had supplanted him. Like other vain and robust men, Gilbey had no capacity for forgiveness whatsoever. He did not propose to forgive this time. Speaking as an elder statesman, without mentioning Roger by name, he expressed his doubts about the nation's defences, about 'intellectual gamblers' who would let us all go soft. 'This is a knife in the back,' an acquaintance in the gallery wrote on an envelope and passed to me.

Gilbey was finishing. 'My lords, I wish for nothing more than that I could assure you that the country's safety is in the best possible hands. It is a long time since I lay awake at night. I have found myself lying awake, these last bitter nights, wondering whether we can become strong again. That is our only safety. Whatever it costs, whether we have to live like paupers, this country must be able to defend itself. Most of us here, my lords, are coming to the end of our lives. That matters nothing to me, nothing to any of us, if only, at the hour of our death, we can know that the country is safe.'

Again, slowly, Gilbey put his hand on his heart. As he sat down, he took from his waistcoat pocket a small pill-box. There were 'Hear hears', and one or two cheers from the benches round him. Gilbey took a capsule, and closed his eyes. He sat there with eyes closed, hand on heart, through the next speech. Then, bowing to the throne, leaning on the arm of a younger man, he left the chamber.

When I had to report this performance to Roger, he took it better than other bad news. 'If it comes to playing dirty,' he said, 'aristocrats have got everyone else beaten, any day of the week. You should see my wife's relatives when they get to work. It's a great disadvantage to be held back by middle-class morality.'

He spoke with equanimity. We both knew that the enemies, both as people and as groups, would become visible from now on. The extreme right, he was saying, was bound to be ten times more powerful in any society like ours, or the American society, than the extreme left. He had been watching them before this. It was not only Gilbey who would be talking, he said.

No, it was not only Gilbey who would be talking, as Caro proved to me a few days later, when she came to have a drink at our flat. She herself, like all her family, had been pro-Suez. At the dinner-table in Lord North Street, she had been outspoken for it, while Roger had not said much. Had they arranged this between themselves, or did they know the moves so well that they did not need to? It was good tactics for Roger to have a wife, and a Seymour, who was talking the party line. Good tactics or not, pre-arranged or not, Caro believed what she said. Once again, people were not clever enough to dissimulate. When Caro talked to me with a bold, dashing, innocent stare, I was furious with her, but I did not doubt that she was honest. She was as much pro-Suez as Lord Gilbey, and for the same reason. What was more, she insisted that Roger's constituents were pro-Suez too, including many of the poor.

She pressed me to visit them, wanted so urgently to take me, that I suspected she might have another motive. She wore me down. One afternoon in November, she drove me down to what she called her 'office'. We had not far to go, for Roger held one of the safe Kensington seats. Caro drove through the remnants of gentility in Queen's Gate, the private hotels, the flats, the rooming-houses, the students' hostels, past the end of Cromwell Road and Earls Court – crowded with the small-part actresses, the African students, the artists, all displaying themselves in the autumn sun, and (I remarked to Caro) as remote from Lord Gilbey's concerns as if he were a Japanese *daimyo*. Caro just said: 'Most of them don't vote anyway.'

Her 'office' turned out to be in one of the back-streets close by Olympia, a back-street of terrace houses, like those I used to walk past in my childhood on the way home. Each Monday afternoon, Caro used, so I gathered, to sit from two to six in the 'front room' of one of her constituency 'chums', a big woman with a glottal Cockney accent, who made us a pot of tea, was on hearty, patting, egalitarian terms with Caro, and cherished her delight at calling a woman of title by her Christian name.

That room, that street, seemed unbusinesslike for Caro. It was the wrong end of the constituency. The seat was safe, the Kensington end would go on returning Roger, if he turned into a gorilla. But down here she was surrounded by the working class. Among the knockabout poor, the lumpen proletariat, she might pick up a vote or two; but the rest, with similar English impartiality and phlegm, would go on voting for another gorilla, provided he was Roger's opponent.

There Caro sat, in the tiny, close-smelling front room, ready to talk to any caller for hours to come. Through the window, the houses opposite stood near and plain, so near that one could see the wood-pocks on the doors. The first of Caro's visitors – perhaps clients was a better word – were Conservative supporters, elderly people living on small private means or pensions, who had made the trip from Courtfield Gardens or Nevern Square, from single rooms in the high nineteenth-century houses, who had come out here – for what? Mostly to have someone to talk to, I thought.

A good many of them were lonely, pointlessly lonely, cooking for themselves, going out to the public library for books. Some wanted to speak of their young days, of gentilities past and gone. They were irremediably lonely in the teeming town, lonely, and also frightened. They worried about the bombs: and though some of them would have said they had nothing to live for, that made them less willing to die. 'Dying is a messy business anyway,' said an old lady who had thirty years before taught at a smart girls' school, putting a stoical face on it. I couldn't have comforted her: dying was a messy business, but this was a hard way to die, frightened, neglected and alone. I couldn't have comforted her, but Caro could, not through insight, not even through sympathy, for Caro was as brave as her brother – but through a kind of comradeship, unexacting, earthy, almost callous, as though saying: We're all dirty flesh, we're all in the same boat.

Those genteel clients, some eccentric and seedy, some keeping up appearances, were pro-Suez all right. That wasn't a surprise. It was more of a surprise when I listened to the later ones. They came from the streets round about, working people finished for the day; they were the sort of mixture you could pick up anywhere, just beyond the prosperous core of the great, muddled, grumbling town; they worked on the Underground and in small factories, they filled in their pools coupons and bet with a street bookmaker. They were members of trade unions and voted Labour. Their reasons for coming along were matter-of-fact – mostly to do with housing, sometimes with schools. In her turn, Caro was brisk and matter-of-fact: yes, that could be taken up, no, that wasn't on.

She gave one or two a tip for a race next day – not as though loftily bestowing a favour, but because she was, if possible, slightly more obsessed with horse-racing than they were themselves. She was playing fair, but once or twice she mentioned Suez, sometimes the others did. It was true what she had stated: there were several who would never have voted for 'her people', they would have said they were against the bosses – but just then, in a baffled, resentful fashion, they were on her side and Lord Gilbey's, not on mine.

When she had said her goodbyes, and we went outside into the sharp night, the stars were bright for London. Behind the curtains, lights shone pallid in the basement rooms. At the corner, the pub stood festooned with bulbs, red, yellow and blue. The whole street was squat, peaceful, prosaic, cheerful. Caro was insisting that I should go back to Lord North Street for a drink. I knew that Roger was in the country making a speech. I knew she was not so fond of my company as all that. She still had something on her mind.

She was driving fast, the eastward traffic was slight on the way home to Westminster.

'You see,' she said. She meant that she had been right.

I wasn't pleased. I began arguing with her; this was a tiny sample which showed nothing, not the real midland or northern working class. But I wasn't sure. Some politicians brought back from their constituencies the same report as hers.

'I hope they're all pleased with the result,' I said. 'I hope you are, too.'

'We ought to have gone through with it,' said Caro.

'You're all clinging with your fingernails on to the past,' I said. 'Where in God's name do you think that is going to take us?'

'We ought to have gone through with it.'

Out of patience with each other, tempers already edged, we sat in her drawing-room. She had been talking all the afternoon, I was tired with having just sat by: but she was restless and active. She mentioned the two boys, both at preparatory schools. Neither of them was 'bright', she said, with an air of faint apology. 'My family was never much good at brains.'

I fancied that when I left she would go on drinking by herself. She was looking older that night, the skin reddened and roughened round her cheek-bones. But it made no difference to her prettiness, and she walked about the room, not with grace, but with the spring, the confidence in her muscles, of someone who loved the physical life.

She went back to the sofa, curled her legs under her, and gazed straight at me.

'I want to talk,' she said.

'Yes?'

'You knew, did you?' She was staring at me as boldly as her brother had done in his club. She went on: 'You know that Roger has had his own line on this?' (She meant Suez.) 'You know it, I know you know it, and it's dead opposite to the way I feel. Well, that's all down the drain now. It doesn't matter a hoot what any of us thought. We've just got to cut our losses and start again.'

Suddenly she asked me: 'You see Roger quite a lot nowadays, don't you?' I nodded.

'I suppose you realise that *no one* has any influence on him?'

She gave her loud, unconstricted laugh.

'I don't mean he's a monster. He lets me do anything I want round the house, and he's good with the children. But when it comes to things outside, it's a different kettle of fish. When it comes to where he's going and how he's going to get there, then *no one* has a scrap of influence on him.'

She said it with submission. Gossips at Basset, and places like it, often said confidently that she ran him. Partly because she was splendid to look at, partly because, as in the incident of Sammikins, Roger behaved to her with deference and chivalry. She's the master in that set-up, the gossips said in knowledgeable whispers, particularly in Caro's smart, rich world.

Caro had just told me who the master was. She said it as though with surprise at her own submission. Also as she spoke, there was a jab of triumph at my expense, for she was insisting that I was a subordinate also. She liked insisting on it – because Caro, who seemed as dashing and as much a gambler as her brother, whom other women grumbled had had all the luck, was jealous of her husband's friends.

'No one's going to push him where he doesn't want to go,' she said, 'it's just as well to get that straight.'

'I've done a certain amount of business with him, you know,' I said.

'I know about the business you've been doing. What do you take me for?' she cried. 'That's why I've got to talk to you. What is it all going to add up to?'

'I should guess', I said, 'that he's a better judge of that than I am.'

'I've not said so to him' – Caro's eyes were fierce – 'because one never ought to say these things or even think them, once he's made up his mind, if one's going to be any help – but I doubt if he's going to get away with it.'

'It's a risk,' I replied. 'But he's gone into it with his eyes open.'

'Has he?'

'What do you mean? Don't you believe in what he's doing?' I asked.

'I've got to believe in it.'

'Well?'

'I can't argue with you. I don't know enough,' she said. 'But I'd follow my instincts, and I don't think he has an even chance of getting away with it. So I want to ask you something.' She was speaking, not in a friendly tone, but with passion.

'What is it?'

'He'll do what he wants in the long run. I've given you fair warning. But you and your friends can make it more difficult for him. Don't. That's what I'm asking you. I want you to give him room to manœuvre. He may have to slide gracefully out of this whole business. That doesn't matter, if he does it in time. But if he gets in it up to the neck, then he might ruin himself. I tell you, you and your friends mustn't make it too difficult for him.'

She was no more intellectual than Sammikins. She rarely read anything, except fashionable memoirs. But she knew this game of high politics better than I did, perhaps better than Roger did himself. She knew it *as* a game, in which one won or lost. It did not count whether Roger had to abandon a policy. What did count was whether his chances of a higher office were going up or down. To that, she was utterly committed, utterly loyal, with every cell of her flesh.

Previously, I had been getting colder to her. But suddenly the passion of her loyalty moved me.

I said, the whole campaign was in his hands. He was too good a politician not to smell the dangers.

'You've got to make it easy for him.'

'I don't think you need worry—'

'How do you expect me not to? What's going to happen to him if this goes wrong?'

'I should have thought' – I was now speaking gently – 'that he was a very tough man. He'd come back, I'm sure he would.'

'I've seen too many future P.M.s,' she said, the edge having left her voice also, 'who've made a mess of something, or somehow or other taken the wrong turn. They're pretty pathetic afterwards. It must be awful to have a brilliant future behind you. I don't know whether he could bear it.'

'If he had to bear it,' I said, 'then of course he would.'

'He'd never be satisfied with second prizes. He'd eat his heart out. Don't you admit it? He's made for the top, and nothing else will do.'

As she gazed at me with great open guiltless eyes, she was immersed in him. Then, all of a sudden, the intimacy and tension broke. She threw her head back in a hearty, hooting laugh, and exclaimed: 'Just imagine him giving up the unequal struggle and settling down as Governor-General of New Zealand!' She had cheered up, and poured herself another drink.

I was amused by Caro's picture of ultimate failure and degradation.

Soon I said that it was time I went home. She tried, insistently, naggingly, to keep me there for another quarter of an hour. Although we were on better terms by now, she was not fond of me. It was simply that, with husband away, children away, she was bored. Like Diana, and other rich and pretty women, she was not good at being bored, and the person nearest to her had to pay for it. When I refused to stay she sulked, but began thinking that she would enjoy gambling her time away. As I left the house, she was ringing round her friends, trying to arrange for a night's poker.

CHAPTER XVII

THE SWITCH OF SUSPICION

I HAD said to Caro that Roger was too good a politician not to smell the dangers. In fact, a nose for danger was the most useful single gift in the political in-fighting: unless it stopped one acting altogether, in which case it was the least. That winter, while others were still vertiginous about Suez, Roger was looking out for opponents, critics, enemies, a year ahead. His policy would be coming into the open then. It was better tactics to let powers like Lufkin get the first taste of it from Roger direct. Patiently he set himself to dine out with them, telling them a little, occasionally letting out a burst of calculated candour.

Moving round Whitehall and the clubs, I got some of the backwash of all this. I even heard a compliment from Lord Lufkin, who said: 'Well, considering that he's a politician, you can't say that he's altogether a fool.' This evaluation, which in both form and content reminded me of the New

Criticism, was the highest praise I remembered Lufkin bestowing on any-one, with the solitary exception of himself.

Towards the end of December, Roger passed one of these forestalling operations on to me. The scientists had fallen behind with their report, but we knew it was going to be delivered early in the New Year; we knew also what it was going to contain. There would be differences in detail between Laurence Astill and Francis Getliffe, but by and large they would all be saying the same thing, except for Brodzinski. He had retained an implacable confidence throughout, absolutely assured both that he was right and that he must prevail. It was clear that he would insist on writing a minority report.

My job, said Roger, was to give him a hint of the future, to pacify him, but to warn him that for the present he couldn't bank on much support, that Government couldn't do much for him.

My own nose for danger twitched. I still reproached myself for not having been open with Douglas Osbaldiston from the start, when he had invited me to do so. I thought it was right to be open with Brodzinski now. But I felt sure that Roger ought to do it.

Roger was vexed and overtired. When I said that I shouldn't have any success, Roger replied that I had been doing these things all my life. When I said that Brodzinski was a dangerous man, Roger shrugged. No one was dangerous, he replied, unless he represented something. He, Roger, was taking care of the industry and the military. Brodzinski was just a man out on his own. 'Are you afraid of a bit of temperament? We're going to run into worse than that, you know. Are you going to leave everything to me?'

It was as near a quarrel as we had had. After I left him, I wrote him a letter saying that he was making a mistake, and that I wouldn't talk to Brodzinski. Feeling superstitious, I went over to the window and then returned to my desk and tore the letter up.

After the next meeting of the scientists, a few days before Christmas, I took my chance to get Brodzinski alone. Walter Luke had walked away with Francis Getliffe and Astill; Pearson was going off, as he did phleg-matically each fortnight, to catch the evening plane to Washington. So I could ask Brodzinski to come across with me to the Athenæum, and we walked along the edge of the pond in the shivery winter dark. A steam of mist hung over the black water. Just after I had heard the scurry, glug and pop of a bird diving, I said:

'How do you think it is going?'

'What is going?' In his deep, chest-throbbing voice, Brodzinski as usual addressed me as Sir Lewis.

'How do you think the committee is going?'

'Let me ask you one question. Why did those three' (he meant Luke, Francis, Astill) 'go away together?'

He was almost whispering in the empty park. His face was turned to mine, his great eyes luminous with suspicion. 'They went away', he answered himself, 'to continue drafting without me being there to intervene.' It was more than likely. If it had not been likely, he would still have imagined it.

'Do you think that I am happy about the committee—?' Once more, the bass, unyielding courtesy.

We walked in silence. It was not a good start. In the club, I took him upstairs to the big drawing-room. There, on the reading desk, was the candidates' book. I thought it might mollify him to inspect it. His name was entered: we had all signed our names in support, Francis, Luke, Astill, Osbaldiston, Hector Rose, the whole lot of us. Somehow everyone knew that he craved to be a member, that he was passionately set on it. We were doing our best. Not merely to soften him, to keep him quiet: but in part, I thought, for an entirely different reason. Despite his force of character, despite his paranoia, there was something pathetic about him.

No, not despite his paranoia, but because of it. Paranoia had a hypnotic effect, even on tough and experienced men. I had come across a first intimation of this earlier in my life, in the temperament of George Passant. It was not entirely, or even mainly, his generosity, his great balloon-like dreams, that drew the young: it was not the scale of his character or his formidable passions. It was that, in his fits of suspicion, of feeling done down and persecuted, he was naked to the world. He called for, and got, sympathy in the way most of us could never do. We might behave better: we might need help out of proportion more: we might even be genuinely pathetic. And yet, by the side of the George Passants, we could never suggest to those round us that revelation, that insight into pathos, which came from seeming innocent, uncorrupt and without defence.

It was like that with Brodzinski. I had told Roger that Brodzinski was a dangerous man: that was a workaday comment, the sort of warning I could keep in the front of my mind. Sitting by him at the end of the Athenæum drawing-room, watching his eyes stray to the candidates' book, I wasn't thinking about warnings: I could feel how once more he was exposed to the brilliance of suspicion, this naked sense of a group of privileged persons, whom he wanted above all to belong to, conspiring together to push him out. One's impulse, even mine, was to make him easier. He ought to be shown that there were no plots against him; one ought to lend a hand. I found myself hoping that the committee would elect him out of turn.

When I offered him a drink, he asked for half a glass of sherry and sipped at it, looking doubtfully at me while I put down a whisky. For a man so massive and virile, he was curiously old-maidish in some of his habits. I said: 'The Minister is extremely grateful for all you've done on his committee. You know how grateful he is, don't you?'

'He is a fine man,' said Brodzinski, with deep feeling.

'I am sure', I went on, 'that before long the Government will want to give you some recognition.'

I knew that it was being arranged for him to get a C.B.E. in the June honours list. I had settled with Roger that I should hint at this.

Brodzinski stared at me with lambent eyes. He understood some of Whitehall politics much better than most Englishmen: but on these matters of honorific etiquette he was mystified. He could not have guessed where Roger or Douglas Osbaldiston, or anyone else, came in. On the other hand, he gave a very English reply.

'It doesn't matter whether I get recognised. All that matters is that we do the right thing.'

'The Minister is extremely grateful for the advice you have given. I know he'll want to tell you so himself.'

Brodzinski sat back in the leather-covered chair, his great chest protruding like a singer's. His face, wide and shield-shaped, was hard with thought, the flap of dusty hair fell to his eyebrows. He was still pre-occupied, I guessed, with the thought of drafting going on without him. Yet he was happy. Roger he had spoken of as a trusted, powerful friend. He was sitting with me as though I were another friend, lesser, but still powerful.

'It will soon be time', he said, 'for the Minister to exert himself.'

I was having to feel my way.

'Of course,' I said, 'what any Minister can do on his own is pretty limited.'

'I am afraid I do not understand you.'

'I mean,' I said, 'you mustn't expect miracles. He's a very able man, as I'm sure you realised a long time ago, and he's prepared to do things that most Ministers wouldn't. But, you know, he can't do much without the support of his colleagues at all levels. He can only do what a great many people think ought to be done – not just himself.'

There was a rim of white all round his irises. His gaze was fixed on me, and stayed so. He said:

'I still do not understand you—' Once more he addressed me in full. 'Or, at least I hope I do not understand you.'

'I am saying that the area of freedom of action for a Minister is smaller, a great deal smaller, than most people can ever understand.'

'I can see that could be so.' He seemed exaggeratedly reasonable, and once more he was optimistic. 'But let us come to practical examples. There are questions – we have been trying to discuss them this afternoon – where there is not unanimity of opinion. There cannot be unanimity of opinion. There will be differences, with some scientists taking Getliffe's view, and some scientists taking mine. Am I correct?'

'There hasn't been unanimity so far, has there?' I was trying the effect of sarcasm, but he went on, set-faced, as though we were already agreed:

'Well then, in such circumstances, the Minister can use his authority on one side or the other: am I correct again?'

'In some circumstances,' I replied, 'he could.'

'In these circumstances, then?' He was throwing in all the weight of his nature, bearing me down. Yet his expression looked as though all was simple, as though difficulties did not exist, and his friends, including me, would give him that he longed for: as though disappointment did not exist on this earth.

I was searching for the words. At last I said: 'I don't think you must count on it.'

'Why not?'

'I've been trying to explain, the Minister is bound to listen to his advisers. You've been giving him one kind of advice. But – you know this, don't you? – the overwhelming majority of opinion is dead against you. The Minster can't say that the pros and cons are about equal, and then just decide.'

'I think I understand. I think I understand clearly.' His heavy hands on his thighs, Brodzinski stared at me. His face had not altered, but his eyes had flared up. The transition was complete, as if the switch of suspicion had, between one instant and the next, been turned on in his mind. A second before, beautiful, expectant clarity: now, the sight of an enemy.

'What do you understand?'

'It is very easy. The Minister is not to be allowed to make up his own mind. These scientists have been carefully picked by other officials. Of course they have. They advise one thing, I advise another. Then other officials surround the Minister. They pick and choose, they are not willing to let the matter be discussed. Of course they are not. I see what I am expected to understand.'

'You mustn't look for sinister explanations.'

'I do not look for them. I am obliged to see them.'

'I'm not prepared', I said, my voice getting harder, 'to listen to suggestions that you have not been treated fairly. Do you really believe that my colleagues have been trying to do you down?'

'I am not speaking about your colleagues.'

'You mean me?'

'I believe there is a saying – If the cap fits, wear it.'

I had become the spider in the web, the origin of persecution. No one likes being hated: most of us are afraid of it: it jars to the bone when we meet hatred face to face. But it was better that I should be the enemy, not Roger.

I had to sound as if I didn't mind being insulted, as though I had no temper of my own. I wanted to lash out and do it better than he did. Natures like his clashed right at the roots with mine: even if he were not being offensive, he would have tempted me to say something hard. But I was doing a job, and I couldn't afford luxuries, certainly not the luxury of being myself. I said, sounding like a middle-aged public man: 'I repeat, the Minister is very grateful for all the effort you've put into this work. I think I ought to say that he has an exceptionally high opinion of you.'

'I hope you are right.'

'He has made it perfectly clear—'

'I hope you are right.' Suddenly his face was full of illumination, as though he were looking over my shoulder. 'Then I shall go straight to him in the future.'

'That may not be possible, when he's occupied—'

'That', said Brodzinski, 'is for the Minister to say.'

With ritual courtesy, he enquired what I should be doing for Christmas. With dignity he thanked me for entertaining him. When I took him to the top of the stairs, he gripped my hand in his immense one. I returned to the drawing-room, and stood preoccupied, not noticing acquaintances about the room, with my back to the fire. I was thinking angrily of Roger. He should have broken the news himself.

A cheerful little old man patted my arm. 'I saw you caballing down there' – he pointed to the end of the room – 'with that scientist chap'.

'Oh yes?' I said.

'Talking a bit of shop?'

'Talking a bit of shop,' I said.

I was wondering just how I could have done it better. One thing was clear: I could hardly have done it worse. I was wondering about Brodzinski's next move.

I was letting myself get worn down by one man. It seemed foolish, right out of proportion, as I stood there by the fire, in the drawing-room of the Athenæum.

It seemed even more foolish, half an hour later, in the drawing-room of my own flat. Francis Getliffe was there before me, having come for dinner before he got the late train back to Cambridge. He was talking to Margaret, who was fond of him, both because she recognised his reciprocal affection, and because she admired what his life had been. Like hers, it had been signally without equivocation. They knew how to talk to each other simply, without parentheses.

The room was bright, the pictures were lively on the walls, it was a home such as in my young manhood I thought I should never have. I mentioned that I had had a scene with Brodzinski. Margaret was smiling, because of the place where it had happened, the club which, unlike my other one, I so rarely used. Francis was impatient. The sooner he delivered the report to Roger, the better: as for this man, he could not see that he mattered. Nor could I, drinking before dinner in my own home.

Francis had quite a different concern. Soon after I arrived, a young man and a girl came into the room, both of them flushed. The young man was Arthur Plimpton, who immediately took charge of the drinks. He made Margaret lie back, and went round with a tinkling tray, refilling our glasses, calling Francis and me by our titles, with his mixture of respect and impudence. The girl was Penelope, Francis's younger daughter.

She was nineteen, but looked older. She was taller than her father, Junoesque and, in a rosy flowering fashion, beautiful. She did not much resemble either of her parents. Where that particular style of beauty came from, no one could explain; if I had not known, it would not have occurred to me that her mother was Jewish.

Arthur had managed to get his way. It had been easy to coax Margaret into inviting them to stay with us for a week. We had plenty of room, now we had added another flat to our own. It had not been so easy for Penelope to accept. Francis, who usually rejoiced in his children's love affairs and marriages, did not seem to rejoice in this. The fact was, that someone had let him know, after Arthur had got inside the family, how rich the young man was. Francis did not like it: or rather, he would have liked them to get married, but could not let anyone see it, even his oldest friends. He would not, even by an ordinary invitation, appear to be encouraging his daughter to marry a fortune. His sense of punctilio was getting stiffer as he grew older: he had all the hard pride of the English professional classes, plus something added of his own.

It amused me, having known Francis since we were both young. I had seen him, less orthodox than now, marrying for love, but also marrying into a rich family. I had seen him defying taboos, a Gentile carrying off a Jewish girl. I had seen him less respectable than now. Other people, meeting him his middle fifties, regarded him as he and I regarded the dignitaries of our own youth – Sir Francis Getliffe, high-principled, decent, full of *gravitas*, a little formal and, yes, a little priggish. I could not regard him so. Even when he was behaving stiffly, I could still hear, as none of us can help hearing with the friends of our youth, the chimes of another time: the 'chimes of midnight', in the empty, lonely streets we had once walked together.

That did not prevent Margaret and me from twitting him, saying that he was showing ridiculous decorum, and ourselves opening our house to Arthur. I was fond of Penelope, who happened to be my goddaughter, but of the pair it was Arthur who was the more fun.

That night at dinner, he had two objectives. One was to absorb the conversation. He could not get over his discovery that Sir Francis, so eminent, so straitlaced about domestic behaviour, was, when he talked about the world, by American standards wildly radical. Arthur could not have enough of it. It shocked him, and gave him a thrill of guilt. Not, I thought, that anything Francis, Margaret or I said would affect him by as much as one per cent. But I thought also, with a certain grim satisfaction, that it would do him no harm to hear us talk about communists as though they were human beings.

Arthur's second objective was less intellectual. It was to get Penelope to himself. Towards the end of the meal, Francis was looking at his watch. He would soon have to leave for Liverpool Street. If Arthur waited half an hour, he and Penelope could slip out without a word. But Arthur was a young man of spirit.

'Sir Francis,' he said, 'we will have to be going ourselves. I must say, it's been a very fine evening.'

'Where are you going?' said Margaret, since Francis did not reply.

'Penny and I are going to dance some place.'

They were both waiting. Penelope, who was not talkative, had an inward-turning smile.

They might be late, Arthur went on, and asked Margaret if they could have a key.

'I'll get her back safe and sound,' Arthur said to Francis.

Francis nodded.

'And I'll send her back to Cambridge in time for Christmas,' Arthur went on, a little lordly, and knowing it.

I joined in, to stop Arthur teasing Francis any more. I said we would all travel to Cambridge together. We were taking our children, as we did each year, to spend Christmas with my brother Martin.

Francis, back in authority again, asked us all to come to his house on Boxing Day. There was to be a great party of Francis's children, a couple of grandchildren, Martin's family and ours.

Just for an instant, Arthur looked appealing. He wanted to be invited. Francis knew it, and glanced at him from under high, quixotic eyebrows. Arthur might be obstinate, but he had met another obstinate man. This time Francis held the initiative. He did not waver. He gave no invitation. He said politely that in five minutes he must be off.

Resilient, Arthur was on his feet.

'We have to go too. Come on, Penny. It's been a very fine evening, Sir Francis.'

They told Margaret they wouldn't want breakfast, and would see her later in the morning. Arthur said good-night to Francis, and Penelope kissed him. Then they went out, a handsome couple, cherishing their secrets, disclosing nothing except happiness, full of the pride of life, full of joy.

CHAPTER XVIII

THE EUPHORIA OF TOUCHING WOOD

On a bright January morning, the telephones kept ringing in my office. Did I know, did anyone know, who was going to be the new Prime Minister? Had anyone been summoned to the Palace? All over Whitehall, all through the maze of the Treasury Building, men were gossiping. To some, in particular to Ministers like Roger, the answer mattered. To one or two it would be decisive. No one in Roger's circle knew what it was going to be. They had not been ready for the resignation. Now the Chancellor was being backed: so was the Home Secretary. Moral sentiments were being expressed, and a good deal of damage being done.

After lunch, we heard that Charles Lenton had been sent for. There had not been such a turnover of fortune for over thirty years. By the end of the afternoon, people in high places were discovering virtues in Lenton that had not before been so vividly perceived. He was a middle-ranking Minister who had, for a short time after the war, been in charge of Hector Rose's department. He was now fifty-five, young to be Prime Minister. He was a lawyer by profession, and people commented that he must be the first Conservative Prime Minister since Disraeli without substantial private means. He was hearty, healthy, unpretentious: he looked amiable and slightly porcine, except that, as a political cartoonist and a smart photographer happily observed, he was born with bags under his eyes. Rose said: 'At any rate, my dear Lewis, we shan't be dazzled by coruscations of brilliance.'

Roger said nothing. He was waiting to see where the influence lay. In the London network, messages about the Prime Minister began flashing like the bulbs on a computer. Whom he listened to, where he spent the weekend, whom he had a drink with late at night.

Within three months, Roger and his friends were certain of one thing. The Prime Minister had set himself up with a confidant. This was not in itself surprising: most men in the 'first place' (as some liked to call the Prime Ministership) did so. But it was more surprising when they realised who the confidant was. It was Reggie Collingwood.

From the outside, the two of them had nothing in common. Collingwood was arrogant, unsocial, in a subdued fashion grand – whereas the Prime Minister was matey and deliberately prosaic, as though his ambition was to look natural in a bowler hat, coming in on the train from Purley.

Yet there it was. At once the gossips were tipping Ministers whom Coilingwood appeared to fancy. They all agreed that Roger's stock was on the way down.

It sounded too near the truth. I had heard from Caro herself that Collingwood had never got on with her family. They were too smart, too much in the high world, for him. Collingwood might have spent a lot of time in the high world, but he did not approve of it. As for Roger, Collingwood had had nothing to do with him. They had not had so much as a drink together. At Basset, during that weekend twelve months before, they had met like remote acquaintances: and then Roger had found himself in, or forced, a quarrel.

Before long, the gossips began to hedge. Monty Cave was brought back into the Government, and promoted to full Ministerial rank. The commentators got busy once more. Was this a gesture towards Roger? Or was the P.M. playing both ends against the middle? Or, a more ingenious gloss, was he showing the left wing of the party that he had nothing against them, before he eased Roger out?

A few days after Cave's appointment, I was sitting in the barber's in Curzon Street when I heard a breathy whisper near my ear. 'Well, what's going to happen tomorrow night?'

As soon as I got out of the chair, I heard some more. Apparently Roger had been summoned to one of those private dinners which busybodies like my informant were beginning to know about: dinners with the Prime Minister and Collingwood and a single guest, which took place, because Collingwood didn't like the Tory clubs, in his own suite at an old-fashioned hotel.

'Well, what are they going to say to him?'

I didn't know. I didn't even know whether the story was true. My informant was a man with a selfless passion for gossip. As I walked down the street in the sunshine, I was thinking bleakly of the old Dostoievskian phrase, that I had heard something 'on not specially reliable authority'.

But it was true. In forty-eight hours we knew, when Caro telephoned Margaret to ask if they could come to dinner that night, with no one present but the four of us.

They arrived very early. The sun was still high over Hyde Park, blinding Caro as she sat down opposite the window. She screwed up her eyes, hooted, told Margaret that she wanted a drink but that Roger needed one first. Roger had scarcely spoken, and Caro's voice, as in her own house, took charge. But Margaret liked her more, and got on with her better, than I did.

Soon they were sitting side by side on the sofa, all of us suddenly quiet. I said to Roger: 'So you saw them last night, did you?'

'Why do you think,' said Caro, 'that we've parked ourselves on you like this?'

From his armchair, Roger was gazing, eyes blank, at the picture over the fireplace.

'How did it go?' I asked.

He muttered, as though he were having to force himself to talk.

I was at a loss. He was not inhibited because Margaret was there. He knew that she was as discreet as I was, or more so. Both he and Caro felt safe with her, and trusted her.

Roger brushed both hands over his eyes, forehead and temples, like a man trying to freshen himself.

'I don't know,' he said. He leaned forward. 'Look here,' he said, 'if I said what the position seemed like tonight – I should have to say that I've got it in the palm of my hand.'

He sounded realistic, sober, baffled. He sounded as though he didn't want us to see, didn't want himself to see, that he was happy.

'Isn't that good news?' said Margaret.

'I can't believe it,' said Roger.

'You can, you know,' said Caro gently.

'You all have to remember' – Roger was speaking with care – 'that things change very fast at the top. I'm in favour now. It may not last twelve months. Things may begin to go the other way. Remember your uncle and what happened to him. You ought to know what to expect,' he said to Caro. 'So ought Lewis and Margaret. They've seen enough. For all we know, I'm at the top of the hill tonight. I may start moving downwards tomorrow. Or perhaps I've already started. We've all got to remember that.'

It was the sort of solemn warning that a sanguine man gives to others, because he feels he ought to give it to himself. Roger sounded so cautious, statesmanlike and wise; he was trying to be all those things; but in his heart he didn't believe a word of it. Behind his puzzled, twisted expression, he was lit up with hope – or almost with hope realised. There were times that evening when he felt that what he wanted to do was already done. There were also times when he was thinking of his next office but one.

Yet, all through the evening, he spoke with self-knowledge, as though he were putting pretentions on one side, almost as though he had been deflated. It was a curious result of success, or the foretaste of success.

We stayed for a long time drinking before dinner. Yes, he had had a reception the night before that he hadn't dared imagine. The P.M. had been cordial; of course the P.M. was professionally cordial, so it didn't mean much. What did mean something was that he had assured Roger of support. As for Collingwood, he had gone out of his way to be friendly; which, from him, who never troubled to be friendly, or couldn't be, had been something no one could have expected.

'The extraordinary thing is,' said Roger, his face puzzled and simple, 'he seems to like me.'

'Why not?' said Margaret.

'Why should he?' said Roger.

He went on:

'You know, it's the first time anyone at the top has crooked his finger at me and said in effect – "My boy, your place is up here." Up to now they've let me crawl up and fight every inch of the way. I'm not the sort of man people feel inclined to help, you know.'

He had spoken with a trace of passion. To others, I was thinking, even to me, that complaint rang strangely. He was too formidable a man for one to think of him as being 'promising', as needing patronage or protection. To most men, to the Collingwoods and their kind, he must have seemed mature and dominant, even before he was forty, long before he had in any sense 'arrived'. Yet Roger did not see himself like that. Perhaps no one saw himself as beyond question, formidable, mature, dominant. Roger knew that, when other men had been helped up, he had been left alone. He spoke as though this had been a wound: as though, years before, it had made him harden his will.

'Never mind,' said Caro, 'they like you, they're telling you you're in.'

Roger said, 'They've left it pretty late.'

As we sat at dinner, he was amiable but absent-minded, until Caro, looking prettier than I had seen her, had been talking about her brother. He broke into a conversation. Across the table, he said to his wife: 'It doesn't matter much being liked, for this kind of life.'

We might have been back in the drawing-room, still discussing the Prime Minister and Collingwood. We hadn't realised, while we talked, that he was daydreaming contentedly away.

For a second, Caro didn't take the reference. Then she misjudged him. She said: 'But they do like you.'

She went on telling him that Collingwood was sincere. She seemed to be reassuring Roger that he got liked as easily as most men. But that wasn't a reassurance he needed. With a grin, part shamefaced, part sarcastic, he said: 'No, that's neither here nor there. I meant it doesn't matter much being liked. For serious purposes, it doesn't really count. Nothing like so much as your relatives have always thought.'

She hesitated. His tone had not escaped her. He had spoken of 'your' relatives as though he had not accepted them, would never accept them, as being his. Yet that was reversing the truth. It had not been easy for him, I had been told, at the time of his marriage. She had loved him to the highest pitch of obstinacy and they had had to put up with her decision. He was not wholly unacceptable, it wasn't as though she had been a wild young girl and he something like a dance-band leader: he was presentable, he would 'do'. But he was not 'one of them'. They would have made him into 'one of them,' if will had been the only element involved; but they could not do it. Years later, there were times when they still couldn't help behaving as though he were the local doctor, or the parson, whom Caro happened to have invited to a meal.

'Making themselves liked, that's how most of them got on,' said Caro.

'Not in the real stuff,' Roger replied. 'What you want is someone who believes in what you do. It's preferable if he doesn't want to cut your throat.'

He was speaking as he had once done, when we were dining at the Carlton Club. It was a theme his mind kept digging into. Personal relations, so Roger went on saying, didn't decide anything in the 'real stuff'. Being one of a group, as with the Whig aristocrats from whom Caro's family descended, decided some things. But in the long run, his job didn't depend on that. In the real issues he wasn't going to get support, just because Reggie Collingwood enjoyed splitting a bottle with him. These things weren't as easy: they weren't as romantic. 'If they like me, and it seems that they may do, they'll take a little longer to kick me out. They might even kick me upstairs. But that's all the benefit I should get out of being liked. While as for support – that's a different cup of tea. They're going to support me for a bit – because it fits in with what they want to do. Because they believe we're on the same side. Up to a point. They're watching me, you know. I tell you, real politics isn't as personal as people think.'

Margaret said: 'Doesn't that make it worse?'

Roger replied: 'Don't you think it's probably better?' His tone was not bantering. It wasn't even specially wise. It was eager. Suddenly I felt in him – what was often hidden, because of his will, his tricks, even the power of his nature – something quite simple. He knew the temptations, the charm of politics, the romantic trappings – but there were times when he wanted to throw them right away. There were times when he could tell himself, and be full of faith, that there was something he wanted to do. Then he could feel that there was a justification for his life. He wanted that grace more than most men: the lumber dropped away from him, he seemed to himself light, undivided, at one.

In the drawing-room, drinking after dinner, tired, content, Roger went on talking about politics. One story had come up the night before, which Collingwood had said he ought to know. A rumour was running round about Cave's appointment. It had reached the clubs; they could expect it in the political columns next Sunday, said Collingwood, who didn't appear to know that in Whitehall we had heard it already. It was that this appointment had been the pay-off for Roger and his associates. Roger had struck a bargain with Charles Lenton when the Prime Ministership fell vacant. He and his friends would support Lenton for the place, but they had fixed the price, and the price was a Ministry for Cave.

'What do you think of that?' asked Roger. He, like Collingwood, seemed to have been surprised by the rumour. Collingwood was an unsociable widower, but I thought there was less excuse for Roger.

'Well,' I said, 'it's not the most terrible accusation I've ever heard.' I was laughing at him. He had been enjoying himself, talking without humbug. All night his mood had been realistic, almost chastened: that was the way he faced the promise of success. And yet, at this mild bit of slander, he felt indignant and ill-used.

'But it's not true!' Roger raised his voice.

'They'll say worse things than that, which won't be true either,' I said.

Roger said: 'No, the point is: politics are not like that. God knows, I've played it rougher than that before now. If necessary I shall play it rough again. But not like that.' He was speaking with complete reasonableness. 'Of course politics can be corrupt. But not corrupt in that fashion. No one makes that kind of bargain. It's not that we're specially admirable. But we've got to make things work, and they couldn't work like that, and they don't. I've never seen anyone make a deal of that kind in my life. It's only people who don't know how the world ticks who think it ticks like that.'

I was thinking, I had once, twenty years before, seen someone propose such a deal. It had happened in my college. The college politicians had turned it down at sight, outraged, just as Roger was, by a man who didn't know 'how the world ticks', by a man who made the world look worse than it was because he had all the cynicism of the unworldly.

We had not drawn the curtains, and through the open windows a breeze was blowing in. For an instant I leaned out. There was a smell of petrol from the Bayswater Road, mixed with the smell of spring. It was a clear night for London, and above the neon haze, over the trees in the park, I could make out some stars.

I turned back to the room. Roger was stretched out, quiet, and happy again, on the sofa. Margaret had asked him a question I did not catch. He was replying without fuss that the decisions had to be taken soon. He might soon cease to be useful. He would be lucky if he had ten years.

CHAPTER XIX

SUDDEN CESSATION OF A NUISANCE

It puzzled me, not that Brodzinski kept pressing for a private talk with Roger, but that all of a sudden he left off doing so. Once he had given me up, letters came into Roger's office. Brodzinski begged for an interview on a matter of grave public concern. He wished to explain his disagreement with his scientific colleagues. He had been alarmed by the attitude of the secretary of the committee.

It was a nuisance, but Ministers' offices were used to nuisances. Roger asked Osbaldiston to see Brodzinski. Douglas, more guarded and official than I had been, gave a reply as though to a parliamentary question: no, the Minister had not reached a conclusion: he was studying both the majority report and Brodzinski's minority report. For a few days, this seemed to reassure Brodzinski. Then the letters began again. Once more I told Roger not to underestimate him.

Roger asked, what could he do? Write to *The Times*? Talk to the Opposition military spokesmen? There we were safeguarded. We had, through Francis Getliffe and others, our own contacts. Francis and I had, for years, been closer to them than to Roger's colleagues. What could the man do? I had to agree. After the talk in the Athenæum, I had come away apprehensive. Now the anxiety had lost its edge. Out of habit, I repeated that Roger ought to have a word with him.

On the Thursday which followed his dinner with the Prime Minister, Roger had been invited to a conversazione at the Royal Society. The day after, he mentioned that he had spent a quarter of an hour with Brodzinski alone.

It looked as though Roger had spread himself. The next letters from Brodzinski said he had always known that the Minister understood. If they could continue the conversation undisturbed, he, Brodzinski, was certain that all the obstacles would be removed. In a few days Roger replied politely. Another letter arrived by return. Then telephone calls. Would the Minister's private secretary arrange a meeting? Could the Minister be told that Brodzinski was on the line? Could he be put straight through?

Suddenly it all stopped. No more telephone calls. No more letters. It was bewildering. I took what precautions I could. We knew his points of influence in the Air Ministry, in the House. Was he pressing them, instead? But no: he seemed not to have been near them. There was no disquiet anywhere, there were not even any rumours hissing round.

The patient young men in Roger's private office allowed themselves a shrug of relief. He had got tired of it at last, they said. Four months of commotion: then absolute silence. From their records, they could date when silence fell. It was the third week in May.

In that same week, I happened to have been enquiring whether certain invitations to accept honours had been sent out. My question had nothing to do with Brodzinski, though I thought mechanically that his invitation must have gone out too. It did not occur to me, not remotely, to connect the two dates.

As the summer began, all of us round Roger were more confident than we had yet been. First drafts of the White Paper were being composed. Francis Getliffe came from Cambridge twice a week to confer with Douglas and Walter Luke. Papers passed between Douglas's office and Rose's. Roger had issued an instruction that the office draft must be ready for him by August. Then he would publish when he guessed the time was right. In private, he was preparing for the month after Christmas, the beginning of 1958.

While we were drafting, Diana Skidmore was going through her standard summer round. On the last day of Ascot week, she invited some of us to a party in South Street. She had heard – as though she had a ticker-tape service about American visitors – that David Rubin was in England. She had not met him: 'He's brilliant, isn't he?' she asked. Yes, I assured her, he was certainly brilliant. 'Bring him along,' she ordered. There had been a time when the Basset circle was supposed to be anti-Semitic. That, at least, had changed.

When Margaret, David Rubin and I stood at the edge of Diana's drawing-room, about seven o'clock on the wet June evening, not much else seemed to have changed. The voices were as hearty as ever: the champagne went around as fast: the women stood in their Ascot frocks, the men in their Ascot uniforms. There were a dozen Ministers there, several of the Opposition front bench, many Conservative members, and a few from the other side.

There was a crowd of Diana's rich friends. She welcomed us with vigour. Yes, she knew that David Rubin was talking to the English nuclear scientists.

'People over here being sensible?' she said to him. 'Come and tell me about them. I'll arrange something next week.' She was peremptory as usual, and yet, because she took it for granted that it was for her to behave like a prince, to open England up to him, he took it for granted too.

How was it, I had sometimes wondered, that, despite her use of her riches, she didn't attract more resentment? Even when she put a hand, with complete confidence, into any kind of politics? She had been drawn back into the swirling, meaty, noisy gaggle: there she was, listening deferentially to her handsome architect. Even in her devoted marriage, she had had a hankering for one *guru* after another. Just as she took it for granted that she could talk to Ministers, so she loved being a pupil. If it seemed a contradiction to others, it seemed natural to her, and that was all she cared about.

Margaret had been taken away by Monty Cave. I noticed Rubin being shouted at hilariously by Sammikins. I walked round the party, and then, half an hour after we came in, found myself by Rubin's side again. He was watching the crowd with his air of resignation, of sad intelligence.

'They're in better shape, aren't they?' He meant that these people, or some of them, had lost their collective confidence over Suez. Now they were behaving as though they had found it again. Rubin knew, as well as I did, that political sorrows did not last long. Political memory lasted about a fortnight. It did not count beside a new love affair, a new job, even, for many of these men, the active glow after making a good speech.

'No country's got a ruling class like this.' David Rubin opened his hands towards the room. 'I don't know what they hope for, and they don't know either. But they still feel they're the lords of this world.'

I was fond of Rubin and respected him, but his reflections on England were irking me. I said he mustn't judge the country by this group. Being born in my provincial town wasn't much different from being born in Brooklyn. He ought to know the boys I grew up among. Rubin interrupted, with a sharp smile:

'No. You're a far-sighted man, I know it, Lewis. But you're just as confident in yourself as these characters are.' Once more he shrugged at the room. 'You don't believe a single thing that they believe, but you've borrowed more from them than you know.'

People were going out to dinner, and the party thinned. Gradually those who were left came to the middle of the room. There stood Diana and her architect, Sammikins and two decorative women, Margaret and Lord Bridgewater, and a few more. I joined the group just as David Rubin came up from the other side with Cave's wife, who was for once out with her husband. She was ash-blonde, with a hard, strained, beautiful face. Rubin had begun to enjoy himself. He might have a darker world view than anyone there, but he gained certain consolations.

No one could talk much, in that inner residue of the party, but Sammikins. He was trumpeting away with a euphoria startling even by his own standards. Just as Diana had lost money at Ascot, he had won. With the irrationality of the rich, Diana had been put out. With the irrationality of the harassed, which he would remain until his father died, Sammikins was elated. He wanted to entertain us all. He spoke with the luminosity of one who saw that his financial problems had been settled for ever. 'All the time I was at school,' he cried, 'm'tutor gave me one piece of advice. He said, "Houghton, never go in for horse-racing. They suck you in."' Sammikins caught sight of David Rubin, and raised his voice once more. 'What do you think of that, Professor? What do you think of that for a piece of advice? Not *à point*, eh?'

David Rubin did not much like being called Professor. Also, he found Sammikins's allusions somewhat esoteric. But he grappled. He replied: 'I'm afraid I have to agree with your friend.'

'M'tutor.'

'Anyway, he's right. Statistically, he must be right.'

'Horses are better than cards, any day of the week. Damn it all, Professor, I've proved it!'

David Rubin was getting noise-drunk. Sammikins, in a more conciliatory tone, went on: 'I grant you this, Professor, I don't know about roulette. I've known men who made an income at roulette.'

The scientific truth was too strong for Rubin.

'No. If you played roulette for infinite time, however you played, you'd be bound to lose.' He took Sammikins by the arm. We had the pleasant spectacle of Rubin, Nobel Laureate, most elegant of conceptual thinkers, not quite sober, trying to explain to Sammikins, positive that he had found the secret of prosperity, distinctly drunk, some aspects of the theory of probability.

Diana said, in her clear, military rasp, that racing was a mug's game. On the other hand, she was sharp with happiness. She wanted to have dinner with the architect. It was only out of duty, as we were all ready to go, that she mentioned the Government.

'They seem to be getting on a bit better,' she said.

There were murmurs of agreement all round her.

'Roger's doing all right,' she said to me. She was not asking my opinion, she was telling me.

She went on: 'Reggie Collingwood thinks well of him.' We were getting near the door. Diana said: 'Yes. Reggie says he's a good listener.'

Diana had passed on the good news, and I went away happy. Objectively, Collingwood's statement was true; but, from a man who could hardly utter about one of the most eloquent men in London, it seemed an odd compliment.

CHAPTER XX

EVENING IN THE PARK

IN September, with the House in recess, Roger kept coming to his office. It was what the civil servants called the 'leave season'. Douglas was away and so, in my department, was Hector Rose. Nevertheless, Roger's secretaries were arranging a set of meetings to which I had to go. As I arrived in his room for one of them, Roger asked in a matter-of-fact tone if I minded staying behind after it was over. He had something he wanted to talk to me about, so he said.

He seemed a little preoccupied as he took the meeting. When he spoke, he was fumbling for the words, as a man does when he is tired and strained. I did not take much notice. The meeting was purring efficiently on. There were some unfamiliar faces, deputy secretaries, undersecretaries, appearing instead of their bosses. The competent voices carried on, the business was getting done.

The cups of tea were brought in, the weak and milky tea, the plates of biscuits. The meeting was doing all that Roger wanted. He might be tired, but he was showing good judgment. He did not hurry them, he let the decisions form. It was past six o'clock when the papers were being packed in the briefcases. Practised and polite, Roger said his good-evenings and his thanks, and we were left alone.

'That went rather well,' I said.

There was a pause, as though he had to remember what I was speaking about, before he replied: 'Yes, it did, didn't it?'

I was standing up, stretching myself. He had stayed in his chair. He looked up without expression, and asked:

'Do you mind if we go for a stroll in the park?'

We went down the corridors, down the stone stairs, out through the main entrance. We crossed over the park beside the lake; one of the pelicans was spreading its wings. The trees were creaking in a blustery wind; on the grass, the first leaves had fallen. It was a dark evening, with clouds, low and grey, driving across from the west. Roger had not spoken since we left the office. For an instant, I was not thinking of him. The smell of the water, of the autumn night, had filled me with a sense, vague but overmastering, of sadness and joy, as though I were played on by a memory which I could not in truth recall, of a place not far away, of a time many years before, when my first love, long since dead, had told me without kindness that she would come to me.

We walked slowly along the path. Girls, going home late from the offices, were scurrying in front of us. It was so windy that most of the seats by the lakeside were empty. Suddenly Roger said:

'Shall we sit down?'

Miniature waves were flecking the water. As we sat and watched them, Roger, without turning to me, said in a curt, flat and even tone:

'There may possibly be trouble. I don't think it's likely, but it's possible.'

I was shocked out of my reverie. My first thought was to ask if any of his supporters, high or low, Collingwood or the back-benchers, had turned against him.

'No. Nothing like that. Nothing like that at all.'

Was he trying to break some news affecting me? I had nothing on my mind, I could not think what it might be. I gave him a chance to tell me, but he shook his head.

Now it had come to the point, the confidence would not flow. He stared at the water. At last he said:

'I have a young woman.'

For the instant, I felt nothing but surprise.

'We've kept it absolutely quiet. Now she's been threatened. Someone's found out.'

'Who has?'

'Just a voice she didn't know, over the telephone,' he said.

'Does it matter?'

'How do we know?'

'What are you frightened of?'

There was a pause before he said:

'If it came out it might do some harm.'

I was still surprised. I had thought his marriage happy enough. A man-of-action's marriage, not all-excluding; but strong, a comfort, an alliance. Some of his worry was infecting me. I felt an irritation, an impatience, that I could not keep quiet. What more did he want? I was asking myself, as simply, as uncharitably, as my mother might have done. A good-looking wife, children, a rich home: what was he taking risks for? Risks, he seemed to think, which might damage his plans and mine. I was condemning him as simply as that, not in the least like one who had seen people in trouble, not like one who had done harm himself.

At the same time, I could not help feeling a kind of warmth, not affection so much as a visceral warmth. In the midst of his anxiety, he had been half-pleased to confess. Not with just the pleasure displayed by men higher-minded than he was, as they modestly admit a conquest – no, with a pleasure deeper than that, something more like joy. Looking at him as he sat, still gazing at the lake, not meeting my eyes, I should have guessed that he had not had much to do with women. But his emotions were powerful and, perhaps, so could his passions be. As he sat there, his face heavy, thinking of the dangers, he seemed comforted by what had happened to him – like a man for whom the promise of life is still there. I set myself to ask a practical question. What were the chances of it coming out?

'She's worried. I've never known her lose her nerve before.'

I said, probably she had never had to cope with a scandal. But the technique was all worked out. Go to a good tough lawyer. Tell everything.

'You've no reason to think that any rumours have gone round already, have you? I certainly haven't.'

Roger shook his head.

'Then it ought to be fairly easy to stop the hole.'

He did not respond, or look at me. He stared into the distance. In a moment, knowing that I was giving him no comfort, I broke off.

I said: 'I'm sure this can be handled. You ought to tell her that. But even if it couldn't be, and the worst came to the worst – is it the end of the world?' I meant, as I went on to say, that the people he lived amongst were used to scandals out of comparison more disreputable than this.

'You're fooling yourself,' he said harshly. 'It isn't so easy.'

I wondered, was he holding something back? Was she very young? 'Is there something special about it?' I said. 'Who is she?'

It seemed that he could not reply. He sat without speaking, and then in a burst of words put me off.

'It isn't important what's done. It is important who does it. There are plenty of people – you know as well as I do – who want an excuse to knife me. Don't you accept that this would be a reasonable excuse?'

'You haven't told me how.'

'There's an old maxim in the Anglican church. You can get away with unorthodox behaviour. Or you can get away with unorthodox doctrine. But you can't get away with both of them at the same time.'

For an instant, his spirits had flashed up. In the same sharp, realistic, almost amused tone, he added:

'Remember, I've never been one of the family. Perhaps, if I had been, I could get away with more.'

What was 'the family'?

The inner circle of privilege, the Caves, Wyndhams, Collingwoods, Diana's friends, the Bridgewaters, the people who, though they might like one another less than they liked Roger, took one another for granted, as they did not take him.

'No,' I said, 'you've never been one of them. But Caro is.'

I brought in her name deliberately. There was a silence. Then he answered the question I had not asked. 'If this thing breaks, Caro will stand by me.'

'She doesn't know?'

He shook his head, and then broke out with violence: 'I won't have Caro hurt.' It sounded more angry than anything he had said. Had he been talking about one worry, about the practical risk that still seemed to me unreal, in order to conceal another from himself? What kind of guilt did he feel, how much was he tied? All of a sudden, I thought I understood at last his outburst on Sammikins's behalf at Basset. It had seemed uncomfortable, untypical, not only to the rest of us but to himself. Yes, it had been chivalrous, it had been done for Caro's sake. But it had been altogether too chivalrous. It had the strain, the extravagant self-abnegation, of a man who gives his wife too many sacrifices, just to atone for not giving her his love.

'Isn't Caro going to be hurt anyway?' I said.

He did not reply.

'This affair isn't ready to stop, is it?'

'Not for either of us. Not for—' He hesitated. He still had not told me the woman's name. Now he wanted to, but at last brought out the pronoun, not the name.

'Can you give her up?'

'No,' said Roger.

Beneath the layers of worry, there was something else pressing him. Part joy: part something else again, which I could feel in the air, but to which I could not put a name – as though it were a superstitious sense, a gift of foresight.

He leaned back, and did not confide any more.

To the left, above the trees, the light from a window shone out – an office window, perhaps in Roger's Ministry, though I could not be sure – a square of yellow light high in the dark evening.

PART THREE

PRIVACY

CHAPTER XXI

BREAKFAST

IT was the morning after Roger had talked to me in the park, and Margaret and I were sitting at breakfast. From the table, I could look down at the slips of garden running behind the Tyburn chapel. I glanced across at my wife, young-looking in her dressing-gown, fresh, not made up. Sometimes I laughed at her for looking so fresh in the morning: for in fact it was I who woke up easily, while she was slumbrous, not at her best, until she had sat beside the window and drunk her first cups of tea.

That morning, she was not too slumbrous to read my expression. She knew that I was worrying, and asked me why. At once I told her Roger's story. I didn't think twice about telling her; we had no secrets, I wanted to confide. She wasn't intimate with Roger as I was, nor with Caro either, and I didn't expect her to be specially concerned. To my surprise, her colour rose. Her cheeks flushed, making her eyes look bluer still. She muttered: 'Damn him.'

'He'll be all right—' I was consoling her; but she broke out:

'Never mind about him. I was thinking of Caro.'

She said:

'You haven't given her a thought, have you?'

'There are two other people as well—'

'He's behaved atrociously, and she's the one who's going to face it.'

As a rule, she was no more given to this kind of indignation than I was myself. Already her temper was high and mine was rising. I tried to quieten us both, and said, in the shorthand we were used to, that Roger wasn't the first person in the world to cut loose: others had done the same.

'If you mean that I damaged someone else to come to you,' she flared up, 'that's true.'

'I didn't mean that.'

I had spoken without thinking.

'I know you didn't.' Her temper broke, she smiled. 'You know, I'd behave the same way again. But I haven't much to be proud of in that respect.'

'Nor have I.'

'You didn't betray your own marriage. That's why I can't brush off Roger betraying his.'

'You say I'm not giving Caro a thought?' Once more we were arguing, once more we were near to quarrelling. 'But how much are you giving him?'

'You said yourself, he'll be all right, he'll come through,' she said scornfully. Just then she had no feeling for him at all. 'Do you know what it's going to be like for her – if they break up?' She went on with passion. 'Shock. Humiliation. Loss.'

I was forced to think, Caro had been happy, she had paraded her happiness. She had done much for him – perhaps too much? Had he never accepted it, or the way her family looked at him?

All that I had to admit. And yet, I said, trying to sound reasonable, let's not make it over-tragic. If it came to losing him, wouldn't she recover? She was still young, she was pretty, she wasn't a delicate flower, she was rich. How long would it take her to get another husband?

'You're making it too easy for yourselves,' said Margaret.

'Who am I making it too easy for?'

'For him. And for yourself.' Her eyes were snapping.

'Losing him,' she said, 'that might be the least of it. It will be bad enough. But the humiliation will be worse.'

She added:

'You've always said, Caro doesn't give a damn. Any more than her brother does. But it's people who don't give a damn who can't bear being humiliated. They can't live with it, when they have to know what it means.'

I was thinking, Margaret was speaking of what she knew. She too, by nature, by training, made her own rules: they were more refined rules than Caro's, but they were just as independent. Her family and all her Bloomsbury connections cared no more what others thought than Caro's did, in some ways less. She knew just how vulnerable that kind of independence was.

She knew something deeper. When she and I first married, she had sometimes been frightened: should we come apart? I might think that I had come home. In her heart, knowing mine, she had not been as sure. She had told herself what she must be ready to feel and what it would cost.

Hearing of Roger and Caro, she felt those fears, long since buried, flood back. Suddenly I realised why the argument had mounted into a quarrel. I stopped my next retort, I stopped defending Roger. Instead, I said, looking into her eyes:

'It's a bad thing to be proud, isn't it?'

The words meant nothing to anyone in the world except ourselves. To her, they were saying that I had been at fault and so had she. At once there was nothing between us. The quarrel died down, the tinge of rancour died from the air, and across the table Margaret gave an open smile.

CHAPTER XXII

'THE KNIVES ARE SHARPENING'

ONE evening in the week that Roger made his confidence, Hector Rose sent his compliments to my office and asked if I could find it convenient to call upon him. After I had traversed the ten yards along the corridor, I was, as usual, greeted with gratitude for this athletic feat. 'My dear Lewis, how very, very good of you to come!'

He installed me in the chair by his desk, from which I could look out over the sun-speckled trees, as though this were my first visit to his room. He sat in his own chair, behind the chrysanthemums, and gave me a smile of dazzling meaninglessness. Then, within a second, he had got down to business.

'There's to be a cabinet committee,' he said, 'by which our masters mean, with their customary happy use of words, something for which the phrase is not appropriate. However, there it is.'

The committee was to 'have an oversight' of some of Roger's problems, in particular the White Paper. It consisted of Collingwood in the chair, Roger himself, Cave, and our own Minister. According to present habit, there would be a floating and varying population, Ministers, civil servants, scientists, attending on and off, which was why Rose had produced his gibe. 'In fact,' he said, 'you and I will no doubt have the inestimable privilege of attending some of the performances ourselves.'

For an instant, Rose's tidy mind was preoccupied with the shapelessness of new-style administration; but I broke in:

'What does this mean?'

'By itself' – he came back to business with a bite – 'it doesn't mean anything. Or at least, anything significant, should you say? The membership seems to be designed to strengthen Mr Quaife's hand. I seem to have heard, from sensible sources, that the Lord President' (Collingwood) 'is a moderately strong backer of Quaife. So, on the face of it, there ought to be certain advantages for policies which Mr Quaife and others appear to have at heart.'

He was baiting me, but not in his customary machine-like manner. He seemed uncomfortable. He folded his arms. His head did not move, but his light eyes fixed themselves on mine. 'You asked me an implied question,' he said curtly. 'I can't be certain, but I have a suspicion the answer is yes.' He added: 'I fancy you do, too. I may be wrong, but I think I ought to warn you that the knives are sharpening.'

'What evidence have you got?'

'Not much. Nothing very considerable.' He hesitated. 'No, I shouldn't feel at liberty to worry you with that.'

Again he had spoken with discomfort, as though – I could neither understand, nor believe it – he was protecting me.

'Do you mean that I'm personally involved?'

'I don't feel at liberty to speak. I'm not going to worry you unnecessarily.'

Nothing would budge him. At last he said:

'But I do feel at liberty to say just one thing. I think you might reasonably communicate to your friends that a certain amount of speed about their decisions might not come amiss. In my judgment, the opposition is going to increase the more chance it gets to form. I shouldn't have thought that this was a time for going slow.' As deliberately as another man might light a cigarette, he smelt a flower. 'I confess, I should rather like to know exactly what our friend Douglas Osbaldiston expects to happen. He has always had a remarkably shrewd nose for the way the wind is blowing. It's a valuable gift. Of course, he's a great friend of both of us, but I think it's fair comment to say that this particular gift hasn't exactly been a handicap to him in his career.'

I had never known Hector Rose behave like this. First, he had told me, not quite 'in terms' (as he would have said himself) but still definitely, that he was supporting Roger's policy. That was surprising. I had assumed that he started, like Douglas and his colleagues, suspicious of it. He might have become convinced by reason: with Rose, more than most men, that could conceivably happen: or else the events of Suez were still working changes in him. Still, it was a surprise. But, far more of a surprise, was his outburst about Douglas.

I had known Hector Rose for nearly twenty years. In all that time, I had not heard him pass a judgment on any of his equals. Not that he did not make them – but keeping them quiet was part of the disciplined life. I had known for years that he probably disliked, and certainly envied, Douglas. He knew that I knew. Yet I was astonished, and perhaps he was too, that he should let it out.

Just then the telephone rang. It was for me: Francis Getliffe had called at my office. When I told Rose he said:

'I think, if he wouldn't mind, I should rather like him to spare me five minutes.'

After I had given the message, Rose regarded me as though, for the second time that evening, he could not decide whether to speak or not. He said: 'You'll have a chance to talk to him later, will you?'

'I should think so,' I said.

'In that case, I should be grateful if you passed on the substance of what I've been telling you.'

'You mean, there's going to be trouble?'

'There are certain advantages in being prepared, shouldn't you say?'

'Including personal trouble?'

'That's going further than I was prepared to go.'

Yet he wanted Francis to know about it, and he also wanted to avoid telling him.

When Francis came into the room, however, Rose was so polite that he seemed to be caricaturing himself. 'My dear Sir Francis, it really is extraordinarily good of you! I didn't expect to have this pleasure—' All the time he was brandishing Francis's title; while Francis, who was not undisposed to formality himself, insisted on calling him 'Secretary'. It sounded absurd, used to it as I was. Yet they respected each other. Rose liked Francis much more than he did me.

Rose did not keep us long. He asked Francis if he were happy about the work of the scientific committee. Yes, said Francis. Was he, if it came to a public controversy – 'and I'm sure you don't need me to tell you, but there may be mild repercussions' – willing to put the weight of his authority behind it?

'Yes,' said Francis, and added, what else could he do?

There were thanks, courtesies, good-byes, more thanks and courtesies. Soon Francis and I were walking across the park to the Duke of York's Steps. 'What was that in aid of?' Francis asked.

'He was telling you that there's going to be a God-almighty row.'

'I suppose we had to expect it, didn't we?'

'More than we bargained for, I fancy.' I repeated what Rose had said to me. I went on: 'He can be so oblique that it drives you mad, but he was suggesting that I'm going to be shot at.'

On the grass, couples were lying in the sunshine. Francis walked on, edgy, preoccupied. He said that he didn't see how that could happen. It was more likely to happen to himself.

I said: 'Look, no one wants to bring bad news. But I've got a feeling, though Rose didn't say a positive word, that he thinks that too.'

Francis said, 'I'm tired of all this.'

We went a few yards in silence. He added:

'If we get this business through, then I shall want to drop out. I don't think I can take it any more.' He began to talk about the international situation: what did I think? Intellectually, he still stuck to his analysis. The technical and military arguments all pointed the same way: peace was becoming much more likely than war. Intellectually he still believed that. Did I? Yet when Quaife and the scientists tried to take one tiny step, not dramatic, quite realistic, then all hell was ready to break loose.

'Sometimes I can't help thinking that people won't see sense in time. I don't mean that people are wicked. I don't even mean they're stupid. But we're all in a mad bus, and the only thing we're all agreed on is to prevent anyone getting to the wheel.'

We were climbing up the steps. He said sharply:

'Lewis, I could do with some advice.'

For a second, I was afraid he was thinking of resigning. Instead he went on:

'I just don't know what to do about Penelope and that young man.'

His tone had become even more worried and sombre. On the way across the park he, who knew more about it than most men, had been gloomy over the military future. Now he spoke as though his daughter had really been the problem on his mind. He spoke exactly as a Victorian parent might have spoken, as though all the future were predictable and secure except for his daughter's marriage, and the well-being of his grandchildren.

He was on his way, he said, to meet her in the Ladies' Annexe of the 'club' (the Athenæum). Would I come too? It might help him out. He hadn't the slightest idea of what had been happening, or what she planned. He did not know whether she and Arthur were secretly engaged, or had even thought of getting married. Arthur had, that summer, returned home to America. Francis did not know whether they had quarrelled.

He did not know – but this he didn't say, for she was his daughter, and both of us were talking more prudishly than if she had been another girl – whether she had been sleeping with Arthur. For myself, in private, I thought it highly probable.

As we sat in the drawing-room of the Annexe, waiting for her, Francis looked more baffled than I had known him. Both he and his wife were lost. Penelope was more obstinate than either of them, and she wasn't given to explaining herself. Unlike his other children, she had never been any good at academic things: she had taken some sort of secretarial course, and she showed about as much interest in Francis's scientific friends as she would have done in so many Amazonian Indians. At present, however, she was prepared to recognise their existence. It had occurred to her that some of them lived in the United States; no doubt one could be persuaded to give her a job.

'I've got to stop it,' said Francis, as we went on waiting. 'I can't have her going over.' He spoke resolutely, like King Lear in the storm, and about as convincingly. He had already ordered a bottle of champagne, with the air of a man trying to keep an exigent girl-friend in a good temper.

At last she came in, with her flouncing walk, flushed, handsome, frowning. 'I thought it was number twelve,' she said. She gazed at us firmly, giving us the blame for her own mistake.

'As you see,' I replied, 'you thought wrong.'

'It used to be number twelve.'

'Never.'

'I remember *going* to number twelve.' She spoke with an extreme display of mumpsimus, persisting confidently in error.

'In that case, either you remember wrong, or you went to the wrong place before.'

She stopped lowering, and gave me an open, happy grin. I could imagine what Arthur and others saw in her.

With a healthy thirst, she put down two glasses of champagne.

Francis's manner to her was courteous but uneasy, very much as when he was talking to Hector Rose. He told her that —— from Oxford was dining with them. 'How old is he?' Penelope sat up.

'Forty-seven or eight.'

Penelope sank back.

'Now if you'd ever seen him,' I remarked, 'you'd certainly have put on a new dress.'

'Of course I shouldn't.' Then a thought struck her. 'Does he know people in America?'

'Why America?' I said, trying to help Francis out.

'Oh, I'm going there this fall or next spring.'

Francis cleared his throat. Screwing himself up, he said:

'I'm sorry, Penny, but I wish you'd get that out of your mind.'

'Why?'

'Because I'm afraid it can't happen.'

'We'll see.'

Francis took the plunge.

'I don't mean that we couldn't find a way for you to earn your keep. I expect we could—'

'Then let's get going!' said Penelope, with enthusiasm.

'That isn't the point. Don't you see it isn't?'

Francis paused: then rushed on:

'Don't you see, we can't let you deposit yourself on young Plimpton's doorstep?'

'Why not?'

Penelope stretched herself luxuriously, with the poised expression of one who has said her last word for the evening.

Francis continued a one-sided conversation, without answers. Didn't she see that they couldn't let her? Didn't she realise that they had to behave like responsible persons?

Suddenly his tone became gentler, and even more embarrassed. He said: 'All that's bad enough, but there's something worse.'

This time she responded:

'What's that?'

'My dear girl, I'm not going to ask you what your feelings are for young – Arthur, or what his are for you. I don't think any of us is entitled to ask that.'

She gazed at him with splendid grey eyes, her face quite unreadable.

'But suppose you do care for him, and something went wrong? You're both very young, and the chances are that something will go wrong. Well, if you've gone over to be with him, and then you're left alone – that's a risk I just can't think of your taking.'

Penelope gave a gnomic smile and said:

'When I go to America I may not see Arthur at all.'

CHAPTER XXIII

VISIT TO A SMALL SITTING-ROOM

IT was still September. In the middle of the morning, the telephone rang on my desk. My personal assistant was speaking: someone called Ellen Smith was on the line, asking to talk to me urgently. The name meant nothing: what did she want? No, said the p.a., she had refused to say. I hesitated. This was one of the occupational risks. Then I said, 'All right, put her through.'

'My name is Ellen Smith.' The voice was brisk and cultivated. 'I've met you once before.'

I said 'Yes?' But did I not remember.

'I think Roger – Roger Quaife – has told you, hasn't he?'

Now I understood.

'He's given me permission,' she went on, 'to talk to you myself. Do you mind?'

Would I call at her flat one evening, when she had got back from her job? That would be better than saying anything on the telephone, didn't I agree? She didn't want to impose on me, but she was worried. She hoped I could bear it.

She sounded precise, nervous, active. I had no impression of her at all. On the way to her flat in Ebury Street, I thought to myself that it was well placed for Westminster – chance or not? But about her, I did not know whether she was single or married, nor anything else.

When she opened the door to me, the first thing I felt was the obvious, the banal irony. She seemed familiar, yet I could not place her. She shook hands with an expression both diffident and severe. She was small and slender, but not at all frail, dark-haired, wearing a white jersey over a black skirt. She was no younger than Caro. By the side of Caro, the confident, the splendid, she would have looked insignificant. One memory, though not about herself, came back with the relevance of someone telling one the time, and I remembered Caro, gay in the drawing-room at Lord North Street, roaring with laughter and saying the woman a wife needs to fear isn't the raving beauty, but that little grey mouse in the corner. It seemed the most cut and dried of ironies to remember that, and then to follow Ellen Smith into her chic, small sitting-room. I still could not recall meeting her, or anything about her.

She poured me a drink. She drew her legs on to the sofa, the tumblers on the table between us.

'It's kind of you to come,' she said.

'Nonsense,' I replied, a little overheartily.

'Is it nonsense?' She looked at me. For an instance I had Caro's eyes in mind, bold, full, innocent. These eyes were not bold, but deeper-set, lit up with attention, lit up with insight. Then the contrast faded out. I was studying her face, not beautiful, not pretty, but fine and delicate. The delicacy, the acuteness of her expression, struck one more when one looked up from her strong shoulders. She smiled, diffidently and honestly. 'This is damned awkward,' she said.

Suddenly a memory flashed back – was it because my fingers were cold against the glass? The Ambassadorial house in Regent's Park, the night of Suez, the wife of J. C. Smith.

So this was she. Yes, it was awkward, though that was not what she meant. Smith, Collingwood's nephew, fanatical, dedicated, so people said about him: I had read some of his speeches and articles: they had a curious gritty violence. They were shot through with a conspiratorial feeling of history and politics: and yet I had met young Conservative members who worshipped him. The wife of J. C. Smith. Yes, it was awkward. I said something muted, such as, the less she fretted the better.

This time her smile was brilliant.

'That's easier said than done, you know.'

I tried to take the edge off both of us. I asked what she had been doing that day. She told me that she had been out as usual at her job. She seemed to be working in a reference library. We mentioned the names of acquaintances, among them Lord Lufkin. I said that I had once worked for him. 'I'm sure that was good for you,' she said with a faint flash of mischief. Strained as she was, her spirits did not take much to revive them. She did not forget about my comfort, either. The glass was refilled, the cigarette-box was open. She broke out: 'I am not fretting about him and me. You do believe that, don't you?'

She went on: 'I'm happy about us. I'm happier than I've ever been in my life. And I think he's happy too. It sounds too conceited to live, but I think he's happy too.'

She had no conceit at all, I was thinking, far too little for her own good.

She had spoken so directly that I could do the same. I asked, where was her husband, what had happened to her marriage? She shook her head.

'I've got to tell you,' she said. 'It sounds ugly. If I heard it about some-one else, I should write her off. I know I should.' She said that, besides Roger, only her husband's parents knew the truth about him. It was to be kept a dead secret. Then she said, flat and hard: 'He's in a mental home.'

It wasn't certain that he would get better, she said. His constituency had been told that he was ill and might not contest his seat at the next election.

'It's been coming on for years. Yes, and that hasn't stopped me. I saw the chance to be happy, and I took it.' She looked at me with an expression honest, guilty and stern. 'I'm not going to make excuses. But you might believe this. It sounds disloyal, but if he hadn't been getting unbalanced I should have left him long ago. I tried to look after him. If it hadn't been for that, I should have left him long before Roger came along.' She gave a sharp-eyed smile, not merciful to herself. 'There's something wrong with a woman who falls for a man she can't endure and then for one she can't marry, isn't there?'

'It could be bad luck.'

'It's not all bad luck.' Then she said, without pretence: 'But, do you know, just now I can't feel that there's much wrong with me. You can understand that, can't you?'

She laughed out loud. One couldn't doubt her warmth, her ardour, her capacity for happiness. And yet I felt that this was not a life for which she was made. Plenty of women I knew in London made the best of this sort of bachelor life in flats like this – though hers was brighter, more expensive, than most of theirs. Plenty of women came back from offices as she did, looked after their little nests, waited for their men. Some of them could take it: light come, light go. Some even felt their blood run hotter because they had to keep a secret, because the curtains were drawn and they were listening – alone – for the snap of the lift-door. Looking at Ellen, I was sure that, though she would bear it in secrecy if she couldn't get him any other way, she was paying a price, maybe higher than she knew.

I asked how long had their affair been going on.

'Three years,' she said.

That set me back. Three years. All the time I had known him well. For an instant I was piqued at having noticed nothing.

There was a silence. Her eyes, dark blue, painfully honest, were studying me. She said:

'I want to ask you something. Very seriously.'

'Yes?' I replied.

'Ought I to get out of it?'

I hesitated.

'Is that a fair question?' I asked.

'Isn't it?'

I said: 'But could you get out of it?'

Her eyes stayed steady. She did not reply. After a moment she said: 'I couldn't do him harm. We've been good for each other. You'd expect him to be good for me, of course, but somehow it isn't all one-sided. I don't know why, but sometimes I think I've been good for him.' She was speaking simply, tentatively: then she broke out: 'Anyway, it would be the end for me if I let him go.'

Her voice had risen; tears had come. With a rough, schoolgirlish gesture, she brushed her cheeks with the back of her fingers. Then she sniffled, and made herself go on in a braver tone. 'But I couldn't do him harm, you know that, don't you?'

'I think I do.'

'I believe in what he's doing. You believe in it, isn't that true?' She said she wasn't 'political', but she was shrewd. She knew where his position was weak.

She gave a sharp smile: 'I'm not fooling you, am I? Naturally I couldn't do him harm. I couldn't bear to damage his career, just because it's him. But I couldn't bear to damage him – because I'm pretty selfish. If he suffered any sort of public harm because of him and me, he'd never really forgive me. Do you think he would?'

I noticed, not for the first time, her curious trick of throwing questions at me, questions about herself which I could not have enough knowledge to answer. In another woman, it would have seemed like an appeal for attention – 'Look at *me*!' – an opening gambit to intimacy, to flirtation. But she was not thinking of me at all as a man, only as someone who might help her. This was her method, not precisely of confiding, so much as of briefing me, so that if the chance came I could be some use.

I said something noncommittal.

'No,' she said, 'it would be the end.'

In an even, realistic, almost sarcastic tone, she added: 'So I get the rough end of the stick, however I play it.'

I wanted to comfort her. I told her the only use I could be was practical. What was happening now? Had she been to a lawyer? What else had she done?

Up till then, she had been too apprehensive to get to the facts. And yet, was that really so? She was apprehensive, all right, but she had spirit and courage. In theory, she had asked me there to talk about the facts. After the years of silence, though, it was a release to have a confidant. Even for her, who had so little opinion of herself – perhaps most of all for her – it was a luxury to boast a little.

The facts did not tell me much. Yes, she had been to a lawyer. He had

had her telephone calls intercepted: once or twice the voice had broken through. Always from call-boxes, nothing to identify it. The same voice? Yes. What sort? Not quite out of the top drawer, said Ellen, just as Mrs Henneker would have said it, as only an Englishwoman would have said it. Rough? Oh, no. Like someone fairly refined, from the outer suburbs. Obscene? Not in the least. Just saying that her liaison with Roger was known, telling her the evenings when he visited her, and asking her to warn Roger to be careful.

Since the check on telephone calls, she had received a couple of anonymous letters. That was why, she said when it was nearly time for me to leave, she had begged me to call that night. Yes, she had shown them to the lawyer. Now she spread them out on the table, beside the tumblers.

I had a phobia about anonymous letters. I had been exposed to them myself. I could not prevent my nerve-ends tingling, from the packed, paranoid handwriting, the psychic smell, the sense of madness whirling in a vacuum, of malice one could never meet in the flesh, of hatred pulsating in lonely rooms. But these letters were not of the usual kind. They were written in a bold and normal script on clean quarto paper. They were polite and businesslike. They said that Roger had been known to visit her between five and seven in the evening, on the dates set down. ('Correct?' I asked. 'Quite correct,' said Ellen.) The writer had documentary proof of their relation ('Possible?' 'I'm afraid we've written letters.') If Roger continued in the public eye, this information would, with regret, have to be made known. Just that, and no more.

'Who is it?' she cried. 'Is it some madman?'

'Do you think,' I said slowly, 'it sounds like that?'

'Is it just someone who hates us? Or one of us?'

'I almost wish it were.'

'You mean—?'

'It looks to me,' I said, 'more rational than that.'

'It's something to do with Roger's politics?' she added, her face flushed with fighting anger, 'I was afraid of that. By God, this is becoming a dirty game!'

I was glad that she was angry, not just beaten down. I said I wanted to take the letters away. I had acquaintances in Security, I explained. Their discretion was absolute. They were good at this kind of operation. If anyone could find out who this man was, or who was behind him, they could.

Ellen, an active woman, was soothed by the prospect of action. Bright-eyed, she made me have another drink before I left. She was talking almost happily, more happily than she had done all the evening, when she said as though without any connection, a frown clouding her face: 'I suppose you know her?'

All of a sudden she got up from the sofa, turned her back on me, re-arranged some flowers – as though she wanted to talk about Caro but wasn't able to accept the pain.

'Yes, I know her.'

She gazed at me: 'I was going to ask you what she was like.' She paused. 'Never mind.'

At the lift-door, when we said good-bye, she looked at me, so I thought, with trust. But her expression had gone back to that which had greeted me, diffident, severe.

CHAPTER XXIV

DESPATCH BOXES IN THE BEDROOM

BASSET in October, a week before the new session: the leaves falling on the drive, the smoke from the lodge chimney unmoving in the still air, the burnished sunset, the lights streaming from the house, the drinks waiting in the flower-packed hall. It might have been something out of an eclogue, specially designed to illustrate how lucky these lives were, or as an advertisement composed in order to increase the rate of political recruitment.

Even to an insider, it all looked so safe.

It all looked so safe at dinner. Collingwood, silent and marmoreal, sat on Diana's right: Roger, promoted to her left hand, looked as composed as Collingwood, as much a fixture. Caro, in high and handsome spirits, was flashing signals to him and Diana across the table. Caro's neighbour, a member of the Opposition shadow cabinet, teased her as though he fitted as comfortably as anyone there, which in fact he did. He was a smooth, handsome man called Burnett, a neighbour of Diana's whom she had called in for dinner. Young Arthur Plimpton was sitting between my wife and a very pretty girl, Hermione Fox, a relative of Caro's. It didn't take much skill to deduce that this was one of Diana's counter-measures against Penelope Getliffe. Arthur, looking both bold and shifty, was in England for a week, intent upon not drawing too much of my attention and Margaret's.

But there was at least one person who was putting on a public face.

Monty Cave's wife had at last left him for good; to anyone but himself it seemed a release, but not to him. The morning he received the final note, he had gone to his department and done his work. That was three days ago. And now he was sitting at the dinner table, his clever, fat, subtle face giving away nothing except interest, polite, receptive – as though it were absurd to think that a man so disciplined could suffer much, could ever have wished for death.

He was a man of abnormal control, on the outside. Mrs Henneker did not know what had happened to him.

When Margaret and I came into the house out of the Virgilian evening, Mrs Henneker had been lurking in the hall. I was just getting comfortable, we were having our first chat with Diana, when Mrs Henneker installed herself at my side. She was waiting for the other two to start talking. The instant they did so, she said, with her sparkling, dense, confident look: 'I've got something to show you!'

Yes, it was my retribution. She had finished a draft of her 'Life', as she kept calling it, the biography of her husband. There was no escape. I had to explain to Margaret, who gave a snort of laughter, then, composing her face, told me sternly how fortunate I was to be in on the beginning of a masterpiece. I had to follow Mrs Henneker into the library. Would I prefer her to read the manuscript aloud to me? I thought not. She looked disappointed. She took a chair very close to mine, watching my face with inflexible attention as I turned over the pages. To my consternation, it was a good deal better than I had expected. When she wrote, she didn't fuss, she just wrote. That I might have reckoned on: what I hadn't, was that she and her husband had adored each other. She did not find this in the least surprising, and as she wrote, some of it came through.

This was a real love-story, I tried to tell her. The valuable things in the book were there. So she ought to play down the injustices she believed him to have suffered, her own estimate of what ought to have happened to him. I didn't say, but I thought I might have to, that she wasn't being over-wise in telling us that as a fighting commander he was in the class of Nelson, as a naval thinker not far behind Mahan, as a moral influence comparable with Einstein – if she wanted us to believe that as a husband he was as good as Robert Browning.

I had spoken gently, or at least, I had intended to. Mrs Henneker brooded. She stared at me. It was near dinner-time, I said, and we had left ourselves only a quarter of an hour to dress. In a stately fashion, Mrs Henneker inclined her head. She had not thanked me for my suggestions, much less commented upon them.

At the dinner table, she was still brooding. She was too much pre-occupied to speak to me. When Arthur, accomplished with elderly matrons, took time off to be polite to her, he did not get much further. At last, after the fish, she burst out, not to either of us, but to the table at large:

'I suppose I must be old-fashioned!'

She had spoken so loudly, so furiously, that everyone attended.

In her briskest tone, Diana said:

'What is it, Kate?'

'I believe in happy marriages. I was happy with my husband and I don't mind anyone knowing it. But my neighbour' – she meant me, she was speaking with unconcealed distaste – 'tells me that I mustn't say so.'

For an instant I was put out. This was what came of giving literary advice. I should never persuade her, nor presumably anyone else, that I had said the exact opposite.

She was put out too. She was indifferent to anyone round her. She said, 'Doesn't anyone nowadays like being married, except me?'

The table was quiet. Roger knew about Monty's state: so did Caro. So did Margaret. I could not prevent my glance deviating towards him. Nor, in that quiet and undisciplined instant, could others. He was sitting with his eyes open and meaningless, his mouth also open: he looked more childlike than clever, foolish, a bit of a clown.

It was Caro who cracked the silence. Her colour had risen. She called out, just like someone offering a bet: 'Damn it, most of us do our best, don't we?' She was teasing Margaret and me, each of whom had been married twice. She laughed at Arthur and Hermione Fox. They had plenty of time ahead, she said, they probably wouldn't do any better than the rest of us.

Arthur gave a creaking laugh. If Caro had been his own age, she would have known exactly how much he fought shy of getting married; she would have had it out of him. He wouldn't have cared. For some, the flash of sympathy between them was a relief.

Except that, for some moments yet, Monty Cave sat with his clown's face. Then his expression, and those of the rest of us, became disciplined again.

With one exception, that Margaret and I speculated about. At the head of her own table, Diana was crying. Even when she gave us orders about how long to stay over the port, the tears returned. When we were alone in our bedroom, Margaret and I talked about it. Yes, she had behaved much as usual after dinner; she still sounded like a curious mixture of Becky

Sharp and a good regimental officer keeping us all on our toes. We both knew that her marriage to Skidmore was supposed to have been an abnormally happy one. Was that why she had cried?

Next morning, meeting me in the hall, she told me that she was too tired to go out with the guns. It was the first time I had known her energies flag. She was still enough herself to give me instructions. I didn't shoot, I might be bored, but I was to keep Monty Cave company in her place. 'He's not to be left by himself just now,' she said. It sounded matter-of-fact and kind. Actually it was kind, but not entirely matter-of-fact. Diana was providing against the remotest chance of a suicide.

Soon the shooting parties were setting out, with me among them. Reggie Collingwood, Caro and Roger walked along together through the golden fields. So far as Collingwood had any casual pleasures, shooting was the favourite one. He approved of Roger for sharing it: while Roger, who had taken on the pastimes of Caro's family when he married her, lolloped tweedily along between them, looking as natural as an Edwardian statesman.

Monty and I veered to the left. When I spoke to him, he answered me, quite sweet-temperedly, but that was all. By the side of the other party, we were funereal. Then quick steps came padding up behind us. I looked round. It was Arthur Plimpton, dressed no more fittingly than I was, but carrying a gun. I did not understand why he had sacrificed a day with a comely young woman, but I was glad to see him. It was possible that he had come out of good nature. He wasn't obtuse, and he couldn't have been in Basset for twenty-four hours without picking up the story of Monty's wife.

'Do you like hunting, sir?' he said cheerfully to Monty.

'No, I never hunt,' said Monty, who had just brought down two birds with a right and left.

'If I may say so, sir, you're doing pretty well for a beginner.' Arthur knew as well as I did that the English did not refer to this form of avicide as 'hunting'. He had used the word out of mischief. He turned out to be a competent shot, about as good as Collingwood or Roger. Of the four of them, Monty was far and away the best. He might be a clever, sad, fat man, whom women were not drawn to: but his eyes and limbs worked like a machine.

At about one o'clock, we all gathered on a mound, eating out of the picnic-baskets. The morning mist had cleared, the light was mellow, clear as Constable's. Caro stretched herself on the turf with the sensuous virtue of one who has taken exercise; she took a swig from a brandy flask and passed it to Roger. The party looked like a tableau out of someone's attempt to present a simpler age.

Collingwood gazed at the shining countryside. 'It's a nice day,' he said.

When, in the dying afternoon, we were sitting in the library up at the house, having just got back for tea, Collingwood felt the phrase could not be much improved. He and Roger and Cave sat in their tweeds round Diana, who was pouring out. 'It's been a nice day,' said Collingwood.

Though it would have taken a great expert in Collingwoodian dialogue to detect this, he was not so patriarchally content as he had been at midday in the sunshine. During the afternoon, the difference between the bags had mounted. By the time we walked home, Collingwood and Roger had had the worst of the day. Collingwood was inclined to blame it on to Roger.

'You seem to have been in good form, Cave,' said Collingwood in the library, with manly frankness, with oblique reproach.

Monty Cave muttered politely, but without interest.

Arthur joined in: 'He was good all day,' and began talking to Cave himself. Arthur was suggesting a two-handed shoot, just the two of them, first thing the next morning.

Collingwood was surveying them. He approved of attempts to 'take his mind off it'. He approved of young men making efforts with their elders. Most of all, he approved of able, rich young men. Drinking whisky instead of tea, he stretched out stockinged legs and gave a well-disposed sigh. Turning to his hostess, he remarked: 'Diana, I must say, it's been a nice day.'

When the despatch boxes arrived, both Diana and he made their routine grumbles, just as they had been doing since the twenties, when he got his first office, and she was starting to run a political house. As Margaret and I were strolling in the courtyard, in the bluish twilight, a government car drove up. A secretary descended, carrying one of the boxes, red and oblong, which we were all used to. We followed him in: this one was for Monty Cave. Within minutes, two other secretaries, carrying two identical boxes, walked through the great hall of Basset, on their way to Collingwood and Roger Quaife.

In the library, Diana, revived, her face less drawn, went through the minuet of grumbles, while she had the satisfaction of seeing three boxes being opened on three pairs of knickerbockered knees.

'I'd better put dinner off till nine?' she said.

'I'm afraid it looks like it,' replied Collingwood. His tone was grave and ill-used: yet he couldn't, any more than Diana, conceal a kind of pleasure, the pleasure, secretive but shining, that they got from being at the centre of things.

Diana had the drill laid on. Dinner to be late, drinks to be sent up at once to the Ministers' rooms. Soon Collingwood was lumbering up the wide staircase, with the step of a man who has to bear too much. The other two followed. I wasn't wanted, and it was some time before I went up to my room. There, as I dressed, Margaret was baiting me through the door, hilarious at the stately ritual downstairs. Did all men in power behave like this? Why? Because otherwise, I replied, they wouldn't reach power, enjoy it, or keep it.

Just then, there was a knock on the door. It was one of the menservants, bearing an envelope, addressed to me in Collingwood's bold Edwardian hand. Inside was a sheet of Basset writing-paper, covered by more of Collingwood's elephantine writing. It said:

'I should be grateful if you could spare us a few minutes of your time. It would be a convenience if you could come without delay.'

I took in the note to Margaret without a word, and left her laughing.

Inside Collingwood's bedroom, which was the biggest in the house, the boxes gaped open on a table, and the great fourposter bed was strewn with papers. All three men were still wearing their outdoor suits, though Collingwood had taken off his jacket. He was sitting on the bed, and the other two had drawn up chairs close by, each holding a glass in his hand.

'Oh, there you are,' said Collingwood. 'We want to get something fixed up.'

Roger explained that they had received a cabinet paper. He said to Collingwood: 'I assume Eliot can see it? He'll get it in his own office on Monday.'

Collingwood nodded.

I ran through it. It was only a couple of pages, typed in triple spacing on one of the large-letter machines, as though specially designed for longsighted elderly men. It came from the Minister of Labour. It said that if a change in weapons policy was at any time contemplated, the Minister wished the labour position to be established from the beginning. That is, a sudden stop, even in a single isolated project, such as A, would mean unemployment for seven thousand men, of whom three thousand were specialists, and difficult to assimilate. This would be embarrassing for the Minister. Any more fundamental change in weapons policy would produce large pockets of unemployment. Unless the changes were spread over several years, they would be unacceptable.

It sounded official, cautious, reasonable. But everyone in the room knew that it meant more. It was a sighting-shot: and it was a sighting-shot, as it were, by proxy. It was not really this Minister who was testing Roger's intentions. It was a set of other interests, who were still keeping quiet. Service groups? Big firms? None of us knew, but all of us were guessing.

'They've been getting at him,' said Collingwood.

'It's very easy, as I said before,' Roger leaned back, 'for them to over-play their hands.'

He looked confident, full of weight, springy with resource. Collingwood turned his handsome head and watched him in silence. So far as I could feel it in the air, there had been no argument.

'Well, then, Quaife, I'm with you. I agree, the committee' (he meant the cabinet committee on defence policy, about which Rose had given me the first news) 'ought to meet tomorrow or Tuesday. That's where we want you to help us—' He spoke to me. He gave, as usual, the impression that he was ill at ease and that he didn't care whether he was at ease or not. Everyone at Basset called him Reggie, but he still found it an effort not to speak to those two cabinet colleagues of his as Mr Quaife and Mr Cave. He just managed to use their surnames. As for me, though I had met him a dozen times in the house, he could not become as familiar as that.

He assumed that I was at his disposal for a modest task. They wanted the committee convened over the weekend. As Douglas Osbaldiston was in charge of the machine, that was his job. Would I telephone him and get that in motion before dinner?

It was barely polite. It was certainly not adroit. Yet, within the next ten minutes, I saw, or thought I saw, how he kept his power. Before I arrived, they had been talking about three big firms: how much influence could they pull out? By this time, Roger and Cave spoke of 'pressure groups', or 'lobbies', as though they were Americans.

'If they were solid together, they might be more of a menace,' said Roger. 'But they're not, we haven't given them a chance to be. There are always going to be some Government contracts. For some of our friends, that prospect carried its own simple logic.'

By the side of Roger, braced for the struggle, his voice taking on its taunting edge, Cave looked slack and gone to seed. But he was more at home than he had been all the weekend. He didn't see, he said, any lobby being effective by itself. 'But I should make two qualifications. First, Government must know its own mind. Second, and this isn't quite a platitude, lobbies may be important if they happen to touch opinion deeper than their own. That is, if they touch opinion which hasn't their own axe to grind.'

'Fair comment,' said Roger.

Collingwood stirred, and put one arm round the bedpost. 'I see.' He was speaking to neither of them in particular, making pauses like one reading from a script: but the authority was there. 'If I understand you both right, there isn't much between us. I take it Cave means that we've got to feel our way. I agree to that. We've got to watch whether any of these forces are having any effect on the party. We can't push the party further than it's prepared to go. I'm not presuming to give Quaife any advice. I never give anyone any advice.' He said this as though it were the most exalted claim a man could make. 'But, if I were Quaife, I should wrap up some of his intentions. I shouldn't let them get down to particular consequences until we've carried most of them with us. Carried them further than they thought. But not further than some of us are ready to go. I shouldn't let the White Paper give them much idea which weapons were being struck off straight away. I should wrap it up.' He was still addressing the wall. 'If I were Quaife, I should remember one other thing. I have a feeling that the party needs a lead. And by the party, I mean the country as well. They need to feel that they're doing something new. I have a feeling that, if anyone gives them a lead, they'll forgive him a lot. They may not like everything he's doing, but they'll be ready to forgive him.'

It was a curious speech, I thought, as I listened, and even more so later. A good deal of it was common form, not specially ominous, but carefully uncommitted. The last part was not such common form. He seemed to be inviting Roger to take a risk. As he did so, I had felt for the first time that he was, in his own right, a formidable man. Was he inducing Roger to take one risk too many? He had sounded, in a stony way, sincere. What did he wish for Roger? He had done him good turns. Did he like him? Men like Collingwood did not like or dislike freely. I was still uncertain about his feelings for Roger, or whether he had any feelings for him at all.

Next day, Margaret and I had to leave the house after tea. The weather had not changed. Just as when we arrived, it was an evening so tranquil that the chimney smoke seemed painted on the sky, and in the air there was a smell of burning leaves. Diana stood by herself in the courtyard, waving us off.

It had been a weekend in the country, with unhappiness in the house, and foreboding. As we settled down in the car, though, I felt, not relief to get away, but disquiet. For some of the disquiet I could find reason; but it was still there, swelling, nagging, changing, as though I were back in my childhood after a holiday, returning home, not knowing what I should find nor what I feared.

CHAPTER XXV

A SPEECH TO THE FISHMONGERS

THE committee room looked inwards to the Treasury yard: the rain sloshed down. Past Collingwood's head, on the two sides of the window, quivered the turning plane-leaves. In the chair, Collingwood behaved as he had done before, sitting on the bed at Basset. He was formal with the Ministers: Douglas Osbaldiston he treated like a servant, which Douglas showed no sign of noticing, much less of minding. But Collingwood got what he wanted. Arguments did not continue, except on lines which he approved, and there were not many. He had come to inspect the skeleton of the White Paper. In his view, it ought to be what he called 'a set of balances'.

This suited Roger. It was not the way in which, that summer, before the opposition began to crystallise, we had been making drafts. This way left him some tactical freedom. It sounded as though he and Collingwood, after the bedroom conference, had made a deal. Yet I knew for certain that, since half past eight on the Saturday night, two and a half days before, they had not exchanged a word in private. Enough had been said. They each understood what would follow, and so did Monty Cave and I. This was the way business got done, very rarely with intrigue, not as a rule with cut-and-dried agreements: quite different from the imaginative picture of the cynical and unworldly.

Osbaldiston, who was neither cynical nor unworldly, would have understood it without even a comment, if he had been present on Saturday night. As it was, he was momentarily surprised. He had expected something more dramatic from his Minister, and had been uneasy. Douglas did not approve of anything dramatic, on paper. Now he realised that the White Paper was going to be filled with detail. He was more comfortable with it so.

While Hector Rose, sick with migraine when I reported to him that afternoon, smelt compromise in the air.

'I think I remember, my dear Lewis, mentioning to you that the knives were sharpening. Has it ever crossed your mind that our masters are somewhat easily frightened off?' He looked at me with sarcastic satisfaction in his own judgment. I told him more about the meeting, which he would have attended himself if he had been well. I said that the Air Minister had reserved his position at much too great length. Rose nodded. It would be a month or two before the White Paper could be finished, they had agreed. By that time, Roger had told them casually, just before the end of the meeting, he would have his 'winding-up' ready for them to see. 'That went down?' Rose raised his eyebrows. 'It sounds like a very neat job of papering-over-the-cracks, shouldn't you say?'

But Rose and a good many others were puzzled when, within a fortnight, Roger next spoke in public. Long before the Basset weekend, Lufkin had made him commit himself to the actual engagement. Whether he had changed his mind about what to say, after Collingwood's allocution, I did not know. Whether he had decided to use this occasion, instead of going on to the television screen, I did not know also. It may have been the chance conjunction of Collingwood and Lufkin that led him to give what became known, a little strangely, as the Fishmongers' Hall Speech.

Lord Lufkin was a Fishmonger. Not that he had ever sold a fish: not even in the Hamletian sense. Lufkin had a singular gift for getting it both ways. He disapproved of the hereditary peerage, and had become a hereditary peer. In just the same way, he had nothing but contempt for the old livery companies. It was grotesque, said Lufkin, with acid scorn, for businessmen to take on the names of honest trades they had not a vestige of connection with: and to stand themselves good dinners out of money earned by better men. It was medieval juju, said Lufkin. It was 'atavistic', he said mysteriously, with the spirit that John Knox might have shown when he was less well disposed than usual to Mary Queer. of Scots. None of that prevented him taking all the honours in his own livery, which, by some fluke, was the Fishmongers. That year, he had risen to be the Prime Warden of the Fishmongers. Most of his colleagues enjoyed each honorific job as it came, and would have enjoyed this. Lufkin showed no sign of pleasure: except, I sometimes fancied, at the thought of doing someone else out of it.

He went through his duties. That was why he had invited Roger to the Michaelmas dinner and had arranged for him to speak. That was why Lufkin stood in a great drawing-room at the hall, that November night, dressed in a russet Tudor gown tipped with fur, surrounded by other officials of the livery, dressed in less grand gowns tipped with less grand fur. Above the fancy dress protruded Lufkin's small, neat, handsome twentieth-century head, as he shook hand after hand with an impersonation of cordiality.

With maces carried before him, he led the procession into the hall for dinner. It was a hall not unlike, though larger than, a college hall: and the dinner was not unlike, though larger than, a college feast. Roger sat at the high table, on Lufkin's right hand. I was somewhere down the hall, placed between a banker, cultivated and reactionary, and a Labour M.P., less cultivated but not much less reactionary. I did not know many men there, though across the room I caught sight of Sammikins, leaning back with a glass in his hand. The food and drink were good, but not good enough to go out for. I knew that Roger was going to use the occasion to 'fly a kite'. I had not seen the script, and did not expect much. I was not at all keyed-up. I got the banker off the subject of South Africa, on which he sounded like an unusually illiberal Afrikaaner, on to German translations of Dostoevsky, where I knew nothing, and he a great deal.

Speeches. A long, and very bad one, by the chairman of an insurance company. I drank another glass of port. A short and very bad one by Lufkin, who sat down among dutiful plaudits as though he both expected them and was impervious.

Then the toastmaster cried: 'Pray silence for your guest, the Right Honourable Roger Quaife, one of her Majesty's Privy Councillors, holder of the Distinguished Service Order, Member of Parliament for—'

In the candlelight, looking at the table before me, I saw the sheen of glass, of gold and silver plate. I turned as Roger rose. He looked enormous, after the image left by Lufkin. He began the incantation: 'My Lord and Prime Warden, your Grace, my Lords, Members of the Honourable Livery Company of the Fishmongers, gentlemen—'

He stopped short, and stood there in silence. He went on in a quiet tone: 'We have, all of us here, a good deal to be thankful for. This is an autumn night, and there is no war. An autumn night, and no war. For ten years out of the lives of almost every man here, we could not have said as much. We are lucky now, tonight. We have to make sure that that luck lasts. Some of us have fought in two wars. Most of us have fought in one. I don't need to tell anyone who has fought that war is hell. We have seen better men than ourselves killed beside us. We have seen the way they died. We have seen our dead. But that is not the worst of it. In the wars we fought, there were times when we could still admire our friends: one was terrified oneself, but others were brave. War was stink, and rot, and burning, but human beings were often fine. Individual men still counted. It is hard to imagine how, in any major war which we can now foresee, they can count much again.'

At that point, Roger had to break off into official language and point out how the armed services were still all-important. But soon he was talking in his own voice again. That was the knack – it was more than a knack, it was a quality which had drawn some of us to him – which held his audience. The hall was quiet. He went on:

'We all think, from time to time, of thermo-nuclear war. Of course we do. We should be foolish, as well as wicked, if we didn't. We can dimly imagine what such a war would be like. By its side, any horrors that men have so far contrived to inflict upon other men would look like a tea-party. So we know that this must never happen. Yet, though we know that, we do not know the way to stop it. I have met men of good will, who don't easily give up hope, thinking to themselves that we are all – all mankind – caught in a hideous trap. I don't believe that. I believe that, with courage and intelligence and a little luck, we shall find a way out. I don't pretend it will be easy. I doubt whether there is a total solution. Perhaps we've got to hack away here and there, trying to do comparatively small things, which may make war that much less likely. That is why I am taking the opportunity tonight to ask a few questions. No one in the world, I think, knows the answers to all of them, perhaps not to many. That is a reason why we should at least ask them. Most of all, in this country. Ours is a country which has been as stable as any in the world for the longest time. We are an experienced people. We have been through many dangers. It happens, through no fault of our own, that this new danger, this change in the nature of war, this thermo-nuclear breakthrough, threatens us more vitally and completely than any major power. Simply because, by world standards, we are no bigger than a pocket-handkerchief, and live so close together. This degree of danger, of course, ought not to affect our judg-ment. I know there are some – most of all, old people living alone, and some of the young, who feel this predicament as unfair – who quite naturally, in their own hearts, occasionally feel frightened.'

There had been no noise, almost no coughing, in the hall. I had been aware of the faces round me, some naked with interest, the banker's reflective and morose. Just then, a voice down the end of the opposite table shouted, thick with drink: 'Speak for yourself!'

Sammikins was on his feet, berserk, calling to the interrupter.

'Shut up, you blasted swine!'

'Speak for yourself!' came a drunken voice.

Sammikin's neighbours were pulling him down, as he cried, 'Where have you fought? This man has, you pig!'

Roger held up his hand. He stood, impassive, immobile, without a flicker. He said: 'I'm prepared for anyone to accuse me of being cowardly.

That doesn't matter. It's hard, I sometimes think, for a man with young children not to be. But I'm not prepared for anyone to accuse the people of this country of being cowardly. They've proved the opposite quite enough for any reasonable man. Anything we decide, now or in the future, about our military position, will be done because it seems to us moral and sensible, not because we're frightened, or because, on the other hand, we have to prove that we're not.' He drew the first rumble of 'hear, hears'. He let them run, then held up his hand again.

'Now, after this bit of pleasantry, I'm going to ask the questions. As I say, no one knows the answers. But if all of us think about them, we may some day be able to say something that decent people, people of good will all over the world, are waiting to hear. First, if there is no agreement or control, how many countries are going to possess thermo-nuclear weapons by, say, 1967? My guess, and this is a political guess, and yours is as good as mine, is that four or five will actually have them. Unless it is not beyond the wit of man to stop them. Second, does this spread of weapons make thermo-nuclear war more or less likely? Again, your guess is as good as mine. But mine is sombre. Third, why are countries going to possess themselves of these weapons? Is it for national security, or for less rational reasons? Fourth, can this catastrophe – no, that is going further than I feel inclined, I ought to say, this extreme increase of danger – can it be stopped? Is it possible that any of us, any country or group of countries, can give a message or indication that will, in fact, make military and human sense?'

Roger had been speaking for ten minutes, and he continued for as long again. In the whole of the second half of his speech, he went off again into official language, the cryptic, encyclical language of a Minister of the Crown. The effect was odd, but I was sure that it was calculated. He had tried them deep enough: now was the time to reassure them. They would be glad of platitudes, and he was ready to oblige.

He did not make much of a peroration, and sat down to steady, though not excessive, applause. There was an amiable and inept vote of thanks, and the Prime Warden's procession, maces in front, Roger alongside Lufkin, left the hall.

When I recalled the evening, I thought that few of the people round me realised that they had been listening to what would become a well-known speech. I was not certain that I realised it myself. There was a sense of curiosity, in some of unease, in some of let-down. I heard various speculations on my way out. Most of them were respectful but puzzled.

In the press of men jostling towards the cloakroom, I saw Sammikins, his eyes flaring. He was not far from me, but he shouted: 'I'm sick of this mob! Come for a walk.'

I had a feeling that the invitation was not specially calculated to please his neighbours, who stood stolid and heavy while he pushed through them, lean, elegant, decorations on his lapel.

We had neither of us brought overcoats or hats, and so got straight out before the others, into the night air.

'By God!' cried Sammikins.

He had drunk a good deal, but he was not drunk. Yet it would have been an error to think that he was tractable. He was inflamed with his grievance, his vicarious grievance at the interruption.

'By God, he's' (he was talking of Roger) 'a better man than they are. I know men in his regiment. I tell you, he's as brave as a man can reasonably be.'

I said that no one doubted it.

'Who the hell was that bloody man?'

'Does it matter?' I asked.

'I expect he was a colonel in the Pay Corps. I'd like to ram the words down his fat throat. What in God's name do you mean, "Does it matter?"'

I said, being accused of something one knows oneself to be ridiculous, and which everyone else knows to be ridiculous, never hurt one. As I said it, I was thinking: Is that true? It pacified Sammikins for the time being, while I was brooding. No, I had sometimes been hurt by an accusation entirely false: more so than by some which were dead accurate.

In silence we walked to a corner and paused there for a moment, looking across the road at the bulk of the Monument, black against the moonlight blue of the sky. It was not cold; a south-west wind was blowing. We turned down Arthur Street and into Upper Thames Street, keeping parallel with the wharves. Beyond the ragged bomb-sites, where the willow herb was growing still, since the air raids nearly twenty years before, we saw the glitter of the river, the density of warehouses, the skeletal cranes.

'He's a great man, isn't he?' said Sammikins.

'What is a great man?'

'By God, are you turning on him now?'

I had spoken carelessly, but his temper was still on the trigger.

'Look,' I said, 'I've thrown everything I could behind him. And I'm taking more risks than most of his friends.'

'I know that, I know that. Yes, damn it, he's a great man.'

He gave me a friendly smile. As we walked along what used to be a narrow street, now wide open to the moonlight, he said: 'My sister did well for herself when she married him. I suppose she was bound to make a happy marriage and have a brood of children. But, you know, I always thought she'd marry one of us. She was lucky that she didn't.'

When Sammikins said that he thought she would marry 'one of us', he spoke as unselfconsciously as his great-grandfather might have done, saying he thought that his sister might have married a 'gentleman'. Despite his hero-worship of Roger, that was exactly what Sammikins meant. As he spoke, however, there was something which took my attention more. Caro was more concerned about him, loved him more, than he loved her. Nevertheless, he was fond of her; and yet he saw her marriage in terms of happiness, exactly as the world saw it. Diana, seeing them walking in the grounds at Basset, or as allies at a Government dinner-table, might have seen it so. This despite the fact that both Diana, and even more Sammikins, had lived all their lives in a raffish society, where the surface was calm and the events not so orderly. Listening to Sammikins talking of his sister's marriage, I thought of Ellen, alone in her flat in the same town.

'Yes, she's got her children.' He was going on about Caro. 'And I am a barren stock.'

It was the only self-pity I had known him indulge in, and incidentally, the only literary flourish I had ever heard him make.

There was plenty of gossip as to why he had not married. He was in his thirties, as handsome as Caro in his own fashion. He was chronically in debt, partly because of his gambling, partly because his money, until his father died, was tied up in trusts he was always trying to break. But sooner or later, as well as inheriting the earldom, he would become a very rich man. He was one of the most eligible of bachelors. Diana commented briskly, with the mercilessness of the twentieth century, that there must be 'something wrong with him'. It was said that he liked young men.

All that might easily be true. I suspected that he was one of those – and there were plenty, often young men of his spectacular courage – who didn't find the sexual life straightforward, but who, if left to themselves, came to terms with it as well as simpler men. Half-sophistication, I was convinced as I grew older, was worse than no sophistication: half-knowledge was worse than no knowledge. Label someone a homosexual too quickly, and he will believe you. Tell him he is predestined to keep out of the main stream, and you will help push him out. The only service you can do him – it was a very hard truth – was to keep quiet. So the last thing I wanted that night was to force a confidence. I did not even want to

receive it. I was glad (though faintly cheated, my inquisitiveness unsatis-
fied) when, after a few more laments at large, he gave a strident laugh and
said: 'Oh, to hell with it.'

Immediately he wanted me to accompany him to ——'s (a gambling
club). When I refused, he pressed me at least to come to Pratt's and make
a night of it. No, I said, I must be getting home. Then let's walk a bit, he
said. He said it scornfully, as though despising my bourgeois habit of
going to bed. He did not want to be left alone.

We walked through the streets of the old City. From the bottom of
Ducks Foot Lane, we caught sight of the dome of St Paul's and, as if
adjacent to it, the pinnacles of Dick Whittington's church, white as sugar
icing in the moonlight. The City of London, in its technical sense, as
opposed to the great incomprehensible town, meant little either to him or
to me. It evoked no memories, I had never worked there, all it brought
back were taxi-rides on the way to Liverpool Street Station. I might have
recalled, but I didn't, one walk with Roy Calvert as well as Sammikins
himself. Yet something played on us – the sight of the vast cathedral?
The bomb sites? The absolute loneliness, not another person in the
streets? The false-romantic memory of the past, the history which is not
one's own but lives in the imagination? Something played on us, not only
on Sammikins but on me, who was more sober and less adrift.

We had passed Great Trinity Lane and had turned right: St Paul's
sprang now into open view before us, soot and whitewash.

Sammikins said:

'I suppose Roger is right. If there is another war, it'll be the end of us,
won't it?'

I said yes.

He turned to me:

'How much does it matter?'

He was speaking in earnest. I couldn't make a sarcastic reply. I
answered: 'What else matters?'

'No. I'm asking you. How much do any of us believe in human life?
When it comes to the point?'

'If we don't, then there's no hope for us.'

'Perhaps there isn't,' he said. 'I tell you, aren't we being hypocritical?
How much do any of us care, really care, for human life?'

I was silent. And in a clear tone, neither fierce nor wild, he went on:

'How much do you care? Except for the people round you? Come on.
What is the truth?'

I could not answer straightaway. At last I said:

'I think I do. At any rate, I want to.'

He said: 'I doubt if I do. I've taken life before now, and I could do it again. Of course I care for a few lives. But as for the rest, I don't believe – when you strip away the trappings – that I give a rap. And that's truer of more people than any of us would like to think.'

CHAPTER XXVI

PARLIAMENTARY QUESTION

THE headlines, on the morning after the dinner in Fishmongers' Hall, had a simple but pleasing eloquence. ARMED SERVICES ALL-IMPORTANT: then, in smaller letters, 'No Substitute for Fighting Men. Minister's Strong Speech,' said the *Daily Telegraph* (Conservative). SECURITY COMES FIRST, 'Mr R. Quaife on World Dangers,' said *The Times* (moderate Conservative). SPREAD OF ATOMIC WEAPONS, 'How Many Countries Will Possess the Bomb?' said the *Manchester Guardian* (centre). CHANCE FOR THE COMMONWEALTH, 'Our Lead in Atomic Bomb,' said the *Daily Express* (irregular Conservative). TAGGING BEHIND THE U.S., said the *Daily Worker* (Communist).

The comments were more friendly than I had expected. It looked as though the speech would soon be forgotten. When I went over the press with Roger, we were both relieved. I thought he felt, as much as I did, a sense of anti-climax.

In the same week, I noticed a tiny news item, as obscure as a *fait divers*, in the 'Telegrams in Brief' column of *The Times*.

'Los Angeles. Dr Brodzinski, British physicist, in a speech here tonight, attacked "New Look" in British defence policy as defeatist and calculated to play into hands of Moscow.'

I was angry, much more angry than apprehensive. I was sufficiently alert – or sufficiently trained to be careful – to put through a call to David Rubin in Washington. No, he said, no reports of Brodzinski's speech had reached the New York or Washington papers. They would not carry it now. He thought we could forget about Brodzinski. If he, Rubin, were Roger, he'd play it rather cool. He would be over to talk to us in the New Year.

That sounded undisquieting. No one else seemed to have noticed the news item. It did not arrive in the departmental press-cuttings. I decided not to worry Roger with it, and put it out of mind myself.

A fortnight later, in the middle of a brilliant, eggshell-blue November morning, I was sitting in Osbaldiston's office. We had been working on the new draft of the White Paper, Collingwood having contorted Douglas's first. Douglas was good-humoured. As usual, he took no more pride in authorship than most of us take in the collective enterprise of travelling on a bus.

His personal assistant came in with an armful of files, and put them in the in-tray. Out of habit his eye, like mine, had caught sight of a green tab on one of them. 'Thank you, Eunice,' he said equably, looking not much older than the athletic girl. 'A bit of trouble?'

'The P.Q is on top, Sir Douglas,' she said.

It was part of the drill he had been used to for twenty-five years. A parliamentary question worked like a Pavlovian bell, demanding priority. Whenever he saw one, Douglas, who was the least vexable of men, became a little vexed.

He opened the file and spread it on his desk. I could see the printed question, upside down: under it, very short notes in holograph. It looked like one of these questions which were rushed, like a chain of buckets at a village fire, straight up to the Permanent Secretary.

With a frown, a single line across his forehead, he read the question. He turned over the page and in silence studied another document. In a hard, offended tone, he burst out, 'I don't like this.' He skimmed the file across the desk. The question stood in the name of the member for a south-coast holiday town, a young man who was becoming notorious as an extreme reactionary. It read:

'To ask the Minister of ——' (that was Roger's department) 'if he is satisfied with security arrangements in relation to atomic defence, especially among senior officials?'

That looked innocuous enough: but Douglas's juniors, thorough as detectives, had noticed that this same member had been making a speech in his own constituency, a speech in which he had quoted from Brodzinski's at Los Angeles. Here were the press cuttings, the local English paper, the *Los Angeles Times*, pasted on to the file's second page.

With a curious sense of *déjà vu*, mixed up with incredulity and a feeling that all this had happened time out of mind, I began reading them. Brodzinski's lecture at U.C.L.A: SCIENCE AND THE COMMUNIST THREAT: Danger, danger, danger: Infiltration: Softening, Conscious, Unconscious: as bad or worse in his own country (U.K.) as in the U.S.: People in high positions, scientific and non-scientific, betraying defence; best defence ideas sabotaged; security risks, security risks, security risks.

'This isn't very pleasant,' said Douglas, interrupting me.

'It's insane.'

'Insane people can do harm, as you have reason to know.' He said it with tartness and yet with sympathy. He knew of my first marriage, and it was easy for us to speak intimately.

'How much effect will this really have—'

'You're taking it too easily,' he said, hard and sharp.

It must have been years since anyone made me that particular reproach. Then I realised that Douglas had taken charge. He was speaking with complete authority. Because he was so unpretentious, so fresh, lean and juvenile in appearance, one fell into the trap of thinking him lightweight. He was no more lightweight than Lufkin or Hector Rose.

It was he who was going to handle this matter, not Roger. From the moment he read the question, he showed his concern. Why it should be so acute, I could not make out. At a first glance, Brodzinski was getting at Francis Getliffe, perhaps me, perhaps Walter Luke, or even Roger himself. It would be a nuisance for me if I were involved: but, in realistic terms, I thought, not much more. Douglas was a close friend: but his present gravity would have been disproportionate, if it had just been on my account.

No. Was he, as a high bureaucrat, troubled when open politics, in particular extremist open politics, looked like breaking out? He was both far-sighted and ambitious. He knew, as well as anyone in Whitehall, that in any dog-fight, all the dogs lose: you could be an innocent victim, or even a looker-on: but some of the mud stuck. If there were any sort of political convulsion, his Treasury friends and bosses would be watching him. His name would get a tag on it. It would be unjust, but he would be the last man to complain of injustice. It was his job to see that the fuss didn't happen. If it did, he might find himself cut off from the topmost jobs for life, a second Hector Rose.

There was another reason why he was disturbed. Though he was ambitious, he had high standards of behaviour. He could no more have made Brodzinski's speech than he could have knifed an old woman behind her counter. Although he was himself conservative, more so even than his colleagues, he felt that the P.Q. could only have been asked – and he would have used simple, moral terms – by a fool and a cad. In a heart which was sterner than anyone imagined, Douglas did not make special allowances for fools, cads, or paranoids like Brodzinski. For him, they were moral outlaws.

'The Minister mustn't answer the questions himself,' he announced.

'Won't it be worse if he doesn't?'

But Douglas was not consulting me. Roger was himself 'under fire a bit'. He had to be guarded. We didn't want too many whispers about whether he was 'sound'. It was at just this point in politics where he was most vulnerable. No, the man to answer the question was the Parliamentary Secretary, Leverett-Smith.

What Douglas meant was that Leverett-Smith hadn't an idea in his head, was remarkably pompous, and trusted by his party both in the House and at conferences. He would in due course make, Monty Cave had said with his fat man's malice, a quintessential Law Officer of the Crown.

Within a few minutes, Douglas had been inside Roger's office and had returned.

'He agrees,' he said. Since Douglas must have spoken with the wrappings off, just as he had spoken to me, it would have been difficult for Roger not to agree. 'Come on. You may have to speak for some of the scientists.'

In Roger's room, Douglas had already written on the file the terms of a reply. When we called on Leverett-Smith, two doors down the passage, the pace of business became more stately.

'Parliamentary Secretary, we've got a job for you,' Douglas had begun. But it took longer. Leverett-Smith, bulky, glossy-haired, spectacled, owlish, stood up to welcome us. Very slowly, he read the civil servants' comments as the question had made its way up, Douglas's draft, the newspaper clippings. Again very slowly, in his reverberating voice, he began to ask questions. What was the definition of 'bad security risk' in British terms? What were the exact levels of security clearance? Had all members of the scientific committee been cleared for Top Secret, and for the information *none of us mentioned*?

Leverett-Smith went inexorably on. The method of slow talk, I thought, as Keynes used to say. Had all the civil servants been cleared? What were the dates of these clearances?

Like his colleagues, Douglas kept his relations with the Security organs obscure. He did not refer to documents, but answered out of his head – accurately, but also impatiently. This was not the kind of examination a Permanent Secretary expected from a junior Minister – or, so far as that went, from a senior Minister either. The truth was, Leverett-Smith was not only cumbrous and self-important: he disliked Roger: he had no use for rough-and-ready scientists like Walter Luke, while men like Francis Getliffe or me made him uncomfortable. He did not like his job, except that it might be a jumping-off board. This mixture of technology, politics, ideology, moral conscience, military foresight, he felt odious and not quite respectable, full of company he did not choose to live his life among.

Actually, he lived his life in one of the odder English enclaves. He wasn't in the least an aristocrat, as Sammikins and his sister were: he wasn't a country gentleman, like Collingwood: to Diana's smart friends, he was stodgy middle class. But the kind of middle class in which he seemed never to have heard an unorthodox opinion – from his small boys' school in Kensington, to his preparatory school, to his house at Winchester, to the Conservative Club at Oxford, he had moved with a bizarre absence of dissent.

'I don't completely understand, Secretary, why the Minister wishes me to take this question?'

After an hour's steady interrogation, he made this enquiry. Douglas, who did not often permit himself an expression of God-give-me-patience, almost did so now.

'He doesn't want to make an issue of it,' he said. Then, with his sweet and youthful smile, he added: 'He thinks you would carry confidence with everybody. And that would kill this bit of nonsense stone-dead.'

Leverett-Smith tilted his massive, cubical head. For the first time, he was slightly placated. He was interested to know if that was the Minister's considered judgment. He would, of course, have to consult him to make sure.

Douglas, still smiling sweetly, as though determined to prove that pique did not exist in public business, reminded him that they had only a few hours to play with.

'If the Minister really wishes me to undertake this duty, then naturally I should be unable to refuse,' said Leverett-Smith, with something of the air of a peeress pressed to open a church bazaar. He had a parting shot.

'If I do undertake this duty, Secretary, I think I can accept your draft in principle. But I shall have to ask you to call on me after lunch, so that we can go over it together.'

As Douglas left the room with me, he was silent. Pique might not exist in public business; but, I was thinking, if Leverett-Smith remained in political office at the time when Douglas became head of the Treasury, he might conceivably remember this interview.

Yet although time might have been spent in Leverett-Smith's ceremonies, there had been no compromise. It was Douglas who had got his own way.

The question was down for Thursday. That morning, Roger asked me to go to the House, to see how Leverett-Smith performed. He also asked me, as though it were an absent-minded thought, to drop in afterwards at Ellen's flat for half an hour.

It was a raw afternoon, fog in the streets, ghostly residue of fog in the chamber. About fifty members were settled on the benches, like an ill-attended matinee. As soon as prayers were finished, I had gone to the civil servants' box. There were several questions before ours, a lot of backchat about the reprieve of a murderer whom a Welsh member kept referring to, with an air of passionate affection, as 'Ernie' Wilson.

Then, from the back bench on the Government side, on my right hand, rose the man we were waiting for – young, smart, blond, avid. On being called to ask Question 22, he announced himself, in a manner self-assured and minatory, his head back, his chin raised, as if he were trying to get the maximum bark from the microphones.

Leverett-Smith got up deliberately, as though his muscles were heavy and slow. He did not turn to the back-bencher in his rear: he stood gazing at a point far down on the opposite side below the gangway.

'Yes, sir,' he said, as though announcing satisfaction, not only with security arrangements but with the universe.

The avid young man was on his feet.

'Has the Minister seen the statement made by Professor Brodzinski on November 3rd, which has been given wide publicity in the United States?'

Leverett-Smith's uninflected, confident voice came rolling out:

'My Right Honourable friend has seen this statement, which is erroneous in all respects. Her Majesty's Government has a defence policy which is the responsibility of Her Majesty's Government, and which is constantly being debated in this House. My Right Honourable friend acknowledges with gratitude the services of his advisers on the scientific committees and elsewhere. It does not need to be said that these men are one and all of the highest integrity and devoted to the national interest. As a matter of standard practice, all persons having access to secret information are subjected to rigorous security procedure. And this is the case with each person consulted, on any matter connected with Defence whatsoever, by my Right Honourable friend.'

Subdued, respectful hear-hears. The blond young man was on his feet.

'I should like to ask whether all scientific advisers have gone through security vetting during this past year.'

Leverett-Smith, standing once more, looked for an instant like an elephantine beast being baited. I was afraid that he would ask for notice of the question.

He stood there letting the seconds tick by. Then his voice resounded, once more impregnable.

'My Right Honourable friend regards the publication of the details of security procedures as not being in the public interest.'

Good, I thought. That was all we wanted.

Again, hear-hears. Again, the pestering, angry voice.

'Will the Minister produce the dates on which certain members of this scientific committee, the names of whom I am willing to supply, were last submitted to security vetting? Some of us are not prepared to ignore Dr Brodzinski—'

There were mutters of irritation from the Tory benches. The young man had gone too far.

This time, Leverett-Smith did not take so long to meditate. Solidly he announced to the middle distance: 'This supplementary question is covered by my last answer. The question is also an unworthy reflection on gentlemen who, often at great sacrifice to themselves, are doing invaluable service to the country.'

Vigorous hear-hears. Definite hear-hears, putting an end to supplementaries. Another question was called. Leverett-Smith sat broad-backed, basking in a job well done.

I was waiting for another question, further down the list, addressed to my own Minister. Douglas, who had been sitting beside me, left with a satisfied grin.

Some time later, a debate was beginning. It was not yet time for me to leave for Ebury Street. Then I saw Roger coming into the chamber; he must have picked up gossip outside, for on his way to his seat on the front bench he stopped by Leverett-Smith and slapped him on the shoulder. Leverett-Smith, turning to him, gave a serious contented smile.

Roger lolled in his seat, reading his own papers, like a man working in a railway carriage. At some quip from the Opposition benches that raised a laugh, he gave a preoccupied, good-natured smile.

As another speech began, he looked up from his scripts, turned to the box, and caught my eye. With his thumb, he beckoned me to meet him outside. I saw him get up, whisper to another Minister and stroll out.

In the central lobby, full of visitors, of little groups chatting earnestly, of solitary persons waiting with passive resignation, much like Grand Central Station on a winter night, he came up to me.

'I hear Leverett was pretty good,' he said.

'Better than you'd have been.'

Roger drew down his lip in a fierce chuckle. He was just going to speak, when I caught sight of Ellen walking past us. She must have come from the Strangers' Gallery, I thought, as she gave me the slight smile of a distant acquaintance. To Roger she made no sign of recognition, nor he to her. I watched her move away from us, through the lobby doors.

Roger said: 'She'll be going straight home. We can follow in a few minutes. I think I'll come along with you.'

In Palace Yard, the lamps, the taxi-lights, shone smearily through the fog. As we got near to the taxis, Roger muttered that it was better if I gave the address.

The click of the lift-door opening, the ring of the bell.

As Ellen opened the door, she was ready for me, but, seeing Roger, gave an astonished, delighted sigh. The door closed behind us, and she was in his arms. It was a hug of relief, of knowledge, the hug of lovers who know all the pleasure they can give each other. For her, perhaps, it was a little more. Meeting him only in this room, pressed in by this claustro-phobia of secrecy, she was glad, this once, to throw her arms round him and have someone there to watch. They would have liked to go straight to bed. Nevertheless, it was a joy to her, as well as a frustration, to have me there.

At last they sat on the sofa, I in an armchair. 'That wasn't so bad, was it?' she asked, enquiring about the incident in the House, but her tone so happy that she might have been asking another question. His eyes were as bright as hers. He answered, in the same sort of double-talk: 'Not bad.' Then he got down to business.

'Everyone seems to think that it passed off rather well.'

I said I was sure it had.

She wanted us to tell her: would the question do any damage now? Difficult to say: possibly not, unless something bigger happened. She was frowning. She was shrewd, but she had not been brought up to politics and found the corridors hard to see her way through.

'Well, anyway,' she said, 'it must be the end of Brodzinski. That's something.'

No, we said, that wasn't certain. Never underestimate the paranoid. I was mimicking Roger and also scoring off him, going back to his handling of Brodzinski. Often they stayed dangerous, while saner men went under. Never underestimate them, I said. Never try to placate them. It is a waste of time. They take and never give. The only way to deal with paranoids is to kick them in the teeth. If a chap has persecution mania, the only practical course is to give him something to feel persecuted about.

I was being off-hand, putting on a tough act to cheer her up. But she wasn't putting on a tough act when she said:

'I want him done in. I wish to God I could manage it myself.' He had done, or was trying to do, Roger harm. That was enough.

'Can't you set some of the scientists on to him?' she asked me passionately.

'They're none too pleased,' I replied.

'Hell, what good is that?'

Roger said that she needn't worry too much about Brodzinski. He would still have some nuisance value, but so far as having any practical influence, he might have shot his bolt. It wasn't a good idea, making attacks in America. It might create some enemies for us there, but they would have been enemies anyhow. As for this country, it would damage his credit, even with people who would have liked to use him.

'There'll be plenty more trouble,' he said, 'but as for Brodzinski, I fancy he'll stew in his own juice.'

'You're not going to do anything to him?'

'Not if leaving him alone produces the right answer.' He smiled at her.

'I want him done in,' she cried again.

His arm was round her, and he tightened his hold. He told her that, in practical affairs, revenge was a luxury one couldn't afford. There was no point in it. She laughed out loud. 'You speak for yourself. There would be some point in it for me.'

I had been trying to cheer her up. She was worried for Roger, more worried than either he or I were that night: yet she was full of spirit. Not just because she was with us. She was behaving as though a wound were healed.

At last I grasped it. This attack had nothing to do with her. She was suspicious that, behind the telephone calls, might be someone Roger had known. For a time, she had been ready to blame Brodzinski. The enquiries I had set moving had already told us that this was unlikely. Now she could believe it. It set her free to hate Brodzinski more. She was blazing with relief. She could not bear the danger to come through her. She would, I thought, have lost an eye, an arm, her looks, if she could have lessened the danger for Roger: and yet, that kind of unselfish love had its own egotism: she would have chosen that the danger were increased, rather than it should have come from her.

I told her that the intelligence people hadn't found anything positive. They now had all her telephone calls intercepted.

'All that's done,' she said, 'is to be maddening when he' – she looked at Roger – 'is trying to get through.'

'They've got their own techniques. You'll have to be patient, won't you?'

'Am I good at being patient?'

Roger said, 'You're having the worst of this. You'll have to put up with it.' He said it sharply, with absolute confidence.

She asked me, was there anything else she could do? Had she just got to sit tight?

'It's pretty hard, you know,' she said.

Roger said: 'Yes, I know it is.'

Soon afterwards, he looked at his watch and said he would have to leave in another half-hour. On my way home, I thought of them a little, free together, by themselves.

CHAPTER XXVII

PROMENADE BENEATH THE CHANDELIERS

It needed no one to instruct Roger about gossip. He picked it up in the air: or more exactly, for there was nothing supernatural about it, he read it in the expressions of acquaintances, without a word spoken, as he walked about the House, his clubs, the offices, Downing Street. We all knew, in those November days, that it was boiling up: some of it sheer random gossip – malicious, mischievous, warm with human relish – and some politically pointed.

I had not yet heard a whisper about Ellen, or any other woman. The P.Q. seemed to have fallen dead. One reason why Roger was being talked about was that he was getting precisely the support he could least afford. The Fishmongers' Hall speech, or bits of it, or glosses upon it, had started to pass round. It had made news. It was drawing the kind of publicity which, because no one understood it, the theatre people called 'word of mouth'. Roger had, within two or three weeks, become a favourite, or at any rate a hope, of liberal opinion. Liberal opinion? To some on the outside, certainly to the marxists, it didn't mean much. It might use different language from the *Telegraph*, Lord Lufkin's colleagues, or the Conservative back-benchers, but, if ever there was a fighting-point, it would come down on the same side. Maybe. But this, inconveniently for Roger, was not how it appeared to the *Telegraph*, Lord Lufkin's colleagues, or the Conservative back-benchers. To them, the *New Statesman* and the *Observer* looked like Lenin's paper *Iskra* in one of its more revolutionary phases. If Roger got praise in such quarters, he was a man to be watched.

There was praise from other quarters, more dangerous still. Irregulars on the Opposition benches had begun to quote him: not the official spokesmen, who had their own troubles and who wanted to quieten the argument down, but the disarmers, the pacifists, the idealists. They were not an organised group; in numbers they might be less than thirty, but they were articulate and unconstrained. When I read one of their speeches, in which Roger got an approving word, I thought with acrimony, save us from our friends.

Roger knew all this. He did not speak of it to me; he held back any confidence about what he feared, or hoped, or planned to do. Once he talked of Ellen; and another time, in the bar of a club, he brought me a tankard of beer and suddenly said: 'You're not religious, are you?'

He knew the answer. No, I said, I was an unbeliever.

'Curious,' he said. His face looked puzzled, uncalculating, simple. 'I should have thought you would have been.'

He gulped at his own tankard. 'You know, I can't imagine getting on without it.'

'Of course,' he went on, 'there are plenty of people who like the Church, even though they don't really believe. I think I should still like the Church, if I didn't believe. But I do.'

I asked: just what did he believe?

'I think,' he said, 'almost everything I learned as a child. I believe in God in Heaven, I believe in an after-life. It's no use telling me that Heaven isn't the place I used to think it was. I know that as well as they do. But I can't help believing.'

He went on talking about faith. His tone was gentle, like a man blundering on. He would have liked me to say, Yes, that's how I feel. He was utterly sincere: no one could confide like that and lie. And yet, half suspiciously, at the back of my mind I was thinking, it is possible for a man to confide, quite genuinely, one thing, because he wants to conceal another.

At the back of my mind I was thinking, this wasn't a device, it came to him by nature. Yet it would be just as effective in keeping me away from his next moves.

Up to now, I had shut up the doubt which Hector Rose had not spoken, but had, with acerbity, implied. I knew Roger and Rose didn't, and wouldn't have wanted to. Rose would have been totally uninterested in his purpose, his aspirations, in his faith. Rose judged men as functional creatures, and there he was often, more often than I cared to remember, dead right. He was asking one question about Roger, and one alone: What – when it came to the point – would he do?

Roger told me nothing. In the next week, I received only one message from him. And that was an invitation to a 'bachelor supper' in Lord North Street, the night after the Lancaster House reception.

At Lancaster House, Roger was present, walking for a few minutes arm in arm with the Prime Minister, up and down the carpet, affable under the chandeliers. That did not distinguish him from other Ministers, or even from Osbaldiston or Rose. The Prime Minister had time for all, and was ready to walk arm-in-arm with anyone, affable under the chandeliers. It was the kind of reception, I thought as I stood on the stairs, that might have happened in much the same form and with much the same faces, a hundred years before, except that then it would probably have been held in the Prime Minister's own house, and that nowadays, so far as I remembered accounts of Victorian political parties, there was a good deal more to drink.

The occasion was the visit of some western Foreign Minister. The politicians and their wives were there, the civil servants and their wives. The politicians' wives were more expensively dressed than the civil servants', and in general more spectacular. On the other hand, the civil servants themselves were more spectacular than the politicians, so that a stranger might have thought them a more splendiferous race. With their white ties, they were wearing their crosses, medals and sashes, and the figure of Hector Rose, usually subfusc, shone and sparkled, more ornamented, more be-sashed, than that of anyone in the room.

The room itself was filling up, so was the staircase. Margaret was talking to the Osbaldistons. On my way to join them, I was stopped by Diana Skidmore. I admired her dress, her jewellery, the big star-sapphires. Underneath it all, she looked strained and pale. But she could assume high spirits; or else, they were as much part of her as the bones of her monkey face. She kept giving glances, smiling, recognising acquaintances as they passed.

She gazed at the Prime Minister, now walking up and down with Monty Cave. 'He's doing it very nicely, isn't he?' she said. She spoke of the Prime Minister rather like a headmaster discussing the performance of the best thirteen-year-old in a gymnastic display. Then she asked me: 'Where's Margaret?' I pointed her out, and began to take Diana towards her. Though Diana knew far more people at the reception than I did, she had not met the Osbaldistons.

She said she would like to, vivacious and party-bright. Before we had gone three steps, she stopped:

'No. I don't want to meet anyone else. I've met quite enough.'

For an instant, I wondered if I had heard right. It wasn't like her break-down at her own dinner-table. Her eyes were bright with will, not tears.

We were in the middle of the party. Yes, since that night at Basset, her backbone had stiffened again. She had been miserable when we talked of marriage. She wasn't used to being miserable without doing something about it. She couldn't go on living alone in that great house, she said. She wanted someone to talk to her. The pupillages she went through, the times when, like an adoring girl, she changed the colour of her thoughts – they weren't enough. Love affairs wouldn't be enough. She wanted someone all the time.

'You're no good,' she said, practical and open. 'You've got a wife.'

In the great drawing-room, most of the faces looked happy. Happier than in most gatherings, I thought. Then I saw Caro walking out on Roger's arm, an impressive smiling couple, unselfconscious, used to catching the public eye. Were there others there with this kind of secret? There were bound to be some: if one knew these lives, there would be some surprises. But not, perhaps, so many as one might think. In this drawing-room the men and women were vigorous and hearty. 'Peach-fed' I had heard them called, though not by themselves. There were some love affairs floating round. But most of them didn't chafe against the limits of the sexual existence. Often they got more out of it than those who did. But they didn't live, or talk, or excite themselves, as though there were, there must be, a sexual heaven round the corner. Perhaps, I some-times thought, that was a pre-condition for the active life.

Anyway, most of them were happy. That night, they seemed to be getting a special happiness out of one another's reflected glory: even the Prime Minister, though the glory reflected was his own. It was one of their rewards. What others were there?

In the hall, after Margaret and I had made our good-byes, we waited while car after car, government car, firm's car, were shouted for by name. Lord Bridgewater: Mr Leverett-Smith: the Belgian Ambassador: Sir Hector Rose. Margaret asked me why I was smiling. I had just remem-bered that I had once asked Lord Lufkin what rewards he thought he got, for a life which many people would have judged arduous beyond compare. Power, of course, I said. We took that for granted. The only other thing, I had suggested, was transport. He had not used a public vehicle in London for a generation: transport was always laid on. In the midst of his dog's life, he travelled as though on a magic carpet. Lord Lufkin had not been amused.

When I saw the other men, brought together for dinner in Lord North Street the following night, I thought Roger had made a tactical mistake. Monty Cave was there, Leverett-Smith, Tom Wyndham: both Rose and Osbaldiston, and also Francis Getliffe. It was easy to see the rationale. Cave was Roger's closest political ally, Leverett-Smith and Wyndham had had to know what was going on. The rest of us had all through been close to Roger's policy. But everyone there, except Francis, had attended the reception the night before. If I had been Roger, I should have waited for the afterglow from the charmed circle to fade; then they might not mind so much the risk of being out of it.

As I sat at the dinner-table, islamic except for Caro at the far end, I began to wonder what Roger's intentions were. He wasn't likely to speak openly, in front of Hector Rose or Douglas, or several of the others. He and Caro, who was working like an ally who had been rehearsed, seemed to be casting round for opinions: just how were the reactions coming in? They weren't asking specific questions. They were sitting back, waiting for any information that was collecting in the room.

Just as when Roger talked to me about religion, I could not rely on my judgment of him, or even be sure, because it was flickering, what my judgment was. Was this the way he would start, if he were looking for an opportunity to withdraw? Perhaps he was not making a tactical mistake after all.

Certainly – and this was clear and explicit – he was giving everyone present the chance to come out with his doubts. He was not only giving them the chance, he was pressing them to do so.

After dinner, Caro did not leave. She was one of the junta, she sat over the port like the rest of us. Before the port was put on the table, something happened that I did not remember having seen in that house or anywhere else. The maids took off the tablecloth, then laid the wine-glasses on the bare and polished rosewood. It was, so she said, an old nineteenth-century custom which had been kept up in her father's house. The glasses, the silver, the decanters, the rounded pinkness from a bowl of roses, were reflected in the table-top: perhaps that was what her ancestors had enjoyed, perhaps that was how she imagined them sitting, forming Victoria's governments, handing out the jobs.

Sliding a decanter to Francis on his left, Roger said casually that everyone there knew pretty well who was for them and who against. For any sort of decision, one had to know that. Then he added, in the most detached of tones, rather like a research student at the Harvard School of Government: 'I sometimes wonder how much freedom any of us have to make decisions? Politicians I mean. I wonder if the limits of freedom aren't tighter than one's inclined to think.'

Hector Rose must have been sure of what he had expected all along, that Roger was preparing a loophole of escape. But Rose took up the argument, as though he were being either judicious or perverse.

'With respect, Minister, I think they're even tighter than that. The older I grow, the more public decisions I have assisted at – in the French sense, I need hardly say – the more I believe that old Count Tolstoy was in the right of it.'

Tom Wyndham looked stupefied but obstinate, as though Hector's opinions – obviously Russian-influenced – might well be subversive.

'It's slightly instructive to ask oneself' – It was rare for Rose to go out to dinner, but he seemed, as he aged, suddenly to be enjoying company – 'exactly what would be the effect on the public decisions, if the whole of your delightful party, Lady Caroline, were eliminated at one fell swoop? Or in fact, which I don't think is really very likely, if we extended the operation and eliminated the whole of Her Majesty's Government and the higher civil service? With great respect, I strongly suspect that the effect would be precisely nil. Exactly the same decisions would be taken within negligible limits, and they would be taken at almost exactly the same time.'

Douglas joined in. He was not averse to disagreeing with Rose, and yet they shared their service solidarity. They did not want the talk to become too concrete: so Douglas took his cue from Rose. He didn't believe in predestination quite so much, he said. Perhaps other men could do the same jobs, make the same choices: but one had to act and feel as though that wasn't so. When one was at the centre of things, said Douglas, one did make the choices. No one believed in predestination when he was making a choice.

He looked round the table. For an instant, his off-hand air had quite gone. 'And that's why we wanted to be at the centre of things.'

'*We*, my dear Douglas?' asked Rose.

'I wasn't speaking only for myself,' said Douglas.

No, but it was as true for him and Hector Rose as it was for any politician, Collingwood included.

Monty Cave, sitting opposite to me half-way down the table, had been watching Roger with quick eyes. His dinner-jacket rumpled, so that his body looked stubbier than it was, Monty caught everyone's attention. Turning away from Douglas and Rose, he asked Roger, in a quiet and confidential tone:

'Weren't you saying – something else?'

'What do you mean?'

'I mean,' said Monty, and suddenly he could not resist the malicious fat grin, 'weren't you saying something a little nearer home?'

'What do you think, Monty?'

'I thought you were telling us that in politics, what's going to be plumb right ten years hence may be plumb wrong now. That is unfortunately true. We all know that.'

'Well?' Roger had no expression.

'I may have misunderstood you, but I thought you were asking us whether there was the faintest chance that mightn't be the present situation.'

'Was that the impression I gave you?'

'In which case,' said Monty, 'wouldn't you be in favour of going into reverse? Wouldn't you tend to be just a little cautious?'

'Do you really think he's been so cautious?' Caro interrupted, from the end of the table. Her eyes were gleaming, her colour was high. She looked angry and splendid.

'I wasn't suggesting it was easy,' said Monty.

'But you were suggesting that he was getting cold feet. Doesn't anyone realise that for months he's been playing his hand to the limit? The only question is, where does he go from here?'

'Where does he?' said Monty.

There was a flash of hostility between them. He was attracted to her, afraid of her. On her part, he was too subtle, not virile enough. Her anger was genuine. She was fighting for Roger, she was ready to let fly; but she knew – as though by instinct – how to let fly in the way that did most good. She was leaving nothing to chance. She had seen plenty of disloyalties round dinner-tables such as this. She wanted to make sure of Leverett-Smith and Tom Wyndham: she was trying to prove to them that Roger was being pushed on by wilder men.

She was high-hearted, and her anger was genuine. How much so was this attack of Cave's? I didn't know whether he and Roger had an understanding. It had been convenient for Roger, it had suited his tactics, for the attack to be made.

'In my judgment—' Leverett-Smith began, with extreme pomposity.

'Yes, Horace?' Caro leaned towards him with two kinds of charm, the aristocratic embrace, the embrace of a pretty woman.

'In my judgment, we ought to remember that sometimes the more haste, the less speed.' He produced this thought as though it contained the wisdom of the ages. Caro continued to smile admiringly.

'Have we been forgetting that?' she said.

'Do enlighten us,' said Monty.

'I'm inclined to think that we've been moving perceptibly faster than opinion round us. It's right that we should move faster, otherwise we shouldn't be giving proper leadership. The problem as I see it,' Leverett-Smith went on, 'is to judge how much faster it is safe to go.'

'Quite,' Monty commented.

His contempt was palpable. I thought he was wrong to dismiss Leverett-Smith as a negligible man. He was as sententious as a man could plausibly be: but he wasn't budgeable. Thinking of the future, I wished he were more negligible, more budgeable. It might be a misfortune for Roger not to have someone malleable in that job.

Caro went on devoting herself to him and Tom Wyndham. She was good with them. She could sympathise with their doubts, the hesitations deep in their conservative flesh – partly because, though she would not have admitted it to anyone but Roger, and not to him, once he had committed himself, those hesitations were her own.

Tom Wyndham was still wistfully wishing that the battleship were the decisive weapon.

'I know it isn't, of course,' he said.

'I'm so glad of that,' said Monty Cave.

Tom persisted, red-faced and puzzled. Since the last war, everyone had gone on changing their minds on what you could fight with. He expected it was all right. But still, he said, 'It takes the chaps' (he meant the serving officers, and also his friends in the House) 'time to get used to things changing like this.'

Francis Getliffe broke in, sounding aloof as he apologised with formality to Wyndham and Leverett-Smith. But he sounded not only aloof, but impatient.

'There isn't much time,' he said. 'The time-scale of politics you know about, it's your business to. But the time-scale of applied science is something like ten times faster. If you're going to wait too long before everyone agrees, then the overwhelming probability is that there won't be anything left to wait for.'

Roger stared at him. Hector Rose gave an impassive smile. Then I put in my piece. If we got really stuck (I was deliberately identifying myself with Roger's policy) we still had one recourse. We had been trying to struggle through by the channels of 'closed' politics – the corridors, the committees. If they got blocked, we could take it into the open. The only even quarter-way open statement had been the speech in Fishmongers'

Hall. We all knew why this was so: the problems were, or at least we made them, technical: most of the facts were fogged by security: these were the decisions which in our country, in all countries, we had become used to settling by a handful of men, in secret. For many reasons, this was forced on us. But there might come a time when someone would have to break it. This mightn't be the time. But even the threat that it was, I said without emphasis, could have an interesting effect.

I didn't expect these remarks to be popular. They weren't. To Douglas, who loved me, they were shocking and best forgotten. To Rose, who didn't, they were the token of why I had never quite fitted in. Even Francis didn't like them much. As for the politicians, Cave was reflecting: he was the only man there who might have considered whether in fact there did exist – in a rich and comfortable country – the social forces to call upon.

Leverett-Smith said, 'I can't associate myself with that suggestion.'

Caro was frowning. There was no debate. Someone changed the subject, and it was a few minutes later that Roger said: 'None of this is easy, you know.'

Since his exchange with Cave he had not spoken. He had sat at the end of the table, sipping his port, pre-potent, brooding. Now he took charge. He showed his worry, he did not pretend. He knew that he had to carry everyone round that table with him. Listening, I thought I had never heard him put on a better performance. Performance? That was true and not true. This might not be all he intended, but it was a good deal. There were ambiguities which might be deliberate: there were also some which he didn't know himself.

As we said good-night, his influence was still pervasive. He seemed to have gained all he wanted.

On the way home, and in cooler blood next morning, I wondered what each man thought Roger had actually said. What you wanted to hear, you heard, even with people as experienced as these. Ask them to write down their accounts, and the answers would have a certain ironic interest. And yet, Roger had said nothing untruthful or even disingenuous.

As for myself, I was further from predicting his actions than I had been since Rose gave his first warning. Of course, Roger was leaving a channel of retreat: he would be crazy not to do so. Of course, he must have faced the thought – and Caro must have brought it into the open – that there was still time to back down, throw the stress of his policy just where solid men could be comfortable, then take another Ministry and gain considerable credit into the bargain. So much was clear. I was sure of nothing else.

CHAPTER XXVIII

A NAME WITHOUT MUCH MEANING

ONE morning in December, I received a report. It was brought by one of my acquaintances in Security. I was not allowed to see it, but I was used to their abracadabra. He gave me the name I wanted, and took the report away with him.

The name I wanted was that of Ellen's persecutor. When I heard it, I said: 'Oh, yes?' It sounded matter-of-fact, like the name of a new house-keeper. It sounded – as facts tend to sound, whenever you are mixed up in a secret investigation (I had thought the same not long before, during the affair at my old college) – as probable or improbable as anything else. Yet, when I was left alone, it seemed very odd. Nothing like what I should have expected. Odd, but not melodramatically odd. I hadn't been told, as in an old-fashioned thriller, the name of Hector Rose or the Prime Minister, or Roger himself. Dully odd. Within five minutes, I rang up Ellen telling her I wanted to see her before one o'clock.

'What about?' But she did not need to ask.

Over the telephone, I made her give me a promise. I couldn't say anything, I told her, unless she did. When she had this information, she must do nothing with it, nothing of any kind, until we had agreed.

'I suppose so,' she said, in a strong reluctant voice.

We had to find somewhere where we could safely meet. It was the Christmas holidays, and at my flat the children would be home. Hers? No, she said: for once, I thought, not practical.

Briskly, she fixed a rendezvous, in an art gallery near Burlington Gardens. There I found her, alone, in the middle of the inner room, on the single chair. Round the walls were slabs and flashes of colour on canvases of enormous size. It occurred to me, walking to her in the deserted gallery, that we might have been two solitary devotees of Action painting: or a middle-aged official, a smartly dressed, youngish woman, at a first assignation. As she saw me, her eyes were open, dark, apprehensive, waiting.

'Well?' she said.

I wasted no time.

'Apparently,' I replied, 'it's Hood.'

For an instant, she couldn't believe that she had heard right, or that the Hood of whom I spoke was the man we both knew slightly, the little, pleasant-faced dispenser of drinks, cherry-cheeked, Pickwickian, who had a job, not one of the top jobs, but two or three rungs down on the commercial side, with one of Lufkin's rivals. I told her I had met him last at Lufkin's birthday party, when he had been exhaling with admiration at each utterance that Lufkin made, and raising his hands high as if to applaud a *diva*.

'I've seen him in the library,' she repeated several times. She went on: 'But he can't have anything against me! I've hardly talked to him alone.'

She was searching for something personal, a snub, a pass she hadn't noticed or had not responded to, but she couldn't flatter herself, she couldn't gain even that tiny bit of consolation.

'Perhaps seeing me there somehow put him on to us. How did he get on to us? Does anyone know?'

I said it didn't matter. To her, in that moment, it mattered so much that she could think of nothing else. Then she cried: 'I've got to have it out with him.'

'No.'

'I've got to.'

'That's why I made you promise,' I said, 'an hour ago.'

She looked at me with violence, with something like hate. She was craving for action as though it were a drug. To be kept from it was intolerable. It was like a denial of the whole self, body and soul, body as well as soul.

Passionately she argued. It could do no harm, she said. It could do no good, I replied: it might be dangerous. Now that we had identified him, some of the menace was gone. If it was simply a personal grudge, which I said again that I didn't believe, he didn't count, except for nuisance value. She could live with that.

But if not a personal grudge, was he acting on his own? If not, for whom? Suddenly Ellen went into a brilliant fugue of paranoia. She saw some central intelligence marshalling enemies: enemies watching them, planning, moving in, studying each aspect of Roger's life and hers. This was one move, Brodzinski's was another. Who was directing it all?

I couldn't pacify her, or persuade her that it wasn't true. I didn't myself know what was happening. In that empty room, the reds in the pictures pushing out towards us, I began to feel in a web of persecution myself.

She wanted to shout, cry, fly out, make love to Roger, anything. Her colour was high – but, as though in a moment-by-moment change, just as a child changes when in illness, when I looked again I saw she had turned pale.

She went very quiet. The passion had died away. She was afraid. At last I got her to talk again: 'If this goes on, I don't know whether I can stand it.'

The truth was, she did not doubt her own fortitude, but his. 'I don't know whether *he* can stand it.' That was what the words really meant. She could not bring herself to say that she had a new fear about why she might lose him. Some of those fears she could confess, as she had done at our first meeting, when she told me that if he lost his political career because of her, he would not forgive her. This was a new fear, which she could not confess, because it seemed a betrayal. But though she worshipped Roger, she knew him. She believed that these persecutions wouldn't stiffen him, but would drive him back into safety – back to the company of his colleagues, to the shelter of Lord North Street.

She could not stop herself from telling me:

'It's being away from him that matters now.' She meant, not being with him every hour of every day. 'When he comes to me he enjoys himself, you know. So do I.' She said it with her usual realism, her lack of fuss. 'But it's not enough now.'

She said: 'I'd give up everything, I tell you, I could live on nothing – I could do anything you like – if only I could be close to him the whole time. I could give up going to bed with him, if I had to, if I could just be near him, night and day, and day after day.'

PART FOUR

TOWARDS A CHOICE

CHAPTER XXIX

MEMORIAL SERVICE

THE bells of St Margaret's, Westminster, tolled under the low cloud-lid, into the dark noon. It was three days after Christmas, the House was in recess, but the Prime Minister and Collingwood, top-hatted, in morning suits, walked under the awning into the porch. So did three other Ministers, a group of elderly peers, then Roger and Monty Cave. People on the pavement were not paying much attention; top-hats, a handful of bigwigs, some sort of service.

I sat in the middle of the church, where, by some optical illusion, the light seemed brighter than out of doors: over the altar, the stained glass gleamed and glowed, like the glass in the front door at home when I was a child, or in the door at the Osbaldistons'. The vigorous, shining faces round me were composed into gravity, but there was no grief. It was part of the ceremonial, ceremonial which they enjoyed, part of the charm of their lives. Collingwood spent some time on his knees. The other Ministers and members sat in the two front rows, doing what was expected of them, doing what their successors would do for them, when their own memorial services came round.

In fact, the one they were commemorating that morning would not have considered that enough was being done. He had been a modest old man, but he had had the sharpest sense of the fitness of things. The church was only half full. Not much of a turnout, he would have said. Much worse, he would have been baffled that the service wasn't being held in the Abbey. 'Giving me a consolation prize,' he would have said.

This was the memorial service to old Thomas Bevill, who had died before Christmas at the age of eighty-eight. When he was a Minister at the beginning of the war, I had been one of his personal staff. That had been my introduction to the official life, and I knew him better than most of the other mourners did. No one, least of all himself, could have called him a great man; and yet I had learned much from him. In a limited sense of the word, he was a politician, a born politician. He knew which levers to pull and how to pull them, more exactly than anyone I had met in Government, with a skill one meets more often in people working in a smaller world, such as Arthur Brown in our college.

Bevill was an aristocrat, and it was part of his manner to appear like a bumbling amateur. He was as much an amateur as one of the Irish manipulators of the American Democratic machine. Bevill had a passion for politics. Like most devoted politicians, he was realistic about everything in them – except his own chances. He had been sacked, politely but firmly, in 1943, at the age of seventy-four. Everyone but himself knew it was the end. But he delayed taking his peerage, still hoping that another Conservative government would call him back. He kept his hand in with one or two non-party appointments, including the Chairmanship of the Atomic Energy Board. Then new Conservative governments came, but the telephone did not ring. At last, at eighty-four, he accepted his viscounty, even then hating it, even then going round asking his friends whether, when the P.M. went, there mightn't be the chance of one more job. When he was told no, his blue eyes ceased to look mild, and became hot and furious. But he surrendered. For the last four years, Thomas Bevill had entered another avatar, under the style of Lord Grampound.

This was the end. He would get mentioned, as a very minor figure, in some of the official histories. He wouldn't rate a biography of his own. I looked at the order of the service – Thomas Bevill, first Viscount Grampound – and felt curiously sad. The dignitaries round me were mumbling the responses. Beside the Prime Minister and Collingwood stood Roger, assured among the assured, his fine voice audible.

I felt, yes, alienated as well as sad. Why, I should have been hard put to it to say. This was the kind of leave-taking any ruling society gave to one of their own. As for Thomas Bevill, I should not have said that I loved him much. He had been an ally of mine in days past, but that had been in the way of business. He had been kind to me, as he always was to his colleagues, out of instinctive policy, unless there were overmastering reasons for not being kind. That was about the size of it. He was a tough old Tory politician, patriotic to the core – and also, the nearer one got to the core, snobbish, despite his unassuming mask, and also callous. Yet I was not really thinking of him like that. Standing among the sound of confident official voices, I was out of it – just as he was out of it, because he was, like any one of us when our time comes, being so easily dismissed.

The service ended, and the congregation trooped out, euphoric, healthy-looking, duty done. I did not hear a word spoken about the old man. The

Prime Minister, Collingwood and Roger got into the same car. As the car drove away, Monty Cave was watching it. He remarked to Sammikins, whom I had not noticed at the service: 'We're going on again after lunch.'

He meant, the cabinet committee had been meeting that morning, and had not finished. This was, we already knew, intended to be their final meeting, and so none of their advisers, none of the scientists or civil servants, except Douglas, was present. Monty, with his clever, imbedded eyes, watched the car turn out of Parliament Square.

'Well timed, don't you think?' he said to Sammikins.

Abruptly, as though he resented the invitation while he was giving it, he asked us whether we were doing anything for lunch. As we drove round to Cave's house in Smith Square, which I had not visited before, Sammikins was talking away in undiscouraged form, although both Cave and I were silent. Had he asked us just because he was lonely, I was thinking, or because there was something he intended, or felt obliged, to say?

The tall, narrow house sounded empty as we went in. In the dining-room I looked out of the window through the tawny winter air at the ruined church. It might have been part of a Gothick fancy. Yet the room itself was bright and elegant; on one wall was a fine Sisley, of poplars and sunny water, on another a still life by Nicholas de Staël, pastel fruit in a white dish.

I asked him about another picture. He was vague: he didn't know the painter. He was better read than most men, but he seemed not to have any visual sense. He was living in a museum of his wife's taste.

The maid brought in avocado pears, cold chicken, tongue, cheese. Cave ate greedily: Sammikins did not eat so much, or with such relish, but he appropriated the bottle of hock. Cave and I had adopted the habit, common among the younger administrators, of not drinking before the evening.

'This is the nicest sort of meal,' Sammikins burst out, 'why do we waste our time sitting down to bloody great set luncheons?'

Monty Cave smiled at him: yes, with affection: yes, perhaps with an envy for the dash, the abandon, he himself had never had. He said, as though casually, with his mouth full, 'Well, we've had a not uneventful morning.'

He said it more to me than to Sammikins. I knew that he was devious, subtle, cleverer than any of us. I suspected that he was not being casual. Certainly I wasn't. I asked:

'How did it go, then?'

'Oh, you know how these things usually go.'

It wasn't exactly a snub, but it was maddening. It was deviousness carried to the point of perversity. I looked at him, the bones of his chin sunk into the flesh, his eyebrows like quarter moons, his eyes watchful, malicious and in that slack face and body, disconcertingly bold. He said:

'Old Roger's taken to making jokes in meetings, nowadays. In cabinet, as well as in this one. Rather good jokes, I must say, but I don't think Reggie sees them.'

Sammikins gave his brazen laugh, but Cave had one sly eye on me, and went on:

'I sometimes wonder a little whether it's wise for politicians to make too many jokes. What do you think? I mean, it sometimes looks as though they're getting worried and are trying to put a bit too much of a face on it. Do you think that's possible?'

'Do you think Roger's getting worried?' I asked.

'I shouldn't have thought so. I can't for the life of me imagine why, can you?'

At that, even Sammikins, not listening so intently as I was, looked baffled.

We all knew that Roger was in his private crisis of politics. Cave knew it as well as any man alive. Suddenly I wondered whether, with extravagant indirectness, he was hinting at something which was not political at all. Was he really suggesting that Roger had another concern, different in kind? He was an observant and suspicious man, and he might have had his suspicions sharpened by unhappiness. Had he guessed that another marriage was in danger?

'No,' I said to Cave, 'I can't imagine why. Unless things went worse this morning than you've told us. And you're wondering if he's got to back down. And of course you too.'

'Oh, no, no, no,' Cave said rapidly. His whole face was transformed by a smile which seemed to come from within, evanescent, amused, youthful. 'I assure you, it's all gone easier than I expected. Of course, the White Paper hasn't really got all that many teeth in it, has it? Unless someone is going to read it in a way Reggie Collingwood wouldn't approve.'

He added: 'Roger was exceptionally good. It was one of the times when he does look the biggest man among us – you know what I mean. It's true, he did just drop one hint, not very loudly and he threw it away – that, in certain circumstances, he conceivably might want to say a word or two in public. It was nothing like as vulgar as threatening to resign, you understand.' Cave smiled again. 'I may be wrong, of course, but I rather got the impression that some of our colleagues took the point.'

With a glint in his eye, Cave said to me, in a very quiet tone: 'So far as I remember that last party of Caro's, Roger might have learned that trick from you, mightn't he?'

It was just on two. The meeting was to start again in half an hour, and soon he would have to be going. We walked upstairs to the drawing-room, also bright, also hung with paintings. But what struck the eye was a large photograph of his wife. It made her look handsomer than she really was: clear-featured, vivid, strong. Not right for him, not conceivably right for him, as anyone studying that face would have guessed. But there it stood. He must have seen it every night when he came in alone. One had a feeling, both of pity and discomfort, that he was living, not only with, but on his sorrow.

With a directness that I could not have matched, nor most of us, Sammikins marched up to the photograph and said:

'Have you heard from her?'

'Only through her solicitors.'

'What about?'

'What do you think?' said Cave.

Sammikins turned on him and said, in a hard, astringent tone, 'Look here, the sooner you say good-riddance, the better it'll be for you. I don't suppose you care about that. But the better it will be for her, too, and you do care about that, worse luck. And the better it'll be for everyone around you.'

He might have been an officer dealing with marital trouble in the ranks. Somehow it didn't sound like a wild young roisterer talking to an eminent man. It was not embarrassing to listen to.

'Never mind,' said Cave gently, with a touch of gratitude, speaking quite genuinely, as Sammikins had spoken. Soon he was saying good-bye, on his way to Great George Street. I thought he was genuine again when, in sympathy and reassurance, he said to me: 'Don't worry about this afternoon. It's all going according to plan.'

But he could not resist one last twist, dig, or mystification:

'The only question is, whose plan?'

CHAPTER XXX

A SENSE OF INSULT

ON Sunday afternoon, a couple of days after the memorial service, Margaret and I were sitting at home. The children had gone out to Christmas parties and we were peaceful. Then the telephone rang. As she answered it, I saw her look surprised. Yes, he is in, she was saying. Apparently the other person was trying to make a date with me: Margaret, protective, suggested that we should be alone, so wouldn't it be better to come in for a drink? There was a long explanation. At last, she left the receiver off and came to me with a commiserating curse. 'Hector Rose,' she said.

Over the telephone, his voice sounded more than ever glacial. 'I am most extremely sorry to disturb you, my dear Lewis, I wouldn't have done so if I hadn't a rather urgent reason. Do make my apologies to your wife. I really am very, very sorry.'

When the polite wind-up had finished, it came out that he needed to see me that same afternoon. He would give me tea at the Athenæum at half past four. I didn't want to go, but he pressed me, all flah-flah dropped, clear and firm. Then, arrangements made, the apologies and thanks started over again.

Seeing our afternoon broken, Margaret and I were cross. I told her that I could not remember him doing this on a Sunday, not even in the busiest time of the war: he must be coming in specially himself, from right beyond Highgate: it occurred to me that I had never been inside his house. Margaret, not placated, was scolding me for not saying no.

She took it for granted, as I did, that the summons had something to do with Roger's White Paper. Yet we had heard, on the Friday night, that Cave's prediction had been correct, and that the cabinet committee had agreed. Margaret said: 'Whatever it is, it could wait till tomorrow morning.'

Leaving the comfortable room, leaving my wife, going out into the drizzling cold, I felt she was right.

It was not perceptibly more encouraging when my taxi drew up in front of the club. The building was in darkness: there, on the pavement, in the slush and the half-light, stood Hector Rose. He began apologising before I had paid my driver. 'My dear Lewis, this is more than usually incompetent of me. I am most terribly sorry. I'd got it into my head that this was one of the weekends we are open. I must say, I'm capable of

175

most kinds of mistake, but I shouldn't have thought I was capable of this.' The courtesies grew more elaborate, at the same time more sarcastic, as though beneath them all he was really blaming me.

He went on explaining, with the same elaboration, that perhaps the consequences of his 'fatuity' were not irretrievably grave: since 'the club' was closed, the Senior would by agreement be open, and we could perhaps, without too much inconvenience, have our tea there. I was as familiar with these facts as he was. Fifty yards from us, just across the Place, the lights of what he called the 'Senior' (the United Service Club) streamed through the first flutter of sleet. All I wanted to do was cut the formalities short and get into the warm.

We got into the warm. We sat in a corner of the club drawing-room and ordered tea and muffins. Rose was dressed in his weekend costume, sports jacket, grey flannel trousers. Still the formalities were not cut short. This was so unlike him that I was at a loss. As a rule, after the ceremonies had in his view been properly performed, he got down to business like a man turning on a switch. His manner was so artificial, so sharply split from the personality beneath, that it was always difficult to pick up his mood. And yet, as he went on describing great labyrinthine curves of politeness, I had a sense, a distressing sense, that he was under strain.

We drank the tea, we ate the muffins. Rose was expressing, for my benefit, a mannerly interest in the book reviews in the Sunday papers. He had noticed something on a subject that was bound to interest my wife, to whom again, his regrets for intruding that day—

Usually I was patient: but I could wait no longer. I said: 'What's all this about?'

He gazed at me with an expression I could not read.

'I suppose', I said, 'that something has happened about Roger Quaife. Is that it?'

'Not directly,' said Rose, in his brisk, businesslike tone. So at last he was engaged. He went on:

'No, so far as I know, that's all right. Our masters appear to be about to sanction what I must say is an unusually sensible White Paper. It's going to cabinet next week. It's a compromise, of course, but it has some good points. Whether our masters stick to those when they get under shot and shell – that's quite another matter. Will our friend Quaife stick to it when they really get at him? I confess I find it an interesting speculation.'

He was speaking from his active, working self: but he was still watching me.

'Well, then?' I said.

'I do think that's reasonably all right,' he said, glad to be talking at a distance, like an Olympian god who hadn't yet decided on his favourite. 'I don't believe you need have that on your mind.'

'Then what do I need to have on my mind?' Again I could not read his expression. His face was set, authoritative, and, when he wasn't forcing smiles, without pretence.

'As a matter of fact,' he said, 'I've been having to spend some time with the Security people.' He added sharply: 'Far too much time, I may say.'

Suddenly, comfortably, I thought I had it. Tuesday was New Year's Day. Each year, Rose sat in the group which gave out honours. Was it conceivable that something had leaked, from our office? I asked: 'Have some of the names slipped out?'

Rose looked at me, irritated. 'I'm afraid I don't quite understand you.'

'I meant, have some of the names in next week's list got out?'

'No, my dear chap, nothing like that. Nothing like that at all.' It was rare for him to let his impatience show through. He had to make an effort to control it, before he spoke calmly, precisely, choosing his words:

'I didn't want to worry you unnecessarily. But I think I remember telling you, some months ago, about representations from various quarters, which I said then that I was doing my best to resist. When would that be?'

We both had good memories, trained memories. He knew, without my telling him, that it had been back in September, when he warned me that 'the knives were sharpening'. We could both have written a précis of that conversation.

'Well, I'm sorry to have to tell you, but I haven't been able to resist indefinitely. These people – what do they call them, in their abominable jargon? "pressure groups"? – have been prepared to go over our heads. There's no remedy for it. Some of our scientists, I mean our most eminent scientists advising on defence policy – and that, I need hardly tell you, is our friend Quaife's policy – are going to be put through a new security investigation. I fancy the name for this procedure, though it is not specially elegant, is "double checking".'

Rose was speaking with bitter distaste, distaste apparently as much for me as for the pressure groups, as he went on with his exposition, magisterial, orderly, and lucid. Some of this influence had been set in motion by Brodzinski, working on the members whom he knew. Some might have started independently. Some had been wafted over via Washington – prompted, perhaps, by Brodzinski's speeches, or his friends there, or possibly by a re-echo of the question in the House. 'We could have resisted any of these piecemeal,' said Rose. 'Though, as you may have noticed, our masters are not at – shall I say, their most Cromwellian – when faced with a "suggestion" from our major allies. But we could not resist them all combined. You must try to give us the benefit of the doubt.'

Our eyes met, each of us blank-faced. No one apologised more profusely than Rose when apologies were not needed: no one hated apologising more when the occasion was real.

'The upshot is,' he went on, 'that some of our more distinguished scientists, who have done good service to the state, are going to have to submit to a distinctly humiliating experience. Or alternatively, be cut off from any connection with the real stuff.'

'Who are they?'

'There are one or two who don't matter much to us. Then there's Sir Laurence Astill.'

I could not help smiling. Rose gave a wintry grin.

'I must say,' I said, 'I think that's rather funny. I wish I could be there when it happens.'

'I have an idea,' said Rose, 'that he was thrown in to make things look more decent.'

'The others?'

'One is Walter Luke. Between ourselves, since he's a chief Government scientist, I take that distinctly ill.'

I swore.

'But still,' I said, 'Walter's a very tough man. I don't think he'll mind.'

'I hope not.' He paused. 'Another is a very old friend of yours. Francis Getliffe.'

I sat silent. At last I said:

'This is a scandal.'

'I've tried to indicate that I don't regard it with enthusiasm myself.'

'It's not only a scandal, but it's likely to be serious,' I went on.

'That was one of my reasons for dragging you here this afternoon.'

'Look,' I said, 'I know Francis very well. I've known him since we were very young men. He's as proud as a man can be. I doubt, I really do doubt, whether he'll take this.'

'You must tell him he's got to.'

'Why should he?'

'Duty,' said Rose.

'He's only been lending a hand at all because of duty. If he's going to be insulted into the bargain—'

'My dear Lewis,' said Rose, with a flash of icy temper, 'a number of us, no doubt less eminent than Getliffe, but still reasonably adequate in our professions, are insulted in one way or another towards the end of our careers. But that doesn't permit us to abdicate.'

It was almost the only personal complaint I had heard him make, and then half-veiled. I said:

'All Francis wants is to get on with his research and live in peace.'

Rose replied:

'If I may borrow your own debating technique, may I suggest that, if he does so, there is slightly less chance that either he or any of the rest of us will live in peace?'

He continued sharply:

'Let's drop the nonsense. We all know that Getliffe is the scientific mind behind Quaife's policy. For military things, I think we're all agreed that he's the best scientific mind we have. That being so, he's just got to swallow his pride. You must tell him so. I repeat, that was one of my reasons for giving you this news today. He'll probably hear of this unpleasantness tomorrow afternoon. You must soften the blow before he hears, and persuade him. If you believe in this policy so much – and I thought, forgive me, that there were certain indications that you did – you can't do any less.'

I waited for a moment, then said, as quietly as I could:

'What I've only just realised – is that you believe in this policy so much.'

Rose did not smile or blink, or show any sign of acquiescence.

'I am a civil servant,' he said. 'I play according to the rules.' Briskly he asked me:

'Tell me, how embarrassing is this going to be for Francis Getliffe?'

'How sensibly do you think they'll handle him?'

'They will be told – they may just possibly even know – that he's an important man.' He went on, the sarcasm left behind: 'He has the reputation of being far to the left. You know that?'

'Of course I know that,' I replied. 'He was a radical in the thirties. In some ways he still thinks of himself as a radical. That may be true intellectually. But in his heart, it isn't.'

Rose did not answer for some instants. Then he pointed with his foot over to my right. I turned and looked. It was an oil-painting, like a great many in the drawing-room, of a Victorian officer, sidewhiskered, high-coloured, pop-eyed, period that of the Zulu Wars.

'The trouble with our major allies,' he said, 'is that they methodically read every speech Francis Getliffe has ever made, and can't believe that any of us know anything about him. One of the few advantages of living in England is that we do know just a little about one another, don't you agree? We know, for instance, the not entirely irrelevant fact that Francis Getliffe is as likely to betray his country as' – Rose read the name under the painting without emphasis, but with his bitterest edge – 'Lieutenant-General Sir James Brudenell, Bart., C.B.'

He was still speaking under strain. It had not grown less, but greater, after he had broken the news about Francis. There was a jagged pause before he said:

'There's something else you'll have to warn Getliffe about. I confess I find it offensive. But modern thought on this kind of procedure apparently requires what they like to call "research" into the subject's sexual life.'

Taken unawares, I grinned. 'They won't get much for their trouble,' I said. 'Francis married young, and they've lived happily ever after.'

I added: 'But what are they going to ask?'

'I've already suggested to them that it wouldn't be tactful to bring up the subject to Sir Francis Getliffe himself. But they'll feel obliged to scurry round his acquaintances and see if he's liable to any kind of blackmail. That is, I take it, to find out whether he has mistresses, or other attachments. As you know, there is a curious tendency to assume that any homosexual attachment means that a man is probably a traitor. I must say, I should like them to tell that to —— and ——.'

For once, Rose, the most discreet of men, was not at all discreet. He had given the names of a particularly tough Minister and of a high public servant.

'I must say,' I echoed him, 'I should like someone to tell Francis that it was being seriously investigated whether he had homosexual attachments or not.'

The thought was not without humour.

But then I said:

'Look here, I don't think he's going to endure this.'

'He's got to,' said Rose, unyielding. 'It's intolerable, but it's the way we live. I must ask you to ring him up tonight. You must talk to him before he hears from anyone else.'

There was a silence.

'I'll do my best,' I said.

'I'm grateful,' said Rose. 'I've told you before, this was one reason why I had to talk to you today.'

'What's the other reason?' I had been dense, but suddenly I knew.

'The other reason, I'm afraid, is that the same procedure is to be applied to you.'

I exclaimed. My temper boiled up. I was outraged.

'I'm sorry, Eliot,' said Rose.

For years he had called me by my Christian name. Now, telling me this news, he felt as much estranged as when we first met. He had never really liked me. Over the years, we had established colleague-like relations, some sort of respect, some sort of trust. I had given him a little trouble, because, in an irregular position, I had taken liberties which a career civil servant could not, or would not, think of taking. Things I had said and written hadn't been easy for him. He had 'picked up the pieces', not good-humouredly, but according to his obligation. According to the same obligation, he had recommended me for official honours. Now, at last, he hadn't been able to protect me, as, by his sense of fitness, he should have protected a colleague. He felt something like dishonoured, leaving me exposed. As a consequence, he liked me less than he had ever done.

'It doesn't make it any more agreeable,' he said stiffly, 'but this has nothing to do with suggestions from our allies. They have asked questions about Getliffe, but nothing about you. No, you seem to have some enemies at home. I take it that isn't exactly a surprise to you?'

'Do you expect me to stand for it?'

'I have to say to you what I said about Getliffe.'

After a while, during which we sat mute opposite each other, he said, strained, cold, hostile:

'I think I ought to make it as smooth for you as I can. If you don't care to submit to this business, then I will make an excuse, which shouldn't be beyond human ingenuity, and someone they're less interested in can take over the defence work. Not of course' – with an effort, punctilio returned – 'that anyone else could be so valuable to us, my dear Lewis.'

'Do you seriously think I could take that offer?'

'I made it in good faith.'

'You knew I couldn't possibly accept?'

Rose had become as angry as I was. 'Do you really believe that I haven't resisted this business for weeks?'

'But it has still happened.'

Rose spoke with deliberate fairness, with deliberate reasonableness:

'I repeat, I'm sorry. As a matter of historical fact, I have been arguing your case and Getliffe's most of the autumn. But yesterday they gave me no option. I also repeat, I want to do anything in the department's power to make it smooth for you. If I were you, I think I should feel very much as you do. Please forget about telephoning Getliffe. It was inconsiderate of me to ask you that, when I had to talk about something which was even more unpleasant for you. And, incidentally, for me. There's no need to decide anything tonight. Let me know tomorrow what you would like done.'

He had spoken with fairness. But I was a reproach, sitting there. All he wanted was for me to get out of his sight. As for me, I could not manage even the grace of his fairness.

'No, there's no choice,' I said roughly. 'You may as well tell these people to go ahead.'

CHAPTER XXXI

RECOMMENDATION BY A PRUDENT MAN

THAT night I did my duty, and rang up Francis in Cambridge. I was angry with him, just as Rose had been with me, because I had to persuade him. I was angry because he was so stiff-necked and hard to persuade. I was angry with Margaret, because out of love and her own high-principled temper she was saying what I wanted to say: that Francis and I should each of us resign and leave them to it.

But I felt something else, which I had not felt before, or not since I was a very young man – the intense, mescalin-vivid sense of being watched. When I picked up the receiver and asked for the Cambridge number, I was listening (was the line tapped?) to sounds on the aural threshold. The clicks and tinkles seemed to me as though they had been picked up by an amplifier.

It was the same for days to come. I remembered a refugee, years before, telling me one of the prices of exile. One had to think about actions which, before one left home, were as unconscious as dreaming. Now I knew what that meant. I found myself looking round before I took a taxi. Though the light was dim, the trees of the park appeared to be preternaturally sharp; I felt I could have counted each twig. The top-light of another taxi shone like a beacon.

Early in the week, Ellen telephoned: she had that morning received another anonymous letter: she and Roger wanted to talk to me together. Once more the world outside seemed over-brilliant. As we talked of where to meet, we sounded reasonable, to each other and to ourselves, but we weren't quite. We had lost our sense of fact, just as people do when they are hypnotised by secrets: just as my brother and I had once done, when, in the war, worried by what we knew, we had gone into the middle of St James's Park so as not to be overheard.

In the end – it was like being young and poor again, with nowhere to take one's young woman – we dropped in, one by one, into a pub on the Embankment. When I arrived, the lounge was empty and I sat at a table in the corner. Soon Roger joined me. I noticed that, despite all the photographs, no one behind the bar recognised him. Ellen came in: I went and greeted her, and brought her to the table.

She gave Roger her severe introductory smile, but her skin was glowing and the whites of her eyes as clear as a child's. She looked as though strain and suspicion were good for her, as though energy was pumping through her. Of the three of us, it was Roger who seemed physically subdued. Yet, as I read the new letter Ellen had brought out of her bag, he was watching me with eyes as alert as hers.

The letter was in the same handwriting, but the words had run close together. The tone was threatening ('you haven't much longer to make him change his mind') and, for the first time, obscene. It was a curious kind of obscenity – as though the writer, setting out for a hard-baked business purpose, had gone off the track, had become as obsessed as someone scrawling in a public lavatory. The obsession slithered on, insinuating, sadistic, glassy-eyed.

I didn't want to go on reading, and pushed the letter away over the glass table-top.

'Well?' cried Ellen.

Roger sank back in his chair. Like me, he was shocked, and at the same time didn't like being shocked. In a deliberately off-hand tone he said: 'One thing is fairly clear. He doesn't like us very much.'

'I'm not going to stand it,' she said.

'What else can we do?' Roger asked her, in a placating voice.

'I'm going to do something.' She appealed to me – no, announced to me: 'Don't you agree, this is the time to do something?'

In the past minute, I had realised that for the first time they were split. That was why I had been asked there that night. She wanted me on her side: and Roger, as he sat back in his chair, giving sensible, cautious reasons why they had to go on enduring this in silence, believed that I had to be on his.

He had spoken with caution, but without much authority. The words came slowly. As for this man, there was no sign that the threats would come to anything. Let it alone. Pretend they were unmoved. It was a nuisance they could live with.

'That's easy for you,' said Ellen.

He stared at her. It was nearly always wrong, he said quietly, to take steps when you couldn't see the end.

'This man can be stopped,' she insisted.

'You can't be sure.'

'We can go to the police,' she said sharply. 'They'll protect us. Do you know that he could get six months for this?'

'I dare say so.' Roger looked at her with a touch of exasperation, as if she were a child being obtuse about her sums. 'But I am not in a position to appear in a witness-box as Mr X. One has to be singularly anonymous for that particular activity. You must see that. *I* can't be Mr X.'

She was silent for a minute. 'No. Of course you can't.'

He put his hand on hers for a second.

Then she flared up again. 'But that isn't the only way. As soon as I knew who he was, I knew he could be stopped. He'll crumple up. This is my business, and I'm going to do it.' Her eyes were wide open with passion. She fixed her glance on me.

'What do you think, Lewis?'

After a pause I replied, turning to Roger:

'It's a slight risk. But I fancy it's probably time to take the offensive.'

I said it with every appearance of reason, of deliberate consideration, and perhaps as persuasively as I ever said anything.

Roger had been talking sense. Ellen was as gifted with sense as he was: but she was made for action, her judgment was always likely to leave her if she couldn't act. I ought to have known that. Maybe, with half my mind, I did know. But my own judgment had gone, for reasons more complex than hers, and much more culpable. As I grew older, I had learned patience. The influence I had on people like Roger was partly because they thought me a tough and enduring man; but this wasn't as natural as it seemed, nor so much all of a piece. I had been born spontaneous, excessively so, emotional, malleable. The stoical public face had become real enough, but the earlier nature went on underneath, and when the patience and control snapped, was still, in my middle age, capable of breaking through. This was dangerous for me, and for those round me, since fits of temper, or spontaneous affection, or sheer whims, filtered through the public screen, and sounded as disciplined, as reliable, as some part of my character had now become, and as I should have liked the rest of it to be. It didn't happen often, because I was on my guard: but occasionally it happened still, as on that evening. No one but Margaret knew it, but for days, since the dialogue with Rose, my temper had been smouldering. Like Ellen, I had gone into the pub craving for action. Unlike her, though, I didn't sound as though I needed it. The craving came out through layers of patience, mixed with all the qualifications and devices of discipline, as though it were the reasonable, considered recommendation of a wise and prudent man.

Yes, I said, we were all being shot at. There were great advantages in absorbing the attacks, in showing passive strength. It made enemies worry about what one had in reserve. But one mustn't stay passive for ever. If so, they ceased to worry, and treated one like a punchball. The whole art was, to stay silent, to select one's time, and then pick them off. Perhaps the time had come, or was coming. This attack on Ellen – there the man was wide open. If he had any connection with others, which we were no nearer knowing, it would interest them to hear that he had been coped with; anyway, this was the thing to do. Roger gave up, with only a token struggle. Except in little things, as Caro had once told me, he was the hardest of men to influence. In all our connection, I had scarcely once persuaded him: certainly not over-persuaded him. Sitting there, round the little table, it did not occur to me that I was over-persuading him. I felt as reasonable as I sounded. Almost at once, the three of us were talking, not of whether anything should be done, but of what.

Later on, when it was all over, I wondered what responsibility I had to accept. Perhaps I was being easy on myself – but had it made much difference, what I said that night? Surely it had been Ellen's will, or more precisely, her desire, which had been decisive? For once, Roger had wanted to slump into acquiescence and let her have her way. He gave the impression, utterly unlike him, of being absent – not from strain so much as from a kind of comfort. He did not even speak much. When he did speak, he said, as though it were one of his most pointed reflections,

'I must say, it will make things smoother, when we don't hear from him again.'

Ellen hissed at him like a cat.

'By God, that's helpful!' she cried. She broke into a grin, a lop-sided grin, furious and loving. As for him, he would be absent until he could take her in his arms.

The truth was, I now accepted, that the love was not one-sided. He loved her in return. It wasn't a passing fancy, such as a man of Roger's age and egotism might often have. He admired her, just as he admired Caro, and oddly enough for some of the same reasons: for these women were not so unlike as they seemed. Ellen was as upright as Caro, and as honourable: in her way, she was as worldly, though she had more grievances about the world. Perhaps she was deeper, nearer to the nerve of life. I believed that Roger thought they were both better people than he was. And, of course, between him and Ellen there was a link of the senses, so strong that sitting with them was like being in a field of force. Why it was so strong, I should probably never know. It was better that I shouldn't. If one reads the love-letters that give the details of a grand passion, they make one forget that the passion can still be grand.

There was one other thing. Just as Ellen's judgment and mine had been distorted, so was his. He loved her. But in a fashion strange to him, he felt he had no right to love her. Not only, perhaps not mainly, because of his wife. People thought of him as a hard professional politician. There was truth in that. How complete the truth was, I still didn't know. I still wasn't sure which choices he would make. And yet I was sure that he had a hope of virtue. He wanted perhaps more strongly than he himself could tell, to do something good. Somehow, as though he was dragged back to the priests and prophets, he would have felt more certain of virtue, more fit to do something good, if, like the greatest politicians, he could pay a price. It sounded atavistic and superstitious, as I looked at the two of them, the sharp, self-abnegating woman, the untransparent hulk of a man: yet, somewhere in my mind, was nagging the myth of Samson's hair.

Ellen and I, with Roger mostly silent, were arguing what was to be done. Private detectives? No, no point. Then I had an idea. This man was employed by one of Lord Lufkin's competitors. If Lufkin would talk to the other chairman – 'Have you ever seen that done?' said Roger, suddenly alive.

Yes, I said, I had once seen it done.

It would mean telling Lufkin everything, Roger was saying.

'It would mean telling him a good deal.'

'I'm against it,' said Ellen.

Roger listened to her, but went on: 'How far do you trust him?'

'If you gave him a confidence, he'd respect it,' I said.

'That's not enough, is it?'

I said that Lufkin, cold fish as he was, had been a good friend to me. I said that he was, in his own interest, without qualification on Roger's side. I left them talking it over, as I went to the bar to get more drinks. As I stood there, the landlady spoke to me by name. I had used that pub for years, since the time during the war when I lived in Pimlico. There was nothing ominous in her addressing me, but her tone was hushed.

'There's someone I want to show you,' she said.

For an instant I was alarmed. I looked round the room, the sense of being watched acute again. There weren't many people there, no one I knew or could suspect.

'Do you know who that is?' she whispered reverentially, pointing to the far end of the bar. There, sitting on a stool, eating a slice of veal-and-ham pie, with a glass of stout beside the plate, was a commonplace looking man in a blue suit.

'No,' I said.

'That', said the landlady, her whisper more sacramental, 'is Grobbelaar's brother-in-law!'

It might have sounded like gibberish, or alternatively as if Grobbelaar were a distinguished public figure. Not a bit of it. Distinguished public figures were not in the landlady's line. In that pub, Roger stayed anonymous and, if she had been told his name, she would have had no conception who he was. On the other hand, she had a clear conception who Grobbelaar was, and so had I. Grobbelaar had been, in fact, an entirely respectable South African, but an unfortunate one. About five years before, living, so far as I could remember, in Hammersmith, he had been murdered for the sake of a very small sum, about a hundred pounds. There had been nothing spectacular about the murder itself, but the consequences were somewhat gothic. For Grobbelaar had been in an amateurish fashion dissected, and the portions made into brown-paper parcels, weighted down with bricks, and dropped, at various points between Blackfriars and Putney, into the river. It was the kind of grotesque crime which, unbeknown to the landlady, foreigners thought typical of her native town, the fate which waited for many of us, as we groped our way through endless streets, in a never-ending fog. It was the kind of crime, true enough, which brought the landlady and me together. As she gave me this special treat, as she invited me to gaze, she knew that she was showing me an object touched by *mana*. It was true enough that this brother-in-law was another entirely respectable man, who had not had the slightest connection with the gothic occurrences. Did he, as an object of reverence, seem a little remote? Had the *mana* worn just a shade thin? The landlady's whisper was in a tone which meant that *mana* never wore thin.

'That', she repeated, 'is Grobbelaar's brother-in-law.'

I went back to our table with a grin. Ellen had noticed me conferring with the landlady; she looked at me with apprehensive eyes. I shook my head and said, 'No, nothing.'

They had decided against Lufkin. The straightforward method was to write a couple of lines to the man himself, saying without explanation that she wished to receive no further communications from him, and that any further letters would be returned. Nothing but that. It implicated no one but herself, and it told him that she knew.

At that we left it, and sat in the cheerful pub, now filling up, with the landlady busy, but her gaze still drawn by the magnet in the blue suit at the end of the bar.

CHAPTER XXXII

SYMPTOMS

THE White Paper was published at last; the House had not reassembled. This concatenation was not just an amiable coincidence. We wanted official opinion to form, the more of it the better. There was our best chance. As soon as the Paper, Command 8964, came out, Roger's supporters were trying to read the signs.

The newspapers didn't tell us much. One paper cried: 'Our Deterrent To Go?' To our surprise, the slogan did not immediately catch on. Most of the comments of the defence correspondents were predictable: we could have written them ourselves. In fact, to an extent, we had written them ourselves, for two or three of the most influential correspondents were friends and disciples of Francis Getliffe. They knew the arguments as well as he or Walter Luke. They understood the White Paper, though it deserved fairly high marks for deliberate obscurity. They accepted that, sooner or later, there was only one answer.

The danger was that we were listening to ourselves. It was the occupational danger of this kind of politics: you cut yourself off from your enemies, you basked in the echo of your own voice. That was one of the reasons why the real bosses stayed more optimistic than the rest of us. Even Roger, more realistic than other bosses, knowing that this was the moment, knowing that he had to be certain what the back-benchers were saying, had to force himself to visit the Carlton or White's.

The cabinet had, as a compromise, accepted the White Paper. But Roger knew – inarticulate men like Collingwood could sometimes make themselves very clear – that they meant the compromise to be kept. If he tilted the balance, if he put his weight on the side of his own policy, he was in danger. The Prime Minister and his friends were not simple men, but they were used to listening to men simpler than themselves. If the back-benchers became suspicious of Roger, then simple men sometimes had grounds for their suspicions. It was by his own party that he would be judged.

As for me, I liked hearing bad news no more than Roger did. But for the next fortnight, I called on acquaintances and used my clubs as I had not done since I married Margaret. I did not pick up many signs. With those I did pick up, I was not sure which way they pointed. Walking along Pall Mall, one wild windy January night, I was thinking that on the whole it was going a shade worse, but not decisively worse, than I reckoned on. Then I went up the steps of a club where I was not a member but was meeting a Whitehall colleague. He was the head of a service department, and after a few minutes with him I was encouraged. As he talked, one eye to his watch, needing to catch a train back to East Horsley for dinner, the odds seemed perceptibly shorter. I caught sight of Douglas Osbaldiston walking through the colonnades. My host said good-bye, and I stayed for a word, what I thought would be a casual word, with Douglas. As he came out into the light, I saw his face, and I was shocked. He looked ravaged.

Before I could ask him, he broke out: 'Lewis, I'm nearly off my head with worry.' He sat beside me. I said, 'What is it?'

In reply, he said one word. 'Mary.' The name of his wife. Then he added that she might be very ill.

As though released, he told me of her signs and symptoms, hyper-attentively, almost with fervour, just as a sick person tells one about his own. About two weeks before – no, Douglas corrected himself, with obsessive accuracy – eleven days before, she had complained of double vision. Holding her cigarette at arm's length, she had seen a replica alongside it. They had laughed. They were happy together. She had always been healthy. A week later, she said that she had lost feeling in her left arm. Suddenly they had looked at each other in distress. 'We've always known, ever since we were married, when either of us was afraid.' She had gone to her doctor. He couldn't reassure her. Forty-eight hours before, she had got up from a chair and been unable to control her legs. 'She's been walking like a spastic,' he cried. That morning she had been taken to hospital. He couldn't get any comfort. It would be a couple of days before they gave him any sort of answer.

'Of course,' he said, 'I've got the best neurologists in the place. I've been talking to them most of the day.' It had been a consolation to use influence and power, to find out the names of the specialists, to have them brought in government cars to his office. That day, Douglas had given up being unassuming.

'I suppose you know what we're afraid of?' he asked in a quiet tone.

'No.' I failed him. All through his description I had been at a loss.

Even when he brought out the name of the disease, it was his manner which harrowed me most. 'Disseminated sclerosis,' he said. He added, 'You must remember reading about Barbellion's disease.'

Then, quite suddenly, he was full of an inexplicable hope.

'It may not be anything of the sort,' he said robustly, almost as though it were for him to cheer me up. 'They don't know. They can't know yet awhile. Don't forget, there are several possibilities which are more or less benign.'

He had a surge of happiness, of confidence in the future. I did not know how soon his mood would change. Not liking to leave him in the club, I offered to take him home to my wife, or to go with him to his own house, deserted now. He gave an intimate smile, some of the freshness returning to his face. No, he wouldn't hear of it. He was perfectly all right, nothing could happen that night. He was staying at the club, he would go to bed with a good book. I ought to know he wasn't the man to take to the bottle by himself.

All he said in that patch of euphoria was, for him, curiously indirect, but when I said good-bye, he gripped my hand.

During the next few days, at meetings, in the office, speculations about Roger got sharper. Parliament would be sitting again in a week. Before Easter there would, Rose and the others agreed, have to be a full-dress debate on the White Paper. But they did not agree either on the strength of Roger's position nor on his intentions. Rose, very distant from me at this time, merely gave a polite smile.

On the fourth morning after I had met Douglas at his club, his secretary rang up mine. Would I please go along at once?

As soon as I entered his room, I had no doubt. He was standing by the window. He gave me some sort of greeting. He said: 'You were worried about her too, weren't you?' Then he burst out: 'The news is bad.'

What had they said?

He replied, no, it wasn't exactly what they had expected. It wasn't disseminated sclerosis. But that wasn't much improvement, he said, with a quiet and bitter sarcasm. The prognosis was as bad or worse. It was another disease of the central nervous system, a rarer one. They could not predict its course with accuracy. The likelihood was, she would be dead within five years. Long before that, she would be completely paralysed. He said, his expression naked and passionate:

'Can you imagine how horrible it is to know that? About someone you've loved in the flesh?' He added: 'About someone you still love in the flesh?'

For minutes I stayed silent, and he broke out in disjointed, violent spasms.

'I shall have to tell her soon.

'She's been kind all her life. Kind to everyone. Why should this happen to her?

'If I believed in God, I should throw him back his ticket.

'She's good.

'She's got to die like this.'

At last, when he fell silent, I asked whether there was anything I could do.

'There's nothing', he said, 'that anyone can do.' Then he said, in a level tone, 'I'm sorry. I'm sorry, Lewis. She'll need her friends. She'll have a lot of time to see her friends. She'll want you and Margaret, of course she will.'

There was a pause. He said:

'Well, that's all.'

I could feel the effort of his will. His voice tightened and he added:

'Now I should like to talk some business.'

He held up his copy of the White Paper, which had been lying on the blotter.

'I want your impression. How is this going down?'

'How do you think?'

'I've been occupied with other things. Come on, what is your impression?'

I replied: 'Did anyone expect absolutely universal enthusiasm?'

'It hasn't got it, you mean?'

'There are some malcontents.'

'From what I've been able to pick up,' said Douglas, 'that may be putting it mildly.'

As he sat there unrelaxed, the nerve of professional expertness showed through. It was not the White Paper which worried him. It was the interpretation which he knew, as well as I did, Roger wished to make and to act upon. He had never liked Roger's policy: his instincts were too conservative for that. It was only because Roger was a strong Minister that he had got his way so far: or perhaps because Douglas wasn't unaffected by Roger's skills. But now Douglas neither liked the policy nor wanted to gamble on its chances. Just as he hadn't wished to be linked with a scandal when the parliamentary question came up, so he didn't wish to be linked with a failure.

As he shut out his suffering, his tormented thoughts of his wife, this other concern leaped out.

'It could be,' I said. He was much too astute a man to be bluffed.

'It's no use deceiving ourselves,' said Douglas. 'Anyway, you wouldn't.

There is a finite possibility that my Minister's present policy may be a dead duck.'

'How finite?'

We stared at each other. I couldn't get him to commit himself. I pressed him. An even chance? That would, before this conversation, have been my secret guess. Douglas said:

'I – I hope he's sensible enough to cut his losses now. And start on another line. The important thing is, we've got to have another line in reserve.'

'You mean—?'

'I mean, we have to start working out some alternative.'

'If that became known,' I said, 'it would do great harm.'

'It won't get known,' he replied, 'and it will have to be done at once. We shan't have long. It's a question of thinking out several eventualities and making up our minds which is going to be right.'

'In this business,' I said, 'I've never had much doubt what's right.'

'Then you're lucky.'

For the moment, he was back in his off-hand form. Then he went on driving himself, clear, concentrated. He had said 'which is going to be right' without any fuss, meaning which policies would, according to the climate of opinion, be both sensible and practicable. He proposed that afternoon to begin writing the draft of a new plan, 'just to see how it looks'. Then, if trouble came, the department would have something 'up its sleeve'.

In everything he said or intended, he was entirely straightforward. His code of behaviour was as rigid as that of Rose. He would inform Roger that afternoon of precisely what he intended to do.

In one respect, however, he differed from Rose. He did not indulge in any hypocrisy of formality or protocol. It never occurred to him to pretend – as Rose had always pretended, and sometimes managed to believe – that he had no influence on events. It never occurred to him to chant that he was simply there to carry out the policy of his 'masters'. On the contrary, Douglas often found it both necessary and pleasant to produce his own.

As I went down the corridors back to my own office, I was thinking of his interview with Roger that afternoon.

CHAPTER XXXIII

A MAN CALLED MONTEITH

It was late that same afternoon when I received a note from Hector Rose – not a minute, but a note in his beautiful italic handwriting, beginning 'My dear Lewis', and ending 'Yours ever'. The substance was less emollient. Rose, who did not lack moral courage, and who was sitting three doors down the corridor, had shied away from telling it in person.

'Could you possibly make it convenient to come to my room at ten a.m. tomorrow? I know that this is both unpleasantly early and at intolerably short notice: but our friends in ――' (a branch of Security) 'are apt to be somewhat pressing. They wish to have a personal interview with you, which is, I believe, the last stage in their proceedings. They have asked for a similar arrangement with Sir F. Getliffe in the afternoon. I take it you would not prefer to approach F.G. yourself, and we are acting on that assumption. I cannot tell you how sorry I am that the notice should be so short, and I have already had a word to say about this.'

That night, as I let myself go to Margaret, taking comfort from her fury, I didn't find Rose's preoccupation with timing funny. I felt it was another dig, another jab of the needle. When I entered his room, at precisely five minutes to ten the next morning, he had something else to brood about and was as brusque as I was.

'Have you seen this?' he said, without any of his greetings. 'This' was an editorial in one of the popular papers. It was an attack on the White Paper, under the heading: ARE THEY THROWING AWAY OUR INDEPENDENCE?

The paper went on asking: Do they intend to sell us out? Do they intend to stop us being a great power?

'Good God alive,' cried Rose, 'what kind of world are they living in? Do they think that if there were a single way in heaven or earth which could keep this damned country a great power, some of us wouldn't have killed ourselves to find it?'

Savagely, he went on swearing. I could scarcely remember hearing an oath from him, much less a piece of rhetoric. 'Do these silly louts imagine', he burst out, 'that it's specially easy to accept the facts?'

He looked at me, his eyes bleak.

'Ah well,' he said, 'our masters will have a good deal on their plate. Now, before Monteith arrives, there is something I wanted to explain to you.' Once more, smooth as a machine, he was on the track of protocol. 'Monteith is going to conduct this business himself. We thought that was only fitting, both for you and Getliffe. But there was some difference of opinion about the venue. They thought it was perhaps hardly suitable to talk to you in your own room, as being your home ground, so to speak. Well, I was not prepared to let them invite you to their establishment, so we reached a compromise that Monteith should meet you here. I hope that is as much to your liking as anything can be, my dear Lewis, in these somewhat egregious circumstances.'

He allowed himself that one flick. It was as near a token of support as he could manage. I nodded, and we gazed at each other. He announced, as though it were an interesting piece of social gossip, that he would soon vacate the room for the entire day.

Shortly afterwards, the private secretary brought in Monteith. This time Rose's greetings were back at their most profuse. Turning to me, he said: 'Of course, you two must have met?'

In fact we hadn't, though we had been present together at a Treasury meeting. 'Oh, in that case,' said Rose, 'do let me introduce you.'

Monteith and I shook hands. He was a brisk, strong-boned man, with something like an actor's handsomeness, dark haired, with drifts of white above the ears. His manner was quite unhistrionic, subdued and respectful. He was much the youngest of the three of us, probably ten years younger than I was. As we made some meaningless chat, he behaved like a junior colleague, modest but assured.

After Rose had conducted the ceremony of chit-chat for five minutes, he said: 'Perhaps you won't mind if I leave you two together?'

When the door closed, Monteith and I were left looking at each other.

'I think we might sit down, don't you?' he said. Politely he showed me to an armchair, while he himself took Rose's. There was a bowl of blue hyacinths in front of him, fresh that morning, witness to Rose's passion for flowers. The smell of hyacinths was, for me, too sickly, too heavy, to stir up memories, as it might have done, of businesslike talks with Rose going back nearly twenty years. All the smell did was to give me a discomfort of the senses, as I sat there, staring into Monteith's face.

I did not know precisely what his function was. Was he the boss? Or a grey eminence, working behind another boss? Or just a deputy? I thought I knew: Rose certainly did. But, with a passion for mystification, including self-mystification, none of us discussed those agencies or their chains of command.

'You have had a most distinguished career, Sir Lewis.' Firmly, Monteith addressed me. 'You will understand that I have to ask you some questions on certain parts of it.'

He had not laid out a single note on the desk, much less produced a file. Throughout the next three hours, he worked from nothing but memory. In his own office, there must have been a dossier a good many inches high. I already knew that he had interviewed, not only scientists and civil servants who had been colleagues of mine during the war and after, not only old acquaintances at Cambridge, such as the former Master and Arthur Brown, but also figures from my remote past, a retired solicitor whom I had not seen for twenty-five years, even the father of my first wife. All this material he had stored in his head, and deployed with precision. It was an administrator's trick, which Rose or Douglas or I could have done ourselves. Still, it was impressive. It would have been so if I had watched him dealing with another's life. Since it was my own life, I found it at times deranging. There were facts about myself, sometimes facts near to the bone, which he knew more accurately than I did.

My earliest youth, my father's bankruptcy, poverty, my time as a clerk, reading for the Bar examinations – he had the dates at command, the names of people. It all sounded smooth and easy, not really like one's past at all. Then he asked: 'When you were a young man in ——' (the provincial town), 'you were active politically?' Speeches at local meetings, the I.L.P., schoolrooms, the nights in pubs: he ticked them off.

'You were then far out on the left?'

I had set myself to tell the absolute truth. Yet it was difficult. We hadn't many terms in common. I wasn't in complete control of my temper. Carefully, but in a sharpened tone, I said: 'I believed in socialism. I had all the hopes of my time. But I wasn't a politician as real politicians understand the word. At that age, I wasn't dedicated enough for that. I was too ambitious in other ways.'

At this, Montieth's fine eyes lit up. He gave me a smile, not humorous, but comradely. I was dissatisfied with my answer. I had not been interrogated before. Now I was beginning to understand, and detest, the pressures and the temptations. What I had said was quite true: and yet it was too conciliatory.

'Of course,' said Monteith, 'it's natural for young men to be interested in politics. I was myself, at the university.'

'Were you?'

'Like you, but on the other side. I was on the committee of the Conservative Club.' He said this with an air of innocent gratification, as though that revelation would astonish me, as though he were confessing to having been chairman of a nihilist cell.

Once more he was efficient, concentrated, ready to call me a liar.

The thirties, my start at the Bar, marriage, the first days of Hitler, the Spanish Civil War.

'You were strongly on the anti-Nationalist side?'

'In those days,' I said, 'we called it something different.'

'That is, you were opposed to General Franco?'

'Of course,' I replied.

'But you were very strongly and actively opposed?'

'I did what little came easy. I've often wished I'd done more.'

He went over some committees I had sat on. All correct, I said.

'In the course of these activities, you mixed with persons of extreme political views?'

'Yes.'

He addressed me formally again, and then – 'You were very intimate with some of these persons?'

'I think I must ask you to be more specific.'

'It is not suggested that you were, or have been at any time, a member of the Communist Party—'

'If it were suggested,' I said, 'it would not be true.'

'Granted. But you have been intimate with some who have?'

'I should like the names.'

He gave four – those of Arthur Mounteney, the physicist, two other scientists, R—— and T——, Mrs Charles March.

I was never a close friend of Mounteney, I said. (It was irksome to find oneself going back on the defensive.)

'In any case, he left the Party in 1939,' said Monteith, with brisk expertness.

'Nor of T——.' Then I said: 'I was certainly a friend of R——. I saw a good deal of him during the war.'

'You saw him last October?'

'I was going to say that I don't see him often nowadays. But I am very fond of him. He is one of the best men I have ever known.'

'Mrs March?'

'Her husband and I were intimate friends when we were young men, and we still are. I met Ann at his father's house twenty odd years ago, and I have known her ever since. I suppose they dine with us three or four times a year.'

'You don't deny that you have remained in close touch with Mrs March?'

'Does it sound as though I were denying it?' I cried, furious at seeming to be at a moral disadvantage.

He gave a courteous, noncommittal smile.

I made myself calm, trying to capture the initiative.

I said:

'Perhaps it's time that I got one or two things clear.'

'Please do.'

'First of all, though this isn't really the point, I am not inclined to give up my friends. It wouldn't have occurred to me to do so – either because they were communists or anything else. Ann March and R—— happen to be people of the highest character, but it wouldn't matter if they weren't. If you extend your researches, you'll find that I have other friends, respectable politically, but otherwise disreputable by almost any standards.'

'Yes, I was interested to find how remarkable your circle was,' he said, not in the least outfaced.

'But that isn't the point, is it?'

He bowed his fine head.

'You want to know my political views, don't you? Why haven't you asked me? – Though I can't answer in one word. First of all, I haven't altered much as I've got older. I've learned a bit more, that's all. I'll have another word about that a little later. As I told you, I've never been dedicated to politics as a real politician is. But I've always been interested. I think I know something about power. I've watched it in various manifestations, almost all my working life. And you can't know something about power without being suspicious of it. That's one of the reasons why I couldn't go along with Ann March and R——. It seemed to me obvious in the thirties that the concentration of power which had developed under Stalin was too dangerous by half. I don't think I was being emotional about it. I just distrusted it. As a matter of fact, I'm not emotional about the operation of politics. That is why I oughtn't to give you any anxiety. I believe that, in the official life, we have to fall back on codes of honour and behaviour. We can't trust ourselves to do anything else.'

He was gazing straight at me, but did not speak.

'But I want to be open with you,' I said. 'In terms of honour and behaviour, I think you and I would speak the language. In terms of ultimate politics, we almost certainly don't. I said that I'm not emotional about the operations of politics. But about the hopes behind them, I'm deeply so. I thought it was obvious that the Revolution in Russia was going to run into some major horrors of power. I wasn't popular with Ann March and R——- and some of my other friends for telling them so. But that isn't all. I always believed that the power was working two ways. They were doing good things with it, as well as bad. When once they got some insight into the horrors, then they might create a wonderful society. I still believe that. How it will compare with the American society, I don't know. But so long as they both survive, I should have thought that many of the best human hopes stand an excellent chance.'

Monteith was expressionless. Despite his job, or perhaps because of it, he did not think about politics except as something he had to give a secret answer to. He was not in the least a speculative man. He coughed, and said:

'A few more questions on the same subject, sir. Your first wife, just before the war, made a large donation to a certain communist?'

'Who was it?'

He mentioned a name which meant nothing to me.

'Are you sure?' I asked.

'Quite sure.'

I knew absolutely nothing of him.

'If you're right,' I said, 'it wasn't for ideological reasons.'

Just for an instant, he had stripped away the years. I was a youngish man, distraught, with a wife I had to look after: still capable of jealousy, but schooled to watching her in search of anyone who might alleviate the inner cold: still appalled because I did not know where she was or whom she was with, at the mercy of anyone who dropped news of her: still listening for her name.

There was a silence. With a stiff sensitivity he said: 'I have informed myself about your tragedy. I need not ask you anything more about her.'

He broke out sharply: 'But you yourself. You attended meetings of ——?' He gave the title of what, not at the time but later, we had come to call a 'Front' organisation.

'No.'

'Please think again.'

'I tell you no,' I said.

'This is very curious.' His manner throughout had been professional. He had kept hostility out: but now there was an edge. 'I have evidence from someone who remembers sitting next to you. He remembers exactly how you looked. You pushed your chair back from the table and made a speech.'

'I tell you, there is not a word of truth in it.'

'My evidence is from someone reliable.'

'Who is it?'

Monteith answered, 'You ought to know that I can't reveal my sources.'

'It is utterly and absolutely untrue.' I was speaking harshly and angrily. 'I take it you've got it from one of your ex-communists? I take it that most of your information comes that way?'

'You've no right to ask those questions.'

I was suffused with outrage, with a disproportionate bitterness. After a moment I said:

'Look here, you ought to be careful about these channels of yours. This isn't specially important. So far as I know, this Front you're speaking of was quite innocuous. I had plenty of connections far more committed than that. I've told you so, and I'm prepared to go on telling you so. But, as it happens, I never went anywhere near that particular group. I repeat, I never went to a meetings of theirs, or had any communication with them. That is flat. It has to be accepted. Your man has invented this whole story. I also repeat, you ought to be careful of his stories about other people. This one doesn't matter much to me. But there may be others which could do more harm – to people who are more helpless.'

For the first time, I had shaken him. Not, I later thought, by anger: he must have been used to that. More likely, because his technical expertness was being challenged. He had had a good deal of experience. He knew that I, or any competent man, would not have denied a point so specific without being dead sure.

'I will look into it,' he said.

'I suppose you'll give a report of this interview to Hector Rose?' I said.

'That is so.'

'When you do, I should like you to mention this matter. And say that you are doing so at my request.'

'I should have done that in any case.'

Just then he was talking, not like an interrogator, but as though we were all officials together, getting to work on 'a difficult one'. 'It's very curious.' He was puzzled and distracted. When he went on with his questions, the snap had left him, like a man who is absent-minded because of trouble at home.

My record over the atomic bomb. Yes, I had known about it from the start. Yes, I had been close to the scientists all along. Yes, I had known Sawbridge, who gave away some secrets. Yes, he and my brother had been to school together. But Monteith was doing it mechanically; he knew that in the end it was my brother who had broken Sawbridge down.

Monteith was watchful again, as he talked of what I had done and thought about the dropping of the first bomb.

'I've made it public. You've only got to read, you know,' I said. 'And you'll find a certain amount more on the files.'

'That has been done,' replied Monteith. 'But still, I should like to ask you.'

Hadn't I, like many of the scientists, been actively opposed to the use of the bomb? Certainly, I said. Hadn't I met the scientists, just before Hiroshima, to see how they could stop it? Certainly, I said. Wasn't that going further than a civil servant should feel entitled to? 'Civil servants have done more effective things than that,' I said, 'I often wish I had.'

Then I explained. While there was a chance of stopping the bomb being dropped, we had used every handle we could pull: this wasn't improper unless (I couldn't resist saying) it was improper to oppose in secret the use of any kind of bomb at any time.

When the thing had happened, we had two alternatives. Either to resign and make a row, or else stay inside and do our best. Most of us had stayed inside, as I had done. For what motives? Duty, discipline, even conformity? Perhaps we had been wrong. But, I thought, if I had to make the choice again, I should have done the same.

After that, the interrogation petered out. My second marriage. Hadn't my father-in-law, before the war, before I knew either of them, belonged to various Fronts? asked Monteith, preoccupied once more. I didn't know. He might have done. He was an old-fashioned intellectual liberal. Official life – nothing there, though he was curious about when I first knew Roger. It was past one o'clock. Suddenly he slapped both palms on the desk.

'That is as far as I want to go.' He leaped up, agile and quick, and gave me a lustrous glance. He said in a tone less formal, less respectful than when he began:

'I believe what you have told me.' He shook my hand and went out rapidly through the outer office, leaving me standing there.

It had all been very civil. He was an able, probably a likeable, man doing his job. Yet, back in my office through the January afternoon, I felt black. Not that I was worrying about the result. It was something more organic than that, almost like being told that one's heart is not perfect, and that one has to live carefully in order to survive. I did not touch a paper and did no work.

Much of the afternoon I looked out of the window, as though thinking, but not really thinking. I rang up Margaret. She alone knew that I should not shrug it off. She knew that in middle age I was still vain, that I did not find it tolerable to account for my actions except to myself. Over the telephone I told her that this ought to be nothing. A few hours of questions by a decent and responsible man. In the world we were living in, it was nothing. If you're living in the middle of a religious war, you ought to expect to get shot at, unless you go away and hide. But it was no use sounding robust to Margaret. She knew me.

I should bring Francis back to dinner, I said, after they had finished with him. This she had not expected, and she was troubled. She had already invited young Arthur Plimpton, once more in London: partly out of fun, partly out of matchmaking.

'I'd put him off,' she said, 'but I haven't the slightest idea where he's staying. Shall I try to get him through the Embassy?'

'Don't bother,' I told her. 'At best, he may lighten the atmosphere.'

'And there might be something of an atmosphere,' she replied.

No, it was no use sounding robust to Margaret – but it was to Francis. As we drove home, under the lights of the Mall, he did not refer to my interrogation, although he knew of it. He believed me to be more worldly, less quixotic, than he was: which was quite true. He assumed that I took what came to me as all in the day's work.

As for himself, he said: 'I'm sorry that I let them do it.'

He was very quiet. When we got into the flat, Arthur was waiting in the drawing-room, greeting us politely. He went on: 'Sir Francis, you look as though you could use a drink.' He took charge, installed us in the arm-chairs, poured out the whisky. He was more adept than Francis's own sons, I was thinking. Which didn't make him more endearing to Francis. But just then, Francis was blaming him, not only for his charm, but for his country. As Francis sat there, silent, courteous, he was searching for culprits on whom to blame that afternoon.

With Arthur present, I couldn't talk directly to Francis: nor, when Margaret came in, could she. She saw him, usually the most temperate of men, taking another drink, very stiff: she hated minuets, she longed to plunge in. As it was, she had to talk about Cambridge, the college, the family. Penelope was still in the United States – how was she? Quite well, when they last heard, said Francis, for once sounding not over-interested in his favourite daughter.

'I heard from her on Sunday, Sir Francis,' said Arthur, dead-pan, like a man scoring an unobtrusive point.

'Did you,' Francis replied, not as a question.

'Yes, she put in a transatlantic call.'

Margaret could not resist it. 'What did she say?'

'She wanted to know which was the best restaurant in Baltimore.'

Arthur had spoken politely, impassively, and without a glint in his eye. Margaret's colour rose, but she went on. What was he going to do himself? Was he going back to the United States? Yes, said Arthur, he had settled on his career. He had arranged to enter the electronic industry. He talked about his firm-to-be with dismaying confidence. He knew more about business than Francis and Margaret and I all rolled together.

'So you'll be home again soon?' asked Margaret.

'It'll be fine,' said Arthur. Suddenly, with an owlish look, he said: 'Of course, I don't know Penny's plans.'

'You don't,' said Margaret.

'I suppose she won't be back on this side?'

For once Margaret looked baffled. In Arthur's craggy face, the blue eyes shone dazzlingly sincere: but under the flesh there was a lurking grin.

When he left us – out of good manners, because, listening, he had picked up in the air what was unspoken – I felt saddened. I looked at Francis, and saw, not the friend I had grown up with, but an ageing man, stern, not serene, not at all at peace. I had first met him when he was Arthur's age. It had been pleasant – or so it seemed that night – to be arrogant and young.

'Francis,' said Margaret, 'you're being rather stupid about that boy.'

Francis gave an unprofessorial curse.

There was a silence.

'I think,' he spoke to her with trust and affection, as though it were a relief, 'I've just about ceased to be useful. I think I've come to the limit.'

She said, that couldn't be true.

'I think it is,' said Francis. He turned on me. 'Lewis oughtn't to have persuaded me. I ought to have got out of it straightaway. I shouldn't have been exposed to this.'

We began to quarrel. There was rancour in our voices. He blamed me, we both blamed Roger. Politicians never take care of their tools, said Francis, with increasing anger. You're useful so long as you're useful. Then you're expendable. No doubt, said Francis bitterly, if things went wrong, Roger would play safe. In a gentlemanly fashion, he would go back to the fold: and in an equally gentlemanly fashion, his advisers would be disgraced.

'You can't be disgraced,' said Margaret.

Francis began to talk to her in a more realistic tone. They wouldn't keep him out just yet, he said. At least, he didn't think so. They wouldn't dare to say that he was a risk. And yet, when all this was over, win or lose, somehow it would be convenient for them not to involve him. The suggestion would go round that he didn't quite fit in. It would be better to have safer men. As our kind of world went on, the men had to get safer and safer. You couldn't afford to be different. No one could afford to have you if you showed a trace of difference. The most valuable single gift was the ability to sing in unison. And so they would shut him out.

We went on quarrelling.

'You're too thin-skinned,' I said, at my sharpest.

Margaret looked from him to me. She knew what in secret I had felt that day. She was wondering when, after Francis had gone, she could make a remark about the thinness of other skins.

CHAPTER XXXIV

THE PURITY OF BEING PERSECUTED

THE next evening, Margaret and I got out of the taxi on the Embankment and walked up into the Temple gardens. All day news had come prodding in, and I was jaded. The chief Government whip had called on Roger. Some back-benchers, carrying weight inside the party, had to be reassured. Roger would have to meet them. Two Opposition leaders had been making speeches in the country the night before. No one could interpret the public opinion polls.

Yes, we were somewhere near a crisis, I thought with a kind of puzzlement, as I looked over the river at the lurid city sky. How far did it reach? Maybe in a few months' time, some of the offices in this part of London would carry different names. Was that all? Maybe other lives stood to lose, lives stretched out under the lit-up sky. Roger and the others thought so: one had to think it, or it was harder to go on.

Those other lives did not respond much. A few did, not many. Perhaps they sent their messages to the corridors very rarely, when the dangers were on top of them: otherwise, perhaps the messages came not at all.

Back towards the Strand, the hall of my old Inn blazed out like a church on a Sunday night. We were on our way to a Bar concert. In the Inn buildings, lighted windows were shining here and there, oblongs of brilliance in a bulk of darkness. We passed the set of chambers where I had worked as a young man. Some of the names were still there, as they had been in my time. Mr H. Getliffe: Mr W. Allen. On the next staircase, I noticed the name of a contemporary: Sir H. Salisbury. That was out of date: he had just been appointed a Lord Justice of Appeal. Margaret, feeling that I was distracted, pressed my arm. This was a part of my life she hadn't known; she was apt to be jealous of it, and, as we walked past the building in the sharp air, she believed that I was homesick. She was wrong. I had felt something more like irritation. The Bar had never really suited me, I had not once thought of going back. And yet, if I could have been content with it, I should have had a smoother time. Like Salisbury. I shouldn't be in the middle of this present crisis.

The hall was draughty. Chairs, white programmes gleaming on them as at a church wedding, had been set in lines and then pushed into disorder, as people leaned over to talk. The event, though it didn't sound it, was an occasion of privilege. Several members from both front benches were there: Lord Lufkin and his entourage were there; so was Diana Skidmore, who had come with Monty Cave. As they shouted to one another, white-tied, bedecked, no one would have thought they were in a crisis. Much less that any of them resented, as I did, the moment in which we stood. They were behaving as though this was the kind of trouble politicians got into. They made jokes. They behaved as if these places were going to stay their own: while as for the rest – well, one could be reminded of them by the russet light of the city sky.

They weren't preoccupied with the coming debate, except to make some digs at Roger. What they were really interested in at this moment – or at least, what Diana and her friends were really interested in – was a job. The job, somewhat bewilderingly, was a Regius Professorship of History. Diana had recovered some of her spirits. There was a rumour that she had determined to make Monty Cave divorce his wife. Having become high-spirited once again, Diana had also, once again, become importunate. Her friends had to do what she told them: and what she told them was to twist the Prime Minister's arm. The P.M. had to hear her candidate's name from all possible angles. This name was Thomas Orbell.

It was not that Diana was a specially good judge of academic excellence. She would have been just as likely to have a candidate for a bishopric. She treated academic persons with reverence, as though they were sacred cows: but, though they might be sacred cows, they did not seem to her quite serious. That didn't stop her getting excited about the claims of Dr Orbell, and didn't stop her friends getting excited for him or against. Not that they were wrapped up in the academic life. It was nice to toss the jobs round, it was nice to spot winners. This was one of the pleasures of the charmed circle. Margaret, who had been brought up among scholars, was uneasy. She knew Orbell and did not want to spoil his chances. She knew that he had left my college, and now held a readership at Newcastle. She was certain that he wasn't good enough.

'He's *brilliant*,' said Diana, herself resplendent in white, like the fairy on a Christmas tree.

In fact, Diana's enthusiasm, the cheerful, cherubim-chanting of a couple of her ministerial friends, Margaret's qualms, were likely all to be beside the point. True, the Prime Minister would listen; true, he would listen with porcine competence. Orbell's supporters might get words of encouragement. At exactly the same moment, a lantern-jawed young man in the private office, trained by Osbaldiston, would be collecting opinions with marmoreal calm. My private guess was that Tom Orbell stood about as much chance for this chair as he did for the headship of the Society of Jesus.

In the library after the performance, where we had herded for sandwiches and wine, I noticed Diana, her diamonds flashing, talk for a moment to Caro alone. Just before we left, Caro spoke to me and passed a message on.

Diana had been talking to Reggie Collingwood. He had said they would all have to 'feel their way'. It was conceivable that Roger would have to 'draw in his horns' a bit. If so, they could look after him.

It sounded, and was meant to sound, casual and confident. But it was also deliberate. Collingwood wasn't given to indiscretion. Nor, when it came to confidences, was Diana. This remark was intended to reach Roger: and Caro was making sure that it reached me. As she told me, she took me by the arm, walking towards the door, and gazed at me with bold eyes. This was not a display of affection. She did not like me any better, she was no warmer to Roger's advisers, as she walked on my arm, her shoulders, because she was a strapping woman, not far below my own. But she was making certain that I wasn't left out.

The Bar concert had taken place on a Thursday night. On the Saturday morning I was alone in our drawing-room, the children back at school, Margaret off for a day with her father, now both ill and valetudinarian, when the telephone rang. It was David Rubin.

This was not, in itself, a surprise. I had heard the day before that he was over on one of his State Department visits. I expected that he and I would find ourselves at the same meeting on Saturday afternoon. That turned out to be true, and David expressed his courteous gratification. But it was a surprise to hear him insisting that I arrange an interview with Roger. Apparently he had tried Roger's office the day before and been rebuffed. It was odd enough for anyone to rebuff him: much odder for him to come back afterwards. 'This isn't just an idea of visiting with him. I want to say something to him.'

'I rather gathered that,' I said. Over the phone came a reluctant cachinnation.

He was flying out next morning. The interview would have to be fixed for some time that night. I did my best. First of all, Caro would not put me through to Roger. When at last I made her, he greeted me as though I had brought bad news. Did I know that Parliament met next week? Did I by any chance remember that he was preparing for a debate? He wanted to see no one. I said (our voices were petty with strain) that he could be rude to me, though I didn't pretend to like it. But it was unwise to be rude to David Rubin.

When I saw Rubin that afternoon, for the first time in a year, he did not look so formidable. He was sitting at a table, between Francis Getliffe and another scientist, in one of the Royal Society's rooms in Burlington House. The room smelt musty, lined with bound volumes of periodicals, like an unused library. The light was dim. Rubin, lemur-like circles under his eyes, looked fastidious and depressed. When I passed a note along, saying that we were due at Lord North Street after dinner, he gave a nod, as from one who had to endure much before he slept.

He had to endure this meeting. He was by now too much of a government figure to hope for a great deal. He was more pessimistic than anyone there. It was not an official meeting. Everyone in the room, at least in form, had attended as a private citizen. Nearly all were scientists who had been, or still were, concerned with the nuclear projects. They were trying to find a way of talking directly to their Soviet counterparts. Several men in the room had won world fame – there were the great academic physicists, Mounteney, who was chairman, Rubin himself, an old friend of mine called Constantine. There were also departmental scientists, such as Walter Luke, who had demanded to take part.

All three Governments knew what was going on. Several officials, including me, had been invited. I remembered other meetings in these musty-smelling rooms, nearly twenty years before, when scientists told us that the nuclear bomb might work.

David Rubin sat like one who has listened often enough. Then, all of a sudden, he became interested. Scientific good will, legalisms, formulations

– they vanished. For the door opened, and to everyone's astonishment, there came into the room Brodzinski. Soft-footed, for all his bulk, he walked to the table, his barrel chest thrust out. His eyes were stretched wide, as he looked at Arthur Mounteney. In his strong voice, in his off-English, he said, 'I'm sorry to be late, Mr Chairman.'

Each person round the table knew of his speeches in America and knew that Francis and Luke had been damaged. Men like Mounteney detested him and all he stood for. For him to enter, and then make his little apology – it irritated them all, it was a ridiculous anticlimax.

'I don't understand,' said Arthur Mounteney, 'why you're here at all.' His long and cavernous face was set. He couldn't produce a soft word among his friends, let alone now.

'I was invited, Mr Chairman. As I suppose my colleagues were, also.'

This I took to be true. Invitations had gone to the scientists on the defence committees as well as to the scientific elder statesmen. Presumably Brodzinski's name had remained upon the list.

'That doesn't mean there was any sense in your coming.'

'I'm sorry, Mr Chairman. Am I to understand that only those of a certain kind of opinion are allowed here?'

Walter Luke broke in, rough-voiced: 'That's not the point, Brodzinski, and you know it. You've made yourself a blasted nuisance where we can't get at you. And every bleeding scientist in this game is having the carpet pulled from under him because of you.'

'I do not consider your attitude is correct, Sir Walter.'

'Come off it, man, who do you take us for?'

This was unlike the stately protocol of a meeting chaired by Hector Rose.

Francis Getliffe coughed, and with his curious relic of diffidence said to Mounteney: 'I think perhaps I ought to have a word.'

Mounteney nodded.

'Dr Brodzinski,' said Francis, looking down the table, 'if you hadn't come here today I was going to ask you to call on me.'

Francis was speaking quietly, without Mounteney's bleakness or Walter Luke's roughneck scorn. He had to make an effort, while they could quarrel by the light of nature. Nevertheless, it was Francis whom we all listened to, Brodzinski most of all.

Brodzinski, although nobody had thought, or perhaps wished, to invite him (since the normal courtesies had failed) to sit down, had found himself a chair. He sat in it, squarely, heavy as a slab of rock and as impervious.

'It's time you heard something about your behaviour. It's got to be made clear to you. I was going to do that. I had better do it now. You must realise there are two things your scientific colleagues hold against you. The first is the way you have behaved to some of us. That is not important in the long run: but it is enough to make us prefer not to have any personal dealings with you. You have made charges about us in public and, as I believe, more charges in private, that we could only meet by legal action. You have taken advantage of the fact that we are not willing to take legal action against a fellow scientist. You have said that we are dishonest. You have said that we have perverted the truth. You have said that we are disloyal to our country.'

'I have been misrepresented, of course,' said Brodzinski.

'Not in the least.'

'I have always given you credit for good intentions, Sir Francis,' said Brodzinski. 'I do not expect such treatment from you.'

His expression was pure, persecuted and brave. It was the courage of one who, even now, believed in his locked-in self that they would see how right he was. He felt no conflict, no regret nor remorse, just the certainty that he was right. At the same time, he wanted pity because he was being persecuted. He was crying out for pity. The more they saw he was right, the more they would persecute him.

Suddenly a thought came to me. I hadn't understood why, the previous summer, he had given up attempting to see Roger: as though he had switched from faith to enmity. It must have been the day the offer of his decoration arrived. He had accepted the decoration – but he could have felt, I was sure he could have felt, that it was another oblique piece of persecution, a token that he was not so high as the Getliffes of the world, a sign of dismissal.

'I had to make some criticisms,' he said. 'Because you were dangerous. I gave you the credit for not realising how dangerous you were, but, of course, I had to make some criticisms. You can see that, Dr Rubin.'

He turned with an open, hopeful face to David Rubin, who was scribbling on a sheet of paper. Rubin raised his head slowly and gazed at Brodzinski with opaque eyes.

'What you did', he said, 'was not admissible.'

'I did not expect any more from you, Dr Rubin.' This answer was so harsh and passionate that it left us mystified. Rubin believed that Brodzinski had remembered that he was a Gentile talking to a Jew.

'You said we were dangerous,' Francis went on. 'I've finished now with your slanders on us. They only count because they're involved in the other damage you've done. That is the second thing you must hear about.

It is the opinion of most of us that you've done great damage to decent people everywhere. If we are going to use the word dangerous, you are at present one of the most dangerous men in the world. And you've done the damage by distorting science. It is possible to have different views on the nuclear situation. It is not possible, without lying or irresponsibility or something worse, to say the things you have said. You've encouraged people to believe that the United States and England can destroy Russia without too much loss. Most of us would regard that suggestion as wicked, even if it were true. But we all know that it is not true, and, for as long as we can foresee, it never will be true.'

'That is why you are dangerous,' said Brodzinski. 'That is why I have to expose myself. You think you are people of good will. You are doing great harm, in everything you do. You are even doing great harm, in little meetings like this. That is why I have come where I am not welcome. You think you can come to terms with the Russians. You never will. The only realistic thing for all of us is to make the weapons as fast as we know how.'

'You are prepared to think of war?' said Arthur Mounteney.

'Of course I am prepared to think of war. So is any realistic man,' Brodzinski replied. 'If there has to be a war, then we must win it. We can keep enough people alive. We shall soon pick up. Human beings are very strong.'

'And that is what you hope for?' said Francis, in a dead, cold tone.

'That is what will happen.'

'You can tolerate the thought of three hundred million deaths?'

'I can tolerate anything which will happen.'

Brodzinski went on, his eyes lit up, once more pure: 'You will not see, there are worse things which might happen.'

'I have to assume that you are responsible for your actions,' said Francis. 'If that is so, I had better tell you straightaway I cannot sit in the same room with you.'

Faces, closed to expression, looked down the table at Brodzinski. There was a silence. He sat squarely in his chair and said:

'I believe I am here by invitation, Mr Chairman.'

'It would save trouble if you left,' said Arthur Mounteney.

With exaggerated reasonableness, Brodzinski said:

'But I can produce my invitation, Mr Chairman.'

'In that case, I shall adjourn the meeting. And call another to which you are not invited.'

Later, that seemed to Rubin a masterpiece of Anglo-Saxon propriety. Brodzinski stood up, massive, stiff.

'Mr Chairman,' he said, 'I am sorry that my colleagues have seen fit to treat me in this fashion. But I expected it.'

His dignity was absolute. With the same dignity, he went soft-footed, strong-muscled, out of the room.

CHAPTER XXXV

A CHOICE

A FEW hours later, in David Rubin's bedroom, he and I were having a snack before we went on to Roger's house. The room was modest, in a cheap, genteel Kensington hotel: the snack was modest too. Rubin had the entrée to heads of state, but, despite the *Tailor and Cutter* elegance of his clothes, he lived more simply than an embassy clerk. He was a poor man, he had never earned money, apart from his academic salary and his prizes.

He sat without complaint in the cold bedroom, nibbling a stale sandwich, sipping at a weak and un-iced whisky. He talked about his son at Harvard, and his mother who would scarcely have known what Harvard was, who had not spoken English in the home, and who had been ambitious for David – just as rapaciously as my mother for me. He spoke a little sadly. Everything had come off for him, spectacular achievement, happy marriage, the love of children. He was one of the men most venerated in the world. Yet there were times when he seemed to look back to his childhood, shrug his shoulders and think that he had expected more.

We had each been talking without reserve, like passengers at sea. He sat there, in elegant suit, silk shirt, hand-made shoes, shook his head, and looked at me with sad, kind eyes. It occurred to me that he had not given me a clue, not so much as a hint, why he was so insistent on talking to Roger that night.

When we arrived at Lord North Street, it was about half past nine and Roger and Caro were still sitting in the dining-room. It was the place where Roger, nearly three years before, had interrogated Rubin. As on that evening, Rubin was ceremonious – bowing over Caro's hand: 'Lady Caroline' – greeting Roger. As on that evening, Roger pushed the decanter round.

At Caro's right hand, Rubin was willing to drink his glass of port, but not to open a conversation. Caro looked down the table at Roger, who was sitting silent and impatient with strain. She had her own kind of stoicism. She was prepared to chat with Rubin, in a loud brassy fashion, about his flight next day, about whether he hated flying as much as she did. She was terrified every time, she said, with the exaggerated protestations of cowardice that her brother Sammikins went in for.

All four of us were waiting for the point to come. At last Roger could wait no longer.

'Well?' he said roughly, straight at Rubin.

'Minister?' said David Rubin, as though surprised.

'I thought you had something to tell me.'

'Do you have time?' said Rubin mysteriously.

Roger nodded. To everyone's astonishment, Rubin began a long, dense and complex account of the theory of games as applied to nuclear strategy. Talk of over-simplification – this was over-complication gone mad. It was not long before Roger stopped him.

'Whatever you've come for,' he said, 'it isn't this.'

Rubin looked at him with an expression harsh, affectionately distressed. Suddenly his whole manner changed from the incomprehensibly devious to a brutal-sounding snap.

'I came to tell you to get out while there's time. If not, you'll cut your own throat.'

'Get out of what?'

'Out of your present planning, or design, or whatever you like to call it. You don't stand a chance.'

'You think so, do you?' said Roger.

'Why else should I come?'

Then Rubin's tone became once more quiet and reasonable:

'Wait a minute. I couldn't make up my mind whether to let it go. It's because we respect you—'

'We want to hear,' said Caro. This wasn't social, it wasn't to make him comfortable. It was said with absolute attention.

Roger and Rubin sat blank-faced. In the room, each sound was clear. To an extent they liked each other: but that didn't matter. Between them there was something quite different from liking or disliking, or even trust. It was the sense of actuality, the sense of events.

'First of all,' said Rubin, 'let me make my own position clear. Everything you've planned to do is sensible. This is right. Anyone who knows the facts of life knows that this is right. For the foreseeable future, there can only be two nuclear powers. One is my country, and the other is the Soviet Union. Your country cannot play in that league. As far as the economic and military side go, the sooner you get out the better. This is correct.'

'You told us so,' said Roger, 'in this very room, years ago.'

'What is more,' said Rubin, 'we will want you out. The way our thinking is shaping up, we will decide that these weapons ought to be concentrated in as few hands as possible. Meaning, us and the Soviets. This is right also. Before long, I'm ready to predict that you'll be under some pressure from us—'

'You're saying it in different terms, and for slightly different reasons.' Roger spoke without either intransigence or suggestibility. 'But you're saying what I've been saying, and what I've been trying to do.'

'And what you can't do.' Rubin's voice hardened as he added: 'And what you must get out of, here and now.'

There was a pause. Then, as though he were being simple, Roger asked: 'Why?'

Rubin spread out his hands.

'I'm a scientist. You're a politician. And you ask me that?'

'I should still like to hear the answer.'

'Do I have to tell you that a course of action can be right – and not worth a second's thought? It's not of importance that it's right. What is of importance, is how it's done, who it's done by, and most of all, when it's done.'

'As you say,' said Roger, 'one's not unfamiliar with those principles. Now I wish you'd tell me what you know.'

Rubin stared down at the table.

'I mustn't say that I know,' he said at last. 'But I suspect. A foreigner sometimes picks up indications that you wouldn't give such weight to. I believe you're swimming against the tide. Your colleagues will not admit it. But if you swim too far, they wouldn't be able to stay loyal to you, would they?'

Rubin went on: 'They're not fools, if you don't mind me saying so. They've been watching you having to struggle for every inch you've made. Everything's turned out ten per cent, twenty per cent, sometimes fifty per cent, more difficult than you figured on. You know that better than any of us. Lewis knows.' For an instant under the hooded lids, I caught a glance, glinting with *Weltschmerz* and fellow-feeling. 'Everything's turned out too difficult. It's my view of almost any human concern, that if it turns out impossibly difficult, if you've tried it every way, and it still won't go, then the time has come to call it a day. This is surely true of intellectual problems. The more I've seen of your type of problem the more I believe it's true of them. Your colleagues are good at keeping a stiff upper lip. But they're used to dealing with the real world. I suspect that they'll be compelled to think the same.'

'Do you *know*?' Roger spoke quietly, and with all his force.

Rubin raised his head, then let his eyes fall again. 'I've made my own position clear to everyone I know in Washington. They'll come round to thinking that you and I were right. But they haven't arrived there yet. They don't know what to think about your weapons. But I have to tell you something. They are worried about your motives for wanting to give them up.'

'Do you think we ought to care about that?' cried Caro, with a flash of arrogance.

'I think you'll be unwise not to, Lady Caroline,' said Rubin. 'I don't claim they've analysed the situation. But as of this moment, they're not all that interested in what you do – as long as you don't seem to be sliding out of the Cold War. This is the one thing that they're scared of. This is the climate. This is the climate in which some of them are anxious about you now.'

'How much have they listened to Brodzinski?' I said angrily.

'He hasn't helped,' said Rubin. 'He's done you some harm. But it's deeper than that.'

'Yes,' said Roger, 'it's deeper than that.'

'I'm glad you know.' Rubin turned to Caro. 'I told you, Lady Caroline, you'll be unwise not to care about this. Some of our people are feeling tense about it. At various levels. Including high levels. Some of that tension is liable to be washed across to this side. Maybe some of it has been washed across already.'

'That wouldn't be so astounding,' said Roger.

'Of course, it's frustrating to disengage oneself,' said Rubin. 'But the facts are very strong. So far as I've observed anything on this side, you've only to play it cool and put it aside for five, ten years. Then you'll be right at the top here, unless my information is all wrong. And you'll be swimming with the tide, not against it. As for Washington, they'll be begging you to do exactly what you can't do now.' Rubin gave a sharp, ironic smile. 'And you're the one person in this country who will be able to do it. You're a valuable man. Not only to Britain, but to all of us. This is why I'm giving you this trouble. We can't afford to waste you. And I am as certain as I am of anything that if you didn't take one step backwards now, you would be wasted.'

For an instant, none of us spoke. Roger looked down the table at his wife and said: 'You hear what he says?'

'You've heard too, haven't you?' said Caro.

All the social clangour had left her voice. It held nothing but devotion. She was speaking as they did when they were alone. They had said very little, but enough. Roger knew what she thought, and what answer she wanted him to give. Their marriage might on his side be breaking, but it still had its language. The message was simple. She was, though Rubin did not know it, his supporter.

Right through Roger's struggle, she had been utterly loyal. One expected nothing else: and yet, one knew what she was concealing. In her heart she couldn't give up her chauvinistic pride. Just as she had flared out against David Rubin, when he reminded them that the English power had sunk, so she couldn't accept that the great days were over. Her instincts were as simple as my mother's would have been.

But that wasn't the main force which drove her to Rubin's side, made her cheeks glow and eyes shine as she answered Roger. For Rubin had just offered Roger a prospect of the future: and that was her prospect too. It would have seemed to her absurd, finicky, hypocritical and above all genteel, not to want the top place for Roger. If he didn't want that, she would have said, then he ought not to be in politics at all. If she didn't want that for him, she ought not to be his wife.

'I agree with almost everything you've said.' Roger spoke directly to Rubin. 'You've made it very clear. I'm extremely grateful to you.' His tone was subdued, reasonable, a little submissive. At that moment he sounded like one willing to be converted, or perhaps already converted, arguing for the sake of self-respect. 'You know,' he said, with an abstracted smile, 'I've thought out some of these things for myself. You'll give me credit for that?'

Rubin smiled.

'Of course,' Roger went on, 'if you want to get anywhere in politics, you've got to be good at pushing on open doors. If you can't resist pushing on closed ones, then you ought to have chosen another job. That's what you're telling me, isn't it? Of course you're right. I shouldn't be surprised if you hadn't wasted some energy on closed doors in your time. Much more than I ever have. But then, of course, you're not a politician.'

It might have been a gibe, I couldn't tell. If so, it was a gentle one. Roger was speaking without strain or edge. He said: 'My one trouble is, I can't help thinking the present situation is slightly different. I think, if we don't bring this one off now, we never shall. Or we shan't until it's too late. Isn't that the only difference between us? Perhaps you can tell me that it isn't so.'

'The honest answer is,' said Rubin slowly, 'that I don't know.'

'You believe everything will drift along, with no one able to stop anywhere?'

'I don't know.'

'Most of us understand the situation. Can none of us affect it?'

'Does any one person matter very much? Can any one person do very much?'

'You're a wise man,' said Roger.

There was a long pause. Roger spoke with complete relaxation, so that it was surprising to hear how strong his voice sounded. He said:

'You're saying, we're all caught. All the world. The position has crystallised on both sides. There's nothing for any of us to do. That's what you're saying, isn't it? All we can do is stick to our position, and be humble enough to accept that there's practically nothing we can do.'

'In detail there may be a little,' said Rubin.

'That's not much, is it?' Roger gave a friendly smile. 'You're a very wise man.' He paused again. 'And yet, you know, it's pretty hard to take. In that case, one might as well not be here at all. Anyone can just wait until it's easy. I don't think I should have lived this life if that were all.'

For a moment his tone had been passionate. Then it became curiously formal and courteous as he added:

'I'm most grateful for your advice. I very much wish I could accept it. It would make things easier for me.'

He looked up the table and said to Caro, as though they were alone:

'I wish I could do what you want.'

It seemed to me that had Caro known she was fighting for her marriage, she would not so openly have implied her opposition to Roger that night. He was guilt-ridden enough to welcome the smallest loophole of escape, just to feel to himself that he could not have gone on, anyway. Yet was that really so? He had known her mind, he had always known it. To her, loyalty to Roger would have seemed less if she had gone in for pretences. She had said nothing new that night. But I believed that her repetition, before Rubin, of what had already been said in private, might have given Roger some vestigial sense of relief, of which he was nevertheless ashamed.

He said, 'I wish I could.'

I wondered when Rubin had realised that Roger was going through with it? At what point, at what word? In intellect, Rubin was by far the subtler; in emotion, he was playing with a master.

There was another oddity. In private, Rubin was as high-principled, as morally fastidious, as Francis Getliffe. And yet (it was a disconcerting truth) there were times, and most important times, when the high-principled were not to be trusted – and perhaps Roger was. For to Roger there were occasions, not common, but not so rare as we all suspected, when morality grew out of action. In private, Rubin lived a better life than most men; and yet he would have been incapable of contemplating walking into obloquy, risking his reputation, gambling his future, as in clear sight Roger was doing now.

I wondered when I myself had realised that Roger was going through with it. In a sense, I had believed it soon after we became intimate, and I had backed my judgment. Yet simultaneously, I had not trusted my judgment very far. In the midst of his obfuscation, I had been no surer than anyone else that he would not desert us. And so, in that sense, I had not realised, or at least had not been certain, that he was going through with it until – until that night.

When did Roger realise it? He would not have known, or been interested to know. Morality sprang out of action, so did choices, certainly a choice as complex as this. Even now, he might not know in what terms he would have to make it nor from what motives it would come.

How much part, it occurred to me again, had his relation with Ellen played?

'I can't accept your advice, David,' said Roger, 'but I do accept your estimate of my chances. You don't think I'm going to survive, do you? Nor do I. I'd like you to understand that I agree.'

He added, with a hard and radiant smile:

'But it isn't absolutely cut and dried even now. They haven't quite finished with me yet.'

Until that moment he had been speaking with total realism. Suddenly his mood had switched. He was suffused with hope, the hope of crises, that hope which just before a struggle warms one with the assurance that it is already won. With the anxious pouches darker under his eyes, Rubin gazed at him in astonishment, and something like dismay.

He felt, we could all feel, that Roger was happy. He was not only happy and hopeful, he was also serene.

PART FIVE

THE VOTE

CHAPTER XXXVI

SOMETHING OUT OF CHARACTER

THE light on Big Ben was shining like a golden bead in the January evening; the House had reassembled. It was a season of parties. Three times that week my wife and I went out before dinner, to Diana's house on South Street, to a private member's flat, to a Government reception. The faces revolved about one like a stage army. Confident faces, responding to other confident faces, as though this parade was preserved for ever, like a moment in time. Ministers and their wives linked themselves with other Ministers and their wives, drawn by the magnetism of office: groups of four, groups of six, sturdy, confident, confidential backs presented themselves not impolitely, but because it was a treat to be together to the room. Roger and Caro were there, looking as impregnable as the rest.

There was an hallucination about high places which acted like alcohol, not only on Roger under threat, but on whole circles. They couldn't believe they had lost the power till it had gone. Even when it had gone, they didn't always believe it.

That week and the next, mornings in the office were like wartime. Roger was sitting in his room, never looking bored, sending out for papers, asking for memoranda, intimate with no one, so far as I knew, certainly not with me. Ripples of admiration and faith were flowing down the corridors. They reached middle-grade civil servants who, as a rule, wanted only to get home and listen to long-playing records. As for the scientists, they were triumphing already. Walter Luke, who had believed in Roger from the beginning, stopped me in a gloomy, lavatory-like passage in the Treasury where his uninhibited voice reverberated round: 'By God, the old bleeder's going to get away with it! It just shows, if you go on talking sense for long enough, you wear 'em down in time.'

When I mentioned Walter's opinion to Hector Rose, he said, with a frigid but not unfriendly smile: '*Sancta simplicitas.*'

Even Rose was not immune from the excitement. Yet he found it necessary to tell me that he had been in touch with Monteith. The piece of false information, which I had protested about, had been checked. Rose had satisfied himself that it was an honest mistake. He told me this, as though the first imperative for both of us was that the official procedures should be proved correct. Then he felt free to pass on to Roger's chances.

During those days I talked once or twice to Douglas, but only to try to comfort him about his wife. The prognosis had been confirmed: she would become paralysed, she would die within five years. At his desk he sat stoically writing upon official paper. When I went in, he talked of nothing but her.

February had come, it was warm for the time of year, Whitehall was basking in the smoky sunlight.

By the end of the month, Roger was due to make his speech on the White Paper. We were all lulling ourselves with work. All of a sudden the lull broke. It broke in a fashion that no one had expected. It was a surprise to the optimistic: but it was even more of a surprise to the experienced. It didn't look much, in the office. Just a note on a piece of paper. Harmless looking, the words.

The Opposition had put down a motion to reduce the Navy vote by ten pounds.

It would have sounded archaic, or plain silly, to those who didn't know Parliament. Even to some who did, it sounded merely technical. It was technical, but most of us knew it meant much more. Who was behind it? Was it a piece of political chess? We did not believe it. Roger did not pretend to believe it.

Our maximum hope had been that, when the House 'took notice' of the White Paper, the Opposition would not make much of the debate, or force a division. This hadn't seemed unrealistic. Some of them believed that Roger was as good – as near their line – as anyone they could expect. If he lost, they would get something worse. They had tried to damp down their own 'wild men'. But now the switch was sudden and absolute. They were going for him, attacking him before his White Paper speech. They were ready to give up two of their supply days for the job. They must have known something about Roger's side. They must have known more than that.

Roger had scarcely seen me, since the night at his house with Rubin. Now he sent for me.

He gave a smile as I entered his room, but it wasn't a comradely one. He had kept his command intact, and his self-control: but, so it seemed, at the price of denying that we knew each other well. We were talking like business partners, with years of risk behind us, with a special risk present now: no closer than that: his face was hard, impatient, over-clear.

What did I know about it? No more than he did, probably less, I said.

'I doubt if you can know less,' he said. He broke out: 'What does it mean?'

'How in God's name should I know?'

'You must have an idea.'

I stared at him without speaking. Yes, I had an idea. I suspected we were fearing the same thing.

'We're grown men,' he said. 'Tell me.'

I did so. I said it looked to me like a classical case of fraternisation behind the lines. That is, some of his enemies, on his own back benches, had been making a bargain with their Opposition counterparts. The Opposition back-benchers had pressed their leaders to bring the vote. They would get support – how much support? – from the Government side. It was more decent that way. If Roger made a compromising speech, his colleagues and party would stay with him. But if he were too unortho-dox – well, if a Minister were too unorthodox to be convenient, there were other methods of dislodging him: this was one which gave least pain to his own party.

'Yes,' he said, 'I think you're quite likely right. That may be it.'

He had spoken neutrally. He went on, in an impatient, active tone: 'Well, there's nothing for it. We've got to know.'

He meant, we had to know, not only whether we were right, but if so, who the enemy were. One or two dissidents in his own party he could write off: but thirty or forty – and the more so if they were respected members – would mean the end.

Unless he behaved as Collingwood and his colleagues would have done, and denied that he meant to do anything at all. For an instant, the tempta-tion flickered again. Then he shut it away. He was set.

He was estimating the odds, and also our sources of information. He would be talking to the whips himself that day and to friends in the party. The trouble was, he said, still talking cold sense, this didn't sound like a respectable revolt. He hadn't received a letter of regret, and no one had spoken to him face to face. We should have to go in for subterranean talking ourselves. Some of my Opposition friends might know something. So might the press.

'You'd better find out,' said Roger, as briskly as though he were himself only remotely concerned, but was advising me for my own good.

From two sources I learned much the same story. An Opposition front-bencher whom I had known at Cambridge told it to me: a journalist took me along to El Vino's to meet a couple of lobby correspondents. Next day, I had some news – not hard news, but more solid than a rumour – for Roger.

Yes, the correspondents had confirmed, our guess had something in it. There had been chaffering (one journalist claimed to know the place of the meeting) between a group of Opposition members and a few Conservatives. The Opposition members were mostly on the extreme right wing of the Labour Party, though there were one or two pacifists and disarmers. I kept asking who the Conservatives were, and how many. There, just at the point of fact – the rumour got wrapped in wool. Very few, one of my informants thought – maybe only two or three. No one who counted. One was, they were sure, the young man who had asked the parliamentary question about Brodzinski's speech. 'Oddballs', my acquaintance kept repeating in the noisy pub, as the drinks went round, as though he found the phrase satisfactory.

It wasn't bad news, so far as it existed. Considering our expectations, we might have been consoled. But Roger did not take it so. We were grown men, he had said. But it was one thing to face the thought of a betrayal, even a little one: another to hear that the thought was true. He was angry with me for bringing the news. He was bitter with himself. 'I've never spent enough time drinking with fools,' he cried. 'I've never made them feel they're important. It's the one thing they can't forgive.'

That evening, he did something out of character. Accompanied by Tom Wyndham, he spent hours in the smoking-room at the House, trying to be matey. I heard the story from Wyndham next day, who said in a puzzled fashion: 'It's the first time I've known the old boy lose his grip.' The great figure, clumsy as a bear, standing in the middle of the room, catching acquaintances' eyes, downing tankards of beer, performing the only one of the personal arts at which he was downright bad. In a male crowd, he was at a loss. There he stood inept, grateful for the company of a colleague who was no use to him, until Tom Wyndham led him away.

He had lost his head. Within twenty-four hours he had regained it. He was outfacing me, daring me to suggest that he had been upset. This time, smoothly in charge, he was doing what ought to be done. One of his supporters had summoned a meeting of the private members' defence committee. No one at that meeting would have guessed that he had, even for a single evening, not been able to trust his nerve. No one would have guessed that he could stand inept, lost, among a crowd of acquaintances.

Reports came flicking through the lobbies that Roger was 'holding them', that he was 'in form', 'back again'. I saw one of my journalist informants talking, as though casually, with a smart, beaming-faced member fresh from the meeting.

Once, to most of us, it had merely been a matter of gossipy interest, to identify the leaks, the sources of news. Now we weren't so detached. This, as it happened, was good news.

I took the journalist back to El Vino's. He was so eupeptic, so willing to cheer me up, that I was ready to stand him many drinks. Yes, Roger had carried them with him. 'That chap won't be finished till he's dead,' said my acquaintance, with professional admiration. After another drink, he was speculating about Roger's enemies. Four or five, he said: anyway, you could count them on one hand. Men of straw. The phrase 'oddballs' had a tendency to recur, giving him a sense of definition, illumination, perfection, denied to me.

CHAPTER XXXVII

THE USE OF MONEY

On the Sunday afternoon, my taxi drove through the empty, comfortable Cambridge streets, across the bridge by Queen's, along the Backs towards my brother's house. There he and Francis Getliffe were waiting for me. I hadn't come just to make conversation, but for a while we sat round the fire in the drawing-room: the bronze doors were not closed, and through the far window the great elm stood up against the sky.

'I must say,' I said, 'it all looks remarkably placid.'

Martin's controlled features broke into a grin.

'I must say,' he jeered at me.

'What's the matter?'

'Do you realise that's exactly what used to infuriate you when big bosses came down from London and met you in the college, and told you what a peaceful place it was?'

His eyes were bright with fraternal malice. He told me one or two of the latest stories about the new Master's reign. Some of the college officers were finding it appropriate to write him letters rather than expose themselves to conversation. Martin gave a bleak smile. 'You live in a sheltered world, you know,' he said.

I wished that he had been with us in the Whitehall struggles. He was a harder man than Francis, tougher and more apt for politics than most of us. It took, even for me, an effort to remember that he was one of the few scientists who had got out of atomic energy and made a sacrifice for conscience' sake. There he was, having chosen a dimmish career as a college functionary: it seemed likely that that was where he would stay. And yet, in his middle forties, he gave out an air not only of detachment but content.

His wife, Irene, brought in the tea-tray. By now time had played on her one of its pyknic practical jokes. She had become mountainous, the flesh had blown up as though she were a Michelin advertisement. She must have weighed fifty or sixty pounds more than when I first met her, before the war. Her yelp of a laugh was still youthful and flirtatious. Her spirits had stayed high, he had long ago won the battle of wills in their marriage, she had come totally to love him, and also was content.

'Plotting?' she said to me. She behaved to me, she had done for years, much as she did to Martin, as though knowing one brother she knew the other: as though neither of us was as sedate as he seemed.

'Not yet,' I said.

As we drank our tea I asked Francis, just to delay my mission, whether he had heard from Penelope.

'As a matter of fact,' he replied, 'I had a letter a couple of days ago.'

'What's she doing?'

He looked puzzled: 'That's what I should like to know.'

'What does she *say*?' Irene burst in.

'I'm not quite sure,' said Francis.

He looked round at the three of us, hesitated, and then went on: 'Look here, what do you make of this?' He pulled an envelope out of his pocket, put on his long-sighted glasses, and began to read. He read, I couldn't help thinking, as though the letter were written in a language like Etruscan, in which most of the words were still unknown.

' "Dearest Daddy,

' "Please do not *flap*. I am *perfectly* alright, and *perfectly* happy, working like a beaver, and all is fine with Art and me, and we haven't any special plans, but he may come back with me in the summer – he isn't sure. There's no need for you to worry about us, we're just having a lot of fun, and nobody's bothering about marriage or anything like that, so do stop *questioning*. I think that you and Mummy must be *sex-maniacs*.

' "I have met a nice boy called Brewster (*first* name), he dances as badly as I do so that suits us both. His father owns *three* night clubs in Reno but I don't tell Art that! ! ! Anyway it is not at all serious and is only a bit of fun. I may go to Art's people for the weekend if I can raise the dollars. I don't always want him to pay for me.

' "No more now. Brew is fuming (much I care) because he's double-parked and says he'll get a ticket if I don't hurry. Must go.

' "Lots and lots of love,

' "Penny." '

'Well,' said Francis, taking off his glasses. He broke out irritably, as though it were Penny's major crime: 'I wish she could spell "all right".'

The rest of us did not find it prudent to meet one another's eyes.

'What do you do?' said Francis. 'What sanctions has one got?'

'You could cut off supplies,' said Martin, who was a practical man.

'Yes,' said Francis indecisively. After a long pause he went on: 'I don't think I should like to do that.'

'You're worrying too much,' cried Irene, with a high, delighted laugh.

'Am I?'

'Of course you are.'

'Why?' He was turning to her for reassurance.

'When I was her age, I could have written a letter just like that.'

'Could you?' Francis gazed at her. She was good-natured, she wanted him to be happy. But he did not find the reassurance quite so overwhelming as she had expected; her youth wasn't perhaps the first model he would have chosen for his daughter.

When she left us, I got down at last to business. It was simple.

For Quaife to survive was going to be a close-run thing. Any bit of help was worth the effort. Could they whip up some scientific support for him – not from the usual quarters, not from the Pugwash group who had dismissed Brodzinski, but from uncommitted men? A speech or two in the House of Lords: a letter to *The Times* with some 'respectable' signatures? Any demonstration might swing a vote or two.

I was still making my case at the moment that Irene returned, apologising, smelling a secret. There was someone on the telephone for me, a long-distance call. With a curse I went off into the lobby under the stairs: a voice came down the line that I didn't recognise, giving a name that I didn't know. We had met at Finch's, the voice was saying. That meant nothing. The pub on the Fulham Road, came the explanation, quick, impatient. They had traced me to my home, and so to Cambridge. They thought I should know what to do. Old Ronald Porson had been arrested the night before. What for? Importuning in a lavatory.

I felt – first – sheer blind irritation at being distracted. Then a touch of pity, the black pity of the past. Then, most of all, the tiredness of the ties one couldn't escape, the accretion of the duties, the years, the acquaintanceships. I muttered something, but the brisk active male voice pressed on. They didn't know the ropes as well as I did.

I collected myself. I gave the name of a solicitor. If they hadn't got one already, they must make Porson listen to this man and do what he was told. Yes: this young friend of Porson's sounded efficient, they were all trying to look after him. The 'old man' hadn't a penny, the voice said. Was I prepared to contribute? Of course, I said, anxious to be away: they must tell the solicitor that I would meet the bill. I felt tired, relieved, as I put the receiver down, trying to put the message out of mind.

As I went back to the hearth, Martin looked at me.

'Anything wrong?' he said.

'Someone in trouble,' I replied. No, not anyone close. No one he knew.

I said impatiently, 'Let's get on.' I had made a proposal, we had been interrupted, there was not much time.

As we sat round the fire Martin did most of the talking. I knew, without our having spoken together, what he thought. He did not believe that we stood more than an outside chance. He did not believe that any government could bring off more than a poor compromise. He believed that any government would have to repudiate a man who tried to do more. But he did not tell me so. He had been close enough to decisions to know the times when it was better not to be told. Instead, he was ready to help: and yet, as he said, he wasn't eminent enough as a scientist to carry weight. Somehow, he remarked, the high scientific community had lost either its nerve or its will. There were plenty of people like himself, he went on, ready to be active. But the major scientists had retired into their profession – 'There's no one of your standing,' he said to Francis, 'who's ready to take the risks you took twenty years ago.' It wasn't that a new generation of scientists hadn't as much conscience or more: or as much good will: or even as much courage. Somehow the climate had changed, they were not impelled. Had the world got too big for them? Had events (Martin repeated a phrase which I had once heard, surprisingly, from Hector Rose) become too big for men?

Neither Martin nor I was willing to admit it. After sitting silent, Francis said, at any rate one had to go on acting as though it were not true.

Yes, he said, shrugging himself free, suddenly speaking as though he were a younger man, in command again, he thought my idea was worth trying. Yes, he agreed, it was no use Martin approaching the most senior scientists. He, Francis, would have to take on another job: he would do it himself. We were not to hope for much. He had used his influence too many times, and there was not much of it left.

As we went on talking, I was only half-thinking of the scientists. I could not get rid, completely or for long, of the thought of Porson. There was something I had heard in the voice over the telephone: something that the voice, confident as it sounded, hadn't uttered. They would have liked to ask me to come back, so I could help him myself.

Years before, that was what I should have done. By now this kind of compulsion had grown dim. I was the worse for it. For most of us, the quixotic impulses might stay alive, but in time the actions didn't follow. I had used money to buy off my fellow-feeling, to save trouble, to save myself the expense of spirit that I was no longer impelled to spend.

CHAPTER XXXVIII

'A SMALL ROOM AND A GAS-RING'

LORD LUFKIN summoned Margaret and me to a dinner-party at twenty-four hours' notice, just as he summoned many guests. He had done the same for thirty years, long before his great success had come: he had done it during the years when he was hated: and still his guests had obeyed.

That February night – it was in the week after my visit to Cambridge – we trooped dutifully into Lufkin's drawing-room in St James's Court. No one could have called it a cheerful room. Lufkin had had it panelled in dark pine, and there was not a picture on the walls except a portrait of himself. No one went to Lufkin's expecting a cheerful party. His gifts as a host were negative. Yet in that room there were standing a couple of Ministers, a Treasury boss, the President of the Royal Society, a fellow tycoon.

Lufkin stood in the middle, not making any small talk, nor any other size of talk; not shy so much as not feeling it worth while. He took it for granted that he was holding court. The interesting thing was, so did everyone round him. In the past, I had sometimes wondered why. The short answer was, the magnetic pull of power. Not simply, though that added, because he had become one of the top industrialists in England. Much more, because he had complete aptitude for power, had assumed it all his life, and now could back it with everything he had won.

He announced to his guests at large that he had taken over the suite adjoining this one. He ordered a door to be thrown open to show a perspective of tenebrous rooms.

'I decided we needed it,' he said.

Lufkin's tastes were austere. He spent little on himself: his income must have been enormous, but he was pernicketily honest, he didn't use any half-legitimate devices for sliding away from taxes, and he had not made an impressive fortune. On the other hand, as though in revenge, he insisted on his firm giving him all the luxuries he had no liking for. This suite was already too big for him, but he had made them double it. He made them pay for his court-like dinner parties. He made them provide not one car, but half a dozen.

Even so, Lufkin had a supreme talent for getting it both ways. 'I don't regard this flat as my own, of course,' he was saying, with his usual moral certainty.

People near him, hypnotised into agreeing, were sagely nodding their heads.

'I regard it as the company's flat, not mine. I've told my staff that time and time again. This flat is for the use of the whole company.'

If I had been alone with Lufkin, whom I had known much longer than had his other guests, I couldn't have resisted analysing that arcane remark. What would have happened, if some member of his staff had taken him at his word, and booked the flat for the weekend?

'As for myself,' he said, 'my needs are very simple. All I want is *a small room and a gas-ring.*'

The maddening thing was, it was quite true.

Though Lufkin might have preferred a round of toast, we moved into a dinner which was far from simple. The dining-room, through another inexplicable decree, was excessively bright, the only bright room in the flat. The chandeliers flashed heavily down above our heads. The table was over-flowered. The hierarchy of glasses glittered and shone.

Lufkin, himself content with a whisky and a soda for the meal, looked on with approbation as the glasses filled with sherry, hock, claret, champagne. He sat in the middle of his table, his skull-face still young, hair neat and dark in his sixties, with the air of a spectator at what he regarded as a well-conducted dinner. He did not trouble to speak much, though occasionally he talked in a manner, off-hand but surreptitious, to Margaret. He enjoyed the presence of women. Though he spent most of his time in male company, with his usual cross-grainedness he never liked it much. It was half-way through the meal when he addressed the table.

His fellow-tycoon had begun talking of Roger Quaife and the White Paper. The Ministers were listening, attentive, deadpan, and so was I. Suddenly Lufkin, who had been sitting back, as though utterly detached, his knife and fork aligned, three-quarters of his pheasant left uneaten, intervened.

In his hard clear voice he said:

'What's that you were saying?'

'I said, the City's getting bearish about some of the long-term consequences.'

'What do *they* know?' said Lufkin, with inspissated contempt.

'There's a feeling that Quaife's going to run the aircraft industry into the ground.'

'Nonsense,' said Lufkin, at his bleakest. He had caught my eye. Even Lufkin was not usually as rude as this without a purpose. I had suspected that this dinner wasn't such an accidental gathering as it seemed.

'There's nothing in that.' He spoke as one who does not propose to say any more. Then he condescended to explain himself.

'Whatever happens, Quaife or no Quaife, or whether they throw you out at the next election' – he gave a sardonic smile at the Ministers – 'and the other chaps come in, there's only room in this country for a couple of aircraft firms, at most. More likely than not, two is one too many.'

'I suppose you mean,' said the other industrialist with a show of spirit, 'that you ought to be the only firm left in?'

Lufkin was the last man in existence to be worried about being *parti-pris*: or to have qualms because he was safe with a major contract: or to question whether his own interests and the national interests must necessarily coincide.

'An efficient firm', he said, 'ought to be ready to take its chance. Mine is.'

That sounded like the cue. Again Lufkin, looking at no one in particular, caught my eye.

He said:

'I might as well tell you. I'm a hundred per cent pro Quaife. I hope you'll see' – he was speaking to the Ministers – 'that *these people*' (by which Lufkin meant anyone he disapproved of) 'don't make the job impossible for him. No one's ever done it properly, of course. With your set-up, there isn't a proper job to do. But Quaife's the only chap who hasn't been a hopeless failure. You might as well remember that.'

Having given what, for him, was lavish praise, Lufkin had finished. Dinner proceeded.

The women left us, Margaret casting at me, over her shoulder, a look of one who is doomed. I had known Lufkin, in that room, keep the men talking over the port for two hours while the women waited. 'You wouldn't suggest that I was conversationally inept, would you?' Margaret had said to me after one of these occasions. 'But several times tonight I dried. We talked about the children, and then about the servant problem, and then about the cleaning of jewellery. I found it hard to be chatty about that. You'd better buy me a tiara, so I can join in next time.' That night, however, Lufkin passed the decanter round twice and then remarked, as though it were self-evident, 'I don't believe in segregating the sexes. Anachronistic.'

As the Ministers, the tycoon, the Second Secretary, the P.R.S., were moving into the drawing-room, Lufkin called out sharply:

'Wait a minute, Lewis. I want a word with you.'

I sat down opposite to him. He pushed a bowl of flowers aside so that he could stare at me.

There were no preliminaries. He remarked:

'You heard what I said about Quaife?'

'I'm grateful,' I replied.

'It isn't a matter for gratitude. It's a matter for sense.'

It wasn't getting easier to be on terms with Lufkin.

'I'd like to tell him,' I said. 'He can do with some moral support.'

'You're intended to tell him.'

'Good.'

'I don't say something about a man in one place, and something else in another.'

Like a good many of his claims for himself, this also was true.

His eyes, sunk deep in his neat, handsome head, swivelled round to me. 'That's not the point,' he said.

'What do you mean?'

'That's not why I sent them away.'

For an instant there was a silence, a negotiator's silence. Like one tired of stating the obvious, he let out:

'Quaife's been a damned fool.'

I did not reply. I sat, not showing excessive interest, gazing at him. He gave a sharp recognitory smile.

'I ought to tell you, I know about this woman of his,' he said. 'He's been a damned fool. I don't care what you think about his morals. A man doesn't want to get mixed up with a woman when he's trying something big.'

Lufkin seldom missed an opportunity to apportion blame. But his tone had become less aloof. I still did not reply, nor change my expression.

Once more, Lufkin smiled. 'My information is,' he said, 'that the man Hood is going to blow the news wide open to Quaife's wife. And to Smith's connections. Any day now. This being, of course, the most helpful occasion.'

This time, I was astounded. I showed it. All my practice at coping with Lufkin had failed me. I knew he sat at the centre of a kind of intelligence service; business and curiosity got mixed up; his underlings fed him with gossip as well as fact. But this seemed like divination. I must have looked like one of my aunts, confronted with a demonstration of spiritualist phenomena. Lufkin gave a grin of triumph.

Later on, I thought it was not so mysterious. After all, Hood was employed by a firm closely similar to Lufkin's. Between the two, there was contact, something like espionage, and personal intimacies at every level. There was nothing improbable in Hood's having a drinking companion, or even a confidential friend, on Lufkin's staff.

'It's likely to be true,' said Lufkin.

'It may be,' I said.

'This man,' said Lufkin, 'needs all his energy for the job in hand. I don't know, and I don't want to know, how his wife will take it. But it isn't the kind of trouble any of us would want hanging over us when we're fighting for our skins.'

He was a tough ally. For his own sake, he wanted Roger to survive. But he was speaking with unusual sympathy, with something like comradely feeling. Once or twice in my own life, I had known him come out of his carapace and show something which was not affection, but might have been concern. It had happened only when one was in trouble with wife or children. No one knew much about his own marriage. His wife lived in the country and there was a rumour that she was afflicted. He could have had mistresses, but if so they had been concealed with his consummate executive skill. None of this we were likely to know for sure until after he was dead.

My instructions were clear. I was to warn Roger, and then look after him. That being understood, the conference was over, and Lufkin got up to join his guests. As he did so, I asked about Hood. Was he being used by others? Were there people behind him?

'I don't believe in chance,' said Lufkin.

As for the man himself, was he obsessed?

'I'm not interested in his psychology,' said Lufkin. 'I'm not interested in his motives. All I'm interested in, is seeing him on the bread-line.'

We did not speak again on our way to the drawing-room. There the party, in Lufkin's absence, had begun to sound a little gayer. He damped it down by establishing us in groups of three with no chance of transfer. For myself, I was preoccupied, and I noticed Margaret glancing at me, a line between her eyes, knowing that something was wrong. In my trio, I heard, as though she were a long way off, the wife of one of the Ministers explaining in minute detail why her son had not got into Pop, a subject which, at the best of times, I should have found of limited interest.

One might have thought that Lufkin's dinner-parties broke up early. But they didn't, unless Lufkin broke them up himself. That night it was half past eleven before, among the first uprising of departures, I managed to get in a word with Margaret. I told her that Lufkin had been warning me, and about what.

Looking at me, she did not need to ask much. 'Ought you to go and see him?' she said, speaking of Roger.

I half-wanted to leave it till next day. She knew that I was tired. She knew that I should be more tired if I didn't act till next morning. She said, 'You'd better go to him now, hadn't you?'

While Margaret waited with Lufkin, I telephoned Lord North Street. I heard Roger's voice, and began:

'Lufkin's been talking to me. There's something I've got to tell you.'

'Yes.'

'Can I come round?'

'You can't come here. We'll have to meet somewhere else.'

Clubs would be closed by this time: we couldn't remember a restaurant near by: at last I said, anxious to put down the telephone, that I would see him outside Victoria Station and was leaving straightaway.

When I told Lufkin that I was going to Roger, he nodded with approval, as for any course of behaviour recommended by himself. 'I can lay on transport,' he said. 'Also for your charming wife.'

Two cars, two drivers, were waiting for us in the street. As mine drew up under the Victoria clock, I did not go into the empty hall, booking-offices closed as in a ghost station, but stayed outside on the pavement, alone except for some porters going home.

A taxi slithered from the direction of Victoria Street, through the rain-glossed yard.

As Roger came heavily towards me, I said:

'There's nowhere to go here.' For an instant I was reminded of Hector Rose greeting me outside the darkened Athenæum, months before.

I said there was a low-down coffee bar not far away. We were both standing stock-still.

Roger said, quite gently, 'I don't think there is anything you can tell me. I think I know it all.'

'My God,' I said, in bitterness, 'we might have been spared this.'

I was angry, not with Hood, but with him. My temper had broken loose because of the risks we had run, of what we had tried to do, of the use he had made of me. He gave a grimace, of something like acquiescence.

'I'm sorry,' he said, 'to have got everyone into a mess.'

Those were the kind of words I had heard before in a crisis: apathetic, inadequate, flat. But they made me more angry. He looked at me.

'Never mind,' he said. 'It's not lost yet.'

As we stood there in front of the station, it was not I who was giving support and sympathy. It was the other way round.

In silence we walked across the station yard, through the dripping rain. By the time we were sitting in the coffee bar, under the livid lights, I had recovered myself.

We sipped tea so weak that it tasted like metal against the teeth. Roger had just said, 'It's been very bad,' when we were interrupted.

A man sat down at a table, and remarked 'Excuse me', in a voice that was nearly cultivated, not quite. His hands were trembling. He had a long, fine-drawn face, like the romantic stereotype of a scientist. His manner was confident. He told us a hard-luck story of considerable complexity. He was a lorry-driver, so he said. By a series of chances and conspiracies, his employers had decided to sack him. Not to put too fine a point on it, he was short of money. Could we see him through the night?

I didn't like him much, I didn't believe a word of it, above all I was maddened by his breaking in. Yet, as I shook my head, I was embarrassed, as thought it were I who was doing the begging. As for him, he was not embarrassed in the least. 'Never mind, old chap,' he said.

Roger looked at him and, without a word, took out his wallet and gave him a ten-shilling note. The intruder took it civilly, but without any demonstration. 'Always glad of a little encouragement,' he said. He made polite goodbyes.

Roger did not watch or notice. He had given him money not out of fellow-feeling, nor pity, nor even to be rid of him. It had been the kind of compulsion that affects men who lead risky lives. Roger had been trying to buy a bit of luck.

Suddenly he told me straight out that Caro would 'put a face on things' until the struggle was over. She would laugh off the rumours which would soon, if Lufkin's intelligence were correct, be sparking round all

J. C. Smith's connections. Caro was ready to deny them to Collingwood himself.

But there was some other damage. Many people, including most of the guests at Lord North Street, and Diana Skidmore's friends, would have expected Caro – and Roger also – not to make much of the whole affair. Yes, Ellen had behaved badly, a wife ought to stick to her sick husband. Roger wasn't faultless either. Still, there were worse things. After all, Caro had lived in the world all her life. Her friends and family were not models of the puritan virtues. Caro herself had had lovers before her marriage. Like the rest of her circle, she prided herself on her rationality and tolerance. They all smoothed over scandals, were compassionate about sins of the flesh by the side of which a man having a mistress, even in the circumstances of Roger and Ellen – was nothing but a display of respectability.

That day, since Caro first read the unsigned letter, none of that had counted, nor had ever seemed to exist. There was no enlightenment or reason in the air, just violence. They hadn't been quarrelling about his public life, nor the morality of taking a colleague's wife: nor about love: nor sex: but about something fiercer. He was hers. They were married. She would not let him go.

He too, felt the same violence. He felt tied and abject. He had come away, not knowing where to turn or what to do.

So far as I could tell, there had been no decision. Or rather, there seemed to have been two decisions which contradicted each other. As soon as the crisis was over, win or lose – Caro gave her ultimatum – he had to choose. She would not endure it more than a matter of weeks, months at the most. Then he had to look after his own career. It must be 'this woman' or her. At the same time, she had said more than once that she would not give him a divorce.

'I don't know,' he said. His face was blank and open. He did not look like a man a few days away from his major test.

For a while we sat, drinking more cups of the metallic tea, not saying much. Then he remarked:

'I told her' (he meant Ellen) 'earlier in the day. I promised I'd ring her up before I went to bed. She'll be waiting.'

Blundering, as though his limbs were heavy, he went off to look for a telephone behind the bar. When he came back he said flatly:

'She wants me to go and see her. She asked me to bring you too.'

For an instant, I thought this was not meant seriously.

'She asked me,' he repeated. Then I thought perhaps I understood.

She was as proud as Caro: in some ways, she was prouder. She was intending to behave on her own terms.

The rain had stopped, and we went on foot to Ebury Street. It was well past one. At her door, Ellen greeted us with the severeness which I had long ago forgotten, but which took me back to the first time I saw her there. Once we were inside the smart little sitting-room, she gave Roger a kiss, but as a greeting, no more. It wasn't the hearty conjugal kiss I had seen before, the kiss of happy lovers used to each other, pleased with each other, sure of pleasure to come.

She offered us drinks. Roger took a whisky, so did I. I pressed her to join us. As a rule, she enjoyed her drink. But she was one of those who, in distress, refuse to accept any relief.

'This is atrocious,' she said.

Roger repeated to her what he had told me. She listened with an expression impatient, strained and intent. She was hearing little new, most of it had been said already over the telephone. When he repeated that his wife would 'see him through' the crisis, she burst out in scorn:

'What else could she do?'

Roger looked hurt, as well as angry. She was sitting opposite to him across the small table. She gave a laugh which wasn't a laugh, which reminded me of my mother when an expectation came to nothing or one of her pretentions was deflated, when she had, by laughing, to deny the moment in which she stood.

'I mean, you have to win. She couldn't spoil that!'

He said nothing. For a moment he looked desperately tired, fretted, drained, as if he had lost interest in everything but the desire to be alone, to switch off the light, turn his face into the pillow and sleep.

Shortly afterwards she cried:

'I'm sorry, I shouldn't have said that.'

'I haven't the right to stop you.'

'It was disloyal.'

She meant, disloyal to him, not to Caro: and yet her emotions towards Caro were not simple. All three of them were passionate people. Under the high-spirited surface, she was as violent as Caro. If those two had met that night, I thought more than once, the confrontation might have gone any way at all.

She sat back and said: 'I've been dreading this.'

'Don't you think I know?' Roger replied.

There was a long silence. At last Ellen turned to me and said in a sharp, steady tone: 'I'm willing to give him up.'

'It's too late for that,' said Roger.

'Why is it?' She looked straight at him. 'You trust me, don't you? I've got that left, haven't I?'

'I trust you.'

'Well then, I meant what I said.'

'It's too late. There were times when I might have taken that offer. Not now.'

They were each speaking with stark honesty. On his side, with the cruelty of a love-relation which is nothing but a love-relation: where they were just naked with each other, with neither children, nor friends, nor the to-and-fro of society to console them, to keep them safe. On her side, she was speaking from loneliness, from the rapacity with which she wanted him, and, yes, from her own code of honour.

Their eyes met again, and fell away. Between them, at that instant, was not love: not desire: not even affection: but knowledge.

As though everything else was irrelevant, she said in a curt, businesslike manner: 'Well, you'd better settle how you're going to handle it next Thursday morning.'

She meant, the cabinet, at which Roger's debate would, though possibly only perfunctorily, come up. Once she had been envious of Caro for knowing the political life as she did not. Now she had learned. Whom could he trust? Could he sound his colleagues before the meeting? Could I find out anything in Whitehall? Whom could he trust? More important whom couldn't he trust?

We talked on for a couple of hours. The names went round. Collingwood, Monty Cave, the P.M., Minister after Minister, his own Parliamentary Secretary, Leverett-Smith. It was like sitting in Cambridge rooms twenty years before, 'counting heads', before a college election. It was like that. The chief difference was that this time the stakes were a little higher, and the penalties (it seemed to me that night) more severe.

CHAPTER XXXIX

POLITICAL ARITHMETIC

DURING those days before the debate, Roger, whenever he went into the House or the Treasury building or Downing Street, was under inspection: inspection often neither friendly nor unfriendly, but excited by the smell of human drama: the kind of inspection that I remembered my mother being

subjected to, in the provincial back streets, when we were going bankrupt.

As they watched him, Roger behaved well. He was a brave man,
physically and morally, people were saying. It was true. Nevertheless, on
those mornings he could not bring himself to read the political correspondents' gossip-columns. He listened to accounts of what they said, but
could not read them. Though he walked through the lobbies, bulky and
composed, cordial to men whom he suspected, he could not manage to
invite the opinions of his own nearest supporters. He sat at his desk in the
office, staring distantly at me, as though his articulateness and self-
knowledge had both gone.

I had to guess what requests he was making: yes, he would like to know
where his Parliamentary Secretary, Leverett-Smith, stood, and Tom
Wyndham too.

This was one of the jobs I fancied least. I had no detachment left. I also
did not want to hear bad news. I did not want to convey it. It was easy to
understand how leaders in danger got poor information.

In fact, I picked up nothing of much interest, certainly nothing that
added to disquiet. Tom Wyndham was, as usual, euphoric and faithful.
He had been one of Roger's best selections. He continued to carry some
influence with the smart young ex-officers on the back benches. They
might distrust Roger, but no one could distrust Tom Wyndham. He was
positive all would turn out well. He did not even seem to understand what
the fuss was about. As he stood me drinks at the bar of White's, I felt, for
a short time, reassured and very fond of him. It was only when I got out
into the February evening that it came to me, with displeasing clarity,
that, though he had a good heart, he was also remarkably obtuse. He
couldn't even see the chessboard, let alone two moves ahead.

With Leverett-Smith next morning – it was now five days before the
Opposition motion – the interview was more prickly. It took place in his
office, and to begin with, he showed mystification as to why I was there at
all. Not unreasonably, he was put out. If the Minister (as he always called
Roger) wished for a discussion, here was he, sitting four doors down the
corridor, from 9.30 in the morning until he left for the House. His point
was reasonable: that didn't make it more gratifying. He looked at me with
his lawyer's gaze, and addressed me formally, like a junior Minister
putting high civil servants in their place.

'With great respect— ' he kept saying.

We should never have got on, not in any circumstances, least of all in
these. We had hardly a thought or even an assumption in common.

I repeated that for Roger next week was the major crisis. This wasn't an occasion for protocol. We were obliged to give him the best advice we could.

'With great respect,' replied Leverett-Smith, 'I am confident that neither of us needs to be reminded of his official duty.'

Then he began something like a formal speech. It was a stiff, platitudinous and unyielding speech. He didn't like me any better as he made it. Yet he was revealing more sense than I gave him credit for. It was 'common ground' that the Minister was about to undergo a supreme test. If he (Leverett-Smith) had been asked to give his counsel, he would have suggested – *festina lente*. Indeed, he had so suggested, on occasions that I might conceivably remember. What might provoke opposition if done prematurely, would be accepted with enthusiasm when the time was ripe. Nevertheless, in the Minister's mind the die was cast, and we all had to put away our misgivings and work towards a happy issue.

We should certainly have six abstentions, Leverett-Smith went on, suddenly getting down to the political arithmetic. Six we could survive. Twenty meant Roger was in peril, unless he had reassured the centre of the party. Thirty-five, and he would, without any conceivable doubt, have to go.

'And you?' I asked quietly, and without hostility.

'I consider,' said Leverett-Smith, formally but also without hostility, 'that that question should not have been put. Except by the Minister himself. If he weren't overwrought, he would know that, if I had been going to disagree with my Minister, I should have done so in public before this and I should naturally resign. So it oughtn't to need saying that now, if the worst comes to the worst, and the Minister has to go – which I still have good hopes is not going to happen – then as a matter of principle I shall go with him.'

Spoken like a stick, I thought. But also like an upright man. The comparison with Roger, in the same position three years before, flickered like a smile on the wrong side of the face.

I was able to report to Roger that afternoon without needing to comfort him. He listened as though brooding: but when he heard of Leverett-Smith's stuffy speech, he shouted out loud. He sounded amused, but he wasn't really amused. He was in one of those states of suspicion when any piece of simple human virtue, or even decency, seems more than one can expect or bear.

He was wrapped up in his suspicions, in his plans for the counter-attacks, like a doctor confronted with an X-ray picture of his own lungs.

He did not even tell me, I did not know until I got home to Margaret, that Caro had invited me to their house the following night.

She had not telephoned, she had dropped in at our flat without notice.

'She obviously had to talk to somebody,' Margaret said, looking upset, 'and I suppose she didn't want to do it with her own friends, so she thought it had better be me.'

I did not ask her what Caro had said, but Margaret wanted to tell me about it.

Caro had begun:

'I suppose you know?' – then had launched into a kind of strident abuse, half-real, half-histrionic, punctuated by the routine obscenities she would have heard round the stables at Newmarket. It was not so much abuse of Ellen, though there was some of that too, but of life itself. As the violence began to wear itself out, she had begun to look frightened, then terrified. She had said, her eyes wild, but with no tears in them, 'I don't know how I shall bear being alone. I don't know how I am to bear it.'

Margaret said, 'She does love him. She says she can't imagine not hearing his key in the lock, not having the last drink with him at night. It's true: I don't know how she is going to bear it.'

CHAPTER XL

AN EVENING OF TRIUMPH

It was just before ten when we got out of the taxi in Lord North Street. We had been invited, not to dinner, but for an after-debate supper. The door shone open for another guest, light streaming across the lances of rain.

I felt Margaret's hand tighten in mine. When we had first entered this house, it had seemed enviable. Now it was threatened. Some of us, going up the stairs that night, knew, as well as Roger and Caro themselves, of both the threats.

She greeted us in the drawing-room, eyes flashing, jewels flashing, shoulders splendid under the lights. Her voice wasn't constricted; she hugged Margaret, perhaps a little more closely than usual, she brushed my cheek. I knew, as we kissed, that this was a performance, gallant as it was. She had never liked me much, but now, if it weren't for her obligation, she would have put me out of sight for good. She had either found out, or had decided for herself, that I had been in Roger's confidence. She might be generous and reckless, but she would not forget her wrongs. This one was not to be forgiven.

The clock had struck the hour. There were already three or four people in the drawing-room, including Diana Skidmore.

'They've not got back yet,' said Caro, in her loud, casual tone, as though this were any other parliamentary night, 'they' being the politicians.

'They've had quite a day, bless their hearts. I haven't seen Roger since he went to cabinet this morning. Have you seen any of them, Diana?'

'Not to speak of, you know,' Diana replied, with a smile as bright, and as communicative, as her emeralds.

'Isn't Monty Cave making a great speech tonight?' Caro went on.

'I suppose he would have to say something, wouldn't he?' said Diana.

Caro told Diana that Monty would be along soon, in a tone which implied that Diana knew already. Diana responded with a question:

'Is the P.M. coming?'

Caro replied boldly: 'I couldn't get him.' She added, as though she wouldn't be outfaced:

'Reggie Collingwood promised to look in. If they're not too late.'

It seemed clear – had the news reached Diana yet? – that Caro was trying to do her last service for Roger. She was not just seeing him through, she was doing more than that. She was calling up all her influence, until the debate. She was helping him to win, as thoroughly as if they had been happy.

And yet, though it was chivalrous, though she would truly have done it if she were losing him next week, did she expect, completely expect, to lose him? As I listened, she didn't seem as if she had quite let go. Did she still hope that if he won, if his career were once more assured, he would have to stay with her? On her own terms? Given a future as brilliant as it had looked the year before, how much of it would he risk or sacrifice?

It would be astonishing if at times, brilliant with certainty, she did not hope like that. For myself, I was at a loss to know whether she was right or wrong.

I wondered also what chances she believed he had of winning. She was radiant with fighting energy. She would go on beyond the last minute. But, though she wasn't subtle, she was shrewd and had seen much. She had been trying to get signals of encouragement from Diana and had received none. That must have been as patent to Caro as it was to Margaret and me. Not that Diana had finally given Roger up. She knew he was in extreme trouble, that was all. She was playing safe. Maybe she did not want to embarrass her closest political friends, like Collingwood; maybe she had heard from him the first whisper of a scandal: but, deeper than that, she was acting out of instinct.

The *beau monde* wasn't kind, Caro had once said to me on a carefree night. If it were kind, it would soon cease to be *beau*. It was tolerably good-natured, until you were really in trouble. Then you were on your own.

I wondered how many worlds were any better. If you were in trouble in the public eye, who was going to guard you? All the worlds I knew, not only the *beau*, but the civil servants, the academics, the writers, the industrialists, the scientists, huddled together to protect themselves. If you became exposed, they couldn't do much. It was the odd acquaintance, sometimes the wild, sometimes the sober who had concealed the fact that he was afraid of nothing and no one, who came out and took the risks and stood by one's side.

Car in the street below. Heavy footsteps on the stairs. Roger came in, came in alone.

I had an instant's anxiety, as though Caro's guests had let her down, as though her gesture had gone for nothing and we were left with a useless supper-party, like so many Baltic Deputies.

Then, with a disproportionate relief, so that I gave a broad and apparently unprovoked grin in Diana's direction, I saw Cave at the door, with Collingwood's hand on his shoulder.

'Give Monty a drink,' cried Roger, in his broadest, heartiest voice. 'He's made the speech of a lifetime!'

'He'll make better speeches some day,' said Collingwood, with an air of the highest congratulation, rather like Demosthenes commenting on a hitherto tongue-tied pupil.

'Give him a drink!' cried Roger. He was standing by his wife. Their faces were open, robust, smiling. They might have been a serene couple, rejoicing, because they were so successful, in a great friend's success. Looking round, I should have liked to know how many of the others saw them so, and how much they knew.

As we sat down at the dinner-table downstairs, I was on edge and guessing. So were others. Some of the decisions – one could feel the crackle in the air – were not only not revealed, they were not yet taken. If Collingwood had heard the news about his nephew's wife, he showed no sign of it. His phlegm was absolute. Diana's self-control, Caro's flaming courage – they were tightened, because people round the table knew that nothing was settled; were waiting to see in what might pass as a convivial evening, where others would – Arthur Brown's old phrase returned to me – 'come down'.

Cave held up a glass to the candlelight, viewed it with his round, sombre, acute eyes, and sat forward, the rolls of chin sinking into his chest. He kept receiving compliments, Collingwood's magisterial and not specially articulate, Roger's hearty but increasingly forced. Cave's glance darted towards them, his eyes sharply scrutinising, in the podgy, clown-like face. Diana was flattering him, with a hortatory rasp, as though irritated that he didn't know how good he was.

About his triumph in the House that evening, there was no ambiguity at all. It had no connection with Roger's policy or what was to come. Cave had, in a routine debate, wound up for the Government. To anyone outside the Commons, what he said would either be unnoticed or forgotten within days: but on the parliamentary stock exchange, the quotation in Cave had rushed up many points. On a normal evening, there would have been no more to it than that. Roger might have been expected to feel that particular blend of emotions appropriate to an occasion when a colleague, friend, rival and ally had just had a resplendent professional success.

As we listened that night, this wasn't all. There was no mystery about the triumph in the evening: but there was considerable mystery about the cabinet a few hours before. Not that Collingwood or the others would in company have talked about cabinet proceedings. Nevertheless, Caro and Diana, neither of them over-theoretical or over-delicate, were used to picking up the signs. Of course, they assumed, Roger's debate next week had been talked about that morning. Of course the cabinet had taken steps. Caro asked Collingwood a question about the vote next Tuesday, with as much fuss as she would have asked about the prospects of a horse.

'We've been thinking about that, naturally,' he said. He added gnomically: 'Not that we're not always busy. We can't spend too much time on one thing, you understand.'

He volunteered a piece of information. The proper operations had been set going. A three-line whip had gone out. Three or four dissidents were being worked on.

There was no side-talk round the table. Everyone was attending. Everyone knew the language. This meant that, in formal terms, the Government was not backing down. This was the maximum show of pressure on its party. It could do no more.

But also, I was thinking, as I listened to Collingwood's grating, confident voice, it could do no less. They had gone too far not to bring out the standard procedure now. We were no nearer to knowing what had happened that morning.

Conceivably, Collingwood and the other Ministers could not have told us, even if they had wanted to. Not because of secrecy; not because some had their own different designs: but simply because of the way cabinet business was done.

Word had come out from the cabinet room that Lenton was, when he wanted to be, an efficient chairman. More than most recent Prime Ministers, he often let Ministers introduce topics, encouraged an orderly discussion round the table, and even took a straw-vote at the end. But this didn't always happen.

Lenton was efficient and managerial. He was more self-effacing than most Prime Ministers. He was also a ruthless politician, and he knew a Prime Minister's power. This power had increased out of all proportion since Collingwood entered politics. The Prime Minister, they used to say piously, was the first among equals. It might be so, but in that case, the first was a good deal more equal than the others.

It wasn't a matter of *charisma*. It wasn't even a matter of personality. The awe existed, but it was practical awe. The Prime Minister had the jobs in his hand. He could sack anyone, and appoint anyone. Even a modest man like Lenton did just that. Any of us, on the secretariat of committees, who had seen any Prime Minister with his colleagues, noticed that they were frightened of him, whoever he might be.

If he didn't want a decision in cabinet, it took a bold man to get one. In office, men tended not to be bold. Lenton, who could be so business-like, had become a master of talking round a subject, and then leaving it in the air. It looked sloppy: little he cared: it was a useful technique for getting his own way.

Perhaps that, or something like it, had happened that day. None of us except Collingwood knew what the Prime Minister thought of Roger or his policy. My guess, for some time past, had been that he thought the policy was rational but that it couldn't be pressed too far. If Roger could placate, or squeeze by, the solid centre of the party, then it would be good for the Government. They might win the next election on it. But if Roger had stirred up too much opposition, if he went beyond his brief and campaigned only for the Getliffe portions of the White Paper, he needn't be rescued. Roger was expendable. In fact, it was possible that the Prime Minister would not be heartbroken if Roger had to be expended. For that pleasantly modest man had some of the disadvantages of modesty. He might not be over-fond of seeing, in cabinet, a colleague much more brilliant than himself, and some years younger.

I fancied that little had been said, either in cabinet or in meetings tête-à-tête. Maybe the Prime Minister had spoken intimately to Colling-wood, but I doubted even that. This kind of politics, which could be the roughest of all, went on without words.

That night, Collingwood, bolt upright on Caro's right hand, showed no sign of embarrassment, or even of the disfavour one can't totally suppress towards someone to whom one is doing a bad turn. His quartz eyes might have been blind. So far as he was capable of cordiality, he was giving it, like a moderate-sized tip, to Monty Cave. Cave was the hero of the evening, Cave looked on the short list for promotion. But Collingwood bestowed a smaller, but judicious, cordiality upon Roger. It was hard to believe that he bore him rancour. This was the behaviour, straight-forward, not forthcoming, of someone who thought Roger might still survive, and who would within limits be content if he did so.

He was just as straightforward when Caro pressed him about who would speak in the debate. Roger would have the last word, said Colling-wood. The First Lord would have to open. 'That ought to do,' said Collingwood. To Caro, to me – did Diana know already? – this was the first sharp warning of the night. The First Lord was a lightweight; it sounded as if Roger was not being given a senior Minister to help him out.

'Are you going to speak, Reggie?' said Caro, as unabashed as she had ever been in Roger's cause.

'Not much in my line,' said Collingwood, as though inadequacy in speech were a major virtue. He rarely spoke in the House, and then mumbled through a script so execrably that he seemed unable not only to speak, but to read. Yet he managed to communicate to the back-bench committees. Perhaps that was what he meant when he looked up the table at Roger and said, with self-satisfaction, 'I've done something. I've done something for you already, you know.'

Roger nodded. But suddenly I noticed, so did others, that his eyes were fixed on Monty Cave. The pretence of heartiness, the poise, the goodwill, had all drained away from Roger's expression. He was gazing at Cave with intense anxiety, not with liking, not with anything as final as enmity, but with naked concern.

We followed his glance. Cave gave no sign of recognition. The rest of us had finished eating, but Cave had cut himself another slice of cheese. His lips, fat man's lips, glutton's lips, child's lips, were protruding. He looked up, eyes hard in the soft face.

Just for an instant even Caro's nerve failed. There was a silence. Then her voice rang out, full, unquailing: 'Are *you* going to speak, Monty?'

'The Prime Minister hasn't asked me,' said Cave.

This meant that he couldn't speak, even if he wanted to. But there was a note in his voice, quiet, harmonious, that rasped the nerves.

Caro could not help asking him:

'Isn't there anything else you can do for Roger?'

'I can't think of anything. Can you?'

'How should we handle it, then?' she cried.

Suddenly I was sure that this question had been asked before. At the morning's cabinet? It was easy to imagine the table, Lenton droning away with deliberate amiability, not letting the issue emerge, as though there weren't an issue, as though no policy and no career depended upon it. It was easy to imagine Cave sitting silent. He knew as well as any man alive that Roger needed, not just his acquiescence, but his support. There was he, the bright hope of the party *avant-garde* its best debater, maybe the future leader. They were waiting for him. He knew what depended on it.

'How should we handle it, Monty?'

'I'm afraid it all depends on Roger. He's got to settle it for himself,' he said in a soft, modulated, considered tone, along the table to Caro.

It was out now. For years Cave's attitude to Roger had been veiled. He had disagreed with some of Roger's policy in detail: but yet, he should have been on the same side. He knew why he was making pretexts for minor disagreements. Much more than most politicians, Cave knew himself. He hadn't forgiven Roger for holding back over Suez. Far more than that, Roger was a rival, a rival, in ten years' time, for the first place. By keeping quiet, Cave might be able to see that rival done for.

For once,. though, it was possible that the career did not come first. Cave might have concealed from others, but not from himself, that he profoundly envied Roger. In the midst of all else, he was letting the envy rip. Envy, most of all, of Roger's careless masculine potence: envy, because Roger did not have women leave him: envy of what, with a certain irony, he thought of as Roger's sturdy, happy marriage. From the sadness of his diffident, frustrated sexual life, he regarded Roger. The contrast made him cruel. As he gave his answer to Caro, his voice was soft with cruelty.

She did not think it worth while pressing further. Soon afterwards the party broke up, although it was only half past twelve. Yet, even then, as they said goodbye, Roger kept hold of himself. He might suspect, he was capable of suspecting anything by now, that Cave had in secret stimulated the attack upon him. But reproach, anger, scorn – he could afford none of them. Cave would keep his hostility quiet. In public, he would behave like a colleague. Once more, Roger congratulated him on the evening's feat. As Roger did so, Collingwood patted him on the shoulder.

Below, the cars were driving away. In the drawing-room, Margaret and I were getting up to go. Now that we were alone, Roger looked at his wife and said, with a curious harsh trustfulness:

'Well, it couldn't be much worse, could it?'

'It might be better,' said Caro, bitter and honest.

The moment after, up the stairs came a rapid, stumbling tread. Sammikins marched into the room and gave a brassy hail. He was wearing a dinner-jacket, unlike anyone at the supper-party: a carnation shone in his lapel. He had been drinking, hard enough for his eyes to stare with fierce, wild, arrogant happiness. 'It's too late,' said Caro.

'I shan't stay long,' he shouted. 'I want a drink.'

'You've had enough.'

'You don't know what I've had.' He spoke with the glee of one who had come, not only from drinking, but from bed. He laughed at her, and went on in a confident cry: 'I want to talk to your husband.'

'I'm here.' Roger sat forward on the sofa.

'By God, so you are!' Sammikins again asked for a drink. This time Caro poured him a whisky, and told him to sit down.

'I'm not going to. Why should I?' He gulped his drink and stared down at Roger.

He announced at the top of his voice:

'It won't do!'

'What do you mean?'

'I can't go along with you next week. It sticks in my throat.'

For an instant I had thought, so had Margaret, that he was denouncing Roger for breaking up the marriage. But he couldn't have known yet about that. If he had known, his sister had protected him too much – his side of their relation was too defiant – for him to care.

Caro had stood up. She took his arm and said passionately: 'No, no, you mustn't go back on him now.'

Sammikins shrugged her off. He shouted down at Roger:

'I shan't abstain. That's a boring thing to do. I shall vote against you.'

Roger did not look up. He snapped his fingers against his thigh.

After a pause, he said in a steady, tired, reflective tone: 'I shouldn't have thought this was the best possible time to betray me.'

Sammikins's face lost its fierce joy. More quietly and considerately than he had so far spoken, he replied: 'I'm sorry about the timing.' Then he broke out: 'I don't like the word "betray".'

'Don't you?' asked Roger, expressionless.

'Two can play at that game. Who are you betraying?'

'Will you tell me?'

'I'll give you credit that you don't mean to. But how are you going to leave this blasted country? You've got your reasons, of course, everyone's got their reasons. We can't play with the big boys, I grant you that. But we've got to be able to blow up someone. Ourselves, if that's the only way out. Otherwise the others will blackmail us whenever they feel inclined. We shall be sunk for good.'

Slowly Roger raised his head, but did not speak.

Sammikins went shouting on. 'You're wrong, I tell you! You're wrong. It's simple. War's always been simple. You're too clever by half. You've just got to think of one simple thing, just to see that we're not sunk for good. It's a pity you didn't have a chap like me, I'm not too clever by half – somewhere on top – just to say "Oi, oi. You're being too clever, your job is to see we're not getting sunk for good."'

'I suppose you're the only patriot we've got?' Roger's voice had turned thick and dangerous. At the end of that day, which he had endured without a lapse, he was suddenly moved, shaken, enraged. It was not that Sammikins's defection, in practical terms, counted much. He was a 'wild man', he had been written off long before as irresponsible, a political play-boy. If he went into the lobby against his brother-in-law, all that meant would be a paragraph in the gossip columns. It was not the defection which stabbed Roger – but the personal betrayal, for he had an affection, almost a paternal affection, for the younger man. The personal betrayal, and yes, the reason for it, the half-baked, drunken words. All through, Roger had been nagged at by the regrets, even the guilt, of someone living among choices where the simple certainties weren't enough. For Roger in particular, with his nostalgia for past grandeur, it was tempting to think of a time when you could choose, without folly, to make the country both powerful and safe. He had thought in terms as old-fashioned as that. He had often wished that he had been born in a different time, when reason did not take one into decisions which denied the nostalgic heart.

'You've only got to keep your eye on the ball and remember the simple things,' Sammikins shouted.

Roger had risen to his feet, a massive bulk in the room.

'No one else tries to remember the simple things?'

'They decide what will happen to us,' said Sammikins.

'Do you think no one else cares what will happen to us?'

'I hope they do.'

Sammikins had not spoken in his loud, confident voice. This time it was Roger who shouted:

'Get out!'

After all his disciplined performances, the fury boiling up and over was astonishing – no, less astonishing than unnerving to hear. The thick, driven cry filled the room. Roger began to move, hunched, on to the other man.

I was standing up too, wondering how to stop the fight. Sammikins was athletic, but Roger was four or five stones heavier, and far stronger. With a bear-like heave, he threw Sammikins against the wall. Sammikins slid very slowly down it, like a coat collapsing from a peg, till he was on the floor. For a moment he sat there, head hanging, as if he had forgotten where he was, or who any of us were. Then, with an athlete's lightness, he sprang up – from crossed ankles – and stood erect with hardly a stagger, eyes staring. Caro got between him and Roger. She clung to her brother's hand.

'For God's sake, go,' she said.

'Do you want me to?' he said, with a curious, injured dignity.

'You must *go*.'

Head back, he moved to the door. From the far end of the room he said to Caro, 'I expect I'll want to see you—'

'This is my house,' shouted Roger, 'get out of it!'

Caro did not reply to Sammikins. She went to Roger's side, and, like a united front of husband and wife, they listened to the footsteps lurching down.

CHAPTER XLI

QUARREL IN THE CORRIDOR

NEXT day, when I called in Roger's office, he sat calm and stoical, like a man without passions, as though any story about an outbreak of his was one's own invention and couldn't be referred to. Yet once more his tic returned: in a distant, cold, almost inimical manner, he asked me to report what the papers were rumouring that morning. 'There's not much,' I said.

'Good.' His face, his voice, became smooth. He was for the moment over-easily reassured, like a man jealous in love, snatching at the bits of news which comfort him.

There was a report in one paper about a meeting of a few back-benchers and some scientists, which seemed to have ended in the scientists quarrelling – that was about all, I said.

Immediately, again like a jealous man, he started on the detective work of anxiety: who could they be? Where? This was the ultra-conservative paper, they were enemies, we knew which member slipped them the gossip. Yet this man, who was venal but abnormally amiable, had already written to Roger pledging his support. Was he reneging at the last minute? I shook my head. I was positive that he was all right. Not that he minded collecting his retainer from the paper.

'One of these days,' said Roger, relieved and savage, 'we'll get men like him expelled from the House.'

What about the scientists? I said. Who were they, anyway? He wasn't interested. Nothing could interest him except the lobbies, now. As I left him, he was working out, repetitiously, unable to shake off the obsession, who these members were, and whether he could count on their votes.

Back in my own room, I wasn't much better. The debate was to begin on Monday afternoon. They would vote the night after that. Four days and a half before it would be over. I pulled down a file from my in-tray. There was a minute written in the most beautiful handwriting, in the most lucid prose. I did not feel like reading it.

I sat there day-dreaming, not pleasantly. Once I rang up Margaret, asking if there were any news, though what I expected I hadn't an idea.

A knock sounded on my door, not the door leading to my assistants, through which visitors should come, but the corridor door, usually inviolable. Hector Rose came in, perhaps for the second time since we had been colleagues, paying me a visit unannounced.

'Forgive me, my dear Lewis, I do apologise many, many times for interrupting you like this—'

'There isn't much to interrupt,' I said.

'You're so much occupied that there's always something to interrupt.' He gazed at the empty desk, at the in-tray with its stack of files. He gave a faint, arctic smile. 'In any case, my dear Lewis, forgive me for disturbing some of your valuable meditations.'

Even now, after all those years, even in stress, I didn't know the response to his singular brand of courtesy. The bright young Treasury officials, certain by this time that he would soon be retiring, and that they would never, as they once imagined, have to answer to him, had invented a quip, the sort of quip which, like a premature obituary, gets circulared when a formidable man is passing out: 'With old Hector Rose, you've got to take the smooth with the smooth.'

Little they knew.

After some more apologies he sat down. He looked at me with bleached eyes and said: 'I thought you ought to know that I had the curious experience of meeting your friend Dr Brodzinski last night.'

'Where?'

'Oddly enough, with some of our political acquaintances.'

Suddenly, the item in the newspaper flashed back, and I guessed:

'So you were there!'

'How have you heard?'

I mentioned the paper.

Rose gave a polite smile and said: 'I don't find it necessary to read that particular journal.'

'But you were there?'

'I was trying to make that clear, my dear Lewis.'

'How did you get invited?'

Again he smiled politely: 'I made it my business to be.'

He cut out the flourishes, and with sarcastic relevance told me the story. Brodzinski, in a last attempt to whip up opposition to Roger's policy, had made an appeal to some of his Tory contacts. Instead of again attacking Roger directly, he had done it through an attack on Walter Luke. He had told some of the extreme right, the pro-Suez relics, that it was Luke's advice which had led Roger into bad judgment. So Brodzinski had been asked to dine with a small splinter group. So, by a piece of upright pig-headed good manners, had Walter Luke. So, through his own initiative, had Hector Rose.

'I wasn't prepared to have the excellent Luke thrown to the wolves,' he said. 'Also, I thought I might as well listen to what was going on. I have a certain influence with Lord A——' (the leader of the splinter group, and the man responsible for the pig-headed good manners. It sounded improbable that he should be a friend of Hector Rose's, but in fact – in the minuteness of the English official world – they had been at school together.)

Between Brodzinski and Luke, there had been a lurid row. Lord North Street was not the only place, the night before, where eminent persons came to physical violence. 'How these scientists love one another,' said Rose. He added: 'Brodzinski could certainly be sued for defamation, if Luke cared to go to law.' With crisp detachment he gave a few examples.

'Is anyone going to believe *that*?'

'My dear Lewis, don't you agree that if anyone is accused of anything, literally anything, most of our friends believe it?'

He went on: 'While I am about it, you might drop a word to our potentially supreme colleague. Douglas Osbaldiston. There appears to be no doubt that Brodzinski has been trying to spill this particular poison into his ear.'

Once before – just once, in that disciplined life where personal relations were left unstated – Rose had let fall his feelings about Douglas. He did not let himself be so direct again, not even when I said that Douglas, whatever Rose thought of him, was honest and fair.

'I am perfectly certain,' said Rose, half-bowing as he spoke, 'that our colleague has been utterly correct. In fact, I gathered that he had refused to grant Brodzinski an interview at the present juncture. No one could be more correct, could he? Our colleague has every qualification for the perfect public servant. But still, I do suggest you drop a word. He is just a shade inclined to believe in reconciliation for its own sake. When all this is settled, he might find it was wiser and safer to have Brodzinski in rather than out. I should regard that as reconciliation carried to a somewhat excessive extent. Our colleague has a slightly greater veneration than I have for the general good sense of everybody in this part of London.'

Our eyes met. For this occasion, we were allies. He said: 'By the way, one fact seems to be generally known.'

'Yes?'

'That he's not a hundred per cent happy about his master's policy, or shall I say his master's ultimate intentions about policy?' Rose was not given to underlining. That morning he was thinking of Tuesday's voting, not with Roger's concentration, for that was total, but with something as channelled as mine. Name by name, he gave his prognosis about last night's party. There had been twelve members present. All but one were on the extreme right, and so possible enemies of Roger. Of these, three would vote for him, including Lord A—— (Rose was, as he might have said himself, most correct. He did not give a vestigial hint that he, a functionary, could possibly have used any persuasion.) Of the others, a maximum of nine would certainly abstain. 'It's beginning to look uncomfortable,' said Hector Rose. He broke off, and went on about the vote. There were bound to be more abstentions. I told him, not the full story of Sammikins, but that he would vote against.

Rose clicked his tongue. He looked at me as though he were going to give a verdict. Then he shook his head, and in a cool tone remarked:

'I take it you will let your friend Quaife know at once. That is, about the information I was able to collect. I needn't tell you, you'll have to do it discreetly, and I'm afraid you mustn't reveal your source. But he ought to know about these abstentions. You can tell him the people by name, I think.'

'What good can that do him?'

'What do you mean?'

'Do you believe that, if he saw them now, he could possibly persuade them back?'

'No,' said Rose.

'Well then, all he can do is make his speech. He'll make a better speech the more hope he's got left.'

'My dear Lewis, with great diffidence, I think he ought to be able to reckon up his opponents—'

'I repeat,' I said with force, 'what good can that do?'

'You're taking a responsibility on yourself.' Rose stared at me, surprised, disapproving. 'If I were he,' he said, 'I should want to be told every scrap of news, however bad it was, until the end.'

I stared back. 'I believe you would,' I said.

It wasn't necessarily the toughest and hardest-nerved who lived in public. Yet sometimes I wondered whether a man as tough and hard-nerved as Rose could imagine what the public life was like, or how much it would have tested him.

He got up. 'Well, that's all the bad news for the present.' He made the grim, Greek-messenger joke, said this seemed as far as we could go, and began his paraphernalia of thanks and apologies.

As soon as he had gone, I looked at the clock. It was nearly twenty to twelve. This time I didn't brood or wait. I went out, through my private office, into the corridor, past the doors of my own department, round three sides of the Treasury quadrangle, on my way to Osbaldiston. I didn't notice, as I had done times enough, the bizarre architecture, the nineteenth-century waste of space, the gigantic unfilled hole in the centre of the building, like a Henry Moore sculpture pretending to be functional. I didn't even notice the high jaundiced walls, the dark stretch of corridor up to the next bend, the compartments where the messengers sat on stools reading the racing editions, the labels on the doors just visible in the half light, Sir W—— H——, G.B.E., Sir W—— D——, K.C.B. It was just dark, domesticated, familiar: a topological journey: the doors passing me by like the stations seen from an underground train.

Before I got into the last straight, which led to Douglas's office, I saw him coming round the corner, head forward, a docket of papers in his hand. 'I was looking for you,' I said.

'I've got a meeting,' Douglas answered. He wasn't evading me. There was not time to return to his room. We stood there in the corridor, talking in low voices. Occasionally, in the next few minutes, doors opened, young men walked briskly past us, throwing a glance in the direction of their boss. Some would know that he and I were close friends. They might have thought that we were settling a bit of business before the meeting, or alternatively, in the way of the top stratum, at once the casual and machine-like, saving time and an inter-departmental minute.

It wasn't going quite like that. As we kept our voices down, I was watching his face with a mixture of affection, pity and blind anger. It had changed since his wife's illness. Now it had the special pathos of a face which, still in essence anachronistically youthful, was nevertheless beginning to look old. Once he had been untouched as Dorian Gray, a character whom he resembled in no other particular, but now all that was gone.

Three times a week, Margaret went to sit with his wife in hospital. By this time, when she wanted to smoke, Mary had to be fed her cigarette. 'How paralysed can you get?' she said, with a euphoria and courage that made it worse to watch.

Douglas had come to stay with us some nights, when he couldn't stand any more either the lonely house or the club. Once he had told us, with bitter, unguarded candour, that there were not two hours together in any day when he didn't think of her lying there, not to move again, while he was free.

All that was out of my mind. I was saying:

'How much do you know of the latest attack on Quaife?'

'What are you talking about?'

'Do you realise that they're going for anyone who has the slightest connection with him? Now it's Walter Luke—'

'You can't have a war,' said Douglas, 'without someone getting hurt.'

'I suppose you're aware,' I said angrily, 'that you've been giving aid and comfort to these people?'

'What are you saying now?' All of a sudden, his face had become stony. He was as enraged as I was: the more so, because we had in private so often been open with each other.

'I'm saying, it's well known that you don't agree with Quaife.'

'Nonsense.'

'Can you tell me that?'

'I do tell you that, and I expect you to believe it,' said Douglas.

'What do you expect me to believe?'

'Listen to me,' he said. 'You've felt yourself entitled to your private view. Not so private, if I may say so. So have I. I've made no secret of it. I haven't left my Minister in any doubt. I think he's wrong, and he knows that as well as I do. But no one else knows it, except you, and one or two people I can trust.'

'So do others.'

'Do you really think I'm responsible for that?'

'It depends what you mean by responsible.'

His face had darkened up to the cheekbones.

'We'd better try to be rational,' he said. 'If my Minister wins, then I shall do my best for him. Of course, I shall be carrying out a policy in which I don't believe. Well, I've done that before and I can do it again. I shall try to make the thing work. Without false modesty, I shall do it as well as anyone round here.'

All that he said was absolutely true.

'You think he can't win?' I said.

'And what do you think?'

His gaze was sharp, appraising. For a second we might have been in a negotiation, listening for a point at which the other would give way.

'You've done a certain amount to make it harder,' I let fly again.

'I've done exactly what I've told you. No more, and no less.'

'You're better at singing in unison than some of us, aren't you?'

'I don't understand.'

'You realise that the line you're taking is the line that a good many powerful persons want you to take? Most of them don't really want Roger Quaife to get away with it, do they?'

With a curious detachment he replied: 'That is possibly so.'

'If he doesn't win, you'll be sitting pretty, won't you? You will have scored a nice new piece of credit for yourself? You'll have everything waiting for you?'

He looked at me without expression. He said, in a quite friendly voice: 'One thing. You know I've had my own view all along about this business. Don't you believe it was an honest view?'

I had to say, Yes, of course I did.

I burst out, without remembering that I had once heard Cave make the same accusation to Roger: 'But all you've done or not done – you must have realised that it wouldn't exactly impede your progress, mustn't you?'

In my fury, I was astonished to see him give a smile – not an intimate smile, but still genuine.

'If we worried about that sort of consideration, Lewis, we should never do anything, should we?'

After glancing at his watch he said, in a businesslike tone:
'You've made me a bit late.'

He went off towards his meeting, quickly but not in a rush, head thrust forward, papers in hand, along the corridor.

CHAPTER XLII

VIEW FROM THE BOX

IN the middle of the afternoon, my p.a. came in with a letter marked 'Urgent'. It must have been delivered by hand, she said. The handwriting on the envelope looked like a woman's, but I did not recognise it. Then I found that the note was signed 'Ellen'. I read:

> 'I expect you will be at the debate Monday and Tuesday. I have got to stay away, of course. I can't even communicate with him until it's all over. Will you please – I have to ask you this – let me know how things are going? I trust you to tell me the bare truth, whatever it is. I shall be in the flat alone, on both evenings. Please ring up, whatever you have to tell me.'

I thought of her that evening, as Margaret and I went out to the theatre, just as an anaesthetic against the suspense. Roger was at home working at his speech, Caro with him. Ellen was the loneliest of all. I talked of her to Margaret. There she was, hearing nothing of him. Once she had feared that, if his career was broken, she would lose him. Now the blackmail had come out, now Caro had confronted him, Ellen must have the contradictory fear. Yet I was sure that she prayed for his success. Margaret said: 'She's not as good as you think she is.'

I said: 'She tries to be.'

Margaret had met Ellen only socially, and then in the past, with her husband. It was Caro whom Margaret knew and loved, as I did not, Caro whom she had tried to comfort. Now, as we stood in the foyer of the Haymarket, avoiding the sight of acquaintances because we wanted to be together, she asked if the position was clear-cut – was Ellen facing that dilemma, either getting him, or seeing him prevail? I said, I didn't believe that either of them knew. There could be something in it? I didn't answer her.

'If there's the slightest bit in it,' said Margaret, 'I'm grateful I was never tested that way about you.'

Monday came and dragged, like one of the days in my youth when I was waiting for the result of an examination. Hector Rose sent his compliments, and informed me that he expected to be in the box (that is, the civil servants' stall) for the last hours of the debate the following night. Otherwise I had no messages of any kind all that morning.

I hesitated about ringing Roger up. I detested being wished good luck myself, and I decided that he, also, would like to be left alone. I did not want to go to a club for lunch, in case I met Douglas or anyone else involved. I was tired of pretending to write or read. Instead, while the others were at lunch, I did what I should have done as a young man, and walked blankly round St James's Park in the sunshine, catching, and being tantalised by, the first scent of spring; then through the streets, calling in at bookshops, nibbling away at time.

In the afternoon, the office clock swept out the minutes with its second hand. There was no point in leaving until half past four: I did not wish to sit through question time and statements. I rang my private secretary, and went with obsessive detail into next week's work. After that, I had a session with my p.a., making sure that she knew where I would be each hour of that day and the next. At last it was four twenty-five. Not quite the starting-time, but I could permit myself to go.

Then, as I was hurrying down the corridor, I heard a voice behind me. It was my p.a., eager, comely, spectacled. My own devices had gone back on me: she knew the time too well. A lady was on the telephone, said Hilda: she said she had to speak to me immediately, it was desperately important, she couldn't wait a minute. Thwarted, anxious, not knowing what to be anxious about, I rushed back. Was Caro going to break some news? Or was it Ellen, or from home?

It was none of them. It was Mrs Henneker.

'I should never have believed it possible.' Her voice came strongly over the 'phone. What was it? I asked.

'What do you think?'

I did not feel inclined for guessing-games. It turned out that she had had a letter by the afternoon post, five minutes before, from a publisher. They had actually told her they didn't consider her biography of her husband would be of sufficient interest to the general public. 'What do you think of that?'

She sounded almost triumphant in her incredulity.

Oh well, I said, there were other publishers – trying to put her off, maddened because I was not out of the room.

'That's not good enough!' Her voice rang out like a challenge.

I would talk to her sometime in the nearish future.

'No.' Her reply was intransigent. 'I think I must ask you to come round straightaway.'

I said I had important business.

'What do you call this, if it isn't important?'

It was utterly and absolutely impossible, I said. I was occupied all the evening, all the next day, all the week.

'I'm afraid,' she said sternly, 'I consider this entirely unsatisfactory.'

I said, incensed, that I was sorry.

'Entirely unsatisfactory. Can't I make you understand what has happened? They actually say – I'd better read you the whole letter.'

I said I hadn't time.

'I believe in putting first things first.'

I said goodbye.

Just as I got to the end of the corridor, I heard my telephone ringing again. I was quite sure it was Mrs Henneker. I walked on.

Down in Great George Street, the evening light bland and calm, I still felt menaced by that monomaniac voice, as though that was the cause of my worry, and not what I was going to listen to in the House. Looking up, I could see the informatory light shining above Big Ben, with a clear violet sky beyond. Though I had seen it so often, it stirred a memory, or at least a disquiet, the reason for which seemed mixed with the monomaniac voice. I was tugging at the roots of memory, but they would not be pulled out. Was it the night my wife and I went to dine at Lord North Street and, arriving too early, had walked round by St Margaret's? The light had been shining that evening, too; yet there had been no disquiet, we had been at leisure, and content.

In the central lobby, busy with cavernous activity, members were meeting constituents, acquaintances, taking them off to tea. When I got into the officials' box, I could have counted less than a hundred members in the chamber. There seemed as yet no special excitement in the air. The Opposition opener was speaking, like a man who is settling down to a steady lecture. He was prosy but confident, saying nothing new. It was a standard speech, gaining nothing, losing nothing. For a while I felt the needle pass away.

On the front bench, Roger was leaning back, fingers entwined, hands under his chin: Tom Wyndham sat dutifully behind him. There were three other Ministers on the front bench, Collingwood among them. A few members entered, others left. Figures were dotted here and there on the empty benches, some not listening. It might have been a borough council, assembled out of duty, for a discussion of something not specially earth-shaking, such as a proposal for a subsidy to the civic theatre.

In the box, Douglas and two other Whitehall acquaintances were already sitting. Douglas, who was writing a note on the small desk flap, gave me a friendly smile. They were all professionals, they had been here before. The climax was a long way off. This was just the start, as perfunctory as the first hour of a county cricket match, or the exposition of a drawing-room comedy.

During the opening speech I went along to the Speaker's Gallery. There Caro and Margaret were sitting together. 'He's not doing any harm,' whispered Caro. They were going back to Lord North Street for a sandwich some time. They knew I shouldn't eat till the sitting was over. 'Come along then, and pick up Margaret,' said Caro, in another whisper. Now that at last we were all in it, all immersed, she could put hostilities aside until another day. Her glance turned on me, bold and full, just as her brother's did when he gambled. No one could expect her to be happy. Yet she wasn't in the true sense anxious, and in her excitement there was a glint, not only of recklessness, but of pleasure.

Back in my place at Douglas's side, I listened to the First Lord making the first reply. He too was competent, more so than I had been told. He was using much the same language as the Opposition spokesman. In fact, I found myself thinking, as the words rolled out like the balloons from characters in comic strips, an observer from Outer Mongolia would have been puzzled to detect the difference between them. 'Deterrence' was a word they both used often. The First Lord was preoccupied with 'potential scaling-down', not scaling-down in the here and now, but 'potential scaling-down if we can have the assurance that this will influence others'. He also talked of 'shield and sword', 'striking power', 'capability'. It was a curious abstract language, of which the main feature was the taking of meaning out of words.

As I listened to their speeches and those which followed, I wasn't interested in speculation, or even the arguments as such. We had heard them all, for years. So I was listening, with concentrated and often obsessed attention, not to the arguments, but simply to what they meant in terms of votes next night. That was all. For all those hours, it was enough. The House grew fuller during the early evening, then thinned at dinner-time. Until nine o'clock there were no surprises. A Labour party back-bencher expressed views close to Francis Getliffe's or mine. When it came to the vote there would, we already knew, be plenty of abstentions on the Labour side – how many we were not certain, but too many for comfort. Though these abstentions meant support for Roger's policy, it was once again the support he could not afford. A Labour party front-bencher expressed views that a member of Lord A——'s splinter group, or an American admiral, might have found reactionary. Lord A—— himself made a Delphic speech, in which he stated his suspicions of the Government's intentions and his determination to vote for them. Another ultra-conservative, whom we had counted as lost, followed suit.

To the surprise of everyone round me, the first hours of the debate didn't produce much animus. It was a full-dress parliamentary occasion. Everyone had heard the passions over the issue and the personality seething for weeks. They were waiting for violence, and it hadn't come.

Then, precisely at nine, the member for a county division was called. When I saw him rise, I settled back without any apprehensions at all. His name was Trafford, and I knew him slightly. He wasn't well off, he lived on a small family business. He wasn't on the extreme right, he wasn't smart. He didn't speak often, he asked pertinacious questions: he was not likely to be invited to Basset. I had met him because, in his constituency, there were people who had known me when I was young. I thought he was dull, determined, over-anxious to do all the listening.

He got up, heavy-shouldered, raw-skinned. Within a minute, he was ripping into an attack. It was an attack which, from the first sounding note, was virulent. He was a loyal supporter of the Government, he said: he hoped to be so in the future: but he couldn't support this particular policy and this particular Minister. The policy was the policy of an adventurer. What else was this man? What had he done? What was his record of achievement? All he did was play the field, look out for the main chance, find the soft option. This was the kind of adventurer's progress he was leading the country into. Why? What were his credentials? What reason had he given us for trusting him? Trust him? Trafford's tone got more violent. Some of us compared him with a man we could truly trust, the Honourable Member for Brighton South. We wished that the Honourable Member for Brighton South were in his place tonight, bringing us back to our principles. We believed that he had been a victim of his own high standards.

As the constituency of Brighton South was shouted out, I could not recall the member's name. I whispered a question to Douglas. 'J. C. Smith,' he said.

So it had got so far. The abuse went on, but the accusation became no more direct. It couldn't have been understood, except by those who knew already; yet the hate was palpable. Was this man Trafford one of Smith's disciples? It might be so. How far were they in touch with Hood, how far was he their weapon?

My own suspicion had crystallised. I did not believe that he was just a man unbalanced, on his own. Or rather, he might be unbalanced, or have become so, as he carried the persecution on. But I believed that there were cool minds behind it. There was evidence that he had a fanatical devotion to his own aircraft firm, the kind of devotion, passionate and pathetic, of one who didn't get the rewards himself, but hero-worshipped those who did. There could have been people shrewd enough to use him, shrewd enough to know that he got excitement from the sexual life of others.

I thought that there were cool minds behind him. But it seemed to me that these were business minds. They might have their links with Smith's disciples; but it didn't sound like the work of those disciples, not even the work of this man himself, snarling in the chamber.

Adventurers were dangerous, he was saying. They might be ingratiating, they might have attractions for all those round them, they might be clever, but they were the ruin of any government and any nation. It was time this Government went back to the solid virtues, and then Trafford and his friends and the whole country would support them once more.

It wasn't a long speech. Twice he was shouted into silence, but even Roger's partisans were embarrassed and for a time hypnotised by his venom. Roger sat through it, expressionless.

I hadn't heard such an outburst in the House before. What harm had it done? For a few, for Collingwood, the reference to Smith wouldn't be missed. The attack came from a quarter we should least have chosen, the respectable middle-of-the-road of the Tory members. Had it been too violent for men to take? That seemed the best hope. When two of Hector Rose's dinner companions got up to say they couldn't support the Government, they were noticeably civil and restrained, and one paid a compliment to Roger's character.

When the House rose, I couldn't trust my judgment. A policeman was shouting 'Who goes home?' as I telephoned Ellen, not knowing what to say. I heard her quick, breathcatching 'Yes', and told her all had gone as we expected, except – again a 'Yes?' – except, I said, for one bit of venom. I couldn't tell what the effect would be. It had been meant to kill. It might result in nothing worse than a single unexpected abstention. 'You're not holding back?' she said. I had to tell here there had been a hint about her husband: not many would have grasped it. Down the telephone came a harsh sigh: What difference would it make? Was it going to tip the balance? Her voice had risen. I said, in flat honesty, that no one could tell: I believed, for better or worse, it wouldn't count. I added, meaninglessly, Try to sleep.

Through the sparkling, frosty night, I hurried round to Lord North Street. On the stairs I heard laughter from the drawing-room. As I got inside, I saw with astonishment that Caro, Margaret and Roger were all looking cheerful. A plate of sandwiches was waiting for me, since I had not eaten all day.

'What have you been doing to Trafford?' Roger asked, as though to put me at my ease.

'Do you understand it?' I cried.

'Whatever does he hope for?' Caro spoke with genuine full-throated scorn, not pretending. She must have heard each overtone of the insinuation, but she laughed like one saying – 'If that is the worst they can do!'

'Have you had any repercussions?' I asked.

'Not one.' Roger spoke with studious interest, with the euphoria which sometimes breaks through in the middle of a crisis. 'Do you know, I can't begin to imagine why he did it. Can you?'

I couldn't answer.

'If no one can supply any motive – Why, I shall soon be forced to think that he meant what he said.' His tone was unforced, free from rancour. He gave a laugh, like a man easy among his friends. He had drunk little, he was keyed up for action next day. He was hoping more simply than he had hoped for weeks.

CHAPTER XLIII

THE MEANING OF NUMBERS

NEXT morning I woke early and lay listening to the papers as they thudded on to the hall floor. They didn't settle either what I feared or what I hoped. *The Times* was playing down the whole debate: on the middle page, Trafford only got a couple of lines. The *Telegraph* gave bolder headlines and more space: if one knew the language, one knew that they were anti-Roger. But they also muffled Trafford's attack. The *Express* was angry with the chief Labour speaker. I dressed and went up Albion Street to buy the other morning papers. I came back to breakfast, neither Margaret nor myself out of our misery, either for good or bad. In the morning light, she was ashamed of herself for having been so elated the night before.

I wondered whether Roger, too, had hated the morning. I wondered whether Caro had tried to give him comfort, as Margaret did to me. She knew, better than I did, that time and the hour ran through the roughest day.

Nothing happened – that didn't make the day smoother – until, once more at tea-time, I was within a few minutes of leaving for the House. Then a telephone call came through; this time, not from Mrs Henneker. Instead, a friend of Sammikins had a piece of news. He had just come away from the Lords. He wanted to tell me that old Gilbey had, ten minutes before, taken a hand.

By this time, Lord Gilbey was very ill. He hadn't been able to make a public appearance for twelve months, and his doctors were surprised that he had lived at all. Yet that afternoon he had been impelled to make a public appearance, even if it were his last. He had arrived in the Lords. The subject for his intervention could not have seemed promising, for some peer, ennobled for scientific eminence, was moving for papers on the state of the country's technological education. This hadn't deterred Gilbey. Standing up, frail, face death-blanched, he had supported the motion with passion. He didn't understand technology, but he wanted it, if that was the price of keeping us strong. He was for anything, whether it was technology or black magic, if competent persons like the Noble Lord proved that it was necessary to keep us strong and make us stronger. He would assert this to his dying day, which wouldn't be far off.

He had spoken for five minutes, an old soldier's attack on *adventurers*, men who were too clever for their good or ours. Adventurers in high places, careerists in high places. He begged Noble Lords to beware of them. He wanted to make this plea, even if it were for the last time.

It was pure revenge. He might die before the summer, but hatred for Roger would live as long as he did. It didn't sound like a hero's end: and then I thought that it might be just his willingness to end like this which had made him a hero.

I was relieved to be back in the box, relieved to sit beside Hector Rose instead of Douglas. On this night it was better to have the company of an ally who wasn't a friend than the other way round. Arms folded across his chest, Rose watched with a trained, cold gaze. As, at intervals of half an hour, three members whom he had designated by name got up with hostile speeches, he permitted himself to say: 'According to plan.' Yet, even to him, fresh as he was, the debate was not giving any answer. The tone had become more bitter on both sides. The benches were full now, members were squatting in the aisles. There were echoes of Trafford; words like 'gambler', 'adventurer', 'risk', 'surrender', snapped into the chamber, but all from men we had already written off. Several speakers sat down, leaving it vague how they intended to vote. When a Labour ex-Minister began a preamble on strategy, Rose said quietly: 'I give him forty minutes. Time for us to eat.'

I didn't want to leave.

'No, you must.'

Douglas had made the same estimate about the speaker's staying-power. As we reached the Hall together, Rose gave him lavish and courteous greetings, but pointedly did not invite him to come along with us.

We hurried through the yard, across to a Whitehall pub. There Rose, who normally had delicate tastes in food, put down a large hunk of cheese and a scotch egg, and inspected me with satisfaction as I did the same. 'That will keep us going,' he said dutifully.

We hadn't spoken about the debate. I said the one word: 'Well?'

'I don't know, my dear Lewis, I don't know.'

'Any chance?'

'He'll have to pull something out of the bag himself, shouldn't you have thought?'

He meant, in the final speech.

I wanted to scratch over the evidence, to reckon the odds, but Rose wouldn't have it.

'It doesn't seem profitable,' he said. Instead, he had his own recourse. He drew out a stiff, plain pocket-book, such as I had often seen him use in meetings, and began to write down numbers. Maximum possible number of members on the Government side, 315. He jotted down the figure, without an enquiry or a doubt. Unavoidable absences, illness, and so on – the whips appeared to expect eight. Available votes, 307. Rose did not hesitate: cabinet dubious, Minister not sticking to the rules, he couldn't afford defections. 290 votes, and he might be safe: 17 abstentions. (From the debate, we now knew there would be at least nine, and one vote, Sammikins's, against.)

Anything under 280, and he was in great danger.

Anything under 270, and it was all over.

Rose went on with his own kind of nepenthe. He didn't think the Opposition vote was relevant, but in his clear, beautiful script he continued to write figures. Maximum: 280. Absences: 12. Abstentions: perhaps 25.

The Government majority was certain, but not significant. Roger could survive provided he received the 290 votes from his own side, plus or minus 10. That would be the figure which all informed persons would regard as decisive that night.

Rose looked up with the pleasure of one who has performed a neat operation. It struck me, even in the suspense, that the figures would be hard to explain to anyone not steeped in this kind of parliamentary process. The figures looked blank, the margins negligible. They would decide at least one career, maybe others, conceivably a good deal else.

When we returned to our places, the ex-Minister had only just finished. More speeches, the House becoming packed. The shouts of laughter were louder, so were the protests, but most of the time there was a dense silence. It was a dense, impatient silence. Men looked at Roger, sitting heavily on the front bench, chin in hand. The last perfunctory 'hear-hears' after the last Opposition speech damped down. Again the silence. Voice from the chair – 'Mr Quaife.'

At last. Roger stood up, heavy, moving untidily but without strain. He was much the biggest man on either front bench. Once again, as when I first met him, in his clumsy, powerful, formidable presence, he gave me a reminder of Pierre Bezukhov. There was loyal applause behind him. He looked relaxed, abnormally so, troublingly so, for a man in his chief trial. He began with taunts. He had been accused of so many things, he said. Some of them were contradictory, they could not all be valid. Of course, wise persons remarked that, if you wanted to hear the truth about yourself, you listened to what your enemies said. Splendid. But that principle didn't apply only to him. It applied to everyone. Even, believe it or not, to other Honourable Members, in some cases Honourable and Gallant Members, who had so reluctantly volunteered their character-sketches of himself. He listed four of the ultra-conservatives. He did not refer, even by an intonation, to Trafford. It might be a good idea if each of us accepted just what his enemies said; it might make us better, and the world too. It would certainly rub into us that we were all miserable sinners.

It was good-natured. The House was laughing. Once or twice a barb darted out. Suddenly one heard him, not so Pierre-like, but clear, hard, piercing. Though his friends cheered, I was not easy. It might be too light a beginning. In a sense, it seemed too much above the battle. I looked at Hector Rose. Almost imperceptibly, he gave a shake of the head. In the House, in the galleries, people were saying that this was the speech of the debate. As he got down to the arguments, he was using the idiom of a late-twentieth-century man. He had thrown away the old style of parliamentary rhetoric altogether. Compared with the other speeches from both the front benches, this might have come from a man a generation younger. It was the speech of one used to broadcasting studios, television cameras, the exposure of the machine. He didn't declaim: he spoke about war, weapons, the meaning of a peaceful future, in his own voice. This was how, observers said later, parliamentarians would be speaking in ten years' time.

I scarcely noticed. I was thinking, was this the time that he might choose to break loose? Once or twice he had threatened to cut the tangle of these arguments, and to try to touch something deeper. Would it help him? We were all children of our time and class, conditioned to think of these decisions (were they decisions? were we just driven?) in forms we couldn't break. Could anyone break them? Were there forces which Roger or anyone in that House, or any of the rest of us, could release?

If he had thought of trying, he put the idea behind him. He was talking only to the House. And yet, within ten minutes, I knew that he wasn't withdrawing, that he had forgotten temptations, ambiguities and tricks. He was saying what he had often concealed, but all along believed. Now that he had to speak, he gave an account, lucid and sharp, of the kind of thinking Francis and his colleagues had made their own. He gave it with more force than they could have done. He gave it with the authority of one who would grip the power. But it was only right at the end that he said something which dropped, quietly, unofficially, into the late night air. 'Look,' he said. 'The problems we're trying to handle are very difficult. So difficult that most people in this country – people who are, by and large, at least as intelligent as we are – can't begin to understand them. Simply because they haven't had the information, and haven't been taught to come to terms with them. I'm not sure how many of us can comprehend what our world is like, now that we're living with the bomb. Perhaps very few, or none. But I'm certain that the overwhelming majority of people who are, I repeat, at least as intelligent as we are, don't have any idea. We are trying to speak for them. We have taken a great deal upon ourselves. We never ought to forget it.'

I was feeling admiration, anxiety, the exhilaration of anxiety. Now it had come to it, did I wish that he had compromised? His colleagues could get rid of him now: the bargains and balances of the White Paper didn't allow for this. The chance, the only chance, was that he might take the House with him.

'It has been said in this House, these last two nights, that I want to take risks. Let me tell you this. All choices involve risks. In our world, all the serious choices involve grave ones. But there are two kinds of risk. One is to go on mindlessly, as though our world were the old world. I believe, as completely as I believe anything, that if this country and all countries go on making these bombs, testing these bombs – just as though they were so many battleships – then before too long a time, the worst will happen. Perhaps through no one's fault – just because we're all men, liable to make mistakes, go mad, or have bad luck. If that happens, our descendants, if we have any, will curse us. And every curse will be justified.

'This country can't be a super-power any longer. I should be happier if it could. Though it is possible that being a super-power is in itself an illusion, now that science has caught up with us. Anyway, we can't be one But I am certain that we can help – by example, by good judgment, by talking sense and acting sense – we can help swing the balance between a good future and a bad future, or between a good future and none at all. We can't contract out. The future is finely poised. Our influence upon it is finite, but it exists.

'That is why I want to take one kind of risk. It is, in fact, a small risk, which may do good, as opposed to a great risk which would certainly do harm. That is still the choice. That is all.'

Roger sat down, heavy-faced, hands in his pockets. For an instant, a long instant, there was silence. Then applause behind him. How solid was it? Was it uncomfortable? There were one or two cheers from the back benches on the other side. Ritual took over. The lobby bells rang. I noticed Sammikins stand up, head high and wild, in the middle of his friends, going out defiantly to vote against them. Half a dozen members sat obstinately on the Government benches, most of them with arms crossed, parading their determination to abstain. That told us nothing. There might be others, not so forthright, who would go out and not pass through the lobby.

The members returned. Some were talking, but the noise level was low. There was a crowd, excited, tense, at the sides of the Speaker's chair. Before the tellers had passed the despatch box, a hush had fallen. It was a hush, but not a high-spirited one. The voice came:

'Ayes to the right, 216.' (There had been more Labour abstentions than Rose had allowed for.)

The voice came again.

'Noes to the left, 271.'

Rose looked at me with cold sympathy. He said, precisely: 'I consider this unfortunate.'

In the chamber, it took longer for the result to sink in. The chairman repeated the numbers in a sonorous bass, and announced that the Noes had it.

Seconds later, half a minute later, a chant opened up from the Opposition. 'Resign! Resign!'

Without fuss, the Government front bench began to empty. The Prime Minister, Collingwood, Monty Cave, went out of the House together, passing close by us in the box. Cries followed them, but the shouts were focused on Roger. He was sitting back, one arm stretched out behind him, talking, with apparent casualness, to the First Lord and Leverett-Smith.

'Resign! Resign!'

The yells broke on him. Once, he gave a wave across the gangway, like a Wimbledon player acknowledging the existence of the crowd.

Taking his time, he got up. He didn't look either at his own back-benchers or at the others. 'Resign! Resign!' The shouts grew louder. His great back moved slowly down the aisle, away from us. At the Bar he turned and made his bow to the chair. Then he walked on. When he was out of sight, the shouts still crashed behind him.

CHAPTER XLIV

'YOU HAVE NOTHING TO DO WITH IT'

NEXT morning, headlines, questions in the papers: rumours in Whitehall. In my office, the scrambled, yellow-corded telephone kept ringing. No message from Roger had reached the Prime Minister's secretary.

Collingwood was reported to have said: 'This dance will no further go.' (The only historical reference the old man knew, said a cultivated voice at the other end of the wire.) He was said to be bearing Roger no malice, to be speaking of him with dispassion. He had heard – this I did not know for certain until later – about Roger and his nephew's wife. He took the news with stony lack of concern. 'I regard that as irrelevant,' he said. He turned out to have no feeling whatsoever for his nephew. That had been one of the unrealistic fears.

That morning, there was a strong rumour, which came from several sources, that some of Roger's supporters were calling on the Prime Minister. They were trying to arrange for the Prime Minister to interview him. He hadn't resigned yet. Another rumour: he was backing down. He wouldn't resign. He would announce that he had stressed one part of the White Paper at the expense of the whole. He had been wrong, but now faithfully accepted the compromise. He would go on implementing the compromise policies: or alternatively, he would take a dimmer job.

I heard nothing from him. I imagined that he was like the rest of us when the worst has happened, in moments still tantalised by hopes, almost by fulfilment, as though it had gone the other way: just as, when Sheila had betrayed me when I was a young man, I walked across the park deceived by gleams of happiness, as though I were going to her bed: just as, when an operation has failed, one lies in hospital and, now and then, has reveries of content, as though one were whole again.

He would be living with temptations. He wasn't different from most of those who have obtained any kind of power, petty or grand. He wanted to cling to it up to the end, beyond the end. If he went out now, untouched, unbudging, that was fine, that was in the style he would like for himself. And yet, he knew politics too well not to know that he might never come back. It would be bitter to behave as if he had been wrong, to be juggled with, put in an inconspicuous ministry for years: but perhaps that was the way to win. Would they let him? He must be thinking of the talks that day. Others would be counting the odds, with more degrees of freedom than he had. It might be good management to make sure that he was disposed of. Some might be sorry, but that didn't count. If they gave him a second chance, it wouldn't be because of sympathy, or even admiration. They owed him no support. It would be because he still had some power. They must be weighing up just how much influence he still possessed. Would he be more dangerous eliminated, or allowed to stay?

In the afternoon I attended a departmental meeting, Rose in the chair. He hadn't spoken to me that morning; he greeted me with overflowing politeness, as though I were a valuable acquaintance whom he had not seen for months. No one round the table could have guessed that we had been sitting side by side, in anxiety, the night before. He got through the business as accurately, as smoothly, as he would have done when I first sat under him, nearly twenty years before. Next year, he would be sixty, taking his last meeting in this room. He would go on like that till the last day. This particular afternoon, it wasn't even interesting business: it had to be done.

As soon as I returned to my room, my p.a. came in.

'There's a lady waiting for you,' she said. She looked inquisitive and apologetic. 'I'm afraid she seems rather upset.'

I asked who it was.

'She says her name is Mrs Smith.'

When I had told Ellen the result over the telephone, late the previous night, she had gasped. I had heard a gulp of tears before the receiver crashed down.

That afternoon, as she sat down in the chair beside my desk, her eyes were open, bloodshot, piteous and haughty. They reminded me of someone else's so hauntingly that I couldn't at first listen to what she was saying. Then, down the years, I had it. They were like my mother's, after an intolerable wound to her pride, as on the day my father went bankrupt.

She asked: 'What is he going to do?'

I shook my head. 'He's told me nothing.'

'I haven't been able to see him.'

She was crying out for sympathy, and yet she would reject it.

I said, as astringently as I could make myself:

'Yes, it's bad. It's part of the situation.'

'I mustn't see him till he's decided, one way or the other. You understand, don't you?'

'I think so.'

'I mustn't influence him. I mustn't even try.'

Then she gave a crisp, ironic, almost cheerful laugh, and added:

'Do you believe I could?'

I had seen her so often under strain. This day was the worst. But – just in that moment – I could feel how she behaved with Roger. Given a chance, she was, more than most of us, high-spirited and gay.

'Tell me something,' she said. 'Which is better for him?'

'What do you mean?'

'You know well enough.' Impatiently she explained herself. She might have been thought-reading my own speculations earlier that day. Until she met Roger, she was politically innocent. Now she could follow, by instinct, love and knowledge, the moves, the temptations, the choices. Her insight had told her much what mine did: except that she was certain that, if Roger wanted to climb down, they would welcome him.

'Which is better for him?'

'If I knew, which I don't, ought I to tell you?' I said.

'You're supposed to be a friend of his, aren't you?' she flared out.

'Fortunately,' this time I could let the temperature drop, and smile sarcastically back, 'I just don't know which is better.'

'But you think you do—'

I said: 'If we forget your side of it, then I think he'd probably, not certainly but probably, be wiser to stay if he can.'

'Why?'

'If he's out of politics, won't he feel he's wasting his life?'

'It means humiliating himself and crawling to them.' She flushed. She was hating 'them' with all the force of her nature.

'Yes, it means that.'

'Do you know that underneath he's a very proud man?'

I looked at her and said, 'Hasn't he learned to live with it?'

'Has anyone? Don't you believe that I'm proud too?'

She was speaking without constraint, self-effacingness stripped off, codes of behaviour fallen away. Her face had gone naked and wild.

'Yes,' I said, 'I believe that.'

'If he does throw it up and comes to me, will he ever forgive me?'

It was a new fear, different from that which she had once confided in her own flat, yet grown from the same root. Then she had been afraid that, once he had failed, he would blame her and be unable to endure her. Now that fear had gone. She believed that, whatever happened, he would need her. Yet the doubt, the cruelty, the heritage remained.

'You have nothing to do with it,' I said. 'If he had never fallen in love with any woman at all, he would have been in precisely the same position as he is today.'

'Are you dead sure?'

I said immediately, 'I am dead sure.'

I was saying what I almost believed. If she had not been sitting beside me, wounded and suspicious, waiting for the slightest qualification, I might have been less positive. Roger had stood much less of a chance of getting his policy through – I became convinced later, looking back – than we imagined when we were living in the middle of it. It was hard to believe that a personal chance, such as their love affair, had had any effect. And yet – their love affair had had an effect on him: without it, would he have acted precisely as he had?

'I am dead sure,' I repeated.

'Will he ever believe it?'

For an instant, I did not answer.

'Will he ever believe it?'

She was thinking of Roger coming to her, marrying her: the plain life, after Caro's home, the high hopes gone: the inquest on the past, the blame. She sat there for a moment or so, not speaking. Ellen, so self-effacing in public as to be inconspicuous, was filled with the beauty of violence, and perhaps with the beauty given her by the passion for sheer action, even if it were action destructive to herself, to all her hopes.

'I'm telling myself,' she said, 'that I ought to get out of it, now. Today.'

I said: 'Could you?' She stared at me, her eyes once more piteous and haughty. She asked: 'What is he going to do?'

CHAPTER XLV

A GOOD LETTER

SOME time after I had seen Ellen into a taxi, I was clearing up work in my office. The sky outside the window was already dark, the secretaries had gone home, all was quiet. The private phone buzzed. Would I call in on Roger before I left?

Through the corridors, deserted now, I trod out the long, maze-like walk. One or two doors were open, lights of offices shone out: always the offices of the top echelon, staying late. Douglas was working, but I did not look in to say good-night. I went straight into Roger's room. From the reading-lamp shone out a cone of light which glared off the paper, was sopped up by the blotting-pad. Roger stood up, looming against the window. For the first time since we had been introduced, years before, he gripped my hand.

'Well?' he said.

I was taken aback by his vigorous, active manner. This was like a conversation which one had rehearsed in one's head and which was going wrong. I muttered something lame, about it being a pity.

'Never mind about that,' he said.

'Well?' he said again. He snapped his fingers.

For an instant I thought he wanted me to take the initiative. It might have been the beginning of a business deal. But I was mishearing him. He went on:

'It's time I thought it out again from the beginning, isn't it?' He gave out a special kind of exhilaration. The exhilaration of failure: the freedom of being bare to the world.

He was certain where he was, because there was nothing else to be certain of. I thought I knew him. Ellen knew him better. But the way we had seen him that day was not the way he saw himself. The hedges, the duplicities of his nature – either they did not exist for him that day, or he saw through them. This was nothing like the night when David Rubin had begged him to back down, and Roger had played with him.

Across the pool of light, he began to talk. To begin with, as though it were obvious and had to be put out of the way, he said that he would have to go. There was no argument. He was out: so was what he had tried to do.

Then he broke out: 'But not for good. Not for long. Someone's going to do it. Maybe I still can.'

It was the last thing I expected. He was talking with a curious impersonality about the future. He did not mention his wife or Ellen, as though ruling out his self-bound concerns, the concern of his own guilt. He did say, as an objective fact, as part of the situation, that he would be on his own: without influence, without powerful friends. Even without money. He would have to start again. 'It will be harder,' he said. 'It'll be harder than if I'd never done anything at all.'

He looked at me with a caustic, open smile.

'You don't think I stand a chance, do you?'

Kindnesses, personal relations, had dropped away. I answered: 'Not much.'

'Someone's going to do it. All we want is time, and luck, and something in the air. Someone's going to do it.'

Just as when he had been at the peak of his power, when it seemed that the Prime Minister and Collingwood were befriending him, he talked about the political process with relaxation, with detachment. Could anyone else have done better than he had done? Could he have avoided the mistakes that he had made? What about mine? If we had handled Brodzinski better? How far did personalities count? Nothing like as much as one liked to think. Only in those circumstances when the hinge is oiled, but the door may swing or not. If that isn't the situation, then no personality is going to make more than an ineffectual noise.

He wasn't asking for comfort. He wasn't even asking for my view. He was speaking as though to himself, in the quiet room. He said, If one goes too far, one's ruined. If one doesn't go at all, one might as well not be there.

He said, Trying may have value. Even when it has failed. The situation will never be quite the same again. He said (I remembered when he had first said it): The first thing is to get the power. The next thing is to do something with it. He said: Someone is going to do what I tried to do. I don't know whether it'll be me.

He spoke with simplicity, almost with purity. It was hard for anyone outside to find within him that pure and simple feeling. He cared, less than many men, what his own feelings were. He had felt most temptations and passions, but not that kind of self-regard. And yet, he wanted something for himself. When he said, he wanted to get power and 'do something with it', he meant that he wanted a justification, a belief that he was doing something valuable with his life. He also wanted a justification, in an older and deeper sense. He wanted something like a faith, a faith in action. He had lurched about until he found just that. Despite his compromises and callousnesses – or to an extent intertwined with them – he had believed in what he was doing. Those round him might suspect him, but there, and there alone, he did not suspect himself.

The irony was that, if our suspicions had been true, he would have been a more successful politician. He might even, within the limits of those years, have done more good.

It was getting on for eight o'clock. All of a sudden, Roger's manner changed. He pushed one foot against the desk and said, as though we were at work once more: 'I want you to read this.'

All this time, a letter had been waiting in front of him. It began, 'Dear Prime Minister', in his own bold holograph, and continued in typescript. It was a good letter. There was not a sign of reproach or rancour, either overt or hinted at. It said that Roger had been honoured to be the Prime Minister's colleague. He was sorry that his policy had evoked so much dissension, and that he had emphasised parts of it to an extent which his colleagues could not share, so that both it and he had now become liabilities to the Government. He continued to believe in his policy. He could not persuade himself that it had been wrong. Since he could not honestly change his mind, there was only one course open to him, which he was sure the Prime Minister would sympathise with and understand. He hoped to be of some use to the Prime Minister and the Government as a private member.

There the typing ended. In Roger's hand, half-way down the third page, was written, black and firm: 'Yours ever, Roger Quaife.'

As soon as I lifted my eyes he said: 'Will that do?'

'It's good,' I said.

'It will be accepted, you know' (he meant the resignation).

'Yes, it'll be accepted,' I said.

'With slightly excessive haste.' We gazed at each other across the desk.

'Well,' he said, 'you'd better see it go.'

One of the red despatch boxes was standing beside the telephones. From his hip-pocket he brought out a bunch of keys and unlocked it. He did it with the ceremonial air of a man who is enjoying a privilege. Not many men had ever revelled more in having the liberty of the despatch boxes, of being in possession of such a key. He was enjoying the privilege, the physiognomic charm of office, even then.

Punctiliously he placed the letter in the box, and relocked it. He pressed a button, and his private secretary – who this last week could have had no time to call his own – opened the door.

'Will you see this goes to the Prime Minister?' said Roger. He spoke in a matter-of-fact tone.

The young man, thirtyish, a high-class civil servant on the climb, acknowledged it with similar matter-of-fact politeness. It might have been any of the messages he had transmitted for Roger these last years, or would go on transmitting for years to come, although he must have been wondering now whether this was the end, and who his new master would be.

The door closed. Roger smiled.

'I might have changed my mind,' he said. 'That would have been unfortunate.'

His voice, his whole expression, had gone tired. He had to force himself to speak again, to produce a spurt of vigour.

'I'm sorry', he sa i, 'to have got some of our friends into trouble.' He was trying to speak with warmth, with intimacy: but he couldn't do it any more. He tried again when he said: 'I'm sorry to have done you harm.'

'That's nothing.'

'I'm sorry.'

After that, he did not want to make another effort. He sat back, waiting to sit in that room alone. As I was leaving he said: 'I shan't be available for some time. I'm going away.'

CHAPTER XLVI

ANOTHER CHOICE

My own choice was clear. Margaret and I dismissed it in half an hour and then, friction-free, stood ourselves a drink. It seemed to both of us that we might be on the eve of a holiday, cases packed and labelled, the car ordered for nine in the morning, the ship awaiting us, rest in the sun.

I waited three days. In that time, Roger's resignation was announced and the name of his successor. It was all assimilated in the papers, Whitehall, the clubs, as though it had happened months before. I waited three days, then asked for an appointment with Hector Rose.

It was a quarter past ten in the morning. In the park below the mist was clearing. On Rose's desk a bowl of hyacinths breathed out the scent of other interviews, of headaching lunches long ago.

I said, the moment I sat down: 'It's time for me to go now.'

The elegant posturing was washed away; his concentration was complete.

'You mean—?'

'I mean, I've outlived my usefulness here.'

'I should have thought', said Rose, 'that that was overstating the case.'

'You know as well as I do that I'm identified with this *débâcle*.'

'To an extent,' Rose replied, arms folded, 'that is unfortunately true.'

'It is entirely true.'

'I don't think, however, that you need take it too tragically.'

'I'm not taking it tragically,' I said. 'I'm just commenting, I have to do business for you with people we both know. In their view, I've backed the wrong horse. Fairly openly. It wouldn't have mattered so much doing it openly, if it hadn't been the wrong horse.'

Rose gave an arctic smile.

'It's simple,' I said. 'I should be no good with these people any more. It's time to go.'

There was a long silence. Rose considered, his pale eyes still on me, unblinking, expressionless. At last he began to speak, fluently but with deliberation.

'You have always had a tendency, if I may say so with respect, to permit yourself a certain degree of over-simplification. I can see that you have occasionally acted in a fashion which would have been, shall I say, unusual, if you had been a career civil servant. That has applied particularly in the matter of the unfortunate Quaife. But I might remind you that there have been other examples, during the course of your valuable activities. I think you should acknowledge that the service is not so finicky as our critics are fond of telling us. The service has been prepared to put up with what might be, by some standards, a certain trifling amount of embarrassment. It has been considered that we have gained through your having taken some rather curious liberties. In fact, we have formed the firm opinion that your presence was very much more advantageous than your absence. I dislike stressing the point, but we have expressed our appreciation in the only way open to us.'

I said, 'You've treated me generously. I know that.'

He bowed his head. He continued, just as precisely: 'I can see that, after these recent events, it wouldn't be in your interests or ours for you to undertake certain commissions for us, including perhaps some which you would have carried through with your usual distinction. I suggest, though, that this is really not serious *sub specie aeternitatis*. It ought not to be beyond the wit of man to make a slight redistribution of your functions. We shall still retain the benefit of your services, at places where we continue to need them. And where, you will understand, though this isn't an occasion for flattery, we can't comfortably afford to dispense with them yet awhile.'

He was speaking with fairness, and perhaps with justice. He was also speaking as he might have done at any time during our twenty years' connection. Within a few months he would himself be retiring from the service – the service which had not given him his full reward, certainly not his desire. If I left a vacant niche, it would soon be no concern of his. Nevertheless, he was still saying 'we', taking care of service needs years ahead. He hadn't, by so much as a flick, recognised that for a short time, for a few days and hours, we had been, not colleagues, but allies. That was wiped out. He was speaking with absolute fairness, but between us there had come down once more, like a curtain, the utter difference in our natures, the uneasiness, perhaps the dislike.

I thanked him, paused, and said: 'No. But that doesn't alter the position. I want to go.'

'You really want to go?'

I nodded.

'Why?'

'I want more time. You know I have wanted that for years.'

Yes, he knew as well as I did that I was worried lest some of my books shouldn't get written.

'Is that all?'

'Perhaps not.'

'You are thinking of taking a hand—'

'There are some things I want to help get done. I shall have to be a private citizen again.'

'Will it be so very private, my dear Lewis?' Rose was watching me carefully.

He asked: 'I take it, there is no financial problem?'

I said no. He knew it in advance. He wasn't above a dash of envy because I had been lucky. By this time, my writing had brought in largish sums. Himself, though he had been expensively educated, he had no money. When he retired, he would have to live on his pension.

'You intend to go?'

'Yes.'

He gazed at me. When it came to men's actions, he was a good judge. He shrugged his shoulders.

'Right,' he said. 'Well, it remains for us to make it as painless as possible.'

There was another silence, not a long one.

He said, without emphasis: 'I should like to put one consideration before you. If you resign now, it won't pass unnoticed. You are fairly conspicuous. There will be those who will be malicious enough to draw certain conclusions. They might even hint that your departure is not unconnected with recent differences of opinion. And it wouldn't be altogether easy to prove them wrong.'

He went on: 'That would be somewhat embarrassing for us. No doubt you will make your own view heard in your own good time. But I suggest you have some obligation to give us a decent interval. You've been working with us for a long time. It wouldn't seem proper if you made matters awkward for us by a dramatic resignation.'

I did not reply. Rose went on:

'I also suggest it wouldn't be good for you. I expect it affects you very little. You have other things to occupy you. I understand that. But still, you've done your service to the state. It would be a pity to spoil it now. Whoever one is, I think it's wrong to leave a job with hard feelings. It's bad for the soul to leave under a cloud.'

I could not tell whether he was being considerate. His manner, which had become more than ever frigid, made the words sound scornful or artificial. Yet he was insistent.

I said:

'How long should I stay?'

'The end of the year? Is that asking too much?'

I said I would do it. Rose accepted the bargain, businesslike, without thanks. It was only when I went towards the door that he began to thank me profusely, not for meeting his wishes or accepting his advice, but for the somewhat more commonplace feat of walking along the corridor to see him.

CHAPTER XLVII

NIGHT SKY OVER LONDON

IT was a warm summer night, a year and a half after Roger's resignation, when Margaret and I arrived at South Street for a party at Diana's. Not that either of us was thinking of the past. This was just an engagement, it wasn't more significant than others, it was part of the to-ing and fro-ing. The children were at school, we were free, it was pleasant to drive round the park through the soft indigo evening.

In the drawing-room upstairs, the guests clattered and drank, keeping eyes alert for the latest entrant. There was a simmer of pleasure as they moved around, the pleasure of being inside the circle, like being in a party on shipboard, with the sea pattering below. It was all still going on, I thought. Going on as, for most of them, it had always been: and as, in their expectations, it always would.

I was curious, as at any of Diana's parties, about who was in favour now. Collingwood stood by the fireplace, sempiternal, satisfied, unvocal. For a while Monty Cave, who had been promoted that spring, was at his side. Cave had now outdistanced his competitors: all Diana's influence was behind him: he was being talked of as the next Chancellor. People were continuing to speculate whether Diana would marry him, but, in spite of her resolve to break away from loneliness, she, who wasn't used to dithering, went on doing so. She was hard-baked enough about the power game, but she couldn't make herself hard-baked about a second marriage. She was still capable of dreams of love. Her will deserted her. She had had a happy marriage and longed for another. She was not ready for one which was not real.

Lenton came in, did not stay long, but found time to talk, modestly, unobtrusively, to his hostess. As Prime Minister he might be busy, but he was teaching some lessons to men who thought him commonplace. One was, never make enemies if you can help it, and above all, never make enemies by neglect. Before he went, he had beamed, porcine and attentive, at each of his supporters. I noticed him whispering to Douglas Osbaldiston, whom I had not seen at Diana's before, and who, years before, when his wife was well and we were better friends, used to tease Margaret and me about our excursions into the high life.

Diana kept up with the times, I thought. She used not to pay attention to top civil servants, but here was not only Douglas, but one of his co-equals at the Treasury. Douglas had duly returned there, and had one of the top jobs created for him. All that Hector Rose, now retired, had wished for from the service, Douglas had obtained. Margaret continued to visit his wife in hospital, and, in the months since I left Whitehall, he had frequently dined with us. Yet, between him and me, the breach wasn't healed. He had tried; the coldness was one-sided, the fault was mine.

From the ruck of the party, Sammikins halloo'ed at me. He was looking for someone to take to Pratt's, to finish off the evening. He wasn't having any luck: he had just been turned down for the sixth time, he announced at the top of his voice, his laugh ringing out like a spirited but inappropriate imitation of Roland's horn at Roncesvalles. Caro went by at that moment, magnificently pretty, looking as though she were carefree. She tapped her brother on the shoulder, threw a cordial word to Margaret, then spun round at the greeting of somebody else and addressed herself to him with vivacity. She did not come near me, nor Margaret, again that night.

I felt my arm gripped. It was Lord Lufkin. He said in a meaningful and grinding tone: 'That man Hood.' The tone was meaningful, but for an instant I was lost. Quite lost. The party lapped and hooted round me. All this was still going on. I had forgotten. But Lufkin did not forget.

'I've got him,' he said.

Lufkin was obsessive enough to go in for revenge. No one else in his position would have done the same. It seemed fantastic that a great tycoon should have spent his energy – not just for a day, but for weeks and months – working out plans for getting a middle-rank employee of another firm dismissed from his job. Yet that was precisely what he had done. He did not regard it as revenge, but as natural justice. When he spoke of it, he did not exhibit triumph or even relish. It was something he had to do, and was able to do. It was part of the rightness of things.

In the roundabout of the party, among the groomed and prosperous faces, for the first time that night I thought of Roger. He was not there. He would not have been invited. If he had been invited, it was not likely that he would have come. Margaret had asked him and Ellen often to our house, but they had accepted only once. Face to face, he was as warm and easy-natured as he had ever been: and yet he shied, like one with an active phobia, from the places and people he had known best in his period of power.

He was still in the House. But, now the divorces had gone through and he had married Ellen, his constituency party would not run him at the next election. He had not lost his hope. He and Ellen were living modestly, in an ambience quite unlike that of Lord North Street. His income, such as it was, came from two or three directorships which Lufkin had stiffly but judiciously put in his way. As for the marriage, we had not seen them at close enough quarters to be anything like certain, but Margaret, prejudiced against it, had nevertheless come to believe that it was firm and good.

Ellen she had not quite brought herself to like. This was partly out of feeling for Caro and partly, I thought to myself with a degree of inner amusement, because in some of the qualities of their natures, she and Ellen were not altogether dissimilar. Both were active, both were capable of violent feeling, both were natural partisans, though Ellen had nothing of the easy flow inbred in Margaret. 'She is a one-man dog, you know,' Margaret had once said to me with a rueful grin, 'she hasn't anything left over for the rest of us. And that I find a little hard to take. Still, it's not hard for him to take, and I suppose that's the important thing.'

Parting from Lufkin, I went through the heat and dazzle, out to the balcony in search of her. There she was, in a group with Francis Getliffe and others, and I took her aside. Lufkin's news filled my mind, absented me from the party. I felt as though I had suddenly recaptured a long-dead grief or joy, and I had to tell her.

She listened, looking at me and then, into the brilliant room. She knew, more quickly than I did, that I was not really telling her about Lufkin or Hood, but about Roger's failure and our own. I was really speaking of what we had tried, and failed, to do.

'Yes,' said Margaret, 'we need a victory.'

Her spirit was strong. She was looking back into the room. Just as I had done earlier, she was thinking how it all went on. 'We need a victory,' she said. She was not giving up, nor letting me.

Francis Getliffe joined us. For an instant Margaret and I stopped talking, awkwardly. We might have been caught gossiping about him, using his name in malice. Francis wasn't with us any more. He had given up. Not that he had changed his opinions: but he could not endure another struggle. He had retired to his house in Cambridge and to his research. Already, that evening, he had talked about a new idea with as much excitement as when he was young.

Defeat can cut into friendships, I was thinking, as much as being on different sides. Francis and I had been intimate for thirty years. Yet now part of the spontaneity had had to go, not much, nothing like so much as with Douglas, but still enough to notice. It was a tiny price to pay for having gone through the struggle: but still, it was a price.

We talked a little, the three of us, of the college and Cambridge. We went to the end of the balcony. Over the garden, over the rooftops, shone the rusty, vivid night-sky of London, the diffused recognition of all those lives. We talked, more eagerly now, of our children, with the special tenderness of old friends who have seen each other's families growing up. The memory of the struggle, even the reason for it, dimmed down. We talked of the children, and were happy. The only puzzle remaining to us that night was Penelope. She and Arthur Plimpton were both in the United States and they had both got married, but not to each other. Francis gave a grim, quixotic smile and thought it was a joke against himself.

Under the town's resplendent sky we talked of the children and their future. We talked as though the future were easy and secure, and as though their lives would bring us joy.

The Sleep of Reason

The Sleep of Reason

1963 – 64

CONTENTS

Contents

PART FOUR. RESPONSIBILITY

PART FIVE. THE FLOW RETURNING

The Sleep of Reason

PART ONE

TRICKS OF TIME

CHAPTER I

VISIT TO A GRANDFATHER

THAT afternoon I had been walking with my son in what for me were familiar streets, streets of the town where I was born. I had taken him there only once before, when he was an infant. Now he was nearly fifteen, and we spoke the same language. I was taunting him because he had seen the 'pretty England' and nothing of the rest; until that afternoon he had never seen a provincial town like this. He grinned. Whose fault was that? he said.

And yet the town was not so unpretty: shops glittered and shone, well-dressed women walked the pavements, fresh-skinned girls in their spring frocks: cars jarred and halted, bumper to stern, hoods dazzling in a burst of sunshine. Once I had heard a fellow citizen called Sawbridge saying, with equal disapproval of the United States and his native town, that you could put the place down in the middle of America and no one would know the difference. It was nearly accurate, not quite. You could still, if you knew your way about, trace some of the streets of the old market town: narrow harsh streets with homely names, like Pocklington's Walk, along which I had gone to work forty years before, craving not to be unknown, craving to get out of there. That I did not explain to my son Charles, who was discreetly puzzled as to why we were wandering through a quarter which, to any unbeglamoured eye, was sombre and quite unusually lacking in romance.

However, when we returned to one of the bright shopping streets, and someone greeted me by name, he did ask, after we had passed on: 'What does that feel like?'

Probably it had not been an acquaintance from the past: this was 1963, I had left the town for good in the twenties: probably it was what Charles was used to, a result of photographs or the mass media. But he was perceptive, he guessed that being picked out in this place might pluck a nerve. Nevertheless, he was surprised by my reply.

289

'To tell you the honest truth,' I said, 'it makes me want to hide.'

He glanced at me sidelong with dark searching eyes. He knew that, as a rule, I was not self-conscious and was used to the public life. He did not understand it. But if he didn't understand it, neither did I. I couldn't have explained what I had just said. It seemed perverse and out of character. Yet it was quite true.

Charles thought of pressing me, then decided against. The clock on the town hall said a quarter to four; it was time for us to make our way to my father's house, or to be more exact, my father's room. Charles had seen his grandfather only once, on his one other visit to the town, when he was three years old. To anyone outside, that must have sounded as though we had been heartless, not only without instinctive ties but without responsibility. After all, I had been lucky, my wife and family lived a privileged life. How could I bear neglecting the old man? In fact, my father had his own views. He seemed, and was, the most affable and gentle of human beings. But he just wanted to be left alone, to get on with his own mysterious concerns, whatever they were and if they existed. My brother Martin had tried to persuade him to live with them in Cambridge: I had wanted to have him in London. Not a bit of it. With simple passive resistance, he refused to move. He would not even take money. I had made more than enough, but he would not accept a penny, except for a bottle of port at Christmas. With his old age pension and the rent from his lodger, he had, he said, quite enough for his needs.

He was, I thought, the most self-sufficient man I had come across. He was amiably and genuinely uninterested in his grandchildren. Even that afternoon, I had had to force him to let Charles and me come to tea. I was having to pay visits to the town every three months or so, on a piece of minor duty. This particular visit coincided with Charles being at home on holiday. So I brought him up for the day, and had insisted that my father invite us. After all, he was in his late eighties: I had my share of piety (from which my father seemed singularly free), and it might be Charles's last chance to talk to him.

We took the bus out to the suburbs, on what in my childhood would have been the old tram route: red brick, the gaol, the gasworks, less change here than in the middle of the town. And when we got off and walked into the back-streets, there was less change still: the doctor's house, the cluster of shops, the chapel, the terraced houses up the rise. Not that I was stirred by memory: I had seen it too recently for that. Instead, I looked up at the clouds, low on the south-west wind, breathed in the soft spring air, and said:

'I like this Atlantic weather.'

'Meteorological fiend,' said my son, with a friendly gibing smile. He had developed the theory that I, the child of cities, could not resist an obsessive interest in climatic phenomena: and that this was not shared by all who heard the results, including himself. It was the kind of sarcastic banter that came easily to him. I answered in kind, pointing out that at least one person had shared my meteorological enthusiasm, and that was one of the few men whom I actively detested.

He was smiling, as we went past the two-storey terrace, front doors opening on to the pavement. It was no use preparing him for what he was going to meet: he would certainly find my father odd, possibly a strain, but that he would have to take. At the end of the row we came to a pair of larger houses, joined together. I pointed to the nearer one, and told him that was where I was born. It was dilapidated, but, to judge from the television aerials on the roof, inhabited by a couple of families. On the strip of earth inside the railings – which my mother used to call the front garden – the laburnum tree had become a blackened stump.

With a concentrated gaze Charles studied the front-room window, the peeling paint, the carved inscription between the houses, *Albert Villas 1860*, and said nothing at all. Then he asked:

'Could we go in, do you think?'

'I don't think so, do you?'

'Perhaps they wouldn't like it.'

The next house along the road had been built in the same period, but was larger and stood on its own. In my childhood it had belonged to my Aunt Milly's husband: he had been a building contractor in a small way, and they were less poor than we were, and had often (offending my mother's pride) been obliged to support us. When my mother died, by this time nearly forty years before, my father had gone to live with Aunt Milly, who was his sister. There he had stayed. Aunt Milly's husband died, then she herself. They were childless, and, though she had willed their savings to various temperance societies, the house had come to my father. He had promptly let it off, keeping one room for himself: and there he had lived for the last twenty years.

I led the way to that single room – down an entry, through a gate, into a yard paved with flagstones. The architecture of Aunt Milly's house, like that of my mother's, was bizarre, as though space didn't matter and the more levels the better, so that there was a one-storey range, with a twenty-foot-high chimney, floors at yard-level: while five steps up was a french window, opening straight into my father's room, which led into the main body of the house. Behind the french window one could see a glow on the ceiling, fluctuating, not very bright although the afternoon was dark, which must come from my father's fire.

'There he is, I expect,' I said to Charles.

We went up the steps, and I rapped on the window. (There was a much quicker and more orthodox method of entry through the front door, but my father did not like being a trouble to his lodger.) Shuffle of steps. Rattle of handles. The two sides of the window opened, and in between them, facing us, my father stood.

'Well, I declare,' he said.

His first action was to peer up at Charles, making tunnels with his fingers over his spectacles as though sighting some far-distant object.

'I shall want a telescope to look at him,' my father said.

I was six feet, and Charles was only an inch or two shorter. My father was a little man. In my childhood he had claimed to five feet four: but now, with extreme old age, he had shrunk an inch or more. Standing there, old wide trousers flopping on his boots, his head seemed to come no higher than our chests.

'I want a telescope, that's what I do.' He went on clowning. He had always clowned, as far back as I could remember; he had been cheerful in his clowning then, just as he was now.

After we had sat down in the crowded little room – Charles on a chair on one side of the fireplace, my father on the other, me on the sofa where he slept at night – he was still talking about telescopes, but in a different vein.

'You know, Lewis, I've always thought I should like one.'

I asked him why: I knew that tone by heart.

'Well, you never know what you might find out.'

He had day-dreamed all his life. Just for an instant he was the supreme astronomer, discovering – at an advanced age and to his own mild surprise – new secrets of the universe. Or perhaps overturning established conceptions, an activity for which he had always had a secret fancy. All through my boyhood he had read travel books, often the same book over and over again: then he was the fearless single-handed explorer, going where no white man had ever trodden – he had a special feeling that the Amazonian jungle was the place for him. I had discovered, on my last visit, that he still borrowed travel books from the library at the corner of the road. As he sat in his chair, I could see a dozen or so books on the shelf behind him: they seemed the only books in the room, the only ones he possessed or had borrowed. How many of those were about travel? Or what other sorts of daydreams did he have?

'You never know what you might find out,' he chortled. 'But I expect I should find out something wrong!'

He went on chortling with satisfaction. He hadn't spoken out of self-pity, or at least, if he had, it was a singular kind of self-pity, which consisted of referring to himself as though he were the most ludicrous of jokes.

He was, as usual, happy. Sitting beneath the mantelpiece, on which stood a marble clock flanked by photographs, some of the choral society of which he had been secretary so long, together with one of my mother, he did not look his age. His hair was white, but he had lost none of it: his great drooping moustache still, amid the white, kept a touch of ginger: the lenses of his spectacles, which he could not manage to put on straight, had not been changed since middle age. His pop eyes remained innocently amused. By some genetic fluke, he had missed the deep blue irises which were dominant in the family: his father had had them and all the rest of us: Charles's, as he watched my father vigilantly across the fireplace, in that light looked not indigo but black. My father's had not faded, but were very light, which made him appear more innocent. Sitting down he also appeared bigger than he was, since his legs were short and his head out of proportion large.

A kettle was boiling on the hob between them. My father had so far paid no attention to Charles, except once or twice to address him, with impersonal cheerfulness, by my Christian name or my brother Martin's. Charles, on the other hand, was paying complete attention to him. Charles had met a lot of people, some formidable, many what the world called successful: but his grandfather was different from any. This was a test, not only of instinctual ties, but also of insight. At the same time Charles, I had no doubt, was listening to my father's soft midland accent, of which Charles could hear the vestigial overtones in me.

'Well, young man,' said my father, abandoning nomenclature as he spoke to Charles, 'I expect you're ready for your tea, aren't you? I know I am.'

Politely Charles admitted that he was.

'I'm always ready for my tea,' said my father. 'If I can't do anything else, then I can always get rid of my tea.'

He hooted with obscure gratification, and sang a few bars of a song I didn't know, in a voice still disconcertingly strong. Efficiently, neat-fingeredly, like a man used to looking after himself, he made the tea.

'One, two, three spoonfuls – and one for the pot,' he chanted. He shuffled round the room, and produced the tea things. He produced also a large plate of cakes, jam tarts, custard tarts, éclairs, marzipan. 'I always say,' my father remarked, 'there's nothing like something sweet to your tea.'

I did not agree, but Charles did. He might be perceptive beyond his years, but he had a healthy fifteen-year-old appetite: and so, while I drank a cup of tea and smoked a cigarette, the grandfather and grandson, with over seventy years between them, sat on opposite sides of the fireplace – in silence, except for appreciative lip-noises under the moustache – eating cakes. Not just one cake each, but two, three, four, half-a-dozen.

When they had finished the plateful, my father sighed with content and turned mild eyes on me.

'You made a mistake there, Lewis. They went down all right, confound me if they didn't.'

Then he seemed to feel that some concession was called for.

'Still,' he said, 'you've got on well, I must say that.'

He had, I was sure, only the haziest notion of my life. He may have realised that I had played some part in affairs: he ought to have known that I was no longer poor, for I had told him so. Certainly he had never read a word I had written. Charles, still vigilant, was wearing a surreptitious smile. Unlike my father, Charles knew a good deal about what had happened to me, the rough as well as the smooth. He knew that, since I left the official life, some attacks had followed me, one or two predictable, and one based upon a queer invention. Charles did not, as some sons would, imagine that I was invulnerable: on the contrary, he believed that this last situation he would have handled better himself.

'I often wish,' my father continued, 'that your mother had lived to see how you've got on.'

Yes, I did too. Yes, I thought, she would have revelled in a lot of it – the title, the money, the well-known name. Yet, like Charles – though without the sophistication – she would have known it all; once again, the rough as well as the smooth. Anyone who raised a voice against me, she, that fierce and passionate woman, would have wanted to claw, not as a figure of speech but in stark flesh, with her own nails.

'That's how I like to think of her, you know,' my father said, pointing to the mantelpiece. 'Not as she was at the end.'

I got up, took the photograph down, and showed it to Charles. It was a hand-tinted photograph, taken somewhere round 1908, when they were a little better off than ever after, and when I was three years old. My mother used to call it the 'garden' photograph, and, when she was dying, asked me to remember her as she looked there. She was wearing a dress with leg-of-mutton sleeves: her black hair and high colouring stood out, so did her aquiline beak of a nose. She looked both handsome, which she could be, and proud, which she always was, sometimes satanically so. As I remarked to Charles, it wasn't a bad picture.

What my father had said might have sounded sentimental, like a gentle old man lamenting the past and the only woman, the only happiness, he had ever known. On the contrary. My father was as little sentimental as a man could reasonably be. The truth was different. What he had said, was a plain statement. That was how, when he thought of her at all – he lived in the present and their marriage was a long time ago – he preferred to think of her. But it had been an ill-tuned marriage: for her, much worse than that. He had been the 'wrong man', she used to confide in me, and in my childhood I took this to mean that he was ineffectual, too amiable for the world's struggle, unable to give her the grandeur that somehow she thought should be hers by right. Later I thought, remembering what I had submerged, that there was more to it. I could recall bitter words over a maid (yes, on something like £250 a year, before the first world war, she kept a maid): I guessed, though I should never know for certain, that under his mild and beaming aspect there was a disconcerting ardour, which came as a surprise, though a pleasant one, to himself. As their marriage got worse, he had, when I was quite young, found his own consolations. Since she died, it had puzzled me that he had not married again. Yet again I guessed that in a cheerful covert fashion he had found what he wanted: and that, on a good many nights, he had returned to this little room raising his robust baritone with a satisfaction, as though singing meaninglessly to himself, which as a child I did not begin to understand.

Charles was still looking at the photograph. My father made an attempt to address him by name, gave it up, but nevertheless spoke to him:

'She always used to tell me "Bertie, don't be such a donkey! Don't be such a donkey!" Milly used to do the same. They always used to say I was a donkey!'

The reminiscence seemed to fill him with extreme pleasure. Charles looked up, and felt called upon to smile. But he gave me a side glance, as though for once he was somewhat at a loss.

The clock on the mantelpiece, in measured strokes, struck five.

'Solemn-toned clock,' said my father with approval. 'Solemn-toned clock.' That was a ritual phrase which I must have heard hundreds, perhaps thousands, of times. When she was hopeful, and her hopes though precarious were inextinguishable, it used to make my mother smile: but in a crisis it made her break out in jangled nerves, in disappointment at all the hopes frustrated. That evening, however, the sound of the clock set my father going: now he was really on his own; so far as he had any self-esteem, here it was. For the clock had been presented to him after a period of service as secretary to a male voice choir: and he had been secretary to similar choirs ever since, for nearly sixty years in all. This had been the theme of his existence, outside himself, and he proposed to talk about it. Which, with amiable, pattering persistence, he duly did. It was all still going on. Not so flourishing as in the past. What with television – he had refused to let us buy him a set, though there was a sound radio in a corner of the room – people weren't so willing to give the time as in the old days. Still, some were keen. There had been changes. Male voice choirs weren't so popular, therefore he had brought in women. (That I had known; it had been the one political exertion of my father's life; it took me back for an instant to my speculations of a few moments before.) He had managed to keep a group of twenty or so together. Nowadays they met for rehearsal each Sunday after service at St Mary's, one of the churches in the town.

It was a quiet little obsession, but it gave him all the enjoyment of an obsession. I didn't want to cut him short, but at last he flagged slightly. I could ask a question. Wasn't St Mary's a longish journey for him? It must be all of three miles.

'Oh,' he said, 'I get a bus that takes me near enough.'

'But coming back late at night?'

'Well, one of our members, Mr Rattenbury' – (I wondered if Charles noticed that 'Mr' which my father had applied to each of his male acquaintances all his life) – 'he usually gives me a lift.'

'But if you don't get a lift?'

'Then I just have to toddle home on my own two pins.'

He rose from his chair, and exemplified – without complaint, in fact with hilarity – very short steps on very short legs.

'Isn't that a bit much?' At his age, that was an understatement, but I couldn't say any more. Even at this, his face was clouded, and I wasn't going to spoil his pleasure.

'It's a bit slippy in winter, you know. But I get here. I shouldn't be here now if I didn't, should I?'

That struck him as the most clinching of retorts. He was delighted with it. It set him off chanting loudly: Anyway – the summer – is – coming – anyway – the – spring – is – here.

Then he seemed to feel that he had certain responsibilities for Charles

which he had not discharged. He had given him cakes. Was that enough?
My father looked puzzled: then suddenly his face shone with preternatural
worldliness.

'Young man,' he said, 'I want to give you a piece of advice.'

Charles leaned gravely towards him.

'I expect,' the old man said, 'your father gives you some money now
and then, doesn't he?'

Charles misunderstood, and was a shade embarrassed. 'I'm quite all
right for money, thank you very much, sir.'

'Of course you are! Of course you are! I'm going to give you a piece of
advice that I gave your father a long time ago.' Now I myself remembered:
he had the memory for detail long past that I had seen before in the very
old. 'I always tell people,' he said, as though he were day-dreaming again,
this time of himself as the successful financier, deferred to by less experienced men, 'I always tell people that you never ought to go about
without a few pound notes sewn in a place where you're never going to
lose it. I told your father a long time ago, and I hope he listened to me,
that he ought to have five of his pound notes sewn into the seat of his
trousers. Mind you, five pounds doesn't go as far now as it did then. If I
were you, I should get someone to sew fifteen or twenty pounds into the
seat of your trousers. I expect you can lay your hands on twenty pound
notes, can't you? Well, you do what I tell you. You never know when
they'll come in useful. You must think of me when you find they've got
you out of a tight corner.'

Charles, his face controlled, promised that he would.

My father exuded content. Charles and I stretched our legs, getting
ready to go. When we were putting on our coats, opening the french
window so that the evening air struck cold into the stuffy, odorous little
room, I told my father that I would drop in during my next visit to the
town.

'Oh, don't put yourself out for me, Lewis,' he said, as though he quite
liked my company but even more preferred not to be disturbed. With his
beaming innocent smile he waved us out.

Charles and I didn't speak until we had emerged from the entry back
into the road. There was a light, I noticed, two houses along, in what
had been our old 'front room'.

It had been raining, the sky was bright again. Charles gave me a curious
smile.

'Life goes on,' he said.

I took him the longer way round to the bus stop, past the branch library, past the red brick church (1900-ish, pitchpine and stained-glass windows, scene both of splendours and miseries for my mother), down the hill to the main road. From the grass in the garden-patches there came a fresh, anxiety-lifting, rainwashed smell. We were each of us silent, not uncomfortably so, but still touched by the afternoon.

After a time Charles said:

'It wasn't exactly what I expected.'

'You mean, he wasn't?'

'No, I didn't mean that, quite.'

I asked him another question, but he shook his head. He was pre-occupied, just as I had been in the middle of the town, and this time it was he who did not want to be pressed.

On the top of the bus, on the way to the railway station, he made one reference to my father's practical advice, smiled, and that was all. We chatted on the station, waiting for his train: he was going home alone, since I had an appointment in the town next day. As we were chatting, quite casually, the station's red brick glaring at us, the sulphurous smoke swirling past, just for once that day, memory, direct memory, gave me its jab. I was standing in that station, years before, going to London, nerves tingling, full of hope.

The train was coming in. Charles's education had been different from mine, but he was no more inhibited than I was, and we hugged each other in the Russian fashion as we said goodbye.

CHAPTER II

A YOUNG WOMAN IN LOVE

AFTER leaving my son, I took a taxi to the Vice-Chancellor's Residence. In my youth, there wouldn't have been such a place or such a person: but in the fifties the old College of Art and Technology, where I had once attended George Passant's lectures, had been transmogrified into one of the newest crop of universities. In fact, it was for that reason that I made my periodical visits to the town. The new university had adopted – out of an obstinacy that derived entirely from its Head – something like a Scottish constitution, with a small executive Court, consisting of aca-demics, local dignitaries and a representative elected by the students: since I could, by a certain amount of stately chicanery, be regarded as an old member, they had elected me. I was happy to go there. For years I had been free of official business: this was no tax at all, it did not distract me from my work: occasionally, as in those for the next day, the term's agenda contained a point of interest. But I was happy really because I had reached a stage when the springs of my life were making their own resonances clear, which I could hear, sometimes insistently, not only with my family but with people I had known.

In the April evening, the taxi chugged along in the stream of outbound traffic, past the hedges and gardens of the prosperous suburb, the gravel drives, the comfortable bourgeois houses, the lighted windows. These were houses I had walked by as a boy: but to this day I had not often been inside. I knew much poorer houses, like my father's, where I had been an hour before: and, because of the way things had gone, I had spent some time in recent years in grander ones. But somehow that specific sector had eluded me, and with it a slice of this comfortable, affluent town.

Was that why, as I stood outside the Residence and saw the bright drawing-room, blinds not drawn, standard-light by the window, I felt a pang, as though I were an outsider? It seemed so for an instant: and yet, in cold blood, I should have known it was not true. I was still capable of walking down any street, seeing a lighted window, and feeling that same pang, which was made up of curiosity, envy and desire: in that sense, one doesn't age: one can still envy a hearth-glow, even if one is returning to a happy home: it isn't a social chance, but something a good deal deeper, that can at untameable moments make one feel for ever youthful, and, as far as that goes, for ever in the street outside.

I went in, and became, as though a switch had been turned, at home. Vicky Shaw greeted me. Yes, my bag had been taken upstairs. Her father, was, as usual, working late. I was to come and have a drink.

Sitting in an armchair in the drawing-room (which was not at all magical, soft-cushioned but with tepid pictures on the walls), I looked at her. Since her mother died, Vicky had been acting as hostess for her father, although she had just qualified as a doctor and had a job at the infirmary. She was just twenty-four, not handsome, her face a shade too equine to be pretty, and yet comely: long, slight: fair hair swept back and knotted. I was very fond of her. She did not make me feel – as on those visits, despite the time-switch on the drive outside, I sometimes did – that I was an ageing man with a public face. And also she had the special radiance, and the special vulnerability, of a young woman for the first time openly in love.

I expected to hear something of that. But she was direct and often astringent; there was business to get through first. She was a devoted daughter, but she thought that her father, as a Vice-Chancellor, was a bit of an ass. His enemies were trying to ease him out – that she knew as well as I did. He was giving them opportunities. Tomorrow's case would be used against him, unless I could work on him. She didn't have to tell me about it: I had heard from the appellants themselves. A couple of young men had been found bedding a girl each in a room in one of the hostels. The disciplinary committee, which meant in effect Arnold Shaw himself, had next day sent all four down for good. They had appealed to the Court.

'He may get away with it there,' Vicky said, 'but that won't be the end of it.'

Once again, both of us knew. He put people off. They said that he was a shellback, with no sympathy for the young.

'Of course,' she said, 'he was wrong anyway. He ought to have told them to go and do it somewhere else. But he couldn't do that, you know.'

I found it impossible to keep back a vestigial grin. Arnold Shaw could bring himself to say that about as easily as John Calvin in one of his less libertarian moods.

'Why in God's name, though,' she said, 'didn't he play it cool?'

Did she have to ask me? I replied.

Reluctantly she smiled. She knew, better than anyone, that he was incorruptible: rigid: what he believed, he believed. If everyone else in the country were converted to sexual freedom, he would stay outside the swim: and be certain that he was right.

She put more whisky into my tumbler. She said:

'And yet, you know, he was a very good father to me. Even when I was little. He was always very kind.'

'I shouldn't have thought you were difficult to bring up,' I told her.

She shook her head. 'No. I wasn't all that disciplined.' She broke off: 'Anyway, do your best with him tonight.'

I said she mustn't bank on anything I could do. With a frown, she replied: 'He's as obstinate as a pig.'

There was nothing else useful to say. So, businesslike, she cut off short, and told me who was coming to dinner. It was a small party. The Hargraves, the Gearys – yes, I had met Hargrave on the Court, I knew the Gearys well – and Leonard Getliffe. As she mentioned the last name, I glanced at her. She had the delicate skin common among her own kind of blonde, and she had flushed down to the neck-line.

Leonard Getliffe was the eldest son of my friend Francis, whom I had met almost as soon as I first went to London from this town: ever since, our lives had interweaved. But their connection with the university was no credit to me, only to Arnold Shaw. Since Francis gave up being an influence in Whitehall, at the time of Quaife's failure and mine, his scientific work had gone better than in his youth, his reputation had grown. And, though probably not as a consequence, he had recently been made a life peer. So Arnold Shaw, whose academic standards were as rigorous as his moral ones (and who, incidentally, was by no means averse to titles), had schemed for him to be the second Chancellor of the University: and for once Arnold had brought something off. He had brought something else off too, more valuable to the place: for he had persuaded Leonard, before he was thirty, to take a professorship. Leonard was, in the jargon of the day, a real flier. He was more gifted than his father: he was, so David Rubin and the others said, one of the best theoretical physicists going. All he needed was a bit of luck, they said, talking of luck exactly as people did in more precarious fields: then they would be tipping him for a Nobel prize. He might be more gifted than his father, but he was just as high principled. He could do his theoretical work anywhere; why not try to help a new university? So, when Arnold Shaw invited him, he had without fuss left Trinity and come.

Vicky was blushing. She met my glance, and her eyes were blue, candid and distressed. It might have seemed that she was pining for him. The opposite was true. He was eaten up with love for her. It had happened a year before, almost as soon as they met, perhaps on the first day. He was begging her to marry him. Her father passionately wanted the marriage: the Getliffes would have welcomed it. All their children were married by now, except Leonard, their eldest and their particular star. The only person who didn't want the marriage was Vicky herself. She couldn't respond. She was a kind girl, but she couldn't see any way to be kind. Sometimes, when she saw him, she felt – there was no repressing it – plain irritated. Often she felt guilty. People told her this was someone of a quality she would never meet again: they told her she was interfering with his work. She knew it. For a while it had been flattering, but that wore off. Once, when I had been staying in the Residence, she had broken out:

'It's not fair! I look at myself in the glass. What have I got to produce this sort of passion? No, it's ridiculous.'

She had little conceit. She could have done with more, I thought. She wanted to shrug the responsibility off, and couldn't. She was honest, and in some ways prosaic. But she didn't seem prosaic when she talked about the man she loved.

She had fallen in love herself – but after she had met Leonard Getliffe. The man she loved could scarcely have been more different from Leonard. I knew him, I knew him better than she did, or at least in a different fashion, for he was my nephew, Martin's son.

She wanted to tell me. Yes, she had seen Pat last week. In London. They had gone to – she brought out the name of a Soho restaurant as though it were embossed, just as she brought out the name of Pat. We had all done it, I thought: the facts, the names of love are special facts, special names: it made the air bright, even to hear. But it also made the air uneasy.

After all, I was looking at him with an uncle's eyes, not with those of an adoring young woman. I thought he was an engaging youth, but I had been astonished when she became enraptured. To begin with, he was only twenty, four years younger than she was. True, he was precocious, and she probably the reverse. Yet I had seen my brother, a steady-natured man, but also a possessive father, trying to cope with that precocity. It had taught my brother what fatherhood could mean. Pat's name wasn't even Pat. He had been christened after me, but had re-named himself when he was an adolescent. He had rebelled against his first school, and been lucky to survive a second. Martin had managed to get him a place at our Cambridge college: he had given up after a year and gone to London to paint. How he managed to get support out of Martin or anyone else, I didn't know: but I thought there weren't many means that he would consider inappropriate. Had he any talent? Here for once Vicky, in the midst of her delight, became half-lucid. 'I do hope', she said, 'that he's as good as he wants to be. Sometimes I worry because he might get bored with it.'

Then she asked me favours: could they come and see us at our London flat? Could I bring him down to the university some time? She was innocent and shameless: yet anyone would have said that she was one of the stablest of young women, and it would have been true. That was why it was a liberation to abandon herself like this. If he arrived that moment, I was thinking, she would be proud to throw her arms round his neck.

I asked for another drink. With a shake of her head, coming back to other people's earth, she poured me a small one.

'Go slow on that,' she said, tapping the glass, talking to me like an affectionate and sensible daughter. 'You'll get plenty tonight. Remember, you've got to stay up with him [her father] when they've all gone.'

Once more she was businesslike, thinking of her duty. How could I handle him? We were talking tactics, when Arnold Shaw himself entered the room. At first sight, he didn't look a martinet, much less a puritan.

He was short, well padded, with empurpled cheeks and a curving, malicious, mimic's mouth. He kissed his daughter, shook my hand, poured himself a lavish scotch, and told us: 'Well, that's polished off the paper for today.'

He was an obsessively conscientious administrator. He was also a genuine scholar. He had started life as an inorganic chemist, decided that he wasn't good enough, and taken up the history of chemistry, out of which he had made a name. In this university the one person who had won international recognition was young Leonard Getliffe. After him, a long way after, in a modest determined fashion, carrying on with his scholarship after he had 'polished off the paper', came the Vice-Chancellor himself. It ought to have counted to him for virtue. It might have done, if he could have resisted making observations about his colleagues and his fellow Vice-Chancellors. It wasn't long since he had told me about one of the latter, with the utmost gratification: 'I wouldn't mind so much that he's never written a book. But I do think it's a pity that he's never read one.'

That night he moved restlessly about the drawing-room, carrying glasses, stroking his daughter's hair. The dinner was a routine piece of entertaining, part of the job which he must have gone through many times: but he was nervous. As soon as the first car drove up the drive, he became more nervous and more active. When the Gearys came in, he was pushing drinks into their hands before they could sit down. Denis Geary, who had been a small boy at my old school just before I left it, gave me a good-natured wink; he was the headmaster of a new comprehensive school, nominated to the Court by the local authority, a relaxed and competent man, not easily put out. The Hargraves followed them in, not as relaxed, knowing no one there except through Court meetings and dinners such as this: both of them diffident, descendants of Quaker manufacturers who had made tidy – not excessive – fortunes in the town. Mrs Hargrave, true to her teetotal ancestry, asked timidly for a tomato juice, which with a flourish Arnold Shaw produced. Then Leonard Getliffe entered, dark-haired, white-faced, handsome in a Mediterranean fashion (I could still recall him playing in his grandfather's house as an infant, misleadingly fresh and fair): he couldn't help his eyes searching for Vicky as he shook hands.

Arnold Shaw was settling them all down, braced on the balls of his feet: there was a buzz of titular enunciation. The mention of Lord Getliffe – Professor Getliffe's father, Arnold Shaw found it desirable to explain – was frequent: there was a good deal of Sir Lewis-ing. But he was not only being nervous, active and snobbish, but also peremptory. The party still had the first drinks in hand, Shaw had only just sat down himself at last, when he gave an order.

'About the Court meeting – discussion tonight forbidden,' he announced.

His bright hot eyes swept round the room. Some were relieved, one could feel, but not Denis Geary.

'That's going a bit far, Vice-Chancellor,' he said. He was hawk-nosed, grizzled, tough as well as harmonious, no man's pushover. He was also a figure in local progressive politics: he had come prepared to argue, not just to dine out.

'Absolutely forbidden.'

'With respect—' Denis began.

'Host's privilege,' said Arnold Shaw.

Denis looked over at me, gave a slight shrug.

'If you say so,' he said with a good grace. He knew when not to force an issue: recently I had often thought that he could have been a good politician on a bigger scale.

'Nothing contentious tonight,' said Arnold Shaw, rubbing it in. 'We're going to enjoy ourselves.'

That was one of the inapposite remarks, I thought, as we went in to dinner, and I sat on Vicky's right hand. For Denis Geary, at any rate, despite his good manners, the night had become pointless. For his wife also: she spoke in a soft midland voice like my father's but was as firm as her husband. As dinner began, at my end of the table I had to exert myself to keep any sort of conversation going. And yet the meal was superb. Arnold Shaw indulged in food and drink; in the Residence both were better than at any private house I knew, out of comparison better than at great houses such as Basset. Dinner that night was as good as ever: borshch, whitebait, tournedos Rossini: while Arnold Shaw was jumping up and down, going round the table with decanters, buttling. There was plenty of buttling to be done: he loved wine, and was more knowledgeable about it than any of my old Cambridge colleagues: wine-drinking of that quality didn't happen nowadays among my friends.

The food and drink ought to have acted as a social lubricant. But they didn't. To most of the party they were an embarrassment. The Hargraves were rich, but they went in for austerely simple living. The Gearys weren't at all austere but didn't understand fine wine or the wine badinage that Shaw insisted on exchanging with me. I was a light eater, though out of politeness I was doing my best. Leonard was gulping down the drink, hoping to see Vicky before the night was over. As so often, Arnold Shaw could not put a foot right.

In fact, he was proceeding, I could hear down the table, to put two feet wrong. He at least was enjoying his meal, and even more his wine: he was not a heavy drinker, I had never seen him drunk, but alcohol made him combative. He was choosing the occasion to parade himself as an extreme reactionary; in particular an extreme reactionary about education. He flourished his views, vigorous and bantam-bright, in front of the Gearys, who in the terms of that period believed the exact opposite, and the Hargraves, who spent their money on benefactions. 'You're all wrong about education,' he was saying. 'Quite wrong. Education isn't social welfare. You're quite wrong about universities. A university isn't anything like what you think. Or it oughtn't to be.' He went on, with a kind of ferocious jocularity, temper not far beneath the surface, making himself clear. A university was a place of learning. No more, no less. The senior members existed to add to knowledge. If they couldn't do that, they shouldn't be there. Some of them had to teach. The students existed only to be taught. They came to learn. They weren't there for social therapy. They weren't there to be made useful to the state: that was someone else's job. Very few people could either add to knowledge, or even acquire it. If they couldn't, get rid of them. He wanted fewer university students, not more. Fewer and better. This university ought to be half its present size.

I heard Hargrave, who didn't speak often, say that he couldn't agree. I heard Denis Geary arguing patiently, and turned my head away. I met Vicky's frown, troubled and cross. I tried to distract her, but she was tense, like someone conducting an intolerable interview, waiting to call time.

For myself, I couldn't intervene: Shaw thought that I was not stupid, but misguided, perhaps deliberately so, and that provoked him more. I let my thoughts drift, wondering why, when I was young, I hadn't known Denis Geary better. He was a good man, and his character had worn well: he had become more interesting than many who had once, for me, outshone him. But, of course, one doesn't in youth really choose one's friends: it is only later, perhaps too late, that one wishes, with something like the obverse of nostalgia, that it had been possible to choose.

The men alone, the port, more of the political testimony of Arnold Shaw. But, despite the luxurious meals, parties at the Residence had a knack of finishing early. All the guests had left, with suitable expressions of reluctance, by 10.45.

Tyres ground on the gravel, and Arnold returned to the drawing-room, lips pursed in triumph.

'I call that a good party,' he proclaimed to Vicky and me, challenging us to deny it. Then he said to Vicky, affectionate, reproachful: 'But I must say, you might have kept young Getliffe behind a bit—'

I had to save her. I said:

'Look, Arnold, I do rather want a word with you.'

'About what?'

'You know about what, don't you?'

He glared at me with hot, angry eyes. He decided that there was nothing for it, and said with increasing irascibility that we had better go to his study.

Before I had sat down, beside the reading-lamp in front of the scholar's bookshelves, ladder close by, he said:

'I warn you, it's no use.'

'Listen to me for a minute.'

'It's no use.'

'I'm thinking of you,' I said.

'I don't want anyone to think of me.'

What I had just told him happened to be true. I was not exerting myself and not crossing wills, entirely – or even mainly – for Vicky's sake. I should have been hard put to it to define my feeling for him, but it contained strata both of respect and affection. Whether he believed that or not, I didn't know: he was not used to being liked: if someone did appear to like him, it affected him with something between exasperation and surprise.

He poured out whiskies for us both, but became more ugly-tempered still. It was the kind of temper that is infectious, and I had to make myself keep my own. I told him that tomorrow's meeting wasn't just a matter of form: if he pressed for the Court to confirm his verdict, then he would certainly get a majority: some would vote against, certainly Geary, probably Leonard Getliffe and two or three of the younger academics. I should, I said in a matter-of-fact tone, vote against it myself.

'Vote against anything you like,' he snapped.

'I shall,' I said.

He would get a clear majority. But didn't he realise that most of the people voting for him nevertheless thought he had been too severe?

'That's neither here nor there.'

'It is, you know,' I said.

I tried another tactic. He must admit, I said, that most of the people we knew – probably most people in the whole society – didn't really regard fornication as a serious offence. In secret they didn't regard it as an offence at all.

'So much the worse for them,' he said.

How could he be so positive? I was getting rougher. Most people couldn't find any moral sanction for such an attitude. I couldn't. Where did he get his?

'That's my business.'

'Not if it affects us all.'

'I'm not going to talk about my moral sanctions. I'm not going to talk about fornication in general.' His cheeks had gone puce. 'We're talking about a university, which you seem to have forgotten. We're talking about a university which I'm in charge of. While I'm in charge of it, I'm not going to allow promiscuous fornication. I don't see that that needs explaining. It gets in the way of everything a university stands for. Once you turn a blind eye, you'd make nonsense of the place before you could look round.'

Then I used my last resource. I said that I too was concerned for the university: and that he was valuable to it. He would never get any credit for that. But he had a single-minded passion for academic merit. As a Vice-Chancellor he couldn't do some things, but he could do one superlatively: that is, he was a connoisseur of academic promise with as great accuracy as he was a connoisseur of wine. It wasn't an accident that this obscure university had put in a bid for Leonard Getliffe. And Leonard Getliffe, though much the best of his collection, was not the only one. He had backed his judgment, appointed three full professors in their twenties and thirties: so that the university was both better staffed, and more adventurously staffed, than any of its class.

I hadn't been flattering him. That was the fact. For the first time I had touched him. The smouldering rage dropped down for an instant, and he said:

'Well, I've got hold of some good men.' He said it humbly.

If he left the place, no one else would have the same gift, I said. And it was possible that he would have to leave. You couldn't fight all your opponents on all fronts. He was making opponents of people who needn't be: they thought that he wasn't living in the climate of his time: he gave them some excuse.

'I've no use for the climate of my time. To hell with it,' he said.

All I wanted him to do – I was being patient – was to make some compromise. The slightest compromise. Even just by permitting the four students to withdraw, as though of their own free will.

'I'll compromise when I can,' he said. 'Not when I can't.'

I told him, as straight and hard as I was able, that if ever there was an occasion to offer a token compromise, then tomorrow was the time. With an angry pout, eyes flat and fixed, he shook his head.

I had had enough, and sat back, silent. Then he said, not so much in a conciliatory manner but as though he wanted me to understand:

'I'll tell you this. You say they may want to get rid of me. That's their business. They won't find it so easy as they think. But if I decide that I'm doing the place more harm than good, then I shall go next day.'

He had spoken in a brisk tone, his anger quite subsided, rather as though he were stating his plans for his summer holiday. In precisely the same tone, he added:

'I shall decide. And I shan't ask anyone else.'

Even more briskly, he said good-night, and at something like a trot went out of the room and upstairs. I noticed that the lights were still on in the drawing-room, and there I found Vicky waiting up.

'Any change?' she asked.

'None,' I said.

She swore. 'He's hopeless.'

Then she, who usually was considerate, who noticed one's physical state, went on as though I were neither jaded nor tired. Couldn't I still do something tomorrow? I was used to this kind of business: couldn't I find a way to smooth things over?

I'd try, of course, I said. But in real conflicts, technique never counted (that was a lesson I had learned long ago in my own college, and then in Whitehall the same lesson, because politics anyhow didn't alter its shape); when people clashed head on it was no use being tactful. I let myself say that, discouraging her because she was nagging at me, and I needed just to go to bed.

She seemed selfishly, or even morbidly, preoccupied about her father. But it was not truly so. No, she was compensating to herself because she did not want to think of him at all. She was dutiful, she could not shrug off what a daughter ought to feel and do. It was another kind of love, however, which was possessing her. She wanted to guard her father's well-being, she wanted to get her conscience clear – so that she could forget it all and lose herself, as though on the edge of sleep, in thoughts of happiness.

CHAPTER III

MEETING

MEETINGS. To twist an old statement, all happy meetings are like one another: every unhappy meeting is unhappy in its own fashion. But was that true? I had been to plenty of unhappy meetings in my time. Whether they were trivial or secret or (by the world's standards) important, they all had a family resemblance. So had the Court meeting that Wednesday morning.

It began uncomfortably quiet, the good-mornings muted in the long room. The room was both extravagantly long and as light as though we were sitting in the open air, since one side was all window, looking southwards on to an arena-like court. The unrelieved lightness of the room – I had thought, on occasions before this one – drew people apart, not together. It was like the whole range of the university buildings, handsome, stark, functional, slapped down at prodigious expense in the fields, four miles outside the town. The Victorian buildings of the old college, where I had first listened to George Passant, had been abandoned, turned over to offices in one of the streets where my son and I had walked the previous afternoon. No dark rooms now: no makeshifts: no, the wide campus, the steel, concrete and glass, the stretches of window, at the same time bare, luxurious, unshadowed, costly.

Arnold sat at the end of the table, behind him on the wall – incongruous in the midst of the architectural sheen – a coloured plaque of the university arms. There were ten people on each side, Hargrave, who had some honorific title in the university, on the Vice-Chancellor's right, Geary two or three places down, looking at ease and interested. I sat on Arnold Shaw's left, and on my side sat Leonard Getliffe and several other academics, most of them under forty. The rest of the Court were older, hearty middle-aged local politicians and businessmen, four or five well-dressed strong-built women.

Item Number 3 on the agenda read, with the simple eloquence of official documents, *Appeal by Four Students against Decision of Disciplinary Committee*. The first two items were routine, and Arnold Shaw, who was a quick decisive chairman, wiped them off. Then he said, in the same unexpansive fashion, not encouraging comment or setting people free to talk, that they all knew the background of the next piece of business: he had circulated a memorandum: the students had appealed to the Court, as was their constitutional right: they had now asked to appear before the

Court in person. Whether they had this right as well was open to question: there was no ruling and no precedent. But Sir Lewis Eliot, as the students' representative on the Court, had presented an official request from the student body – that the four students should be given the privilege. He, Arnold Shaw, had with some dubiety granted it. As to the case itself, the facts were not in dispute. There was nothing to be said about them. We had better have the students in straightaway.

Better for them if they had not come, I had thought all along. I had tried to persuade them, for I had interviewed the four of them more than once. But the young man Pateman, who was the strongest character among them, was also a good deal of a sea-lawyer: there were other sea-lawyers among the union leaders: they were insisting on appearance before the Court as an inalienable right. I found it distinctly tiresome. So far as the four had any chance at all, that would worsen it if they came and argued: I knew the impression they would make: I knew also that one of the girls had already lost her nerve.

As Arnold Shaw had said, picking up the official phrase, the facts were not in dispute. They could hardly have been less in dispute. About 3.0 a.m. on a winter morning (actually it happened early in March) the assistant warden of one of the women's hostels had gone into a sitting-room. It was pure coincidence that she should have done so; she was having a sleepless night, and thought she remembered seeing a magazine there. She had switched on the light; on the sofa lay one naked pair, on an improvised bed another. What conversation then took place didn't seem to have been put on record. The assistant warden (who was both sensible and embarrassed) knew both girls, they were members of the hostel and had their own rooms upstairs. Presumably she found out the men's names at once: at any rate, next day she had no option but to report them. It was as simple as that.

We had better have the students in straightaway, Arnold Shaw was saying. He pressed a bell, told the attendant to bring Miss Bolt.

Myra Bolt came in. She was a big girl, pretty in a heavy-featured, actressish way: at close quarters she rolled her eyes and one noticed that her skin was large-pored. She was quite self-possessed that morning. I had not yet seen her otherwise: it wasn't she whose nerve had snapped. She was hearty and loud-voiced, and her parents were much better off than those of most of the students. Her father was a stockbroker who had a country house in Sussex. It was easy to imagine her, a little younger, taking riding lessons and being eager to have a roll in the bushes with the groom. She had not exactly boasted or confided, but let me know that something of that kind had duly taken place. At this time, she was twenty, in her second year, academically not much good.

The table was bad for interviewing, far too long, the candidate (or, that morning, the appellant) much too far away. Arnold Shaw, though a good chairman, was a bad interviewer. He just snapped out questions, his mind channelled as though he were wearing blinkers. That morning he was not only a bad interviewer but a hostile one, and he wasn't going to pretend otherwise.

'Miss Bolt,' he said. 'We understand that you have representations to make to the Court. What are they?'

Myra Bolt wasn't overawed, but she wasn't specially used to formal speeches. I had told them the kind of questions to expect, but not that one, not as the first.

'Well—' she began inconclusively, like someone saying goodbye at a railway station.

I thought that I had to step in. She wasn't a favourite of mine: there was only one of the four whom I was really fond of, and it wasn't she. But it was my job to see they got a hearing. I said – 'Vice-Chancellor, I wonder if I can help the Court a little, and Miss Bolt? Perhaps I could take her through what the students wish to say?'

How often had I seen others start a clash like that, voices smoothed down by official use? Arnold Shaw glanced at me with aggressive eyes – but he couldn't have stopped me easily. He seemed to like having an adversary, me in particular. He nodded, and projected my name.

I began by one or two innocuous questions: how long had she been living in the hostel? How well did she know the other girl, Joyce Darby? Not all that well, said Myra: just to have coffee with, or go out with for a drink. I had two objectives: I wanted to domesticate the whole business, to make them look more acceptable, so that they might express some sort of regret (which I knew that two of them at least, Myra among them, weren't inclined to do). Then I wanted them to make a responsible case about their careers: what would happen to them if they were thrown out of this university, and so couldn't get into another? The more professional it all sounded, the easier for them – and, I had hoped until the night before, the easier for Arnold Shaw.

How had they ever got into it? They didn't usually have this kind of party, did they? I was speaking casually. Myra answered: no, there'd never been anything like it before. She added:

'I suppose we all got carried away. You know how it is.'

'Had you been drinking?'

'A bit. I must say, it was a bit off.'

That was mollifying. But she was preoccupied – as she had been when I talked to her – by the fact of the two couples in the same room, what in her language they called an orgy.

'If David and I had gone off in my car that evening, and the other two in somebody else's, then I don't suppose we should have heard another word about it.'

That was less mollifying. Across the table, nearer to Myra, one of the women members of the Court broke in. She had a beaky profile, fine blue eyes, and a high voice. She said, in a sharp, sisterly, kindly tone:

'You didn't think you were doing anything wrong?'

'That depends on how you look at it, doesn't it?'

'But how do you look at it?'

'Well,' said Myra, 'I'm sorry other people got dragged in. That wasn't so good.'

The woman member nodded. 'But what about you?'

'What about me?'

'I mean, do you think you've done anything wrong?'

Myra answered, more lucidly than usual: 'I don't think there's anything wrong in making love, if you're not hurting anybody else.' She went on: 'I agree with Mrs What-do-you-call her, wasn't she an actress, that it doesn't matter what people do so long as they don't stop the traffic.'

It was like her, in her bumbling fashion, to get the reference wrong. Some of the Court wondered, however, where she had picked it up. Probably from one of their student advisers, trying to rehearse them.

But, bumbling or not, when Denis Geary asked her about the consequences of the punishment, she did her best. Denis was playing in with me, as competently as my brother Martin had done, in not completely dissimilar proceedings at our own college, now nearly ten years before: he was experienced, he knew the tone of the people round this table much better than I did: he didn't sound indulgent or even compassionate: but what did the punishment mean? To herself, she said, nothing but a headache. She could live at home or get a job with one of her father's friends (what she meant was that she would find someone, probably someone quite unlike her student fancies, to marry within a year or two). But to the others, who wanted careers, it meant they couldn't have them. Unless some other university would take them in. But they were being expelled in squalid circumstances: would another institution look at them? David Llewellyn, for instance (he had been Myra's partner: she didn't pretend to love him, but she spoke up for him) – he wanted to be a scientist. What chance would he have now?

'Has any member of the Court anything further to ask Miss Bolt?' Arnold Shaw looked implacably round the table. 'Have you anything further you wish to say, Miss Bolt? Thank you.'

With the next girl, I had one aim and only one, which was to get her out of the room with the least possible strain. She wasn't in a fit state to be interviewed. That she showed, paradoxically helping me, by beginning to cry as soon as Arnold Shaw asked his first formal question. 'Miss Darby, we understand—' She was a delicate-looking girl, actually a year older than Myra, but looking much younger. She appeared drab and mousey, but dress her up, make her happy, and she would have her own kind of charm. She came from a poor family in industrial Lancashire, a family which had been severe with her already. She was a bright student, expected to get a First, and that, together with her tears, made Shaw gentler with her. All she said was: 'I was over-influenced. That's as much as I can tell you.'

It was not gallant. In secret (it sounded hard, but I had seen more of her than the others had) I thought that she was not only frightened, which was natural enough, but self-regarding and abnormally vain.

She spoke in a tiny voice. Quite gently, Shaw told her to speak up. She couldn't. Whether she was crying or not, she wouldn't have been able to. Anyone used to interviewing would have known that there are some people who can't. Anyone used to interviewing would also have known that – despite all superstitions to the contrary – the over-confident always get a little less good treatment than they deserve, and girls like this a little more.

Someone asked her, who had influenced her? She said: 'The rest of them.' She wouldn't, to do her justice, put special blame on Dick Pateman, her own lover. One of the academics who had taught her, asked her what, if she continued with her degree work, she hoped to do? She wanted to go on to a Ph.D. What on? Henry James. She began to cry again, as though she felt herself shut out from great expectations, and Arnold Shaw was in a hurry to ask the dismissive questions.

It had done harm: it might have been worse. David Llewellyn, though he was as nervous as she was, gave a good performance. This was the one I liked, a small neat youth, sensitive and clever. When one compared him and Myra, there was no realistic doubt about who had done the seducing. Probably she was his first woman (they had been sleeping together some months before the party), and I expected that he was

proud of it and boasted to his friends. But how he got led into the 'orgy'
I couldn't understand, any more than if it had been myself at the same
age. When I had asked him, he looked lost, and said:

'Collective hysteria. It can't have been anything else.'

After his name was announced, people round the table may have been
surprised to hear him talk in a sub-cockney accent. His parents, I had
discovered, kept a small shop in Southend. Of the four of them, only
Pateman lived with his family in the town. But then, the great majority
of the university's students came from all over the country, to be put
up in the new hostels: just as the local young men and women travelled to
other parts of the country to be put up in identical hostels elsewhere. It
might have seemed odd, but not to anyone acclimatised to the English
faith in residential education.

Llewellyn did well, without help from me or Geary. He was ready to
apologise for what had happened: it had given trouble, it had stirred up a
scandal. The circumstances were bad. So far as they were concerned, he
had no defence. The party was inexcusable. He was nervous but precise.
No one pressed him. If they had, he would have been honest. His private
sexual behaviour was his own affair. On that he and Myra had made a
compact: and their student political adviser was backing them. But
Llewellyn didn't require any backing. He was ambitious, and shaking
for his future. He had his own code of belief, though. An attempt by
Shaw or one of the others to make him deny it would have got nowhere.

However, that didn't happen. Leonard Getliffe, not preoccupied as on
the night before, asked him some questions about his physics course:
Leonard, sharp-witted, was talking like a master of his job, but without
any condescension at all: the answers sounded sharp-witted also.

In the silence, after he had left and we were waiting for Pateman, someone said:

'I must say, that seems a pity.'

Across the table, Leonard Getliffe said: 'He has talent.'

For the next quarter-of-an-hour, Dick Pateman sat at one end of the
table arguing with the Vice-Chancellor and the others. Pateman's head
was thrown back, whether he was listening or speaking: he had staring
light eyes in deep orbits, a diagonal profile, and a voice with no give in it.
Less than any of the others, he did not want to make human contact:
with his contemporaries, this gave him a kind of power; he seemed to
them uninfluenceable, waiting only for them to be influenced. It was the
kind of temperament which wasn't necessarily linked with ability – he
was not clever, he ought to have been finishing his degree but had been

dropped back a year – but which is sometimes dangerous and not often negligible. It did not seem negligible at the table that morning – though his logic-chopping and attempts at legalism were stirring up Arnold Shaw's contempt, which Pateman met by a contempt, chilly and internal, of his own.

On the surface it might have sounded like a trade-union boss negotiating with an employer. On one side stood the student body, Pateman was grating away (I had anticipated this, tried to stop it, could only sit by): on the other 'the authorities'. It was necessary for matters of discipline to be settled by the two sides in combination.

'Nonsense,' said Arnold Shaw.

Shaw's temper was seething. The young man seemed to have no temper. He went on:

'If that's the attitude the authorities take up, then the students will have to join forces with students of other universities—'

'Let them,' said Arnold Shaw.

So it went on. The authorities had no right to impose their own law unilaterally on the students, said Pateman. The students had their own rights.

'In that sense,' said Shaw, 'you have none at all.'

Pateman said that they were free citizens. They paid their fees. They were prepared to collaborate in drafting laws for the university, and would abide by them. They expected that the authorities had their own rights about examinations. Everything else should be settled by mutual consent. Or, alternatively, the students should simply be subject to the laws of the land. In the present case, there was no suggestion that anything had been done contrary to the laws of the land.

'Look here,' said Denis Geary, 'this isn't very profitable.'

'I was speaking for the students—'

'You'd better speak for yourselves. You've behaved like damned fools, and messy damned fools, and you know it. You'd better give us one good reason why we should be spending our time here this morning—'

Young Pateman gave something like a smile. He must have realised, since Geary was well known in the town, that here was one of their best hopes: he didn't mind, he was enough of a politician to be easy with rough words.

'I don't take back the students' case,' he began, and Geary broke in:
'Drop that.'

'I should have thought the practical thing you've got to consider this morning,' Pateman went on, in precisely the same ungiving tone, 'is whether you want to ruin us.'

'Ruin's a big word,' said Geary.

'What else do you think you're doing?'

The Vice-Chancellor was interrupting, but Denis Geary had his own authority and went on:

'I want to know one thing. How much do you feel responsible?'

'What do you mean, responsible?'

'If it hadn't been for you, would this have happened?'

'I don't know about that.'

'You're the oldest of this group, aren't you?'

'Joyce is older than I am. So is David.'

'Never mind about calendar age. You're a grown man, aren't you?'

He was young enough to be softened, for an instant. Geary asked:

'Do you think it's a good idea to get hold of youngsters like this—'

'It depends on the co-operation I get.'

The answer was brash. Geary used more force:

'But you ought to feel responsible, oughtn't you?'

'I don't know about that.' Pateman was repeating himself.

'You do feel responsible, though, don't you?'

There was a long pause. Pateman said, slowly, his voice more grating still: 'I don't want to see anyone ruined.'

Geary glanced at me, a partner's glance. That was the most he could extract. I touched the Vice-Chancellor's sleeve. He didn't want to let Pateman go, but he acquiesced.

Coffee was brought in. It was about a quarter past eleven, and we had started at ten. Motion: that the Court confirms the decision of the Disciplinary Committee.

In the unconfined, hygienic room the air was tight. Not, so far, with anger: remarks were quiet: there was curiosity, unease, something else. I heard, or thought I heard, someone whispering about *the university premises*. Arnold Shaw stared down the table. He wasn't pleased to have lost his leadership during the hearings: he was asserting it now.

'There is a motion before the Court,' he said. 'Before I put it, I should like to hear whether anyone wishes to discuss it.'

Pause. One of the academics spoke up: 'Some of us are wondering, I think, Vice-Chancellor, whether it isn't possible to make distinctions between these students—'

Shaw sat, high coloured, without answering. Others were doing that. It was a line some were eager for. Surely one of the girls had been dominated. Didn't she deserve different treatment (I noticed that the handsome blue-eyed woman, though she sat silent, had her own view of

Joyce Darby)? No one had any use for Pateman. There was a great deal of talk, scrappy, some of it merciful. Someone said : 'Whosoever shall cause one of my little ones—' and trailed off. I caught the word 'degenerates'. It was left for Leonard Getliffe to make a special case.

'I should like the Court to give consideration to young Llewellyn. I can speak for the physics department. He's worth saving. I said before, he has talent. He's certainly the best student I've taught here. I don't know about the general position. I mean, I can't reach absolute conclusions about student behaviour. I should say, in terms of character as I understand it, he is a decent young man.'

Leonard was speaking politely but without concessions. On his clever conceptualiser's face there was a half-smile, a mannerism which some found irritating. It meant nothing. He spoke like a man sure of himself. Underneath the fine nerves, he was more virile than most. If Vicky had been an older woman, she would have been bound to perceive it. Yet it had quite escaped her. I wondered if, free that morning from his obsessive love, he had time to be bitter because it was weakening his manhood, just as, younger than he was, but in this same town, and for the identical cause, I had been bitter myself.

I wondered also if he felt envy for the culprits. Envy because, instead of being prisoners of love, they took sex as though it didn't matter. Or because they just took sex as it came. At various places round the table, through the curious unease, through both the mercifulness and the disapproval, there had been those stabs of envy.

He went on:

'There is another point. I admit that it's a slightly more abstract one. The more people the university sends down, the less penalty it really is. That is, the importance of the gesture is inversely proportional to the number involved. If you send the whole university down, no one will care. If you send one person down, then that is a genuine penalty.'

He had spoiled his case, I thought irritably. That was what the theoreticians called cat-humour. Why didn't they keep it for their seminars?

One of his colleagues, more worldly than he was, thought the same. 'Never mind that,' he said. 'Vice-Chancellor, going back to Professor Getliffe's first point, there does seem to be some feeling for discretionary treatment on behalf of two of these students. We should like to ask, rather strongly, whether that isn't possible?'

Shaw had been quiet, like a discreet chairman letting the discussion run. Now he looked round, took his time, and said:

'No. I have to tell the Court it is not possible.'

There were noises of disappointment, but he was in control.

'No. The Court must face the position. This is all or nothing. If you ask me for the reason, I give it you in one word. Justice.'

Denis Geary said that justice could be unjust, but for once he was overweighted.

'No,' said Arnold Shaw. 'It would be wrong to distinguish between these four. Morally wrong. There are no respectable grounds for doing so. Age. Some people might think that a respectable ground, though I should beg to differ. In any case, the students whom some members want to favour are the two oldest. Academic ability. We are not judging a matter of academic ability. We are judging a matter of university discipline and moral behaviour. No one wants to deprive the university of able students. We haven't enough. But you can't make a special dispensation for the able when they've committed exactly the same offence. Personally I am sorry that Pateman ever became a student here – but to dismiss him and let others stay, who are precisely as guilty on the facts, simply because they might get better classes in their degrees – well, I could have no part in it. I'm surprised that anyone could find it morally defensible. Finally, influence. It's easy to think we know who is responsible. We don't. We can have our suspicions – but suspicions aren't a basis for just action. Anyone who is certain he knows what happens between two people is taking too much on himself. In this case, it would be utterly unjustified to go behind the facts. I repeat, I for one could have no part in it.'

Quiet. It was time to turn the argument. I said, perhaps I might put another point of view. 'Do,' said Arnold Shaw, firm and beady-eyed.

I was deliberately cool. I didn't want to get entangled in the legalities of the case, I remarked. So far as they went, the Vice-Chancellor's statement was unanswerable. And everyone round the table understood the position in which the Disciplinary Committee had found themselves. All that any of us wished to say was, weren't we making too heavy weather of it? The committee had been obliged to take action: that was accepted. But wasn't the penalty, now we had had time to realise the repercussions, too severe? Send the students down for the rest of the academic year, and no one would have asked a question. But were we really intending to cut them off from finishing their university education anywhere? It wouldn't have happened at other institutions or American colleges that I knew. Wouldn't it be fairly easy for the committee to have another look, just as an act of grace?

Arnold Shaw turned half-left towards me: 'Sir Lewis, you've just said that this wouldn't have happened at other institutions?'

'Yes,' I replied, 'I did say that.'

'You were a don yourself once, weren't you?'

That was a rhetorical question.

'Might I ask,' said Arnold Shaw, 'what would have happened at your own college if undergraduates had behaved like this?'

I answered that I couldn't recall a case.

'The question,' he persisted, 'seems to me a fair one.'

Sometimes, I said, I had known blind eyes turned.

'The question,' Arnold Shaw went on, 'still seems to be a fair one. In your college. Two of your own undergraduates and two women. Or in a room in Newnham. What about it?'

He had won that point, I was thinking to myself. I had to remember a time when Roy Calvert nearly missed a fellowship, because he was suspected, as a matter of gossip, not of proof, to be keeping a mistress.

'I grant you that,' I said with reluctance. 'Yes, they'd have been got rid of.'

Then I recovered myself. 'But I want to remind you that that was getting on for thirty years ago. The climate of opinion has changed since then.' I was trying to work on the meeting. 'So far as I can gather the sense of this Court today, the general feeling, is very different from what it would have been thirty years ago. Or even ten.'

Some murmurs of support. One or two noes. I was right, though. The tone that morning had been calmer and more relaxed than in our youth most of us could have imagined.

'I've told you before, I don't believe in climates of opinion,' said Shaw. 'That seems to me a dangerous phrase. But even if opinions have changed, are you maintaining that moral values have changed too?'

I had had too much practice at committees to be drawn. Arnold Shaw wore a curving, sharp-edged smile, enjoying the debate, confident that he had had the better of it. So he had. But, with some, he was doing himself harm. They wanted a bit of give-and-take, not his brand of dialectic.

I was having to make my next, and final, move. I looked across at Denis Geary, the only useful ally there, wishing that we could confer. I was trying to think of two opposite aims at once, which was a handicap in any kind of politics. On the one hand, I didn't want Shaw to do himself more harm (about that Geary would have been indifferent): if we pressed it to a vote, the Vice-Chancellor would get his support, but – as I had told him flatly the night before – it would be remembered against him. On the other hand, I wasn't ready to surrender. For the students' sake? For the sake of the old-Adam-ego, for after all I was fighting a case? That didn't matter. Someone was saying, and this time the words were clear: 'If only it hadn't happened *on the University premises.*'

I had been reflecting only for moments. There wasn't time to delay. But I found myself infected by a subterranean amusement. Arnold Shaw had made me think back to my college in the thirties: and, hearing that single comment, I was thinking back again. A college meeting. Report of a pyromaniac. He had set fire to his sitting-room once before, and that was thought to be accidental. Now he had done it again. One of the senior fellows, our aesthete, old Eustace Pilbrow, raised his voice. The young man must be got out of college at once. That day. But he must be found (since Pilbrow was a kind man) *a very good set of lodgings in the town.*

'Vice-Chancellor,' I said, returning to the occasion, 'I have a simple proposition to make.'

'Yes?'

'I suggest we take no formal action at all. Let's leave it over till the next meeting of the Court' (which was due to take place two months ahead, in June).

'With respect, I don't see the force of that.' Shaw's lips were pouting.

'There is a little force in it.' I explained that to me, and I thought to some others, the formality and the procedures were not important. We should be content, if we could save some chance for the students' careers. Given two months, Leonard Getliffe could talk to his physicist colleagues in other universities: come clean about the events: some department might be willing to take Llewellyn in. And so with the others. Many of us had contacts. Then, if and when they were placed elsewhere, the Court would be happy, and needn't worry about consequences.

'Not satisfactory,' said Arnold Shaw, but Geary broke in:

'Vice-Chancellor, in the circumstances nothing is going to be satisfactory. But I must say, I've never heard of a compromise which made things so easy for the powers-that-be. You're not being voted against, you're just being asked to wait a minute.'

'It's not even rational.'

'Vice-Chancellor,' Geary was speaking heavily, 'it will be difficult for me, and I know I'm speaking for others, if you can't accept this.'

Hargrave coughed. Under his white hair with its middle parting, his face, often quietly worried, looked more so. He was more distressed by the hearing than anyone there. He rarely spoke on the Court, but now he forced himself.

'It's usually right to wait, if one is not hurting anyone.'

'You've listened to those four this morning,' said Shaw.

Hargrave kneaded his temples, like one with a migraine, and then said with surprising firmness,

'But if we wait a little, we shan't hurt anyone, shall we?'

Even then, I doubted whether Shaw was going to budge. At last he shook his head.

'I don't like it,' he said. 'But if you want me to put your motion' (he turned to me) 'to the Court, I'm willing to do so. As for myself, I shall abstain.'

With bad grace, he sat in the chair while the hands went up. Only three against. There was a susurration of whispers, even giggles, as people stirred, ready to leave.

It wasn't a rational compromise, Arnold Shaw had complained. But then he was expecting too much. I had twice heard an elder statesman of science announce, with the crystalline satisfaction of someone producing a self-evident truth, that sensible men usually reached sensible conclusions. I had seen my brother cock an eyebrow, in recognition of that astonishing remark. I had myself reported it, dead pan, to others – who promptly came to the conclusion that I believed it myself.

It was not even a rational compromise. I packed up my papers, quite pleased with the morning's work. Others were talking, glad to have put it behind them. They were used, as people were in a society like ours, highly articulated, but so articulated that most lives touched only by chance, to hearing names, even to meeting persons in the flesh, once, twice, then not again. To most of the Court, the four we had interviewed were strangers, flickering in and out. Myra Bolt, David Llewellyn – they had swum into others' consciousness that morning, like someone sitting next to one in an aircraft, talking of where he had come from and where he was going to. To people round the table, the names they had heard weren't likely often to recur. That seemed entirely normal to them, just as it so often seemed to me.

CHAPTER IV

A SIMPLE HOME

YET for me, later that day, one of the names flickered, not out, but in again. I had arranged to spend another night at the Residence, in order to have my ritual drink with George Passant, and was sitting alone in the drawing-room after tea. Vicky had not returned from hospital, and

Arnold Shaw had gone to his vice-chancellarial office for another of his compulsive paper-clearing spells.

I was called to the telephone. This was Dick Pateman, a voice said, lighter and more smooth than it sounded face to face: he was anxious to see me. He knew about the result, or rather the non-result? Yes, he had been told: he was anxious to see me. Well, I accepted that, it was all in the job. In any case, I couldn't stay with him long. Where, I asked? At the Residence? Not much to my surprise, he said no. Would I come to his own home? I asked for the address, and thought I remembered the road, or could find it.

Getting off the bus at the park gates, I looked down into the town. There was a dip, and then a rise into the evening haze: lights were coming out, below the blur of roofs. On the left, down the New Walk, I used to go to Martineau's house. I must have looked down, at that density of lights and roofs, many times in those days: not with a Rastignac passion that I was going to take the town, any more than I had felt it looking down at London roofs (that was too nineteenth-century for us), but with some sort of pang, made up of curiosity and, perhaps, a vague, even sentimental, yearning.

I had been over-confident about my local knowledge, and it took me some time to identify the road. This was a part of the town which in the last century had been a suburb, but was so no longer; it certainly wasn't a slum, for those had gone. It was nothing in particular; a criss-cross of tidy streets, two-storeyed houses, part working-class, part the fringe of the lower middle. I asked my way, but no one seemed clear. So far as I could remember, I had never set foot in those particular back-streets: even in one's native town, one's routes were marked out, sharp and defined, like the maps of underground railways.

At last I saw the street-sign; on both sides stood terraced houses, the same period, the same red brick, as those my son and I had passed on the way to my father's room. At the end of the road some West Indians were talking on the pavement. That would have been a novelty years before. So would the sight of cars, at least three, waiting outside houses, including the house I was searching for. The window of the front room gave on the pavement: as in the window of the Residence the night before, a light was shining behind the curtains.

When I rang the bell, Dick Pateman opened the door. His greeting was off-hand, but I scarcely noticed that, since I was puzzled by the smell that wafted out, or one component of it. I was used to the musty smell of small old houses, I had known them all my childhood, and that was present here – but there was also something different in kind, not repulsive but discomforting, which I couldn't place.

Behind the closed door of the front room, pop music was sounding: Dick Pateman took me to the next, and only other, door. This would be (I knew it all by heart) the living-room or kitchen. As I went in, Dick Pateman was saying: 'This is my father and mother.'

That I hadn't bargained on. The room was cluttered, and for an instant my only impression was of the idiosyncratic smell, much stronger. I was shaking hands with a man whose head was thrown back, his hand stretched out, in a gesture one sometimes sees displayed by grandiose personages.

My eyes became clearer. Mr Pateman was taller than his son, with high square shoulders and a heavily muscled, athletic body. His grip on my hand was powerful, and his forearms filled his sleeves. His light blue eyes met mine unblinkingly, rather as though he had been taught that, to make a good impression, it was necessary to look your man straight in the eye. He had sandy hair, pale eyebrows and a sandy moustache. Under the moustache two teeth protruded a little, his under-lip pressed in, with the suggestion of a slight, condescending smile.

'I've never met you,' he said, 'but I've heard a great deal about you.'

I said that he was not to believe it. Mr Pateman, humourlessly, without any softening, said that he did.

Then I shook hands with Mrs Pateman, a tiny little woman, a foot shorter than her husband or son, wrinkled and dark-skinned. She gave me a quick, worried, confiding smile.

As we sat down, I didn't know why I had been enticed like this, how much the parents knew, nor how to talk to them.

The room was crammed with heavy nineteenth-century furniture. There was a bookcase with a glass window in the far corner, and a piano on the other side. A loose slack fire was smouldering in the grate, and the air was chilly. On the table, upon a white openwork cloth spread upon another cloth of dark green plush, with bobbled fringe, stood a teapot, some crockery, and what looked like the preparations for a 'high tea', though – by the standards of my mother's friends – a meagre one. Everything was clean: and yet, about the whole room, there hung a curiously dusty air, less like the grime of neglect than some permanent twilight.

Mrs Pateman asked whether she could help me to some food. When I answered her and said no, her husband smiled, as though I were proving satisfactory.

He himself was eating tinned salmon. He said: 'Well, we're giving them something to think about, I'm glad to say.'

I was still at a disadvantage. This was obviously a reference to the morning's meeting, and he seemed as invulnerable as his son. If he had been a softer man, worried or even inconsolable because his son's future was in danger, I should have been more at home. I should have been more at home with Mrs Pateman, who was watching the two of them with shrewd, puzzled anxiety. But, in the presence of the father, it wasn't in the least like that.

'The best we can do now' – I was feeling my way, speaking to Dick Pateman – 'is to try and get you fixed up elsewhere. As soon as we can.'

'That's not very satisfactory,' said Dick Pateman.

'No,' said Mr Pateman.

'It's a bad second best,' said Dick – as though he were arguing with me at the end of the long table.

'Some of us', said Mr Pateman, 'aren't prepared to see our children get the second best.'

I didn't want to show impatience, though it was displeasingly near. Above all, I didn't want to give pain, certainly not to Mrs Pateman. I couldn't speak frankly. With an effort, I said: 'You'll have to regard this as nothing more or less than a friendly talk. I can't do much. I might be able to give you a little advice, simply because I know the rules of this game, but that's all.'

Mr Pateman faced me with a set cunning look, which declared that he was not to be taken in. He assumed that I was a man of influence, he had an unqualified faith in what he called 'pulling strings'. The more I disclaimed being able to act, the more convinced he was of my Machiavellian power.

Dick argued, so did his father.

I was becoming certain that he didn't know much, nothing like the full story. Not that Dick had deceived him. He didn't want to know, he didn't even want to hear. He was positive that he was right. Obviously his son was being badly used: which meant, and this was how he translated it, that he himself was being badly used. He was a churchgoer, he pointed out to me, assuming, with an air of pitying superiority, that I wasn't. With a family in distress, I should have expected to feel protective, even though I hadn't asked to be there, even though I didn't like them. But Mr Pateman made that impossible. By some extraordinary feat of character or moral legerdemain, he took it for granted that all I had to do was my simple duty. So far as there was any pity flowing, he was pitying me.

It was a long time since I had met a man so self-righteous. And yet his son was self-righteous too. That was what had exacerbated the Court, that billiard-ball impregnability in circumstances where self-righteousness didn't appear to be called for. With a prepotent father like that, some sons would have been worn down. Not this one. There did not seem any tenderness, or even much communication, between them. They treated each other like equal powers, each censorious, each knowing that he was right.

The person I was curious about was Mrs Pateman, not bullied, but excluded from the talk. What could it be like to live here?

Mr Pateman made a practical point, as though I were responsible. If Dick had to transfer to another university (did Dick himself believe it would be all that easy, I was thinking? when was the right time to stop them hoping too much?) he wouldn't be able to make a contribution to the housekeeping. As it was, he had been doing so out of his student grant.

'The grants are miserable, I suppose you know that,' said Dick, ready to argue another grievance.

'Take him away,' said Mr Pateman, 'and he won't be able to pay a penny. There'll be nothing coming in.'

I had nothing to say on this topic, but Mr Pateman needed to finish it off. 'It's diabolical,' he said.

Soon afterwards a young woman came in, unobtrusively, slipping into the room. This must, I thought, be Dick's sister, whom I had just heard of, no more than that. Although she had only recently come in from work and could not have known of the Court result, she did not make any enquiry, nor even look at her brother. Instead, she was asking for jam. There wasn't any jam today, said Mr Pateman. There must be jam, she was saying. She was sounding peevish when, with a grandiloquent air, Mr Pateman presented me. She was not much bigger than her mother. She had fine eyes, but she turned them away from mine in a manner that could have been either shy or supercilious. In a delicate fashion, she was pretty: but, although she was perhaps only two years older than her brother, she had that kind of femininity which throws a shadow before it: her face was young, yet carried an aura, not really a physical look, of the elderly, almost of the wizened.

They called her Kitty. There was also a mention of someone named Cora: in the conversation I gathered that she and Cora shared, and slept in, the front room. It must have been Cora who had been playing records when I entered the house, which I had only just realised was so packed with people. I had another thought, or half-memory, from something I had heard not long before. Wasn't this Cora the niece of George Passant, the daughter of one of his sisters who had died young? I asked Kitty: she looked away, gave a sidelong glance, as though she wanted to resist answering me straight.

'I think she is,' she said, with what seemed a meaningless edge of doubt.

Could I have a word with her? George was a lifelong friend; by a coincidence, I should be meeting him in half an hour. It was not such a coincidence, though I didn't tell her so.

Kitty did some more shuffling, then said:

'I'll see if she can come.'

In the time Kitty was out of the room, Mr Pateman had returned to the 'diabolical' results of administrative decisions. Then the two young women returned, Cora first. She was tallish, with blunt heavy features, short straight hair; under a plain straight-hanging dress, she was strong-shouldered and stoutly built. I couldn't see much look of the Passant family, except perhaps a general thick-boned nordic air. I said that I knew her uncle. She gave an abrupt yes. I said I owed him a lot. She said:

'I like George.'

There were a few more words spoken, not many. She volunteered that she didn't see George much, nowadays. She said to Kitty:

'We ought to go and clear things up. The room's in a mess.'

As they went out, I did not anticipate seeing them again. More people evanescing: it had been the condition of that day. By the side of the two Pateman males, those self-bound men, the girls didn't make demands on one, not even on one's attention. True, I felt cold and shut in: but then, the little room was cold and shut in. It was a relief that it was not now so full of people. This 'simple home', as Mr Pateman called it, in one of his protests about Dick's contribution, pressed upon me. I was growing to dislike the sharp and inescapable smell, strong in the little room, strongest near to Mr Pateman himself. I had now isolated it in my nostrils, though I did not know the explanation, as a brand of disinfectant.

Mrs Pateman was clearing away the tea, Dick – whose manners could not have been regarded as over-elaborate – had gone out, shortly after the girls, and without a word. It was still early, but I could decently leave; I was anticipating the free air outside, when Mr Pateman confronted me with a satisfied smile and said:

'Now, we can talk a little business, can't we?'

Immediately I took it for granted that he was, at last, going to speak seriously about his son. That made me more friendly: I settled in my chair, ready to respond.

'I'm not very happy about things,' he said.

I began to reply, the best practical step was to find Dick a place elsewhere—

He stopped me. 'Oh no. I wasn't thinking about him.'

'I don't understand.'

'He'll be all right,' said Mr Pateman. 'I've done my best for my family and I don't mind saying, no one could have done more.'

He looked at me, as usual so straight in the eye that I wanted to duck. He wasn't challenging me, he was too confident for that.

'No,' he went on, 'I'm not very happy about *my* position.'

So that was it. That was why I had been invited, or enticed, to the house that evening.

'Do you realise,' he asked, 'that those two young people in the next room are both bringing in more than I am?'

I asked what he was doing. Cashier, he said, in one of the hosiery firms, a small one. Curiously enough, that was a similar job to my father's, years before. The young women? Secretaries. Fifteen or sixteen pounds a week each, I guessed?

'You're not far off. It's a lot of money at twenty-two or three.'

Mr Pateman did not appear to have the same appreciation of the falling value of money as my father, that unexpected financial adviser. But I happened to know the economics of this kind of household, through a wartime personal assistant of mine and her young man. Though Mr Pateman could not realise it, that acquaintanceship, in which I hadn't behaved with much loyalty, made me more long-suffering towards him and his family now.

'How much are they paying you for their room?' I said.

'If you don't mind,' Mr Pateman answered, throwing his head back, 'we'll keep our purses to ourselves.'

Anyway, I was thinking, he couldn't extract a big amount from them – even though, as I now suspected, he was something of a miser, a miser in the old-fashioned technical sense. I had been watching his negotiations with the tea-table food. Between them, the two young women must have money to spend: they could run a car: it was strangely different from my own youth in this town, or the youth of my friends.

'My position isn't right,' said Mr Pateman, 'I tell you, it isn't right.'

It was true to this extent, that a middle-aged man in a clerical job might be earning less than a trained girl.

'All I need', he went on, 'is an opportunity.'

I had to hear him out.

'What have you got to offer?'

'If I get an opportunity,' he said, with supreme satisfaction, 'I'll show them what I've got to offer.'

I said, he had better tell me about his career. How old was he?

Fifty last birthday.

'I must say,' I told him, 'I should have thought you were younger.'

'Some people', said Mr Pateman, 'know how to look after themselves.'

Born in Walsall. His parents hadn't been 'too well endowed with this world's goods' (they had kept a small shop). They had managed to send him to a grammar school. He had stayed on after sixteen: the intention was that he should one day go to a teachers' training college.

'But you didn't?'

'No.'

'Why not?'

A very slight pause. Then Mr Pateman said defiantly:

'Ah, thereby hangs a tale.'

For the first time that evening, he was dissatisfied with his account of himself. I wondered how often I had heard a voice change in the middle of a life story. A platitude or a piece of jargon suddenly rang out. It meant that something had gone wrong. His 'tale' seemed to be that he wanted to make money quick. He had had what he called a 'brainwave'. At twenty he had become attached to a second-hand-car firm, which promptly failed.

'Why did it fail?'

'It isn't everyone who is fortunate enough to have capital, you know.'

Then he had become a clerk in an insurance office in Preston.

'You may be thinking I've had too many posts. I was always looking for the right one.'

He had got married ('I'm a great believer in taking on one's responsibilities early'). Unfit for military service. Both children born during the war.

Another brainwave, making radio sets.

'My ship didn't come home that time either,' said Mr Pateman.

'What happened?'

'Differences of opinion.' He swept his arm. 'You know what it is, when the people in command don't give a man his head.'

'What would you have done if they had given you your head?'

'They never intended to. They asked me there on false pretences. My schemes never got beyond the blueprint stage.'

A new venture – this time in patent medicines. It looked as though all was well.

'Then we met a very cold wind. And I don't want to accuse any-one, but my partner came better than I did out of the financial settle-ment.'

By that time, in his early forties, he had lived in a dozen towns and never made more, I guessed, than a few hundred a year. He descended further, and for eighteen months was trying to sell vacuum cleaners house-to-house. He brought it out quite honestly, but as though with stupefaction that this should have happened to him. Then – what he admitted, with a superior smile, had seemed like a piece of luck. An acquaintance from his radio days had introduced him to his present firm. He had moved to the town, and this house, five years before. It was his longest continuous job since his young manhood.

'And I'm still getting less than my own daughter. It isn't right. It can't be right.'

I should have liked to avoid what was coming. Playing out time, I asked if his firm knew that he was considering another move. He gave a lofty nod.

'Are they prepared to recommend you?'

'They certainly are. I have a letter over there. Would you like to read it?'

It did not matter, I said. Mr Pateman gave me a knowing smile.

'Yes, I should expect you to read between the lines.'

I was saying something distracting, meaningless, but he was fixing me with his stare:

'I want an opportunity. That's all I'm asking for.'

I said, slowly: 'I don't know what advice I can possibly give you—'

'I wasn't asking for advice, sir. I was asking for an opportunity.'

Even after that higgledy-piggledy life, he was undefeated. It was easy to imagine him at the doors of big houses, talking of his vacuum cleaners, impassively, imperviously, not down and out because he was certain the future must come right.

Nevertheless, I was thinking of old colleagues of mine considering him for jobs. Considering people for jobs had to be a heartless business. No man in his senses could think Mr Pateman a good risk. They mightn't mind, or even be interested in, his odder aspects. But he carried so many signs that the least suspicious would notice – he had been restless, he had quarrelled with every boss, he had been unrealistically on the make.

Still, nowadays there was a job for anyone who could read and write.

Mr Pateman was, in the mechanical sense, far from stupid. He had a good deal of energy. At his age, he would not get a better job, certainly not one much better. He might get a different one.

He was sitting with his hands on his knees, his head back, a smile as it were of approbation on his lips. He did not appear in the least uneasy that I should not find an answer. The slack fire smoked: the draught blew across the room: among the fumes I picked out the antiseptic smell which hung about him as though he had just come from hospital.

'Well, Mr Pateman,' I said. 'I mustn't raise false hopes.' I went on to say that I was out of the official life for good and all. He gazed at me with confident disbelief: to him, that was simply part of my make-believe. There were two places he might try. He could possibly get fitted up in another radio firm: I could give him the name of a personnel officer.

'Once bitten, twice shy, thank you, sir,' said Mr Pateman.

Alternatively, he might contemplate working in a government office as a temporary clerk. The pay would be a little better: the work, I warned him, would be extremely monotonous: I could tell him how to apply at the local employment exchange.

'I don't believe in employment exchanges. I believe in going somewhere where one has contacts at the top.'

He seemed – had it been true before he met me? – to have dreamed up his own fantasy. He seemed to think that I should say one simple word to my old colleagues. I tried to explain to him that the machine did not work that way. If the Ministry of Labour took him on, they would send him wherever clerks were needed. He could tell them that he had a preference, but there was no guarantee that he would get what he wanted.

Anyone who had been asked for such a favour had to get used to the sight of disappointment – and to the different ways men took it. There were a few who, like Mr Pateman now, began to threaten.

'I must say, I was hoping for something more constructive from you,' he said.

'I'm sorry.'

'I don't like being led up the garden path.' His eyes were fixed on mine. 'I was given to understand that you weren't as hide-bound as some of them.'

I said nothing.

'I shall have to consider my course of action.' He was speaking with dignity. Then he said: 'I expect that you're doing your best. You must be a busy man.'

I got up, went into the back kitchen, and shook hands with his wife. She could have overheard us throughout: she looked up at me with something like understanding.

Mr Pateman took me down to the passage (the record player was still sounding from the front room), and, at the door, threw out his hand in a stately goodbye.

CHAPTER V

TIME AND A FRIEND

OWING to the single-mindedness of Mr Pateman, I was a few minutes late for my appointment with George Passant. I arrived in the lounge of the public house where we had first drunk together when I was eighteen, nearly forty years before: the room was almost empty, for the pub was no longer fashionable at night and George himself no longer used it, except for these ritual meetings with me.

There, by the side of what used to be a coal-fire and was now blocked up, he sat. He gave me a burst of greeting, a monosyllabic shout.

As I grew older, and met friends whom I had known for most of my lifetime, I often thought that I didn't see them clearly – or rather, that I saw them with a kind of double vision, as though there were two photographs not accurately superposed. Underneath, there was not only a memory of themselves when young, but the physical presence: that lingered in one's sight, it was never quite ripped away, one still saw them – through the intermittence of time passing – with one's own youthful eyes. And also one saw them as they were now, in the present moment, as one was oneself.

Nowadays I met George three or four times a year, and this double vision was still working. I could still – not often, but in sharp moments – see the young man who had befriended me, set me going: whose face had been full of anger and hope, and who had walked with me through the streets outside on nights of triumph, his voice rebounding from the darkened houses.

But, more than in any other friend, the present was here too. There he sat in the pub. His face was in front of me, greeting me with formal welcome. It was the face of an old, sick man.

Not that he was unhappy. On the contrary, he had been happier than most men all his life, and had stayed so. Not that he behaved as though he were ill. On the contrary, he behaved as though he were immortal. If I had been studying him for the first time, I should have been doubtful about guessing his age. His fair hair was still thick, and had whitened only over his ears, though it was wild and disarranged, for his whole appearance was dilapidated. His face was lined, but almost at random, so that he had no look of mature age. His mouth often fell open, and his eyes became unfocused.

He was actually sixty-three. I had tried to get him to discuss his health, but he turned vague, sometimes, it seemed to me, with a deliberate cunning. He spoke casually about his blood pressure and some pills he had to take. He admitted that his doctor, whose name he wouldn't tell me, had put him on a diet. From what I noticed, he didn't even pretend to keep to it. He still ate gargantuan meals, somehow proud of his self-indulgence, topping off – in a fashion which once had been comic but was now frightening – a meal larger than most of us ate in two days with four or five cream-cakes. He drank as much, or more, than ever. He had always been heavy, but now was fat from his upper chest down to his groin. He must have weighed fifteen stone.

None of that had interfered with his desire for women. I had an uncomfortable suspicion that, as he grew old, he wanted younger girls: but with the same elderly cunning with which he dissimulated his health, he had long ago concealed those details from me. I knew that his firm of solicitors had pensioned him off a couple of years before. Once again, he was vague in telling me the reasons. It might have been that his concentration had gone, as his body deteriorated. It might have been that what he called his 'private life', that underground group activity by which he had once started out to emancipate us all, had become notorious. And yet, in this middle-sized town, none of the members of the Court that morning would have been likely even to have heard his name.

He kept his strange diffident sweetness. When he forced himself, his mind became precise. He liked seeing me. Yet, I had to admit it (it was an admission that for years I had shut out), he had become quite remote. Whenever we met, he asked the same set of hearty mechanical questions, as he did that night. How was Margaret? Well, I said. Splendid, said George. Was I writing? Yes, I said. Splendid, said George. How was Charles? Getting on fine, I said. Here the formula took a different course. 'I'm not concerned about his academic prospects. I take those for granted,' said George. 'I'm asking you about his health.'

'He's very tough,' I said.

'I hope you're certain about that,' said George, as though he were a family doctor or the best-qualified censor of physical self-discipline.

'He's fine.'

'Well, that's slightly reassuring,' said George. 'It's his health that I want to be convinced about, that's the important thing.'

That conversation, in very much the same words, took place each time we met. It expressed a kind of formalised affection. But it had set in a groove something like ten years before. So far as there was meaning in the questions about Charles, they referred to the fact that he had been seriously ill in infancy. Since then he had been as healthy as a boy could be: but George, who wanted to show his interest, couldn't find an interest in anything that had happened to him since.

'Drink up!' cried George. I had another pint of beer, which, except with him, I never drank.

I should have liked (I had enough nostalgia for that) to settle down to talk. I mentioned my singular experience with Mr Pateman. George, happy with some internal reverie, gave a loud but inattentive laugh. I said that I had, for a moment or two, come across his niece. At that he showed some response, as though breaking through the daydream which submerged him.

'I'm afraid I haven't been able to see much of my family,' he said.

I understood his language too well to ask why not. There were esoteric reasons manifest to him, though to no one else. He had had three sisters: all had married, and one, Cora's mother, was now dead. Another one was living in London, and the third stayed in the town. All three of them had borne nothing but daughters; I had met none of George's nieces until that afternoon, and he himself seldom referred to them.

'This one [Cora] seems to be pretty bright,' he said. 'She even tagged along with some of my people not so long ago—'

'My people' were the successors to the group of which, in my time, he had been the leader and inspirer. All the years since he had been surrounded by young men and women, his own self-perpetuating underground.

'What happened?'

'Oh, somehow she seemed to lose touch.' He went on: 'I've never enquired into the lives of any of my family. And I've never told them anything about my own.'

He said that with the simplicity of Einstein stating that 'puritanical reticence' was necessary for a searcher after truth.

I started to speak about a concern of mine. After all, he was my oldest friend, and it had been a jagged year for me, as my father didn't know but my young son did – and as George had barely noticed. When I got out of public life, soon after Roger Quaife's defeat, I had expected to get out of controversy also. But it hadn't happened like that. Some of the enmity had followed me, and had got tangled up with my literary affairs. A few months before, I had been accused, in somewhat lurid circumstances, of plagiarism. This had made the news, and kept recurring. As I told George, understating the whole business, if you live in public at all, you have to take what's coming: but, though I could imagine almost any other kind of accusation against me having some sort of basis, this one hadn't. That, however, didn't make it any more pleasant.

My brand of sarcasm washed over him.

'I remember seeing something or other in the papers,' he said. 'Of course, I couldn't take part. Who's going to listen to a retired solicitor's clerk? Anyway, as you say, you've nothing to complain about.'

That was not what I had really said: he had forgotten my tone of voice. 'If anyone's got anything to complain about,' said George, warming up, 'I have. Do you realise that I've spent forty-two years in this wretched town, and they've kept me out of everything? They've seen to it that I've never had a responsible position in my whole life. They've put a foot across my path ever since I was a boy. And at the end, if you please, they don't say as much as thank you and they give me a bit more than they need just to stop feeling ashamed of themselves.'

In the first place 'they' meant his old firm of solicitors. But 'they' also meant all the kinds of authority he had struggled against, detected conspiracies among, found incomprehensible and yet omnipotent, since he was a boy. All the authority in the country. Or in life, as far as that went. It sounded like persecution-mania, and he had always had a share of it. Yet, like many people with persecution-mania, as my wife had said of Donald Howard, he had something to feel persecuted about. Perhaps the one allured the other? Which came first? He was the cleverest man whom I had seen, in functional terms, so completely wasted. But now I had seen more, I speculated on the kind of skill, or whether there was any, which would have been needed not to waste him – or not to let him waste himself.

'I never got anything, did I?' he said, with a gentle puzzled smile.

'No, you didn't.'

'I suppose I didn't want it very much.' Just for an instant, all the paraphernalia of his temperament was thrown aside, and that dart of candour shot out.

'Anyway,' he shouted, in a great voice, not the voice of a sick man, 'they won. *They won.* Let's have another drink on it.'

He was happy and resigned. Did he realise – probably not, he was too happy to go in for irony – that, in a different sense, it was he who had won? All those passionate arguments for freedom – which meant sexual freedom. The young George in this town, poor, unknown, feeling himself outside society, raising the great voice I had just heard. 'Freedom from their damned homes, and their damned parents, and their damned lives.' Well, he had won: or rather, all those like him, all the forces they spoke for (since he was, as someone had said during one of his ordeals, a 'child of his time') had won. How completely, one could not escape at the Court that morning. The freedom which George had once dreamed about had duly happened: and, now it had happened, he took it for granted. He didn't cherish it as a victory. He just assumed that the world was better than it used to be.

I had expected that we should have a meal together – but George was looking at his watch.

'I'm afraid', he said, 'that I'm rather pressed tonight.'

He had the air, which one sometimes saw in businessmen or politicians, of faint estrangement from those not regulated by a timetable.

I did not ask where he was going. I said I should attend the Court in June, and that we could meet as usual. Splendid, said George. Splendid, he repeated, with immense heartiness. He got up to leave me. As he went to the door, I noticed that he was making one, though only one, concession to his physical state: he was walking with abnormal slowness. It was deliberate, but from the back he looked like an old man.

When I myself left the pub, I didn't stroll through the streets, as I often liked doing. That meeting with George had had an effect on me which I didn't understand, or perhaps didn't want to: it hadn't precisely saddened me, but I didn't want my memory to be played on. It was better to be with people whom I hadn't known for long, to be back in the here-and-now. So I returned to the Residence: this time the drawing-room lights, seen from the drive, were welcoming. The sight of Vicky was welcoming too. They had had an early dinner, she said, and her father had gone off to his manuscripts. She said: 'When did you eat last?'

Not since breakfast, I replied. She chuckled, and said that I was impossible. Soon I was sitting in front of the fire with a plate of sandwiches. Vicky curled up on the rug. I was tired, but not unpleasantly so, just enough to realise that I had had a long day. It was all familiar and comfortable, the past pushed away, no menace left.

Vicky wouldn't talk, or let me, until I had eaten. Then she said that her father had told her about the Court proceedings. She knew the result, and she was relieved: anyway, we had time to work in: perversely, she was enough relieved to be irritated with me.

'You two [she meant her father and me] had an up-and-a-downer, didn't you?'

'Not exactly.'

'That's his account, anyway.'

I told her that I thought I deserved a bit of praise. She said:

'I must say, I should like to knock your heads together.'

It appeared that Arnold Shaw had told her of a violent argument, in which he had prevailed. Actually, she was pleased. Pleased because she was protective about her father and trusted me. She was hopeful about the next moves. I said that the academics were being sensible, and I myself would try to involve Francis Getliffe.

She was sitting on her heels, her hair shining and her face tinted in the firelight.

'Bless you,' she said.

I had not mentioned Leonard Getliffe's name, but only his father's. That was enough, though, to set her thoughts going, as if I had touched a trigger and released uncontrollable forces. Her expression was softened; when she spoke her voice was strong, but had lost the touch of bossiness, the doctor's edge.

Could she make a nuisance of herself again? she said. She knew that I understood: questions about Pat had formed themselves. My first impulse, before she had said a word, was of pity for Leonard Getliffe.

Though I knew, and she knew that I knew, she started off by seeming unusually theoretical. Was a marriage, all other things being good, likely to be affected if the wife was earning the livelihood? Even for her, the most direct of young women, it was a pleasure to go through a minuet, to produce a problem in the abstract, or as though she were seeking advice on behalf of a remote acquaintance. I gave a banal answer, that sometime I had known it work, sometimes not. In my own first marriage, I added, my wife had contributed half the money: and, though it had been unhappy, it had not been any more unhappy, perhaps less, because of that. She hadn't heard of my first marriage: and after what I had just said, she still really hadn't heard. She said:

'So you're not against it?'

I said, once more banal, that any general answer had no meaning. Then I asked:

'Are you going to get married then?'

'I hope so.'

I had another impulse, this time of concern for her. She was speaking with certainty. I wished that she was more superstitious, or that she had some insurance against the future.

'You see,' said Vicky, 'I can earn a living, though it won't be a very grand living, while we see if he can make a go of it. Is that a good idea?'

'Isn't he very young—' I began carefully, but she interrupted me.

'There is a snag, of course. You can't do a medical job with young children around. I'm too wrapped up in him to think about children now. You know how it is, I can't believe that I shall ever want anything but him. I have to tell myself, of course I shall.' She gave a self-deprecating smile. 'I'm just the same as everybody else, aren't I? I expect I shall turn into a pretty doting mother.'

'I expect you will,' I said. I was easier when she got down from the heights.

'If we wanted to start a family in three or four years' time, and we oughtn't to leave it much later, because I shall be getting on for thirty, then he might not be able to keep us, might he?'

Practical plans. Delectable practical plans. As delectable as being on the heights, sometimes more so.

'However good he is,' I said, 'it's hard to break through at his game—'

'I know,' she said. 'Well, what else can he do on the side?'

I said it would be difficult for his father to allow him anything. Martin had a daughter still at school, and, apart from his Cambridge salary, not a penny. As for myself—

'Oh, I couldn't possibly let you give us money.'

Her young man quite possibly could, I thought. I nearly said it: but she, like George in the pub an hour or two before, would not have recognised my tone of voice.

In any case, there was something that I ought to say.

'Look, Vicky,' I began, as casually as I could, hesitating between leaving her quite unwarned and throwing even the faintest shade upon her joy, 'I told you a minute ago, he is a very young man, isn't he?'

'Do you know, I don't feel that.'

'Your character's formed,' I went on. 'You're as grown-up as you'll ever be.' (I wasn't convinced of that, but it was a way to talk of Pat.) 'I'm not so sure that's true of him, you know.'

She was looking at me without apprehension, without a blink.

'I mean,' I said, 'parts of people's character grow up at different rates. Perhaps that's specially so for men. In some ways Pat's mature. But I'm not certain that he is in all. I'm not certain that he's capable of knowing exactly what he wants for his whole life. He may be too young for that.'

She smiled.

'You're wrong,' she said.

She smiled at me affectionately, but like someone in the know, with a piece of information the source of which cannot be revealed.

'He's a very strong character,' she said.

All my hesitation had been unnecessary. I hadn't hurt her. She was no less fond of me, and also no less joyous. She was totally unaffected. She was confident – but that was too weak a word, for this was the confidence of every cell in her body – that she knew him as I could never do, and that was right.

We did not say much more about Pat that night. Some time afterwards, while we were still sitting by the fire, Arnold Shaw came in, rubbing his hands.

'Couple of hours' good work,' he announced. 'Which is more than most of my colleagues will do this term.'

With the utmost friendliness and good nature, he asked me if I had spent a tolerable afternoon, and invited me to have a nightcap. Vicky was watching us both with a blank expression. She had heard him talk of a bitter quarrel: if I knew Arnold Shaw's temper, he had denounced me as every kind of a bad man: here he was, convivial, and treating me as an old friend. She admired him for being a museum specimen of a seagreen incorruptible (in that she was her father's daughter): here he was, looking not incorruptible but matey and malicious, and certainly not seagreen. Here we both were, drinking our nightcaps, as though we wanted no one else's company. Yet she didn't for an instant doubt that he would never budge an inch, and that I too would stick it out. Here we were, exchanging sharp-tongued gossip. It struck her as part of a masculine conspiracy which she could not completely comprehend.

When Arnold Shaw was disposed to think of a second nightcap, she roused herself and, daughter-like, doctor-like, said that it was time for bed.

CHAPTER VI

DESCRIBING A TRIANGLE

BACK in our flat, the sunlight slanting down over the Hyde Park trees, my wife was listening to me. I had been telling her about the past two days:

we had our own shorthand, she knew where I had been amused and where I was pretending to be amused.

'It's a good job you've got some stamina, isn't it?' she said.

It sounded detached; it couldn't have been less so. She was happy because I was well and not resigned, any more than she was herself. She had always looked younger than her age, and did so still. Her skin remained as fine as Vicky Shaw's. The only open signs of middle age were the streaks of grey above her temples. I had suggested that, since she looked in all other respects so young, she might as well have them tinted. She had been taken aback, for that was the kind of intervention which she didn't expect from me. But she said no: it was the one trivial thing she had refused me. She wore those streaks like insignia.

In some ways she had changed during our marriage: or rather, parts of her temperament had thrust themselves through, in a fashion that to me was a surprise and not a surprise, part of the Japanese-flower of marriage. To others, even to friends as perceptive as Charles March or my brother, she had seemed over-delicate, or something like austere. It was the opposite of the truth. Once she had dressed very simply, but now she spent money and was smart. It might have seemed that she had become vainer and more self-regarding. Actually, she had become more humble. She didn't mind revealing herself, not as what she had once thought suitable, but as she really was: and if what she revealed was self-contradictory, well then (in this aspect true to her high-minded intellectual ancestors, from whom in all else she had parted) she didn't give a damn.

Earlier, she used to think that I enjoyed 'the world' too much. Now she enjoyed it more than I did. At the same time, in the midst of happiness, she wanted something else. She had thrown away the web of personal relations, the aesthetic credo, in which and by which her father, whom she loved, had lived his life. That was too thin for her: and as for the stoical dutifulness of many of my political or scientific friends, she could admire it, but it wasn't enough. She would have liked to be a religious believer: she couldn't make herself. It wasn't a deep wound, as it had been for Roy Calvert, for she was stronger-spirited, but she knew what it was – as perhaps all deep-natured people know it – to be happy, to count her blessings, and, in the midst of content, to feel morally restless, to feel that there must be another purpose to this life.

With Margaret, too clear-sighted to fabricate a purpose, this gave an extra edge to her responsibilities. As a young woman she had been responsible, with a conscience greater than mine: now she was almost superstitiously so. Her father, who had been ill for years – she wouldn't go out at night without leaving a telephone number. Her son by her first marriage. Charles and me at home. Her sister. Margaret tried to disguise it, because she knew her own obsessions: but if she had believed in prayer, she would have prayed for many people every night.

So she took it for granted that I ought to do my best for Arnold Shaw and Vicky. She took it for granted that I should be as long-suffering as she could be – for after the years together some of my behaviour had shaded into hers, and hers into mine. Further, she was herself involved. She seemed controlled, whereas I was easy and let my emotions flow, so that people were deceived: her loves and hates had always been violent, and below the surface they were not damped down. She was exhibiting one of them now, against my nephew Pat. She thought he was a waster. She was sorry for any woman who married him. Yet, although she scarcely knew Vicky, she believed me when I said that she was totally committed.

There wasn't much one could do in others' lives: that was a lesson I had taught her. But there was no excuse for not doing the little that one could: that was a lesson she had taught me. At the least, I could put in a word for Arnold Shaw. It would be better for both of them if he kept his job. It was worth going to Cambridge, just to get Francis Getliffe's support, Margaret agreed. We didn't like being parted, but she couldn't come, while her father was so ill: for some time past she had been tied to London, and consequently in the last twelve months I had spent only six or seven nights away from home.

This time I need not stay in Cambridge more than one night – and that I could put off until Charles went back to school. There were a few days left of his holidays, and he was still young enough to enjoy going out with Margaret and me to dinner and the theatre, the pleasant, safeguarded London evenings.

Those days passed, and I was in a taxi, driving out along the Backs to the Getliffes' house, within a week of my visit to the Court. So that, by chance, I had completed the triangle of the three towns that I knew best – in fact, the only three towns in England in which I had ever lived for long. The sky was lucid, there was a cold wind blowing, the blossom was heavy white on the trees: it was late afternoon in April, the time of day and year that I used to walk away from Fenner's. This was the 'pretty England' with which I had baited my son, the prettiest of pretty England. Nowadays when I saw Cambridge, I saw it like a visitor, and thought how beautiful it was. And yet, when I lived there, I seemed scarcely to have noticed it. It had been a bad time for me, my hopes had come to nothing, I was living (and this had been true of me until I was middle-aged) as though I were in a station waiting-room: somehow a train would come, taking me somewhere, anywhere, letting my hopes flare up again. But that wasn't what I remembered first about Cambridge: instead, it was the distractions, or even the comforts, that I had found. One of the most robust of men, who was given to melancholy, told a fellow-sufferer to light bright fires. Well, I had had enough to be melancholy about, but what I remembered were the bright fires. There had been times when I didn't know what was to become of me: yet it had been a consolation (and this was the memory, unless I dug deeper against my will) to call on old Arthur Brown, drink a glass of wine, and get going on another move in college politics. Even if I had been content, I should nevertheless, I was sure, have got some interest out of that power-play. I enjoyed watching personal struggles, big and small, and I couldn't have found a better training-ground. But, all that admitted, if I had been content, I shouldn't have become so passionately absorbed in college politics. They were my refuge from the cold outside.

The Getliffes' drawing-room was, as usual, untidy and welcoming: perhaps a shade more untidy than it used to be, since now they had half-a-dozen grandchildren. It had been welcoming in the past, even when my relations with Francis had been strained, once when we were ranged on different sides, and again more recently when, led by Quaife, we had been on the same side and lost. It had been welcoming even when he was torn by ambition, when his research was going wrong or his public campaigns had wrecked his nerves. One could see the traces of those tensions in his face to this day, the lines, the folds of tinted flesh under his eyes. But the tensions had themselves all gone. Of my close friends, he had had the greatest and the most deserved success. Quite late in life, he had done scientific work with which he was satisfied. That was his prime reward. The honours had flowed in: he was no hypocrite, and he liked those too. There had never been anything puritanical about his radicalism. On a question of principle, he had not made a single concession: his integrity was absolute: but, if orthodoxy chose to catch up with him, well, then he was ready to enjoy sitting in the House of Lords.

The stiffness, the touch of formality which looked like pride and which had developed during the worst of his struggles, had almost vanished. Sometimes in public it could recur. I had recently heard some smart young debunker pass a verdict on him. The young man had met him precisely once, but felt morally obliged to dispose of an eminent figure.

'He's the hell of a prima donna, of course, but he does know how to land the jobs.' I hadn't been infuriated so much as stupefied. Each of us really is alone, I thought. And now I was greeting my old friend and his wife, in their own home, in the happiest marriage I had ever seen.

I embraced Katherine. She had, with unusual self-discipline, been dieting recently and had lost a stone or two: but she remained a matriarch. When Francis was surrounded by the three married children and assorted grandsons and granddaughters, he became a patriarch. Yet now he and Katherine were smiling at each other with – there was no need to diminish or qualify the word – love. They had been married for well over thirty years: it had been a lively active marriage, the support – more than support, the inner validity in all his troubles. They had gone on loving each other, and now, when the troubles were over, they did so still.

It would have been easy, one would have expected, to envy Francis. He had had so much. And yet, curiously enough, he had not attracted a great deal of envy. Nothing like as much as our old colleague, Walter Luke: not as much as I had at times myself. What makes a character envy-repellent? On the whole, the people I had known who attracted the least envy were cold, shut in, mildly paranoid. But none of that was true of Francis, who was – at least in intimacy – both kind and warm. So was she, and they were showing it that evening.

Though Katherine complained that she hated entertaining, and had given that as a reason why Francis should not become Master of the college (the hidden reason was that he shrank from the in-fighting), this house had, with the years, taken on a marked resemblance to the ground floor of an American hotel. One son and one daughter lived in Cambridge; and they, their children, their friends, their friends' children, paid visits as unpredictable as those in a nineteenth-century Russian country house. In the midst of the casual family hubbub, the Getliffes took care of others: they knew that Margaret would want news of her son Maurice, and so, along with a party of young people, some of whom I couldn't identify but who all called Francis by his Christian name, he had been brought in for a pre-dinner drink. By one of the sardonic tricks of chance, it was just that same considerate kindness which had brought ill-luck to their eldest son: for, on a similar occasion, when Leonard first brought Vicky Shaw to see them, they had invited my nephew Pat: and it was in this drawing-room that she had fallen in love.

In a corner of the room, I was talking to Maurice about his work.

'I wish I were brighter,' he said with his beautiful innocent smile, as he had said to me before, since for years Margaret and I had had to watch him struggle over one scholastic hurdle, then another. He bore no malice, even though the rest of us found these hurdles non-existent. He was fond of his step-brother, who was a born competitor. Sometimes I couldn't help thinking – it was a rare thought for me – that he was naturally good. He had been a beautiful child, and now was a good-looking young man. I should have guessed, when I first saw him as an infant, that by now he would appear indrawn: but that had proved dead wrong. He had turned out good-looking in an unusual fashion, as though the world hadn't touched him: fair, unshadowed, with wide-orbited idealist's eyes. Yet the world probably had touched him, for those were the kind of looks that at school had brought him plenty of attention. And he would get the same from women soon, I thought. He gave affection very easily: he might be innocent, but he accepted all that happened round him. He liked making people happy.

Margaret was devoted to him. Partly with the special devotion, and remorse, that one feels for the child of a broken marriage: partly because there was something of her own spirit in him. But none of her cleverness, nor of his father's.

I was trying to discover how things were going. He was in his first year. He hoped to become a doctor, like his father. Psychologically, that would be a good choice for him. He wanted to look after others: given the faith which he, like Margaret, didn't find, he would have made a priest.

The trouble was, the college had told us that he was unlikely to get through the Mays (the Cambridge first-year examinations). I was inquiring what he thought, and which subjects were the worst.

'I'm afraid I'm pretty dense,' he said.

'No, you're not,' I said. I let some impatience show. Often I felt that, just as he accepted everything else, he accepted his own incompetence.

'You believe I'm doing it on purpose, don't you?' He was teasing me. He and I had always been on friendly terms. He wasn't in the least frightened of me: nor, so far as I had seen, of anyone else. He had his own kind of insight.

At last the Getliffes and I were left alone. For once there was no one else present when we went into dinner. Francis, who had seen me spend a long time with Maurice, began talking about him.

'I'm afraid', he said, 'he isn't going to make it.'

'He's very nice,' said Katherine.

'He's not even stupid,' said Francis. 'I know, it must be a worry for you both.'

The two of them were not only loving parents, they took on the duties of parents at one remove. It seemed like a way of giving thanks for their own good fortune. The problems of friends' children – not only those of intimate friends like us – they spent their time upon. About Maurice, Francis had had interviews with his tutor and supervisors. Francis and Katherine hadn't known the inside of a broken marriage: but their sympathy was sharp, they could feel for both Margaret and me; in different senses, it made us more vulnerable through Maurice.

They were sympathetic, but also practical. With a creased, unsentimental smile, Francis said that, come hell, come high water, we had to get the young man through some sort of course. Damn it, he had to earn a living. His supervisors said he didn't seem to possess any approach to a memory. He couldn't memorise anything. 'I should have thought,' said Francis, 'that's going to make medicine pretty well impossible. The anatomy they learn is sheer unscientific nonsense, but still they've got to learn it.'

He gave me some consolatory examples to tell Margaret, of intelligent people who had nothing like a normal memory, and there we had to leave it, Katherine reluctantly, for she, like all her relatives I had once known so well, couldn't resist coming back to test an aching tooth.

The dinner was good. Francis, who had been so gaunt and Quixote-like right into his mid-fifties, was at last beginning to put on a little weight. I was comfortable with them both, and more than that. But I should have to leave in an hour or two, for I was staying with my brother. It was time to discharge what I had come for.

'Francis,' I said, 'I wonder if you can give a hand about old Arnold Shaw.'

He had heard most of the immediate story – though neither he nor Katherine were above enquiring about the details of the students' goings on. I told him that the present issue was effectively settled: it looked as though two or three of the students would be placed elsewhere: and then Shaw would get a confirmatory vote and, in form, a victory. But, I said, it might be an expensive victory. He had plenty of enemies before. Now there would be more. There might come a point, not too far off, when his position became untenable. Could Francis use his influence as Chancellor? Could he talk to the academics in private? And to some of the dignitaries? After all, he could speak with real authority. He just had to tell them that, in spite of his faults, Shaw was doing a good job.

Francis had been listening as carefully as he used to listen in Whitehall. He passed the decanter round to me, and watched me fill my glass. He said:

'I don't think I can tell them that.'

'Why not?'

'Quite simply, I don't believe he is.'

'Oh come,' I said. Incautiously, I hadn't been prepared for this. 'Look, I know he's an awkward customer, I have to stand more of it than you do, but after all he has put the place on the map.'

'I don't believe', said Francis, 'that a man ought to be head of a university if he gets detested by nearly all the students and most of the staff.'

It was years since I had seen him in action: I had half-forgotten how decisive he could be.

'Remember', I said, 'that he's brought in the staff – at least, he's brought in all of them that are any good.'

'He is a good picker.' Francis was irritatingly fair. 'Yes, that's been his contribution. But now he's got them, he can't get on with them. It's a pity, but the place will be at sixes and sevens so long as he's there.'

He added:

'It's a pity, but he's cut his own throat.'

'He's got some human quality,' I said.

Katherine broke in:

'You said that before. About the other one. And we said his wife was appalling. So she was, but I suppose she was attached to him in her own fashion. When he died, it was just before Penelope had her second baby, she stayed with the coffin and they had to pull her away from the grave.'

For the moment, I had lost track. Who was she talking about?

'And then she died within three months, though no one troubled to know about her, and so no one knew what was the matter. As for Walter Luke, it didn't do him any harm. He went to Barford and got into the Royal Society and nearly got killed—'

'No connection,' Francis smiled at her, though he looked as mystified as I was.

'And finished up perfectly well and got decorated and had another child.' She ended in triumph:

'You did make a frightful ass of yourself that time, Lewis.'

That was a phrase her father used to brandish. I had been quite bemused, but now I had it. She was indulging, as she did more often, in a feat of total recall, just as her father used to. What she had been saying referred to an argument about the Mastership in that house, no less than twenty-six years before. It was the candidate I had wanted, Jago, who had died, and his wife after him – but that was not twenty-six years before, only two. When Katherine got going she existed, just as her father had, in a timeless continuum when the present moment, the three of us there at dinner, was just as real, no more, no less, than the flux of memory.

Francis was slower than I to take the reference. Then he gave her a loving grin, and said to me:

'She's right, you know. You did make an ass of yourself that time.'

It was true. It had been bad judgment. But, though my candidate had lost, though it was so long ago, Katherine and Francis often liked to remind me of it.

'Two can play at that game,' I began, ready to try rougher tactics, but in fact Katherine's performance had taken the sting from the quarrel, and also, realistically, I knew that Francis, once he had taken up his stance, would be as hard to move as Arnold Shaw himself. So when he said that I was now making the same mistake, that I got more interested in people than in the job they had to do, I let it go. It wasn't without justice, after all. And it wasn't without justice that he spoke of Arnold Shaw. Something would have to be done for him, if and when he resigned: the university would give him an honorary degree: he could be found a research appointment to help out his pension. That would be better than nothing, I said. Then I mentioned that I had met Leonard, and the three of us were at one again.

'I'm getting just a little tired', said Francis, 'of people telling me that as a scientist he is an order of magnitude better than I am.' But he said it with the special pride of a father who enjoys his son being praised at his own expense. To give an appearance of stern impartiality, as of one who isn't going to see his family receive more than their due, he said that their second son, Lionel, wasn't in the same class. 'I don't think he's any better than I am,' said Francis judiciously. 'He ought to get into the Royal before he's finished, though.'

I said that they were abnormally lucky: but still, the genes on both sides were pretty good. Francis said, not all that good. His father had been a moderately competent barrister at the Parliamentary Bar. Katherine said: 'There's not been a single March who's ever produced an original idea in his life. Except perhaps my great-uncle Benjamin, who tried to persuade the Rothschilds not to put down the money for the Suez canal.'

Anyway, said Francis, who wanted to talk more of Leonard, a talent like his must be a pure sport. High level of ability, yes, lots of families had that – but the real stars, they might come from anywhere, they were just a gift of fate. 'It must be wonderful', he said, half-wistfully, 'to have his sort of power.'

They were so proud of him, as I should have been, or any sentient parent. They were pleased that he was as high-principled as they were: he had recently defied criticism and appointed Donald Howard, who had once been a fellow of the college, to his staff, just because he had been badly treated – although Leonard didn't even like the man. Yet, despite their close family life, they seemed to know little or nothing of his unhappiness over Vicky. 'It's high time he got married,' said Katherine, as though that were his only blemish, an inexplicable piece of wilfulness. They wondered what sort of children he would have.

After Francis had driven me to the college gate, I walked through the courts to the Senior Tutor's house. I had walked that same way often enough when Jago was Senior Tutor. Now I was accustomed to it again, since my brother, after Arthur Brown's term, got the succession. Lights were shining, young men's voices resounded: the smell of wistaria was faint on the cool air: it brought back, not a sharp memory, but a sense that there was something I knew but had (like a name on the tip of the tongue) temporarily forgotten.

My brother's study was lit up, curtains undrawn, and there he and Irene were waiting for me. She fussed round, yelping cheerfully: Martin sat by the fireside in his slippers, sharp-eyed, fraternal, suspecting that there was some meaning in this visit.

Another home, another marriage. A settled marriage, but one which had arrived there by a different route from the Getliffes'. She had been a reckless, amorous young woman: in their first years she had had lovers, had cost him humiliation and, because he had married for love, much misery. But he was the stronger of the two. It was his will which had worn her down. It was possible – I was not certain – that as she grew to depend upon him utterly, she in her turn had been through some misery. I was not certain, because, though he trusted me more than anyone else and occasionally asked me to store away some documents, he preserved a kind of whiggish decorum. If there had been love affairs, they had been kept hidden. Anyway, their marriage had been settled for a long time past, and Martin's anxiety had its roots in another place.

On my way down to Cambridge, I hadn't been confident that I should get him to talk. As soon as I entered his study we were easy together, with the ease of habit, and something stronger too. But he had been controlled and secretive all his life, and in middle age he was letting secretiveness possess him. I still didn't know whether I should get an answer, or even be able to talk at all.

By accident, or perhaps not entirely by accident, for she understood him well, it was Irene who gave me the chance.

We had begun by gossiping. Nowadays the college changed more rapidly than it used to in my time. There were twice as many fellows, they came and went. Many of my old acquaintances were dead. Of those who had voted in the 1937 election, only Arthur Brown, Francis and Nightingale were still fellows. Some I had known since hadn't stayed for long. One who hadn't stayed – it was he whom Irene was gossiping about – was a man called Lester Ince. He had recently run off with an American woman: an American woman, so it turned out, of enormous wealth. They had each got divorces and then married. The present rumour was that they were looking round for a historic country house.

'A very suitable end for an angry young man,' said Martin, with a tart smile. I was amused. I had a soft spot for Lester Ince. It was true that, since he had started his academic career by being remarkably rude, he had gained a reputation for holding advanced opinions. This had infuriated both Francis and Martin, who believed in codes of manners, and who had also remained seriously radical and had each paid a certain price.

'He's quite a good chap,' I said.

'He hasn't got the political intelligence of a cow,' said Martin.

'He's really very amiable,' I said.

'If it hadn't been for that damned fool,' Martin was not placated, 'we shouldn't have been in this intolerable mess.'

That also was true. Before Crawford, the last Master, retired, it had been assumed that Francis Getliffe would stand and get the job. That would presumably have happened – but Francis had suddenly said no. The college had dissolved into a collective hubbub. Lester Ince had trumpeted that what they needed was an *independent man*. The independent man was G. S. Clark. Half the college saw the beauty of the idea: G. S. Clark was an obsessed reactionary in all senses, but that didn't matter. Martin, who was an accomplished college politician, did his best for Arthur Brown, but the Clark faction won by a couple of votes. It had been one of the bitter elections.

'It's got to the point,' Martin was saying, 'that when the Master puts his name down to dine, half-a-dozen people take theirs off.'

'What about you?'

'As a rule,' said Martin, without expression, 'I dine at home.'

That had its own eloquence. He was both patient and polite: and once he had been on neighbourly terms with Clark. Yes, he replied to my question, they were saddled with him for another dozen years.

Irene was more interested in Lester Ince's future.

'Think of all that lovely money,' she said.

She told me about the heiress. It appeared that Lester Ince had at his disposal more money than any fellow (or ex-fellow, for he had just resigned) of the college in five hundred years.

'Money. We could do with a bit of that,' she said.

She said it brightly, but suddenly I felt there was strain, or meaning, underneath. To test her, I replied: 'Couldn't we all?'

'*You* can't say that to us, you really can't.' Her eyes were darting, but not just with fun.

'Is anything the matter?' I wasn't looking at Martin, but speaking straight to her.

'Oh, no. Well, the children cost a lot, of course they do.'

Their daughter Nina, who was seventeen that year, went to a local school: she was a gentle girl, with a musical flair which her brother might have envied, and had cost them nothing. It was Pat on whom they had spent the money – and, I guessed, more than they could spare, although Martin was financially a prudent man. It was Pat about whom she was showing the strain. She had to risk offending Martin, who sat there in hard silence.

I risked it too.

'I suppose it'll be some time before he's self-supporting, won't it?' I asked.

'Good God,' she cried. 'We shouldn't mind so much if we were sure that he would ever be.'

She went on talking to me, Martin still silent. I must have known young men like this, mustn't I? What could one do? She wasn't asking much: all she asked was that he should come to terms, and begin to behave like everyone else.

This was the strangest game that time had played with my sister-in-law. It had played a game with her physically, but that I was used to: she had been a thin, active young woman, and then in her thirties, although her face kept an avid girlish prettiness, she had, as it were, blown up. But that was a joke of the flesh, and this was odder. For only a few years before, as she contemplated her son, she was delighted that he seemed 'as wild as a hawk'. She had enjoyed the prospect of a son as 'dashing' as the young men with whom she had herself racketed round. Now she had it. And she was less comfortable with it than respectable parents like the Getliffes might have been.

She seemed specially horrified about his debts, though, again oddly, she had no idea how big they were.

'Don't worry too much about that,' I said. 'Perhaps I can help.'

'That isn't necessary.' For the first time since his son was hinted at, Martin spoke.

Irene looked at him: either she did not choose, or did not dare, to talk any further. In a moment, with a bright yelping cry, she announced that she was tired. 'You boys can sit up if you want, don't mind me,' she said, on her way to the door.

Martin was sitting with his shoulders hunched, his fingers laced together on one knee. His scalp showed where the hair was thinning: between us, in the old grate, gleamed one bar of the electric fire. Behind Martin was a bookcase full of bound scientific journals, photographs of teams he had played for in his athletic days: as I glanced round, in the constrained and creaking quiet, on his desk I noticed the big leather-covered tutors' register which Arthur Brown used to keep.

Then he began to talk, in the tone of a realistic and experienced man, as though we were talking, not having to explain ourselves, about an acquaintance. He interrupted himself, seeming more deliberate, to light a pipe. It was easy to exaggerate these things, wasn't it? (He might have been echoing my talk with Vicky.) People grew up at different rates, didn't they? Young men who were sexually mature often weren't mature in other ways. And young men who were sexually mature found plenty of opportunities to spend their time. 'Most of us', said Martin, in a matter-of-fact, ironic fashion, 'would have welcomed a few more such opportunities, wouldn't we?'

In an aside, he mentioned my first marriage. When I met Sheila, I was nineteen: if I had known more about women – Martin said, with dry intimacy – I should have been spared a lot.

'In his case' (he did not call his son by name), 'it's the other way round.' He was looking away from me, with his forehead furrowed.

'I don't know where I made the mistake. I wish I knew where to blame myself.' Quite suddenly his realism had deserted him. His tone had changed. His voice, as a rule easy and deep, had sharpened. If he had sent his son to a different school – they hadn't been clever at handling him, they had certainly misunderstood him. If he had never started at the university – that was Martin's fault. It was just the kind of harking back that Martin must have listened to many times in that room: from parents certain that their young man was fine, that circumstances had done all the havoc, or his teachers, or a particular teacher, or their own blindness, lack of sympathy, or bad choice.

'There's only one rule,' I said, trying to console him. 'Whatever you do is wrong.'

'That's no use. I've got to make sure where I've made the mistakes – so that I can get him started now.'

Not only his realism had deserted him, so had his irony. That last remark of mine, which he might have told himself in secret, listening to parental sorrows, was just a noise in his ears. For neither I nor anyone else could be any good to him. Irene, who was an affectionate mother, worried about her son, but practically, not obsessively; Martin's love was different in kind. People sometimes thought him a self-contained and self-centred man: but now, more than in sexual love, he was totally committed. This had been so all through his son's life. It was a devotion at the same time absolutely possessive and absolutely self-abnegating.

It was possible that Martin might not have been so vulnerable if his own life had gone better. He had started with ambitions, and he had got less than he or the rest of us expected. Here he was, as Senior Tutor, dim by his own standards, and that was, in careeristic terms, the end. Martin was a worldly man, and knew that he was grossly undercast. He had seen many men far less able go much further. To an extent, that had made him wish to compensate in the successes of his son. And yet, I thought it might have happened anyway: it was men like himself, stoical and secretive, who were most often swept by this kind of possessive passion.

It was a kind of passion that wasn't dramatic; to anyone outside the two concerned, it was often invisible, or did not appear like a passion to all: and yet it could be weighted with danger, both for the one who gave the love and for its object. I had seen it in the relation of Katherine Getliffe's father with his son. It had brought them both suffering, and to the old man worse than that. It was then that I picked up the antique Japanese phrase for obsessive parental love – darkness of the heart. Nowadays the phrase had become too florid for my taste; nevertheless, that night, as I listened to Martin, it might still have had meaning for someone who had known what he now felt.

I had seen this passion in old Mr March. But I had felt it in myself. I had felt it for one person, and – in his detached moments the reflection might strike him as not without its oddity – that was Martin. Sitting there in his study, we were middle-aged men. Although I was nine years the older, it many ways he was the more set. But when we were young, that wasn't so; I was deprived of the children whom I wanted, and, less free than I had later become, I transferred that parental longing on to him. Once again, it had brought us suffering. It had separated us for a time. It had helped bring about crises and decisions in his career, in which he had made a sacrifice. As he spoke of his son, I didn't bring back to mind that time long past: yet, for me at least, it hung in the air: I did not need telling, I did not need even to observe, that this parental love can be, at the same moment, both the most selfless and the most selfish of any love one will ever know.

I couldn't give him any help. In fact, he didn't want any. This was integrally his own. When he had brushed off my offer of money, he had done it in a way quite unlike him. Usually he was polite and not over-proud. But this was his own, and I didn't offer money again that night. The only acceptable help was that I might arrange some more introductions for his son.

At last I was able, however, to talk about Vicky: and he replied simply and directly, more so than he had done that night, as though this were a relief or a relaxation. Did he know her?

'Oh yes, she's been here.'

'What do you think of her?'

'She's in love with him, of course.'

'What about him?' I asked.

'He's fond of her. He's been fond of a good many women. But still – he's certainly fond of her.'

He was speaking quietly, but with great accuracy. It struck me that he knew his son abnormally well, not only in his nature but in his actions day to day. Whatever their struggles or his disappointments, they were closer, much closer, in some disentangleable sense, than most fathers and sons. It struck me – not for the first time – that it took two to make a possessive love.

'She's expecting him to marry her, you know,' I said.

'I think I realised that.'

'She's a very good young woman.'

'I agree,' said Martin.

'I've got a feeling that, if this goes wrong, it may be serious for her. I'd guess that she's one of those who doesn't love easily.'

'I think I'd guess the same.' Martin added, quite gently: 'And that's not a lucky temperament to have, is it?'

'God knows,' I said, 'I don't blame the boy if he doesn't love her as she loves him.'

'He's a different character. If he does love her – I can't say for sure – it's bound to be in a different way, isn't it?'

'Of course,' I said, 'I don't blame him if he doesn't want to be tied.'

'It might be what he needs,' said Martin. 'Or it might be a disaster.'

'I tell you, I don't blame him. But if she goes on expecting him to marry her – and then at the end he disappears – well, it will damage her. And that may be putting it mildly.'

'Yes.'

'She is a good young woman, and she doesn't deserve that.'

'I hope it doesn't happen.'

'And yet,' I said, 'you don't care, do you? You don't really care? So long as he isn't hurt—'

Martin replied:

'I suppose that's true.' Since we were speaking naturally, face to face, a flicker of his sarcasm had revived. 'But it isn't quite fair, is it? One can't care *in that way* for everyone, now can one? I'm sure you can't. You wait till your son has a girl who is besotted on him.'

He gave me a friendly, fraternal smile.

'In any case,' he want on, 'whatever do you want me to do?'

'No. I don't think there is anything you could do.'

'I'm certain there isn't.'

'But if he's going to drop her in the long run, it would probably be better for her if he did so now.'

'I couldn't influence him like that,' said Martin. 'No one could.' Again he smiled. 'Coming from you, it doesn't make much sense, anyway. I don't pretend to know what's going to happen to them. You seem to have made up your own mind. But you may be wrong, you know. Haven't you thought of that?'

CHAPTER VII

A QUESTION OF LUCK

THE afternoon was so dark that we had switched on the drawing-room lights. The windows were rattling, the clouds loomed past. It was the middle of June, and Charles was at home for a mid-term holiday. He lay on the sofa, without a coat or tie, long legs at full stretch. Margaret was out having her hair done: I had finished work, and Charles had just mentioned some observation, he told me it was Conrad's, about luck.

Of course, I was saying. Anyone who had lived at all believed in luck. Anyone who had avoided total failure had to believe in luck: if you didn't, you were callous or self-satisfied or both. Why, it was luck merely to survive. I didn't tell him, but if he had been born twenty years earlier, before the antibiotics were discovered, he himself would probably be dead. Dead at the age of three, from the one illness of his childhood, the one recognition-symbol which his name evoked in George Passant's mind.

Charles had set me daydreaming. When I thought of the luck in my own life, it made me giddy. Without great good luck, I might shortly be coming up for retirement in a local government office. No, that wasn't mock-modest. I had started tough and determined: but I had seen other tough, determined men unable to break loose. Books? I should have tried. Unpublished books? Maybe. By and large, the practical luck had been with me. On the other hand, I might have been unlucky in meeting Sheila. And yet, I should have been certain to waste years of my young manhood in some such passion as that.

Something, perhaps a turn of phrase of Charles's or a look in his eye, flicked my thoughts on to my brother Martin. He had been perceptibly unlucky: not grotesquely so, but enough to fret him. If I had had ten per cent above the odds in my favour, he had had ten per cent below. Somehow the cards hadn't fallen right. He had never had the specific gift to be sure of success at physics: unlike Leonard Getliffe, whose teachers were predicting his future when he was fifteen. Martin ought to have made his career in some sort of politics. True, he had renounced his major chance; it seemed then, it still seemed, out of character for him to make that sacrifice, but he had done it. I believed that it was a consolation to him, when he faced ten more dim years in college: he had a feeling of free will.

But still, he had all the gifts for modern politics. You needed more luck in that career, of course, than in science, more even than in the literary life. Nevertheless, if Martin had been a professional politician, I should have backed him to 'get office', as the politicians themselves called it. He would have enjoyed it. He would have liked the taste of power. He would have liked, much more than I should, being a dignitary. And yet, I supposed, though I wasn't sure, that he didn't repine much: most men who had received less than their due didn't think about it often, certainly not continuously: life was a bit more merciful than that. There were about ten thousand jobs which really counted in the England of that time. The more I saw, the more I was convinced that you could get rid of the present incumbents, find ten thousand more, and the society would go ticking on with no one (except perhaps the displaced) noting the difference. Martin knew that unheroic truth as well as I knew it. So did Denis Geary and other half-wasted men. It made it easier for them to laugh it off and go on working, run-of-the-mill or not, it didn't matter.

Charles said:

'You remember at Easter, when we came away from your father's, what I said? I told you, it wasn't quite what I expected.'

He had a memory like a computer, such as I had had when I was his age. But his conversational openings were not random, he hadn't introduced the concept of luck for nothing.

'Well?' I said, certain that there was a connection, baffled as to what it was.

'I expected to think that you'd had a bad time—'

'I told you, I had a very happy childhood.'

'I know that. I didn't mean that. I expected to think that you'd had a bad start.'

'Well, it might have been better, don't you think?'

'I'm not sure.' He was smiling, half-taunting, half-probing. 'That's what I was thinking when I came away. I was thinking you might have had better luck than I've had.'

I was taken by surprise. 'What do you mean?'

'I mean, you were a hungry boxer. And hungry boxers fight better than well-fed boxers, don't they?'

However he had picked up that idiom, I didn't know. In fact, I was put out. I was perfectly prepared to indulge in that kind of reflection on my own account: but it seemed unfair, coming from him.

'I should have thought', I said, 'that you fight hard enough.'

'Perhaps. But I've got to do it on my own, haven't I?'

He spoke evenly, good-temperedly, not affected – though he had noticed it – by my own flash of temper. He had been working it out. I had had social forces behind me, pressing me on. All the people in the back-streets who had never had a chance. Whereas the people he had met in my house and grown up among – they had been born with a chance, or had made one. Achievement didn't seem so alluring when you met it every day. He was as ambitious as I had been: but, despite appearances, he was more on his own.

I was talking to him very much as nowadays I talked to Martin. Sometime I thought he bore a family resemblance to Martin, though Charles's mind was more acute. Yes, there was something in what he said. I had made the same sort of observation when I met my first rich friends. Katherine Getliffe's brother Charles – after whom my son was named – had felt much as he did. The comfortable jobs were there for the taking: but were they worth it? Books were being written all round one: could one write one that was worth while? Whereas I was twenty-three or more before I met anyone who had written any kind of book. 'And that', I observed, 'was a remarkably bad one.'

Charles gave a friendly grin.

When I first went into those circles, yes, I had comforted myself that it was I who had the advantage. For reasons such as he had given. And yet – I had had to make compromises and concessions. Too many. Some of them I was ashamed of. I had sometimes been devious. I had had to stay – or at any rate I had stayed – too flexible. It was only quite late in life that I had been able to harden my nature. It was only quite late that I had spoken with my own voice.

'But all that', said Charles, 'kept you down to earth, didn't it?'

'Sometimes,' I said, 'too far down.'

'Still, it has come out all right.' He insisted: 'It's all come out more than all right, you can't say it hasn't?'

'I suppose I'm still more or less intact,' I said.

He knew a good deal about what had happened to me, both the praise and blame. He was a cool customer, but he was my son, and he probably thought that I was a shade more monolithic than I was.

'Don't overdo it,' he said.

'I thought I should have a placid old age. And I shan't.'

'Of course you will in time. Anyway, do you mind?'

I answered: 'Not all that much.'

'The important thing is, you must live a very long time.'

That was said quite straight, and with concern. His smile was affectionate, not taunting. The exchange was over. I said:

'Of course, if it will make things easier for you, I can disown you tomorrow. I'm sure you'd get a nice job in the sort of office I started in.'

We were back to the tone of every day. The clouds outside the window were denser, Margaret had not yet come in. Charles fetched out a chess set, and we settled down to play.

Not that afternoon, perhaps at no moment I could isolate, I realised that there was another aspect in which I was luckier than Martin. Anyone who knew us in the past, in the not-so-remote past, would have predicted that, if either of us were going to be obsessively attached to his son, it would be me. I should have predicted it myself. I was made for it. All my life-history pointed that way. I had deliberately forewarned myself and spoken of it to Margaret. But, though I was used to surprises in others' lives, I was mystified by them in my own. It hadn't happened.

When first, a few hours after he was born, I held him in my arms, I had felt a surge of animal insistence. His eyes were unfocused and rolling, his hands aimlessly waving as though they were sea-plants in a pool: I hadn't felt tender, but something like savage, angrily determined that he should live and that nothing bad should happen to him. That wasn't a memory, but like a stamp on the senses. It had lasted. In the illness of his infancy, I had gone through a similar animal desolation. Soon, when he learned to drive a car, I should be anxious until I heard his key in the lock and saw him safely home.

But otherwise – I didn't have to control myself, it came by a grace that baffled me – I didn't want to possess him, I didn't want to live his life for him or live my own again in him. I was glad, with the specific kind of vanity that Francis Getliffe showed, that he was clever. I got pleasure out of his triumphs, and, when he let me see them, I was irritated by his setbacks. Since there was so little strain between us, he often asked my advice, judging me to be a good professional. He had his share of melancholy, rather more than an adolescent's melancholy. As a rule, he was more than usually high-spirited. The tone of our temperaments was not so very different. I found his company consoling, and often a support.

I could scarcely believe that I had been so lucky. It seemed inexplicable and, sometimes, in my superstitious nerves, too good to be true. Call no man happy until he is dead, as he himself liked quoting. Occasionally I speculated about an event which I should never see: whether my son, far on in his life, would also have something happen to him which was utterly out of character and which made him wonder whether he knew himself at all.

CHAPTER VIII

RED CAPSULES

Two evenings later – Charles was still at home, but returning to school next day – a telegram was brought into the drawing-room, as we were having our first drinks. Margaret opened it, and brought it over to me. It read: Should be grateful if you and Lewis would visit me tonight Austin Davidson.

Austin Davidson was her father. It was like him, even in illness, to sign a telegram in that fashion. It was like him to send her a telegram in any case: for he, so long the champion of the twenties' artistic *avant garde*, had never overcome his distrust of mechanical appliances, and in the sixteen years Margaret and I had been married, he had spoken to me on the telephone precisely once.

357

'We'd better all go,' said Margaret, responsibility tightening her face. She didn't return to her chair, and within minutes we were in a taxi, on our way to the house in Regent's Park.

Charles knew that house well. As we went through the drawing-room where Margaret had once told me I could be sure of her, I glanced at him – did he look at it with fresh eyes, now he had seen how his other grandfather lived? In the light of the June evening, the Vlaminck, the Boudin, the two Sickerts, gleamed from the walls. Charles passed them by. Maybe he knew them off by heart. The Davidsons were not rich, but there had been, in Austin's own phrase, 'a little money about'. He had bought and sold pictures in his youth: when he became an art critic, he decided that no financial interest was tolerable (Berenson was one of his lifelong hates), and turned his attention to the stock market. People had thought him absent-minded, but since he was forty he hadn't needed to think about money.

In his study, though it was a warm night, he was sitting by a lighted fire. Margaret knelt by him, and kissed him. 'How are you?' she said in a strong maternal voice.

'As you see,' said her father.

What we saw was not old age, although he was in his seventies. It was much more like a youngish man, ravaged and breathless with cardiac illness. Over ten years before he had had a coronary thrombosis: until then he had lived and appeared like a really young man. That had drawn a line across his life. He had ceased even to be interested in pictures. Partly, the enlightenment that he spoke for had been swept aside by fashion: he had been a young friend of the Bloomsbury circle, and their day had gone. But more, for all his stoicism, he couldn't come to terms with age. He had gradually, for a period of years, got better. He had written a book about his own period, which had made some stir. 'It's not much consolation,' said Austin Davidson, 'being applauded just for saying that everything that was intellectually respectable has been swept under the carpet.' Then he had weakened again. He played games invented by himself, whenever Margaret or his other daughter could visit him. Often he played alone. He read a little. 'But what do you read in my condition?' he once asked me. 'When you're young, you read to prepare yourself for life. What do you suggest that I prepare myself for?'

There he sat, his mouth half-open. He was, as he had always been, an unusually good-looking man. His face had the beautiful bone structure which had come down to Margaret, the high cheek-bones which Charles also inherited. Since he still stumbled out to the garden to catch any ray of sun, his skin remained a Red Indian bronze, which masked some of the signs of illness. But when he looked at us, his eyes, which were opaque chocolate brown, quite different from Margaret's, had no light in them.

'Are you feeling any worse?' she said, taking his hand.

'Not as far as I know.'

'Well then. You would tell us?'

'I don't see much point in it. But I probably should.'

There was the faintest echo of his old stark humour: nothing wrapped up, nothing hypocritical. He wouldn't soften the facts of life, even for his favourite daughter, least of all for her.

'What can we do for you?'

'Nothing, just now.'

'Would you like a game?' she said. No one would have known, even I had to recall, that she was in distress.

'For once, no.'

Charles, who had been standing in the shadows, went close to the fire.

'Anything I can do, Grandpa?' he said, in a casual, easy fashion. He had become used to the sight of mortal sickness.

'No, thank you, Carlo.'

Austin Davidson seemed pleased to bring out the nickname, which had been a private joke between them since Charles was a baby, and which had become his pet name at home. For the first time since we arrived, a conversation started.

'What have you been doing, Carlo?'

'Struggling on,' said Charles with a grin.

There was some talk about the school they had in common. But Austin Davidson, though he had been successful there, professed to hate it. How soon would Charles be going to Cambridge? In two or three years, three years at most, Charles supposed. Ah, now that was different, said Austin Davidson.

He could talk to the boy as he couldn't to his daughter. He wasn't talking with paternal feeling: he had little of that. All of a sudden, the cage of illness and mortality had let him out for a few moments. He spoke like one bright young man to another. He had been happier in Cambridge, just before the first war, than ever in his life. That had been the *douceur de la vitesse*. He had been one of the most brilliant of young men. He had been an Apostle, a member of the secret intellectual society (Margaret and I had learned this only from the biographies of others, for he had kept the secret until that day, and had not given either of us a hint).

'You won't want to leave it, Carlo.' Davidson might have been saying that time didn't exist, that he himself was a young man who didn't want to leave it.

'I'll be able to tell you when I get there, shan't I?' said Charles.

Again, all of a sudden, timelessness broke. Davidson's head slumped on to his chest. None of us could escape the silence. At last Davidson raised his head almost imperceptibly, just enough to indicate that he was addressing me.

'I want a word with you alone,' he said.

'Do you want us to come back when you've finished?' asked Margaret.

'Not unless you're enjoying my company.' Once again the vestigial echo. 'Which I should consider not very likely.'

On their way out Margaret glanced at me and touched my hand. This was something he would not mention in front of Charles. She and I had the same suspicion. I said, as though a matter-of-fact statement were some sort of help, that I would be back at home in time for dinner.

The door closed behind them. I pulled up a chair close to Davidson's. At once he said:

'I've had enough.'

Yes, that was it.

'What do you mean?' I said automatically.

'You know what I mean.'

He looked straight at me, opaque eyes unblinking.

'One can always not stand it,' he said. 'I'm not going to stand it any longer.'

'You might strike a better patch—'

'Nonsense. Life isn't bearable on these terms. I can tell you that. After all, I'm the one who's bearing it.'

'Can't you bear it a bit longer? You don't quite know how you'll feel next month—'

'Nonsense,' he said again. 'I ought to have finished it three or four years ago.' He went on: he didn't have one moment's pleasure in the day. Not much pain, but discomfort, the drag of the body. Day after day with nothing in them. Boredom (he didn't say it, but he meant the boredom which is indistinguishable from despair). Boredom without end.

'Well,' he said, 'it's time there was an end.'

He was speaking with more spirit than for months past. He seemed to have the exhilaration of feeling that at last his will was free. He wasn't any more at the mercy of fate. There was an exhilaration, almost an intoxication, of free will that comes to anyone when the suffering has become too great and one is ready to dispose of oneself: it had suffused me once, when I was a young man and believed that I might be incurably ill. At the very last one was buoyed up by assertion of the 'I', the unique 'I'. It was that precious illusion, which, on a lesser scale was a consolation, no, more than a consolation, a kind of salvation, to men like my brother Martin when they make a choice injurious (as the world saw it) to themselves.

'You can't give me one good reason,' he said, 'why I shouldn't do it.'

'You matter to some of us,' I began, but he interrupted me:

'This isn't a suitable occasion to be polite. You know as well as I do that you have to visit a miserable old man. You feel better when you get outside. If I know my daughter, she'll have put down a couple of stiff whiskies before you get back, just because it's a relief not to be looking at me.'

'It's not as simple as that. If you killed yourself, it would hurt her very much.'

'I don't see why. She knows that my life is intolerable. That ought to be enough.'

'It isn't enough.'

'I shouldn't expect her', said Davidson, 'to be worried by someone's suicide. Surely we all got over that a long while ago.'

'I tell you, it would do more than worry her.'

'I thought we all agreed', he was arguing now with something like his old enthusiasm, 'that the one certain right one has in one's own life is to get rid of it.'

When he said 'we all', he meant, just as in the past, himself and his friends. I had no taste for argument just then. I said no more than that, as a fact of existence, his suicide would cause a major grief to both his daughters.

'Perhaps I may be excused for thinking', he said it airily, lightheartedly, 'that it really is rather more my concern than theirs.'

Then he added:

'In the circumstances, if they don't like the idea of a suicide in the family, then I should regard them as at best stupid and at worst distinctly selfish.'

'That's about as untrue of Margaret as of anyone you've ever known.'

It was curious to be on the point of quarrelling with a man so sad that he was planning to kill himself. I tried to sound steady: I asked him once again to think it over for a week or two.

'What do you imagine I've been doing for the last four years?' This time his smile looked genuinely gay. 'No, you're a sensible man. You've got to accept that this is my decision and no one else's. One's death is a moderately serious business. The least everyone else can do is to leave one alone.'

We sat in silence, though his head had not sunk down, he did not seem oppressed by the desolating weight that came upon him so often in that room. He said:

'You'll tell Margaret, of course. Oh, and I shall need a little help from one of you. Just to get hold of the necessary materials.'

That came out of the quiet air. He might have been asking for a match. I had to say, what materials?

Davidson took out of his pocket a small bottle, unscrewed the cap, and tipped on to his palm a solitary red capsule.

'That's seconal. It's a sleeping drug, don't you know.'

He explained it as though he were revealing something altogether novel – all the time I had known him, he explained bits of modern living with a childlike freshness, with the kind of Adamic surprise he might have shown in his teens at the sight of his first aeroplane.

He handed the capsule to me. I held it between my fingers, without comment. He said:

'My doctor gives me them one at a time. Which may be some evidence that he's not quite such a fool as he looks.'

'Perhaps.'

'I could save them up, of course. But it would take rather a long time to save enough for the purpose.'

Then he said, in a clear dispassionate tone:

'There's another trouble. I take it that I'm somewhere near a state of senile melancholia. That has certain disadvantages. One of them is that you can't altogether rely on your own will.'

'I don't think you are in that state.'

'It's what I think that counts.' He went on: 'So I want you or Margaret to get some adequate supplies. While I still know my own mind. I suppose there's no difficulty about that?'

'It's not altogether easy.'

'It can't be impossible.'

'I don't know much about drugs—'

'You can soon find out, don't you know.'

I said that I would make enquiries. Actually, I was dissimulating. I twiddled the seconal between my fingers. Half an inch of cylinder with rounded ends: the vermilion sheen: up to now it had seemed a comfortable object. I was more familiar with these things than he was, for

Margaret used them as a regular sleeping-pill. Perhaps once or twice a month, I, who was the better sleeper, would be restless at night, and she would pass me one across the bed. Calm sleep. Relaxed well-being at breakfast.

Up to now these had been innocent objects. Though there were others – mixed up in my response as for the last few minutes I had listened to Davidson – which I had not chosen to see for many years. Another drug: sodium amytal. That was the sleeping-drug Sheila, my first wife, had taken. Occasionally she also had passed one across to me. She had killed herself with them. Davidson must once have known that. Perhaps he had not remembered, as he talked lucidly about suicide. Or else he might have thought it irrelevant. At all times, he was a concentrated man.

When I told him I would make enquiries, he gave a smile – a youthful smile, of satisfaction, almost of achievement.

'Well then,' he said. 'That is all the non-trivial conversation for today.'

But he had no interest in any other kind of conversation. He became withdrawn again, scarcely listening, alone.

When I returned to the flat, Margaret and Charles were sitting in the drawing-room. Margaret caught my eye: Charles caught the glance that passed between us. He too had a suspicion. But it had better remain a suspicion. Margaret had had enough of parents like some of her father's friends, who in the name of openness insisted on telling their children secrets they did not wish to hear.

It was not until after dinner that I spoke to Margaret. She went into the bedroom, and sat, doing nothing, at her dressing-table. I followed, and said:

'I think you'd guessed, hadn't you?'

'I think I had.'

I took her hands and said, using my most intimate name for her:

'You've got to be prepared.'

'I am,' she said. Her eyes were bright, but she was crying. She burst out:

'It oughtn't to have come to this.'

'I'm afraid it may.'

'Tell me what to do.' She was strong, but she turned to me like a child.

All her ties were deep, instinctual. Her tongue, as sharp as her father's, wasn't sharp now.

'I've failed him, haven't I?' she cried. But she meant also, in the ambiguity of passionate emotion, that he had failed her because his ties had never been so deep.

'You mustn't take too much upon yourself,' I said.

'I ought to have given him something to keep going for—'

'No one could. You mustn't feel more guilty than you need.' I was speaking sternly. She found it easy to hug guilt to herself – and it was mixed with a certain kind of vanity.

She put her face against my shoulder, and cried. When she was, for an instant, rested, I said:

'I haven't told you everything.'

'What?' She was shaking.

'He wants us to help him do it.'

'What do you mean?'

'He's never been too good at practical things, has he?' I spoke with deliberate sarcasm. 'He wants us to find him the drugs.'

'Oh, no!' Now her skin had flushed with outrage or anger.

'He asked me.'

'Hasn't he any idea what it would mean?'

Again I spoke in our most intimate language. Then I said: 'Look, I needn't have told you. I could have taken the responsibility myself, and you would never have known. There was a time when I might have done that.'

She gazed at me with total trust. Earlier in our marriage I had concealed wounds of my own from her, trying (I thought to myself) to protect her, but really my own pride. That we had, with humiliation and demands upon each other, struggled through. We had each had to become humbler, but it meant that we could meet each other face to face.

'Can you imagine,' she cried, 'if ever you got into his state – and I hope to God that I'm dead before that – can you imagine asking young Charles to put you out?'

All her life, since she was a girl, she had been repelled by, or found quite wanting in human depth, the attitude of her father's friends. To her, they seemed to apply reason where reason wasn't enough, or oughtn't to be applied at all. It wasn't merely that they had scoffed at all faiths (despite her yearning, she had none herself, at least in forms she could justify): more than that, they had in her eyes lost contact with – not with desire, but with everything that makes desire part of the flow of a human life.

'Tell me what to do,' she said again.

'No,' I replied, 'I can't do that.'

'I just don't know.' Usually so active in a crisis, she stayed close to me, benumbed.

'I will tell you this,' I said. 'If it's going to hurt you too much to give him the stuff, that is, if it's something you think you won't forget, then I'm not going to do it either. Because you'd find that would hurt you more.'

'I don't know whether I ought to think about getting hurt at all. I suppose it's him I ought to be thinking about, regardless—'

'That's not so easy.'

'He wants to kill himself.' Now she was speaking with her father's clarity. 'According to his lights, he's got a perfect right to. I haven't any respectable right to stop him. I wish I had. But it's no use pretending. I haven't. All I can do is make it a bit more inconvenient for him. It would be easy for us to slip him the stuff. It would take him some trouble to find another source of supply. So there's no option, is there? I've got to do what he wants.'

The blood rushed to her face again. Her whole body stiffened. Her eyes were brilliant. 'I can't,' she said, in a voice low but so strong that it sounded hard. 'And I won't.'

I didn't know what was right: but I did know that it was wrong to press her.

Soon she was speaking again with her father's clarity. The proper person for him to apply to for this particular service would be one of his friends. After all – almost as though she were imitating his irony – there was nothing they would think more natural.

Obviously he had to be told without delay that we were failing him. 'He'll be disappointed,' I said. 'He's looking forward to it like a treat.'

'He'll be worse than disappointed,' said Margaret.

'I'd better tell him,' I said, trying to take at least that load from her.

'That's rough on you.' She glanced at me with gratitude.

'I don't like it,' I said. 'But I can talk to him, there's no emotion between us.'

'There's no emotion between him and anyone else now, though, is there?' she said.

Once more she stiffened herself.

'No, I must do it,' she said.

She looked more spirited, brighter, than she had done that night. Hers was the courage of action. She could not stand the slow drip of waiting or irresolution, which I was better at enduring: but when the crisis broke and the time for action had arrived, when she could do something, even if it were distasteful, searing, then she was set free.

So, with the economy of those who know each other to the bone, we left it there. We returned to the drawing-room, where Charles, who was reading, looked at us, curiosity fighting against tact. 'You're worried about him, I suppose,' he allowed himself to say.

CHAPTER IX

TRICK OF MEMORY

ALL through those weeks, I was being badgered by messages from the Pateman family. One had arrived during Charles's break; another the evening after Austin Davidson made his request, the same day that Margaret went to him with our answer. Dick Pateman's messages came by telephone, in the form of protracted trunk calls (who paid the bills? I wondered): he had been found a place at a Scottish university, but that made him more dissatisfied. But his dissatisfaction was not so grinding as that of his father, who wrote letters of complaint about his son's treatment and his own. There was, I knew it well, a kind of blackmail of responsibility: once you did the mildest of good turns, natures such as these – and there were more than you imagined – took it for granted that you were at their mercy. Well, after the June Court, I had decided to pay them a last visit and say that that was the end.

Meanwhile, Margaret had faced her father: and the result was not what we expected. True, he had been bitter, he had been intellectually scornful. He regarded what he called her 'mental processes' as beneath contempt. And yet, she could not be sure, was he also feeling relieved, or perhaps reprieved? At any rate, he seemed both more active and less despairing: and physically, after his announcement to us and his quarrel with her, he had, for days which lengthened into weeks, something like a remission. If that had happened to anyone else, he would have thought it one of fate's jokes, though in slightly bad taste. During Margaret's visits, daily though uninvited, he produced ironies of his own, but didn't speculate on that one. As for her, she dared not say a word, in case this state were a fluke, something the mind-body could hold stable for a little while, before the collapse.

On the day of the Court meeting, which was 22 June, I arrived at the station early in the afternoon and went straight out to the university. The Court was to meet at 3.0: the proceedings would be formal: but (so I had heard from Vicky) Leonard Getliffe and two of the younger professors had decided that, since it wasn't necessary for them to

366

attend, they wouldn't do so. Arnold Shaw had expressed indifference: he was going to get his vote of support, there would be no dissension. Had the man no sense of danger? I thought. The answer was, he hadn't. Among his negative talents as a politician, and he had many, that was the most striking. If one had watched any kind of politics, big or little, one came to know that a nose for danger was something all the real performers had. They might lack almost every other gift, but not that. Trotsky, like Arnold Shaw, whom he didn't much resemble in other respects, had singularly little nose for danger. He got on without it for a few years. If he had had it, he might have held on to the power for longer.

Thus I was sitting in Leonard Getliffe's office (they used the American term by now) in the physics department. Outside, it was a bright mid-summer afternoon, just like the weather twenty-two years before, when Leonard was nine years old, the day we heard that Hitler's armies had gone into Russia. A motor-mower was zooming over the lawn, and through the open window came the smell of new-cut grass. In the room was a blackboard covered with symbols; there were three or four photographs, among them I recognised Einstein and Bohr: on the desk, notebooks, trays, another photograph, this time of Vicky Shaw. Not a flattering one. She wasn't photogenic. In the flesh she had both bloom and vital force, but in two dimensions she looked puddingy.

There the picture stood, in front of him. I said, wouldn't he reconsider and come along to the Court? After all, we had done what we could for the students. Yes, said Leonard, even Pateman had got fitted up. 'The Scots can cope with him now,' I said.

'No, not the Scots.' Leonard gave the name of a university close by, only twelve miles away. 'They've accepted him' said Leonard.

'Are you sure?'

'I don't see why he should invent the story, do you?' Leonard's grey eyes were regarding me cat-humorously through his glasses. 'Especially as it stops us exerting ourselves.'

No doubt that was why I hadn't been badgered on the telephone for several days. It hadn't been thought necessary to tell me that I wasn't to trouble myself further.

'Well then,' I said. 'It's only a formality today. Why not come along?'

'It's only a formality,' said Leonard. 'Why come along?'

'You know as well as I do. Just to patch things up.'

'In that case, it's not precisely a formality, is it?'

It resembled an argument with his father – over tactics, or principles, or choices – such as we had had since we were young men. But it wasn't quite like that. Leonard was just as immovable, but gentler and at the same time more certain. The matter had been mishandled. He and his colleagues (but I now felt sure that his was the authority behind them) weren't willing to appear placated, until they had made their own terms. They weren't being noisy. They were merely abstaining. It was the quietest form of protest. Maybe others would understand.

'What about the Vice-Chancellor?'

'He's only got to see reason, hasn't he?' said Leonard.

Vicky had told me that, if she had appealed to him to go easy on her father, he would have done it. She (for once confident) was sure that she could do anything with him. But that was the one appeal she couldn't make. One oughtn't to use love like that, unless one can pay it back. And also I, having heard her secrets, couldn't use it either: she had said so, direct as usual. Well, that did credit to the decency of her feelings. And yet, for once confident, she was for once over-confident. Listening to him, I didn't believe that, if she had promised to marry him tomorrow, she would have changed one of his decisions about Arnold, or even his tone of voice.

Was it possible that, miserable about her, he – who was as decent as she was, and no more malicious – was taking it out of her father? I didn't believe that either. It was hard to accept, but personal relations often counted not for more, but for far less than one expected. There were people who in all human affairs, not only politics but, say, the making of a painter's reputation, who saw a beautiful spider's web of personal connections. Such people often seemed cunning, abnormally sophisticated in a world of simple men: but when it came to practice, they were the amateurs and the simple men were the professionals.

'Can't you really go a step or two to meet him?' I asked.

'I think it is for him to meet us.'

Dead blank. So, killing time before the Court, I chatted about some of the scientists I knew of his father's generation – Constantine, O–, B–, Mounteney. As usual, I found an obscure amusement in the way in which Leonard and his contemporaries discussed fellow-scientists twenty or thirty years older than themselves. Amiable dismissal: yes, they had done good work; once, they deserved their awards and their Nobels: but now they ought to retire gracefully and cease cluttering up the scene. Mounteney – 'It's time', said Leonard, 'that he was put out to grass.' With the same coolness Leonard remarked that he himself, at thirty-one, might very well be past his peak. His was probably the most satisfying of all careers, I said: and yet, for the reason he had just given, I was glad that it had not been mine.

Somehow, casually, I mentioned Donald Howard. It was good of Leonard to have found him a niche. No, merely sensible, said Leonard. Of course, he added vaguely, you knew something about the affair in your college, didn't you? Yes, I knew something, I said (I felt sarcastic, but Leonard, like other conceptual thinkers, had a thin memory, didn't store away the things he heard). I even knew Howard a bit. Would I like to see him for a minute? Out of nothing but curiosity, I said yes. Leonard spoke to the apparatus on his desk, beside Vicky's picture. Within minutes, Howard came, head bent, into the room. He shook hands, conventionally enough. He wasn't quite as graceless as I remembered, though he had some distance to go before he became Lord Chesterfield. His shock of hair, which used to push out from his brow, had been cut: he looked more like the soldier that most of his family had been. He wasn't cold to me, but equally he wasn't warm. Did he like living in the town? He'd seen worse, he said, without excess. How did he enjoy the university? It was better than a technical college, he said, without excess. He seemed to think that some conversational initiative of his own was called for. What was I doing in this place, he ventured? I had come down for the Court, I replied. I shouldn't have thought that was worth anyone's time, said Howard. After that, he felt that he had done his duty, and escaped.

Leonard grinned at me.

'How good is he?' I asked.

'Oh, he's better than Francis [the Getliffe family, like Edwardian liberals, called their parents by their first names] used to think. By a factor of two.' Leonard went on to say that at the time of his dismissal from the college, and during the research which led up to it, Howard had been paralytically lacking in confidence: so much that it made him look a scientific fool. But that he wasn't. Now he had been given a 'good problem' and was having some success, he showed a certain amount of insight. He'd never be really first-rate: he'd probably never make the Royal Society, said Leonard, as though that were the lowest limit of man's endeavour. But he could develop into a competent professor, conscientious with his students and with half-a-dozen respectable scientific papers to his name.

That sounded like a firm professional judgment. When I asked about other parts of Howard's life, Leonard had picked up or remembered little. He didn't know – as I had heard and believed to be true – that Howard had ceased to be a fellow-traveller. He hadn't gone through a dramatic conversion, he had just moved without explaining himself into the centre of the Labour Party. About his marriage – yes, Leonard did know, coolness breaking, showing the tentative nervous interest of a man who should be married himself, that Howard had divorced his wife. She had gone off with Eric Sawbridge, who, unlike Howard, had stayed a communist, pure and unbudgeable, and wouldn't budge until he died. He had served nine years in gaol, after passing on some of the early atomic information, and had come out unchanged.

'One of the bravest men I ever knew,' I said to Leonard.

'Francis says the same,' Leonard replied. But to him all this, all those crises of conscience which had riven his scientific predecessors, all the struggles, secret and public, in which his father and I had spent years of out lives, seemed like history. If he had been our age, he would have felt, and done, the same as we did. As it was, he signed the 'liberal' letters, but otherwise behaved as though there were nothing else that a man of goodwill could do.

It was getting on for three, and I got up.

'I still can't persuade you to come?' I said.

'I'm afraid not, Lewis,' he answered, with an unyielding but gentle smile.

In the Court room, one side wide open to the afternoon sun, in fact so open that curtains had to be drawn to avoid half the table being blistered, the first item on the agenda took three minutes. And those three minutes were the stately minuet. *Resolution of confidence in Disciplinary Committee.* The secretary reported that three of the students had found accommodation elsewhere: Miss Bolt had announced her engagement, and did not wish to undertake further study. 'Any discussion?' said Arnold Shaw, sharp eyes executing a traverse. Not a word. 'May I ask for a motion?' This had been prearranged: resolution of confidence, moved by a civic dignitary, seconded by an academic. 'Any further discussion?' Not a word. 'Those in favour?' Denis Geary looked across at me while hands were going up. No, there was no point in indulging oneself, though he, unlike me, wasn't interested in protecting Arnold Shaw. His hand went up, so did mine. 'Unanimous,' said Shaw, giving a pursed smile, with a satisfaction as great as Metternich's after one of his less commonplace manœuvres.

The whole of the rest of the proceedings was dedicated to the October congregation. Flummery, of course; but then people, even serious people like Denis Geary, enjoyed flummery: there were wafts of pleasure, as well as mildly dotty practical suggestions, in the air. Lord Getliffe would preside. Honorary degrees would be presented. The Court had already approved the names of the honorary graduands. Dinner. Speeches. Who should speak? That particular topic took up a long time. I sat absent-minded, while the general enjoyment went on. At last (though it was actually only about half past four) I got out into the summer air. Would I have tea? Shaw was pressing me. No, I had an engagement soon. That was embroidering the truth. For the first time on any of my visits to the town, George Passant had sent me a note – like all the letters I had ever received from him, as short and neat as a military despatch – saying that he was otherwise occupied and couldn't meet me for our usual drink. All I had to do was call on the Patemans, when the father was home from work, and settle my account. Then I could go to the Residence, obligations fulfilled, though (I was still thinking of Leonard) not in a fashion anyone could congratulate himself upon.

Still, it was pleasant to walk by myself round the campus (that word also had swept eastward) in the still sunshine. The students were dressed differently from those I used to know: young men and girls in jeans, long hair, the girls' faces unpainted and pale. Transistor radios hung from a good many wrists. Pairs were lolling along, arms round each others' waists: that too wouldn't have happened in my college before the war. I stretched myself on the grass, not far from such a group. The conversation, how-ever, as much as I could catch, was not amorous but anxious. They nearly all carried examination papers with them. This was the time of their finals: they had just been let out of a three-hour session: they were holding inquests. Dress changed: social manners changed: sexual manners changed: but examinations did not change. These boys and girls – they must have been round twenty-one, but they were so hirsute that they looked younger – were at least as obsessed as any of us used to be. They had another paper next morning. One girl was saying that she must shut herself up that night, she needed to put in hours and hours of work. Wrong, I wanted to say: real examinees didn't behave like that: don't look at a book, don't even talk about it. But I kept quiet. Whoever listened to that kind of advice? Or to any other kind of advice, except that which they were already determined to take?

It was pleasant in the sun. I was timing myself to arrive at the Patemans' house at six. Now that I knew the way, I managed it to the minute. But Mr Pateman was not there. His wife let me in, the passage dark and smelly as I entered from the bright afternoon. From the front room the record player was, just as last time, at work. In the parlour high tea was laid.

The room was empty except for Kitty, who, cutting a slice of bread, gave a little beck of recognition.

'He's not in yet, I'm afraid,' said Mrs Pateman again.

'I told him the time I should be coming.' She was the only woman of the household whom I liked: I couldn't let myself be rough with her.

'The doctor doesn't have his surgery till six, you see,' Mrs Pateman began a flustered explanation.

'I'm sorry,' I had to say. 'I hope there's nothing much the matter?'

'Of course there isn't.' Kitty gave a fleering smile. 'There's never anything the matter with him—'

'You didn't ought to say that about your father.' Mrs Pateman seemed overwhelmed in this house, this 'simple home' which even to me was uncomfortably full of egos. Kitty shrugged, looked at me under her eyebrows, and informed me that Dick was camping, and wouldn't be back for a week. She said it in a manner which was little-me-ish and at the same time hostile, no, not so much hostile as remote from all of them. She might be resenting his having a higher education, while she, appreciably cleverer, had been kept out of one. I found her expression, partly because of its mobility, abnormally difficult to read. I guessed that she might, despite the fluttering, be as hard as the others. That was as far – and perhaps even this I imagined or exaggerated – as I could see that night.

Taking her slice of bread, she went back with light scampering steps to the front room, where I assumed that Cora Ross was waiting. Mrs Pateman, naturally polite, embarrassed, continued to explain about her husband. He was always one for going to the doctor in good time. He had a stiffness in his throat which he thought might be associated with a backache (a combination, I couldn't help thinking to myself, unknown to medical science). He was always careful about what she, echoing him, called 'germs'. That accounted, I realised, for the disinfectant smell which hung about this room, even in his absence. He must add, to his other unwelcoming characteristics, a chronic hypochondria.

At last he came in, head thrown back, hand outstretched. He gave me a stately good evening, and sat down to his corned beef and tomato ketchup. Meanwhile his wife was saying:

'He didn't find anything, did he, Percy?'

'Nothing serious,' he said with a condescending smile. 'I'm a great believer', he turned to me, 'in taking precautions. I don't mind telling you, I should recommend anyone of your age to be run over by his doctor once a month.'

I said that I couldn't stay long. I wanted only to finish up this business of his son. I hadn't heard until that day that he had been accepted by— (the neighbouring university). That completed the story, and they ought to consider themselves fortunate.

'No,' said Mr Pateman, not angrily but in a level, reasonable fashion. 'I can't be expected to agree with that.'

'I do expect you to agree with that.' I had come to break this tie. To be honest, I didn't mind a quarrel: but I wasn't getting it.

'Well then, we shall have to agree to differ, shan't we?'

'Your son', I said, 'is a remarkably lucky young man. If he were here – by the by, I have not had a word from him about his news – if he were here I should tell him so. He might have been thrown out for good. As it is, this is exactly like going on at the university here as though nothing had happened.'

'Ah,' Mr Pateman smiled, an all-knowing patronising smile. 'There I have to take issue with you. Do you realise that this place is twelve miles away?'

'Of course I do.'

'How is he going to get there?'

I muttered, but Mr Pateman continued in triumph:

'Someone is going to have to pay his fare.'

I stared at him blank-faced. With a gesture, he said:

'But I'll grant you this. It's not so bad as Scotland. No, it's not so bad as Scotland. So we'd better let bygones be bygones, hadn't we?'

He was victorious. For the moment, he was sated. I thought – not then but later, for on the spot I was outfaced, deflated, like one working himself up to a row and finding himself greeted with applause – how people say comfortably that persecution never works. Read a little history, and you find that persecution, more often than not, is singularly effective. The same with paranoia. You might think it was a crippling affliction: live some of your life, and you find that paranoia too, more often than not, is singularly effective. Certainly the streak possessed by the Patemans, father and son, had won them, in this business, what they wanted. It also made Mr Pateman that evening feel powerful as most of us never do. Paranoia of that kind is only placated for an interval, and then, like sexual jealousy, starts up again. But while it is placated, it – again like sexual jealousy – gives a reassurance which is utterly possessing, as though all enemies were conquered or annihilated, a reassurance of non-enmity that those of us who are not paranoid will never know.

Before I left, Mr Pateman favoured me with his views on civil servants.

It was no thanks to me, but he was enjoying some new 'brainwave' about a move for himself. He reiterated, he couldn't remain a cashier much longer. 'I'm like a bank clerk shovelling money over the counter and not having any for himself.' But he had listened to me enough to visit the Employment Exchange. As he had foreseen, he said with satisfaction, they had been useless, totally useless.

'You know what civil servants are like, do you?'

I told him I had been one, during the war and for years later.

'Present company excepted.' He gave a forgiving smile. 'But you've had some experience outside, you ought to know what civil servants are like. Rats in mazes. You switch on a light and they scramble for the right door.'

I said goodbye. Mr Pateman, standing up and squaring his shoulders, said that he was glad to have had these talks. I asked if the new job he was thinking of was an interesting one.

'For *some* people,' he said, 'every job is an interesting one.'

He volunteered no more. His lips were complacently tight, as though he were a cabinet minister being questioned by a back-bencher of dubious discretion.

Sitting in the Residence drawing-room, a few minutes to go before dinner, I told Vicky that I had had a mildly punishing day. 'Poor old thing,' she said. I didn't say anything about Leonard Getliffe or the Pateman parlour, but I remarked that it was bleak to miss my customary drink with George. She shook her head: she didn't know him, he was just a name from the town's shadows.

'Anyway,' she said, 'you might meet another old friend tonight.' She asked – would I let her drive me out into the country, for a party after dinner? Would that be too much for me? What was this party, I wanted to know. Parents of friends of hers, prosperous business people, not even acquaintances of mine. 'But they want to collect you, you know. And it'd be a bit of a scoop for me to produce you.' Vicky gave a cheerful grimace. She had a tendency, characteristic of realistic young women, to find any symptom of the public life extremely funny. I found that tendency soothing.

Before she had time to tell me who the 'old friend' was, Arnold Shaw joined us, beaming with eupeptic good-humour. 'Excellent meeting today, Lewis,' he said. He was feeling celebratory, and had opened one of his better bottles of claret for dinner. At the table, the three of us alone, he did not once refer to the controversy. It was over, in his mind a neat, black, final line had been drawn. He talked, euphorically and non-stop, about the October congregation. Arnold loved ceremony, protocol, anything which distinguished one man from another. If the President of the Royal Society came to receive an honorary degree, should he, or should he not, on an academic occasion, take precedence over a viscount who was not receiving a degree?

As he propounded this intricate problem, Vicky was smiling. She was still amused when he went on to what for him was the fascinating topic of honorary degrees. Here he took great trouble, and, as so often, received no credit from anyone, not even her. If a university was going to give honorary degrees at all, he had harangued me before now, it ought to be done with total purity. He would make no concessions. As so often, no one believed that he was a pure soul. Yet he had done precisely what he said. No local worthies. No putative benefactors. No politicians. Men of international distinction. No one else.

'I'm glad you mentioned the man Rubin,' he said to me. 'I've made enquiries. They say he's good. No, they say he's more than good.'

'Well, Arnold, the fact that he got a Nobel prize when he was about forty', I said, 'does argue a certain degree of competence.'

Arnold let out his malicious chuckle.

'Leonard Getliffe thinks a lot of him. And that young man isn't very easily pleased.' He was glancing meaningfully at his daughter. 'I always know I shall get an honest opinion from Leonard on this sort of business. Yes, he's absolutely honest, he really is a friend of mine.'

His glance was meaningful. So, in a different sense, was mine. I hadn't told Vicky about my conversation with Leonard: now I was glad that I hadn't; it would have done no good and turned her evening sour. I sipped at the admirable wine. Why was Arnold so innocent? Hadn't he noticed the abstentions from the Court? Why were he and Leonard so pure? Under the taste of the wine, a vestigial taste of black currants – a vestigial reminder of a worldly man, unlike those two, a man nothing like so pure, Arthur Brown, looking after his friends in college, giving us wine as good as this, years ago.

As soon as we had settled in her car and Vicky was driving up the London Road, out of the town, I asked who was the old friend? The old friend I was to meet?

'They didn't want to tell either of you, so that it would be a surprise.'

'Come on, who is it?'

'I think her name is Juckson-Smith.'

'I've never heard of her,' I said.

'They said you used to know her.'

'I've never heard the name.'

'Have I got you on false pretences?' Vicky glanced sideways from the wheel, to see if I was disappointed. 'Juckson-Smith – I think they call her Olive.'

Then I understood. I had not seen her for thirty years. Once there had been a sort of indeterminate affection, certainly not more, between us. She had been a member of George Passant's group, the only one of us from a well-to-do family. Those had been idealistic days, when George ranged about the town, haranguing us with absolute hope about our 'freedom'. But after I left the town, some of them worked out their freedom: Olive took a lover, and under his influence got mixed up in the scandal which – to me at least, who had to watch it – had been a signpost along our way.

She had, so far as I had heard, cut off all connections with the town. Her family was respectable, and it was not a pretty story. She had married Jack Cotery, her lover, and some time during the war, I had been told that they had parted. Presumably she had married again. All this had happened many years before, and except to a few of us, might be submerged or forgotten.

Myself, I wasn't remembering much of it, memory didn't work like that, as Vicky drove past the outer suburbs, into the country, past the midland fields, every square foot man-made and yet pastoral in the level light. It was past nine, but the sun was still over the horizon. Swathes of warm air kept surging through the open window, as we passed, slowing down, tree after tree.

'You do know her, then?'

'I knew her first husband better. He was rather an engaging man.'

'Why was he engaging?'

'You might have liked him.' No, I shouldn't have said that. Jack Cotery was just the kind of seducer whom this young woman had no guard against. I hurried on: 'He had a knack of reducing everything to its lowest common denominator. He often turned out to be right, though I didn't enjoy it.'

I began to tell her an anecdote. But this was one that I didn't mind recalling. My spirits had become higher. When I was in high spirits, and letting myself go, Vicky found it hard to decide whether I was serious or not. She drove on, her expression puzzled and even slightly mulish, as I indulged myself talking about Martineau. Martineau, when I was in my teens, had been a partner in one of the town's solidest firms of solicitors – the same firm of which George Passant was managing clerk. He was a widower, and he kept something like a salon for us all. Then, over a period of two or three years, round the age of fifty, he became invaded by religion, or by a religious search: he started wayside preaching, and before long gave up all he had, except for what he could carry, and went off as a tramp. At my college I used to receive postcards from various work-houses.

'Did you?' said Vicky, as though it were an invention.

He joined a religious community, and soon left that to become a pavement artist on the streets of Leeds. The pictures he drew were intended to convey a spiritual message. After a while, he moved to London and operated in the King's Road. The average daily take in Chelsea was three times the take in Leeds: I picked up some information about the economics of pavement artistry in the late thirties.

'Did you?' said Vicky once more.

The point was, I said, Jack Cotery had insisted from the start that all Martineau wanted was a woman. Jack had discovered that his wife had been an invalid, he had had no sexual life right through his forties. Jack said that if he and my Sheila went off together, that would cure them, if anything could. I thought that was too reductive, too brash by half. The trouble was, about Martineau it turned out to be right. (Just as it turned out to be right that, soon after I went to bed with Sheila, my obsessive jealousy left me. It had seemed over-simple, and at that time I wanted life to be more elaborate and grandiose than the fact had proved.)

'What happened?' Suddenly Vicky was interested.

Very simple. At the age of sixty Martineau met, Heaven knows how, a very nice and mildly eccentric woman. They got married within three weeks and had two children in the shortest conceivable time. Martineau gave up pavement artistry (though not religion) and returned to ordinary life. Very ordinary: because he became a clerk in exactly the type of solicitors' firm in which he had been a partner and given his share away. My last glimpse of him: he had been living in a semi-detached house in Reading, running round the garden bouncing his daughter on his back. He had exuded happiness, and had survived in robust health until nearly eighty.

'I can understand that,' said Vicky, driving past the golden fields.

'Can you?'

'I shouldn't be so edgy if I weren't so chaste.'

'You're not very edgy.'

'I'm getting a bit old to sleep alone.'

'You know,' I said, 'it isn't the answer to everything.'

'It's the answer to a good many things,' she said.

Yes, she would have taken Jack Cotery's comments more equably than I had done at her age.

From the road, a mile or two further on, one could see a house standing a long way back upon a knoll, as sharp and isolated as in a nineteenth-century print. That was where we were going, said Vicky. It was a comely Georgian façade: once, I supposed, this had been a squire's manor-house. Not now. Not now, as we drove up the tree-verged drive, car after car parked right to the door: no poor old Leicestershire squire had ever lived like this. In fact, we didn't enter the house at all, but went round, past the rose-gardens, to the swimming pool. There, standing on the lawn close by, or sitting in deck chairs, must have been sixty or seventy people. Some were in the water: waiters were going about with trays of drinks. I met my hostess, middle-aged, well dressed. I met some guests, middle-aged, well dressed. I found myself trying to remember names, just as if I were in America. For an instant, looking down from the pool over the rolling countryside, I wondered how I could tell that I wasn't in America. This might have been Pennsylvania. This was a style of life that was running round the fortunate of the world. One difference, perhaps, but that was only a matter of latitude: in Pennsylvania it wouldn't have been bright daylight at half past nine.

I had a drink, answered amiable questions, received an invitation or two: one man claimed to have played cricket with my brother Martin. My hostess rejoined me and said:

'You know Olive Juckson-Smith, don't you?'

I said, yes, I used to. She said, do come and meet her, it'll be a surprise.

We made our way, through the jostling party, the decibels rising, the alcohol sinking, to a knot of people at the other side of the pool. My hostess called: 'Olive! I've got an old friend for you.'

The first thing I noticed was that Olive's hair had gone quite white. She was my own age, so that oughtn't to have disturbed me, though for a moment, after all those years, it did. She had been, in her youth, a handsome nordic girl, bold-eyed and strong. Her eyes still shone light-blue, but her face was drawn: she had lost a lot of weight: though her arms were muscular, her body had become gaunt. The first moment was over, the shock had gone. But I was left with the expression that greeted me. It was one of hostility – no, more than that, something nearer detestation.

'How are you?' I asked, still expecting (it was the mild pleasure I had been imagining on the way out) to meet an old friend.

'I'm well enough.' Her answer was curt, as though she didn't want to speak at all.

'Where are you living now?'

She brought out the name of a northern town. She was fashionably turned out. I guessed that she and her husband were as well off as my hosts. I didn't know whether she had had children, and I couldn't begin to ask. I said, trying to remain warm:

'It's a long time since we met, isn't it?'

'Yes, it is.' Her voice was frigid, and she hadn't given even a simulacrum of a smile.

My hostess was becoming embarrassed. To ease things over, she said to Olive that I had done a good many things in the time between. 'I've heard of some of the things you've done,' Olive said to me, her face implacable.

To start with, I had thought that she was hating me because I reminded her of a past she wanted to obliterate, in which I had, quite innocently, been involved. But that seemed to be the least of it. For suddenly she began to attack me, and soon to denounce me, for parts of my public life. I had been a man of the left. My 'gang', people like Francis Getliffe and the others (she knew a number of them by name, as though she had been monitoring all we said and wrote) had done their best to bring the country to ruin. We were all guilty, and I was as guilty as any man.

If she had merely become conservative, there would have been nothing astonishing in that. It had happened to half the friends, perhaps more than half, with whom I had knocked about in my youth. But she had become fanatically so. And, for the paradoxical reason that I had lived a good deal among politicians, I was all the worse prepared to cope. In Westminster and Whitehall, in political houses such as Diana Skidmore's Basset, your opponents didn't curse you in private. Sometimes, at the time of Munich or Suez, one thought twice about accepting a dinner invitation – but I had never, not once, been blackguarded like this. Except, now I came to think of it, by one of my cousins, who, discovering that I had made a radical statement, told my brother Martin that he had crossed my name out of his family Bible.

There was nothing to do. I caught the eye of Vicky, who was standing not far off, made an excuse and joined her group. Then I moved round the pool, from one cordial person to another, cordial myself. They were drinking, so was I, it was like any party anywhere. Except that, when I next encountered Vicky, I said that I didn't want to stay too long: as soon as we decently could, I should like to slip away. She was enjoying herself, but she nodded. Before half past eleven, she was driving back into the town. Over the dark fields, the sky was dark at last.

'That wasn't a success, was it?' she said.

'Not by the highest standards,' I answered.

'I'm sorry.'

'I'm sorry to have dragged you away.' She didn't get enough treats, I was thinking: but she made the most of any that happened to her. She had been happy by the pool-side, as though she were a child, fascinated by her first party. Nevertheless, she had witnessed some of the scene with Olive, and she had come away without a question. As I had told Martin, she was a good girl.

Never mind, she was saying, she would be taking her holiday in September, she would be in London with Pat, there would be plenty of parties. She broke off:

'Was she always like that?'

'When she was your age, people might have thought she was a lot like you.'

'Oh, that's not fair!'

'I was going on to say that they would have been dead wrong. Sometimes she seemed to think about others, but I fancy she was always self-absorbed.'

'Of course,' said Vicky in her level tone, 'I suppose I am rather conservative. Most doctors are, you know.'

'But you won't get conservative like that. If you meet Maurice' – I was choosing someone with whom she was friendly – 'in thirty years' time, you won't tell him he's the worst man in the world.'

She chuckled, then said:

'Was it nasty?'

'No one likes being hated. I've known people who pretended not to care—'

'You do have to put up with some curious things, don't you?'

She said it in her kind, aseptic fashion, and for the rest of the drive we talked about her father. When we came to the suburbs, she had to stop at a traffic light, behind another car. There was a lamp-standard on the pavement, brightening the leaves of the lime tree close beside. Quite suddenly, without warning or cause, I had something like an hallucination. The number-plate of the car in front, either to my eyes or in my mind, I could not distinguish whether the transformation was visual or not, was carrying different, fewer figures. NR 8150. Those were the figures in my mind. That was the number of Sheila's father's car, when we were twenty. She disliked driving and seldom used it. She had driven me in it only once or twice, and nowhere near this road. The car meant nothing to either of us, and I had not thought of its number in all those years. There it was. Vicky was asking me something, but all I could attend to was that number.

It was a trick of memory that seemed utterly unprovoked. At dinner the taste of claret had brought back an instant's thought of Cambridge, but that was the kind of sensuous trigger-pressing all of us often know. It was possible that I was hyper-aesthetised to some different form of memory after the confrontation with Olive: but it didn't strike home like that, the scene with Olive had been in the here-and-now, this was as though time itself had played a trick.

Vicky had put a hand on my arm.

'Are you all right?' she was saying.

'Perfectly.'

I was speaking the truth. I had remembered a number, that was all.

PART TWO

ARRESTS OF LIFE, FIRST AND SECOND

CHAPTER X

AN EDGE OF DARKNESS

SUMMER, autumn, 1963. It was a placid time for us, more so than for a long time past. My name had gone out of the news: Margaret's father stayed, by what seemed like one of fate's perversities, in better health and spirits. The world outside was more placid too. Sometimes we talked of South-East Asia, but without the smell of danger. Even suspicious and experienced men, like Francis Getliffe, were allowing themselves a ration of hope.

We turned inwards to the family – and there Margaret had a little to worry about, nothing dramatic, just a routine worry, as she watched her children's lives. Maurice had failed in his first-year examination: by a concession which in abstract justice should not have been granted, he was being allowed back for his second year. He took it with as little pique as ever. When Charles cursed a piece of work he had brought back for the holidays, Maurice said: 'Now you realise that you ought to be stupid, like me.'

Then he had gone off for the whole summer to work as an attendant in a mental hospital. It was not a job many young men would have taken, but he was happy. He had the singular composure which one sometimes meets in the self-abnegating. At night, when we were alone, Margaret often talked about him. Ought he to care so little for himself? Wouldn't it be better if he had more drive, and yes, a dash of envy? She was worrying, but she felt a twisted joke at her own expense. She had come to admire the selfless virtues: and now with her first-born – whom she loved differently from Charles – she was wishing that, instead of trying to be of some good to the helpless, he would think about his future and buckle down to his books.

Yet, when they were together, he was protective towards her. Just as he was protective towards Vicky, the evening that she and Pat spent with us in the flat. It was late in September, Charles had gone back to school, the two of them came for an early drink and stayed to dinner, Maurice had not yet returned from his hospital.

Pat, who knew well enough that Margaret disapproved of him, began making up to her the moment he came in. I found the spectacle entertaining, partly because I had a trace of softness about my nephew, partly because Margaret was not entirely unsusceptible. He entered, put Vicky down in one chair, made Margaret keep her place in another while he took charge of the drinks. It was all quick, easy and practised: and yet, in the serene evening, the mellow light, there was at once a stir and crackle in the room.

He was a shortish young man, shorter than his father, who was himself inches less tall than Charles or me. He had strong shoulders like his father's, and similar heavy wrists. His hair curled close to his forehead, he had sharp eyes, a wide melon mouth. No one could have called him handsome, or even impressive. When he made a sidelong remark to Vicky, who didn't show amusement easily, she was laughing with sheer delight.

I observed them as he bustled round with the whisky and the ice-jug. She was elated. As for him, his spirits were usually so high that it would be hard to detect a change. Frequently he called her darling, he said that 'we' had been to the theatre last night, that 'we' were going to a friend's studio tomorrow. He was using all the emollients of a love affair. She was looking at no one else in the room: while he was sparking with energy to make Margaret like him.

He was sitting between her and Vicky, and I opposite to them, with my back to the light. Eyes acute, he was searching Margaret's face to see when he drew a response. Her father? Yes, he seemed a little better, said Margaret. 'That's all you can hope for, isn't it?' said Pat, bright and surgent. Once, when he was brasher, he would have been asking her to let him call on Austin Davidson: but now Pat not only knew her father's condition, he knew also that she had been exposed all her life to young painters on the climb. With the same caution, he didn't refer, or pay attention, to the great Rothko, borrowed from her father, on the wall at their back, which from where I sat beamed swathes of colour into the sunset. Pictures, painting, Pat was shutting away: as he leaned towards her, he was leaving himself out of it. He tried another lead. Maurice? Yes, he knew about the hospital. 'I'm sorry he missed the Mays' (he was speaking of the examination). 'But still, it doesn't matter all that much, now does it?'

'It's a nuisance,' said Margaret.

'Aren't you being old-fashioned, Aunt Meg?' When I heard him call her that, which no one else ever did, I felt he was getting surer. 'You all believe in examinations, like my father, don't you now?'

'Well, he's got to get through them – if he's going to do what he wants.'

'But does he want to? Are you sure he does?'

'Don't you think he wants to be a doctor?' Margaret was asking a question, a genuine question.

'I don't know. I'm not sure that he does. But I'll bet you this, he'll find something, either that or something else, that he really wants to do.'

He looked eagerly at Margaret, and spoke with authority. 'I suppose you realise that all the people my age think he's rather wonderful? I mean, he's influenced a lot of us. Not only me. You know what I'm like. But if I'd stayed at Cambridge, and it wasn't a tragedy for anyone that I didn't, you know, he would have been one of the better things—'

'I know he's kind—'

'I mean more than that.'

For the moment at least he had melted her. Next day she would have her doubts: she was too self-critical not to: and yet perhaps the effect wouldn't wear off. I was thinking, you can't set out to please unless you want to please. He had his skill in finding the vulnerable place, and yet this wasn't really skill. He couldn't help finding the way to give her pleasure. Men like Arnold Shaw would view this activity, and the young man himself, with contempt. In most of the moral senses, men like Arnold were beyond comparison more worthy. Nevertheless, they would be despising something they could never do.

I was thinking also, how old should I guess Pat to be, if I didn't know? Certainly older than he was, older than Vicky: but he had, apart from his mouth, the kind of lined, small-featured face which stays for years in the indeterminate mid-twenties. He was taking two drinks to our one, but there again his physical temperament was odd. He showed the effect of alcohol when he had finished his first glass – and then drank hard, and didn't show much more effect, for hours to come. He seemed to live, when quite sober, two drinks over par: with alcohol, he climbed rapidly to four over par, and stayed there.

They were talking about doctoring.

'I've always thought I should have enjoyed it,' Margaret was saying to Vicky. 'I often envy you.'

'I don't know about that,' said Vicky.

'Oh, you must.'

'No,' Vicky persisted with her stubborn honesty. 'I don't think I had a vocation. It's a job—'

'It's a job where you're doing some good, though.'

'You don't feel that so much if you're dealing with out-patients nine to five,' said Vicky. 'I might have enjoyed being a children's doctor. Because they're going to get better, most of them.'

'Maurice's father once told me something similar. He's in that line himself. Did you know?' I put in. It was easier for me to say it than for Margaret.

'Yes, I should have liked it too,' Margaret said.

'But you don't need to be too disappointed if Maurice doesn't, isn't that right?' Pat turned to her again. 'You're sure you haven't been guiding him, without meaning too?'

He told her that might be why Maurice couldn't – really couldn't, for all his sweetness and good will – force himself to work. Did Margaret believe it? Perhaps she would have liked to. And, though Pat was continuing to efface himself, he would have liked to believe it too. For in secret, and sometimes not so much in secret, he put the blame for his own academic disasters down to his father's fault. If Martin hadn't wanted him to be a scholarly success—

As we sat at the dinner table, Pat continued to talk comfortingly to Margaret. I didn't interrupt. As Margaret knew, or would remember when the well-being had dropped, I couldn't accept those consoling explanations: but I didn't propose to break the peace of the evening. As for Vicky, it was the peace of the evening that she was basking in. Pat was doing well. He was being listened to. They didn't go to many dinner parties with middle-aged couples. It was all unexacting and safe. It was like a foretaste of marriage.

Happily, Vicky put in another word about child-doctoring. It had improved, out of comparison, since before the war. Children's health was better in all classes. It was lucky to have been born in the 1950s. Then she mentioned that people a mile or so from my father's house would next week be escorting their children back and forth from school. A boy of eight had disappeared a day or two before; there was a wave of anxiety going round. 'I hope they find him,' said Vicky.

Margaret remarked that once, when Maurice was a child, she had been beside herself when he was an hour late. Then Pat broke in and told her another story of Maurice at Cambridge.

While Pat and Margaret talked to each other, Vicky was able to pass some information on to me. Her glance sometimes left me and flicked across the table: she wanted a smile, she gave a smile back: but that didn't prevent her telling me the news. It was worrying news, and she had to tell me before the evening was over. But she didn't sound worried, her words were responsible while her face was not. Anyway, she had gathered (not, so far as I could learn, from Leonard Getliffe) that there might shortly be another resolution before the Court. The three academics, Leonard and two others, who had kept away from the vote of confidence, were growing more dissatisfied. At the least, they wanted some definition of the Vice-Chancellor's powers. No, they were being careful, they were hoping to find a technique that didn't hurt him – but they meant business.

Did Arnold know? I asked. He was quite oblivious, Vicky said. She tried to warn him, but he behaved as though he didn't want to know.

Would I make sure to come to the next Court? That was on the day of the congregation in October? Yes, I said, I intended to come.

'You might be able to make him understand,' she said.

'I doubt it.'

'You may have to tell him the truth.'

I swore.

'But you will come? You promise me?'

'Of course I'll come.'

She was content. After that, we returned to the drawing-room, and were chatting like a family circle when, towards ten o'clock, Maurice came in. He kissed his mother, kissed Vicky, than sank down into an armchair with a tired easy-going sigh. When Margaret asked him, he said that he had been sitting with a schizophrenic patient all afternoon. It took a bit of effort, he said: until this holiday he hadn't known what schizophrenia could mean. He was wearing a shabby suit, his face – unlined in spite of his fatigue – pallid by the side of Pat's doggy vigour. Margaret had a plate of sandwiches ready for him, and he began to scoff them. He glanced at Pat, who was by this time at least his customary four drinks over par. 'I'm a long way behind, aren't I?' said Maurice, with his objective smile. Margaret gave him a whisky, which he put down at speed.

'Better,' he said. It surprised some people, but he wasn't at all ascetic about alcohol. Whether he was ascetic about sex, I couldn't (it was strange to be so baffled with someone one had watched since infancy) have sworn.

Before long, he and Pat and Vicky were talking together. Any one of them was easy with Margaret or me, didn't feel, or let us feel, the gap of a generation: but together they were drawn by a gravitational pull. Curiously, their voices got softer, even Pat's, which could be strident when he was confronting his elders. Was it fancy, or did they and their friends whisper to each other more than we used to do?

Yes, Maurice said to them, he would be going back to Cambridge in a fortnight to 'have another bash'. A singular phrase, I thought, for that gentle young man, not one which the professionals in the family would find encouraging. Vicky was giving him some advice about medical examinations. Maurice listened acceptantly and patiently. Soon he switched off: what were they going to do? Well, Vicky said, her holiday would be over in a few days, she'd be returning to the hospital. Pat said that he'd be staying in London: he'd got some sort of job (it sounded as though he had collected a little money too), he'd be able to paint at nights and weekends.

'You'll be separated again, won't you?' said Maurice.

'It can't be helped,' said Vicky.

'How do you manage?'

'Oh, we have to manage,' she said.

'I suppose', said Maurice, 'you get on the phone and tell each other when you're free.'

He meant – so I thought – that it was Pat who told her when he was free.

'It's nice when we do see each other,' said Pat, just as evenly as Maurice was speaking.

'I should have thought', said Maurice, 'that it was an awful strain.'

'We're getting used to it,' she said.

'Are you?'

'Are you worried about me, Maurice?' Vicky asked.

'Yes, I am.' He answered with absolute naturalness.

'Oh, look, I'm pretty tough.'

'I don't think you ought to rely on that for ever. Either of you.'

He spoke to Pat. 'What do you think?'

Pat replied, with no edge in his voice: 'Perhaps you're right.'

At dinner there hadn't been a word about their plans, partly because Pat was repressing all his own concerns, partly because neither Margaret nor I felt we could intrude. But Maurice hadn't been so delicate, and no one was upset. It might be a happy love affair, but he had picked up (as, in fact, we had also, in the midst of happiness and peace) that there was something inconclusive in the air. As for their plans, they seemed that night to have none at all. So Maurice, less involved in this world than any of us, told them that it was time they got married.

To me, as I listened to the quiet voices, the odd thing was how they took it. Pat: with no sign of resentment, as though it were a perfectly reasonable conversation about how they were going to get back to

Islington when they left the flat. Well, Pat wasn't touchy. But Vicky? She too wasn't resentful, or even apprehensive. She seemed to take it as a token of kindness, but not really relevant to her and Pat. She might have been nervous about this intervention, if she hadn't been so certain that, just because she and Pat were themselves, in due course he would marry her. She had, I thought, a kind of obstinacy which no one outside could shift – obstinacy or else a faith (it was here, and nowhere else, that she showed something like conceit) in her own judgment.

Anyway, the three of them remained on the best of terms, and Maurice and Pat had another drink or two before the end of the evening.

When Maurice had gone back to Cambridge and Margaret and I were alone, she reminded me more than once of that initiative of his. She was proud of how uninhibited he was, particularly when she was worrying about him again. And also she thought he had been right. She was a little ashamed of herself, of course, for having been melted by Pat's blarney. She was, like Maurice, altogether on Vicky's side. It would be bad for her if the affair dragged on like this.

So we talked, on pleasant October evenings. There wasn't much on our minds. I was working hard, but not obsessively. On a Friday night Charles rang up, according to habit, from school. All well. I told him that, the following Wednesday, I had to go to the Court and congregation. 'Multiplying mummery,' came the deep mocking voice over the wire. Politics too, I said. That's more like it, said Charles.

The next morning I woke up, drowsy and soothed, looking forward as I came to consciousness to a leisurely weekend alone with Margaret. I was lying on my right, and through a gap in the curtains the misty morning light came in over the Tyburn gardens. As I looked at the gap, I noticed – no, I didn't notice, it hit me like a jolt in a jet plane 30,000 feet up, the passage up to that instant purring with calm – a veil over the corner of my left eye. A black veil, sharp-edged. I blinked. The veil disappeared: I felt a flood of reassurance. I looked again. The veil was there, covering perhaps a quarter of the eye, not more.

Margaret was sleeping like a child. I got out of bed and went to the window, pulling a little of one curtain back. Outside was a tranquil autumn haze. It was the kind of morning in which, years before, it had been good to be back in England after a holiday abroad. On my left side the black edge cut out the haze. I blinked. I went on testing one eye, then the other. It was like pressing on a tooth to make sure it is still aching. The veil remained. Now that I was looking out into the full light, there was a penumbra, orange-brown, along its edge, through which I had some sort of swirling half-vision, as through blurred smoked glass. The veil itself was impenetrable. No pain.

I tiptoed out to the bathroom, and looked at myself in the glass. A familiar eye looked back. There wasn't a mark on it, the iris was bright, the white wasn't bloodshot. The lines in my face had deepened, that was all.

I went back to bed, trying to steady myself. I was more frightened, or not so much frightened as nervously exposed, than I liked being. Later on, people made excuses for me, told me it wasn't so unnatural: the eye is close to the central nervous system, and so, they said cheeringly, eye afflictions often have their psychological effects. But I wasn't thinking of explanations or excuses then. All I wanted was to talk sensibly to Margaret.

She was still sleeping. As a rule, she slept heavily in the early morning, and woke confused. Again I left the bed, found our housekeeper already stirring, and asked for breakfast as soon as she could bring it. Then I sat looking down at my wife. I said, 'I'm sorry, but I should like you to wake up now.'

CHAPTER XI

OBJECTIVITY?

As I put my hand on her shoulder, she struggled through a dream, through layers of sleep. She managed to say, is anything the matter? I replied that a cup of tea would be arriving soon. She asked the time, and when I told her, said that it was too early. I said that I was just a little worried. What about, she said, still not awake, then suddenly she caught my tone of voice. What about? she said, only to act, slipping out of bed into her dressing-gown, watching me, her face wide open.

While she had a cup of tea, smoked her first cigarette, I described my symptoms. Or rather my symptom, for there was only the one. 'What can it be?' said Margaret. I was asking her the same thing. For a moment we looked at each other, each suspecting that the other had some guess or secret knowledge. Then we knew that we were equally lost.

She didn't think of saying that it might pass. We were too much at one for that. Over breakfast she was wondering what advice we could get. Clearly we needed an eye specialist. What about the man whose son was at Charles's school? No sooner had she thought of the name than she was riffling through the telephone directory. Mansel. Harley Street. No answer there. Home address. She got through, and, listening, I gathered that Mr Mansel was away. At an eye-surgeons' conference in Stockholm. He would be back very late tomorrow, Sunday, night.

'That's probably time enough,' I said.

She said: 'I want to know what you've got.'

I argued, with the perverse obstinacy of shock, that he was said to be first-rate and that at casual meetings we had both liked him. We could ring him up on Monday morning: that would, I said again, be time enough.

'I want to know,' she said. Couldn't we find a doctor who might have an idea? The curious thing was we hadn't needed a doctor professionally for ten years or more. Since my breakdown as a young man, I had been abnormally healthy, and so had she. So far as we had a doctor, it was my old friend Charles March, but we met him only when he came to dinner.

Still, she would talk to him, she said. Once more I listened to her on the telephone. Dr March was on holiday, was he? Back in a fortnight? He had a locum, of course? Could she have his telephone number?

'No, leave it now,' I said.

She did not mention the name of her first husband. He was an excellent doctor, she had complete faith in him – but no, she couldn't, she couldn't, she couldn't disturb, not the peace of the moment, but the insulation of the moment in which we sat together.

But there were other doctors. Later it seemed to us inexplicable – or out of character for either of us, especially her, so active and protective – that we spoke to none of them through that long weekend. She was used to a kind of pointless stoicism which sometimes, in bad trouble, came over me. As a rule, if we expected harsh news, she wanted to find out the worst and get it over: my instinct was to wait, it would come soon enough, other miseries had passed and so might this. That weekend, though, she behaved as I did myself. I was worried enough but, perhaps because I had a physical malaise to preoccupy me, she was worse. For once, she did not want to brave it out and discover our fate.

During the morning, I went into the study and found her there. In a hurry, she put her hand over what she was reading. It was a medical dictionary. I had come for exactly the same purpose. I gave her a smile. It was the sort of grim joke old Gay's saga-men would have enjoyed. She smiled back, but she was having to control her face.

Before lunch we went for a walk in the park. It was a day of absolute calm, the sun warm enough to tinge the skin, the mist still lying in the hollows. The grass smelt as welcoming as on a morning in childhood.

Margaret, clutching my arm, was watching me shut and open my left eye.

'How is it?'

'No better,' I said. In fact, it was worse. The veil had spread and now covered between a third and a half of the eye. The orange penumbra flickered dizzily as I tried to gaze into the benign autumn sky. When I closed the eye, I could walk as comfortably as on the afternoon before, the time that Margaret and I had taken a stroll in the same beautiful weather.

It was a long weekend. I couldn't write or even read: as for looking at television, that became an exercise in calculating whether the veil was creeping further. We talked a good deal, but only about what had happened to us, us together, us alone. Those we were interested in, or responsible for, we didn't talk about at all. The exchanges of habit, as soothing as a domestic animal one loved, those we had thrown away: not a word about Charles's next Sunday at home. Some time before the Sunday morning Margaret had made her own diagnosis. I didn't ask to know it. And yet at moments, as in all strain, time played tricks. We were back on Friday evening, having our drinks after Charles's telephone call. This hadn't happened. And then Margaret was watching me as I opened my eye.

On Monday morning, after a drugged and broken night, I woke early. I found Margaret looking at me. With a start I stared at the window. The veil was black: no larger, but like a presence on the nerves. I turned towards her, and said: 'Well, we shall soon know.'

'Yes, we shall,' she said, steady by now.

When could I decently ring this man up? She was even prepared to smile at the 'decently': now the time had come, we had something to do.

Over breakfast we decided on nine o'clock. But when I tried his office, I heard that he had been in hospital since six. 'Mr Mansel gets on without much sleep,' said his secretary, with proprietorial pride. I could get him there: which, fretted by the delays, in time I did.

'I'm sorry, I didn't arrive home till late last night. They gave me your message.' The voice was brisk, light, professional. 'What's gone wrong with your eye?'

I told him. 'That's a very clear description,' the voice said with approval, rather as though I were a medical student walking the wards and making a report. I had better see him that morning. He was doing an operation at 9.30. He would be at Harley Street by 11.30. Too early for me?

No, not too early, we thought as the minutes dragged. I couldn't block out the bad eye enough to read the newspapers. Margaret went through them for me: nothing much: a Kennedy speech: oh yes, the body of that child who was missing, the one in your home town, that's just been found, poor boy: an old acquaintance called Lord Bridgwater (once Horace Timberlake) had died on Saturday. We were not interested. Margaret sat beside me in silence and held my hand.

Just as, still silent, she held my hand in the taxi on the way to Harley Street. It was only a quarter-of-an-hour's trip from the north side of the park. We hadn't been able to discipline ourselves; we arrived at 11.10. No, Mr Mansel wasn't in yet: empty waiting-room, the smell of magazines, old furniture, the smell of waiting. All Margaret said was that, when he examined me, she wanted to be there.

At last the secretary entered, comely, hygienic, and led us in. Mansel was standing up, greeting me like a young man to an older; the room was sparkling with optical instruments, and Mansel himself was as sharp as an electronic engineer. Although our sons were in the same year at school, he was not more than forty, tall, thin, handsome in an avian fashion. Did he mind my wife staying? Not in the least. He showed her to a chair, me to another beside his desk. He had in front of him a card about me, name, age, address, clearly filled up: he asked a question.

'Should you say your general health was good?'

I hesitated. 'I suppose so,' I said with reluctance, as though I were tempting fate.

No illnesses? Latest medical examination? Long ago. 'Then we won't waste any time on that,' he said with impersonal cheerfulness, and chose, out of a set of gadgets, what looked no more complicated than a single lens. Left eye? Firm fingers on my cheek, lens inches away, face close to mine. His eyes, preternaturally large, like a close-up on the screen, peered down: one angle, another, a third.

He took perhaps a minute, maybe less.

'It's quite straightforward,' he said. 'You've got a detached retina.'

'Thank God for that,' I heard Margaret say.

'As a matter of fact,' he said coolly, 'I could have diagnosed it over the telephone.'

'If you had,' I said, sarcastic with relief, 'it would have saved us a bad couple of hours.'

'Why, what did you think it was?'

Margaret and I glanced at each other with something like shame. Ridiculous fears we hadn't spoken. Fears uninformed. Fears out of the medical dictionary. Brain tumour, and the rest.

Mansel was speaking as though cross with us.

'I understand. It's easy to imagine things.' Actually, he was cross with himself. He hadn't been sensitive enough. He wouldn't make that mistake again. He wasn't only a technician, I thought, he was a good doctor. From her corner by the surgical couch, Margaret broke out: 'Mr Rochester.'

'What?' I said.

'He must have had exactly your condition. Don't you remember?'

The point seemed to me well taken. Mansel found this conversation incomprehensible, and got down to business. He would have to operate, of course. What were the chances? I asked. Quite good. Statistically, I pressed him. Not worse than 75 per cent, not better than 85 per cent, he said with singular confidence. I wasn't to expect too much: they ought to be able to give me back peripheral vision.

'What does that mean?'

'You won't be able to read with it. But you'll have some useful sight.'

If he could have operated on Saturday, he said, in an objective tone, just after the eye went, he might possibly have done better: it was too late now. Still, he had better get me into hospital that afternoon, and perform next morning.

'That's a little difficult,' I said. To myself, my voice sounded as objective as his. I felt collected, exaggeratedly collected, as though, after the anticlimax, I had to compete on equal terms.

'Why is it difficult?'

I said that I had an engagement on Wednesday which I was anxious to keep. He interrogated me. I explained that I wouldn't have thought twice about the formal ceremony at the university, but there was a Court meeting which I had given a serious promise to attend. Margaret, her face intent but hard to read, knew that I was referring to Vicky and her father.

'Some promises have to be broken,' said Mansel.

'I have some responsibility this time. Some personal responsibility, you understand.'

'Well, I can't judge that. But I've got to give you medical advice. You ought to have this operation tomorrow. The longer we put it off, the worse the chances are. I've got to tell you that.'

He was a strong-willed man. Somehow I had half-memories of the times I had clashed with men like this, both struggling for what I used to think of as the moral initiative.

'I'm not going to be unreasonable,' I said. 'But you must be definite about the chances. Is that fair?'

'I'll be as definite as I can.'

'If we delay three days, what difference will it really make?'

'Some.'

'Would it, say, halve the chances? In that case, of course, it's off.'

His will was crossed by his professional honesty. He gave a frosty smile.

'No. Nothing like that.'

'Well then. Can you put it into figures again? Tomorrow you said it would be an 80 per cent chance. What would it be on Thursday?'

'A little worse.'

'How much worse?' I said.

'Perhaps 10 per cent.'

'Not more than 10 per cent?' I went on, 'Less rather than more?'

'Yes,' said Mansel without palaver. 'I should say that was true. Less rather than more.'

Then I asked, would he mind if I had a word with my wife alone? With his courtesy, which was both professional and youthful, he said that he would be delighted: he was sure she would be the wisest of us all.

We looked into the waiting-room, but there were by now several people in it. So, her fingers interwoven with mine, we walked up and down the pavement outside the house. The mist had lifted, the air was pearly bright.

'Well,' I said, 'what do I do?'

'I must say,' said Margaret, 'I'd be happier to see you tucked up in hospital.'

'And yet, if you were me, you wouldn't even hesitate, would you?'

'That's a bit unkind.'

'No. The idea that you wouldn't take a tiny bit of risk—'

She understood, without question, that I wasn't being quixotic, as she might have been. If she had been asked, she might have said that I was showing defiance, taking my revenge for feeling helpless. In both of us as we grew older, there emerged a streak of recklessness which she had always had and which I loved in her. But this wasn't a time, we took it for granted, to discuss motives. We had both grown tired of the paralysis of subjectivism, when every action became about as good or about as bad as any other, provided that you could lucubrate it away.

She knew that if she asked me to go into hospital that night, I should do so. She understood me, and didn't ask.

We returned to Mansel's consulting-room. He stood up, polite and active, looking expectantly at Margaret.

'No,' I said. 'I'm at your service any time from Thursday morning.'

'Right,' said Mansel, without a blink or sign of disapproval. 'You'll go in some time that afternoon, will you? I'll deal with you early on Friday.'

CHAPTER XII

MONOCULAR VISION

WITH Margaret there to look after me, I arrived at the university robing-room half an hour before the morning ceremony. She had fitted me with a patch which shut out my left eye, and when Francis Getliffe saw it – he was already dressed in his chancellarial regalia – he walked across to us, frowning with concern. When Margaret explained what had happened, he said angrily:

'You ought never to have come.'

'Francis,' I said, 'you know perfectly well why I've come.' On the agenda for the Court that afternoon, over which he was to preside, there was an innocent-looking item standing in his son's name. Shaw still hadn't picked up the significance, so far as I had heard: but Francis knew, so did the group of young professors, and so did I.

We couldn't speak any more, the room was bumbling with a kind of backstage movement of human beings in fancy dress. Scarlet hoods, azure hoods, chef-like hats of French universities: hoods of this university, all invented by Shaw himself, one of which, the D.Sc., was a peculiarly startling yellow-gold. Soon I was in fancy dress myself, regarding the scheme with monocular detachment: I could see perfectly well, as well as with two eyes, but somehow the sheer fact of physical accident kept me in a bubble of my own. People I knew, Shaw, Leonard Getliffe, Geary, did not look quite real. Nor did my old acquaintance, Lord Lufkin, who, since he was to be invested with a hood later in the morning, stood subfusc, among the blur of colours, in a black gown. He was getting on for seventy by this time, and had at last been persuaded, or perhaps financially coerced, into retiring. But that hadn't take the edge off his public persona. He had taken to going about with someone I saw at his side in this milling, behooded mob; a man of fifty who acted as something like Lufkin's herald, producing pearls of wisdom from Lufkin's past, while the master himself stood by in non-participating silence.

That morning we came together in the crush. Untypically, Lufkin kissed Margaret's cheek. 'I'm glad to see your charming bride,' said

Lufkin, who disapproved of American business idioms and often used them.

He was not above taking an interest in my misfortunes. Once more we had to explain.

'If they're going to use the knife on you,' said Lufkin creakingly, 'you'd better get the best man in London. I always believe in getting the best man in London.'

'He's always said that,' said the herald, pink-faced, well tubbed, plump beside his hero's bones.

'Who is your man, then?' Lufkin said.

I produced the name of Mansel.

'Never heard of him,' said Lufkin, as though that removed Mansel from the plane of all created things.

After a patch of conversational doldrums, he had another thought.

'I have it,' he said. He turned to the herald. 'Go and ring up—.' Lufkin gave the name of the President of the Royal College of Surgeons – 'and find out how this fellow's thought of.'

The herald trotted off. The curious thing was, as Margaret and I had discovered, that he was a successful solicitor, and not Lufkin's solicitor at that. He had appointed himself Lufkin's handyman, not for money or any other sort of benefit (Lufkin's patronage had gone by now), but just because he loved it.

Lufkin considered that he had done his duty to me, and passed on. His parting shot, as he gazed at some honorary graduands, was:

'I never have believed in giving people degrees they haven't worked for.'

In which case, one would have thought, he ought not to have been present to receive one himself that morning. Most men would have thought so: but not Lufkin.

The academic procession got into line, a mace-bearer led us, caps dipping, hoods glaring, into the university hall. It might have been any one of two thousand academic processions that year in the English-speaking world, all copied, or not so much copied as refabricated, from processions of corporations of clerics four hundred years before. It wasn't really a tradition, it was man-made. Man-made, not woman-made, Margaret used to say: women couldn't have kept their faces straight long enough to devise colleges and clubs, the enclaves and rituals which men took shelter in.

Anyway, with solemnity this particular ritual pattered on. We climbed up the steps on to the platform, we took off our caps to Francis Getliffe,

Francis Getliffe took off his cap to us. We sat down. For a moment or two the order of proceedings was interrupted, for some students had become amused by the patch over my eye and started to cheer. Then Francis Getliffe delivered the invocation: more standing up, sitting down, taking off of caps.

At last the public orator was beginning to make his speech in praise of Lufkin. The orator stood towards the edge of the dais, and Lufkin, standing opposite, did not turn his face towards him. Lufkin just remained there, immutable, with an assessing expression – just as he used to sit at his own table, in the days of his industrial power, surrounded by his court of cherubim and seraphim. He listened now, as he used to listen then, to the story of his virtues and achievements, as though he could, if he felt inclined, point out where certain important features were being omitted. About his virtues, Lufkin's view of his own character was different from any other person's: about his achievements, the maddening thing was, he was right. He made his claims for himself, and he sounded like, and perhaps sometimes was, a megalomaniac: yet objectively the claims were a little less than the truth.

Lufkin was duly hooded, the citations fluted on, an orientalist was being celebrated: I was only half-listening, with my eye regarding David Rubin, whose turn was still to come. At each academic pun, a smile crossed his clever sad Disraelian face. One might have thought that he enjoyed this kind of jocularity or that he was intoxicated by the occasion, never having been honoured before. If one did think either of those things, one couldn't have been more wrong. I had known him for a good many years, and I sometimes thought that I now knew him less than at our first meeting: but I did know one thing about him. He felt, underneath his beautiful courtesy, that his time was being wasted unless it was spent in his own family or with one or two colleagues whom he accepted as his equals. He had been adviser to governments, he had had all the honours in his own profession, he was courted by the smart, and he was so unassuming that they believed they were doing him a favour: it must have seemed, people said, a long way from his Yiddish momma in Brooklyn. Not a bit of it. His skin was like parchment, there were panda-like colorations under his eyes, he had never looked satisfied either with existence or himself. But, satisfied or not, Rubin was one of the aristocrats of this world. He walked among us, he was superlatively polite, and (like Margaret's forebears) he didn't give a damn.

Another citation; looking out over the hall, I felt, or imagined, that my sound eye was getting tired. I didn't observe that a note was being passed up to Lufkin: in fact, during that ceremony no one but Lufkin would have had a note passed to him. I was surprised to be tapped on the arm by my neighbour and be given a piece of paper. On it was written, in a great sprawling hand, the simple inscription: *Mansel is all right. L.*

Rubin, last on the list, had returned to his seat with his scroll; Francis Getliffe gave the valedictory address, and Margaret led me away. I had begged myself off the mass luncheon, and she and I ate sandwiches in an office. I told her, not that she needed telling, that I should be glad when the Court was over. She knew that I couldn't rely on my energy that afternoon, that I, who had been to so many committees, was nervous before this one.

Because I was nervous, I arrived in the Court room too early, and sat there alone. I read over the agenda: it was a long time since any agenda had looked so meaningless. Item No. 7 read: *Constitution of Disciplinary Committee*. It would take a couple of hours to get down to it. Previously I had thought that Leonard Getliffe and his friends had been well advised, the tactics were good: now the words became hazy and I couldn't concentrate.

The others clattered in noisily from the luncheon, some of them rosy after their wine. Francis Getliffe took the ornamental chair, looking modestly civilian now that his golden robes were taken off. Arnold Shaw, flushed and bobbish, sat on his right hand. Francis was just going to rap on the table when his son came and whispered to me: 'I'm very sorry that you had to come.' Civil of him, I thought without gratitude. Did he know that, if you are in any kind of conflict, the first law is – be present in the flesh?

Francis Getliffe cleared his throat and said that, before we began, he would like to say how sorry the entire Court was to hear of my misfortune, and how they all wished me total success in my operation. Several voices broke in with 'my lord chairman', saying how they wished to support that. I duly thanked them. Down below the words I was cursing them. Just as energy had seeped away, so had good nature. The last thing I could take was either commiseration or kind wishes.

As though at a distance from me, the meeting lumbered into its groove. Lumbered, perhaps, a little more quickly than usual, for Francis, though a stately chairman, was surreptitiously an impatient one. Someone by my side crossed, one by one, five items off. The sixth was *Extension to Biology Building*, and even Francis could not prevent the minutes ticking the afternoon away. The voices round me didn't sound as though they could have enough of it. The U.G.C.! Architects! Appeals! Claims of other subjects! Master building plan! Emotions were heated, the voices might have been talking about love or the preservation of peace. Of all the academic meetings I had attended, at least half the talking time, and much more than half the expense of spirit, had been consumed in discussions of building. Whatever would they do when all the buildings were put up? The answer, I thought, though not that afternoon, was simple: they would pull some down and start again.

At length I heard the problem being referred (by an exercise of firmness on Francis's part) to the Buildings Sub-Committee. Sharply Francis called out 'Item No. 7.' I gripped myself: I had to be with them now. It was hard to make the effort.

Focusing on Francis, I was puzzled that he didn't ask the Vice-Chancellor to leave us. Whether Shaw knew it or not, he was going to be argued over.

Instead Francis gazed down the table.

'Professor Getliffe,' he said to his son, 'I think you have something to say on this matter.'

'Yes, my lord chairman,' Leonard said to his father. 'My colleagues and I want to suggest that we postpone it. We should like to postpone it until next term.'

'That would give me a chance,' said Shaw briskly, automatically (Good God, I was thinking again, still not reacting, how many months would he have survived in Whitehall?) 'to send round a paper on the present arrangements for discipline. And how I propose to make one or two changes.'

'Thank you, Vice-Chancellor,' said Francis, who might have been thinking as I did. 'Anyway,' he addressed the room, 'I must say, I think there is some merit in Professor Getliffe's suggestion, if it appeals to the Court. I know this seems an important piece of business to some of us, and it would be a mistake to rush it. I'm anxious that everyone should have the opportunity to give us his views. I believe Sir Lewis is interested, isn't that so?'

'Yes, I am rather interested.'

'Well then. We hope you'll be able to attend the Court next term. Completely recovered. Then I shall propose we might set aside the first part of the meeting for this business. We shall very much want to hear your opinion.'

I said, yes, I should try to attend the Court. In temper, in ultimate let-down, I could keep to the official language. Would anyone to whom the official language might as well have been Avar or Estonian, realise that they were considering me, that this was a put-up job between father and son?

Leaving the meeting in time to escape conversation, I got a university car to myself to take me to the Residence. There, among the smell of leather (to me an anxious smell), I sat in a state both harsh-tempered and depressed. The let-down, yes. The wasted effort, yes. The physical discomfort, yes. But this was a state, concealed from others, that I used to know, and didn't often now. The bizarre thing was, I had got my way. Through the Getliffes' indulgence I had won Shaw four months' grace. If I had been at my most competent, I shouldn't have done better than that. I might easily have done much worse (there would be time, there was still the residue of a planner working within me, to lobby Denis Geary and some of the others). I should never know whether – if the Getliffes hadn't treated me with pity – I could have made my effort that afternoon at all.

When Margaret saw me enter our bedroom at the Residence, she said, 'You've been doing too much.' I said, 'I've been doing nothing at all.' Before I told her the story, she made me lie on the bed: then, reassured, she let me talk. This time I wasn't using the official language: Margaret was used to me when I wasn't giving events the benefit of the doubt. She sat beside me, looking down with a curious expression, clear-eyed.

She told me it was six o'clock, nearly time to dress for the dinner that night. Was I going to be able to manage it? I nodded. She didn't protest: she just remarked that a drink would help, and she would find one. Soon she returned, with Arnold Shaw following her, in his shirt sleeves and carrying a tray, enjoying himself as butler. He poured a large whisky for her, and an even larger one for me. He splashed in soda, spooned the ice. Then, as he picked up the tray, ready to depart, he said to me, with a wise reproving frown: 'It was irresponsible of you. To come here today. It was irresponsible, you know.'

The door shut behind him, quick executive feet pattered down the passage. I took a gulp at my glass, and then I laughed. It was a sour laugh, but it was at least a laugh.

Margaret joined in. 'I've been wanting to do that for quite some time,' she said. 'I've been wondering just when you wouldn't mind.'

Since I couldn't knot a tie easily one-eyed, she did it for me, and I went down before her into the drawing-room. David Rubin and Francis Getliffe had already arrived, and as I joined them Rubin was saying that sometimes, this autumn, he had felt his intellectual analysis might be wrong. He meant, his analysis of the chances of peace. It had always been blacker than either of ours, more pessimistic than that of anyone we met. Yet he knew as much as we did, and more. He said he was inclined to trust his analysis, not his feelings: said it with a shrug and began to cachinnate. He was not the lightest of company when the cachinnation broke out and he was predicting the worst. Still, he said, sometimes he felt he might be wrong. If so, he went on sarcastically, it wouldn't be any thanks to people like us. We had, all three of us, done our best, we had spent months and years of our lives, we had tried to find ways of action. It hadn't affected the situation, said Rubin, by .001 of 1 per cent. If things did go right, it would be no thanks to us: it would be due to something as random and as incalculable as a change in the weather.

Others came up to us. Francis was being less fatalistic, when David Rubin took me aside. In a corner of the room he indicated my patched eye and said:

'This is a nuisance, Lewis.'

It sounded brusque. But it wasn't so. He looked at me with monkey-sad eyes, incongruous above his immaculate dinner jacket (his colleagues gossiped, why should a man of his morbid pessimisim appear to be competing as the Best-Dressed Man of the Year?). His eyes were sad, his nerve-ends were as fine as Margaret's. He wasn't going to harass me with sympathy, or with alternative plans for surgical treatment.

'Yes,' I said, without any bluff.

'These retinas are getting rather common.'

I asked him why.

'Quite simple. We're all living longer, that's all. You've got to expect bits of the machine to break down.'

He had judged it right, he was being a support.

'You've played your luck, you know,' he said.

He went on: he had a check-up every six months. When did I last have a check-up?

I said something about American hypochondria.

'Maybe,' said Rubin, with astringent comradeship. 'They'll find something sooner or later. Let's see, you're ten years older than I am. But remember, I did my best work before I was thirty. I bet you, I've felt older than you have – I bet you I have done for years.'

But, when we had gone into dinner, the courses clattering in the most lucullan of all Arnold Shaw's feasts, I sat with Rubin's brand of consola-tion wearing off. The amnesia of the first drinks wore off too: going into hospital next day, I had to stop drinking early in the meal, though I didn't want to. The mechanics of politeness jangled on: I turned from the honorary graduate's wife on my right to the one on my left and back again: they found me dull: I just wanted the day to end.

There was one diversion, though. Vicky had led the women out, and the rest of us had re-seated ourselves at Shaw's end of the table. Shaw was in excelsis. He had made four distinguished scholars honorary graduates. There was also Lufkin, who had been forced upon him by the engineers, but still he was good enough. Shaw saw them all round him. He was a man of uncomplicated pleasures, and he was content. He was also content because he had given them splendid wine, and drunk a good deal of it himself. Again, Lufkin was an exception. True to his bleak rule, he had drunk one whisky before dinner, another with the meal, and now, while the others were enjoying Shaw's port, he allowed himself a third. But it was he who dominated the table. He was explaining certain circumstances, to him still astonishing though they had happened a couple of years before, surrounding his retirement.

'I decided it was right to go. Before there was any risk of being a liability to my people. Not that I wasn't still at my best, or I should have got out long before.' He sat there skull-faced, still youthful-looking. He delivered himself as though indifferent to his audience, completely absorbed in his own drama, projecting it like something of transcendental importance and objective truth.

'What do you imagine happened?' It was the kind of rhetorical question no one could answer, yet by which men as experienced as Rubin and Francis Getliffe were hypnotised.

'Nothing happened.' Lufkin answered himself with stony satisfaction. He went on:

'I made that industry.' It sounded gigantesque: it was quite true. He had possessed supreme technological insight and abnormal will. He had made an industry, not a fortune. He had more than enough money for his needs, but he had nothing to spend it on. By the standards of his industrial colleagues, he was not a rich man. 'I made that industry, and everything inside it. I used to tell my people, *I am your best friend.* And they knew, *I was their best friend.*'

Heads, hypnotised, were nodding.

'What did they do?' Silence again. Again Lufkin answered himself. 'Nothing.' He spoke with greater confidence than ever. 'When any of my managers retired, the whole works turned out. When my deputy retired, the whole organisation sent a testimonial. What did they do for me?'

This time he didn't give an answer. He said:

'I wasn't hurt. I was surprised.'

He repeated:

'I wasn't *hurt*. I was *surprised*.'

When we joined the women, it was only minutes before Margaret spoke to Vicky and Arnold Shaw and took me off to bed. Alone in our room, I said to her: 'Paul Lufkin is lonely.' I was wondering, how used were the others to this singular display of emotion? Horizontal fission, we used to call it. Lufkin sincerely believed that he wasn't hurt. And yet, even he must realise at least that he felt lost. After great power for thirty years, power all gone. After a lifetime of action, nothing to do. Once he had talked of retiring to Monaco. Now, so far as I knew, he lived in Surrey and came to London once a week for the committee of a charity. 'Paul Lufkin is lonely,' I said.

'He's not the only one,' said Margaret.

I asked what she meant.

'Didn't you realise that Vicky was waiting for a telephone call all night, poor girl?'

In the solipsistic bubble in which I had gone through that day, I had scarcely noticed her.

'Did she hear?'

Margaret shook her head.

'That nephew of yours. I'm afraid he's throwing her over, don't you think so?'

'It doesn't look good.' I was sitting on the bed, just having taken off the eye-patch. I was trying to speak about Vicky, but the black edge cut out the light, the orange fringe was giddily swimming, and I let out that complaint only for myself.

CHAPTER XIII

HOMAGE TO SUPERSTITION

THE next morning, tea trays on our bed. Margaret sketched out the day's timetable. There was a train just after one, we could be in London in a couple of hours: that would bring us to the hospital before tea. The less time I had in the dark, the better, I said. I knew that I should have to lie on my back, both eyes blindfolded, to give the retina hours to settle down.

When I had agreed to Margaret's programme, I said:

'In that case, I think I'd like to see my old father this morning.'

For an instant, she was caught open-mouthed, her looks dissolved in blank astonishment. Her own relation with her father had been so responsible. She had sometimes been shocked by mine. She had never seen me in search of a father, either a real one or a surrogate, in all our time together. She gazed at me. She gave a sharp-eyed, intimate smile and said:

'You know, it isn't much more than having a few teeth out, you do know that?'

It sounded like free association gone mad, but her eyes were lit up. To others I seemed more rational than most men; not to her. She had lived with a streak of superstitiousness in me as deep as my mother's, though more suppressed. She had watched me book in, year after year, at the same New York hotel, because there I had heard of a major piece of luck. She had learned how I dreaded any kind of pleasure on a Tuesday night because one such evening I had enjoyed myself and faced stark horror on the Wednesday morning. Sometimes I infected her. She wasn't sorry, she was relieved, to hear this atavistic desire of mine. It might be a longish operation, Margaret had said: there was a shrinking from unconsciousness which was atavistic too. She, as well as I, wasn't disinclined to make an act of piety, to make this sort of insurance for which one prays as a child. The fact that it was an incongruous act of piety might have deterred her, she had more sense of the fitness of things, but she took me in my free- dom, and didn't wish it to deter me.

So, by the middle of the morning, she had said our goodbyes, and we were driving out through the back-streets along which, the preceding spring, I had walked with Charles. The cluster of shops, the chapel, the gentle rise. When I was a boy, cars didn't pass those terraced windows once a day; and even that morning, when the university Daimler stopped outside Aunt Milly's old house, there were curious eyes from the 'entry' opposite.

I led Margaret in by the back way. Passing the window of my father's room, I stood on tiptoe but could see only darkness. When I went up the steps to the french window, I found the room was empty. We returned along the passage. I rang at the familiar front door (pulling the hand bell, perhaps it was still the same bell, as when I came back one night, late from a school debate, found our own house empty and rang Aunt Milly's bell: there was my mother pretending to laugh off a setback, lofty in her disappointed pride). The bell jangled. After a time footsteps sounded, and a middle-aged man in his shirt-sleeves opened the door. I had seen him before, but not spoken to him: he was always referred to by my father as Mr Sperry. He was called my father's 'lodger', though he occupied the entire house except for the single room.

I told him my name and said that I was looking for my father. Mr

Sperry chuckled. He was long and thin, with a knobbly Adam's apple and a bush of hair. He had a kind, perplexed and slightly eccentric face. I thought I remembered hearing that he was a jobbing plumber.

'I expect the old gentleman's doing his bit of shopping,' he said.

'When do you think he'll be back?'

Mr Sperry shook his head. 'It's wonderful how he does for himself,' he said. He had the most gentle manners: but it was clear that, though he had occupied the house for ten years, he didn't know much about my father, and was puzzled by what little he did know. 'I can't tell you when he'll be home, I'm sure. Would you care to come in?'

I exchanged a glance with Margaret. I said we hadn't many minutes, there was a train to catch; we'd just hang about outside for a little while. That was true: and yet, kind as Mr Sperry was, he was a stranger, and I didn't want to sit in childhood's rooms with him.

Standing outside the car, Margaret and I smoked cigarettes. It would be bad to miss my father now. I kept looking along the road to the library, down the rise to the chapel. Then Margaret said:

'I think that's him, isn't it?'

I was watching the other direction. She was pointing to a tiny figure who had just turned into sight, by the chapel railings.

She wasn't certain. Her eyes were perfect: she could make out that small figure as I could not: but she couldn't be certain because, owing to my father's singularity, she had met him only twice.

Slowly, with small steps, the figure toddled on. Yes, it was my father. At last I saw him clearly. He was wearing a bowler hat, beneath which silky white hair flowed over his ears: his overcoat was much too long for him, and his trousers, as wide as an old-fashioned Russian's, billowed over his boots. At each short step, a foot turned outwards at forty-five degrees. He was singing, quite loudly, to himself. He seemed to be looking at nothing in particular. He was only four or five houses away when he noticed us.

'Well, I declare,' he said.

Away from him, how long was it since I had heard that phrase? It was like listening at a college meeting when I was a young man: one heard usages, long since dead, such as this one of my father's, stretching back three generations. 'I declare,' he repeated, gazing not at me but at Margaret, for he kept his appreciative eye for a good-looking woman.

I explained that we had had to attend a university function the day before, and thought we would look him up. It would be easier if he had a telephone, I grumbled.

'Confound it,' said my father, speaking like a national figure who would not dare to have an entry in the directory, 'I should never have a minute's peace. Anyway '– he fumbled over Margaret's name, which he had forgotten, but went on in triumph – 'You tracked me down, didn't you? Here you are, as large as life and twice as natural.'

We followed him in, down the passage again, up the steps to the french window, saying that we would stay just a quarter-of-an-hour. In the dark little room, my father switched on a light. To my mother, who had never seen it in that house or her own, electric light had been one of the symbols of a higher existence: and anyone who thought that proved her unspiritual didn't know what the spirit was.

He offered to put the kettle on, and make us some tea. No, we didn't want to drink tea at twelve o'clock in the morning. But he had to give us something. At last, with enormous gratification, he produced from a cupboard a bottle about one-third full of tawny port. 'I've always liked a drop of port,' he told Margaret, and proceeded to tell her a story about going out with the waits at Christmas 'when Lena was alive', being invited into drawing-rooms and figuring as the hardened drinker of the party. That was one of the daydreams in which I didn't believe. I looked out into the stone-flagged yard. There was a stump of a plum-tree still surviving near his window. As far back as I could remember, that tree had never borne any fruit.

My father was talking with animation to Margaret. So far he hadn't commented on the patch over my eye. Either he hadn't noticed, or he thought that it was the kind of idiosyncrasy in which I was likely to indulge. I interrupted him:

'As a matter of fact, I've got to have a minor operation tomorrow.'

'You've ruptured yourself, have you?' he said brightly, as though that was the only physical mishap he could imagine happening to anyone. It had happened, apparently, to Mr Sperry.

'No,' I said with a faint irritation, tapping my patch. 'I've got a detached retina.'

My father had never heard of the condition. In fact, he had only the haziest notion of where the retina was. Margaret, very patient with him, drew a diagram, which he studied with an innocent expression.

'I expect he'll be all right, won't he?' he asked simply, as though I wasn't there.

'Of course he will. You're not to worry.'

Not, I couldn't help thinking, that he seemed overwhelmed by anxiety.

'I've never had any trouble with my eyes, you know,' he was ruminating.

'I've got a lot to be thankful for, by gosh I have.' In fact he had kept all his senses into his late eighties. He surveyed me with an air of preternatural wisdom or perhaps of cunning.

'You ought to take care of your eyes, that you ought. I tell people, I must have told you once upon a time, be careful, you've only got one pair of eyes. That's it. You've only got one pair of eyes.'

'At this moment,' I said, 'I've got exactly half of that.'

This was a kind of grim comment in which Martin and I, and young Charles after us, occasionally indulged ourselves. My father was much too amiable a man to make such comments: but whenever he heard them – it had been true in my boyhood, it was just as true now – he appeared to regard them as the height of humour. So he gave out great peals of his surprisingly loud, harmonious laughter.

'Would you believe it?' he asked Margaret. 'Would you believe it?' He kept making remarks about me, directed entirely at her, as though I were a vacuum inhabited only by myself. 'He's a big strong fellow, isn't he? He'll be all right, won't he? He's a young man, isn't he?' (I was within a week of my fifty-eighth birthday). 'I wish I were as young as he is.'

At that reflection, his face, usually so cheerful, became clouded.

'I'm not so young as I used to be,' he turned his attention from Margaret to me. 'I don't mind for myself, I poddle along just as well as ever. But people are beginning to say things, you know.'

'What people?'

'I'm afraid they're beginning to say things at the choir.'

I felt a stab of something like animal concern, much more as though he were my son than the other way about.

'What are they saying?'

'They keep telling me that they're sure I can manage until Christmas. I don't like the sound of that, Lewis, I don't like the sound of that.'

'Do they know how old you are?'

'Oh no. I haven't told them that.' He regarded me with the most extreme shrewdness. 'If anyone asks, I just say I'm a year older than I was this time last year.'

He burst out:

'They're beginning to ask if the walk home isn't too much for me!'

It wasn't an unreasonable question, addressed to a very old man for whom the walk meant a couple of hours on winter nights. It wasn't an unreasonable question: but I hoped that that was all. I said, I was ready to arrange for a car, each time he had to attend the choir. Anything to prevent them getting rid of him. Anything.

'That's very good of you, Lewis,' he said. 'You know, I don't want to give it up just now.'

His tone, however, was flat: and his expression hadn't regained its innocent liveliness. My father might be a simple old man, but he had – unlike that fine scholar and man of affairs, Arnold Shaw – a nose for danger.

CHAPTER XIV

THE DARK AND THE LIGHT

A VOICE was saying:

'You're waking up now.'

It was a voice I had not heard before, from close beside me. I had awakened into the dark.

'What time is it?' It was myself speaking, but it sounded thick-tongued in the dark.

'Nearly three o'clock.'

'Three o'clock when?'

'Three o'clock in the afternoon, of course. Mr Mansel operated this morning.'

Time had no meaning. A day and a bit since that visit to my father, that had no meaning either.

'I'm very thirsty.'

'You can't have much. You can have a sip.'

As I became conscious, I was aware of nothing but thirst. I was struggling up to drink, a hand pressed my shoulder. 'You mustn't move.' I felt glass against my lips, a trickle of liquid: no taste, perhaps a dry taste, a tingle in the throat: soda-water?

'More.'

'Not yet.'

In the claustrophobic dark, I was just a thirsty organism. I tried to think: they must have dehydrated me pretty thoroughly. Processes, tests, injections, the evening before, that morning, as I lay immobilised, blinded: reduced to hebetude. This was worse, an order of magnitude worse, than any thirst after a drunken night. I didn't want to imagine the taste of alcohol. I didn't want to touch alcohol again. Lemon squashes: lime juice: all the soft drinks I had ever known: I wanted them round me as soon as I got out of here, dreaming up a liquid but teetotal elysium.

Through the afternoon I begged sip after sip. In time, though what time I had no idea, the nurse said that my wife had come to see me. I felt Margaret's hand in mine. Her voice was asking after me.

'I don't like this much,' I said.

She took it for granted that it wasn't discomfort I was complaining of. Yesterday's superstition, today's animal dependence – those I was grinding against.

'It won't be long,' she said.

'Too long.'

Her voice sounded richer than when I could see her: she told me Mansel had reported that the operation had gone according to plan. It would have been easier if he could have done it earlier in the week ('obstinate devil,' I said, glad to be angry against someone). It had taken nearly three hours – 'One's playing with millimeters,' he had said, with a technician's pride. He wouldn't know whether it had worked or not for about four days.

'Four days.'

'Never mind,' she said.

'That's easy to say.'

'There isn't much I can say, is there?' she replied. 'Oh, they're all convinced you're remarkably well. That's rather a comfort, isn't it?'

I didn't respond.

'At least,' she said, 'it is to me.'

Patiently she read to me out of the day's papers. At last she had to leave me, in the dark.

Yet, though my eyes were shut and blindfold, it wasn't the familiar dark. It wasn't like being in a hotel room on a black night, thick curtains drawn. It was more oppressive than that. I seemed to be having a sustained hallucination, as though deep scarlet tapestries, colour glowing, texture embossed and patterned, were pressing on both my eyes. I had to get used to it, until the nightly drug put me to sleep, just as I had to get used to my thoughts.

Early next morning, time was still deranged; when I switched on the bedside radio it was silent. I heard Mansel's greeting and felt skilled fingers taking off the bandages, unshielding the eye. Five minutes of light. The lens, the large eye peering, the aseptic 'It looks all right so far', the skilled fingers taking the light away again. A few minutes of his shop: it was a relief to get back into someone's working life. What hours did he keep? Bed about 10.0, up at 5.30, first calls, like this one, between 6.0 and 7.0. Training like a billiards player, he couldn't afford to take more than one drink a night: three operations that morning, two more after lunch. He enjoyed his job as much as Francis Getliffe enjoyed his: he was as clever with his hands. Nearly all his techniques were new. Thirty years ago, he told me, they couldn't have done anything for me at all.

That was an interlude in the day. So was Margaret's visit each afternoon, when she read to me. So was the radio news. Otherwise I lay there immobile, thinking, or not really thinking, so much as given over to a plasma of mental swirls, desires, apprehensions, resentments, sensual reveries, sometimes, resolves. It wasn't often that this plasma broke out into words: occasionally it did, but the mental swirl was nearer to a dream, or a set of dreams. Dreams in which what people called the 'unconscious' lived side by side with the drafting of a letter. Once when I was making myself verbalise, I thought – as I had often done – that the idea of the unconscious as 'deep' in our minds had done us harm. It was a bad model. It was just as bad a model as that of a 'God out there', out in space, beyond the clouds. We laughed at simple people and their high heavens, existing in our aboriginal three-dimensions: yet, when we turned our minds upon our own minds, we fell into precisely the same trap.

Thoughts swirled on. To anyone else, even to Margaret, I should have tried to make some sort of show of sarcasm. To myself, I hadn't the spirit. I didn't like self-pity in myself or others. There were times, in those days, when I was doing nothing but pity myself. I had known that state before, ill and wretched, as a young man. I had more excuse then. This wasn't enough excuse for one's pride to break. Yet I couldn't pretend.

Margaret asked if I wanted other visitors. None, I said, except her. That was an attempt at a gesture. Yes, I should have to see Charles March: as he was my doctor, I couldn't keep him out. When he came in on the second morning, I told him, putting on an act, that it was absurd anything so trivial should be such a bore.

In his kind harsh voice (voices came at me out of the dark, some from nurses whom I had never seen) he replied:

'I should find it intolerable, don't you think I should?'

He was closer in sympathy than any of my friends, he could guess how I was handling my depression. As though casually, he set to work to support me by reminding me of the past. He had been thinking only the other day, he said – it gave him a certain malicious pleasure – of the way we had, in terms of money, exchanged places. When we first met, he had been a rich young man and I was penniless. Now he was living on a doctor's income and I had become distinctly well-to-do.

'It would have seemed very curious, the first time you came to Bryanstone Square, wouldn't it?'

The irony was designed to provoke me. The voice went on:

'You've had an interesting life, Lewis, haven't you?'

'I suppose so,' I said.

'All those years ago, if you had been told what was going to happen to you, would you have compounded for it?'

'Would you have done, about yourself?'

'I wasn't as insatiable as you, you know. In most ways, yes.'

I didn't have to explicate that answer. He hadn't chosen to compete. His marriage, like mine to Margaret, had been a good one. He had two daughters, but no son. He envied me mine. But he was trying to be therapeutic, he didn't want to talk about himself.

'You had a formidable power in you when you were young, we all knew that. We were all certain you'd make your name. You can't say you haven't, can you? But it must have been surprising when it happened. I know some of it's been painful, I couldn't have taken what you've had to take. Still, that was what you were made for, wasn't it?'

I heard the friendly smile, half-sardonic, half-approving.

'You didn't find your own nature', he was saying, 'altogether easy to cope with, did you?'

'You know I didn't.'

'You started out subtle and tricky as well as rapacious. You had to make yourself a better man. And the trouble with that sort of effort is that one loses as well as gains. We're both more decent than we were at twenty, Lewis, but I'm sure we're nothing like so much fun.'

At that I laughed. That was the primordial Charles March. He might have become more decent, but his tongue hadn't lost its sadistic edge.

'Still, I've told you before,' he went on, 'it's impossible to regret one's own experience, don't you agree?'

'I used to agree with you. Which you thought entirely proper, of course.' Just for an instant I had caught the debating tone of our young manhood. Then I said: 'But in this I'm beginning to wonder whether you are right.'

He was glad to have revived me a bit, to have led me into an argument: but he was taken aback that I had spoken with feeling, and that my spirits had sunk down again. Quickly he switched from that subject, although he stayed a long while, casting round for other ways of interesting me, before he left.

Claustrophobia was getting hold of me. It had been a nuisance always.

The scarlet tapestries pressed upon my eyes, the pillows were built up so that I couldn't move my head more than a few degrees.

Blindness would be like this. Did one still have such hallucinations? Was it the absolute dark? Of all the private miseries, that was one I was not sure I could endure. None of us knew his limits. Once, when young Charles was conceived, I thought it might be beyond my limit if the genes had gone wrong, if he were born to a suffering one could do nothing about.

I shouldn't be able to read with my left eye. That was practical. If this could happen to one eye, it could happen to the other. Peripheral vision (Mansel's voice). Useful vision. A great deal of my life was lived through the eye. How could I get on without reading? Records, people reading to me. It would be gritty. How could I write? I should have to learn to dictate. It would be like learning a new language. Still.

The machine wearing out (Rubin's voice). People talked about getting old. Did anyone believe it? Ageing men went in for rhetorical flourishes: but were they real? One didn't live in terms of history, but in existential moments. One woke up as one had done thirty years before. Certainly that was true of me. Men were luckier than women. There was nothing brutal to remind one of time's arrow. Perhaps men like Rubin, physicists, mathematicians, remembered they had had great concepts in their youth: never again, the power had gone. I had seen athletes in their thirties, finished, talking like old men and meaning it. But for me, day by day, existence hadn't altered. Memory faltered a little: sometimes I forgot a name. The machine wearing out.

As I pushed one fact away, another swam in. Living in public. Attacks. That year's attack, people saying that I had stolen other men's writing. They could have accused me of many things, but, as I had told George Passant, not of that. That I couldn't have done. You had to make yourself a better man (Charles March's voice). Yes, but even when I was as he first knew me, when I was 'tricky and rapacious', that I could never have done. Not out of virtue, but out of temperament. It was one of my deficiencies – and sometimes a strength – that I had to stay indifferent to what I didn't know at first-hand. Yet the accusation hurt. It seemed to hurt more than if it had been true.

In the red-dark: motionless: there came – for instants among the depression or the anger – a sense of freedom. This was as low as I had gone. There was a kind of exhilaration, which I had known just once before in my life, of being at the extreme.

Then the vacuum in my mind began to fill itself again.

Early in the fifth morning, Mansel's greeting. The clever fingers: the reprieve of light. The lens, the large eye. He was taking longer than usual, examining from above, below, and the right.

Crisply he said:

'I'm sorry, sir. We've failed. The retina hasn't stuck.'

It was utterly unanticipated, I had prepared myself for a good deal, not for this. At the same time it sounded – as other announcements of ill-luck had sounded – like news I had known for a long time.

'Well,' I said, 'this is remarkably tiresome.'

'That's putting it mildly,' said Mansel. He spoke in bad temper, blaming himself and me, just as I heard scientists taking it out of their lab-assistant after an experiment had gone wrong. He was re-calculating. There was an element of chance in these operations. There was an element of human error. He couldn't trace the fault.

'Anyway, inquests are useless,' he said snappily. He became a doctor, a good doctor, again.

'There's no reason why you should be uncomfortable any longer,' he said, taking the cover off my good eye. We shall have to look after that one, he remarked, in reassurance. It would have to be inspected regularly, of course. He would ring up my wife, so that she could take me home. I should feel better there. It would do me good to have a drink as soon as I arrived.

'What will happen to this?' I pointed a finger towards the left eye.

'For the present, it will probably be rather like it was before we operated. Then, if we did nothing further – I shall have to talk to you about that, you understand, but not just now – if we did nothing further, it would gradually die on you. That might take some time.'

After he had gone, I sat up in bed and drank a cup of tea. Lying flat, I had been scarcely able to eat a sandwich, and I was hungry. Obviously Mansel wanted to try another operation. It was dark to face the thought of going through all that again. Just to get some minor vision. A little sight was better than no sight. The bad eye would die on me. That might be the right choice. He was a strong-willed man, he wouldn't have me let it go without a conflict. In my way I was stubborn too. I had to make my own forecasts.

Yet, in the middle of indecision, I got an animal pleasure out of being in the light. My left eye Mansel had bound up again, but the other was free. It was good to see the roofs outside, and a nurse's face. She had spoken to me each morning, and now I saw her. If I had met her in the street, I should have thought she looked sensible enough, with the map of Ireland written on her. But now her face stood out, as though I had not seen a face before.

It was she who told me that I had a visitor. I looked at my watch. Still not ten o'clock. I thought Margaret had been in a hurry. But the nurse held the door open, not for her, but for young Charles.

'How are you?' I asked mechanically.

'No, how are *you*?' he said.

I asked if he had seen Margaret. I was hoping that she had broken the news to him. No, he had come straight from school: he had begged the morning off to visit me.

He sat by the bedside, watching me. I saw his skin, fresh from an adolescent shave. I had to come out with it. I said, more curtly than I intended:

'It hasn't worked.'

His face went stern with trouble.

'What does that mean?'

I answered direct:

'I think it means that I shall go blind in that eye. But you're not to worry—'

'Good God, why aren't I to worry? What's your sight going to be—'

I interrupted, and began to talk as reassuringly as Mansel. The good eye was perfectly sound. One could do anything, including play games, with one eye. Nature was sensible to give us two of everything. 'We're got to take reasonable precautions, obviously,' I went on. 'Mansel will have to check that eye, we shall lay on a routine—'

'How often?'

'Once a month, perhaps—'

'Once a week,' said Charles fiercely. I had never seen him so moved on my behalf.

I tried to distract him. Going back to one of the reflections that rankled when I lay in the dark (going back and deliberately domesticating it), I produced the kind of question that normally made him grin. Being accused of something which is untrue – one feels a sense of moral outrage. But being accused of something which is dead true – one also feels a sense of moral outrage. Which is the stronger? I told him a story of Roy Calvert and me, travelling with false passports in the war, masquerading as members of the International Red Cross – and being accused by French officials at the airport of being frauds. Just as in fact we were. I had never felt more affronted in my life, more morally wronged.

Charles gave a faint absent smile, and then his face became stern again.

I had a suspicion that he was hiding some trouble of his own. Love, perhaps – or equally possible, some essay that in his professional fashion he thought had been undermarked. In any case, he would have kept his own secrets: but that morning he wanted to conceal the expression on his face. Could he take me home? It was foolish to bring Margaret all this way. He would ring her up while I dressed.

Soon he was leading me through the corridors – the hospital smell threatening, the walls echoing and gaunt. He was supporting me, unnecessarily, on his arm, as he led me through the corridors down to the waiting taxi.

CHAPTER XV

SUAVE MARI MAGNO

BACK in the flat, with Charles returned to school, I lay on the sofa, not talking much. Now at last I was beginning to feel it. Margaret, unselfregarding, gave me books that might snag my attention and brought in trays when I didn't want to sit down to meals.

It went on like that for three days. On the morning after I left hospital, Mansel came in and took off the bandages, saying that the operation cut had healed. He also said that I should probably be more visually comfortable if I went on wearing a patch over the eye.

So I lay about in the drawing-room during those days, not able to rouse myself. Occasionally I inched up the patch for an instant, shutting the good eye, puzzled by the impact of light and what I did or did not see.

Exactly four days after Mansel had stood over my hospital bed and clipped out the verdict, I woke. It was half past seven. Out of habit I looked towards the chink of light between the curtains. I had taken off the patch when I went to bed. I closed the good eye and with the left eye open stared towards the chink. I dropped the eyelid, looked again. I did that several times, as if performing an exercise or doing an optical experiment. Then I got up, as I had nearly a fortnight before, pulled one of the curtains aside, shut my good eye again, and looked. Just as I had done nearly a fortnight before, I went back to bed. This time, I didn't disturb Margaret, but waited for her to wake. At last she did so. Even then I did not speak at once, but waited until she was alert.

I said:

'Something odd has happened.'

'What is it now?' Her voice was quick and anxious.

'No, nothing bad.' I went on carefully, as though my words might be quoted: 'The eye seems to have cleared itself up. At least, there doesn't seem to be any black veil this morning.'

She cried out:

'What can you see?'

'I can see a bit. Not very well. But anyway I do seem to have a full field of vision.'

It might be temporary, I warned her, trying to warn myself. In fact, for a couple of days past, I had been wondering each time when I squinted past the patch, where the black edge had gone to: Just for the moment, the eye appeared to be behaving something as Mansel had promised me it would, if the operation worked. I could see the shape of the room, Margaret's face, I could make out the letters in the masthead of *The Times*, nothing else. Above all, there was no blackness pressing in. That made me hopeful, unrealistically in relation to what the eye could do.

'It would be better than nothing.' Again I was choosing the words.

Margaret also was trying to be cautious. Action was neutral, action didn't mean false hope: the best thing she could do was telephone Mansel. He could come at half past one, she reported. Margaret and I talked the morning away, waiting until he arrived, spotless as David Rubin, always busy, never in a hurry, sacrificing the solitary sandwich and the half-hour off in his obsessive day.

Lying flat, I was part of the familiar routine. The lens, the scrutinising eye. It went on longer than usual, longer than the morning of decision four days before.

'Well, I'm damned,' said Mansel. He broke out: 'Look, I am glad! You're quite right. The retina has got itself back somehow.'

He had spoken simply, like one who was enjoying someone else's good luck. Then he became professional once more, professional with a problem on his mind.

'You haven't much to thank me for. I think you ought to understand that. I've never seen anything quite like this. By all the rules that retina ought to be floating about. But there's a great deal we don't understand in this business. We're really only at the beginning. It's a great deal more hit-and-miss than it ought to be. I hope it will be a bit more scientific before I've finished.'

He was preoccupied with the problem, absent-minded as he gave me instructions. Inspections. This might be a fluke, he had better see me within the week. Premonitory symptoms, flashes of light before going to sleep: I must see him at once. His mind still absent upon the physics of the retina, he told me to avoid any risk of knocks on the head – such as in boxing or association football. I said mildly that those risks weren't in my case so very serious. Mansel had the grace to give a sheepish youthful grin.

'You must think I've made a mess of things,' he said. He said it with the detachment of a man who knew that he was a master of his job: and who assumed that I knew it too.

After he had departed, Margaret burst out crying. Her nerves were strong when we were in trouble. Trouble over, she was left with the aftermath. Comforting her, I didn't feel any aftermath at all. This had been an arrest of life. It was already over. I went for a walk in the park that afternoon, looking with mescalin-sharp pleasure (sometimes shutting my good eye) at the autumn grass. I felt full of energy, eager to escape from the solipsist cage in which I had been confined for those last days. Life goes on, young Charles had told me consolingly after we paid that visit to my father. Had he ever heard of an arrest of life? When would he know one? Anyway, it was time to get back into the flow.

Though I didn't often write in the evening, I put in a couple of hours' work before dinner. Later, I was busy with the letters that had stayed unread. Often I became irked by claims upon my time, other people's dilemmas: not that night. I was back with them again.

As I read, I called out the news to Margaret. Nothing to vex either of us, as it happened. Just the balm of getting back into good nick, as Martin and the other games players used to say. A note from Maurice's tutor – no, nothing worrying, in fact he seemed to be doing a little better. W—— (the tutor) would like a chat about future plans for him, just that. Margaret wasn't listening to any arrangements of W——'s: she was suffused with a tender, unprotected, abjectly loving smile. At the most vestigial suggestion of good news – practical good news – about Maurice, she blushed as she did when she was first in love. How did one become a favourite child? Why had I, not Martin, been my own mother's? Margaret loved young Charles because he was himself and because he was mine. But she took his academic skill for granted, just as she did her own. She could judge his ability with detachment. After all, she came from a family of professionals, where, when one got a first, someone like her father or one of his brothers came up and said, Well, it's nice for you to know you're not altogether a fool. Maurice she loved, though, with all her tenacious passion. She loved him in a light of his own. She responded like the simplest mother who had scarcely heard of universities and who was bedazzled to find her child was there. If Maurice could struggle through to any kind of degree she would be so proud.

Yes, of course I would see W——, I was saying. But I wasn't prepared to go out of London yet awhile. After the past fortnight, I needed to get back into my own particular nick. Four hours' work from ten a.m. each morning, no lunch anywhere. Then I was at anyone's disposal for the rest of the day. W—— could call the next time he was in London.

Margaret blushed again. When I took the most prosaic administrative step on Maurice's behalf, she was over-grateful. She asked if I had got through my pile of letters, and then produced another from her bag. 'This is from Vicky,' she said. 'I wasn't to trouble you with it unless you were quite well.'

She went on:

'She rang up this afternoon. When you were out on your walk. She's been ringing up every day.'

As she handed me the letter, she said:

'If you'd been free, you know, that girl would have fallen for you.'

'No,' I said, 'for once you're wrong.'

'I'm not jealous.'

'No, you're not jealous, but you're wrong.'

Margaret was happy, affectionate and obstinate. In snatches as I went through the letter, I persisted: I should have been the first to know. What Vicky needed was not someone to love (we had seen her taste), but a father to talk to. If a young woman had Arnold Shaw as a father, it wasn't entirely unnatural that she should need to talk to someone else.

The letter was actually concerned with Arnold. I wasn't to make any effort until I had had a holiday (Vicky could not resist giving me some medical advice). But afterwards, if I could talk to people at the university before the Lent term Court it might be a precaution. As far as she could gather, feeling hadn't changed. The last Court meeting had gained time, but hadn't altered the situation.

'I must say,' I cried, 'everything seems preposterously normal.'

At the end of her letter, Vicky wrote that she might be coming to London before Christmas, but she wasn't sure.

'That means that she's hoping he will ask her,' said Margaret. 'That's normal, too.'

We looked at the big round handwriting, the oddly stilted, official-sounding phrases. 'I wonder what her love-letters are like?' said Margaret. Sitting together on the sofa, we discussed whether there was anything we could do for her. Of course there wasn't. But it was a luxury to show concern. To be just to us both, we each felt some concern. We were fond of her, and respected her. Yet, warming us both that night, there was an element of *suave mari magno*. We were on the shore, watching the rough sea and someone else being tossed about in the storm. We had been through it ourselves, alone and together. That night we were by ourselves, in our own home, trouble past. It was a luxury to show concern.

Back in the flow, it wasn't long before I was talking to Francis Getliffe about the university quarrels. It happened in a private room at Brown's Hotel. We were attending a dinner party, but not a social one. We had been attending that same kind of dinner party for a good many years past. This was a group of eminent scientists, in which I was included because I had worked with them for so long. They had been meeting several times a year to produce ideas on scientific policy. They were entertained, with some lavishness, by a wealthy businessman who was both sweet-natured and a passionate follower of the Opposition politicians. The scientists didn't pay much attention to the lavishness, being most of them abstemious: but they were interested in the politicians, for by that autumn it was certain that there would be an election next year and probable that the Opposition would win it. This group of scientists had been men of the left all their lives; and they still hoped that, if that happened, some good things could be done.

There they sat round the table, our host's good wine going, very slowly, down uncomprehending crops. Constantine, his head splendid and at the same time Pied Piper-ish: Mounteney, granitic, determined not to be appeased: Francis Getliffe: Walter Luke: my brother Martin: several more: our host and a couple of the Opposition front bench. Most of the scientists had international reputations, two were Nobel prizewinners, and all except Martin were fellows of the Royal. At one instant, while Constantine was talking – which didn't differentiate it from a good many other instants – I had a sense that I had been here before.

I was seeing the haze of faces as in a bad group picture – striking faces most of them – of my old acquaintances. Very old acquaintances: for they had all (and I along with them) been at common purposes for getting on for thirty years. We had, as young men, sat round tables like this, though not such expensive ones, trying to alarm people about Hitler: then preparing ourselves for war: then, when the war came, immersing ourselves in it. That had been, in the domain of action, their apotheosis. They had never been so effective before or since. But they hadn't given up. Nearly all of them had risked unpopularity. Some, most of all Constantine, had paid a price. Some, like Francis, had become respectable, though politically unchanged. The truth was that the youngest at the table was Martin, a year off fifty. Why was the evening such a feat of survival? There was scientific ability about, comparable with theirs, but either the younger professionals didn't take their public risks, or there was something in the climate which didn't let such rough-hewn characters emerge.

That night, they didn't sound in the least like sheer survivals. There were candles lit on the dinner table, but they insisted on the full lights above. One or two, like Francis, were talking good political sense. As usual, Mounteney didn't infer, but impersonally pronounced, that if the politicians and I were eliminated, then some progress might be made. Two of the less cantankerous had brought memoranda with them. The chief politician was listening to everyone: he was as clever as they were, yet when they were at their most positive he didn't argue, but stowed the ideas away. They thought they were using him: he thought he could use some of them. That made for general harmony. All in all, I decided, it wasn't a wasted evening.

After the rest had gone, Francis and Martin, not so frugal as their colleagues, stayed with me for a final drink. But Martin, when I mentioned Arnold Shaw, did not take any part in the conversation. He and Francis, though they were sometimes allies, were not friends. There had always been a constraint between them, and now, for a simple reason, it was added to. Francis had come to know of the misery that Vicky was causing his son. Francis also knew that she was infatuated with Pat, whom he thought a waster. In all that imbroglio, Francis could not help remembering that Pat was Martin's son: and – with total unfairness from a fair-minded man – he had come to put the blame on Martin and regard him with an extra degree of chill.

As I tentatively brought in the name of Arnold Shaw, I drew a response from Francis which surprised me. In his own house in the spring, he had had no patience with me. This night, sitting by the littered table in Brown's, he answered with care and sympathy. 'Of course,' he said, 'I still think you over-rate the old buffer. You're putting yourself out too much, I'm certain you are. But that's your lookout—'

I said that I hadn't any special illusions about Arnold: but I didn't want him to be pushed out in a hurry, hustled out by miscellaneous dislike.

'Leonard doesn't dislike him,' Francis was saying. 'He thinks he's a damned bad Vice-Chancellor, but otherwise he's rather fond of him.'

He looked at me with a considerate smile, and went on:

'I don't believe you're going to alter the situation there. It's gone too deep. But what do you really want?'

I replied, I too accepted that there wouldn't be peace until Arnold left. The decent course was to make it tolerable for him, to ease him out, with a touch of gratitude, over the next three years.

Francis shrugged. 'Nice picture,' he said. But, in a friendly fashion, he continued: 'Look, I think the only hope is for him to come to terms with the young Turks. I don't imagine it will work, mind you, but I'm sure it's the only hope.' That is, according to Francis, Shaw would have to take the initiative (as anyone fit to be in charge of an institution, he added tartly, would have done long ago). He would have to face Leonard and his colleagues, no holds barred. They were used to harsh argument, they would respect him for it. Couldn't I pass on the word, that this was worth trying? 'You know, if he doesn't try it,' said Francis, 'there'll be the most God-almighty row.'

Francis was speaking as though he were on my side: yet in principle he wasn't. And when he disagreed in principle, he wasn't often as sympathetic as this. It occurred to me that he might be affected by my physical mis-adventure. Most people when you were incapacitated or ill tended insensibly to write you off. They took care of you in illness, but did less for you in action. Your *mana* had got less. With a few men, particularly with strong characters like Francis – perhaps by a deliberate effort – the reverse was true. They seemed to behave, or tried to behave, as though your *mana* had increased.

After we had said good-night to Francis, who was staying at the Athenæum, Martin and I sat in the dark taxi, swerving in the windy dark through empty Mayfair streets. Nothing eventful had happened to him, but we went on talking in my drawing-room, talking the small change of brothers, anxiety-free, while the windows rattled. He had nothing to report about Pat, but for once he spoke of his daughter Nina. Yes, she seemed to have a real talent for music, she might be able to make a living at it. She was a great favourite of mine, pretty, diffident, self-effacing. If the luck had fallen the other way, and Pat had had that gift, Martin would have been triumphant. But he was composed and happy that night, and, though he was an expert in sarcasm, that specific sarcasm didn't get exchanged.

CHAPTER XVI

DECISION ABOUT A PARTY

Now I had started moving about again in London, I had to pay a duty visit to Austin Davidson. It was not such an ordeal as it had been, Margaret told me. She, except when I was in hospital, went to him each day. In fact, when we called at tea-time, passing by the picture-hung walls, he was able to meet us at his study door and return to his armchair without help or distress, though he waited to get his breath before he spoke.

In the study, strangely dark, as it always seemed, for a connoisseur of visual art, the only picture I could make out hung above his chair. I thought I had not seen it before: a Moore drawing? The December night was already setting in, the reading-lamp beside Davidson lit up nothing but our faces.

He looked at me from under his eyebrows: from the cheek-bones, the flesh fell translucently away. His eyes, opaque, sepia, bird-bright, had, however, a glint in them.

'I'm sorry about your catastrophe,' he said.

'It's all over,' I replied.

'You notice that I used the word catastrophe?'

'Yes,' I said.

'Old men get a remarkable amount of satisfaction out of the physical afflictions of their juniors.' He gave his old caustic grin. 'There's nothing to make an old man feel half his age – as much as hearing that someone twenty years younger has just died.'

It might have been an effort. If so, it was a good one. It wasn't a new thought, but it had the note of the unsubdued, unregenerate Davidson. Margaret and I were laughing. If most men had said that – certainly if I had – it would have sounded guilty. Not so with him. It sounded (just as his talk about his own suicide had sounded) innocent and pure.

He leant back, brown eyes sparkling. He was delighted that he could entertain us. For the next couple of hours, except when he heard himself gasping, he forgot to be morose. Another friend of his came in, whom Margaret and I had often met, a man about my age called Hardisty. He had been a disciple of the set to which Davidson belonged: he was clever, miscellaneously cultivated, good-looking apart from being as nearly bald as a man can be: he believed that Davidson and his friends had been the new Enlightenment, and that it would be a long time before there was another. He did most of the talking, while Davidson nodded, for they formed a united front. Neither Margaret nor I wanted to be abrasive, so we left them to it, Davidson occasionally making some reflection which gave Hardisty a chance to eat a tea young Charles wouldn't have thought contemptible. Savoury toast: Chelsea buns: éclairs. Davidson's house-keeper had provided tea for us all. The rest of us ate nothing, but the tea disappeared, and Hardisty chatted away between mouthfuls, the sort of man who did not put on weight.

Davidson recalled when, just before the 1914 war, he had seen his first Kandinsky. It had been uncivilised of the Russians not to understand that that was a step forward. Yes, said Hardisty, perfectly in tune, art, any art, had its own dynamic, nothing could stop it. You mightn't like it, you mightn't understand it, but since the first abstracts were painted nothing could have stopped the art of our time. A little later, he said, just as easily, morals had their own dynamic too. In a few years, for example, we should all regard drugs, or at least most drugs, as we now regarded alcohol. It was much too late for any of us to start on them, he said, brimful of health, but still—. Again Davidson nodded. Yes, he said, it was interesting how the taboos had been vanishing in his own lifetime.

'In my young days at Cambridge, don't you know,' he went on, 'homo-sexuality was a very tender plant.'

Hardisty gave an acquiescent smile. For as long as Margaret and I could remember, he had been living with another man. This partner I had seen only once: I had an idea that he didn't fit into our sort of company: but the arrangement had been as stable as most marriages. Certainly Hardisty was a happy man.

'By and large, this has been a dreadful century,' Davidson was saying. 'But in some ways we have become a bit more civilised.'

He seemed satisfied, either by the reflection or because he had not been too tired by the effort to talk. 'Do you know,' he said to his daughter, 'I think I'm going to allow myself a drink?'

On the way home, Margaret, just because his spirits had lifted (she had begun to feel justified in not giving way to him that summer) looked youthful and gay: youthful, gay, maternal, as though she had just heard that Maurice had passed an examination.

We kept another social engagement that week, this time at one of Azik Schiff's theatre parties. As the taxi joggled for position in front of the Aldwych, the lights were washing on to the streaming pavement, but an attendant, hired by Schiff, was waiting with an umbrella, another atten-dant, hired by Schiff, was waiting in the foyer to lead us to our place.

Our place, to begin with, was a private room which led out of the near-stage box. Waiters were carrying trays loaded with glasses of champagne. On the table were laid out mounds of pâté de foie gras. In the middle of it all stood Schiff, looking like an enormous, good-natured and extremely clever frog. By his side stood his wife Rosalind, looking like a lady of Napoleon's Empire. Her hair was knotted above her head, her mouth was sly, her eyes full. She was wearing an Empire dress, for which, in her fifties, she didn't have the bosom. On each of her wrists, thin and freckled, glittered two bracelets, emerald and diamond, ruby and diamond, sapphire and diamond, and (as a modest concession) aquamarine. Jewellery apart, skin-roughening apart, she had not changed much since I first met her. For she was an old acquaintance: she had been Roy Calvert's wife. But, although immediately after Roy's death I had written to her for a time, it was not on her initiative that, a few years before this theatre party, we had met again. It was on her second husband's.

No doubt Azik thought that, in some remote fashion, I might be useful. I didn't mind that. He had the knack, or the force of nature, to think one might be useful and still have plenty of affection to spare for one on the side. I had a lot of respect for him. He had had a remarkable, and to me in some ways an inexplicable life. In the thirties, when Roy Calvert had been working in the Berlin oriental libraries, Azik also had been in Berlin, a young student, ejected from the university under the Hitler laws. He had escaped to England with a few pounds. Somehow he had completed an English degree, very well. Somehow, when the war came, he escaped internment and fought in the British army, also very well. He finished the war in possession of several decorations, a first-class honours degree, and what he had saved out of his pay. He was thirty-three. He then turned his attention to trade, or what seemed to be a complex kind of international barter. Eighteen years later, by the time of this party, he had made a fortune. How large, I wasn't sure, but certainly larger than the fortunes of Charles March's family or the other rich Jewish families who had befriended me when I was young.

It seemed like a conjuring trick, out of the power of the rest of us, or like an adventure of Vautrin's. I once told him that if our positions had been reversed, and I had had to become a refugee in Berlin, I should – if I had been lucky – have kept myself alive by giving English lessons, and I should have gone on giving English lessons till I died. Azik gave an avuncular smile. Obviously he thought rather the same himself.

He was not in the least like my old March friends. They had become indistinguishable, by my generation, from rich upper-middle-class gentile families, rather grander Forsytes. Azik was not indistinguishable. To begin with, he went to synagogue, whether he believed or not. He was a devoted Zionist. He would not have considered anglicising his first name. Unlike the Marches, who, in common with their gentile equivalents, had taken to concealing their money, Azik enjoyed displaying his. Why not? He was an abundant man. No one could be less puritanical. So long as he could leave young David – Rosalind, late in life, had given him a son, by this time ten years old – well off, he liked splashing money about as much as making it. Anyway, he created his own rules: he wasn't made to be genteel: sometimes I thought, when people called him vulgar, that in following his nature he showed better taste than they. As another oddity, he was politically both sophisticated and detached. He made large contributions not only to Israel but to the Labour Party: and in private treated us to disquisitions as to what social democratic governments were like and exactly what, if we got one next year, we could expect from ours.

His entertainments were no more understated than the rest of him. He had a passion for the theatre, and he had a passion for trade. So he mixed the two up. Theatre boxes, plus this gigantic running supper: snacks before the play, snacks in the intervals, snacks after the play. Other people went to ambassadors' parties: ambassadors got used to going to his. There were several present in the private room that night. It was no use being finicky. There was more Strasbourg pâté on view than I remembered seeing. One waded in, and ate and drank. It bore a family resemblance to a party at a Russian dacha, when the constraints had gone, the bear-hug was embracing you, the great bass voices were getting louder and the lights appeared to be abnormally bright.

While listening with one ear to a conversation on my left (a Hungarian was asking Azik what effect on world polititics Kennedy's assassination would have – it had happened a fortnight before), I talked to Rosalind. Once she had made up to me because I was Roy Calvert's closest friend: all that was forgotten. I was one of many guests, but she liked to please. How were my family? Like a businessman, or a businessman's wife, she had docketed their Christian names. She always read everything about us, she said, with a dying fall. That was more like old times. At close quarters she looked her age: the skin under her eyes was delicately lined. (I heard Azik saying robustly that he didn't believe single individuals affected world politics. Whatever had been going to occur before Kennedy's death, would occur, for good or bad.) She was using a scent, faint but languorous, that I didn't recognise. Even before she married her first rich man, she had always been an expert on scents.

'Unless I get another glass of champagne, I shall just collapse,' she said, with another dying fall. That was still more like old times. Soon she was talking about Azik, with adoration, but her own kind of adoration. Except that the name happened to have changed, she might have been talking about Roy Calvert thirty years before. To an outsider's eyes, they seemed distinctly different men. A good many women had thought Roy romantic. Rosalind had adored him. She had learned something about his profession, and could talk as the wife of a scholar should. When she spoke of him, there was no one else in this world: and there was also, in the midst of the worship, a kind of debunking twinkle, as though she alone could point out that, though he was everything a woman could wish for, he could do with a bit of sense.

On the other hand, Azik was not a romantic figure, except in the eyes of someone like Balzac. It would be stretching a point to suggest that he had an over-delicate or tormented nature. But once again, when Rosalind spoke of him, there was no one else in this world. Once again she had learned something about his profession, and could talk as the wife of an international *entrepreneur* should. And once again, in the midst of the worship, there was a kind of debunking twinkle, as though she alone could point out that, though he was everything a woman could wish for, he could do with a bit of sense.

It was a great gift of hers, I thought, to fall in love so totally just where it was convenient to fall in love. Though she wasn't an adventuress, she had done better for herself than any adventuress I had met. Roy had been well off, at least by our modest academic standards of the time (I had seen his father's name over a hosiery factory when I walked to school as a boy): Azik was perhaps ten times richer. She had loved each of them in turn. She herself said that night, in the sublime flat phrase of our native town: 'No, I can't say that I've got much to complain about.'

In the throng of the party Muriel joined us, Roy Calvert's daughter, born a few months before he was killed, so that she was now twenty-one. I had seen her, intermittently, in the last few years. As a child she promised to get the best out of both her parents' looks, but, though she had a kind of demure attractiveness, that hadn't happened. Her nose was too long, her eyes too heavy-lidded. Usually those eyes were averted, her whole manner was demure: but when she asked a question, one received a green-eyed sharp stare, perhaps the single physical trait that came from her father. No, there was another: her face one wouldn't notice much, now she was grown up, but when she walked she had his light-footed upright grace.

Rosalind chatted on about Azik's exploits. Muriel, eyes sidelong, put in a gentle comment. On the face of it, she thought Rosalind was under-rating him. Whether this was Muriel's way of amusing herself, I didn't know.

The bells were ringing, we went into our box. Azik's passion for the theatre was an eclectic one, and we were seeing a play of the Absurd. Within a few minutes I tried, in the darkness of the box, to make out the hands of my wrist-watch: how long before the first interval? In time it came. Back into the private room. Back to more champagne, the table re-stocked, dishes of caviare brought in. But back also to a sight I had had no warning of. One of the diplomats had taken charge of Margaret, I was in another group with Azik – when I saw, in the corner of the room, dinner-jacketed like the rest of us, my nephew Pat. He was talking, head close to head, with Muriel. I put my hand on Azik's massive arm, and drew him aside. I indicated the couple in the corner, and in an undertone said:

'How do you know that young man?'

'It was impossible to fit him into the boxes,' said Azik, misunderstanding me, as though apologising for not doing his best for Pat. 'So I asked if he would not mind to join us for our little drink—'

'No,' I said. 'I meant, how did you come to know him?'

'I must say,' replied Azik, 'I think he presented himself to my wife. Because his father was such a great friend of Calvert.'

He moved his great moon face nearer to mine, with a glance of friendly cunning. Did he have any suspicions about that story? In fact, it was quite untrue. Martin had known Roy Calvert only slightly: they might have walked through the college together, that was about all. Of course, it was conceivable that Pat had picked up a different impression. Family legends grow, he must have heard a good deal about Roy both from me and his father. As for Rosalind, I doubted whether she had known, let alone remembered, many of Roy's Cambridge friends.

'I did not raise objection,' Azik said. He added, putting a finger to the side of his squashed and spreading nose: 'Remember, I am a Jewish papa.'

I told him, I sometimes felt I should have made a pretty good Jewish papa myself. But some of our thoughts were in parallel, with one at right angles.

'Your brother's is a good family, I should say,' said Azik.

I would have disillusioned him, if it had been necessary. But it wasn't. He knew as well as I did that the Eliots were not a 'good family' in the old Continental sense. He knew precisely where we came from. But he meant something different. Azik saw, much more clearly than most Englishmen, what the English society had become. It was tangled, it was shifting its articulations, but in it men like Martin had their place.

I asked Azik whether he had seen much of Pat.

'Ach, he is very young,' said Azik, with monumental good nature and a singular lack of interest. Our thoughts still did not meet. Azik began to speak, quietly but without reticence, about money, Muriel's money. 'I have to be careful, my friend. Mu came into something of her own this year.' Calvert (as Azik always called Roy) had not had much except a big allowance: but what he left had been 'tied up' for Mu. 'He was a very careful man,' said Azik with a kind of respect. 'However, that is chicken-feed.' Azik, totally unprudish about money, unlike most of my rich English acquaintances, told me the exact sums. 'But Calvert's father, no, that isn't such chicken-feed.' Rosalind had been bequeathed a life-interest in half of it; the rest had been in trust for Muriel, and had now come to her. 'Fortunately, she has her head screwed on.'

Before we parted, Azik could not resist explaining to me how different his own dispositions were. 'I have made over a capital sum to Rosalind with no strings attached. So she can walk out on me tomorrow if she can't stand me any longer.' He gave an uxorious chuckle. As for David, well, need anyone ask? Though I did not need to ask, Azik insisted on telling me of a magniloquent settlement.

After another instalment of the Absurd, we returned for the second interval in the private room. This time, seeing that Pat had reappeared and was once more close to Muriel, I went straight to them.

'Hello, Uncle Lewis,' said Pat, treacle-brown eyes wide open and cheeky. 'Who'd ever have thought of seeing you here?'

'Daddy would have hated it if you weren't here, you know that, Sir Lewis,' said Muriel, precisely. She was utterly composed.

I asked them how they liked the play. Muriel smiled, lashes falling close to her cheeks. Pat began: 'I suppose we can't communicate, at least that's the idea, isn't it?'

Yes, that was the idea.

He looked at Muriel. 'But I can communicate with you sometimes, can't I?'

'I think', she said, 'I can communicate with Daddy.'

For a moment, I had cursed myself for mentioning the play. It was true that for two acts it had been expressing non-communication: but at the end of the second, as though for once human beings could make themselves clear to one another, there had been a lucid, and in fact a lyrically eloquent description of *fellatio*. I had been with Pat in company where he would have found this an occasion too hilarious to resist. But no, now he was holding his tongue: was he being protective towards her, or was it too early to frighten her?

I watched her, her eyes meekly cast down. She did not appear to be in need of protection. She was composed, more so than he was. I knew that Rosalind, like other mothers whose own early lives had not been unduly pure, had taken extreme care of her. She hadn't gone unsupervised, she had had to account for any date with a young man. And yet I should have guessed – though I wouldn't have trusted any of my guesses about her very far – that she was one of those girls who somehow understand all about the sexual life before they have a chance to live it.

'Uncle Lewis,' said Pat, 'are you open on New Year's Eve this year?'

This time he was really being brash. I had to answer that I had been pretty much occupied that autumn, we hadn't made up our minds. That was, in literal terms, true. But Margaret and I had got into the habit of asking our families and close friends for New Year's Eve: neither of us had suggested breaking it. The point was, he was begging for the two of them – as though Vicky, who had been invited the year before, could be dropped, or as though they might all have an amicable time together.

'I think', put in Muriel, quick, sure-footed, 'Daddy said that we're having dinner with you soon, aren't we?' (She meant Azik, Rosalind and herself.)

Yes, I said.

'That will be nice.'

Pat looked at me, as though he would have liked to wink. He wasn't used to anyone as cool as this – who could, so equably, declare his proposition closed.

As Margaret and I were given a lift home in one of the diplomatic cars, acquaintances beside us, we couldn't have our after-the-play talk. In the lift, going up to our flat, she was silent, and stayed so until she had switched on the drawing-room lights and poured herself a drink. She asked if I wanted one, but her tone was hard. Sitting in the chair the other side of the fireplace, she said:

'So that's the way it is!'

Her face was flushed: the adrenalin was pouring through her: she was in a flaming temper.

'What do you mean?'

'You know what I mean.'

'I haven't any idea.'

'You have,' she said. 'Your nephew. What does he think he's up to?'

'How should I know?'

'It's intolerable,' she cried. I was thinking, yes, she was kind, she took to heart what Vicky might go through: but also Margaret was no saint, she was angry because she herself had, at intervals, been taken in by Pat. I was getting provoked, because of the disparity we both knew between Margaret's kind of temper and my own. I had to make an effort to sound peaceful.

'Look here, I don't know much about this girl [Muriel], but if it's any consolation to you, I fancy that she can look after herself—'

'I shouldn't be surprised,' she said. But she said it with edge and meaning.

We were on the verge of a quarrel. I said:

'I don't understand.'

'I was thinking of her father.' She went on, with exaggerated reasonableness. 'Of course he was in a higher class than your nephew Pat. But shouldn't you have said that there might be some sort of resemblance—?'

'Nonsense.' This was an old argument. With the gap in age between us, she had felt shut out from parts of my youth. At times she was jealous of the friends who had known me when I was a young man. Francis Getliffe and Charles March – with those she was on close terms. George Passant, she had worked to understand. But Roy Calvert, who was dead, whom she could never know, she could not help believe that I had inflated, had given a significance or an aura that he could not conceivably, in her eyes, have possessed.

'Well, Pat does set out to be a miniature Byronic hero, doesn't he?'

'Roy Calvert', I said, 'had about as much use for Byronic heroes as I have.'

'But still,' she said, 'you do admit that he succeeded in bringing misery to everyone, literally everyone, so far as I've ever heard, who had any relations with him?'

I sat without speaking.

'I know you claim that he had a sort of insight. But I can't convince myself that the spiritual life, or the tragic sense, or whatever they like to call it, is a bit like that.'

Like her, I spoke with deliberate carefulness, as though determined either to take the bite out of my voice or not to overstate my case.

'I'm not sure that nowadays I should see him quite in the same way. But of one thing I am perfectly certain. Of all the men and women I've ever known, he was the most selfless. He's the only one, and he suffered for it, who could really throw his own self away.'

Not then, but sometimes, I wondered what I should think of Roy if I met him for the first time now. But against Margaret I couldn't admit as much.

We were quarrelling. We had learned, early in our marriage, that it was dangerous to quarrel. If I had been like her, there would have been no danger in it. Her temper was hot: the blood rushed: it was soon over. But with me, usually more controlled, temper, once I had lost it, smouldered on.

Margaret, watching me, knew this bitter streak in me and knew it more acceptantly than I did myself.

'If you say that,' she said, 'then I've got to take it.'

I accused her of making a concession. I said that neither of us wanted the other to make concessions which were not genuine. Between us there couldn't be that kind of compromise—

'Perhaps it was not quite genuine,' she said with a difficult smile. 'But – what am I to do?'

Somewhere, filtering towards my tongue, were words that would make us both angrier. Suddenly, as though by some inexplicable feedback, I said in a mechanical tone:

'Pat was sucking up for an invitation to our party. For both of them.'

Margaret gave a shout of laughter, full-throated, happy laughter.

'Oh God,' she cried. 'What on earth did you say?'

'Oh, just that we hadn't decided whether we were going to give one.'

'It must be wonderful to be tactful, mustn't it?'

Margaret went on laughing. We were certainly going to give a party, she said. After all (her mood had changed, she was still flushed, but now with gaiety), we had a lot to be thankful for, this past year. My eye. Young Charles's successes. Maurice's survival. Her father better. Various storms come through. It would be faint-hearted not to give a party. But one thing was sure, she said. He was not going to bring that girl. Was that all right? Yes, I said, caught up by her spirits, that was completely all right. Without a pause between thought and action, she went to the study, brought back a sheet of paper, and, although it was late, began writing down a list, a long list, of names.

CHAPTER XVII

EVENING BEFORE THE PARTY

FOR the next four days, Margaret enjoyed planning the party. It had become a token of thanksgiving. Every evening we sat in the drawing-room and added some more names. The list grew longer; we knew a good many people, most of them in professional London, but wider spread than that. We had changed the date to Christmas Eve. This was partly because there was another New Year's party, to which we felt inclined to go: but also because we calculated that Pat would be back with his family in Cambridge, and so we could invite the Schiffs. That calculation, however, went wrong. Martin and Irene decided to come for the night, and, together with their children, to have Christmas dinner with us next day. Margaret swore: would nothing get rid of that young man? But she was in high spirits, the party occupying her just as it might have done when she was a girl. There weren't enough refusals, I complained. The senior Getliffes couldn't come, but Leonard could. Others accepted from out of London. There's nothing like an operation to make people anxious to see one, I said.

Still, it was agreeable, when Maurice had come down from Cambridge and Charles had returned from school, to have the four of us sitting before dinner, talking about this domestic ritual. Maurice had young men and girls he wanted to invite, some of them lame ducks. Charles had schoolfriends who lived in the London area. Throw them all in, we agreed. The age-range of the party would be about sixty years. As we sat there in the evening, the week before Christmas, I thought that in contrast to Maurice's untouched good looks, Charles already appeared the older. He had just won a scholarship, very young: but sometimes, as on the morning he visited me in hospital, he seemed preoccupied. I noticed that, instead of staying in bed late, as he used to do in the holidays, he got up as early as I did, riffling through the letters. I had been older than that, I thought, when I was first menaced by the post. But he was controlled enough to live a kind of triple life: his emotions were his own, but, as the Christmas nights came nearer, curtains not yet drawn at tea-time, black sky over the park, he sat with us teasing Margaret, dark-eyed, ironic, enjoying the preparations as much as she did.

It was the afternoon of 23 December, about five o'clock. Margaret had not come back from visiting her father, the boys were out. I was, except for our housekeeper, alone in the flat. I had been reading in the study, the light from the angle-lamp bright across my book. There were piles of papers by the chair, a tray of letters on the room-wide desk, all untidy but findable, at least by the eye of memory; all the grooves of habit there. The telephone rang. I crossed over to the far side of the desk. 'This is George.' The strong voice, which had never lost its Suffolk undertone, came out at me. I exclaimed with pleasure: I had not seen him for months. 'I'd rather like to have a word,' the voice went on robustly. 'I suppose you're not free, are you?'

I replied that I was quite free: when would he like—? 'I can come straight round. I shan't be many minutes.'

Waiting for him, I fetched the ice and brought in a tray of drinks. I was feeling comfortably pleased. This was a surprise, a good end to the year. I hadn't seen him for months, I thought again, no, not since the April Court. That hadn't been my fault, but it was good that he should invite himself. He might come to the party the following night, that would be better still; there was something, not precisely nostalgic but reassuring, in going back right through the years. My brother hadn't really known me when I was in my teens: but George had, and he was the only one, when I was in the state young Charles was approaching now.

I let him in, and took him to the study. Would he have a drink? I hadn't seen him in full light, I had my back towards him as I heard a sturdy yes. I splashed in the soda, saying that it was too long since we had had an evening together.

Then I sat down opposite him.

'I ought to explain. This isn't exactly a social visit,' he said.

I began to smile at the formality, so like occasions long ago when he wished to discuss my career and behaved as if there were some mysterious etiquette that he, alone among humankind, had not been properly taught. I looked into his face as he lifted the glass, ice tinkling. He was staring past me; his eyes were unfocused, which was nothing new. His hair bushed out over his ears, in blond and whitening quiffs, uncut, unbrushed. The lines on his forehead, the lines under his eyes, made him appear not so much old as dilapidated: but no more old or dilapidated than when I had last seen him in our traditional pub.

Over the desk, on his right, the window was uncovered, and I caught a glimpse of his great head reflected against the darkness.

It was all familiar, and I went on smiling.

'Well, what's the agenda?' I asked.

'Something rather unpleasant has happened,' said George.

'What is it?'

'Of course,' said George, 'it must be some absurd mistake.'

'What is it?'

'You know who I mean by my niece and the Pateman girl?'

'Yes.'

'They've been asking them questions about that boy who disappeared. The one who was done away with.'

For an instant I was immobilised. I was as incapable of action as when I stood at the bedroom window, blinked my eye, and found the black edge still there. That edge: the noise I had just heard, the words: they were all confused.

Without being able to control my thoughts, I stared at George, wishing him out of my sight. I heard my voice, hard and pitiless. Who were 'they'? What had really happened?

George, face open but without emotion, said that detectives had been interviewing them: one was a detective-superintendent. 'He seems to have been very civil,' said George. Statements had been taken in the Patemans' house. The young women had been told that they might be questioned again.

'Of course,' said George, 'it's bound to be a mistake. There's a ridiculous exaggeration somewhere.'

I looked at him.

'There must be,' I said.

'I'm glad you think that,' said George, almost cheerfully.

From the instant I had heard the news, and been frozen, I had taken the worst for granted. With a certainty I didn't try even to rationalise. Yet here I was, giving George false hope. When, thirty years before, he had faced me with his own trouble – trouble bad enough, though not as unimaginable as this – I had been maddened by his optimism and had tried to destroy it. Here I was doing the opposite. But it was not out of kindness or comradeship. Even less out of gratitude. I couldn't find a thought for what he had once done for me. Forebodings from the past, linked with this new fact, at the same time incredible and existential, drove out everything else. I wanted not to see him, I wanted to agree with him and have him go away

I tried to do my duty.

'I suppose,' I said, 'I've got to ask, but I know it isn't necessary, you can't be touched in any way yourself?'

'Well '– George's tone was matter-of-fact – 'they've been in on the fringe of our crowd. If anyone wanted to rake up stories of some of the crowd, or me as far as that goes, it might be awkward—'

'No, no, no. Not in this sort of case.' This time my reassurance was honest, impatient.

'That's what I thought myself.' He spoke amiably but vaguely: he had once been a good lawyer, but now he seemed to have forgotten all his law. He went on:

'I ought to have kept more of an eye on them, I grant you that. But the last two or three years, since my health went wrong, I've rather gone to pieces.'

He said it with acquiescence, without remorse: as though 'going to pieces' had been a vocation in itself.

'What steps have you taken? About those two. What practical steps?' I heard my own voice hard again.

'Oh, I've put them in touch with solicitors, naturally.'

'What solicitors?'

'Eden & Sharples. I didn't need to look any further.'

Just for a moment, I was touched. Eden & Sharples was the present name of the firm of solicitors where George had been employed, as managing clerk, all his working life. When he was a young man of brilliant promise, they hadn't been generous to him. Sometimes I used to think that, had they treated him better, his life might have been different. Yet even now, made to retire early, pensioned off, he still thought of the firm with something like reverence. In this crisis, he turned to them as though they were the only solicitors extant. It was misfits like George – it was as true now as when I first met him – who had most faith in institutions.

'Well then,' I said. 'There's nothing else you can do just now, is there?'

That was a question which was meant to sound like leavetaking. I hadn't offered him another drink: I wanted him to go.

He leaned forward. His eyes, sadder than his voice, managed to converge on mine. 'I should like to do something,' he said. 'I should like to ask you something.'

'What is it?'

'I told you, I've rather gone to pieces. I can't look after this business. I'm relying on you.'

'I don't see what I can do.'

'You can make sure – if things get more serious, which is ridiculous, of course – you can make sure that they get the best advice. From the senior branch of the legal profession.' George brought out that bit of solicitor's venom, just as he used to do as a rebellious young man. But he was more lucid than he seemed. As so often, he both believed and disbelieved in his own optimism. He was anticipating that they would go to trial.

'I can't interfere. You've got to trust the solicitors—'

Once more, George had become lucid. He could admit to himself how the legal processes worked. He said:

'I just want to be certain that we're doing everything possible. I just want to be certain '– he looked at me with resignation – 'that I'm leaving it in good hands.'

I had no choice, and in fact I didn't want any. I said:

'All right, I'll do what I can.'

'That's very nice of you,' said George.

I had to give him his second drink. He did not say another word about the investigation. For a few minutes he chatted amicably, made his formal enquiry about Charles, and then announced, with his old hopeful secretive restlessness, that he must be off.

When I had seen him to the lift, I went straight into the bedroom, so as to avoid meeting either of the boys. There I sat, neither reading nor thinking, until Margaret returned. She was taking off her hat as she opened the door. At the sight of me she said:

'What's happened?'

I told her, dry and hard.

'This is dreadful.' Still wearing her coat, she had come and put her arms round me.

'I'm sorry for George,' she said.

'I don't know who I'm sorry for.'

She was listening to each inflexion. Even she could not totally divine why I was so much upset. George was my oldest friend, but she knew that we met seldom and couldn't really talk. Even so, even if the relation had been closer, George himself was not in danger or involved. It was all at one remove, startling that it should come so near, perhaps—

'You won't tell the boys tonight, will you?'

'They'll read it in the papers—'

'Don't tell them tonight, though.'

She meant, she didn't want their spirits quenched before tomorrow's party.

'You'll find', I said, 'that they can take it. People can take anything. That's the worst thing about us. Those two will take it. Maurice will take it because he's naturally good – and Charles because, like us, he isn't.'

I had spoken roughly, and she frowned. She frowned out of bafflement and concern. Still she could not divine why I was so much upset. Nor could I. I couldn't have given a reason, either to her or to myself, why this had struck me like another arrest of life. Not so near the physical roots as the blinded eye – but somehow taking hold of more of my whole self, stopping me dead.

Maybe (I tried to explain it as I lay awake, later that night) a physical shock, one could domesticate, it was part of the run of this existence, it wasn't removed from Margaret and my son, it was in the nature of things. But George's announcement didn't happen to one, it didn't happen even when one heard it and, at the same instant, foresaw what was to come. Nevertheless, I couldn't reach, any more than Margaret, what I really felt.

CHAPTER XVIII

THE CHRISTMAS GREETING

JUST before nine on Christmas Eve, as we sat round waiting, Charles wanted to arrange a sweepstake on the first guest to arrive. Martin, Irene and Pat had been dining with us: Pat, to whom parties were like native air, was making sure that the hired waiters knew their job. Standing in the drawing-room, decorous, empty, expectant, paintings throwing back the light, Margaret, Irene and Martin were taking their first drinks. As for me, I should have to be on my feet for the next few hours: anyway, it was better not to drink that night.

If Charles's sweep had been arranged, no one would have won it. The bell rang on the stroke of nine: the first guest entered: it was Herbert Getliffe, whom only I knew and whom most of the others had scarcely heard of. He entered, a little dishevelled, his glance at the same time bold and furtive. He was in his mid-seventies by now, years older than his half-brother Francis. When I first entered his chambers (and found myself exploited until I learned the tricks of one of the trickiest of men), most people prophesied that he would be a judge before he finished. Herbert would have prophesied that himself: it was his ambition. But it hadn't happened. He had, fairly late in life, got on to the snakes instead of the ladders. He might pour out his emotions, but he was pathologically tight with money. That put him on the final snake. For, although it was hushed up, he had been over-ingenious with his income-tax returns. After that, no judgeship. He had carried on with his practice until a few years before. He made more money, and, when his wife died, saved it by living in a tiny Kensington flat and inviting himself out to meals with his friends. They did not mind having him, for, though his ambition had failed him, his ebullience hadn't. As he grew old, most of us – even while we remembered being done down – became fond of him.

With great confidence, he called my wife Marjorie. He seemed under the impression that she was an American. Breathlessly, with extreme gusto, he told her a story of his daughter, who was living 'in a place called Philadelphia'. His style of conversation had become more mysteriously allusive: Margaret, who had met him just once before, looked puzzled. Helpfully he explained: 'Pa. U.S.A.'

In the morphology of such a party, four people had come in by ten past nine, and then something like fifty in the next few minutes. Expectancy left the rooms, the noise-level climbed. I had to walk round, looking after the strangers. An African friend of Maurice's, lost among the crowd. As I talked about his work, I saw Douglas Osbaldiston, fresh-faced, still young-looking, standing among a group of young women. There were long tables, laid with food and glasses, in each of the bigger rooms: but within half an hour a hundred bodies stood round them, more were coming, one had to push one's way. I couldn't spend time with my own friends. Lester Ince, who had been drinking before he arrived, introduced me to his new wife, ornamental, a couturier's triumph. She was full of enthusiasm for any of Lester's acquaintants, but he was chiefly occupied with hilarity because I was going about with a glass of tomato-juice.

In the crowd, the noise, trying to spot the lonely, I put last night's news out of mind. Yet once – as though it were unconnected – I was thinking, as I introduced Vicky to Charles March, that Christmas Eve was an unlucky night. Why had we fixed on it? There had been one Christmas Eve, at another party, which even now I couldn't forgive.

I shook hands with Douglas Osbaldiston in the press. Friendly, kind, competent, he asked about an acquaintance: could he help? Was any night a lucky night for Douglas? He was at the top of the Treasury by now, as had been predictable long before. Some of the young people in these rooms thought about him as the high priest – unassuming, yes, but stuffy and complacent – of what they still called 'the Establishment'. Early next morning, as on every morning, he would go to his wife's bedside. The paralysis had, after six years, crept so far that she could not light a cigarette or turn the pages of a book. He had loved her as much as anyone there would ever love.

In the innermost room, one of the Opposition front bench, who had attended the scientists' dinner, was holding court. No, not holding court, for he was as matey and unassuming as Douglas himself. Standing there, listening to the young, chatting, tucking away names in a computer memory.

In another room Monty Cave, who had in July become a Secretary of State, held his own court. It had needed staffwork by Martin, assisted by Pat – who had been amiable to Vicky but became over-conscientious in his party duties – to keep the front benches apart. Not because the two of them were political opponents, but because they were personal enemies. We didn't want a battle of practised distaste, even though Monty, who was not a favourite with many, would come off worst.

Gilbert Cooke, plethoric, hot-eyed, like a great ship in sail, burst through to me. He was in search of my son Charles, intent on talking about the old school. But when I saw them together, Charles was politely slipping away. Their school was for Gilbert the most delectable of topics of conversation, but Charles did not share that view, especially if there were comely girls close by. For Charles, whatever letter he was waiting for in the mornings, was on the look-out that night. There was a daughter of Charles March's, shy and pretty, whom he knew I should have liked him to take out. Instead I kept noticing his head close to that of Naomi Rubin, David Rubin's youngest, who was working in London and who was years older than Charles. She looked bright, nothing like so pretty as the March girl: but she was listening, and I didn't doubt that he was dissembling about his age.

There were swirls through the rooms as a few people left or others came in late. Caro, who used to be Roger Quaife's wife, made an entrance with her new husband. It was surprising that she came, for normally she moved entirely in a smart circle with which Margaret and I had only a flickering acquaintance. Her second husband, unlike Roger, came from an ambience as rich and rarefied as her own – though to some that was concealed under the name of Smith. He was cultivated, much more so than Caro, and, of all those I had talked to that night, he was the only one who could identify our paintings.

We were standing in the dining-room, which had at that stage of the party become the central lobby, so congested that I found it hard to direct Smith's Hanoverian head to a newly acquired Chinnery, when I heard scraps of a conversation, loud and alcoholic, nearer the middle of the room.

'That's all we need to say,' Edgar Hankins was declaiming, in the ele- giac tone he used for his literary radio talks. His rubbery, blunt-featured face was running with sweat. 'That's all we need to say. Birth, copulation and death. That's all there is.'

He was declaiming to, or at least in the company of, Irene. Once, and it had overlapped the first years of her marriage to Martin, she had been in love with him. All that was long since over. She gave a cheerful malicious yelp (was there, out of past history, just the extra edge?), and replied:

' "He talks to me that never had a son".'

It was true (aside, someone was complaining about quotations from the best authors) that Hankins, who had married after their love affair, had no children. Hankins, with elevated reiteration, answered:

'Birth, copulation and death.'

'If you must have it,' cried Irene triumphantly, 'birth, copulation, children and death! That's a bit nearer.'

Hankins went on with his slogan – as though he had reached one of the drinking-stages where the truth is ultimately clear and only needs to be pronounced. As I pushed away, seeing someone alone, I heard Irene's antiphon.

'Birth, copulation, children and death! If anyone leaves out the children, he doesn't begin to know what it's all about.'

Quite late, about a quarter to twelve, when the rooms were beginning to thin, Sammikins, in a dinner jacket with a carnation in his buttonhole, walked in. He asked loudly after his sister Caro, who had already left. Their father had died a couple of years before, and Sammikins had come into the title. So he had had to give up his seat in the Commons, which to him, though to no one else, appeared his proper occupation. He told me – or rather he told the room – that he had lost 'a packet' at poker an hour or two before. I hadn't seen him for months: I thought he looked drawn and that the flesh had fallen in below his cheekbones. When I got him to myself, I asked how he was.

'Just a touch of alcoholic fatigue, dear boy,' he said in his brazen voice. But he was quite sober. Apart from me and some of the very young, he seemed the only person present who had not had a drink that night.

Many people in the swirl were well and happy. Some, I knew, were heartsick. With Douglas, from a cause that couldn't be cured. Others, like Vicky, who couldn't restrain herself from begging ten minutes alone with Pat, might some day look on at this kind of party, just as the content now looked at her. Leonard Getliffe had been and gone. There must have been others there, not only among the young, who – without the rest of us knowing – were putting a face on things. It was part of the flux.

Just as it was part of the flux that, in the public eye, some were having the luck and some the opposite. Douglas, in spite of his organic grief, had reached the peak in his job. The master-politician was confident that, before this time next year, he would have reached the peak in his. An American playwright, who had been modestly drinking in a corner, had just had a spectacular success. And there was another success, the most bizarre of all. Gilbert Cooke, who had been fortunate to be kept in the civil service after the war, had managed to become deputy head of one of the security branches. It couldn't have been a more esoteric triumph: except to Douglas, one dared not mention the name of the post, much less of its occupant. I had not the slightest conception of how Gilbert had made it. For him, who was not able even to suggest that he had been promoted, it was his crowning glory.

Whereas Herbert Getliffe was not the only one for whom the snakes had been stronger than the ladders. Edgar Hankins's brand of literary criticism, which had been rooted in the twenties, had gone out of fashion. He could still earn a living, one saw his name each week, he still wrote with elegiac eloquence: but the younger academics sneered at him, and in the weeklies he was being referred to as though he were a dead Georgian poet. There was another turn-up for the book (Sammikins, in another context, had just been blaring out those words), the most unjust of all – as though anything could happen either way. Walter Luke had stepped in for half an hour, grizzled, crisp. Yes, he had got honours, but what did they mean? Apart from Leonard Getliffe, he had a greater talent than anyone there. But for years past he had thrown up everything to lead the project on plasma physics. Now, so all the scientists said, it was certain that the problem would not be solved for a generation. Walter Luke knew it, and knew – making jaunty cracks at his own expense – that he had wasted his creative life.

At midnight, as I was saying some goodbyes at the hall door, another guest, the last of all, emerged from the lift. It was Ronald Porson. He hadn't been invited by me – but he was one of those, living alone in bed-sitters in the neighbourhood, whom Maurice and the local parson went to visit. The parson had been at the party, but had left some time before to celebrate Christmas mass. I guessed, from the first sight, that I should need some help with Porson, but Maurice was nowhere near.

He came lurching up. In the passage light there was the gleam of an MCC tie.

'Good evening, Lewis,' he said in a domineering tone. I asked him to come in. As we walked into the dining-room, he said:

'I was told you had a champagne party on.'

Not quite, I said. But there was the bar over there—

'I insist,' said Porson, 'I was told it was a champagne party.'

As a matter of fact, I said, there were lots of other liquids, but not champagne.

'I insist,' began Porson, and I told him that, if he wanted champagne, I would find a bottle. He had come to pick a quarrel: I didn't mind his doing so with me, but there were others he might upset. Immediately he refused champagne, and demanded gin.

'I don't like large parties,' said Porson, looking round the room.

'Can't be helped,' I replied.

He took a gulp. 'You've got too many Jews here,' he announced.

'Be careful.'

'Why should I be?'

Martin, who had been watching, whispered, 'You may need a strong man or two.' He beckoned Sammikins, and they both stood near. Porson was in his seventies, but he could be violent. None of us, not even the clergyman, knew how he survived. He had eked out his bit of capital, but it had gone long since. He had once been convicted of importuning. But all that happened to him made him fight off pity, and become either aggressive or patronising or both.

'Who is he?' He pointed to Sammikins.

I said, Mr Porson, Lord Edgeworth.

'Why don't you do something about it?' Porson asked him.

'What are you talking about?'

'Why don't you do something about this country? That's what you're supposed to sit there for, isn't it?' Porson put out his underlip. 'I've no use for the lot of you.'

'You'd better calm down,' said Sammikins, getting hot-eyed himself.

'Why the hell should I? I had an invitation, didn't I? I *suppose* you had an invitation—'

Then Maurice came up, and greeted him amicably. 'Hallo, young man,' said Porson.

'I expected you'd be in church,' said Maurice.

'Well, I thought about it—'

'You promised Godfrey' (the parson) 'you would, didn't you?'

'To tell you the bloody truth,' said Porson, 'it's a bit too spike for me.' He began, self-propelled on to another grievance, on what 'they' were doing to the Church of England, but Maurice (the other's rage dripped off him) said he would drive him round, they would still arrive in time for the Christmas greetings. Gentle, unworried, Maurice led him out: although the last I saw, looking through the hall towards the lift, were Porson's arms raised above his head, as though he were inspired into a final denunciation of the whole house.

About an hour later, the crowd had gone, Pat and the waiters had cleared the glasses from the drawing-room, the windows were open to the cold air. Again in the morphology of parties, there was still the last residue remaining, not only remaining but settling down. Edgar Hankins reposed on cushions on the drawing-room floor: so did the playwright: Margaret and I sat back in our habitual chairs. Martin and Irene, since they were staying with us, remained too. Their daughter had gone to bed, Pat had disappeared, but Charles wanted to look as though the night were just beginning. Also fixtures, unpredictable fixtures, were Gilbert and Betty Cooke.

Martin, cheerful, said to me:

'Look, you're about eighteen drinks behind the rest of us. Won't you have one now?'

I hadn't been able to tell him about George Passant's news. It would have been a relief to do so. But now I was tired, sedated by the to-and-fro of people, not caring: yes, I said, I might as well have a drink. When he brought it to me, it was very strong. That was deliberate, for Martin was a vigilant man.

Someone cried 'Happy Christmas!'

From the floor Edgar Hankins, who was far gone, raised a dormouse-like head.

'Not the English greeting,' he muttered, fluffing the words.

'What's the matter?' said Irene.

'Not Happy Christmas. Insipid modernism. Vulgar. Genteel taste. Merry Christmas – that's the proper way. Merry Christmas.'

Hankins subsided. Gilbert Cooke, with Charles sitting beside him, could at last indulge his insatiable passion for talking about their school. Charles wanted to hold inquiries about people at the party, but was trapped.

For a few minutes Betty and I were in conversation, quietly, with talk all round us. We were fond of each other, we had been for years. In bad times for us both, we had tried to help each other. Her love affairs had gone wrong: she was diffident but passionate, she hadn't the nerve to grab. We had thought, certainly I had, that she deserved a better man than Gilbert, or at least a different one. Yet somehow the marriage had worked.

That night, as we whispered, she was watching me with her acute, splendid eyes, the feature which, more in middle age than youth, gave her a touch of beauty.

'You've had enough,' she said.

I protested.

'Now, now, now,' she said. 'I used to notice one or two things, didn't I?'

I had to give a smile.

'I'll get rid of them,' she said, glancing round the room. It was the sort of practical good turn which, even in her bleakest times, she had often done for me.

Next morning I woke up early. Through the window came the sound, very faint, of church bells. I stretched myself, feeling well, with the vague sense, perhaps some shadow of a memory from childhood, of a pleasing day ahead. Then, edging into consciousness, suddenly shutting out all else – as sharp, as absolute as when, a few weeks before, I had awakened in well-being and then seen the veil over my eye – was the brute fact. There was nothing to keep away or soften what George had told me; and what I felt as I listened, I felt waking up that morning, as though the passage of hours hadn't happened, or couldn't do its work.

PART THREE

QUESTIONS WITHOUT ANSWERS

CHAPTER XIX

A FAIR QUESTION

A MILKY blue sky, a bland and sunny afternoon, very mild for the second week in January. There was a blazing fire in the Residence drawing-room, and I was sitting on the window-seat. Neither Vicky nor Arnold Shaw had been in the house when I arrived an hour before, but all the matter-of-fact comforts had been arranged and, looking out at the bright day-light, I did not want to leave them. In fact, I had an appointment with Eden & Sharples, George's old firm, at half past three.

My old colleagues who had to live the disciplined official life had taught me, not that I was good at it, to cut off my thoughts. Douglas Osbaldiston went each morning to see the wife he loved, able to move only her lips and eyes: he arrived at the Treasury as immersed in the day's timetable as when he was happy. At times it was better to think of the timetable. I was to call on my father that night. That would be no tax: I had received a letter from him just after Christmas (he had written to me not more than half-a-dozen times in my whole life) saying that he would like to see me.

I had one more thing to do before I went to the solicitors. As soon as the young women were charged, which happened on the last day of December, I had telephoned George, telling him that I would keep my promise, but that in return I needed to know about his health. It sounded harsh, or even irrelevant: George was angry and then evasive: I insisted. I couldn't explain, but I had to know what I was taking on, and where I could draw the limits: how much responsibility was he fit for himself?

So, in the hall at the Residence, I did some more telephoning. George had at last given me his doctor's name. He had also undertaken to tell the doctor that I was authorised to enquire.

Over the telephone I heard a jolly, lubricated, courteous voice. Yes, Passant was a patient of his. Yes, he knew about me, of course, but he didn't remember Passant mentioning my name. I said (George, whom I

445

shouldn't see till next day, had either forgotten or been deceitful) that I was a very old friend.

'Well, anyway, I'm glad to talk to you.' The voice was forthcoming, relaxed. 'He hasn't any close relations, has he?'

I said that he had two sisters alive, but, so far as I knew, saw nothing of them.

'He's not as well as he ought to be, you know.'

I asked what was the matter.

'Physically, he's a good deal older than his age.'

Was he really ill?

'No, I can't say that. But I can't say either that he's a specially good life.'

Was he in a condition to take serious strain?

That the doctor couldn't guess. Passant was a happy man. His arteries, though, were hardening: his blood pressure, despite medication, stayed high.

'He's his own worst enemy, you know.' The voice was kind, that of someone fond of George. 'He's a very self-indulgent chap, isn't he? We all like a drop to drink, but I fancy that he takes more than most of us. And I'm certain that he eats too much. If you could persuade him to lose a couple of stone, he might live ten years longer. He ought to have a wife to look after him, of course.' It was all compassionate, brotherly, down-to-earth: but this was one patient out of many, he had no idea of George's secret life. Nevertheless, he went on talking. It was a relief to know that George had someone who thought about him. 'He's a good soul, isn't he? Do what you can to make him sensible, won't you?'

It was a relief to the doctor, maybe, that there was someone who thought about George. Yet, an hour later, standing in the outer office at Eden & Sharples, where I had often waited for him, I was asking questions as though this were a routine visit to a solicitor's. Mr Eden was expecting me? Mr Eden was sorry, the secretary said, he had been called away at short notice. Could I see someone else? Yes, Mr Sharples would be free in a minute. I looked round the office: still frowsty, shelves of books, metal boxes with clients' names painted in white. Although the practice was going on, I should have guessed that it had diminished, that there must be twenty bigger firms in the town by now.

The present Eden was the nephew of the senior partner whom I had known. Neither of them had been over-energetic; this one (though I wasn't quite a stranger) was avoiding a distasteful interview that afternoon. Probably George had always inflated the standing of the firm. It must have made, I thought mechanically, a fair living for the two partners, not much more.

The inner door opened, and a big man, taller than I was and much more massive in the shoulders, stood on the threshold. He uttered my name as though it were a question.

'Come you in,' he said.

It was meant to sound cordial. In effect, it sounded like the standard greeting of someone indrawn.

I sat down in an armchair in his office, which had once been Martineau's. More shelves of law books. Double windows, so that there was no noise from the street beneath.

Sharples took the chair behind his desk. He was in his forties, handsome in a sombre, deep-orbited fashion. He had the forearms of a first-class batsman, and the hair grew thick and dark down to the back of his hands.

'Well –' he addressed me by name again, gazing at me under his eyebrows – 'what can we do for you?'

He seemed both formal and awkward.

I said: 'I think I mentioned in my letter, anyway I'm fairly sure that Aubrey Eden knows, that I'm a friend of George Passant's.'

Sharples said:

'Mr Passant left our employment some time ago.'

That told me enough of his attitude to George.

'If it weren't for that connection,' I said, choosing the words, 'I shouldn't have any right to be here at all.'

'We're very glad to see you. Any time you care to come.'

'You are acting for these two women, Passant's niece and the other one, aren't you?'

He looked at me with deep, sad eyes. He detested George, but he was determined to be courteous to me. In his own manner, he was a courteous and not unfriendly man. On the other hand, he was equally determined not to say a word out of place.

After a pause, he replied:

'That is not quite accurate.'

'What isn't quite accurate?'

'We are acting for Miss Ross, that's true.' That was the minimum he could tell me: it wasn't a professional secret, it would be on the record by now. 'But we're not acting for Miss Pateman.'

'You mean, you've passed that on to another solicitor?'

'You will find that another firm is handling her case.'

'Why is that?'

'You're familiar with our trade, Sir Lewis.'

In fact, the answer was obvious. There might be a conflict of interest between the two. It was standard procedure to give them different lawyers from the start.

'Can you tell me this,' I said (it was like talking to a wall), 'have you briefed counsel yet?'

He paused again, then said:

'Yes.'

'Who?'

Once more he was working out that I could get the information elsewhere. At length he produced a name, Ted Benskin. It was a name that I recognised, for during the few years I practised at the Bar, I had been a member of the Midland Circuit, and still, rather as men read about their old school, I watched for news of it. Not that Benskin had been a contemporary of mine. He was one of the crop of young men who had become barristers after the war and who were now making reputations for themselves.

'He took silk not long ago, didn't he?' I said.

For once Sharples could answer without brooding. In 1960, he said. He then added that Benskin was well thought of.

I asked: 'Have they got a counsel for Miss Pateman [I was falling into Sharples's formality] yet?'

'I'm afraid I oughtn't to answer that.'

That seemed like the end of the conversation. I tried one more slant: had he any idea, assuming that the case went for trial, who would be leading for the Crown? The question was not innocent. If the case was grave enough, or had roused enough horror, then the Attorney-General might elect to appear himself. Sharples was on guard.

'It isn't very profitable to speculate, I should have thought,' he said. 'We'd better cross that bridge when we come to it.'

Against the far wall, visible to both of us, stood an old grandfather clock. It said a quarter to four. I had been shown into the room at 3.35. The interview was over. He seemed more embarrassed than at the start, now that we were both silent: I found it hard to jerk myself away. I turned to the window on my right, watching the traffic pass soundlessly below, where the tramlines used to run, and pointed to the building opposite. I told Sharples that I had worked there as a youth. 'Did you, by Jove?' he said with excessive interest and enthusiasm.

When I went out into the street, my timetable had gone all wrong: my next date, the only one that evening before I went to my father's, was not until six o'clock. There was a stretch of empty time to kill, and I didn't want a stretch of empty time. Absently (I didn't expect much from the next meeting, I didn't know where to find hard news, it was a foggy meaningless suspense, without the edge of personal anxiety) I walked a few hundred yards into Granby Street, in search of a café that I remembered. There was still a café somewhere near, but neon-strips blared across the ceiling, people were queuing up to serve themselves. Close by, a block of offices was going up, the landmarks were disappearing, this street was reaching above the human scale. I went on another few hundred yards and crossed into the market place. There, all seemed familiar. The shops grew brighter as the afternoon darkened: doors pushed open, smells poured out, smells of bacon, cheese, fruit, which didn't recall anything special to me – perhaps there was too much to recall. For an instant all this gave me a sense of having cares sponged away. Best of all, the old grinding machine was working on, the smell of roast coffee beans flooded out, bringing reassurance and something like joy.

But even there, where we had once entered past the machine and into the café, there was no café left. I walked along the pavement, opposite the market stalls. Alongside me, facing me, women in fur coats, redolent of bourgeois well-being, just as the whole scene was, were bustling along. The cafés of my youth might have vanished, but such women had to go somewhere, after their shopping, for a cup of tea: so I finished up in a multiple store, scented and heated as Harrods, where I found a restaurant full of well-dressed women, most of them middle-aged, myself the only man. There was not a face in the room that I recognised, though once I might have passed some of those faces in the streets.

Over my tea, reading the local evening paper, I was preparing myself for Maxwell. It was one way of pushing away the suspense, any practical thought was better than none. Otherwise, I hadn't any reason to think he would help me. In the days after Christmas, beating round for any kind of action, I had remembered that he had become the head of the local C.I.D. I had known him, very slightly, when I was pleading one or two criminal cases and he was a young detective-sergeant. Then I had met him again, during the war, after he had been transferred to the special branch. Why he had moved again, back to ordinary police work, I hadn't any idea. I hadn't seen him since just after the war; this present job must be the last of his career.

There were bound to be half-a-dozen of his subordinates busy on a case like this. The police weren't stingy about manpower. It would be detective-inspectors who had done the investigations, not their boss. He might not know much, but he would certainly know something. That was no reason, though, why he should talk to me. I was not a special friend of his. Further, I should have to declare that I had some sort of interest. He was far too shrewd, and also too inquisitive, a man not to discover it. If I had been there out of random or even out of sadistic curiosity, I should have stood a better chance.

I had asked him to meet me at a pub in the market place. There, in the saloon bar, immediately after opening time, I waited. But I didn't have to wait long. The door swung open, and Maxwell entered with a swirl and a rush of air. He was a man both fat and muscular, very quick on small, strong, high-arched feet. He turned so fast, eyes flashing right and left until he saw me, that the air seemed to spin round him. 'Good evening, sir,' he said. 'How are you getting on?'

I said, come and have a drink.

We sat in an alcove, tankards on the table in front of us. When he lifted his tankard, wishing me good health, Maxwell's eyes were sighting me. He had a strange resemblance to my old colleague Gilbert Cooke. Maxwell, too, was smooth-faced and plethoric, so much so that a doctor might have worried, though he was athletically active for a man in his mid-fifties. His great beak nose protruded violently from the smooth large face. His eyes were of the colour that people called cornflower blue, and so wide open that they might have been propped. The resemblance to Gilbert was so strong that it had previously, and had again that night, a curious effect on me: it made me feel that I knew him better than I did. Because I had an affection for Gilbert, I felt a kind of warmth, for which in reality I had no genuine cause, for this man. In upbringing, though, they weren't at all the same. Gilbert was the son of a general, while Maxwell's mother had been a charwoman in Battersea. He had himself started as a policeman on the beat, and one could still hear relics, by now subdued, of a south-of-the-river accent.

'Are you getting on all right?' he began – and he didn't know what to call me. When we had some dealings together in the war, he had come to use my Christian name. Now my style had changed; he was uneasy, and cross with me because he was uneasy. That was the last thing I wanted, to begin the evening. Not for the first time, I cursed these English complications. I told him, as roughly as I could, to drop all that. Underneath his inquisitive good manners he could be rough himself, as well as proud. He gave a high-pitched laugh, drained his tankard, called me plain Lewis, and whisked off to fetch two more pints, although I was only half-through mine.

He went on with his enquiries about my fortunes. I retaliated by asking about his; all was well, he had just had a grandson. But with Maxwell the questions tended to flow one way.

'What are you here for, anyhow?' he eyes were unblinking and wide.

'That's almost what I've come to ask you.'

'What's that, then?'

'Your people have been dealing with this murder, haven't they? I mean, the boy who disappeared.'

He stared at me.

'What's the point?' he asked.

I thought it better not to hedge. 'I happen to know a relative of one of those young women—'

'Do you, by God?'

Across the table his big face was looking at me, open, not expressionless, but with an expression I couldn't read. His reactions, like his movements, were very quick. He was wondering whether to tell me that he couldn't speak. Yes or no. I had no idea of the motives either way.

As though there hadn't been a hesitation, he said:

'You'd better come to the office. Too many people here.'

He looked round the bar with his acquisitive glance, the same glance, I guessed, that he had used as a detective in London pubs, picking up gossip, talking to his informers, just as much immersed in the profession of crime as if he were a criminal himself. Nowadays he was too conspicuous a figure to do that magpie collecting job. Yet the habit was ingrained. Leave him here, and he would find someone who would gossip and information, irrespective of value (perhaps about the domestic habits of commercial travellers), would be docketed away.

'When you've finished your beer—' Now that he had made up his mind, he was eager to be off.

Through the familiar market place he walked with short quick steps, faster than I should have chosen. Then up the street where the recognition-symbols were disappearing: the pavements were crowded, every third or fourth face seemed to be coloured; I mentioned to Maxwell that when I was a boy it was an oddity to see a dark skin in the town.

'Mostly Pakistanis,' said Maxwell. 'Don't give much trouble.'

Keeping up his skimming steps, he was telling me, as it were simultaneously, that the police headquarters weren't far off and that the town had less than the nation's average of crime. On one side of the street were a few shops whose names hadn't changed: on the other, a building vast by the side of its neighbours, bare and functional. Maxwell jerked his thumb.

'Here we are,' he said, taking my arm and steering me across, as though the traffic didn't exist.

In the great entrance hall, policemen said Good-evening, Superintendent. The lift was painted white, so was the fourth floor corridor. Maxwell opened a door, whisked through a stark office where sat men in plain clothes, opened another door into his own room. After all the austerity, it was like going into a boudoir. The furniture, I imagined, was official issue, though, at that, he had a couple of armchairs. There were flowers on his desk and on a long committee-table. Flanking the vase on his desk stood two photographs, one of a middle-aged woman and one of a baby.

'That's the grandson,' said Maxwell. 'Have you got any yet?'

'No,' I said.

'They'll give you more pleasure than your children,' said Maxwell. 'I promise you they will.'

We had sat down in the armchairs. He pointed to a cigarette-box on the desk, then said, without changing his tone of voice:

'I want you to keep out of this.'

I replied (despite his quiet words, the air was charged): 'What could I do anyway, Clarence?'

He looked at me with an intent expression, the meaning of which again I couldn't read.

Suddenly he said:

'Who is this relative?'

He was speaking as though we were back in the pub, the past twenty minutes wiped away.

'Cora Ross's uncle. A man called Passant.'

'We know all about him.'

I was taken aback. 'What do you know?'

'It's been going on a long time. Corrupting the young, I should call it.'

I misunderstood. 'Is *that* why you want me out of the way?'

'Nothing to do with it. We can't touch Passant and his lot. Nothing for us to get hold of.'

'Then what are you warning me about?'

For once his response wasn't quick. He seemed to be deliberating, as in the pub. At last he said,

'Those two women are as bad as anything I've seen.'

'What have they done?'

'You'll find out what they've done. I tell you they are bad. I've seen plenty, but I've never seen anything worse.'

I had heard him speak pungently before, but not like this. His feeling came out so heavy that I wanted to divert it, to return to the matter-of-fact.

'You can prove it, can you?' I said.

'We've brought them in, haven't we?' At once he was a professional, cautious, repressed, telling me that I ought to know the police didn't arrest for murder unless they were sure.

'And can you prove it?'

'We can prove enough,' he said in a businesslike fashion, a good policeman at the end of his career, one who had brought so many cases to the courts. 'You can trust us on that.'

'Yes,' I said, 'I can trust you on that.'

'They'll go down for life, of course. There's just one dodge they might pull. And you know that as well as I do.' He stared at me, with meaning and, at last I realised, with suspicion.

He said, in a level, controlled tone:

'I'm going to tell you something. I mean every word of it. Those two are as sane as you or me. When we had them in here and found out what they'd done, if I could have got away with it, I'd have put a bullet in the back of both their necks. It would have been the best way out.'

Once more I wanted to get back to something matter-of-fact, or innocent.

'They'll get life, you said. This isn't a capital murder, then?'

At this time we were still governed by the 1957 Act, a compromise under which the death penalty was kept, but only for a narrow range of murders, depending on the choice of weapon and the victim: that is, poisoning was not capital, unless you poisoned a police officer; but murder by shooting was.

'No,' said Maxwell.

'How did they do it?'

'They beat him to death. In the end.'

'You may as well tell me—'

'We don't know everything. I doubt if we ever shall know.'

I said, once again, tell me.

'We're pretty sure of this. They played cat-and-mouse with him. He wasn't a very bright lad. They picked him up at random, they don't seem to have had a word with him before. They've got a hide-out in the country, they took him there. They played cat-and-mouse with him for a weekend. Then they beat him to death.'

He wasn't being lubricious about the horrors, as I had heard other policemen or lawyers round the criminal courts, telling stories of killings which I remembered clinically, as though they had happened to another species: I had to remember them clinically just to remember them at all, and yet I believed that, despite appearances, I was less physically squeamish than Maxwell.

'The worst they can get for that', he said, 'is life. Which doesn't mean much, they'll be let out all right, you know that. But it's the worst they can get, and by God they're going to get it.'

'The alternative is—'

'The alternative is a nice comfortable few years in a blasted mental hospital. Diminished responsibility. They'll try that. What do you think I've been talking to you about tonight?'

Yes, he had been suspecting me. He had seen me in action as an official, he could imagine me going round to doctors, talking to them about 'diminished responsibility', which was another feature of the 1957 Act.

'Yes, they'll try that, Clarence,' I said. 'On the strength of what you tell me, any competent lawyer would have to.'

'They don't want any help,' he said.

'But don't you think they'll get it—'

'I told you something else a minute ago. Those two are as sane as you and me.'

'How are you so certain?'

'I've seen them.'

'That's not enough—'

'If you'd seen them and talked to them as I have, you'd be certain too. You'd be as certain as that you're sitting there.'

He went on:

'If anyone pretends they didn't know what they were doing, then we've all gone mad. We might as well give up the whole silly business. Will you listen to me?'

He was more intense. And yet, I had been misjudging him. Yes, he was inclined to see conspiracies, he thought I might be one of those standing in his way. He was a policeman: he had 'brought them in', he wanted his conviction. But, staring open-eyed at me in the flowery office, he didn't want only, or even mainly, that. Strangely, he was making an appeal. It was deeper than his professional pride, or even moral outrage. He wanted to feel that I was on his side. He wanted to drag me, with all the force of his great strong body, on to what to him was the side of the flesh, or (to use a rhetorical phrase which he would have cursed away) of life itself.

In a sharp but less passionate tone, he asked:

'You don't believe in hanging, do you?'

'No.'

He gazed at me, unblinking.

'Don't you think you might be wrong?' he asked.

'I've made up my mind.'

He still gazed at me.

'I'll give you one thing,' he said. 'I don't believe in all the crap about deterrence. It deters some of them from carrying guns, that's about all. Nothing in the world would have deterred those two.'

'And you go on saying they're quite sane.'

'By God I do. They just thought they were cleverer than anyone else. They just thought, I expect they still think, they're superior to anyone else and no one would ever find them out or touch them.'

There was a silence.

'I can't get away from it,' he said. 'There are some people who aren't fit to live.'

I replied: 'We're not God, to say that.'

'I didn't know you believed in God.'

'It might be easier if one did,' I said.

Maxwell shook his head. 'Either those two aren't fit to live,' he said, 'or else the rest of us aren't.'

'Why did they do it?' I broke out. 'Have you any idea why they did it?'

'I think it was a sort of experiment. They wanted to see what it felt like.'

His lip was thrust out, his face, interrogating, confronted mine. After a moment, he said: 'I told you, when we had them in and discovered what they'd done, I'd have put a bullet in them both. What would you do with them? That's a fair question, isn't it? What would you do with them?'

I had a phantom memory of another conversation, a loftier one, in which a character more tormented than Maxwell asked a similar question of someone better than me. But I was living in the moment, and I had no answer ready, and gave no answer at all.

CHAPTER XX

TWO CLOCKS

As I looked up from the road outside my father's house, the winter stars were sharp. I had gone there straight from the police headquarters:

455

looking up at the stars, I had a moment of relief. I was getting ready for the mutual facetiousness which, as a lifetime habit, I expected with my father.

When I got inside his room, though, it wasn't like that. First, there was something unfamiliar about the room itself which, to begin with, I couldn't identify. Then his voice was toneless as he said hello, Lewis. He was watching a kettle beginning to boil on the hob. He was ready to make himself a cup of cocoa, he said. Would I have one?

No, I said (the flicker of how I usually addressed him still showing through), I wasn't much given to cocoa.

'I don't suppose you are,' said my father.

His spectacles were at their usual angle from forehead to cheek, the white hair flowed over the wings. Through the lenses, his eyes were lugubrious.

'How are you getting on?' he said, not half-heartedly, nothing like so much as half.

'How are *you* getting on?'

'They've given me the sack, Lewis.' Suddenly his eyes looked magnified: tears began to glisten down his face. They were the tears, as abject and shameless as a child's, of extreme old age. And yet, watching them, I wasn't shameless myself, but the reverse. I had never seen him cry before. Not in all his misfortunes or his humiliations: not when he went bankrupt, or when my mother died.

I said: Hadn't he told the people at his choir that I would provide transport? That it was all arranged? In fact, immediately after my last visit and before the operation, I had, through Vicky, made contact with a car-hire firm in the town. They were to produce a car and driver any time he asked. I had written to my father, spelling out precisely what he had to do. I had had no answer: but then, that was nothing new.

'I did tell them,' said my father, sniffling, defensive, as though I were angry with him for incompetence, as his wife and sister used to be. 'I did tell them, Lewis.'

'Well then?'

'It was no good.

'They had me on a piece of string,' he added, lachrymose but acceptant.

It turned out, he went on to explain, that they persuaded him not to find his own car. They drove him forth and back every Sunday night until Christmas. Then they told him – one of the older men had to break the news – that it was 'getting too much' for him.

'It wouldn't have done any good, Lewis. Even if you'd driven me yourself. They thought it was time to get rid of me. They thought it was time I went.'

I couldn't comfort him. Wouldn't they let him go on somehow, wouldn't it be something if he just attended the choir, when he felt like it?

'It's no use. There's nothing I can do any more.'

He went on:

'I told you what they were up to. You can't say I didn't tell you, can you?'

For an instant, that pleased him. He said:

'I suppose you can't blame them. They've got to think about the future, haven't they?'

'You've got to think about yourself.'

He answered:

'I haven't got anything to think about.'

As I heard that, I was left silent.

'Mind you,' he said, 'they made a bit of a fuss of me. They had a party, and they drank my health. Sherry, I think it was. You'd have enjoyed that, Lewis, that you would. And what do you think they gave me?'

I shook my head.

'Over there,' he pointed.

The little room had struck strange: but in the dim light, taken up by my father's wretchedness, I hadn't noticed the clock in the corner, although it had been ticking, I now realised, heavily away, racket-and-whirr. It was a large old-fashioned grandfather clock, glass-fronted, works open to sight. When I drew my chair nearer, I could see that it was a good specimen of its kind, with gold work on the face and gilt inlays in the woodwork. They had made a handsome, perhaps a lavish, present to the old man.

'Two clocks,' said my father, indicating the familiar one, on the mantelpiece. 'That's what I got.'

'They can't have known you'd had another one—'

'I've only had two presentations in my livelong days,' he said. 'Both clocks.'

I couldn't be sure whether he was ready to clown, or making an effort to. I said, anyway, they had spent a lot of money this time, the gift was well meant.

'They don't even tell the same time,' said my father. 'You ought to hear them strike, they go off one after the other. When they wake me up in the morning, I think, confound the clocks.'

Not for the first time, I was beating round for something to interest him. Wouldn't he at least let me send him a television set? No, he said with meek obstinacy, he would never look at it. How did he know till he tried? He did know. Everything else I could think of, record-player, books, he met with the same gentle no. Wasn't there anything at all I could get for him?

'Nothing I can think of, thank you, Lewis,' he said.

Absently, quite remote from me, he seemed to be thinking again about his clocks.

'I don't know why people should fancy that I always want to know the time. Time doesn't matter all that much now, does it?'

He went on:

'After all, I shouldn't be surprised, I might go this year.'

He was speaking without inflection, and in fact as though I were not present. He didn't say much more, apart from offering to put the kettle on again and make some more cocoa, or tea if I preferred it. Whether he was glad to have told me of his demission, I couldn't guess, but he was calm and affable as we said goodbye.

Outside the house, I remembered the visit with my son Charles the previous spring. When I thought of the old man, I should have been grateful for my son's company, all of us part of the flow. But then Maxwell's question drilled back into my mind: that was what I was here for: no, it was better to be alone.

CHAPTER XXI

'IS IT AS EASY AS THAT?'

THE following afternoon, there was a light in George Passant's sitting-room at three o'clock. When I lived in the town, that light had often welcomed me late at night: he had taken lodgings in this dark street of terraced houses – similar to the Patemans' and less than half-a-mile away – as soon as he got his job in the firm of solicitors, and had kept them ever since. Though I had not visited him there for a good many years, it was my own choice, and a deliberate one, to go that afternoon. I did not want to meet in a pub, and give him an excuse to have a drink and break – restlessly? secretively? – away. At least that would have been my rationalisation. Perhaps I did not want to be reminded of hearty evenings and the grooves of time.

At the front door he greeted me with his robust, cordial, impersonal shout. Although he had kept the same lodgings for so long, I couldn't help but notice that those lodgings had changed for the worse. There was a violent, attacking smell of curry percolating the whole house, reaching inside his own sitting-room. Once he had been looked after by a landlady. When she died, her heirs had split up the house into tiny apartments: George had no one to cook a meal for him, and in his sixties was more uncomfortable than as a young man. I glanced round his sitting-room, littered with papers, pipes, ashtrays, undusted, newsprint on the floor. Like my father, he was having to 'make do' for himself. Unlike my father, he didn't produce a vestige of order, but seemed to imbue the derelict room with an air of abandon or even of intent.

Over the mantelpiece stood a steel engraving of the Relief of Lady-smith, which had been there getting on for forty years before. Since his parents died, a few of his personal documents had accrued to him and been hung round the walls: his Senior Oxford certificate, the records of his solicitor's examinations (showing him always in the highest class), a photograph of himself when he first qualified, and a diploma stating that he had been incorporated as a member of the Independent Order of Rechabites. I knew the Rechabites from my own childhood; they were one of the teetotal movements that sprang up in the nineteenth century, just as the upper fringe of the working class tried to become respectable; my own Aunt Milly had held high office in the organisation, just as she had in any teetotal organisation within her reach. Once, long ago, after a night when George and I had been racketing round the town, we had discovered that each of us had 'signed the pledge' before the age of ten. I was as hilarious as he was, and as determined to celebrate with another drink. But, in cold history, the pubs were already shut.

As I sat down, on the other side of the fireplace in which glowed one bar of an electric fire, I looked into his face. The skin under his eyes was dark and corrugated: that had been so for long enough. I couldn't be sure that there was any change in him at all, any visible change, that is, from the night before Christmas Eve. He said, in a loud but formal tone:

'Well, how do you think things are going?'

I answered:

'Worse than anyone could have imagined.'

His reply was automatic:

'Oh, I'm not entirely prepared to accept that.'

'You must.'

'You can't expect me to assume that whatever your set of informants have been telling you—'

'George,' I said, 'there have been times when I've let you comfort yourself. I may have been wrong, I don't know. Anyway, this time I can't.'

I told him that I had had an interview with the superintendent. George interrupted, protesting about 'these policemen'. But as so often his optimism, and the lack of it, seemed to co-exist in the same instant. When I said 'You must listen to me', he fell silent, his eyes blank.

I told him, just as clinically as I had remembered killings in Maxwell's office, what the police believed the two young women had done. His face was frowning and deliquescent with pain. Physically, he had always been easily moved: he could be upset by the thought of suffering trivial by the side of this.

When I finished (I was as curt as I could be) he said:

'Do you believe this too?'

'Yes.'

George gazed at me with a helpless expression, the sound of his breathing heavy, and said, as though it was all he could find to say:

'It's very bad.'

There were no words for me either. But I could not let him slip, as I had once seen him in a disaster of his own in that same room, into the extreme lethargy which was more like a catatonic state.

After a time, I said:

'There's almost nothing that anyone can do.'

'I'm leaving it to you,' he said.

'I can't do anything.'

'You're not backing out, are you?'

I did not reply at once. I said:

'No. For what it's worth, I'm not.'

For an instant his face shone with one of his old, expansive smiles. Then he asked:

'Will you go and see her? My niece, I mean?'

I said, as gently as I could manage:

'I think that's your job, you know.'

He replied:

'I'm afraid I'm not up to it any more.'

Looking at him, I knew that I had no option. This might be a surrender of his, he might, if forced, still be capable of an effort. But I was obliged to do what I had come for. She must be in the local gaol, I assumed.

George nodded. I wasn't certain whether any but relatives would be allowed to visit her. If it could be arranged, I would go.

George thanked me, but as though he took it for granted. Ever since he collected his first group of young people round him, ever since he was to them – which included me – the son of the morning in this town, he had been used to a kind of leadership. Even now he felt it natural that anyone who had been close to him should do as he asked.

There was something I wanted to find out. As if casually, I said:

'How well do you know her?'

George's voice was more animated than it had been that afternoon. 'Oh, about as well as some of the others on the fringe of our crowd. She was rather interesting at one time, but then she began to slip out of things. And of course there were always a lot of lively people coming on—'

'What is she like?'

George responded with an air of distraction, even irritation, speaking of someone far away:

'She didn't join in much. I suppose she used to listen. I thought she took things in.'

'Is that all?'

'I didn't notice anything special, if that's what you mean. Of course, some time or other she took up with the Pateman girl. Some of the young men seemed to like the Pateman girl, I never could see why.'

'George,' I was speaking with full urgency by now, 'you must have talked to your niece, you must know more about them than this?'

He said, suddenly violent:

'I refuse to take any responsibility for either of them. You know what I've told them. I told them what I've told everyone else, that they ought to make the best of their lives and not worry about all the neutered rubbish round them who've denied whatever feeble bit of instinct they might conceivably have been endowed with. Do you think I cared if they lived together? Not that I knew for certain, but if they did they were just acting according to their nature. And that's more than you can say for the people you've chosen to spend your time among. I suppose you're trying to put the responsibility on to me. If they'd never been told to make the best of their lives, they'd have been just as safe as everyone else, would they? None of this would ever have happened to them? I won't accept it for a single instant. It's sheer brutal hypocritical nonsense. If that's all you've got to say, I'm not prepared to be attacked any more.'

As his voice died down, I replied:

'I didn't say it.'

After his outburst, he sank back, exhausted, drained.

I went on:

'But there is something I ought to say. It's quite practical.'

'What's that?' he said without interest.

'The police know a good deal about your group. For God's sake be careful.'

'How have you heard this?' His attention had leapt up: his eyes were cautious and veiled.

'Maxwell told me.'

'What did he say?'

'He only talked vaguely about corrupting the young. But they've been watching you.'

'What do they call corrupting the young?'

I said:

'Never mind that. For God's sake don't give them the slightest chance—'

When I was a young man, I had failed him by not being harsh enough. Now, too late, I meant to be explicit. After this case, the police would have no pity. They were well informed. Either he ought to break up the group once for all: or else it had to be kept legally safe. No drugs (not that I had heard any rumour of that). No young girls. No homosexuality.

George gave a dismissive nod. 'I'll see about it.'

'Do you mean that?'

Once more he nodded.

'You've got to mean it,' I said.

'I'm sorry if I've got people into a mess,' he replied.

I had heard others, in the deepest trouble, speak as flatly as that: strangely enough, Roger Quaife, a man as different from George as one could be, when he saw his political hopes collapsing.

Yet, from George that afternoon, it was a response that seemed extraordinary: inadequate, detached, as though he were not at all involved or had no need to look into himself. All along, perhaps, even when I first knew him, he had been alienated (though at that time we didn't use the word) from the mainstream of living: now he had become totally so. I had to believe, against my will, that nothing could have changed him. It wasn't just chance, or the accidents of class and time. For now I was forced to see him as if I had met him when I myself had learned something: just as sometimes when Margaret wasn't making me defend my early heroes, I found myself thinking of Roy Calvert.

George. If I had met him in middle life.

There were plenty who had lived alongside him, who thought they shared his hopes – like my brother Martin or me, when we were in our teens – who, whatever had happened to us, were not alienated at all. But George had gone straight on, driven by passions that he didn't understand or alternatively were so pre-eminent that he shrugged off any necessity to understand them. I was not sure, though I guessed, how he had been spending his later years. He was a man of sensual passion. Of that there was no doubt, he was more at its mercy than most men. But equally it was sensual passion more locked within himself, or his imagination, than most men's. He was in search, not really of partners, but of objects which would set his imagination alight. But that solipsistic imagination (as self-bound as mine when I was lying in the hospital dark) was linked – and that may have been the most singular thing about him – to a peculiarly ardent sexual nature. And so he had finally come to desire young girls, one after another, each of them lasting just as long as they didn't get in his imagination's way. It had meant risks. Yet he seemed to be stimulated by the risks themselves. There had been his disaster, where I had been a spectator, of years before. That hadn't stopped him. There had been, though I didn't learn the details until after his death, warnings and near-catastrophes since. In secret, after each one, he seemed driven, compelled, or delighted to double his bets.

It was a sexual temperament which only a man in other respects abnormally controlled could have coped with. That he wasn't, and – so it seemed – in his later life didn't want to be. In the past I had thought that, despite his gusto and capacity for joy, he too had known remorse and hadn't cared to look back at the sight of what he had once been. I had thought so during the time, long before (it was strange to recall, after my last meeting with her), when Olive and I were friendly, and she, who gave none of us the benefit of the doubt, jeered at me for giving it to George. I had believed that she didn't understand faith or aspiration, that she looked at men as strange as George through the wrong end of the telescope. That was true: and yet her view of George wasn't all that wrong, and mine had turned out a sentimentality. Curiously enough, it would have seemed a sentimentality to George himself. To borrow the phrase he had just employed, he had lived 'according to his nature'. For him, that was justification enough. He wasn't one who felt the obligation to re-shape his life. *Of course* he could look back at the sight of what he had once been. If I – because of comradeship or my own moral needs – wished to invest him with the signs of remorse, then that was my misfortune: even if, as I sat with him that afternoon, it meant the ripping away of – what? part of my youth, or experience, or hope?

I still had an answer to get out of him, though part of it had come through what he hadn't said.

'The legal line, I take it, will be pretty obvious,' I said. 'The defence for those two, I mean.'

'I thought you were suggesting that there wasn't any,' said George, withdrawn again.

'Oh, it'll all depend on their state of mind, won't it?'

Intentionally, I said it in a matter-of-fact tone, like one lawyer to another. But George ceased to be lack-lustre, he straightened himself, his voice was brisk with action.

'Of course it does!' he cried. 'I suppose everyone realises that, you'd better make sure they do.'

I said, it looked as though counsel would have no other choice.

'Of course, they must be mad,' said George.

'You didn't say so, when I asked you about them, did you?'

I had said that as an aside, and George took no notice.

'Of course, they must be mad,' he repeated, with an increase of vigour.

'What makes you think so?'

'That's the answer,' George shouted.

'Did you ever see any signs in either of them, which make you think so?'

'Damn it, man,' he said, 'I'm not a bloody mental doctor.'

'What sort of signs did you see?'

'I tell you, I'm not a mental doctor.'

I asked: 'Why do you think they are mad?'

George stared at me, as he used to when he was young, face protesting, defiant, full of hope.

'I'm assuming they've done what you say,' he said. 'No sane person could have done it. That's all.'

'Is it as easy as that?'

'Yes,' he cried. 'It's as easy as that. They're criminal lunatics, that's what they are. Only lunatics could behave as they did. They're nothing to do with the rest of us—'

I had to tell him: 'The police don't think so. They think they're as sane as any of us.'

George cursed the police, and said: 'They're not bloody mental doctors either, are they?'

'I expect,' I said, 'that those two are being watched by doctors all the time.'

'Well,' he said, fierce and buoyant, 'we've got to bring in our own. I can rely on you, can I, that the lawyers get hold of the right people—'

He went on, as though he had realised the truth from the moment I broke the news; the comforting and liberating truth. He was active as I had not seen him for a long time. Happy again, he went on examining me about the defence.

'It stands to reason,' he cried, 'they must be as mad as anyone can possibly be.'

Soberly, firmly, he began to talk about the trial. The committal proceedings wouldn't take long. He wasn't going to ask me to come. But when it came to the assizes, George said, he would have to attend himself.

'It won't be very pleasant, I accept that,' he said.

He asked, with a half-smile:

'Can you be there?'

I said, 'What use would that be?'

'I should feel better if you were somewhere round, you know,' he said.

CHAPTER XXII

OUT OF PRISON

IT occurred to me that Maxwell, for reasons of his own, would be in favour of my paying a visit to the gaol. So, back at the Residence, I rang him up. Passant wanted me to talk to his niece, I said: he wasn't in a fit state to do it himself: it wasn't a job I welcomed, but what was the drill? Maxwell said that he would speak to the governor. If she wouldn't see me, they couldn't force her, that was the end of it.

Later in the evening, the telephone rang, and Vicky, who was sitting with me, went into the hall to answer it. In a moment she returned and told me: 'It's for you. Police headquarters.'

I heard Maxwell's voice, sounding higher pitched than when one met him in the flesh. All fixed. I could go to the gaol at four o'clock the following afternoon. She hadn't shown any interest. They had asked if she objected, and she said she didn't mind whether I went or not.

When I got back to the drawing-room, Vicky enquired:

'All right?'

'I suppose so,' I said.

She knew why I was staying in the town, but she hadn't asked about any of the details. She assumed that I was trying to help old friends. She

465

might have noticed that I was unusually silent. Perhaps not: she had her own concerns, she didn't think there could be anything wrong with me. In any case, she was not inquisitive.

Instead she was talking in high spirits about her father's dinner party next day. Her spirits were high because she had heard from Pat (who, I thought, either got fond of her in absence or was keeping her in reserve) that week. She was also pleased because her father, instead of resisting the advice which I relayed from Francis Getliffe, had, contrary to all expectation, taken it. He had actually invited Leonard and his other young academic critics to dinner. It was to be an intimate dinner so that he could put his 'cards on the table', as he had told both of us euphorically, implying that we should have to keep out of the house. Vicky was herself euphoric. She couldn't help but think of Leonard and her father as clever, silly, squabbling men, and now perhaps they would take the opportunity to stop making idiots of themselves.

Next afternoon, just before four, I was outside the main gate of the gaol. Above me the walls stretched up, red brick, castellated, a monument of early nineteenth-century prison architecture – and a familiar landmark to me all through my childhood, for I passed it on the route between home and school. Passed it without emotion, of course: it just stood there, the gates were never open. And yet, even before the inset door did open that afternoon, let me in, closed behind me, I felt the nerves at my elbows tight with *angst* – the sort of tightness one felt visiting a hospital, perhaps, as though one were never going to escape? No, more shameful than that.

A policeman met me, gave me the governor's compliments, told me the governor was called away to a meeting but hoped that next time I would have a glass of sherry with him. The policeman led me up flights of stone stairs, right up to the top of the building, along a corridor, white-painted, to a door marked CONFERENCE ROOM.

'Will you wait here, sir?' said the policeman. 'We'll get her along.'

The room was spacious, with a long table: it was dark here, but through the window I could see the russet wall of the prison, and over the wall the bright evening sky.

After a time there were footsteps outside, and two women entered. One was in police uniform: in the twilight she seemed buxom and prettyish. Should she switch on the light? she asked. Yes, it might be better, I replied. Her voice sounded as uneasy as mine.

The exchange of domesticities went on. Should she send for a cup of tea? I hesitated. I heard her ask her companion – though with the room now lit up, I had glanced away – whether she would like a cup of tea.

Some sort of affirmative. You can sit down, said the policewoman to her companion. I took the chair on the other side of the table: and then, for the first time, I had to look at her.

'May I give her a cigarette?' I called to the policewoman, who had gone right to the end of the room.

'Yes, sir, that's allowed.'

I leant over the table, as wide as in a board-room, and offered a packet. The fingers which took the cigarette were square-tipped, nails short, not painted but neatly varnished. I had not really looked at her before, not in the few minutes in the Patemans' living-room; her eyes met mine just before I held out a match, and then were half-averted.

Her face was good-looking, in a strong-boned, slightly acromegalic fashion, more like her uncle's than I had thought, though unlike him she did not have a weight of flesh to hide her jaw. Her hair, side-parted, cut in a thick short bob, was the same full blonde. But it was her eyes, quite different from his, from which I could not keep my own away. George's were a light, almost unpigmented blue, the kind of colour one sees only in nordic countries: hers were a deep umber brown, so heavily charged that, though they stayed steady while averted from me, they seemed to be swimming in oil.

'What have you come here for?' she asked.

'George asked me to.'

'What for?'

I didn't answer until two cups of tea had been placed on the table. I sipped mine, weak, metallic-tasting, like Whitehall tea.

I had to submerge or discipline what I felt. Going into the gaol, preparing for this visit, I had been nervous. In her presence, I still was. It might have been anxiety. It might have been distaste, or hatred. But it was none of those things. It was something more like fear.

'He wanted me to see if there was anything I could do for you.'

'I shouldn't think so.'

She had been wearing a half-smile ever since I looked at her. It bore a family resemblance to the expression with which George, at our last meeting and often before that, asked me for a favour, but on her the half-smile gave an air, not of diffidence, but of condescension.

'He asked me to come,' I repeated.

'Did he?'

'He wanted me to see if you needed anything.'

My remarks sounded, in my own ears, as flat as though I were utterly uninterested: and yet I was longing to break out and make her respond.

(*What have you done? What did you say to each other? When did that child know?*)

'I like George,' she said.

'Did you see much of him?'

'I used to. How is he?'

'He's not too well.'

'He doesn't look after himself.'

The flat words faded away. Silence. The other questions were making my pulses throb (*Who suggested it? Didn't you ever want to stop? Are you thinking of it now?*) as, after a time, I asked, in the stiff mechanical tone I could not alter:

'How are they treating you?'

'All right, I suppose.'

'Have you any complaints?'

A pause. Her glance moved, not towards me, but down to her lap.

'This dress they've given me is filthy.'

It was a neat blue cotton dress, with a pattern of white flowers and a pocket. I could see nothing wrong with it.

'I'll mention that,' I said.

Another pause.

'Anything else?' I asked.

'I shouldn't mind seeing a doctor.'

'What's the matter?'

She wouldn't reply. Was she being modest? I looked at her body, which, contradicting her face, was heavy, deep-breasted, feminine. (*Did you ever feel any pity? Will you admit anything you felt?*)

'I'll tell them.'

Flat silence. Forcing myself, I said:

'I used to be a lawyer. I'm not sure if you know that.'

She gave the slightest shake of her head.

'If I can be any help—' (*Did you do everything they say? What have you done?*)

'We've got our lawyers,' she answered, with what sounded like contempt.

'Have you talked to them?'

'They've asked me a lot of questions.'

'Are you satisfied?'

'It didn't get them very far,' she said.

Silence again. I was trying to make another effort, when she said:

'Why have we got different lawyers?'

For an instant I thought she was confused between solicitors and barristers, and started to explain; but she shrugged me aside and went on:

'Why have Kitty and me got different lawyers?'

'Well, the defence for one of you mightn't be the same as for the other.'

'They're trying to split us up, are they?'

'It's common practice—'

'I thought they were. You can tell them they're wasting their time.'

She went on, bitter and scornful:

'You can go and tell the Patemans so.'

I began, this must have been the solicitors' decision, but she interrupted:

'Yes, those Patemans have always wanted to come between me and Kitty. That's all they're good for, the whole crowd of them.'

Her anger was grating. She went on:

'You wanted to know if there was anything you could do for me, didn't you? Well, you can do this. You can tell that crowd they're wasting their time.'

She went on, nothing was going to split her and Kitty. With bitter suspicion, she said:

'I suppose you'll get out of it, won't you? You won't go and tell them so.'

I said, if it was any comfort to her, I would.

'I should like to see their faces when you did.'

Once more, angrily, she said that I should slip out of it. I said without expression that I would tell them.

'I hate the whole crowd of them,' she said.

After that, she seemed either exhausted or more indifferent. My attempts to question her (the internal questions were dulled by now) became stiffer still. I gave her a cigarette and then another. To eke out the minutes, I kept raising the cup to my lips, saving the last drops of near-cold tea.

At last I heard the policewoman moving at the far end of the room (for some time we had been left alone). 'Afraid your time is up, sir.' I heard it with intense relief. I said to Cora that I would come again, if she wanted me.

She didn't say a word: her half-smile remained. Outside the gaol, in the fresh night air, I still felt the same intense relief, mixed with shame and lack of understanding. The great walls, which dominated the road in daytime, were now themselves dominated by the neon lights. I didn't clearly remember, five minutes afterwards, what it was like inside.

Some time later, when I met Vicky in the town – I was taking her out for dinner in order to leave the Residence free for Arnold Shaw's private party – she did not so much as ask me what I had been doing. Some young women would have noticed that I was behaving with a kind of bravado, but Vicky took me for granted. Which was soothing, just as it was to see her happy. The small-talk of happiness, merely the glow, still un-damped, of a letter from Pat. The pleasure of sitting at a restaurant-table opposite a man. The pleasure, incidentally, of a very good meal. She had nominated an Italian restaurant which had not existed in my time, and she tucked into hearty Bolognese food with a young and robust appetite. When I lived in the town, we couldn't have eaten like this, even if we had had the money, but since the war people had learned to eat. Restaurants had sprung up: there was even good English cooking, which I had never tasted as a boy. Other things might go wrong, but food got better.

The pink-shaded lamp made her face look more delicate, as faces look when the light is softening after a sunny day. She was talking more than usual, and more excitedly. Once I wondered if she was wishing – as a good many have wished in the lucky lulls in a love affair – that time could stand still. No, I thought. She was too grave, too positive, not appre-hensive enough for that.

We had to spin the evening out. Arnold Shaw's dinner party had started early, but we were not to arrive back until eleven. 'Anyway,' said Vicky, 'it'll be nice to have them stop nattering at each other, won't it? He ought to have patched it up months ago.' Although I was dawdling over our bottle of wine, I couldn't do so for another hour and more.

'What shall we do?' I said.

'I know,' said Vicky with decision.

'What?'

'Don't you worry. Leave it to me.'

After we left the restaurant, she led me down a couple of side-streets past a window which was darkened but, as in the war-time blackout, had a strip of light visible along the top edge. On the door, also in dimmed light, was the simple inscription HENRY'S.

'We go in here,' said Vicky.

Inside it was as dark as in a smart New York restaurant. If it hadn't been so dark, Vicky and I might have looked more incongruous, for her skirt was much too long and my hair much too short. But the young people, lolling about at crowded tables drinking coffee, were too polite or good-natured to notice. They pushed along, made room for us, settled us down. It was not only dark, the noise was deafening: a record-player was on full blast, couples were twisting on a few square yards of floor. It was so noisy that some young man, hair down to his shoulders, had to point to a coffee-cup to inquire what we wanted.

Soon afterwards the same young man patted Vicky's knee and jerked his thumb towards the floor. To my surprise, she gave an enthusiastic nod. When she started to dance, she appeared much older than anyone there: she wasn't dressed for the occasion, she was as out of place as someone arriving in a lounge suit at a function with all the others in white tie and tails. But, again to my surprise, she danced as one who loved it: she had rhythm from the balls of her feet up to her pulled-back hair: she had more animal energy than the boys and girls round her. It was a strange fashion to end that day, watching Vicky enjoy herself.

'Nice,' she said in the taxi going home. It occurred to me that all this was a legacy of Pat's, and that she might be thinking of him.

It was not, however, quite the end of that day. When we arrived at the Residence, the windows were shining but there were no cars standing in the drive. We seemed to have timed it right, said Vicky efficiently. As we went into the hall, Arnold Shaw came out of the drawing-room to greet us. His colour was high, his melon-lips were pursed and smiling. They've gone? she asked. He nodded with vigour, and said, expansively, come in and get warm.

In the bright drawing-room, used glasses on the coffee-tables, Shaw stood on the hearth-rug, braced and grinning.

'You've been in prison this afternoon, Lewis, haven't you?' he said to me. He said it with taunting good-nature, eyes bright, as though this was the sort of eccentric hobby I should indulge in, having no connection with serious living.

I said that I had.

'Well, I'm out of prison myself, you'll be glad to know,' he announced. 'And that means that I'm going to give us all a drink.'

At a quick and jaunty trot he left the room. As we waited for him, Vicky was happily flushed but didn't speak. For me, his one casual question had triggered other thoughts.

He returned balancing a tray on which shone two bottles of champagne and three tulip glasses. While he was twisting off the wire from one bottle, Vicky burst out:

'So everything is all right, is it?'

'Everything is all right,' he said.

The cork popped, carefully he filled a glass, watching the head of bubbles simmer down.

'Yes,' he said, 'I shall be going at the end of the term.'

'What?' cried Vicky.

'I'm resigning,' he said, filling another glass. 'I've told them so. Of course they'll treat it as confidential until I get the letter off tomorrow. I had to explain the protocol—'

'Oh, blast the protocol,' said Vicky. Tears had started to her eyes.

I had been jolted back into the comfortable room, into their company.

'You can't do it like this, Arnold,' I began.

'You'll see if I can't. It's the right thing to do.'

'You must give yourself a bit of time to think.' I was finding my way back to an old groove, professional concerns, the talk of professional men. 'This is an important decision. You've got to listen to your friends—'

'Quite useless.' He spoke with mystifying triumph. 'This is final. Full stop.'

Vicky, cheek turned into her chair, was crying. For once, she was past trying to boss him: she wasn't often like a child in his presence, but now she was. She couldn't make an effort to dissuade him. She didn't seem even to listen as I said:

'Hadn't you better tell us what has happened?'

'It's simple,' said Arnold Shaw. 'They were all very friendly—'

'In that case, this is a curious result.'

'They were all very friendly. No one minded speaking out. So I asked them whether, if I went on as Vice-Chancellor, I had lost their confidence.'

'And they said—'

'They said I had.'

'In so many words?'

'Yes. In so many words.' Arnold re-filled his glass, looking at me as though he were master of the situation.

'I must say, it all sounds very improbable,' I told him.

'They were absolutely direct. I respected them for it.'

'You must find respect very easy.'

'I don't like double-dealing,' said Arnold Shaw.

'But still – why have you got to listen? These are only three or four young men—'

'No good, Lewis.' Shaw's expression was happy but set. 'They're my best young professors. Leonard is alpha double plus, but the others are pretty good. They're the people I've brought here. They're going to make this place if anyone can. A Vice-Chancellor who has lost the confidence of the men who are going to make the place hasn't any business to stay.'

'Look here, there are some other arguments—'

'Absolutely none. It's as clear as the nose on your face. I go now. And I'm right to go.'

Arnold, like one determined to have a celebration, poured champagne into my glass. He was so exalted that he scarcely seemed to notice that his daughter was still silent, huddled in her chair. At a loss, I drank with him, for an instant thinking that of all well-meant interventions Francis Getliffe's had been the most disastrous. It was the only advice I could remember Arnold Shaw taking. Without it he would have battered on, unconscious of others' attitudes, for months or years. Yet, though unlike my old father he had no nose for danger, he took it far more robustly, in fact with elation, when he was rubbed against it. Of course, he was many years the younger man. My father, when his own dismissal came, had nothing else to live for. But still – it was an irony that I didn't welcome – it was often the unrealistic who absorbed disasters best.

'I remember, Lewis, I told you one night in this house,' Arnold pointed a finger, 'I told you I should decide when it was right to go. No one else. It didn't matter whether any of the others, or any damned representations under heaven, were aiming to get rid of me. If I thought I was doing more good than harm to this place, then I should stay and they would have to drag me out feet first. But I told you, do you remember, that the moment I decided, myself and no one else, that I was doing more harm than good, then I should go, and that would be the end of it. Well, that's the position. I can't be any more good in this job. So I go at the earliest possible time. That's the proper thing to do.'

He was just as intransigent as when he was resisting any compromise or moderate suggestion in the Court. He was more than intransigent, he felt victorious. He was asserting his will, and that buoyed him up: but more than that, he was behaving according to his own sense of virtue or honour, and it made him both happy and quite immovable. He had scarcely listened to anything I said: and, as for Vicky, perhaps she realised at once when first she heard his news and began to cry, how immovable he was.

At last she had roused herself and, eyes swollen, began to talk about their plans. Yes, they would be moving from the Residence, they would have to find another house. She didn't say it, but she was becoming protective again. How much would he miss his luxuries, and much more, all the minor bits of pomp and ceremony? Would he be impregnable, when once he knew that he had really lost his place? Vicky said nothing about that, but instead, in a factual and prosaic manner, was calculating how much income they would have.

Arnold insisted on opening the second bottle of champagne, I didn't want it, but he was so triumphant, in some way so unshielded, that I hadn't the heart to say no.

CHAPTER XXIII

THE FRONT ROOM

THE Patemans' house was not on the telephone, and I sent a note that I should call on them at half past six, at Cora Ross's request, before I caught my train back to London. That was the day after my visit to the gaol. The clear weather had broken, it was raw and drizzling in the street outside, the street lamps shone on the dark front window, curtains left undrawn.

Mrs Pateman let me in. The light in the passage was behind her, and I could not see her face. She said nothing except that my overcoat was wet. I put down my suitcase and went into the parlour, into claustrophobia and the disinfectant smell. There, sitting at the table, plates not cleared away, were both Mr Pateman and his son. Dick nodded, Mr Pateman, head thrown back, gave me a formal good-evening. I sat down by the slack fire, no one speaking. Then Mr Pateman said, in a challenging, more than that, attacking tone:

'I hope you're bringing us good news, sir.'

'I'm afraid not,' I said.

He stared at me.

'I don't want you to make any mistake from the beginning. I don't credit a single word that anyone brings up against my daughter.' He was hostile and at the same time his confidence seemed invulnerable. But now I could, though the room was dim, watch Mrs Pateman's face: it was washed youthful by fear. I said:

'I've got nothing to say about her.'

'I didn't expect it,' said Mr Pateman. 'Some of us don't need telling about our children.'

'I've only come', I said, 'to give you a message from her friend.'

'Mind you,' said Mr Pateman, ignoring me, 'I know that certain people want to drag her through the courts.' With confidence, with the brilliance of suspicion, he went on: 'I have my own ideas about that.'

I tried to speak gently, in the direction of his wife:

'You'll have to prepare yourselves for the trial, you know.'

'Thank you,' said Mr Pateman, 'we are prepared for more than that. My daughter's room' – he pointed towards the front of the house – 'is waiting for her as soon as this trial is over. It's waiting for her empty, with not a penny coming in.'

How soon would the trial be? Mrs Pateman asked in a timid voice. I explained that they would be sent from the police court to the assizes – that would be two or three months ahead. To my surprise, Mr Pateman accepted this information without protest: perhaps he had discovered it already. Would he accept a different kind of information, if I warned him that his hopes were nothing but fantasy and that he was going to hear the worst? I might have warned him, if we had been alone: in the presence of his wife, certainly frightened, maybe clinging to his hopes, I hadn't the courage to speak.

'I've only come', I repeated, 'to give you a message from Cora Ross.'

'I don't want anything to do with that woman,' said Mr Pateman.

'It was just this – when it comes to the trial, she wants you to know, they're going to be loyal to each other.'

'I shouldn't expect anything else. From my daughter,' said Mr Pateman with complete opacity, dismissing the news as of no interest, getting back to his own suspicion: 'I never liked the look of that woman, she was a bad influence all along. I always had my own ideas about her.'

He stared at me accusingly:

'I don't want to say this, but I've got to. I never liked the look of that woman's uncle. He's a friend of yours, sir, I've been told?'

'That's true,' I said.

'I don't want to say this, but he's been the worst influence of all. Even if he is a friend of yours, he's a loose liver. There's bad blood in that family, and it's a pity my daughter ever came anywhere near them. That's why certain people want to drag her through this business. They think anyone who goes round with that woman must be as bad as she is. And that woman wouldn't have turned out as bad if it hadn't been for her uncle.'

'I don't agree with that,' said Dick Pateman, who had been sitting with an expression as aggressive as his father's.

'Some of us', said Mr Pateman, 'have spent a lifetime summing people up.'

'Passant would have been all right,' Dick went on, 'if only they'd given him a chance.'

'I can't agree.'

Dick continued. 'They' were to blame, 'the whole wretched set-up', the racket, the establishment, society itself. We should have to break it up, said Dick. Look what they had done to his father. Look at what they were doing to him. His discontent was getting violent (I gathered he was having more trouble with examinations at his new university). Kitty would be happy in a decent society. There was nothing wrong with her. As for Cora Ross, if she'd 'done anything', that was their fault: no one had looked after her, she'd never been properly educated, she'd never been found a place.

I didn't answer. What did he believe about the crime? Certainly not the naked truth. He was more lucid than his father, and more angry. He seemed to accept that Cora Ross was involved. But his indignation comforted him and at the same time deluded him. It removed some of the apprehension he might have had about his sister. So much so that I had to ask one question: had he talked to her solicitors? No, he said, his father had done that.

All the news in that home, then, had come from Mr Pateman. He and Dick must have sat in the parlour arguing with no more sense of the fatality than they showed tonight. It was intolerable that they should be so untouched. The dark little room, with its single bulb, pressed upon one. We were shut in, they didn't mind being shut in. Their faces were as bold as when I had first seen them. The disinfectant smell seemed to become stronger, mixed with the sulphuretted smell of the slack fire.

'Yes,' said Mr Pateman, 'I've done my best with those people' (the solicitors to whom Eden & Sharples had sent Kitty's case).

He confronted me with glass-bright eyes.

'And thereby hangs a tale,' he announced.

For an instant, I thought he was going to give some of their opinions. He said:

'They're running up their bills, those people are. I want to know, where is the money coming from?'

It was a question for which I was totally unready. I hadn't even asked George about the legal costs for his niece. In the midst of shock, I hadn't given it the vestige of a thought. Yet it was certain that George couldn't afford to pay himself. His friends in the town were better off than they used to be: perhaps they had already supported him, but I didn't know.

'It will cost some money,' I said.

'That doesn't get me very far.'

I said that the whole expenses wouldn't be less than several hundred pounds.

'You're not being very helpful, sir.'

I said: 'I'm just telling you the facts.'

'Do you think it's helpful to mention a sum like that to me, after the way I've been treated?'

I said (I was recalling that the structure of legal financing had changed since the time I practised) that they were not to worry. Legal aid would be forthcoming. In a case like this, no one had to think about solicitors' and barristers' fees.

'Oh no,' said Mr Pateman, 'we've already been granted legal aid. So has the other one, they tell me.'

'Then what are you worrying about?'

'Charity,' said Mr Pateman with a superior smile. 'I don't like my family receiving charity.'

My patience was snapping. 'You can't have it both ways—'

'I always believe in exploring avenues,' he went on, still invulnerable.

'I don't know what you're thinking of.'

'Newspapers. That's what I'm thinking of.'

Yes, he had heard of newspapers paying for the defence in a murder case, and getting an article out of it afterwards. Wasn't that true?

'Do you really want that to happen?' I asked.

'It would recoup us all for some of our losses. It would mean my daughter was paying her way.'

He appeared to want, though he didn't specifically say so, advice about the popular press, or perhaps an introduction. I had no intention of giving either, and got up to leave; once more Dick nodded and Mr Pateman and I exchanged formal good-nights. In the passage Mrs Pateman, who had followed me out, plucked at my sleeve.

'Please,' she whispered. 'Come in here a minute.'

With quick scurrying steps (such as I had noticed in my glimpses of her daughter) she opened the door of the front room. It looked, as soon as the standard lamp was switched on, bright, frilly, feminine: the lamps gleamed behind painted Italian shades: from the passage one could see straight across the room to a long, low dressing-table, looking-glass shining under the lights. The floor was swept and polished, just as on an afternoon when the young women were returning from their work. And yet I had an instant of holding-back before I could cross the threshold, an instant which was nothing but superstitious, as though I were entering a lair.

Furtively she closed the door behind us. I sat on one divan, Mrs Pateman on the other, which lay underneath the window: in the black uncovered glass one of the lamps was reflected full and clear. Close to me stood the latest model of a record-player. There were other gadgets, well cared for, stacked neatly on the shelves, a tape-recorder, a couple of transistor radios.

Mrs Pateman gave me a wistful, ingratiating smile.

'Are you sure?' she said.

Taken aback, I stammered a reply:

'Am I sure of what?'

'Are you sure what's happened?'

The eyes in the small, wrinkled face were fixed on mine.

I said 'No'. She was still gazing at me.

'It's a good job he doesn't believe she's done anything, isn't it?'

'Perhaps it is,' I answered.

'He won't believe it whatever happens. It's just as well. He couldn't face it if he did.'

She said it simply. She was speaking of the husband who dominated her as though he were sensitive, easily broken, the soul whom she had to protect.

'Are you sure yourself?' she asked again, just as simply.

I hesitated.

'I should have to be absolutely sure to tell you that.' It was as near a straight answer as I could give. It seemed to satisfy her. She said:

'I can't bear to think of her in there.'

The words sounded unhysterical, unemotional, almost as though she were referring to a physical distress.

'I can understand that.'

'She's got such nice ways with her when she tries, Kitty has.'

I mentioned – we were both being matter-of-fact – that I had met her once or twice.

'And she often did good things for people, you know. She was always free with her money, Kitty was.'

She added:

'Her father used to tell her off about that. But it went in one ear and out of the other.'

Her face was so mobile, for an instant there was the recollection of a smile.

'I've been worrying about her a long time, as far as that goes.'

'Have you?'

'I thought there was something going wrong with her. But I couldn't find out what it was. It wasn't just having a good time—'

'Did she talk to you?' I put in.

She shook her head.

'That's the trouble with children. They're your own and you want to help them and they won't let you.'

She went on, without any façade at all:

'I don't know where I went wrong with her. She always kept herself to herself, even when she was a little girl. She had her secrets and she never let on what they were. I didn't handle her right, of course I didn't. She was the clever one, you know. She's got more in her head than the rest of us put together.'

'You mustn't blame yourself too much,' I said.

'Wouldn't you?'

I replied in the same tone in which she asked:

'Yes, if anything bad happened to my son, I know I should.'

'I can't bear to think of her in there,' she repeated.

'I'm afraid you've got to live with it.'

'How long for?'

'You don't need me to tell you, do you?'

Her face was twisted, but no tears came. All she asked me was that, if I saw her during the trial, I should tell her any news without her husband knowing. She wouldn't understand the lawyers, she said, it would be over her head. That was all. Very quietly she opened the door of the room, and then the front door. She whispered a thank you, and then saw me out into the street without another word.

CHAPTER XXIV

QUARREL WITH A SON

THE sky over Hyde Park, as Margaret and I sat together in the afternoons, was free and open, after the Patemans' parlour. The lights of the London streets were comfortable as we drove out at night. It might have been the only existence that either of us knew. But Margaret was watching me with concern. She saw me go into the study to work each morning: she didn't need telling that I had never found it harder. She didn't need telling either that I was making excuses not to dine out or go into company.

One night, she had persuaded me to accept an invitation. At the dinner-party, her glance came across to me more than once, seeing me behave in the way she used to envy when she herself was shy. Back in our own flat, she said:

'You seemed to enjoy that.'

I said that for a time I had.

'You've still got more than your share of high spirits, haven't you?'

'Other people might think so,' I said. 'But they don't know me as well as you do.'

'I think so too,' she replied. 'It's been lucky for both of us. But—'

She meant, she knew other things. A little later, after we had fallen silent, she said, without any warning:

'What's the worst part for you?'

'The worst part of what?'

'You know all right. The worst part of all this horror.'

I met her eyes, brilliant and unevadable. Then I looked away. It was a long time before I could find any words. It was as hard to talk as in the dark period before we married, when we each bore a weight of uncertainty and guilt.

'I think', I said haltingly at last, 'that I'm outraged because I am so close to it. I feel it's intolerable that this should have happened to me. I believe it's as selfish as that.'

'That's natural—'

'I believe it's as petty as that.' Yet to me that outrage was as sharp as a moral feeling.

'But you're not being quite honest. And you're not being quite honest at your own expense.'

'It's surprising how selfish one is.'

'Particularly,' she said, 'when it's not even true. I don't believe for a moment that that is the worst of it for you.'

She added: 'Is it?'

I was mute, not able to answer her, not able to trust either her insight or my own.

On another topic, however, which came up more than once, it was not that I wasn't able to answer her, but that I wouldn't. Just as, during my conversation with Cora Ross, so flat and banal, there had been questions pounding behind my tongue, so there were with Margaret. *What did she do? What did they say to each other? What was it like to do it?* For me in the gaol, for Margaret in our drawing-room, those questions boiled up: out of a curiosity which was passionate, insistent, human, and at the same time corrupt. She was no purer than I was, and more ready to ask. I felt – with what seemed like a grotesque but unshakeable hypocrisy – that she oughtn't even to want to know. I didn't give her, or alternatively muffled, some of the information that I actually possessed. I showed her the reports of the committal proceedings which, although they made a stir in the press, were tame and inexplicit.

Throughout those weeks I took no action which had any bearing on the case. It would have been easy to talk to counsel, but I didn't choose. I had one of George's neat impersonal notes, telling me the name of a psychiatrist who was to be called in his niece's defence. It would have been easier still to talk to this man. He was a distant connection of Margaret's, her mother having been a cousin of his. They both came from the same set of inter-bred academic families, and I had met him quite often. He was called Adam Cornford, and he was clever, tolerant, easy-natured, someone we looked forward to seeing. He was also, I told myself, a man of rigid integrity: nothing that I or anyone else said to him would alter his evidence by a word. That was true: but it wasn't the reason why I shied away from speaking to him and even – as though he were an enemy whose presence I couldn't bear – avoided going to a wedding at which he might be present.

My mood, I knew, was wearing Margaret down. I told her so, and told her I was sorry. She didn't deny it. If I could have been more articulate, it would have been easier for her. She accepted – there was no argument, she took it for granted – that I should have to attend the trial. But she thought I oughtn't to be left alone there, with no one to turn to. Would it be useful if she came herself? She would come for part of the time anyway, if her father didn't need her. Who else? There weren't many people, as I grew older, to whom I gave my intimacy. Charles March, or Francis – but they were too far away from the roots of my youth. Without my knowing it at the time, Margaret rang up my brother Martin. He would understand it as the others couldn't. Her relation with Martin had always been close: they couldn't have been each other's choice, and yet there was a tie between them as though it might have been pleasant if they had. She talked to him with that kind of trust. Yes, he was ready to hang about the trial in case I wanted him. But – and again I didn't know it at the time – she found, as they talked, that he too, underneath his control and irony, seemed unusually affected.

One Sunday, when we had fetched Charles from school to have lunch at home, Margaret mentioned the date of the trial. The assizes would be beginning in April: how long would the trial take? Anyone's guess, I was saying: probably three or four days, perhaps a week or two, depending on how the defence played it. Margaret told Charles that meant he might not be seeing much of me during the Easter holidays. I said, he could possibly endure that extreme deprivation. Charles gave a preoccupied grin.

After lunch, he and I were alone in the drawing-room. He was looking out of the window: it was a serene milky day in late February, smoky sunshine and mist, the branches on the trees just showing the first vestigial thickening.

Charles turned away and said:

'So you're going to this trial, are you?'

'Yes, I must.'

'Why must you?'

'One of those women is a niece of old George's, you know.'

'I knew that.' He was sitting on the arm of a chair: his face was clouded. 'But you can't do any good.'

'I can't desert him now,' I said.

'You won't do any good. You won't make any difference to him.'

'Perhaps a little,' I said.

'I doubt it,' said Charles. In a hard, minatory tone he went on: 'I don't think you ought to go.'

'I don't understand you.'

'This trial will have all the press in the world. They'll be after you.'

'I shall just be there in the court, that's all—'

'Don't fool yourself. You're a conspicuous figure.'

'They might notice I was there,' I said. 'Still—'

'This is going to be the horror of horrors. Don't fool yourself. You ought to have learned by now that you'll land yourself in trouble. Don't you realise that someone is going to link you up with the Passants? There'll be a lot of mud flying round. Some of the mud will stick. On you.'

His expression was so dark that my temper was rising. I tried to seem casual.

'I think you're exaggerating,' I said. 'But even if you weren't, does it matter all that much?'

'I should have thought you'd had enough of it,' he replied, not with kindness so much as reproach.

'Look here, I've known George since I wasn't much older than you are today. Do you really expect me to leave him absolutely alone *now*?'

'If you could do any good, no.'

'Whether I can do any good or not—' I was speaking harshly.

'That's sentimental. You're taking a stupid risk which won't do any good to him and will do you some harm. There's no justification at all.'

'Good God, Carlo,' I cried. 'You're talking like a chief whip—'

'I don't care what I'm talking like. I'm telling you, you're being sentimental, that's all.'

'You really think I ought to abandon an old friend just to avoid a bit of slander—'

'That's not a good piece of translation.'

'Put it any way you like.'

'I'll accept it your way. And I say – if you can't be any good to him, the answer is yes.'

I was bitterly angry with him. Was it because he reminded me – too nakedly – of an aspect of myself when young, when I was rapacious and at the same time calculating the odds? Was it also because, with a cowardice of the nerves, I should have liked to agree with him and follow his advice?

'Do you believe', I said, my temper grinding into my voice, 'that you'll be able to live your own life without taking this kind of risk? My God, if you can be that cold, what sort of life are you going to have?'

Charles had become angry in his turn. His skin, which, different from mine or Margaret's, didn't colour in the sun, took on a kind of pastel flush. He said:

'I shall take more risks than you ever did.'

'Say that when you've done it.'

'I shall take more risks than you did. But I shall know what I'm taking them for.

'As for being cold,' he went on, eyes black with resentment, 'I think you're wrong. I'm not sentimental, if that's what you mean. I never shall be. I'm not going to waste so much of myself.'

For some time we sat in mutinous silence, each of us hurt, each of us throwing the blame upon the other. Then Margaret entered, the low sunlight streaming on to her face, which unlike ours was tranquil and bright. In an instant, though, she felt the fury in the room. It astonished her, for she had scarcely heard Charles and me exchange a bad-tempered word.

'Whatever's the matter with you two?' she burst out.

'Carlo's been telling me that I oughtn't to go to the trial,' I said, shrugging it off.

'No,' she spoke to Charles, 'he's right to go.' She said it soothingly, but Charles, smothering his pride, began to tease her: why was she always so certain of her moral position? The teasing went on, light and easy. He could talk so easily because of the difference between them. That afternoon he couldn't have talked to me like that. He didn't give a glance in my direction. He was responding to her with fondness and detachment. He couldn't have told, or wanted to know, how he was responding to me: and nor in reverse could I.

CHAPTER XXV

A QUIET OPENING

As Margaret and I approached the old Assize Hall, there was a smell of moist grass, sweet and taunting. It was the kind of April morning which, when one is happy, is lit up with hope: on the patch of lawn beside the steps, dew sparkled in the wave of sunlight. In front of the Georgian façade, policemen were standing, faces fresh in the clear light. The smell of grass returned, sweet and seminal. Looming behind the building was a gothic wall, a relic of the historic town: we were half-a-mile away from the shopping streets, and close to the quarter where I had taken Charles for a walk the year before.

The entrance hall was high, bright from the lofty windows, crowded, people hurrying past. There were spectators making their way into the court-room, policemen in plain clothes, rooted on thick legs, policemen in uniform stationed by the doors. At the far end of the hall barristers, in gowns but not yet wearing their wigs, pushed to and from the robing-room. The hall fell into shade, as the spring wind outside drove clouds across the sun. Then bright again. On the wall-panels stood out the arms of the county regiments. Across the far end, near where the barristers appeared and disappeared, a long trestle table carried a couple of tea-urns and plates of sandwiches, cakes, and sausage rolls, as though at an old-fashioned church fête.

Margaret was seeing all that for the first time. She had never been inside this place before – in fact, she had never been inside a criminal court. The curious thing was, I seemed to be seeing it for the first time too. And yet, when I was studying law in the town, I had gone into this entrance hall a good many times. Later, when I was practising, I had appeared in several cases at these assizes, using that same robing-room at the far end, walking through to the court-room in the way of business. Once, in the minor financial case which had involved George Passant: often we had forgotten that, or at least acted, despite the premonitions, as though it had signified nothing.

In all those visits, I seemed to have noticed very little. Was it that I had been blinkered by my own will? When I had been a 'hungry boxer', to use Charles's phrase, there were scenes I had wanted to rush through, like one passing in a train.

That morning, just as Margaret was looking round, so was I. One or two acquaintances said good-morning, knowing me by sight. I was more familiar to them than they to me. It reminded me that my presence wasn't unobserved. So it did when a young man came up, telling me that he worked in the Deputy Sheriff's office. The Deputy Sheriff would be pleased to find places for us, in his own box, near to the bench. I glanced at Margaret. We were waiting for George Passant: we should have to sit in the public court beside him. I thanked the young man and explained that we should have other people with us. Margaret said, surprising me, that if her husband was on his own later in the trial, he would certainly take advantage of the offer.

It was about twenty past ten. Through the door of the entrance hall George Passant trod slowly in. He was wearing an old bowler hat, as he used to do on formal occasions, though there had not been many in his life: underneath the bowler, his hair bushed wildly out. Before he saw us, his face looked seedy and drawn. But at the sight of Margaret he took off his hat, and broke into a smile – almost of pleasure, of astonished pleasure. He gave a loud greeting, asked how we were, asked after Charles's health. It might have been a meeting on one of his visits to London, running into us by a lucky chance, somewhere between our flat and the Marble Arch.

I went to one of the doors leading into the court-room. A policeman told me it was quite full down below but that perhaps there was still room in the gallery. We climbed up the stairs, and there, at the extreme wing, found seats which looked down into the packed and susurrating court. Packed, that is, except for a gaping space in the dock and for the empty bench.

From the gallery, we looked down at the line, not far away, of the backs of barristers' wigs. Behind them the solicitors, Sharples massive among them, were sitting, one of them leaning over to talk to his counsel. The court-room was small and handsome, dome-roofed, the eighteen twenties at their neatest. It struck lighter than in my time: that I did, all of a sudden, notice. Turning round, I saw that a vertical strip of window, floor to ceiling, had been unblocked. The whole court might have been a miniature Georgian theatre in a county town, except that light was streaming in from the back of the auditorium.

Without noise (only those used to the courts had heard the order, *put them up*) a policewoman had appeared in the dock, coming up from the underground passage. It happened so unobtrusively that Cora Ross's head also came up before people were looking. A catch of breath. Then Kitty Pateman was sitting beside her, another policewoman following behind.

The court-room was quiet. Heads were pushed forward, trying to get a glimpse of them. It wasn't a natural silence. Something – not dread, more like hypnosis – was keeping us all still.

Cora Ross sat straight-backed in the dock. She was wearing a chocolate dress with white sleeves. That, together with her thick bobbed hair, made her look severe, like some pictures of Joan of Arc. Her face was turned towards Kitty, with a steady undeviating glance. Kitty's glance, on the other hand, was all over the place. To say she didn't look at Cora wasn't true. She looked at everyone, her eyes darting round lizard-quick. She must have seen her parents, whom I had identified just below. She showed no recognition, but her expression was so mobile that it was impossible to read. She seemed prettier than I remembered, in her small-featured peaky fashion: the skin of her neck and forehead, though, appeared stretched, ready to show the etchings of strain. She was wearing a pale-blue blouse of some silky material. She rested her elbows on the front of the dock but shifted about as though she could not find a comfortable position; from above, I could see that one of her legs was entwined with the other.

The silence didn't last long. From the side door, a couple of barristers hurried in, took their seats, muttered something matey, desultory, to their colleagues, one of them wearing an apologetic smile.

The court-room clock, high up at the back of the gallery, had turned half past ten. Margaret touched my hand. She didn't know how casual the timekeeping of a court could be: but she did know that I was irked by unpunctuality, more so when I was anxious, more so still that morning. We had to wait another five minutes before we heard the ritual cry. As we were all rustling to our feet, the assize procession entered, close by the box where Margaret and I had been invited to sit. The old judge limped to his place of state: he was old, but as he faced us, in his red robe and black waistband, he had the presence of a strong and active man. With an amiable, Punch-like smile he made a becking bow to the court in front, to the jury on his left.

He had been a high-court judge for many years. The last of the gentlemen judges, so legal acquaintances of mine used to call him. He lived like a country squire, but he was still doing his duty on the assize round – a *red* judge, my mother would have said with awe – at the age of getting on for eighty. Just as through a chance resemblance I felt I knew Detective-Superintendent Maxwell better than I did, so I felt with this man, Mr Justice Fane, whom I had actually met only once, at an Inn guest-night. For he reminded me of a man of letters who had done me a good turn: the nutcracker face with the survival of handsomeness, the vigorous flesh, the half-hooded eyes, tolerant, worldly, self-indulgent, a little sad. He didn't pretend to be a great lawyer, so my informants said. But he had tried more criminal cases than anyone on the bench, and no one had been more compassionate.

In a full, effortless voice, the Clerk of Assize, just below the judge's place was speaking to the prisoners:

'Are you Cora Helen Passant Ross?'

'Yes.'

'Are you Katharine Mavis Pateman?'

'Yes.'

'Both of you are charged together in an indictment for murder. It is alleged that you, Ross, and you, Pateman, on a day unknown between 20 September 1963, and 9 October 1963, murdered Eric Antony Mawby. Ross, are you guilty or not guilty?'

'Not guilty,' said Cora Ross in a hard, unmodulated tone.

I had heard that indictment a fair number of times (Kitty Pateman was pleading not guilty, her voice twittering and bird-like): when I was a pupil in chambers in London, with nothing to do, I had attended several murder cases. But there was a difference that morning. In the court-room – although all of us knew the shadow of horror behind those charges – the air was less oppressive. There was none of the pall upon the nerves, at the same time shameful and thrilling, which in those earlier murder trials I had sensed all round me and not been able to deny within myself. For there was no chance of these two being sent to their own deaths. That was the chance which had, at least in part, in earlier days enticed us to the courts. Yes, young lawyers like myself had gone there to pick up something about the trade: yes, there was the drama: but we had also gone there as men might go, lurking, ashamed of themselves, into a pornographic bookshop. In the mephitic air, the sentence of death would be coming nearer.

That morning, the air was not so dense. There was one specific sensation less. In fact, as the jury were being sworn, I thought that there had been an attempt, despite the excitement in the press, to damp down other sensations. As I had learned some time before, the Attorney-General was not taking charge of the prosecution himself. It had fallen to the leader of the Midland Circuit, and when, just after eleven, he began his opening speech, he was as quiet and factual as if he were proposing an amendment to the Rent Act. The judge had spoken just as quietly a moment before, in telling the jury what the timetable would be: 10.30 –

1.0, then 2.30 – 4.30. 'We shall not sit longer, because of medical advice in relation to Miss Pateman, you understand.'

We had heard no mention of that, and later discovered that she had nothing worse than an attack of rheumatism. The judge was being elaborately considerate: just as, when he called her Miss, he seemed to be rebuking the old custom of the courts, which the Clerk had had to follow, of charging prisoners by their bare surnames.

Bosanquet began: 'My Lord and Members of the Jury, on 20 September last year, 1963, a child disappeared. His name was Eric Mawby. He was eight years of age. He was an only child, and he lived with his parents at 37 Willowbrook Road, which is part of the housing estate in — (he mentioned one of the outer suburbs). You will hear that he told his mother that he was going to play in the recreation ground about half-a-mile away from their house. You will also hear that, on most summer and autumn evenings, at about half past five o' clock, he went to the same recreation ground for an hour or so's play. He was always expected back before seven o'clock, and had never failed to do so until the evening of 20 September, which was a Friday.'

To a foreigner, this lead-in could have sounded like English under-statement. But a foreigner might not have known the transformation in English rhetoric, both in parliament and in the law courts, since about the middle of the thirties, when Bosanquet was starting to practise. He was using the tone of speech which was becoming common form. He had actually joined this circuit not long after I gave it up and accepted the College fellowship. He had already been referred to in court as 'Mr Recorder', which had made Margaret give me a puzzled glance: he worked, besides having his solid practice, as Recorder, which meant in effect judge of a lower court, in a city close by. As he stood a couple of yards away from the dock on his right hand, he was looking at the jury with an expression unmoved and unassuming. Distorted by the wig, as some faces are, his appeared preternaturally foreshortened, round and Pickwickian.

The quiet unaccented voice went on:

'He did not return by seven o'clock that evening. His parents became anxious, as any of us with children would be. They made enquiries of their neighbours and their neighbours' children. At nine o'clock they got in touch with the police. At once there was set in motion the most thorough of searches, of which you will hear more. I think you will agree that the police forces at all levels deserve many congratulations for their devotion and efficiency in this case. There was no news of Eric for over a fortnight, although many thousands of reports had been investigated and already certain lines of investigation were in train. But Eric had not been found, and there was no direct news of him. When the news did come, it was the worst possible. His body had been discovered through a very remarkable piece of fortune, if I may use the word in happenings such as these. It was the only piece of fortune that the police had throughout their massive investigations. There is, I think, no reason to doubt that, without this accident, they would shortly have discovered the burying place. However, something else happened. Very early in the morning of 9 October, a pack of hounds belonging to the—' – he gave the name of a local hunt – 'were out cubbing in a wood or covert to which the nearest village is Snaseby, though that is some distance away. The wood is known locally as Markers Copse.'

Like most people, perhaps everyone, in the court, I had heard of the incident which he was – without a trace of acceleration – coming to. During the police court proceedings, it had been carried, more than any single feature of the case, all over the press. He was telling us nothing new. But up till now I hadn't read or heard the name of the exact spot. Now I did hear it, and it meant something to me. The place was a few miles out of Market Harborough, where, as a boy, I used to stay with my uncle Will. On these holiday visits I went walking over the countryside and sometimes followed the hunt on foot (which my uncle approved of, considering it in some obscure fashion good for his estate agency). I knew Markers Copse well enough. There had been, and presumably still was, an abandoned church down in the next fold of the gentle, rolling country: a church with an overgrown graveyard, relic of a village long deserted. Below the church ran a stream, in which a friend and I often went to fish. It had been pretty country, lonely, oddly rural: sometimes I, who was used to townscapes, had liked to imagine that I was back in the eighteenth century.

'In Markers Copse, then, in the very early morning of 9 October, Mr Coe, the huntsman, took his hounds. In a short time he found that two of them had got loose from the pack. They were well-trained hounds and he was naturally irritated. He had to go some distance through the copse to find them. They were smelling, apparently without any reason, at a patch of earth between two of the trees. Mr Coe couldn't understand their behaviour. It took him considerable effort, and a good deal of discipline, to draw them away. Later that same day, when his work was done, Mr Coe was still puzzled by their behaviour. He is an extremely experienced huntsman and knows his hounds. He will tell you that he felt silly, but he had to make sure whether there was any explanation or not. So he went back that evening to Markers Copse with a neighbour and a couple of spades. He could remember the precise location where the hounds had been smelling. He and his neighbour started to dig. It didn't take them long to find the body of Eric Mawby – although the grave was fairly deep and had been carefully prepared.'

Bosanquet's expression hadn't changed, nor had his stress. Conversationally he informed the jury:

'You will hear medical evidence that the child had been dead since approximately the time that he disappeared. You will also hear, however, that he did not die on that first night and probably not for forty-eight hours afterwards. The pathological experts will tell you that he had received mortal injuries, through his skull having been battered in, though with what precise implement or implements it is impossible to say. The pathological experts will also tell you that there were signs of lacerations and other wounds on his body, not connected with the mortal blows, which may have been inflicted many hours before death.

'That is something of what happened to Eric, though I am afraid that I shall have to tell you more later. I now come to the connection between him and the defendants in the dock.'

He made the slightest of gestures to his right, but continued to gaze steadily at the jury.

'So far as is known, Eric had not spoken to either of them before the evening of 20 September. He may never have seen them before. There is evidence, however, that they had seen him. These two young women share a room in the house of Miss Pateman's parents. They have also, for two years past, rented a cottage in the country, where they have been accustomed to go at weekends. You will hear more, I am afraid, of Rose Cottage. It is near Melton Mowbray, and some considerable distance from Markers Copse. It has, however, become not uncommon, as you will hear, for their acquaintances, or members of a circle to which they belong, to rent cottages similar to theirs at convenient distances from the town, and they are known to have visited one in the Market Harborough direction, in fact in Snaseby.'

That was a reference, which some besides me must have picked up, to George Passant's group. Bosanquet left it there, and went on:

'It may sound as though Miss Ross and Miss Pateman were living a luxurious life. I might remind you that they were each drawing good salaries, Miss Pateman as a secretary, Miss Ross as a trained clerical worker. They had left school with their O-levels, Miss Pateman with seven and Miss Ross with four, and in the normal run of things they were regarded as valuable employees whose security wasn't in doubt. For two years past they had been able to run a car, a Morris saloon. As it happens, that car had its own part, a negative but finally a significant part, in the story of Eric's disappearance.'

Patiently, meticulously, he described the police investigations. They had interviewed some thousands of people who might have seen Eric on the evening of 20 September. There had been several hundred reports from others who thought they had (or, though he didn't say it, couldn't resist either exhibiting themselves or taking the sadistic bait). Witnesses, sound and level-headed, were almost certain that they had seen Eric walking off with a pair of men or a single boy. Others believed they had noticed him catching a bus. Several had caught sight of him in various makes of car. These stories took weeks to sift, and all turned out to be false.

The careful words tapped gently into the court. The minute hand was getting round to twelve. The judge leaned forward and asked:

'Is all this quite necessary, Mr Recorder?'

'There is a great deal of complexity, my lord.'

'But do we need all of it?'

'I'm inclined to think it may be as well.'

The voices were courteous, silky and just perceptibly tense. There might be some past history between the two men: or was the judge simply impatient? He knew, of course, everything the lawyers knew. No one on either side believed there could be any challenge to the facts. He had presumably expected that there would be a short opening speech, after which the defence, instead of trying to disprove the facts, pleaded diminished responsibility at once. Bosanquet stood there, amiable, obstinate. This was his case: he wasn't going to be hurried or budged. It might be that he had a double motive. I thought, and later had it confirmed, that he must have heard that the defence were still uncertain about their plea: though at that time I didn't guess the reason. And also he could be insuring against the medical evidence, once diminished responsibility was brought in: by being so rational himself, he was underlining how calculated the crime had been, just as he had, as though by accident, reminded everyone that the two women were of more than average intelligence.

Without altering his pace, he persevered. Many reports of persons who thought themselves eye-witnesses had been analysed and discarded. But two, which had been received in the third week of the investigation, had something in common. In both, the witnesses thought they had seen a child sitting between two people in the front seat of a car, with a woman driving. One of these sightings had taken place not far from the recreation ground. The child, as Mrs Ramsden would testify, appeared to be smiling and waving, the other adult's arm round his neck and shoulders. Was the other adult a man or a woman? That Mrs Ramsden hadn't been sure of, since the face was obscured by dark glasses. The second sighting had been a mile away from Rose Cottage. Mr Berry, who was working in his garden, had seen a car travelling very fast: he had noticed a child on the front seat but could not be positive about the other occupants. He had several times before observed Miss Ross and Miss Pateman driving to Rose Cottage: but he did not bring these occasions to mind, and this was not the car he had seen previously. It was in fact a brown Austin, and the number plate was not noticed at either sighting, or else was obscured.

'Those were the first indications which brought the defendants within the scope of the enquiry. I have to remind you that the police had many leads which seemed far more positive and more worth pursuing. But the police routine could not overlook even the most unpromising of suggestions. And so, as a matter of routine, Miss Ross and Miss Pateman were interviewed for the first time on 6 October, that is, three days before Eric's body was found. They were, as you will hear, both calm and co-operative. They expressed themselves as horrified by the disappearance and anxious to help. They denied any knowledge of the boy, but were very willing to account for their movements in the weekend of 20–2 September. Their car had, as it happened, needed repairing, and they had left it in their usual garage. So they had gone out to Rose Cottage by bus and spent their usual quiet weekend. On the Saturday morning Miss Ross had done a little shopping in the village. They had returned to the Patemans' house by the last bus on Sunday night.

'All this sounded quite natural. As a matter of routine the police checked one or two details of their account. Miss Ross was remembered as shopping in the village as usual on the Saturday morning. No one had noticed anything unusual, outside their ordinary weekend habits. In the same way, an enquiry was made at their garage, the Wyvern Garage in Whitehorse Street, and their car had duly been left there for repair during the weekend, as they had stated. But here Detective Constable Hallam, whom you will hear in evidence, asked some further questions. He wanted to know what had been wrong with the car. The answers did not satisfy him. The garage proprietor, Mr Norman, had been slightly puzzled himself. There had been a small jamming in the gear-change, but only of the kind which experienced car-owners like the defendants could put right in a few minutes themselves. This was simply a straw in the wind, but Detective-Constable Hallam was not satisfied.'

The enquiries went on, Bosanquet leaving nothing out. The car was conspicuous, it was well known in the neighbourhood. It occurred to the detective-constable to discover whether it had ever been noticed on the other side of the town, in the vicinity of Eric Mawby's house. He had found witnesses who had seen such a car patrolling, not one evening but three or four evenings consecutively, the route between Eric's house and the recreation ground.

'This was still a straw in the wind,' said Bosanquet, with no emphasis at all. 'But Detective-Constable Hallam's superiors thought it justified a visit to the Patemans' house, at a time when Miss Ross and Miss Pateman were present. We have now come to December last, when, of course, Eric's body had already been discovered. At this second interview Miss Ross and Miss Pateman were not as co-operative as at the first. They refused to discuss the repairs to the car, and after a while refused to answer further questions.'

Silence. The hallucinations of fact. Cora had her gaze still turned on Kitty, who had begun, in a frenetic fashion, to scribble notes and push them forward to her solicitor. She was writing as assiduously as the judge himself.

'There followed a third interview, this time at Rose Cottage,' Bosanquet said. 'During the questioning of Miss Ross and Miss Pateman, which was being conducted by Detective-Inspector Morley, other officers were searching the cottage and the garden. For some time this search revealed nothing. The cottage was swept and garnished. But in due course one of the officers, Detective-Sergeant Cross, discovered a small metal object pushed into the corner of a shelf. He recognised it as an angle joint which might have come from a Meccano set. He asked them to explain why it was there. At that point Miss Pateman said or screamed something across to her companion – something like, though no one can be definite about the exact words, "You blasted fool".

'Neither of the defendants produced any explanation about the presence of this Meccano unit. They said it had nothing to do with them. After a further interval officers searching the garden found, buried in the bushes, the box of what appeared to be a new Number One Meccano Set, containing most of its components, and carrying on the lid a tab from the Midland Educational Company. At this stage the defendants were separated, cautioned, and brought back to police headquarters for further enquiries.'

Bosanquet glanced at his wrist-watch. As though under suggestion, others of us did the same. It was ten minutes to one.

'By this time, since the officers had spent some hours at Rose Cottage, it was Saturday afternoon. Nevertheless the manager of the Midland Educational Company was immediately contacted, and search, of course, continued at the cottage. The bill for the purchase of a Number One Meccano Set was traced, bearing the date of 18 September last year, that is, two days before Eric's disappearance. The shop assistant who had made this transaction was visited at her home. She was able to remember the purchaser as someone answering to the description of Miss Ross.

'Meanwhile Miss Ross was being examined alone by Detective-Superintendent Maxwell. He will tell you that she was still denying knowledge of the Meccano set, although in a parallel examination Miss Pateman was providing explanations, such as, that it was a long-forgotten present which had never been delivered. The detective-superintendent was given the information from the Midland Educational Company. He told Miss Ross and asked her to account for it. Then she said: "Yes, we took him out to the cottage that Friday night. We borrowed a car to do it." '

In a tone indistinguishable from that in which he quoted her, he spoke to the judge:

'I'm inclined to think, my lord, this might be a convenient time to break off.'

'As you like, Mr Bosanquet.'

The politeness, the bowing judge, the ritual, Cora's fair head disappearing underground. When I had followed George and Margaret downstairs, the entrance hall was full, people were pushing towards the refreshment table. Outside, in the spring air, cameras clicked. Some were press cameras, but the journalists had not emerged yet, and I led the other two away, trying to hurry George's invalid pace. I heard some whispers and thought I could pick one out as 'that's her uncle'.

We walked, Margaret in the middle, George's heavy slow step with feet out-turned delaying us. Neither Margaret nor I could find anything to say. Instead, George spoke:

'It's nasty,' he said.

His words, like all the words spoken that morning, could not have been more matter-of-fact.

'It's nasty, of course,' he repeated.

'I'm sorry, George,' said Margaret.

He smiled at her, a diffident, gentle smile.

'Still,' he went on, 'wait till you hear the answer.'

Margaret couldn't reply, nor could I. Was he whistling up his old unextinguishable optimism, or was he just pretending? Wait till you hear the answer. I had heard politicians growl that identical phrase across the floor of the Commons, after the bitterest attack from the other side.

'I must say,' said George, 'I thought that—' – he brought out his curse as though the word had just been invented or as though the carnal reality were in front of his eyes – 'was unnecessarily offensive.'

Now he wasn't pretending. He was speaking out of the hates of a lifetime. I didn't answer. This was no time to argue, though in fact I thought the exact opposite. I thought also that Bosanquet, in his own fashion, was a master of his job.

'Well,' said George, 'where are we going to eat?'

Margaret and I looked at each other, hesitating. We didn't want much, she said. George, with a kind of boisterous kindness, said that we must eat something. He knew of a good place.

It turned out to be a pub which sometimes we used to visit (he showed no sign of remembering that) at the end of a night's crawl. Nowadays it served hot lunches: and there, in a small and steaming room upstairs, George, giving out an air of old-fashioned gallantry, placed Margaret in a chair and insisted that she eat some steak-and-kidney pie. His pleasure was extreme, pathetic, when she was ready to join him in drinking a double whisky.

He was fond of her, because she never blamed him. He had told her a good deal about his life, and found that she casually accepted it. 'I hope that's really all right for you,' he said, looking at her plate of meat and pastry, like a proud, considerate, but slightly anxious host.

It was not we who were trying to support him, but the reverse. He might be behaving so out of a residue of robustness greater than most men's – or out of indifference or a lack of affect. All we knew was that he was behaving like a brave man. He even told a long complicated funny story, so quirky that it didn't seem unfitting that day.

He did ask me – in an aside – whether Bosanquet (whom he never referred to by name, but always by the Anglo-Saxon curse, as though it were a kind of title) was going to 'drag in' any of the crowd. George hadn't missed the single oblique reference. I said that it seemed unlikely. Perhaps the people who lent the car might be mentioned – were they connections of George's?

George shook his head, his expression for an instant lost and suffering, and said that he didn't know. 'I don't want anyone else to get into a mess,' he muttered, repeating the words that had chilled me in his sitting-room.

He turned his attention to Margaret again, trying to think of another treat for her, before we returned to the Assize Hall. Again the crowded entrance, the barristers in the court-room seen from above, the ascent of those two into the dock. A little delay, only three minutes this time. The ritual bowing. Bosanquet on his feet, beginning:

'My lord, and members of the jury, we now turn for a moment to certain statements of Miss Pateman—.'

CHAPTER XXVI

TEACHING A CHILD TO BEHAVE

'Miss Pateman made a number of statements to police officers during the period when Miss Ross was being examined by Detective-Superintendent Maxwell,' said Bosanquet in a level tone, without a flick of sarcasm. 'On the following day Detective-Superintendent Maxwell decided to take her out once more to Rose Cottage and question her himself. By this time, of course, the search in and round the cottage had been intensified. Traces of blood, small traces, had been found in the bedroom. This blood, as you will hear from experts of the Forensic Laboratory, did not belong to the blood groups of either Miss Ross or Miss Pateman. It did, however, belong to the blood group of Eric Mawby. In the garden were found the remains of a nylon blouse not completely burnt, a blouse which witnesses recognised as having been worn by Miss Ross. On this were detectable some stains of the same blood group.

'In due course, as Detective-Superintendent Maxwell interrogated her –' (How long had they been alone together? When was she told that Cora had broken down?) – 'Miss Pateman withdrew her denials that the child had never been inside the cottage. She now told what appeared to be a coherent and self-consistent account of those events. She and Miss Ross had for some time past wanted to have a child alone, by themselves, to be in control of. She gave a reason for this desire. They wanted to teach it to behave.'

For the first time in the long and even speech, Bosanquet laid a stress, it sounded like an involuntary stress, upon the words. In an instant he had controlled himself. 'They had accordingly, so it appears, picked out a boy at random. For some time they had driven round the city, in places where they were not familiar, looking for a suitable subject. It was the misfortune of Eric Mawby and his parents that they settled on him. They decided on the weekend of 20 September. They bought the Meccano set two days before in order to give him something to do. They picked him up on the Friday evening without difficulty. According to Miss Pateman's account, Eric was pleased to go with them.' Bosanquet paused. 'That we cannot, of course, deny or establish. We also cannot establish at what stage exactly they began to ill-treat him. Possibly early on the Saturday. You will hear expert evidence about the many wounds on his body. He suffered them, according to expert judgment, many hours before death. These body wounds were healing when he was finally beaten to death by at least seven blows on the head, probably with something like a poker or a metal bar and also with a wooden implement.

'About the wounds on the body, Miss Pateman said that they had – what she called "punished" him. They wanted to teach him to behave.

'I should say that neither she or Miss Ross have ever admitted that they actually killed him. They had each given accounts of what happened to Eric on the Sunday night. The accounts are different. One is, that he was put on a bus to take him back to the town. The other, which is Miss Ross's, is that they drove him back themselves in the borrowed car, and dropped him at the corner of the road leading to his parents' house. Needless to say, neither of these stories deserves a moment's thought. That same night, and early the following morning, that same car was seen, as will be sworn by two witnesses, very close to Markers Copse. Further, when the car was ultimately examined – I must tell you that its real owners had no conceivable connection with this crime – there was evidence of blood, blood of Eric's group, on the floor of the back seat.'

He turned to the judge, and remarked:

'I think I need go no further at present, my lord. It would be my duty, if there were any conceivable doubt about the facts of this case, to make the position clear to members of the jury. But there is no doubt. We know most of what happened to Eric Mawby from the Friday evening until the time that he was buried. I haven't any wish to add to the intolerable facts you are obliged to listen to. You can imagine for yourselves the suffering of this child. There is no doubt about the way he was killed, nor about who killed him. All I need say is that this has been proved to be a deliberate, calculated, premeditated crime. That is enough.'

During the last few minutes of Bosanquet's speech, I had flinched – and this was true of Margaret and everyone round me – from looking at the two women in the dock, although, keeping my gaze on Bosanquet, I could not help noticing with peripheral vision the fingers of Kitty obsessively scribbling her notes.

A witness was being sworn, a man in his twenties, soft-faced, soft-voiced. It turned out that, with the indifferent businesslike bathos of the legal process, he was being examined about the loan of his car.

The box was on the judge's right hand, a couple of yards away from where Bosanquet had been standing: so that prosecutor, dock, witness, were all exposed to the same light. The young man's fair hair shone against the panelling.

'Your name is Laurence Tompkin? You are a schoolteacher employed by the local education authority? You know both the defendants?'

Yes, said the young man in a gentle, ingratiating manner, as of one who was trying to win affection, but he knew Miss Ross better than Miss Pateman. Do you remember either of them saying they might want to borrow your car? Yes, he remembered that, it was Miss Ross. When was that? In the early summer, last year. In the summer, not September? No, much earlier, more like June. What did she say? She just said they might want to borrow it some time, she wanted to be sure that it was available. Then, some time later she did borrow it? Yes. For a weekend in September? Yes. Can you tell us the date? The weekend beginning 20 September. Was the car returned? Yes. When? The following Monday. Did you notice anything odd about it? There seemed to be a lot of mud on the number plate, although it had been a sunny weekend. You didn't examine the floor of the car, down below the back seat? No, he didn't think of doing so.

Benskin, Cora's counsel, got up to speak for the first time that day. He was a small man, with a long nose and a labile merry mouth: his voice was unexpectedly sonorous. He was asking a few questions for appearance's sake. He had, of course, understood Bosanquet's tactics, that is, to demonstrate the long laid planning before the boy's death. As for the defence's own tactics, a good many of us were puzzled. They seemed to be in a state of indecision or suspense.

It would be perfectly reasonable to ask a friend, said Benskin, whether he could lend a car? Perfectly reasonable to ask, as a kind of insurance, if one was having any trouble with one's own? Even if the trouble didn't become serious for weeks? As for the return of the car, if Miss Ross and Miss Pateman drove it back to the town late on the Sunday night, they couldn't conveniently have returned it, could they? It was perfectly reasonable to park it outside their own house, and return it next day?

Having registered his appearance, Benskin sat down, with a grim half-smile to his junior. Kitty Pateman's counsel did not get up at all.

The young man left the box. He was one of George's group: he had not been asked how he could afford a car, or whether he shared it with anyone, or whether he also shared a cottage, or at what kind of parties he and Cora Ross had met. No one had a reason, so it appeared, to disturb that underground. This had been the guess that I made to George. I glanced at him, heavy-faced, mouth a little open: perhaps, even after the prosecutor's ending, not so many minutes before, he felt – as we all do in extreme calamities, when a minor selfish worry is taken away – some sort of relief.

Another witness, this time the manager of the garage where the women's own car had been left for repairs. When had it been deposited? 19 September. What was supposed to be wrong?

At this the judge, shifting himself from one haunch to the other as he spoke, became restive.

'Surely we are going into very great detail, aren't we, Mr Recorder?'

'With your permission, my lord, I wish to establish the whole build-up before the child was abducted.'

'I suggest we are all ready to take a certain amount for granted.'

'This is a complicated structure, my lord.' Bosanquet spoke mildly, but he didn't budge. 'I require my pieces of bricks-and-mortar.'

'Spare us anything you don't require,' said the judge, with a nod which was resigned but courteous.

The garage manager's mystification: she (Cora Ross) could have put it right in ten minutes. She was a first-class mechanic herself.

Next witness, Detective-Constable Hallam. He was raw-boned, quite young, and as he stood in the box his head was bent down towards his hands. His pertinacity about the car. 'I was not satisfied,' he said, for once raising his head. His manner was stern but guilty-seeming, he hesitated over answering matter-of-fact questions. Gradually Bosanquet's junior, young Archibald Rose, dug the story out of him. How he hadn't been satisfied. How at the garage he thought something was strange. How he made enquiries all along the half-mile between Eric's home and the recreation ground, asking if a green Morris had ever been seen. When had the car first patrolled that route? (That couldn't be answered, but it might have been as much as a month before 20 September.)

The young constable, who had been a halting, unhappy witness, was given a special word of approval. Without him, it might have taken much longer to look in the direction of Rose Cottage.

Statements from persons who had noticed a green Morris, read in a strong voice by the Clerk of Assize. 'I saw this car when I was getting home from work, but did not take its number. . . .'

A detective-sergeant in the box, the first search of the cottage. The piece of Meccano. Exhibit. A plain-clothes policeman, standing by the clerk, with a stiff robot-like movement held up his hand. From where I sat, just a glint of metal. Then he exposed it on his palm. The gesture was as mechanical as the plaything. An ordinary object, prosaic and innocent: yet it did not seem quite real, or else had its own aura. An object like Davidson's capsule, or the blank space in Palairet's notebook.

'Was this the piece of Meccano you discovered in Rose Cottage . . . ?'

'It was.'

Another detective-sergeant (the cottage and garden had been crowded with them). The Meccano box. Exhibited. The plain-clothes policeman went through his drill.

'Was this the box you discovered in the garden of Rose Cottage . . . ?'

'It was.'

The shop-assistant at the Midland Educational Company. The bill for a Number One Meccano Set.

'Is this bill dated 18 September?'

'Yes, sir.'

'Do you remember selling this set?'

'Yes, I do.'

'To whom did you sell it?'

'To the one sitting there—' She glanced at Cora and away again.

'That was on Wednesday, 18 September?'

'Yes, sir.'

Bosanquet asked her to make sure of the date. 'I'm sorry to press this, my lord, but you will see what I am establishing—' The judge turned to the jury. 'Bricks-and-mortar,' he said. He sounded affable and half-sardonic: but he was being fair to Bosanquet, underlining that this was evidence of intent. Following him, Benskin tried to shake the identification, but the girl was both gentle and strong-willed, and he got nowhere.

Witnesses, names, occupations, addresses, came, went, were forgotten, a random slice of the town. One stood out, a Mrs Ramsden, who testified about seeing a boy being driven in the car. She was plump, with a sharp nose poking out of the flesh: as a girl she must have had a cheerful, impertinent prettiness. As soon as she gave evidence, she gave the impression (much more so than any of the policemen) of being a natural witness. She was one of those people, and there were very few, who seemed to be abnormally observant and at the same time scrupulous. Yes, she had seen a brown Austin driving out of the city on the evening of 20 September. What time? She could be fairly exact: she was hurrying home for a television programme: about 5.45. Where was this? Not far from the recreation ground? A few hundred yards away. What did she notice? A small boy sitting between two people in the front seat. She didn't know Eric: from the photographs, it could have been him, it looked very like him, she couldn't be more positive than that. A woman was driving the car. The other person in the front seat? Might have been a man or woman. Fair-haired, wearing dark glasses. What was the boy doing? He seemed to be waving. He might have been struggling? He might have been, but she didn't think of it at the time. She thought that he was laughing. The person with dark glasses had an arm round him? Yes, round his neck. Like this? Bosanquet beckoned one of the plain-clothes policemen, who, sheepish and redfaced, had his neck encircled by counsel's arm. There was a titter, tight and guilty, the first that afternoon. Both defence counsel cross-examined. Kitty's, a young silk called Wilson, his actor's face hard, masculine, frowning, was trying to demonstrate that the boy had gone willingly. Benskin, that the kidnapping might have taken place much later. To most people in the court, none of this could matter, it only dragged out the strain. All those who were used to courts of law would have known by now, though, that they were struggling with their instructions, though I for one couldn't be certain what any of them were hoping for.

When Mrs Ramsden had left, the judge coughed, and said in an amiably testy fashion: 'I see the clock has stopped.' Heads turned to the back of the court. 'I make it,' said the judge, 'very nearly half past four. I don't want to go much beyond the half-hour, Mr Bosanquet. I hope you can be brief with the next witness. After all, no one challenges the fact that the boy was taken by car to Rose Cottage. That is so, Mr Benskin, Mr Wilson?'

For the first time, Bosanquet conceded the point. He left the witness – who swore to sighting the car near Rose Cottage on the Friday evening – to his junior, and within minutes the judge was bowing himself out of court.

It had been difficult to feel, since the end of Bosanquet's speech, how much people in the court-room had been anaesthetised by the sheer mechanics of the trial. We soon knew. As we walked with George through the entrance hall, there was an air of hostility which, like a blast of freezing wind, tightened the skin. Then came, not loud, but menacing and sustained, the sound of hissing. George threw his head erect, jamming his hat further back so that his forehead was exposed. The hisses went on. They were not directed at him as a person (at the time I didn't think of it: all I wanted was to lead him through the angry crowd). He wasn't well enough known in the town for that. But he was connected with those two, and this was enough.

We got him into the street. There were no taxis anywhere near, and we had to walk half a mile, people following us, women shouting at him, before we found one. On the way to the station, where Margaret had to catch a train back to London, none of us spoke. When we came in sight of the station building, the red brick glared like a discord in the spring sunshine.

While I paid off the taxi, George stood mute by Margaret's side. Then he said:

'Well, I'd better leave you now.'

No, we each told him, he must wait and see her off.

'I'd better leave you now,' George repeated.

We looked into his face. It was wild, his eyes gazing past us: and yet, how was it different from lunch-time, what did his expression mean?

'I don't want you to, you know,' said Margaret.

'I think I'd better. I've got some things to do.'

Without even glancing at each other, we thought we couldn't press him any further. 'I'll see you tomorrow, then?' he said to me. 'Of course,' I replied. He said to Margaret: 'It was very nice of you to come,' and kissed her.

When we were alone in the booking hall – the smell of damp wood and train smoke so familiar to me, but that evening bringing back neither homesickness nor meaning – Margaret said:

'That must be the worst of it over, mustn't it?'

Her eyes were sharp with pain. All I could say was that I didn't know.

Down in the refreshment-room, gazing at me across the marble table, she was saying that she was glad I was staying with the Gearys. That had happened because Vicky and her father had by this time left the Residence. Margaret had spent the previous night with me at the Gearys' house; she had liked them and trusted them more than she usually trusted at first sight. She wasn't being entirely protective; she would have welcomed their good nature for herself as well as for me; she had been appalled by that day in the court. Before she went through it, she had imagined what it would be like. She had believed that she would be stronger than I was. Now she didn't want (and this was true of the reporters and police officers, more used to the horrors of fact than the rest of us) to be alone.

We were sitting there fidgeting with the glasses on the table, as we might have been in a love affair that was going wrong, articulateness deserting us, pauses between the words.

She said:

'Could we have taken it?'

After a gap, I said:

'I've told you, sometimes I am afraid that one can take anything.'

'I wasn't thinking only of the little boy.'

I nodded.

'I was thinking of the parents. If it had been ours—'

I didn't need to reply.

In time, she went on:

'And I was thinking of the parents of the others. The ones who did it. If they had been ours—'

Slowly I said:

'Perhaps there, life's a bit more merciful. Somehow one might cover it up or make excuses—'

'Do you really believe that?'

When the London train drew in, she clung to me on the platform until the whistle shrilled.

The Gearys' house was right on the outskirts of the town, in a district which had been open fields when I was a boy. Small gardens lay in front of the neat semi-detached pairs on both sides of the road: junior managers lived there, as well as modest professional men like Denis Geary. He and his wife were waiting for me in their sitting-room, bright, well kept, reproductions of Vermeer and Van Gogh on the walls, on the mantelpiece photographs of their children, groups of the family on holidays abroad.

A copy of the local evening paper under the bookshelf. Headlines about the trial. As he stood up, handsome, grizzled, Denis pointed to it.

'Now,' he said, 'you've got to forget all about it.'

He was years younger than I was. But he was talking benevolently, as though I were a junior teacher on his staff, coming to him with some domestic trouble.

I said that it wasn't so easy.

'Lewis, you've got to forget about it.' He went on, it might have happened anywhere, it had absolutely nothing to do with the normal run of things, we just had to wipe it out of our minds.

I wasn't used to being spoken to paternally. Not many men had ever tried to father me. But Denis was one of this world's fathers, and I didn't resent it.

'He's right, you know,' said Alison Geary.

'I promise you', said Denis, 'that we'll look after anything practical when it's all over. We'll look after old George as far as we can.'

Yes, they would visit the Patemans and the two young women, wherever they were sent. It was all in the line of duty. They had visited criminals before now, they took it as naturally as talking to me.

Denis said: 'Now forget it and have a drink.'

They had observed, at those dinners at the Shaws', that I enjoyed drinking. They had laid in more liquor than would be expected in a headmaster's house and more, I couldn't help thinking, than they could comfortably afford. But I wasn't saving their pockets when I told them that, in times of trouble, I drank very little. It was true. They were so kind that I was confiding in them.

'I think I can understand that,' said Denis. He said it with fellow-feeling, as though he had gone through dark nights. Just for an instant, I wondered if he were more complex than he seemed. Heartily he came back: 'Still, you must have a little.'

They set to work to distract me both then and through dinner, which, as on the night before, was a delectable English meal. The Vice-Chancellorship – Denis guessed that I might still be made interested in jobs. They hadn't yet found a successor to Arnold Shaw. They had offered the post to Walter Luke, but he had turned it down. Why? Denis replied, straight-faced: 'He said that he didn't want to become a stuffed shirt.' I couldn't resist a grin: that sounded like the authentic Walter. Someone asked him if there were other reasons. Denis said, still straight-faced: 'He said he couldn't improve on the one he had already given.'

Comprehensive education – they were both campaigning for it, it meant that our old school, Denis's and mine, would cease to be a grammar school. 'But it's the only answer,' said Alison eagerly. 'It really is.' She was as devoted a radical as her husband; she brought out all the arguments of the day. The lives we were wasting: we three had been lucky in our education, though we hadn't thought so, we had been lucky, compared with the neighbours round us. This was the only answer. It was also good politics; the public wanted it, whatever the Tories said, and that was nothing against it; but the point was, it was right.

Although she had been talking to distract me, she was committed. Her bright sepia eyes were shining: it was easy to imagine her, quick-stepping, full-bodied, tapping at the voters' doors.

She couldn't raise an argument. She spoke about their children. The daughter had been married that winter. Did they like the man? He's a very good chap, said Denis, we think they're very happy. Where were they living? He was a schoolteacher in the town, said Alison.

'Well, you did the same,' said Denis, with an uxorious grin.

'He's an extremely nice man,' said Alison. 'He'll make her a good husband.' Then, as though she couldn't help it, her face changed. It began to wear an expression I had not seen in her before – was it wistful or shamefaced ?

'But I always used to think she'd do something different, after all.'

'She's going to be happy,' Denis told her, like one repeating himself.

'Yes. She's a pretty girl,' Alison turned to me, 'though I am her mother.'

From the photographs, that I could believe.

'She's got a lot of imagination too. She always used to be reaching after something wonderful. I used to think that she'd finish up by marrying – well, someone like André Malraux.'

It seemed a curious dream: even though Alison, determined to be practical, explained that she meant, naturally, a younger version of M. Malraux. The Gearys' marriage was one of the happier ones: but what Alison dreamed for her daughter, she must, of course, once have dreamed for herself.

They didn't stop working to snag my interest until, very early, I went up to my room. Through the open window came faint scents of the spring. Clouds rushed across the sky, unveiling stars. At the bottom of the garden there were no houses in sight, only a range of trees. The moon, rising above one level branch, was just turning from silver to gold. In some moods that sight would be a comfort or a cheat, telling one that there was an existence more desirable than ours.

I might have remembered, though I didn't, someone who refused to take false comfort. We did not exist outside out of time. Those were only words which drugged us, which made us blind to our condition. He said to me, on just such a night as this, that he hated the stars.

I stayed at the window, looking out at the night sky.

CHAPTER XXVII

AN IMPERMISSIBLE TERM

THE next morning, I arrived early in the entrance hall. Through a side door I could see the court-room, already nearly full. There was not such a queue outside as on the first day. Lawyers hustled by, swinging their brief-cases, on the way to robe. Then, as I stood about, George Passant, also early, joined me. After his loud greeting, which hadn't varied in all the years, his first remark was:

'I've been thinking, I don't think I shall fag to come in today.'

I was so surprised that I hardly noticed the old-fashioned slang.

'You won't?'

'I don't see any point in it today.'

His manner was bold, defiant, diffident, like a young man's. As I looked at him, I didn't understand. Other people in the hall were looking at him, but there was no demonstration. One might have thought he was frightened of another crowd like that of the night before, but I knew that wasn't true. His courage was absolute, as it had always been. He was saying that tomorrow or next day, they might be getting somewhere. Then I believed I had it. He had been working out the progress of the trial. This morning or afternoon, which he wanted to escape, the medical evidence would come into court. That, though he couldn't tell me and was brazening it out, he wasn't able to endure.

'I think that I shall stay,' I said.

'Well then,' said George with relief, 'I'll see you later on.'

After I had watched him leave, I asked a policeman to take a message to the Deputy Sheriff, enquiring whether he could still find me a place. Before the answer came back. I saw, and this was another surprise, for at that time I hadn't been told of the telephoning between him and Margaret, my brother Martin. He wasn't smiling, but he said: 'I thought you mightn't mind a bit of company.'

I recognised the clerk from the morning before, polite and welcoming. Yes, of course there were two seats. Yes, of course the Deputy Sheriff would be delighted to invite Dr Eliot. The clerk led us down a corridor behind the court, narrow and white-painted, past the judge's room, out to the official box.

From there our line of sight was only just above the level of the lawyers' wigs. We had to look up to see the crowd in the rake of the court, heads lit up by the long windows behind them. The row of barristers, the next row of solicitors – suddenly they reminded me of ministers on the front bench in the Commons, their PPS's whispering to them: I might have been watching them, as I had done often enough from the civil servants' box, but the angle was different, for it was like being on the wrong side of the Speaker's chair.

Somehow we were in an enclosure with the professionals, part of the machine. An official sitting beside us gave us piles of typescript, records of the police-court hearing, depositions.

The two women came up into the dock, their faces, beyond the lawyers, on a level with ours. Cora stared straight at me, without a sign of recognition. As she turned quarter-face to her left, listening to Kitty, she seemed like a painting I had once seen in the Uffizi, with a visage stormy, troubled, handsome (later I was puzzled to discover that the painting was, of all things, Lorenzo di Credi's Venus). Martin, who had not seen either of them before, sat forward, tense. Kitty was saying something, eyes sharp and flickering. At the end she gave a quick, surreptitious, involuntary smile. Her skin appeared to have darkened, not become paler, through imprisonment, and now she looked older than her partner.

Through the door just beside our box, the procession entered. As he finished his bow to the jury, beaming, affable, the judge gave me an appraising glance.

The first part of the morning was routine: so much routine that there was a sense of let-down in the court, but Bosanquet was as undeterred as a batsman playing himself in for his second hundred. Questions from the judge: placid answers from Bosanquet, this was a matter of 'filling in some pieces'. So there was evidence leading to the weekend of 20–2 September. Identification of Cora in the village. A good deal of car and transport evidence. Proof that the story of a bus back to the town, late on the Sunday night, was a fabrication. Sighting of the car near Markers Copse on the same Sunday night. Sighting of the car, close to the cottage, early the following morning. Examination of the car (this was the first apperance of the forensic scientists). Blood on the floor, close to the back seat. Category of blood.

Martin, like Margaret, had not attended a criminal trial before. He wasn't prepared for the patches of doldrums, the pauses for the judge to catch up with his longhand, the flatness of facts, or even the sheer numbers of the witnesses who came and went, names, addresses, occupations, units in the lonely crowd, just as we to them were units too. (How many people did one know? Intimately? A hundred, if one was lucky. Slightly? Perhaps ten thousand, if one had lived a busy life.) The witnesses came and went: so had the students before the university court the year before, most of us expecting never to see them again. There, but only by chance, I had been wrong: it hadn't been my last sight of the Patemans. So that, as I looked back, that ridiculous set-piece appeal not only loomed stiffer and more formal than this present trial, but also took on a significance, a kind of predictive ominousness, that it hadn't in the slightest degree possessed when I was sitting through it.

Already half past twelve. The court stirred. The prosecution was coming to the discovery of the body. Archibald Rose began to examine Mr Coe, the huntsman. The evidence was, of course, a matter of form, since no one could contest it: but it took some effort to drag it out. Mr Coe didn't appear at all like the romantic picture of an open-air worker: his face was pallid, his hair jet black, his cheeks sunken. In addition, he was one of those witnesses who, when told to speak up, find it – just as my least favourite student had done – as impossible as a tone-deaf person asked to sing a tune. Archibald Rose had a fine resonant performer's voice: in a cheerful reproving tone he kept saying – 'You're not to speak to me, you must speak to my lord and the jury.' Mr Coe looked lugubriously across to the jury box, raised his volume for a sentence, and then let his chin descend into his chest. My place was within touching distance of the jury, and though I had sharp ears I was missing one word in two. The judge broke in: he was a hunting man, and, though Coe didn't become more audible, he nodded his head once or twice less sombrely, as though sensible men were talking about sensible things. It was a famous pack, the judge was saying, one of the best packs in the shires, wasn't it? The judge had never seen or heard of hounds behaving as those two had done that morning, had Mr Coe? If they hadn't been so cussed, would Mr Coe have thought of returning to the spot?

Coe gave a happy smile when told that he could leave the box, so happy that others smiled in response.

Exhibit. Policeman holding up a small plastic bag, testifying that within were the clothes found on the body. There was also a polythene wrapper, which, for some reason not explained, had been used to cover the boy's head. The bag was opened: not many had attention to spare for the sight of bits of clothing; all round, as though there never had been any other and as though it would last for ever, was the charnel smell.

'Please remove that,' said the judge. 'And we will wait a moment before the next witness.'

The next witness had to be taken care of, for it was Eric Mawby's mother. She should have given evidence the previous afternoon, but – so the Deputy Sheriff's assistant, sitting at his desk in our box, told us as we waited, the smell still in our throats – she had not been well enough to attend. However, when she did step into the box, she was erect, and her voice was firm. She was a tall woman, with a high-nosed, proud, imperious face. As the judge asked after her health and told her she would not be questioned for long, she replied like one who enjoyed having attention paid to her.

Yes, Eric always went to play in the summer and autumn before his father came home for his tea (tea in that home must have meant a sub-stantial meal). He always went to the recreation ground, which was a good safe place. Yes, he was always expected back by a quarter to seven. Yes, he was a good obedient boy, he'd never been more than a few minutes late. But that Friday night when he didn't return— Enquiries. The police.

Bosanquet was asking her as few questions as he could manage: but he had to say: 'On 9 October, did the police tell you that a boy's body had been found?'

'Yes, they did.'

'Did they ask you to identify the body?'

'They did.'

'It was your son's body, Mrs Mawby?'

'It was Eric.' Her head was thrown back, her tone was not so much piteous, or even angry, as commanding.

'And the clothes – they were his clothes?'

'Yes, they were his things.'

Bosanquet thanked her, and finished. Defence counsel shook their heads. The judge thanked her, congratulated her on her courage, and gave her his sympathy. 'Thank you, my lord,' she said, taking pity from no one, proud to act as though she were used to courts.

On the way out down the corridor – the court rose after her evidence – Martin was saying that our mother would have behaved something like that. As soon as we reached the entrance hall, Archibald Rose, the junior prosecution counsel, approached us, looking boyish now that he had taken off his wig. 'Hallo, I was watching out for you.' He introduced himself; he was the nephew of my old chief Hector Rose. He said that Clive Bosanquet and he wondered if we would like to lunch with them.

In Rose's car we drove into the centre of the town, talking about acquaintances. All four of us had been drilled in the compact English professional world, where, if you didn't know someone, you at least knew someone else who did.

Sitting in the restaurant, the lawyers studied the menu. They had been working hard, they were hungry. Bosanquet allowed himself one drink. Close to, his expression was sadder and more authoritative than it seemed in court.

'What do you think of all this?' he said across the table, meaning the case.

I shook my head.

'If you'd stayed at the bar, you'd have done this sort of job, you know.'

'Do you all get used to it?' asked Martin with hard sympathy.

'Do you imagine anyone ever gets quite used to something like this?' Bosanquet was as direct as we were. Despite his comfortable senatorial frame, there was not much padding about him. Young Rose, whose spirits were less heavy, tried to talk of another case. Bosanquet spooned away at a plate of soup.

He looked up.

'I've had about enough of it,' he said.

He went on:

'I'm afraid I've got to bring it all out. I warn you, this afternoon isn't going to be pleasant.'

A week before, he told us, he had thought that they could 'smother some of the horrors'. They weren't good for anyone to hear. But – he had to go on.

'Look here,' I interrupted, 'I've been puzzled all along. What are the other side expecting?'

At that, Bosanquet and Rose glanced at each other, and Bosanquet suddenly got away from his revulsion and began to talk like a man at his ease. This was professional, this was clean. Neither of them could understand it. Something had gone wrong. The case was proved to the last inch. The defence counsel knew it, of course. Their only line was to make the best deal they could about the women's mental states ('We shall go for them there, anyway,' said Archibald Rose). Ted Benskin was a first-rate lawyer. Bosanquet was certain that was how he wanted to plead. But something had gone wrong.

'I shan't be surprised if they don't cut their losses any moment now.' (That is, accept the prosecution's case and make their plea.) 'I tell you, no one will be better pleased than me. As it is, I've got to plod on through all this filth.'

He gave a sweet, irritated smile.

'And old Jumbo doesn't make it any easier. I wish he wouldn't try to run my case for me.'

'Old Jumbo' was Mr Justice Fane. This too was professional, this was clean – in a different compartment from blood, cruelty, the smell of death. Just as Mansel was intent upon his professional problems while I, in a different compartment, was speculating about going blind. Bosanquet was happier now. Everyone loved old Jumbo, he was saying. He had been kind to Bosanquet himself all through his career. But there was no doubt about it, he hadn't much of a lawyer's sympathy with a well-built case.

Bosanquet was assessing the old judge like a man who, in the nearish future, might become a judge himself. It would be a good end to his career: and, unlike Mr Justice Fane, he had no private means. As with a writer or an actor, he wasn't secure from illness or old age. The barrister's life had altered since my time, they told me. How much had I made in my first year? Under a hundred pounds. Nowadays one would make a decent income, getting on for two thousand. Rose said that he had done so himself. But he appeared to have some money – which surprised me, for his uncle had none, and his father was a suffragan bishop. Anyway, Rose had acquired a house in the country when he joined the circuit. He was inviting us all there, including the defence lawyers, in a couple of nights' time.

Martin, lacking my nostalgic interest in legal careers, put in a question. He said, getting back to a preoccupation of his own:

'Have you any idea which of those two was the prime mover?'

Bosanquet said, once more clouded:

'No, we don't know.'

'I suppose it might have been the butch,' said Rose.

'We don't know,' said Bosanquet. He said it in a subdued tone, but with authority. 'There are plenty of things about this case that we don't know.' He addressed Martin, who might not have realised how much information police and lawyers possessed, but couldn't prove or use: 'But we do know two things. They had planned this, or something like this, literally for months beforehand. And they were going to kill, right from the beginning. That was the real point all along.'

Martin nodded.

'It's ten past two,' said Bosanquet, without changing his tone. 'We ought to be going.'

The afternoon began quietly. In the dock Kitty was sitting, pen in hand, but for the moment not writing. The first witness, examined by Rose, was an experimental officer from one of the midland forensic laboratories, an unassertive friendly man, his manner similar to those of the meteorologists who predicted the weather after the television news. Yes, he had examined samples of blood after Eric Mawby's body was discovered. These came from another laboratory ('We shall have a deposition to establish', said Archibald Rose, more emphatic than his senior, 'that these samples were taken from relics of dried blood still remaining on his head wounds and also on his clothes.') It had been possible to determine the blood group. The blood group was the same as that already given in evidence for specimens of blood found on the floor and walls of Rose Cottage.

Another experimental officer. Blood found on a piece of clothing, a woman's nylon blouse not completely burnt, in the garden of Rose Cottage. Identical blood group.

Deposition about taking samples of blood from K. M. Pateman, C. H. P. Ross. Another witness, from another laboratory, tested these samples (at this stage, the scientific tests seemed mysteriously ramified). Neither belonged to the same group as that of the other specimens.

All muted, abstract as a chart of last year's trade returns, except for Rose's ringing voice.

A new witness mounted into the box, and Bosanquet stood up himself. Laurence McQuillin. Home Office pathologist. His arms were folded, he was short, sturdy, unvivacious as a Buddha. He was practised at giving evidence, and he also enjoyed exposition: so that, though he was extremely positive, people did not react against him, but wanted to listen. Bosanquet must have examined him before, and carefully let him give an answer about the problems presented by a body buried for three weeks. 'In some matters,' said McQuillin, 'there is an area of doubt. I shall indicate to my lord and the jury where the conclusions have to be tentative.'

'But you have reached some definite conclusions?'

'I have.'

One definite conclusion was that the boy's body showed two types of injury. The first type was wounds which could not have caused death and which had, with reasonable certainty, been inflicted some considerable time before death. These wounds included lacerations on the back, buttocks and thighs. The exact number could not be decided. Well over twenty. There were also cuts on the breast and groin. A number of burns on the upper arms and shoulders. Not less than ten. Marks on the ankles and wrists.

'What were these wounds inflicted with?'

'There must have been different instruments. The lacerations on the back and buttocks could have been caused by a stick. If so, it must have been used with severe force.'

'And the others?'

'The cuts would have needed a sharp instrument. A knife could have been used. Or scissors.'

'The burns?'

'I cannot be certain. They are quite small in area. Perhaps a lighted cigarette end, but that is only a speculation.'

The marks on the ankles and wrists were minor. They were consistent with the child's arms and legs having been tied, but that also was a speculation.

'None of these injuries had any connection with the victim's death?'
'None at all.'

McQuillin added to his answer: they would have caused extreme pain, but a healthy child, or a healthy adult for that matter, would have recovered physically in a comparatively short time.

'How do you reach your conclusion that they were incurred a considerable period before death?'

There were two reasons, McQuillin said. One was simple and didn't require technical explanation. Blood, in considerable quantity, had been found on the outside of the boy's clothes. This had come from the head wounds. Almost none had seeped through to the inside of his shirt and shorts. On the other hand, some of the body wounds, not all, but many of the lacerations as well as the cuts, had resulted in the effusion of blood. There was no trace of this blood on the inside of his clothes. He had been killed when he was fully dressed. Thus he must have received the body wounds some time before: possibly, and in fact probably, over a period of hours: presumably while he was naked.

The second reason was technical – McQuillin described the physiology of flesh wounds, and their rate of healing. If the body had been discovered sooner, he could have been precise about the relative time of the head and body wounds. As it was, all indications pointed in the same direction, that there were hours between them.

'There is no other explanation for those body wounds than the one you have given?'

'I see no other explanation except systematic torture.'

McQuillin had not raised his voice. The judge, leaning forward, spoke even more softly.

'I think it is better for us, Doctor McQuillin, if you restrict yourself to your scientific findings.'

'I am sorry, my lord,' said McQuillin.

'I understand,' said the judge.

The head injuries – these had been the cause of death? He was killed, said McQuillin, by multiple head injuries, multiple fractures of the skull. There had been seven blows, and possibly more. Any one of several blows would have been sufficient to cause death. One group of five had been delivered by something like a heavy poker or an iron bar. The others, by a solid obtuse weighted surface, such as the anterior wooden portion of an axe-handle. Yes, the bleeding would have been copious. 'Nothing bleeds so copiously as the scalp,' McQuillin added. 'There must also, with such wounds, have been a discharge of brain tissue. And fragments of bone thrown out, though these have not been found. The vault of the skull showed a number of gaps.'

The blows had been delivered from in front (here McQuillin beckoned a policeman, like a lecturer carried away by his subject and needing to illustrate it), or at least the first one had been. The head had been held back by the hair – like this – possibly not by the person delivering the blow. The remainder of the blows could have followed when the body had sunk to a kneeling or recumbent position—

Benskin interrupted. 'This doctor in my submission is going beyond the evidence of a medical expert.'

The judge said: 'Mr Benskin, I think I agree with you. Doctor, you have told us your conclusions about the cause of death? You are quite certain about them?'

'I am quite certain, my lord.'

'Then I hope we might leave it there, Mr Bosanquet.'

Bosanquet stood, thinking, and said: 'I am content.'

Both defence counsel cross-examined. They were sharp and edgy about the doctor's reconstructions. Neither of them was free from the miasma which had during his evidence settled on the court. It was a miasma which both rotted the nerves and at the same time held them stretched. Glances at the dock were furtive. The doctor had been imagining how the blows had been struck. Creeping glances at the two women. They knew whether he was right.

Head wounds, body wounds – the lawyers were doing their job, they had to bring the descriptions back before us. To some there, those could be nothing but names by now. But not to Wilson, the youngest of the silks. He sounded angry: he could not, less so than Benskin, insulate himself: he took it out of the doctor, partly because it was tactically right, but also because he genuinely, and for his own sake, wanted to disbelieve. The head wounds – no one doubted they had been inflicted, no one doubted they were the cause of death. But surely the doctor's reconstruction was entirely fanciful? In any case, it was not relevant: if it had been relevant, anyone's reconstruction would have been worth about as much, which was next to nothing at all?

'I have had some experience of these matters,' said McQuillin impassively.

'I repeat, your reconstruction is fanciful. But that is not the point. The death happened, we all know that. I suggest to you, your conclusions about the body wounds are also fanciful?'

'I have recorded my findings. I could give further conclusions about those wounds.'

'They might have been incurred very near the time of death—?'

'I regard it as most unlikely.'

'It is not impossible?'

'In giving scientific evidence, it is often wrong to say something is impossible.'

'That is, your picture of long-sustained wounding – I might remind you that you used an impermissible term for which my lord reproved you – your picture goes right beyond the medical evidence?'

'In my judgment, it is the only one that fits the facts.'

Wilson could not leave it alone. Questions about lacerations, cuts, bloodstains, the whole pathological examination over again.

At last the judge said: 'Mr Wilson, I shouldn't put obstacles in your way if I thought we were getting any further. But I do suggest that the jury has as much information as we can give it. And perhaps this is getting burdensome for us all.'

He said it aseptically. Wilson, face flushed, wiped his forehead, continued with more questions about flesh-wounds, and then sat down.

Bosanquet's re-examination was brief. He remarked that the doctor had been a long time in the box, and asked if, as a result, he wished to modify any of his statements of fact or his conclusions. McQuillin was as impassive as when he first answered to his name. He had given considered opinions, he answered. He did not wish to change in the slightest anything he had said.

It was well after half past four, the court had over-run for the first time in the trial: the judge had watched the clock, but not interrupted.

CHAPTER XXVIII

ANOTHER QUESTION

WHEN at last Martin and I got out into the air, we heard a voice behind us calling. It was Edgar Hankins who, nowadays turning his hand to non-literary journalism, was writing special articles on the trial for a Sunday paper. He came running after us, his face cheerful, rubbery, sweating.

'Let's all go and have tea and then a drink,' he said.

Before I could reply, Martin said:

'No, not now. Lewis and I have something to talk about.'

Hankins dropped back, his face still not having forgotten the smile of invitation. I hadn't often heard Martin impolite before: his tone had been colder than when I offered to help out financially over his son. As a rule with Hankins, because of their past history, he was specially considerate. He didn't speak until we were sitting in his car. Then, before he started it, he said:

'I couldn't bear his brand of nonsense tonight.'

He went on:

'You know, we could write it for him. Great throbbing pieces about how we're all guilty. So really no one is guilty. So really everything is as well as could be expected in an admittedly imperfect world.'

Neither of us said much more – Martin's face was hard and angry, he made another aside about 'saccharine rhetoric' – until, a little later, he re-joined me in the bar of his hotel.

It was a bar which we both knew: though, since I had left the town for good when he was a schoolboy, we had never before sat there together. It was still a meeting-place for men coming out of their offices on the way home to the prosperous suburbs: the income level had always been higher than in the pubs which George and I most often used. Though the bar had stayed geographically in the same place, it had been transmogrified, like the hotel and most of the town itself. It had become plushier and, in the American style, much darker, lights gleaming surreptitiously behind the sandwich-bar. But the people looked much the same, hearty middle-aged men, bald or greying, a good many of them carrying their weight on athletes' muscles: from some of these Martin, as we sat in a corner alcove, kept getting shouts of greeting. For while I might be recognised from photographs, he had more acquaintances here, they had played games together before the war. Amiable impersonal back-chat: how are you getting on, I'm an old man now, I can't get my arm over any more, you never did get it very high, I shall soon be taking to bowls. Some of them had made money, Martin mentioned, when we weren't observed. There was a lot of quiet money in this town. There were also one or two casualties in that bar, boyhood friends who were scrabbling for a living or who had taken to drink. Most of them, though, had come through into this jostling, vigorous, bourgeois life. All round us he could see the well-being, the survival, and sometimes the kindness of the flesh.

Was that any sort of reassurance to him? I was wondering. We had said little to each other: to an extent, we did not need to. I had let slip a remark about the time-switch at Auschwitz, and he had picked it up, just as Margaret would have done, or often young Charles. I didn't have to explain. I meant – someone had said it before me – that at Auschwitz one could not help being invaded by the relativity of time. The relativity which was at once degrading and ironic. That is, on the same day, *at the same moment*, people had been sitting down to meals or begetting children while, a few hundred yards away, others had been dying in torture. It had been the same with this boy's death. While he was beginning to suffer fright and worse than fright, the rest of us had, at the same moment, through the switch of time, been living as healthily as those men round us in the bar, talking or making love or maybe being preoccupied with what seemed a serious worry of our own. Martin understood without my saying so. He did not understand (I did not want to explain, perhaps because it reminded me of another death) that I had been, in court, working out the hours of the boy's suffering. That might have been going on – in all probability it had been going on – during a happy dinner party at our London flat, when Margaret and I were looking forward to the children's future, making a fuss of Vicky, and being entertained by Martin's own son.

Martin did not know that. But he knew something else, when I mentioned Auschwitz. For he and I and others of our age had seen the films of the concentration camps just after the troops had entered and when the horror came before our eyes like a primal, an original, an Adamic fact. Yes, with what we possessed of decency and political sense we had made our plans, so that, if people like us had any part in action at all, this couldn't happen again: and we had gone on spending, though men like Rubin told us that we were wasting our time, a good deal of our lives in action. And yet, while we watched those films, we had, as well as being appalled, felt a shameful and disgusting pleasure. It was almost without emotion, it was titillating, trivial and (just as when Margaret asked me questions in our drawing-room) seepingly corrupt. We were fascinated (the sensation was as affectless as that) because men could do these things to other men.

The wretched truth was, it had been the same in the court-room that afternoon. Not only in us, but in everyone round us. But it was enough to know it for ourselves.

So, when I spoke, as though casually, of Auschwitz, Martin did not ask any questions. He nodded (raising one hand to a greeting from the other side of the bar), and looked at me with a glance which was grim but comradely.

In time he said:

'What people feel doesn't matter very much. It's what they do we have to think about.'

It sounded bleak, like so much that he said as he grew older. Yet, as we sat there, old acquaintances pushing by him, he was as much at the mercy of his thoughts as I was, maybe more so. We were different men, though we had our links of sympathy. What we had learned from our lives, we had learned in different fashions: we had often been allies, but then events had driven us together: perhaps now, in our fifties, we were closer than we had ever been. But Martin, whom most people thought the harder and more self-sufficient of the two, had once had the more brilliant and the more innocent hopes. I had started off in this town in the first blaze of George's enlightenment. Let the winds of life blow through you. Live by the flow of your instincts. Salvation through freedom. Like any young man, I had got drunk on those great cries. It wasn't through any virtue of mine, but simply because of my temperament and my first obsessive love affair, that I couldn't quite live up to them. But there was another side to it. George, like many radicals of his time, believed, passionately believed, in the perfectibility of man. That I could never do, from the time that I first met him, in my teens. Without possessing a religious faith, I nevertheless – perhaps because I wasn't good myself – couldn't help believing in something like original sin.

With Martin, it had gone the other way. He had in his youth, though he had never been such an intimate of George's and nothing like so fond of him, accepted the whole doctrine. He really did have the splendid dreams. Rip off the chains, and he and everyone else would break through to a better life. He enjoyed himself more as a young man than I had done. He had gone through the existence where ideals and sex and energy are all mixed up – perhaps, even now, when people thought him sardonic and restrictive, there were times when he thought of that existence with some sort of regret. It hadn't lasted. He was clear-sighted, he couldn't deny his own experience. His vision of life turned jet-black. Yet not completely, not so completely as he spoke or thought. It was what people did that mattered, he had just said, as he had often said before: if that was true, then what he did sometimes betrayed him. After all, it had been he – alone of all of us – who had broken his career, just when he had the power and prizes in his clutch. Conscience? Moral impulse? People wondered. They might have accepted that of Francis Getliffe, not of Martin. But it was he who had done it. Just as it was he who, under the carapace of his pessimism, pretending to himself that he expected nothing, invested so much hope in his son, was wide open to danger through another's life.

The bar was noisy, but neither of us wanted to leave. The place had been familiar, part of commonplace evenings, to each of us – though it had taken something not commonplace but unimaginable to seat us there together. Martin's acquaintances downed their liquor. Most of them were middle-aged, not thinking about their age, carried along, like us, by the desire to persist. They looked carefree. For all we could tell, some of them were also at the mercy of their thoughts. One, whom I knew slightly, had reminded me of a photograph in a newspaper that morning: of Margaret and me walking with George Passant, a straggle of women demonstrating behind. Did I know 'that crowd', did I know those two women? The questions had been edged. Martin had answered for me, guarded and official, Passant had been a friend of ours when we were young men. Otherwise the rest of them said their good-evenings, wanted to know whether we were staying long, offered us drinks. Someone enquired, why don't you come back and live here, not a bad place, you know, we could do with you.

Martin said:

'If you hadn't had your connections here, just by chance – would this have meant much to you?'

He was talking of what we had listened to that afternoon.

'Should you have thought about it much?' he went on.

'Should we?' I replied. For Martin, in his unexpressive manner, was using the second person when he meant the first.

'I can't be sure.'

'Could we have shrugged it off? Some people can, you know.'

I told him about the Gearys, who weren't opaque, who longed, more than most of us, to create a desirable life. Yes, they could dismiss it: they could still look after both the innocent and guilty: but it seemed to them only an accident, a freak, utterly irrelevant to the desirable life they longed for or to the way they tried to build it.

'That's too easy,' said Martin.

I said, most of our wisest friends would see it as the Gearys did.

'I should have thought,' said Martin, 'we'd had enough of the liberal illusions.'

'Those I'm thinking of aren't specially illusioned.'

'Anyone is illusioned who doesn't get ready for the worst. If there's ever to be any kind of radical world which it's possible to live in, it's got to be built on minimum illusions. If we start by getting ready for the worst, then perhaps we stand a finite chance.'

Though to many it seemed a contradiction in his nature, Martin had remained a committed radical. In terms of action, we had usually been at one.

Someone sent over tankards of beer, smiling at us. With public faces, Martin and I smiled back.

'Tell me,' said Martin, 'those two aren't mad, are they?'

'I'm not certain we know what madness means.'

'Are you evading it?'

'Do you think I should choose to, now?'

I went on:

'Do you think I should? All I can tell you is, no one round them thinks they're mad.'

He said: 'They look – like everyone else.'

I replied:

'I'm certain of one thing. In most ways, they feel like everyone else. The girl Kitty is in pain. She can't get comfortable, she's just as harassed as any other woman with sciatica having to sit under people's eyes. I'm certain they wake up in the morning often feeling good. Then they remember what they've got to go through all day.' It had been like that, I said, when I had the trouble with my eye. The moments of waking: all was fine: and then I saw the black veil. I said that in the existential moments tonight, as they ate their supper and sat in their cells, they must be feeling like the rest of us.

'I suppose you're right,' said Martin.

'The horror is,' I said, 'that they are human.'

The dialogue was going by stops and jerks: soon it fell into doldrums, like an imitation of the doldrums of the trial. We dropped into chit-chat, not even the ordinary family exchange. Neither of us mentioned – and this was very rare – our children. Martin spoke (although I knew nothing of botany and cared less) about a plant he had identified on Wicken Fen. Sometimes we were interrupted, the bar was only beginning to empty. Still we didn't want to leave. Somehow we seemed protected there. We fetched sandwiches, so as not to have to depart for dinner.

In the middle of the chit-chat, Martin made another start.

'Human beings are dangerous wild animals,' he said. 'More dangerous than any other animals on earth.'

I didn't disagree. But I added that perhaps there were some slight, slighter than slight, possibilities of grace. 'You have to give us the benefit of the doubt. We need that, the lot of us, to get along.'

'I think you've given us all far too much benefit of the doubt,' said my brother.

Maybe. And yet I believed that in the end I was more suspicious than he was.

Later, as we still sat, talking about someone who had just left the bar, Martin suddenly interrupted:

'What do you hope will happen to those two?'

'What do you mean?'

'I mean, what verdict are you hoping for?'

I had explained the legal situation, and how I couldn't understand why diminished responsibility hadn't been brought in before now. Otherwise they might as well have pleaded guilty of murder and have done with it. He had already asked about diminished responsibility: what were the chances that the defence could win?

'Do you hope they win?' Martin pressed me.

I hesitated for a long time.

'I just don't know,' I said.

It would be easier, of course, for their families, I went on, it would be easier for George, it would save some pain.

'It would be easier for everyone,' said Martin. He asked, in a hard and searching tone·

'And you still don't know?'

'Do you?' I replied.

It was his turn to hesitate. At last he shook his head.

By this time there were, besides ourselves, only a couple of men left in the room. It had become cavernous and quiet: now the aquarium light obtruded from behind the counter. Soon, said the barman, there would be another crowd, the after-dinner crowd, coming in. In that case, Martin said, he felt inclined to stay, he didn't specially want to move yet awhile. Neither of us suggested going out, so that we could be alone, the two of us together.

PART FOUR

RESPONSIBILITY

CHAPTER XXIX

A MOTHER'S REMARK

ON the third morning, which was a Wednesday, Martin and I returned to our seats in the official box, having lingered about uselessly for George. In the court-room the chandelier lights were switched on, the clouds pressing towards the windows were dense and purplish, there was a hubbub of wind and rain. Outside it was a dramatic, a faintly apocalyptic, day: but inside the court the proceedings were subdued, voices were quiet, nothing dramatic there.

In fact, police officers were giving routine evidence about the statements made by the two women. Statements which contradicted each other, but that was no news, we had heard it already. We had heard also the elaborations, the different versions, the excuses for past lies, that Kitty had made as the police played on her. None of this was new. It was all delivered flatly, with nothing like the confidence and projection of the medical witness the afternoon before. But it had the curious intimacy that sometimes descended on law courts – an intimacy in which the police, the criminals, the lawyers, the judge, seemed to inhabit a private world of their own, with their own understandings, secrets and even language, shutting out, like an exclusive club, everyone who hadn't the right of entry.

In the middle of the morning – the gale was blowing itself out, the windows were lighter – Detective Superintendent Maxwell went into the witness box. He was, I knew well enough, a formidable man: but he didn't look or sound formidable as he stood there, opposite to us, across the court. He looked less bulky, his eyes less probing and hot: he gave his evidence as flatly as the others, unassertively, almost gently.

'Yes, sir, when she was making her fourth statement the defendant Miss Pateman told me that they had picked him up at 5.45 on the Friday night.'

Bosanquet asked, in a similar tone, what she had said. 'She said that he was glad to go with them.'

That had been included, in identical words, in Bosanquet's opening. So had her explanation of the child's wounds. Leaning confidently on the box-rail, Maxwell said: 'She told me, We wanted to teach him to behave. She told me again, We had to teach him to behave.'

He sounded like an uncle talking of a game of parents-and-children. I hadn't seen any man conceal his passions more.

The judge put in, also in an unassertive tone:

'You went just a little fast for me, Superintendent. Was it – She – told – me – we – had – to – teach – him – to – behave?'

The judge's pen moved anachronistically over his paper. Then Bosanquet again – When did they begin to ill-treat him? 'She never gave me the exact time. All she said was, We started as we meant to go on.'

I was watching Kitty's face, just then washed clean of lines. Was she out of pain? Her expressions changed like the surface of a pond. She was writing another of her notes.

Maxwell had led her through the Saturday and Sunday hour by hour. 'We put him to bed at half past nine on the Saturday, Miss Pateman told me. I asked her, what sort of condition was he in then? She said, We gave him three aspirins and a glass of milk before he went to bed.' You couldn't elicit how badly he had been hurt by that time, said Bosanquet neutrally. Just as neutrally, Maxwell said, no, she hadn't made a positive statement. On the Sunday, she did tell him, they had been obliged to be strict. But they had let him look at television at Sunday tea-time. 'What sort of condition was he in then, I asked her, but she never replied.'

The defence was raising no objection. There must be an understanding, or they must have a purpose, I thought.

It hadn't been established, it still wasn't clear, at what time on the Sunday night he had been killed. It might even have been early on the Monday morning. 'I asked her,' Maxwell said, 'did you tell him what was going to happen to him. She said he had asked them once, but they didn't say anything.'

Again, the judge remarked that his pen wasn't keeping up. Maxwell, constraining himself so tightly, was speaking unnaturally fast. When the judge was satisfied, Maxwell went on:

'I think – I should like to have permission to refer to my notes –' studiously, horn-rimmed glasses on his prow-like nose, he read in a small pocket-book – 'that on that occasion Miss Pateman stated that they hadn't any knowledge themselves of what did happen to him.'

There was a sudden flurry of confusion. Comparison of statements, Kitty's fourth and fifth: the judge had mislaid Cora's second. Bosanquet steered his way through: had Miss Pateman given any account of the actual killing? No, replied Maxwell. In one statement she said that early on the Sunday evening they had put him on a bus. That contradicted statements, not only by Miss Ross, but by Miss Pateman herself. On another occasion she said that she didn't know, or seemed to have forgotten, what had happened on the Sunday night.

'Will you clarify that?' said Bosanquet. 'She actually said she *seemed to have forgotten*—?'

'You will find that in her statement number five.' For an instant Maxwell's eyes flashed.

'What did you say, when you heard that?'

'I said,' Maxwell replied, once more in his most domestic tone, 'Now listen, Kitty. I can't make any promises, but it will save us a lot of worry, you included, if we get this story straight.'

'How did Miss Pateman respond?'

'She said, I will only tell you, I've given you the story as far as I remember it. I don't remember much about anything that Sunday night.'

Bosanquet was passing to Maxwell's interviews with Cora. The first breakdown: the first admission (it was she who had made it, not Kitty) that they had taken the child out to the cottage that Friday. All quiet and matter-of-fact. Then Benskin was on his feet, jester's face smiling at Bosanquet. 'If my learned friend will permit me. My lord, Mr Wilson and I have agreed that we shall not challenge this evidence for the Crown. Perhaps it would be advisable for us to indicate—'

The judge gave a sapient nod. 'Will you please come up, Mr Benskin, Mr Wilson? Mr Recorder?' The barristers moved to the space immediately below the judge's seat, and there they and the judge and the Clerk of Assize were all whispering in what, to most people in court, seemed a colloguing mystery. In our box, the Deputy Sheriff's assistant gave us a knowledgeable glance. 'About time, too,' he murmured. It was, we assumed, what those on the inside had expected all along: they were changing their plea: it would have been tidier, so he was saying, if they had started clean on the first morning. Meanwhile wigs were nodding below the judge, the old man was half-smiling.

At that moment we heard a loud unmodulated shout. It was Cora, standing in the dock, palms beating on the rail. 'What the hell do you think you're doing with us? What right have you got?' She was jeering at them with fury and contempt; she began to swear, sweeping round at all of us, the oaths coming out unworn, naked, as in one of George's outbursts. The air was ripped open. Most people in the court hadn't heard until that moment what anger could sound like. 'We'll answer for ourselves. We don't want you, you—' again the curse crackled. 'Do you think we need to explain ourselves to a set of—?'

Kitty was pulling at her arm, urgently, eyes snapping. The judge spoke to Benskin, and raised his voice, which showed, for the first time, the unevenness of age. 'Miss Ross, you are doing yourself no good, you must be quiet.'

'Do you mean to say anything will do us good among you crowd—'

Very quietly, Benskin had moved to the dock. For an instant she stood there, towering over him: then we heard a rasp of command, and there was a nervous relief as she sat down. Whispers from Benskin, low and intense, which none of us could pick up. ('He's a very tough man,' the official was commenting to Martin.) Shortly he was back in his place, facing the judge. 'My lord, I wish to express regret, on behalf of my client,' he said, with professional smoothness, like a man apologising for knocking over a glass of sherry.

'Very well,' said the judge. Then he spoke to the jury: 'I have to tell you that you must dismiss this incident from your minds. And I have to tell everyone in court that it must not be mentioned outside, under penalties of which I am sure you are well aware.' He spoke to the jury again, telling them that he now proposed to adjourn the court until the following morning. This was because the defence would then open their case, admitting the facts about the killing, but claiming that the defendants acted with diminished responsibility. 'That means, you understand, that they still plead not guilty to murder, and, because of their mental condition, under our present law, are seeking to prove to you that their crime should be regarded as manslaughter.' The judge lingered over this piece of exposition, courteous, paternal, with the savour of an old professor, famous for his lectures, who may soon be delivering the last one. The jury were to realise that the trial would from now on take a different course. The defence would not attempt to disprove the Crown evidence as to the nature of the killing. So that the jury need not worry themselves about certain questions of detail which had already taken up some time, such as precisely when the child was killed. The legal position would, of course, be explained to them carefully by counsel and by himself in his summing-up. He realised that this trial was an ordeal for them, and perhaps they would benefit by an afternoon free. 'And perhaps,' he turned to the two in the dock, without altering his tone or his kindness, 'you also will be able to get a little rest.'

During the morning I had noticed Mrs Pateman in the court-room, without her husband. I followed her out, and said that if she cared, I could visit her that afternoon. As I spoke to her (she was looking frightened, her eyes darting round like her daughter's) I noticed that two journalists were watching us. As we knew already, young Charles's forecasts hadn't been entirely wrong.

Going back to Martin, I found him among a knot of lawyers in the hall, all simmering with gossip and rumours. Yes, naturally the defence had wanted to make this plea from the beginning. The only resistance had come from the two women. Or really, said someone, with the satisfaction of a born insider, from one of them. It had been the woman Ross who hadn't co-operated with the psychiatrists. Co-operated about as much as she did in court this morning. The gossip sparked round.

She said that she despised them.

The other one had been willing to play.

But they'd stuck together up to now. If Ross wasn't agreeable, then Pateman wouldn't insist.

Tagging on behind the master, as usual.

The previous two nights, their solicitors had been working on them. So had Ted Benskin. Last night they thought that Ross had given way. If they wanted to switch the case, she'd go along.

Did she go along this morning? You saw her hit the ceiling.

Among the buzz, a quiet voice said that he was wondering whether that wasn't a put-up job. The quiet voice came from a young man, possibly a law student, about the age I had been when I first attended this assize.

He meant, if they were going to prove she wasn't responsible, she had given them something to go on, hadn't she?

An older man said, he didn't believe anyone could act as well as that. She just cracked.

She was horrifying, said another.

If you'd been to many criminal trials, said one of the clerks, you'd be ready to believe anything. She might have been acting, she might not. Everything seemed about as likely or unlikely as anything else. (That thought must have occurred to many in the middle of violent events: or even when hearing that a man like Sawbridge was being watched for espionage.)

Ted Benskin will have to put her in the box, won't he?

A couple of hours later, I was walking along the street, now familiar, now repelling, to the Patemans' house. The smell of curry. The wind, still high, whistled down an entry. Pencilled cards, names of tenants, beside one front door: pop music from a bedroom.

When I rang the bell, Mrs Pateman was there, as though she had been waiting in the passage.

'It's very good of you, I'm sure,' she said.

In the little sitting-room, the fire was bright, as I hadn't seen it when Mr Pateman was there to supervise. Her attempt to welcome me, perhaps? The disinfectant was not so pungent, but the room was still pressingly dark, although through the single window which gave on to the backyard one could see that the sun was coming out. We were alone in the house.

'He's gone off to work today,' she said. She was answering a question I hadn't asked: in his absence, she seemed less diminutive. 'I told him to. It keeps his mind off it, if he's got something to do.'

As for her son, I knew already that, from the day Arnold Shaw's resignation was announced, he had been absenting himself from his new university in order to campaign at his old one. Full restitution for the four dismissed students! Dick Pateman had organised placard-carrying processions (the dismissals were a year old now, and the two bright students were doing well elsewhere). The university gave out the news that, at the summer convocation, the ex-Vice-Chancellor was to receive an honorary degree. More processions by Dick Pateman and his followers. No degree for Shaw! Insult to student body! All this was happening during the police-court proceedings against Dick's sister, and in the weeks before the trial. Could anyone be so fanatical? asked charitable persons such as the Gearys. And they found something like menace in it.

I was trying to explain to Mrs Pateman about the trial. It was all changed now, she understood that, didn't she? The lawyers were going to admit that the boy had been killed.

'They did it, did they?' She seemed less shrewd than on the evening she took me into the empty front room.

'Never mind what happened. You won't hear much more about it.'

'They took him there, didn't they?'

I said, now the whole point was, whatever had happened, they mightn't have been responsible for what they did.

'They're going to say', said Mrs Pateman, flickering-eyed, 'that she's not all there?' With a gesture curiously like a schoolgirl's, she tapped a forefinger against her temple.

'Something like that.' I told her that they would put it in their own language, it would sound strange.

'She did something, of course she did. And they're going to say she's not all there.'

She looked at me with an expression open, confiding, and somehow free from apprehension.

'I can't take it in,' she said.

Margaret and I had been wrong, or at least half-wrong, when we sat in the station buffet imagining her feelings. So far as I could reach her, she wasn't covering up or making excuses. But she spoke as though she were shut off from the facts, or as though they hadn't entered or touched her.

She asked:

'What will they do to her?'

I said it depended on which way the trial now went. If this new plea didn't succeed, she would go to prison ('they'll say for life, but you understand, it doesn't mean anything like that'): if the plea did succeed, then it would probably be a mental hospital.

'When will they let her out?'

'They'll have to be satisfied, you know, that she's not going to be a danger to anyone else.'

'She won't be, they needn't vex themselves about that.'

For an instant I misunderstood her. I thought she was shielding her daughter.

She went on:

'I'm not saying anything for her, she's done whatever she has done. But she's got her head screwed on, has Kitty. She'll be careful, she won't let the police get hold of her again.'

Now that I had understood her, I was astonished. On the instant, that struck me as the strangest thing I had yet heard during the trial.

She glanced at me, her eyes for once meeting mine. She said:

'I can't take it in. I suppose it's a blessing that I can't.'

Yes, she was grateful, but she hadn't been able to pray, she said. She hadn't been able to pray much for a long time.

'He's been praying every day,' she told me. He had taken to going to early-morning service, and then at home, in their bedroom, he prayed out loud each night. He was praying for help against all their dangers and against all the enemies who were working to do harm to him and his.

From her account (was there, even that afternoon, while she was lost and numbed, a trace of slyness?) it seemed he could still believe that Kitty was a victim, so was he; they had been conspired against.

'Sometimes I get frightened about him,' she said.

Not of him, though that must sometimes, perhaps often, have been true. But she was frightened for him. He might hear something in this trial that he couldn't reject or alter. He might not be able to protect himself. She had been worrying for years, worrying since the children had been young, about how much (it was her own phrase) his mind could stand.

CHAPTER XXX

FANTASY AND ACTION

THAT evening Martin and I did not talk in private, for we were having supper with the Gearys. I mentioned that George, for the second day running, had not turned up in court. Within minutes Denis was on the telephone to one of his staff, asking him to find out whether Passant was 'all right'. It didn't take half an hour before the reply came back. There was nothing the matter with him, Denis called to us from the receiver: he would return to the trial when it wasn't a 'waste of time'. That sounded like a direct quotation. I was glancing at Martin as Denis sat down again, giving out a satisfaction similar in kind to Lord Lufkin's in his days of glory, demonstrating how smoothly his organisation worked. We picked up the conversation, quite remote from George, all friendly in the bright clean room. Martin was so disciplined that I couldn't tell where his real thoughts were. It might have been that he had the same difficulty about me.

Next morning, once more in the official box, we were listening to Benskin's opening. It was short and subdued. Subdued out of his normal style, for he had more taste for drama than the other barristers in the case. But he was deliberately adapting himself to the tone of the trial. He had a reputation for wit, and that he had also to suppress. His expression was stiff, the humour strained out of it, as he faced the jury. 'My lord told you yesterday that my learned friend Mr Wilson and I are, on behalf of our clients, asking you to take a new consideration of this crime. I am speaking here in agreement with Mr Wilson, because there is no shade of difference between us, nor, and I want you to remember this, between Miss Ross and Miss Pateman. We do not dispute that this young boy was killed – and everyone in court must want to express the most profound sympathy to his mother and father. We do not dispute that Miss Ross and Miss Pateman were the agents of that killing. That having been admitted by us without reserve, you can dismiss from your minds any minor matters of controversy. I have just stated the central, plain and simple fact. But we now wish to prove to you that, while they were agents for this killing, Miss Ross and Miss Pateman were not responsible for their actions in the sense that you and I would be, if we performed such actions. My lord will instruct you about the nature of the law in relation to diminished responsibility. But perhaps it will be some assistance to you if I read to you from Clause 2 of the Homicide Act 1957. *Persons suffering from diminished responsibility.* He shall not be guilty of murder if he was suffering from such abnormality of mind (whether arising from a condition of arrested or retarded development of mind or any inherent causes or induced by disease or injury) as substantially impaired his mental responsibility. . . . You will notice that the definition is wide. Abnormality of mind – leading to impairment of mental responsibility. If I may, I would like to say a few words about how that clause applies to these two young women and this case. My lord will, I know, correct me if he finds I am at fault. When we claim, and we have no doubt that we shall prove it to you, that they perpetrated this killing with diminished responsibility, or impairment of responsibility, we do not intend to state that, either at the time or now, they were or are clinically insane. You have all probably heard of the old M'Naghten rules under which a defendant was only free from guilt if at the time of his offence he couldn't tell right from wrong. We do not state that either, for these two young women. What we do state is something different, about which we all have to think as clearly and with as little emotion as we can. Let me put it this way. If you and I perform a criminal action, or any other action as far as that goes, we can be assumed to do it in a state of complete responsibility. Or, if you like, free choice. If, for instance, I suddenly assault Mr Bosanquet with this heavy inkwell in front of me' (just for an instant that old-Adam-buffoon was leaking out) 'you will consider me, and I hope rightly consider me, fully and completely responsible for that action. And that is true of you and me in every action, decision and choice right through our lives.' (Benskin had taken a First in Greats, but he wasn't proposing to puzzle the jury with any of the textbook questions.) 'That', Benskin went on, 'is the normal condition of normal people. It is true of you and me. It is true of nine hundred and ninety-nine people out of one thousand in the world round us. There are some, however, of whom it is not true. You will know this from your own experience. There are some whom we cannot consider responsible for all their actions. Through some defect of personality, or what the Act calls abnormality of mind, they cannot stop performing actions which may be foolish or may be anti-social or may be hellish. We suggest to you – I am only saying we suggest because we are certain – that that is the case with the two young women in the dock. Their actions have been hellish. I should be the last person to minimise how appalling and unspeakable they are. But we suggest that Miss Ross and Miss Pateman were not responsible for these actions. Clearly we want the help of eminent experts who will give us their professional judgment about these young women's personalities and mental condition. I shall begin straightaway by calling Dr Adam Cornford.'

Adam Cornford. Qualifications. First classes, research fellowship at Trinity, membership of the Royal College of Physicians, psychiatric training. Few groups had ever had more academic skills than his family and Margaret's and their Cambridge relatives. Like a number of tnem, like Margaret herself, he looked abnormally young for his age. He was actually forty-six, within months of Margaret's age. His hair was fair, he was good-looking in a fashion at the same time boyish, affable and dominating. His voice, as with Austin Davidson, was light and clear.

From the beginning, he spoke unassumingly, without any affectation, but also like a man who hadn't considered the possibility of being outfaced. Yes, he had been asked to examine Miss Ross. He ought to explain that he hadn't been able to make as complete a psychiatric examination as he would have wished. At their first meeting, she wouldn't communicate. We'll come to that later, said Benskin. She did talk to you at later meetings?

To some extent, said Adam Cornford. Then he went on, stitch-and-thread through the questions, Cornford easy but conscientious, Benskin as clever, trying to smudge the qualifications down. Miss Ross was in intelligence well above the average of the population. She was not in any recognised sense psychotic. She had some marked schizoid tendencies, but not to a psychotic extent. A great many people had schizoid tendencies, including a high proportion of the most able and dutiful citizens. Those tendencies were often correlated with obsessive cleanliness and hand-washing, as with Miss Ross. It was important not to be confused (Cornford threw in the aside) by professional jargon: it was useful to psychiatrists, but could mislead others. Schizophrenia was an extreme condition, which Miss Ross was nowhere near, and she was no more likely to be afflicted by it than many young women of her age.

'Nevertheless, Doctor Cornford, you would say her personality is disturbed?'

'Yes, I should say that.'

'You would say that she has a personality defect?'

'I've never been entirely happy about the term.'

'But, in the sense we often use it in cases such as this, it applies to her?'

'I think I can say yes.'

'She has in fact an abnormality of mind?'

'Again, in the sense the law uses that expression, I should say yes.'

All of a sudden there was a quiet-toned legal argument. Cornford had been called as a witness to the mental state of Cora Ross: he said that he could do it 'in any sort of depth' only if he could discuss her relation with Miss Pateman. By permission of her lawyers, he had been able to conduct professional interviews with Kitty Pateman: who, so Cornford said, had been much more forthcoming than her partner and had given him most of the knowledge he had acquired. Wilson (this had, it was clear, been prearranged) told the judge that he welcomed Dr Cornford giving any results of his examination of Miss Pateman. The judge asked Bosanquet if he wished to raise an objection. For some moments, Bosanquet, hesitated: he wasn't spontaneous, he was hedging on protocol: it was, I thought, his first tactical mistake during the trial.

'I should like to give the defence every opportunity to establish the prisoners' states of mind, Mr Recorder,' said the judge.

'The position is very tangled, my lord.'

'Do you really have a serious objection?'

'Perhaps I needn't sustain it against your lordship.' Politely, not quite graciously, Bosanquet gave an acceptant smile.

Cornford had listened, he said, to both of them about their relationship. It was intense. Probably the most important relationship in either of their lives. That was certainly so with Miss Ross. She had said, in a later interview, when she was putting up less resistance, that it was all she lived for.

Benskin: I have to put this question, Doctor Cornford. This was an abnormal relationship?

Cornford (harmoniously): I shouldn't choose to call it so myself.

Benskin: Why not?

Cornford: I don't like the word abnormal.

Benskin: Most people know what it means.

Cornford: Most people think they do. But persons in my profession learn to doubt it. If you ask me whether there was a sexual element in the relation of Miss Ross and Miss Pateman, then the answer is, of course, yes. If you ask whether there was any direct sexual expression, then the answer is also yes.

But it was easy to misunderstand some homosexual relations, Cornford said. Persons outside thought the rôles were easily defined. Often they were not. In this case Miss Ross appeared to be playing the predominantly masculine rôle. When that happened, it could throw a weight of guilt upon the other partner: for Miss Pateman was behaving like a woman, without the full satisfactions, without the children, that in her feminine rôle she was ready to demand. That might be particularly true of her, because in her family the women seemed to be expected to be submissively feminine, more than ordinarily so (was that the total truth? had Cornford had any insight into Mrs Pateman?). Perhaps that was why she had sought a relation with a woman – so as to be feminine, and rebel against males, at one and the same time. But in doing so, she took upon herself more guilt, more a sense of loss and strangeness, than Miss Ross.

For Miss Ross had lived an isolated life, without those intense family pressures. Her father had deserted her mother, her mother had died young. She had been supported by an uncle. In adolescence she had been somewhere near, without being part of, a circle without many constraints. They were committed to a creed of personal freedom. She had made acquaintances there, but not close contacts. Perhaps she was too indrawn a character, or perhaps she was already finding it necessary to make a masculine compensation.

She had, said Cornford, an unusual degree of immaturity. For example, she preserved every scrap of printed matter – programmes of cinema-shows they had attended together, even bus tickets – relating to Miss Pateman. That sometimes happened in an intense relation, but he had never seen it carried to this extent. She had drawers full of objects which Miss Pateman had touched, including handkerchiefs and sheets.

In a different fashion, Miss Pateman showed her own, not quite so unusual, signs of immaturity. She kept up a large collection of dolls, and apparently took one or two with her whenever she left home.

Through the questions and answers – Benskin was skilfully feeding him – Cornford, unflustered, equable, drew his psychological profiles. It sounded, to listeners in court not used to this kind of analysis, strangely abstract, a dimension away from the two women's bodies in the dock. Several times, in the midst of the articulate, lucid replies, I glanced at them. Cora had her head thrown back, almost for the first time in the trial. So far as she was showing emotion, it looked something like pride: but beside her Kitty was frowning, her face crumpled with anger, her eyes sunk and glittering, as in a patient with a wasting disease, when the skin is bronzing and the eyes sinking in.

Benskin Q Cornford A. The two young women found each other, they responded to complementary needs, they were driven to escape from unsatisfactory environments. Very soon they began to live in a private world. A private world with their own games, rules, fancies. That was very common in many intense relationships. It was part of a good many marriages. It could be a valuable part. A married couple got great exaltation from living in a world made for two. This happened frequently in intense homosexual relationships. Sometimes it gave them unusual depth and strength. But it had dangers, if the relationship was overloaded with guilt. As in the case of Miss Ross and Miss Pateman. When there was a component of bad sex rather than good sex. When the sexual expression was not full or free or sufficient in itself. That needn't happen in a homosexual relation: far more often than not it didn't: very occasionally it did. It was rarer, but not unknown, in heterosexual relations also.

Benskin: Can you explain the dangers you are referring to, Doctor?

Cornford: One of them is sometimes called *folie à deux*. That is, the partners may incite each other to fantasies which neither would have imagined if left to him or her self.

Benskin: And these fantasies may be transferred into action?

Cornford: In extreme cases, there is a danger that that may happen.

We didn't know, said Cornford, why the gap between fantasy and action — which in most of us is wide and never crossed — should in those extreme cases cease to exist. If we did know that, we should understand more of the impulses behind some criminal actions. If he were going to admit the term personality defect, he might apply it to those impelled to carry such fantasies into action.

Benskin: That would apply to Miss Ross?

Cornford: That would apply equally to Miss Ross and Miss Pateman.

They had certainly made fantasies about having children in their charge. That was not uncommon in relations like theirs, overshadowed by guilt: especially so when one of the partners was a woman deprived, or a mother *manquée*, like Miss Pateman. There was a strong maternal aspect in her feeling for Miss Ross. In many such relationships, similar fantasies existed. They had played imaginary games of parents and children (that reminded me of the Superintendent's homely tone). But it was an extreme case of *folie à deux* that led them to translate that game into a plan—

They had made fantasies about ultimate freedom. They had heard of people who talked about being free from all conventions: they had met people who prided themselves on not obeying any rules. They felt superior because they were breaking the rules themselves: that was not inconsistent with unconscious guilt, in fact it often went hand-in-hand with it. But they excited each other into being freer than anyone round them. They made fantasies about being lords of life and death. They thought of having lives at their mercy. That again was not unknown – particularly in relations with a coloration of what he (Cornford) had previously called 'bad sex'. But it was very rare for the impulse to be so uncontrollable as to carry over into action.

Guilty relationships, the more so if the guilt was not conscious, had a built-in tendency to lead to further guilt. One had done something which one couldn't thrust away or live with peacefully or reconcile with one's nature: with many people in that position, there grew a violent impulse to do something which one could face even less. Guilty relationships pushed both partners further to the extreme. All guilt had a tendency towards escalation.

That might be true, I was thinking: it was certainly true of some that I had known. A few people, dissatisfied with their lives, tried to re-shape them. But there were many more like George, who couldn't take his pleasures innocently, who felt, at least when he was young, attacks of remorse – and yet couldn't help getting more obsessed with the chase of pleasure, never mind the risks, never mind who got hurt. He knew that those who accused him or mourned over him were right: well, to hell with them, he'd give them twice as much to be right about.

The gap between fantasy and action. Those who jumped it – Benskin got back to business – had some serious – in the terms of the Act – abnormality of mind? There was some fencing about definitions. Cornford, so confident in his own line, was intellectually a conscientious and modest man. He wasn't prepared to trust himself in semantics or metaphysics, he said.

Benskin: But if we accept from you that personality defect or abnormality of mind is not an exact term, you would tell us that Miss Ross had features of her personality which drove her into living out her fantasies?

Cornford: I should say that.

Benskin: And that really does mean an abnormality of mind, doesn't it?

Cornford: In the legal sense, I should say yes, without question.

Benskin: Also she couldn't control that part of her personality?

Cornford: I should say that too.

Benskin: That is, while planning and performing those criminal actions, she had far less responsibility for them than a normal person would have?

Cornford: I'm a little worried about the words 'normal person'.

Benskin: Like most of the people you meet, not as patients, doctor, but

in everyday life. Compared with them, her responsibility was impaired?
Very much impaired?

Cornford: Yes, I can say that.

Wilson asked permission to put the same questions about Miss Pateman.
After Cornford had given an identical reply, Benskin finished by saying:

'I should like you to give a clinical opinion. How well, in your judgment,
would Miss Ross's mental state respond to treatment?'

For once Cornford hesitated: but he wasn't hesitating because –
although it was true – this was a long-prepared question by the defence.

He said: 'I can't be as certain as I should like.'

'You told us, you found her difficult to examine?'

'Quite unusually.'

'And the first time, she wouldn't co-operate at all?'

'No.'

'What happened?'

'She told me she had nothing to say.'

'In what terms?'

'Pretty violent ones.'

If one had heard her outburst in court, one could imagine the scene.
Cornford's handsome face was wearing a faint, uncomfortable smile. He
was upset as a doctor: he had his share of professional vanity: and
perhaps, of physical vanity too.

Later meetings had been easier, but it had been hard throughout to
get her to participate.

'What sort of indication is that? About her mental state being treat-
able?'

'Usually it is a bad sign. When a patient hasn't enough insight to
co-operate, then the prognosis is bad.'

Benskin thanked him and sat down. Wilson did not ask similar questions
about Kitty Pateman. Cornford might have said that Kitty Pateman had
more insight, and, though the whole tone of his evidence had been in her
favour, at least as much as Cora's, that final word could have done her
harm.

Bosanquet must have seen the chance to divide the two. But he didn't
take it. His duty was to get them both. It was more than his duty: it was,
as I knew by now, what he believed to be right. Further, as he began to
cross-examine Cornford, I gained the impression that beneath the stubborn
phlegm Bosanquet was irritated. Cornford had the knack, just as Davidson
and the older generation of their families had, of provoking a specific kind
of irritation. They were clever, they were privileged, to outsiders it seemed

that they had found life too easy: they were too sure of their own enlightenment. Bosanquet hadn't found life at all easy: despite his name, his family was poor, he had been to a north-country grammar school. He wasn't sure of his own enlightenment or anyone else's, after living in the criminal courts for thirty years. His first questions were, as usual, paced out and calm but – I thought my ear was not deceiving me – his voice was just perceptibly less bland.

Bosanquet: Doctor Cornford, you have been telling us about the gap between fantasy and action, haven't you?

Cornford: Yes, a little.

Bosanquet: We all have fantasies, you were saying, weren't you, of violent actions. That is, we all have fantasies of putting someone we dislike out of the way?

Cornford: I can't be certain that we all do. But I should have thought that it was a common experience.

Bosanquet: Granted. But not many actually do put someone they dislike out of the way?

Cornford: Of course not.

Bosanquet: As you were saying, the gap between fantasy and action is not often crossed?

Cornford: Precisely.

Bosanquet: And you suggest, when it is crossed, people are driven by forces out of their control, that is, they are not responsible?

Cornford: That is rather further than I intended to go.

Bosanquet: Or, at any rate, their responsibility is diminished?

Cornford: In many cases, not necessarily all, yes, their responsibility is diminished.

Bosanquet: I don't think we have heard you make exceptions before. What exceptions would you make?

Cornford: I don't want to go into the nature of responsibility in general. That's too wide to be profitable.

Bosanquet: But you are prepared to talk about responsibility in particular cases? Such as the present one?

Cornford: Yes, I am.

Bosanquet: This case is, even to those of us who have had more experience of such crimes than we care to remember, a singularly horrible one of sadistic killing. You will agree with that?

Cornford: I am afraid so.

Bosanquet: And you have stated your opinion that the two women who performed it were acting with diminished responsibility?

Cornford: Yes. I have said that.

Bosanquet: And you would say exactly the same of any similar case of sadistic killing?

Cornford: I can only talk as a psychiatrist of this particular case about which I have been asked to express a professional opinion.

Bosanquet: But you would be likely to give the same opinion in any comparable case? Of killing just for the sake of killing?

Cornford: I can't answer that question without knowing the psychiatric background of such a case.

Bosanquet (sternly): I have to ask you as an honest and responsible man. In any such case, where a person or persons had been living in a morbid fantasy world, and then carried out those fantasies in action, you would be likely to say that that was an example of diminished responsibility?

Cornford (after a pause): I should be likely to say that.

Bosanquet: That is really your professional position?

Cornford: That is going too far. It might, in a good many cases, be my professional position.

Bosanquet: Thank you, Doctor Cornford. I should like to suggest to you that this is a curiously circular position. You are saying that, when people commit certain terrible crimes, they wouldn't do this unless there was no gap between fantasy and action: and that therefore they *ipso facto* are acting with diminished responsibility. That is, the very fact of their committing the crimes implies that they are not responsible. Isn't that what you are saying?

Cornford: It is not so simple.

Bosanquet: Isn't it precisely as simple? Committing the crime is proof, according to your position, that they are not responsible. How else are we to understand you?

Cornford: I'm not prepared to generalise. In certain cases, where I can explore the psychological background, I may be convinced that committing the crime is, in fact, a sign of lack of responsibility.

Bosanquet: Surely that is making it very easy for everyone? Don't you see that, if we accept your view, if we accept that people don't commit crimes when they are responsible, we can dispense with a good deal of our law?

Cornford: It is not for me to talk about the law. I can only talk as a psychiatrist. I can only talk about specific persons whom I have examined.

Bosanquet kept at him, but Cornford was quite unruffled. He was intellectually too sophisticated not to have gone through this argument, and what lay beneath it, in his undergraduate days. But he was in court, he was determined not to leave his home ground. And further, he had no patience with what he regarded as pseudo-problems. Free will, determinism, the tragic condition, all the rest, if there had been any meaning to them we should have found the answers, he thought, long ago. He was as positive-minded as Martin, but in the opposite sense. We should each of us die, but he liked making people better while they were alive. He was a good doctor as well as a psychiatrist: he was benevolent as well as arrogant, and his world was a singularly sunny one.

Through the morning and afternoon (the cross-examination was going on after the lunch break) I kept thinking that, in private, he was more variegated than this. He had a touch, as he remarked in his harmonious clinical manner, of the manic-depressive. In the box, however, he was more uniform and consistent than anyone we had heard, reminding me of one of those theologians who set out with sharp good will to reconcile anything with anything else, every fact of life being as natural as every other, everything being overwhelmingly and all-embracingly natural: reminding me also of a military spokesman giving a battle commentary on what might have seemed to be a disaster (and which actually was), explaining it away and encouraging us about the prospects to come.

His profiles-of all our lives, I thought, would have sounded just as sensible, a little sunnier than those lives had been to live. One could imagine how he would have described mine, or Margaret's, or Sheila's, or Roy Calvert's. But one couldn't imagine it all: he had his own insight, lucid, independent. He would have told us things we didn't recognise or admit in ourselves. He would certainly have been more penetrating, and wiser, about George Passant than I had been. If Sheila had been a patient of his, he would have worked his heart out to reconcile her to her existence. He could not have admitted that to her – and at times to the rest of us, though not to him – it was not tolerable to be reconciled. He would have thought that she was resisting treatment: while she would have gone away, not ready to have her vision blurred, even if it meant living in a nightmare.

When he left the box, it was something like a star going off the stage, to be succeeded by a competent character actor. This was the psychiatrist called on behalf of Kitty Pateman, a dark, worried man whose name was Kahn, not so eminent in his profession, nothing like so articulate. In fact, for the rest of the afternoon, he told very much the same story and gave the same opinion. A clear case of abnormality of mind and substantial impairment of responsibility. He gave, to me at least, a strong impression of self-searching and difficult honesty. He did produce one new piece of evidence. At eighteen, a year or two before she met Cora Ross, Kitty had had, without her parents knowing, an affair with a married man. The details were not clear, but Dr Kahn testified that she had suffered a traumatic shock. In his view this had been one of the causes which had driven her into her relation with Cora Ross.

CHAPTER XXXI

TALK ABOUT FREEDOM

THAT was the evening when Martin and I were due for the party at Archibald Rose's house. Driving slowly past the thickening hedges, Martin did not want to talk about the trial. Instead, he was asking me, how much had this bit of the county changed since we were boys? Not much, we thought. It was still surprisingly empty. Now and then a harsh red brick village interrupted the flow of fields. It was a warm day, unusually so for April, windless and pacifying: looking out into the sunshine, one felt anthropocentrically that the pastures, rises and hollows, were pacified too.

Unlike the house to which Vicky had driven me the previous summer, this one lay half-hidden, down beside a wood. When we got inside, there were other dissimilarities, or really perhaps only one: there was nothing like so much money about. Children were running round, Rose's wife, a young woman in her twenties, greeted us, noise beat cheerfully out from what in the nineteenth century might have been used as the morning-room. This had once been a dower house, and was still called that; it hadn't been much restored: from the morning-room, where the party had already begun, the windows gave on to a rose-garden. It was a room which, like the smell of soap in the morning, wiped away *angst*, or certainly the lawyers seemed to find it so. They were all there, the two defence counsel and their juniors, Clive Bosanquet, the Clerk of Assize, the judge's clerk, various young men who could have been pupils in chambers. Glancing through the crowd, I didn't notice any of the solicitors. Plates of cold chicken, duck, tongue, ham, stood on the side-table, glasses, bottles of red and white wine. The Roses weren't as rich as Vicky's business friends, but they spread themselves on entertaining. Rose's wife, one child holding on to her hand, was cheerful among all the men. The lawyers were walking about, plates and glasses in hand, munching, drinking, and above all talking. Martin and I might have been inhibited, as we drove out, from talking about the trial: not so these. For a good part of that evening, they were talking of nothing else. During the war and after, Martin had spent plenty of time with high civil servants: he was used to their extremes of discretion: with Rose's uncle Hector, for instance, one had to know him, literally for years, before he would volunteer an opinion about a colleague (which, in his case, was then not specially favourable). Martin hadn't seen lawyers relaxing in private during a trial. Ted Benskin, more than ever glinting with grim mimicry, came up and asked what we thought of Cornford's evidence. Bosanquet was standing by. Martin, not certain of the atmosphere, feeling his way, gave a noncommittal reply.

'We should all like to know,' said Ted Benskin. 'I'm damned if I do.'

A young man (I took him to be a pupil of Bosanquet's, not long down from the university) said: either we are all responsible for our actions, or else no one is.

'I wish,' said Bosanquet, gazing at him like a patient, troubled ox, 'I wish I were as certain about anything as you are about everything.'

'But if you were on that jury,' said Archibald Rose, more positive than his leader, 'you wouldn't follow the Cornford man—'

Bosanquet said, not eagerly but with weight:

'No. I couldn't do that.'

'If you were old Jumbo,' said someone, 'and summing up, what would you tell them?'

'What will old Jumbo tell them, anyway?'

Someone else said: if we're not responsible for abominable actions, then we're not responsible for good ones. If you explain one set away, then you explain the other. It's the ultimate reduction.

Ten Benskin said:

'Anyway, I've got to put my woman in the box. I wish I could get out of it, but I can't. Clive knows that.'

Bosanquet gave a professional smile. If Cora Ross didn't give evidence for herself, the inference was, it was because she might appear too sane.

'It's worse for Jamie here,' said Benskin. He pointed to Wilson, who was standing a little apart, looking handsome, hard, distracted. After a while, simply because he looked so miserable, I went into a corner and spoke to him alone. None of them was unaffected: but he was more affected than any. At a first glance in court, I had thought him insensitive. It was one of those impressions such as that which Margaret often produced, which were the opposite of the truth.

'Yes, of course, I've got to call her,' he was telling me. 'And I'm afraid she'll destroy anything the psychiatrists say.

'You've met her, haven't you?' he went on. 'I'm afraid she'll seem perfectly lucid. Mind you, I think some of these people are dead wrong,' he nodded towards the middle of the room. 'I accept one hundred per cent what Adam Cornford said. Don't you?'

'You've talked to her yourself?' I asked.

'Of course,' he said, set-faced. 'When I'm defending people, I always insist on getting to know them personally.'

He added:

'It's not pleasant to be tried for anything. Whoever you are and whatever you have done.'

Back among the central crowd, I let Ted Benskin re-fill my glass, while Martin was listening to some of the tougher lawyers. Freedom. Ultimate freedom. They had picked up the phrase from Adam Cornford. They didn't know, as Martin and I did, how once it had been a slogan in George's underground. But they knew that the two women had used it to excite each other. (I could remember a passage from George's diary. 'The high meridian of freedom is on us now. In our nucleus of free people, anyway – and sometimes I think in the world.' That was written in 1930, and I had read it two years later. I hadn't imagined, any more than he had, what was to come.)

'It's done a lot of harm, propaganda about freedom,' said someone.

'Freedom my arse,' said the Clerk of Assize with simpler eloquence.

'Keep your heads, now,' said Ted Benskin. 'I tell you, my children are happier than we ever were. And I think they're better for it.'

'We need a bit of order, though,' said Bosanquet.

'You're getting old, Clive.'

'Order is important.' Bosanquet was as unbudgeable as in court. 'This country is getting dirtier and sillier under our eyes.'

'Happiness isn't everything,' said someone. 'Perhaps it isn't the first thing.'

'I tell you,' said Benskin, 'if ever there was a time to keep our heads, this is. By and large, there's been more gain than loss.'

Other lawyers rounded on him. How could anyone spend his life in the criminal courts, and believe that? Benskin replied that he did spend his life in the criminal courts: that he proposed to go on doing so, and give them all a great deal of trouble: and that he still believed it.

There were a number of strong personalities round us, clashing like snooker balls: Benskin was ready to go on clashing all night. As he stood there, shorter than the rest of us, with his urchin grin, one of the clerks began to speak of 'topping' (he was using the criminals' slang for hanging). The 1957 Act was a nonsense. You couldn't have categories of murder. Why was the murder in this case non-capital, whereas if they had shot the child—?

Mrs Rose, who by this time had put her family to bed, said with a firm young woman's confidence that she was in favour of capital punishment. Good for you, shouted one of the lawyers. So far as I could tell, there was a majority in support – certainly not Wilson, not a couple of the pupils. Benskin hadn't given an opinion. It was Bosanquet who spoke.

'No,' he said, as steady as ever. 'I've always been against it. And I still am.'

Some rough comments flew about, until, in a patch of quietness, a voice said without inflection:

'Even in a case like this?'

'Yes,' said Bosanquet. 'In a case like this.'

Tempers were getting higher – Benskin, who seemed to have a passion for buttling second only to Arnold Shaw's, was uncorking another bottle – when Archibald Rose mentioned that day's appointments to the bench. It might have been a host's tact: he had been disagreeing with his leader: anyway, whether it was a relief or a let-down, it worked. Two new appointments to the High Court. One was (I hadn't noticed it in *The Times* that morning) an old acquaintance of mine called Dawson-Hill. Bosanquet, who might reasonably have expected the job himself, was judicious. Benskin, who mightn't, being years too young, wasn't. 'We don't want playboys up there,' he said. 'He's just got there because he's grand, that's all—'

'But why is he all that grand?' I asked. I was genuinely puzzled. It was one of those English mysteries. Everyone agreed that Dawson-Hill was grand or smart or a social asset, whatever you liked to call it. But it was difficult to see why. His origins were similar to Rose's or Wilson's in this room, perhaps a shade better off: nothing like so lofty as those of Mr Justice Fane, and no one thought Fane excessively smart.

'That bloody school,' said Benskin, meaning Eton.

'He went to our college,' said Martin. 'And that's about as grand as the University Arms.'

'He must have made a mistake that time,' said Benskin with a matey grin. 'Anyway, you can't deny it, any of you, no dinner party in London is complete without our dear D-H.'

As he drove down the path, away from the party, Martin remarked:

'To say that was a popular appointment would be mildly overstating the case, wouldn't it?'

Gazing over the wheel into the headlight zone, he wore a pulled-down smile. The back-chat about Dawson-Hill had softened the evening for him. He was a man whose emotional memory was long, sometimes obsessive, at least as much so as mine. Often he found it harder for his mood to change. For the past three days he hadn't been able to shrug off what he had been listening to. It had lightened him to be in the company of men who could. Driving on, he was asking me about them, half-amused, half-envious. They were less hard-baked than he expected, most of them, weren't they? Yes, I said, criminal lawyers seemed to have become more imaginative since my time. But the jobs mattered, Martin was smiling, they were pretty good at getting back out of the cold? Archibald Rose had been talking to him seriously about when he should take silk. They were pretty good at getting back on to the snakes-and-ladders, weren't they? Of course they were, I said. I nearly added – but didn't, since I was feeling protective towards my brother, as though we were much younger – that I had heard him written off as a worldly man.

Through the dark countryside, odd lights from the wayside cottages, I was thinking, he must know it all. How often had we said, political memory lasted about a fortnight. Legal memory lasted about a day after a trial. You had to forget in order to get along. It made men more enduring: it also made them more brutal, or at least more callous. One couldn't remember one's own pain (I had already forgotten, most of the time, about my eye), let alone anyone else's. In order to live with suffering, to keep it in the here-and-now in one's own nerves, one had to do as the contemplatives did, meditating night and day upon the Passion: or behave like a Jewish acquaintance of Martin's and mine, who, before he made a speech about the concentration camps, strained his imagination, sent up his blood-pressure, terrified himself, in confronting what, in his own flesh, it would be truly like.

When the car stopped in front of the Gearys' house, Martin got out with me. It was bright moonlight, still very warm. Martin said: 'It's a pleasant night. Do you want to go to bed just yet?' We made our way through the kitchen, out into the garden. Upstairs a light flashed on in the Gearys' bedroom, and Denis yelled down, Who's there? I shouted back that it was us. Good, Denis replied: should he come and give us a drink? No, we had had enough. Goodnight then, said Denis thankfully. Lock up behind you and don't get cold.

We sat on a wooden seat at the end of the garden. On the lawn in front of us, there were tree-shadows thrown by the moon. It reminded me of gardens in our childhood, when, though the suburb was poor, there was plenty of greenery about. It reminded me of Aunt Milly's garden, and I said:

'After all, it's the twentieth century.'

For a moment, Martin was lost, and then he gave a recognising smile. It had been a phrase of hers which obliterated all threats, laughed off the prospect of war (I could hear her using it in July 1914, when I was eight years old), and incidentally promised the triumph of all her favourite causes, such as world-wide teetotalism. She had used it indomitably till she died.

After all, it was the twentieth century. We had heard others, who had found their hopes blighted and who had reneged on them, call it (as Austin Davidson did, and most of his friends) this dreadful century. Neither Martin nor I was going to know what our children would call it, when they were the age we had reached now.

Martin lit a cigar. The smell was strong in the still air. After a time he said:

'There was a lot of talk about freedom.'

'You mean, among the lawyers? Tonight?'

'Not only there.'

Not able to stop himself, he had returned to the two women. Ultimate freedom. The limitless talks. More than most people, certainly more than any of the lawyers or spectators at the trial, Martin and I could re-create those talks. For we had heard them, taken part in them. 'What is to tie me down, except myself? It is for me to will what I shall accept. Why should I obey conventions which I didn't make?' It was true that, when we had heard them, those declarations were full of hope. George's great cries had nothing Nietzschean about them. They were innocent when they proclaimed that there was a fundamental 'I' which could do anything in its freedom. When you started there, though, Martin said, in an even, sensible tone, you could go further. Wasn't that what the man Cornford was getting at with his 'escalation'?

'Do you believe,' asked Martin, 'that – if it hadn't been for all the hothouse air we used to know about – those two mightn't have done it?'

He spoke without emotion, rationally. The question was pointed for us both. We were gazing out to the moonlit lawn, like passengers on the boatdeck gazing out to sea. Without looking at him, I spoke, just as carefully. It was impossible to prove. Was there ever any single cause of any action, particularly of actions such as this? Yes, they must have been affected by the atmosphere round them, yes, they were more likely to go to the extreme in their sexual tastes. Perhaps it made it easier for them to share their fantasies. But between those fantasies, and what they had done, there was still the unimaginable gap. Of course there were influences in the air. But only people like them, predisposed to commit sadistic horrors anyway, would have been played on to the lethal end. If they had not had these influences, there would have been others.

'Your guess is as good as mine,' I said. 'But I think that wherever they'd been, they'd have done something horrible.'

'Are you letting everyone off?' he said.

'I was telling you, I don't know the answer, and nor does anyone else.'

'I grant you that,' said Martin.

We were not arguing, our voices were very quiet. He said – in a quite different society, more rigid, more controlled, was there a chance that they would never have killed? He answered his own question. Maybe there might be less of these sexual crimes. Perhaps such a society could reduce the likelihood. 'But, if you're right,' he said, 'no one could answer for those two.'

He had turned to me, speaking quite gently. He thought that I might be making excuses for us all: yet they were excuses he wanted to accept. He also knew that I was as uncertain as he was.

All of a sudden, his cigar-tip glowing in the shadow, he gave a curious smile. In an instant, when he spoke again, I realised that he had been thinking of a different society. 'I have seen the future. And it works.' That had been Steffens's phrase, nearly fifty years before. When Martin repeated it, there was in his tone the experience of all that had happened since. He went on, in the same tone, not harsh, not even cynical: 'I have seen freedom. And it rots.'

In some moods, he might have said it with intention. But not that night; it was one thought out of many, often contradicting each other, that he couldn't keep out of his own mind and could suspect in mine. In fact, he took the edge off his last words almost at once. Anyway, he was saying, unabrasively, as though he too had had his memory shortened, as though he were just content with the calm night, there was something in what Ted Benskin had said, wasn't there? Authority might have disappeared, there wasn't much order about, but our children, like Ted's, seemed happy. Not that there had been much paternal authority in our family; Martin was smiling about our father. 'Whereas,' he said, 'young Charles has to put up with you.'

Martin knew Charles very well, in his independence, his secret ambitions, and his pride. They were unusually intimate for uncle and nephew. In some aspects, their temperaments were more like each other than either was like mine.

Martin leaned back, giving out an air of bodily comfort: we seemed to have regressed to a peaceful family night.

'By the by,' he said, 'I meant to have a word with you about my boy' – (he never liked calling Pat by his name of protest).

This wasn't altogether casual, I knew as I said yes. He had been holding it back all week.

'You told me once, it must have been getting on for a year ago, about that nice girl. Vicky,' Martin went on.

'What about her?'

'I think someone ought to make her realise that it's all off.'

'Are you sure?'

'I shouldn't be saying this,' said Martin, 'unless I really was sure.'

'It's for him to do it,' I said, both angry and sad. I wanted to say (the old phrase came back, for which we hadn't found a modern version) that it would break her heart.

'He's genuinely tried, I really am sure of that too. I don't often defend him, you know that.' Martin, who did not as a rule deceive himself, spoke as though he believed that was the truth. 'But he has genuinely tried. She's been hanging on long after there's been nothing there. It's the old story, how tenacious women can be, once they're in love.'

'It's absolutely over for him? He won't go back and play her up again?'

'I guarantee he won't.'

'He's not above leaving a thread he likes to twitch. When he's got nothing better to do.'

'Not this time,' said Martin.

'Why are you so sure?'

'I'm afraid that he's made up his mind. Or someone else has made up his mind for him.'

Martin was speaking with kindness of Vicky, more than kindness, the sympathy of one who was fond of women and who might have felt his eyes brighten at the sight of this one. But he was also speaking with obscure satisfaction, as though he had news which he couldn't yet share but which, when he forgot everything else, gave him well-being, and, as he sat there beside me in the garden, something like animal content.

CHAPTER XXXII

QUALITY OF A LEADER

BACK in court the following morning, we were listening to more psychiatrists, as though this were the normal run of our existence and the family conversation in a garden as unmemorable as a dream. These were the psychiatrists called by the prosecution, and we knew in advance that there would be only two. That was planned as the total evidence in rebuttal, and they were as careful and moderate as the defence doctors, without even the occasional wave of Adam Cornford's panache. In the result, though, through the moderate words, they were each saying an absolute no.

Obviously by pre-arrangement – as I whispered to Martin, sitting at my side in the box – neither Benskin nor Wilson pressed the prison psychiatrist far. Bosanquet had questioned him about his knowledge of the prisoners: yes, he had had them under observation since they were first arrested. He was a man near to retiring age, who had spent his whole career in the prison service: he had seen more criminals, psychotics, psychopaths, than anyone who had come into court, and yet he still spoke with an air of gentle surprise. Miss Ross and Miss Pateman had shown no detectable signs of mental disorder. Some slight abnormality, perhaps, nothing more. Medically, their encephalograms were normal. He had conducted prolonged interviews with Miss Pateman: Miss Ross had, under examination, not usually been willing to discuss her own history. So far as he could judge, they were intelligent. Miss Pateman had asked for supplies of books from the prison library. Their behaviour was not much different, or not different at all, from other prisoners held on serious charges. Miss Pateman exhibited certain anxiety symptoms, including chronic sleeplessness, and her health had caused some concern. Miss Ross had a tic of obsessive hand-washing, but this she admitted was not new or caused by her being in prison. Neither had at any time been willing to speak of the killing. Occasionally Miss Ross went in for something like talking to herself, monologues about what appeared to be imaginary scenes, in which she and Miss Pateman figured alone.

'None of this has made you consider that they are not responsible for their actions?'

'No.'

'From all your observations, you would not consider that they acted in a state of diminished responsibility?'

548

'No. I'm afraid I can't give them that.'

'After your long experience, you are positive in your opinion?'

'I am.'

It was while Benskin, in his first questions, was asking the doctor to say what he meant by a 'slight abnormality of mind', that Martin, plucking my sleeve, pointed to the body of the court. Since the morning before, when the medical evidence had begun, the attendance had fallen off, as in a London theatre on a Monday night: the gallery was almost empty that morning, and the lower ranges only half-full: but there (he had not been present at the beginning of the session, he must have entered during the Crown examination) sat George. His great head stood out leonine; he was staring at the witness box with glaucous eyes.

I scribbled on the top of a deposition-sheet *We shall have to sit with him this afternoon.* As Martin read that, he nodded, his brow furrowed, all the previous night's relaxation gone.

Benskin was asking, weren't those opinions subjective, wasn't it difficult or impossible even for an expert to be absolutely certain about some mental conditions? Could anyone in the world be certain about some mental conditions? Weren't there features of the doctor's observations, given in his examination-in-chief, which might be regarded as pointers to deep abnormality—? Just for an instant, Benskin (who often suffered from the reverse of *l'esprit de l'escalier*, who thought of the bright remark, made it, and then wished he hadn't) was tempted away from his own strategy. He began to ask when 'our expert' had last been in touch with professional trends? Had he read—? Benskin shook himself. The jury wouldn't like it, this was an elderly modest man, the sooner he was out of the box the better. The tactic was to reserve the attack for the heavyweight witness. Disciplining himself, anxious at having to waive a marginal chance, Wilson kept to the same line. He asked a few questions about Miss Pateman's state of health, her record of psychosomatic illness, and then let the doctor go.

The heavyweight witness was a Home Office consultant, brought in as a counterpoise to Adam Cornford. When Bosanquet asked 'Is your name Matthew Gough?', that meant nothing to almost everyone in court, and yet, before he answered the question at all, during the instant while he was clambering up to the box, he had been recognised, as no one else had been recognised in the whole trial. The fact was, he appeared often on television, under the anonymous label of psychiatrist, giving his views – articulately, but with as little fuss as Cornford in court – on crime, delinquency, abortion, homosexuality, drugs, race relations, censorship and the phenomena relating to Unidentified Flying Objects. On the television screen he gave the impression of very strong masculinity. In the witness-box this impression became more prepotent still. He was dark haired, vulture faced, with a nose that dominated his chin. Despite his peculiar kind of anonymous fame, which brought him some envy, his professional reputation was high. He wasn't such an academic flyer as Adam Cornford, but his practice – in a country which didn't support many private psychiatrists – was at least as large. He was said to have had a powerful and humane influence upon the Home Office criminologists. I had heard also that he was – this came as a surprise in his profession – a deeply religious man.

In the box, his manner was kind, not assertive, but with a flow of feeling underneath. He had, he answered, spent a good many hours with each of the two women. He had found Miss Ross – in this he was odd-man-out from the other doctors – as communicative as Miss Pateman, sometimes more completely so. It was true that occasionally she put up total 'resistance': but his judgment was that this was deliberate, and could be broken when she wanted. Not that he blamed her, that was one of her protective shields, such as we all had. To the puzzlement of many, he differed flatly from the others in his attitude to Cora Ross; he seemed to find her more interesting, or at least more explicable, than Kitty. Miss Ross's father had left her mother when she was an infant; not much was known about him, Miss Ross's memory of him was minimal and her mother was dead: there was some suggestion that he had been (and possibly still was, for no one knew whether he was alive) mentally unstable. He had been an obsessive gambler, but that might have been the least of it. Miss Ross had been left alone in her childhood more than most of us: it had been an unusually lonely bringing-up. Perhaps that had conduced both to her immaturity (about which he agreed with Cornford) and to the sadistic fantasies, which she had certainly been possessed by since an early age: but that was common to many of us, so common that the absence was probably more 'abnormal' than the presence.

Without emphasis Bosanquet led Matthew Gough over the descriptions Cornford had given. It was a good examination, designed to show that Gough was as unprejudiced as the other men. Yes, Miss Ross had lived on the fringe of a free-living group. If she had been less timid or inhibited, that might have 'liberated' her. Actually it had driven her further into herself. It was hurtful to live in a Venusberg without taking part oneself.

As for her relation with Kitty, he had some doubts about Cornford's analysis. He wouldn't dismiss it altogether: but 'guilt' used in that fashion was a technical term. He wasn't easy about this concept of the escalation of guilt. Many homosexual or perverse relations were quite free of it. 'Bad sex', in Cornford's sense, was very common: it did not often lead to minor violence, let alone to sadistic killing; it was very dangerous, and unjustified, to try to define a simple causation.

Bosanquet : You would not accept then, Dr Gough, that this relation in any way diminished their responsibility?

Gough : No.

Bosanquet : Or that any other feature of their personal history did so?

Gough : No.

On Kitty Pateman, he said one puzzling thing (which I half missed, since just at that time the judge's clerk entered our box, giving me his lordship's compliments, and asking if I would care to lunch with him on the coming Monday). He was speaking about her environment: while Cora had grown up solitary, Kitty had lived her whole childhood and youth in a close family life – as intense, I was thinking, as the fug in that stifling sitting-room. That was a good environment, said Gough. Stable, settled, affectionate. This must have been his own interpretation of Kitty's account – or had she misled him? Gough was disposed to believe devotedly in family life, I was thinking. It was then that he surprised me. But even in a stable family, he said, there could be wounds – which only the person wounded might know. Was he being massively fair-minded, or had he picked up a clue?

In the specific case of Miss Pateman, it seemed that she might have had an excessive attachment to her father. But he, Gough, could not regard that as a cause of her later actions. That was over-simplifying. Her relation with Miss Ross, her part in the crime – no one could identify the origins.

Bosanquet : You discussed the crime with her, Doctor?

Gough : With each of them. On several occasions.

Bosanquet : Were they willing to describe it?

Gough : Up to a point.

Bosanquet : Will you elaborate that, please?

Gough : They were prepared to describe in detail, almost hour by hour, how they planned to kidnap the boy. They told me about what happened at the cottage and how they brutalised him. But they wouldn't go beyond the Sunday afternoon. Miss Pateman said they had finished punishing him by then. Neither of them at any time gave any account of how they killed him.

Bosanquet: Were they at this stage still pretending that they hadn't done so?

Gough: I think not.

Bosanquet: Why wouldn't they speak of what they did to him after the Sunday afternoon, then?

Gough: They each said, several times, that they had forgotten.

Bosanquet: That is, they were concealing it?

Gough: Again I think not. I believe it was genuine amnesia.

Bosanquet: You really mean, they had *forgotten* killing that child?

Gough: It is quite common for someone to forget the act of killing.

In his last question Bosanquet had, quite untypically, inflected his voice. For once he was at a loss. We realised that he was getting an answer he didn't expect, and one that the defence might return to (Benskin was muttering to his junior). In an instant, Bosanquet had recovered himself: with steady precision he brought out his roll-call of final questions, and the doctor's replies fell heavily into the hush.

'It has been suggested by some of your colleagues,' said Bosanquet, 'that a sadistic killing of this kind couldn't be performed by persons in a state of unimpaired responsibility. You know about that opinion?'

'Yes. I know it very well.'

'How do you regard it?'

'I respect it,' said Gough. 'But I cannot accept it.'

'This kind of planned cruelty and killing is no proof of impaired responsibility, you say? I should like you to make that clear.'

'In my judgment, it is no proof at all.'

'People can perpetrate such a crime in a state of normal responsibility?'

'I believe so. I wish that I could believe otherwise.'

He added those last words almost in an aside, dropping his voice. Very few people in court heard him, or noticed the sudden lapse from his manner of authority. Later we were remarking about what had moved him: did he simply feel that, if to be cruel one had to be deranged, there would be that much less evil in the world? And he found that thought consoling, but had to shove it away?

'And that was true of the actions of Miss Pateman and Miss Ross?'

'I believe so.'

'You are certain?'

'Within the limits of my professional knowledge, I am certain.'

'You would not agree that either of them had a real abnormality of mind?'

'We must be careful here. In each of them there is a degree of abnormality. But not enough, in the terms of the Act, to impair substantially their mental responsibility.'

'Their responsibility was not impaired? Not substantially impaired?'

'No.'

'That is true of neither of them?'

'Of neither of them.'

That was the last answer before the lunch-time break. Hurrying out of court in order to catch up with George, we saw him walking away, not looking back. When I called out, it was some time before he heard or stopped. He didn't greet us, but as we drew near him, stared at us with a gentle, absent-minded, indifferent smile. He gave the impression that he had not noticed we had been present in the court. Instead of insisting on showing us a place to eat, as he had done with Margaret and me on the first morning, he scarcely seemed to know where he was going. He was quite docile, and when Martin suggested having a sandwich in a snack bar George answered like a good child, yes, that would be nice.

As the three of us sat on backless chairs at the counter, George in the middle, he did not speak much. When he replied to a question, he did not turn his face, so that I could see only his profile. Trying to stir him, I mentioned that, the previous day, the defence doctors had given strong evidence, precisely contrary to what he had just heard.

'Yes, thank you,' said George. 'I rather assumed that.'

He was just as polite when he replied to Martin, who made some conversation on his other side. I brought out the name of Bosanquet, hoping to hear George curse again. He said:

'He's leading for the prosecution, isn't he?'

After that, he sat, elbows on the counter, munching. One could not tell whether he was daydreaming or lost in his own thoughts: or sitting there, dead blank.

When we led him back into the court-room, Martin and I exchanged a glance. It was a glance of relief. There was a larger crowd than in the morning, but still the lower tiers of seats were not full, and we sat, George once more between us, three rows back from the solicitors, gazing straight up into the witness-box. Then, the judge settled, the court quiet, Gough took his place. At once Benskin was on his feet, neat and small, wearing a polite, subdued smile.

'I put it to you, Doctor,' he began, 'we agree, do we not, that Miss Ross suffers from a defective personality?'

'To an extent, yes.'

'You agree that she has a defect of personality, but as a matter of degree you don't think that it brings her within the terms of the Act?'

'I certainly don't consider that she comes within the terms of the Act.'

'But it is a matter of degree?'

'In the last resort, yes.'

'I suggest, Doctor,' Benskin said, 'that any opinion in this matter of degree, about defect of personality or of responsibility – in the sense we are discussing them in this case – any opinion is in the long run subjective?'

'I am not certain what you mean.'

'I think you should be. I mean, that of a number of persons as highly qualified as yourself, some might agree with your opinion – and a proportion, possibly a high proportion, certainly wouldn't. Isn't that true?'

'I have said several times', said Gough, showing no flicker of irritation nor of being drawn, 'that I can speak only within the limits of my professional judgment.'

'And many others, as highly qualified as yourself, would give a different professional judgment?'

'That would be for them to say.'

'You would grant that neither you nor anyone else really has any criterion to go on?'

'I agree that we have no exact scientific criterion. These matters wouldn't cost us so much pain if we had.'

'That is, your expert opinion is just one opinion among many? You can't claim any more for it than that?'

'I am giving my own professional judgment.'

'I put it to you, Doctor,' said Benskin, flicking his gown round him as though it were a cape, 'that your judgment shows a certain predisposition. That is, you are more unwilling than many of your colleagues to accept that people can suffer from diminished responsibility?'

'I do not know that you are entitled to say that. I repeat, I have given my professional judgment. I am responsible for that, and for no one else's.'

'But cannot a professional judgment betray a certain predisposition, Doctor? Or prejudice, as we might say in less lofty circles?'

The judge tapped his pen on the desk. 'I think you would do better to avoid words which might suggest that you are imputing motives, Mr Benskin. You are asking Dr Gough about his general attitude or predisposition, and that is permissible.'

'I am obliged to your lordship.' Benskin gave a sharp smile. 'Then I put it to you, Doctor, that you have betrayed a certain predisposition? That you never considered it probable that Miss Ross – or Miss Pateman – were not fully responsible? And you ignored important signs which point the other way?'

'Will you be more specific?'

'Oh yes. I was intending to. You said in evidence that Miss Ross, and Miss Pateman also, had actually forgotten the act of killing. You said, I think these were your words, that it was genuine amnesia. To most of us that would appear to indicate – very sharply – an abnormal state of mind. Impaired responsibility maybe. But not to you, Doctor?'

Gough said, in a tone not argumentative but sad:

'I couldn't regard it so.'

'Why not?'

'I think I also said, this condition is surprisingly common.'

'Surprisingly common?'

'That is, among people who have done a killing, it is common for them to have forgotten the act.'

'Does that signify nothing about them?'

Gough said:

'It is specially common among people who have killed a child. In my experience, I have not once known any case when they could recall the act.'

Benskin had gone too far to draw back. Quietly he said:

'Might not that suggest then a special state of mind, or lack of responsibility, in such cases?'

Gough answered:

'I am afraid not. Not in all such cases. In my experience, that would not be true.'

Benskin was pertinacious. He knew he had lost a point, and was covering it up. He was cleverer than the doctor, quicker witted though not as rooted in his own convictions. I thought later, there were not many better counsel for this type of defence.

Hadn't Doctor Gough glossed over, or explained away, all the other indications of abnormal personality? Their fantasy life: the gap between fantasy and action: Benskin was using Cornford's analysis, jabbing the rival case straight at Gough, trying to make him deny it or get involved in psychiatrists' disputes. Fairly soon Benskin won a point back. Gough hadn't become rattled, he seemed to be a man singularly free from self-regard: but he wasn't so good as Benskin, or as Cornford would have been, in seeing a chess-move ahead. In replying to a question about their fantasy-fugues, Gough let drop the observation: 'But of course they are both intelligent.'

Benskin did not let an instant pass. His eyes flashed at his junior, and he said:

'Ah, now we have it, perhaps. You are predisposed [there was a stress on the word] to believe that persons of adequate intelligence are automatically responsible for their actions?'

'I didn't say that.'

'That is, defects of personality don't really matter, abnormalities of mind don't really matter, if people have a reasonable I.Q.?'

'I repeat, I did not say that.'

'Doctor, it was the implication of your remark.'

'In that case, I shall have to withdraw it.'

'I shall have to ask my lord to make a note of what you actually said. And this gets us in a little deeper, Doctor Gough. I suggested, and you didn't like the suggestion, that you were predisposed to think that Miss Ross and Miss Pateman were fully responsible – perhaps because they were intelligent? No, never mind that. I am now asking you, what sort of persons, in what sort of circumstances, would you ever admit not to be fully responsible? Are there any?'

'I have examined some. And given testimony on their behalf.'

'And what were they like? Were they imbecile?'

'One or two were,' said Gough without hedging. 'By no means all.'

'And the rest. They were grossly and obviously inferior mentally to the rest of us, were they?'

'Some were. Not all.'

'You will see the force of my questions, Doctor. I am not misrepresenting your position – or predisposition – am I? You are extremely reluctant to admit that persons can be afflicted with a lack of responsibility. And can commit criminal actions in that state. You are reluctant to admit that, aren't you?'

'I have given my testimony in favour of some unfortunate people.'

'When they are so pitiable that it doesn't need a doctor to tell us so, isn't that so? But you won't give any weight, as your colleagues do, to a history like Miss Ross's and Miss Pateman's – which isn't as obvious but is, I suggest to you, Doctor, precisely as tragic?'

As he delivered that question, Benskin sat down with a shrug, so as to cut off Gough's reply.

Emotions in the court, provoked and stimulated by Benskin, had risen higher. Mrs Pateman, who was sitting in the row in front, gave me a flickering, frightened glance, so like her daughter's. Whispers were audible all round us, and I could see two of the jury muttering together. As soon as Wilson took his turn to cross-examine, the restlessness became more uncomfortable still: but it seemed to be directed against him, as though the women in the dock had – in the fatigued irritable afternoon – been forgotten. To most spectators, Wilson sounded histrionic, hectoring and false. When he demanded with an angry frown, a vein swelling in his forehead, whether the doctor had deliberately refrained from mentioning Miss Pateman's adolescent breakdown, it rang out like a brassy, put-on performance. The truth was, he was sincere, too sincere. Benskin had enjoyed the dialectic and been in control of himself throughout: but Wilson wasn't, he had become involved, in a fashion that actors would have recognised as living the part. Which almost invariably, by one of the perverse paradoxes, gave an effect of sublime artificiality upon the stage: as it did that day in court. Wilson was totally engaged with Kitty. He felt for her and with her. He believed that she had not had a chance, that all her life she had been fated. So he couldn't repress his anger with Matthew Gough, and almost no one perceived that the anger was real. He even rebuked Gough, Gough of all people, for being flippant. It sounded the most stilted and bogus of rebukes: yet Wilson meant it.

Kitty, who had given up her obsessive note-making since the psychiatric evidence began, listened – often sucking in her lips as though she were thirsty – to her counsel's angry voice. I wondered if she realised that he was struggling desperately for her. I wondered if she was cool enough to speculate on what influence he was having. For myself, I guessed – but my judgment was unstable, I kept foreseeing different ends – that he was doing her neither harm nor good.

That was what I told George as the three of us sat at tea, in the same scented, women-shoppers' café as I had visited in January, the day that I first heard the physical facts of the case. The central heating was still on, though it must have been 70 degrees outside: the hot perfumed air pressed on us, as George asked me: 'Well. What about it?'

I said, things were back where they were. Bosanquet had wasted almost no time at all in re-examining Matthew Gough: he had merely to repeat his opinion. Diminished responsibility? No. Gough, contradicting Cornford, spoke as scrupulously as Cornford himself had spoken the day before.

Now all the evidence was in – except what the two said when they went into the box themselves.

'That won't make much difference,' I said.

557

'Whatever she says, it can't do her any good,' George replied. He lifted his eyes and gazed straight at me.

'What are her chances, then?'

After a moment, I answered:

'Things might go either way.'

George shook his head.

'No. That's too optimistic. You're going in for wishful thinking now.'

I felt – and it was true of Martin also – nothing but astonishment, astonishment with an edge to it, almost sinister, certainly creepy. We had heard George hopeful all his life, often hopeful beyond the limits of reason: now on that afternoon, the trial coming to its close, we heard him reproaching me.

There was another surprise. His manner – one could have said, his mind and body – had totally changed since lunchtime, only three hours before. Then he had been lolling about in a state of hebetude, getting on for catatonic, as helplessly passive as a good many people become in extreme strain. Now he was talking like an active man. In the hot room the sweat was pouring down his cheeks, his breathing was heavy, beneath his eyes the rims were red: but still he had brought out reserves of fire and energy, which no one could have thought existed, seeing him not only that morning but for months past, or even years.

'You're being too optimistic,' he said, with something like scorn mixed up with authority. 'I can't afford to be.'

'George,' said Martin, 'there's nothing you can do.'

'Nonsense,' said George, with an angry shout. 'The world isn't coming to an end. Other people have got to go on living. Some of them I've been responsible for. I don't know whether I'm any further use. But I've got to go on living. What in God's name is the point of telling me that there's nothing I can do?'

Martin said, he meant that there was nothing George could do for his niece.

Still angry, George interrupted him:

'If they send her to a hospital, then I suppose there's a finite possibility that they'll cure her, and I shall have to be on hand. That's obvious to either of you, I should have thought. But as I've told you' – he was speaking to me as though I were a young protégé again – 'that's the optimistic plan. It's over-optimistic, and that's being charitable to you. If they send her to gaol—'

I said: 'I agree, that may happen.'

'Of course it may happen,' he said harshly. 'Well, in that case, I don't expect to be alive when she comes out.'

Was he recognising his state of health? If so, it was the first time I had heard it.

'So I'm afraid that I should have to regard her as dispensable, so far as I am concerned. She won't be out while I'm alive. There are other people I shall have to think about. And what I ought to do myself. That means a second plan.'

Neither Martin nor I could tell whether this was make-believe. He was talking with the decision, buoyed up by the thought of action, such as he used in his days of vigour. He was also talking like the leader which – in his own bizarre and self-destructive fashion – he had always been. When he said that Cora was 'dispensable' (just as when he did not so much as mention Kitty Pateman's name, since she was no concern of his), he was showing – paradoxically, so it seemed – a flash, perhaps a final one, like the green flash at sunset, of the quality which made people so loyal to him. For a leader of his kind needed gusto, and he had had far more than most men: needed generosity of spirit, and no one that I knew had lavished himself more: needed a touch of paranoia, to make his followers feel protective: needed something else. And the something else, when I was young, I should have called ruthlessness. That was glossing it over. It was really more like an inner chill. By this time, I had seen a number of men whom others without thought, as it were by instinct, looked upon as leaders. Some in prominent places: one or two, like George, in obscurity and the underground. Of these leaders, a few, not all, attracted loyalty, sometimes fanatical loyalty, as George did: and they were alike in only one thing, that they all possessed this inner chill. It was the others, who were warm inside, more plastic and more involved, who got deserted or betrayed.

CHAPTER XXXIII

REVENANT

ON the Saturday morning in our drawing-room, Margaret was asking me about my father. A beam of sunlight edged through the window behind me, irradiated half a picture on the far wall, a patch of fluorescent blue. It was all easy and peace-making. Yet it felt unfamiliar that I wasn't catching the bus down to the Assize Hall.

I had returned very late the night before, and we hadn't talked much.

Yes, I told her now, Martin and I had been to visit the old man (actually, we had gone straight from that teatime with George). He had complained vaguely that he wasn't 'quite A.1': but, when we asked what was the matter, he either put us off or didn't know, saying that 'they' were looking after him nicely. 'They' appeared to consist of the doctor and a district visitor who came in twice a week. My father spoke of her with enthusiasm. 'She goes round all the old people who haven't got anyone to look after them,' he said, expressing mild incredulity at the social services. We had told him that it was his own fault that he hadn't someone to look after him, it was his own mule-like obstinacy. But he scented danger, with an old man's cunning he suspected that we were plotting to drag him away. 'I should curl up my toes if anyone shifted me,' he said. His morale seemed to be high. Incidentally, he had with fair consistency called Martin and me by each other's names: but he had done that in our childhood, he was no more senile now than when I last saw him.

Margaret gave a faint smile, preoccupied as to whether we ought to leave him there, how far had we the right to interfere.

Just then Charles, still on holiday, entered in a new dressing-gown, smelling of shaving-soap. Over the last year he had suddenly become careful of his appearance. He said hallo, looking at me with scrutinising eyes. He didn't remind me of his warning, but I hadn't any doubt that he had searched the papers each day. And his forecasts had proved not so far from the truth. There had been references to my presence at the trial, some just news, a few malicious. An enterprising journalist had done some research on my connection with George Passant. He had even latched on to Gough's casual comment the day before. 'Venusberg trial – Lewis Eliot again with boyhood friends.'

Not waiting for Charles to be tactful, I asked if he had noticed that.

He nodded.

'Well?' he said.

'One gets a bit tired of it. But still—'

Margaret gave a curse. I didn't tell him, but he certainly knew that it was true for me, that no one I had known, including the hardest political operators, ever quite got used to it. Instead I said (using reflectiveness to deny the here-and-now, the little sting), that this kind of comment, the mass media's treatment of private lives, had become far more reckless in my own lifetime.

Charles was not much impressed. This was the climate which he had grown up in and took for granted.

'Have you done any good?' he asked.

I thought of George at tea the day before.

'Very little,' I said. 'Probably none at all.'

Charles broke into a broad smile. 'Anyway, we've got to give you credit for honesty, haven't we?' He teased me, with the repetitive family gibes. Margaret was laughing, relieved that we hadn't reverted to our quarrel. Why did I insist on getting into trouble? Even when I wasn't needed? Fair comment, I said, thinking of George again.

I hadn't seen Charles at all the night before, and he hadn't had a chance to enquire about the trial itself. At last he did so. What was it really like?

I looked at them both. I repeated what I had said to Margaret, just before going to sleep.

'It's unspeakable.' Then I added: 'No, that's foolish, we've been speaking about it all the week. But not been able to imagine it.'

I didn't want to talk to him as I had done to Martin: perhaps I should have been freer, if it hadn't been for the sexual heaviness that hung over it all. True, there wasn't much, in verbal terms, that I could tell Charles: he had listened for years to people whose language wasn't restrained, and I was sure the same was true with him and his friends. But together we didn't talk like that. There was a reticence, a father-and-son reticence, on his side as well as mine, when it came to the brute facts, above all the brute facts of this case.

So I said, it had been appalling to listen to. Like an aeroplane journey that was going wrong: stretches of tedium, then the moments when one didn't want to believe one's ears. I couldn't get it out of my experience, I told him.

'I haven't had as much of it as you have,' said Margaret. 'But that's true—' she turned to Charles.

Once more, as with Martin, I was remembering Auschwitz. To these two, I did not need to say much more than the name.

A couple of summers before, when the three of us had been travelling in Eastern Europe, I had left Margaret and Charles in Kraków, and had driven off to the camp with an Australian acquaintance. We had walked through the museum, the neat streets, the cells, in silence. It was a scorching August day, under the wide cloudless Central European sky. At last we came to the end, and were walking back to the car. My acquaintance, who hadn't spoken for long enough, said:

'It's a bastard, being a human being.'

Often this last week, I'd felt like that, I said to Charles. I was certain that his uncle Martin had as well.

Charles was silent, regarding me with an expression that was grave, detached and unfamiliar.

After a few moments, I went on:

'Did you know', I said, 'that there was a medieval heresy which believed that *this* is hell? That is, what we're living in, here and now. Well, they may have a point.'

Charles gazed at me with the same expression. Almost imperceptibly, he shook his head. Then in a hurry, as though anxious not to argue, trying to climb back upon the plane of banter, he asked me, why was it that unbelievers always knew more about theological doctrine than anyone else? However had I acquired that singular fact? He was being articulate, sharp-witted, smiling, determined not to become serious himself again, nor to let me be so.

After tea the following afternoon, when I was in one of the back rooms, Charles called out that there was someone for me on the telephone.

Who was it? He wouldn't say. Soft voice, Charles added – slight accent, north-country perhaps.

I went into the hall, picked up the receiver, asked who was there, and heard:

'This is Jack.'

'Jack who?'

'The one you've known longest.'

'Sorry,' I said.

'It's Jack Cotery,' came the voice, soft, reproachful. 'Are you free, Lewis? I do want to see you.'

I was extremely busy, I said. All that night. I shouldn't be at home the following day.

'It is important, it really is. I shan't take half-an-hour.' Jack's tone was unputoffable, wheedling, unashamed, just as it used to be.

'I don't know when.'

'Only half-an-hour. I promise.'

I repeated, I was busy all that night.

'You're alone now, aren't you? I'll just come and go.'

He had hung up before I could reply. When I rejoined Charles, he asked who had been speaking. A figure from the past, I said. A fairly disreputable figure. What did he want? 'I assume', I said, 'that he's trying to borrow money.' Why hadn't I stopped him? Charles enquired, when he discovered that Jack Cotery was coming round. Irritably I shook my head, and went off to assemble a tray of drinks, reminded of how – with pleasure – I had done the same for George, that evening the previous December.

As soon as I heard the doorbell ring, I went and opened the door myself.

'Hello, Lewis,' breathed Jack Cotery confidentially.

I had seen him last about ten years before. He was my own age to the month: we had been in the same form at school. But he was more time-ravaged than anyone I knew. As a young man his black hair was glossy, his eyes were lustrous, he had a strong pillar of a neck: he had only to walk along the street to get appraising glances from women, to the envy of the rest of us. Now the hair was gone, the face not so much old as unrecognisably lined, still a clown's face but as though the clown hadn't put his make-up on. Even his carriage, which used to have the ease of someone who lived on good terms with his muscles, had lost its spring. But his glance was still humorous, giving the impression that he was making fun of me – and of himself.

I led the way into the study, put him in the chair where George had sat when he first broke the news.

'Will you have a drink?' I said.

'Now, Lewis.' He spoke with reproach. 'You ought to know that I never was a drinking man.'

In fact, that had been true. 'I'm a teetotaller nowadays, actually,' said Jack, as though it were a private joke. 'Also a vegetarian. It's rather interesting.'

'Is it?' I said. I turned to the whisky bottle. 'Well, do you mind if I do?'

'So long as you take care of yourself.'

Sitting at the desk, glass in front of me, I looked across at his big wide-open eyes.

'Shall we get down to business?' I said. 'There isn't much time, I'm afraid—'

'Why are you so anxious to get rid of me, Lewis?'

'I am pretty tied up—'

'No, but you are anxious to get rid of me, aren't you?'

He was laughing, without either rancour or shame. I couldn't keep back some sort of a smile.

'Anyway,' I said, 'is there anything I can do for you?'

'That isn't the right question, Lewis.' Once more, he seemed both earnest and secretly amused.

'What do you mean?'

'The right question is this: Is there anything *I* can do for *you*?'

Once I had had some practice in learning when he was being sincere or putting on an act: although, often, he could be doing both at once, taking in himself as well as me. It was a long while since I had met anyone so labile, and I was at a loss.

'I've been following this horrible case, you see,' Jack went on. 'I'm very sorry you are mixed up in that.'

'As a spectator.'

'No, Lewis, not quite that. Remember, I knew you a long time ago. I understand why you had to go—'

'Do you?'

'I think I do. Trust your old friend.' He put a finger to the side of his nose, in a gesture reminiscent of Azik Schiff talking of millions or of Jack himself, in old days, thinking how to make a quick pound. 'You weren't able to forget how George used to shout at us at midnight outside the gaol. And we used to walk down the middle of the tramlines, later on at night, when the streets were empty, dreaming about a wonderful future. So when the future came, and it turned out to be this, you thought you had to stand by George. You weren't going to let him sit there alone, were you?'

'That's rather too simple,' I said. Also too sentimental, I was thinking: had he always made life sound softer than it was?

'You see, Lewis, you're a kind man.' That was more sentimental. I wanted to stop him, but he went on: 'I've heard people say all kinds of things about you. Often they hate you, don't they? But they don't realise how kind you are. Or perhaps they do, and it makes them hate you more.'

'I wish I could believe you,' I said. 'But I don't. I strongly suspect that, if I'd never existed, no one would have been a penny the worse.'

'Nonsense, man. I'm an absolute failure, aren't I?'

'I don't know what that means.'

'I do. I'm no use, if you put me up against the people you live among now. But I can see some things that they wouldn't see if they lived to be a thousand. Perhaps because I've been a failure. I can see one or two things about you. I tell you this. You've lived a more Christian life than most of the Christians I know.'

It was my turn to say nonsense, more honestly than he had done. It was an astonishing statement, ludicrous in its own right, and also because Jack, when I knew him, took about as much account of Christianity as he did of Hamiltonian algebra.

'Oddly enough,' he said, 'that's what I came to tell you. Just that.'

It was possible – I was still suspicious, but of course I wanted to believe – that he was not pretending and had come for nothing else. A little later

I discovered that he had made a special journey from Manchester – 'on the chance of catching you'. It would have been more sensible, I said, to have rung up or written. 'You know,' said Jack, 'I always did like a bit of surprise.'

Perhaps it had been nothing but an impulse. But he had come to hearten me. Once or twice, when we were young men, he had taken time off from his chicanery or amours, to try to find me a love affair which would make me happier. The tone was the same, he liked bringing me comfort. That afternoon, I might have wished that the comfort was harder and nearer the truth – but none of us gets enough of it, we are grateful for it, whatever its quality, when it comes.

In his soft and modulated voice, Jack was talking, sadly, not nostalgically, about our early days. 'No, Lewis, we all did each other harm, I'm sure we did. I was a bad influence on George, I know I was. And he wasn't any good for me. Of course, you didn't see the worst of it. But you suffered from it too, clearly you did.'

He said, eyes wide-open, as when he was playing some obscure trick: 'You know, I began to realise something, not so long ago. I thought – look here, I shouldn't like to die, after the life I've lived.'

After a moment, I mentioned that, the summer before, I had met his first wife, Olive. He said:

'Would you believe it, I've almost forgotten her.'

I knew that he had married again, and asked about it.

'No,' said Jack. 'I extricated myself, some time ago.'

Just for an instant, his remorseful expression had broken, and he gave a smile that I had often seen – shameless, impudent, defiant. Or it might have been an imitation of that smile.

'Have you got anyone now?'

'I've given all that up.'

'How long for?'

'Absolutely and completely,' said Jack. 'For good and all. You see, I've taken to a different sort of life.'

He explained that nowadays he spent much of his spare time in church. He explained it with the enthusiasm that once he used to spend on reducing all human aspirations down to the sexual act – and with the same humorous twitch, as though there was someone behind his shoulder laughing at him. How genuine was he? Sometimes one could indulge one's suspiciousness too much. Would there be another twist, was this the end? Of that I couldn't guess, I didn't believe anyone would know the answers, until he was dead.

'Let's be honest,' said Jack. 'I didn't just come to tell you you'd lived a Christian life. There's something else—'

Right at the beginning, I had been counting on a double purpose. Now it came, and the laugh was against me.

'I think you ought to be a Christian – in faith as well as works. I really do.'

He asked, had he over-run his time? Could he have a few more minutes? I hadn't expected that afternoon to end with Jack expending all his emotion trying to convert me. The old arguments flicked back and forth. The old theological questions. Then Jack said, you'd find it a strength, Lewis. You'd find it made this hideous business easier to take. Strangely, that was what I had said myself to Superintendent Maxwell. But now, as I replied to Jack, I did not believe it. Faith did not mean that one acquiesced so quietly, did it? Surely it was deeper than that? The question of suffering, the other extreme questions, stood in front of real believers: nothing I had read of them suggested that they were any more reconciled. I should have respected them less if they had been.

At last Jack went away. I offered to introduce him to my wife and son, but he reminded me, with a not quite saintly grin, how pressed I was for time.

When I joined Charles in the drawing-room, he said:

'Well, how much did he want to borrow?'

'As a matter of fact,' I said, 'the subject didn't crop up.'

CHAPTER XXXIV

REFLECTIONS OF A TIRED MAN

GOING back to the trial by an early train, I stood outside the Assize Hall, not certain whether the others would arrive. Then Martin's car drew up: he said good-morning as he had done for days past, as though we had been pulled back and couldn't be anywhere else. I had seen politicians meet in the Yard like that during a time of crisis, glad that there was someone else who couldn't escape, making a kind of secret enclave for themselves. It was a beautiful morning. Close by, the church clock struck the quarter. A few minutes later, as we were getting ready to go into court, we saw George walking towards us, walking very slowly in the hazy sunshine.

As he came up the slope, he said:

'Anyway, it won't be long now.'

I replied:

'Not very long.'

'It ought to be over by tomorrow night.' George seemed to be entirely preoccupied by the timetable. When I mentioned that, later in the morning, I should have to leave them and sit in the official box, since I was lunching with the judge, he said: 'Oh, are you?' He wouldn't have been less interested if I had said that I was lunching with the Archbishop of Canterbury. He went on ticking off the last stages of the trial – 'I don't see', he said, 'how they can keep it going beyond tomorrow.'

In the court-room, more crammed that morning than during the psychiatrists' evidence, Cora Ross went into the box. She stood there, hair shining, shoulders high and square, as she faced Benskin. She had taken on an expression which had something of the nature both of a frown and a superior smile: her eyes did not meet her counsel's but (as I recalled from the conversation in prison) were cast sidelong, this time in the direction of Kitty. It was clear from the beginning that Benskin had one of the most difficult of jobs. He didn't want her to appear too balanced or articulate: on the other hand, the jury mustn't have any suspicion that she had been rehearsed in seeming abnormal or was herself deliberately putting it on. There had already been whispers that her outburst in court the previous week was a clever piece of acting. And, of course, he was loaded with an intrinsic difficulty. Even if he had been trying to prove that she was mad, not irresponsible, how did sensible laymen expect mad persons to answer or behave? Had they ever seen anyone within hours of a psychotic suicide? Looking, talking, seeming, perhaps feeling, more like themselves than they would ever have believed?

Benskin was much too shrewd not to have worked this out. In fact, he wasn't going to give her the opportunity to talk much. Not that he need have been so cautious, for she was responding as little, as deadeningly, as she had done to me. She sounded as though she were utterly remote, or perhaps more exactly as though there was nothing going on within her mind. Light, practised, neutral questions – not friendly, not indulgent, for Benskin had chosen his tone – made no change in her expression: each was answered by the one word, no.

He had begun straightaway upon the killing. Did she now remember any more about it? No. Had she anything to say about it? No. Could she describe the events of the Sunday evening? No.

'You don't deny, Miss Ross, that you were associated with the killing?'

'What's the use?'

But she still had nothing to say of how it happened? No. Or when? No. She had no memory of it? No. Had she ever had blocks of memory before? She didn't know. Did she remember meeting Miss Pateman for the first time? Yes. When? At the — café, in a crowd. (I didn't glance at George: it was one of his favourite rendezvous.) Did she remember setting up house with Miss Pateman? Yes. When? 17 November 1961. The answer came out fast, mechanically. But she had no memory of the boy's death? No.

'I have to press you, Miss Ross. Has it quite vanished?'

Cora gave something like a smile, stormy, contemptuous. Her reply wasn't immediate.

'No,' she said.

'You mean, you have some recollection?'

'Something happened.'

'Can you say anything more definite?'

'No.'

He went on; when she said 'something happened', what did that mean? She returned to saying no. It might have been, so people thought afterwards, that she had given away more than she intended: or, as Matthew Gough believed, that there was only a vague sense of tumult, of whirling noise, remaining to her, something like the last conscious memory of a drunken night.

But she didn't deny, Benskin asked, that there had been planning to get the boy out to the cottage? No. The planning had taken place, she hadn't forgotten it? No. Then what had she to say about that?

'When you set out to do something, you do it.'

'Someone must have thought about it for quite a time beforehand?'

She answered, head thrown back:

'I thought about it.'

'Can you tell us how you discussed it with Miss Pateman?'

'No.'

When he repeated some versions of this question, she merely answered No. Here, I at least was sure that this was a willed response: she could have told it all if she chose.

'Well. What state of mind were you in, can you tell us that?'

'No.'

'Come, Miss Ross, you must realise that you have done terrible things. Do you realise that?'

She stared to one side of him, face fixed, like the figurehead on an old sailing ship.

'If you had heard of anyone else doing such things, you would have thought they were atrocious beyond words. Isn't that so?'

Again she stared past him.

'So can't you tell us anything about your state of mind, say the fortnight before?'

'No.'

'You said, a moment ago, you set out to do something. Meaning those atrocious things. Why did you set out—'

She said:

'I suppose you get carried away.'

Benskin said:

'Miss Ross, we really want to understand. Can't you give us an idea what you were thinking about, when you were making those plans?'

'I thought about the plans.'

'But there must have been more you were thinking about?'

'That's as may be.'

'Can't you give us an idea?'

'No.'

Benskin said:

'Miss Ross, aren't you sorry for what you've done?'

Cora Ross replied, not looking directly at Kitty:

'I'm sorry that I dragged her into it.'

Suddenly, as though on impulse, Benskin nodded, sat down, examination over. Some lawyers thought later that he ought to have persevered: to me, sitting in the silent, baffled court-room, his judgment seemed good. On his feet, Bosanquet asked his first question in a voice as always quiet, but not so punctiliously unemotional:

'Miss Ross, you have just told my learned friend that you are sorry to have involved Miss Pateman. Is that all you are sorry for?'

'I'm sorry I dragged her in.'

'You know perfectly well that you have done what have just been called atrocious things. Aren't you sorry for that?'

No answer.

'You mustn't pretend, Miss Ross. You must have some remorse. Are you pretending not to understand?'

'You can think what you like.'

Bosanquet was, of course, meeting precisely the opposite difficulty to her own counsel's. If he drew dead responses like that last one, or any response which seemed outside human sympathy, then he might, paradoxically, be helping her. Momentarily he had himself been shocked. With professional self-control, he started again, quite calmly.

(Remorse. I was distracted into thinking of genuine remorse. Whenever I had met it, in myself or anyone else, there had always been an element of fear. Fear perhaps of one's own judgment of what one had done: often, far more often, of the judgment of others. I wondered if this woman was one of those, and they existed, who were incapable of fear.)

Carefully, on his new tack, Bosanquet was setting out to domesticate her life. She had lived with her mother until she died? Yes. She had had a normal childhood? She had gone to school like everyone else? She had never been under medical inspection? She had not been in any sort of trouble? She had done satisfactory work at school, she had been good at games? No one treated her as different from anyone else?

'In fact,' said Bosanquet, 'no one had any reason to consider that you were?'

'I was.' For once she had raised her voice.

Bosanquet passed over that answer, repeating that no one treated her differently—?

'I'll answer for myself.' It was an angry shout, like the tirade to the court the week before, mysterious-sounding. She might have been giving out a message – or just stating how, to her own self, she was unique.

With a smooth and placid transition, Bosanquet moved on to her ménage with Miss Pateman. They were living very comfortably when they pooled their resources, weren't they? Their incomes added together came to something like £1,600, didn't they? They paid Miss Pateman's father £200 for their room? It was an eminently practicable and well-thought-out arrangement, their joint establishment, wasn't it?

It was at this stage that I made my way out of court and round to the official box, so that I missed a set of questions and answers. From the court record, when I read it later, Bosanquet was making it clear that their domestic planning was far-sighted and full of common sense. There were exchanges about insurance policies and savings. Altogether they had been more competent than most young married couples, and as much anticipating that their relation would last for ever.

When I slipped into my place in the box, Bosanquet had just finished asking:

'So you managed to live a pleasant leisurely life, didn't you?'

'We did our jobs.'

'But you had plenty of leisure outside office hours?'

'I suppose so.'

'What did you do with your leisure?'

'The usual things.'

'Did you read much?'

'She was the reading one.'

As Bosanquet tried to discover what Cora Ross read, the answer seemed to be nothing. Certainly no books, scarcely a newspaper. Music she listened to, for hours on end: all kinds of music, apparently, pop, jazz, classical. Television, often the whole evening through. Films of any kind, but more often on television in their room (they had another set at Rose Cottage) than by going to a cinema. Yes, sometimes they went to a cinema: no special kind of film, they went to see stars that they 'liked' – a word which had a sexual aura round it.

Music, the screen. She had been drenched and saturated with sound. No printed words at all: or as little as one could manage with, in a literate society. In an earlier age, would she have wanted to learn from books?

'You had everything sensibly organised, Miss Ross,' said Bosanquet in his level tone. 'Then you thought you might do a little sensible organisation about – something else?'

'No.'

'Think a moment. What you did to this boy, beginning with the kidnapping, that required a good deal of organisation?'

'No.'

'It required just as much careful thinking as the way you planned your household accounts?'

'No.'

'We know already how you sensibly allocated your combined income. A certain proportion to the drinks bill—'

'She didn't drink.'

'No, you were a careful household. But you gave exactly the same sort of attention when you decided to make away with a harmless child?'

Sensible, careful, organised: Bosanquet was reiterating the words, letting no one forget how competent they were. It made an extraordinary picture, just because it was so commonplace: the two of them coming back to this room, Cora allowing herself a couple of evening drinks (a bottle of whisky lasted them a fortnight). It made too extraordinary a picture, for there were many in court, uneasy, disturbed, feeling that their life together, even well before the crime, couldn't have been quite like that. Yet at times it might or must have been.

'You did a great deal of careful planning – when you decided it was a good idea to make away with a harmless child?'

'No.'

'Of course you did. You have told your own counsel so. We have all heard how you picked on that child weeks beforehand. You organised the whole operation just as thoughtfully as you did your household, isn't that so?'

'No.'

'Do you deny that you planned it?'

She raised her head. 'I thought about one or two things.'

'You planned it step by step?'

No answer.

'Every inch along the way?'

With a kind of scorn or irritation, she said: 'It wasn't like that.'

'You planned it very lucidly, Miss Ross. It's not for me to find an answer to why you did so. Were you getting bored with everything else in your life together?'

'No.' Her face was convulsed.

'Were you ready for anything with a new thrill?'

'No.'

'Well then. What put this abominable idea into your head?'

For some instants it seemed that she was not going to answer. Then, as though she were wilfully getting back into the groove, or as though it were an answer prepared beforehand, she repeated what she had said to Benskin:

'You get carried away.'

Bosanquet, looking up at her, said again that it was not for him to find an answer. He returned to the planning, extricating each logistic point, sounding as temperate as though it were a military analysis. By this time – perhaps it was a delayed reaction – Cora had lost her temper. Her monosyllables were shouted, her expression changed from being wild and riven to something like smooth with hate. Then she sank back into sullenness, but her fury was still smouldering. When he finished with her, her gaze for once followed him: she stared down upon him, face pallid, minatory, deadened.

Benskin half-rose, then thought better of it, and left that impression of her standing there.

There was not time to begin Kitty's examination before lunch. After the judge's procession had departed, I went out, and found his clerk waiting for me. A car was ready to drive me to the judge's lodgings, in the old County Rooms in the middle of the town: he would be following at once with another guest.

In fact, as I walked into his dining-room, white-panelled, perhaps later than Georgian, but light and lively on the eye, the judge was hallooing cheerfully behind me. 'We caught you up, you see,' said Mr Justice Fane.

Do you two know each other? he was saying. Yes, we did, for his other guest was Frederick Hargrave, whom I kept meeting on the University Court. For an instant I was surprised to see him there, he looked so quiet, unassuming, insignificant beside the judge's bulk: I had to recall that Hargrave (whose grandfather and father had lived in the town like simple Quaker businessmen) was a deputy lieutenant of the county and not unused to entertaining circuit judges.

Still wearing his red gown – he had taken off only his wig – Mr Justice Fane stood between us, as tall as I was, weighing two or three stone more, very heavily boned and muscled, offering us drinks. No, that's no use to you, he corrected himself, speaking to Hargrave: his manners were just as cordial and attentive out of court as in. So Hargrave was equipped with ginger-beer, while the judge helped me to a whisky and himself to a substantial gin and tonic.

'It's very good of you both to have luncheon with me today,' he said. 'I don't like being lonely here, you know.'

As we stood up, there was some talk of common acquaintances: but the judge, like the barristers at Rose's house, couldn't keep from living in the trial.

'You haven't listened to much of it, have you?' he said to Hargrave, who replied that he had attended one afternoon.

'It can't have been a pleasant experience for you, Eliot,' said the judge.

'Terrible,' said Hargrave in a gentle tone.

'I think it's as terrible as anything I've seen,' the judge added. In a moment, he went on:

'I don't know what you think. All this talk of responsibility. We are responsible for our actions, aren't we? I'm just deciding whether to have another gin-and-tonic. Eliot, if you give me five pounds on condition that I don't have one, I'm perfectly capable of deciding against. That's my responsibility, isn't it? As you don't show any inclination to make the offer, then I shall, with equal responsibility, decide to have another one. And I shall bring it to the table, because it's time we started to eat.'

That was a Johnsonian method of dealing with metaphysics, I thought as we sat down, one on each side of the massive old man. The long table stretched away from us, polished wood shining in the airy elegant room.

The judge told us he had ordered a light meal, soup, fish, cheese. He and I were to split a bottle of white burgundy. He was brooding, he was drawn back – as obsessively magnetised as any of us, despite his professional lifetime – to the morning in the court.

'She tried to be loyal, didn't she?' he said to me.

I said yes.

The judge explained to Hargrave, who had not been present.

'The Ross girl was loyal to her friend this morning. She tried to take all the blame she could.'

'I'm glad to hear that,' said Hargrave.

'I don't believe her,' said the judge.

'I meant, it shows there's some good in her, after all,' Hargrave insisted, at the same time diffident and firm.

'I don't believe that she was so much in charge.' The old man was wrapped in his thoughts. Then he looked up, eyes bright, hooded, enquiring.

'Do you know what went through my mind, when I was listening to that young woman in the box? And remember, I've been at this business not quite but almost since you two were born. I couldn't help pitying anyone in her position. You can't help it. But ought you to pity her? Think of what she'd done. She'd helped get hold of that little boy. I expect they promised him a treat. And they took him out there and tortured him. That was bad enough, but there was something else. He must have been frightened as none of us has ever been frightened. Just remind yourself what it was like, your first days at prep school. You were eight years old and you'd got some brutes pestering you and you didn't see any end to it. Well, that poor child must have gone through that a million times worse. All I hope is that he didn't realise that they meant to kill him. I don't know about you, Eliot, but I can't imagine what he went through. Perhaps it's a mercy not to have enough imagination. So I ask myself, ought you to pity her?'

'I think you ought,' said Hargrave.

'Do you?'

'I think we shall all require pity, judge,' Hargrave went on with his surprising firmness, 'when our time comes.'

'Ah, you're a reformer, you believe in redemption. Are you a reformer, Eliot?'

'Of course he is,' I had never seen Hargrave so assertive. He spoke across to me: 'You're on the side of the poor, you always have been—'

'That's different,' I replied. 'I'm afraid I'm not a reformer in your sense.'

'You don't believe', the judge asked Hargrave, 'that any human being is beyond hope, do you?'

'Certainly not.'

'You should look at those two. And I tell you, the Ross girl isn't the worst of them. I've got a suspicion that the little one is a fiend out of hell.'

That was startling. Not because no one had said it before: the old man knew no more about them than anyone else, he might not be right. But he hadn't said it with loathing, more with a kind of resignation. It was that which shook both Hargrave and me, as we gazed at him, forking away at his sole, looking like a saddened eagle.

In time Hargrave recovered himself.

'You're asking me to believe in evil,' he said.

'Don't you?'

(Listening to Hargrave, I wasn't comfortable. Yet he didn't obtrude his faith: was I imagining a strand of complacency which wasn't there?)

'No. We've all seen horrible happenings in our world, we've seen horrible happenings here. But, you know, in the future people are going to do better than we have done. It wouldn't be easy to go on, would it, if one wasn't sure of that?'

The judge didn't wish to argue. Perhaps he too was uncomfortable with faith, or too considerate to disturb it. He may have known that Hargrave had done more practical good than most men, more than Mr Justice Fane and I could have done in several lifetimes.

'I don't know that I believe in evil,' he contented himself by saying. 'But I certainly believe in evil people.'

He cut himself a very large hunk of the local cheese. He had made a heartier lunch than Hargrave and I put together.

'It'll soon be over now,' he said, like an echo of George Passant earlier that morning and sounding for the first time like a tired and aged man. Then he had a businesslike thought. 'Unless Clive Bosanquet makes an even longer speech than usual. Clive is a good chap, but he will insist on not leaving any stone unturned. Within these four walls – if in any doubt he thinks it better to turn them back again. And that does take up a remarkable amount of time, you know.'

With the comfort of habit, he was mapping out the progress of the trial. His own summing-up wouldn't be over-long, he assured us. Nevertheless, he was tired, and it needed all his friendliness and good manners to prevent him from letting the meal end in silence.

CHAPTER XXXV

THE LIMIT

THAT afternoon, with Kitty Pateman in the witness box, was for me both the most mystifying and most oppressive of the trial. The court-room was as packed as it had been on the first two days: the three of us were sitting in the body of the court, with the Pateman family (Mr Pateman had reappeared that afternoon, and Dick attended for the first time) a few yards away, both men rigidly upright, the back of Mr Pateman's head running straight down into his collar. Mrs Pateman turned once, caught my eye, and gave what, strain playing one of its tricks, looked exactly like a furtive but excited smile. A beam of sunlight began to fall directly on to people's faces on the far side of the upper rows; as they fidgeted and tried to shut out the light, nerves were getting sharper, for I was not the only one who felt an inexplicable intensity all through the afternoon.

No one in that court but me had heard the judge's remarks about Kitty Pateman. As I sat listening to her, several times it came back to me, and it did nothing but add to the disquiet. For a strange thing was, that as the hours passed and Kitty talked, I couldn't get any nearer forming an opinion as to whether that remark had truth in it or not.

There were other strange things. Much of the time I, along with other observers, was certain that she was acting, and Jamie Wilson, without realising it, was helping her to act. His examination didn't sound, and didn't stay in the memory, like the ordinary questions-and-answers of a trial. It was much more like a conversation in which she was playing the major part, and a part which was quick-tongued, elaborate and strange.

Glance flitting to the jury box, the judge, once to her family, she described what she called her 'first breakdown', words hurrying out. Sometimes she could recall it all, sometimes she couldn't: she had told the psychiatrists, but not everything, because she got flustered, and she didn't like to mention that she had heard voices. Yes, voices when she was eighteen, which she thought someone was managing to produce in her radio set, tormenting her. Or perhaps taking charge of her, she didn't know at the time, she was frightened, she thought she might be going 'round the bend' or else something special was happening to her. She heard the voices over a period of months: sometimes they came just like a telephone message. They told her all sorts of things. They were advising her against her father. He was her enemy. He was keeping her at home, he was planning to keep her at home until her brother had grown up: he wanted her to be a prisoner. They told her to trust 'this man' (the man whom Dr Kahn had mentioned). She had thought that he was meant to be her escape. But he wasn't, it had been a disaster. The voices told her that he was her enemy, like her father. She was intended for something different, no one was going to imprison her. But then they stopped speaking to her, and she hadn't heard them for years.

The light voice fluted on: I was too intent to get any sense of how others were responding, even Martin – though later I heard a good many opinions, some mutually contradictory, about this part of her evidence. For myself, I had no doubt, on the spot or later, that most of it was a lie. At least the story of her voices was a lie. She was clever enough to have picked up accounts of people's psychotic states: of how some had precisely that kind of aural hallucination, certain that they were spoken to (in earlier times they would have heard the messages in the air, nowadays they emanated from machines) over the wires. She might even have known such a person, for they weren't uncommon. But I didn't believe that it had happened to her. She was mimicking the wrong kind of breakdown. If she were ever going to become deranged – or ever had been – it would be in a different fashion.

But that wasn't all, it was merely clinical, and only made her seem more ambiguous and shifting than before. For when people lied as she was lying, they usually couldn't help showing some stratum of the truth. She invented stories of what those voices told her about her father: they said something – though nothing like all – of what she felt for him herself. In the voices, which perhaps as she invented them seemed both romantic and sinister, and flattered her imagination, you could smell something much more down-to-earth, the antiseptic smell of the Pateman house. And you could hear something not so down-to-earth, but which emerged from that same house, and was seething in her imagination – 'something special' was happening to her, she was 'intended for something different'.

People afterwards said they hadn't often seen a face change so much. At times she looked young and pretty, at others middle-aged. In the box, which gave her height, she had lost her air of hiding away, and no one thought her insignificant. She made an impression which separated her from the lookers-on, and yet didn't repel them, almost as though she touched a nerve of unreality. Certainly it was an impression which Clive Bosanquet, as soon as he began to cross-examine, wanted to dispel.

In his level tone, he asked:

'Miss Pateman, when did you first make plans to kill a child?'

She looked at him and replied without a pause:

'I don't think I thought anything like that. No, that would give the wrong idea. You see, no one does anything cut-and-dried, you understand—'

Bosanquet was determined to stop her going off on another conversational flight.

'Miss Pateman, there is no doubt that you planned, methodically and over a period of weeks or months, to kill a child. Apparently it needn't have been Eric Mawby, you picked on him at random. I am asking you, when did you first make plans to kidnap and kill a child?'

'Well, kidnapping is one thing that we might have talked about—'

'I asked, Miss Pateman, when did you first make plans to kidnap and kill a child?'

'I was saying, we might have talked about catching hold of one for a little while, you know, we talked about all sorts of things, you know how it is, anyone can make a suggestion—'

'When did this happen?'

'It might have happened at any time, I couldn't tell you exactly.'

'It might not have happened at any time, Miss Pateman. When did it happen?'

The judge was regarding her, and spoke as considerately as ever in the trial. 'You must try to tell us, if you can.'

'Well, if I had to put a date to it, I suppose it would be about the time when I had this second breakdown.'

Her counsel had let her introduce 'this second breakdown' and then gone no further, as though he and she assumed, and the court also, that she had been living in a haze. But Bosanquet – for once less imperturbable – was having to struggle to clear the haze away. What was this second breakdown? She realised that it had not been adduced in the medical evidence? She had not at any time during this period considered consulting a doctor? She had been working effectively at her job, and living her life as usual in the room at home and out at the cottage?

'You don't know about breakdowns unless you're the one having them, no one could know, not even' – and then she added, with a curious primness – 'Miss Ross.'

'You were entirely capable of doing everything you usually do?'

'No one who's not had a breakdown can understand how you can go on, just like a machine, you know—'

'You were entirely capable of making very careful detailed plans, everything thought out in advance, to abduct this child and kill him?'

'But that's just what I was saying, you can go on, and you don't know what's happening—'

'You didn't know what was happening when you brutalised this child? And killed him? A child, Miss Pateman, who if you were a year or two older might have been your own?'

'No, he wasn't, that's got nothing to do with it, it didn't matter who he was.'

That reply, like many that she had made, might have been either fluent or incoherent, it was difficult to know which. Just as it was difficult to know whether Bosanquet's thrust of rhetoric, so different from his usual method that it must have been worked out, had touched her. Were the psychiatrists right, how much was she deprived, how much had she wanted to live as other women? How much did those dolls of hers signify? As she lied and weaved her answers in and out, most of us were as undecided as when we heard her first word. Bosanquet brought up the remark – to many the most hideous they had listened to in court – 'we wanted to teach him to behave'. What did that mean? Wasn't that the beginning of the plan? *Who said it first?*

'Oh, it was just a way of explaining afterwards, I don't think anyone actually said it. I'm sure I didn't, that's not the way you speak to each other, is it, even if you aren't living through a breakdown.'

'You found the idea so attractive that you planned everything methodically to abduct the child and then go on to ill-treat him and murder him?'

'No, that's not the way things go, you know how it is, you say lots of things that you don't mean, ever, we used to say, wouldn't it be nice if one could do things, but we didn't meant it.'

Her answers were shifting and shimmering like one translucent film drawn across another: underneath them there were marks when a fragment of their day-to-day life appeared, and then was obfuscated again. The two of them in that front room at the Patemans': yes, someone had said 'it would be nice if we could do things': it might have seemed like an ordinary sexual come-on, voice thick, eyes staring. Who had spoken first? Did that matter? In the witness-box, Kitty Pateman was not making the attempt to shield Cora as Cora had done her. She was most intent on seeming crazed. It still had the elaboration, almost the compulsion, of a piece of acting, yet sometimes one felt that, through pretending to be crazed, she had hypnotised herself into being so. Had she – or both of them – pretended like that before? In retrospect, when our minds were cooler, one thing struck most of us. She had far more imagination than Cora. But imagination of a kind which one sometimes meets in the sexual life, at the same time vatic and obscene. She might have, and almost certainly had, prophesied to herself a wonderful life through sex, more wonderful than sex could ever give her: and simultaneously she would never leave a sexual thought alone.

Martin said later that her imagination – or else her nervous force – had tis effect on him. Despite the beams of sunlight, the court-room seemed shut-in as a greenhouse.

But Bosanquet was not a suggestible man. As with Cora, though this was technically the harder job, he wanted to domesticate her answers. He went through a similar routine about their workaday lives. Once or twice she tried a fugue again, but then gave up. Here she couldn't sound unbalanced. Mostly her replies were shrewd and practical. Then he asked her about the books she read. Yes, she read a lot. She produced a list of standard authors of the day. 'Sometimes I go a bit deeper.' 'Who?' 'Oh well –' she hesitated, her glance flickered – 'people like Camus—'

At that, I should have liked to question her, for I suspected that she was lying again: not this time because of some thought-out purpose, but simply because she wanted to impress. She might even be, I thought, a pathological liar like Jack Cotery in his youth.

For once Bosanquet was taken aback. He was a good lawyer, but he wasn't well up in contemporary literature. He recovered himself:

'Well, what do you get out of them?'

Again she hesitated. She answered:

'Oh, they go to the limit, don't they; I like them when they go to the limit.'

I was now sure that she had been bluffing: somehow she had brought out a remark she had half-read. But it gave Bosanquet an opening. He didn't know about Camus, but he did know that she wanted to show how clever she was. *Hadn't she enjoyed showing how clever she was – when they were planning to capture the child? Hadn't she felt cleverer than anyone else, because she was sure that she could get away with it?* She had said a good deal to her counsel about being 'different' and 'special' – *wasn't that a way of proving it?*

She was flustered, the current of words deserted her.

'No. It wasn't like that. That was my second breakdown, that's all.'

She spoke as though she was astonished and ashamed. She gave the impression that he had hit on the truth which she was trying, at all costs, to conceal. Yet Bosanquet himself, and others of us, knew that wasn't so. Certainly she had enjoyed feeling clever, set apart, someone above this world – but none of us, looking at her, could conceive that that was all.

And yet, of all the questions put to her in the witness-box, these were the ones which upset her most. He picked up a phrase of hers – *she had gone to the limit, hadn't she? Wasn't killing a child going to the limit?* That didn't upset her: she got back into her evasive stream. Then he said:

'After it had all happened. Didn't you feel cleverer than anyone else, because you thought you had got away with it?'

Again she couldn't answer. This time she stood as mute as Cora.

'Didn't you talk it over together? You'd brought off something very special, which no one else could have done, didn't you tell yourselves that?'

'No. We never said anything about it.'

That, I suspected again, but without being sure, was another lie. It was possible that 'going to the limit' had *disappointed* them, grotesque as the thought might be.

Bosanquet left her standing there quietly, not flying off with an excuse which would smear over the picture of the two of them sitting together, congratulating each other on a scheme achieved. At once Wilson set her going again, fugue-fluent, on her breakdowns, first and second, and we listened without taking in the words.

About an hour later – still heavy after the afternoon of Kitty Pateman – I called at the Shaws' new house. During the weekend I had rung up Vicky, asking if I could see her: I wanted to get it over, after my talk with Martin, as much for my sake (since I still detested breaking bad news) as hers. The house was in a street, or actually a cul-de-sac, which I remembered well from my boyhood and which had altered very little since, except that there used to be tramlines running past the open end. On both sides the houses showed extraordinary flights of pre-1914 fancy; most were semi-detached in various styles that various human minds must have thought pretty: one stood by itself, quite small, but decorated with twisted pinnacles, and led into by a porch consisting mainly of stained glass. In the patch of front garden the only vegetation was an enormous monkey-puzzle. When I was a child, I didn't notice how startling the architecture was: I probably thought it was all rather comfortable and enviable, because the people who lived there – it was only half a mile away from our house – were distinctly more prosperous than we were. One of them, I recalled, was a dentist. It looked that afternoon as though the social stratum hadn't changed much, a good deal below that of the Gearys' neighbours, considerably above that of the streets round George's lodgings. The Shaws' house was one of a pair confronting one at the end, unobtrusive by the side of the art nouveau and suburban baroque, but built at the same time, front rooms looking over a yard of garden down the street, perhaps six rooms in all.

When I rang the bell, it was Arnold Shaw who opened the door. After he had greeted me, his first words were:

'This is a long way from the Residence.' He wore a taunting smile.

'That's just what I was thinking,' I replied.

He led the way into the front room. Vicky jumped up and kissed me, knowing that I had come for a purpose, looking at me as though trying to placate me. Meanwhile her father, oblivious, was pouring me a drink.

'I needn't ask you what you like,' he said in his hectoring hospitable tone. There was an array of bottles on the sideboard. However much Arnold had reduced his standard of living, it hadn't affected the liquor.

I gazed round the room, about the same size as our old front room at home. The furniture, though, was some that I recognised from the Residence.

'It's big enough for me,' said Arnold Shaw defiantly.

I said, of course.

'Anything else would be too big.'

With the enthusiasm of an estate agent, he insisted on describing what he had done to the house. There had been three bedrooms: he had turned one of them into a study for himself. 'That's all I need,' said Arnold Shaw. They ate in the kitchen. No entertaining. 'No point in it,' he said. 'People don't want to come when you've got out of things.'

He hadn't mentioned the trial: to me, at that moment, it was lost in another dimension. Not noticing Vicky, half-forgetting why I was visiting them, I felt eased, back in the curiosities of every day. It was a relief to be wondering how Arnold was really accepting what his resignation meant, now that he was living it. He was protesting too much, he was putting on a show of liberation. I nearly said, all decisions are taken in a mood which will not last: he would have known the reference. And yet, the odd thing was, although he probably put on this show for his own benefit each day of his life, he was also, and quite genuinely, liberated. Or perhaps even triumphant. I had seen several people, including my brother Martin, give up their places, some of them, in the world's eyes, places much higher than Arnold Shaw's. Without exception, they went through times when they cursed themselves, longing for it all back, panoplies and trappings, moral dilemmas, enmities and all: but, again without exception, provided they had made the renunciation out of their own free will, underneath they were content. Free will. For one instant, listening to Arnold, I was taken back to that other dimension. Free will.

The Limit

Arnold had, or thought he had, given up his job of his own free will. He felt one up on fate. It was a similar superiority to that which some men felt, like Austin Davidson, in contemplating suicide: or alternatively in bringing off a feat which no one else could do. Just for once, in the compulsions of this life, one didn't accept one's destiny and decided for oneself.

It didn't sound as exalted as that, with Arnold Shaw grumbling about his pension and discussing the economics of authorship. The university had treated him correctly but not handsomely (that is, they hadn't found him a part-time job): he was hoping to earn some money by his books. His chief work would be appearing in the autumn, he had the proofs in his study now: it was the history of the chemical departments in German universities, 1814–60. It was the last word on the subject, said Arnold Shaw. I didn't doubt it. That was the beginning of organised university research as we know it, said Arnold Shaw. I didn't doubt that either. It ought to be compulsory reading for all university administrators everywhere: how many would it sell? Ten thousand? That I had to doubt a little, and he gave me an angry glare.

Forgiving me, he filled my glass again. Then he said, aggressively, jauntily:

'Well, I'd better get back to those proofs. This won't help bring in the dibs.'

As he shut the door and I was still amused by that singular phrase, Vicky had come to the chair beside me.

'Have you got any news?'

She was looking with clear, troubled, hopeful eyes straight into mine.

'I'm afraid I have.'

'Have you seen him?'

I shook my head.

'Oh well.' Her expression was sharp, impatient again, hope flooding back. 'How do you know?'

'I'm afraid I do know.'

'He hasn't told you anything himself?'

'I shouldn't come and say anything to you, should I, unless I was sure?'

'What are you trying to say, anyway?' Her tone was rough with hate – not for him, for me.

'I think you've got to put him out of your mind. For good and all.'

No use, she said. She had flushed, but this was not like the night when her father broke the news of his resignation, she was nowhere near tears. She was full of energy, and with the detective work of jealousy, easy to recognise if one had ever nagged away at it, wanted to track down what my sources of information were. Had I seen him at all? Not for months, I said. Had I been talking to his friends? Did I know them? Young men and young women? The only one of his friends that I knew at all, I said, was my stepson Maurice. He had been home for the vacation, but he hadn't said a word about Pat.

She couldn't accept even now, not in her flesh and bone, that he had deceived her. When she loved, she couldn't help but trust. Even when she didn't love, she found it easier to trust than distrust, in spite of her sensible head. She trusted me that afternoon (even while she was giving me the sacramental treatment of a bearer of bad news) but it was only with her head that she was believing me.

I asked her when she had last heard from him. She had written to him a good many times since Christmas, she said. She didn't tell me, she let me infer, that she hadn't heard from him.

'I can't do any more,' she said. 'I don't think I can write again.'

That didn't seem like pride, more like a resolve. We had all been through it, I told her. It was very hard, but the only way was not to write, not to be in any kind of contact, not even to hear the name.

'No,' she said. 'I've got to know what's happening to him.'

'It's a mistake.'

She said:

'I still feel he might need me.'

That was the last refuge. She was obstinate as her father: she had no more sense of danger – and she had her own tenderness.

Crossly, for I was handling it badly, I said:

'Look here, I really think you ought to give a second thought to Leonard Getliffe.'

I was handling it badly, and that was the most insensitive thing I had done. Nothing I could have said would have made much difference: all the tact in the world, and you can't soften another's disasters. But still, I was handling it specially badly, perhaps because I had come to her from the extremes of death and horror, and, by the side of what I had been listening to, I couldn't, however much I tried, get adjusted to the seriousness of love. Some kinds of vicarious suffering diminished others: unhappy love affairs – in absolute honesty, did one ever sympathise with total seriousness unless one was inside them? – seemed among the more bearable of sufferings. So that I was, against my will, less patient than I wanted to be. Having met Leonard Getliffe at the Gearys' for a few minutes the week before, which made me think perfunctorily of Vicky, I had merely wished – with about as much sympathy as Lord Lufkin would have felt – that they would get on with it. And now Leonard's name had found itself on my tongue.

She gave a cold smile.

'No,' she said.

'I'm pretty sure you underestimate him.'

'Of course I don't. He's a great success—'

'I don't mean in that way. I'm pretty sure you underestimate him as a man.'

She gazed at me in disbelief.

'Once you set him free, I bet you he'd make a damned good husband.'

'Not for me,' she said.

She added:

'It's no use thinking about him. There's no future in it.'

She had blushed, as I had seen her do before when Leonard was mentioned. She still could not understand how she had inspired that kind of passion. Once more she used that bit of old-fashioned slang: there was no future in it. She was utterly astonished at being the one who was loved, not the one doing the loving. She was not only astonished, she was disturbed and curiously angry with Leonard because it was a position she couldn't fit.

Then, as I became more impatient, she tried to prove to me that, of the two, it might be Pat who needed her the more.

CHAPTER XXXVI

LET-DOWN OR FRUSTRATION

At the close of Kitty Pateman's evidence, the judge had announced that, on the following morning, the court would begin half an hour early, at ten o'clock, in the hope of finishing the case that day. When the morning came, and we sat there knowing that the verdict was not far away – the two women back in the dock, Kitty not scribbling any more, the triptych of Patemans in front of us – the proceedings were low-keyed and the three final speeches by counsel were all over by noon. It wasn't that they were hurrying, but all they could do, in effect, was repeat the medical arguments for and against. The evidence for mental abnormality wasn't disputed, said Benskin. What had been disputed was how much this abnormality impaired their responsibility: as he had put it to the Crown witness, Dr

Gough, it was a matter of degree: and yet surely, after all the evidence, the impairment wasn't in doubt? Could anyone, said Jamie Wilson, having heard Kitty Pateman's history and *having seen and listened to her in the witness-box* (that was the boldest stroke that either he or Benskin made), believe that she was capable of a free choice? That her state of mind allowed her to control what she had done? All that her doctors said showed that this was incredible, and all that she said herself made it more incredible still.

Clive Bosanquet spoke for longer than the other two, but for less than an hour. More than ever, he was meticulously correct. Prosecuting for the Crown, he said, he had the duty to bring home to the jury the attention that they ought to pay to the prisoners' plea: there had not been many cases where such a plea had been thoroughly argued: no one, certainly not the Crown, wished to dismiss that plea if these women were mentally irresponsible. But – and then he examined point by point what Cornford had said, how Matthew Gough had rebutted it, and what 'responsibility' had to mean. The unassertive voice went in, not with passion, but with attrition. At one stage he said that it would be possible, or at least theoretically possible, for the jury to admit the plea for one of the women and reject it for the other: but neither defence counsel had wished to argue this, and the prosecution did not admit it: the two were inseparably combined, and what applied to one, as all the technical evidence demonstrated, would apply to the other: it had to be all or nothing. That was all. With a gesture, he got on with the attrition.

All through those speeches, I couldn't listen as I usually did. It was not till I read them later than I appreciated what had actually been said. Odd phrases stuck out, tapped away at circuits in the mind that I couldn't break. Free choice. Who had a free choice? Did any of us? We felt certain that we did. We had to live as if we did. It was an experiential category of our psychic existence. That had been said by a great though remarkably verbose man. It sounded portentous: it meant no more than the old judge declaring robustly that he could decide – it was in his power and no one else's – whether to take a second gin-and-tonic. It meant no more: it also meant no less. We had to believe that we could choose. Life was ridiculous unless we believed that. Otherwise there was no dignity left – or even no meaning. And yet – we felt certain we could choose, were we just throwing out our chests against the indifferent dark? We had to act as if it were true. As if. *Als/ob*. That was an old answer. Perhaps it was the best we could find.

Morality. Morality existed only in action. It arose out of action: was formed and tested in action: expressed itself in action. That was why we mustn't cheapen it by words. That was why the only people I knew – they were very few – who had any insight into the moral life, talked about it almost not at all. I had seen Rogert Quaife act in his final choice: no one would have called him a specially good man: yet there was more discrimination in the way he acted than in all the exhortations I had ever heard.

On the stroke of twelve, the judge started to sum up. Suddenly I was listening with acute attention, absent-mindedness swept clean away. I watched the old, healthy, avian face as he turned, with his courteous nod, towards the jury box: I was listening, knowing already what his opinion was.

'Members of the jury, it is now my duty to sum this case up for you.' All through the trial his voice had shown, except in one rebuke, none of the cracks or thinning of age, and as he talked to the jurors, so easily and unselfconsciously, it was still unforced and clear: but his accent one had ceased to hear except in old men. It belonged to the Eton of 1900, not cockney-clipped like the upper-class English two generations later, but much fuller, as though he had time to use his tongue and lips. 'This, I think, is the seventh day on which you have listened with the utmost patience to the evidence and the speeches. And, at the end of it all, the issue in this case comes down to the point of a pin. It is agreed by everyone, I think, that these two young women have some degree of mental abnormality: is it enough to impair substantially – I have to remind you of that word – their mental responsibility? Are Miss Ross and Miss Pateman not responsible for the deeds, I need not tell you they are terrible deeds, that they have committed? Or, to make the point sharper still, are they not fully responsible, so that we have to make special allowance for them and accept their plea? Which is, you will remember, one of diminished responsibility. Either you will accept that, and bring in a verdict accordingly: which means, you understand, that they will be treated like mental patients who have perpetrated the crime of manslaughter. Or else you will decide that they were responsible for what they have done, and find them guilty of murder. In which case it will be necessary for me to pass the statutory sentence.'

Almost from the start of the summing-up, Cora had been yawning. It looked like insolence: I believed that it was her first sign of nerves. The judge went on:

'I do not for one instant pretend that that decision is easy for you. As learned counsel have carefully explained to you, this whole conception of diminished responsibility is relatively new to our law. And you have also been told that it has no really sharp and precise definition in medical or scientific terms. You have actually heard doctors of great distinction, mental doctors or psychiatrists, whatever we like to call them, taking absolutely contrary positions about the degree of responsibility of these two young women. Dr Cornford and Dr Kahn have told us – and I am sure that no one here would doubt their absolute professional integrity – they have told us that these women were less than fully responsible, so much less as not really to be answerable for their actions, when they killed the child. On the other hand, Dr Gough and Dr Shuttleworth, again with integrity that no one can doubt, have given their judgment, which is that Miss Ross and Miss Pateman were as responsible as any of us, when we perform any deed for good and ill. No, perhaps I have gone a little further than those doctors did. But they were quite positive that these young women's responsibility was not substantially impaired.

'Members of the jury, this is not going to be easy for you. I shall try shortly to give you what little help I can. But I have no more knowledge of these young women's minds than you have. I shall try to remind you what the doctors said, and what Miss Ross and Miss Pateman said themselves. You have listened to it all, and so have I. And it is for you, and you alone, to make the decision.

'But, right at the beginning, I have to tell you two things. I have just said that it is for you, and you alone, to make the decision. I have to repeat it, so that you will never forget it during your deliberations. This issue must not be decided by doctors. I should tell you that, and tell you it time and again, even if the doctors' opinions were not divided. It is not in the nature of our law to have judgment by professional experts. We listen to them with gratitude and respect, but in the end it is you who are the judges. In such a case as this, it would, in my view, be specially wrong for the issue to be decided by doctors. For I am convinced that none of these eminent men would consider stating that they had reached any final certainties about the human mind. Perhaps those certainties never will be reached. Sometimes, for the sake of our common humanity, I find myself hoping that they won't. At any rate, no one can be certain now. It is for you to reach a decision as to whether these young women – as my learned friend Mr Benskin put it very clearly – are or are not responsible for these criminal actions, in the sense that you are yourselves for what you do. It is your decision. You will have to be guided by your experience of life, your knowledge of human nature, and I must say, by something we sometimes undervalue, by your common sense.

'Now one other thing, before I try to draw your minds back to the evidence. You have had to listen to the story of an abominable crime. When one thinks of the treatment of that young boy before he died, and then of his death, one finds it hard – and here I am speaking for myself, as an ageing man – one finds it hard to cling to one's faith in a merciful God.

'But now I have to ask you to do something which you may think impossible. You must do your best, however. I want you to put the nature and details of this crime out of your consideration. You are concerned only with whether these women are, or are not, fully responsible. It would be the same question, and the same problem, if they had committed some quite minor offence, such as stealing half-a-dozen pairs of stockings or a suitcase. It would be the same problem. I ask you to approach the decision in that spirit. I know that it will be difficult. I am asking you to banish the natural revulsion and horror that you must have felt. Forget all those thoughts. Think only of whether these young women were responsible for what they have done.'

One would have to be something like clairvoyant, I was thinking, to listen to him now – and then guess right about how he spoke in private. And yet he was as relaxed, speaking to the jury, as when he spoke to Hargrave and me in his dining-room. It was the habit of a lifetime to be calm and magisterial, to let nothing of himself slip out. Except perhaps a distaste for all the theorists who didn't live in his own solid world. As he went on, underneath the fairness, underneath the amiable manners, he once or twice inflected his voice, just towards the edge of sarcasm, when he discussed the psychiatrists' 'explanations'. Or did I imagine the inverted commas? He was not a speculative man: in secret, he hadn't much use for intellectual persons. But that had been so all through his career. It was nothing new that day, it didn't affect his judgment, it would have been hard to tell whether he was trying to lead the jury at all.

That was Margaret's impression, as we sat at lunch, the four of us. She had travelled up during the morning, in order to be with us at the end, and had heard nearly all the summing-up, which the judge had still to finish.

'He's not pushing them one way or the other, is he?'

George gazed at her.

'Perhaps he doesn't think it's necessary,' he said. He wasn't speaking bitterly: or apathetically: not with much emotion, just as a matter of fact, like one who took the result for granted. He was not looking drawn. The rest of us were showing signs of suspense, but not George. He gave out an air of resolve or even of obscure determination. It was he who took the initiative, telling us it was time to return. 'Last sitting,' he said in a loud, vigorous, exhorting cry.

In the court-room, full but not as jam-tight as on the first day, smelling in the warm afternoon of women's scent, sweat, the odour of anxiety, the judge turned again to the jury box, with a smile that was social, not quite easy or authoritative.

'Members of the jury, thanks to the exertions of the lady who has been taking the shorthand notes, I have been supplied with a transcript of what I said to you this morning, and I see that I have made three very stupid little mistakes.' They were, in fact, small mistakes which most of us had either not noticed or discounted as slips of speech, such as transposing the doctors' names: but the judge was flustered, irritated with himself and those he was talking to. Perhaps he had the streak of vanity that one met in men who had not competed much and who weren't used to being at a disadvantage: perhaps he didn't like being reminded that he had reached one of the stages in old age when he could still trust his judgment, but not his memory. At any rate, he wanted to shorten his summing-up, he was distrustful of quoting names, he had to make an effort to assert himself. 'Let us get our feet on the ground. We are dealing with reality, and this is certain—' He went on with an adjuration that, I fancied, he might have used before. 'You have been dealing with an avalanche of words. This is nobody's fault, of course. It is the only way that it could be done. But you are not dealing with things of imagination. You are dealing with actual lives, actual things that really happened.' Then he was in command again. He told them that he agreed totally with Bosanquet, and by implication with the other counsel: there was no ground for discriminating between the two. He repeated, slowly and masterfully, that it must be the jury's decision, and not the doctors'. They must detach themselves from their hatred of the crime, and consider as wisely as they could what substantial impairment (he reiterated the words three times) of responsibility meant and what responsibility those two young women bore. At that, he gave his benevolent paternal beck to the jury. 'It is in your hands now,' he said.

The judge's procession left: the heads of the two women dipped out of sight. It was about ten to three. Slowly, in jerks and spasms, the courtroom emptied. As soon as we got outside into the hall, Margaret lit a cigarette, as in an interval at the theatre. In the rush, we all found ourselves near the refreshment-table, where I brushed against Archibald Rose, wig in hand, eating a sausage roll.

'Now we shan't be long,' he whispered to me, in a casual detached tone. None of the others had heard that remark: but each of us, certainly George, was behaving as though Rose was right, as though the jury would be returning soon. We talked very little. It was a good many minutes before George said: 'Well, I suggest we might as well have a cup of tea.' We lingered over it, so weak and milky, like the tea I had tasted in the gaol. The hall was less crowded, people were edging away. We drank more cups of tea. All of a sudden the delay seized hold of me. I didn't know about the others, but later Margaret and Martin told me it was the same for them.

At half past four I said: 'Let's go for a stroll.' George said that he wouldn't bother, found a chair in the now half-deserted hall, sat down and lit a pipe. The others were glad to escape into the free air. Neither of them dissenting, we went away from the Assize Hall, not just round the block, but on into the centre of the town, getting on for a mile away. Margaret knew what I was doing: so probably did Martin. I was trying to cheat the time of waiting – so as to get back when it was all over. We had lived through times of waiting before this. I might have recalled that other time with George in this same court: but curiously, so it seemed to me in retrospect, I didn't. Maybe my memory blocked it off. Instead, it was much more like times that each of us had been through: meaningless suspense: bad air trips, making oneself read thirty pages before looking at one's watch: Martin knowing that his son was driving, not told when he might arrive.

'What does all this mean?' Martin said, without any explanation, after we had walked a few hundred yards.

'It must mean that the jury are arguing,' I replied.

'I wouldn't have believed it,' he said. He had taken it for granted that the defence didn't stand a chance.

'Would you?' Margaret asked me.

'No.' I was wondering who might have done. Perhaps the Patemans. Were they hopeful now?

It could be, Martin supposed, that one or two jurors were holding out. None of us had any idea, then or later, what happened in that jury-room.

We reached the opulent streets, women coming out of shops, cherishing new chair-sets, complexions matt in the clear sunlight. It would take us twenty minutes to walk back, said Martin.

In sight of the Assize Hall, we made out the policemen on the steps. We hurried into the entrance hall: there were a few people round the refreshment-table, others scattered about, George still sitting down. He gave us his open, inattentive smile. 'Nothing's happened,' he said.

During the next hours, we couldn't cheat the time of waiting any more. Except that I had a conversation with a colleague of Edgar Hankins, a bright-eyed, preternaturally youthful-looking man. We had met occasionally at parties, and in the hall he drew me aside. He wanted, he was full of his own invention, to discuss the treatment of criminals sane and not-so-sane. If we assumed that the two young women were sane, which he believed, then he believed equally that they would never do anything again. In that case, they were no danger to society. So what was the of the kind justification for keeping them in gaol? It was pure superstition, he was saying. I had always found his kind of brightness boring, and that evening, time stretching out, I found it worse than that. When I returned to Margaret and Martin, they asked what we had been talking about, but I shook my head.

At last – and yet it seemed unexpected – we heard that the jury were coming back. When we went into the court-room, we saw it gaping, nearly empty: the time was nearly eight o'clock, most of the spectators hadn't been able to see the end. The two women walked up to the dock, Kitty's eyes darting – with something like a smile – to her family. Cora had brushed her hair, which shone burnished as the court lights came on. The jury trampled across the room, making a clatter; it was as though one had not heard the noise of feet before. As they settled in their box, I saw one of them, a middle-aged woman with thick arms, gaze intently at Cora Ross.

The judge took his place and bowed. Then the old routine, in the Clerk's rich voice.

'Members of the jury, who will speak as your foreman?'

A grey-haired man said: 'I will.'

'Mr Foreman, do you find the prisoner, Cora Helen Passant Ross, guilty or not guilty of murder in this indictment?'

'Guilty.'

The same question, about Katharine Mavis Pateman.

'Guilty.'

'And those are the verdicts of you all?'

'Yes, they are.'

'Cora Helen Passant Ross, you stand convicted of the felony of murder. Have you anything to say why you should not now be given judgment according to law?'

Cora stood erect, shoulders squared, her expression unmoved. 'No,' she said, in a loud voice. Kitty Pateman followed her with a quieter, perfunctory no.

The judge looked at them, and said clearly but without inflection:

'The sentence is a statutory one, and it is that you, and each of you, be sentenced to imprisonment for life.'

He did not say anything more. He gave them a nod, polite, almost gentle, dismissing them. They were taken below for the last time.

Neither in the court-room, talking to the solicitors and to his junior, nor outside in the hall, when the final ritual was over, would Clive Bosanquet accept congratulations: he had too much emotional taste to do so, in a case like this. He looked, however, modestly satisfied: while Jamie Wilson, speaking to no one, rushed ahead of the others to the robing-room, his face surly with self-reproach. Leaning against the refreshment-table, Benskin chatted with vivacity to other lawyers and gave us a cheerful wave. Of all the functionaries at the trial, the only one I actually spoke to, as we made our way to the entrance-hall, was Superintendent Maxwell. He spun his bulk round, came up to me in soft-footed steps, and said, in a quiet high mutter: 'Well, they didn't get away with it. Now we've got to keep the other prisoners off them. I don't envy anyone the job.'

I didn't hear many comments, among the relics of the crowd. There was none, absolutely none – and there hadn't been during the last minutes in court – of the gloating fulfilment which years before I had felt all round me, and in myself, when I heard the death sentence passed. You could call it catharsis, if you liked a prettier name. There was none of that. So far as there was a general mood, it seemed to be almost the opposite, something like anti-climax, let-down, or frustration.

In the tone, firm and yet diffident, in which he always used to issue his invitations, George said to the three of us:,

'I should like you to come round to my place for half an hour.'

Before any of us replied, my sleeve was being gently tugged and Mrs Pateman was saying, very timidly: 'I wonder if you could have a word with him, sir. It might settle him down. I don't know what's going to happen to him, I'm sure.'

She was quite tearless. In fact, she didn't mention her daughter, only her husband, who was standing at the side of the hall, gesticulating as he harangued Dick Pateman. As she led me towards them, she asked me if I would 'humour him a bit'. She said that she didn't know how he would get over it.

When he saw me, his gaze was fixed and angry. He seemed possessed by anger, as though that were the only feeling left.

'I can't have this,' he said.

I said that I was sorry for them.

'I can't let it go at this,' he said.

I attempted to soothe him. Couldn't they all go and try to sleep, and then talk to the solicitors tomorrow?

That made him more angry. His eyes stood out, his fists clenched as though he were going to hit me.

'They're no good to us.'

'Well then—'

'I want someone who'll take care of people who are ill. My daughter's ill, and I insist on having something done about it.'

'That's what we want,' said Dick Pateman.

I said, she would certainly be under medical supervision—

'I'm not going to be put off by that. I want the best people to take care of her and make her better.'

Again I tried to soothe him.

'No,' he shouted into my face. 'I can't leave it like this. I shall have to talk to you about how I can get things done—'

He was threatening me, he was threatening everyone. And yet he was crying out for help. The curious thing was, I was more affected by his appeal than by his wife's. She had known a good many sorrows: this was another, but she could bear it. Whatever else came to her, she would go on enduring, and nothing would break her. But she didn't believe that was true of her husband and her son. Standing with him, listening to their threats (for Dick joined in), I thought she could be right. To be in their company was intolerable: in many ways they were hateful: and yet they were helpless when there was nothing they could do. Their only response to sorrow, the chill of sorrow, was to fly out into violence. Violence without aim. Shouts, scowls, threats. What could they do? They were impotent. When they were impotent, they were nothing at all.

I told Mr Pateman that I had no knowledge of the prison service or of prison doctors but that, if he ever wanted to talk to me, he was welcome to. He didn't thank me, but became quieter. Any bit of action was better than none. Getting a promise out of me, however pointless, showed that he was still effective, and was a comfort to him.

CHAPTER XXXVII

FORGETTING

'I SHOULD like you to come round to my place for half an hour,' George had said, before Mrs Pateman took me away. When I rejoined the three of them, they were waiting to walk out to Martin's car. As we drove across the town, up past the station, all of us in silence, I was thinking again, yes, that was how George used to invite us – when he was asking us, not to a pub, but to his 'place', as though it were a baronial hall.

In the sharp spring night, transistor radios were blaring and people lolled about the pavement, when we drew up outside the door. Inside his sitting-room, as he switched on the light, the newspapers and huddle sprang to the eye, and one's nostrils tingled with the dust.

'Now,' he said, as, panting, he cleared litter from the old sofa to make a place for Margaret. There were only two chairs. Martin put me in one of them, and himself sat on the sofa-end. 'Now,' said George. 'Is there anything I can get you?'

Margaret glanced at me, looking for a signal. She was tired, after the long, nerve-ridden day. She would have liked a drink. But, though she knew George well, she had really no idea about his style of life. Even in her student days, she hadn't seen a room like this. No, she said, he wasn't to bother. If she had asked for a drink, I thought, she would probably have been unlucky. For George, who drank more than anyone round him, had – at least in my experience, in the time I knew him best – scarcely ever drunk at home.

'I can easily make some tea,' said George.

'Never mind,' said Martin. 'We've drunk enough tea for one day.'

George looked at the three of us, as if to make sure that the formalities had been properly observed. That gave him pleasure, even now, as it had always done. Then he took the vacant chair at the side of the fireplace, pulled down his waistcoat, and said:

'Well. I thought you ought to be the first to hear.'

He was addressing me more than the others, but not personally, rather as a matter of etiquette, because he had known me longest.

He said:

'I'm going away.'

'What do you mean?'

'I mean that I shan't put a foot inside this damned town again.' He stared past me. 'It's quite useless to argue,' he went on, though in fact none of us were arguing. 'I made my plans as soon as I saw that business of hers' (he meant Cora, but couldn't, or didn't, refer to her by name) 'could only come to one end. Incidentally, I thought that you were all deceiving yourselves about that. I never believed that any jury in the country would do anything different.'

He said:

'It's horrible, I don't require anyone to tell me it's horrible, but there's no use wasting time over that. I've had to think about my own position. I've got plenty of enemies in this wretched town. I'm perfectly prepared to admit that, according to ordinary standards, I deserve some of the things they want to bring up against me. But I've got enemies because I wouldn't accept their frightful mingy existence and wouldn't let other people accept it either. And all these sunkets want is to make the place too hot to hold me.' This didn't have the machine-like clank of paranoia, which one often heard in him. 'Well, now the sunkets have something to use against me. They can breathe down my neck until I die. It doesn't matter to them that she hasn't spoken to me for a couple of years. They can smear everything I do. They can control every step I take. By God, it would be like having me in a cage for crowds to stare at.'

Martin gave me a glance. Neither of us could deny it.

George said:

'That's not the worst of it. If it were just myself, I think I might conceivably stay here and take my medicine. But there is the whole crowd. Everyone who has ever come near to me. You heard what they did to young — in the witness box. They'll all be under inspection as long as I am here. Their lives won't be worth living. When I go away, it won't be long before it all calms down again. They'll be all right, as soon as people have forgotten about me.'

Again, neither Martin nor I could say that he was wrong. It was Margaret who said:

'That's very generous, George. But are you sure you're really well enough?'

'Well enough for what?'

'Well enough to uproot yourself like that.'

George gave her a shifty, defiant smile, and said:

'Oh, if I'm not up to the mark, I shall get in touch with some of you.'

Had he thought of where he might be going? *Of course*, what did she take him for? For the first time that night, George broke into laughter, loud laughter. For days past – perhaps when he had been absent from the court, and perhaps, I now suspected, for a longer period than that – he had been making logistic plans, like the administrator he might have been. It would take him no time at all to 'clear up his effects'. He didn't propose to stay in England. He had never travelled much: as a matter of fact, apart from a weekend in Paris and a few days in Ostend, he had not, in sixty-four years, travelled at all. Yet, it was one of his schematic hobbies, he knew the geography, railways, timetables of Europe far better than the rest of us.

'Well, now I've got a bloody good chance to look round,' he cried.

He intended to start in Scandinavia, for which he had a hankering, because he had once met a Swede who looked remarkably like himself.

'I'm sorry to nag,' said Margaret. 'But, before you go, do ask your doctor. You know, you're not very good at taking care of yourself, are you?'

'I shall be all right.'

'Or let us find you a doctor in London, won't you?'

'You're not to worry about me.'

He answered her with child-like impenetrable obstinacy: nothing was going to stop him now.

Margaret, used to her father and the sight of illness, thought it was kinder to say no more. Then Martin and I, almost at the same instant, mentioned money. Up till then, the grudges, bad luck, resentments of a lifetime had been submerged: all of a sudden, they broke through. *Of course* he was bound to be short of money. After that ineffable firm (Eden & Sharples, and George's curses crashed into the room) had fobbed him off with his miserable pension. Seven hundred and fifty a year; that was all he received for a life's work. When he had saved them from their own contemptible incompetence. If it hadn't been for him, they would have been extinct long ago! Seven hundred and fifty a year. In exactly one year's time, he added, with savage, mirthless hilarity, he would get his old age pension. Then he would have nearly a thousand a year. The glorious reward for all his efforts in this mortal life!

Anyone from outside might have thought that George was morbidly preoccupied with money, miserly in the fashion of Mr Pateman. That was dead wrong. No one had minded about it less, or given it away more lavishly. In that storm of protest, it wasn't money that was making him cry out.

But he had his streak of practicality, and I had to answer on those terms.

'Are you going to be able to cope?' I said.

'Can't you work it out for yourselves?'

'You must let us help.'

'No. It's rather too late to impose upon my friends.'

He had spoken with stiff pride. Then, to soften the snub, he gave his curiously sweet and hesitating smile.

Martin half-began a financial question, and let it drop. There was a silence.

'Well,' said George.

None of us spoke.

'Well,' said George again, like one of the students before the Court, as though he were seeing us off at a railway station. Martin and I, used to his habits in days past, realised that he was anxious for us to go. Perhaps he had someone else to see that night. As we stood up, George said, amiably but with relief:

'It was very good of you all to come round.'

Margaret kissed him. Martin and I (it wasn't our usual way, we might have been saying good night in a foreign country) shook him by the hand.

When Martin stopped the car in front of the Gearys' house, the drawing-room lights, curtains undrawn, shone out into the front garden: there were other luminous rectangles in the houseproud road. Denis Geary met us at the door.

'Here you are! It's not so late, after all.'

I had rung up from the Assize Hall to say that they weren't to wait supper for us, we couldn't tell when we should be home. Alison Geary was hurrying us into the bright warm room, saying that we couldn't have eaten much. Margaret replied that she was past eating, but, at her ease as she wasn't at George's, added that she was pining for a drink. 'It's ready for you,' said Denis, pointing to the sideboard. They had been preparing for us all the evening. Martin, who was ravenous, tucked into a plateful of cold beef: we sat, not at the table, but in easy chairs round the room; outside the french windows, stars sparkled in the cold clear sky. 'That's better,' said Denis to Margaret, who was now starting on some bread and cheese. 'You all looked a bit peaked when you came in. We'd been expecting that,' said Alison. Margaret smiled at them, and gave a grateful-sounding sigh.

We hadn't been sitting there for long before we told the Gearys about George's decision. Is he really going? Alison wanted to know. Yes, we said, we were certain that he meant it. Margaret added that he wasn't fit to go off alone, his physical state was worse than any of us imagined. Denis looked at her; 'I'll see if I can check on that,' he said.

'I don't think he'll thank you for it,' I told him.

'I tried,' Margaret said.

George was going, we said to Denis. He didn't intend to listen to anything that got in his way. I thought – but Margaret believed he could be deceiving himself – that he knew he wasn't a good life.

'So we can't stop him, you think?' said Denis, frowning, chafing to be practical. Then he added gently, having seen, more continuously than we had, the whole course of George's existence:

'Perhaps it's all for the best.'

Soon afterwards he said:

'Anyway, this town isn't going to be quite the same without him.'

He said it without any expression on his elder statesman's face. It might have been a platitude. None of us was feeling genial, no one smiled. But Denis, though he was a very kind man, was not without a touch of irony.

He refilled our glasses. He looked across at his wife, as though they were colloguing. Then, in exactly the same tone, firm and sympathetic, in which he had greeted me on the first night of the trial, he spoke to the three of us:

'Now then. You've got to put all this behind you.'

For an instant, no one answered.

'All of it,' Denis went on. 'The whole hideous business you've been listening to. You've got to forget it. You've got to forget it.'

Very quietly, speaking to an old friend whom he respected, Martin said:

'I absolutely disagree.'

All of a sudden, in the bright comfortable room, we were back in the argument – no, it wasn't an argument, it was at once too much at random and too convergent for that, we agreed more than we disagreed, the dialectic existed only below the words – which I had been having with Margaret for a long time past and with Martin on those nights together during the trial.

It was wrong to forget. We had forgotten too much. This was the beginning of illusions. Most of all (this was Martin, speaking straight to Denis Geary) of the liberal illusions.

False hope was no good. False hope, that you hold on to by forgetting things.

The only hope worth having was built on everything you knew, the facts you didn't like as well as the facts you did. That was a difficult hope. For the social condition, it was the only hope that would give us all a chance. For oneself—

Was anyone tough enough to look at himself, as he really was, without sentimentality or mercy, all the time?

For an instant I thought, though I didn't report it, of something that had happened to me during the trial. When Kitty Pateman was being cross-examined, when we all might have expected to forget our own egos, I found myself shutting my eyes, flooded with shame. It was entirely trivial. I had suddenly remembered – I had no idea what trigger set it off – an incident when I was about eighteen. My aunt Milly had just been making a teetotal pronouncement, her picture was in the local paper, and I was talking to some friends. One of them suspected that she was a connection of mine: I swore blind that I had never seen her in my life.

It wasn't the memory itself that rocked me, now that it returned in the Gearys' sitting-room. Who hasn't stood stock-still in the street, blinking away some petty shame which has just jabbed back to mind? No, what shook one was the sheer perseverance and invading-power of one's self-regard. Whenever we made attempts to loose ourselves, that confined us. And yet, in brutal terms, it also saved us to survive.

Reason. Why had so much of our time reneged on it? Wasn't that our characteristic folly, treachery or crime?

Reason was very weak as compared with instinct. Instinct was closer to the aboriginal sea out of which we had all climbed. Reason was a precarious structure. But, if we didn't use it to understand instinct, then there was no health in us at all.

Margaret said, she had been brought up among people who believed it was easy to be civilised and rational. She had hated it. It made life too hygienic and too thin. But still, she had come to think even that was better than glorifying unreason.

Put reason to sleep, and all the stronger forces were let loose. We had seen that happen in our own lifetimes. In the world: and close to us. We couldn't get out of knowing, that it meant a chance of hell.

Glorifying unreason. Wanting to let the instinctual forces loose. Martin said – anyone who did that, either hadn't much of those forces within himself, or else wanted to use others' for his own purpose. And that was true of private leaders like George as much as public ones.

(Were others thinking, as I did, of those two women? Was it true of one of them?)

Midnight had passed. Margaret and Alison were trying to look after each other. Margaret knew that the Gearys were not, like the rest of us, buoyed up by the energy of strain. We were feeling tireless, as one does in the crisis of a love affair, ready to walk all night. The Gearys had had nothing to make them tireless: Margaret said it was time to go to bed. But Alison had a sense that we were getting a curious kind of nepenthe, even when we were speaking as harshly as we could. We weren't being considerate: at times we should have said that we didn't mind reawakening our own distress or anyone else's: and yet, it seemed that we were producing the opposite effect. It was like being made hypocrites by accident. Whatever we said, however hard our voices sounded, just by being together we were creating an island of peace.

No, said Alison, he (Denis) didn't have to go to school tomorrow. She would make us a pot of tea. To herself, she thought it was good for us to go on sitting there.

We shied off tea, which had been offered to us enough that day. Then Denis ordered us to have another drink. Martin refused, saying he had to drive his car back to Cambridge before the morning. Margaret settled down in her chair, wakeful, but all of us quiet by now.

Denis said: 'We can only do little things, can't we? But we must go on doing them. At any rate, I must. There's no option. I shall have to go on doing the things that come to hand.'

Martin nodded. They spoke about old acquaintances, whom they had known when they were in the same form together. Denis broke off:

'Look here, I'm the Martha of this party. Much more than she is.' He put his hand over his wife's. 'There's a certain amount of debris to be cleared up. You'd better remind me what I ought to do.' A call on George before he left – he was ticking off: 'those Patemans': inquiries about the prisons. That all?

Then, leaning forward, he surprised us – it came out without any lead at all – by asking what was the name of that old man, who, living in riches, said he felt like a beggar holding out his hand for another day of life. Was that going to happen to us all? When did it begin to happen? He was in his early fifties, but, half-smiling, he wanted an answer. I was the oldest there, but I shook my head.

'I've got an uncomfortable idea', said Denis, 'that some day it is going to happen to me.'

PART FIVE

THE FLOW RETURNING

CHAPTER XXXVIII

THE COST OF MR PATEMAN

YOU'VE got to forget it, Denis Geary had said, that night in his house after the trial. But, for at least a couple of prosaic reasons, it wouldn't have been easy, even if we had been different people: one of those reasons was the result of some activities of Denis himself. He had duly paid his call on George Passant, who had mentioned that, once he left the country – which he did within a week – there was no one to visit Cora. Perhaps it might be arranged for me to do so? It was the most off-hand of legacies. I did not hear a word from George direct, although he had passed on a *poste restante* address.

I got in touch with Holloway prison, and was told that Cora was totally uninterested: she was, by her own choice, living in solitary confinement, and would scarcely speak to the doctors or prison officers. A few weeks later, I had a telephone call from the governor. 'Now she says that she wouldn't mind seeing you some day. It won't be pleasant for you, but I expect you must be prepared for that.'

It was a bright afternoon late in May as I drove through the low indistinguishable North London streets, which after living in the town so long I had never seen: betting shops, little shabby cafés with chalk-scrawls on blackboards outside, two-storey terrace after two-storey terrace, then porticoed houses, oddly prosperous, in sight of the pastiche castle itself. In a public garden the candles stood bright on the flowering chestnuts, but when I got out of the car in front of the gaol the air blew bitterly cold from the arctic, the late spring cold that we were getting used to.

As I was signing my name in the visitors' book, I should have been glad to get as used to prisons, hospitals, any institutions where the claustral dread seized hold of me: even now, I couldn't get rid of that meaningless anxiety. The corridors, the stone, the smells: the sight of other visitors taken passively off. By a mistake of my own, I was led to the wrong

602

reception room, something like a café, plastic-topped tables with trolleys pushing between them. It was a general visiting day, the tables were already full, I was wondering if I could have picked out prisoners from the relations who came to see them. Some wearing their remand dresses, blue and pink, as Cora had done in the local gaol. As I waited, standing in the corner, I noticed one woman chain-smoking, with a packet of cigarettes in front of her. It looked as though she was determined to get through it before the hour was up.

In a few minutes one of the staff found me.

'Oh no,' she said, with a commanding smile, like a hospital nurse's, 'we couldn't let her in here. It wouldn't be safe.'

With anyone inside for her kind of crime, she was explaining, the other prisoners would try to 'do' her. It was as Maxwell had said. Cora was making a rational choice in opting for solitary. It showed that she had thought out how to preserve her own life.

'It's a headache for us,' said the deputy. 'And it's going to be a headache as long as she's here.'

Each time they took her out for exercise, it meant a security operation; to the same extent, but in exact reverse, as if she were a prisoner about whom plans were being made for an escape. As for herself, she gave no trouble. She didn't grumble, her cell was immaculate. Apart from what they had on-paper, the prison staff knew nothing more about her.

The deputy, who name was Mrs Bryden, took me to another block and opened the door of a very small room, perhaps ten feet by six: inside were a table and two chairs, the backs of both chairs almost touching the walls, which were papered but had no decorations of any kind. On the table, curiously dominant, the only other object in the room, stood a single ashtray. 'You've an hour to yourself,' said Mrs Bryden. 'Two officers will be waiting in the corridor outside to take her back.'

The door opened again, and, one of those officers on either side of her, Cora stood in the doorway. She was wearing one of her own dresses, one which she had worn on the first day of the trial. She nodded as Mrs Bryden greeted her and said goodbye to me.

As the two of us sat there alone, I offered her a cigarette, grateful right at the beginning – as in a hospital visit – for anything which got some seconds ticked away.

I had to break the silence.

'You know George has gone away?' My voice sounded loud and brusque.

Again she nodded.

While I was thinking of another opening, she said:

'I liked George.'

'He'll come back some time.'

'Will he?' she said, without reaction.

Another interval. My tongue wouldn't work any better – maybe worse – than when I saw her before the trial.

'What's it like in here?'

Her glance met mine, slid viscously away, pale-eyed in the heavy handsome face. She gave a contemptuous shrug.

'What do you think it's like?' she said. Then her tone became a violent mutter:

'There's the soap.'

'What?'

'The soap. It's diabolical. Every morning when I go to wash, it makes me want to throw up.'

I listened to a long, unyielding, gravelly complaint about the soap. It sounded as though she had a sensitive nose. Against my will, I felt a kind of sympathy.

'Why don't you tell them?'

'They wouldn't care.'

She gave up complaining, and sank into muteness again. Inventing one or two questions, I got nothing but nods. Calmly she asked:

'Will they let me see her?'

'I don't know.' I did know: but it wasn't for me to tell her, or at least I rationalised it so.

Another patch of muteness. Again calmly, she said:

'What's the position about letting us out?'

I said, surely her solicitors had told her already. She said yes, and then, with implacable repetitive calm and obstinacy, asked the question once more.

Well, it spun the time out to explain. The sentence, as she knew, I said, was a statutory one: but, as she also knew, it didn't mean what it said. In some years, no one could tell quite when, the authorities would be reviewing their cases: if there was thought to be no danger, then they might be released.

'How long?'

'In some cases, it's quite a short time.'

'They won't do that for us. People will be watching what happens to us.'

That was more realistic than anything I had heard from her before.

Raising her voice, she asked: 'I want to know, how long do you think they'll keep us in?'

I thought it was a time to speak straight. 'If they're sure there's no danger, my guess would be something like ten years.'

'What are you talking about, danger?'

'They'll need to be sure you won't do anything of the same kind again.'

She gave a short despising laugh.

'They needn't worry themselves. We shan't do anything like that again.'

For an instant I recalled that colleague of Hankins, too clever by half, making bright remarks before the verdict. Then, more sharply, Mrs Pateman talking of her daughter.

'We shan't do anything like that again,' said Cora.

She added:

'Why should we?'

I couldn't reply. Not through horror (which at that moment, and in fact throughout that interview, I didn't feel): through something like loneliness, or even a sense of mystification that led into nothing. It was a relief to ask her commonplace questions – after all, if my guess was right, when she came out she'd still be a young woman, wouldn't she? Not much over thirty, perhaps? What did she intend to do?

'I haven't got as far as that,' she said.

But she had. It came out – she wasn't unwilling to let it – that she had been making plans. The plans were practical. They would go and live somewhere else, in a large town, perhaps London. They would change their names. They might try to change their appearance, certainly they would dye their hair. They wouldn't have much difficulty, if the labour market hadn't altered, in getting jobs. They would have to cover up for not having employment cards, but still they'd manage. In all she said, there was no vestige of a sign that she was thinking of re-shaping her life – no more than George ever had, though about that I had once believed otherwise. She had no thought of finding another way to live. I was listening for it, but there was none at all. All she foresaw, or wanted to foresee, was picking up where she had left off.

Throughout she had been using the word 'we'. It was 'we' who were going to find another place to settle in. Was that going to happen in ten years' time? How would she endure it, if it didn't happen? It was difficult to have any prevision of what Kitty would be like. She might be imagining a different kind of life. If she were capable of that, when the time came she would throw Cora away as though she didn't recognise her face.

The hour wore on. I was trying, when she dropped her chin, to catch a glance at my wrist-watch below the table.

'I don't know how to pass the time,' she said. She hadn't observed me: she was saying it – not as a complaint, but as a matter of fact – about herself. What did she do all day? I couldn't make out. Sometimes 'they' let her listen to the radio.

'It's all right for her,' she said, once more as a matter of fact, without envy. 'She'll be doing a lot of reading.'

She repeated:

'I don't know how to pass the time. She'll be learning things.'

She seemed to be thinking of tomorrow and the next day, not of the stretch of years.

My time, not hers, was nearly up. I said that I should have to go. As though she were imitating the judge after he had sentenced them, she gave me a dismissive nod.

Meanwhile, I had been having another reminder, which, except by disconnecting the telephone, I could not escape. I had told Mr Pateman – in his frenetic state, when his wife led me to him – that he was at liberty to talk to me. He took me at my word. When we had returned to London, on the first evening, the telephone rang. A personal call: would I accept it, and reverse the charges? Mr Pateman's grinding voice: 'I can't let it go at this.' His daughter was ill. They hadn't listened to what the doctors said. They were behaving like rats in mazes. Something must be done about his daughter. Something must be done about people in her condition. What about the authorities 'high up': when could I get them moving? Patiently that first night, I said that neither I nor any other private citizen could do anything at all: this was a matter of law – 'I can't be expected to be satisfied with that.' When should I be coming to the town again, so that he could explain his 'point of view'? Not for some time, I had no engagement there: in any case, I said, I knew very well how he felt. No, he had to explain exactly.

The conversation was not conclusive. Three or four times a week the call came through: reverse the charges? The same voice, the same statements, often identically the same words. Rats in mazes. Authorities high up. His point of view. He wasn't rude, he wasn't even angry, he just went grinding on. Once he had found words which contented him, he felt no need to change them.

It was no use Margaret answering the telephone, and saying that I was out. He was ready to ring up again at midnight, 1 a.m., or very early the following morning. We thought of refusing to accept the calls: but that we couldn't bring ourselves to do. Whatever his wife had feared, whether it was that he might become clinically deranged, seemed not to be happening to him now. In hectoring me, in grating on with his ritual, he had found an activity which obsessed and satisfied him. He might even have lost contact with what the object of it was. Over the telephone I couldn't see – and didn't want to see – his face. I suspected that he was beginning to look as when I had first seen him, the dislocation going, the confidence of *folie de grandeur* flooding back.

Yet each night we became fretted as we waited for the telephone to ring. And, there was no denying it, we found ourselves showing a streak of miserliness, as though we were being infected from the other end of the line. It was ridiculous. Margaret had never counted shillings in her life. We spent more on cigarettes in a week than those reverse charges could possibly amount to. Nevertheless, with the experience of the trial only a few weeks behind us, we scrutinised our telephone bill with indignation, calculating what was the cost of Mr Pateman.

CHAPTER XXXIX

A YOUNG MAN ON HIS OWN

A FEW days after my visit to the prison, Charles and I were sitting under a weeping willow on the river-bank. It was a fine afternoon, and I had gone down to his school to settle what he should do during the next academic year. Not that there was much to settle, for he had made up his mind months before. He had cleared off all the examinations, and it was time to go. The only issue remaining was not when, but where. He was only a little over sixteen, and he had to fill in three terms before he went to the university. He was taking the chance to start off on his travels, and it was some of those plans that we had been discussing.

'You might even write a letter occasionally,' I said.

He grinned.

It would have seemed strange in my time, I said, to be going off on one's own at his age. In fact, among my friends, it would have been not only strange, but unimaginable. Of course, we didn't have the money—

'Do we really grow up faster, do you think?'

'In some ways, yes, you do.'

I added:

'But, for what it's worth, I wanted to get married before I was twenty.'

The Sleep of Reason

'Who to?'

'My first wife.'

'You didn't marry her for six – or was it seven – years afterwards, did you?'

'No.'

'If it had happened when you were twenty – what would it have been like?'

'It couldn't have been worse than it turned out.'

Charles gave a grim, saga-like smile, similar to his uncle's. But I was thinking that, though he knew the facts of my life with extreme accuracy, he didn't know how torn about I'd been. He wouldn't have believed that I had gone through that long-drawn-out and crippling love. He saw me as balanced and calm, a comparatively sensible ageing man. Sometimes I was amused. I permitted myself to say:

'You haven't the monopoly of temperament in this family, you know.'

It was easy to talk to him, as to Martin, on the plane of sarcasm. As we sat there, I mentioned the telephone activities of Mr Pateman. 'You've brought it on yourself,' said Charles, operating on the same plane. An acquaintance of his sculled by, and Charles gave an amiable wave – rather like, since he was leaving so soon, Robin Hood gazing on the exploits of the budding archers. When the swell had passed, the river was mirror-calm, the willow leaves meeting their reflections in the water. It was something like an afternoon with C. L. Dodgson, I said to Charles, and went on to tell him that I had talked to Cora Ross in Holloway.

'Haven't you packed all that up by now?'

'Not quite.' I added, sometimes it seemed that I never should.

He leaned forward, confronting me.

'I think you're wrong.'

'What do you mean, I'm wrong?'

'This is an incident. If it hadn't been for sheer blind chance, it wouldn't have been an incident that mattered to you. All along, you've given it a significance that it doesn't possess.' He was speaking lucidly, articulately, but with force and something like antagonism.

'I could have found other incidents, you know. Which would have affected me in the same fashion.'

'That's because you're looking for them,' said Charles. 'Do you remember, that weekend I was at home, you were breathing hell-fire and damnation about Auschwitz? I disagreed with you then. You noticed that, did you? And I still disagree with you.'

'Auschwitz happened.'

608

'Many other things have happened. Remember, Auschwitz happened years before I was born. I'm bound to be interested in what's happening now—'

'That's fair enough.'

'Of course there are awful things. Here and now. But I want to find them out for myself.'

'Retracing all our mistakes in the process?'

'That's *not* fair enough.' He said it politely, but as though he had been thinking it out alone and his mind had hardened. 'I don't think I'm easily taken in. My generation isn't, you know. We've had to learn a fair amount.'

'It's curious how you talk about "your generation",' I said. 'We never did.'

He wasn't distracted. 'Perhaps that's because we know that we have a difficult job to do. You don't deny that, do you?'

I said, that would be the last thing I intended.

He was referring to his friends by name. As a group, they were abler, very much abler, than those I had known as a boy. Some of them would take the world as they found it: become academics, conventional politicians, civil servants: that was easy, they had no problem there. But one or two, like himself, were not so content. Then what do you do? 'We should like to find something useful. Perhaps I ought to lower my sights, but I don't feel inclined to, until I've had a shot. And I don't think it would be very different, even if I hadn't got you on my back—'

He threw in that remark quite gently. I said that he could forget me.

He said, still gently but with a flick of sarcasm, that he would do his best to. That was the object of the exercise.

No, not really the object, but the first condition, he corrected himself. He wanted to throw in his weight where it would be useful: and he wanted to be sure it was his weight and no one else's.

It had the ring of a youth's ambition, at the same time arrogant and idealistic, mixed up with dreams of happiness. Some of it sounded as though it had been talked out with friends. Most of it, I thought, was solitary. He seemed spontaneous and easy-natured, but he kept his secrets.

He said that he had no more use for 'doctrines of individual salvation' than I had. (I wondered where they had picked up that expression?) Any of those doctrines was dangerous, he said: they nearly always meant that, either actively or passively, one wished harm on to the world. Of course, he wanted for himself anything that came. What did he want? He was imagining something, but kept it to himself. He returned to saying that, whatever he found to do, it was going to be hard enough: so he couldn't afford to carry any excess luggage with him.

'I want everything as open-ended as it can be, isn't that right?' he said. 'I don't want to set limits yet awhile. Limits about people, I mean. So that's why I can't take this trouble of yours as tragically as you do. Do you mind that?'

All I could answer was to shake my head. I was sure by now that he had come to this meeting resolved to make his declaration: once he had got it over, he was in high spirits. Cheerfully he stretched himself, sucking a stem of grass. It was almost time, he said, for us to move off into the town for tea. 'Tea's not much good to you, is it?' he said. 'Well, afterwards we'll go to a hotel and I'll stand you a Scotch. Just to celebrate the fact that this is the last time you'll have to come down to this establishment—' he spread out a hand towards the river, the fields, the distant towers across the meadows.

I asked whether he would miss it at all: but I guessed the answer, for here we were very much alike.

'Who knows?' he said.

Yes, I knew, the places, the times, one was nostalgic for were not the obvious ones, not even the happy ones.

'Anyway,' he went on, 'I can always send them home thoughts from abroad.'

A moment later he said:

'It will be good to be on the move.'

Then, before we stirred ourselves, he enquired about how we should be getting on at home. Maurice would presumably still be round: he was close to his mother, and that was fine. 'He's very sweet,' said Charles, who, like others of what he called his generation, wasn't ashamed of what mine would have considered saccharine expressions. He was fond of his half-brother, and sometimes, I thought, envied him, just because he seemed so untainted by the world. What would happen to him? 'I wish', said Charles, 'that he could get through his damned examinations.' Was there nothing we could do?

Charles was busy about others' concerns, joyful, vigorous, since in independence he was setting off on his own. It would be good to be on the move, he had said. I wasn't resenting the rapacity and self-absorption of his youth, perhaps one couldn't in a son when the organic links were strong, when one had known in every cell of one's body what that state was like. I should worry about his remaining alive, until I myself was dead. It was strange, though – not unpleasant, a kind of affirmation, but still strange – to see him sitting there, as much on his own as I was now or had ever been.

CHAPTER XL

DEATH OF AN OLD MAN

As Margaret and I sat over our breakfast, the telephone rang. Good God, I said, was it Mr Pateman again? – not so amused as Charles had been, hearing of this new addition to our timetable. Margaret answered, and as she stood there nodded ill-temperedly to me: it was a trunk call, from the usual place. Then her expression altered, and she replied in a grave and gentle tone. Yes, she would fetch me. For an instant she put a hand on mine, saying that it was about my father.

'This is Mr Sperry here.'

'Yes?'

'I'm afraid I've got bad news for you, I'm very sorry, I'm sure. Old Mr Eliot—'

'Yes?'

'Early this morning. He passed away.'

Again I said yes.

'I was with him when he went.'

Mr Sperry was asking me about the funeral. 'I'm doing what I can,' he said. I replied that I would arrive at the house by lunchtime. Mr Sperry, sounding more than ever apologetic, said that he had a piece of business then. Could I wait till half past three or four? 'It doesn't matter to him now, does it? He was a fine old gentleman. I'm doing what I can.'

Returning to the breakfast table, I repeated all this to Margaret. She knew that she would be desolated by her own father's death: she was tentative about commiserating with me about the death of mine. Somehow, even to her, it seemed like an act of nature. He was very old, she said: it sounded like a good way to die. It was a pity, though, that instead of having only his lodger with him, there was none of us. 'I'm not sure that he even wanted that,' I said.

We found ourselves discussing what he would have wanted in the way of funerals. It was so long since I had talked to him seriously – I had talked to him seriously so seldom, even when I was a child – that I had no idea. I suspected that he wouldn't have cared a damn. I forgot then, though later I remembered, that once he had expressed a surprisingly positive distaste for funerals in general, and his own in particular. He was rueful that if he died before his wife (he had outlived her by over forty years) she would insist on 'making a fuss'. But I forgot that.

Neither Margaret nor I felt any of that singular necrophilic confidence with which one heard persons express certainty about what a dead relative would have 'liked'. I had once stood with a party at Diana Skidmore's having drinks round her husband's grave, carefully placed near a summer-house on his own estate. Diana had been positive that there was nothing he would have liked more than to have his friends enjoy themselves close by: she was equally positive that he would, curiously enough, have strongly disliked golf balls infringing the airspace over the grave.

Margaret and I had no such clear idea. My father must have a funeral. In church? Again we didn't know. As one of his few gestures of marital independence, he had always refused to attend church with my mother, who was devout. I was pretty sure that he believed in nothing at all. Yet, for the sake of his choir practices, he had frequented church halls, church rooms, all his life. When I rang up Martin to tell him the news, I asked his opinion. Rather to my surprise, for Martin was a doctrinaire unbeliever, he thought that maybe we ought to have a service in the parish church. Quite why, he didn't or couldn't explain. Perhaps some strain of family piety, perhaps a memory of our mother, perhaps something more atavistic than that. Anyway, wherever his impulse came from, I was relieved, because I had it too.

This was a Wednesday, late in June. Martin's family would all travel the next day, and so would Margaret and Charles. The funeral had better be on Friday, if I could arrange it. That was what I had to tell Mr Sperry, as we sat in Aunt Milly's old 'front room' that afternoon – the room where, with indignant competence, she laid down the battle-plans for the tee-total campaigns. But I couldn't tell Mr Sperry about the funeral at once, for he had a good deal to tell me.

It was a dank close day, and when he opened the door he was in his shirt-sleeves. As though he wouldn't have considered it proper to speak of 'the old gentleman' dressed like that, he immediately put his jacket on. The Venetian blinds in the front room were lowered, a crepuscular light filtered through. Mr Sperry gazed at me with an expression that was sad and at the same time excited by the occasion.

'I'm very sorry, I'm sure,' he said, repeating his greeting at the door. I thanked him.

'Of course, it has to come to us all in the end, doesn't it? He had a long innings, you've got to remember that.'

Yes, I said.

'Mind you, he's been a bit poorly since the winter. But I didn't expect him to go like this, and I wonder if the doctor really did, though he says it might have happened any time.'

From his first words, he had been speaking in a hushed whisper, the tone in which my mother always spoke of death. In the same whisper, he went on:

'There was someone, though, who knew his time had come.'

He said: 'The old gentleman did. Himself.'

'When?'

'Last night.'

He paused. Then, more hushed: 'I was just getting in from a job, I had been looking after Mrs Buckley's drainpipe, it must have been getting on for half past six, and I heard him call out, Mr Sperry, Mr Sperry. He had a good strong voice right up to the end. Of course I went in, he was lying on his sofa, it was made up to sleep in, you know, he said, Mr Sperry, I wonder if you'd mind staying with me tonight. I said, yes, Mr Eliot, of course I will if you want me to. I said, is there anything the matter? He said, yes, stay with me please, I think I'm going to die tonight. That's what he said. So I said, do you mind if I go and get a bit to eat? He said, yes, you have your supper, and I went and had a bit of salmon, and came back as soon as I could. He said, I wonder if you'd mind holding my hand. So I stayed there all night. I kept asking him, do you want anything else, but he wouldn't say.'

I asked, was he in pain.

'He didn't say much after I got back, he didn't seem to want to. Sometimes he gave a kind of shout. I didn't think he was going, but he did. I wish I'd sent for the doctor sooner, Mrs Sperry and me, we blame ourselves for that. His breathing began to make a noise, then the sun came up. I'm sorry to say—'

I said, 'You did all that anyone could do.'

'It was full light before he went. The doctor got here a few minutes after.'

He added:

'I got her [Mr Sperry didn't explain who that was] to lay him out this morning. He didn't look very nice before, and I didn't think you'd want to see him like that.'

He said:

'I never heard anyone say a bad word about him.'

That was a formal epitaph, such as I used to hear in my childhood in that road. But Mr Sperry, as well as keeping his sense of propriety about a death, had also been totally efficient. The death certificate had been signed: the undertaker would be calling to see me later that evening. At last I had the opportunity to tell Mr Sperry that we wanted a church service. Mr Sperry was ready to cope with that. It meant that I ought to go round to the vicar's and fix a time, before the undertaker came. All the old gentleman's 'bits of things' had been sifted through and collected in his room. So far as Mr Sperry knew or could discover, he had not left a will.

'Why should he?' I asked. Yet, in fact, he owned the house: it was dilapidated now, not worth much, a thousand at most. Anyway, whatever arrangement Mr Sperry had with him (I later found that Mr Sperry was paying £2.2.6 a week), that must go on. Mr Sperry would not have brought up the subject – certainly not until after the funeral – but he was relieved.

He said:

'Now you'd like to see him, I'm sure.'

He took me into the hall, opened the door of my father's room, touched my sleeve, and left me alone. As I crossed the threshold into the half-dark, I had a sense, sudden, dominating, of *déjà vu*. I could just make out the short body lying on the sofa, then, though all the superstitious nerves held my fingers back, I switched on the light, and looked at him. Strangely, he appeared much more formidable than in life. His head had always been disproportionately larger than the rest of him: as it lay there above the sheets, it loomed strong and heavy, the clowning all gone now that the spectacles were off and the mild eyes closed. His moustache had been brushed and didn't droop any more. It might have been the face of a stranger – no, of someone bearing a family resemblance, a distant relative whom I hadn't often seen.

Standing by the sofa, I stayed and looked at him. It took an effort to move away, as I went to inspect the other side of the room, where Mr Sperry had neatly stacked my father's 'bits of things'. There were a couple of old suits: a bowler hat: a few shirts and pairs of long woollen pants: another night shirt, as well as the one his body was dressed in. An umbrella, one or two other odds and ends. No papers or letters of any kind that I could see (he must have destroyed all our letters as soon as he read them). A couple of library books to be returned, but otherwise not a single book of his own. The two clocks – but they had not been moved, one still stood on the mantelpiece, presentation plaque gleaming the other in the corner. That was all. He hadn't liked possessions: but still, not many men had lived till nearly ninety and accumulated less.

I went back and looked at him. All of a sudden, I realised why I had had that overmastering sense of *déjà vu*. It wasn't a freak, it was really something I had already seen. For it was in that room that, for the first time in my life, at the age of eight, I had seen a corpse. My grandfather, when he retired, had lived in this house with Aunt Milly, and he had died here (it was early in 1914). I had come along on an errand for my mother. I couldn't find Aunt Milly, and I ran through the house searching for her and rushed into this room. Just as when I entered today, it was half-dark, chinks of light round the edges of the blinds: there lay my grandfather in his coffin. Before, afraid, I ran away, I saw, or thought I saw, the grey spade beard, the stern and massive face. He had been a man of powerful nature, and perhaps my father's comic acts, which lasted all his life, had started in self-defence. And yet in death – if I had really seen my grandfather as I imagined – they looked very much the same.

When I put the room into darkness again, and rejoined Mr Sperry, he asked me:

'How did you like him?'

'Thank you,' I replied.

Satisfied, he gave me the vicar's address. They couldn't afford to live in the vicarage nowadays, said Mr Sperry. That didn't surprise me: the church had been built after I was born, the living had always been a poor one. The vicar I remembered must have been a man of private means: he and his wife had lived in some state, by the standards of the parish, and he shocked my mother, not only by his high church propensities (he's getting higher every week, she used to whisper, as though the altitude of clergymen was something illimitable) but also by rumours of private goings-on which at the time I did not begin to understand. Parties! Champagne, so the servants reported! Women present when his wife was away! My mother darkly suspected him of having what she called an 'intrigue' with one of the teachers at the little dame-school which she sent me to. My mother was shrewd, but she had a romantic imagination, and that was one of the mysteries in which she was never certain of the truth.

There was nothing of all that about the present incumbent. He was living in a small house near the police station, and politely he asked me into a front room similar to Mr Sperry's. He was a youngish, red-haired man with a smile that switched on and off, and a Tyneside accent.

I told him my name, and said that my father had died. At once, both with kindness and with the practice of one used to commiserating in the anonymous streets with persons he did not know, he gave me his sympathy. 'It's one of the great losses, when your parents go. Even when you're not so young yourself. There's a gap that no one's going to fill.' He was looking at me with soft brown eyes. 'But you've got to look at it this way. It's sad for you, but it isn't for him, you know. He's just gone from a nasty day like this '– he pointed to the grey cloud-dark street – 'and moved into a beautiful one. That's what it means for him. If you think of him, there's nothing to be sad about.'

I didn't want to answer. The vicar was kind and full of faith. Young Charles, I was thinking, might have called him sweet.

I went on to say that, if it could be managed, we should like the funeral in two days' time, on Friday. 'Excuse me, sir,' said the vicar, 'but could you say, have you any connection with this parish?'

That took me aback. Without thinking, I hadn't been prepared for it. My mother, hanging on to the last thread of status after my father's bankruptcy: her stall at the bazaar, her place at the mothers' meeting: she had felt herself, and made others feel her, a figure in that church until she died. Yet that was long ago. He had never heard of her, or of any of us. When I mentioned my name, it had meant nothing at all.

Of course, he said (both of us embarrassed, as I began lamely to produce the family credentials) he would be glad to take the funeral. Was there anything special that I required? A musical service? An organist? Once more that day I found myself thinking, as simply as my mother would have done, of what the old man might have 'liked'. He had loved music: yes, we would have an organist. In that case, said the vicar, the service couldn't happen till early evening on Friday, when the 'lady who plays the organ for us' got out of work. They couldn't afford a regular organist nowadays, he said: the church was poorer than it had been when I lived here, not many people attended, there were no well-to-do members of his congregation. The only one in my time (at least he seemed well-to-do to us) would have been the local doctor. 'The present doctors don't come to church,' said the vicar, with his switched-on, acceptant smile.

As I left his house, it was like walking home when I was a child. The church might have become poorer, but the houses – though many of them were the same houses – looked more prosperous: in front of several of them cars were standing, which, when my mother and I walked that quarter of a mile from church, we never saw. One of my father's neighbours was trimming the patch of grass between his front wall and the road. Others glanced at me from their windows: they must have known my father, at least by sight, but not me.

As soon as I got back to Mr Sperry, he asked me, in his obsessive, considerate fashion, what I would care to do until the undertaker came. Without knowing why, I said that prehaps I could sit in the garden for a few minutes. At once Mr. Sperry let me out, past the barren plum tree which Charles had seen from his grandfather's window, through the paved yard, down the steps into the garden. There, from a little shed, Mr Sperry brought out a deckchair, and said that he would call me when the undertaker arrived. For the second time, not exactly timidly but like one to whom physical contact didn't come easy, he touched my arm.

I knew the geography of that garden as well as that of ours at home, which in fact I could see over a couple of low walls, not more than thirty yards away: the apple-trees had been cut down, under whose shade I used to sit reading on summer nights like this. Aunt Milly's garden had always been better kept than ours, thanks to the devotion of her husband. It was this one I had been reminding Martin of, when we returned to the Gearys' after that lawyers' dinner in the middle of the trial. It occurred to me that, since I ceased to be poor, I hadn't had a garden of my own to sit in: that was a luxury (the thought might have pleased my mother) which I had enjoyed only in our bankrupt house.

In the moist air, the smells of the night stocks and roses were so dense that they seemed palpable. For, though Aunt Milly's husband had been a conscientious gardener, Mr Sperry was a master: which, now I had watched him in action, didn't surprise me. I couldn't remember seeing a garden of this size so rich. Phlox, lupins, delphiniums, pinks on the border, rambler-roses on the wall: a syringa-bush close to the bed of stocks. The scents hung all round me, like the scents of childhood.

From my chair, looking up at the house, I could see the french windows of my father's room. They stood dark-faced, the curtains drawn since that morning. It was up the steps to those french windows that I had led Charles, over a year before. I should not go up that way again.

CHAPTER XLI

ANOTHER FUNERAL

SUNLIGHT shining on the lacquer, the empty hearse stood outside the church. Martin's car, and the one that I had hired, were drawn up in line. We had arrived early, and had been waiting on the pavement, near the iron palings which guarded a yew tree and the 1908 red brick. Irene and her daughter were wearing black dresses, and Margaret was in grey:

Martin, Pat, Charles and I had all put on black ties. The Sperrys, though, who had just walked slowly along the road from what used to be my father's house, were in full mourning, or at least in clothes such as I remembered at funerals in this church, he in a black suit with an additional and almost indistinguishable armband, she in jet from her hat to her shoes. As they passed us, they said a few soft words.

One or two other people were approaching, perhaps members of his old choir, who had sent a wreath. The solitary cracked bell began to toll, and I took Margaret, our feet scuffling on the gravel (was that sensation familiar to Martin too?) towards the church door. The pitch-pine. The smell of wax and hassocks. The varnished chairs. In my mother's heyday, we used to stop at a row immediately behind the churchwardens', which she had appropriated for her own. But we couldn't now, since the church, small as it was, was full of empty space. There were the under-taker and his four bearers. The Sperrys. The seven of the family, walking up the aisle. Three others. I didn't know, but it might have been about the size of the congregation on Sunday mornings nowadays. With the organ playing, we moved up to the second row: there, all of us except Margaret having been drilled in anglican customs, we pulled out the hassocks and went down on our knees. It was a long time since I had been to any kind of service, longer still to a church funeral. On its trestle behind the altar-rails, the coffin rested, wreath-covered, brass-handled, short, unobtrusive.

While the organ went on playing, I glanced at the hymn board, record of last Sunday's evensong, and began mechanically – as though the boyhood habit hadn't been interrupted by a week, organ music booming on lulled but uncomprehending ears – juggling with the numbers in my head. Once that game had made the time go faster, helping on the benediction.

The vestry door had opened and shut: the vicar was standing in front of the altar. His voice was as strong as the Clerk of Assize's at the trial, without effort filling the empty church.

I am the resurrection and the life, saith the Lord: he that believeth in me, though he were dead, yet shall he live: and whosoever liveth and believeth in me shall never die.

At one time I knew those words by heart. I couldn't have told whether I was listening now.

We brought nothing into this world, and it is certain we can carry nothing out. The Lord gave, and the Lord hath taken away: blessed be the name of the Lord.

I couldn't have told whether I was listening now. Even at Sheila's

funeral, my first wife's, though I was ill with misery, I couldn't concentrate, I was dissociated from the beautiful clerical voice – and yes, from
the coffin resting there. Yet this time I half-heard, It is certain we can
carry nothing out. Just for an instant, I had a thought about my father. I
wondered if the same had come to Martin, whom I had told about his
possessions. No one had had much less to carry out.

*For a thousand years in thy sight are but as yesterday: seeing that is past
as a watch in the night.*

*In the morning it is green, and groweth up: but in the evening it is cut down,
dried and withered.*

*For when thou art angry, all our days are gone: we bring our years to an
end, as it were a tale that is told.*

*The days of our age are threescore years and ten: and though men be so
strong, that they come to fourscore years: yet is their strength then but labour
and sorrow, so soon passeth it away, and we are gone.*

That was being said over my father in his late eighties. It must have
been said also at the funeral of Eric Mawby, aged eight.

First Corinthians Fifteen. By this time I was scarcely trying to listen,
or even to follow the words in my prayer book. At school I had studied
Corinthians for an examination, and I couldn't keep my mind from drifting
to my father's forebears, who had listened to that passage, there was no
escaping it, generation after generation for hundreds of years.

The last enemy that shall be destroyed is death.

Not my grandfather. That deep Victorian agnostic had never been
inside a church after he left school at the age of ten. Yet – one couldn't
trust a child's memory, I might be romanticising him, but I didn't think
so – he was pious as well as agnostic, he had a library of nineteenth-
century religious controversy, and then decided, just as Martin might
have done, that he didn't believe where he couldn't believe. He would
have made a good nineteenth-century Russian. I was sure, and here I did
trust my memory, that he was a clever man. He would have got on with
his grandchildren and with Charles.

*What advantageth it me, if the dead rise not? Let us eat and drink, for
tomorrow we die.*

But his father and grandfather: they hadn't had the education he had
hacked out for himself. He believed, he told me when I was five and could
read quite well, that that was more than they could do. So far as he knew,
his grandfather could only make his mark. Yet, he insisted, they were
strong, intelligent men. He was bitter about them, and the muteness
from which they came. Small craftsmen one generation: then back to

agricultural labourers (not peasants, for England had had no peasants for long enough), no history, no change, further back than the church registers went. There was none of the social moving, the ups-and-downs, that had happened on my mother's side. The Eliot families must have gone to the funeral services in the village churches, and listened to this Pauline eloquence for at least a dozen generations. Some of that gene-pool was in us. Gone stoically, most of them, I thought. As with us, phrases stuck in their memories. As with me as a child, the rabbinical argumentation washed over them.

Death is swallowed up in victory. O death, where is thy sting? O grave, where is thy victory? The sting of death is sin: and the strength of sin is the law.

How old was I, when I first became puzzled by that last gnomic phrase? We had all listened to it, the whole line of us, life after life, so many lives, lost and untraceable now.

The vicar led the way out of church; following him, the bearers' shoulders were firm under the coffin. Margaret and I walked behind, then Martin and Irene, then the grandchildren. As the coffin was slid into the hearse, windows so clear that there might have been no glass there, the undertaker stood by, rubicund, content that all was in order, holding his top hat in a black gloved hand. 'Easy on,' muttered one of the bearers at the last shove.

Slowly the little procession of cars drove down the side street into the main road. On the pavement people passed casually along, but one old man stopped in his walk and took off his hat. The parish church, being so new, had never had a graveyard: and in fact all the parish graveyards in the town had been full for years. My mother had been buried in the big municipal cemetery, and it was there, along the sunny bus route, cars rushing towards us and the suburbs, that we were driving. But my mother, as she had died young, had not arranged to reserve a grave beside her: and that was a matter to which my father would not have given a thought. So his coffin was carried to the opposite side of the great cemetery, new headstones glaring in the sun, flower vases twinkling, angels, crosses, such a profusion of the signs of death that it gave an extra anonymity to death itself: as in one of the wartime collective graves, where all that one took in was that the victims of a siege were buried here.

In a far corner, a neat rectangle had been marked out, and below the edge of turf, one could see the fresh brown earth. Wreaths away, coffin lowered (again one of the bearers muttered), and we stood round.

There were no prayer books to follow now. Rich voice in the hot evening.

Man that is born of a woman hath but a short time to live, and is full of misery.

In the midst of life we are in death.

I had noticed which of the bearers was holding bits of earth in hand. At the end of the appeal he was waiting to hear *suffer us not, at our last hours, for any pains of death, to fall from them.* Promptly he stepped forward and, with a couple of flicks, threw down the earth upon the coffin.

Opposite to me, across the grave, Charles's mouth suddenly tightened. He had not heard that final sound before.

For as much as it hath pleased Almighty God of his great mercy to take unto himself the soul of our dear brother Herbert Edward here departed: we therefore commit his body to the ground; earth to earth, ashes to ashes, dust to dust, in sure and certain hope of the Resurrection to eternal life ... the voice went on, it was soon all over, the collect and the blessing.

We were very near one entrance to the cemetery, and before long were standing there, shaking hands. Our voices, which had been so subdued as we waited for the bell to toll and on the road to the cemetery, suddenly became loud. I heard Martin's, usually quiet, sound hearty as he thanked the vicar. I shook hands with the undertaker and the bearers, one of whom kept rubbing his hand on his trousers, as though he couldn't get rid of the last particle of earth. Margaret was telling the Sperrys, once again, how grateful we were for their kindness.

Thanks given and re-given, we stood about, not knowing what to do. No one wanted to make a move. Pat's face, more labile than any of ours, was suiting itself to sadness, just as it did to a party. Charles, tall by his cousin's side, politely answered questions from Mr Sperry. The truth was, we were at a loss. I had made a mistake, or forgotten something. After funerals such as this, my mother and her friends had always departed to a meal, spending on it often much more than they could afford. Singular meals, so far as I remembered – ham, chicken (bought for this special occasion), blancmanges, jellies, cakes. A bottle of what my mother always called Port Wine. When I was Charles's age, that seemed to me as naïve as it would to him. Yet maybe it was wise. It made an end. As we stood about at the cemetery gate, this was no sort of end.

Glancing round with bright, apprehensive eyes (the same treacle-brown eyes that one could see in her son and daughter), Irene said:

'Well, perhaps we ought to be thinking of—' her voice trailed off.

Martin, once more over-hearty, was saying to the Sperrys: 'Now are you all right for transport? Are you sure you're all right? Or else I can get you home—' The vicar and the undertaker assured him that they had room for the Sperrys.

More thanks. At last that party moved towards the hearse, and we to our own cars. My niece said to me, through the hair which obscured half her face: 'That's over, isn't it, Uncle Lewis?' She might have said it by way of comfort. Charles, who was walking with her, flashed me a hard and searching look, as though I had mismanaged things.

CHAPTER XLII

A BIT OF NEWS

WE were all staying at the hotel which Martin had used during the trial. There were too many of us to go to friends: and in fact, we shouldn't have chosen to. Without a word passed between us, Martin and I hadn't wanted to see a person we knew on this last family occasion in the town. Let it be as obscure as the old occasions. The local paper had printed a one-inch paragraph about our father's death, and that was all.

As our party was walking past the reception desk towards the lifts, Martin hung behind.

'Get down before the rest, for a few minutes,' he said to me, very quietly.

'Where?'

'Oh, the old bar.'

It was the bar, aquarium-lit, in which he had spoken to me with pain and ruthlessness in the middle of the trial. I was down a little before him, and when he entered and we looked at each other, I hadn't forgotten and knew that nor had he. This time the bar was emptier: it was later, the pre-dinner drinkers had sifted away. Just one single acquaintance called out to Martin: 'You here again?' Here again, Martin, affably, impersonally, called back.

The alcove, where we had talked before, was vacant. We sat ourselves there, and I asked him what he would drink. No, he said, the drinks were on him. As he carried them to our table, I watched his face, set, controlled: yet somehow, as I had seen once or twice in his life, it was illuminated from within, like one of the turnip heads in which we used to place candles when we were boys.

'I have a bit of news,' he said.

'Yes.'

'Pat is going to get married.'

'Is he, by God?'

Then I asked, who to: but I thought I knew.

'Muriel. Roy Calvert's Muriel.'

Martin was so happy that I had to be happy for him. I said, using our own cipher, well, Pat might have done worse.

'He might have done worse,' said Martin, all cautiousness gone.

It would have seemed strange thirty years before, I said, to think of his son marrying Roy Calvert's daughter. Actually (though I didn't bring it back to mind) he and Roy had never been more than acquaintances. If Roy were alive now, he would have been fifty-three.

'It's hard to imagine him like that, isn't it?' said Martin.

'Anyway, you're obviously glad.'

'I'm very glad.'

The engagement would be announced the following Monday, he said. He didn't want any mention of it at dinner that night.

'Why ever not?'

He shook his head.

'Whatever could be more natural?' I meant, an old man dies, his grandson gets married: after all that we had said, and felt, in this alcove a few weeks before, we were back in the flow of things. It mightn't be very grand: there was the splendid, of which we had seen a little, there was the hideous, of which we had seen enough: yet this was neither, it was what we lived in, in order to endure.

'I don't think Irene would like it,' he said.

Well, I said, he knew his wife better than I did. But didn't he remember her at the Christmas Eve party, shouting out birth, copulation, children, death, as though that was the biography of us all?

'At that party,' Martin broke in, 'you knew what we were in for? About the trial?'

'I had an idea.'

'I only realised later that you must have done.'

He went back to talking of Irene.

'She's more conventional than I am, you know.'

That sounded strange, after the life she had led. But he was certain. She wouldn't consider it proper to celebrate an engagement on the day that we had buried our father.

'Also,' he added, 'I don't think she's too happy about the marriage, anyway.'

In that case, I said, she was pretty hard to please. The girl was attractive: she was said to be clever, not surprising for Roy's daughter: she had a small fortune of her own. They wouldn't have to support Pat any further, presumably. Martin, with a brotherly grin, said he had thought of that.

'To be perfectly honest,' I said, 'I'm surprised you didn't get more obstruction from the other side.'

'The young woman', said Martin, 'made up her mind.'

He added:

'But still, Irene doesn't really like it.' He shrugged. 'That doesn't count. It's going to happen soon.'

'When?'

'Very soon. In about a month.'

'What's the hurry?'

Martin smiled. After a moment, he said, off-hand:

'Oh, the good old-fashioned reason.' His smile spread, masculine, lubricous, paternal. He gazed across the table. 'In any case, it's time there was another generation.'

He explained, he explained with elaborate detail, that they had been planning to marry weeks before she became pregnant – they were already planning it when we sat in the Gearys' garden and he warned me about Vicky (whose name had not been mentioned in our alcove that night), and some time before that. All the while Pat had been in some sort of conflict with his father, and still so intimate that Martin knew it all. Again, I thought, it takes two to make a possessive love. Pat might be one of the more undesirable sons, but he wanted his father. Whereas, if Martin had had Charles for a son, he would have been spared most of the suffering and found that the son had slipped away.

That night in the Gearys' garden, Martin had – in the midst of all that had gone wrong – been sustained by a kind of content. Talking to me in the alcove, the night after the funeral, he felt more than content, he felt sheer simple joy.

'It will be the making of him,' he repeated. No one could have thought Martin a simple man. What he had been saying to me, over the past weeks, wasn't simple: it wasn't comfortable, it didn't leave him much, or me either. He meant it, he continued to believe it, it was what he had to say. Yet that night he was full of joy, because of one of the simplest of all things.

Last Things

Last Things

1964 – 1968

CONTENTS

PART ONE. RESOLUTIONS

PART TWO. ARREST OF LIFE, LAST BUT ONE

Contents

PART THREE. ENDS AND BEGINNINGS

PART ONE

RESOLUTIONS

CHAPTER I

RETURNING HOME

As the car passed the first houses away from London Airport (the September night had closed down, lights shone from windows, in the back seat one heard the grinding of the windscreen-wiper) Margaret said:

'Is there anything waiting for us?'

'I hope not.'

She meant bad news. It was the end of a journey, the end of a holiday, coming home. We had each of us felt that edge of anxiety all our lives: not only when there was something to fear in a homecoming, but when, as now, there was no cause at all. As a child of eight, I had rushed from the day's outing full of dread, back to my mother's house, expecting what fatality I couldn't name. I had known that happen often enough since, and so had Margaret. It used to get hold of me, coming home across the Channel, just about the time that I could see the cliffs. But that was a long time ago, before the war: travel had changed by now: and, if it was going to happen – often it didn't, but that night Margaret and I were trapped by the old habit – it was along the motorway, the airport left behind.

Yes, people had learned to call it *angst*, appropriating a stronger word. In fact, this state, except that it hadn't a cause, was much more like what games-players called the needle, or what others felt when they went into an examination room or knew they were due to make a speech. Curiously enough, the top performers never lost it. You had to be a little nervous, so they said, to be at your best. It wasn't all that dreadful. One learned to live with it. And perhaps, as one grew older, it was a positive reassurance to find the nerves at one's elbows tightening and to be reminded that it was possible to be keyed up as one used to be.

Still, Margaret was unusually silent, not leaving much interval between cigarettes, willing the car into London. It wouldn't have soothed her, or me either, to tick off the worries and reason them away. The neon names of factories high above the road: the standard airport journey, it might have been anywhere in the world: point A to B, the topology of our time. It was familiar to us, but it seemed long. The east-bound traffic in the Cromwell Road was thick for eight o'clock at night.

In Queens Gate, bars of gold on the streaming pavements. A wait at the park gates. The glint of the Serpentine, the dark trees. At last, our block of flats.

Margaret said, 'The driver will help you in, I'll go ahead.' While I was bringing the bags out of the lift, I saw our door open and heard her voice and the housekeeper's. All was well, came loud Italian repetitions. Margaret's father – no, no bad news. All was well. A letter from Mr Maurice waiting for her. A postcard from Mr Charles. All was well. The housekeeper embraced the whole of Margaret's family sense and obligations.

In the drawing-room, lamps reflected in the black sky over the park, Margaret and I exchanged sheepish smiles. Pouring out drinks, she said, 'Well, there doesn't seem anything disastrous for the moment, does there?' She was touching wood, but she was happy. We sat on the sofa, the bright pictures welcoming us, letters on the coffee-table close beside our glasses; as the last reflex of the journey home, she riffled through them, but left them still unopened. If there had been anything wrong with her father, there would have been a message from Helen. He was too much an invalid to leave alone, and her sister had come to London to be on call, so that we could take our holiday. It had been our first holiday by ourselves for months or years. It was peaceful, but also strange, to sit there in the empty flat.

Any earlier summer, one of the boys or both would have been returning with us. Margaret leaned back, her colour quite returned. Neither of us wanted to stir. At last she picked out an envelope from the pile, the letter from Maurice, her son by her first marriage.

She read, eyes acute but without expression. Then she broke out, 'He seems very well and cheerful.' She looked at me with delight: she knew that I, like everyone in the family, was fond of Maurice. As for her, her face was softened, love shining through, and a curious kind of pride, or even admiration.

The letter, which was several pages long, came from nowhere more remote than Manchester. Maurice was working as an assistant in a mental hospital. Without complaint. Without self-concern – though, as he had done it before in vacations, he knew there weren't many more menial jobs. It was that lack of self-concern which Margaret admired, and might have wished for in herself and hers. Yet there was a twist here. For the truth was, she couldn't really come to like it. All her family were clever, people who might denounce life's obstacle race and yet, as it were absent-mindedly, contrived to do distinctly well at it. Maurice, her first child, whom she loved with passion, happened to be a sport. As a child, he hadn't been free from storms: and then in adolescence (the only boy I had ever seen change that way round) he became more tranquil than any of us.

He was not in the least clever. He had that summer failed his examinations, for the second year running, at Cambridge. She had hoped that he might become a doctor, but that was out. Maurice himself accepted it with his usual gentle amusement. He thought he ought to try to be as useful as he could. 'I don't know much,' he had said, talking of the hospital, 'but I suppose I can look after them a bit.'

In secret, Margaret was distracted. She knew that his friends, as mystified as she was, were beginning to believe that he was one of nature's innocents or saints. But could you bear your favourite child to be one of nature's saints?

Meanwhile, I had been reading the postcard from Charles, her son and mine. He was not at all innocent, and he was extremely able. He looked older than his half-brother, though he was still not seventeen. He had had a brilliant career at school, and had decided, independent, on his own, to spend a year abroad before he went to Cambridge. He was writing from Bukarest. 'Romanian is interesting, but I'd better economise on languages if I'm going to have one or two good enough. People won't talk Russian here; and when they do aren't usually very competent. Plum brandy is the curse of Eastern Europe. On the other hand, standards of primness – behind closed doors – markedly and pleasingly low.' It reminded me of the postcards I used to receive from another bright young scholar, Roy Calvert, a generation before.

'Well,' I said, after Margaret had passed over Maurice's letter, 'you pay your money and you take your choice.'

I was pretending that I was more detached than she was. She knew better.

For herself, Margaret couldn't help remembering Charles as an affectionate small boy. Now he was as self-willed as we had been. In the past she had imagined the time when her sons were grown up, and nothing but a comfort. She said, realism deserting her, 'If only each of them could give the other a little of what he doesn't have.'

She was harking back to them, reading Maurice's letter again (would he look after his health?), as we picked our way through the rest of the mail. Five or six days of it. The ordinary professional letters. An invitation from the Lester Inces for the following weekend. A note from the wife of my nephew Pat, married that summer, child expected in January, hoping to see Margaret. Invitations to give lectures. Letter from a paranoid, asking for help against persons persecuting her by means of wireless messages. Two lines on a postcard from old George Passant, sent from Norway. Agenda of a meeting.

That was all. Nothing exciting, I said. That was the last thing we wanted, said Margaret, as we went in to eat at leisure, by ourselves.

We had arrived back on Tuesday. The next Monday morning we were again returning home, this time in a train, autumn fields bland in the sunshine, no shadow over us: in fact, in contented, mocking spirits, amused by the weekend. For we hadn't been able to resist the Inces' invitation. Margaret's sister had been willing to stand in for another week, I was glad of a little grace before I started a new book. More than that, we had been inquisitive. The young took up our attention now, and it was a relaxation to have a look at middle-aged acquaintances.

In fact, it turned out fun to see Lester Ince installed in his second avatar, in his recently established state. It was, as it had unrolled before our eyes those last two days, a remarkable state. He had run off – or she had done the running off – with an American woman who was not merely rich, but as her friends said, rich-rich. They had raced through their divorces in minimum time, and they had simultaneously been looking for a stately home. They had found it: one of the most famous and stateliest of homes: nothing less than Basset. Basset, where Diana Skidmore used to perform as a great hostess, and where Margaret and I, though nowhere near the smart life, had sometimes been among the guests. But that had been in the fifties, getting on for a decade ago (this was 1964), and Diana had got tired of it. No one seemed to be certain why, but, just as decisively as she once talked to ministers, she announced that she had had enough, and closed the house within a month. She was reported to be living, quite simply, in a London flat, seeing only her oldest friends. Basset had stayed empty for several years.

Then came the Inces. They had heard of it: they inspected it: they bought it. Together with associated farms, tenantry, trout-streams, pheasant-shooting and outspread acres. Basset had become more opulent, so the knowing ones said, than ever in its history; Margaret and I had regarded it all, that weekend, with yokel-like incredulity, or perhaps more like American Indians confronted with the twin miracles of Scotch whisky and firearms. In my less stupefied moments, I had been trying to work out how many hundred thousands of pounds they had spent.

Lester Ince as landowner. Lester Ince in a puce smoking-jacket, at the head of his table in the great eighteenth-century dining-room, ceiling by Thornhill: Lester pushing the decanter-runners round, after the women had left us. Well, one had to admit, there were considerable bonuses. The food in Diana's time had always been skimpy, and usually dim. Not now. There used not to be enough to drink. Lester Ince, who remained a hearty and kindly man, had taken care of that.

Still, it seemed a slight difference of emphasis away from the Lester Ince who was a junior fellow of my old college only ten years before. He had written a highly regarded work on the moral complexities in Joseph Conrad: but his utterances, almost as soon as he was elected, had been somewhat unexpected. He had surveyed his colleagues, and decided that he didn't think much of them. Francis Getliffe was a stuffed shirt. So was my brother Martin. The best college hock Lester firmly described as cat's pee. The comfortable worldliness of Arthur Brown was even less to his taste. 'I should like to spill the crap about this joint,' someone reported him saying in the combination room: at that stage, he had a knack of speaking what he thought of as American demotic.

As a result of this kind of trenchancy, he became identified as one of the academic spokesmen of a new wave. This was protest. This was one of the voices of progressive opinion. Well, there seemed a slight difference of emphasis now.

To a good many, particularly to those who couldn't help finding leaders and then promptly losing them, the conversation at Basset that weekend might have been disconcerting. This used to be one of the major political houses. A number of ministerial careers had been helped, or alternatively hindered in Diana Skidmore's drawing-room. It was possible that policies – though did any of us know how policies were really made, in particular the persons who believed they made them? – had at least been deviated. Basset was not a political house any longer. But, in spite or because of that, it had become far more ideological than it had ever been. Diana's Tory ministers hadn't indulged much in ideology: the Inces and their friends were devoted to it. The old incumbents didn't talk about the Cold War: now, there were meals when the Basset parties talked of nothing else.

That was election autumn, both in America and England. Ince's wife thought that we were not sufficiently knowledgeable about the merits of Senator Goldwater. He mightn't have everything, but at least he wasn't soft on communism. As for our general election, if the Conservatives didn't come back, there was a prospect of 'confiscatory taxation', a subject on which Lester Ince spoke with poignant feeling.

Once or twice we had a serious argument. Then I grew bored and said that we had better regard some topics as forbidden. Lester Ince was sad; he believed what he said, he believed that, if they listened, people of goodwill would have to agree with him. However, he was not only strong on hostly etiquette, he was good-natured; if the results of his political thinking put us out, then we ought to be excused from hearing them. 'In that case, Lew,' he said, with a cheerful full-eyed glint from his older incarnation, 'you come to my study before you change, and we'll have a couple of snifters and you can talk about the dear old place.'

He meant the college, for which, though it had treated him well, he still felt a singular dislike. In actual truth, he had altered much less than others thought, less even than he thought himself. Protest? Others had been sitting in the places he wanted. Now he had settled his ample back-side in just those places, and it was for others to protest. When young men seemed to be rebelling against social manners, I used to think, it meant that they would, in the end, not rebel against anything else.

In the train, Margaret and I agreed that we each had a soft spot for him. Anyway, it wasn't every day that one saw an old acquaintance living like a millionaire. As the taxi took us home from Waterloo, we were thinking of persons, acquaintances of his roughneck years, who might profitably be presented with the spectacle of the new-style Basset. The game was still diverting us as we entered the flat.

Beside the telephone, immediately inside the hall, there stood a message on the telephone pad. It read, with the neutrality and unsurprisingness of words on paper:

'Mr Davidson [Margaret's father] is seriously ill. Sir Lewis is asked for specially, by himself. Before he goes to the clinic, please call at 22 Addison Road.'

As with other announcements that had come without warning, this seemed like something one had known for a long time.

CHAPTER II

GOD'S OWN FOOL

IN Addison Road, Margaret's sister was staying with some friends. As she kissed me, her expression was grave with the authority of bad news. Silently she led me through the house, down a few steps, into a paved garden. It was not yet half past eleven – I had not been inside my flat for more than minutes – and the sky was pearly with the morning haze. She said:

'I'm glad you came.'

For a long time, we had not been easy with each other. She had been stern against Margaret's broken marriage and put most of the blame on me. All that was nearly twenty years before, but Helen, who was benign and tender, was also unforgiving: or perhaps, like some who live on the outside uneventful lives, she made dramas which the rest of us wanted to coarsen ourselves against. She was in her early fifties, five years older than her sister: she had had no children, and her face not only kept its youth, like all the others in her family, but did so to a preternatural extent. It was like seeing a girl or very young woman – with, round her eyes, as though traced in wax, the lines of middle age. She dressed very smartly, which that morning, as often, seemed somehow both pathetic and putting-off: but then it didn't take much to make me more uneasy with her, perhaps because when I was to blame, I hadn't liked being judged.

She was looking at me with eyes, like Margaret's, acute and beautiful. She hadn't spoken again: then suddenly, as it were brusquely, said:

'Father tried to kill himself last night.'

As soon as we read the message, Margaret – distressed that he didn't want her – had tried to find an explanation: and so had I, on the way here. But, obtusely so it seemed later, neither of us had thought of that.

'He asked me to tell you. He said it would save unnecessary preambles.'

That sounded like Austin Davidson first-hand. I hadn't met many men as uncushioned or as naked to life. He despised the pretences that most of us found comforting. He despised them for himself, but also for others, quite regardless of what anyone who loved him might feel. That morning Helen said (she had lavished less care on him than had Margaret), almost in his own tone, 'He's never thought highly of other people's opinion, you know.'

She told me how it had happened. As we all knew, he had been in despair about his illness. Until his sixties, he had lived a young man's life: then he had a thrombosis, and he had been left with an existence that he wouldn't come to terms with. A less clear-sighted man might have been more stoical. Austin Davidson, alone in Regent's Park except for Margaret's visits, had sunk into what they used to call accidie. A tunnel with no end. There had been remissions – but his heart had weakened more, he could scarcely walk, and at last, at seventy-six, he wouldn't bear it. Somehow – Helen didn't know how – he had accumulated a store of barbiturates. On the previous evening, Sunday, about the time that I was drinking pre-dinner 'snifters' with Lester Ince, he had sat alone in his house, writing notes to his daughters. Then he had swallowed his drugs, washed them down with one whisky, and stood himself another.

But he had done it wrong. He had taken too much. A few hours later, stupefied by the drug, he had staggered about, violently sick. While vomiting, he had fallen forward, gashing his forehead against the handle of the W.C. Near by, he had been discovered at breakfast-time, covered with blood but still alive. They had driven him to the —— clinic.

'Fortunately,' said Helen, 'he seems to be surprisingly well. I don't know whether I ought to say fortunately. He wouldn't.'

She had destroyed the two notes unopened. He had been at least half-lucid when she talked to him in his hospital room. He had asked, several times, to see me, without Margaret. So Helen had been obliged to give the message.

'I wish', I said, 'that he had asked for her. She minds a great deal.'

'That's why he'd rather have you, maybe,' said Helen.

The midday roads were dense with cars, and it took forty minutes before the taxi reached the clinic. On the way, I had been wondering what I should find, or even more what I should manage to say. I was fond of Austin Davidson, and I respected that bright, uncluttered mind. But it wasn't the respect that one might feel for an eminent old man. It was an effort to think of him as my father-in-law. Except when the sheer impact of his illness weighed one down, he seemed much more like a younger friend.

It was the clinic in which, during the war, I had first met Margaret. I thought I remembered, I might be imagining it, the number of my room. At any rate, it was on the same ground floor, at the same side, as the one I was entering now.

In his high bed, flanked by flowers on the tables close by – the ceiling shimmered with subaqueous green reflected from the garden – Austin Davidson looked grotesque. His head, borne up by three pillows, was wrapped in a bandage which covered his right eye and most of his fore-head: even at that, there was a bruise under the right cheekbone, and the corner of his mouth was swollen. More than anything, he gave the appear-ance of having just been patched up after a fight. Among the bandages, one sepia eye stared at me. I heard his voice, dulled but the words quite clear.

'You see God's own fool.'

I felt certain that he had prepared that opening, determined to get it out.

'Never mind.'

'If one's got to the point' – he was speaking very slowly, with pauses for breath and also to hold his train of thought – 'of doing oneself in – the least one can do – is to make a go of it.'

'Lots of people don't make a go of it, you know.' To my own astonishment, at least in retrospect, for it was quite spontaneous, I found myself teasing him: dropping into a kind of irony, as he did so often, putting himself at a distance from the present moment. The visible side of Davidson's face showed something like the vestige of a grin, as I reminded him of German officers during the war. Beck took two shots at himself, and then had to get someone to finish him off. Poor old Stülpnagel had blinded himself, but without the desired result. 'You would expect them to be better at it than you, wouldn't you? But they weren't.'

'Too much fuss. Not enough to show for it.'

He was drowsy, but he did not seem miserable. To an extent, he had always liked an audience. And also, was there even now a stirring of, yes, relief? Had he wanted, had the flesh wanted, to persist – it didn't matter how much he denied it?

'Tell them. No more visitors today. Margaret can come tomorrow. If she wants.'

'Of course she will.' Margaret was his favourite daughter; but he had never appeared to realise that his detachment could cause her pain.

'She's prudish about suicide.' His voice became louder and much more clear. 'I simply can't understand her.'

After a moment:

'Extraordinary thing to be prudish about.'

Then he began to ramble, or the words thickened so that it was hard to follow him. *Sources of supply.* That might mean the way he got hold of his drugs. Some people wouldn't act as sources of supply. Prudish. Glad to say, others weren't like Margaret—

It might have been strange to hear him, even in confusion, engaged in a kind of argument, scoring a dialectical triumph over Margaret. But it didn't seem so. I was easier with him than she was: easier with him than with my own father, at least on the plane where Davidson and I were able to talk. Not that Davidson managed to be any cooler than my father. In fact, in his simple fashion, without trying, he had been as self-sufficient and as stoical as Davidson would have liked to be.

There had been nothing histrionic about my father's death a few months before. On the last evening, in his own small room, he had asked his lodger, who was almost a stranger, to sit with him. 'I think I am going to die tonight,' so the lodger had reported him saying. He was right. It wasn't given to Austin Davidson to die as quietly as that.

Even in stupor Davidson kept making gallant attempts to carry on the argument. Then I thought he had fallen asleep.

Out of semi-consciousness he made another effort.

'I'm always glad to see you, Eliot.'

I had heard him say goodbye even to his daughter in those cool terms, but it was the use of my surname which startled me.

It sounded like a regression to the time when we first met, before I married Margaret, when he was going about in his vigorous off-hand prime. But as I went away, I wondered if it hadn't been a further regression, back to the pride, arrogance and brightness of his youth, when he and his friends felt themselves the lucky of this world, but, with manners different from ours, did not think of calling each other by their Christian names.

CHAPTER III

A THEME RESTATED

THE next time I saw him was on the Wednesday, since Margaret and I decided to share the visits, each going on alternate days. It was a tauntingly mellow September afternoon, like those on which one looked out of classroom windows at the start of a new school year.

Half-sitting in his bed, pillows propping him (that was to be his standard condition, to reduce the strain on his heart), Austin Davidson had been spruced up, though underneath the neat diagonal bandage across his eye there loomed another deep purple bruise which on Monday had been obscured. His hair, thick and silver grey, had been trimmed, the quiff respectfully preserved. Someone had shaved him, and he smelt fresh. He was wide awake, greeting me with a monocular, sharp, almost impatient gaze.

'I should like some intelligent conversation,' he said.

To understand that, one needed to have learned his private language. Since he first became ill, he seemed to have lost interest in, or at least be unwilling to talk about, the connoisseurship which had been the passion of his life. He wouldn't read his own art criticism or anyone else's. He chose not to look at pictures, not even his own collection, as though, now the physical springs of his existence had failed him, so his senses, including the sense that meant most to him, were no use any more.

Instead, he fell back on his last resource, which was something like a game. But it was a peculiar sort of game, to some of his acquaintances unsuitable, or even fatuous, for a 'pure soul' like Davidson. For it consisted of taking an obsessive day-by-day interest in the Stock Exchange. It was an interest that had given him pleasure all his life. Like all his circle, he had heard Keynes, with his usual impregnable confidence, telling them that, given half an hour's concentrated attention to the market each morning, no man of modest intelligence could avoid making money. Unlike others of his circle, Davidson believed what he was told. Certainly he was a pure soul, but he enjoyed using his wits, and playing any kind of mental game. This also turned out to be a singularly lucrative one. He had been left a few thousand pounds before the First World War. No one knew how much he was worth in his old age; on that he was reticent, quite uncharacteristically so, as about nothing else in his life. He had made over sizeable blocks of investments to his daughters, but he had never given me the most oblique indication of how much he kept for himself.

So 'intelligent conversation' meant, in that bedroom at the clinic, an exchange about the day's quotations. He became almost high-spirited, no, something more like playful. It was a reminder of his best years, when he seemed so much less burdened than the rest of us.

Listening to him, I had to discipline myself to take my part. In any circumstances, let alone these, I didn't serve as an adequate foil. I could act as a kind of secretary, telephoning his stockbroker from the bedroom, so that Davidson could overhear. He wasn't satisfied with academic discussions: that would have been like playing bridge for counters. But I discovered that his gambles were modest, not more than £500 at a time.

Apart from my secretarial duties, I wasn't a good partner. I didn't know enough. I assumed that, until he died, I should have to try to memorise the financial papers more devotedly than I had ever thought of doing.

Though he spun it out, and I followed as well as I could, that day's effort dwindled away. Pauses. Then a long silence. His eye had ceased to look at me, as though he were turning inward.

After the silence, his voice came back:

'I shan't get out of here. Of course.'

He wasn't asking for false hope. He made it impossible to give.

I asked: 'Are you sure?'

'Of course.'

Another pause.

'They won't let me. People always interfere with you.' He was speaking without inflection or expression.

'The one thing they can't interfere with is your death. Not in the long run. You have to die on your own. That's all there is to it, you know.'

He added:

'I told Margaret that.'

Yes, he had told her. But he wasn't aware of – and wouldn't have been concerned with – her response, to which I had listened as we lay awake in the middle of the night. It wasn't the cool, such as Davidson, who felt most passionately about death. Margaret, whose appetite for living was so strong, had to pay a corresponding price. She wouldn't have talked, as more protected people might, of any of those figures which, by pretending to face the truth, in fact make it easier to bear. The swallow coming out of darkness into the lighted hall, and then out into the darkness again. That was too pretty for her. So were the phrases about silence and the dark. Whatever they tried to say was too near to say like that.

She struggled against it, even while she was searching for the C major of this life. The C major? In sexual love? In the love of children? She knew, as an innocent man like Davidson never could have done, that you could hear the sound and still not have dismissed the final intimation. And, by a curious irony, having a father like Davidson had made that intimation sharper: made it sharper now.

That was why, lying awake in the night repeating to me his acerb remarks about his fiasco, she wasn't reconciled. She was torn with tenderness, painful tenderness, mixed up with what was nothing else but anger. It was a combination which she sometimes showed towards her own children, when they might be doing themselves harm. Now she couldn't prevent it breaking out, after her father tried to commit suicide, and then talked to her as though it had been an interesting event.

In the dark, she kept asking what she could do for him, knowing that there was nothing. At moments she was furious. With all the grip of her imagination, she was re-enacting and re-witnessing the scene of Sunday evening. The capsules marshalled on Davidson's desk (he was a pernick-etily tidy man): the swallows of whisky: the last drink, as though it was a modest celebration or perhaps one for the road. It might have been a harmless domestic spectacle. Capsules such as we saw every day. An old man taking a drink. But, just as in the trial I had had to attend earlier that year, objects could lose their innocence. For Margaret the capsules and the whisky glass weren't neutral bits of matter any more.

They were reminders, they were more than that, they were emblems. Emblems of what? Perhaps, I thought, as I tried to soothe her, of what the non-religious never understand in the religious. Margaret, though she didn't believe, was by temperament religious. Which meant, not as a paradox but as a condition, that she clung – more strongly than her father could have conceived possible – to the senses' life, the species' life. So, when that was thrown away or disregarded, she felt horror: it might be superstitious, she couldn't justify it, but that was what those emblems stood for.

Her father, however, settled her in his own mind by saying again, as though that was the perfect formulation, that she was prudish about suicide. After a time during which neither he nor I spoke, and he was looking inward, he said, quite brightly:

'Most of you are prudish about death. You're prudish about death.'

He meant Margaret's friends and mine, the people whom, before his illness, he used to meet at our house. They were a different generation from his, most of them younger than I was (within a month I should be fifty-nine).

'You're much more prudish than we were on that fairly relevant subject. Of course you're much less prudish about sex. It's a curious thought, but I suspect that when people give up being prudish about sex they become remarkably so about everything else.' (I had heard this before: in his lively days, he used to say that our friends dared not talk about money, ambition, aspiration, or even ordinary emotion.) 'Certainly about death. You people try to pretend it doesn't exist. I've never been able to bear the nineteenth century' – the old Bloomsbury hatred darted punctually out – 'but at least they weren't afraid to talk about death.'

'It's the only thing in one's whole life that is a hundred per cent certain.'

'It's the only thing one is bound to do by oneself.'

Later, after he had died – which didn't happen for over a year – I was not sure whether he had really produced those two sayings that afternoon. The difficulty was, I had so many conversations with him in the clinic bedroom; they were repetitive by their nature, and because Davidson was such a concentrated man. Talk about the Stock Exchange: then his thoughts about dying and death. That was the pattern which did not vary for weeks to come, and so the days might have become conflated in my memory. It often seemed to me that the other themes of his life had been dismissed by now, and there was only one, the last one, which he wanted to restate. *You have to die on your own.* And yet, he had never said that. I was inventing words for him. Perhaps I was inventing a theme that was, not his, but mine.

I hadn't felt intimations of my death as deeply as Margaret. But, like all of us, intermittently since I was a young man, as often as a young man as when I was ageing, I had imagined it. What would it be like? There were the words we had all read or uttered. You die alone. *On mourra seul.* The solitude. I thought I could imagine it and know it, as one does being frightened, appalled or desirous.

There it was. It wasn't to be evaded. Perhaps that was why I invented words for Davidson which he didn't utter. And read into him feelings which I couldn't be certain that he knew.

But certainly he said one thing, and did another, which I was able to fix on to that afternoon.

'Nearly all my friends are dead by now,' he said. 'Most of them had moderately unpleasant deaths.'

I was thinking, of those who had mattered to me, Sheila and Roy Calvert had died, though not naturally. Many of my acquaintances were reaching the age-band where the statistics began to raise their voice. Looking at us all, one couldn't prophesy about any single casualty, but that some of us would die one way or the other – within ten, fifteen years – one could predict with the certainty of a statistician. Only a fortnight before, while Margaret and I were still abroad, I had heard that Denis Geary, that robust schoolfellow of mine who had been a support to us a few months before, had gone out for a walk and been found dead.

'Of course,' said Davidson, 'there's only been one myth that's ever really counted. I mean, the after-life.'

'It's a pity one can't believe in it,' he said.

'Yes.' (Not then, but afterwards, I remembered kneeling by Sheila's bed after her funeral, half-crazed for some sign of her, not even a word, just the shadow of a ghost.)

'It's a pity it's meaningless. I don't know why, but one doesn't exactly approve of being annihilated. Though when it's happened, nothing could matter less.'

One wouldn't ask for much, Davidson was saying, just the chance to linger round, unobserved, and watch what was going on. It was a pity to miss all that was going to happen.

That was one of the few signs of sentimentality I had seen him show. Soon he was remarking sternly, as though reproving me for a relapse into weakness, that it was not respectable to talk about an after-life. There wasn't any meaning in it: there couldn't be. It was the supreme wish-fulfilment. 'Which, by the way,' he said, brightening up, 'has done the wretched human race a great deal more harm than good.' He went on, still half-reproving me, telling me to think of the horrors that had been perpetrated in the name of the after-life. Torturing bodies to save souls. Slaughter to get one's place in heaven. 'If people would only accept that this is the only life there is, they might be a shade more civilised.'

No, I didn't want to argue: he was getting some sort of comfort from his old certainties. It seemed a perverse comfort. Yet he still believed in the enlightenment he grew up in, the lucky oasis, the civilised voices, the privileged Edwardian hopes.

Then he did something which also might have seemed perverse, if he had preserved the consistency of which he was so proud. It was a warm afternoon, and he was covered only by a single sheet. Suddenly, but not jerkily, he pulled it aside, and with eyes glossy-brown as a bird's, oblivious of me, gazed down towards his feet. Against blue pyjama-trousers, his skin shone pale, clear, not hairy: the feet were large, after the thin legs, with elongated, heavy-jointed toes. For some time I could not tell what he was studying so observantly. Then I noticed, over the left ankle, a small roll of swelling, so that the concavity between ankle-bone and talus had been filled in. On the right foot, the swelling might have been grosser; from where I sat, it was difficult to make out.

Davidson went on gazing, as intently, as professionally, as he used to look at pictures.

'The oedema's a shade less than this morning. Quite a bit less than yesterday,' he said. He said it with a satisfaction that he couldn't conceal. or didn't think of concealing. Throughout his illness, for years past, he must have been studying his ankles, observing one of the clinical signs. Even now, night and morning (perhaps more often when he was alone) he went through the same routine. But it wasn't routine to him. Sunday night – he had swallowed the capsules. All he said to me since, he meant. Nevertheless, when he inspected his ankles and decided the swelling was a fraction reduced, he felt a surge of pleasure, not at all ironic. No more ironic than if he had been in middle age and robust health, and had noticed a symptom which worried him but which, as he tested it, began to clear away.

CHAPTER IV

DOMESTIC EVENING, WITHOUT INCIDENT

VISITING her father every other day, Margaret's behaviour, like his, began to show a contradiction which really wasn't one. She couldn't help becoming preoccupied with a future birth, with the child my nephew's wife was expecting in four months' time. Margaret had not previously given any sign of special interest in Muriel, and so far as she had a special interest in Pat it was negative, or at least ambivalent. Sometimes she found him good company, but when he had gone away she thought him worthless. And yet Margaret took to visiting them in their flat, and then invited them to dinner at our own, together with Muriel's mother and stepfather.

That was a surprise in itself, a surprise, that is, that Azik Schiff should come. He was himself inordinately hospitable and in his own expansive fashion seemed to like us all. But he was also very rich: and like other rich men, did not welcome hospitality unless he was providing it himself. However, he had accepted, and as we waited for them all I was saying to Margaret that one of the advantages of being rich was that everyone tended to entertain you according to your own standards. Just as all gourmets were treated as though the rest of us were gourmets. It seemed like a natural law, a curiously unjust one. Certainly the food and drink which had been set up for that night we shouldn't have produced for anyone less sumptuous than Azik.

The young couple arrived a few minutes before the other two, but as soon as Azik entered the drawing-room he took charge. None of us had dressed, but he was wearing, as though in competition with Lester Ince, a cherry-coloured smoking-jacket. He gave Margaret not a peck but a whacking kiss, and then stood on massive legs evaluating the room, in which he had never been before. In fact, he was more cultivated than any of us: the pictures he understood and approved of: but he was puzzled that, apart from the pictures, the furniture was so ramshackle. He had guessed our financial position – that was one of his gifts – and knew it as well as I did. Why did we live so modestly? He didn't ask that question, but he did enquire about the flat. Yes, we had a lot of rooms, having joined two flats together. How much did we pay? I told him. He whistled. It was cheaper than he could have reckoned. He couldn't help admiring a bargain: and yet, as he proceeded to explain, living like that was good tactics, but bad strategy.

'You should buy a house, my friends,' he said paternally (he was several years younger than I was) as at last he settled down on the sofa, his chest expanded, as usual looking like a benevolent, ugly and highly intelligent frog.

Rosalind, his wife, braceleted, necklaced, bejewelled with each anniversary's present, was looking at me with something like an apprehensive wink. She had known me when she was Roy Calvert's mistress and later his wife: that was years before Margaret and I first met. Rosalind had known me when I was cagey and secretive, and it was a continual surprise to her that I didn't mind, or even encouraged, Azik to interfere in my affairs. She was always ready to help me evade his questions, even after all the times when she had seen him and me get on so easily.

No, I said to Azik, if one has been born without a penny, one never learned to spend money. Azik shook his great head. 'No, Lewis,' he said, 'there I must take issue with you. That excuse is not satisfactory. It doesn't do credit to your intellect. First, I have to remind you that your lady bride' (he beamed at Margaret: Azik spoke a good many languages imperfectly, and one of those was American business-English) 'was not born without a penny. So there should be a corrective influence in this family. Second, I have to remind you that I also was born without a penny. I have to say that I have never found it difficult to spend money.' With which Azik expounded on a 'certain little difference' between the tailor's shop near the old Alexanderplatz where he was born, and his present home in Eaton Square.

Someone said (when Azik was projecting himself, he filled the room, and it wasn't easy to notice who else was trying to edge in) was it true, the old story, that if one had been born rich and then had everything taken away one never minded much?

Azik pronounced that he had known some who suffered. People were almost infinitely resilient, I was beginning, but Azik went on with a shout: 'You and I, Lewis, say we've lost everything tomorrow morning. You aren't allowed to publish a word. These children don't believe it, but we should make do. You'd pretend that nothing had happened and go and get a job as a clerk. As for me' – he put a finger to the side of his nose – 'I should make a few shillings on the side.'

He was benevolent and happy, parodying himself, showing off to Rosalind, whom he adored. None of us had such a flow of spirits, nor was so harmoniously himself. There might have been one single discontinuity, only one, and even that I could have exaggerated or imagined.

It happened when Margaret asked about the second drinks. On the first round she and I had had our usual long whiskies, and so had Pat: Azik had had a small one. He refused another, and watched our glasses being filled again.

Suddenly, quite unprovoked, he said:

'No Jew drinks as you people do.'

'Oh, come off it, Azik,' I said. I mentioned something about parties in New York—

'They are not real Jews. They are losing themselves'.

Real Jews, Azik went on, took sex easy, took wine easy: they didn't go wild, as 'you people' do. I had never heard anything like that from him before. He might be overpowering, but he didn't attack. We all knew that he kept up Judaism; he went, not to a reformed synagogue, but to a conservative one, even though he said that he had no theology. All of a sudden, just for that instant (or was I reading back to my first Jewish friends?) Judaism seemed the least natural, or the least comfortable thing about him – as though it were a proud hurt, an affront to others.

He relaxed into paternal, prepotent supervision.

'Ah well,' he said, 'enjoy yourselves.'

He was the only one to enquire about young Charles. Last heard of in Persia, I said, on his way to Pakistan. We had heard nothing for a fortnight.

'You must be worried, Lewis,' he said, with a rush of fellow-feeling. I said, 'a little': the dinner-party had distracted me until then.

'Oh, he'll be all right. He lands on his feet,' said Pat.

'That you should not say.' Azik turned sternly on to Pat, who for once looked outfaced, sulky, quite aware that he had shown jealousy of his cousin, glancing at his young wife, whose face was reposeful, as though she had not noticed anything at all nor heard of Charles.

As we sat at the dinner-table, I was paying attention to Rosalind. Beautifully accoutred as she was, she had nevertheless let her hair go grey: that must have been a deliberate choice, for, before she married Azik, she had kept it undeviatingly dark. She knew what was required of the elegant wife, no longer young, of a great tycoon. Her thin, freckled hands displayed her rings. As before, she sometimes gave me a look – sidelong from her cameo face – as though we shared an esoteric private joke. But all she talked about was Azik's business, and how next week she would have to entertain the Foreign Minister of Brazil. 'It's all in the game, you know,' she said, with a dying fall which sounded sad and which was nothing of the kind. I sometimes wondered whether she ever thought that, if it had not been for fatality, she would still be married to a distinguished, perhaps an unbalanced, scholar (it was hard to imagine what Roy Calvert would have become in his fifties). Probably she didn't. Rosalind lived on this earth. She might sigh over memories, but she would sigh contentedly and get on with the day's work, which was to keep Azik cheerful and well.

On my left, her daughter Muriel was quiet, cheekbones and jawline softened by pregnancy. Then I caught a flash of her eyes, as though she were surreptitiously making fun of Rosalind or me or both. It was the kind of green-eyed disrespectful flash I had seen often enough in her father, whom she had never known. She was polite to me as she was to everyone, maddeningly polite, but I didn't begin to understand her. She had not once asked me a question about her father, though she must have known that I had been his closest friend. One day, out of curiosity or provocation, I had tried to talk about him. 'Did you think that?' she had said decorously. 'Oh, I must ask Aunt Meg' (as she called Margaret, of whom she seemed to be fond). Again, she must have known that Margaret and Roy had never met.

When, for an instant, Pat engaged his mother-in-law in conversation, Muriel asked a few soft-voiced questions about the autumn theatres. She knew that I wasn't much interested, and rarely went. Was she being obtuse, or amusing herself? She was abnormally self-possessed and strong-willed, that was all I knew about her. Like a good many other men, I found her – in some inexplicable and irritating fashion – very attractive.

Just then – we had finished the fish, Azik was smelling his first glass of claret, for which, in spite of his earlier strictures, he had considerable enthusiasm – I heard Pat utter the name of Margaret's father. Startled, turning away from Muriel, I looked down the table. Pat was smiling at Margaret with something between protectiveness and triumph. His brown eyes were shining: he had his air of doggy confidence, of one who managed to please but wasn't easily put down.

'Yes,' he was telling her, 'he was in better spirits, I'm sure he was.'

'You mean, you've seen him?'

'Of course I have, Aunt Meg.'

It became clear that Pat was telling the truth, which could not invariably be assumed. It also became clear that Austin Davidson had talked with his innocent candour, and that Pat knew everything we knew, and had – certainly to his wife and her mother – passed most of it on. Pat had paid, not one visit, but several: for an instant Margaret looked stupefied, astonished that her father had told us nothing of this. But why should he? He had other visitors besides ourselves, but he didn't think it relevant to mention them.

The greater mystery was how Pat had learned that Davidson was in the clinic at all, and how he had got inside the place himself. As for the first, he was one of those natural detectives or intelligence agents, whom I had come across, and been disconcerted by, more than once in my life: and, further, he had always been specially inquisitive about Davidson, and anxious to know him. Not from motives which were entirely pure: Pat was an aspiring painter, and he believed that an eminent art critic, even though retired, must have retained some useful acquaintances. Anyway, insatiably curious and also on the make, Pat had somehow obtained the entrée to Davidson's bedroom, quite possibly using my name without undue fastidiousness.

Once there, it was no mystery at all that Davidson had encouraged him to come again. Pat was on the make, he was a busybody, a gossip, often a mischief-maker and several kinds of a liar: but he was also kind. In the presence of the isolated old man, Pat would try to enliven him, using all his resources, which were considerable: for he was more than kind, to many people he was a life-giver. The unfairness was, he had that talent far more highly developed than persons of better character: when I came to think of it, life-givers of Pat's species had, so far as I had met them, usually been people who wouldn't pass much of an examination into their moral nature. That had been true of my boyhood friend Jack Cotery, whom in a good many ways Pat resembled. It was probable, I thought, that Pat's visits were more of a help to Austin Davidson than either Margaret's or mine.

'You must believe me,' Pat said to Margaret, 'he's looking forward to things now, he's picking up, you'll see.'

'I've known him longer than you have, haven't I?' said Margaret.

'That's why you don't see everything about him now,' Pat replied, with his mixture of tenderness and cheek. No, he insisted, you have to notice that Davidson was eager for his little pleasures: he was allowed five cigarettes a day, and each one was an occasion; so were his cups of tea. He had made his own timetable to live by. He would go on living for a long time yet.

He had put that 'other business' behind him, Pat was persuading her. It had been an incident, that was all. Margaret did not believe him, and yet wanted to. In spite of herself, she was feeling grateful. Pat had heard all about Davidson's plan to kill himself. And yet he could forget it, from one minute to the next: it wasn't that he was too young to understand, for often the young understood suicide better than the rest of us. Perhaps he was just too surgent. Anyway, his optimism came from every cell of his body. He was positive that Austin Davidson would survive and that his life was worth living.

Azik, left out of this conversation, was giving his wife uncomfortable glances. Not that he hadn't listened to it all before; not that he was embarrassed for Margaret, or found his son-in-law unduly brash; more, I thought, because Azik had the delicacy of the very healthy, who did not much relish the echoes of mortality. Finally he said to Margaret that he would send her father more flowers, and addressed me down the table on the subject of next week's general election. Yes, it would be a near thing. The American election wouldn't be. Things looked a bit more promising all round, said Azik: for about that time, a year or two before and after, he, like other detached and unillusioned men, was letting himself indulge in a patch of hope. That was the case with Francis Getliffe and with me: with Eastern European and American friends, including even David Rubin, the least optimistic of men. In world-outlook, there was more hope about than at any time since the twenties. We did not enjoy being reminded of that afterwards, but it was so.

About our local affairs, Azik was repeating what he often told us: it didn't much matter who got in. He proceeded to lecture us, with the relish of a born pedagogue, on the limits of political free will. Margaret was grinning surreptitiously in my direction: she enjoyed hearing me being treated as an innocent. Like me, she was fond of Azik, and his ingrained conviction that we were ignorant, though not entirely unteachable, was one of the endearing things about him. But she couldn't resist asking him if he wasn't being disingenuous. After all, it was common knowledge that he had made lavish contributions to Labour party funds.

Azik was imperturbable. 'That's doesn't affect the issue, my friends,' he said. 'That is a little piece of insurance, you understand?'

Did we? Azik liked playing the game all ways. He was a shrewd operator. If a Labour government came to power, there were advantages in having friends at court. Yet that, I thought, was altogether too simple. Azik wished to pretend to us, and to himself, that he calculated all the time: but he didn't, any more than less ingenious men. He was an outsider, and he was, in some residual fashion, of which he was half-ashamed, on the side of other outsiders. For all his expansiveness, the luxury in which he revelled, he was never ultimately at ease with his fellow-tycoons. He had once told me that, coming to England as an exile, he had felt one irremovable strain: you had to think consciously about actions which, in your own country, you performed as instinctively as breathing. He was also another kind of exile: rich as he had become, he had to think consciously about his actions when he was in the company of other rich men.

It sometimes occurred to me – not specially at that dinner-table – how differently he behaved from the Marches, who had been the first rich family to befriend me when I was young. They too were Jewish: they were not, and never had been, anything like so plutocratic as Azik had become. And yet, though they were slightly more sceptical about politics than their Gentile counterparts, their instincts were the same. After generations in England, they thought and spoke like members of the English haute bourgeoisie, like distinctly grander and better-connected Forsytes. If, when I first knew them, anyone had made contributions such as Azik's to the wrong party, some of the older members might have been capable of saying (though I didn't remember hearing the phrase in the March houses) that he was a traitor to his class.

Nevertheless, after dinner, Azik did recall to me one of those patriarchs, my favourite one. We were sitting in the drawing-room, brandy going round. It was quite early, not long after ten, but Pat had begun to fuss ostentatiously over his wife. Twice he asked her, wasn't it time for him to take her home? Coolly, demurely, she said that she was perfectly well.

'Of course she is,' said Margaret. 'This isn't an illness, don't you realise that?'

'If it is,' said Rosalind, 'it's a very pleasant one.'

There was an unexpected freemasonry. Margaret and Rosalind agreed that, when they were carrying their children, they had never felt better in their lives. They also agreed that they wished they could have had some more. Azik gave them a condescending hyper-masculine smile, as though women were women, as though (he must have known, when he listened to his wife's confidences, that she and Margaret had less in common even than he and I, and liked each other a great deal less) he wasn't above remarking that they were sisters under the skin.

'That's all very well,' he projected himself again. 'But I say young Pat's right. He has to be careful.' He gave his wife a beaming glance. 'You don't have your first grandchild every day. He has to be careful. As far as that goes, I must say, I'm not happy that they're being careful enough. I don't like the sound of that doctor of theirs. They ought to have the best man in London—'

Azik had been studying the *Medical Directory*, in search of their doctor's qualifications, and was deeply suspicious as a result. It was then that I had a memory of old Mr March, Charles March's father, the patriarch whom we used to know as Mr L., going through the same drill. When his daughter was expecting a baby, or his relatives were ill, or even their friends, Mr March would carry out sombre researches into doctors' careers, and emerge, with indignation, prophecies of disaster and fugues of total recall, expressing his disapprobation and contempt for what he called *practitioners*, and above all for the particular practitioner in charge of the case.

Even Azik couldn't let himself go in his freedom as totally as Mr L. Yet for an instant the images got superposed, the two of them, abundant, paternal, unrestrained, acting as they felt disposed to act.

With a good grace, Muriel got ready to go. Her step was still elegant and upright: as she said good-bye, she gave Margaret a smile which was secretive, lively, amused. Gallantly, like someone who would be glad to execute an imitation of Sir Walter Raleigh but hadn't the excuse, Pat draped a cape over her shoulders.

When they had left and we heard Pat drive the car off down below, Azik had a word to say about their living arrangements, the Chelsea flat, paid for out of Muriel's money, for she kept them both. For once Azik had no immediate suggestions for improvement. Then, having disposed of the topic of his stepdaughter, he introduced another one, like a child saving the jam to the last, that of his own son. This was the only child Azik and Rosalind had between them, born when she was over forty. One never met Azik without, in the end, the conversation coming round to David, who had already been the subterranean cause of Azik's sympathy about Charles. And, in fact, the conversation, at least with Margaret and me, tended to repeat itself, as it did that night. David was high-spirited and very clever. He was at a private day-school in London: Azik wanted him to go later to a smart boarding-school. If so, we kept telling him, he ought to be at a boarding-school now. It would be harder for him, much harder, to leave home at thirteen or fourteen. 'No,' said Azik, as he had done before, 'that I could not do. I could not lose him now.'

It was the old argument, but Azik enjoyed any argument about his son. It even kept him up later than he intended. David. The possibilities with David. David's education. Azik went over it all again, before his gaze at his wife began to become more intense, more uxorious, and he felt impelled towards his power-base, his home.

CHAPTER V

RED CARPETS

THE chamber of the House of Lords glowed and shone under the chandeliers, the throne-screens picked out in gold, the benches gleaming red, nothing bare nor economical wherever one turned the eye, as though the Victorian Gothic decorators had been told not to be inhibited or as though someone with the temperament of Azik Schiff had been given a free hand to renovate the high altar of St Mark's.

It was a Wednesday afternoon, about half past five, the benches not half-full, but, as peers drifted in from tea, not so startlingly empty now as they had been an hour before. I had come to hear Francis Getliffe make a speech, and he had found me a seat just behind the Bar, at ground level. I had heard him speak there several times, but that afternoon there was a difference. This time, as he rose from the back benches, he was on the right hand of the throne, not the left. The election, as we had guessed at the dinner-party with the Schiffs, a month before, had been as tight as an election could be — but it had been decided, and a Labour government had come to power. So, for the first time, Francis was speaking from the Government side.

He had never been a good speaker, and he was using what looked like a written text. He wasn't a good reader. But he was being listened to. The debate was on defence policy, and it was well-known that he was a grey eminence: no, not so grey, for his views had been published, in his time he had gained negative popularity because of them. Ever since he was a young man, in fact, he had been an adviser to Labour politicians. As he grew older, no one had more private influence with them on scientific–military affairs. That was when they were in opposition, but now he was being attended to as though this were an official statement.

As a matter of fact, it was as guarded as though it might have been. Francis was both loyal and punctilious, and, though he had to speak that afternoon, he wasn't going to embarrass his old colleagues. One had to know the language, the technical detail, and much back history, to interpret what he was, under the courtesies, pressing on them. Under the courtesies – for Francis, whose politeness had always been stylised, had taken with gusto to the stylisation of that chamber. In his speech he was passing stately compliments across the floor to 'the noble Lord, Lord Ampleforth'. One needed a little inside information to realise that Lord Ampleforth, who was something like Francis's opposite number on the

Tory side, was a man with whom Francis had not agreed on a single issue since the beginning of the war; or that Francis was now telling his own Government that, in three separate fields, the exact opposite of Lord Ampleforth's policies ought to be their first priority.

Polite hear-hears from both sides as Francis sat down. Lord Lufkin, sprawling on the cross-benches, looked indifferent, as though certain he could have done better himself. In the back tier of the Opposition benches, I saw the face of Sammikins, hot-eyed, excited, but (since I last met him, twelve months before) startlingly thin.

The courtesies continued. Lord Ampleforth, who spoke next, paid compliments to the noble Lord, Lord Getliffe, 'who brings to your Lordships' house his great scientific authority and the many years of effort he has devoted to our thinking on defence'. Lord Ampleforth, who despite his grand title had started his career as a radio manufacturer called Jones, was a rougher customer than Francis and more of a natural politician: he drew some applause from his own side when he expressed 'a measure of concern' about Francis's 'well-known' views upon the nuclear deterrent. Even so, one again needed a little inside information to grasp what he really felt about Francis. It helped perhaps to know that he had, during the time of the previous Government, rigorously removed Francis from his last official committee. More courtesies. The noble Lord's international reputation. The wisdom he brought to our counsels. Assurances of support in everything that contributed to the country's security.

As soon as Lord Ampleforth finished, Francis got up from his place and nodded to me as he went out, so that I joined him in the lobby. He gave me a creased saturnine smile. As we walked over the red carpet down the warm corridor – so red, so warm that I felt rather like Jonah in one of his more claustrophobic experiences or alternatively as I had done after an optical operation, with pads over both eyes – Francis remarked:

'That chap reminds me of a monkey. A very persistent monkey trying to climb a monkey-puzzle tree. That is, if they do.'

All I knew of monkey-puzzles was the sight of them in front of houses more prosperous than ours, in the streets where I was born. However, Francis was not occupied with scientific accuracy. Lord Ampleforth had climbed, he was saying, over all kinds of resistance: on the shoulders of, and in spite of their efforts to throw him off, better men than himself. Including a number of the scientists we knew.

'He'll go on climbing,' said Francis with cheerful acerbity. 'Nothing will ever stop him. Not for long.'

Affable greetings along the corridors. Congratulations to Francis on his speech. Lord Ampleforth had an astonishing gift, Francis was saying, for ingratiating himself with his superiors, and an equally astonishing gift for doing the reverse with those below.

We entered the guest-room. More mateyness, from men round the bar, more congratulations on the speech. I couldn't help thinking that they might have found Francis's present line of thought more stimulating. But he was popular there. As we sat in a window seat looking over the river, lights on the south bank aureoled in the November mist, people greeted him with the kind of euphoria that one met in other kinds of enclave, such as a college or a club.

One of the new Ministers, from a table close by, was engaging Francis in earnest, low-voiced conversation. So, getting on with my first drink, I gazed from our corner into the room. It wasn't altogether novel to me: when Francis was in London, I sometimes met him there: but my first visit had been much further back, in the thirties, when I had been invited by an acquaintance called Lord Boscastle. So far as I could trust my memory, it had been different then. Surely there had been less people, both in the chamber and round this room? Somewhat to his surprise, Lord Boscastle's first speech for twenty years had not been much of a draw.

Had the place really been socially grander, or was that a young man's impression? I remembered noticing, even in the thirties, that there were not many historic titles knocking about. Lord Boscastle, who bore one and was a superlative snob, had once remarked, with obscure and lugubrious satisfaction, that the House was quintessentially middle-class. Well, that night, there were still three or four historic titles on view. One of them was sitting at the bar, with a depressed stare imbibing gin. There was another, at a table surrounded by his daughters: my maternal grandfather had been a gamekeeper on his grandfather's estate. A number, though, had come up from the Commons, or their nineteenth-century ancestors had; some had been successes in politics, some had missed the high places, and some had never hoped for much. There were several life peers, as Francis was, and some women. Round the room one could hear a variety of accents: about as many as in the Athenæum, which was a meritocratic club, and a good deal more than in the other club I sometimes used.

Most of these people might have seemed strange to their predecessors in the Lords a hundred years before. No doubt the professional politicians (and there had been plenty of professional politicians there in the nineteenth century, even if, like Palliser, they were landed magnates too) would have found plenty to talk about to the modern front-benchers:

there was no tighter trade union in England, then or now. But still, it was like our college, Francis's and mine. The fabric of the building hadn't altered: the survival of politeness in which Francis had been indulging in the Chamber, that hadn't altered either, not by a word. The forms remained the same, while the contents changed. It had perhaps been a strength sometimes, this national passion for clinging on to forms, nostalgic, pious, wart-hog obstinate. Alternatively, it could have released our energies if we had cut them away. And yet, for this country that had never been on, there had never been a realistic chance. Bend the forms, make them stretch, use them for purposes quite different from those in which they had grown up: that had been the way we found it natural (the pressures were so mild we didn't feel them, as mild as the soft English weather) to work. Sometimes I wondered whether my son and his contemporaries would find it natural too.

I mentioned as much to Francis that night. I had recently heard from Charles, and so could think about him at ease. His was a generation that to Francis, whose children were older, seemed like strangers.

The loudspeaker boomed out – 'Defence debate. Speaking, the Lord ——.' Within two minutes of this news, the population flowing into the guest-room had markedly increased. Among the deserters was Lord Ampleforth, pushing his way towards the bar, heavy shoulders hunched. Glancing across to our corner, he nodded to Francis, a flashing-eyed, recognitory nod, as from one power to another. Francis called out:

'Interesting speech, Josh.'

We watched Josh acquire his whisky, and glance round the room.

'Looking for someone useful,' Francis quietly commented. Apparently, whatever Josh was in search of, he didn't find it. He swallowed his drink at speed, gave another flashing-eyed nod to Francis, patted two men on their shoulders, and went out, presumably back to the Chamber, even though Lord —— was still up.

Francis, settling back in his chair by the window, did not feel obliged to follow. He was comfortable, ready to sit out the next few speeches, until out of courtesy he returned for the end of the debate. If it hadn't been for his own choice, he wouldn't have been as free as that; he would have been on the front bench, waiting to wind up for the Government. For, the weekend after the election, he had had an offer. Would he become a Minister of State? To take charge of the nuclear negotiations? He had told me before he replied, but he wasn't asking for advice. He had said no.

There was one objective reason. He knew, just as I knew, without the aid of Azik's benevolent instruction, how little a Minister could do. The

limits of free action were cripplingly tight, tighter than seemed real to
anyone who had not been inside the process. We had both watched, been
associated with, and gone down alongside a Tory Minister, Roger Quaife,
who had tried to do what Francis would have had to try. And Quaife had
been far more powerful than Francis could conceivably be. The limits of
freedom for this Government would be much narrower than for the last.
Francis would fail, anyone would fail. He had done a good deal in the line
of duty – but this, he said bleakly, was a hiding to nothing. If he had asked
my opinion, I should have agreed.

But that wasn't all. He had been an influence for so long. He had been
criticised, at times in disfavour, privately defamed – but always, like other
eminent scientists called in to give advice, covered by a kind of mantle of
respect. That closed and secret politics was different from politics in the
open. Francis hadn't been brought up in open politics. At sixty-one (he
was two years older than I was) his imagination and thin skin told him
what it would be like. Francis had plenty of courage, but it was courage
of the will.

But that was not all either, or even most of it. His major reason for
saying no, almost without a thought, was much simpler. It was just that
he had become very happy. This hadn't always been so. His marriage –
that had been good from the beginning. If he hadn't been lucky there, if
he hadn't had the refuge of his wife and children, I had sometimes
thought, he would have broken down. Even now, though his face looked
younger than his age, his hair still dark, carefully trimmed on the forehead, by a streak of vanity, to conceal that he hadn't much dome on the
top of his fine El Greco features, he bore lines of strain and effort, bruise-
like pouches left by old anxiety under his eyes. For many years his
creative work hadn't gone well enough, according to the standards he set
himself. Then at last that had come right. In his fifties he became more
serene than most men. To those who first met him at that time, it might
have seemed that he was happy by nature. To me, who had known him
since we were very young, it seemed like a gift of grace. His home in
Cambridge, his laboratory, where, since he was a born father, the research
students loved him as his children did, his own work – what could anyone
want more? He just wished to continue in the flow of life. Yes, in the flow
there were the concerns of anyone who felt at all: his friends' troubles,
illnesses, deaths, his children's lives. His elder son, more gifted than
Francis himself, was eating his heart out for a woman who couldn't love
him; his favourite daughter, in America, was threatening a divorce. He
took those concerns more deeply just because he felt so lucky and thus

had energy to spare. That was the flow, all he wanted was for it to stretch ahead: he wasn't going to break out of it now.

So he had refused. Some blamed him, thinking him over-proud or even lacking in duty. The job had gone to an old wheel-horse of the party, who was given it for services rendered. 'He won't last long,' said Francis that night, ruminating on politics after the departure of Josh. 'There's talk that they may want to rope you in. Well, you've always had to do the dirty work, haven't you?'

He grinned. He had spoken quite lightly, and I didn't pay much attention. I should have asked a question, but we were interrupted by acquaintances of Francis enquiring if they might join us, and bringing up their chairs. Two of them were new members on his own side, the other a bright youngish Tory. They were all eager to listen to him, I noticed. He was relaxed and willing to oblige. But what they listened to would have puzzled those who had known him only in his stiffer form, fair-minded and reticent in the college combination room.

For Francis was giving his opinions about the people who had worked on the atomic bomb. His opinions weren't at all muffled, he wasn't bending over backwards to be just: he had an eye for human frailty and it was sparkling now. 'Anyone who thinks that Robert Oppenheimer was a liberal hero might as well think that I'm a pillar of the Christian faith.'

'X [an Englishman] never had an idea in his head. That's why he gave everyone so much confidence.'

'Y [an American] is an anti-Semitic Jew who only tolerates other Jews because the Russians don't.'

Some of Francis's stories were new to me. Several of his characters I had met. I had thought before, and did so again that evening, that since he became content he had shown it differently from most other men. A good many, when they had been lucky, felt considerable warmth and approval for others who had been lucky too. Somehow it added to their own deserts. Well, Francis was not entirely above this feeling: but more and more he felt a kind of irreverence, or rather gave his natural irreverence, carefully concealed during his years of strain, its head. Buttoned-up, stuffed, deliberately fair – so he had seemed to most people when he thought that he mightn't justify himself. His wife Katherine knew him otherwise; so did his children; so did I, and one or two others. But with everyone else he was determined not to show envy, not even to let his tongue rip, at the expense of those who were enjoying what he so much longed for. Those who did better creative work than his had to be spoken about with exaggerated charity. It made him seem maddeningly judicious, or too good to be true. He wasn't. As he became happy, he became at the same time more benign and more sardonic. I didn't remember seeing that particular change in anyone else before.

He was talking about David Rubin. Yes, he was one of the best physicists alive, he was a better man than most of them. It wasn't decent for anyone to be so clever. But the trouble with Rubin, Francis said, was that he enjoyed being proved right more than doing anything useful. He had never believed that any of us could do anything useful. If he knew that we were all going to blow ourselves up in three hours' time, David would say that that had always been predictable and remind us that he had in fact predicted it.

I was enjoying myself, but I had to leave. As I retraced my way over the red carpets, I was hoping for a glimpse of Sammikins, just to ask how he was. I had an affection for him: he was a wild animal, brave but lost. He hadn't come into the guest-room for a drink, which was strange enough. I wanted to glance into the chamber, to see if he was still sitting there, but an attendant reminded me that that wasn't allowed, guests had to pass without lingering on to the red carpet on the other side.

CHAPTER VI

MARRIAGE, ELDERLY AND YOUTHFUL

MARGARET had had her suspicions for some time, but they were not confirmed until the evening of Hector Rose's dinner-party. She and I had arranged to meet in a Pimlico pub, because she was coming on from Muriel Eliot's flat and Rose (among the other unexpected features of his letter) had given an address in St George's Drive. As soon as Margaret arrived, I didn't need telling that she was distressed – no, not brooding, but active and angry. Her colour was high, her eyes brilliant, and when I said, 'Something the matter,' it was not a question.

'Yes.'

'What is it?'

She looked at me, seemed about to break out, then suddenly smiled.

'No. Not yet. Not here.'

Her tone was intimate. We both understood, she didn't want to spoil the next few minutes. It wasn't just an accident that we were meeting in this pub. The place had memories for each of us, but not particularly pleasant ones, certainly not unshadowed ones. We used to drink there, early in the war, when I was living in Dolphin Square, close by: right at the beginning of our relation, long before we married, when we were already in love but in doubt whether we should come through. Sitting there now, more than twenty years later, or walking round the corner to the square, we felt as we had done before, the Dantesque emotion in reverse. No greater misery, he said, than to recall a happy time in sadness: turn that the other way round. At some points our sentimentalities were different, but here they were the same. The scenes of the choked and knotted past – if we had any reasonable pretext, as on that night, we went and looked at them with our present eyes.

Margaret had asked for bitter, which she rarely drank nowadays. The pub was humming with background music, in the corner lights on a pin-table flashed in and out, all new since our time. But then we had not noticed much, except ourselves.

She gazed round, and smiled again. She said:

'Well, what's it going to be like tonight?'

We hadn't the vestige of an idea. The week before I had received a letter in a beautiful italic hand that once had been so familiar, when I used to read those minutes of Rose's, lucid as the holograph itself. The letter read:

'My dear Lewis, It is a long time since I said good-bye to you as a colleague, but I have kept in touch with your activities from a distance. When I read your work, I feel that I know you better than during our period together in the service: that gives me much regret. It is unlikely that you could have heard, but I have recently remarried. It would give us both much pleasure if you and your wife could spare us an evening to come to dinner. [There followed some dates to choose from.] I have retired from all public activities, and so you will be doing a kindness if you can manage to come. Yours very sincerely,

                                                            Hector Rose'

In the years when I had worked under Rose in Whitehall, and they were getting on for twenty, I had never met his wife. It was known that he lived right at the fringe of Highgate: when he entertained, which wasn't often, he did so at the Athenæum: there was no mention of children: he kept his private life locked up, as though it were a state secret. Underneath his polite, his blindingly polite manners, he was a forbidding man, in the sense that no one could come close. He was as tough-minded as any of the civil service bosses, and I came to admire his sheer ability more, the longer I knew him. But that façade, those elaborate manners – they were so untiring, so self-invented, often so ridiculous, that one felt as though one were stripping off each onion-skin and being confronted by a precisely similar onion-skin underneath. There were those who thought he must be homosexual. I couldn't have guessed. By this time he was sixty-six, and reading his letter Margaret and I decided that he must have married a second time for company (I remembered reading a bare notice of the death of the first wife, with the single piece of information that she, like Rose himself, had been the child of a clergyman). Otherwise, the only inference we could draw came from his last sentence. Rose used words carefully, as a master of impersonal draftsmanship, and that sounded remarkably like a plea. If so, it was the only plea I had ever known him make. He was the least comfortable of companions, but no one was freer from self-pity.

So, as Margaret and I walked, with our own perverse nostalgia, across the end of the square, past the church and the white-scarred planes, along the street for a few hundred yards, we couldn't imagine what we were going to. When we came outside the house itself, it was like the one that I had lived in towards the end of the war, under the eye and landladyship of the ineffable Mrs Beauchamp: a narrow four-storey building, period latish nineteenth century, ramshackle, five bells flanking the door with five name-cards beside them. Rose's was the ground-floor flat: it couldn't be more than three or four rooms, I was reckoning as I rang the bell. It was another oddity that Rose should live in this fashion. He had no private means, he might not have earned much since he retired from the Department, but his pension would be over £3000 a year. That didn't spread far by this date, but it spread farther than this.

But, when he opened the door, all was momentarily unchanged. Strong, thick through the shoulders, upright: his preternatural youthfulness had vanished in his fifties, but he looked no older than when I saw him last.

'My dear Lewis, this is extraordinarily good of you! How very kind of you to come! How very, very kind!'

He used to greet me like that when, as his second-in-command, I had been summoned to his office and had performed the remarkable athletic feat of walking the ten yards down the corridor.

He was bowing to Margaret, who had met him only two or three times before.

'Lady Eliot! It's far far too long since I had the pleasure of seeing you—'

His salutations, which now seemed likely to describe arabesques hitherto unheard of, had the knack of putting their recipient at a disadvantage, and Margaret was almost stuttering as she tried to reply.

Bowing, arms spread out, he showed us – the old word ushered would have suited the performance better – into the sitting-room, which led straight out of the communal hall. As I had calculated when we stood outside, they had only one main room, and the sitting-room was set for dinner, napery and glass upon the table, what looked like Waterford glass out of place in the dingy house. Round the walls were glass-fronted bookshelves, stacked with volumes a good many of which, I discovered later, were prizes from Marlborough and Oxford. A young lecturer or research student at one of the London colleges, just married, might have been living there. However, neither Margaret nor I could attend to the interior decoration when we had the prospect of Rose's wife herself.

'Lady Eliot,' said Rose, like a master of ceremonies, 'may I present my wife? Darling, may I introduce Sir Lewis Eliot, my former colleague, my distinguished colleague.'

As I muttered 'Lady Rose' and took her hand, I was ready for a lot of titular incantations, wishing that we had Russian patronymics or alternatively that Rose had taken to American manners, which seemed unlikely. It was going to be tiresome to call this woman Lady Rose all night. She was alluring. No, that wasn't right, there was nothing contrived about her, she was simply, at first sight, attractive. Not beautiful: she had a wide mouth, full brown eyes, a cheerful uptilted nose. Her cheeks seemed to wear a faint but permanent flush. She must have been about forty, but she wouldn't change much; at twenty she wouldn't have looked very different, a big and sensuous girl. She was as tall as Rose, only two or three inches shorter than I was, not specially ethereal, no more so than a Renoir model.

Margaret gave me the slightest of marital grins, jeering at both of us. Our reconstruction of the situation . . . elderly people 'joining forces', marriage for company. If that was marrying for company, then most young people needed more of it. As for Rose's putative plea, the only reason for reviving our acquaintance seemed to be that he wanted to show her off, which was simple and convincing enough.

In actual fact, as company in the conversational sense, she wasn't a striking performer, as I discovered when we set out to talk. She was superficially shy, not at all shy deeper down. She was quite content to leave the talk to us, beaming placidly at Rose, as though signalling that she was pleased with him. I picked up one or two facts, such as that there had been another husband, though what had happened to him was not revealed. If there had been a divorce, it had been kept quiet. I couldn't gather how she and Rose had ever met: she didn't belong to any sort of professional world, she came perhaps – there was a residual accent – from origins like mine. I knew that when Rose left the service he had taken a couple of directorships: my guess was that he had come across her in one of those offices; she might have been his secretary.

Well, there they were, eyes meeting down the table. 'Jane darling, would it be troubling you if you reached behind you—' The one aspect which baffled me completely was why they should be living like students. It might have been one of the games of marriage, in which they were pretending to be young people starting out. If so, that must have been his game, for she would have been satisfied wherever they had lived.

She was an excellent cook. On nights when we had worked late together, Rose and I used to split a bottle of wine, and he had recollected that.

He was talking with elaborate animation to Margaret about the differences between Greats in his time at Oxford, and the philosophy in hers at Cambridge. Jane listened and basked. As for me, I was engaged in a simple reflection. A woman had once told me that she didn't know, no one could possibly know, what a man was like until she had gone to bed with him. It was the kind of comment that sounded wise when one was young, and probably wasn't. And yet, looking at that pair, remembering how so many people had pigeonholed Rose, myself among them, I felt that this once there might be something in it.

Table pushed back after the meal, for the room was small though high-ceilinged, we sat round the grate, in front of an electric fire. Rose and his wife had finished drinking for the evening, but hospitably he had put a decanter of port on the floor. Some more fine glass, from the archdiaconal or even the Highgate home. I mentioned former colleagues. I tried to get him to say something about his career.

'Oh, my dear Lewis, that's really water under the bridge, water distinctly under the bridge, shouldn't you agree? I don't know whether Lady Eliot has ever had the misfortune to be exposed to the reminiscences of retired athletes,' he was gazing, bleached-eyed, at Margaret, 'but I assure you that mine would be, if anything, slightly duller.'

'I don't believe that,' said Margaret, who still found him disconcerting.

'But then, my dear Lady Eliot, if you'll permit me, you haven't spent getting on for forty years in government departments.'

'Do you regret it?' I said. I had learned long since that one had to tackle him head on.

'Regret in what particular manner? I'm afraid I'm being obtuse, of course.'

'Spending your life that way.'

Rose gave his practised, edged, committee smile. 'I follow. I should be inclined to think that, with my attainments such as they are, I shouldn't have been markedly more useful anywhere else. Or perhaps markedly less.'

'That's a bit much, Hector,' I broke out. I said that, when I first reported to him and for years afterwards, he had been tipped to become head of the civil service. That hadn't happened. He had finished as a senior permanent secretary, one of the half-dozen most powerful men in Whitehall, but not at the absolute top. Most of us thought he had been unlucky, and in fact badly dealt with. (I noticed that this seemed to be news to his wife, who had blushed with something like gratification.) Did he mind?

'I doubt if it would have affected the fate of the nation, my dear Lewis. I think you will agree that the general level of our former colleagues was, judged by the low standard of the human race, distinctly high. That is, granted their terms of reference, which may, I need hardly say, be completely wrong, a good many of them were singularly competent. Far more competent than our political masters. I learned that when I was a very lowly assistant principal, just down from Oxford. And I'm afraid I never unlearned it. Incidentally, out of proportion more competent than the businessmen that it was my misfortune to have to do official business with. Of course my experience has been narrow, I haven't had Lewis's advantages, and my opinion is *parti pris*.' He was speaking to Margaret. 'So you must forgive me if I sound parochial. But, for what it is worth, that is my opinion. That is, the competition among my colleagues was relatively severe. So a man who by hook or by crook became a permanent secretary ought to feel that he hadn't any right to grumble. He's probably been more fortunate than he deserved. There was an old Treasury saying, Lewis will remember, that in the midst of a crowd of decent clever men anyone who became a permanent secretary had of necessity to be something of a shit.'

Rose delivered that apophthegm as blandly as his normal courtesies. His wife chortled, and Margaret grinned.

'Well,' said Rose, 'I qualified to that extent.'

'Hector,' I said, 'you haven't answered my question.'

'Haven't I, my dear Lewis? I really do apologise. I am so very, very sorry.'

We gazed at each other. We were less constrained that night than we had been during the years in the office. And yet he was just as immovable, it was like arguing with him over a point on which I was, after all the paraphernalia, going inevitably to be overruled.

Rose was continuing, in his most unargumentative tone.

'Recently I had the pleasure of introducing my wife to the Italian lakes. Actually we chose that for our honeymoon—'

'Lovely,' said Jane.

'Yes, we thought it was a good choice. And, as a very minor bonus, I happened to come across an inscription which might interest you, Lewis. Perhaps, for those whose Latin has become rusty, I may take the liberty of translating. It is pleasantly simple. GAIUS AUFIDIUS RUFUS. HE WAS A GOOD CIVIL SERVANT.

'Don't you think that is remarkably adequate? Who could possibly want a more perfect epitaph than that?'

I knew, and he knew that I knew, that he was parodying himself. I nodded my head, in acquiescent defeat. Impassively he let show a smile, but, unlike his committee smile, it contained a degree of both malice and warmth. Then he gave us, his wife for the first time assisting in the conversation, a travelogue about Como and Garda, the hotels they had stayed in, the restaurants they would revisit when, the following spring, they proposed to make the same trip again. This honeymoon travelogue went on for some time.

Then, when we got up and began our good-byes, Rose encircled us with thanks for coming. At last we got out into the road, waiting for a taxi: the two of them, while they waved to us, stood on the doorstep close together, as though they were ready to be photographed.

As we drove past Victoria through the Belgravia streets, Margaret, in the dark and sheltering cab, was saying:

'How old is she?'

'Late thirties?'

'Older. Perhaps she's too old.'

'Too old for what?'

'A child, you goat.' Her voice was full of cheerful sensual nature. 'Anyway, we'd better watch the births column next year—'

She went on:

'Good luck to them!'

I said yes.

She said:

'I hope it goes on like that.' She added: 'And I hope something else doesn't.'

We had both enjoyed the bizarre but comforting evening, and I had remembered only intermittently (and that perhaps had been true for her) that she had news to break. Now she was angry again – at me, at herself, at the original cause – for having to fracture the peace of the moment.

'What is the matter?'

'Your nephew.'

666

Muriel had told her the story that afternoon. Pat was having other women, certainly a couple since the marriage, with the baby due in the New Year. It was as matter-of-fact as that.

'He's a little rat,' said Margaret.

With the lights of Park Lane sweeping across us, I remarked:

'You can't do anything.'

'You mustn't defend him.'

'I wasn't—'

'You want to, don't you?'

I had never been illusioned about Pat. And yet Margaret was reading something, as though through the feel of my arm: an obscure male free-masonry, or perhaps another kind of resistance she expected, whenever her judgments were more immediate and positive than mine.

We didn't say much until we were inside our bedroom.

'It's squalid,' said Margaret. 'But that makes it worse for her.'

'I'm sorry for her.'

'I'm desperately sorry for her.'

Her indignation had gone by now, but her empathy was left.

'I know,' I said. I asked how Muriel was taking it.

'That's the curious thing,' Margaret gave a sharp-eyed, puzzled smile. 'She seems pretty cool about it. Cooler than I should have been, I tell you, if you'd left me having Charles and done the same.'

A good many women would have been cooler than that, I told her.

She burst out laughing. But when I repeated, how had Muriel reacted, her face became thoughtful, not only protective but mystified and sad. In her composed, demure fashion, Muriel had been evasive about her husband during previous visits; this time she had come out with it, still composed but clinical. Not a tear. Not even a show of temper.

'What do they think they're playing at?' said Margaret. 'He wasn't in love with her, we never believed he was. He was after the main chance, blast him. But what about her? It doesn't make sense. She must love him, mustn't she?

'After all,' she went on, 'she's only twenty-two.'

A silence.

Margaret said: 'I don't understand them, do you?'

She was upset, and I tried to comfort her: and yet for her it was no use being reflective or resigned. For, though this mess was quite far away from her – it wasn't all that dramatic or novel, and Muriel was no more than a young woman she knew by chance – it had touched, or become tangled with, some of her own expectations. None of us had expected more from all the kinds of love than Margaret. With her father, those afternoons as she sat by him in his loneliness, she had felt one of them finally denied: and with her sons also, as she grew older, there was another kind of isolation. Maurice passive, gentle, but with no flash of her own spirit coming back: Charles, who had spirit which matched hers, but who responded on his own terms. She had invested so much hope in what they would give her: and now, despite her sense, her irony, she sometimes felt cut off from the young. That was why Pat and his deserted wife became tokens for her: they made romantic love appear meaningless: all her expectations were dismissed, as though she belonged to another species. It wasn't like that, I tried to tell her, but I did no good. Unlike herself, so strong in trouble close to hand, that night – on the pretext or trigger of an acquaintance's ill-treatment – she felt lonely and unavailing.

'Never mind,' I said, 'you'll feel different when Carlo [our name for Charles] is back.'

'What will he be like then?' she said.

She asked, would he understand the situation of Pat and Muriel better than we did. Neither of us could guess. It was hard to believe that he had much in common with either.

CHAPTER VII

FAIR-MINDEDNESS

ON the afternoon of Christmas Day, Margaret and I were sitting in our drawing-room, along with Maurice, who had the day off from his hospital. Over the park outside, the sky was low, unbroken: no rain, not cold, a kind of limbo of a December day. We had put off the Christmas meal until the evening, since my brother Martin and his wife and daughter were driving down from Cambridge. No newspapers, no letters, a timeless day. I suggested that we should go for a walk: Margaret looked at the cloud-cover, and decided that it wasn't inviting. Maurice, as usual glad to oblige, said that he would come with me.

We didn't go into Hyde Park, but instead turned into the maze of streets between our flat and Paddington. Or rather I turned that way, for Maurice didn't assert himself, and happily took what came. It wasn't that he was a weak character: in his own fashion, he was a strong one; but it was a fashion so different from mine, or my own son's, that I was no nearer knowing what he wanted, or where his life would go. Since he came to me, at the age of three, when I married Margaret, he and I had always got on well: there hadn't been the subliminal conflict of egos that had occasionally broken out in my relation, on the surface ironic and amiable, with young Charles. Sometimes it seemed that Maurice didn't have an ego. I had been concerned, because it made Margaret anxious, about his examination failures. I had also been concerned, because I was enough of a bourgeois born, about whether he would ever earn a living. Which had a certain practical interest, since otherwise I should have to go on supporting him.

He walked at my side, face open, good-looking, not feminine but unhardened for twenty-one. As usual, he was unprickly, free from self: yet, I had often wondered, was that really true? It was the puzzle that one sometimes met in people who asked very little for themselves. They cared for others: they did good works and got nothing and claimed nothing: they had no rapacity or cruelty: so far as human beings could be, they were kind. Nevertheless, occasionally one felt – at least I did – that underneath they had a core more impregnable than most of ours. Somehow they were protected. Protected as some men are by shields of vanity or self-regard. Certainly Maurice made one feel that he was in less danger than any of us. Maybe it was that, more than his kindness, which made him so comfortable to be with.

Under the monotone sky, the high houses, also monotone, similar in period to the one where the Roses were living, more run-down. In the square, neon signs of lodging-houses. Church built when the square was opulent (a million domestic servants in London then, and the slum-poor nowhere near these parts), Christmas trees lit up outside. Sleazy cafés on the road to Paddington station. A few people walking about, slowly, in the mild gloom. A scrum of West Indians arguing on the pavement. Christmas decorations in closed shops. Here and there on the high house-fronts, lighted windows.

Once or twice Maurice reminded me of stories which he had told about those streets, for he knew them well. In his holidays he used to join a friend of his, the vicar of a local parish, on pastoral visits, making a faintly comic pair, the vicar stout, becassocked and birettaed, Maurice as thin as a combination of the idiot prince and a first-class high-jumper. It was their way of enjoying themselves, and they had been inside many more rooms in the Paddington hinterland than the vicar's duty called for. Yes, some of the sights weren't pretty, Maurice had reported, unshockable: you could find most kinds of vice without going far. Also most kinds of suffering. Not the mass poverty of the thirties, that had been wiped out. But alcoholic's poverty, drug addict's poverty, pensioner's poverty. Being poor when you're old, though, that's not the worst of it, Maurice had said. It's being alone, day after day, with nothing to look forward to until you die. For once (it had happened one night when he returned home, a couple of years before), Maurice had spoken with something like violence. Genteel poverty behind lace curtains. A lucky person had a television set. If anyone feels like being superior about television, when they're old they ought to live alone without one. You know, Maurice had gone on, they look forward to seeing Godfrey (the vicar) and me. I suppose one would if one were alone. Of course we can't do much. We can just stay talking for half an hour. Anyway, Godfrey isn't much good at conversation. But I suppose it's better than nothing.

As we walked along, solitary figures passing us in the empty streets, lighted windows in the houses, I was thinking, he had been behind some of those windows. They weren't as taunting when one got inside as when one gazed at them from the street as a young man. For an instant, I was, not precisely remembering, but touched by a residual longing from other Christmas days long past, when I had also gone out for walks on deserted pavements, just to kill time, just to get through the day. That had been so in the provincial town, after my mother died: slipping out after Christmas dinner, necessarily teetotal, at Aunt Milly's, I used to tramp the streets as the afternoon darkened, gazing up garden paths at bright and curtained sitting-rooms, feeling a kind of arrogant envy. That had been so again, my first year in London: my friends all at home, no George Passant to pass the evening with, and I with nothing to do. The streets must have looked much as they did that day with Maurice, but that I had forgotten or repressed, and where I finished up the night.

'Not exactly cheerful,' I said, as though commenting on the present situation, indicating a young man who was dawdling past us.

'Poor old thing,' said Maurice, who really was commenting on the present situation. 'He doesn't look as if he's got anywhere to go—'

For any connoisseur of townscapes, that afternoon's had its own merit. The unvaried sky lay a thousand feet above the houses: the great city stretched all round one, but there was no sense of space: sky, houses, fairy lights on Christmas trees all pressed upon the lost pedestrians in the streets. Yes, the townscape had its own singular merit, but it was good to be back (did Maurice feel this too?) among the lights of our own drawing-room, able to find our own enclave.

To be realistic, it was not quite such a well-constructed enclave as it might have been. At least, not when we sat down to dinner. Physically all was well. The food was good, there was plenty to drink. But in Margaret, and in me watching her, the nerves were pricking beneath the skin. One reason everyone round the table knew. That was the first Christmas Charles had not been at home. He would not be seventeen for some months. In his own fashion he would be celebrating the festival in Karachi: for the time being he was, so far as we knew, static and safe. Then he would start his journey home, all over land, travelling alone, picking up rides. The whole Eliot family was there, eating the Christmas dinner, except the youngest.

The whole Eliot family, though, that was a second reason for constraint, which perhaps, I couldn't be certain, Martin and his wife didn't realise. They had duly arrived, with their daughter Nina, while Maurice and I were out on our afternoon walk. We hadn't seen any of them since the summer, at Pat's wedding, but this family party had been planned long since. So, as a matter of course, Pat and Muriel had been invited. After Muriel's disclosures, Margaret had asked her if she still wanted the pair of them to come. Yes, Muriel replied, without expression. There they were at dinner, Muriel on my left, by this time heavily pregnant, hazel eyes sharp, face tranquil, Pat on Margaret's left, working hard to be a social stimulant.

It was difficult to know whether anything was being given away. Once Pat tried his brand of deferential cheek on Margaret: she was polite, but didn't play. Pat, whose antennae, always active, were specially so that night, must have known what that meant. But his father and mother did not seem to notice. Maurice tried, like a quiet impresario, to make the best of Pat's gambits. Margaret didn't like dissimulating, but when she was keeping a secret she was as disciplined as I was. From the other end of the table, all I could have told – if she hadn't warned me – was that she laughed very little, and that her laughter didn't sound free. While Pat, whose brashness was subdued, kept exerting himself to make the party bubble, Martin was attending to him, with a faint amused incredulous smile which I had seen creep on him before in his son's company – as though astonished that anyone so unguarded could be a son of his.

By my side, Irene didn't often meet Pat's quick frenetic brown-eyed glance, so like her own, but instead kept me engaged with Cambridge gossip. As she did so, I heard Muriel, voice clear and precise, taking part in repartee with Pat: no sign of strain, no disquiet that I could pick up. Later, I observed her talking to Nina, her sister-in-law, inconspicuous in her parents' presence, more so in Pat's. She might be inconspicuous, but she was a very pretty girl, so far as one could see her face, for she had hair, in the fashion of her contemporaries, which trailed over one eye. Also in the fashion, her voice was something like a whisper, and I couldn't hear any of her replies to Muriel. Of the two, I was judging, most men would think her the prettier: but perhaps most men would think that Muriel provoked them more.

In the drawing-room after dinner, Muriel announced that, as this was a family Christmas party, she proposed to put off her bedtime. Very dutifully, Pat argued with her – 'Darling, you know what —— [her doctor] said?'

'He's not here, is he?' said Muriel, and got her way. They didn't leave until half past eleven: it was midnight before Martin and I sat by ourselves in my study, having a final drink.

Now at last it seemed to me like an ordinary family evening, peace descending upon the room. We hadn't talked, except with others present, all that night: nor in fact since the summer, the day of our father's funeral. Martin proceeded to interrogate me, in the way that had become common form since we grew older. Nowadays his workaday existence didn't change from one term to another, while mine was still open to luck, either good or bad. So that our roles had switched, and he talked to me like a concerned older brother. How was the new book going? I was well into it, I said, but it would take another year. Was there anything in this rumour about my being called into the Government? He was referring to a piece of kite-flying by one of the parliamentary correspondents – *New Recruits?*

I knew no more about it than he did, I told him, and mentioned the conversation with Francis Getliffe in the Lords' bar. This correspondent wrote as though he had been listening, or alternatively as though the House of Lords was bugged. As had happened often during my time in Whitehall, I had the paranoid feeling that about half the population of Parliament were in newspaper pay.

I had heard nothing more, I repeated to Martin. I supposed it was possible. They knew me pretty well. But it would be a damned silly thing for me to do. 'Oh, if they do ask you, don't turn it down out of hand,' said Martin, watchful, tutorial, as cautious as old Arthur Brown. He went on, he could see certain advantages, and I said with fraternal sarcasm, that it was a pity he ever withdrew from the great world. Great World, I rubbed it in. We both knew enough about it, partly by experience, partly by nature. Martin gave his pulled-down grin.

He would like just one more drink, he said, and went over to the sideboard. Then, as he settled back in his chair, glance turned towards his glass, he said, in a casual tone:

'I don't think Irene knows anything about these goings-on.'

'What do you mean?' It was a mechanical question. I had understood.

'That young man of ours playing round.' Pat's Christian name was actually Lewis, after me, and Martin seldom referred to him by his self-given name. Suddenly Martin looked full at me with hard blue eyes.

'I gathered you had heard,' he said.

'Yes.'

'I'm sure she doesn't know.'

That seemed to give him an obscure satisfaction. Irene had never liked the marriage, although it had taken Pat off their hands, providing him with the money he had never earned.

'Did you realise', I asked, 'that we knew – before tonight?'

'Never mind that.' He wouldn't answer, and left me curious. He might have picked it up in the air, for he was a perceptive man. But I thought it sounded as though he had been told. By whom? He was not intimate with his daughter-in-law. Strange as it seemed, it was more likely to be his son. Martin felt for his son the most tenacious kind of parental love. It was, Martin knew it all by heart, so did Margaret, so did Azik Schiff, so did Mr March and old Winslow long before we did, the most one-sided of human affections, the one which lasts longest and for long periods gives more pain than joy. And yet, one-sided though such a relation as Martin's and his son's had to be, it took two to make a possessive love. With some sons it couldn't endure; if it did endure, there had to be a signal – sometimes the call for help – the other way. Pat had cost his father disappointment and suffering: there had been quarrels, lies, deceits: but in the midst of it all there was, and still remained, a kind of communication, so that in trouble he went back, shameless and confiding, and gave Martin a new lease of hope.

The result was that Martin, who was usually as quick as any man to see the lie in life, who had an acute nose for danger, was talking that night as though I were the one to be reassured. He did it – I had heard him speak of his son in this tone before – with an air of apparent realism. Yes, there must be plenty of young men, mustn't there, who think of amusing themselves elsewhere in the first year of marriage. No one was ever really honest about the sexual life. How many of us made fantasies year after year? There weren't many who would confess their fantasies, or admit or face what their sexual life had been.

I didn't interrupt him, but he could have guessed what I was thinking. Did he remember, earlier that year in our native town, how we had talked during the murder trial? Talked without cover or excuses, unlike tonight.

There was a gap between fantasy and action, the psychiatric witnesses had been comfortably saying. It was a gap that only the psychopaths or those in clinical terms not responsible managed to cross. That made life more acceptable, pushed away the horrors into a corner of their own. Martin wouldn't accept the consolation. It was too complacent for him, he had said, as we sat in the hotel bar, talking more intimately than we had ever done.

Now, Martin, swirling the whisky in his glass, looked across the study from his armchair to mine.

'I agree,' he said, as though with fair-mindedness, 'not so many people act out their fantasies. But still, this business of his must be fairly common, mustn't it? You know, I'm pretty sure that I could have done the same.'

Shortly afterwards, he made an effort to sound more fair-minded still.

'Of course,' he said, 'we've got to face the fact that he might turn into a layabout.'

He used the objective word, his voice was sternly objective. Yet he was about as much so as Francis Getliffe complaining (with a glow of happiness concealed) that people said his son Leonard was a class better as a scientist than himself. Both of them liked to appear detached. It made Martin feel clear-minded, once he had suggested that the future might be bad. But he didn't believe it. He was still thinking of his son as the child who had been winning, popular, anxious to make people happy – and capable of all brilliant things.

'I thought they were getting on all right tonight, didn't you?' said Martin. 'He'll shake down when the baby is born, you know. It will make all the difference, you'll see.'

He gave a smile which was open and quite unironic. Anyone who saw it wouldn't have believed that he was a pessimistic man.

CHAPTER VIII

SIGHT OF A NEW LIFE

THE New Year opened more serenely for Margaret and me than many in the past. True, each morning as the breakfast tray came in, she looked for letters from Maurice or Charles, just as one used to in a love affair, when letters counted more. And, as in a love affair, the fact that Charles was thousands of miles away sometimes seemed to slacken his hold on her.

Distance, as much as time, did its own work. Reading one of Charles's despatches, she was relieved that he was well: but she was joyful when she heard from Maurice. Sometimes I wondered, if she and I could have had other children, whom she would have loved the most.

The flat was quiet, so many rooms empty, with us and the housekeeper living there alone. Mornings working in the study, afternoons in the drawing-room, the winter trees in the park below. Visits to Margaret's father, back to the evening drink. Once out of the hospital, it was all serene, and there was nothing to disturb us. As for our acquaintances, we heard that Muriel was moving into Azik Schiff's house to have her baby – Eaton Square, Azik laying on doctors and nurses, that suited him appropriately enough. Margaret kept up her visits to her, as soon as she was installed, which was towards the end of January, with the baby due in a couple of weeks.

About six o'clock one evening, the birth expected any day now, there was a ring at our hall-door. As I opened it, Pat was standing on the threshold. There wasn't likely to be a more uninvited guest. I knew there couldn't be any news, for Margaret had not long returned from Eaton Square. He entered with his shameless smile, ingratiating and also defiant.

'As a matter of fact, Uncle Lewis,' he said, explaining himself, 'I would rather like a word with Aunt Meg.'

He followed me into the drawing-room, where Margaret was sitting. She said good-evening in a tone that he couldn't have thought indulgent (it was the first time she had seen him since the Christmas dinner), but he went and kissed her cheek.

'Do you mind,' he said, bright faced, 'if I help myself to a drink?'

He poured himself a whisky and soda, and then sat on a chair near to her.

'Aunt Meg,' he said, 'I've come to ask you a favour.'

'What do you mean?'

'I want you to let us call this child after you.'

For once Margaret was utterly astonished, her face wide open with surprise, and yes, for an instant, with pleasure.

Her first response was uncollected. 'Why, you don't know whether it's going to be a girl.'

'I'm sure it will be.'

'You can't be sure—'

'I want a girl. I want to call it after you.'

His tone was masterful and wooing. Watching with a certain amusement from the other side of the room (I had not often seen anyone try this kind of blandishment on her), I saw her eyes sharpen.

'Whose idea was this?'

'Mine, of course, what do you think?'

Margaret's voice was firm.

'What does Muriel say?'

'Oh, she's in favour. You'd expect her to be in favour, wouldn't you?'

'I don't know, she might be.' Margaret hadn't altered her expression. 'But she hasn't quite your reasons, after all.'

'Oh come, Aunt Meg, I just want to show how much I feel for you—' For the first time he was protesting – as though he had just recognised that he was no longer in control.

'When did you think this up?'

'A long time ago, months ago, you know how you think about names.'

'How long ago did you hear that Muriel had told me?'

'Oh that—'

'You don't like being unpopular, do you?'

'Come on, Aunt Meg, you're making too much of it.'

'Am I?'

He threw his head back, spread his arms, gave a wide penitential grimace, and said:

'You know what I'm like!'

She looked at him with a frown, some sort of affection there:

'Is that genuine?'

'You know what I'm like, I've never pretended much.'

'But, when you say that, it means you're really satisfied with yourself, don't you see? Of course, you want to make promises, you want us all to be fond of you again, that's why you're here, isn't it? But really you don't feel there's anything gone wrong—'

'Now you're being unfair.'

Even then, he wasn't ready to be totally put down. Apologetic, yes – but, still, people did things, didn't they? People did things that hurt her and perhaps they couldn't help themselves. Like her father. There were others who didn't feel as she did. Somehow Pat had discovered, it must have been from Davidson himself, that once he had applied to us for drugs. Still, he found someone else, didn't he, said Pat, not brashly but with meaning. 'It's no use expecting us to be all the same.'

Margaret told him that he was making things too comfortable for himself. For a time they were talking with a curious intimacy, the intimacy of a quarrel, more than that, something like understanding. It was easy to imagine him, I thought, behaving like this to his wife when she had found him out, penitent, flattering, inventive, tender and in the end unmoved.

But Margaret didn't give him much. Soon, she cut off the argument. She wasn't responsible for his soul or his actions, she said: but she was responsible for any words of hers that got through to Muriel. It sounded as though she wanted to issue a communiqué after a bout of diplomatic negotiations, but Margaret knew very well what she was doing. Pat, as a source of information, particularly as a source of information about his own interests, was not, in the good old Dostoevskian phrase, a specially reliable authority. He was not, Margaret repeated, to give any version of this conversation. He was not to report that Margaret would like a girl to be called after her. Margaret herself would mention the proposal to Muriel the next time she saw her.

Pat knew the last word when he heard it. With a good grace, with a beaming doggy smile, he said, Taken as read, and helped himself to another drink. Soon afterwards, he knew also that it was time for him to go.

Did he expect to get away with it, I was speculating, not intervening, although Pat had tried to involve me once or twice. Like most bamboozlers or con men, he assumed that no one could see through him. More often than not (I had watched it in men subtler than he was), bamboozlers took in no one but themselves. In fact, Margaret had seen through him from the start. Of course, the manœuvre was a transparent one, even by his standards. He had studied how to slide back into favour; he may have thought of other peace-offerings, before he decided which would please her most. Incidentally, he had chosen right. But a woman didn't need to be as clear-sighted as Margaret to see him coming, gift in hand.

So he had, with his usual cheek, put his money down and lost it. Lost most of it, but perhaps not all. Margaret thought him as worthless as before, perhaps more so: she knew another of his tricks; he had even ceased to be interesting; and yet, despite herself, sarcastic at her own expense, she was, after that failure of his, left feeling a shade more kindly towards him.

Muriel, as usual polite and friendly, did not give away her thoughts about the baby's name, so Margaret told me. 'I've got an idea she's made her own decision,' said Margaret. If that were so, we never knew what it was. For the child, born a few days later, turned out to be a boy. He was to be called, Margaret heard the first time she saw him, Roy Joseph. And those names were certainly Muriel's own decision, Margaret was sure of that. In fact, Muriel had said that she would have liked to call the boy after her stepfather, but you couldn't use Azik if you weren't a Jew. So she fell back on Roy, after her own father, and threw in Joseph, which was one of Azik's other names.

Anyway, whatever the marriage was like, this was a fine little boy, said Margaret, and took me to see him on her next visit, when he was not yet a week old.

The first time I went inside a prosperous house in London nearly forty years earlier, I had been greeted by a butler. In Azik Schiff's house in Eaton Square, one was also greeted by a butler. That didn't often happen, in the London of the sixties. But even Azik, many times richer than old Mr March, couldn't recruit the footmen and the army of maids I used to meet in the March household. Still, the Eaton Square house was grander, differing in kind from those most of our friends lived in – the comfortable flats, the Kensington, Chelsea, Hampstead houses of professional London. So far as that went, Azik wouldn't have considered adequate for his purposes the politicians' houses in Westminster, a good deal richer, that I used to know.

Azik, as he liked to announce, was fond of spending money. In the hall at Eaton Square, the carpets were deep: round the walls there were pictures which might have belonged to the antechamber of a good, though somewhat conventional, municipal gallery. That was true of Azik's pictures throughout the house. His taste wasn't adventurous, as Austin Davidson's had been. Azik had bought nothing later than the Impressionists, except for one Cézanne. He had been cautious, out of character for him, perhaps not trusting either his judgment or his eye. But he had a couple of Sisleys, a Boudin, a Renoir, a Ruysdael – he might have been cautious, but we coveted them each time we went inside his house.

Getting out of the lift, which was one of Azik's innovations, Margaret led me to the master bedroom on the third floor, the whole of which Azik had made over to his stepdaughter. Inside the high light bedroom (through the window one could see the tops of trees in the private garden), Muriel was sitting up in bed, a great four-poster bed, a wrap round her shoulders, looking childish, prim, undecorated. She said, Good afternoon, Uncle Lewis, with that old-fashioned correctness of hers, which often seemed as though she were smiling to herself or pretending to drop a curtsy.

'It's very good of you to come,' she said.

I said no.

'Aunt Margaret likes babies. It can't be much fun for you.'

Margaret put in that I had been good when Charles was a baby.

'That was duty, though,' said Muriel, looking straight at me.

I was, as often, disconcerted by her, not sure whether she had a double meaning, or whether she meant anything at all.

She made some conversation about Charles, the first time I had heard her mention him. Then there was a hard raucous cry from a room close by, from what must have been the dressing-room.

'Yes, that's him,' she said, with composure.

'Oh, come on, let's have him in,' said Margaret.

'That will be boring for Uncle Lewis, though.'

With other young women, that might have seemed coy. Not so with her. I told her that I hadn't expected to wait so long. She gave a grin which made her look less decorous, and pressed the bell by her bedside.

As a nurse carried in the baby, Margaret said:

'Let me have him, just for a minute.'

She pressed the bundle, arms slowly waving, to her, and looked down at him, with her expression softened by delight.

'I do envy you,' she said to Muriel, and from the tone I was sure that remark had been made before. Yet Margaret's pleasure was as simple as it could be, all the life in her just joyful at the feel of life.

She passed the child to his mother, who settled him against her and said, in a clear voice:

'Hallo, old man.'

It might have happened, it almost certainly must have happened, that my mother showed me Martin soon after he was born. But if so I had totally forgotten it, and everything to do with his birth, except that I had been sent to my aunt's for a couple of days. No, the only days-old baby I remembered seeing was my son. The aimless, rolling eyes, the hands drifting round like an anemone's fibrils. As a spectacle, this was the same. Perhaps the difference, to a photographic eye, was that this child, under the thin flaxen hair, had a high crown to his head, the kind of steeple crown Muriel's father had once possessed.

But when I first saw my son it hadn't been with a photographic eye. It hadn't even been with emotion, but something fiercer and more animal, so strong that, though it was getting on for seventeen years ago, it didn't need bringing back to memory; it was there. That afternoon in Muriel's bedroom, perversely, I did watch the pair of them, mother and baby, with something like emotion, the sort of emotion which is more or less tender, more or less self-indulgent, which doesn't trouble one. My brother's grandson. Roy Calvert's grandson. Would this child ever know anything about Roy Calvert, who had passed into a private mythology by now? How much did I recollect of what he had been truly like?

This child would live a different life from ours, and, of course, with any luck, live on when our concerns, and everything about us, had been long since swept away. Did one envy a life that was just beginning? Pity for what might happen, that was there. Pity was deeper than the thought he would live after one. But, yes, the impulse for life was organic; in time it would overmaster all the questions; it would prevail over pity; all one would feel was the strength of a new life.

CHAPTER IX

PIECES OF NEWS

SEVERAL afternoons that April, Margaret and I walked through the empty flat to an empty bedroom, making quite unnecessary inspections in time for Charles's return. It was the room he had occupied since he was three years old: not the one where we had watched him in his one grave illness, because after that, out of what was sheer superstition, we had made a change. This was the room, though, to which he had come back on holidays from school.

From the window, there was the view over Tyburn gardens which I had seen so often, waking him in the morning, that now I didn't see at all. The shelves round the room were stacked with books, which, with a streak of possessive conservatism, he refused to have touched: the geological strata of his books since he began to read, children's stories, C. S. Lewis, Henry Treece, other historical novels, Shakespeare, Latin texts, Greek texts, Russian texts, political treatises, modern histories, school prizes, Dostoevsky. Under the shelves were piles of games, those also not to be touched. Once or twice Margaret glanced at them as the wife of Pastor Brand might have done. We didn't know where he was, nor precisely when to expect him. There had been a cable from Constantinople, asking for money. He had had to stop for days in an Anatolian village; that was all the news.

'Well,' said Margaret, looking at the childhood room, 'I think it's how he likes it, isn't it? I hope he will.'

On the bright chilly April days we were listening for the telephone. But, while we were waiting for news of him, we received other news which we weren't waiting for: two other pieces of news for which we were utterly unprepared, arriving in the same twenty-four hours.

The first came in the morning post, among a batch of press cuttings. It was an article from a paper, which, though it was well-known, I didn't usually read. The title was simply *Secret Society*, and at the first glance was an attack on the new Government's 'back-room pundits'. There was nothing specially new in that. The Government was already unpopular with the press: this paper was thought of as an organ of the centre, but a lot of abuse was coming from the centre. Like most people who had lived or written in public, I was used to the sight of my own name, I was at the same time reading and not reading. Lord Getliffe. Mounteney. Constantine and Arthur Miles. Sir Walter Luke. Sir Lewis Eliot. . . .

The writer didn't like us at all, not any of us. That didn't matter much. What did matter was that he had done some research. Some of his facts were wrong or twisted, but quite a number true. He had done some neat detective work on the meetings ('grey eminence' meetings) which we used to hold, through the years when the present Government was in opposition, in Brown's Hotel. He reported in detail how Francis had been offered a post in October; he knew the time of Francis's visit to Downing Street, not only the day but the hour. But what made me angry was the simple statement that the same offer might soon be made to me.

Whatever I said, I shouldn't be believed, I told Margaret. No correction made any difference. That was an invariable rule of public life.

'It's a nuisance,' she said.

'It's worse than that. If they were thinking of asking me, they wouldn't now.'

'That doesn't matter. You know it doesn't.'

'Even things I don't specially want, I don't like these people sabotaging. Which, of course, is the whole idea.'

Margaret said – and it was true – that I was upset out of all proportion.

That afternoon, Margaret went out, and it was after tea-time before she joined me in the drawing-room. She looked at me: she knew, better than anyone, that my moods, once set, were hard for me to break, and that I had been regressing to the morning's news.

'I've something else for you,' she said.

I replied, without interest. 'Have you?'

'I've been to see Muriel.'

That didn't stir me. I said again: 'Oh, have you?'

'She's got rid of Pat.'

At last I was listening.

'She's got rid of him.'

'Does she mean it?'

'Oh yes, she means it. It's for good and all.'

Margaret said, she hadn't begun to guess. Nor had I. Nor, so far as we knew, had Azik or Rosalind. Possibly not the young man himself. It was true, Muriel had remained at Eaton Square, a couple of months now since the baby was born: but that seemed to us like a spoiled young woman who enjoyed being looked after. Not a bit of it. During that time she had, with complete coolness, telling no one except her solicitor, been organising the break. Her solicitor was to dispose of the Chelsea flat: he was to buy a house where she would take the baby. She had sent for Pat the evening before, just to tell him that she didn't wish to see him again and that an action for divorce would, of course, go through. So far as Margaret could gather, Muriel had been entirely calm during this interview, much less touched by Pat's entreaties, wiles, sorrows and even threats than Margaret herself on a less critical occasion. It seemed to me strangely like Muriel's father disposing of a college servant. In a methodical, businesslike fashion she had, immediately he left, written him a letter confirming what she had just said.

'I've never seen anything like it,' said Margaret.

We felt, for the moment, nothing but surprise. It was clear that Muriel had made her decision months ago, kept it to herself, not altered it by a tremor, and worked out her plans. She didn't seem heartbroken: she didn't even seem outraged: she merely behaved as though she had had enough of him. As we talked, Margaret and I were lost, neither of us could give any kind of insight, or even rationalisation. Why had she married him? Had she been determined to escape from a possessive mother? Her life, until she was over twenty, had been shielded, by the standards of the day. Rosalind was both worldly and as watchful as a detective, and it had been difficult for Muriel not to stay a virgin. Perhaps Pat had been the most enterprising young man round her. Certainly he had contrived to seduce her: but there might have been some contrivance on her part too, so that she became pregnant and stopped any argument against the marriage. Yet all that seemed too mechanical to sound true. Was she one of those who were sexually avid and otherwise cold? Somehow that didn't sound true either. Was it simply his running after women that made her tired of him? Or was that an excuse? She might have plans for the future, but if so those too she was keeping to herself. She might be looking for another husband. Alternatively, it seemed as likely that she had no use for men. Neither Margaret nor I would trust our judgment either way. She had her child, and that she must have wanted; Margaret said that in a singular manner, on the surface undisturbed, she was a devoted mother.

While we were still talking, still mystified – it must have been between six and seven – there were Italian cries, our housekeeper's, penetrating to us from rooms away, cries that soon we made out as excited greetings, which came from the front door. 'Here he is! Here he is!' she was shouting, and Charles entered the room.

As Margaret embraced him, she broke out:

'Why didn't you let us know?'

'Anyway, I'm here.'

He needed a shave, he was wearing a jacket, roll-top sweater and dirty jeans. It was the first time I had seen him sunburnt, and he wasn't over-clean after the travel. He looked healthy but thin, his face, high-cheekboned, masculine, already set in the pattern that would stay until he was old. He stretched out on the sofa, long feet protruding over the end.

I asked him to have a drink. After islamic countries, he was out of practice, he said: yes, he would like a gin. He began to describe his route home: we wanted to hear, we were glad to have him there, we were trying to throw off the beginning of the day. He was in high spirits, like one who has made a good voyage. Suddenly he threw his legs off the sofa, sat up straight, gazed at me with alert eyes.

'You're looking sombre,' he said.

Of Margaret and me, I was the one whose face he could read the quicker.

I said something evasive and putting off.

'You've got something on your mind.'

I hesitated, said no again, and then reached out for the press cutting.

'I suppose you'll have to see this sooner or later,' I said as I handed it over.

With a scrutinising frown, Charles read, and gave a short deep curse.

'They're not specially fond of you, are they?'

'One thing I'm worried about', I said, 'is that all this may rebound on you.'

'I shall have worse than that to cope with.'

'It may be a drag—'

'Never mind that.'

'Easier said than done,' I told him.

'You're not to worry about me.' Then he said, in an even tone:

'I told you years ago, didn't I, I won't be worried about.' He said it as though it were a good-natured domestic gibe: that was ninety per cent of the truth, but not quite all.

Then, he tapped the cutting, and said he hadn't read English newspapers for months until that day. He had got hold of the morning's editions on the way over. There was one impression that hit him in the eye: how parochial, how inward-looking, this country had become, Parish-pump politics. Politics looked quite different from where he had been living. 'This isn't politics,' he said, looking contemptuously at the cutting. 'But it's how this country is behaving. If we're becoming as provincial as this, how do we get out of it?'

He was saying that vigorously, with impatience, not with gloom. In the same energetic fashion, he said:

'Well then, is that all the bad news for the present?'

That was an old family joke, derived both from Hector Rose and from the time when Charles himself began to read Greek plays.

'The rest isn't quite so near home,' I answered. 'But still, it's bad news for someone. You tell him,' I said to Margaret.

As he heard about Muriel, he was nothing like so impatient. He was concerned and even moved, more than we had been, to an extent which took us by surprise. So far as I knew, he had had little to do with his cousin, and both Pat and Muriel were five years older than he was. Yet he spoke about them as though they were his own kind. Certainly he did not wish to hear us blaming either of them. He didn't say one word of criticism himself. This was a pity – that was as far as he would go. Still with stored-up energy, poised on the balls of his feet, he declared that he would visit them.

'They might tell me more than they've told you,' he said.

'Yes, they might,' said Margaret. 'But Carlo, I'm sure it's gone too far—'

'You can't be sure.'

Margaret said that it was Muriel who had to be persuaded, and there weren't many people with a stronger will. Charles wasn't being argumentative, but he wouldn't give up: and, strangely enough, his concern broke through in a different place, and one which, taken by surprise, we had scarcely thought of.

'If they can't be stopped,' he remarked, 'it's going to be a blow for Uncle Martin, isn't it?'

There had always been sympathy between Martin and Charles, and in some ways their temperaments were similar, given that Charles's was the more highly charged. Charles knew a good deal about Martin's relation with his son, even though it was one that he wouldn't have accepted for himself and would, in Pat's place, have shrugged off. But now he was thinking of what Martin hoped for. Incidentally, where would Pat propose to live? The studio, where he had conscientiously worked at his painting, would be lost along with the Chelsea flat. But there Charles showed a spark of the irony which had for the past half-hour deserted him. He admitted that even he couldn't pretend that Pat was not a born survivor.

CHAPTER X

POSSIBLE HEAVENS

THROUGH the following days and weeks, right into the early summer, there was plenty of to-ing and fro-ing – the bread and butter of a family trouble, trivial to anyone outside – of which I heard only at second or third hand. I knew that Pat had been to see Margaret two or three times, begging her to intercede, or, in his own phrase, 'tell her I'm not so bad'. Margaret had, I guessed, been kind and taken the edge off her tongue: but certainly she had told him there was nothing she could do.

Charles spent several evenings with both Muriel and Pat, but kept the secrets to himself, or at least from his mother and me. All I learned was that at one stage he invoked Maurice, at home for a weekend from the hospital. The two of them, and Pat's sister Nina, now studying music in London, met in Charles's room at our flat, and I believed that Maurice, who had an influence over his contemporaries, went out to make a plea, though to which of them I didn't know. One day Martin telephoned me, saying that he was in London and was having a conference with the Schiffs: he made an excuse for not coming to see me afterwards. That was a matter of pride, and it was just as I might have behaved myself.

On an afternoon early in June, I took Charles with me on one of my routine visits to his grandfather. In the taxi, I was warning Charles that he wasn't going to enjoy it: this wouldn't be like his last sight of my own father, comic in his own eyes, happy in his stuffy little room. He had been stoical because he didn't know any other way to be: while Austin Davidson was putting on the face of stoicism, but – without confessing it to anyone round him – was dying, but bitterly. I was warning Charles: in secret I was preparing myself for the next hour. For, though those visits might have seemed a drill by now, I couldn't get used to them. The cool words I had trained myself to, in reply to Davidson's, like rallies in a game of ping-pong: but there hadn't been one single visit when, as soon as I got out of the clinic into the undemanding air, I didn't feel liberated; as though solitariness and an inadmissible boredom, by the side of someone I admired, had been lifted from me. That was as true or truer, nearly a year later, as when I first saw him after his attempt at death.

In the sunny green-reflecting bedroom, Austin Davidson was in the familiar posture, head and shoulders on high pillows, looking straight in front of him, feet and ankles bare. He didn't turn his eyes, as the door opened. I said.

'I've brought Carlo to see you.'

'Oh, have you?'

He looked round, and slowly from under the sheet drew out a thin hand, on which stood out the veins and freckles of old age. As Charles took it, he said:

'How are you, grandpa?'

Davidson produced a good imitation – perhaps it was more than that – of his old mephistophelian smile.

'Well, Carlo, you wouldn't want me to tell you a lie, would you?'

Their eyes met. They each had the same kind of cheekbones. Even now, it was easy to see what Davidson had looked like as a young man. But, though I might be imagining it, I thought his face had become puffier these last few weeks; some of the bone structure, handsome until he was old, was being smeared out now.

Charles gave a smile, a smile of recognition, in return.

'Also,' said Davidson, 'you wouldn't like me to give you an honest answer either, don't you know?'

Charles gave the same firm smile again, and sat down by the bed, on the side opposite to me. For a while Austin Davidson seemed pleased with his own repartee, or, perhaps more exactly, with the performance he was putting up. Then he began to show signs, which I hadn't expected, of something like disappointment, as though he were a child who, out of good manners, couldn't protest at not being given a treat. That was a surprise, for he had, even in illness, displayed a liking for Charles, and had occasionally asked for his company. Not that Davidson had much family sense, few men less: but of his descendants and relatives, Charles, I fancied, appeared most like the young men Davidson had grown up with. Yet now he wished that Charles was out of the way.

Then, when Davidson couldn't resist a complaint: 'I suppose it's too much to expect Carlo to take an intelligent interest—' I had it. Charles couldn't pick up the reference: but by now Davidson, always obsessive, had become addicted to our afternoon ritual, first what he called 'intelligent conversation' (that is, about the stock market), and then his reflections on dying. His interests had narrowed to that. It still seemed to me harrowing that in that clinical room, afternoon following afternoon, we talked about Stock Exchange prices. I had to tell him what he had gained or lost by his last investment. It was purely symbolic: money had not mattered much to him, except as an intellectual game, and nothing could matter less now. Yet there was something triumphant about his interest, as though he had proved that one could be pertinacious to the end.

However, that afternoon, with Charles present, he was deprived. For a time he fell into silence, indrawn. Whether he was wondering if he ought to talk about death in front of Charles, I didn't know. Probably he didn't trouble himself. Austin Davidson used to feel, as only a delicate man could feel, that it was invariably wrong to be over-delicate. At any rate, after a while he produced a question.

'Carlo. If you believed in an after-life, which by definition is impossible, which of the various alternatives so far proposed for the after-life would you prefer?'

Davidson's sepia eyes were shining, as though gratified to be talking again.

'Meaning what in the way of alternatives?' Charles was good at catching the tone.

'Any that you've ever heard of.'

Charles considered.

'They're all pretty dim,' he said.

'Granted. There's not much to be said for the human imagination.'

'I suppose there may be something outside this world—'

I thought, Charles wasn't used to the Edwardian brand of unbelief.

'That hasn't any meaning. No, people have always been inventing heavens. All ridiculous. Now you're asked to name the one you fancy.'

Gazing at the old man, Charles realised that he had to play this game according to the rules.

'Well then,' he said. 'Valhalla.'

Davidson gave a genuine smile.

'Not so good, Carlo. Just like a regimental mess.'

'Good stories,' said Charles.

'My God. Listening to rather stupid hearties talking about battles for all eternity.'

'That would be better than listening to harps, wouldn't it?'

'I put it about equal. But all that boozing—'

Like nearly all his circle, Davidson had never gone in much for drink. I recalled, years before I met Margaret, being taken by a Cambridge friend to a party in Gordon Square. The hosts – we now knew from the biographies – had been intimates of Davidson's and brother Apostles. The thinking might have been high, but the entertainment was austere.

'One would get used to it after the first thousand years, I think.'

They kept up the exchange, Charles doing his share as though this were a natural piece of chit-chat. Whether it cost him an effort, I couldn't be sure. His face was grave, but so it had to be to match Davidson's fancy, while Davidson's spirits, so long as they could go on talking, were lighter than I had felt them for weeks past. After the two of them had exhausted the topic of putative heavens, Davidson didn't relapse into the dark silence, when it seemed his eyes turned inward, that I had sat through so often in that room. Instead, and this was very rare, for even Margaret he scarcely mentioned when I visited him, he brought a new person into the conversation.

'Oh that young man, what's he called, your nephew—' he said to me, and I supplied the name. 'Yes. He came in here the other day. He's been to see me once or twice, don't you know.'

Yes, I knew.

'I gather he's having some sort of trouble with his wife.'

It was an extraordinary place to come and confide, but Pat, I thought, wasn't above searching for comfort or allies anywhere.

I said that his wife had turned him out.

'Can't someone make her be sensible? It's all remarkably uncivilised.'

His tone was stern and complaining. That was a word of condemnation, one of the very few he ever used. He began to talk about his own friends. They tried to get the maximum of pleasure out of their personal relations. If this meant triangles or more complicated geometrical figures, well then, one accepted that too. Of course jealousy sometimes intruded: but jealousy had to be kept in its place. They believed in pleasure, said Davidson. If you didn't believe in pleasure, you couldn't be civilised.

Davidson wasn't wandering, I hadn't heard him do so since the first morning in the clinic. Lucidly he returned to his starting-point. Muriel was being uncivilised. Of course, Pat might have gone in for a certain amount of old-fashioned adultery. What of it? He wanted to preserve the marriage.

'I should have thought', said Davidson, 'that he was a man of fundamentally decent feeling.'

I should have liked to discover what Charles made of that judgment. He had been listening with absorption to Davidson speaking of his friends: at Charles's age, though this was his grandfather talking, that period, that coterie, must already have passed into history and have seemed as remote, as preserved in time, as the pre-Raphaelites. Would they have a glamour for Charles? Or would he detest their kind of enlightenment, what Davidson had just called being 'civilised', as much as his mother did?

We had stayed in the bedroom – I was used to looking at my watch below Davidson's eye-level in that room – half an hour longer than I set myself. But when I began to move, muttering the 'Well—' which begins to set one free, he said he would like us to stay a little longer. He realised we were unlikely to share his opinion, he remarked with a flicker of the old devil, but he was having a mildly diverting afternoon.

CHAPTER XI

REPLICA OF A GROUP

IT was getting on for a month later, on an afternoon when Margaret was taking her turn to visit Austin Davidson, that Azik Schiff rang up: would I call round at his house, he wanted (using an idiom known only to Azik) to include me in the picture.

High summer in Eaton Square, trees dense with foliage, leaves dark under the bright sun, car-bonnets flashing. The major rooms in Azik's house were on the second floor, a kind of *piano nobile*, and there in the long drawing-room, standing in front of his Renoir, Azik greeted me. He gave his face-splitting frog-like smile, called me 'my friend', put his arm round my shoulders and conducted me to a sofa where Rosalind was sitting. Then there was conferring about whether it was too late for tea, or too early for a drink. Both of them, Azik in particular, were making more than their normal fuss of me, trying to wrap me round with warmth.

When we were settled down, welcomes insisted on, Azik put his hands on his thick thighs, and said, like one at home with negotiations:

'Lewis, my friend, you are not a principal in this matter. But we thought you ought to be informed.'

'After all, you're his uncle, aren't you?' Rosalind said appeasingly, but as though raising an unnecessary doubt.

I said, I had heard so many rumours, I should be grateful for some facts.

'Ah, it is the young who have been talking.'

'Not to me,' I said.

'Your son is a fine young man.'

I explained, I hadn't a clear idea what he had been doing.

'It makes no difference,' said Azik. 'It is all settled. Like that—' he swept his arm.

'She's as obstinate as a pig, she always was,' said Rosalind.

Azik gave a brisk businesslike account. Nothing had affected Muriel. Not that that was different from what I had expected: I imagined that she had stayed polite and temperate all through. While others had been arguing with her, giving advice, making appeals, she had been quietly working with her solicitor. The Chelsea flat had been sold ('at a fair price', said Azik): she had bought a house in Belgravia, and moved into it, along with child and nurse, the day before. The transaction had gone through so fast that Azik assumed that it must have been started months ago.

'Remember, my friend, she is well provided for. She is independent with her money. We have no sanctions to use against her. Even if we were sure of our own ground.'

All of a sudden, Rosalind went into a tirade, her face forgetting the gentility of years and her voice its dying fall. She began by being furious with her daughter. After all her, Rosalind's, care. Not to be able to keep a man. To get into a mess like this. No gratitude. No consideration. Making her look like an idiot. But really she was being as protective, or as outraged at not being able to be so, as when her daughter was a child. Rosalind's sophistication had dropped clean away – her marriages, her remarkable talent for being able to love where it was advantageous to love, her climb from the suburbs of our native town to Eaton Square, her adventures on the way, all gone.

She had forgotten how she had campaigned to capture Muriel's father, who, when one came down to fact, had not been much more stable with women than Pat himself. As for Pat, Rosalind felt simple hate. Twister. Gigolo. Expecting to be paid for his precious ——. Rosalind's language, when she was calm, could be slightly suggestive, but now there was no suggestion about it. One comfort, he had got what was coming to him. Then he went whining round. Rosalind began to use words that Azik perhaps had never heard, and that I hadn't since I was young. Mardy. Mardyarse. How any child of hers, Rosalind shouted, could have been taken in by a drip like that ——.

'She has to make her own mistakes, perhaps,' said Azik, in a tone soothing but not quite assured, as though this violence in his wife was a novelty with which he hadn't had much practice.

Rosalind: Who is she going to pick up next?

Azik: We have to try and put her in the way of some nice young men.

Rosalind: We've done that, since she was seventeen. And look what happens.

Azik: We have to go on trying. These young people don't like being managed. But perhaps there will be a piece of luck.

Rosalind: She'll pick another bit of rubbish.

Azik: We must try. As long as she doesn't know we're trying.

The dialogue went on across me, like an argument in the marriage bed, Rosalind accusing, Azik consolatory. It wasn't the first of these arguments, one felt: perhaps the others, like this, faded away into doldrums, when Azik, still anxious to placate his wife, had time to turn to me.

'There is something I have already said to Martin,' he told me. 'Now I shall say it to you, Lewis, my friend.'

I looked at him.

'I should be sorry if this business of these young people made any break between your family and ours. I must say, I should be sorry. It will not happen from our side.'

He spoke with great dignity. Uxorious as he was, he spoke as though that was his decision, and Rosalind had to obey. Loyally, making herself simmer down, she said that she and I had known each other for thirty years. On the other hand, I was thinking, I should be surprised if she went out of her way to meet Martin in the future.

Just after I had replied, telling him that I felt the same – I should have had to return politeness for politeness, but it happened to be true – young David ran into the room. He was a handsome boy, thin and active, one of those genetic sports who seemed to have no resemblance to either of his parents, olive-skinned. His father looked at him with doting love, and the boy spoke to both of them as though he expected total affection, and gave it back. He was just at the age when the confidence between all three was still complete, with nothing precarious in it, as though the first adolescent storm or secret would never happen. At his school his record was as good as Charles's had been at the same age, six years before. In some ways, I thought, this boy was the cleverer. It was a triumph for Rosalind, much disapproved of by persons who regarded her as a kind of Becky Sharp, to produce for Azik when she was well over forty a son like this.

As for me, watching (the bonds between the three of them were so strong there wasn't really room for an outsider there) the happiness of

that not specially Holy Family, I couldn't have found it in me to begrudge
it them. But I was thinking of something else. When they had been talking
of Muriel, Rosalind had behaved in what Austin Davidson would have
called an uncivilised fashion: in fact he would have thought her strident
and coarse, and had no use for her. While Azik had been showing all the
compassionate virtues.

Well, it was fine to be virtuous, but the truth was, Rosalind minded
about her daughter and Azik didn't. To everyone round them, probably
to his wife, possibly even to himself, he seemed a good stepfather,
affectionate, sympathetic, kind. I had even heard him call himself a
Jewish papa, not only in his relation to his son but to his stepdaughter.
One had only to see him with that boy, though, to know what he was like
as a father -- and what he wasn't to Muriel. Of course he was kind to her,
because there weren't many kinder men. He would do anything practical
for her: if she had needed money, he would have been lavish. But as for
thinking of her when she was out of his sight, or being troubled about her
life, you had just to watch his oneness – animal oneness, spiritual oneness –
with his son.

If that had not been so, if his imagination had been working, working
father-like, on her behalf, it was unthinkable that he wouldn't have been
more cautious about Pat. At the time (it had happened so quickly, we had
all been puzzled how Pat came to know Muriel) I had thought he was
taking Pat very easily. Yet Azik was no fool about people. He just wasn't
truly interested, neither in Pat nor in the girl herself. If it had been a
business deal, or even more anything concerned with Azik's son, Pat
would never have slid inside the house. As it was, he got away with it:
until he discovered, what no one had imagined, that the young woman was
more ruthless than he was.

Which began to have other consequences we hadn't expected. As soon
as they knew of Muriel's resolve, Charles, Maurice and other friends of
theirs had been working to bring about a reconciliation. There was a
feeling, a kind of age-group solidarity, that Pat had to be helped. He was
living in his father's house in Cambridge; occasionally he came to London,
and we heard that he was lent money by some of the young people.
Nevertheless, as the summer went on, he was – as it were insensibly –
pushed to the edge of their group. One didn't hear any of them say a harsh
word about him: but one ceased to hear him much talked about at all.
Whereas Muriel one always saw, when, as occasionally they did, they
invited older people to their parties.

Muriel's own house was modest but smart, the house of a prosperous young married couple, except for the somewhat anomalous absence of a husband. But, instead of entertaining there, she went to the bedsitting-rooms in which most of that group lived, such as Nina's in Notting Hill. There seemed to be about a couple of dozen of them drifting round London that summer. Charles, waiting to go up to Cambridge, was the youngest, though some of the others had been at school with him. Young men and girls sometimes called in at our flat for a drink. They were friendly, both with an older generation and each other. They didn't drink as much as my friends used to at their age: there were all the signs that they took sex much more easily. Certainly there didn't appear to be many tormented love affairs about. A couple of the girls were daughters of my own friends. I sometimes wondered how much different was the way they lived their lives from their parents' way: was the gap bigger than other such gaps had been?

Often I was irritated with them as though I were the wrong distance away, half involved, half remote: and it was Charles's self-control, not mine, which prevented us from quarrelling. He was utterly loyal to his friends and when I criticised them didn't like it: but he set himself to answer on the plane of reason.

All right, their manners are different from yours: but they think yours are as obsolete as Jane Austen's. If they don't write bread-and-butter letters, what of it? It is an absurd convention. If (as once happened) one of them writes on an envelope the unadorned address Lewis Eliot, again what of it?

He wouldn't get ruffled, and that irked me more. Take your friend Guy Grenfell, I said. They had been at school together. Guy was rich, a member of a squirearchical family established for centuries. He might grow his hair down to his shoulders, but once, when he came to an elderly dinner-party, he behaved like the rest of us, and more so. Yet when he was in the middle of their crowd, he appeared to be giving a bad imitation of a barrow boy. Was this to show how progressive he was?

Charles would not let his temper show. Guy was quite enlightened. Some of them were progressive. . . .

I jeered, and threw back at him the record of Lester Ince and his *galère*. They were just as rude as your friends. Look where they finished. I brought out the old aphorism that when young men rebel against social manners, they end up by not rebelling against anything else.

We shall see, said Charles. Angry that I couldn't move him, I had let my advocacy go too far: but, still, there were times when, unprovoked, I thought – are these really our successors? Will they ever be able to take over?

Those questions went through my mind when, one day in July, I received the news of George Passant's death. It had happened weeks before, I was told, very near the time that I had been having that family conference with Azik in Eaton Square. In fact, so far as I could make out the dates, George had had a cerebral hæmorrhage the night before, and had died within twenty-four hours. This had taken place in a little Jutland town, where he had exiled himself and was being visited by one of his old disciples. Two or three more of his disciples, faithful to the last, had gone over for the funeral, and they had buried him in a Lutheran cemetery.

It might have seemed strange that it took so long for the news to reach me. After all, he had been my first benefactor and oldest friend. Yet by now he was separated from everyone but his own secret circle in the provincial town: while I, since my father's death, had no connections in the town any more. There was nothing to take me there, after I resigned from the University Court. It wasn't my father's death that cut me off, that was as acceptable as a death could be: but after the trial there were parts of my youth there that weren't acceptable at all, and this was true for Martin as well as for me. Some of those old scenes – without willing it, by something like a self-protecting instinct – we took care not to see. I still carried out my duty, George's last legacy, of visiting his niece in Holloway Prison. Occasionally I still had telephone calls, charges reversed, from Mr Pateman, but even his obsessional passion seemed not to have been spent, but at least after a year to be a shade eroded.

So far as I could tell, there had been no announcement of George's death, certainly not in a London paper. He had been a leader in a strange and private sense, his disciples must be mourning him more than most men are mourned, and yet, except for them, no one knew or cared where he was living, nor whether he was alive or dead.

I heard the news by telephone – a call from the town, would I accept it and reverse the charges? I assumed that it was Mr Pateman, and with my usual worn-down irritation said yes. But it was a different voice, soft, flexible, excited, the voice of Jack Cotery. I had seen him only twice in the past ten years, but I knew that, though he had a job in Burnley, he still visited the town to see his mother, who was living in the same house, the same back-street, whose existence, when we were young and he was spinning romantic lies about his social grandeur, he had ingeniously – and for some time with success – concealed. Had anyone told me about George, came the eager voice. He, Jack, had just met one of the set. The poor old thing was dead. Jack repeated the dates and such details as he had learned. Until George died, there was someone with him all the time: he knew what was happening, but couldn't speak.

'I don't know what he had to look forward to,' Jack was saying. 'But he loved life, in his own way, didn't he? I don't suppose he wanted to go.'

To do Jack credit, he would have hurried to tell me the news, even if he hadn't had an ulterior motive. But that he had. The last time he visited me, he had been trying to convert me to organised religion. Now, over the telephone, he couldn't explain, it was very complicated, but he had another problem, very important, nothing bad, but something that mattered a very great deal – and it was very important, so, just to come out with it, could I lend him a hundred pounds? I said that I would send a cheque that evening, and did so. After what I had been listening to, it seemed like paying a last debt to the past.

Guy Grenfell and other companions of Charles were in the flat, and as I joined them for a drink I mentioned that I had just heard of the death of an old friend. Who, said Charles, and I told him the name. It meant nothing to the others, but Charles had met George year after year, on his ritual expeditions to London. Charles's eyes searched into my expression. 'I'm sorry,' he said. But, though he had never told me so – he was too considerate for that – I was certain that in secret he had found George nothing but grotesque. Diffidence. Formality. Heartiness. Repetitive questions ('Are you looking after your health?'). Flashes of mental precision. Slow-walking, hard-breathing figure, often falling asleep in an armchair, mouth open. Once, coming in drunk, he had fallen off a chair. That was what Charles had seen, and not many at his age would have seen more. He could not begin to comprehend the effect that George had once had on me and my first friends.

The irony was, that the 'freedoms' George – and all the other Georges of his time – had clamoured for, had more or less come true. The life that Charles's own friends were leading was not that much different from what George had foreshadowed all those years ago. A lot of the young men and girls in the Earls Court bedsitters would have fitted, breathing native air, into George's group. Gentle. Taking their pleasures as they came. Not liking their society any more than George had done. Making their own enclaves. The passive virtues, not the fighting ones. Not much superego (if one didn't use older words). The same belief, deep down, that most people were good.

That would not suit Charles for long, any more than it had suited me. And yet it had its charm. It seemed at times like an Adamic invention, as though no one had discovered a private clan-life before. That was true even with the more strenuous natures among them, like his own. It might have been true, I thought, of Muriel.

So much so that when – some weeks after the news about George, to whom I didn't refer again – I told Charles that his friends went in for enclave-making, just as much as the bourgeois they despised, he didn't like it. Once more he felt curiously protective about the whole circle, more so than I remembered being. But he was still not prepared to quarrel and he suspected there might be something in what I said. He had also seen more subsistence poverty than any of us. All over the advanced world, people seemed to be making enclaves. I thought that wasn't simply a fantasy of my own. The rich like Azik and some of our American friends; the professionals everywhere; the apparently rebellious young; they were all drawing the curtains, looking inwards into their own rooms, to an extent that hadn't happened in my time. The demonstrations (that was the summer when the English young, including Charles's friends, started protesting about Vietnam), the acts of violence, were deceptive. They too came from a kind of enclave. They were part of a world which, though it could be made less comfortable, or more foreboding, no one could find a way to shake.

Charles listened carefully. This wasn't an argument, though I had touched on the rift of difference between us. Since he had left school and gone on his new-style grand tour, he had been released, happy and expectant. Inside the family, we had no more cares, possibly less, than most of our own kind. It had been an easy summer, with time to meet his friends and our own. Except that we had to be ready for the death of Margaret's father, we had nothing that seemed likely to disturb us, not even an examination or a book coming out.

'How many of your prophecies have gone wrong?' said Charles, without edge, with detachment.

'Quite a few.'

'How right were you in the thirties?'

'Most of the time we [I was thinking of Francis Getliffe and others] weren't far off. Anyway, a lot of it is on the record.'

'In the war? What did you think would be happening now?'

I paused.

'There I should have been wrong. I thought that, if Hitler could be beaten, then things would go much better than in fact they have.'

'I hope', said Charles, 'that you turn out wrong again. After all, some of us might see the end of the century, mightn't we?'

He gave a smile, meaning that he and his friends by that time would only be middle-aged.

CHAPTER XII

RESULT OF AN OFFER

THE Lords were having a late-night sitting, Francis told me over the telephone (it was the last week in October), a committee stage left over from the summer. He would be grateful if Margaret and I would go along and have supper with him there, just to help him through the hours. Yes, we were free: and it was conceivable that Francis wanted more than sheer company, for one of the political correspondents (not our enemy of the spring) had that morning reported that Lord Getliffe had been called to Downing Street the day before. The same correspondent added with total confidence that S——, the old Commons loyalist who had been given the job when Francis previously refused it, would be going within days. He was being looked after – a nice little pension on one of the nationalised boards.

It sounded like inside information. Just as Hector Rose and my old colleagues used to ask in Whitehall, often with rage, I wondered how ever it got out. Possibly from S—— himself. Politicians, old Bevill used to say, were the worst keepers of secrets. They will talk to their wives, he added with Polonian wisdom. He might have said, just as accurately, they will talk to journalists: and the habit seemed to be hooking them more every year, like the addiction to a moderately harmless drug.

As we came out of Westminster underground, the light was shining over Big Ben, there was a smell – foggy? a tinge, or was one imagining it, of burning wood? – in the smoky autumn air. Francis, waiting for us in the peers' entrance, kissed Margaret and led us up the stairs, over the Jonah's-whale carpets, straight to the restaurant; we were rescuing him, he said, the parliamentary process could be remarkably boring unless you were brought up to it, man and boy. In fact, he was already occupying a table, one of the first to establish himself, though some men, without guests, were walking through to the inner room. Under the portraits, under the tapestries, taste following the Prince Consort, I noticed one or two faces I vaguely knew, part of a new batch of life peers. Not then, but a little later, when we were settling down to our wine and cold roast beef, there came a face that I more than vaguely knew – Walter Luke, grizzled and jaunty, saying 'I didn't expect to see you here, Lew,' as he passed on. It would have been a fair reply that, a short time before, no one could have expected to see *him* there. But here he was, as though in honour of science – and, because there already existed a Lord Luke, here he was as Lord Luke of Salcombe.

Francis, who had always been fond of Walter Luke, was saying, once he had got out of hearing, that no one we knew had been unluckier, no one of great gifts, that was. If things had gone right, he would have done major scientific work. But all the chances, including the war, had run against him. After all of which, said Francis, he got this curious consolation-prize.

Yet he had seemed in highish spirits. As the room filled up, no more divisions till half past eight, most people seemed in highish spirits. Greetings, warm room, food, a certain amount of activity ahead, the kind of activity which soothed men like a tranquilliser. For an instant, I recollected my conversation with Charles in the summer. Enclaves. Perhaps it was right, it was certainly natural, for any of us to hack out what refuges we could, some of the time: none of us was tough enough to live every minute in the pitiless air. This was an enclave *in excelsis*.

As the noise level rose, and no one could overhear, I asked Francis if he had seen the paragraph about him that morning.

'I was going to tell you about that,' he said.

'How true is it?'

'Not far off.'

I asked: 'So S—— is really going?'

'To be more accurate, he's actually gone.'

'And you?'

'Of course, I had to say what I did before. I had to tell him I'd made up my mind.'

That was what I expected.

The Prime Minister had been good, said Francis. He hadn't pressed too much. But after S——, he needed someone with a reputation abroad. Francis added:

'I think you'd better make up your own mind, pretty quickly.'

After our talk the previous autumn, that also wasn't entirely unexpected, either to Margaret or me. Despite the attempt to forestall it. There weren't many of us who had this sort of special knowledge: and even fewer who had used it in public. One could make a list, not more than three or four, of men likely to be asked. It might have sounded arrogant, or even insensitive, for Francis to assume that he was number one on the list, and the rest of us reserves. But it didn't sound so to Margaret or me.

This wasn't a matter of feeling, about which Francis had been delicate all our lives: it was as objective as a batting order. He was a scientist of international reputation, and the only one in the field. His name carried its own authority with the American and Soviet scientists. That was true of no one else. He would have been a major catch for the Government, which was, of course, why they had come back to him. Now, as he said, they had to fill the job quickly. It would do them some harm if they seemed to be hawking it round.

'Well, that's that,' he said, dismissing the subject. He was so final that I was puzzled, and to an extent put out. After those hints, it seemed bleak that he should turn quite unforthcoming. I glanced at Margaret and didn't understand.

Within a short time, however, we were talking intimately again, the three of us. Getting us out of the dining-room early, Francis, with tactical foresight, was able to secure window seats in the bar: there we sat, as the debate continued, the bar became more populated, the division bell rang and Francis left us for five minutes and returned. That went on – the division bell interrupted us twice more – until after midnight, and in the casual hubbub Francis was telling us some family information we hadn't heard, and asking whether there was any advice he could give his elder son.

It was one of the oldest of stories. A good many young women might have wondered why Leonard Getliffe hadn't come their way. He was the most brilliant of the whole Getliffe family, he had as much character as his father, to everyone but one girl he was fun. And that one girl was pleasant, decent but not, to most of us, exciting. He had been in love with her for years. He was in his thirties, but he loved her obsessively, he couldn't think of other women, in a fashion which seemed to have disappeared from Charles's circle once they had left school. Whereas she could give him nothing: because she was as completely wrapped up in, of all people, my nephew Pat.

When Pat had deserted her and married Muriel, the girl Vicky (she wasn't all that young, she must now be twenty-six) had – so Francis now told us – at least not discouraged Leonard from getting in touch with her again. Since I hadn't visited Vicky and her father since my own father's death, that was some sort of news, but it was commonplace and natural enough.

'I must say, of course I'm prejudiced,' Francis broke out, 'but I must say that she's treated him pretty badly.'

Margaret, who knew Vicky and liked her, said yes, but it wasn't very easy for her—

'I mean,' said Francis, 'she never ought to have done that. Unless she was trying to make a go of it.'

Margaret said, she mightn't know which way to turn. There were plenty of good women who behaved badly when they were faced with a passion with which they didn't know how to cope.

'If I thought she was really trying—' Then Francis let out something quite new. In the last couple of months, perhaps earlier, Pat had been seen with her.

None of the young people had got on to that. Yet, the moment we heard, it seemed that we ought to have predicted it. Vicky was a doctor, she could earn a living, she would keep him if he needed it. Further, perhaps even Pat wasn't just calculating on his bed and food: perhaps even he wasn't infinitely resilient, and after Muriel wanted someone who set him up in his self-esteem again; after all that, he might just want to be loved.

But at that time I wasn't feeling compassionate about my nephew. Like other persons as quicksilver sympathetic as he could be, as ready to expend himself enhancing life, he had been showing an enthusiasm for revenge quite as lively as his enthusiasm for making others cheerful: and he had been searching for revenge against Margaret, feeling, I supposed, that she had done him harm. Anyway he had spread a story which was meant to give Margaret pain. Whether he believed it, or half-believed it, I couldn't decide. He had one of those imaginations, high-coloured, melodramatic and malicious, that made it easy to believe many things. The story was that, hearing Austin Davidson talk of his 'sources of supply', the people who had provided him with drugs to kill himself, Pat had found out their names. They were Maurice and Charles.

To most of us, this bit of gossip wouldn't matter very much: probably not to the young men themselves. But I knew – it was no use being rational where reason didn't enter – that it would matter to Margaret. To her it would be something like a betrayal, both by her father and her sons. She would feel that she had lost them all. Maybe Pat guessed what she would feel.

For the time being, I stopped the story from reaching Margaret, which didn't make me think more kindly of Pat, for it meant both some tiresome staffwork, and also my being less than open with her. So I had to get the truth from Davidson himself before she found out. That, in itself, meant a harsh half-hour. By this time he seemed to be failing from week to week: unless he led the conversation, it was hard to get him to attend. I had to force upon him that this was a family trouble, and might bring suffering for Margaret. He was silent, a long distance from family troubles or his daughter's pain. For the first time in all those visits, I broke into his silence. He must trust me. He must make an effort. Who had given him the drugs?

At last Davidson said, without interest, that he had made a promise not to tell. That threw me back. I had never known him break a confidence: he wouldn't change his habit now. After a time, I asked, would he answer two questions in the negative? He gazed at me without expression. Had it been Maurice? With irritation, with something like boredom, Davidson shook his head. Had it been Charles? The same expression, the same shake of the head. (On a later visit, when he was less collected, I was led to infer that the truth was what we might have expected: the 'source of supply' had nothing to do with any of the family, but was an old friend and near-contemporary of his called Hardisty.)

So that had been settled. Nevertheless, when Francis brought in the name of my nephew, it took some effort to be dispassionate. There were few things I should have liked more that night than to say we could all forget him. There was one thing I should have liked more, and that was to believe that Vicky and Leonard would get married out of hand.

Francis asked us point-blank:

'Does he stand a chance?'

Margaret and I glanced at each other, and I was obliged to reply, in the angry ungracious tone with which one kills a hope:

'I doubt it.'

Apparently Leonard, the least expansive of Francis's children and the one he loved the most, had come to his father with a kind of oblique appeal – ought he to take a job at the Princeton Institute? That wasn't a professional question; Leonard could name his own job anywhere; he was mutely asking – it made him seem much younger than he was – whether it was all hopeless and he ought at last to get away.

'You really think that she'll go back – to that other one?'

'I'm afraid so.' She would not only go back, she would run to him, the first time he cricked a finger. Knowing (but also not knowing, as one does in an obsessive love) everything about him. On any terms. She was worth a hundred of Pat, Margaret was saying. On any terms. Nothing would stop her. Would we try to stop her, if we could? It was not for me to talk. I had taken Sheila, my first wife, on terms worse than any this girl would get. I had done wrong to Sheila when I did so: that I had known at the time, and knew now without concealment, after half a lifetime. But if I could have stopped myself, granted absolute free will, should I have done so?

Even now, after half a lifetime, I wasn't certain. If I had made the other choice, despite the suffering, despite the years of something like maiming, I might have been less reconciled. And that, I thought, could very well prove true for this young woman. If she married Pat (which I regarded as certain, since he wasn't exactly a spiritual athlete and wouldn't give up his one patch of safe ground) she would go through all the torments of a marriage without trust. If she didn't, she would go through another torment, missing – whoever else she married – what she couldn't help wanting most of all. No, I wouldn't have stopped her. She might even come out of it better than he did. Sometimes there were ironies on the positive side, one of them being that the faithful were often the more strongly sexed and in the end got the more fun.

It wasn't often that Francis, who had gone to extreme trouble about our children or Martin's, had come for any sort of comfort about his own. But sometimes the kind liked to receive kindness, and he didn't want us to leave until the House was up.

In the taxi, as it purred up the midnight-smooth tarmac, under the trees to Hyde Park Corner, Margaret was saying, what a bloody mess. That triangle, Vicky, Leonard, Pat. People anything like Pat – even if they were more decent than he was – always did more destruction than anyone else. She broke off: 'Was Francis sounding you out? Early on. Was he really making you the offer? Had they asked him to?'

No, I said, I didn't think it would be done like that.

'Anyway, I hope that doesn't happen; you know, don't you?'

That was all she said, before returning to brisk comments upon Pat.

It did happen, and it happened very fast. Late the following night, just as we were thinking it was time for bed, the telephone rang. Private secretary at Downing Street. Apologies, the sharp civil servant's apologies that I used to hear, from someone whom I used to meet. Could I come along at once? Logistic instructions. I was to be careful not to use the main entrance. Instead, I was to go in through the old Cabinet Offices in Whitehall. There would be an attendant waiting at the door.

It all sounded strangely, and untypically, conspiratorial. Later I recalled what Francis had said about 'hawking the job round': they were taking precautions against another visitor being spotted: hence presumably this Muscovite hour, hence the eccentric route. The secretary had asked whether I knew the old office door, next to the Horseguards. Better than he did, it occurred to me, as I went through the labyrinth to the cabinet room: for it was in the room adjoining the outside door, shabby, coal-fire smoking, that I used to work with old Bevill at the beginning of the war.

I was back again, going past the old offices into Whitehall, within twenty minutes. Time, relaxed time, for the offer and one drink. I had asked, and obtained, forty-eight hours to think it over. Outside, Whitehall was free and empty, as it had been in wartime darkness, when the old Minister and I had been staying late and walked out into the street, sometimes exhilarated because we had won a struggle or perhaps because of good news on the scrambled line.

When I opened the door of our drawing-room, Margaret, who was sitting with a book thrown aside, cried out:

'You haven't been long!'

Then she asked me, face intent:

'Well?'

I said, cheerful, buoyed up by the night's action:

'It's exactly what we expected.'

Margaret knew as well as I did the appointment which Francis had turned down: and that this was it.

She said:

'Yes. I was afraid of that.'

For once, and at once, there was strain between us. She was speaking from a feeling too strong to cover up, which she had to let loose however I was going to take it. She had been preparing herself for the way in which I should take it: if you didn't quarrel often, quarrels were more dreaded. But even then she couldn't – and in the end didn't wish to – hold back.

'What's the matter?' I was put out, more than put out, angry.

'I don't want you to make a mistake—'

'Do you think I've decided to take the job?' I had raised my voice, but hers was quiet, as she replied:

'Haven't you?'

It had never been pleasant when we clashed. I didn't like meeting a will as strong as my own, though hers was formed differently from mine, hers hard and mine tenacious: just as her temper was hot and mine was smouldering. Also I didn't like being judged – some of my secret vanity had gone by now, but not quite all, the residual and final vanity of not liking to be judged by the one who knew me best.

Just to add an edge to it, I thought that she was misjudging me that night. Not dramatically, only slightly – but still enough. It was true – she had heard me amuse myself at others' expense as they solemnly professed to wonder whether they should accept a job they had been working towards for years – that most decisions were taken on the spot. When one asked for time to 'sleep on it', old Arthur Brown's immemorial phrase, when one asked for the forty-eight hours' grace of which I was bad-temperedly telling Margaret – one was, nine times out of ten, ninety-nine times out of a hundred, merely enjoying the situation or alternatively searching for rationalisations and glosses to prettify a decision which was already made.

That wasn't quite the case with me that night. I had in my mind all the reasons why I should say no. So far Margaret was wrong. But only a little wrong. What I wanted was for her to join in dismissing those reasons, take it all lightly, and push me, just a fraction, into saying yes.

Reasons against – they were the same for me as for Francis, and perhaps by this time a shade stronger. He had said that he couldn't do much – or any – good. I was as convinced of that as he was, whoever did the job: more so because I had lived inside the government apparatus, as he had never done. That hadn't made me cynical, exactly (for cynicism came only to those who were certain they were superior to less splendid mortals): but it had made me Tolstoyan, or at least sceptical of the effect that any man could have, not just a junior Minister, but anyone who really seemed to possess the power, by contrast to the tidal flow in which he lived. Some sort of sense about nuclear armaments might one day arise: what Francis and David Rubin and the rest of us had said, and within our limits done, might not have been entirely useless: but the decisions – the apparent decisions, the voices in cabinets, the signatures on paper – would be taken by people who couldn't avoid taking them, because they were swept along, unresisting, on the tide. The tide which we had failed to catch.

That wasn't a reason for not acting. In fact, Francis and his colleagues believed – and so did I – that, in the times through which we had lived, you had to do what little you could in action, if you were to face yourself at all. But it was a reason, this knowledge we had acquired, for not fooling ourselves: for not pretending to take action, when we were one hundred per cent certain that it was just make-believe. If you were only ninety per cent certain, then sometimes you hadn't to be too proud to do the donkey work. But, if you were utterly certain, then pretending to take action could do harm. It could even drug you into feeling satisfied with yourself.

By this time, our certainties had hardened, that nothing useful could be done in this job. The year before, when Francis was offered it, we thought we had known all about the limits of government. We had flattered ourselves. The limits were tighter than self-styled realistic men had guessed. Azik Schiff couldn't resist saying that he had warned us about social democracies. Vietnam was hag-riding us. Bitterly Francis said that a country couldn't be independent in foreign policy if it wasn't independent in earning its living. That remark had been made in the presence of some of Charles's friends, and had scandalised them. To many of us, the window of public hope, which had seemed clearer for a few years past, was being blacked out now.

All this was objective, and I didn't need so much as mention it to Margaret. Nor the other reason against, which was more compelling than with Francis. He had his research to do, and I had my writing. He had the assurance that any good scientist possessed, that some of what he had done was right (it was no use quibbling about epistemological terms; in the here-and-now, in Francis's own existence that was so). No writer had that assurance: but, exactly as his work was a private comfort, no, more than comfort, justification, so was mine. And – this was a difference between us – I had more to finish than he had, perhaps because I had started later. I had never liked talking about my books, and should never have considered writing anything about my literary life. I had had my joys and sorrows, like any other writer. In fact, most writing lives were more alike than different, which made one's own not specially interesting, except to oneself. After all, the books were there.

However, quite as much as ever in my life, as much as in the middle of the war, this preoccupation remained with me. It had been steady all through, it hadn't lost any of its strength. In the middle of the war, I had been a youngish man, I hadn't the sense of losing against time. I had been too busy to write anything sustained, but I could, last thing at night, read over my notebooks and add an item or two. It had been like going into a safe and quiet room. If I took this job, I could do the same, but I wasn't youngish now. I should have liked to count on ten years more to work in.

Ten years with good luck. Margaret knew that was what I was hoping for. She couldn't bring herself to talk about my life-span. She did say that this would mean time away from writing. Francis, she forced herself to say, had talked about a year or two in office: and he had said that he couldn't afford a year or two. She didn't ask a question, she made the statement in a flat, anxious tone, the lines deep across her forehead.

Yes, in every aspect but one, Francis and I were in the same situation, or near enough not to matter. So that the answer should also be the same. There was just one difference. I should like to do the job. I should enjoy it. It was that, precisely that, which Margaret hated.

She had been utterly loyal throughout our married life. She had tried not to constrict me, even when I was doing things, or showing a vein within myself, which she would have liked to wipe away. It wasn't that she thought that I was an addict of power. If that had been so, she felt that I should have acquired it. And she had learned enough by now to realise that this job I had been offered carried no power at all: and that the more you penetrated that world, the more you wondered who had the power, or whether anyone had, or whether we weren't giving to offices a free will that those who held them could never conceivably possess.

Nevertheless, she would have liked me to be nowhere near it. Her own principles, her own scrupulousness, couldn't have lived in that world, any more than her father's could. She despised, as much as he did, or his friends, the people who got the jobs, who were ready to scramble, compromise, muck in. She couldn't accept, she resented my accepting, that any society under heaven would need such people. She was put off by my interest, part brotherly, part voyeuristic, in them – in the Lufkins, the Roger Quaifes, even my old civil service colleagues, who were nearer in sympathy to her. When I told her that they had virtues not given to her father's friends, or to her, or to me, she didn't wish to hear.

'It's all second-rate,' she had said before, and said again that night.

Here was I, out of spontaneity (for, though I had trained myself into some sort of prudence, I was still a spontaneous man), or just for the fun or hell of it, ready to plunge in. I should even have enjoyed fighting a by-election: but that wasn't on, no government with a majority of three could risk it. Anyway, if I said yes, I should enjoy making speeches from the despatch-box in the Lords.

To her, who loved me and in many ways admired me – and wanted to admire me totally – it seemed commonplace and vulgar. As our tempers got higher, she used those words.

'That's no news to you,' I said.

'Yes, it is.'

'In your sense, I am vulgar.'

'I won't have that.'

'You've got to have it. If you mean that I'm not superior to the people round us, then of course I'm vulgar.'

'I don't want you to behave like them, that's all.'

The quarrel went on, and I, because I was not only angry but raw with chagrin (on the way home, I had been expecting a bit of applause, ironic applause maybe: she spoke about temptation, but she might, so I felt, have granted me that this particular temptation didn't come to all that many men), was having the worst of it. I betrayed myself by bringing up an argument which in my own mind I had already negated: the necessity for action, for any half-way decent man in our own time. I even quoted Hammarskjöld at her, though none of us would have used his words. She looked at me with sad lucidity.

'You've been sincere in that, I know,' she said. 'But you're not being sincere now, are you?'

'Why not?'

'Because this isn't real, as you know perfectly well. It isn't going to be any use, and if it were anyone else you'd be the first to say so.'

Since that was precisely what in detachment I had thought, I was the more angry with her.

'Well,' she said at last, without expression, 'I take it that you are going to accept.'

I sat sullen, keeping back the words. Then I crossed over to the sideboard and poured myself a drink, the first either of us had had since I returned. Once more I sat opposite to her, and spoke slowly and bitterly (it was a conflict which neither of us had the language for, after twenty years).

I said, that if anything could have made me decide to accept that night, it was her argument against. But she might do me one minor credit: I hadn't lost all my capacities. It would be better to decide as though she had said nothing whatever. There were serious arguments against, though not hers. I should want some sensible advice, from people who weren't emotionally committed either way. There I was going to leave it, for that night.

It was already early morning, and we lay in bed, unreconciled.

CHAPTER XIII

ADVICE

As we were being polite to each other at breakfast, I repeated to Margaret that I should have to take some advice. She glanced at me with a glint which, even after a quarrel, wasn't entirely unsarcastic. One trouble was, I had made too many cracks about others: how many times had she listened to me saying that persons in search of advisers had a singular gift for choosing the right ones? That is, those who would produce the advice they wanted to hear.

No, I said, as though brushing off a comment, I thought of calling on old Hector Rose. He knew this entire field of government backwards: he was a friendly acquaintance, not even specially well disposed: he would keep the confidence, and was as cool as a man could reasonably be.

Margaret hadn't expected that name. She gave a faint smile against herself. All she could say was that he would be so perfectly balanced that I might as well toss up for it.

When I telephoned Hector at the Pimlico flat, his greetings were ornate. Pleasure at hearing my voice! Surprise that I should think of him! Cutting through the ceremonial, I asked if he were free that morning: there was a matter on which I should like his opinion. Of course, came the beautiful articulation, he was at my disposal: not that any opinion of his could be of the slightest value—

He continued in that strain, as soon as I arrived in their sitting-room. He was apologising for his wife and himself, because she wasn't there to receive me, to her great disappointment, but in fact she had to go out to do the morning's shopping. As so often in the past, facing him in the office, I felt like an ambassador to a country whose protocol I had never been properly taught or where some customs had just been specially invented in order to baffle me. I said: 'What I've come about – it's very private.'

He bowed from the waist: 'My dear Lewis.'

'I want a bit of guidance.'

Protestations of being at my service, of total incompetence and humility. At the first pause I said that it was a pleasant morning (the porticoes opposite were glowing in the autumn sunshine): what about walking down to the garden by the river? What a splendid idea, replied Hector Rose with inordinate enthusiasm – but first he must write a note in case his wife returned and became anxious. Standing by my side, he set to work in that legible italic calligraphy. I could not help seeing, I was meant to see.

Darling, I have gone out for a short stroll with Sir L. Eliot (the old Whitehall usage which he had inscribed on his minutes, often, when we were disagreeing, with irritation). *I shall, needless to say, be back with you in good time for luncheon. Abiding love. Your H.*

It was so mellow out of doors, leaves spiralling placidly down in calm air, that Hector did not take an overcoat. He was wearing a sports coat and grey flannel trousers, as he might have done as an undergraduate at Oxford in the twenties. Now that we were walking together, it occurred to me that he was shorter than he had seemed in his days of eminence: his stocky shoulders were three inches below mine. He was making conversation, as though it were not yet suitable to get down to business: his wife and he had been to a theatre the night before: they had an agreement, he found it delectable to expatiate on their domestic ritual, to get out of the flat two evenings a week. The danger was, they had both realised when they married – Hector reported this ominous fact with earnestness – that they might tend to live too much in each other's pockets.

It was like waiting for a negotiation to begin.

When we turned down by the church, along the side of the square towards the river, I jerked my finger towards one of the houses. 'I lived there during the war,' I said. 'When I was working for you.'

'How very remarkable! That really is most interesting!' Hector, looking back, asked exactly where my flat had been, giving a display of excitement that might have been appropriate if I had shown him the birthplace of Einstein.

We arrived at the river-wall. The water was oily smooth in the sun, the tide high. There was the sweet and rotting smell that I used to know, when Margaret and I stood there in the evenings, not long after we first met.

On one of the garden benches an elderly man in a straw hat was busy transcribing some figures from a book. Another bench was empty, and Hector Rose said: 'I'm inclined to think it's almost warm enough to sit down, or am I wrong, Lewis?'

Yes, it was just like one of his negotiations. You didn't press for time and in due course the right time came. The official life was a marathon, not a spring, and one stood it better if one took it at that tempo. People who were impatient, like me, either didn't fit in or had to discipline themselves.

Now it was time, as Hector punctiliously brushed yellow leaves from off the seat, and turned towards me. I told him of the job – there was no need to mention secrecy again, or give any sort of explanation – and said, as usual curt because he wasn't, what about it?

'I should be obliged if you'd give me one or two details,' said Hector. 'Not that they are likely to affect the issue. But of course I am quite remarkably out of things. Which department would this "supernumerary Minister" be attached to?' The same as S——, I said. Attentively Hector inclined his head. 'As you know, I always found the arrangements that the last lot [the previous government] made somewhat difficult to justify in terms of reason. And I can't help thinking that, with great respect, your friends are even worse, if it is possible, in that respect.'

'This Minister' would have a small private office, and otherwise would have to rely on the department? A floating, personal appointment? 'Not that that is really relevant, of course.'

He was frowning with concentration, there was scarcely a hesitation. He looked at me, eyes unblinking, arms folded on his chest. He said:

'It's very simple. You're not to touch it.'

When he came to the point, Hector, who used so many words, liked to use few. But he didn't often use so few as this.

Jolted, disappointed (more than I had allowed for), I said, that was pretty definite, what was he thinking of?

'You're not immortal,' said Hector, in the same bleak, ungiving tone. 'You ought to remember that.'

We gazed at each other in silence.

He added:

'Granted that no doubt unfortunate fact, you have better things to do.'

He couldn't, or wouldn't, say anything more emollient. He would neither expand his case, nor withdraw. We had never been friendly, and yet perhaps that morning he would have liked to be. Instead, he broke off and remarked, with excessive pleasure, what a beautiful morning it was. Had I ever seen London look so peaceful? And what a kind thought it was for me to visit a broken-down civil servant! As usual with Hector's flights of rhapsody and politeness, this was turning into a curious exercise of jeering at himself and me.

There was nothing for it. Very soon I rose from the bench – the old man in the straw hat was still engrossed in esoteric scholarship – and said that I would walk back with Hector to his flat. He continued with mellifluous thanks, apologies, compliments and hopes for our future meetings. The functional part of the conversation had occupied about five minutes, the preamble half an hour, the coda not quite so long.

When I returned home, Margaret, who was sitting by the open window, looking over the glimmering trees, said:

'Well, you saw him, did you?'

Yes, I replied.

'He wouldn't commit himself, would he?'

No, I said, she hadn't been quite right. He hadn't been specially non-committal.

'What did he think?'

'He was against it.'

I didn't tell her quite how inflexibly so, though I was trying to be honest. The next person I turned to for advice didn't surprise her. This was what she had anticipated earlier in the morning. It was my brother Martin, and I knew, and she knew that I knew, on which side he was likely to come down. That proved to be true, as soon as I got on the line to

Cambridge. Why not have a go? I needn't do it for long. It would be a mildly picturesque end to my official career. Martin, the one of us who had made a clear-cut worldly sacrifice, kept – despite or because of that – a relish for the world. He also kept an eye on practical things. Had I reckoned out how much money I should lose if I went in? The drop in income would be dramatic: no doubt I could stand it for a finite time. Further – Martin's voice sounded thoughtful, sympathetic – couldn't I bargain for a slightly better job? They could up-grade this one, it was a joker appointment anyway, Ministers of State were a fairly lowly form of life, that wasn't quite good enough, he was surprised they hadn't wanted Francis or me at a higher level. Still—

Margaret, who had been listening, asked, not innocently, whether those two, Hector Rose and Martin, cancelled each other out. I was as non-committal as she expected Rose to be, but to myself I thought that my mind was making itself up. Then, not long afterwards, we were disturbed again. A telephone call. A Government back-bencher called Whitman. Not precisely a friend, but someone we met at parties.

'What's all this I hear?'

'I don't know what you mean,' I replied.

'Come on. You're being played for, you know you are.'

'I don't understand—'

'Now, now, of course you do.'

In fact, I didn't. Or at least I didn't understand where his information came from. Was it an intelligent bluff? The only people who should have known about this offer were the private office, Margaret, Hector Rose, Martin. They were all as discreet as security officers. I had the feeling, at the same time euphoric and mildly paranoid, of living at the centre of a plot, microphones in the sitting-room, telephones tapped.

More leading questions, more passive denials at my end.

'You haven't given your answer already, have you?'

'What is there to give an answer to?'

'Before you do, I wish you'd have dinner with me. Tonight, can you make it?'

He was badgering me like an intimate, and he had no claim to.

I said that I had nothing to tell him. He persisted: 'Anyway, do have dinner with me.' Out of nothing better than curiosity, and a kind of excitement, I said that I would come.

I duly arrived at his club, a military club, at half past seven, and Whitman was waiting in the hall. He was a spectacularly handsome man, black-haired, lustrous-eyed, built like an American quarter-back. He had won a Labour seat in 1955, and held it since, something of a sport on those back benches. A Philippe Égalité radical, his enemies called him. He had inherited money and had never had a career outside politics, though in the war he had done well in a smart regiment.

'The first thing', he said, welcoming me with arms spread open, 'is to give you a drink.'

He did give me a drink, a very large whisky, in the club bar. Loosening my tongue, perhaps – but he was convivial, expansive and not over-abstinent himself. Nevertheless, expansive as he was, he didn't make any reference to his telephonic attack: this evening had been mapped out, and, like other evenings with a purpose, the temperature was a little above normal. More drinks for us both. He was calling me by my Christian name, but that was as common in Westminster as in the theatre. I had to use his own, which was, not very appropriately, Dolfie.

Gossip. His colleagues. The latest story about a senior Minister. A question about Francis Getliffe. The first lead-in? Dolfie in the Commons had, as one of his specialities, military affairs. We moved in to dinner, which he had chosen in advance. Pheasant, a decanter of claret already on the table. An evening with a purpose, all right, but he was also a man who enjoyed entertaining. More chat. We had finished the soup, were were eating away at the pheasant, the decanter was getting low, when he said:

'By the way, are you going into the Government, Lewis?'

'Look,' I said, 'you do seem to be better informed than I am.'

'I have my spies.' He was easy, undeterred, eyes shining, like a man's forcing a comrade to disclose good news.

'You don't always trust what they tell you, do you?'

'A lot of people are sure that you're hesitating, you know—'

'I really should like to know how they get that curious impression. And I should like to know who these people are.'

His smile had become sharper.

'I don't want to embarrass you, Lewis. Of course I don't—'

'Never mind about that. But this isn't very profitable, is it?'

'Still, you could tell me one thing, couldn't you? If you've accepted today, it will be in the papers tomorrow. So you won't be giving anything away.'

I was on the edge of saying, this discussion would get nowhere, it might as well stop. But I could keep up my end as long as he could, one didn't mind (not to be hypocritical, it was warming) being the object of such attention. Further, I was getting interested in his motives.

'I don't mind telling you,' I said, 'that there will be nothing in the papers tomorrow. But that means nothing at all.'

'Doesn't it mean you have had an offer?'

'Of course not.'

'Anyway, you haven't accepted today?'

'I've accepted nothing. That's very easy, unless you have something to accept.'

Whether he had listened to the qualification, I was doubtful. His face was lit up, as though he were obscurely triumphant. With an effort, an effort that suddenly made him seem nervous and over-eager, he interrupted the conversation as we took our cheese. More chat, all political. When would the next election be? The Government couldn't go on long with this majority. With any luck, they'd come back safe for five years. Probably ten, he said, with vocational optimism. His own seat was dead secure, he didn't need to worry about that.

It was not until we had gone away from the dining-room, and had drunk our first glasses of port in the library, that he began again, persuasive, fluent, with the air of extreme relief of one getting back to the job.

'If it isn't boring about what we were saying at dinner—'

'I don't think we shall get any further, you know.' I was still cheerful, still curious.

'Assuming that an offer – well, I don't want to make things difficult' (he gave a flashing, vigilant smile) – 'assuming that an offer may come your way—'

'I don't see much point, you know, in assuming that.'

'Just for the sake of argument. Because there's something I want to tell you. Very seriously. I hope you realise that I admire you. Of course, you're an older man than I am. You know a great deal more. But I happen to be on my own home ground over this. You see, you've never been in Parliament and I have. So I don't believe I'm being impertinent in telling you what I think. You see, I know what would be thought if anyone like you – you, Lewis – went into the Government.'

He was speaking now with intensity.

'It wouldn't do you any good. Anyone who admired you would have to tell you to think twice. If they were worried about your own best interests.'

He said:

'It's a mistake for anyone to go into politics from the outside. It's a mistake for anyone to take a job in the Government unless he's in politics already. A job that people in the Commons would like to have themselves. I beg you to think of that.'

Yes, I was thinking about that, with a certain well-being, as I left him for a moment in order to go to the lavatory. As usual, as with a good many warnings, even when they were least disinterested, there was truth in what he said. And yet, in a comfortable mood, enhanced by Whitman's excitement and the alcohol, I felt it would be agreeable – if only I were dithering on the edge – not to be frightened off. There was a pleasure, singularly unlofty, in being passionately advised not to take a job which one's adviser wanted for himself. As, of course, Whitman wanted this. Not that I had heard him mentioned. On the contrary, the gossip was that he was too rich, and too fond of the smart life, to be acceptable to his own party.

That didn't prevent him craving for office. Just as old age, or what an outsider might have thought a time of satiety, didn't prevent men clinging to it, as I had seen in old Thomas Bevill or, earlier in my first glimpse of the office-hanging life, Charles March's uncle Philip. The appetite – and it was an appetite – was as strong in Dolfie Whitman as in any of them.

On the way back from the lavatory, those thoughts still drifting amiably through my mind, I saw the back of someone I believed I recognised, moving very slowly, erect, but with an interval between each step, towards the lift. I caught him up, and found that, as I had thought, it was Sammikins. But his face was so gaunt, his eyes so sunk and glittering, that I was horrified. Horrified out of control, so that I burst out:

'What is the matter?'

He let out a kind of diminuendo of his old brazen laugh. His voice was weak but unyielding, as he said:

'Inoperable cancer, dear boy.'

I couldn't have disentangled my feelings, it was all so brusque, they fought with each other. Affronted admiration for that special form of courage: sheer visceral concern which one would have felt for anyone, sharpened because it was someone of whom I was fond: yes (it wouldn't hide itself, any more than a stab of envy could), something like reproach that this apparition should break into the evening. Up to now I had been enjoying myself, I had been walking back with content, with streaks of exhilaration: and then I saw Sammikins, and heard his reply.

Could I do anything, I said unavailingly. 'You might give me an arm to the lift,' he said. 'It seems a long way, you know.' As I helped him, I asked why I hadn't been told before. 'Oh, it's not of great interest,' said Sammikins. The irritating thing was, he added, that all his life he had drunk too much: now the doctors were encouraging him to drink, and he couldn't manage it.

I was glad to see the lift-door shut, and a vestigial wave of the hand. When I returned to the library, Whitman, who was not insensitive, looked at me and asked if something had gone wrong.

An old friend was mortally ill, I said. I had heard only in the last few minutes.

'I'm very sorry about that,' said Whitman. 'Anyone close?'

'No, not very close.'

'Ah well, it will happen to us all,' said Whitman, taking with resignation, as we had all done, the sufferings of another.

He ordered more drinks, and, his ego reasserting itself, got back to his plea, his warning, his purpose. Politics (he meant, the profession of politics) was a closed shop, he insisted, his full vigour and eloquence flowing back. Perhaps it was more of a closed shop than anything in the country. You had to be in it all your life if you were going to get a square deal. Any outsider was bound to be unpopular. I shouldn't be being fair to myself unless I realised that. That was why he had felt obliged to warn me, in my own best interests.

I found myself sinking back into comfort again, my own ego asserting itself in turn. There were instants when I was reminded of Sammikins, alone in a club bedroom upstairs. Once I thought that he too, not so long ago, had been hypnotised by the 'charm of politics', just as much as this man Whitman was. The charm, the say-so, the flah-flah, the trappings. It made life shine for them, simply by being in what they felt was the centre of things.

Yet soon I was enjoying the present moment. It began to seem necessary to go on to the attack: Whitman ought to be given something to puzzle him. So I expressed gratitude for his action. This was an exceptionally friendly and unselfish act, I told him. But – weren't there two ways of looking at it? In the event, the unlikely event, of my ever having to make this choice, then of course I should have to take account of all these warnings. I was certain, I assured him, that he was right. But mightn't it be cowardly to be put off? In that way, I didn't think I was specially cowardly. Unpopularity, one learned to live with it. I had had some in my time. One also had to think of (it was time Whitman was properly mystified) duty.

No, Whitman was inclined to persuade me that this was not my duty. He would have liked me to stay longer: there were several points he hadn't thoroughly explained. He gazed at me with impressive sincerity, but as though wondering whether he could have misjudged me. As he saw me into a taxi, he might have been, so it seemed, less certain of my intentions than when the evening began.

CHAPTER XIV

END OF A LINE

On the Friday morning I said to Margaret that the forty-eight hours would be up that night, and I should have to give my answer.

'Do you know what it's going to be?'

'Yes,' I said, in a bad and brooding temper.

She was not sure. She had seen these moods of vacillation before now. Perhaps she had perceived that I was in the kind of temper that came when one was faced by a temptation: saw that it had to be resisted: and saw, at the same time, that if one fell for it one would feel both guilty and liberated. But we were not in a state for that kind of confidence. I was still resentful that she had been so positive. The only comment that I could take clinically had been Hector Rose's: Hector had his share of corrupt humanity, but not in his judgment: and this was a time when corrupt humanity got in the way. He was, of course – as in lucid flashes I knew as well as he did – dead right.

Yet still, though I had made up my mind, I acted as though I hadn't. Or as though I were waiting for some excuse or change of fortune to blow my way. I took it for granted that Margaret couldn't alter her view, much as she might have liked to, for the sake of happiness.

The only time when we were at one came as I told her about Sammikins. She too had an affection for him, like mine mixed up – this was long before his illness – of respect, pity, mystification. He had virtue in the oldest sense of all: in any conceivable fashion, he was one of the bravest of men. And his gallantry, from the time we had first met him, in former days at Basset, had been infectious. Since when we had learned more, through some of our police acquaintances, about his underground existence. Pick-ups in public lavatories, quite promiscuous, as reckless in escalating risks as he was in war. He had been lucky, so they said, to keep out of the courts. Sometimes, without his knowing it, his friends, plus money and influence, had protected him. When he came into the title, he hadn't become more cautious but had – like George Passant chasing another kind of sensation – doubled his bets.

'What a waste,' said Margaret. Strangely enough, before he was ill, he might in his strident voice have said that of himself, but not so warmly.

When we had ceased to talk of Sammikins, I became more restless. I went into the study and started to write the letter of refusal which I could as well have drafted on the Wednesday night. But I left it unfinished, staring out over the park, making a telephone call that didn't matter. Then I went and found Margaret: it might be a good idea if I went to Cambridge for the night, I said.

Temper still not steady, I asked her to call Francis at his laboratory. I was showing her that it was all innocent. While she was close by, I was already talking to Francis – I should like to stay in college that night, no, I didn't want to bother him or Martin, in fact I should rather like to stay in college by myself. Perhaps he would book the guest-room? Francis offered to dine in hall – yes, if it wasn't a nuisance. No, don't trouble to send word round to Martin, I shall see him soon anyway. Nor old Arthur Brown, this wasn't a special occasion. But young Charles – if he would drop in my room soon after hall? Francis would get a message round to Trinity. 'There,' I said to Margaret. 'That ought to be peaceful enough.'

Autumn afternoon. The stations paced by: the level fields, the sun setting in cocoons of mist. From the taxi, the jangled Friday traffic, more shops, brighter windows, than there used to be. When I entered the college, the porter on duty produced my name with a question-mark, ready with the key, but not recognising me by sight.

As I crossed the court, I recalled that, when I was first there, at this time of year there would have been leaves of Virginia creeper, wide red leaves, squelching on the cobbles and clinging like oriflammes to the walls. Since then the college had been cleaned, and these first court walls were bare, no longer grey but ochre-bright, looking as they might have done, not when the court was built (there had been two façades since then), but in the eighteenth century.

That was a change. But it made no difference to the curious tang that the court gave one in October, quite independent of one's deeper moods, springy, pungent, a shade wistful. Was that climatic, or was it because the academic year had the perverse habit of beginning in the autumn? Anyhow, it had been pleasurable when I lived there, and was so visiting the place that night.

The guest-room lay immediately under my old sitting-room, and it was up the stairs outside that callers used to climb, as light-footed as Roy Calvert, or ponderous as Arthur Brown, during various bits of college drama. Not that I thought twice, or even once, about that. It was fairly early in the evening, but I had some letter-writing to do. It was already too late to get a written answer to the private office by the time I had promised: but all day I had been half muddling through, half planning that I could telephone the secretary (that is, the principal private secretary) in time enough, and have the letter reach him tomorrow.

I waited till seven o'clock before I called on Francis. The first hall-sitting was noisy, rattle of plates, young men's voices, the heavy smell of food, as I pushed through the screens. In the second court, the seventeenth-century building stood out clean-lined under a fine specimen of a hunter's moon, rising over the acacia. Francis's lights were shining, from rooms which in my time had been the Dean's. But, now Francis had stripped off the hearty decorations, they were handsome to look at as soon as one stepped inside, moulded panelling, Dutch tiles round the fireplace. Francis gave me a friendly cheek-creased smile, and then, absent-mindedly, as though I were an undergraduate, offered me a glass of sherry. When I said that, except in Cambridge, I didn't touch that dispiriting drink once a year, Francis's smile got deeper; but he wasn't surprised, he was waiting for it, to hear me continue without any break at all.

'I've got the offer of your job, you know,' I said.

'Yes,' said Francis. 'I was given a pretty firm hint about that. Otherwise I wouldn't have said anything on Tuesday night.'

We were sitting on the opposite sides of the fireplace. Francis looked at me, eyes lit up over the umber pouches (misleading perhaps, that anyone now so content should carry indelibly all those records of strain) and asked:

'Well, what about it?'

I hesitated before I replied. Then I said:

'I'm inclined to think that I ought to give the same answer as you did.'

'I don't want to persuade you either way. I just don't know which is better for you.'

He was speaking with affectionate, oddly gentle, concern. Maybe I had expected, or hoped, even with the letter written, that he would say something different. But I should have known. When he had seemed curt or uninterested in the Lords bar, that was nothing like the truth. He cared a good deal for what happened to me. On the other hand, or really on the same hand, he was too fine-nerved to intrude – unless he was sure that he was discriminating right. Only once or twice in the whole of our lives had he intervened into my private choices. On politics, of course he had. On pieces of external behaviour, yes. But almost never when it would affect my future. The only time I could bring back to mind that night was when he told me, diffidently but exerting all his strength, that whatever the cost and guilt I ought, after Margaret and I had parted and she had married someone else, to get her back and marry her myself.

None of my friends, certainly no one I had known intimately, was as free from personal imperialism as Francis. He didn't wish to dominate others' lives, nor even to insinuate himself into them. Sometimes, when we were younger, it had made him seem – side by side with the personal imperialists – to lack their warmth. As they occupied themselves with others, the imperialists were warm for their own benefit. In the same kind of relation, Francis, within the human limits, wasn't concerned with his own benefit. That was a reason why, after knowing him for a lifetime, one found he wore so well.

'I think I probably ought to turn it down.' I still said it as something like a question.

'I just don't know for you.' Francis shook his head. 'I dare say you're being sensible.'

A little later, he observed, with amiable malice:

'Whatever you do, you'll be extremely cross with yourself for not doing the opposite, won't you?'

Soon we left it. We could have retraced the arguments, but there was nothing more to say. The quarter chimed from one of the churches beyond the Fellows' Garden. Francis, opening a cupboard to pick up his gown, said:

'By the by, the Master's dining tonight. You can't say I don't sacrifice myself for you.'

Francis was speaking of G. S. Clark. Francis detested him, and even Martin took his name off the dining-list when he found the Master's on it. Clark was a man of the ultra-right (the present gibe was that he monitored all B.B.C. programmes, marking down the names of left-wing speakers, including the Archbishop of Canterbury), and he and his supporters had taken over the college government, so that Martin, as Senior Tutor, was left without power and on his own.

The college bell began to ring, undergraduates were running along the paths, Francis and I walked to the combination room. It was already full, men, most of them young, pushing round the table, panel-lights glowing over their heads. When I was a fellow, there had been fourteen of us; now, in 1965, the number was over forty; more often than not, they told me, the high table overflowed. Before the butler summoned us into hall, the Master welcomed Francis and me with simple cordiality. 'We don't often have the pleasure,' he said. He had been a cripple since infancy, and had a fresh pink-skinned juvenile face as though affliction, instead of ageing him, had preserved his youth. His smile gave an impression both of sweet nature and obstinacy. Martin and Francis had certain comments to make about the sweet nature. Everyone agreed that he was a strong character, so much so that, although he dragged his useless leg about, no one thought of him as a cripple, or ever pitied him.

By his side stood his chief confidant, an old enemy of mine, the ex-Bursar, Nightingale. To my surprise, he insisted on shaking me strongly by the hand.

In fact, the forms were being preserved. As soon as grace was ended and we settled down at high table, at our end, the senior end, conversation proceeded rather as though at an international conference with someone shouting 'restricted' when a controversial point emerged. The immemorial college topics took over, bird-watching, putative new buildings, topics in which my interest had always been minimal and was now nil. I turned to my left and talked to a young fellow, whose subject turned out to be molecular biology. He seemed very clever: I suspected that, when he heard the name of one bird trumping another, when he listened to that beautiful display of non-hostility, he was amused. With him and his contemporaries, so Francis and others told me, there was a change. A change for the better, said Francis. These young men were much more genuine academics than their predecessors: most of them were doing good research. They mightn't be such picturesque examples of free personality as those I used to sit with; but a college, Francis baited me, didn't exist to be a hothouse of personality. These young men were high-class professionals. I should have liked to know what they thought of relics of less exacting days.

When we arrived back in the combination room, Francis asked me if I wanted to stay for wine. No, I said, the young men were hurrying off; and anyway Charles would presumably be calling at the guest-room soon. With a nod, not devoid of relief, Francis led me out into the first court. He said:

'What was all that in aid of?'

He meant, why had I wanted to dine in hall. I couldn't have given a coherent answer: it wasn't sentiment, it had something to do with the confusion of that day.

Francis asked me to let him know when the decision was made.

'Oh, it is made,' I said.

'Good,' said Francis, and added that he had better leave me alone with Charles. 'He won't give you any false comfort.' Francis broke into an experienced paternal grin before he said good-night.

A hard rap at the guest-room, Charles punctual but interrogatory. 'Hallo?'

I thought that he felt he was being inspected: it was his first term, and though he had made himself a free agent so early he was cagey about being visited or disturbed.

'This is nothing to do with you, Carlo,' I said.

'Oh?'

'It's entirely about me. I wanted to tell you the news myself.'

'What have you been doing now?'

'Nothing very sensational. But I've just sent off a letter.'

He was watching me, half-smiling.

'Refusing a job,' I went on, 'in the Government.'

'Have you, by God?' Charles broke out.

I explained, I should have to make a telephone call later that evening. They wanted to receive an answer that night, and the letter would confirm it. But Charles was not preoccupied with administrative machinery. Of course – he was brooding in an affectionate, reflective manner – it had always been on the cards, hadn't it? Yes, it could have been different if I had been an American or a Russian, then perhaps I might have been able to do something.

'Still,' he said, 'it isn't every day that one declines even this sort of job, I suppose.'

He said it protectively, with a trace of mockery, a touch of admiration. He was still protective about my affairs, bitter if he saw me criticised. And he also felt a little envy, such as entered between a father and son like us. But, when I envied him, it was a make-believe and a pleasure: when he envied me, there was an edge to it. I had, for better or worse, done certain things, and he had them all to do.

'I'm rather surprised you did decline, you know,' said Charles. 'You've chanced your arm so many times, haven't you?'

There was the flash of envy, but his spirits were high, his eyes glinting with empathetic glee.

'I've always thought that was because you didn't have the inestimable privilege of attending one of our famous boarding-schools,' he said. 'There's precisely one quality you can't help acquiring if you're going to survive in those institutions. I should call it a kind of hard cautiousness. Well, you didn't have to acquire that when you were young, now did you? And I don't believe it's ever come natural to you.'

'Yes, you're right.'

So he was, though very few people would have thought so.

I was thinking, when he was looking after his friends, or even me, he could show much sympathy. When he was chasing one of his own desires, he was so intense that he could be cruel. That wasn't simply one of the contradictions of his age. I expected that he would have to live with it. That evening, though, he was at his kindest.

'So I should have guessed that you'd plunge in this time,' he said, with a cheerful sarcastic flick. 'And you didn't. Still capable of surprising us, aren't you?'

'That wasn't really the chief reason,' I played the sarcasm back.

'For Christ's sake!' he cried, by way of applause. 'Anyway, not many people ever have the chance to say no. I'm going to stand you a drink on it.'

We went out of the college and slipped up Petty Cury towards the Red Lion, just as before the war – especially in that autumn when the election of the Master was coming close and we didn't want to be traceable in our rooms – Roy Calvert and I used to do. Neither Charles, nor undergraduates whom he called to in the street, were wearing gowns, as once they would have been obliged to after dusk: but they were wearing a uniform of their own, corduroy jackets and jeans, the lineal descendants of Hector Rose's morning attire, that reminder of his youth.

While I sat in the long hall of the pub, Charles rejoined me, carrying two tankards of beer. He stretched out his legs on one side of our table, and said:

'Well, here's to your abdication.'

I was feeling celebratory, expansive and at the same time (which didn't often happen in Cambridge) not unpleasantly nostalgic. It was a long time since I had had a drink inside that place. It seemed strange to be there with this other young man, not so elegant as Roy Calvert, nothing like so manic, and yet with wits which weren't so unlike: with this young man, who, by a curious fluke, had that year become some kind of intimate – in a relation, as well as a circle, mysterious to me – of Roy Calvert's daughter.

After a swallow of beer, Charles, also expansive, though he had nothing to be nostalgic about, said:

'Daddy' (when had he last called me that?), 'I take it this is the end of one line for you, it must be.'

'Yes, of course it must.'

'It never was a very central line, though, was it?'

I was trying to be detached. Living in our time, I said, you couldn't help being concerned with politics – unless you were less sentient than a human being could reasonably be. In the thirties people such as Francis Getliffe and I had been involved as one might have been in one's own illness: and from then on we had picked up bits of knowledge, bits of responsibility, which we couldn't easily shrug off.

But that wasn't quite the whole story, at least for me. It wasn't as free from self. I had always had something more than an interest, less than a passion, in politics. I had been less addicted than Charles himself, I said straight to the attentive face. And yet, one's life isn't all a chance, there's often a secret planner putting one where one has, even without admitting it, a slightly shamefaced inclination to be. So I had found myself, as it were absent-mindedly, somewhere near – sometimes on the fringe, sometimes closer in – a good deal of politics.

When had it all started? This was the end of a line all right. Perhaps one could name a beginning, the night I clinched a gamble, totally unjustified, and decided to read for the Bar. That gave me my chance to live among various kinds of political men – industrial politicians, from my observer's position beside Paul Lufkin, academic politicians in the college (as in that election year 1937, fresh in my mind tonight), and finally the administrators and the national politicians, those who seemed to others, and sometimes to themselves, to possess what men thought of as power.

Charles knew all that. He thought, if he had had the same experience, he would have gone through it with as much interest. But he didn't want to discuss that theme in my biography, now being dismissed for good and all. He was occupied, as I went to fetch two more pints, with what lessons he could learn. We had talked about it often, just as on the night he returned home in the summer. Not as father and son, but as colleagues, fellow-students, or perhaps people who shared a taste in common. Many of our tastes were different, but here we were, and had been since he grew up, very near together.

Closed politics. Open politics. That was a distinction we had spoken of before, and stretched out in gawky relaxation Charles came back to it that night. Closed politics. The politics of small groups, where person acted upon person. You saw it in any place where people were in action, committees of sports clubs, cabinets, colleges, the White House, boards of companies, dramatic societies. You saw it perhaps at something like its purest (just because the society answered to no one but itself, lived like an island) in the college in my time. But it must be much the same in somewhat more prepotent groups, such as the Vatican or the Politburo.

'I fancy,' said Charles, 'you've known as much about it as anyone will need to know.'

That was said very simply, as a compliment. He was right, I thought, in judging that the subject wasn't infinite: the permutations of people acting in closed societies were quite limited, and there wasn't all that much to discover. But I also thought that he might be wrong, if he guessed that closed politics were becoming less significant. I might have guessed the same thing at his age – that wasn't patronising, some of his insights were sharper than mine – but it would have been flat wrong. For some reason about which none of us was clear, partly perhaps because all social processes had become, not only larger, but much more articulated, closed politics in my lifetime had become, not less influential, but much more so. And this had passed into the climate of the day. Many more people had become half-interested in, half-apprehensive about, power groups, secret decisions. There were more attempts to understand them than in my youth. It was only by a quirk of temperament, and a lot of chance, that I had spent some time upon them, I told Charles: but, just for once, he could take me as a kind of weather-vane.

Yes, he granted me that: and where did we go from there?

As we left the Lion, and walked through the market place, he began to speak freely, the words not edged or chosen, but coming out with passion. The real hope was open politics. It must be. If any of his generation – anywhere – could make open politics real again.

Yes, the machinery mattered, of course it mattered, only a fool ignored it – but there was everything to do. It just wasn't enough to ward off nuclear war or even to feed the hungry world. That was necessary but not sufficient. People in the West were crying out for something more.

Although it was after ten when we reached Trinity, the gate stood open (Charles, unlike me, had not seen it closed at that time of night) and two girls were entering in front of us. The Great Court spread out splendid in the high moonlight: as we passed the sundial, its shadow was black-etched on the turf: Charles was oblivious to the brilliant night or to any other vista. Hadn't one of my old friends, he was asking, once said that literature, to be any good, had to give some intimation of a desirable life? Well, so had politics. Far more imperatively. All kinds of people were feeling something like this. It was what the advanced world, the industrialised world, the whole of the West was waiting for. Someone had to try. Someone who understood the industrialised world: that was there for keeps. Someone who started there. A Lenin of the affluent society. Someone who could make its life seem worth while.

'It may not be possible,' said Charles, after we climbed the stairs to his room, his fervour leaving him. 'Perhaps it never will be possible. But someone has to try.'

I glanced out of his window, which looked over the old bowling-green, neatly bisected, light and dark, by a shadow under the moon. Not wanting to break the current (I hadn't often heard him so emotional, in the old non-marxist sense so idealistic), I asked if this was what, when some of his contemporaries were protesting, they were hoping to say or bring about.

'Oh that. Some of them know what they're doing. Some are about as relevant as the Children's Crusade.'

If they had been listening to his tone, which was no longer emotional, I couldn't help thinking that certain contemporaries referred to would not have been too pleased.

'Mind you, I shall go out on the streets again myself over Vietnam.'

He gazed at me with dark searching eyes. 'First, because on that they're right. Second, because we may need some of those characters. And if you're going to work with people, you can't afford to be too different.'

That was a good political maxim, such as old Bevill might have approved of. Charles had not for a long while spoken straight out about the career he hoped for: in fact, I thought that he was still unsure, except in negatives. It would have been easy for him to become an academic, but he had ruled that out. He would work like a professional for a good degree – but that was all he had volunteered. As we were in sympathy, unusually close, that night, I said:

'Is this what you're planning for yourself?'

I didn't have to be explicit. The kind of leader he had been eloquent about, the next impulse in politics.

He gave a disarming, untypically boyish smile.

'Oh, I've had my megalomaniac dreams, naturally I have. The times I used to walk round the fields at school. But no. That's not for me.'

For an instant, I was surprised that he was so positive. 'Why not?'

'Look, you heard me say, a minute ago, that it may not be possible. The whole idea. Well, anyone who's going to bring it off would never have said that. He's got to be convinced every instant of his waking life. He's got to think of nothing else, he's got to eat and breathe it. That's how the magic comes. But that's what I couldn't do. I'm not made for absolute faith. I'm probably too selfish, or anyway I can't forget myself enough.'

He had more self-knowledge, or at least more knowledge of his limits, I realised, than I had at his age, and older. But he was young enough to add with a jaunty optimistic air:

'On the other hand, I wouldn't say that I mightn't make a pretty adequate number two. If someone with the real quality came along. I could do a reasonable job as a tactical adviser.'

A little later, still comfortably intimate (it was one of the bonuses of that singular day) Charles and I walked back through the old streets to the gate of my own college. I had told him that I should have to hurry to put through the telephone call; and so he left me there, saying, with a friendly smile, 'Good luck.' We each had our superstitions and he would never have wished me that if I had been waiting for news, any more than I should have done to him before an examination. It was just a parting gift.

I had brought with me the private secretary's home number, but I had to wait a good many minutes before I heard his voice.

'Hallo, Lewis, are you all right?' I had known him when I was in Whitehall and he one of the brightest young principals. I apologised for disturbing him so late.

'I should have been worried if you hadn't. Well, what do you want me to report?'

I gave all the ritual regrets, but still I had to say no. A letter was on its way. Very slight pause, then the clear Treasury voice. 'I was rather hoping you'd come down the other way.' Like most aides-de-camp, he tended to speak as though it was he I had to answer to. I could have a few more hours to think it over, he said, there might be other means of persuasion. At my end, another slight pause. Then, quickly, brusquely: 'No, this is final, Larry.' One or two more attempts to put it off – but Larry was used to judging answers, and, though he was duplicating Hector Rose's career, he didn't duplicate Hector Rose's ceremonial. 'Right,' came the brisk tone. 'I'll pass it on. I am very sorry about this, Lewis. I am very sorry personally.'

All over. No, not quite all over. There was something else to do. I went into my bedroom, and there, shining white on the chest of drawers, was the letter I had not yet sent. I had told a lie to my son. Not a major lie – but still, quite pointlessly, for underneath the resolve was made, I hadn't brought myself to send the letter off. Had I really hoped that Francis Getliffe would dissuade me, or even Charles, or that there would be some miraculous intervention which would give me the chance to change my mind, pressure from a source unknown?

Probably not. It was just because the wavering was so pointless that I felt a wince of shame. It wasn't the crimes or vices that made one stand stock still and shut one's eyes, it was the sheer sillinesses that one couldn't stop. Vacillations, silly bits of pretence – those were things one didn't like to face in oneself: even though one knew that in the end they would make no difference. I wondered whether young Charles, who seemed so strong, went through them too.

It wasn't that night but later, when I recalled that I behaved in the same manner, ludicrously the same manner, once before. At the time that I was sending my letter of admission to the Bar and a cheque for two hundred pounds (to me, at nineteen, most of the money that I possessed).

Then, just as today, the resolve was formed. Everyone I knew was advising me against, but nevertheless, as with Charles, my will was strong and I went through with the risk. But only after nights of hesitations, anxieties, withdrawals: only after a night when I had boasted of the gamble, talking to my friends rather in the vein of Hotspur having a few stiff words with reluctant troops. I explained how the letter – which committed me – had been sent off that day. Then, at midnight, after the celebration, I had returned to my bedsitting-room and found the letter waiting there, the sight of it reproaching me, telling me there was still time to back out.

Then I had been nineteen. Now I was sixty. That had been, in Charles's phrase, the beginning of one of my lines (the first letter went off at last, and I duly read for the Bar). Tonight was the end of that line. Delaying a little less than I had done at nineteen, a few hours less, I went out into the empty moonlit street to post the letter.

CHAPTER XV

WAKING UP TO WELL-BEING

MARGARET, glad about the outcome, more glad because the quarrel had dissolved, believed with Francis Getliffe that I should be cross with myself. I might have believed that also: certainly I was incredulous, as though I were observing astonishing reactions in some Amazonian Indian when I found how equable I was. True, I had my jags of resentment. As I opened the paper one morning and saw the job had been filled – it had gone to Lord Luke of Salcombe, which added a touch of irony – I pointed to the announcement and said to Margaret:

'Now look what you've done.' On the moment, I was blaming her, it was the kind of gibe which wasn't all a gibe: but I shouldn't have made it if I hadn't been serene underneath.

It would be a singular apotheosis for Walter Luke, making speeches from the despatch-box in the Lords. Only a few years before he had been denouncing politicians and administrators with fervent impartiality. Stuffed shirts! Those blasted uncles! Out of inquisitiveness and perhaps fellow-feeling, I went along to hear his first ministerial speech. Walter's cubical head looming over the box: the rich West Country intonation that he hadn't lost. As for the speech itself, it was competent, neither good nor bad. His civil servants had put in all the safeguards and qualifications which used to evoke his considerable powers of abuse. Walter uttered them now with every appearance of solidarity, as though they were great truths. But, then, so should I have had to utter them.

That afternoon, walking past Palace Yard in one of the first autumn fogs, I was again mystified that I should be so serene. Work was going well, but there I wasn't at the mercy of my moods; it would have gone as well if I had been cursing myself. Margaret and I were entertaining more than we usually did, catching up with friends and acquaintances, the Marches, the Roses, the Getliffes, Muriel, Vicky Shaw and her father. That was agreeable: but it wasn't the origin of my present state.

The secret lay – though I should never have predicted it – in the sheer fact of saying no, in what Charles called my abdication. Certainly I had seen others, among them my brother Martin, gain a gratification out of giving up 'the world' – in Martin's case, when he was very much in it and with the prizes dangling in front of him; he had become content, or even happy, out of great expectations denied. But that wasn't so with me. This job of Walter Luke's – orating in the fog-touched chamber – hadn't been part of my own expectations. No, the satisfaction came, if I understood it at all, from one's own will. In most of the events of a lifetime, the will didn't play a part. We were tossed about in the stream, corks bobbing manfully, shouting confidently that they could go upstream if they felt inclined. Somehow, though, the corks, explaining that it would be foolish to go upstream, went on being carried the opposite way.

Very rarely one was able to exercise one's will. Even then it might be an illusion, but it was an illusion which brought something like joy. It could happen when one was taking a risk or remaking a life. Sometimes I speculated whether people at the point of suicide felt this kind of triumph of the will. I should have liked to think that Sheila went out like that. What did Austin Davidson feel as he swallowed his pills and took what he believed to be his last drink?

Earlier, it would have been easy to ask him. No one would have been less embarrassed than Davidson, and he would have given an account of classical lucidity. During one of my visits that November, I began telling him of my experience, in the hope that I might lead on to his own. But I hadn't realised, nor had Margaret, seeing him so often, how much further away he had slipped. When I told him that I had been offered the job, he said, eyes vacantly staring:

'Did they give you a book?'

I wanted to leave it, but he insisted. I said, no, since I had refused, I didn't get anything: and then, slowly, sickeningly slowly to one who had been so clever, I tried to explain. Government. Ministers. Politics.

He strained to comprehend, cheeks flushed. He managed to say:
'No serious man has anything to do with politics.'

With relief at getting a little communication, I said that was a good apostolic pre-1914 sentiment. Then I hurried on, abandoning any attempt to try a new question. I went back to the familiar conversational forms. Those he could still understand, and, for some of the time (it was the longest of hours), take part in.

As soon as I returned home, I asked Margaret – what had been her impression of him earlier that week? Much as he usually was, she replied: not taking much interest, but he hadn't done for months. I told her that I thought I saw – I might be imagining it – a difference. If I'd seen him for the first time that afternoon, I shouldn't have given him long to go.

'Of course it may just be a bad day,' I said. 'But I think you ought to be prepared.'

She nodded. 'Yes, I am.'

Prepared, perhaps, both for loss and for relief. The strain of the long illness told on her more than on me, because it was she who loved him. If you loved – instead of being fond of – someone taking a long time to die, there were times when you wanted the release. What had been my mother's phrase for it? A happy release. One of those hypocritical labels which half-revealed a truth. Then, when the release came, you felt the loss more, because it was mixed with guilt. As with so many consequences of love, what you lost on the swings you lost also on the roundabouts.

Meanwhile, I believed that I knew a way to give him pleasure. I had tried it once before – any more often, and he would have been suspicious. He was physically capable of reading, so the doctors said, and yet he refused even to glance at a newspaper. Still, one had to allow for remote chances. It meant a certain amount of contrivance, and a visit to my stockbroker.

Late the following week – I had seen him in the interval – I entered the familiar, the too familiar, hospital room, catching the smell of chrysanthemums and chemicals, with underneath the last echo of cigarette-smoke and faeces. From the bed Davidson muttered, but it was not until I was facing him that he looked at me. Instead of sitting at the end of the bed, I carried a chair round to his left-hand side. It was becoming forlorn to expect that he would begin a conversation. I had to start straight off:

'You've not lost your touch, you know.'

'What are you talking about?' he said in a dull tone.

'I was telling you, you haven't lost your touch. You've made me quite a bit of money.'

The bird-brown eyes flickered. 'I don't understand.'

'You did some listening to financial pundits in your time, didn't you? Well, you're not the only one.'

He gave the sketch of a smile.

'Do you remember telling me about a year ago' – actually it was slightly longer, soon after he was taken into the clinic – 'that you guessed that it was time to go into metals? Particularly nickel. And you produced some rules about the right kind of share. I tell you, I did some listening. And took some action.'

'Unwise. You forgot the first rule of investment. Never act on tips from an enthusiastic amateur.' He was shaking his head, but there was colour in his voice.

'You're about as much an amateur as the late lamented Dr W. G. Grace.'

This esoteric remark, to begin to understand which one had to be born (*a*) in England, (*b*) not later than 1920, made him laugh. Not for long, but audibly, sharply.

'So I took some action. I thought you might as well know the exact score – here's a letter from my broker. Would you like to read it—?'

'No, you read.'

The letter said – 'The purchase of Claymor Nickel has turned out very profitable for you. We bought on Oct. 14, 1964, 3000 shares, which then stood at 21/6. The price this morning is 47/9. This shows a gross gain of just under £4000. If you wish to sell, there will as you know be a capital gains tax of 30%, but the net profit will still be £2600 approximately. However, in our opinion the price is likely to rise still higher.'

I broke off: 'I said, you haven't lost your touch, have you?'

'One can't help being right occasionally, don't you know.' But he was very pleased, so pleased that he went on talking, though he had to stop for breath. 'Anyway, I've not made you poorer, which is more than one can say of most advice. That is, unless you've taken some other tips from me which have probably been disastrous—'

'Not one.'

'I must admit, it's agreeable to be some trivial use to you. Even when one's finishing up in this damned bedroom. It's not unpleasant to be some trivial use—'

'I don't call it trivial—'

Davidson lifted his head a few inches from the pillows. His expression was lively and contented. In a tone in which one could hear some of his old authority, which in fact was curiously minatory, he said: 'Now you ought to get out of that holding. Tomorrow. They may go higher. But remember, tops and bottoms are made for fools. That was the old Rothschild maxim, and they didn't do too badly out of it.'

'Right,' I said obediently.

'There's another point. I should consider that your unit of investment was too large. £3000 – that was it, wasn't it? – is far too much for this kind of risk. It came off this time, but it won't always, you follow. You've heard the units that I use myself—'

'I had more faith in you.'

'You oughtn't to have that much faith in anyone—'

I had not heard him take so much part in the duologue for many months. His manner, despite the heavy breathing, stayed minatory and on the attack: but that meant he was enjoying himself or at least self-forgetful. He even asked me to pour him a small whisky, although it was not yet four in the afternoon. It might have been a device to make me stay, for he insisted – suddenly reminding me of Charles as a child, importuning me to talk to him before he went to sleep – that I pour another for myself.

When at last I was outside the clinic, standing in the Marylebone Road looking for a taxi, I felt a little more than the usual emancipation. The afternoon had been easy: of course it was good to be out: slivers of rain shone, as though they were frozen, past the nearest street-lamp, and then bounced from the glistening pavement. I felt some of that zest – disgraceful and yet not to be denied – which came from being well in the presence of someone who couldn't be well again. The lift in one's step, which ought for decency's sake to be a reproach, just wasn't: it was good to breathe the dank autumnal air. It was not unpleasant, even, to stand in the rain waiting for a taxi. For an instant, a surreptitious thought occurred to me: it was rather a pity that I hadn't, in cold fact, bought shares on the old man's judgment. Either those or any others. The trouble was, I believed too much in his maxim about enthusiastic amateurs. If I hadn't, if I had trusted him, I should have been a good deal better off.

That visit took place on a Monday. It was not on the following morning, but on the Wednesday that I woke up early, so early that the window was quite dark. I lay there, comfortable, not sure whether I should go to sleep again or not. It was pleasant to think of the day ahead, lying relaxed and well. Perhaps I dozed off. Light was coming through the curtains. As in a sleep-start, I jerked into consciousness. There was a blackout over the far corner of my left eye.

I knew what that meant, too well. I went to the windows, pulled a curtain, looked out over the Tyburn garden to a clear early morning sky.

Trying to cheat the truth, I blinked the eye and opened it again. Yes, for an instant the blackout seemed dissolved. Comfort. Then it surged back again. A clear black edge. Against the lightening sky, a little smoky film beyond the edge.

I couldn't cheat myself any longer. I knew what that meant, too well. The retina had come loose once more. Perhaps the veil didn't spread so far as the other time. But I was complaining, Good God, this is rough, could I face going through all that again?

Margaret was still quiet in her morning sleep. There was no point in waking her. Minutes didn't matter, and I could tell her soon enough.

CHAPTER XVI

INTO OBLIVION

BEFORE breakfast, Margaret rang up Mansel, the ophthalmologist who had operated on me before. We had learned his timetable by now, since he had been inspecting my eyes each month or so. He would call in, Margaret told me, about eleven, on his way from the hospital to Harley Street.

As we sat waiting, I said to Margaret:

'He'll want to have another shot.'

'Let's see what he says.'

'I'm quite sure he'll want to.' I added: 'But I'm not so sure that I can bear it.'

I wasn't thinking of the operation, in itself that didn't matter, but of the days afterwards, lying still, blinded, helpless in the dark. Though I had managed to control it, I had always had more than my share of claustrophobia. As I grew older, it got more oppressive, not less; and lying blinded for days brought on something like claustrophobia squared. The previous time had been pretty near my limit: or so it seemed looking back, even more than when I was going through it.

Margaret wanted to distract me. She said how this would have been more than a nuisance if I had been in the Government.

'It's a good thing you didn't take that job,' she said.

'If I had taken it, this mightn't have happened,' I replied.

Oh come, Margaret said, glad to have found an argument, that was taking psychosomatic thinking altogether too far. But I didn't respond for long.

When Mansel arrived, he was as usual brisk and elegant, busy and unhurried.

'I'm sorry to hear about this, sir,' he said to me.

We had come to know each other well, but it was a curious intimacy, in which he, almost young enough to be my son, insisted on calling me Sir, while I insisted on calling him by his Christian name. I admired him as a superb professional, and he listened to my observations as possibly useful to his clinical stock-in-trade.

While making conversation to Margaret, he was without fuss disconnecting a reading-lamp, fixing a bulb of his own. The drawing-room was just as good as anywhere else, he said to her with impersonal cheerfulness. He had brought a case with him, packed with White Knight equipment invented by himself: but, searching into the back of my eyes, he had never used anything more subtle than an ordinary lens. As he did now, lamp shining on the eye, Mansel asking me to look behind my head, to the left, down, all the drill which I knew by heart.

He didn't waste time. Within half a minute he was saying:

'There's no doubt, I'm afraid. Bad luck.'

Not quite in the same place as before, he remarked. Then, with some irritation, he said that there hadn't been any indication or warning, the last time he examined me, only a month before. If we were cleverer at spotting these things in advance, he went into a short professional soliloquy. It would have been easy enough to use photolysis: why couldn't we get a better warning-system?

'No use jobbing back,' he said, as though reproaching me. 'Well, we shall have to try and make a better go of it this time.'

I glanced at Margaret: that was according to plan.

'Look, Christopher,' I said, 'is it really worth while?'

His antennae were quick.

'I know it's an awful bore, sir, I wish we could have saved you that—'

'What do I get in return? It's only vestigial sight at the best. After all that.'

Mansel gazed at each of us in turn, collected, strong-willed.

'All I can give you is medical advice. But anyone in my place would have to tell you the same. I'm afraid you ought to have another operation.'

'It can't give him much sight, though, can it?' Margaret wanted to be on my side.

'This sounds callous, but you both know it as well as I do,' said Mansel. 'A little sight is better than no sight. There is a finite chance that the other eye might go. We're taking every precaution, but it might. Myopic eyes are slightly more liable to this condition than normal eyes. Any medical advice is bound to tell you, you ought to insure against the worst. If the worst did come to the worst, and you'd only got left what you had yesterday in the bad eye – well, you could get around, you wouldn't be cut off.'

'I couldn't read.'

'I'm not pretending it would be pleasant. But you could see people, you could even look at TV. I assure you, sir, that if you'd seen patients who would give a lot even for that amount of sight—'

Margaret came and sat by me. 'I'm afraid he's right,' she said quietly.

'Would you like to discuss it together?' Mansel asked with firm politeness.

'No,' I said. 'Intellectually I suppose you are right. Let's get it over with.'

I said it in bad grace and a bad temper, but Mansel didn't mind about that. He had, as usual, got his way.

He and Margaret were talking about the timetable.

'If it's all right with you, sir,' Mansel turned to me, 'there's everything to be said for going into hospital this morning.'

'It's all one to me.'

'Well done,' said Mansel, as though I were an industrious but not specially bright pupil. 'Last time, you remember, you had an engagement you said you couldn't break. That delayed us for three or four days. I thought it was rather over-conscientious, you know.'

I wasn't prepared to bring those episodes back to mind: any more than to recall a visit to my old father, purely superstitious, just to placate the fates before an operation. Which my father, with his remarkable gift for reducing any situation to bathos, somewhat spoiled by apparently believing that I was suffering from a rupture, the only physical calamity which he seemed to consider possible for a grown-up man.

I was too impatient to recall any of that. I was thinking of nothing but the days laid out in the post-operational dark. I had no time for my own superstitions or anyone else's chit-chat: I was in a hurry to get back into the light.

Within an hour I was already lying on my back, with the blindfolds on. Margaret had driven with me to the hospital, while I gazed out at people walking busily along the dingy stretch of the City Road: not a glamorous sight unless anything visible was better than none. To me, those figures in the pallid November sunshine looked as though they were part of a mescalin dream.

In the hospital, I was given the private room I had occupied before. Someone – through a mysterious performance of the bush telegraph which I didn't understand – had already sent flowers. As she said good-bye, Margaret remarked that last time (operations took place in the morning) I had been quite lucid by the early evening. She would come and talk to me just before or after dinner tomorrow.

After she had left, I assisted in the French sense in the hospital drill. In bed: eyes blacked out: I even assisted in the receipt of explanations which I had heard before. Some nurse, whom I could recognise only by voice, told me that both eyes had to be blinded in order to give the retina a chance to settle under gravity; if the good eye was working, the other couldn't rest.

Helpless. Legs stretched like a knight's on a tomb: not a crusader knight's because I wasn't supposed to cross them. Just as Sheila's father's used to stretch, when he was taking care of himself.

'Mr Mansel is very liberal,' said another nurse's voice. With some surgeons, a few years before, I should have had sandbags on both sides of my head. So that it stayed dead still. For a fortnight.

Tests. Blood pressure – that I could recognise. Blood samples. Voices across me, as though I were a cadaver. Passive subject, lying there. How easy to lose one's ego. Persons wondered why victims were passive in the concentration camps. Anyone who wondered that ought to be put into hospital, immobilised, blinded. Nothing more dramatic than that.

Once or twice I found my ego, or at least asserted it. The anaesthetist was in the room, and a couple of nurses. 'I've been here before, you know,' I said. 'The other time, when I came round, I was as thirsty as hell.'

'That's a nuisance, isn't it?' said the anaesthetist.

'I suppose you dehydrate one pretty thoroughly.'

'As a matter of fact, we do.' A genial chuckle.

'Can anything be done about it? Tomorrow afternoon?'

'I'm afraid you will be thirsty.'

'Is it absolutely necessary to be intolerably thirsty for hours? They gave me drops of soda water. That's about as useful as a couple of anchovies.'

'I'll see what can be done.'

'That's too vague,' I said. 'Look here, I don't complain much—'

I wrung some sort of promise that I might have small quantities of lime-juice instead of soda water. That gave me disproportionate satisfaction, as though it were a major victory.

In the evening, though when I didn't know, for already I was losing count of time, Mansel called in. 'All bright and cheerful, sir?' came the light, clear, upper-class voice.

'That would be going rather far, Christopher,' I said. Mansel chortled as though I had touched the heights of repartee. He wanted to have one more look at my eye. So, for a couple of minutes, I could survey the lighted bedroom. As with the figures in the City Road, the chairs, the dressing-table, the commode stood out, preternaturally clear-edged.

'Thank you, sir,' said Mansel, replacing the pads with fingers accurate as a billiards-player's. 'All correct. See you early tomorrow morning.'

How early, again I didn't know, for they had given me sleeping-pills, and I was only half-awake when people were talking in the bedroom. 'No breakfast, Sir Lewis,' said the nurse, in a firm and scolding tone. 'Nothing to drink.'

Someone pricked my arm. That was the first instalment of the anaesthetics, and I wanted to ask what they used. I said something, not clearly, still wanting to be sentient with the rest of them. In time (it might have been any time) a voice was saying: 'He's nearly out.' With the last residue of will, I wanted to say no. But, as through smoke whirling in a tunnel, I was carried, the darkness soughing round me, into oblivion.

PART TWO

ARREST OF LIFE, LAST BUT ONE

CHAPTER XVII

NOTHING

IN the dark, a hand was pressing on mine. A voice. The dark was close, closer than consciousness. What was that hand?

A voice. 'Darling.'

The sound came from far away, then suddenly, like a face in a dream, dived on me. How much did I understand?

'All's well.' It might have been a long time after.

Perhaps the words were being repeated. Until – consciousness lapping in like a tide, coming in, sucking back, leaving a patch still aware – I spoke as though recognising Margaret's voice.

'Why are you here?'

'I just dropped in.'

'Is it evening?'

'No, no. It isn't tea-time yet.'

That was her voice. That was all I knew.

Was there a memory, something else to hold on to?

'Didn't you say you'd come in the evening?'

'Never mind. I thought I'd like to see you earlier.'

Utterly soothed, like a jealous man getting total reassurance or a drunk hearing a grievance argued away. That was her hand, pressing down on mine. I began to say that I was thirsty. Other voices. Coolness of glass against my lips. A sip. No taste.

'You were going to give me lime-juice.' I held on to another memory.

'I'm sorry,' that must be a nurse, 'it isn't here.'

'Why isn't it here?'

Unsoothed again, a tongue of consciousness lapping further in. Darkness. Suspicion.

I was aware – not gradually, it happened in an instant – of pain, or heavy discomfort, in my left side, as though they had put a plaster there.

'What's happening?' I said to Margaret. I could hear my voice like someone else's, thick, alarmed, angry.

Voices in the room. Too many voices in the room. My right ankle was hurting, with my other foot I could feel a bandage on it. Margaret was saying 'Everything's all right,' but other voices were sounding all round, and I cried out:

'This isn't my room.'

'The operation's over.' That was Mansel, cool and light. 'It's gone perfectly well.'

'Where am I?'

Mansel again. 'We're just going to take you back.'

Once more I was soothed: it seemed reasonable, like the logic of a dream. I didn't notice motion – ramps, lifts, corridors didn't exist; I must have returned to somewhere near the conscious threshold. It might have been one of those drunken nights when one steps out of a party and finds oneself, without surprise, in one's own bed miles away.

I had been in a big room: I was back in one where the voices were close to me, which soothed me because, with what senses I had left, it was familiar: I didn't ask, I knew I had slept there the night before.

I was awake enough, tranquil enough, to recognise that I was parched with thirst. I asked for a drink, finding it necessary to explain to Margaret (was she still on my right?) that I was intolerably dry. The feel of liquid on a furred clumsy tongue. Then the taste came through. This was lime-juice. Delectable. As though I were tasting for the first time. All in order: lime-juice present according to plan: reassurance: back where I ought to be.

Someone was lifting my left arm, cloth tightening against the muscle.

'What are you doing?' I shouted, reassurance destroyed at a touch, suspicion flaring up.

'Only a little test.' A nurse's voice.

'What are you testing for?'

Whispers near me. Was one of them Margaret's?

Mansel: 'I want to know your blood pressure. Standard form.'

'Why do you want to know?'

'Routine.'

In the darkness, one suspicion soothed, faded out, left a nothingness, another suspicion filled it. Did they expect me to have a stroke? What were they doing? Ignorant suspicions, mind not coping, more like a qualm of the body, the helpless body.

'Everything is all right,' Margaret was saying quietly.

'Everything is not all right.'

A patch of silence. They were leaving me alone. Neither Margaret nor Mansel was talking. For an instant, feeling safer, I asked for another drink.

Time was playing tricks, my attention had its lulls, it might have been minutes before a hand was pulling my jacket aside, something cold, glass, metal against the skin.

'What are you doing now?' I broke out again.

'Another test, that's all.' Mansel's voice didn't alter.

'I've got to know. I'm not going on like this.'

Fingers were fixing apparatus on my chest.

'What's gone wrong?' Again, that didn't sound like my own voice. 'I've got to know what's wrong.'

Clicks and whirrs from some machine. My hearing had become preternaturally acute and I could hear Mansel and Margaret whispering together.

'Shall I tell him?' Mansel was asking.

'You'd better. He's noticed everything—'

There was movement by the side of my bed, and Mansel, instead of Margaret, was speaking clearly into my ear.

'There's nothing to worry about now. But your heart stopped.'

The words were spaced out, distinct. They didn't carry much meaning. I said dully, 'Oh.'

I gathered, whether Mansel told me then or not I was never sure, that it had happened in the middle of the operation.

I asked: 'How long for?'

'Between three and a half and three and three-quarter minutes.' I thought later, not then, that when Mansel told one the truth, he told the truth.

'We got it going again,' Mansel's voice was cheerful. 'There's a bit of a cut under your ribs. You're fine now.'

He was at pains to assure me that the eye operation had been completed. It was time, he said, for him to let my wife talk to me.

Replacing Mansel's voice was Margaret's, steady and warm.

'Now you know.'

I said, 'Yes, I know.' I added:

'I bring you back no news from the other world.'

Margaret went on talking, making plans for a fortnight ahead ('You'll be out of here by then, you understand, don't you?'), saying there would be plenty of time to argue about theology. She sounded calm, ready to laugh: she was concealing from me that she was in a state of shock.

Just as my remark might have concealed my state from her. In fact, it had been quite automatic. It could have seemed – perhaps it did to Margaret – as carefully debonair, as much prepared for, as her father's greeting to me after his messed-up attempt at suicide. You see God's own fool. I might have been imitating him. Yet I hadn't enough control for that. Anything I said slipped out at random, as though Margaret had put sixpence in a juke box and we both had to listen with surprise to what came out.

Later, when I thought about it in something like detachment, it occurred to me how histrionic we all could be. Perhaps we had to be far enough gone. Then, though it might be right outside our ordinary style, we put on an act. For Austin Davidson, who had always enjoyed his own refined brand of histrionics, it came natural to rehearse, to bring off his opening speech. I was about as much unlike Davidson as a man could reasonably be: but I too, though as involuntarily as a ventriloquist's dummy, had put on an act. Probably we should all have been capable of making gallows jokes, in the strictest sense: we should all, if we were about to be executed in public, have managed to make a show of it. It might have been different if one was being killed in a cellar, with no audience there to watch.

It might have been different. It was different for me, when I had to get through that night. Margaret left me: so did Mansel, and another doctor, one with a strong deep voice. Not that I was left alone: there were nurses in the room, busy and quiet, as I lay there in the hallucinatory darkness, in full surrender to the state which perhaps I had concealed from Margaret. It was one of the simplest of states, just terror.

I had learnt enough about anxiety all through my life. Worse, I had been frightened plenty of times – in London during the war, on air journeys, visits to doctors, or during my illness as a young man. But up to that night I hadn't known what it was like to be terrified. There was no alleviation, no complexity, nor, what had helped in bad times before, an observer just behind my mind, injecting into unhappiness and fear a kind of taunting irony, mixed up with hope. No, nothing of that. This was a pure state and apart from it I had, all through that night, no existence. All through that night? That wasn't how I lived it. The night went from moment to moment. There mightn't be another.

Soon after Mansel's good-night, fingers were cool against my arm again, a susurration, a whisper, the rustle of paper.

'All right?' I muttered, trying to ask a casual question, craving for some news.

'You go to sleep,' said a nurse's voice, calm and muted.

Within minutes – I was drugged but not asleep, I couldn't count the time – fingers on my arm, the same sounds in the dark.

'What is it?' I cried.

'Try to sleep.'

I dozed. But there was something of me left – the will or deeper – which was frightened to give way. Sleep would be a blessing. But sleep was also oblivion. Fingers on my arm once more. Once more I tried to ask. To them I made no sense. To myself I wanted to talk rationally, as though I were interested, not terrified. I couldn't. Time after time, between sleep and consciousness, the fingers at my arm.

It became like one of those interrogations in which the prisoner is not allowed to rest. I couldn't understand that they were taking my blood pressure three times an hour.

Once, between the tests, I was aware of my left eye. Staring into the darkness, which wasn't the darkness of a black night, but, as I recalled from the operation two years before, was reddened, patterned, embossed, I saw a miniature light, like a weak bulb, very near to me, as though it were burning in the eye itself. I was aware of that without giving it a thought: I might have been a man desperately busy, preoccupied with a major and obsessive task, not able or willing to divert himself with something as trivial as the condition of his eye.

It was abject to have no interest – or even, so it seemed, no time, as though every second of the night was precious – for anything but fright. I made an effort to address myself rationally, as I had tried to speak to the nurses. Perhaps I was trying to put on an act to myself as I did to others. Under trial, we all wished to behave differently from how we felt, there was a complementarity which made us less ashamed. Waiting for the nurse's fingers, I wanted to reason away the terror, exorcising it by words, thinking to myself, as I rarely did, in words, using words to stiffen (or blandish or deceive) myself as one might use them on another.

What was I frightened of?

Death? Death is nothing. Literally nothing. I ought to know that by now.

Dying? Nothing was easier than dying. Not always maybe. But if it happened as it had that morning, nothing was easier. If I went out now, it would be as easy.

What was I frightened of?

Not that night, but afterwards, when I was remembering dread, not existing in it, I might have given an answer. At least I knew what didn't matter, what hadn't drifted for an instant through my mind. Listening by the side of Austin Davidson's bed, I had heard him say that what chilled him was to realise that he would never hear the end of any story that had interested him: nor even be present as a spectator, or the most tenuous shadow of a ghost. Yes, he was being honest. But one could feel that at any time in one's life, thinking about death. Davidson knew he would die soon, but still he wasn't in the presence of annihilation. If he had been, he would have been lonelier, less lofty, than that. I could answer only for myself: yet there I would have answered for him too. One had no interest left, except in the absolute loneliness. Questions that had once been fascinating – they had no meaning. Politics, the world, what would men think about one's work: that was a blank. Friends, wife, son, all the future: that was as dead a blank.

Sometimes, in health, as I couldn't help recalling after a visit to Austin Davidson, I had imagined what dying would be like. You die alone. I thought that I had imagined it as real. Nonsense, I had fooled and flattered myself. It was so much less takable, near to, identical with, the fright of the flesh itself. Had it been like this for my old father? He had asked for his lodger's company: his lodger held his hand: he must have been quite alone.

What was I frightened of? When I was remembering it, not living it, I might have said, of nothing. Of being nothing. On the one side, there was what I called 'I'. On the other, there was nothing. That was all. That was what it reduced to. In the abyss between the two was dread.

Yet maybe, when I was remembering, I, like Austin Davidson, made it more delicate than the truth.

Beside the bed, a voice I hadn't heard before. Without noticing, I had been the other side of the sleep threshold. This was a different nurse, a different voice, they were coming in shifts. Whispered figures, but louder whispers, almost enough to catch. Out of the dark, I recalled the other figures, Mansel's figures, the only ones that anyone had told me. Three and a half minutes, three and three-quarters. Trying to think. Another of the night's cold sweats. The grue down the spine. I could have read or heard – or had my memory gone? – that three minutes was enough to damage the brain. The sweat formed at the temples, dripped down. I had to try. What did I remember? My telephone number. Births and deaths of Russian writers – Turgenev 1815–83. Dostoevsky 1821–81. Tolstoy 1828–1910. They came clicking to mind, just as they always did. Poetry. I began the first lines of *Paradise Lost*, then stuck. That was nothing new, I was calming myself. It was young Charles who had the photographic memory. Characters in *Little Dorrit* – Clennam, Mrs Finching, Merdle,

Casby, Tite Barnacle – they came out quick enough. What about prob-lems? The old proof of the prime number theorem, that once made me wish I had gone on with mathematics. Yes, I could work through that. There didn't seem (it was the only reassurance through the night) any damage yet awhile.

The small light in my left eye had gone out. I was in the red-dark. Sometimes, nearer sleep, the tapestries took themselves away and the darkness deepened. The previous time that I had been in that condition, I had thought that blindness would be like this, and I wasn't sure that I could endure it. Now I wasn't thinking of blindness. That was a specula-tion one made when one could afford to, like Davidson's regret about what he was going to miss. Thoughts became simpler as they narrowed: there wasn't room for luxury, even the luxury of being anxious. Only one dread was left, the final one.

Fingers at my arm, jolts into half-waking: like a night in the prison cell it went on. Once I asked the time. Someone told me, half past two.

CHAPTER XVIII

'YOU'VE GOT TO FORGET IT'

A NURSE was giving me a sponge, waking me, asking if I would like to freshen myself. Mr Mansel was on his way, she said. Then his crisp, light-toned voice.

'Good morning, sir. I hope you've had a good night.'

'Not exactly, Christopher. Rather like being in a sleeper on the old Lehigh Valley—'

During the night I had had reveries about blaming him, about letting all the fright and anger loose. Yet I found myself replying in his own aseptic fashion.

He said, professionally cheerful:

'Sorry about that. We thought you might sleep through it.'

'If they'd have let me alone for one single damned hour, perhaps I could—'

'That was just a precaution.' Mansel told me what they had been doing. 'We wanted to see that everything was working. Which it is.'

'I suppose that's some consolation.' Nevertheless, while he was talking I felt safe.

'I think it should be, sir. Now let's have a look at the eye.'

The clever fingers took off the pads, and I blinked into the bright, solid, consoling room. Outside the window, the sky was black, before dawn on a winter morning. If I could stay in the light, perhaps the night would be behind me.

Mansel's face, smelling of shaving-soap, was only inches away. His eye, magnified by the lens, was searching into mine. After a minute or so, he said:

'It's early days yet, of course. I don't want to raise false hopes, but it may have gone better than last time.'

'That's a somewhat minor bonus in the circumstances, don't you think?'

'Not at all,' Mansel answered. 'We've had a bit of unexpected trouble, of course we have. That's all the more reason why we want to get the eye right at the end of it.'

Quickly, carefully, he put me back into the dark. I wished to say that his professional concern was not shared by me. I had meant to tell him – I had composed the speeches at one stage of the night – that, if I could get out of this hospital alive, it didn't matter a curse what happened to the eye. We never ought to have risked the operation. A tiny gain if all went well. If all didn't go well – that I could tell them about as I lay there that night, side strapped up under my heart, nurses keeping watch. I had been against this operation from the first, and he had overruled me. Anger got mixed up with fright, was better than fright, I had meant to project the anger on to Mansel. Yet I did nothing of the sort. The principle of complementarity seemed to work whenever I had an audience, and I behaved like a decent patient. Though once again in the dark, respite over, the night's thoughts came flooding back.

Mansel's voice was amiably exhorting me to have a cup of tea and some breakfast. I said, making the most of a minuscule complaint, that it was nearly impossible to eat lying rigid. Mansel was attentive: I was blinded, but perhaps my face still told him something. 'We may be able to make things easier for you soon,' he said. Meanwhile people would be coming in shortly to perform another test. In a couple of hours Mansel himself would return, together with a colleague.

What did that mean? I was as suspicious as in the afternoon before. If only they would tell me all the facts – that was what all sophisticated people cried out in their medical crises. Later, I wondered how much one could really take. How much should I have been encouraged if they had let me know each blood-pressure reading all through the night?

Once again apparatus was being fixed to my chest, the chill of glass, the whirr of a machine. Then, for some time, I could hear no one in the room. Out of a kind of bravado, I called out.

'Yes, sir,' came a chirping, quiet voice, a nurse's that I hadn't heard before. 'Do you want anything?'

'No, as a matter of fact, I don't,' I had to say.

I couldn't talk to her: I remained with suspiciousness keeping me just one side of the edge of sleep. It took Mansel's greeting to startle me full awake.

'Here we are again, sir!'

I could distinguish other footsteps besides his.

'I want to introduce a friend of mine – ' Mansel again – 'Dr Bradbury. Actually he was here last night, but you were slightly too full of dope to talk to him. He's a heart specialist, as a matter of fact. That's because it's easier than coping with eyes, isn't it, Maxim?'

As soon as I heard Maxim reply, I recognised the voice. It had been present among the commotion – all mixed up by the shock, disentanglable now – of the night before. It was very deep (they were exchanging gibes about which line brought in the easy money), as deep as my brother's or Charles's, but without the bite that lurked at the back of theirs. This was just deep and warm.

A hand gripped mine, and a chair scraped on the floor beside the bed.

'The news is good.' Slow, gentle, warm, emphatic. 'The first thing is, I want you to believe me. The news is good.'

I felt excessively grateful, so grateful that my reply was gruff.

'Well, what is it?'

'Your heart is as sound today as it was yesterday morning. We've looked at it as thoroughly as we know how, and we shouldn't be able to detect that anything had happened. I couldn't tell you this unless I was sure.'

Mansel (quietly): 'I can guarantee that.'

'I need hardly say,' I remarked, 'that I hope you're right.'

'We are right, you know.' Deep, gentle voice. 'I expect you want to ask, then why did it happen? The honest answer is, we haven't the slightest idea. It was simply a freak.'

'A freak which might have been mildly conclusive,' I said.

'Yes, it might. I have to tell you again, we haven't the slightest idea why it happened. All we know is that it did. After you'd been on the operating-table for an hour and a half. I'm not sure whether Christopher has told you—'

Mansel: 'No, not much.'

'Well, I think you ought to know. Christopher tried to start the heart again by external massage. That didn't work. Then he decided – and he was perfectly right – that he hadn't much time to spare, so he did it from inside. Fortunately, although he's an eye-man, he's quite a competent surgeon.'

Undergraduate teasing, in the midst of all the energy he was spending upon me.

'I've got a certain amount of faith in him,' I caught the same tone.

Mansel cachinnated.

'So you should have.' This was Maxim. 'Now I want you to listen to something else. This has been an unusual experience, and that's rather an understatement, isn't it? It's an experience which could do harm to a good many people. You have to be pretty robust to take it in your stride. Robust psychologically – we can look after you physically, you're absolutely all right there. I should guess you're a tough specimen all the way round, and Christopher gives you an excellent report. But this is going to call for as much toughness as you can find. You've got to put it behind you. Straightaway. Today.'

It was a long time since anyone had spoken to me as paternally as this. I hadn't yet seen his face, and, as it happened, I never did see it. He might very well be young enough, as Mansel was, to be my son. Yet I felt, not only gratitude so strong as to be uncomfortable, but also acquiescence, or even something like obedience.

'You've got to forget it.' The voice was even warmer, even more urgent. 'That's what I'm really telling you. The only danger is that you'll let it stay with you. You've got to forget it.'

Curiously enough, that was what another strong-natured patient man had told us, at the end of the murder trial eighteen months before. He had also spoken like a father. But, after we had listened, my brother had said that that meant living in illusion: it might have been more comfortable, but it would have been wrong. You've got to forget it. This time, if I could obey, it presumably would do no harm to anyone, it wouldn't mean false hope, it wouldn't be wrong. And yet, as I thanked Maxim, I added that I wasn't much good at forgetting things.

'Well, you'll have to train yourself. This was just an incident. Don't let it make life dark for you. I'm going to tell you again, you've got to forget it.'

I heard him get up from the bedside, and then he and Mansel, at the far end of the room, engaged themselves in a professional argument mixed with backchat. I couldn't follow much, the two voices, phone and antiphone, light and clear against deep bass, were kept low. But they each seemed to have a taste for facetiousness which wasn't mine. Somehow I gathered that Maxim was not Bradbury's baptismal name but had been invented by Mansel, who took great credit for it. As for the argument, that was about me.

'Nothing secret,' Bradbury called out, considerate and kind. 'We're just wondering when to get you up.'

Though I didn't appreciate it, they were meeting a dilemma. What was good for the heart was a counter-indication for the eye, and vice versa. For the heart, they would like me sitting up that day: to give the eye the best chance, the longer I lay immobilised, the better.

'Well, I'll see how it looks tomorrow,' I heard Mansel tell him, and Bradbury came nearer the bed to say good-bye.

'I probably shan't have to see you again,' he said. 'I'm very pleased with you. Do remember what I've told you.'

The door clicked shut behind them. With that voice still comforting me, I needn't fight against sleep any more. In a moment, seconds rather than minutes, as though I were going under the anaesthetic again, I was flat out.

When I woke, I first had the sense of well-being that came after deep sleep. Then suddenly, eyes pressed by the darkness, I remembered what had happened. That wasn't the first time I had wakened happy and then been sickened by the thought of what lay ahead; there had been a good many such times since I was young: but this was the darkest.

My side hurt a little, so little that I should scarcely have noticed. That brought it all back. It had happened once. It could happen again. I was as frightened as I had been in the night. Perhaps more than that.

I tried to steady myself by recalling Bradbury's words. This was cowardly; it was unrealistic; he said that all was well. If he had been back in the room, I should have been reassured. Totally reassured, effusively grateful once more But now he had left me, I could see through all the lies: either I had been deceiving myself, he hadn't said those words, or else I could see through his reasons for saying them. They knew that it would happen again Perhaps that day or the next He thought I might as well have the rest of my time in peace.

CHAPTER XIX

PRIVATE LANGUAGE

MARGARET was speaking to me and holding my hand It couldn't have been many minutes since I awoke, but I had lost all sense of time In fact, she had arrived about eleven o'clock; Mansel and Bradbury had made their call quite early, not long after eight.

I muttered her name. She kissed me and asked:

'How is it now?'

'It's too much for me.'

Her fingers stiffened in mine, gripped hard. After the other operation, or even after Mansel broke the news the previous evening, she had heard me make some sort of pretence at sarcasm; she had come in expecting it now. She had come in, waiting to break down and confide what she had gone through: the telephone call as she sat in the flat at midday: just – would she come round to the hospital at once. The taxi-ride through the miles of streets. Kept waiting at the hospital. No explanation. A long five minutes – so she told me later. (She remembered as little of them afterwards as if she had been drunk.) At last Mansel at the door, looking pallid. Then he said it was all right. Sharp clinical words to hearten her. After that, the operating-theatre, where she sat waiting for me to come round.

Now she had come, needing release from all that: to be met by a tone which brought back all her misery, and, instead of giving her comfort, took it away. She had known me harsh and selfish enough in petty sufferings: but that was different from this flatness, this solitude.

At once she was talking protectively, with love.

'Of course it's not. Nothing ever is—'

'I shan't get over this.'

I wasn't trying to hurt her, I was alone, I might as well have been talking to myself.

'You will, you've had a bad time, but of course you will. Look, my love, I've been talking to them—'

'I don't trust them.'

'You've got to. Anyway, you do trust me—'

Silence.

She said urgently:

'You do trust me?'

At last I answered:

'No one knows what it's like.'

'Don't you think I do?'

Getting no reply, she broke out, and then subdued herself.

'Let's try to be sensible, won't you? I have talked to those two. I'm telling you the absolute truth, you believe that?'

'Yes, I believe that.'

'They're completely certain that there's nothing wrong. You're perfectly healthy. There won't be any after-effects. I made sure that they weren't hiding anything. I had to know for my own sake, you understand, don't you? They're completely certain.'

'That must be pleasant for them.'

'You ought to give them credit, they're very good doctors.'

'I'm not much moved by that.'

'You're not willing to be moved by anything, are you?'

'I haven't time to be.'

She drew in her breath, but didn't speak. Then, after we had each been quiet, my temper seethed out – with the anger that I had fantasised about discharging on Mansel, but which I couldn't show to him or anyone else, except to her. For it was only to her – who knew all about the pride, the vanity, the ironies, even the discipline with which I covered up what I didn't choose for others to see – that I could speak from the pitiful, the abject depth.

'Why do you expect me to listen to them?' I shouted. 'Do you really think they've been so clever? They even admit that they haven't any idea why they nearly put me out yesterday. Why should anyone believe what they say about tomorrow? They won't have any more idea when I've had it for good. You expect me to believe them. Remember it was they who let me in for this.'

'It's no use blaming them—'

'Why isn't it? It was an absurd risk to take. Just for a minor bit of sight which is about as good as yours when you're seeing through a fog. Just for that, they're ready to take the chance of finishing me off.'

'No, dear.' After the harsh cries I had made, her voice was low. 'That isn't right. Christopher Mansel wasn't taking a chance. It would all have gone normally – except for once in ten thousand times.'

'That's what they've told you, is it? How have they got the impertinence to say it? I tell you, they don't know anything. It was an absurd risk to take. We never ought to have allowed it. I blame myself. You might think back. I didn't like it at the time. Mansel persuaded me. We ought to have stopped it.'

'That wouldn't have been reasonable.'

'Do you think that what they've achieved is specially reasonable? We ought to have stopped it.'

I went on:

'You ought to have helped me to stop it.'

'That's not fair,' she cried.

'It's the fact.'

'No, it's not fair. Are you blaming me?'

'I'm blaming myself more.'

Reproaching me for other times when I had thrown guilt on to her, she was angry as well as wounded. For a time it became a quarrel: until she said, tone not steady:

'Look here, I didn't come for this. Whatever are we doing?'

'Exchanging views.'

She laughed, with what sounded like relief. I had spoken in something near the manner she was used to, when I was ironing an argument away. It came as a surprise to her – and so much so to me that it passed me by. To me, it seemed that we had moved into the doldrums of a quarrel (like Azik and Rosalind that afternoon in Eaton Square), when we had temporarily ceased lashing out, but were waiting for the animus to blow up again. But Margaret, listening to me raging, accepted the anger and the cruelty; sometimes she had seen that in me before; she had not seen me as frightened as this morning, but that too she accepted. And so, she was ready to notice the first change of inner weather, long before I recognised it myself. She was sure that I was, at least for the time being, through the worst. Casually she chatted, mentioning one or two letters that had arrived at home, pouring herself a drink: in fact, she was watchful, prepared to talk me to sleep or alternatively to take the initiative.

She did take the initiative, in a language that no one on earth but she and I could understand:

'I've got a lunch date on Saturday,' she said. 'I expect I shall forget it.'

If I didn't or couldn't respond, she would drop it. This was an exploration, a tentative.

'You'd better not,' I said.

'It hasn't been imprinted on my memory.'

At that, I laughed out loud. She knew she was home. For this was a secret code, one of our versions of the exchange about the cattleya, more complicated than that but just as cherished. It went back to a time in the middle of the war, before we were married. On Saturday afternoons I used to go to her bedsitting-room: there was a particular Saturday afternoon about which we had made a myth. The coal fire. The looking-glass.

Lying in bed afterwards, watching the sky darken and firelight on the ceiling. The curious thing was, that apparently historical Saturday afternoon didn't really exist. There were plenty of others. Once or twice, in the wartime rush, she had forgotten the place for lunch and I had had to follow her to her room. Many times we had enjoyed ourselves there. Yes, there had been a coal fire and a looking-glass. Nevertheless, we each remembered the detail of different Saturdays, and somehow had fused them into one. One that became a symbol for all the pleasure we had had together, and a signal to each other. Often the mood was formalised. 'What did I tell you about the fire?' To that there was a ritual reply, also part of the myth. In the hospital that morning, she made the ritual speeches, and I followed suit. Soon she was crying:

'You're *much* better.' This also was part of the drill, but for that special moment it was true.

Resurrection, she was saying, not touching wood at all. Until the middle of the afternoon, she remained by my bedside. When she left me it was I who began to touch wood. She had gone, the reassurance had gone, it seemed strange, almost unnatural, that the vacuum hadn't filled. Should I soon be terrified again? I threw my thoughts back, not to Margaret, but to last night, as though I wanted to learn whether it would return. No, my moods were unstable, I hadn't any confidence in them, but I wasn't frightened. Perversely, I wanted to ask why I wasn't. Anything I felt or told myself now, I thought, would be part of a mood that wouldn't last.

Still, the evening – occasionally I enquired about the time – lagged on between sleep and waking. They were taking my blood pressure every three hours, but one nurse told me that that would finish next day. During the night I slept heavily, and woke only once, when they took another reading.

I didn't know where I was, until I understood the darkness in front of my eyes. Then the night before returned, but rather as though I was reading words off a screen, without either fright or relief: with a curious indifference, as though I hadn't energy to waste.

CHAPTER XX

OBITUARY

SPONGE in my hands, warm water on my face, Mansel's voice, the flurry of early morning.

'They tell me you've slept, sir.'

'Better, anyway,' I said, as though it were bad luck to admit it.

Eye uncovered, the lights of the room, three dimensions of the commode, standing out like a piece of hardware by Chardin. Mansel's face close to mine. In a short time, he said:

'Good. Qualified optimism still permitted.'

After he had blindfolded me once more, his voice sounded as in a prepared speech.

'Now we have to make a decision, sir.'

My nerves sharpened. 'What's the matter?'

'Nothing. It's a choice of two courses, that's all. You heard me and Maxim discuss it yesterday, didn't you?'

'I heard something.'

'You're getting on well, you know. The point is, if we're going to get you generally fit as soon as may be, you probably ought to sit up most of today. Now that may, just possibly, disturb the eye. I'm beginning to think, I may as well tell you, that we're very likely too finicky about keeping eye patients still. I suspect in a few years it will seem very old-fashioned. But I have to say that some of my colleagues wouldn't agree. So, if we let you up, one has to warn you, there is – so far as the retina goes – a finite risk.'

I was beginning to speak, but Mansel stopped me.

'I'm not going to let you make the choice. Though I fancy I know which it would be. No, I don't think there is any reasonable doubt. Your general health is much more important than a margin of risk to the retina. Which I don't want you to get depressed about. With a little good fortune, we ought to keep that in order too.'

He could see my face.

'And it will be distinctly good for your morale, won't it?'

Mansel gave an amiable, clinical chuckle. 'Though it's stood up pretty well, I give you that.' He didn't know it all, but he knew something. I was thinking, perhaps not even Margaret knew it all.

After he had given instructions that the nurses were to get me up during the morning, he was saying good-bye. Then he had another thought.

'I wanted to ask you. Which is the hardest to put up with? Having to lie still. Or having to live in the dark.'

'You needn't have asked,' I said. 'Having to live in the dark is about a hundred times worse.'

'I thought so. I have had patients who got frantic at being fixed in one position. But you manage to put up with that, don't you? Good morning, sir.'

When Charles March arrived, I was already sitting up in an armchair. They had told me that he had visited the hospital twice in the last twenty-four hours, being not only an old friend but also my doctor. Each time he came, I had been asleep. Now I apologised, saying that I hadn't been entirely responsible for my actions. Charles replied that he had dimly realised that that was the case.

I suspected that he was gazing straight into my face. How much did it tell him? There weren't many more observant men. He said, in a matter-of-fact doctor-like fashion, that he was glad they had got me up. Mansel, in the middle of his professional circuit, had found time to telephone Charles twice about my condition, and had also written him a longish letter.

'If either of us were as efficient as that young man,' I said, 'we might have got somewhere.'

It was not long after, and we were still chatting, not yet intimately, that I heard Margaret's footsteps on the floor outside. As she came in, she exclaimed in surprise, and approaching my chair, asked how I was, said in the same breath that they must be satisfied with me to let me out of bed. Then went on:

'How is he, Charles?'

'I think he looks pretty good, don't you agree?'

For some time neither of them enquired, even by implication, about my state of mind: I soon believed that they were shying off it. Margaret had seen enough the day before; and Charles, who had once known me as well as any of my friends, was being cautious. We talked about our children and relatives; it was casually, in the midst of the conversation, that she remarked:

'What are you going to do with yourself all day, sitting here?'

'Exactly what I should do lying there.' Blindly I moved a hand in what I thought to be the direction of the bed. 'It's even a slight improvement, you know.'

'Of course it is.' Margaret sounded quick, affirmative, like one correcting a piece of her own tactlessness.

Then I said: 'No. There's going to be a difference.'

'What do you mean?'

'I'm not going to sit here all day doing nothing. I'd like you to get some people in. If I can't see them, I might as well hear them.'

'So you shall.' But Margaret, busy with practical arrangements, saying that she would pass the word round by tomorrow, promising that she would send in some bottles of Scotch, was nevertheless puzzled as well as pleased. So was Charles: for they both knew that this was quite unlike me, that in illness – as in my first operation – I wanted to hide like a sick animal, seeing no one except my family, and them only out of duty. I couldn't have enlightened them. It was one of the occasions when one seemed to be performing like a sleep-walker. If I had been forced to give an explanation, I should probably have said – very lamely – that I realised, as on the day before, that this mood, or any other mood, wouldn't last, but that I wished to commit myself to it. Perhaps I could fight off regressions, the return to that night, the sense of – nothing, once I had announced that I intended to have people round me.

Later Charles told me that that was very near his own interpretation. He thought that I was trying to hold on to something concrete, so as to ward off the depressive swing. With Margaret it was different. Of the three of us, she alone thought that I was stabler than I myself believed, and that she could see – unperceived, or even denied, by me – not only a new resolve, but underneath it a singular, sharp but indefinable change.

If she had been beside me in a waking spell that night, she mightn't have been astonished at what I felt. First I spoke out loud, to see if there were a nurse in the room. Then I realised that the blood-pressure watch had been called off, they were leaving me alone. That didn't frighten me or even remind me. On the contrary, I was immediately taken over by a benign and strangely innocent happiness. I didn't for an instant understand it. It was different in kind from any happiness that I had known, utterly different from the serenity, the half-complacent satisfaction, in which I had gone about after refusing the Government job. Perhaps the nearest approach would be nights when I had wakened and recalled a piece of work which had gone well. But that wasn't very near – this didn't have an element of memory or self-concern. It was as innocent as nights when I woke up as a child and enjoyed the sound of a lashing storm outside. It was so benign that I did not want to go to sleep again.

After Mansel had examined me next morning, he was ruminating on what he called 'morale'. Mine was still keeping up, he thought, with his usual inspectorial honesty. A doctor never really knew how a patient would react to extreme situations.

'You're very modest, Christopher,' I said.

'No, sir. Just open-minded, I hope.'

Both of us ought to be interested in my morale, he said I spent some time at it, I remarked, but Mansel was not amused. Tomorrow, he said, there might be another minor decision for us to make.

Taking me at my word, Margaret had telephoned the previous afternoon to say that I could expect some visitors. The first, in the middle of the morning, was Francis Getliffe. His tread sounded heavy, as it used to sound up my staircase in college, for so spare a man. I greeted him by name before he reached me, and he responded as though I had performed a conjuring trick.

'One's ears get rather sharp,' I said.

'You're putting up with it better than I could.'

'Nonsense. Little you know.'

'Yes, you are. You can cope with it, can't you?' His tone was affectionate but hesitant. Perhaps, I thought (for I hadn't seen him with anyone incapacitated before), he was one of those inhibited when they had to speak to the blind or deaf. I said that it was tiresome not being able to see him.

'I bet it must be.' But that was an absent-minded reply; he was thinking of something else. As he talked, still hesitantly, I realised that Margaret must have told him the whole case-history. Not that he referred to it straight out: he was skirting round it, trying not to touch a nerve, wanting to take care of me. He felt safer when he was on neutral ground, such as politics. The world was looking blacker. We agreed, in all the time we had known each other, there had been only three periods of hope – outside our own private lives, that is. The twenties: curiously enough, wartime: and then the five or six years just past. But that last had been a false hope, we admitted it now.

'If anyone', said Francis, 'can show me one single encouraging sign anywhere in the world this year, I'd be very grateful.'

'Yes,' I said. Things had gone worse than expectations, even realistic or minimum expectations. As Einstein in old age had said, there seemed a weird inevitability about it all. Very little that Francis and I had done together had been useful.

'This country is steadier than most. But I can't imagine what will have happened before we're ten years older. I'm not sure that I want to.'

It was all sensible: yet was he just talking to play out time? I broke out:

'Forty-eight hours ago, I should have been quite sure that I didn't want to.'

He said something, embarrassed, kind, but I went on:

'It would have seemed quite remarkably irrelevant. It rather restricts one's interests, you know, when you're told you might have been dead.'

'Do you mind talking about it?'

'Not in the slightest.'

'I couldn't if I were you.'

Strangely – as I had been realising while the earlier conversation went on, impersonal and strained – that was the fact. What I had said, which wouldn't have troubled Charles March or my brother, risked making him more awkward still. It was a deliberate risk. Francis, who was a brave man, physically as well as morally, was less hardened than most of us. His courage was a courage of the nerves.

While he had been talking, so diffidently, I had recalled an incident of the fairly recent past. At that time it was not unusual, if one moved in the official world, to be asked to prepare an advance obituary notice of an acquaintance – all ready for *The Times*. I had done several. One day, it must have been three or four years before, someone announced himself on the telephone as a member of the paper's staff. Agitation. He had found that by some oversight, on which he elaborated with distress, there was no obituary of Francis Getliffe. How could this be? 'It would be terrible,' said the anxious voice, 'I shouldn't like to be caught short about a man like Getliffe.'

While I was reflecting on that peculiar expression, I was being pressed to produce an obituary – in forty-eight hours? at latest by the end of the week? Francis was in robust health when last seen, I said, but the voice said, 'We can't take any risks.' So I agreed and set to work. Most of it was easy, since I knew Francis's career as well as my own, but I wasn't familiar with his early childhood. His father had married twice, and I had heard almost nothing about his second wife, Francis's mother. So I had to ring up Cambridge. Francis was out, but his wife Katherine answered the phone. When I told her the object of the exercise, she broke into a cheerful scream, and then, no more worried than I was myself, gave businesslike answers. She would pass the good news on to Francis, she said. She had listened to some of his colleagues fretting, in case their obituary should be written by an enemy.

I had met Francis in London shortly afterwards. Without a second thought, I told him the piece was written and presumably safe in *The Times* files. I asked him if he would like to read a copy. Without a second thought – taking it for granted that he would like what I had written, and also taking it for granted that he would behave like an old-style rationalist. For in that respect Francis often behaved like a doctrinaire unbeliever of an earlier period than ours; like, for example, old Winslow, who refused to set foot in college chapel except for magisterial elections, and then only after making written protests. Francis likewise did not go into chapel even for memorial services; his children had not been baptised and, when he was introduced into the Lords, instead of taking the oath he affirmed.

Whereas men like my brother Martin, who believed as little as Francis, would go through the forms without fuss, saying. as Martin did, that if he had been a Roman he would have put a pinch of salt on the altar and not felt that he was straining his conscience.

So innocently I asked Francis if he would care to read his obituary. 'Certainly not,' Francis had said, outraged. Or perhaps hag-ridden, like a Russian seeing one trying to shake his hand across the threshold, or my mother turning up the ace of spades.

When, as Francis was taking care to avoid any subject which might disquiet me, I recalled that incident, it occurred to me that someone must have written my own obituary. I expected to feel a chill, but none came. It was curious to be waiting for that kind of dread, and then be untouched.

After I had been brusque, cutting out the delicateness, Francis became easier. He said:

'This mustn't happen again, you know.'

'It's bound to happen again once, isn't it?'

'Not like that. I was horrified when Margaret told me. I must say, she was very good.'

She had had the worst of it, Francis was saying. Almost as though I had done it on purpose, it crossed my mind. No, that was quite unfair. Francis, whom acquaintances thought buttoned-up and bleak, was speaking with emotion. He had been horrified. I was too careless. Did I give a thought to how much I should be missed?

Though I was to most appearances more spontaneous than Francis I shouldn't, if our positions had been reversed, have told him so simply how much I'd miss him.

I nearly gave another grim answer such as even that seemed a somewhat secondary consideration, but it would have been denying affection. Of the people we had grown up with, we had scarcely, except ourselves, any intimates left. Some had died: others the chances of life had driven away, just as Francis had been parted from his brother-in-law Charles March.

And I, who felt the old affinity with Charles March each time we met, nevertheless had ceased to be close to him, simply because there was no routine of living to bring us together. While Francis and I, during much of our lives, had seen each other every day at meetings. It sounded mechanical, but as you grew older that kind of habit and alliance was a part of intimacy without which it peacefully declined.

Francis's tone altered, he began to sound at his most practical. He proposed to talk to some of his medical friends in the Royal. This never ought to have happened, he said. It was no use passing it off as a fluke or an accident. There must be a cause. What sort of anaesthetic had they used? This all had to be cleared up in case I was forced some day into another operation. There had to be a bit of decent scientific thinking, he said, with impatience as well as clarity – just as he used to speak, cutting through cotton-wool, at committee tables during the war.

That could be coped with. And also, he went on, half-sternly, half-persuasively, it was time I took myself in hand. I had worked hard all my life: it was time I made more of my leisure. 'I'm damned well going to enjoy my sixties, and so ought you,' he said. He was leading up to a project that he had mentioned before. The house in Cambridge, full of children, happy-go-lucky, called by young Charles and his friends the Getliffe steading, he couldn't bear to leave, he would stay there in term-time always. But he and Katherine were hankering after another house, more likely to get some sun in winter, maybe somewhere like Provence. Why shouldn't we find a place together? They would occupy it perhaps four months a year, and Margaret and I in spring and autumn?

We couldn't travel far while Margaret's father was alive, I replied, as I had done previously. No, but that couldn't be for ever. Francis was set on the plan, more set than when he first introduced it. It would be good for his married children and their families. It would be good for ours – young Charles, Francis said, would be mysteriously asking to have the house to himself, and leaving us to guess whom he was bringing there.

He was so active, so determined to get me into the sunshine, that I was almost persuaded. It might be pleasant as we all became old. But I held on enough not to make the final promise. I wasn't as hospitable as Francis, nor anything like as fond of movement. Anyway, now the plan had crystallised, I didn't doubt that he would carry it through, whether I joined in or not. It had started as a scheme largely for my sake: but also Francis, decisive and executive as ever, was carving out a pattern for his old age.

CHAPTER XXI

SILENCE OF A SON

BEFORE evening, the room was smelling of flowers and whisky. The flowers were due, in the main, to Azik Schiff, who hadn't come to visit me himself but whose response to physical ailments was to provide a lavish display of horticulture. More flowers than they'd ever seen sent, said the nurses, and my credit rose in consequence. Though I could have done without the hyacinths which, since my nose was sensitive to begin with and had been made more so by blindness, gave me a headache, the only malaise of the day.

As for the whisky, that had been drunk before lunch by Hector Rose and his wife and after tea by Margaret and a visitor who hadn't been invited, my nephew Pat. When Margaret was sitting beside my chair and she was reading me the morning's letters, there were footsteps, male footsteps, that I didn't recognise. But I did recognise a stiffening in Margaret's voice as she said good-afternoon.

'Hallo, Aunt Meg. Hallo, Uncle Lew. Good to see you up. That's better, isn't it, that really is better.'

It was a situation in which, given enough nerve, he was bound to win. Whatever he didn't have, he had enough nerve. Though he might have been slandering Margaret and her children, she couldn't raise a quarrel in a hospital bedroom. And he was reckoning that I was quite incapacitated. There he might have been wrong: but, as usual in Pat's presence, I didn't want to say what a juster man might have said. Margaret stayed silent: and I was reduced to asking Pat how he had heard about me.

'Well-known invalid, of course.'

'No,' I said, 'we've kept it very quiet. On purpose.'

'Not quiet enough, Uncle Lew.' Pat's voice was ebullient and full of cheek.

Margaret had still said nothing, but I listened to the splash of liquid. Presumably he was helping himself to a drink. He said, irrepressible, that he couldn't reveal his sources – and then gave an account, almost completely accurate, of what had happened since I entered the hospital. Massage of the heart. Margaret being sent for.

'It must have been terrible for you, Aunt Meg.'

Margaret had to reply.

'I shouldn't like to go through it again,' she said. The curious thing was, his sympathy was genuine.

'Terrible,' he said again. Then he couldn't resist showing that he knew the name of the heart specialist, and even how he had telephoned Margaret on the first night.

That was something I hadn't been told myself. As before with Pat, just as in the past with Gilbert Cooke, I felt uncomfortably hemmed in, as though I was being watched by a flashy but fairly successful private detective. Actually, I realised later that there was no mystery about Pat's source of information. There was only one person whom it could have come from. My brother Martin had been asking Margaret for news several times a day. And Martin, who was as discreet as Hector Rose in his least forthcoming moments, who had, when working on the atomic bomb, never let slip a secret even to his wife, on this occasion, as on others, could, and must, have told everything to his son.

Pat might be said to have outstayed his welcome, if there had been any welcome. Talking cheerfully, the bounce and sparkle not diminishing, he stayed until Margaret herself had to leave. But there had been, aided by alcohol, some truce of amicability in the room. Margaret had taken another drink, and Pat several more. It was I who was left out: for to me, who wasn't yet drinking, there might be amicability in the room, but there was also an increasing smell of whisky.

Later that night, when I had been put back to bed, the telephone rang on the bedside table. Gropingly, my hand got hold of the receiver. It was Margaret.

'I don't want to worry you, but I think you'd better know. It's not serious, but it's rather irritating.'

Normally, I should have demanded the news at once. But in the calm in which I was existing, as yet inexplicable to me but nevertheless very happy, I wasn't in a hurry. I asked if it were anything to do with Charles, and Margaret said no. I said: 'You needn't mind about worrying me, you know.'

'Well,' came her voice, 'there's an item in one of the later editions. I think I'd better read it, hadn't I?'

'Go ahead.'

The item, Margaret told me, occurred in a new-style gossip column, copied from New York. It read something to the effect that I had been undergoing optical surgery, and that there had been complications which had caused 'grave concern'.

When she rang up to break the news, Margaret assumed that this would enrage and worry me. She had seen me and others close to me secretive about their health. One of the first lessons you learned in any sort of professional life was that you should never be ill. It reduced your *mana*. When I was a young man, and just attracting some work at the Bar, I had been told that I was seriously ill. I had gone to extreme lengths to conceal it: if I had died, it wouldn't have mattered anyway – and if, as it turned out, I didn't, well then I had been right.

Nowadays I was removed from the official life: but even to a writer it did harm – an impalpable superstitious discreditable harm – if people heard that your death was near. You were already on the way to being dispensed with. The way they talked about you – 'did you know, poor old X seems to be finished' – was dismissive rather than cruel, though there was a twist of gloating there, showing through their self-congratulation that they were still right in the middle of the mortal scene.

So Margaret anticipated that this bit of news would harass me – and, before I went into hospital, she would have been right. Now it didn't. I said:

'Oh, that doesn't matter.'

'We'd better do something, hadn't we?'

I was reflecting. The lessons I had learned seemed very distant; but still they had been learned, and one might as well not throw them away.

'Yes,' I said. 'I suppose we'd better be prudent. I'll make Christopher Mansel send out a bulletin.'

'Shall I talk to him tonight?'

'It can wait until he comes in tomorrow morning.'

When Margaret had rung off, I lay in bed, not thinking of Mansel's bulletin, but contentedly preoccupied with a problem which gave me a certain pleasure. Whoever had leaked that news? It couldn't be the doctors. It couldn't be my family. Someone in the hospital? Just possibly. Someone whom Margaret had talked to, trying to enlist visitors for me? Possibly.

No, the answer was too easy. There was one person who stood out, beautifully probable. Motive, opportunity, the lot. I would have bet heavily on my nephew Pat. He had his contacts with the young journalists. Once or twice before, our doings had been speculated about knowledgeably in the gossip columns. Pat was not above receiving a pound or two as a link-man. There was not much that Pat was above.

The next morning, as Mansel said good-morning, I told him about the rumour and said that I wanted him to correct it.

'Right, sir. There are one or two things first, though.'

After he had examined the left eye, he said:

'Promising.' He paused, like a Minister answering a supplementary question, wanting to give satisfaction, so long as it wasn't the final commitment: 'I think I can say we shall be unlucky if anything goes wrong this time.'

Quick fingers, and the eye was shut into darkness again.

'That'll do, I think.' Mansel was gazing at me as though he had made an excellent joke.

'What about the other eye?' I said.

'You can have that, if you like.' He gave a short allocution. What I had said the day before was what he expected most patients to say. He had already decided to leave the good eye unblinded. It was more convenient to have me in hospital for a few more days: I should stand it better if I had an eye to see with. The advantages of blinding both eyes probably weren't worth the psychological wear and tear. 'I'm pretty well convinced', said Mansel, 'that we've got to learn to do these operations and leave you one working eye right from the start.'

I said that I should like to stand him a drink, but in his profession, at 6.45 in the morning, that didn't seem quite appropriate. I said also that, if he would leave me one eye, he could go through the entire eye-operation again. Without any frills or additions, however.

Mansel was scrutinising me.

'You could face it again, could you?'

'If it's not going to happen, one can face anything.'

He seemed to make another entry in his mental notebook – *behaviour of patient, after being allowed vision.*

'Well, sir, what about this statement? That's really your department, not mine, you know.' It was true, he was not so brisk, masterful and masterly when he sat down and started to compose.

Ballpoint pen tapping his teeth, he stayed motionless, like Henry James in search of the exact, the perfect, the unique word. After a substantial interval, at least fifteen minutes, he said, with unhabitual diffidence, with a touch of pride:

'How will this do?'

He read out the name of the hospital, and then—

'Sir Lewis Eliot entered this hospital on 27 November, and next day an operation was performed for a retinal detachment in the left eye. As a result there are good prospects that the eye will be restored to useful vision. During the course of the operation, Sir Lewis underwent a cardiac arrest. This was treated in a routine manner. In all respects, Sir Lewis's progress and condition are excellent.'

'Well, Christopher,' I said, 'no one could call you a sensational writer.'

'I think that says all that's necessary.'

'Cardiac arrest, that's what you call it, is it?'

I hadn't heard the phrase before. Though, by a coincidence, when my eye first went wrong, two years earlier, I had been reminded of an older phrase, 'arrest of life'. Perhaps that was too melodramatic for a black veil over half an eye. This time, it didn't seem so.

'After all,' I remarked absently to Mansel, 'one doesn't have too many.'

'Too many what?'

'Arrests of life.'

'Cardiac arrests is what we say. No, of course not, most people only have one.'

Unfussed, he went off to telephone the bulletin to the Press Association, while I got up, self-propelled again, and, being able to see, was also able to eat. It was a luxury to sit, free from the solipsistic darkness, and just gaze out of the window – though, even as the sky lightened, it was still a leaden morning, and bedroom lamps were being switched on, high up in the houses opposite.

Mansel had told the nurses not to let me move, except from bed to chair. But the telephone was fixed close by, and I rang Margaret up, telling her to bring reading-matter. That wasn't specially urgent, it was good enough to enjoy looking at things. But this presumably soon ceased to be a treat. Thirty years ago, I was remembering, an eminent writer had given me some unsolicited advice. Just look at an orange, she said. Go on looking at it. For hours. Then put down what you see. In the hospital room there was, as it happened, an orange. I looked at it. I thought that I should soon have enough of – what had she called it? The physiognomic charm of phenomena.

It was a relief when the telephone rang. The porter in the entrance hall, announcing that Mr Eliot was down below. 'We've been told to send up the names of visitors from now on, sir.' Mr Eliot? It could be one of three. When I heard quick steps far down the corridor, my ear was still attuned. That was Charles.

He came across the room and, in silence, shook my hand. Then he sat down, still without speaking. It was unlike him, or both of us together, to be so silent. There was a constraint between us right from the beginning.

With my unobscured eye, I was gazing at him. He gazed back at me. He said:

'I didn't expect—'

'What?'

'That they'd let you see.'

'New technique,' I said, glad to have a topic to start us talking. I explained why Mansel had unblinded me.

'It must be an improvement.'

'Enormous.'

We were talking like strangers, impersonally impressed by a medical advance: no, more concentrated upon eye-surgery, more eager not to deviate from it, than if we had been strangers.

Another pause, as though we had forgotten the trick of talking, at which people thought we were both so easy.

At last I said:

'This has been a curious experience.'

'I suppose so.' Then quickly: 'You're looking pretty well.'

'I think I'm probably very well. Never better in my life, I dare say. It seems an odd way of achieving it.'

Charles gave a tight smile, but he wasn't responding to the kind of sarcasm, or grim facetiousness, with which he and I, and Martin also, liked to greet our various fatalities. Was I making claims on him that he couldn't meet? The last time my eye had gone wrong, and it seemed that I was going to lose its sight, he had been fierce with concern. Then he had been two years younger. Now, in so many ways a man, he spoke, or didn't speak, as though his concern was knotted up, inexpressible, or so tangled that he couldn't let it out.

It was strange, it was more than strange, it was disappointing and painful, that he should be self-conscious as I had scarcely seen him. At this time of all times. I thought later that perhaps we knew too much: too much to be easy, that is, not enough to come out on the other side. He had plenty of insight, but he wasn't trusting it, as the constraint got hold of us, nor was I mine.

A father's death. What did one feel? What was one supposed to feel? Sheer loss, pious and organic, a part of oneself cut away – that would have been the proper answer in my childhood: but a lot of sons knew that it wasn't so clean and comfortable as that. When I was growing up, the answer would have changed. Now it meant oneself at last established, final freedom, the Oedipal load removed: and a lot of sons still knew that it wasn't so clean and unambiguous as that. As Charles was growing up, all the Oedipal inheritance had passed into the conventional wisdom, at least for those educated like him: and, like most conventional wisdom, it was half believed and half thrown away.

Probably Charles and his friends weren't so impressed by it as by the introspective masters: Dostoevsky meant more to them than the psychoanalysts did. Not surprisingly to me, for at twenty, older than they were and having lived rougher, I also had been overwhelmed. I had met, as they had, the difficult questions. *Who has not wished his father dead?*

That hadn't meant much to me since, from a very early age, I could scarcely be said to have a relation with my father. From fourteen or so onwards, I was the senior partner, so far as we had a partnership, and he regarded me with mild and bantering stupefaction. Perhaps I had suffered more than I knew because he was unavailing. His bankruptcy in my child-hood left some sort of wound. It was also possible that as a child I knew more than I realised about his furtive chases after women. I had a memory, which might not have been genuine but was very sharp, of standing at the age of seven or eight outside a rubber shop – with my father blinking across the counter, which mysteriously gave me goose-flesh as though it were a threat or warning. Still, all that was searching back with hindsight. During the short part of our lives which we had lived together, we impinged on each other as little as father and son, or even two members of the same family, ever could.

It was not like that with me and Charles. Partly because our tempera-ments were too much the same weight, and, though we were in many respects different, in the end we wanted the same things. And there was a complication, simply because I had lived some of my life in public. That meant that Charles couldn't escape me and that, without special guilt on either side, I got in his way.

That night when he returned home from his travels, I had said in effect that I was leaving him an awkward legacy. He had replied, more harshly than seemed called for, that he wouldn't be worried over. In fact, on the specific point I had been wrong. He didn't mind in the least that, when I died, some of the conflicts and enmities would live on and he would some-times pay for them. That he not only didn't mind but welcomed. For, though he couldn't endure my protecting him, he was cheerful and fighting-happy at the chance of his protecting me. And if he had to do it posthumously, well, he was at least as tenacious as I was.

It was not the penalties that he wanted to escape, but the advantages. He had seen and heard my name too often. There were times when I seemed omnipresent. Anyone of strong nature – from my end, it was a somewhat bitter irony – would have preferred to be born obscure.

Yet perhaps I was making it too easy for myself. Perhaps – if he had never heard my name outside the family – we should still have faced each other in the hospital bedroom with the same silences. Perhaps it was our-selves that we couldn't escape. He might still have expected me to claim more than I did. I should have still felt ill-used, for I believed that I had been unpossessive, had claimed little or nothing, and wanted us to exist side by side.

Was that true? Was that all? My relation with Charles was utterly unlike mine with my own father. That was certain. But, as we sat in that room, the familiar sardonic exchanges not there to bring us together or smooth the minutes away, I felt a shiver – more than that, a menace and a remorse – from the past. For Charles was behaving now very much, nerve of the same nerve, as I had behaved when I sat by my mother at her deathbed.

It was more than forty years before. Instead of a smell evoking the past, the past evoked a smell: in my hygienic flower-lined room, I smelt brandy, eau-de-Cologne, the warm redolence of the invalid's bedroom. Then I had sat with the tight constrained feeling, full of dread, which overcame me when she called out for my love. For I couldn't give it her, at least in the terms she claimed.

'I wanted to go along with you,' she had cried, demanding more for me than I did for myself. 'That's all I wanted.'

I did my best (I was about the same age as Charles was now) to console her. Yet, whenever I felt remorse, I had to recall one thing – whatever I did, I hadn't brought her comfort. She was the proudest of women; she was vain, but she had an eye for truth. She knew as well as I that if one's heart is invaded by another (that was how I used to think, when my taste was more florid, and I didn't mind the sound of rhetoric), then one will either assist the invasion or repel it. I repelled it, longing that I might do otherwise. And she knew.

I had been as proud as my mother, and in some ways as vain. Some of that pride and vanity was exorcised by now: for I had lived much longer than she did, and age, though it didn't kill vanity, took the edge of it away. Like her, I sometimes couldn't deceive myself about the truth. Charles was behaving as I had done. Was it also true that, against my will and anything that I desired, without knowing it I was affecting him as she had me? Had the remorse come back, through all those years, and made me learn what it had been like for her, and what it was now like for me?

Charles's tone changed, as he said:

'There is something I wanted to tell you.'

'What's that?'

'Maurice and Godfrey [Maurice's parson friend] will be coming in later today.'

'That's all right.'

'Yes, but you mustn't put your foot in it, you know.' His eyes had taken on a piercing glint: there was a joke at my expense. Suddenly he had switched – and I with him, seeing that expression – to our most companionable.

'What are you accusing me of now?'

'You might forget that old Godfrey has a professional interest in you, don't you think?'

'Aren't I usually fairly polite?'

'Fairly.'

'Well then. I don't propose to stop being polite, just because the man is an Anglo-Catholic priest.'

'So long', Charles's smile was matey and taunting, 'as you don't forget that he *is* an Anglo-Catholic priest.'

I taunted him back:

'My memory is in excellent order, you'll be glad to know.'

'That's not the point.'

'Come on, what do you want me to say to him?'

'It's what I don't want you to say that counts.'

'And that is?'

'Look here, it isn't everyone who's done a Lazarus, is it?'

'Granted,' I said.

'It's therefore reasonable to suppose that a priest will have a special interest in you, don't you realise? After all, we expect him to have some concern about life after death, don't we?'

'Granted again.'

'Well then, you'd better not say much about first-hand knowledge, had you? I should have thought this wasn't precisely the occasion.'

We had each known what this duologue meant, all along. About his friends' susceptibilities, or his acquaintances' as well, Charles could be sensitive and far-sighted. But also he had constructed a legend about me as a blunt unrestrained Johnsonian figure, in contrast to his own subtlety. It was the kind of legend that grows up in various kinds of intimacy. In almost exactly the same way, Roy Calvert used to pretend to be on tenterhooks waiting for some gigantesque piece of tactlessness from me: on the basis that, just as William the Silent got his nickname through being silent on one occasion, so I had been shatteringly tactless once. With both of them – often Charles acted towards me as Roy Calvert used to – they liked rubbing the legend in. And Charles in particular used this device to make amends. It took the heat out of either affection or constraint or the complex of the two, and gave us the comfort we both liked.

CHAPTER XXII

THE FOUR THINGS

As Charles had prepared me, Maurice and Father Ailwyn duly arrived later that day, round half past four, when I had finished drinking tea. The Quixotic pair came through the door, Maurice so thin that he looked taller than he was, Father Ailwyn the reverse. Since all my family called Ailwyn by his Christian name, I had to do the same, although I knew him only slightly. He gave a shy, fat-cheeked smile, small eyes sharp and uncertain behind his glasses, cassock billowing round thick-soled boots. While they were settling down in their chairs, he was abnormally diffident, not able to make any kind of chat, nor even to reply to ours. Maurice had told me that he was quite as inept when he visited the old and lonely: a stuttering awkward hulk of a fat man, grateful when Maurice, who might be self-effacing but was never shy, acted as a lubricant. Yet, they said, Godfrey Ailwyn was the most devoted of parish priests, and the desolate liked him, even if he couldn't talk much, just because he never missed a visit and patiently sat with them.

With the excessive heartiness that the diffident induced, I asked if he would have some tea.

'No, thank you. I'm not much good at tea.'

His tone was hesitating, but upper-class – not professional, not high bourgeois. Even my old acquaintance, Lord Boscastle, arbiter of origins, might have performed the extraordinary feat of 'knowing who he was' – which meant that his family could be found in reference books.

'I'm pretty sure', said Maurice, 'that Godfrey would like a drink. Wouldn't you now, Godfrey?'

The doleful plump countenance lightened.

'If it isn't any trouble—'

'Of course it isn't.' Maurice, used to looking after the other man, was already standing by the bottles, pouring out a formidable whisky. 'That's all right, isn't it?'

Maurice, taking the glass round, explained to me, as though he were an interpreter, that Godfrey had had a busy day, mass in the morning, parish calls, a couple of young delinquents at the vicarage—

'It must be a tough life,' I said.

Godfrey smiled tentatively, took a swig at his drink and then, all of a sudden, asked me, with such abruptness that it sounded rough:

'You don't remember anything about it, do you?'

For an instant I was taken by surprise, as though I hadn't heard the question right, or didn't understand it. I hadn't expected him to take the initiative.

'Maurice says you didn't remember nything about it. When you came to.'

'I wasn't exactly at my most lucid, of course.'

'But you didn't remember anything?'

'I was more concerned with what was happening there and then.'

'You still don't remember anything?'

I was ready to persevere with evasion, but he was not giving me much room to manœuvre.

'Would you expect me to?' I asked.

'It was like waking from a very deep sleep, was it?'

'I think one might say that.'

Father Ailwyn gave a sharp-eyed glance in Maurice's direction, as though they were sharing a joke, and then turned to me with an open, slumbrous smile, the kind of smile which transformed depressive faces such as his.

'Please don't be afraid of worrying me,' he said, and added: 'Lewis, I am interested, you know.'

'Godfrey said on the way here that he wished he wasn't a clergyman.' Maurice was also smiling. 'He didn't want to put you off.'

I should have something to report to young Charles when next I saw him, I was thinking.

'I'm not going to be prissy with you,' said Godfrey. 'All I'm asking you is to return the compliment.'

I had come off worst and gave an apologetic smile.

'Eschatology is rather a concern of ours, you see. But most believers wouldn't think that you were interfering with their eschatology. They'd be pretty certain to say, and here I don't mind admitting that they sometimes take an easy way out, that you hadn't really been dead.'

Instead of being inarticulate, or so shy as to be embarrassing to others, he had begun to talk as though he were in practice.

'I don't think I've ever claimed that, have I?' I said.

'I should have thought that, by inference, you had. And most believers would tell you that it's very difficult to define the threshold of death, and that you hadn't crossed it.'

'I can accept that—'

'They would tell you that the brain has to die as well as the heart stopping before the body is truly dead. And until the body is truly dead, then the soul can't leave it.'

I still didn't want to argue, but I respected him now and had to be straightforward.

'That I can't accept. Those are just words—'

'They don't mean much more to me than they do to you.'

Again Godfrey's face was one moon-like smile. 'It's a very primitive model, of course it is. At the time of the early church, a man's spirit was supposed to hover over the body for three days, and didn't depart until the decomposition set in.'

Yes, I said, I'd read that once, in a commentary on the Gospel according to Saint John. It was the priest's turn to look surprised. He had expected me to be entirely ignorant about the Christian faith, just as I had expected him to be unsophisticated about everything else. In fact, he was at least as far from unsophisticated as Laurence Knight, my first wife's father, another clergyman, in one of his more convoluted phases.

Godfrey Ailwyn had also one of those minds which were naturally rococo and which moved from flourish to invention and back again, with spiralling whirls and envelopes of thought – quite different from the clear straight cutting-edge mentalities of, say, Francis Getliffe or Austin Davidson in his prime. Quite different, but neither better nor worse, just different: one of the most creative minds I ever met was similar in kind to Father Ailwyn's, and belonged to a scientist called Constantine.

What did Ailwyn believe about death, the spirit or eternal life? I pressed him, for he had brushed away the surface civilities, and I was genuinely curious to know. Though he was willing to spin beautiful metaphysical structures, I wasn't sure that I understood him. Certainly he believed, so far as he believed at all, in something very different from what he called the 'metaphors' in which he spoke to his parishioners. The body, the memory, this our mortal life – if I didn't misinterpret him – existed in space and time, and all came to an end with death. The spirit existed outside space and time, and so to talk of a beginning, or an end, or an after-life – they were only 'metaphors', which we had to use because our minds were primitive.

It was about memory alone that I could engage with him. He would have liked to believe (for once, he wasn't intellectually cool) that some part of memory – 'some subliminal part, if you like' – was attached to the spirit and so didn't have to perish. That was why, with more hope than expectation, he had wanted to cross-question me.

On the terms we had now reached (they weren't those of affection and, though I was interested in him, he wasn't in me, except as an imparter of information: but still, we had come to terms of trust) it would have been false of me to give him any agreement. No, I said, I was sure that memory was a function of the body: damage the brain, and there was no memory left. When the brain came to its end, so did memory. It was inconceivable that any part of it could outlive the body. If the spirit existed outside space and time (though I couldn't fix any meaning to his phrase), memory couldn't. And what possible kind of spiritual existence could that be?

'By definition,' said Godfrey Ailwyn, 'we can't imagine it. Because we're limited by our own categories. Sometimes we seem to have intuitions. Perhaps that does suggest that some kind of remembrance isn't as limited as we are.'

No, whatever it suggested, it couldn't be that, I said. He was a very honest man, but he wouldn't give up that toehold of hope. Did I deny the mystical experience, he asked me. No, of course I didn't deny the experience, I said. But that was different from accepting the interpretation that he might put upon it.

As we went on talking, Maurice, unassuming, bright-faced, poured Godfrey another drink. In time, I came to wonder whether, though Godfrey's mind was elaborate, his temperament wasn't quite simple. So that in a sense, detached from his intellect, he wasn't so far after all from the people he preached to or tried to console, stumbling with his tongue at a sick bed, in a fashion that seemed preposterous when one heard him talk his own language as he had done that afternoon.

Soon they would have to leave, he said, his expression once more owlish and sad. He had to take an evening service. Would he get many people, I asked. Five or six, old ladies, old friends of his.

'Old ladies,' Maurice put in, 'who, if they hadn't got Godfrey, wouldn't have anything to live for.'

'I don't know about that,' said Godfrey, awkward as an adolescent.

I couldn't resist one final question. We had spoken only of one of the eschatological last things, I said. Death. How did he get on with the other three? Judgment, heaven, hell.

Again he looked as though I weren't playing according to the rules, or hadn't any justification to recognise a theological term.

Did he place heaven and hell, like the spirit, outside of space and time? And judgment too? Wasn't that utterly unlike anything that believers had ever conceived up to his day?

His sharp eyes gazed at me with melancholy. Then suddenly the pastiness, the heaviness, the depression did their disappearing trick again, and he smiled.

'Lewis. I expect you'd prefer me to place them all in your own world, wouldn't you? I'm not sure that that would be an improvement, you know. But if you like I'll say that you've made your own heaven and hell in your own life. And as for judgment, well, you're capable of delivering that upon yourself. I hope you show as much mercy as we shall all need in the end.'

When they had departed, I thought that that last remark didn't really fit under his metaphysical arch, but that nevertheless, if he allowed himself an instant's pride in the midst of his chronic modesty, he had a good sound right to do so.

CHAPTER XXIII

LYING AWAKE

WHEN Charles March called in for ten minutes later that same evening, I asked him to do a little staff work. Would he, either on his own account or by invoking Mansel, make an arrangement with the nurses? Up to now, they had forced sleeping-pills upon me each night. I wanted that stopped. Partly because I had an aversion, curiously puritanical, from any routine drug-taking: I would much rather have a broken night or two than get into the habit of dosing myself to sleep. But also I wasn't in the least tired, I was serene and content, I didn't mind lying awake: which in fact I did, luxuriously, looking out one-eyed into the dark bedroom.

Not that it was quite dark, or continuously so. There was a kind of background twilight, contributed perhaps by the street lamps or those in the houses opposite, which defined the shape of the window and chest of drawers close by. Occasionally, a beam from a car's headlights down below swept across the far wall, and I watched with pleasure, as though I were being reminded of lying in an unfamiliar bedroom long ago, at my Uncle Will's in Market Harborough, when as a boy I didn't wish to go to sleep, so long as I could see the walls rosy, then darker, rosy again, as the coal fire flickered and fell.

I was being reminded of something else, what was it, another room, another pattern of light, almost another life. At last I had it. A hotel room in Menton, regular as a metronome the lighthouse-beam, moving from wall to wall: in the dark intervals, the sea slithering and slapping on the rocks beneath. Yes, I had been ill and wretched, wondering if I should recover, maddened that I might die quite unfulfilled, longing for the woman whom I later married and did harm to. Yet the recollection, in the hospital bedroom, was happy, pain long since drained out, as though all that persisted was the smell of the flowers and the sharp-edged lighthouse-beam.

Other unfamiliar rooms. The hotel bedrooms of a lifetime. Why did I feel, not only serene, but triumphant? The half-memories, the flashes, seemed like a conquest. Alone. Not alone. Dense curtained darkness: the sound of breathing from the other bed. Smell of beeswax, potpourri, wood smoke. That might have been Palermo. Sound of a sentry's stamp outside. Travelling as an official. Then unofficial, utter quiet, lights across the canal.

Switch of association. Godfrey Ailwyn had talked of the threshold of death. He hadn't been inhibited, he hadn't worried about delicacy or restraint, and that had pleased me. He had set out to argue that I hadn't been dead. Curious to argue whether, at a point of time, one was or was not dead. That hadn't seemed ominous, became the opposite of ominous now. As, after the recall of nights abroad, I thought (associations, day-dreams, drifting in and out) of some of Godfrey's words, I didn't feel less serene but more so. I hadn't minded him cross-questioning me like a coroner: no, I welcomed it. It was only five nights since I had lain in this room, frozen with dread. Frightened to think back a few hours, to the time they were standing round me and Mansel got to work.

Now – with a change which I hadn't recognised as it was happening, but which had come to feel delectable and complete – I wasn't frightened to think back, there was nothing which gave me a greater sense of calm or of something more liberating than calm. 28 November 1965. That morning, round about half past eleven, I might have died. I liked telling myself that. Nothing had ever been so steadying, not at all bizarre or nerve-racking, just steadying: nothing had set me so free.

I did not have to reason this out to myself, certainly not on that contented night, or make it any subtler than it was. It was just a fact of life, an unpredicted but remarkably satisfying fact, one of the best. When, however, I tried to explain it to others (which I didn't want to for a long time afterwards) I didn't even satisfy myself. It all sounded either too mysteriously lumbering or else altogether too casual. One difficulty was that, to me as the sole recipient, the emotional tone of the whole thing was very light. I tried to spell it out – it made one's concerns, even those which before the relevant morning would have weighed one down, appear not so much silly as non-existent.

After all, one might not have had them any more.

Just as in the dread which I had experienced only once, in the hours of 28/29 November, everything disappeared, longings, hopes, fears, ego, everything but the dread itself: so they disappeared in this anti-dread.

Most of us looked upon our lives – not continuously but now and then – as a kind of journey, progress or history. A history, as the cosmogonists might say, from Time $T = 0$ at birth to $T^1 =$ the final date, which it wasn't given us to know in advance. (I had once heard Roy Calvert say that, if given the chance to see ten years ahead, he wouldn't take it. If he had taken it, he would have seen – nothing.

Who, at any age, younger than Charles, older than me, would dare to look into the mirror of his future?)

Somehow that progress, journey, history had for me become disconnected or dismissed. As though what fashionable persons were beginning to call the diachronic existence had lost its grip on me.

Yet what I really felt was as simple as a joy. As though I had smelt the lilac, and time-travelled back to the age of eleven, reading under the tree at home: as though troubles past or to come had been dissolved, and become one with the moment in which I was watching the cars' lights move across the bedroom wall.

So, when the priest told me to show myself as much mercy as we should all need in the end, that affected me, but not as it might have done six days before. They were kind words: they were good words: once, though I didn't share his theology, they would have made me heavy-spirited as I thought about my past. But now I was freer from myself. Yes, I could still think with displeasure about what I had done, and wish that whole episodes or stretches of years might be wiped away. But I wished that, and still felt a kind of joy, with no *angst* there.

Judgment? Well, thinking with displeasure on what I had done was a kind of judgment. It wasn't either merciful or the reverse. I didn't feel obliged to reckon up an account, as though one ought to tick off the plus and minus scores. Once I had told a friend (perhaps the least moral friend I had ever had) that, if I had never lived, nobody would have been a penny the worse. That was altogether too cut-and-dried for me now. Too historical, in fact: and actually, in terms of history, microscopic history, it was not even true. But on the other hand, when I was recovering from the first operation, and Charles March had said that it was impossible to regret one's own experience, I had on the moment been doubtful, and later to myself (in this same bedroom) utterly denied it. I did regret, sometimes passionately, sometimes with remorse, but more often with impatience, a good deal of my youth. Right up to the time – I was thirty-four – when Sheila killed herself.

I didn't take more of the blame than I had to. It wouldn't have been true, it would have been over-dramatic and, curiously enough, over-vain, to imagine that I could have altered all or many of my actions. I had struggled too hard, and with too much self-concentration: but it would have been impossible not to struggle hard. Nevertheless, in a sense, in a sense which was real although one could explicate it half away, I had been a bad son, a bad friend, a bad husband. To my mother I could, without being a different person, have given more. Yes, I had been very young: but I was already old enough to distrust one's own withdrawals, and to know that one's own needs – including self-protection and the assertion of one's loneliness – could be cruel. And, what took more recognition, could be disciplined.

I had been a bad friend to George Passant – not in later years, when there was nothing to be done except be there, when all he wanted was to spend a night or two in what he thought of as a normal world – not then, but almost as soon as I ceased to be an intimate and left the town for London. It was then that I had blinkered myself. I ought to have known how the great dreams were being acted out, how all the hopes of the son of the morning were driving him where such hopes had driven other leaders before him. I ought to have used my own realism to break up the group or his inner paradise. Perhaps no one could have done that, for George was a powerful character and had, of course, the additional power of his own desires. But I was tougher-minded than he was, and there was a chance, perhaps one chance in ten, that I could have shifted him.

As for being a bad husband to Sheila, it was simply that I shouldn't have been her husband at all. There I had committed the opposite wrong to what I had done (or rather not done) to George Passant. Instead of absenting myself, as from him – or earlier from my mother, I had summoned up every particle of intensity, energy and will. She, lost and splintered as she was, had to take me in the end. After that, I couldn't find a way, there was no way, to make up for it. Now I had seen in my son Charles the same capacity for intense focusing of the whole self, regardless of anyone and anything, regardless in his case of his normal sense or detached kindness. Regardless in mine of the tenderness that I felt for Sheila, independent of love, and lasting longer.

That I couldn't forget. When Austin Davidson played with speculations about the after-life, I had a reason, stronger than all others, for wishing that I could, even in the most ghostly fashion, believe in it: a reason so mawkish and sentimental that I couldn't admit it, and yet so demanding that once, when Davidson and young Charles were bantering away, I couldn't listen. Instead, I wanted to hear – it was as mawkish as that – a voice from the shades saying (clipped and gnomic as so much that Sheila had said in life): 'Never mind. It's all right. You should know, it's all right.'

If I had been given the option, I should have chosen to eliminate the first half of my life, and try again. No one could judge that but myself. Francis Getliffe, who had known me continuously for longer than anyone else, would have been – in the priest's terms – too merciful. He had seen me do bad things, but he hadn't seen those hidden things: and, even if he had, he would still have been too merciful.

For the second half of my life, Margaret had known me as no one else had. At times she had seen me at my worst. But there I should – compared with the remoter past – have given myself the benefit of the doubt. And I thought that she would too. She would have said – so I believed – that I had made an effort to reshape a life. It wasn't easy or specially successful, she might have added to herself: for Margaret was not often taken in, either about herself or me, nor so willing to be satisfied as Francis. But she would have given me the benefit of the doubt, even if she had known me from the beginning. She had a higher sense of what life ought to be than I had: but also she could accept more when it went wrong.

Yet, as I lay in bed, it wasn't the remorse – the tainted patches, the days, the years – that became mixed with this present moment. Instead, other moments, dredged up from the past, flickered into this one. Moments which might originally have been miserable or joyous – they were all content-giving by now. Lying awake as a child, hearing my father and some choral friends singing down below; walking with Sheila on a freezing winter night; sitting tired and ill by the sea, wondering how I could cope with the next term at the Bar; triumph after an examination result, drinking, chucking glasses into the fireplace.

I was vulnerable to memories, I wanted to be, some I was forcing back to mind. They were what remained, not the judgments or the regrets. Again I thought of Charles March in that same conversation two years before, saying, as I listened with eyes blacked out: 'You've had an interesting life, Lewis, haven't you?'

An interesting life. Did anyone think – to himself – of his own life like that? That was the kind of summing-up that a biographer or historian might make: but it didn't have any meaning to oneself, to one's own life as lived. Zest, action growing out of flatness, boredom growing out of zest, achievement growing out of boredom, reverie – joy – anxiety – action. Could anyone sum that up for himself, or make an integral as an onlooker might? True, I had once heard an old clergyman, in his rooms in college, tell me that he had had 'a disappointing life'. He had said it angrily, in a whisky-thickened voice. It had been impressive, though not precisely moving, when he said it: on the spot, he was sincere, he meant what he said. But he had a reason for bursting out: he was explaining to himself (and incidentally to me) why he proposed not to do a good turn to another man. I didn't believe that even he thought continuously of his life in terms like that. He enjoyed his bits of power in the college: he enjoyed moving from his sessions with the whisky bottle to his prophecies of catastrophe. Certainly a biographer – in the unlikely event of his ever having one – could have summarised his existence in his own phrase. It was objectively true. I doubted if it seemed so to himself for hours together. Even as he was speaking to me, his vitality was still active and hostile, he still was capable of dreaming that, by a miracle, his deserts might even now be given him.

Like most of us, he occasionally thought of his life as a progress or a history. Then he could dispose of it by his ferocious summing-up. That was on the cosmogonists' model which had occurred to me before: from $T = 0$, the big bang, the birth of Despard-Smith, to $T = 75$, the end of things, the death of Despard-Smith. A history. A disappointing history. But that wasn't the way in which he, or the rest of us, thought most frequently to himself about his life. There was another cosmogonists' model which, it seemed to me, was much closer to one's own life as lived. Continuous creation. A slice disappeared, was replaced again. Something was lost, something new came in. All the time it looked to oneself as though there was not much change, nor deterioration, nor journey towards an end. Didn't each of our lives, to ourselves as we lived them, seem, much more often than not, like a process of continuous creation?

So, when Austin Davidson in his last illness dismissed the themes which had preoccupied him for a lifetime (except for his game of gambling: 'If I knew I was going to die tomorrow,' he once said, 'I should still want to hear the latest Stock Exchange quotations'), he found others which filled their place: and the days of solitariness, though they might be, and often were, bitter, had their own kind of creation. Even studying his ankles, watching in detail the changes in his physical state, was a fresh awakening of interest, petty if you like, but in its fashion a revival. That was as true for him as it was for my mother, also talking of her ankles in her last illness. Yes, that was a singular outburst of the process of continuous creation. Themes of a lifetime wore themselves out: but we weren't left empty, the resolution wasn't as tidy as that, somehow the psychic heart went on pumping, giving one a new or transformed lease of existence – perhaps restricted, but more concentrated because of that.

Before the operational experience and in the bedroom since, I had been discovering this for myself. In fact, it was something each of us had to discover for himself: you couldn't reach it by empathy, it was too unfamiliar, and perhaps too disconcerting, for that. Not long ago, in full health, I dismissed the third and slightest of the themes – different from Davidson's – which had preoccupied me, the concern, partly voyeuristic, partly conscientious, for political things. That dismissal was final, I didn't doubt it: but now I could imagine, not playing the chess game of politics in any shape or form, but – if a cause or even a whim impelled me – raising my voice with a freedom which I hadn't known before.

Something similar was true of the second theme, which was the kinds of love. Sexual love, parental love (so different that we confused ourselves by giving them the same name), they had never let me go: and often my public behaviour had seemed to me like the performance of a stranger. A pretty good performance, since on the level of action I had some of my temperament under control. Well, those kinds of love – I thought of the last talks with Margaret and my son – were creating within themselves something new, in part unforeseeable by me. Not in marriage, perhaps defying fate we should both think that: but certainly in my relation with my son. I hadn't any foreknowledge of what we should be saying to each other in ten years' time, if I lived so long. That wasn't distressing, but curiously exciting, the more so since that date of 28 November. It was as though I were quite young again, having to learn, with the sense, on the whole a pleasurable sense, of surprise ahead, what a human relation was like.

Third and last, myself alone. My own solitude, different from Austin Davidson or anyone else's. In so much we are all alike: but in one's solitude one is unique. I had been confronted by mine, since the operation, more than in all my life before. In a fashion that had astonished me. And given me a sense of change, and also a kind of perplexed delight, for which I had been totally unprepared. Somehow that was a delight too, as though I had suddenly seen a horizon wide open in front of my eyes.

A clock was striking somewhere outside the hospital. I didn't count the strokes, but there might have been twelve. I was sleepy by now, and turned on to my side. As often immediately before sleep, faces came, as if from a vague distance, into the field of vision under the closed lids: one came very clear and actual, nearly a dream, not yet a dream. It was a face which hadn't any waking significance for me, the matey comedian's face of a barrister acquaintance, Ted Benskin.

CHAPTER XXIV

AN UNDEFEATED VISITOR

NEXT day (for by this time the press had done its work and so, I guessed, had gossip) I was dividing potential visitors into sheep and goats, those I wanted to see and those I didn't. Among the goats, to be kept out with firmness, were those whose motives for inspecting me didn't need much examination – such as Whitman, my back-bencher acquaintance, who was presumably anxious to see that I was safely incapacitated, or Edgar Hankins, looking for a last personal anecdote to put into one of his elegiac post-mortems.

On the other hand, Rosalind was to be welcomed and, a somewhat more surprising enquirer, Lester Ince. Rosalind entered during the morning, bearing more flowers from her husband and, after she had kissed me and sat down, spreading her own aura of Chanel.

'Well, old thing. You don't look too bad.' She had never given up either the slang of her youth or the indomitable flatness of our native town.

How was she? She couldn't grumble. And Azik? He was on one of his business trips. Still, there were compensations. What did she mean? She usually got a present when he went abroad. With lids modestly downcast, with a smile that might have been either furtive or salacious, she held out the second finger of her right hand. On it gleamed a splendid emerald.

'What do you think that cost?' she said, and explained, again modestly: 'I had to know for the sake of the insurance.'

'A good many thousand.'

'Fifteen,' said Rosalind, with simple triumph.

What about her daughter? No, Rosalind didn't see much of her. The divorce would soon be through. Was Muriel intending to marry again? 'She never tells me anything,' Rosalind replied, hurt, aggrieved. She recaptured some of her spirit when she switched to young David. 'He's a different kettle of fish. He tells me everything.'

'He won't always, you know.' Rosalind might be as hard as they came, a child of this world, or, in her own language, as tough as old boots; but there (as she had done already with her daughter) she could suffer as much as the rest of us.

'Perhaps he won't. But he's lovely now.'

Rosalind continued, as usual not frightened of the obvious. We were all getting older. It would be nice when she was an old lady to have a handsome young man to take her out. David would be twenty-one in nine years' time. 'And you know as well as I do,' said Rosalind, 'what that will make me.'

There were few square inches of Rosalind, except for her hair, which had been left to nature unassisted. Couturiers, jewellers, cosmetic-makers had worked for their money, and Azik had duly paid; yet she minded less than many people about growing old.

She also didn't appear to mind overmuch about my misadventures. She had known me so long, she took my continued existence for granted. So far as she showed an interest, she was inclined to blame Margaret, whom she had never liked, for neglecting me.

'You'll have to look after yourself, that's all,' she said. If I wanted any advice, there was always the 'old boy' (one of her appellations for Azik). After which, she said a crisp good-bye and departed like a small and elegant warship succeeded by a wash of scent.

That was still lingering on the air when, a couple of hours later, Lester Ince came in.

'Who's your girl-friend?' he said, sniffing, a leer on his cheerful pasty face. 'That's not Margaret's.'

Lester was one of those men who, solidly masculine, nevertheless were knowledgeable about all the appurtenances of femininity. It made other men more irritated with him, particularly as he seemed – incomprehensibly to them – to have his successes, including his present wife. I had been mildly surprised when I heard that he wanted to visit me. I was a good deal more surprised when he said that he had been thinking about me and had something to propose. He wasn't really a friend: he didn't object to me as vigorously as he did to Francis or my brother, but that wasn't specially high praise. Perhaps he would have been just as concerned if any acquaintance had run into physical trouble. Anyway, his proposal was down to earth. He was offering me Basset for my convalescence.

Although I hadn't the most fugitive intention of accepting (all I wanted was to be left undisturbed at home), I was touched, as one was by a bit of practical good nature: touched enough to pretend that I couldn't make up my mind. Of course, one had to be more apolaustic than I was to be fit for Basset. That was a view which Lester sternly repudiated. Compared with many others, he reproved me, it wasn't a *big house*: as the owner of

Chatsworth might point out that his establishment was diminutive by the side of Blenheim.

My second line of defence was that we couldn't help getting in their way. Lester bluffly answered that they would be leaving after Christmas anyway; they weren't prepared to endure another English winter. I was reflecting, when I first met Lester he was living with his first wife and family in a dilapidated house in Bateman Street: if I knew anything about Cambridge temperatures, the conjugal bedroom wouldn't get about fifty degrees most of the year, and Lester had found it satisfactory for his purposes. Now, however, he behaved like a frailer plant. He had recently acquired a place in the Bahamas. It would be very good for them, he assured me earnestly. Not only to escape the winter rigours, but because there was a danger in living in a house like Basset. They didn't want to become like *birds in a gilded cage*. And they proposed to avoid that danger, I tried to ask without expression, by having their own beach in the Bahamas? Lester gazed at me, also without expression.

After I had promised to give my answer about Basset when I got out of hospital, he explained that there was another great advantage about the new regime. He could rely on getting each winter free for work; he could sit there in the sun and wouldn't be disturbed. It was time he made a start on another book. It was going to be a long-term project. Several years; he didn't believe in premature publication. Subject? Nathaniel Hawthorne and the New England moral climate.

When at tea-time I told Margaret about that conversation, we looked at each other dead-pan. He was the kind of visitor who ought to be encouraged, she said. No strain. Off-handed benevolence. But he used to be a humorist. Was all this a piece of misguided humour? If it were, I said, he deserved his fun. No, Margaret decided, she couldn't remember, even in his unregenerate days, Lester being humorous about himself.

About six o'clock she left, and I was feeling peaceful. No more visitors that day, except my brother Martin after dinner. I went back to a novel I had been reading, a Simenon, and I put Lester's moral discrimination out of my thoughts.

In a few minutes, a knock on the door. A peremptory double knock. Before I had said 'come in', Ronald Porson lurched into the room.

'How in God's name did you get in?' I cried, with something less than grace. I didn't want to be disturbed: I was irritated, I had given instructions that only those whose names were cleared should be sent up.

Porson gave one of his involuntary winks, right eyelid dropping down towards his cheek: the left side of his face twitched in sympathy. As a result, just as when first I met him, back in the early thirties, he produced an effect which was conspiratorial, friendly and remarkably *louche*. As usual, he was smelling of liquor and his speech was slurred.

'I suppose I can help myself, can't I ?' He had already caught sight of the bottle on the chest of drawers.

'Yes, do,' I said without enthusiasm, and repeated: 'How did you get in ?'

Porson turned back with his glass, winked again, this time perhaps less involuntarily, and sat down in the other chair. He was wearing his Old Etonian tie, which he – unlike my former colleague Gilbert Cooke – used only on special occasions. The rest of his appearance was more dilapidated than his normal, and in that respect the standard was very high. Cuffs frayed, buttons off waistcoat, shoes dirty, hair straggling, face puffed out with broken veins. Yet, though he was now seventy-two or three, he did not look his age, as though the battered ruleless life had acted – as it had done also with George Passant, in both cases much to the disapproval of more proper persons – as a kind of preservative and given them an air, among the ruins of their physique, of something like happiness and youth.

Actually Porson had, ever since I first knew him, moved from one catastrophe to another, with a seemingly inevitable and unrelieved decline such as didn't happen to many men. To begin with, he was making a living at the Bar. That soon dropped away, owing to drink, his tendency to patronise everyone he met becoming more aggressive and overpowering the more he failed, and perhaps – for those were less tolerant days – to rumours about his sexual habits. Then he ran through his money and you could trace his progress as his address in London changed. The first I remembered was that of a modestly opulent flat off Portland Place. After that Pimlico, Fulham Road, Earls Court, Notting Hill Gate, stations of descent. At the present time, so far as I knew, he was living in a bed-sitting-room in Godfrey Ailwyn's parish, and the priest and I both guessed he kept alive on national assistance. How he paid for his drink I didn't understand, although it was a long time since I had seen him quite sober. As he grew older, his picking-up became more rampant, and he had spent one term in gaol for importuning. Ailwyn reported that there had been other narrow squeaks.

None of this, none of it at all, prevented him from looking to the future with the expectation of a child wondering what would turn up on his birthday. The last time I had met him, he had been saying, using exactly the same phrase as my mother might have used, very strange for one like

Porson brought up in embassies, that there was still time for his ship to come home.

'How did you get in?'

'I've got one or two chums downstairs.' He winked again, and put a finger to the side of his nose, rather like Azik Schiff parodying himself. Then, suddenly angry, he burst out:

'Good chaps. Better than the crowd you waste your time with.'

'I dare say.' I was used to his temper. It was like handling a more-than-usually unpredictable bathroom geyser.

'Good chums. I've always said, you can get anywhere if you've got good chums.'

Now he was swinging between the maudlin and the accusatory.

'You can't deny. I've always got anywhere I wanted, haven't I?'

In a sense it was true. He had been seen in places where none of the rest of us could ever have had the entrée. Some people could explain it only by assuming a kind of homosexual trade union or information network. Ailwyn had once suggested that he had escaped worse trouble because of a contact in the local C.I.D. Not that that had prevented Ronald Porson, when he found himself in more conventional circles, from denouncing 'Jews and Pansies' as the source of national degeneration. With those he trusted, though, he tended to concentrate on the racial element.

'Well, I'm here, aren't I?' he accosted me, hands on knees. 'Do you know why?'

After I had failed to reply, he said, accusatory again:

'My boy, I'm here to give you a bit of advice.'

'Are you?'

'You haven't always taken my advice. You might have done better for yourself if you had.'

'It's a bit late now,' I began, but firmly he interrupted me.

'It'll be too late unless you listen to me for once. I'm going to give you a bit of advice. You'd better take it. *You're not to enter this hospital again.*'

'It's a perfectly good hospital.'

'It's the best hospital in London,' he shouted, getting angrier as he agreed with me. 'But, damn your soul, it's not the best for you.'

'I've got no grumbles—'

'I tell you, damn you, it's not the best for you. I know.'

'How can you know?'

'It's no use talking to people who only believe in what they can blasted well touch and see.' For an instant he was raging about E.S.P. Then he said, calming himself down, with a look of patient condescension:

'Well, let's try something that you understand. I suppose you admit that you nearly passed out last Friday. As near as damn it. Or a bloody sight nearer. You admit that, don't you?'

'Of course I do.'

'You haven't any option.' He spoke indulgently, contemptuously. 'And what would have been the use of your blasted reputation then?'

I wanted to stop listening, but his face came nearer, bullying, insistent. The left side was convulsed by a seismic twitch.

'It's no use making any bones about it. You know as well as I do. You did pass out last Friday. You've taken that in, haven't you?'

I nodded.

'You're the luckiest man I know. You won't have the same luck next time.'

Again I was trying to put him off, but he overbore me:

'You mustn't come into this hospital again, you understand?'

He added: 'I know you mustn't. I *know*.'

'I'll try not to.'

He stared full-eyed at me, triumphant. He was certain he had made an impression.

'Of course, my boy, *I'm* thinking of you. *You* ought to think of some of the chaps here. In the hospital. What the hell do you fancy they were doing last Friday?'

He paused, and went on.

'I'll tell you. They were peeing their pants. They were afraid it would get into the papers. If I'd been in your place, the papers mightn't have got hold of it. Somehow they know your name.'

(I thought later that that had been a minor mystery to Porson for thirty years. But at the time this was a reflection I hadn't the nerve to make. He had frightened me. To begin with, it had been a *frisson*, the kind of shiver which my mother called 'someone walking across her grave'. Now it was worse than that.)

'It wouldn't have been good for the place,' Porson said, 'if you'd gone out feet first.'

'Well, I didn't.'

'They weren't to know that, were they? I'll tell you something else. They didn't breathe easy until a long time after you'd been brought back. They've told me that themselves. You were all settled down and comfortable and having a good night's rest before they felt sure there wasn't going to be a funeral after all.'

'I hope they stood themselves a drink.'

'I've done that, my boy. They know you're an old friend.'

Later on, I had another reflection, that I had never discovered who 'they' were. Certainly males. Certainly not doctors. I guessed, but never knew for sure, that they must have been porters or medical orderlies. At the time, feeling the sweat prickling at my temples, I had just one concern, which was to get him out of the room.

'Good,' I said. 'You go and stand them another one for me.' I told him where to find my wallet, and soon he was duly pocketing a five-pound note. But even then, enjoying the conversation, he wasn't eager to go. Pressed, I had to invent and whisper another pretext, of the kind that Ronald Porson couldn't resist. A visitor was coming soon – no one knew, my wife didn't know – I couldn't tell even him the name, he'd understand. With a look, both confidential and jeering, of ultimate complicity, Porson weaved towards the door, saying at the threshold:

'So long, my boy. I hope you've been listening to what I said.'

Yes, I had. I wiped sweat away, but I might have come out of a hot bath. I was ashamed that I couldn't be steadier: why should my nerves let me down, just because old Porson blustered away? For days past, ever since the first fright left me free, I had listened to everyone without even a superstitious qualm. I hadn't been putting on a front: I hadn't needed to. Definitions of death, theological death, the different degrees of uneasiness with which people, my wife, my son, approached me. I had become something of an expert on relative uneasiness. Nothing had plucked a nerve. Then, after all that, after the visits of those closest to me, came Porson. Drunk, of course. Officious, as he had been ever since I first met him. Nothing new. I had been through it all before. But he had frightened me.

There was no denying, I had felt the chill. If I could have understood why, I might have thrown it off. I had no clue at all. The thought of Porson's cronies, down in the hospital basement, counting my chances – what was so bad about that? (In cold blood afterwards, I doubted if they had been all that wrought up. Porson enjoyed his overheated fancy. They must have had a little excitement, no more.) There was nothing bad, or even remotely unnatural about it. Yet, when Porson told me, it brought back the dread.

Listening to him, I felt it as on the first night. Now he had gone, I was searching inward, testing how strong it was. It was exactly like the days after the first eye-operation, when I was worried by each speck or floater in the field of vision, wondering whether the black edge was coming back. The dread. It would be hard to have that as a regular visitation. No, perhaps it was not quite like the first night. Perhaps there was already a spectator behind my mind. It wasn't only the fright and nothingness.

Still, as I tried to eat the hospital supper, I was waiting, I didn't know what for, perhaps for the chill again, or some sign that I wasn't in the clear. I was glad that Martin was due to visit me that night.

When he arrived, though, I was for an instant disappointed. For he had brought his daughter Nina with him, enquiring about me in her fashionable whisper as she kissed me, her face hiding behind her hair. As a rule, I should have welcomed her. More and more she seemed the most agreeable girl in Charles's circle, the one who was most likely to make a man happy and enjoy her marriage. Nevertheless, in her presence I couldn't talk directly to my brother. Which was probably, I imagined, why he had brought her. It was a typical quiet tactic of his, meaning that there was nothing good to say about Pat and that Martin wished to evade any discussion. Also, now that Martin at last was compelled to show traces of realism about his son, he was turning to the daughter whom he had so long neglected. He even induced her to tell me about her music: her teachers were certain that she (quite unlike her brother, Martin might have been thinking) would become a good professional.

Martin had seen me once since the operation, enough to satisfy himself, but not alone. Now he was watching me.

'How are you?' he said.

'All right.'

'Only all right?'

'A little tired of death-watch beetles.'

'You've given them a first-class opportunity, you know.' Martin was speaking with a tucked-in smile, but he and I were signalling to each other, and probably Nina didn't recognise the code. 'Anyone special?'

'Old Ronald Porson's been improving the occasion.'

'When?'

'Oh, not long ago.'

Martin nodded. 'That must have been pleasant for you.'

'He was telling me about the preparations downstairs for my demise.'

A slight pause. In his misleadingly soft voice, Martin said:

'It's high time we began to make modest preparations for his.'

'He's inclined to think that he'll outlast me.'

'Thoughtful of him.'

'After all,' I said, 'he'd be the first to point out that he very nearly did.'

'I'm sure he would.'

'Nothing that rejuvenates an old man more, my father-in-law used to say, than to contemplate the death of someone younger.'

'Naturally,' said Martin. Then casually, as though in an afterthought of no interest, he said: 'By the by, did you want to see that old sod?' He didn't explain to his daughter that he meant Porson.

'No. He gate-crashed.'

'I imagined so. Well, I'll see that that doesn't happen again.'

I looked at my brother, face controlled, eyes dark and hard. I speculated as to whether Nina knew that he was smouldering with anger.

'Never mind,' I said. 'I can take him.'

'I can't see any reason why you should. I can see several reasons why you shouldn't.'

That was all. Affectionate good-byes. I expected that it would be some time before Martin left the hospital. For myself, I didn't abstain from my sleeping-pills that night, and wasn't long awake. Then I woke in the middle of the night, feeling calm. Immediately I waited for the fright to grip me. But it didn't: at least, not enough to be more than a reminder, the kind of reminder of mortality that came at any age, from youth upwards, and wasn't the real thing. Testing the black edge, I forced back thoughts of Porson. No, his voice bullied me in a vacuum, I recalled occasions long ago when he had lost a case and still took the offensive against everyone round him, not to himself defeated. I wondered if Martin had discovered who it was that let him in.

CHAPTER XXV

OUTSIDE THE HOSPITAL

THE morning that Margaret came to fetch me home, I had been in that bedroom for eleven days. On the afternoon before, she, who knew how institutions gave me more than my normal claustrophobia, and that I didn't make fine distinctions between prisons and hospitals, they were just places which shut one in, asked how long it felt. I said that often it had seemed no time at all. She wasn't sure whether I was being perverse. But I had already told her of my relapse during Porson's visit. Perhaps, also perversely, that had given her confidence in my state of mind. She hadn't quite trusted the complete serenity, the looking back to 28 November as though that eliminated disquiets past, present and to come: now she knew that the serenity could be broken, she trusted it more.

Dressed, wearing my one club-tie, the M.C.C., as though in retrospective homage to Ronald Porson, I said good-bye to the matron, the ward sister, a posse of nurses. I caught sight of myself in the looking-glass, grinning cordially like an ageing public man.

Walking downstairs, out to the steps in front of the hospital, I was still wearing a blindfold over the left eye, and hadn't stereoscopic vision when I looked down at the steps: so that Margaret, taking my arm, had to guide me, and as I probed with my feet I looked infirm. Infirm enough for a photographer, on the hospital steps, to ask if I wanted help: which didn't prevent him snapping a picture of the descent. When we came into the open air, there were a dozen photographers waiting, shouting like a new estate of the realm, telling us to stand still, move, smile. There was the whirr of a television camera. 'Look as if you're happy,' someone ordered Margaret. 'Talk to each other!' Worn down by this contemporary discipline, we muttered away. What we were actually saying, beneath the smiles, was what fiend out of hell had leaked the time. Someone had tipped off the press. Pat? One of Porson's 'chums'?

As we climbed into the car, I looked back at the hospital façade. Nostalgia for a place where I had been through that special night? No, not in the least. It was different from occasions when I was young, and said good-bye to stretches of unhappiness. When I left the local government office, after my last morning as a clerk, I felt, although or because I had been miserable and humiliated there for years, something like an ache, as though regret for a bond that had been snapped. A little later, when I was a young man, and had been sent to the Mediterranean to recover from an illness, I had, driving to the station for the journey home, looked back at the sea (I could remember now the smell of the arbutus after rain). I had been desolate there, afraid that I might not get better: going away, I felt a distress much more painful than that outside the old office, a yearning, as though all I wanted in this life was to remain by the sea-shore and never be torn away.

None of that now, though this had been the worst time of the three. I regarded the hospital with neutrality; it might have been any other red-brick nineteenth-century building. As one grew older, perhaps the nervous rackings of one's youth died down. Or perhaps, and with good reason, one wasn't so frightened of the future. After all one had had some practice contemplating futures and then living them.

It was pleasant, anxiety-free, to be going home.

PART THREE

ENDS AND BEGINNINGS

CHAPTER XXVI

DISPENSATION

LYING in bed in the hospital, set free by the talisman of 28 November, I hadn't so much as wondered how long this state would last. If I had even wanted to wonder so, it would have been a false freedom. And whatever it was (it might make nonsense of a good deal that I expected or imagined), it was not false. Fortuitous, if you like, but not false.

It transferred itself easily enough into my everyday life, as soon as I got back. In a fashion which would have seemed curiously unfair, if they had known about it, to those who thought that all along I had been luckier than I deserved. For the bad times got dulled, shrugged off as though if 28 November had gone the other way they wouldn't have existed. But, by a paradoxical kind of grace, the reverse didn't apply, the dispensation wasn't symmetrical: on the contrary, the good times became sharper. Shortly after I left hospital, I published a book which I liked and which fell, not exactly flat, but jaggedly. If that had happened in early November, it would have cost me some bad days. As it was, though I didn't pretend to be indifferent (changes in mood are not so complete as that), I had put it behind me almost as soon as it occurred. Shortly afterwards – and this was just as surprising – I found myself revelling, without any barricade of sarcasm or touching wood, in a bit of praise.

There had been a time when I used to declare, with a kind of defiance: you had to enjoy your joys, and suffer your sufferings. As I knew well enough, I had more talent for the latter. I had managed to subjugate the depressive streak in action, and conceal it from others and sometimes myself, but it was there half-hidden: it wasn't entirely an accident that I could guess when Roy Calvert was going to swing from the manic into its other phase. With me, what for Roy was manic showed itself only as a kind of high spirits or an excessive sense of expectation: most of the time, I had to watch, as better and robuster characters had to watch, for the alternate phase. Now the balance had been tilted, and I felt myself closer than I had ever been before to people whom I had once in secret thought thick-skinned and prosaic: people who weren't menaced by melancholy and who were better than I was at enjoying themselves.

It was a singular dispensation to overtake one at sixty, faintly comic, humbling and yet comforting.

When Margaret's father had died, which he did in his sleep in the January of 1966, two months after my operation, she and I were alone together as in the first days of marriage. More alone, for then she had been looking after Maurice in his infancy. Just as when we returned to the flat the previous autumn, it was both a treat and strange to be there by our-selves. We spun time out, lengthening the moments, making the most of them. Work was over for me now by the early afternoon: after that, we were alone and free. I had got rid of any duties outside the home. We had time to ourselves, as we hadn't when we were first married. We were able to look at each other, not as though it were the first time (when one sees nothing but one's own excitement), but as though we were on holiday, waking up fresh in a hotel.

In another sense, it was as fresh when I walked with my son on spring evenings in the park. I was listening to him, not as though he had changed, but as though something had changed between us. Not that I was less interested in him, or in his friends. Actually, I had become more so, but in a different fashion. I was less engaged in competing with them, or proving to Charles that they were wrong. My brother Martin had once said, after his renunciation: 'People matter: relations between them don't matter much.' Whether he ever thought of that, in his troubles with his own son, I didn't know: if so it must have seemed a black joke against himself. But it was somewhere near the way (so I thought, and didn't have a superstitious tremor) in which I was now taking pleasure in Charles's company. I was interested in him and the rest of them, excited, stimulated by their energies and hopes: it was like being given a slice of life to watch and to draw refreshment from, so long as one could keep from taking part oneself.

It didn't seem like an ageing man's interest in the flow of life, or Francis Getliffe's patriarchal delight in his children and grandchildren and those of his friends, the delight of life going on. It didn't even seem so much like a bit of continuous creation, in which through being en-grossed in other lives one was making a new start for oneself. It might, I thought casually, have been all of those things: but if it was I didn't care. I felt closer than that, through being given a privileged position, having those energies under my eyes: it was much more like being engaged with my own friends at the same age, except that I – with my anxieties, perturbations, desires and will – had been satisfactorily (and for my own liberation) removed.

It was at the end of the Easter vacation, when Charles had returned from another of his trips, that he got into the habit of asking me out for an evening walk. He was home only for a week; each day about half past five, active, springy on his feet, he looked at me with eyebrows raised, and we went into the park for what became our ritual promenade. Out by the Albion Gate: across the grass, under the thickening trees, along the path to the Serpentine, by the side of the Row to the Achilles statue, back along the eastern verge towards Marble Arch. Once I had walked that way, less equably, with Roy Calvert. But that I scarcely remembered, much less told Charles. Instead I said, after the second trip, that we might have been two old clubmen going through their evening routine. Charles grinned companionably, and next day started precisely the same course.

His conversation, however, was not much like an old clubman's. He was relaxed, because I was the right distance from him: the right distance, that is, for him to talk and me to listen. I took in more about his friends than I had done before, and believed more, now that I wasn't conducting a dialectic with him. Yes, they were more serious than I had let myself admit. Their politics (his less than the others) might be utopian, but they were their own. They were probably no better or no worse thought out than ours had been, but they came from a different ground.

The results could be curiously different. Charles and his circle were more genuinely international than any of us had been. The minor nationalisms seemed to have vanished quite. They were not even involved in Europe, though most of them had travelled all over it. It was the poor world that captured their imagination: the Grand Tour had to be uncomfortable and also squalid nowadays, said Charles with a sarcastic smile. That was what he had been conducting in Asia before he was seventeen, and this present vacation he had been rounding it off in Africa.

They weren't specially illusioned. They didn't imagine an elysium existing here and now upon this earth, as young men and women of their kind in the thirties sometimes imagined Russia or less often the United States. It was true, dark world-views didn't touch them much. They might hear – in that year 1966 and later – people like Francis Getliffe and me saying that objectively the world looked grimmer than at any time in our lives. They might analyse and understand the reasons which made us say so. But they didn't in the end believe it. They were alive for anything that was going to happen. That was bound to be so: you live in your own time.

Listening to Charles those evenings, I thought that, not only did his friends' opinions have more to them than I had been willing to grant, but so had he. He seemed more of a sport – that is, less like me or Martin, less like anyone on Margaret's side – than I had believed. The family patterns didn't fit. He wasn't so easy to domesticate. There were contradictions in him that I hadn't seen before.

This was striking home all through that week: on one of the last evenings, I could not help but see it clear. We had just crossed the bridge over the water: it was a dense and humid April night, but with no clouds in the darkening sky; Charles suddenly began to press me about, of all subjects, the works of Tolkien. I turned towards him, ready to say something sharp, such as that he ought to know that I had no taste for fancy. His eyes left mine, looked straight ahead.

I met his profile, dolichocephalic, straight-nosed, hair curling close to his head. On the moment he looked unfamiliar, not at all how I imagined him to look. Curious: feature by feature, of course, the genes had played their part, the hair was Martin's, the profile Austin Davidson's: but the result was strange. So strange that I might have been gazing at a young man I didn't recognise, much less understand. The sharp repartee dropped away, I said that naturally I would give this favourite of his a try.

Curious, I was thinking again. He was in many respects more concentrated and practical than I had been at his age, or maybe was now: almost certainly, when he wanted something, he was more ruthless. Yet, if I had no taste for fancy, he had enough for two: whimsies, fantasies, they hadn't been left behind in childhood. With him they co-existed, and would continue to co-exist, with adult desires and adult fulfilments: he was one of those, or would become one, who had the gift of being able to feel guilty with Dostoevsky, innocent with hobbits, passionately insistent with a new girl-friend, all on the same day.

Good, he was saying affectionately, as I promised to read the book.

As we walked on, other contradictions of his became as clear. He had proved his own kind of courage. Whether he had set out to prove it to himself, no one knew: but the fact was, none of my contemporaries, not even those as adventurous as the young Francis Getliffe, would at sixteen have contemplated setting out on solitary expeditions such as his. As for me, it would have seemed about as plausible – for reasons of pennilessness in addition to physical timidity – as trying to round the Horn. Of course, most of Charles's friends travelled further than we did: but he was the one who had made it into a trial of nerve. Not nerve, just patience, he explained with a straight face. All calculated and singularly deliberate, as though he had reverted to one of those nineteenth-century Englishmen with private means, scholarly tastes and inordinate self-will.

And yet, he was nervous, more so than most of us, in another old-fashioned, even a primitive sense. When he had arrived back safe after his second trip and had produced some understatements which were not so modest as they sounded, I asked him how much I should have to pay him to sleep (*a*) in a haunted house, (*b*) in a graveyard. Again straight-faced, he said: 'As for (*a*), more than you could afford. For (*b*), no offers accepted. And I suppose you'd do either for half a bottle of Scotch. Or less. Wouldn't you?'

He was being, as usual, truthful about himself. He was capable of getting frightened by ghost-stories. There were still occasions, after he had been reading, when he carefully forgot to turn off his bedroom lamp.

Walking by his side – lights were coming on in St George's Hospital – I mentioned, as though by free association, the name of Gordon Bestwick. This was a friend of his, whom I had met, but only casually, at Christmas time. Charles, protective about any of his circle, wasn't easy about Gordon's health, and had been suggesting that I should go to Cambridge next term, and meet him again, to see what my opinion was.

'Why did you think of him?' said Charles, clear-voiced.

'Oh, it just occurred to me that he might be more rational than you are.'

Charles chuckled.

'I've told you, he's a bit like you. He's *our* Bazarov, you know.'

That was a complicated private reference. Charles must have picked up from Francis Getliffe, or more probably his wife, the impression that I made on the Marches when they first befriended me. A poor young man: positive: impatient with the anxieties of the rich. Making them feel over-delicate, over-nurtured, frail by the side of a new force. In fact, their impression was in most respects fallacious. My character seemed to them more all-of-a-piece and stronger just because I was poor and driven on: in the long run, much of the frailty was not on their side but mine. Still, they called me after Turgenev's hero and for a while made a similar legend about me. And that was what Charles and his circle were duplicating in their reception of Gordon Bestwick.

Charles had met him at Trinity, both of them scholars in their first year. He came from a lorry driver's family in Smethwick. He was extremely clever; according to Charles, brought up in one of the English academic hothouses, at least as clever as anyone he had known at school. Bestwick was reading economics and had much contempt for the soft subjects, which sounded Bazarov-like enough. I had talked to him only for a few minutes, but no one could have missed noticing his talent. Otherwise he had some presence without being specially prepossessing, and if Charles hadn't forced his name upon me, I doubted whether I should have gone out of my way to see him again.

That evening, as we were turning parallel to Park Lane, Charles reiterated his praise.

'He may easily be the ablest of us,' he said. He was pertinacious, prepared to be boring, about someone he believed in. 'He's certain to be a very valuable character.'

He added, with an oblique smile:

'He's even a very valuable member of the cell.'

They thought of themselves – it didn't need saying – as student revolutionaries: Charles knew that I knew: though he, on that October night when I told him of what he called my abdication, had defined with political accuracy where he stood.

He was gazing to our left, where, in the west, over the London smoke, one of the first stars had come out. Charles regarded it with simple pleasure, just as my father might have done. I recalled night walks when I was in trouble, getting some peace from looking at the stars.

'Old Gordon', Charles remarked with amusement, 'says that we're fooling ourselves about space travel. We shall never get anywhere worth while. He says that science fiction is the modern opium of the people.'

He added:

'Sensible enough for you, isn't he?'

During that conversation, and the others we had that week, Charles did not leave out the name of Muriel. He brought it in along with a dozen more, without either obtruding it or playing it down. He spoke of her as though she were one of the inner group (which included not only school and Cambridge friends, but also one or two studying in London, such as his cousin Nina), but he didn't single her out or ask a question about her.

CHAPTER XXVII

DISCUSSION OF SOMEONE ABSENT

WHEN Muriel herself invited me to her house one evening, shortly after Charles had gone back to Cambridge, she began in very much the same tone as he had used of her: but there came a time when she was not quite so cautious.

She had asked me round for a drink before dinner, on the first Monday of the month, which happened to be a day when Margaret was regularly occupied with her one and only charity. I had been to Chester Row once before, to a party the preceding summer: I had forgotten that Muriel's house was a long way up the road, near the church, not far from where Matthew Arnold used to repose himself, all seventeen stone of him.

The door was smelling of fresh paint, there was a tub of wallflowers outside, a flower-box under the ground-floor windows, everything burnished and neat. The housekeeper told me, in a decorous whisper, as though she had been infected by the house's hush, that Mrs Calvert was waiting for me in the drawing-room upstairs (Muriel had reverted to her maiden name the day that the divorce came through).

In fact, she was standing at the end of the first-floor corridor.

'How very good of you to come, Uncle Lewis,' she called out, light and clear. 'It's such a long way to drag you, isn't it?'

It was not much more than a mile. As usual, following her into the drawing-room, I was put off by her politeness, which seemed like a piece of private fun.

She led me to an armchair beside the window, enquired what she should give me to drink and precisely how I liked it, fitted me with coffee-table, glass and cigarettes, and then sat down opposite me in a hard-backed upright chair. She was dressed with quakerish simplicity, white blouse, dark skirt: and the skirt, though it showed an inch or two of thigh, looked long that year on a woman of twenty-three.

'I'm so sorry that Aunt Meg couldn't come too,' she said. 'It's one of her trust days, isn't it? I ought to have remembered that, it's very bad of me. One oughtn't to be careless like that, ought one?'

It was only then that I suspected she hadn't been so careless. It hadn't occurred to me that she wanted me by myself, or could have any motive for it.

'Do please tell Aunt Meg that I am dreadfully sorry. I want to see her so much.'

Muriel fixed me with an intense, undeviating gaze. I had admired her acute green eyes (which others called hazel, or even yellow) before, but I hadn't met them full on until now. They had a slight squint, such as was required from prize Siamese cats before the trait was bred out. It might have been a disfigurement or even comic, but on the spot it made her eyes harder to escape: more than that, it made one more aware of her presence.

Self-consciously (I was more self-conscious with this girl than I was used to being) I looked round the room.

'How fine this is,' I said.

That was a distraction, but also the truth. It was an L-shaped room, running the whole length of the house, the front windows giving on the street, back window on to her strip of garden, from which an ash-tree extended itself, three storeys high. Edging through the same back window came the last of the sunlight, falling on two pictures, by painters I didn't know, but whom, I thought, she might be helping.

'I'm so glad you like it,' said Muriel. 'I do think it's rather good.'

'We all envy you, you know.'

She gave a slight shrug. 'The Victorian middle classes did themselves pretty well, didn't they?'

'So do you,' I replied.

She didn't like that. For an instant, she was frowning, her face looked less controlled, less young. Her self-possession for once seemed shaken. Then, springing up, graceful, she cried:

'Look! You've never seen the house properly, have you, Uncle Lewis? Please let me show you, now.'

Show me she did, like a house agent taking round a possible though unknowledgeable buyer. It was one of those tall narrow-fronted houses common in that part of London, built (said Muriel precisely) between 1840 and 1845. Built for what kind of family? She wouldn't guess. Professional? A doctor's, who had his practice in the grand houses close by?

Anyway, it must have been more immaculate now than ever in the past. Basement flat at garden level, three rooms for the housekeeper, as spotless-fresh, as uninhabited-looking, as Muriel's drawing-room. Dining-room on the ground floor, table laid for one, silver shining on the rosewood. Second floor, Muriel's bedroom, scent-smelling, cover smooth in the evening light: as she stood beside me, she said there was another room adjacent, which we would come back to – 'that is, if you can bear any more'.

She led the way up to the top storey, light-footed as an athlete. The main room was the nursery and I could hear infantile chortles. She hesitated outside the door. I said that I liked very small children. 'No, forgive me, he'll be having a feed.' Instead she showed me two bedrooms on the same floor. That's where she could put people up, she said. What people, I was wondering. Quick-eyed, she seemed to read my thoughts. American students who were forced out of Berkeley, she said. Those were the last two. They had something to teach us.

She climbed up some iron steps to a balcony garden: she was slim-waisted, she looked slight, but she was nothing like as fragile as she seemed. She gazed across the roofs and gardens before she descended, and took me downstairs again to the second floor. Then she opened the door next to her bedroom: 'Would you really mind sitting here just for a little while?'

It was something between a boudoir and a study. There were plenty of bookshelves: there was a cupboard from which she brought another tray of drinks, though as before she didn't take one herself. But also there were what appeared to be other cupboards for her dresses, a long mirror, a smaller looking-glass in front of a dressing-table. I had noticed another, more sumptuous dressing-table in her bedroom: but I guessed that it was here she spent most of her time. It smelt of her scent, which was astringent, not heady: no doubt Lester Ince would have known the name. On the desk stood a large photograph of Azik Schiff and another which later I should have recognised as of Che Guevara, though at the time I had scarcely seen the face. That night I was wondering if this might be a lover: it wasn't the only time that she sent me on a false direction. There was no picture of her mother, and none of her father, nor any reminder of him at all, except, very oddly, for a copy of the seventeenth-century engraving of our college's first court, hanging in obscurity on the far wall.

'I do hope I haven't tired you,' she said.

I said that it was a beautiful house. I went on: 'You're a lucky girl.'

'Do you really think I am, Uncle Lewis?' The question was deferential, but her eyes were once more staring me out.

'By most people's standards, yes, I think you are.'

'Some people's standards would be different, wouldn't they? They might think it was wrong for anyone like me to have all this.' Her eyes didn't move, but there was a twitch, unapologetic, sardonic, to her mouth. 'You couldn't tell me it wasn't wrong. Could you? It is, you know it, don't you?'

'I wasn't talking about justice,' I said. 'I was talking about you.'

'Isn't that rather old-fashioned of you, though?'

To say I wasn't provoked wouldn't be true. I heard my words get rougher.

'I don't know whether you're unhappy. But if you are, I do know that it's more tolerable to be unhappy in comfort. You try working behind a counter when you're miserable, and you'll see.'

'Aren't you being rather feminine, Uncle Lewis? You're reducing it all to personal things, you know. You can't believe they matter all that much—'

'They matter to most of us.'

'Not if one has anything serious to do.' Her manner was entirely cool. 'Perhaps you don't think I am serious, though. That would be rather old-fashioned of you again. I'm very very sorry, but it would. Because I've got plenty of money. Because I'm living a plushy bourgeois life – not so very different from yours, if I may say so. Then it's artificial if I don't accept this nice cosy world I'm living in. You don't trust me if I want to have a hand in getting rid of it and starting something better. You think I'm playing at being discontented, don't you? Isn't that it?'

I thought, she wasn't stupid, she was suspicious about me, her suspicions were shrewd. As I watched her face, disciplined except for the eye-flash, I had been reflecting on people like Dolfie Whitman, that invigilator of others' promotion. Philippe Égalité radical, his enemies had called him. Rich malcontents. I had known a good many. Some had seemed dilettantes, or else too obviously getting compensation for a private wound. Often they weren't the first allies you would choose to have on your side in a crisis. A few, though, were as unbending and committed as one could be. Such as the scientist Constantine or Charles March's wife. What about this young woman? I was mystified, I couldn't make any sort of judgment. I still had no idea why she wanted me in her house. Surely not to sit alone with her in her study, having an academic discussion on student protest, or any variety of New Left, or the place of women with large unearned incomes in radical movements?

It was time, I felt, to stop the fencing.

'I don't know you well enough to say.' I went on: 'You're cleverer than I thought.'

'Thank you,' she said, gravely, politely, imperturbably, as unruffled as if I had congratulated her on a new dress. It was the manner which I couldn't break through, and which had made me, not patronising as it might have sounded, but harsh and rude.

'For all I know,' I said, 'you may be absolutely in earnest.'

'It would be rather upsetting for you, wouldn't it,' she replied, 'if you found I was.'

'What do you hope for?'

She wasn't at all put off. Her reply was articulate, much what I had heard from friends of Charles's, less qualified and political than from Charles himself. This country, America, the world she knew, weren't good enough: there must be a chance of something better. The institutions (they sometimes called them structures) of our world had frozen everyone in their grip: they were dead rigid by now, universities, civil service, parliaments, the established order, the lot. One had to break them up. It might be destructive: you couldn't write a blueprint for the future: but it would be a new start, it would be better than now.

All that I was used to; the only difference was one thing she didn't say, which I was used to hearing. She didn't talk about 'your generation', and blame us for the existing structures and the present state of things. Whether that was out of consideration, or whether she was keeping her claws sheathed, I couldn't tell.

'What can you do about it? You yourself?'

The question was another attempt to break through. She didn't mind. Her reply was just as calm as before, and this time businesslike. Money was always useful. So was this house. She could help with the supply work. (I had a flickering thought of young women like her doing the same for the Spanish war and the 'party' thirty years before.) Of course she couldn't do much. In any sort of action, though, one had to do what came to hand: wasn't that true?

Yes, it was quite true. In fact, I fancied uneasily that I might have said it myself: and that she was impassively quoting it back at me.

'Why are you in it at all?'

The first flash of anger. 'You won't admit I believe in it, will you?'

It was my turn to be calm. 'I said before, you may be absolutely in earnest.'

'But you really think it's a good way to keep some men round me, don't you? It's a good way to keep in circulation, isn't it?'

The words were still precise, the face demure with a kind of false and taunting innocence. But underneath the smooth skin there was a storm of temper only just held back.

'I might even collect another husband, mightn't I? If I was lucky. Now that would be a reason for being in it, you'd accept that, wouldn't you?'

I said (she was suspicious of me again, this time the suspicion had gone wrong):

'It hadn't even occurred to me. I should have thought, if you did want another husband, you wouldn't have to go to those lengths, would you?'

She gave what for her was an open smile, like a woman, utterly confident with men, suddenly enjoying an off-hand, not over-flattering remark.

'But now you're talking about it,' I went on, 'I suppose you will get married again, some time?'

'I don't know,' she said. 'I just don't know.' Then she added, as though she had spoken too simply: 'It's the only thing I was brought up for, you see. And that isn't a point in its favour, particularly.'

In the same quiet, judicious tone she was blaming her mother for her education, being prepared for nothing but that, protected, watched over. In the quiet judicious tone she wasn't concealing that she disliked her mother – with not just a daughter's ambivalence or rebellion, but with plain dislike. If she hadn't been trained for the marriage stakes, she might have done something. Anyway she had made her own marriage. That hadn't been a recommendation for trying it again. She didn't refer to Pat with dislike, as she did her mother, but with detachment, not mentioning his name. She spoke of her marriage as though it had been an interesting historical event or an example of mating habits which she had happened to observe.

'I don't intend to make a mess of it again,' she said. 'But you needn't worry about me. I shan't die of frustration. I can look after myself.'

It seemed as though she was being blunt: but even when she seemed to be, and maybe was, trying to be direct, she could sound disingenuous at the same time. Was she suggesting, or stating, that she wasn't going to risk another marriage, but took men when she wanted them? Was that true in fact?

There had been a time when I thought the opposite. As I watched her getting rid of Pat, or as the centre of attraction at one of the previous summer's parties, it seemed to me that she might have had bad luck: the bad luck that goes with beauty. Not that her face was beautiful: people looked at her long nose, wide mouth, didn't know how to describe her. Pretty? Alluring? But she behaved like others whom everyone called beautiful. It wasn't good to be so. Those I had met – there were only two or three – had been unable to give love or else were frigid. It wasn't simply the shape of a face that made others decide that a woman had the gift of beauty. They had to feel some quality which set her apart and came from inside. There was nothing supernatural about it: it might very well be a kind of remoteness, a sensual isolation or a narcissism.

Whatever it came from, the gift of beauty – as the old Yeats knew too well – was about the last one would wish for a daughter.

When I had seen Muriel surrounded by Charles and his friends, attention brushing off her, she was behaving as though she need not look at them, but only at herself. As I said, I thought then that she had had that specific bad luck, or, if you like, that fairy's gift.

Now I had changed my mind. I didn't know much about her, there were things which I couldn't know: but I was fairly sure that she was less narcissistic than I had believed and, underneath the smooth, the some-times glacial front, a good deal more restless. She didn't radiate the hearty kind of sexuality that anyone could find in the presence of, for example, Hector Rose's new wife. But she had – I wasn't certain but I guessed – a kind of sexuality of her own. It might be hidden, conspiratorial, insinuating. Some man would discover it (I couldn't tell whether Pat had or not), and then would find the two of them in a sensual complicity. It wouldn't be hearty: it might even seem corrupt. But some man, not put off by whispers or secrets, enjoying the complicity, would find it. He might be fortunate or unfortunate, I couldn't guess that far.

I didn't like her. I never had: and, now that I had seen a little more, I didn't like her any better. She might be easier to love than to like: but, if that was what she induced, it was a bad prospect for her and anyone who did love her so. If I had been younger, I should have shied away.

Yet, in a curious sense, I respected her. Of course, her attraction had its effect on me as on others. But though that sharpened my attention, it didn't surround her with any haze or aura. She was there, visible and clear enough, not specially amiable, certainly not negligible. She was not much like anyone I had known. The links one could make with the past didn't connect with her. She was there in her own right.

Earlier on, as we climbed up and down the house, and again when she talked about the programme of action, she had mentioned Charles. Almost precisely as he had mentioned her, when it would have been artificial, or even noteworthy, not to do so.

Now, shortly after she had switched on the reading-lamp, which, throwing a pool of light upon the desk, also lit up both our faces, she asked a question. It was casual and matter-of-fact.

'By the way, do please tell me, what is Charles going to do?'

'What ever do you mean?'

She was smiling. 'Please tell me. I'm fairly good at keeping quiet.'

I said: 'I'm sure you are. But I've no idea what you mean.'

'Haven't you really?'

I shook my head.

She was still smiling, not believing me. To an extent, she was right not to believe.

'Well then, do forgive me. What is he going to do about his career?'

'I haven't the slightest idea.'

'But you must have.'

'I'm not certain that he has himself. If so, he hasn't told me.'

'But you have your own plans for him, haven't you?'

'None at all.'

She gazed at me, showing her scepticism, using her charm.

'You must have.'

'I'm not sure how well you know him—'

Her expression didn't alter, she was still intent on softening me.

' – it would be about as much use my making plans for him as it would have been for your father. But I haven't the faintest desire to, I haven't had since he was quite young.'

I told her, when he was a child, I watched his progress obsessively from hour to hour. Then I dropped it, determined that I wouldn't live my life again in him. Fortunately, now that I could see what he was really like. I didn't tell her, but now for me he existed, just as she did, in his own right. Embossed, just as persons external to oneself stood out. Like that, except perhaps for the organic bonds, the asymmetry that had emerged for moments in the hospital bedroom.

'That's very splendid,' said Muriel, 'but still you're not quite so simple as all that, are you?'

'I've learned a bit,' I said.

'But you haven't forgotten other things you've learned, I can't believe it. I've heard my father say' (by that she meant Azik Schiff, whereas a few minutes before I had been thinking of Roy Calvert) 'that you know as much about careers as any man in England.'

She went on:

'You won't pretend, I'm sure you won't, that you haven't thought what Charles ought to do. And whatever it is, you know the right steps, you can't get rid of what you've done yourself, can you?'

'I might be some use to one or two of his friends,' I said. 'Such as Gordon Bestwick. But not to him.'

'You're being so modest—'

'No, I know some things about him. And what I can do for him. After all, he's my son.'

She said: 'You love him, don't you?'

'Yes, I love him.'

She was totally still. Sitting there, body erect in the chair, she seemed not to have moved an involuntary muscle, except for the play of smiles upon her face.

I wanted to say something emollient. I remarked:

'I've told him, I shall make him financially independent at twenty-one. That's the only thing I can do.'

Suddenly she laughed. Not subtly, nor with the curious, and not pleasing, sense of secret intention which she often gave: but full-throatedly, like a happy girl.

'It really is extraordinary that that's still possible today, isn't it? Talk about justice!'

'My dear girl, it would have seemed even more extraordinary forty-odd years ago, when I was Charles's age, if someone had done the same for me.'

I explained that, until my first wife died, I had received exactly £300 which I hadn't earned. And even that made a difference. Muriel was not in a position to talk, I told her, waving my hand to indicate the house in which we happened to be sitting. But now she didn't resent being reminded about being an heiress. Somehow that exchange, singularly mundane, about riches, poverty, inherited wealth, had made us more friendly to each other.

Not at the instant when I heard her question about Charles, but soon after, I had realised that this was the point of the meeting. For some reason which she was hiding or dissimulating, it was to ask about his career that she had taken pains to get me to her house alone. Not for the sake of information, but to face me and what I wanted. Why she needed that so much was still a mystery to me.

There was lack of trust on both sides, or something like a conflict or a competition, as though we were struggling over his future. I suspected that she intended to keep him close to their group, cell, movement, whatever they cared to call it: she had power over a good many young men, maybe she had power over him. I didn't know whether she felt anything for him. Did she assume that I was playing a chess game with her, thinking some moves ahead to counter hers? If so, I thought, she was over-rating herself.

Yet Muriel had faced me. Though there was nothing to struggle about, we had been struggling. Underneath the words, precise on her side, deliberately off-hand on mine, there had been tempers, or feelings sharper than tempers, not hidden very deep. Now we were quieter.

'He is very unusual,' she said without explanation.

'In some ways, yes.' I had heard that opinion from his friends, as well as from her: it struck them more than it did me.

'So it matters what he does.'

'It will probably matter to him.'

We weren't crossing wills: this was all simple and direct.

'He is very unusual,' she repeated. 'So it might matter to others.'

'Yes, if he's lucky, so it might.'

CHAPTER XXVIII

TWO PARTIES

CAMBRIDGE in May. Margaret and I walked through the old streets, then along Peas Hill, where in winter the gas flares used to hiss over the book-stalls. The gas flares would have looked distinctly appropriate that after-noon, for a north-west wind was funnelling itself through the streets, so cold that we were bending our heads, like the others walking in our direction: except for one imperturbable Indian, who strolled slow and upright, as though this was weather that any reasonable man would much enjoy. The clouds scurried over, leaden, a few hundred feet high. It was like being at Fenners long ago, two or three of us huddled in overcoats, waiting for ten minutes' play before the rain.

Soon Margaret and I had had enough of it, and turned back. Cambridge in May. It was so cold that the early summer scents were all chilled down: even the lilac one could scarcely smell. We were staying with Martin (I had come up, as I promised Charles, to have a look at his friend Bestwick), and we hurried back to the tutorial house. There in his drawing-room we stood with our backs to the blazing coal-fire, getting a disproportionate pleasure from the wintry comfort and the spectacle of undergraduates haring about in the wind and rain below.

We were not so comfortable in the early evening, when Charles, in order to produce Gordon Bestwick without making him suspicious, had arranged something like a party in Guy Grenfell's rooms. It was the least lavish of parties. As I had noticed before, the young men and women drank very little, much less than their predecessors. Some of their friends smoked pot, and they didn't condemn it, any more than they condemned anything in the way of sex. But they condemned racism, which had be-come, even to contemporaries of theirs who weren't militant at all, the primal sin: which meant that when Grenfell, as a concession to the past, gave Margaret and me small glasses of otherwise unidentifiable sherry, one knew that it was not South African. Most of the group (it might have been because they intended to have a meeting that night, or even because Grenfell, who was well off, was also mean) contented themselves with beer or even the liquid emblem of capitalism, Coca-Cola.

The room was on the ground floor, and very handsome: but it was also very cold. Before the war, there would have been a coal-fire, as in Martin's sitting-room: but now Grenfell's college had installed central heating, and turned it off for the Easter term. I remarked to Bestwick, soon after I met him, that privileged living had become increasingly unprivileged, ever since I was a young man. Just in time to do him completely in the eye, he said, which pleased me, being less stark than I expected. Young men came in and out, sometimes meeting Margaret or me, usually not introduced. There were some good faces, one or two (as in any company of the political young that I had ever seen) with idealists' eyes. There was plenty of character and intelligence moving through the room. A young woman, voice strained with distress, blamed me for Vietnam. One or two asked questions about Russia, which I knew, and China, which I didn't: but were more interested in the second than the first. Charles March's younger daughter passed by, and my niece Nina, who must have made a special trip from London. Someone spoke angrily about students' rights.

It was no use speaking to the young as though you were young yourself. If you did, they distrusted you. Often they suspected you of a sexual motive: and they were sometimes right.

Students. They all called themselves students. Yet the term was scarcely heard in Cambridge when I first arrived there. They wouldn't have been interested in that reflection. They were singularly uninterested in history. Not that that differentiated them much from other generations. We had all believed that we were unique: and these, as much as any.

Did anything differentiate them? On the surface, looks and manners. When one couldn't see, or didn't notice, their faces, some did look unlike anything this century. Guy Grenfell, for instance, grew his hair as long as a Caroline young man. Which seemed odd since his face had the port-wine euphoria, the feminine (but not effeminate) smoothness, of one of his eighteenth-century ancestors, and his manners once more struck me as strangely managed, as though he were determined to forget any he had ever known and was hoping to invent some for Year One, and to find the equivalents of *citoyen* and *tovarishch*. The result was not, as he presumably hoped, that he sounded like my forebears or Gordon Bestwick's, but like his own at their most aggressive, on a foreign railway station in brazen voices hailing a porter.

But all that brushed off (if they were different, and they might be, it was because of their time and place) when I had a word with him alone, or later with Gordon Bestwick. Talking to Grenfell I felt obliged to bolster up his confidence. He was a nice and humble man, inconveniently torn between an embarrassing pride in his antecedents and the necessity of feeling more passionately modern than anyone around him. He wouldn't have felt like that if he hadn't been quite humble: he liked tagging on to people whom he believed with simplicity to be cleverer and better than he was. This led him to displays of exaggerated sensibility. His school had been 'beastly and brutalising'. The mere thought of the army, his family profession, was beastly and brutalising too. He was very much preoccupied with the number of examination suicides at Cambridge, almost as though, frail plant that he was, he couldn't expect both to pass his first-year Mays and to survive. In fact, he was a tough and hardy character, who didn't need so much sympathy as he felt entitled to and modestly induced.

Whereas, in some respects, Gordon Bestwick needed more. With him, not long before Margaret and I were due to leave, I sat down on a window seat. Charles had had the intuition to guess that Bestwick and I would have something in common, and I had been told what to look for. Physically, he was gawky and tall, taller than Charles or Guy Grenfell, themselves over six feet, but he had not been as peach-fed as Grenfell; as he stretched out his legs, the thighs were thin, and there were deficiency lines from nostril to mouth. There were also other lines, premature furrows, on his forehead: his face was not exactly ugly, but plain, with wavy hair already thinning, hard intelligent eyes, square jowls. It was a physical make-up not uncommon in those whose temperament wasn't easy to handle, what with natural force, ability and a component of anxiety. It was the anxiety that Charles had asked me to watch; for Bestwick had been complaining, to Charles alone, of physical symptoms, and Charles had heard something of similar troubles of mine as a young man.

At that time I had been too proud to say a word. My first impression was that Bestwick was at least as proud. All I could risk was to let fall reminiscences about what it was like in my youth to be born poor. Charles had probably told him that I wasn't a dolt. It didn't matter if he thought I was a bore. Reading for the Bar. Gambling on nothing going wrong. Strain. Lying awake at night. Sleep-starts. Pavements giving way under foot. When the game looked in my hands, sent away ill.

If none of that applied to him (his expression was lively, but gave nothing away) he must have thought me a remarkably tedious conversationalist. Before we sat alone, he had been analysing the economic thinking of the old left. Informal, confident, not rude but dismissive. I thought I would test him. Sometimes the brightest demolition men weren't so easy with the biological facts of life. 'Anyway,' I said, 'there wasn't anything much wrong with me. I recovered well enough to have my heart stop last November.'

He gave a grim friendly smile. 'I heard about that,' he said. 'You look as though you're hanging on all right, though. Aren't you?'

He was treating me as an equal, that was good. It was just possible that psychosomatic recollections hadn't been a bad idea. He might have been glad to hear that he wasn't unique. I should have been glad of that, at his age.

We went on talking. An American black had been talking to a knot of admirers earlier on. Now they (American blacks), said Bestwick, were in a genuinely revolutionary situation. While the total of the United States society was nowhere near it, as far away as you could get. So that with Americans of student age, the counterparts of the people in this room, you had a revolutionary climate without a revolutionary situation. Had that ever occurred before?

He was worth listening to, I was thinking. Charles might have over-estimated him, but not excessively. Perhaps his mind was not as precise as Charles's, which, as the mathematical analysts used to say, tended to be deep, sharp and narrow. Bestwick's mind was certainly broader than Charles's, and possibly more massive. It was a pleasure to meet ability like this: a pleasure I used to feel, then for a time lost, and now had begun to enjoy again.

There was something else about him, quite minor, which interested me. His voice was pleasant, his tone was confident but unaggressive, but he hadn't made any audible attempt to change his accent or his manner. If I hadn't known his home town, I should still have guessed that he came from Birmingham or somewhere near. There were the intrusive *g*'s, ring-ging, hang-ging, which I used to hear when I travelled twenty miles west from home. In my time those would have gone. Except for the odd scientist like Walter Luke, people of our origins, making their way into the professional life, tried to take on the sound of the authoritative class. It was a half-unconscious process, independent of politics. Bestwick hadn't made any such attempt. Yet he was a man made for authority. The social passwords had changed. Again it was a half-unconscious process. Perhaps he took it for granted that there wasn't an authoritative class any more, or that it existed only in enclaves, bits and pieces. Curiously enough, I thought, that might not make things easier for him.

Just then Nina came up, smiled at me through her hair, and whispered to Gordon Bestwick. 'When the party's over, we're all going to the Eagle. Is that O.K. for you?'

'Fine,' said Bestwick, and she slipped away. His eyes followed her, and he called out: 'Mind you wait for me.' It sounded masterful: was it as relaxed as when he talked to me?

I had not been told that those two knew each other. On the other hand, he must have been aware that she was a relative of mine. That might have made me more tolerable, I wasn't sure. Anyway, when I said that Charles must bring him to stay with us at the end of term, he was eager, and less certain of himself than he had been at any time before.

Half an hour later, out at the Getliffes' house, the level of comfort rose again. When we moved into the dining-room, the long table was not set for so many places as it often was: only for nine, which slightly took away from the normal resemblance to a Viking chieftain's hall, that resemblance which was responsible for Charles naming it the Getliffe steading. We were used to the sight of Francis at one end of his table presiding over a concourse. That night, as it happened, besides Margaret and me, there were only Martin and Irene, who had followed us out from the college, the Getliffes' second son Peter and his wife, and their elder son, Leonard. Francis was pushing decanters round, gazing down the table with an expression of open pleasure, just faintly tinged with saturnine glee. Everyone there knew each other. Martin and he had, after a good many years of guarded and respectful alliance, at last grown intimate. While Martin, before he and Francis became specially friendly, had long been fond of the Getliffe sons. And there was, as often in that house, something to celebrate. Leonard had been offered a chair in Cambridge, and one that even he, at the top of his profession, was pleased to get. How far he had recovered from his unrequited love, I didn't know, and probably Francis didn't. But he wasn't migrating to Princeton after all, and Francis and Katherine, who liked their dynasty round them, were happy. Peter, settled in a university job, Ruth, the elder daughter, married to another don, now Leonard, persuaded to come back. That left only their youngest, Penelope, who was pursuing an erratic matrimonial course in the United States.

In the warm candle-light – one could hear windows rattling in the wind – Katherine was saying:

'It's funny, your Charles being so high [she put her hand below the table] and ours grown up.'

'He's taller than I am, dear,' I replied, 'and just about to take Part I.'

'No! No! I meant, when you brought him here and Margaret put her foot in it, and that woman from Leeds thought you were a clergyman.'

Katherine was proceeding by free association: that was an occasion something like sixteen years before, though all the details were lost, certainly in my memory and Margaret's, probably in that of the woman from Leeds, and were preserved only in Katherine's. If you wanted to live outside of history, to dislocate time, then Katherine was the one to teach you: but, it happened very rarely, for once that total recall had slipped. At the time of this incident, Charles would have been about two. If so, Leonard, their oldest, had barely left school.

I pointed this out to Katherine, who expostulated, wouldn't admit it, laughed, was disconcerted like an *avant-garde* American confronted by an example of linear thinking. Katherine's thinking, I told her, was far from linear: then had to apologise, and explain with labyrinthine thoroughness (for Katherine didn't easily subside) what the reference meant.

That led, transition by transition, to the party from which Margaret and I had come. Yes, we had been mixing with the local *avant-garde*: or the protesters: or the new left: or the anarchists: or the post-marxists: they had all been there, all they had in common was the Zeitgeist, they wanted different things, they would end up in different places.

'Oh well,' said Francis, 'that has happened before.'

I corrected myself, hearing him take it so facilely. Perhaps I had spoken like that too. I said that for some purposes, just at present, they were at one.

Up and down the table, the others argued with me. There was one feature of that family party; on most issues, either of politics or social manners, we were, with minor temperamental shades, pretty well agreed. Irene had taken on most of Martin's attitudes: Katherine had always been ready to believe that her husband was right. That wasn't true of Margaret, certain of her own beliefs, which weren't quite mine; she would have fitted better in an age when it was natural to be both liberal, or Whiggish, and also religious. Still in terms of action she was close to the rest of us.

As for the young Getliffes, there seemed next to nothing of the fathers-and-sons division. Even that family couldn't invariably have been so harmonious: but certainly on politics they spoke like their father, or like other radicals from the upper middle class – not so committed as he had been, perhaps, but independent and ready to take the necessary risks. They were scientists like Francis, and that gave them a positiveness which sometimes made Margaret, and even me, wish to dissent. Nevertheless, those shades of temperament didn't matter, and on the likely future and what ought to be done – the future of fate and the future of desire – there wouldn't have been many dinner-tables that night where there was less conflict.

Such conflict as did emerge was on a narrow front. The young Getliffes, both in their early thirties, were more cut off from Charles and his society, more impatient with them, than the rest of us.

'It's all romantic,' said Leonard Getliffe at one point. 'I'm not a politician, but they don't know the first thing about politics.'

'That's not entirely true,' I said.

'Well, look. They think they're revolutionaries. They also think that revolution has something to do with complete sexual freedom. They might be expected to realise that any revolution that's ever happened has the opposite correlative. All social revolutions are puritanical. They're bound to be, by definition. Put these people down in China today. Haven't they the faintest idea what it's like?'

That was a point I had to concede. I was thinking, yes, I had seen other groups of young people dreaming of both their emancipation and a juster world. That was how George Passant started out. Well, all, and more than all, of the emancipation he prescribed to us had realised itself – in the flesh – before our eyes. And we had learned – here Leonard was right – you can have a major change in sexual customs and still leave the rest of society (who had the property, who was rich, who was poor) almost untouched.

'The one consolation is,' said Martin, 'human beings are almost infinitely tough. If you did put them down in China, they'd make a go of it. I suppose if we were young today, we shouldn't be any worse off than we actually were. They seem to find it pretty satisfactory.'

He might have been speaking of his son or, nowadays more likely, of his daughter.

'Think of the time I should have had!' Irene gave a yelp of laughter. Her husband laughed with her, troubles long dead, and so did the rest of us. One could have remarked that, considering the restrictions, her actual time had not been so uneventful.

Francis brought out a bottle of port, which nowadays we didn't often drink. Sexual freedom apart, I asked them, did they think there was nothing else in this – assertion, unrest, rebellion, alienation, of the young, you could call it what you liked? It was happening all round the world. Yes, it might be helped by commercialism. Yes, it hadn't either an ideology or a mass political base. But they (the Getliffes) were writing it off fairly complacently; they might be in for a surprise. Of course, if people of that age (I returned to something I had been thinking in Grenfell's rooms) were different at all, it was nothing ultramundane, it was because of their time and place. But somehow their time was working on them pretty drastically. I wasn't much moved by historical parallels. This was here and now. There were sometimes discontinuities in history. On a minor scale, we might be seeing one.

I didn't find it necessary to report that, the previous summer, I should have been arguing on the Getliffes' side, in the opposite sense. Well, I had changed my mind. As completely as all this? Perhaps my experience with young Pateman and his student following had prejudiced me against Charles's friends, or perhaps I had over-reacted to him. Anyway, these weren't another crop of Lester Inces; some day I ought to tell Charles that there I had been wrong.

Most of the dinner-party knew that I wasn't detached, and that I was so interested because of my son. But Francis and Katherine had an affection for him, as well as for us. Martin and Irene too had their reasons for being interested. It was only the young couple and Leonard who were regarding the phenomenon as being a pure exercise in sociology. Since it was a cheerful evening, I didn't suppress a gibe at the expense of Peter and his wife. They already had two children, five and three. A dozen years or so, and it would be their turn next. Either like this, or something different. Possibly stranger still.

That night at the dinner-table, it was natural to think of Francis's grandchildren a dozen years ahead. Francis's life, at times strained, dissident, dutiful had nevertheless held more continuity that most of ours. His father had lived not unlike this. His sons were already doing so. Though Francis's hospitality was all his own, spontaneous and disconcerting to those who knew only his public face. That night he was in cracking spirits, talking of changes he had already seen, prepared to see more, jeering at himself and me for false prophecies, of which there had been plenty, gazing with astringent fondness at his family and friends. It was natural to think of that family going on.

While we were having our evening at the Getliffes, Bestwick and Charles and the others were at work. They were more active than we, or any of their predecessors, had been: or rather, we had talked a good deal but not acted, while they didn't recognise any gap between the two. They weren't ready to wait, as we had waited, until we had won a little, even the most precarious, authority. At eighteen, nineteen, twenty, they were getting down to business. They were doing so that night. Where in Cambridge they met I didn't know, either then or later: nor what was decided, nor who took part. Charles had learnt discretion very early, and so I found had Bestwick, when I knew him better; neither of them at any stage told me, or even hinted at, anything I shouldn't hear. It was only later, from another source, and a most unlikely one, that I could piece together fragments of the story.

CHAPTER XXIX

WALKING SLOWLY IN THE RAIN

'THE only examinations they'd heard of were medical ones. They weren't very good at getting through those.'

It was Gordon Bestwick, talking of his family.

'The same would be true of mine,' I said. 'I doubt if any one of them had ever taken a written examination until I did.'

Bestwick nodded his massive head, but he was faintly irked. He didn't want me to be a partner in obscurity. He had been staying with us for a week, the first time, he said, that he had been inside a professional London home. It might have suited his expectations better if this had been more like my own first visits to the Marches, back in the twenties, butlers, footmen, wealth for generations on both sides. I had a feeling that he was disappointed that we lived so simply.

That evening he was sitting in our drawing-room after dinner, alone with Margaret and me. On the other days since Bestwick's arrival, Charles had prompted me into having a series of guests to dinner, but that night he had some engagement of his own and had begged off. It was late in June, somewhere near the longest day, and the sky was like full daylight over the park.

'Carlo didn't suffer from the same disadvantage, though,' he said.

'If it was a disadvantage,' I replied. 'In some ways you and I may have had the better luck. He thinks so—'

'And it's like his blasted nerve. I don't mind all that much his having been given ten yards start in a hundred, but when he gets explaining that it made things more difficult for him, that's more than I can take.'

Margaret smiled. The two young men were more than allies, they were on comradely terms. Gordon was, so far as I had heard, the only one of Charles's intimates who called him by his family pet name. But there was a mixture of envy and admiration which flowed both ways. Charles would have liked the dominance which he, and other acquaintances of ours older than he, couldn't help feeling in Gordon. One didn't have to be a talent spotter to recognise Gordon's ability, that shone out: but I wondered whether there wasn't something else. One or two chips bristled like iguana scales on his shoulders: but he managed to sink them, when he talked about those who really were deprived. He knew and cared. Privileged men were still vulnerable when they heard that kind of voice.

But those were times when Gordon was on duty. During his week with us, especially when he was talking to Margaret, one saw another aspect. He became attentive and anxious to please. Once or twice, trying to entertain her, he looked not mature, as he did addressing Hector Rose, but younger than his years.

In private Margaret told me that, though she liked him, she didn't find him attractive as a man: and that she believed that would have been the same if she had been his own age. After that I asked Charles how Gordon got on with women. Charles reflected. Perhaps Gordon wasn't his first choice for sexual confidences. 'Oh,' said Charles at length, 'he's a bit of a star, you know, he's had one or two offers. Chiefly from very rich girls—' Charles grinned. But Gordon, he went on, was pretty concentrated, he didn't have much time to spare. The only girl in whom he seemed 'interested' (the peculiarly anaemic word which they used and which their more inhibited predecessors would have thought genteel) was Nina.

It was thundery, as Gordon sat in the drawing-room with us, and Margaret said she had a headache. I invited Gordon to come out for a drink. He looked hesitant as though we weren't being solicitous enough or as though there were an etiquette in which he hadn't been instructed. Margaret said Go on, it'll do you good, and promised, in case Charles returned, to send him after us.

In the heavy air Gordon and I walked through the back-streets, as I had done with my stepson one Christmas Day. The clouds were thickening, but it hadn't yet begun to rain, and outside a pub people were sitting round the open-air tables, at one of which Gordon and I settled down with pints of beer. Lightning flashes from the direction of the park. Growls of thunder far away. Close by the pavement kerb, cars, headlights shining in the murk, passed as on a conveyor belt on their way from Paddington.

It used to be a quiet pub, I remarked to Gordon, when I first lived in Bayswater Road. Now we might as well be sitting in a café in one of the noisier spots in Athens.

'Never been abroad,' he said, big frame relaxed, ingesting bitter.

'Come off it, Gordon. We all know there is no sorrow like unto your sorrow. We also know that you could get large grants to travel any time you chose to ask for them. Which is more than I ever could. You're rather inert physically and rather unadventurous, that's all.'

He was used to some of my techniques by now, and gave a matey smile. I went on baiting him. He blamed too much on to environment and hoped for too much from environment. That had always been the mistake of romantic optimists. If he and his friends were going to hammer some sense into progressive thought, they had to dispose of that mistake. Gordon didn't mind a challenge. He didn't believe in any sort of Calvinism, scientific, intuitive or any other. The only thing you could change was environment. Change the environment of the working class – and he knew what the working class was like, he was born right there, he didn't romanticise them, he didn't want them to stay as they were – and they would become better.

(I was thinking, I had seen George Passant's hopes fork two ways. You've got to forget it, said the sane and decent people but, like my brother Martin I couldn't forget what freedom might end in. And the other fork was what this young man believed and was acting upon. Maybe – in the better moments one wanted to believe – that might be a shade the stronger.)

Granted, I said: but what you could do by changing environment for anyone or any group of people had its limits.

We've got to believe that there are no limits, said Gordon.

In that case you're in for another of the progressive disillusions.

If so, he said, we'll all take that when we come to it: we've got to act as though we can make a new species.

You've got to act like that, but you mustn't expect it.

It does good to expect the best.

There I wasn't with him, I said. If you expect the best, then you're blinding yourself to the truth.

Truth sometimes has to be put into suspended animation.

I don't believe, I said, that you achieve good action – not for long – if the base is anything but true.

It was an old argument, but new facts were flooding in. He knew them as well as I did. He was an honest controversialist, ready to grope and brood. I had never had a great taste for argument, had lost what little I once had: but it was pleasant arguing with him. In the headaching night we drank more beer, talked on, heard from inside the pub the call of time, and then saw the first half-crowns of rain bombing the pavement.

'We'd better hurry,' I said. 'We're going to get wet.'

Running in bursts, sheltering under porticoes, lumbering, panting, we reached the main road. He was more mobile than I was, but not a track performer. The storm had broken, water was sploshing up to our shins. We made a last run to the block of flats. There, under cover of the doorway, we halted, so that I could get my breath.

'Good God,' said Gordon, pointing up the street towards Marble Arch.

There was a solitary figure on the pavement, sauntering very slowly. When it passed into zones illuminated by the arc lamps, one saw it through lances of rain.

'Carlo,' said Gordon.

He came towards us, not altering his pace. Watching him, I caught a fresh smell of wet leaves, bringing peace.

When one saw his face, he was wearing a smile, as though satisfaction were brimming over from inside. For an instant I thought that he was drunk.

'Hallo,' he called, from a couple of yards away.

He was dead sober.

'Christ, man,' Gordon greeted him, 'you're wet through.'

It wouldn't have been possible to be much wetter.

'So I am,' said Charles in a mild tone. He looked at us with something like affectionate surprise. He didn't say any more, but his smile was pressing to return, and he didn't restrain it.

About a fortnight after Gordon had returned home, in the middle of July, Charles insisted on treating Margaret and me to a show and taking us out to supper afterwards. The show had to be a film, since to him and his circle the theatre was an obsolete art-form, which ought to have gone out with the Greeks or certainly with Shakespeare. The show also had to be a film he had seen before so that he could guarantee it. In the cinema he placed himself punctiliously between Margaret and me, whispering to her during the film, showing her an obsessive, and for him unusual degree of filial attention.

Nothing was said that night. It was the next day, after tea, sitting with both of us in the drawing-room, when he said, quietly but with no introduction at all:

'As a matter of fact, I'm thinking of moving into Chester Row. I'm sure you don't mind, do you?' He was speaking to Margaret, with whom his surface conflict had in the past flared up. 'Of course you don't mind, I shall be around, of course.'

'Chester Row?' she said in flat surprise.

'Are you, by God?' I said. I had a picture of him walking in the rain, the other night: slow, smile of joy, smell of wet leaves. I should never know whether I was right. Had he just come away from her? Was he retracing the history of the race? Did he feel that this was a unique achievement, that it had just been done for the first time?

'When are you aiming to go?' said Margaret, as though she were gripping on to practicalities.

'As a matter of fact, if it doesn't put anyone out, I was thinking of moving tonight.'

'How long for?'

'Indefinite.' He gave her a smile, reassuring but secretive.

She began to speak and then thought better of it. Charles was giving out happiness, now that he had broken the news, but wasn't willing to say another word about it. By a curious kind of understanding, almost formal, we all behaved as on the most uneventful of evenings. We looked at the television news at 5.50. Afterwards at dinner Charles made a fuss of his mother. The only references he made to his announcement were strictly practical. He didn't want anyone at all, including Guy Grenfell, Gordon, his cousins (there were good reasons for that at least, I thought), to hear where he was living. He would collect letters every two or three days. As for telephone calls, we were to say that he was out but would ring back, and then pass the message on to Chester Row. He apologised for the nuisance, but it was necessary.

I didn't enquire why. It was true that he often carried security precautions to eccentric lengths. If this had happened to me in comparable circumstances, I couldn't help thinking, I should have been a good deal less self-denying and more boastful.

After dinner Margaret went with him to his room and helped him pack: which reminded me of one of my hypercivilised acquaintances doing precisely the same for her husband, each time he left her for a new girl-friend.

In the bright warm evening the three of us stood outside on the pavement, large suitcase standing beside Charles, waiting until a taxi came along. He waved to us from inside, and then we were left gazing as it joined the traffic-stream to Marble Arch.

Back in the drawing-room, Margaret looked at me.

'Well, that's cool enough,' she cried. She burst out into laughter, full, sisterly, sensual.

I hadn't been sure what she was feeling: at that moment, she was feeling exactly as I was, it wasn't just a fatherly response, she shared it. Nothing subtle, just pleasure, the warmth of sexual pleasure at second-hand. Mixed with approval that he didn't lack enterprise. But mainly we were getting what, if you wanted to be reductive, you could think of as a voyeuristic joy. That was there: but it wasn't quite all: it wasn't quite as self-centred as that. It wasn't in the least lofty, though. We were animals happy about another animal. And to parental animals, the happiness was rich.

In that sense Margaret – and it surprised me a little – felt as I did. If this had been a daughter? No, there was a disparity one couldn't escape. I was certain that I should have been miserable. Perhaps there would have been some sexual freemasonry underneath, but worry would have overwhelmed it. I supposed that would have been true, and presumably more true, of Margaret also.

After a time, in which we had taken an evening drink, Margaret became more pensive.

'I don't think this is going to be good for him, you know.'

'Oh well. If it hadn't been her, it would have been another.'

That sounded platitudinous and non-controversial, but it provoked Margaret.

'But it is her. You can't brush that away.'

'He might have done worse, in some ways—'

'I don't like her.'

'I've told you before, I don't like her either.'

'You like her a lot more than I do,' said Margaret. 'She's a cold-hearted bitch.'

I didn't remind Margaret that once she had been a partisan of Muriel's and had tried to look after her.

'You're not going to pretend, are you,' she burst out, 'that she's in love with him?'

'Does that matter?'

'Of course it matters. Do you think it's good to have your first affair with someone who doesn't give a damn for you?'

'My impression was, she had some feeling for him. I don't understand what it is.'

'She's five years older.' Margaret had flushed, her eyes were bright with temper. 'You all say she's attractive to men, she could have her pick, unless there's something wrong with her. Why in God's name should she throw herself at him? What has he to offer her? He's too young. I could understand it perhaps if he were her own age, then he might be a good prospect—'

She went on:

'I tell you, I can't understand it. Unless – there are just two reasons why she might be doing it. And neither of them is very pleasant.'

'Go on,' I said.

'Well, she might be one of those women who like seducing boys. That would be bad for anyone like him—'

'It's possible.' I stopped to think. 'I shouldn't have thought it was likely, though. I haven't heard her talk about his being young. I doubt if she thinks of him like that.

'Anyway,' I added, 'I'd guess that he'll soon be able to look after himself in that sort of way.'

'If it's not that,' she said, 'it's something worse. She's determined to get him to herself. Away from us. So that she can fix him right inside that wretched movement of theirs. And she's chosen the one certain way to fix him.'

I had already thought something not unlike that myself: this might be the second stage of the struggle. In that case, she had all the advantages.

'Are you happy about that?' Margaret was distressed by now: and, as often happened, her distress turned into anger.

'No.'

'Do you want him to waste himself?'

'You might remember, that I'm not responsible for any of this. Just because I've said one word in her favour—'

Margaret broke into a guilty smile, then hardened again.

'But he may be wasting himself, you can't deny it, can you? If she gets control of him, and makes him sink himself in this nonsense, then he could be a casualty, of course he could. To begin with, if that takes up all his time, his work is going to suffer.'

'He's pretty tough, you know. And he likes doing well. I really do doubt if that will happen.'

'Anyway, it's a waste of anyone like him. He ought to be thinking of something worth while. If he spends his energy on something which anyone of his sense ought to see is useless, and worse than useless, then he can do himself harm. Whatever he wants to do later. It'll take him a long time to recover. Just because this woman has got hold of him.'

I hadn't any answer which satisfied either of us. She was exaggerating, I said, she was making Charles out to be weaker than he was; she was leaving out all that he would do, if Muriel didn't exist. But none of that was comforting. She had made me apprehensive, as I hadn't been for a long time: in a fashion which I had become released from, the future was throwing its shadows back.

CHAPTER XXX

DAUGHTER-IN-LAW

OUR housekeeper, getting it both ways, mourned the departure of the last young presence from the flat and simultaneously showed robust Mediterranean enthusiasm for its cause. When Charles, becoming punctilious towards her as to Margaret, telephoned to say that he would call on us for a meal, he was welcomed by his favourite dishes. This happened regularly twice a week throughout the late summer; Charles came in at six, talked cheerfully through dinner without mentioning Muriel or his way of life, and left at ten. He did take care to dispel one of Margaret's qualms. Yes, he was working: he was too much conditioned not to, he said, teasing her over the exploits of her academic grandfather and uncles. Their reading parties! He was prepared to bet that he did more work by himself than they did smoking their pipes, taking marathon walks, cultivating personal relations and revering G. E. Moore.

All was serene, on the plane of conversation. It was harder for her than for me to accept that most of his existence she couldn't know.

Then, soon after he had returned to Cambridge for the Michaelmas term, she had news of her other son. It was in the middle of an October afternoon when, reading in the study, I heard the door-bell ring. Moments afterwards it rang again, long and irritably. No one was responding. I got up and went to open the door myself.

There, on the landing, stood Father Ailwyn, bulky, white face shimmering over black cassock. He didn't smile: he moved his weight from one foot to the other.

I asked him to come in. His awkwardness infected me. I wasn't fond of uninvited visitors: and also he was one of those of whom I thought kindly when he wasn't there – and uneasily when he was. And yet, I had a regard for him after that talk – or interrogation – in the hospital.

As I led him into the drawing-room, neither of us spoke. When he was sitting down, light falling on the pale plump face, which might have looked lard-like if his growth of beard, clearly visible after the morning shave, hadn't been so dark and strong, he was still mute. Then we managed to exchange words, but his tongue seemed as thick as it usually did, and mine more so.

My first attempt was an enquiry about his parish.

'It doesn't alter much,' he replied.

Stop.

I tried to repeat something I had read about an œcumenical conference.
'No, I don't know anything about that,' he said.

After that he felt that an effort was up to him. Suddenly he asked, with exaggerated intensity, about my eye. I said, all had gone well.

'Is it really all right?'

'It's got some useful sight. That's the best that they could promise me.'

I closed the good eye. 'I can see that you're sitting there. I might just be able to recognise you, but I'm not sure.'

'Very good. *Very* good.' His enthusiasm was inordinate, but that was where it ended. Silence again.

He stared at me, and broke out:

'Actually, I was hoping to see your wife.'

That seemed not specially urbane, even by his standards. Still, it was a diversion, and I went to find her. She was in the bedroom, sitting at her dressing-table in front of the mirror, having not long come back from her hairdresser. I told her that Godfrey Ailwyn was asking for her, and that she had better come and take the weight off me.

But, after they had shaken hands, the weight was not removed. His eloquence was not perceptibly increased. There were now two people for him to gape at awkwardly, instead of one. Margaret, who had had some practice at making conversation, found the questions falling dead.

Ignoring her, Father Ailwyn looked straight and soberly at me.

'I think,' he said, 'I ought to speak to Margaret by herself.'

She gave me a baffled glance as I went out. I was more than baffled, as I sat alone in the study. I had no premonition at all about what he had come to tell her.

It was not long, not more than a quarter of an hour, before Margaret opened the study door.

'You'd better come back now,' she said. She was looking flushed and strained, her eyes so wide open that the lids seemed retracted.

'What's the matter?'

'It's about Maurice.'

'Is he ill?' My thoughts had flashed – not because I had ever imagined it of him, but because of a groove of experience – to suicide.

'Nothing like that.'

I was standing by her, and had put my arm round her.

She went on:

'No. He's going to get married.'

'Oh well—' I was beginning to laugh it off, when she broke in:

'To someone who is handicapped.'

'What does that mean?'

She shook her head, and moved like someone impelled to hear a verdict, towards the drawing-room.

Rising as she entered, Godfrey Ailwyn was clumsy as ever on his feet, but more comfortable, and more authoritative, now that he had done his duty. From their first remark I gathered that he had delivered a letter from Maurice; I wasn't given this to read until later, but it was full of love for Margaret and explained that, though he knew this would cause difficulties and disappointments for her, he proposed to marry someone whom he 'might be some good to'. The wedding and all the arrangements would have to be 'very simple and private' because she wasn't 'used to these things and mustn't be frightened or given too much to cope with'. Godfrey Ailwyn knew all the circumstances and would be able to discuss what should be done.

With Godfrey resettled in his chair, I picked up most of this, and another piece of information, which was that the girl was the sister of a patient in the hospital where Maurice worked.

Margaret was looking at me. There was a question which had to be asked.

'Is she mentally affected?' I said.

'No.'

'You're not keeping anything from us?'

'Lewis,' he replied, 'you needn't have said that.'

He was both stern and wounded, and I apologised.

'Well then, what is wrong with her?'

I didn't know how much Margaret had discovered. I had better make certain.

'She has a limp. It looks like the kind of limp that polio leaves them with, but I believe she's always had it.'

'Is it very bad?'

'One is aware of it. Perhaps it's more distressing to others than to herself. I think, taken alone, no, it is not very bad.'

'Taken alone? You mean there's something else?'

'She is also partially deaf,' said Godfrey. 'I think that is congenital too, and she has never had normal hearing. Of course, that made her backward as a child. But mentally she has caught up. I mustn't give you the impression that she is brilliant. There is nothing wrong with her there, though. What is more serious is that being deaf kept her out of things. She is very uncertain of herself, I doubt if she has ever made friends. And that is why Maurice has changed everything for her.'

'Is that what he means,' said Margaret, voice tight, 'when he says she's handicapped?'

'That is what he means.'

'And that is all he means?' I pressed him.

'That is all he means.'

'You're certain? You do know her?'

'I know her. She's staying at the Vicarage now.'

'Then I can see her?' Margaret broke out.

'I'm afraid not, Margaret,' said Godfrey in a gentle tone, but with cumbrous strength.

'Why not?'

'Maurice thinks we must make everything easy for her. And he knows more about the unlucky, and how to help them, than any of the rest of us will ever know.'

'But I must see her. This is his whole future.'

'Margaret, your son is trying to lead a good life. I don't believe you could alter that, but I beg you to listen to me, you mustn't let him see that it brings you pain.'

Godfrey was speaking to her as though I was not present. After all, Maurice was not my son. Maybe that was why Godfrey, giving the impression of bumbling incivility, first insisted on telling the news to her alone. He was her son, not mine. And Godfrey – one had to remember – did not approve of divorce.

'I wish', said Margaret, her eyes bright with tears held back, 'that he was leading a life like everyone else.'

'If I were you,' Godfrey replied, 'I should wish the same. But I don't think it would be right, do you?'

'I can't be sure. For his sake, I can't be sure.'

My own feeling might have been different from hers, certainly was different from Godfrey's. But this wasn't a time to speculate. Godfrey was continuing to tell us more about her. She was, he thought, a 'nice person' (which, at that moment, seemed one of the flatter descriptions). She was twenty-three, the same age as Maurice. It was not until that point that I learned her name. That may have been true of Margaret also, for Maurice had not mentioned it in his letter. It was, Godfrey said in passing, Diana Dobson. He believed that in her family she was called Di.

'You must remember,' Godfrey told Margaret, 'she comes from the very poor. Her mother is a cleaner in a factory. The father left them long ago. They are as poor and simple as they come. I'm afraid that's another difficulty for you—'

Margaret flared up.

'Do you think *that* would make the slightest difference to me?'

She was angry, seizing a chance to be angry. Godfrey gazed at her with a sad, doughy smile. He said:

'Without meaning to let it, and feeling bad in the sight of God, I have to confess that it always makes a difference to me.'

He must have been speaking of his visiting round in the parish. Maurice once told me that, when he went as companion, he usually enjoyed it, but Godfrey almost never.

Margaret's expression changed. All of a sudden she was open and naïve, as few people saw her. She said, as though it was the natural reply:

'I am sorry, Godfrey. I know you're a good man.'

'No.' Heavily he shook his head. 'I wish I could be. It's your son who is a good man.'

He added:

'I'd often hoped that he'd become a priest. It would be the right place for him. But now there's this marriage instead—'

I was thinking, Godfrey strongly disapproved of divorce: the only thing he disapproved of more strongly was marriage. At least for himself and his friends. No, that was unfair. But it was the kind of unfairness – or slyness or malice if you like – that showed that I was becoming fonder of him.

He and Margaret got down to business. Maurice had given instructions which weren't to be departed from. There were to be no press announcements of the engagement: and none of the wedding, except for a single notice in the Manchester evening paper, for the sake of Diana's relatives. No announcements. He would write himself to his friends. (Why all this? However his friends might behave in other situations, here he could have trusted them: Charles and all the rest would have set out to welcome her. That was part of their creed. They would be far kinder than, in the past, my circle would have been. Yet Maurice was being excessively cautious, like Charles but unlike himself, or anything that he had written to his mother or told to Godfrey: acting – it was hard to believe – as though he were ashamed of it.)

The wedding was to be in Godfrey's church, in a fortnight's time. Here – and this was entirely understandable, for as Godfrey said, it was in order not to harass the girl – there was to be no one invited, except a cousin of Diana's to give her away.

Very quietly Margaret said:

'Am I not to come?'

'He thought she might be more panicky—'

'No.' Margaret's tone was level, unemphatic. 'I shall come. I can sit at the back of the church.'

She did go. I offered to go with her, but she refused. When she returned – the wedding had been early in the morning, and it was not yet eleven o'clock – her expression would to others have seemed controlled.

'That's done,' she said.

She sat on the sofa, smoking, not looking at me.

'You know, one always imagines what one's children's weddings will be like. Do you do that about Carlo's?'

'No, never.'

'Perhaps it's a mother's privilege.' For an instant her tone was sharp-edged. Then she went on:

'I've imagined all sorts of weddings for Maurice. I haven't told you, but I have. So many women would have married him, wouldn't they? But I never imagined anything like this.'

I asked something pedestrian, but she didn't hear.

'He looked very nice. Very handsome. I think he was happy. No, I'm certain he was happy. I used to tell myself, all I wanted was for him to be happy.'

Had she met the girl? Oh yes, Maurice had brought her (Margaret) into the vestry. She and the best man were the witnesses. There had been one other person, a stranger, in the church: not Maurice's father, who had sent flowers and a cheque.

What was the girl like – the question wanted to come out, but I hesitated. Margaret didn't need to hear it. She said:

'She's almost pretty.'

She added:

'She wanted to say something to me, but she could hardly get out a word.'

After a moment, still not letting go:

'I wanted to say something to her, but I wasn't much better.'

Three weeks later, I was able to see Maurice's wife for myself. He brought her to tea one afternoon, and trying to settle her down and to smooth away her shyness (and our own), Margaret and I complained heartily of the misty weather, and made a parade of drawing the curtains and shutting the evening out.

'Oh, never mind,' said Maurice, entirely serene. 'It'll be worse where we live, won't it, darling?'

His wife didn't reply, but she understood, and gave a dependent, trusting smile. I was thinking, as she sat in the armchair, turning towards him, Margaret's description wouldn't have occurred to me. She hadn't a feature which one noticed much, but she wasn't, either in the English or the American sense, homely. Often she wore the expression, at the same time puzzled, obstinate, and protesting that one saw in the chronically deaf. How deaf she was, I couldn't tell. Maurice spoke to her with the words slowed down, deliberately using the muscles of his lips, and she seemed to follow him easily. Sometimes he had to interpret for Margaret or me.

She was wearing a nondescript brown frock. But, as well as her limp catching the eye, so did her figure. Standing still, she looked shapely and trim.

We should have had to quarry for conversation if it hadn't been for Maurice: but he took charge, like an adoring young husband acting as impresario. Each time he spoke to her, she smiled as though he had once more called her into existence.

Yes, they had a place to live in. They were buying a three-bedroom house in Salford, so that Di's mother could live with them. I knew about this in principle, for as our wedding present Margaret and I had paid the deposit. Maurice would continue at his job at the mental hospital. Di would earn some money, typing at home.

'We shall manage, shan't we?' he said to her, with his radiant unguarded smile.

'If we can't,' she said, 'we shall have to draw in our horns.' When she spoke to him, her tone was transmuted: it became not only confident and trusting, but also matter of fact.

All that we could learn about her, through the deafness (our voices sounded more hectoring as we tried to get through, the questions more inane), was that she was utterly confident with Maurice, and not in the least surprised that he had married her.

I did manage to have one exchange with her, but it couldn't have been called specially illuminating. I had been casting round, heavy-footed, for gossip about the Manchester district. I happened to mention the United football team. Her eyes suddenly brightened and became sharp, not puzzled: she had heard me, she gave a sky-blue recognising glance. Yes, she liked football. She supported the United. There wasn't a team like them anywhere. She used to go to their matches – 'until I met him'. It was the first time she had referred to Maurice without directly speaking to him, and they were both laughing. 'I'm not much good to you about that, am I?' said Maurice, who had no more interest in competitive games than in competing at anything himself.

In time, it had seemed a long time, Maurice got up and said:

'Darling, we shall have to go. Old Godfrey will miss us at the service. You know, there mightn't be anyone else.'

They had a little church backchat to themselves. I had never been certain whether Maurice was a believer, or just a fellow-traveller. The girl seemed to be devout.

Then they got up, and Margaret went towards her and embraced her. Looking at Maurice, the girl stood uncertain, not knowing which way to go, while I in turn approached and laid my cheek against hers.

When we heard the lift-door close, Margaret sat down again and sighed: After a while, she said:

'Tell me, Lewis' (actually she used a pet name which meant that she needed me) 'is that a real marriage?'

'I haven't the remotest idea.'

'No, I want to know what you think?'

'For what my guess is worth,' I said, 'I'd say that it probably was.'

'It would be a consolation, if I were certain of that.'

As she had told Godfrey, she wanted Maurice to be like everyone else: or as near like as he could come. Perhaps she was thinking, as she did later, about the nature of goodness. He was behaving, as he so often did, in a way which would have been impossible for most of us. If behaviour was the test, then he did good, and most of us didn't. Margaret and I had often agreed, behaviour was more important than motive. And yet she, as a rule less suspicious than I was, had her moments of suspicion about this son she loved. Was it too easy for him to be good? Was it just an excuse for getting above, or out of, the battle? Did he really feel joyous and whole only with those who were helpless?

She didn't ask me, because she felt that I was likely to be hard. In fact, I shouldn't have been. There was something, I should have said, in what she suspected. He might even desire a woman only when she was disabled and had him alone to turn to. That was why, incidentally, I was ready to believe that his was a real marriage. But also, not in terms of desire but of well-being, he might be at his best himself only when he was with the unlucky and the injured. But that was true of everyone who had his kind of goodness. Did that make it less valuable? Maybe yes. It depended whether you were going to give any of us the benefit of the doubt.

Nevertheless, I thought, when I was a young man, if I had met Maurice and my nephew Pat, I should have been hypnotised by Pat's quick-change performances and attributed to him depths and mysteries which he didn't in the least possess. Whereas I shouldn't have been more than mildly interested in Maurice and should have said that you couldn't behave like that if you were a man.

After having seen more people, nowadays I should be much more sceptical about my 'explanation' of either of them: but I shouldn't be in the least sceptical of one thing, that is which of the two I preferred to have close by. Virtue wore well, after all.

CHAPTER XXXI

A PRACTICAL JOKE?

THERE weren't many dates which Margaret and I celebrated: there was one that November which I couldn't celebrate with her. The twenty-eighth. First anniversary. For her it meant nothing but pain and extreme isolation – the hospital waiting-room, the dead blank, no news. She didn't wish to be reminded. So I called in at my club and, avoiding friends and acquaintances, stood myself a drink.

That was the most private of celebrations. After all, it had been the most private of events.

I knew by now, not that it was a surprise, that traumas didn't last in their first efficacy. This trauma didn't keep me immune from hurt, as it had done for a time, when I had only to recall the date and bring back oblivion. One's character and one's nature weren't so easily modified or tamed. Traumas weren't so magical as that. And yet, they weren't, or this one wasn't, quite unavailing, and the effect took some time to fade right away. Not always but often I could ride over disappointments and worries, just as people more harmonious than I was had been able to do, without effort, all their lives.

That autumn (it hadn't always been so) Margaret was worrying more about Maurice than I was about Charles. Walking alone in the park, I wasn't thinking of what he used to say to me when he accompanied me. Which added to my well-being and perhaps, if he had known, to his.

After Maurice's visit with his wife, Margaret heard of them only by letter. And it was not until December, when his term had ended, that we had a sight of Charles. He called on us ostensibly to pick up letters, but really to invite us to dinner the following week at Chester Row.

As we got ready to go, we hadn't an inkling of what to expect. Margaret said it was like going out when she was a young woman, not on terms with social occasions. She was trying to dissemble that she was more than a little tense. When we arrived, we might not have known what to expect: but, whatever we had expected, it wouldn't have borne any resemblance to this.

The housekeeper, beaming, took our coats from us in the bright hall. 'Mrs Calvert wonders if you would mind going straight up to the drawing-room, Lady Eliot.' Inside which, the first thing we saw was Azik Schiff, sitting on the sofa, looking unusually subdued. Muriel came towards us. 'I'm so very pleased you could come, Aunt Meg,' she said, giving us formal kisses. She was wearing a long frock, so that Margaret appeared distinctly under-dressed: and, I noticed by a sideways glance, so did Rosalind, who was installed in an armchair. I wondered how long it was since Rosalind had gone out to dinner and found herself under-dressed.

'You'll both probably have Scotch, won't you?' said Charles, standing beside Muriel, polite and decorous in a dark suit. Though he and Muriel drank so little, they had provided for all our tastes: both Azik and Rosalind had been given campari, presumably from domestic knowledge acquired by Muriel. As though to make us feel at home, which was the last thing any of their guests were feeling, Charles joined us in taking a whisky, which must have been another display of courtesy.

Two sofas, three armchairs, made an enclave at the street end of the long room. Muriel disposed us and then sat in one of the armchairs, utterly composed, like one presiding over a salon. Charles took his place near to the shelf of drinks: just once I thought or fancied I caught a dark-eyed glance.

They each asked host-like questions, but the conversation didn't flow. Margaret, trying to sound easy, remarked that the room was nice and warm. Yes, said Muriel, the heating system was efficient. 'Actually,' she went on, 'we both like it a little cooler. But it was a case of majority opinion, we thought. So we stepped it up five degrees. I do hope that was right?'

Her eyes fixed themselves earnestly on her mother, then came back to Margaret. Nothing could have been more thoughtful or made them more uncomfortable. 'Don't mind about me,' said Rosalind, out of countenance. '*Of course* we mind about you,' said Muriel in a clear voice. An instant of silence. Up in the square, the church clock struck once: it must have been a quarter to eight.

'How quiet it is here,' I remarked, thinking it was not the most brilliant of conversational openings. Charles said: 'At the weekends' (this was a Saturday night), 'we might as well be living in a small country town.'

I hadn't the presence of mind to enquire when he had ever lived in a country town, small or otherwise. Azik made a contribution, standard Mittel Europa, not Azik's own uninhibited self, about the charms, the variety, the changes every quarter-mile, the village shopping streets, of London.

It went on like that, after we moved downstairs to the dining-room. I sat on Muriel's right, Azik on her left, Rosalind next to me, Margaret next to Azik, Charles at the head of the table.

'Six is the easiest number, isn't it?' Muriel said with demure pleasure.

The food was excellent, soup, grouse, a savoury. They had acquired some good claret, such as Azik and I might have provided. It was all as formal as any small dinner-party we were likely to go to. In fact, it was appreciably more formal, since not many of our friends had the domestic help for this kind of entertaining, nor the peculiar dead-pan style which Muriel found natural and which, that night at least, it amused Charles to adopt. It all seemed – would they have done this for anyone else's benefit? – like an elaborate, long-drawn-out practical joke: the kind of joke in which Muriel's father used to involve himself, so that sometimes it looked as though he had forgotten that it was a joke at all.

The conversation round the dinner-table was stylised also. Azik and Charles had an exchange about Asian politics, on which Azik was know-ledgeable because of his business. They might have been meeting for the first time. Neither gave much away about his political opinions, or whether he had any opinions whatever. Enquiries about Muriel's child, not fended off, politely replied to: yes, he was bright and flourishing. Enquiries from me about Charles's friends: those were fended off, though Charles gave an amiable smile as he did so. The only direct talk, pro-priety for once relaxed, came when Azik produced the precious, the inevitable topic of his son. Next October, 1967, David would be going to his public school. They had finally decided on Westminster: despite all their resolves, they couldn't let him go away from home: he might win a scholarship ('certain to,' said Charles with professional competence), but even so he would enter as a day boy. For a while Azik's parental passion dominated the table and the family relations spread among us all. At the end of the meal, however, we had returned to a discussion of jewellery.

Then Muriel gazed along the table towards Charles.

'Darling,' she called out, 'will you bring the others up when you're ready?'

'Of course,' said Charles.

Margaret gave me a stupefied glance before she went with the other two women out of the dining-room. Now I felt sure that this evening must have been prepared for, though it seemed due more to Muriel's sense of – humour? mischief? even impudence? than to Charles's. He might have thought up a charade, but he wouldn't have carried it so far. He might have considered that last touch inartistic. He knew as well as anyone there that Margaret and I had never separated men from women after dinner since we set up house. Nevertheless, still grave and decorous, he apologised to Azik and me for not being able to offer us port; could we make do with brandy?

Until we left, I didn't hear an intimate word spoken. Chat when the party re-formed in the drawing-room, Charles having kept us below for a precise fifteen minutes. Chat admirably tailored for a dinner-party in a remote diplomatic mission, third secretary and wife doing their duty by elderly compatriots. Once Rosalind asked her daughter: 'What are you doing for Christmas?' – where the 'you' was intended to be in the singular.

'Oh,' said Muriel, 'we shall have a quiet time, I expect; we shan't be going away.' She contrived to make their ménage sound remarkably like the end of *Little Dorrit*. Occasionally their eyes met. Otherwise they behaved, not only as though they were safely married, but as though they had been so for a long time.

Glances at watches. Good-byes. Margaret unusually effusive with thanks for a delightful evening. Ritual of gratitude. Ritual of kisses. Margaret and I back home by eleven o'clock.

The departure of their guests so early might have suggested to Muriel and Charles that the party had not been an uproarious success. Presumably that wasn't weighing on their spirits. And yet, as with so many of Muriel's father's exploits, there was a faint, an almost imperceptible doubt. It was a thousand to one against – but what if they had been serious? What if they had been to obsessive trouble and given their first dinner-party?

In that case, said Margaret, tender to the embarrassments of the young, it would have been a major disappointment. She didn't believe it: but she didn't utterly and absolutely disbelieve it. I laughed at her, and wasn't unaffected myself. Muriel had a gift for disquiet, I thought: that is, she stayed still and here were we, more mystified about them both than we had been before.

We were not the only people who were mystified that night. Two days later, on the Monday afternoon, Azik's secretary telephoned me. Mr

Schiff would be very grateful if I could spare him a few minutes. When? Straightaway, if I could manage it: otherwise – Yes, I was doing nothing, I said, I would come round. Mr Schiff will send a car for you. That wasn't necessary. Oh, Mr Schiff insists—

Mr Schiff did insist, just as Lord Lufkin used to, and as in Lord Lufkin's time I was driven in a Daimler to the office. Driven in state for something like eight hundred yards. For Azik, like other tycoons, had moved his office westwards, into the Park Lane fringe of Mayfair, and now inhabited a mansion which in the nineteenth century had been the town house of a Whig grandee. All, including the car, was as sumptuous as Lord Lufkin's accoutrements used to be: thick carpets on the office floors, Regency decorations restored, regilded. There was just one difference. Of those two, Azik was by far the more outpouring: which wasn't saying much, since very few men were less outpouring than Lufkin. In fact, Azik was lavish by any standard, his tastes were exuberant, as witness his house in Eaton Square. Yet Lufkin's personal office had reminded one of the Palazzo Venezia in one of the Duce's more expansionist phases: whereas Azik's office in Hertford Street, which I had not visited before that day, must have been something like a closet or at best a dressing-room in the old mansion, much smaller, darker, more shut-in than the room of his own secretary, and, apart from a desk and a couple of chairs, almost totally unequipped.

There were no offers of tea, drinks or even cigarettes. Azik did all his hospitality at home. He shook my hand, and immediately asked:

'I wanted to hear, what do you think of our young friends?'

'I suppose you knew about them?'

I meant, did he know, before Saturday night, that they were living together. Azik laid a finger to the side of his nose.

'My dear Lewis, what do you take me for?'

As a matter of historical fact, it had not required superhuman acumen or any other quality with which I was willing to credit Azik. Muriel had, for some purpose of her own, first raised her mother's suspicions and then, after various misdirections, had gone into a fit of apparent absent-mindedness and told her.

'They have presented us with a *fait accompli*, I should say,' Azik put it like a question. 'I don't understand why they wish to remind us of it, do you?'

That was only one of the things I didn't understand, I said. Including the whole situation.

Azik nodded.

'The only certain feature of that situation is that it won't stand still.' He went on, he'd never known a situation with a woman which did stand still, until he married Rosalind: and not always then. He spoke with a shamefaced smile, not so unquenchably the hypermasculine or the Jewish papa.

Then he said:

'Your son is a lucky young man, shouldn't you say?'

'Is he?'

'He loves her, of course. He'd be very hard to please if he didn't. Believe me, I know more about the girl than you do. He's very lucky to love and find everything teed up. We didn't have so much luck, you and I, my friend.'

I said yes. I was thinking – me at Charles's age, walking the town streets, virgin, craving, about to fall in love without return. As for Azik at that age, I knew nothing: it must have been about the end of Weimar, he might perhaps have been wondering whether he would have the chance, not to love, but simply to live.

'Well then,' said Azik. 'It would be more of a blow to him if she dropped him. And if you'll listen to me, I have to assure you, that might happen.'

I had a sudden sense of affront, that he should suggest Charles was going to be ill-treated in love. If he said it about me, well and good – so that I was more off-hand than I need have been, when I replied:

'It has happened to better men than him.' I went on: 'But I've seen no sign of it. Have you? Have you heard anything?'

Azik slowly shook his great head. There was a long pause, as though he were hesitating whether to speak or alternatively was reorganising his case. With the apologetic air of one putting a probing amendment, he said:

'How would you regard it if they got married?'

I wasn't prepared. I blurted out:

'He's far too young—'

'As far as that goes, he is grown up. He has grown up very fast. But I didn't mean now, my friend. Not yet. Not yet.'

'I haven't given it a thought.' That wasn't true. It had passed through my mind as a possibility, one that seemed unlikely and that I didn't like.

'Perhaps you might some day.' He gave me a cheerful, watchful evaluating glance. Another pause. 'I should say, there would be no objection from our side. My side.' (Was that a correction? Did Rosalind, as I could well believe, disagree with him? Was that why we were meeting in his office?) 'There would be no objection. No, I should welcome it.'

'Oh well, there's no hurry,' I said, playing for time.

'I want her to have a good life. She mustn't make another mistake. That was a disaster, the last one. But this time she has chosen something worth while.' He broke into a grin.

'I must say, she is making a habit of being covered by members of your family.' He had been speaking of his stepdaughter with genuine fondness, something like the affection of the flesh: he was still doing so, though I hadn't expected that last remark.

He went on:

'I couldn't have chosen better for her if she'd asked me, this time. You have a fine boy there.'

'So have you with yours.' That was tactical. I wanted to break the conversation up.

'We have both been luckier than we deserve. Oh yes, David will give me something to live for when I'm an old man. And your Charles is a blessing too.' The mention of his son hadn't distracted him for long. He said:

'You needn't wonder why my girl is in love with him.'

'I don't wonder. I doubt it. I don't know.'

'I tell you, Lewis, I do know. I know her. She puts on a front, she wears a mask, she drives you mad. But she feels without anyone seeing. I know. I know because she used to feel for me. She is in love with him.'

This was the direct opposite of anything that Margaret or I had thought. How much did Azik believe it? He was out to persuade me, he did it with fervour. Of course, he was set on making some sort of bargain – though he must have known that I hadn't any control over Charles. Perhaps he wanted something quite simple, such as that I shouldn't use my influence against the marriage, if I were asked. He was pressing her claims, softening me by insisting (he could have known no more than I did, I thought) that she was in love.

'We'd better leave it to them, hadn't we?' I said.

'Tell me, Lewis. We are good enough friends to say anything, I should think. Why are you against her?'

'Wait a minute. Haven't you something to explain to me? Not very long ago you were warning me that she might drop him. Now you're talking about serious love. You can't have it both ways—'

He didn't blink, he gave his wide-lipped frog-like smile.

'Oh yes I can. You see, she has been bitten once. If she feels in danger now, if she's getting in too deep, and doesn't see marriage at the end, then she would pull out and save herself. She won't risk another fiasco. If she thought that was happening she'd be capable of cutting her losses. And breaking both their hearts in the process.'

That was altogether too elaborate, I said. When I was young, I invented some labyrinthine explanations for the way I behaved with Sheila. I shouldn't trust them now. I had come to be suspicious, more than suspicious, of second-order emotions and motives.

Azik shrugged.

'If they come apart, you may have to see who did it.' He broke off: 'But you haven't told me. Why are you against her?'

What I said wasn't all I felt. I was afraid, I was speaking without much emphasis, that if he married young she might confine him.

'What do you mean, confine him?'

'She won't alter. She's set by now—'

'Are you saying her opinions are set? And that young man is going to adopt them? God in Heaven, Lewis, do you know your own son?'

'Not quite that. No, they might confine each other. They both happen to have a passion for politics.' (Did he know that about his stepdaughter?) 'That might restrict them, they might never get out of the groove—'

'Politics schmolitics,' said Azik, who encouraged, irrespective of merit, anything which Gentiles accepted as Jewish jokes.

The meeting, which seemed to have been disappointing for him and was disconcerting for me, ebbed towards, not a conclusion, but an end.

CHAPTER XXXII

STAFF WORK, NEW STYLE

'WE shall have a quiet time, I expect,' Muriel had said in her own drawing-room, when asked about their plans for Christmas. She might have expected it, if she were less shrewd than any of us imagined: what was certain is that she didn't get it.

Otherwise there was not much one could be certain about. What happened to them in the winter of 1966–7 no one knew in detail but themselves. I received a partial account some time afterwards, from, I kept thinking, the one source I shouldn't have contemplated. Much of it seemed honest: but it had the disadvantages of all accounts which were given with hindsight. However, some of it I could check against events which I observed for myself. Like most bits of second-hand history, it left one dissatisfied, possibly both too credulous and too sceptical.

Still, that account was all that I had to work on. Later, I sometimes wondered what I should have said if I had had information at the time. Certainly, that they were expecting too much, that they had fallen into the occupational disease, for politicians of any age, of over-optimism. So that they sometimes seemed romantic, if not silly. But if I had known it all I should also have admitted, perhaps only to myself, that some of them were capable. Once I had underestimated them. I had thought, with something like contempt, whether they were really our successors. I didn't think that any more. They would sit in my contemporaries' chairs soon enough, or perhaps in different chairs which they had constructed for themselves.

To begin with, it seemed – and there was nothing surprising here – that during the Christmas period and the New Year they were preoccupied with, or at least spent much of their time upon, what was now in private jargon called 'the movement'. But they were preoccupied in a complex and sometimes ambiguous fashion. They were taking part in plans for the movement's operations: the interesting thing was, they and their intimates, including Bestwick, had plans within plans, and these often, for security's sake, had to be concealed.

Not that they were unrealistic or undisciplined. It was their own choice to join, as very much the junior partners, with a core of London students. A London college was to be the point of action. The Cambridge group hadn't much to offer, except as a token of good will, rather like a contingent of New Zealanders being attached to American forces. They found a leader whom they would in any case have had to accept: but who in fact had a quality none of them possessed or had come across before. He was already a national figure and was to become more so. I did not meet him until much later, and then only casually: but like most other people I was soon used to seeing his face on television and hearing him talk. His name was Olorenshaw. The television interviewers and commentators called him by his Christian name of Antony, or, when they knew him less well, Tony. However, that was something like affable Ministers strolling through the smoking-room and addressing backbenchers by the wrong first name. All Olorenshaw's friends and comrades called him nothing else but 'Olly', following a good old lower-class habit, much in use among professional games players. Olly actually was a goodish cricketer, and had played in the Bradford League. His father was a journalist on the *Yorkshire Post*, and Olly had been brought up in modest comfort. He was a muscular, shortish, low-slung young man, with a snub-nosed face that one wouldn't have noticed in a crowd.

Yet there was no doubt that he had, to use the fashionable word of that period, *charisma*. Characters as different as Charles, Gordon Bestwick, Grenfell, Muriel, all recognised it and succumbed to it; perhaps some envied it. Quite why he had it, or what it consisted of, none of them could analyse, even later in cooler blood. He was a fair organiser, though not as competent as some of his student colleagues: he had considerable powers of decision. He possessed some knowledge of the theory, Marcusian and so on, which was running round the student world. His intelligence was better than average, but Gordon and Charles couldn't have thought him a flier. He was an impassioned but repetitive speaker.

None of that added up to the effect which he produced. Perhaps the answer was quite simple. He really did feel exactly as others round him felt, and had the gift of voicing it an instant before they recognised it for themselves. That night in Trinity, over a year before, Charles had said – with self-knowledge, with inhibiting self-knowledge – in politics you couldn't afford to be too different from everyone else. In behaviour Charles to some extent acted on that maxim, and Bestwick more so: but not in feeling. Whereas to Olly it came as natural as his strong-muscled walk.

He had no irony, such as Charles in private couldn't suppress. Irony would have been a crippling disqualification for Olly's kind of leadership, and probably for any other. When he heard a battalion of his followers, mobilised and drilled according to plan, chanting Dinshaw-out (Dinshaw was the principal of the college), Johnson-out, Wilson-out, Brezhnev-out, any other disyllable-out, Olly was at one with them, all he wanted was to join in. Charles and others like him might have forced themselves to join in, but they would have felt the discomfort of simultaneously watching performing animals and being performing animals themselves.

In a similar manner, Olly didn't suffer from intellectual reserves. Quite sensibly, he believed that student protests could, before too long, exact their own demands from universities. Equally sensibly, he believed that student protests would end where they began, unless they were supported by, and finally submerged in, the working class. The working class, with students acting as catalysts, was the only force which could break the old order – as an article of faith, Olly believed that that would happen. Gordon Bestwick argued that it was intellectually untenable. Gordon, still living among the English working class, didn't dramatise them. Olly, more prosperous, did. His faith was untouched. Once the working class took over, he was willing not to lead anything or anyone again.

That Christmas, Olly and his London lieutenants met a number of times at Chester Row. They weren't trying to hasten the revolt – the current word was blast-off – at the college. That wasn't necessary, it was coming anyway, they judged it good tactics to let it start, as it were, out of the ruck, with no leaders at all. What they wanted was to be ready with plans and take control just before the count-down.

It was the kind of preparation and patient waiting which would have been familiar enough to any politician, public or private. Their planning of the phases of the revolt, so it appeared in the event, was excellent. Here Gordon, Charles and others who were let into their confidence had nothing to give. They were beginners, and Olly's staff were experienced professionals. Some of them were first-class organisers. It was a mistake to think that young men in their early twenties (most of the London group were round Muriel's age) had much to learn about organisation. That didn't require experience, but energy and some clear minds. These did their job as briskly and unfussily as Hector Rose in middle age might have done it. Where they could still have learned something from Hector Rose was, not in primary organisation but in foreseeing consequences.

Under the cover of those plans, which the Cambridge cell imbibed lessons from, they were also devising one of their own. It was not clear (or at least I never knew) who had the first conception, but Gordon and Charles passed it on to Olly, and Muriel used persuasion on him too. Not that he made difficulties about others' ideas; he was ready to give these bright outsiders a run: that showed one of his strengths. All the evidence suggested that he was quick and active in getting their plan worked out. He thought it valuable enough to call it top secret (they had adopted many of the official forms). A number of followers had to receive logistic instructions, but the only persons Olly informed about the inner purpose were his numbers two and three.

The plan was, in essence, quite simple. The revolt, when under full control, was designed to occupy the main block of college buildings. Food, drink, bedding, new-style chemical closets, even books, were already being stored in a warehouse close by, enough for a stay of one month. As a result of American experience, the principal's office and the administrative floors were to be seized also, in the first hour – which was pencilled in as 4.30 a.m. (shortly before dawn on a summer morning). All that would have been arranged, in precisely the same fashion, without a minute's change in timetable, if the Cambridge cell had not existed. The only addition that they and their sub-plan had brought about seemed innocuous enough. It was that there should be a side foray, needing perhaps a dozen men, to take possession of two offices in the biochemistry department.

That was not so innocuous as it seemed. Almost everyone concerned with secrets, particularly military secrets, lived under the illusion that they are better kept than ever happened. We had learned that in the war. Heads of State rested happily in the conviction that their own Ministers were totally ignorant of the manufacture of nuclear bombs. They probably were: but there were thousands, including humble and entirely unexpected people, who weren't.

Through an identical process, which was set going by words slipping out, occasionally in fits of conscience, but more often because of self-importance or even the sheer excitement and ebullience of living, friends of Gordon and Charles had picked up what to officials would have been a horrifying amount of knowledge about government work on biological warfare. Second-year science students such as Guy Grenfell could make a fairly sharp guess about the operations at the Microbiological Research Establishment at Porton: they could have written out a list of the viruses which were being cultivated, and the diseases which were available as weapons of war.

Further, they wouldn't have had to guess, they knew, which pieces of the work had been sub-contracted to university departments. Here their intelligence was often precise. They knew, for instance, that research upon psittacosis was being carried out, under Ministry of Defence subsidy, at this London college. They knew it. The difficulty was to prove it. That was the point of the sub-plan, which someone had christened Asclepius. Two professors were known – one of the best intelligence contacts was an obscure laboratory assistant – to be in charge. It occurred to Gordon and Charles that, if their offices could be ransacked, there might with good luck be some evidence. They didn't expect much. They had consulted some acquaintances in the civil service and had learned how secret contracts were drawn up. Probably not so much through delicacy as through prudence, they didn't come to me, who if I had chosen could have told them more. They had considered employing a professional safe-breaker. They had made up their minds to look for 'indications'. Even a hint about biological war would be enough, Olly had become vociferous in proclaiming to, 'blow the roof off'. They could get their hands on nothing more useful. There was no propaganda equal to this.

That sounded cynical, just as their operations sounded, because they were thought out. It would be a mistake, however, to imagine that any of them, facing the prospect of biological war, were in the remotest degree cynical. Young men like Gordon and Charles – it is worth remembering, that during this period of planning Gordon was not yet twenty, and Charles a year younger – knew a good deal about power politics. Other states might possess both ultimate weapons and the will to use them. Charles was an amateur of military history, and knowledgeable about it. Nevertheless, when it came to the manufacture of disease, they felt exactly like the simplest of the young people around them. They felt a sheer horror, not in the least sophisticated, naïve if you like, that this should be done. That it was done in their own country didn't soften the horror, but added anger to it.

CHAPTER XXXIII

CONVERSATION IN THE OPEN AIR

THROUGH the spring they were still waiting for their time. While I remained in total ignorance of any of their plans. When I saw Charles, which wasn't often, he was in good spirits, composed and lively, interesting on books he had read. He gave no sign of strain that I perceived. When, months later, I heard something of the story, I wondered how much I had missed or whether he had become a good actor.

One morning in May, Martin rang me up from Cambridge. What about a day at Lord's? I didn't see much inducement, but he pressed me. When I had said yes, I felt cross with him. He must have known that I had given up watching cricket: even if I hadn't, the match, when I looked it up in the papers, had no attractions either for him or me. It wasn't even good weather. Although the sky was bright, it wasn't warm enough to sit with pleasure in the open air.

Waiting for me in front of the pavilion, Martin gave an impassive smile. Not too exciting to be unbearable, he said. We were almost alone, sitting there in the cold sunlight. Above the spring-fresh grass, the stands shone white and empty. Nothing was happening. A few runs, no wickets. From one end a large man with a long run bowled medium-paced inswingers to a legside field. From the other end an almost identical man did almost identically the same. Curious how the game had developed, Martin commented. It was probably still great fun to play. He couldn't pretend it was great fun to watch.

Yet he continued to watch with absorption. The technique was always interesting, he said. All I admitted was that the fielding looked marvellous,

839

out of comparison better than when I followed the game. The score seeped up to twenty-five after an hour's play. One wicket fell, to a good catch at leg-slip.

Just before one o'clock Martin said that we had better have a snack before the rush. I was glad to move, but I couldn't understand where the rush was coming from. In the pavilion bar, under layers of team photographs, stood half a dozen men, one of whom Martin knew. To one of the ledges under the photographs, we carried our sandwiches and glasses. Martin continued to talk cricket. I asked how he had had the inspiration for us to spend the day like this. He looked at me with a fraternal recognitory glance, and then exchanged a word with his acquaintance close by.

As we left the bar, he suggested that we might take a walk round the ground. Through gaps in the stands, one saw the players still moving in the middle, not yet come in for lunch. We arrived at the practice nets, the expanse of turf behind the Nursery end. There was no one anywhere near.

'Yes, there is something,' he said.

I was at a loss. Then I realised that he was replying to my question in the bar, which had actually been entirely innocent, just a mock-complaint.

'I'm not sure how reliable my information is,' he said.

'What is it?'

'Had you heard that Charles and company are trying to crash Porton wide open?'

That was the first intimation I had. Those meetings in Muriel's study, which were later described to me, had not been so much as suspected, and still weren't, either by Martin or me, that morning at Lord's. He had been given – so I discovered – only the slimmest of hints.

It was enough for him. Most people would not have taken so long, wouldn't have eased away time by technical analyses of the game, before they broke the news. But Martin, as he grew older, had developed the habit, not uncommon in men who had seen many things go wrong, of deliberately slowing himself down, of adapting the displeasing to his own pace. It was a habit which I had noticed long before in his predecessor in college office, Arthur Brown.

'I've heard nothing at all,' I said.

'Does it make any kind of sense? Is it in their line?'

'It could be.'

'How would they get hold of anything? I suppose it mightn't be impossible.'

He knew very little more. Martin and I exchanged remarks about biological warfare in our old kind of Whitehall shorthand. We might have been back in wartime, talking about the most recent news of the nuclear bomb. In fact, that was why Martin had led me to the practice ground, where we could speak without being overheard, just as in the war we held some secret conversations in the middle of St James's Park.

'It could be dangerous,' said Martin.

'Who for?' It didn't need asking.

'For anyone who wants to broadcast something he hasn't any right to know.'

'Yes. Meaning Charles.'

'Charles. One or two others as well, I fancy. I'm thinking of Charles.'

We had reached, walking slowly, the rough and piebald grass where, during festive matches, the tents were pitched.

Martin said:

'He might get into desperate trouble. If he gives them a chance to use the law against him, they could take it. He wouldn't stand a chance.'

'They'll try to keep it quiet—'

'He might have gone too far for that.' He was speaking very quietly. 'Good God, he's making a nuisance of himself.'

'That's the least of it.'

'Why in hell does he want to set up as the conscience of the world?'

For an instant, I got away from thoughts of Charles.

'I'm not sure', I said, 'that that comes too well from you.'

Neither of us could forget that when Martin had been in his thirties, years older than Charles was now, he had behaved in a fashion that was (if one had been feeling like sarcasm) comically similar. From inside the nuclear project, he had attempted to write a letter of outrage when the bombs were dropped on Hiroshima and Nagasaki. I had stopped him, at a cost to our relation which had taken some time to put right. Then later, with the headship of the whole English operation open to him, he had, without flurry and almost without explanation, resigned. All Charles's friends would have thought Martin a hard and worldly man: he could be both those things. Yet, among the middle-aged people whom Charles knew, Martin was one of the few who had made a sacrifice.

Hearing my gibe, he gave a grim smile, lips pulled down.

'I should have thought', he said, 'that I was in a privileged position.'

He went on talking of the penalties that anyone breaking official secrets might pay. We both knew all about it. Some careers could be closed, or at least impeded: one would find mysterious obstacles if one attempted most kinds of official life. Martin's concern, and mine, became practical, almost as unethereal as though we were trying to watch over Charles's health.

To some, it would have seemed puzzling, or even unnatural, that Martin should be so much affected. True, he had shown a glint of brotherly malice, of obscure satisfaction, that, after all his troubles with his own son, I should run into one with mine.

But that glint emerged from feelings which contradicted it. Martin had a family sense much stronger than my own. Charles might have existed for years as an incarnate reproach to Martin's son: but he was also the chief hope of the whole family. With any luck, Martin believed, he was going to make his independent name. And Martin imagined him making a name in the official world where Martin could himself have been successful. It was noticeable, I thought, that people living inside what Charles's friends called a 'structure' couldn't easily picture able men fulfilling themselves outside. That had been true of me when I lived, as Martin did now, in a college, or afterwards in Whitehall and Westminster. Somehow these institutions, which had their own charm to those inside, set limits to one's expectations. Enclaves which made for a comprehensible life. When one left them behind, as I had done, it was a bit of a surprise to find that enclaves weren't necessary, and that comprehensibility wasn't such a comfort as one had thought.

So that some of Martin's hopes for Charles I could get on without, and my concerns, as we walked back and forward across the Nursery turf, were less sharp-edged. Yet still I was shaken by thoughts of prosecution – or less than that, plain scandal, almost as my mother would have been. One's self-sufficiency dropped away. One cared where one didn't choose to care: often where one ought not to care. Scandal, notoriety, row. He was proposing to act – so far as I could tell – according to his beliefs. To many – what did I think myself? – they were decent beliefs. Scandal, notoriety, row. I wasn't a stranger to them myself, and had survived.

Yet that wasn't a consolation, as I walked with Martin in the chilly afternoon.

'I'm not certain', Martin was saying, after a period in which we had each been brooding, 'that what I did [he meant, his resignation] was right. If you think of what has happened, it wasn't.'

'You couldn't have predicted that.'

'There's not much excuse for being wrong.'

It was true, we had all been wrong. We had foreseen that if men made nuclear bombs they would use them. There would be the slaughter of many millions. We shouldn't escape a thermo-nuclear war. It was because he couldn't accept his share of that responsibility that Martin abdicated. As it turned out, what we expected was the opposite of the truth. We shouldn't have believed it, but an equilibrium had set in. It might be an unstable peace, but it had been peace for over twenty years. By this time, we were afraid of other fates, but not of major war.

So the most quixotic action of Martin's life looked, in retrospect, like a bad guess.

I said:

'Perhaps it helps the rest of us if one or two people show they don't approve of mass annihilation.'

'I wonder.'

He had been right about Hiroshima, I said. We got hardened to killing with astonishing speed: it was one of the horrifying features of the human animal.

'I dare say', Martin remarked, 'that you and I have become hardened too, don't you think?'

'Does that surprise you?'

'You know, this business that Charles is kicking about, there was a time when I couldn't have taken it, could you?'

'Most people can take anything. Not many kick.'

'Perhaps that will be a comfort to him some day,' Martin said.

'It's the only one he's likely to get.'

What was to be done? 'You could do more harm than good,' said Martin, thinking of his own attempts to guide Pat, who put up no resistance and then found some new manœuvre. With Charles it would be a mistake to try anything remotely subtle: he wasn't labile as Pat was, but he was hard to fool. The only way was to be direct. We arranged that I should write him a letter, saying that this gossip had reached me, and telling him he ought to be aware of the Official Secrets Act. Then Martin, back in Cambridge, would ask him round. They were on good terms, it would be easier, and conceivably more effective, for Martin to talk to him than for me.

The pavilion bell was clanging, and Martin showed a disposition to return to the game. I delayed him, having something else to ask.

'Your information,' I said. 'How did you get it? You haven't told me—'

He hesitated.

'Everything is in confidence, you needn't worry,' I told him, playing a family joke, that he was so secretive that he didn't like telling one the time.

He returned the gibe.

'Within these four walls,' he said, waving a hand towards the bare expanse, mimicking a colleague of ours long since retired.

'Well then,' he went on, 'it was through Nina.'

I exclaimed, and recalled some talk about attachments.

'From the young man Bestwick, I suppose?'

'I think not.'

Martin's reply, unusually brusque, sounded as though he didn't favour Bestwick.

I said:

'I have a lot of use for him, you oughtn't to write him off—'

'I'm not writing him off. I rather wish that it did come from him. But it was from someone else.'

'Why did she tell you?'

'I fancy she was trying to protect him.'

'Not Charles, of course?' She was fond of her cousin, but they had never been close.

'Oh no.'

It seemed that Martin was not certain whom she was protecting. That afternoon, I couldn't identify the name.

But I could identify the way secrets leaked. Just as they got hold of news about Porton, so they had let out their own news. There was a certain perverse symmetry about it. Particularly as Nina was the channel, one of the most trustworthy of girls.

'Look,' I said, 'this mustn't go any further.'

'Nina told me that.' Martin smiled. 'Just to make certain, I told her the same.'

I didn't like what I had to say next.

'You'd better impress on her that she mustn't tell her brother.'

That was the nearest I could go to impressing on Martin that he mustn't tell his son. It was bitter to have to say anything, but after the disclosures of last year I dared not take a risk.

Martin said, without expression:

'I don't think that's necessary. You needn't worry, he won't be told.'

CHAPTER XXXIV

COMMUNIQUÉS FROM HEADQUARTERS

THE results of our communication with Charles were not dramatic. To me he wrote a civil and affectionate answer, saying that since he had now studied the Official Secrets Act, there was some danger that he would get mixed up and include it in his papers in the Mays: while Martin reported over the telephone that Charles had in conversation been completely sensible, but neither admitted nor denied that the rumour was correct. 'If he is considering anything,' Martin said, 'then he's got it worked out every step of the way.' Which had been true of Martin himself, in his days of action.

With that I could do nothing but leave it. There were some disturbances at London colleges throughout May, but they did not amount to much more than shouting in the streets and in the quadrangle at King's. I paid them very little attention, since I still knew nothing of any link between student risings and this warning about Charles. In the same spirit, when the major rising actually started, in the first week in June – at the end of the Cambridge, but not the London, term – I watched the film shots on television with a detached interest, not much more involved than if these events had been taking place in Stockholm or Warsaw.

Which, in everything but language, they might have been. The students, and especially the students milling in the streets, looked as international as airports. Hair, dress, expressions, slogans, pop music – as well as the same hatreds and the same hopes – had broken across frontiers like nothing else in the century. Watching these spectacles, I thought the only local difference was that the police weren't using shields. This was the most international activity I had ever seen.

Pictures of the principal, students at each shoulder, being interviewed on the pavement. Yes, he had been requested not to enter his office. Requested? No reply. Communiqué that night from the *Students' Headquarters. Principal's Office.*

Messages of support from Essex, Oxford, Sussex, Cambridge. That conveyed nothing to me. If I had known, I might have reflected that the sight of young men and girls fighting in a porter's lodge, swearing like George Passant in a rage, some of them being frog-marched by policemen, seemed some distance away from quiet conferences in the boudoir-study at Chester Row, a dozen heads round the table, talking in the low, unassertive voices that were common form, refreshed by some maidenly coffee or Coca-Cola. It was as long a distance as from any staff headquarters to the front line.

For Margaret, who had taken part in 'demos' in her youth, and for me, who had seen the street mobs in Germany, the sight of violence wasn't pretty. Maybe it wasn't to some of the planners. That I didn't know and, since I was uninterested, didn't think about. But I did have a passing thought that there were organising minds behind it.

Anyone who had spent half an hour inside a political movement would have realised that. There was a fair amount of chaos. Some allies, including Muslim liberators and a free-drugs party, must have been an embarrassment. There was some violence which didn't appear premeditated. But too many contingents arrived at what seemed the right time. Too many squads (the serious invaders, as opposed to the irregulars, seemed to work in platoons of round about a dozen) knew what to do. College porters, secretaries, staff, were picked up, led out, put gently enough into cars, all too quickly and smoothly to be true. True, that is, in terms of the student manifestos, or what we heard on the news or on discussion programmes from Olly himself.

Spontaneous. Rising against grievances not attended to for months. Complaints not recognised. Student rights. Participation. He gave us all that, as his face became familiar on the screen. He wasn't smooth. He had what had come to be called a classless accent, meaning one which could belong only to a small but definable class. He had the gift of speaking like a human being who believed what he said and wanted you to believe it too. He didn't appear clever, and sometimes not coherent. Several of my acquaintances said that, if he joined either of the major parties, he would get office before he was thirty.

'Tell me, Antony,' said one of the cordial television interviewers, 'do you expect to get most of your demands?'

'We can't help not get them.'

'But what, I know you're explaining what the students are insisting on straightaway, what do you really expect to get?'

No smile. 'We shall get what we take.'

He wasn't hectored on the screen, as the national politicians might have been.

'Yes, I understand, but that isn't your basis for negotiations, is it, Antony?'

Long, disjointed, sincere speech.

'You mean, do you, Tony, that you want to establish rights for all students everywhere?'

'We're not only struggling for students, but for everyone who's not allowed to speak for himself.'

'That means, doesn't it, that even if and when you reach a satisfactory settlement at the college, you'll still go on protesting—'

'The struggle will go on.'

The principal of the college, interviewed in the same programme two nights later, wasn't so comfortable, nor so respectfully treated. He was a man in his mid-forties, with a neat small-featured face. I hadn't met him, but as he was a physicist and a good one, the Getliffes knew him well. He was said to be fun in private, and to be conscientious and open-minded. Why he had given up science and taken to university administration none of his admirers could understand. Perhaps he couldn't, as on the box he gave an impression – so unjustified, that he ought to bring a slander action against himself, someone said – of being irresolute and even shifty.

Yes, he was in favour of student participation at all levels. They would be welcome on suitable college committees.

'But aren't you on record as saying, Dr Dinshaw, that the students' claim to a place on appointments committees—' Dinshaw: That, of course, was a special case: it wasn't considered in the students' interest to take part in appointments of lecturers or professors.

(Why the hell, said Margaret, doesn't he say that they'd be totally incompetent to judge?)

But didn't Dr Dinshaw agree that the students felt it was very much in their interest? Dinshaw: There were two views about that, after all, there were students and students. The student with whom Dr Dinshaw would have to negotiate, however, had only one view? Dinshaw: The real academics among the students, the ones who would really understand about academic excellence, and that was the important thing about a place of higher education, didn't take part in this kind of student activity.

Of all his remarks, that one sank the principal into most trouble with the press. From then on, the interviewer was needling him. What did the principal understand by the students' wider aims? If they reached a settlement with the college, then Mr Ollorenshaw had pointed out there were claims on behalf of others? At last, badgered, Dinshaw broke out that it wasn't his function to negotiate for the entire human race.

For us, a few minutes' diversion. Each night for a week, there was something about the students. When Charles came round one morning to fetch some clothes, I mentioned that, to begin with, we didn't like to miss the news. But, as a spectator sport, rioting became monotonous. We were getting tired of it. He smiled. I didn't think of asking him whether he knew any of the participants. Instead, he mentioned that he had seen Francis Getliffe, who was off to spend the summer at the house outside Montpellier, which, with his usual decision, leaving me out of it, he had bought that spring.

It might have been two or three days later when, not on television, but in *The Times*, I saw an item of news. One headline ran: STUDENTS CHARGE COLLEGE WORKING ON GERM WAR.

That was it. I needn't have read any more. Angry that I had seen so little, I still didn't see all the connections, or even most of them: but I saw enough. Enough to be waiting for what was coming next.

Actually, the students' announcement was, like most of their official utterances, discreet. It was issued as one of their communiqués from the principal's office, said simply that documents had been found demonstrating that the college microbiological department was under contract to the Ministry of Defence, through the M.R.E. at Porton. The students would insist that all work on biological warfare should be stopped forthwith.

That was ingeniously drafted, I thought. Unless it were a sheer invention, which seemed unlikely, they had got hold of some papers, and the authorities wouldn't know which or how much they gave away.

The signatures, as with all the previous communiqués, were those of Olly and his two adjutants from the college.

Apart from the headlines, the newspaper wasn't spending much space on the announcement. Nor did any of the others that I read. In one leader it was referred to, in an aside, as another sign of 'immature thinking'. The leader went on to ponder whether the grants of student protesters should be withdrawn, and rather surprisingly used this example of immature thinking to conclude that they should not.

There was no reference anywhere to collaboration from outside, or to any Cambridge group. For some reason, perhaps technical, they were being kept in the background, and I was asking myself how much respite that would give.

CHAPTER XXXV

A FOG OF SECRETS

MARGARET was already going to bed when, late the following night, the front door bell rang. I had been sitting in the drawing-room, not certain how much longer I could bear to wait: whether it was wise or not, I should have to talk to Charles. For an instant, I thought this caller might be he. Opening the door, I saw – with disappointment, with let-down – that it was Nina. Rain was trickling from her mackintosh cape and hood.

'I'm so sorry, Uncle Lewis, I don't know what the time is—' she said breathlessly.

'Never mind.'

'But Daddy asked me to give you a message, without fail, he said, tonight.'

'Come in.' The let-down had vanished. I couldn't delay in getting her coat off, bringing her into the drawing-room, meanwhile answering a call from Margaret about who it was.

'Well?' I asked Nina, pressing a drink on her which she wouldn't take. Just then Margaret, in her dressing-gown, joined us, kissed Nina, interposed another wait.

'What did your father say?'

Nine swept dank hair from over her eye. She said:

'I tried to tell him something on the telephone this morning—'

'What was it?'

'Give her a chance,' said Margaret. Nina smiled at her, and then at me. She was shy but firm and self-possessed.

'I told him I'd heard something about people making enquiries at Chester Row, but he stopped me. He wouldn't let me speak on the phone. So I had to go to Cambridge. Then he wouldn't ring you up either, so I had to come back and see you tonight.'

'Yes,' I said, restless with impatience, 'what was this message?'

'He said to tell you – *it looks as though someone like Monteith is already on the job. You must advise them straightaway.*'

I glanced at Margaret. It was all plain. Too plain. Martin's precautions about the telephone had probably been automatic: he had lived with security all through the war and after. So had I, for longer. I had had dealings with Monteith myself, when he was second-in-command of one of the security services. I had dropped out of that claustral system, but I remembered hearing that he had been promoted.

'You were told this morning, were you?' said Margaret. She was quiet but as urgent as I was.

'Yes,' said Nina. The previous evening, two visitors had called at Chester Row. One was a conspicuously fat man (that must be Gilbert Cooke, I broke out, he had taken Monteith's place as number two, the investigation was starting at a very high level).

They had asked all sorts of questions. They had been very friendly and polite—

'They would be,' I commented. There was a technique in interrogation. The next interview, if Gilbert took it himself, wouldn't be quite as friendly.

'Who did they ask?'

'Charles. Muriel. They'd seen Olly already, somewhere else. Oh, and Gordon Bestwick was at Chester Row last night too.'

'What did they seem to be after?'

'How much they knew about b.w. [biological warfare]. Where they'd been for the last week. Had they been inside the college. Had they seen the files from any of the offices. You know.'

I knew, and Margaret also, that Nina herself was remarkably well informed. She was as cool as any of them. She reported that, early in the proceedings, before they were interrogated separately, Muriel had enquired whether she could send for her solicitor, if it seemed a good idea. Charles had stopped her, saying that it was a very bad idea. That was, Margaret and I agreed without a word spoken, good judgment on his part.

They had parted with cordiality. The next step, the fat man had said, was – if they wouldn't mind and if it wasn't too inconvenient – for them to have a talk with his superior. That sounded like Monteith himself: I still couldn't understand – and if I did understand, I was more troubled – why they should be working this enquiry from the top. Normally it would be done by agents very much junior, though Cooke might have been shown the papers.

Those 'talks' were beginning tomorrow: that is, since it was now nearly midnight, in a few hours' time. Olly and the signatories to the communiqué had been 'invited' to attend in the morning, Charles, Muriel, and 'poor Gordon' in the afternoon. They were to go to the Admiralty – which everyone else took for granted, but which seemed to me like a piece of mystification for mystification's sake. Monteith and Cooke had perfectly good offices of their own, together with a dislike for using them.

'Why "poor Gordon"?' Margaret was asking.

'He seems to be taking it harder than the others,' said Nina, with a sort of clinical kindness. Then she told us, now that she had given us the hard news and could be off duty for a moment: 'Do you know, when Daddy heard that all this happened at Chester Row, that was the first time he had realised that Charles and Muriel were living together?'

She gave an innocent smile at the innocence of the elderly.

'What did he think about it?' Margaret said.

'I think he was rather shocked.'

As a matter of fact, about a sexual adventure Martin and a none-too-prim citizen of Antonine Rome would have been about equally shockable. If he disliked this one, it was because the woman had been his son's wife, and he was still capable of blaming her.

I had been thinking, it would be better if Nina, not I, rang up Chester Row. If they were at home, I ought to go there at once. As she was obeying, she hesitated and remarked, as though it were an afterthought:

'I don't think anyone mentioned Guy Grenfell last night. I don't think he's having to go tomorrow.'

Then she went to the telephone. Those last words seemed curiously inconsequential: but Margaret looked at me with eyes indulgent but sharp. She had no doubt that Guy Grenfell was Nina's channel of communication – and very little more that she had brought him into the conversation, partly because she was anxious about him, partly for the pleasure of uttering his name. Uttering his name with people there to hear: she might be self-possessed, an excellent courier, but she wasn't immune to the softer pleasures. Margaret liked her for it. As for me, in the hurry and tension of the evening, I wondered for a moment whether this would come as a surprise to Martin, and whether or not he would approve.

In the hall of our block of flats, I waited, Nina beside me, for a taxi. I was feeling the special chagrin of no transport that came upon one in big towns. It was raining as hard as that night the previous summer when Charles had sauntered slowly home, absent-minded with joy. If we walked to the tube station, I said to Nina, we should get drenched. Did she mind? Don't be silly, Uncle Lewis, she said, taking my arm, as physically relaxed as she was shy, dark hair falling from under her hood, cheeks flushed, looking already naiad-like in the rain. I had an irrelevant thought, it was absurd that on this particular night I should arrive at their house, Muriel's and my son's, just as inspissatedly soaked as when I first arrived, long ago, at Sheila's.

We were, however, rescued. A car drew up – 'Aren't you getting wet?' came a cheerful but not original question. The driver happened to be the one neighbour with whom, after twenty years living there, I was on social terms. Chester Row? No problem. Humming merrily, rosy after a party but driving with care, he took us through the midnight-empty streaming streets.

At the house, Charles opened the door, with Muriel waiting close by, but there was at once a hiatus. He held my coat, but both of them were looking, with glances that were not unfriendly but steady and purposeful, at Nina.

'How are we going to get you home?' said Charles, quite affectionately, giving a good impersonation of an elder brother. He didn't look it, but he was a month younger.

'I think I'd better order a car. We shan't get a taxi tonight,' said Muriel.

They weren't going to talk in front of Nina. They had realised, it didn't take much divining, where my information had come from. They didn't seem to resent my possessing it (in fact they had greeted me with warmth and perhaps relief) but they weren't giving Nina the chance to transmit any more. They had become, and no one could blame them, as security conscious as the men who had been questioning them.

They were doing less than justice, though, both to themselves and Nina. It wasn't through their laxness that she had learned any single fact: as I discovered later, Guy Grenfell had of necessity to know all the secrets, and they couldn't have foreseen that, apparently all of a sudden, he wanted to share everything with this girl. Whereas Nina, who was really as discreet as her father, had spoken only to him. She couldn't do more, because of her obligations to the others, nor less, because of her duty to do her best for Guy.

Anyway, Muriel did not take her upstairs. We all waited down in the dining-room, Charles pouring me a drink, making a kind of family conversation about Irene's sciatica and Maurice's new wife, whom by this time they had all met. Nina, not at all touchy, showed no sign of resentment at being shut out. She had the talent for acceptance which one sometimes found in the happy. We were all listening, me with impatience, for the car to drive up outside.

At last the three of us were alone in the long drawing-room. Charles and Muriel sat on the sofa facing me, his arm round her and fingers interlaced. It was not often that they were demonstrative in public, if by public one meant anyone else's presence, such as mine.

I said:

'Well, I've heard these people came and questioned you. You'd better tell me what they said.'

Their account, though fuller, agreed with what I had been told already once that night. They both had precise memories, and sometimes they reproduced conversations word by word. There was one point of interest, though it was predictable. When they were being interrogated separately, the two agents had left them for a few minutes, obviously to confer, and returned to concentrate on a day, the preceding Wednesday, for which Charles had already given a story of his movements. She had been taken over the same hours, asked where she had been, how much of the time he had been with her, whether she could sketch out her diary of the day. It was an old trick, and I was surprised that Cooke had used it so blatantly. It had got nowhere. Their reconstructions coincided, and they had demonstrably been telling the truth.

'Yes,' I said. 'That's all right. But it's tomorrow that matters.'

'Or rather today,' said Charles looking at his watch. It was now past one o'clock.

'You've been summoned for the afternoon, haven't you?'

They nodded.

'That gives us a bit of time. There are several ways you ought to prepare yourselves—'

'Look,' said Charles, 'I can handle this situation for myself. For us both.'

It sounded like, it was, a flash of adolescent pride, such as he might have shown two or three years before but had long outgrown. It was strange to hear it from him now. For an instant he seemed sham-arrogant, young or even pathetic. I was moved by a once-familiar yearning, now forgotten or submerged.

'Don't be a fool,' said Muriel, squeezing his fingers, calling him by a pet name which I had never heard. 'He knows things we don't. You've got to listen.'

Charles's face was close to hers, as he broke into a slight acquiescent smile.

'The first thing is,' I said, 'don't underestimate them. They don't work the way we do. They don't believe in intuition much. They just go on adding one and one. But they tend to get there in the end.'

I went on:

'Which means, whenever they have a fact right, and they will have a large number of facts right, your best line is to agree with them. Don't deny anything which they can prove. That makes it easier, if you want to deny something which they can't prove.'

'I follow,' said Charles, who was now gazing at me with concentration.

'Don't say any more than you need. You can tell them you disapprove of biological weapons. They'll be used to that. Don't elaborate. Don't go in for systematic theory. Remember their politics are simpler than yours.'

'What do I do?' asked Muriel.

'The same.'

'Won't it look as though he's rehearsed me, though?'

'You can't provide for everything. People aren't clever enough to pretend for long. No, you say the same. Same facts, same timetable, same attitude. That's natural. After all, to some extent I presume it happens to be true.'

Muriel gave a neutral smile. For the first time I noticed a very small dimple on her right cheek, close to her mouth, which didn't appear to have its replica on the other side.

'I want to ask you something,' I said curtly. 'For practical reasons I ought to know. It's almost certainly Charles they're after' (I was addressing myself to Muriel), 'not you. So I ought to know.' Then I spoke straight at him: 'What have you done?'

He leant back, the whites of his eyes visible under the irises. 'That's not so easy to answer—'

'That's nonsense.'

She was coming to his help, saying, 'No, it's really not,' when he sat up and faced me.

'No,' he said, in a level tone, 'I don't mind telling you, but it isn't so easy. I don't want to fake it either way.'

'Well then. Did you extract those letters from the office?'

'No,' he replied. 'Not with my own hands, that is. But that's the trouble, I don't want to pretend that I'm not involved.'

'How much are you involved?'

'I knew about it before and after.'

'But you didn't take the letters?'

'I've told you, no.'

'You had them in your hands?' As I asked, Muriel was shaking her head, but he wasn't looking at her for confirmation.

'Not that either. But I've seen photostats.'

That, though it was clearly true, seemed an odd piece of bureaucratic procedure.

'Have you been inside those offices?' I meant by that, those of the principal and the professors.

'Not at the relevant times.' (That is, when the files were ransacked.) 'But I have been inside them, yes.'

'So have I, so have the others,' Muriel intervened. On the spot, that baffled me. It appeared that each of the Cambridge group had been by himself inside the college. Charles and Muriel, not together but on their own, had been smuggled in at night. Later it occurred to me that Olly might be making certain that they were committed. He had made use of them, very sensibly, as staff officers, and hadn't wasted them as crowd fodder. As for spokesmen, he didn't want too many public faces. But the private faces had to perform some token action: so each of them had made his visit and had, in form, taken part in the occupation. After they had told me of those incidents, so far as I could guess holding nothing back, I said:

'That is all?'

'That is all,' said Charles.

'They will know nearly everything you've said, either of you.' I was talking of Monteith and his people. I emphasised that they would almost certainly know of meetings in this house and of the nocturnal visits. They would probably know that Charles was one of those who had been shown

photostats. It was not impossible that they had had an informer somewhere near: it was not impossible, it was probable that they had one,
though how close to the centre I couldn't guess. It was not impossible
that they knew of Charles's staff work and of the first idea about the b.w.
documents, but that would be very difficult to prove. On that he needn't
volunteer anything.

'It comes to this, doesn't it?' Muriel was speaking, having been subdued
most of the night, acting only as a support for Charles. 'They'll know
that he's connected, we couldn't cover that up if we wanted to, could we?
But that's really all they'll know and I suppose something like that applies
to me.'

'That's the best you can expect,' I said.

Neither of them was soft, but they were lost, and to an extent frightened
because they were groping, in the security fog. I had been in my mid-
thirties when, at the beginning of the war, I had my first taste of that
peculiar chilling swirl. They had walked into it very early. When I
mentioned that there might have been an informer among their circle,
even in this house, they had looked both astonished and, unlike either of
them, dismayed. They had felt an intimation of the mosaic of paranoia,
the shrinking or freezing of one's own nature, that came to any of us when
overwhelmed by secrecy. You had only to feel that paranoia for a short
period in your life, to live just temporarily with security, to understand
what happened to conspirators once they gripped the power and then
realised there might be other conspiracies, this time against themselves.

Quietly, Charles asked:

'What is the worst we can expect?'

'They might know effectively everything that you've said and done.'

'What would that mean? For him?' Though, as the night went on,
Muriel's eyes were becoming reddened with tiredness, they were brilliant.
She had become much more aggressive than he was. She sounded, all the
tricks of politeness gone, as though she were defying me.

I replied, doing my best to seem professional, that it was almost unthinkable they would prosecute. It wouldn't be worth the publicity.
Incidentally they wouldn't like to give away their sources of information.
There would, however, be entries on personal dossiers. There would be
communications about Charles and his friends with persons at Cambridge.
It was conceivable that one or two promising academic careers would be
interrupted.

'Do you think that will happen?' he said.

'Your guess is about as good as mine.'

'If it does, you wouldn't like it, would you?'

'No.'

He said: 'Nor should I.'

He had been speaking intimately, equal to equal. He didn't ask if I understood why he had acted. He might have taken that for granted, or thought it irrelevant. He wasn't trying to be considerate. It was knowledge, of himself and me, that he was speaking from, not emollience.

'You know,' he said, in genuine, unaffected surprise, 'I didn't think I should mind – if it came to trouble. I find that I do.'

Muriel broke in fiercely, as though rallying him, though he was much calmer than she was. It couldn't and didn't matter practically: nothing would break his academic career for long: anyway, it didn't matter, he couldn't really be touched. Anything he had ever talked of doing was quite outside anyone else's power.

I sat silent while she stormed at him, once or twice her gaze flashing towards me.

Charles smoothed back her hair, and said:

'All right. All right. But some of us don't find it quite so easy to escape from the respectable embrace, you know.'

He said it teasing her, with affection. Yet, strangely enough, though he had made remarks which sounded arrogant once or twice that night, that was the only one which struck me so.

A little later, as I was getting ready to go, he said to me, in an altogether different tone:

'I'm sorry if all this is a trouble to you. I know it is.'

I said, taken by surprise at his naturalness, more bluff than I usually was, that there were worse things.

Muriel, brilliant with courtesy returned, said:

'We've been very grateful for all your help, Uncle Lewis, you're much too kind, aren't you? I'm very sorry if we're a trouble to you. I am so very sorry.'

CHAPTER XXXVI

A SELECTED MEETING-PLACE

NEXT evening Gordon Bestwick called on me. By this time they had become obsessively careful about telephoning or any other means of communication short of physical presence: thus Charles hadn't rung me up to report on his interview with Monteith but had sent Gordon round instead.

At least, that was the ostensible reason for the visit, but I soon found that he was consumed with worry. Perhaps Charles thought I might give him some relief.

It was hard work, either when Margaret was present or when she had made an excuse to set Gordon and me free for a walk outside. To begin with, he wouldn't talk at all about the interview that afternoon. Whether they had resolved not to speak to unauthorised persons, and whether they had decided that Margaret was such a one, I couldn't tell. It might have been that she still kept an air of something like privilege, whereas I was nearer to the ground he knew.

If that was so, it was a classic case of misjudgment. For Margaret, used all her life to her relatives making exhibitions of themselves for conscience sake, was the least disturbed of any of us. After all, her father and his friends had received obloquy and worse through being conscientious objectors in the First World War: they had been under inspection twenty years later as premature anti-Fascists, being used as front men by the other side. They were people who had been brought up – and who had had the not negligible encouragement of private means – not to give a damn.

So, though she hadn't much patience with the students' cause, she felt in the nature of things that spirited young men would join it. If they didn't count the risks, well, since her marriage she had come to know so many of my colleagues who (and she had once felt this of me) counted the risks too much. Not that she didn't count the risks for Charles: but she would have said, except when the superstitious flesh was overruling her, that she hoped he wouldn't do so for himself.

She did her best to get Gordon talking as he sat sprawled on the sofa, great formidable head back against the cushions, at times fidgeting upwards as though he were trying to take part. The head wasn't less formidable, but more grotesque, on account of a large acne pustule on his nose. He looked so miserable that we both forgot that he was a man probably stronger, and with the certainty of more powers to come, than either of us. We just saw him lolling there, with the lost-for-ever misery of youth. And it was a double misery. Once he roused himself and asked Margaret when she last saw Nina.

'Last night, actually,' said Margaret, speaking the truth, not knowing whether she should.

'Oh.' A hard noise. I felt a kind of pity, sentimental perhaps, for young men who had no confidence with girls.

Soon afterwards Margaret left us, and immediately I asked him what had happened yesterday. Even then he did not reply at ease. I had to say, my brother and I felt safer, discussing security affairs in the open air. Would he prefer that? When we were walking up the streets towards Lancaster Gate, for the first time his voice lost its dullness.

The interrogations, he said, had lasted about an hour each: there was mention of more to follow. At intervals 'the man' (who had not introduced himself) interjected not as questions but as facts, statements about the examinee – 'where I was, what I had been doing,' Gordon told me. 'Irrelevant, a lot of it. But they had collected stuff about me that they seemed to know better than I did.'

They had been to his school, and to people who knew his family. That was standard technique, I said. It seemed strange to have it brought up now, he replied. That was standard response, everyone felt that, I said. As for what happened, both in the rising and in the plans, they knew plenty.

'They're leaving us guessing in spots. Whether they know or whether they're bluffing. But they know enough to fix us. If we try to fool ourselves about that, we shall make things worse.'

Apparently one or two of the principals, though not Charles or Muriel, were still self-buoyant with optimism (the adrenalin-optimism of action, perhaps; Gordon had spent last night upon them, using his bitterest and most competent tongue). As we walked along, he wasn't saying anything that couldn't have been foreseen. Up a side street, people were carrying their tankards outside a pub, standing on the pavement in the warm air. I asked Gordon if he would like a drink. No, he said, he wasn't feeling much like it. He might be one of those – I could sympathise – who in trouble shied away from any sort of solace.

Except perhaps the solace of making resolutions.

'This is a lesson for us, anyway,' he said roughly, not looking towards me, but as though I were a companion who had to be convinced. 'We mustn't make the same mistake again. We tried to do two things at once, and that's because we were too conceited. We made it all too complicated, it was my fault and Carlo's. It seemed a good idea, but it was an infantile mistake. It mustn't be repeated—'

He meant, and it was probably true, that without the inner plan of seizing official correspondence the rest would have been a total success. Which to the external world it had already been. Olly and his committee were getting their demands piecemeal: by the end of the summer their whole charter would have been met. But that was easy, Gordon was reflecting with harsh realism. Whatever students wanted as students would be given them on a plate. It was child's play to make that kind of impact. But when the impact broke through a bit deeper, got right among the things which the society would hold on to like death, then the forces of resistance suddenly crept round you—

'Damn them to hell,' said Gordon, 'why do they always know when to use their blasted advantages?'

I replied, with the kind of sarcasm that I should have used to Charles, that it didn't seem to me entirely unreasonable. You used your means of offence: established society replied with its own.

'Damn them to hell,' said Gordon. 'I hate them. I hate them and everything they stand for.'

He was not disposed either to dispassion or irony. What was right for him was wicked for the other side. That capacity for anger was a great help to him that day and might, I thought, be a strength in the future. Nearly all men of action possessed it. You had to believe the other side was a hundred per cent wrong, and preferably evil, to be a hundred per cent committed to your own. It was one of the more disagreeable facts of life. I much preferred Gordon when he was sad, trying to cope with a heavy-weight temperament, mind sharp, senses rebelling: but it was his talent for anger which acted like a blood transfusion that evening, lifted him out of sadness or even fright, made one simultaneously less engaged by his company and more certain that he would survive.

It must have been shortly after that night, possibly in the same week, that he met with the rest of the inner circle on two occasions, which, according to the accounts I heard later that year, were more eventful, or at least more tense, than any of their planning sessions in Chester Row.

There had been a geographical change. These two meetings didn't take place in Muriel's study. The whole group had now become hypno-tised by security, as we all did when it percolated round ourselves, as detestable as the smell of gas. They decided that Chester Row, and they were not necessarily wrong, was not security-proof. So they shifted the venue.

Their choice of a second meeting-place seemed to bear the imprint of ingenious minds familiar with political history, possibly Gordon's or Charles's: for, with what must have been a tinge of satisfaction, they chose a setting not likely to be kept under surveillance. That is, they chose the London house, in Halkin Street, of Guy Grenfell's father, chairman of his local Conservative party, Baronet (for political and public services), member of the Carlton, Beefsteak, Pratts, The Turf and White's.

A disinterested observer might have gained a subdued pleasure from the fact that this house, in period, style, structure and market value, was remarkably similar to Muriel's and only just over half a mile away.

Present at both these meetings were Olly, his two deputies, Muriel, Gordon, Charles and Guy Grenfell. The first of them lasted from 9 p.m. till something like one the next morning, the second rather longer. There was little to eat or drink. Before them was a single topic, the security attack on the b.w. disclosure, and how to get out of it with the least damage.

It was possible to think, as some of them did in calmer times, that they exaggerated their danger. Perhaps for the first time they were not behaving like experienced operators. If so, I was partly to blame: for my warnings, which had been overstressed and more darkened by pessimism because I was thinking of Charles, had been taken as a precise, almost official, forecast by Muriel and Gordon, and relayed as such to Olly. So that from the beginning they all assumed that lies or stonewalling weren't going to last them for long: they had, as a minimum, to produce a story which admitted some of the truth. That is, that letters about the sub-contract had been suspected, and deliberately searched for, and then, as was public knowledge, used.

The story ought to be kept as simple as possible. It ought to involve as few persons as possible. Security might know or half-know more than they could reveal, and would conceivably be placated by an account which was less than complete but was self-consistent.

All this was debated, and often repeated, for they were all under strain, at the first session. It seemed that Muriel played more of a leading part than usual. She wasn't as creative as one or two of the others, but she was as acute, particularly for this kind of semi-legal argument, as any of them. She also had influence on Olly, so that in the end she brought him round to a solution. It could all be very simple. It could be just one person's private initiative. And that meant one thing. Someone had to take the rap.

That phrase had been used by Olly – who, like other leaders, had no fastidious objections to a cliché – to sum up the first meeting. It would not be difficult to develop a history of how one person became committed to the idea and executed it. Who? It had, in order to agree with the facts which security were known to possess, to be one of the Cambridge cell. In the end, it reduced to one of the three, Charles, Gordon, Guy.

As I had already been told, the real conception had emerged, not only from those three, but from several others, all drawn together in a sort of invisible college or committee of young men. Who carried it through, that is who was present when the offices were invaded and the files searched, I never knew, nor (I was nearly certain) did my source of all this information. Apart from his own denial, I had some reason, circumstantial but strong, to believe that it was not Charles. I was inclined to think that the balance of evidence pointed to Gordon. In any case, it was very largely chance who had been the actual agent. Olly paid no attention to it when, in the second session, he made them come to a decision. Someone had to take the rap. It had to be the one whom the movement could most easily spare. Olly might not be a brilliant young man: possibly he would not be heard of much again. But in that meeting he showed his quality. Not brought into contact with him (I was told that I should be bored) I thought he sounded something like a junior Parnell. Not bright: not specially articulate, but somehow he could stay still and people waited to listen to him.

The one whom the movement could spare. There was no sentiment about the choice. If it fell on Gordon, he would suffer most, being poor and depending on his grants and the prospect of a fellowship. While Charles was the youngest of the whole party. So far as anyone could see, Olly didn't give even a token consideration to either of those claims. He cut out what old Crawford used to call the personalia. He was cordial and, without making a show of it, ruthless.

None of this was done quickly. Leaders of his type didn't utter laconic orders out of the side of the mouth. It was a long churning conversation, more like a trade union committee than a meeting of the Stavka. The more astute, though, didn't take long to see that the result was already determined. Gordon was the last man to sacrifice, Olly led one of his aides into saying: they needed him for the future, he was their best economic brain, probably the best brain all round that they possessed. On a reduced scale there was some similar opinion in favour of Charles. He wasn't specially popular with Olly: perhaps his ironic tongue, or the fact that some of them thought him unduly lucky, had made enemies. He himself said that he was reasonably expendable: the consequences, in practical terms, would not be all that important to him But the majority would not have it. Whether living with Muriel went in his favour or not, it was impossible to make out. All in all, the positives outweighed the negatives, and they said that he was too useful to lose.

So, slowly, talk gradually converging, never pointed, the party came to look towards Guy Grenfell. Just how it was made clear to him that he had to volunteer remained obscure, even when I was told the story. Almost certainly, there was no direct remark or question. On the other hand, there must have been a number of hints, and not too subtle ones. In his own house, very likely having thoughts of his parents, Guy for a long time managed to avoid seeing them.

It must have been, I thought later, like a drawing-room version of more mortal sacrifices. You couldn't read the diaries of the Scott expedition without realising that it had been hinted, more than once, to Captain Oates that he ought to go. The solemn issue of morphine pills a few days before. No one I knew who had been in any kind of collective danger doubted the tone in which that was done. The finale was grand. They were brave men. Actions weren't the less grand because those who performed them were recognisably like the rest of us.

It took a long time, but Guy brought out his offer. Not in a gallant manner, but with a touch both of truculence and superciliousness. The others responded with relief, but taking it very much for granted. They all knew he had money of his own. They all knew also that he was not a star academic. Charles, who was fond of him and felt he was a richer character than most of them, first repeated his own offer and then acted as impresario in producing enthusiasm for Guy's. The others crowded round with comradely applause. Courtesies over, they set to work composing a history – where Guy was a solitary figure – which security would find it hard not to accept. They did not break up until that was tested and done.

Security either did find it hard not to accept, or, more likely, for their own reasons were glad to pretend to do so. All that outsiders – including me, at the time – knew was that, suddenly, the fuss about biological warfare disclosures died down. There was an official statement, of a muffled nature, saying that no secrets had been revealed and that precautions about the Official Secrets Act in relation to government research establishments were being enquired into, as a routine precaution. The college issued its own statement saying that, in general principle, contracts from government departments were not normally undertaken; that the demands of the students for representation had been met: and further that the college and the students had set up a joint committee to examine any further points in dispute.

Some time in July, Charles and Muriel paid us a call, and with meaning but without explanation said that Guy Grenfell would in September be leaving for Harvard and would complete his studies there.

CHAPTER XXXVII

A GARDEN AND LIGHTED WINDOWS

WHEN Muriel asked over the telephone if I 'could possibly call round' for a drink, and I said yes, neither of us pretended the invitation was just a casual thought. As before that year, she had chosen Margaret's evening away from home: arriving at Chester Row, I should have been surprised to find Charles in. At once, as I entered the drawing-room, Muriel apologised blank-faced for his absence. Then she kissed me, not in the happy-go-lucky English fashion, but as though it were a deliberate, an hieratic gesture. Our cheeks parted, and she was standing upright, her eyes not far below mine: I noticed, which I hadn't before, the first starry lines at the corners, fine and faint on the smooth healthy skin.

She led me to the window seat, where she had been sitting. At the bottom of the window, a few inches were open.

'Is that too much for you?' she asked.

'Not a bit,' I said, amused by the old-fashioned phrase. Actually, the breath of air was warm: outside it was a beautiful night for late September.

Facing me on the seat she said:

'I wanted to tell you, Uncle Lewis.'

'Yes?'

'We're fairly certain now that we're in the clear.'

I nodded. I didn't ask for evidence. On such a matter, I had confidence in her judgment.

'We thought of letting you know before this. But he was keeping his fingers crossed a little.'

'So should I have been.'

'Would you?' She looked at me with a flash of interest, as though searching my lineaments for the most remote resemblance to my son.

There was a momentary silence. She said:

'It really is all right, Uncle Lewis.'

'Excellent.'

As we sat there on the window seat, there was another, and a longer, silence. I was used to her enough by now to feel that this wasn't the only point of the meeting. Her legs were intertwined, one foot jerking from the ankle. It was rare for her not to have her body, as much as or more than her expression, under complete control.

She said:

'I wonder if you could possibly bear to have your drinks in the garden?

It's almost nice enough, perhaps. Of course it's being a terrible nuisance—'

'Let's go,' I replied. She was taking refuge in politeness which didn't sound like politeness, which might have been mocking. But when I began to move, she leapt up, crossed the room to the sideboard, agile with physical relief. She arranged the tray, and preceded me down the stairs, through her back sitting-room, out to the patio garden. Carrying the tray, she was as poised as a shipboard steward. Some women, I thought, with a figure like hers would have been conscious of it, but that impression she had never given me.

At the end of the garden, table and chairs were waiting under an overhanging rose-bush, a bloom or two gleaming out in the twilight. There was a smell, already autumnal, of drying leaves, blended with something less wistful, perhaps – I couldn't place it – a tobacco plant? She poured out a drink for me, and I sat comfortably sipping. The news was good. Whatever she was intending to say, I was ready to wait. It was getting on for seven o'clock in the evening. In the west, towards the King's Road, the sky was still luminous. From the houses on each side of Muriel's, lighted windows were already shining.

Looking at one of them, amber curtains drawn with a chink between them, a standard lamp just visible, for an instant a shape passing across, I felt a curiosity, or something softer like a yearning, which when I was younger I should have thought inadmissible, maudlin and nevertheless undeniable, and which was just as undeniable now. Once, long before, when I was an outsider, gazing at strangers' windows from the nocturnal streets, it might have been explicable that I should have imagined the hearth glow of homes such as I didn't have: when I longed for one to return to. Often I had pretended to myself that it was sheer inquisitiveness about others' lives, trying to feel proud because I wasn't tamed and was on my own. That wasn't altogether false. The inquisitiveness was there also. Walking with Maurice on the sombre Christmas afternoon, two or three years ago, I had been oddly gratified – more than the event deserved – as he pointed to lighted rooms in the derelict squares and told me some of the stories that lay behind.

Yet that evening in Muriel's garden, when curiosity and longing ought both to have been satisfied, I felt the same emotion as I should have felt as a young man. Habits, I had told myself before this, at a time when I had learned less, lived longer than freedoms. Sometimes they told one more about oneself.

We had been sitting quietly. Muriel gazed up the garden at her own house, so that I could see only her profile, which was becoming softened as the light grew dimmer. Then she said:

'I'm sorry, but I think you're misunderstanding me.' Her tone was clear, but (I thought I heard) not quite composed.

'What about?'

'Charles.'

'What about him?'

'You won't see it. But you and I, we're on the same side.'

'Are we?' My voice had become rough and unconceding.

'I think we are.'

She wasn't to be beaten down. Her eyes were fixed steadily on me now. She said:

'You'd like him to make the best of himself, I think you would. And so should I.'

'We might not agree', I replied, 'on what that means.'

'It means, that we should like him to make the most of his talent. Or wouldn't you?' For an instant, she gave a sharp and attacking smile. There was nothing between us, though. Neither age, nor sex, nor subliminal dislike.

'Of course I should.'

'Yes. I'm afraid that he may take one risk too many.'

'You mean, what you've just been doing—'

'No, no, no. We've learned something. That's not the correct way, we shall have to find another method. By the way, I'm not apologising for us. I'm sure he'd be angry with me if I did. And I don't feel like doing so on my own account.'

'What is this risk that he's going to take?'

She shook her head. 'Haven't you noticed that he keeps his secrets?'

'From you?'

'Oh yes. From me.'

'What do you know, then?'

'I don't know. I may be imagining it. You can guess how one does—' Just then, she lost her crispness.

'Well, what are you afraid of?'

'It's not for tomorrow. It's not until he's finished at Cambridge' (that is, until he graduated in the following June). 'Then—'

'Then what?'

'I think he may be deciding to get away from us all.'

'Will he leave you?'

'Men have left women before, haven't they?' She added in a level tone: 'He would also be leaving you.'

'Men have left their fathers before, haven't they?' I replied, copying her. Then, to make amends I said: 'But that's different. He's bound to do that. In fact, he's done it already.'

'When he came to me?'

'Long before.'

'Do you think he's quite as free as that?' Eye-glint in the expressionless face. She went on:

'Who do we believe he's escaping from? You think it must be me, don't you? I rather prefer to think that it's really you.'

I smiled. Even now, when she was speaking in earnest, her kind of subterranean impudence once or twice broke through. I said that it might not be either of us: I had come, I told her, to distrust the subjective explanations. His motive might have nothing to do with anyone but himself.

'I don't care why he's doing it,' she said sharply, 'so long as we can keep him safe.'

'You still haven't told me, safe from what?'

'I wish I knew.'

'No, what are you thinking of?'

She looked away, frowning.

'In some ways, he's cautious, isn't he? He always says he's very timid, but all that means is that he likes working things out in advance. He can be very cool, but he's a gambler too. I think that's what I'm afraid of. He might decide to do something sensational if he thought it was worth the risk.'

She might be right. My nerves were getting tightened in tune with hers. At the same time, I was thinking, it was strange to hear Charles, whom I assumed that I knew well, described by someone who also knew him well.

'I wish,' she said, 'we could find something for him that kept him away from that—'

'What would you like him to do?'

Eye-glint again.

'Just about the same as you would. Something nice and quiet for a few years. Like Gordon Bestwick—' She told me that Gordon was proposing to get a job in academic life, waiting 'under cover' to see where he might go into action. There wasn't any doubt, she said, that some Cambridge college would soon snap him up. There wasn't any doubt that the same would happen to Charles also, if we could persuade him to stay.

'Well, that's what I should like for him, to begin with. There couldn't be anything more respectable than that, could there?'

She gazed straight at me, and went on:

'You used to think that I wanted to get hold of him, didn't you? Just to be useful in campaigns?'

'Yes, I did.'

'You were quite wrong, you know. I doubt if anyone could get hold of him like that. I should never have stood a chance. No, it wasn't that. You can see it wasn't that, can't you?'

I nodded. 'What is it, though?'

She replied:

'I want him.'

After a pause, she added: 'I wanted him before we started. I want him more now.'

She was speaking even more quietly, like a reticent neighbour at a dinner-table asking one to pass the salt. At the same time, there was an undertone of something like blame – no, heavier than that – directed not at him nor me, but at herself. She wasn't convinced, it seemed, that I believed or trusted her. She was playing for me as an ally, she hadn't pretended anything else: now, as though the treaty were not signed and one party had to produce evidence of good faith, she was searching for something to tell me.

It was then that I heard some history. About the meetings in her house, and the undercover plans. She described the sessions in Halkin Street, which were, of course, utterly unknown to me. In fact, there wasn't much of her story I was likely ever to have known: for neither she nor Charles would have spoken without a purpose. Ostensibly her purpose was to persuade me that she hadn't over-influenced Charles, that in their political efforts they had been partners, and that, so far as there was influence, it had been more on his side than hers. That I couldn't judge, though her reporting seemed as precise as his would have been. In any case, the balance of influence didn't interest me so much. I was listening to what she was saying – whether intentionally or not, I didn't know – about herself and Charles.

I remembered hearing Azik Schiff talking about them in his splashy exuberant domestic fashion. His stepdaughter's taste was distinctly more austere. She did not once admit or confess that she was in love. She certainly wasn't rejoicing at the state in which she found herself. She seemed to feel resentful, or at least not pleased with fate, at being emotionally trapped: just as another woman, starting a casual affair, might curse at another trap, that is the more primitive one of being pregnant.

The curious thing was, that about her feeling for Charles Azik had been right: right for the wrong reasons perhaps, but still right. She was in love. Myself, long before, even when I had been frustrated and wretched, I drew a kind of elation out of the state itself: other people were dull dogs, here was I, borne up in a special capsule of my own. Nothing like that was true of Muriel. If I had mentioned my own experience to her, she might have regarded it either as a sign of self-deception or alternatively as though it was as irrelevant as some reminiscence from the Languedoc courts of love.

As we gazed up the garden, lights had sprung out from other windows. Muriel's house had the second and third floors left dark. Her voice sounded more than ever clear. None of us had been sure that we knew much about her. Was it possible, I was wondering, that she was one of those who were abnormally free of sexual guilt, and who, on the other hand, weren't easily touched by what I called love and in my youth boasted about? So that, if they were threatened or overcome by that kind of love, they felt it as a dark and frightening force. If you took sex without guilt or any other consequences or ancillaries, were you at risk? That is, did you fear all the menace of emotion that most of us had taken as part of love? That seemed to be true of some of the old Greeks. Or the Japanese. Might it be true of this young woman, so disciplined, trying to persuade me as we sat in her garden?

It was noticeable that, when she spoke of other human relations, she wasn't inhibited at all. Just as she had once asked me whether I loved Charles, so she spoke without any reserve about her love for her own child. As though parental love wasn't a danger, and we could in tranquillity use the word. Well, she hadn't yet known in full what parental love was like. Perhaps she was right though, in talking as though they were different in kind. As I had thought one night lying in the hospital bedroom, if love was the proper term for what (as I had that evening accepted) she felt for Charles, then though parental feeling could be as desperate, and could bring as great a solace, it ought to be called by a different name.

Talking of how much she loved the infant, she mentioned that Charles was very fond of him.

'He loves children, did you know?' she said.

She added:

'I'd be glad to give him all he wants.'

It sounded casual, but she hadn't said much that was casual all that evening. When I let her see that, if she was right about Charles's intentions, then obviously I would help her if I could, she wasn't satisfied. She couldn't leave it alone, almost as though she were persuading, not me, but him.

CHAPTER XXXVIII

INTERROGATION BY A STATESMAN

WHEN the rumour spread that someone was intending to speak about the summer's disturbances in the Lords, most of us believed it. If acquaintances eagerly brought a vaguely displeasing rumour, it usually turned out to be true. None of Charles's group – all except Muriel were now back for the university term – appeared to be much perturbed: but Charles decided that it ought to be watched.

That was the reason that he and I, one afternoon at the end of October, were sitting in the gallery of the Lords' chamber. I had tried to get tickets from Francis Getliffe, but was told that he hadn't returned to Cambridge: so I had fallen back on Walter Luke, who said that he was down to answer a question that afternoon. As soon as I looked at the order paper, I expected that it was the question Charles and I were waiting for. It was fourth and last on the list. *The Lord Catforth. To ask Her Majesty's Government whether the defence contracts alleged to be disclosed during the disturbances at —— College in June had actually been placed with the college.*

It wasn't a masterpiece of legal drafting: but the civil servants who had to write the official answer would have realised at first sight that it wasn't innocent. I could recall similar questions arriving flagged in my in-tray in days past: and Hector Rose's glacial and courteous contempt for all the trial shots at the answer, including, though for politeness' sake not mentioned, the most senior, being my own.

The civil servants would have known, it was their business to know, something about the questioner. He was a back-bench Labour peer, recently ennobled, who had served a long time in the Commons: a trade unionist who had made a speciality of military subjects, on which he was considerably to the right of the Tory front bench.

It was a Thursday, about five past three. High up in the gallery (there was, as mountaineering books used to say, an uncomfortable feeling of space in front of one) we looked down on a packed house. A house so packed that it might have been one of the perspectiveless collective portraits of historical Lords debates, hung in their own corridors. The scarlet and gold was swamped. Grey heads gleamed, bald heads shone: there were some very young heads also, one or two as hirsute as Guy Grenfell's. This attendance was not, however, in honour of Catforth's question. A debate on Southern Rhodesia was to follow later that day, and there might (or might not) be a vote. For most of those present, the preliminary questions were merely curtain-raisers or minute-wasters; to be endured, just as for parliamentarians anti-climatic business was always having to be endured.

Not so with Charles. He was leaning forward in the gallery, hands clasped round one knee. The fourth question might – it was not likely but it was possible – have its dangers. He was keyed up, but actively so, as, I guessed, he would have been before an examination. If he could have taken part, he would have been happy.

He was also, I supposed, not put off by flummery. He and his friends were disrespectful towards English formalities, but they were used to them. A stately question number two about salmon fisheries in Scotland made him smile, but not so incredulously as if he had been a foreigner. Content changed, forms stayed, I used to think. I was no nearer knowing the answer to an old puzzle of mine, how much of the forms he and his contemporaries would leave intact.

At last the fourth question. 'The Lord Catforth.' A big man, with large spectacles and a black moustache, rose from the middle of the Government benches, opposite to us in the gallery. 'I beg leave to ask—' standard formula, but not mumbled, sententiously uttered.

Walter Luke, who had been putting his feet up from the front bench, stood at the despatch-box. His hair was now steel grey, not pepper and salt, but his face had filled out in his fifties, the lines, instead of being furrows, had become undramatic creases.

In the comfortable West-Country burr, from his official file he read:

Her Majesty's Government are aware that certain allegations were made during the June disturbances. As my honourable friend said in another place on 29 June none of these correspond to the facts as known by him. It is true that from time to time defence contracts have been placed with the college, as with many other university institutions. All such contracts are of a research nature which makes them suitable for work in university laboratories. They are placed in accordance with recognised procedures which have been used for many years, in the case of the college in question since before 1939.

Loyal hear-hears from those near Walter. The civil servants must have calculated, I was thinking, that the wider, the better.

Lord Catforth, on his feet again: *While thanking my noble friend for that answer, it does not appear to answer the question.*

Scattered hear-hears.

Will my noble friend tell us whether any contracts of a specifically military nature relating to biological warfare have been placed with the college?

As soon as I heard that, I was sure that there had been some colloguing with Lord Catforth. Perhaps the whips had got at him. Anyway he was not the man to disapprove of any weapon either already in existence or ever to become so.

And Walter Luke was suspiciously quick in glancing at the answers to possible supplementaries with which he had been briefed.

Lord Luke of Salcombe: *I can assure the House that no contracts of a specifically military nature, either relating to biological warfare, or any other kind of weapon, have been or will be placed with the college under the present Government.*

Louder hear-hears.

Someone gave voice from under the gallery whom I couldn't see.

Does the noble lord deny that there has been a security leak? Can he estimate how valuable the information about biological warfare will be to the Russians—

Order, order.

Now I thought I recognised the voice. Man of the ultra-right. Probably attending to speak about Rhodesia.

Lord Luke of Salcombe: *As I have said to my noble friend, Lord Catforth, there has been no contract of a military nature relating to biological warfare, and so no information about biological warfare could have been or has been elicited.*

Defence spokesman from the Tory front bench, rising quickly:

Can the noble lord assure us that appropriate security precautions have been taken?

Lord Luke of Salcombe: *I can certainly give that assurance.*

The last question had been intended to be helpful. But it didn't, as it was meant to, silence the interlocutor below.

Can the noble lord tell us how much information reaching the public press during the riots carried security classifications?

Lord Luke of Salcombe: *It would not be in the public interest to answer questions which might bear on security matters.*

Very loud hear-hears from both sides of the house.

Voice: *Well then. Was any of the information which reached the public press covered by the Official Secrets Act? I should like a straight answer from the noble lord. Yes or no.*

Lord Luke of Salcombe: *I am not prepared to let the noble lord form my answer for me. My answer is in fact the same as my answer to his last question.*

Voice: *The noble lord seems incapable of giving a straight answer.* (Order, order, and a few hear-hears.) *Perhaps, since we shall be bound to hear in due course, he might conceivably answer this one. Is the Government intending to prosecute any of the persons concerned under the Official Secrets Act?*

Lord Luke of Salcombe: *No, my lords.*

A few cries of why not, and then a venerable figure spoke, with a disproportionately strong voice, from the Government rear.

Lord F.: *Does the Government realise that many of us on this side and throughout the country share our young people's detestation of this atrocity called biological warfare?*

Lord Luke of Salcombe: *We fully realise what my noble friend has said.*

Lord F.: *Further does the Government realise that anything said about biological warfare by any of the young spokesmen during what I prefer to call the events of last June were said in a spirit of genuine and absolutely spontaneous indignation?*

I looked at Charles, so that his glance met mine. The whites of his eyes were as milk-clear as a child's, the irises almost black. For an instant, blinking not winking, the lids came down and opened again.

Lord F. had spent his life in liberal faiths and never lost them, but Walter Luke could have done without him that afternoon.

Lord Luke of Salcombe: *We all know, at any rate, how genuine my noble friend's spontaneous indignation is.*

The voice under the gallery was raised again, but there were grumbles of order, the leader of the House was half-getting up to intervene, until among a hubbub the supplementaries ceased. One of his colleagues was patting Walter on the knee, and – because another was speaking near to a microphone – we heard a bass and presumably confidential 'well done'.

Walter's cheeks were ruddy and shining. Probably not knowing that he had done an old friend a good turn (for Monteith and his apparatus didn't pass on much to Ministers, perhaps in this case the bare results, not names which they regarded as peripheral as Charles's), he had enough reason to be modestly pleased with himself. His permanent secretary was likely to have warned him that 'this might be an awkward one': students by themselves were a delicate subject by now, students plus security were as delicate as you could reasonably get short of espionage. I should have been prepared to bet that the officials had done some conferring with

Walter's political boss (the Secretary of State, Walter's 'honourable friend', who sat in the Commons and for whom Walter, as his number two, answered in the Lords). Any official would have wished that an experienced politician had to cope with that subject, not an amateur such as Walter.

Still, Walter had done well. I hadn't had attention to spare, but now I was thinking, he might have sunk the Government into trouble. He had got away with it. If this had been the Commons, he would have had a rougher time.

Just then I noticed Azik Schiff entering the chamber and jerking his head in the direction of the throne. I hoped that he wouldn't look up towards the gallery. He had been made a peer that summer and for a few weeks had revelled in it. He had still been at his most exuberant, when in Muriel's garden I thought of him and two different kinds of love, thought of him as a happy man with emotions spilling over.

Now I didn't dare to meet him. Certainly not with Charles by my side. Perhaps, if I believed that I could have been any use to Azik, I might have found the courage, or shamed myself into it. As it was, all I wanted was to avoid his eyes.

It was easier (and more selfish and self-protecting) to return to thinking of Walter. Just as when, not so long before, I was planning a Christmas party and George Passant told me that he was in horrifying trouble: then as now, one's first impulse was to escape, one needed to get him out of the house.

Yes, Walter might have got the Government into trouble. Strange how tactful he had been. Transformed from the brash scientific roughneck of his Barford years. As though he were acting. Sweet reasonable public face. Once upon a time he used to make brisk observations about men with public faces. Stuffed shirts. Then, as though no happier phrase had ever been invented, he would repeat it.

But I recalled that as a very young man, when he was first elected a fellow of the college, he had been as tactful as he was this afternoon. Also self-effacing. Perhaps he had overdone the brashness. It was a part that suited him. Now he seemed to be returning to his youth. I wondered whether he was bland to his officials. Or whether they were treated to the middle-period Walter: unregenerate, behaving like a tycoon in a film, cracking insults out of the corner of his mouth. Strange how a man so rigid in character should act parts in his life. No, not so strange. Just because he was so rigid, the transformations had to be hard-edged. With others they happened in the flux of life, merging into one another, like the colours of an iridescent film, merging continuously and still preserving the same and unique film.

It hadn't been only Walter's tact, though: there had been some operating in private, through 'the usual channels' perhaps, or with Walter and his colleagues conducting some informal little talks themselves. Lord Catforth would have been exposed to blandishments. It was clear that the official Opposition had been squared. That was easy to do in a security matter: besides, the official Opposition was at least as gently disposed to young rebels as the Government, probably more so. Almost certainly, Walter Luke would have had a drink with his opposite number on the Tory side. The opposite number would know, without being told, that Walter proposed to obscure the issue and tell a ministerial fraction of the truth. The opposite number also would know that the students' disclosures were factually true. Walter would wrap up his answer so as to avoid a direct lie. In effect, though not in legalistic words, he might be telling one.

Both front benches, and many experienced persons in the House, would know all those things. It would be a mistake to imagine that they felt qualms of conscience. This was how you had to behave, if you were going to govern at all. Walter had taken it as all in the day's work.

I must have been letting loose a smile, for Charles, sitting at my side in the gallery, returned it, though he could not have guessed anything near the reason. I was thinking about him and one of fate's practical jokes. For it was because of him, who had with strong approval seen me shut the last door on politics and so dismiss the most minor of the three themes of what Margaret's forebears would have called my moral life – it was because of him that I was here, returning to the old subject, interested in the machinery as I used to be. No, as I had confirmed to myself in hospital, it wouldn't capture me again, but there it was.

Just as it was because of Charles that I had been reminded of the other themes, stronger than the first. I had been reminded that they could revive, and had – face to face with Muriel I knew it – already done so.

Walter had instructed me that, when we were tired of sitting in the gallery, we were to make our way to the tea-room. If questions had been followed by the Rhodesia debate, it would have taken more force than mine to tear Charles away: but in fact the next item on the order paper was the second reading of a bill to legalise the use by other denominations of certain redundant Anglican churches. Charles's spirit was not so deeply stirred by that, and so soon we sat close to the tea-room tapestry, waiting for Walter Luke.

When he arrived, I had to introduce Charles to him. He was asking us both, before he sat down, had we heard the bit of fun and games? By which he meant his performance. It was an unnecessary question, since he knew we had come for nothing else. We nodded.

'Was it all right?' said Walter.

'Fine,' I said.

'Did you think it was all right?' Walter had turned to Charles.

'Yes, it was excellent, sir.'

'I thought it was all right myself,' said Walter Luke.

He wasn't being jocular at his own expense, comparing his present incarnation with the not-so-distant past, or recalling his one-time animadversions on persons fulfilling public functions such as he now fulfilled. There was no irony about Walter Luke. There never had been. He was enjoying his existence, and he proceeded to make a hearty tea, eating several cakes and pressing them on Charles, very much as my father had done at their only effective meeting.

Walter was asking Charles about Cambridge, and said – and this surprised me, much more than similar apostrophes from Lester Ince – that he had never liked the place. Why not? Well, as soon as he got really going on his research, the Cavendish was proceeding to break up. As for the college, it got on his nerves. Sometimes men like old Winslow made him feel there ought to be a servants' entrance constructed specially for him, Walter. (Loud, crackling laugh which caused heads to turn from near-by tables.) Then there was Roy Calvert. It got you down, living within touching distance of melancholia.

I hadn't realised that the young Walter – he was speaking of himself at twenty-four or -five – had observed so much.

'You knew Roy Calvert then, did you, sir?' Charles asked, polite and expressionless.

'You've heard of him, have you?'

'Just a little. From my father.'

'I was jealous of him sometimes,' said Walter with simplicity. 'Poor chap.'

To him, Charles's question must have seemed pointless. Yet Charles himself he seemed to have taken a fancy to, though he couldn't have found much in common.

After tea, he asked us not to go unless we had to: it was a bit early to start drinking, but we might as well pre-empt a corner in the guest-room.

It was the same tactic that Francis Getliffe had used on my last visit there, and the same window-corner. Walter stood for a moment, spine as upright as though he were in surgical splints, gazing over the river through the autumn drizzle. The necklace of lights on the south bank dimly glimmered. It was not a spectacular vista, but he was gazing at it with proprietorial pleasure, as though he owned it.

When we sat down, the room was nearly empty, though one figure was in solitude drinking gin at the bar. In a comradely, roughly casual but unaggressive tone, Walter said to Charles:

'My lad, what are you going to do with yourself?'

'Do you mean tonight, sir?' Charles, trying to gain time, knew that Walter meant no such thing.

'No. I mean what are you going to do with your life?'

Charles asked, gently:

'What do you think I ought to do?'

'Damn and blast it, old Lewis will be better on that than I am.'

Charles looked at me and said:

'He's been very good.'

It was a gnomic remark, but it sounded genuine and without edge, and I was touched.

Charles went on:

'I should be grateful for some advice, I mean it, you know.'

Charles forgot nothing. He remembered Margaret teasing me after I had refused Walter's present job. And the family exchanges about asking advice. One's truisms had a knack of coming home.

'Well, you're obviously bright, anyway you've proved that. So that you must be sure of what you can do best—'

'Yes. But how many things are worth doing?'

Suddenly Charles's tone had changed. He was now speaking with intensity and force. So much so that Walter dropped his avuncular manner. His horizon-light eyes, set full in the rugged head, confronted Charles's deep-set ones.

'No, not many. That's why most of us just do the things that come to hand. That's what I've done.'

'But is that always good enough?'

'How do I know? Only God would know, if he happened to exist.'

'Would you have liked to do anything different, yourself? If you'd had an absolutely free choice?'

That wasn't disrespectful. There wasn't any offence, umbrage, mock humility or presumption on either side. They were talking with a curious mixture of impersonality and friendliness, something like Mansel and a colleague discussing an eye-operation.

'I used to think,' said Walter, 'that I should like to have done some first-class physics. I never did. Not within bloody miles of it. The war came along and I got shunted from one job to another. They said they were useful. I thought they were useful. That was a hundred per cent copper-bottomed excuse for not doing real physics. And sometimes I looked at myself in the shaving-glass and said Walter my lad you're a fraud. It isn't any blasted excuse at all.'

Charles was listening, hand under chin. Just for an instant, perhaps because of Walter's rolling Devonshire, and his Christian name, the tableau brought back the old Victorian picture, the youth hanging on to the sailor's tale: in my early childhood I had it fixed in my mind that the sailor must be Raleigh.

'Then I began to get my head down to its proper size,' Walter went on. 'All that was just damned silly inflation, I thought. What difference should I have made if I'd stayed in a physics lab every blasted minute of my life? The answer is, damn all. There aren't more than five or six men in the whole history of science who've made a difference that you can call a difference. And that's where you don't belong, Walter Luke.

'Take old Francis Getliffe. He's kept at it year in, year out. He's done some pretty nice work. If I'd stuck at physics as long as he has, I might have done about the same. I should have chanced my arm more than the old boy.' (After hearing Francis, not far from that same spot, express pity for Walter's ill-fortune, there was a certain pleasure in witnessing the same process in reverse. Did Charles know that, of the two, most of their fellow scientists thought that Walter had the bigger talent?) 'Well, if old Francis had never existed or had gone in for theology or stamp collecting or something of the sort, someone else would have come along and done exactly the same work within a matter of months. All that happens is that the old boy gets a hell of a lot of satisfaction. I suppose I might have got that too. But that bloody well doesn't count, what does it matter? When you know that you could be got rid of and no one would feel the difference?'

Walter finished in a cheerful, ruminative, acceptant tone. 'That's the point, isn't it? If your head's the proper size, you see that you're not all that significant. Anywhere. So I finished up here.' Walter swept an arm as though to take in the Palace of Westminster. 'Hell, it's good enough for me.'

'What you're saying', Charles asked him, 'would apply to anything creative, wouldn't it?'

'Unless you were old Will Shakespeare, I should think it did.'

Charles had gone over this argument with me before: not that I disagreed about the fundamentals, though I should have altered the stress. I knew that he had argued it also with his cleverer friends at school since he was thirteen. He said:

'No one wants to do second-hand things, do they? Scholarship's second-hand, even the best of it. Criticism's second-hand—'

'That comes from having a literary education,' Walter burst out in his old-style raucous vein. 'You think a bloody sight too much of criticism if you put it as high as second-hand. Our infernal college' (he turned to me) 'after we'd cleared out elected some damn fool who'd written a thesis on the Criticism of Criticism. Instead of electing him they ought to have kicked his bottom down the Cury.'

Charles smiled, but wasn't to be put off. 'Anyway, no one wants the second-hand things. And there's no use doing first-hand things unless one is superb, is that right?'

'That's a bit stronger than I meant,' said Walter, who, despite his conversational style, was a moderate man.

'Well, is this nearer? You wouldn't allow the old romantic conception of the artist. That is, an artist is justified whatever he does and it doesn't matter much whether he's any good so long as he thinks he is.'

'That's piffling nonsense,' said Walter Luke.

'I believe it's disposed of for ever. Among my generation anyway,' said Charles. 'You've never had any time for it, have you?' He turned to me.

'That's putting it mildly,' I replied.

'Well, we've wiped off quite a lot of possibilities, haven't we?' Charles had the air of one who, very early in a hand at bridge, could name where the cards lay.

'For God's sake, lad, don't let me discourage you from anything.'

Walter was subtler than he seemed or wanted to appear. He had realised some time before that this discussion was not entirely, or perhaps not at all, academic.

'Please don't worry. You wouldn't discourage me from anything if I didn't discourage myself. Most of those things I'd ruled out long ago.'

'I hope you've left something in,' said Walter, boisterous and avuncular again.

'A little.'

'Well, what's it going to be?'

'I can't tell you anything definite yet.'

'Tell me something indefinite, then.'

Charles grinned. Not perturbed, he said: 'I do think that the things worth doing in my time are going to be a bit different.'

'Why? Different to what?' Walter said.

'Different from things that your contemporaries did. I think we ought to do things which will actually affect people's lives. Quite quickly. Here and now. Not in a couple of generations' time. In our own.'

'What does all that add up to?'

'Don't I wish I knew?'

'You're thinking of something like the other end of this place?' Walter jerked a thumb in the direction of the Commons.

'No, not quite that, perhaps.'

'Anyway, you don't know yet, do you?'

'No, not yet.'

'Oh, don't rush yourself. There's plenty of time,' said Walter.

When Charles was expressing indecision, speaking almost bashfully, I doubted it. I didn't believe that Charles had started the conversation for my benefit, either to challenge or (what might have been more likely, as our relation changed) to prepare me. It was a mistake growing out of egotism or paranoia to suspect that all actions were aimed in one's own direction. Even with a person to whom one was close: he could have, and had, his own purposes which were quite independent of one's own. That, I was sure, was true of Charles as they started talking in the guest-room. The mention of Roy Calvert had no reference to me, or to any thought of his that Roy's daughter and I had been dissolving hostilities because of him. He had her on his mind, that was all.

But there had come an opportunity, or a turn in the talk, so that he could say something, not much but something, which he wished me to hear. It might have been easier to do so via Luke, using him as an interpreter, so to speak: quite likely it was: whether out of consideration or semi-secretiveness, or father – son aphasia, of which we all knew the intermittences, scarcely mattered.

The one certain thing was that he had passed on a message. If I asked for its final meaning, I should be evaded. There had been the best of openings to tell me, if he chose. He knew, it didn't need repeating, it would oppress him if repeated, what I wanted for him. Not his happiness: that was for him to get: to wish that would have been mawkish, and though I could be so about acquaintances, I wasn't about those closest to me. But I did wish, in the most elementary and primal fashion, for his well-being.

He knew that well enough. Once when he was nine or ten I had taken

him for a walk, and he had rushed in front of a car. Quick-footed he had
backed away, with not more than inches to spare. The driver cursed, 'You
won't have a long life, you won't.' Charles saw that I was pallid and couldn't
speak. Sometimes when still a child he asked me about it, and got brushing-
off answers. Then he gave up asking. But when my eye went wrong he
took my arm with solicitous and much more than filial care, much more
compensatory than filial, whenever I had to cross a road.

On our corner table, there was a round of drinks. Walter Luke was
giving instruction to Charles about science in the last war, pointing with
blunt fingers at the end of a stiff, strong arm. Charles had returned to his
absorbent posture, chin in hand.

CHAPTER XXXIX

UNINVITED GUEST

ALTHOUGH towards the end of November Margaret received news that
Maurice's wife was pregnant it was not until Christmas that we saw her.
Meanwhile Margaret, whom I have never known beg for favours except
for her elder son, was shamelessly using any influence either of us
possessed to get him a job in London. She wasn't searching for anything
lofty – just the equivalent of what he was doing in the Manchester hospital
or perhaps a clerkship in an almoner's office. 'Though I expect he'd think
that was too soft an option for him, wouldn't he?' she said. She was
smiling, making a decent show of being sarcastic, but underneath the
sarcasm melted away.

Still, she was being practical. When the baby was born, she was determined to be within reach. Expecting what? Her moods oscillated as I
watched them; some moments she was very happy, almost triumphant,
as she had been when she was pregnant herself; at others she was dreading,
with a rational dread with which I was touched myself, that the child
would be born afflicted. Yes, there was a chance, said some of the medical
scientists, told of the mother's family history. Not worse than one in four,
perhaps better than one in sixteen. But these were worse odds than one
got in any of the ordinary risks of life.

Whatever could be done, Margaret was doing. From the beginning the
child was to have the best doctors, whether Maurice and his wife liked it
or not. I told her she was behaving like old Mr March in his heyday (I
should have mentioned Azik Schiff too, if this conversation had happened

three months earlier). Margaret replied, 'You know what I feel about his marriage, you haven't needed telling, have you?' Just for once she was asking for pity or even pitying herself. 'Well, if they get a healthy child, that'll make up for everything. I swear I'll be good to it. And to her as well.'

'So you will if the child is born – unlucky,' I said. 'Even more so.'

I meant it. There were some, including Margaret, who thought that her son Maurice was naturally good. Margaret had more original sin, maybe, but she made herself good by effort. There was no one who would behave better and more patiently – though she wasn't patient by nature – if the baby was what she often feared. She would cherish it and its mother, so that everyone thought such love came easy to her.

She had invited them to stay over Christmas with us, and on Christmas Eve we had what by courtesy one could call a family dinner party – with Margaret and me, Maurice and Diana, Charles and Muriel. Until recently, either on that night or on New Year's Eve we had often filled the flat with a mass all-comers' party. But, because I was surreptitiously still as atavistic or superstitious as my mother, we had killed the custom dead. On 23 December 1963, George Passant had called on me and had, not broken, but declared the news which still at times hag-rode me: which had cut off any thoughts about one whole phase of my youth. The following night, I had had to be host to one of those mass parties. Not again. That was four years before, and the memory was still sharp and shrivelling.

And yet, as we sat at dinner, I would almost have welcomed a crowd of people trampling in soon. Diana took her place at my right hand, sidling in with her head down, giving out an air of being ill-treated, injured, self-regarding and full of conceit. I had suspected it the first time I met her: now I couldn't miss it. Margaret had, half-heartedly to be sure, accused me of being hard on her. That I couldn't take. If I pretended not to see her as I did, who was that a kindness to? I wasn't going to patronise her. In fact, as Margaret had discovered that afternoon, she wasn't at all easy to patronise, even for the most necessary of purposes.

To begin with, she had enjoyed being made such a fuss of, which Margaret was doing, spontaneously and happily, as soon as they arrived. Wonderful about the child. Margaret's sister had no children. Margaret had the two boys. In Margaret's family this would be the first child of the new generation. Diana was frowning to understand, but Maurice did some explaining. When she had gathered in the praise, she tossed her head, just as I remembered girls at a palais-de-danse in the provinces when I was a youth, giving the same response when they were asked for a dance. It didn't mean they were going to refuse. It meant that they would graciously accept, saying in the phrase which I had heard not long since from the lips of Muriel's mother, 'I don't mind if I do.'

Margaret was not used to north-country manners, but she detected that Diana was pleased. On the other hand, she didn't detect that when Diana was pleased she did not become less obstinate but more. So that, immediately the prospect of a move to London was conveyed to her (by this time Margaret had three different offers arranged for), she refused pointblank. 'I don't see why we should.'

Maurice had to placate her. He might have been over-considerate or even too diffident (for it was he who did the wooing), but it was clear he hadn't mentioned the possibility, though his mother had been writing to him about it, and his replies had been grateful and willing.

'It might be a good idea, sweetie,' he said.

'That's as maybe. I don't see why we should.'

Well, they would be nearer to his family and friends. To which she replied, with truculent accuracy, that they would be further from her family and friends.

Doctors, Margaret was speaking of. She could recommend some of the best—

'We've got doctors where we live. Ours aren't that bad.'

By this time Margaret realised that this wasn't shadow boxing. In a mother-cum-sister fashion she began to speak of the flukes of childbirth, how she was certain that Diana wasn't frightened of anything, but it would take a load off her (Margaret's) mind if they took some precautions. She would feel happier – she didn't approve of herself and she didn't expect them to, but they might humour her – if they didn't have the baby on the national health. There was a good nursing home where she had had Charles—

Diana sat with an internal smile, looking deferred to and unmoved.

As a result, when she came to the dinner-table, she was the centre of attention. As usual, she was wearing a dress in dingy chocolate brown, a colour for which she seemed to have a strong predilection.

In my eyes, she was plain, not ugly but plain, and the other young people were all personable, her husband much more than that, the most handsome man of his age whom I had seen in that room. Still, by a process of group hypnosis, it was she whom everyone was making up to and was anxious to please.

I had had a word with Charles on our own before dinner, and told him, for his mother's sake, to do his best. He gave a workmanlike smile, and as he sat by her at the table, I was surprised to see how good his best could be. I had heard from his friends that he took much trouble to help: when he hadn't a purpose of his own, he had, so they suggested, a lot of free energy, which he would dispense on anyone, without much favouritism or horns-and-halo partiality, who seemed to need it.

Certainly he was making more progress with Diana than any of us. I heard him begin on the attractions of London. Well, that might soften her some time, I thought, concerned for Margaret. As for myself, I shouldn't have been sorry for that dinner-party to be broken up. I was sitting between Diana with whom I couldn't communicate and who showed no desire to communicate with me – and Muriel, with whom I could communicate, but who had communicated much that we couldn't mention at that table, so that we were shy and abrupt with each other.

After dinner, Diana was sitting on the sofa between her husband and Charles. She was still being courted by Charles, but his conversational energies were flagging. Maurice watched with an affectionate smile, apparently gratified that she was receiving so much attention. The rest of us scattered round the room, Muriel preoccupied, Margaret once or twice glancing at me as though wishing that she and I had been trained to do simple conjuring tricks. It was about a quarter past nine, just about the time when, before the George Passant trauma, the first big wave of the Christmas party came breaking in. I asked round the room whether anyone would like more to drink. No takers. With someone to join me, I should have been ready to drink a good deal, which nowadays I rarely did.

Then there was a ring at the front door bell. While Margaret and I were speculating – it wouldn't be a visitor, perhaps a Christmas delivery from a shop – Charles went out to answer. A voice from the hall. He returned, looking not self-possessed but clouded, followed by his cousin Pat.

'Hallo, Aunt Meg!' He kissed her cheek. 'Hallo, Uncle Lew!' He made a bow, ceremonious and stately, to his former wife. He shook hands with the other two, and stood in the middle of the room, brown eyes bright, vigilant and defiant, rocking springily on his heels.

'What are you doing in London?' I was the first to speak to him.

'Oh, I just thought there might be a party on.'

That couldn't be true. He knew, as well as anyone there, that the old parties had been suspended for four years past. He didn't even bother to make the pretext plausible.

Where was his wife, Margaret asked. That was his second wife, Vicky, whom we liked much more than we liked Pat. Oh, she was in Cambridge with his father. He (Pat) would drive down and join them late that night.

'Who else do you think is there?' He darted the question at his cousin with the sparkle of one who held the initiative and intended to keep it.

'How do I know?' Charles was gruff.

'A friend of yours.'

Charles made no response.

'A boy called Grenfell.'

'Is he, by God?' Charles couldn't keep back a flash of interest.

'I have a tiny suspicion – of course that may just be me – but a tiny suspicion that my lady mother fancies that he might be rather a good match.'

Smiles, reluctant, wintry, but nevertheless smiles from Margaret and Muriel. Maurice, who had often defended Pat, said amiably:

'What does Nina think?'

'My dear sister doesn't give a thought to such mundane things.' Pause. 'That doesn't mean, though, that she won't snaffle him.'

More shamefaced smiles. His deserts might be small, no guest had ever appeared more often uninvited, but there was no denying that he had brightened the evening. But why had he come? Not to indulge in mild malice at the expense of his family. Not even to bring out miscellaneous items of news, regardless of accuracy. Was he there simply out of inquisitiveness? Or mischief-making? (In the midst of his high jinks, his eyes strayed more than once in the direction of Muriel.) More likely, I thought, it was nothing more than one of his whims.

When he had sat down, taking a chair midway between Muriel and Charles, and been given a glass of the Christmas champagne, he began telling me about my native town. For, since he had at last married Vicky, he had been living there, supported, one presumed, by Vicky's earnings as a doctor. It was strange to have those two as my only link with that place. Particularly as Pat's news, though it might be inaccurate, had a knack of being disconcerting. He had been seeing the Patemans, father and son. With glee he told me that they were inclined to think that I had 'let them down'. Particularly Pateman senior. He had come to the conclusion that I wasn't a 'man you could rely on'. 'Fine words butter no parsnips' was Mr Pateman's considered view of my intervention in his affairs. Unless, and this was more sinister, I had my own reasons for not helping him as he patently deserved.

I cursed. When I thought of the time and trouble, and even the money, that I had spent on that man – the hours in that horrible back room of his, listening to the grating voice.

Margaret and Charles, who knew the whole story, were laughing out loud at me. They couldn't understand how I had put up with him. I was supposed to be realistic: I had heard him speak with disapproval, rancour and hate of everyone who had helped him: and here I was, upset when I found he was doing the same about me.

While they were laughing, I noticed Pat address Muriel directly for the first time. I didn't pick up the question, but across the room came Muriel's clear reply.

'Very well.'

By this time, Charles, cutting his laughter short, was attending. We all heard Pat continue:

'How's the new house?'

'Doing very nicely, thank you.'

Charles put in:

'It's very comfortable to live in.'

If he had been older, he might have left that alone, I thought. He need not have impressed the situation upon Pat – who certainly knew, not only that Charles was living in the house, but also the exact date when he moved in.

'I'm very very glad that's worked, I really am.' Pat was still speaking to Muriel, with great earnestness, as though he had been deeply concerned about the practicability of the house. Yet there was a streak of ambiguity, as if he just conceivably might not be referring to the house at all.

Muriel had been answering with unflurried coolness. I doubted whether an outsider, judging from her manner alone, could have imagined that they had ever been married. It sounded as though he might not have been inside Chester Row, though I knew he had been, at least once, to pay a dutiful visit to the baby. When he did so, his manner wouldn't have varied, it would have been precisely as it was now.

Pat turned, like a friend of the family, to Charles.

'How's the work going, Carlo?'

Just as Charles had seen the beauty of Mr Pateman's behaviour, so I saw the beauty of this. Pat had done no work either at Cambridge or the College of Art, and had been ejected from each: Charles worked like a scholar. Now Pat was enquiring with an expression of faintly worried responsibility, like an elder person concerned about an undergraduate's progress.

'Well enough.' Charles sounded oddly gauche, unable to match Muriel's style.

'Never mind, you won't have to stand it much longer.'

'You needn't worry about me.'

'My dear Carlo, of course we do, we all do, you know that, don't you?'

Charles muttered something. It was a long time since I had seen him at such a disadvantage. The rest of us were embarrassed – or more uneasy than that – at Pat's display. I for one couldn't tell whether it was effrontery for the sake of effrontery or whether there were double meanings.

'Of course you'll soon be going out into the great wide world, won't you?'

'Who knows?' Charles tried to be casual.

'Why shouldn't you?' Pat gave him a knowledgeable nudging smile. 'We all know that there's some money coming to you before long. After all, you'll be twenty-one in a year and a bit, isn't it? Then you can do what you damned well please.'

Here I was taken off guard. The only persons who should have known about the trust for Charles were Margaret, the trustees, who were lawyers, Muriel, whom I had told, and Charles himself.

'You know, you can get married if you want, can't you?' said Pat.

Charles didn't reply.

'You two can get married soon, there's nothing to stop you, is there?'

This had to stop. But neither Margaret nor I were much more effective than Charles. It was Maurice who said: 'Don't bother, Pat, everything will be all right, he'll be fine.'

Whether that would have stopped Pat before, one couldn't tell. Perhaps he had gone as far as he intended. He went on with minor semi-affectionate jabs at Charles, but nothing outrageous. Among those who were listening, there was one curious feature. Muriel was not taut; she wasn't even cool or blank-faced: she was smiling, like one who, used to this kind of scene, was ready to laugh it off.

Not so much later, Diana, who could have thought that the attention had faded from her, announced to Maurice that she wanted to go to bed. Seizing on the excuse, I was on my feet. I heard Pat talking to Muriel and Charles. He could drive them to Chester Row. It would be no trouble, he wouldn't get to Cambridge anyway until the early morning. It was clear that he intended to go into the house with them, as though nothing ought to be allowed to separate the trio.

When we were in our bedroom, door shut, safe by ourselves, Margaret sat on the bed and exclaimed: 'God, what a night.'

I said I'd had more than enough of Christmas Eves.

'I take it', said Margaret, 'that nephew of yours is trying to break up their ménage?'

'It looks like it,' I said.

'Why?'

'He might be after her again himself. It might be sheer devilry.'

'If it wasn't for Martin,' she said, 'I'd get rid of him for good.'

She looked reflective, and went on:

'Once, you know, I'd have been glad for anyone, even if it was that little snake, to get Carlo out of her hands.'

She added:

'I don't know, now I sometimes think I'm getting reconciled to her.'

Before we went to sleep, after we had talked over Maurice and his wife, soothing ourselves with the inquest, Margaret said: 'I wonder if any single one of us got what he wanted tonight?'

CHAPTER XL

CALL NO MAN HAPPY UNTIL . . .

AFTER Christmas we did not see Maurice again, and Charles only for an hour or two, during the rest of the winter. Letters from Maurice were, however, arriving often, and untypically they were businesslike letters; for, to my surprise if no one else's, Margaret had got her way, and Maurice and his wife were moving to London after Easter, well before the child was due. Whether this was a success for Charles's persuasive powers, none of us could tell: but certainly he not only cajoled Diana on Christmas Eve, but had persisted, spending a weekend with them in Manchester to do so.

There was also another kind of cajolery going on. Pat, so we heard, had been seen with Charles in Cambridge, and Muriel told me, as a matter of fact, without explanation, that he had called on her twice when she was alone. She said nothing more, but it had all the appearance of a deliberate campaign. With labile characters such as Pat, the line was precarious (as I had learned with bitterness much earlier in my life) between being a busy-body and being destructive for destructiveness' sake.

In January, I had heard something which made our family seem lucky. For some reason that went out of mind, I had been dining by myself at the Athenæum. Towards the end of my meal, I was staring out of the window at the reflection of the table lights, when someone close by uttered my name. It was Leonard Getliffe.

'I'm very glad to see you, Lewis. I was going to ring you up.'

I asked him to help me finish the wine, which he wouldn't: he sat down on the opposite side of the table.

'I wanted to tell you about my father,' he said.

His clever conceptualiser's face looked cheerful, and at the sight of him I felt so myself.

'He's been ill. Oh, it's coming out all right, we're all delighted. But it's important that the news shouldn't get around.'

I said that I had had some practice in guarding the news of illnesses, including my own.

'We thought of telling you when it happened. Three or four months ago. But we decided that the possibility of leakage was directly proportional to the number of people who knew.'

That might be statistically true, I was thinking. It was also somewhat bleak to tell to a man's oldest friend. But Leonard wasn't really being bleak, he was indulging in what his colleagues called cat-humour.

Francis hadn't been specially well all the summer.

At Viredoux (that was the house in Provence) he'd been coughing a lot, but he said it was bronchitis. He used to have it in Cambridge, you know, that was one of the reasons for taking a *pied-à-terre* somewhere else.

Leonard went on:

'Well, he wasn't feeling quite up to coming back at the beginning of last term. So Katherine persuaded him, he'd always hated the idea of doctors of course, to go and let them look him over in Nîmes.'

'Yes?'

'They found he had a spot on one lung. They operated at once, very skilfully, Francis says. He has a lot of use for their experimental technique. It was perfectly successful. He's convalescing down there now. It'll be a bit of time before he's back to optimum form, but he's remarkably well. His morale is very high and he's fretting about not being back at the lab. He's feeling stronger every day. We're all extremely pleased with him. I think we were more worried than he was, but that's gone now. We want to get him back in Cambridge by April. He's very eager to see you, by the by.'

I tried to show no sign of disbelief as I gazed into the intelligent innocent face. From the moment he mentioned the operation, I had been horrified. Perhaps, I wanted to think, old anxieties were running away with me, Leonard might be right, Francis was not a self-deceiver.

I could not shift my own mood for an instant. I found Leonard's euphoria dismaying, and anything he said of Francis's. After a few flat questions – I did not want to puncture Leonard's well-being, but I could not (for premonition's sake, not honesty's) give any expression of pleasure or relief – I made an excuse, and went home.

As soon as I arrived there, I telephoned Charles March. Since old Mr March's death, Charles had been reconciled to his sister and her husband, but it was the kind of reconciliation in which the years of difference were covered up, not eliminated or transformed. Still, he might have heard from them.

When I asked, that turned out to be true. What did he think, as a doctor?

There was a long pause at the other end. 'I haven't enough to go on, I haven't even seen him. One's opinion isn't much use—'

Charles was growing more hesitant as he passed into his sixties. The fire and devil of his youth – and the unfairness – did not often show. He was more inclined to speak like a responsible citizen who didn't want to be quoted.

'No, but what is it? I want to know what you think, that's all.'

Another long pause.

'If it were you or me, I doubt if we should be as optimistic as they are.'

'No.'

'Mind, sometimes these operations really work.' Charles mentioned some cases of cancer which he had seen.

'How would you put his chances?'

He refused to make a guess. Then he said: 'If what you're afraid of did happen – and you know I'm as afraid of it as you are – then I'm terribly worried for Katherine. She loves her children, but he's been her whole life.'

That same night, I wrote to her, carefully casual, saying I had just seen Leonard and was hoping that all continued well. A reply came about a fortnight later, from Francis himself, as euphoric as Leonard's report had been. Of course, he couldn't expect to get all his strength back overnight; it would take months rather than weeks; but they would expect Margaret and me in Cambridge in the summer. With a blend of invalid concentration and scientific interest, he enclosed a sketch of the original X-ray of his lungs, and a diagram showing how the surgeons had operated.

That letter arrived at the beginning of February. In April – our own family concerns still, so far as we knew, unchanged – came one from Katherine. In her bold and steady hand, it read: 'All the children have had to be told, and I have also written to my brother. I'm sure that Francis would think that you ought to know too. He has not been so well for two or three weeks past, and last weekend went into hospital again. The disease has spread to the other lung and has advanced quickly there. There is nothing to say except that this promises badly. Francis has a desire to return home. The hospital people are trying to resist this, but I cannot see that they have any reason on their side.'

At the end of May, just at the time when the examination results were coming out, a telegram from Cambridge:

'Francis died peacefully this morning Katherine Leonard Peter Ruth Penelope'

The obituary notices were the longest of those for any of my friends, but they were stiff, a record of achievement, as though Francis's public persona had warded off the writers from coming anywhere near him. A few personal notes followed, a surprisingly warm one from L. of S. (Luke of Salcombe), one from me. The funeral was private. That seemed to be the end.

Then in the post arrived the neat little envelope, the printed slip, announcing a memorial service after a Cambridge death. How many services for fellows of the colleges in my time? Vernon Royce, Roy Calvert, Despard-Smith, Eustace Pilbrow, C. P. Crystal, Winslow, Paul Jago, Crawford, M. H. L. Gay. But this was the one I least expected to hear of. Even after I was anticipating Francis's death. For he was the firmest of unbelievers, who didn't attend memorial services for others and would have repudiated one such for himself. True, he had made a kind of apology for not going to Roy Calvert's, but that had been a gesture of consolation to me, perhaps of regret that he had not liked Roy better. When that had happened, and we were all young men, I had not imagined, in the midst of grief, that one day I should be attending a service for Francis himself. Nor could I have imagined that I should feel such a sense of loss.

Staying in Martin's house, within the college precincts, the night before the service, I confessed, what Margaret already knew, that I was sad in a way I didn't look for. After all, at my age one had seen enough of death. Including one's own, said Martin, with his own brand of nordic irony. Including one's own, I agreed. Oh, be quiet, said Irene, who had become fond of me, now that she was middle-aged.

Margaret had spent the afternoon with Katherine, and was silent now.

Through the open window of Martin's drawing-room, we could hear shouts in the court below. Glancing down, I caught sight of a posse of young men jostling along the path, some of them carrying suitcases. Another young man was walking between a middle-aged couple, perhaps his parents. That had been the last of the degree days, one of the less dramatic ritual occasions, graduates kneeling before the Vice-Chancellor and then being congratulated by tutors with meaningless heartiness on a feat which had been public knowledge some weeks before. In my time, the ceremony was becoming obsolescent, the independent young did not bother to attend: yet those below had been participating, somehow it still survived.

Although the sky was clear, turning dense indigo to the east, away from the sunset, it had been raining during the afternoon. The night seemed warmish, which we were not used to in that wet and frigid summer. There blew in wafts of flower scents, strong in the humid air. The smell of syringa, tantalising, aphrodisiac, poignant, prevailed over the rest. It brought back, not a memory, but a kind of vague disquiet: if I could remember an occasion when I had smelt the syringa so – Perhaps in that place? No, I couldn't trace it. Just the scent, unease, the sensual knowledge that there had been other nights like this.

We had already heard from Martin how the memorial service had come about. As soon as Francis was dead, the Master, G. S. Clark, had been pressing condolences upon Katherine. The fact that he had detested Francis, and that Francis had not been over-indulgent in return, seemed only to have enhanced the Master's compassion. In his ardour, he had insisted there should be a service. Katherine believed as little as Francis and must have known his wishes: so had Leonard and the rest of the Getliffe family. The Master had borne them down.

It wasn't that Katherine was as yet deadened by sorrow: on the contrary, having had to watch her husband through the long illness, she had returned to a kind of activity, an illusory vigour that might not last her long. She had argued about the service, and so had the family, but the truth was, they all wanted to agree.

They were holding on to anything that kept Francis in others' minds: or perhaps, more primitive than that, they had the feeling that while his name was being mentioned he was not quite obliterated, his shadow (they would have liked to say his spirit or his ghost) was still there. Just as Martin himself had returned to a primitive piety when our father died, and had proposed that he should be buried according to religious rites in which Martin was the last person to believe.

Once Clark had won the Getliffes over, there followed one of the traditional college struggles, though for kindness's sake Martin had let none of this reach Leonard, not to speak of Katherine. The question was, who was to give the memorial address? In the past this had been the prerogative of old Despard-Smith, the only fellow then in orders. With the result that he had made the oration over Roy Calvert, for whom he cherished extreme and ominous disapproval. Now, by a grisly coincidence, the pattern was repeating itself. There was at present no fellow in orders. So the Master assumed it was his own prescriptive right to make memorial orations. He had every intention of doing so for Francis Getliffe, for whom in life he had scarcely had one amiable thought.

Martin couldn't explain why Clark was so set on this. It might have been he couldn't resist, Martin suggested, 'getting into the act': after all, Francis was an eminent man. Or it might have been Christian charity. Martin, who was no more disposed to give Clark the benefit of the doubt than Francis had been, did not regard that suggestion of his own with favour.

In any case, Clark's address was not to happen. Feeling ran round the college, for Francis had become revered by most of the younger fellows. And Arthur Brown, the elder statesman, seventy-seven years old, was deputed to make representations to the Master. Over Roy Calvert's memorial service, Arthur Brown had tried to displace Despard-Smith, and had failed. This time in old age, the senior fellow since the death of Gay, Arthur was happy to have another go. He was himself, so Martin said, as moved as the young men. He had a good deal of affection, and more respect, for Francis, despite his affiliations with a government which Arthur was increasingly prone to describe in terms that a Russian émigré in 1920 might have considered sensible as applied to Lenin's administration, but perhaps a little over-strong. As for Arthur's opinion of the Master, he would not have mentioned that except to one of his old allies, and they had died or left the college, leaving him alone.

The upshot was that Arthur Brown had emerged from the Lodge, looking contented but flushed, and told the protestors that he would deliver the oration himself. 'It won't be exactly a rabble-rouser,' Martin had said that evening when he told the story, 'but it'll be perfectly decent. Which is more than we had a right to expect.'

Since we arrived, Martin and Irene had been waiting to tell us their own news. Irene had known Francis only as an acquaintance, and wasn't pretending to more than a social sorrow. Martin had lost a friend, and more significantly, an ally, but you could lose friends and allies and still enjoy your joys within the next half-hour. Unlike me, Martin had not known Francis for a lifetime. I was absent-minded, even when they felt that deference to mourning had been duly paid.

I was absent-minded, thinking of that occasion in hospital when Francis had said that if I died he would miss me. At the time it had sounded unusually unrestrained for Francis, and simultaneously a little inadequate and a little sentimental. Now I could test it for myself. He had known better than I had. I was already missing him. No more, no less. It wasn't the fierce and comminatory grief which came like a brainstorm or illness at the death of someone you loved. This was different. Someone you had known for a lifetime. Missing was the right word. To say any more would have been sentimental: but so would to say any less.

Meanwhile, Martin and Irene hadn't been able to suppress their triumph. The day before, Nina had become engaged to Guy Grenfell. All tied up and formal. The announcement would appear in *The Times* later that week. There had been family conferences and negotiations because she was so young.

I had seldom seen my brother look so happy. It seemed that all those disappointments and humiliations over his son had been cancelled. It was a pleasingly sarcastic flick – very much in his own style, though he wouldn't have been grateful for being reminded of it now – that this should happen through the daughter to whom until recently he had given casual affection but not much more.

'Old Grenfell', he said, 'isn't a bad old creature. Eton, and the Brigade, and the City. But he's not very good at chairing a meeting. There was him and his wife, the two of us, and the young couple. It was a pretty fatal combination for getting anything done quickly. There was only one thing to settle, ought they to wait a year or not?'

'I'd been around more than she has before I was her age,' said Irene with a lively lubricious grin.

'You weren't marrying into a respectable family, my girl.' Martin's smile was congratulatory, as though addressed not only to his wife but to Nina's mother.

'We haven't any money, of course,' Martin went on. 'That was made quite clear. It seemed to puzzle Lady G. They have quite a lot of money. That was also made quite clear. And that seemed a very reasonable state of things to Lady G. Somehow it also seemed a rather strong argument to her for them to wait until she's twenty-one. Old G. didn't quite see the logical connection, but he felt there was some force in it.'

He said, face illumined from inside, as it appeared when for once his self-control had slipped:

'But they could have argued till the sun blows up, it wouldn't have made any difference. The girl and boy were fine. I thought Guy was a bit of a wet when she first brought him here, but I couldn't have been more wrong. He was like a rock. Very polite, long hair and all, but like a rock. He was apologetic, but they were going to get married in August. They were absolutely sure. They didn't want to be awkward, but they were absolutely sure. They would make any concessions – they'd even have a smart wedding if that would give any pleasure – they didn't want to disappoint anyone, so long as they were married in August.'

Martin was extracting pleasure, more even than Irene, from the last detail of their daughter's engagement. He was fundamentally a healthy man, despite his pessimism – or perhaps it was because he was healthy that he could let his pessimism rip. My thoughts cast back to Francis: he too had rejoiced when each of his children married: it was part of the flow, there was a proper time to become a patriarch. Now Martin, whom occasionally I still regarded as my young brother, was enjoying that same proper time. It wasn't made worse (as he had commented, executing a complex gibe against himself, worldly people in general and the world-liness of the world) because Guy was, by the standard of Martin's society, a distinctly desirable husband. Martin had had, in all external things and in some closer to him, less luck than most of us. It was good to hear him saying, without any reserve, tight lip all gone, that this was luck he hadn't counted on.

He said something else, which made me feel that I had been facile in thinking about Guy. I had assumed that he was a rich young man who relished talk of world convulsions, so long as they took place in drawing-rooms. I remembered predicting to Charles that he would finish up in a merchant bank. So far, said Martin, there was no sign of that. He was trying to find a job in famine relief. And was being held up, by a beautiful piece of security machinery, because of his part in last year's revolt.

No doubt their elders would go on waiting for Charles's circle to renege. As yet, none had done so. The only half exception was the leader, Olly, who had recently been chosen as a Labour candidate; but as he was standing in one of the richest constituencies in London, he couldn't be said to have compromised with professional politics yet awhile.

Next morning, from Martin's drawing-room, we heard the chapel bell begin to toll. Charles had joined us there, after spending the previous night in his own college, packing ready to depart: he was wearing a black tie, as Martin and I were. As we walked along the paths through the college, other parties were converging on the chapel, women in black, like Margaret and Irene. It was all as it used to be for other memorial services, all as it was for Roy's. Through the great gate, a group of a dozen people were entering, and the first court's flags were jolted by men moving slowly, as though in time with some inaudible march, clothes and gowns dark in the bright shower-washed sunlight. The grass on the lawn was so green, the eyes dazzled.

The chapel, its interior Georgian and seemly, was already full. Seats had been reserved for fellows and sometime fellows and their families, and we took up ours. Opposite sat Katherine, in a grey dress, not in full mourning, the Getliffe sons and daughters, their wives and husbands. Charles and Ann March were close by, and others of Katherine's family. Chairs had been placed in the ante-chapel, under which some early Masters had been buried (and where old Gay had expressed a wish, not honoured, to lie himself). The moulded doors had been left open, and from our seats we could see the ante-chapel also full, with young men standing. Most of the faces, having been so long away from Cambridge, I didn't know. Some of them must have been from Francis's own laboratory, and I recognised one or two senior scientists from the Cavendish. There were several Ministers, officers in uniform, civil servants, reminders of the strata of Francis's public life. One pair I saw, inconspicuous in the distance, Roger Quaife aud his wife.

(It was, I thought later, a slice of official, or functional, England, but not one that the young were familiar with. Few people there were likely to be mentioned in gossip columns and fewer were rich. Some of the scientists had creative work of the highest order to their credit, but a young man as well informed as Gordon Bestwick would scarcely know their names.)

A hymn. A prayer: the kind of prayer, I thought, that one heard at American ceremonies, designed not to give offence to any religion. Another hymn. Then Arthur Brown, surpliced, hooded, bejowled, high-coloured, mounted the pulpit. He mounted with firm heavy steps. He had always been heavy, but getting towards eighty he was hale and still carried his stomach high.

In a strong voice, vowels well rounded, he began. He began much as we expected. Yes, we were thinking, it won't be exciting, but it will be acceptable. About how Francis had been a pillar of the college, the university, the scientific community, the state. About how he was a man so just that some had thought him over-nice. 'But no juster man has ever walked the courts of this college.' About how he was absolutely upright in all his dealings. 'He was the most scrupulous of colleagues. As well as being one of the three or four most eminent members of our society during the present century.'

All that was good enough. Orotund, like Arthur Brown in public. More from the outside than he could be, talking with slow cunning about someone he knew well. Perhaps he had never known Francis well. Or not noticed the struggle between the disciplined and the acerb.

Then Arthur Brown clutched the lectern, looked down the chapel, right out through the doors, with a hard, dark, resolute gaze. 'Now I have to speak in a way which may be painful for some present. But if I did not, it would be hypocrisy on my part, and hypocrisy of a kind which our colleague would have been one of the first to resent. I have to tell you that he was not a Christian. He did not believe in the religion to which this chapel is dedicated, and which some of us here profess. What is more, he did not believe in a religion of any kind. He was an utterly truthful man, and he would not compromise on this matter. So far as I can remember, he entered this chapel only for the purposes of electing a Master, that is only twice in his whole life. I am certain, that if he had honoured us by becoming our Master himself, he would not have felt able to perform any ceremonial duties within the chapel.' Anyone who knew Arthur Brown must have been astonished. All his life he had been confining himself to emollient and cautious words. He had much dislike for the brash or those who said 'something out of place'. Civility meant being careful: one's own convictions and much less one's self-expressions were no excuse for embarrassing others. But now – how much effort had it cost him? – he was letting go. Perhaps with a touch of defiance (that last remark about Francis's not taking the Mastership was not calculated to give pleasure to the present occupant, sitting in the magisterial pew) such as the prudent felt when, just for once, they were not being prudent: but more so out of duty to a dead man.

'And I cannot and will not talk of him in terms of the Christian virtues. It is more appropriate to talk and think of him in terms of a world before Christianity existed.

'He was the absolutely upright man, such as the classical world admired. His life would have been a model to them: it is easy to imagine Lucretius saying that this was how a man should be. I wish to say that to you myself, but I was not prepared to let you hear it on false pretences. He lived a life better than most of us can aspire to, but he did it without the support of any faith.

'I wish to press another thought upon you. He was, in his later years, a very happy man. Earlier he had his struggles – struggles for a better world in which some of us cannot believe, struggles on behalf of his country where we are all grateful to him. He had throughout the blessing of an ideally happy marriage, and he was doubly blessed in a family of exceptional gifts. All our sympathy goes out to his wife and children, but they should have the consolation of being certain how happy they made his life. For years past he lived in an Indian summer. He was not a man easily contented, but he had become totally contented. His scientific work had received full recognition. Only last year he was awarded the Copley medal of the Royal Society, the highest honour that the Society can give. In these past years he had private happiness and the esteem of his peers to an extent which is not granted to many men.

'It is because of that I am presuming to offer what may be another small consolation to those who loved him. Life is always uncertain, as they have too much reason to know. Even that happiness of his might have been broken. There is a word from the classical world which he would have appreciated: *Call no man happy until he is dead.* It is little comfort to those who have lost him, but sometimes perhaps they will be able to tell themselves that he left them with his felicity unbroken.'

I was gazing at Katherine, whose fine features, strong and not congruent with the matronly form, had not stirred. Arthur Brown had been through serious illness: but had he known what it was like to be warned about his death? Or what Francis felt in his last months? Call no man happy . . . what did that sound like to those who had been close by? I had heard very little about the final illness. Either Arthur Brown had forgotten both his realism and his tact, or else he had found out more.

He retired, his tread audible in the silent chapel, from the pulpit to his place. Hymn. Prayer. The fellows began to file out, the Master stopping beside the Getliffes so as to ask them to go first. In the court, knots of people were gathering on the flagstones. The Master nodded to Arthur Brown, but did not speak. Nor did Nightingale, the only other man besides Brown who had remained a fellow from my time to this.

Katherine had, however, shaken Brown's hand, and the Getliffe family were clustering round him. All seemed pleased, and without qualms. In the crowd, Margaret was talking to an old acquaintance, the Getliffes were being joined by colleagues of Francis, and I hung about waiting for a chance to speak with Arthur Brown.

When we were able to move off, the two of us, out of the ruck, I said:

'Well done.'

'I hope Francis would have liked it.'

'I'm sure he would.' Francis wouldn't have been above thinking that, if G. S. Clark and Nightingale were affronted, not only as personal enemies, but also as religious devotees, so much the better. I didn't say that to Arthur, who was a latitudinarian member of the Church of

England: disapproving of 'enthusiasm', though, very much as his nineteenth-century predecessors had done.

'Old friend,' said Arthur, 'he'll leave a gap here, you know. We're dropping off one by one.'

He was speaking with regret, or nostalgia, but not like an old man. He went on:

'I wish you hadn't gone away from us, Lewis. Oh, I know you couldn't have done what you had to do if you'd stayed. But still – this isn't quite the place it was.'

I said, with the whole university expanding, it couldn't be—

'I dare say it's better, but it isn't quite the same. It's not very loyal to criticise, because the college has been enormously kind to me, it's given me so much more than I deserved.' That was not mock modesty, but the real thing: Arthur had never had much opinion of himself.

'But I can't get used to changes. I've reached the stage when I don't really enjoy a person's company unless I've known him for a long time.'

I said: 'I've found young Charles's friends a bit refreshing—'

'Ah. That reminds me.' Suddenly Arthur had brightened up. 'I did want to have a word with you about that young man. Just for your ear alone. He's done perfectly splendidly, of course. It did occur to me that we might manage to construct a vacancy for him here. Mind you, I can't promise anything. I couldn't think of guaranteeing anything until I'd found out how the land was lying. There are some people who mightn't be entirely favourable. But there might be a chance that we should turn out too strong for them—'

With a touch of his old zest, with more than a touch of his old labyrinthine pertinacity, Arthur proceeded to examine how the college might be induced to elect Charles to a fellowship before 'others get in first'. The college had to poach nowadays, especially in subjects like Charles's, which were becoming short of first-class talent. Someone had mentioned another Trinity man called Bestwick, but Arthur didn't at present feel 'so keen about him'.

'Of course,' Arthur reiterated, 'this is entirely between ourselves. I can't possibly promise anything. It might be better if you regarded this conversation as not having happened, at any rate for the time being—'

Then Arthur went up to his rooms, after an affectionate good-bye, still dubious about my discretion and inclined to treat me, as he had always done, as a man of promise not yet old enough or experienced enough to be entirely trustworthy in serious affairs.

Now the court had emptied, Margaret and Martin taking a porter with them to fetch our bags: Charles alone remained, who had earlier transported his own to the porter's lodge. He came and joined me, at the foot of the staircase which I used to climb.

'I expect you're glad that's all over,' he said in a quiet and sympathetic tone, indicating the chapel. I nodded.

He hesitated. We had scarcely been alone together since Francis's death.

'I didn't know him well,' he said. 'But it was a comfort to feel that he was there.'

That was an epitaph of which Francis might have been glad. Charles went on to mention the memorial address. Didn't it deserve very high marks for ruffling dovecotes, and putting cats among pigeons? Wouldn't it be mildly fun to be dining at high table that night? Charles didn't need telling that this had been the most uncharacteristic gesture – almost the only gesture – of old Arthur's peace-loving college life.

He did need telling, though, of something which wasn't at all uncharacteristic, Arthur's desire to manipulate the college machine, this time on behalf of Charles himself. Charles said:

'He's a sweet old man.'

Not always so sweet, when he was in action, I said. Charles was smiling. He gave no indication of whether the offer meant anything to him, yes or no: or even whether he would, in Arthur's own old phrase, sleep on it.

On the other hand, he was disturbed that Arthur seemed to have ruled Gordon Bestwick out.

'What the hell is the matter? If you don't mind me saying it, this isn't a great college. By God, they won't get a chap like Leonard once in ten years—'

Somebody else would take him, I said, but Charles was not appeased.

Couldn't I use my influence with Arthur to get him to think again? I said, neither I nor anyone else had any influence with Arthur. Once his mind was set, he was as obstinate as a mule.

Charles, not satisfied, was wondering about other approaches. It hadn't occurred to him, apparently, that Gordon's reputation as an activist would not be an overpowering inducement to Arthur Brown. Perhaps because Charles did not find his own getting in his way: but then he had been more discreet, and would in any case be forgiven a great deal by Arthur. Anyway, I was relieved that Charles was for once less than acute. I didn't wish to quarrel about politics that day; nor more did he. He was being easy and friendly, ready either to amuse or soothe or just stay at my side.

We walked, very slowly, clockwise round the court. Looking at the lodge and hall, lines clear, stone honey-coloured in the sun, I told him what I thought to myself that October evening nearly three years before. When I first saw those buildings, they were grey with the soot of years, and covered with creeper. Now, the theory was, we saw them as when they were built – except that the windows would have been entirely different, the façade of another kind of stone, and the roof of the hall feet lower. Charles, not specially modernist in visual taste, said:

'I expect it always looked pretty pleasant, though.'

He added:

'It's very handsome, in a quiet way, isn't it?'

He might have said that to please me, but it was true. He might have said also, but that wouldn't have come so easy to him – that it was very English. At least, I had never seen anything like it out of England.

In the bedroom of the lodge, a light had been left on, pale and unavailing in the sunshine.

'You must have walked round here a good few times,' he said:

'Yes, quite a few.'

He smiled. 'In various assorted moods, if I know you.'

'Yes, that too.'

He couldn't have divined it, but without any justification at all, since Martin was there to be visited, I had had a feeling, hard-cut, dismissive, that I was seeing the place for the last time.

CHAPTER XLI

A BEARER OF BAD NEWS

IT was a domestic scene such as we had once been used to, and were no longer. Our drawing-room: lights already on, though the time was only nine o'clock, a few days after midsummer. Outside, a cool cloudy evening, for, since the day of Francis's memorial service, the weather had returned to form. Present, along with me, Margaret and her two sons. It was a family evening which, a few years before, we should have taken for granted and thought nothing of.

As it was, Maurice had come to the flat because his wife had gone into hospital. The baby was a few days overdue, and both he and Margaret were conscious of the telephone beside the door. It was the first time I had seen Maurice show the effects of suspense, or of waiting. In the periods when he had taken examinations, he had, with maddening acceptance, not been anxious about the results, assuming them to be bad: he hadn't ever appeared worried about someone turning up for an assignation, as the rest of us had been, watching the clock on the restaurant wall, making excuses for the non-arrival, with pique, anger and with longing.

Now Maurice, though he made no complaint, seemed no better at waiting than anyone else.

His only sign of the old self-forgetfulness came soon after he had met Charles that evening. Maurice had said, gently but unhesitantly, that he hoped Muriel was well and happy. And that he hoped Charles was 'looking after her'. No one else would have spoken to Charles like that. It might have seemed impertinent, if it hadn't been said with so little self-assertion. Anyway, Charles took it, though he didn't make an explicit reply.

Whether Maurice knew or not, Charles had been sleeping in his old bedroom at the flat since less than a week after we returned from Cambridge.

During the daytime he had been nearly always out, possibly with Muriel: one heard him telephoning her each morning. He seemed in high spirits, with patches of contemplativeness. He gave no indication that he also was in a period of waiting.

That evening, as we sat chatting, chatting to induce the telephone to ring, Margaret occasionally gazed at the two of them – her innocent, her strenuous one – and then at me. She might have been thinking of the time we had talked about them in that room. The events of their growing up, commonplace to everyone else as another family's photographs, at times dramatic, searing rather than dramatic, to us. I recalled (I didn't have to bring it back to memory, it was always there) the morning when we sat there, having been told that Charles, then an infant, was recovering from meningitis. In thanksgiving, we didn't speak about him but about Maurice. We repeated, just as we had said in the hospital, *we must save him from everything we can.* Margaret had been as good as her vow: her love for Maurice had deepened, not grown less, deepened with the trouble he had caused her, not through conflict but through ineptitude or lack of self. As for me, I had tried to follow her. What will could do, I had done. Other men, I thought again that evening, would have done better.

Two days later, the child, a girl, was born. The first medical reports were encouraging. As a newborn baby, she seemed everything she ought to be. Of course, some disabilities they couldn't test for, yet. It would be weeks or months before they knew. So that one of Margaret's anxieties was not eliminated, though for the time being assuaged. She couldn't let herself go, but, trying to suppress it, she was full of joy.

The baby was born on 2 July. The medical opinions reached her next day. That same evening, I was entertaining a foreign acquaintance at a club. When I arrived home, it was quite early, not yet half past ten, but the drawing-room lights were switched off. Margaret called from our bedroom.

She was not undressed, but was sitting on the chair in front of her dressing-table.

'Carlo has been talking to me,' she said. 'I think he's gone off to tell Muriel.'

'What is it?'

'He asked me to tell you. Of course he'll see you tomorrow.'

'What is it?'

I knew her face so well, yet it was difficult to read. Her eyes were bright, her cheeks a little flushed. In a temper she sometimes looked like that, but at that moment her temper was cool. 'He's come out with his plans. I ought to say that he was extraordinarily nice. He even waited to talk until he knew that I wasn't anxious about the baby.' (Just as, I had a recollection, my first wife had once delayed telling me the most wounding news – until I was in good health.) 'Mind you, I fancy he's been certain himself for quite a time.'

'What is it?'

She made me sit down on the bed. She said:

'My love, a part of this you're not going to like. Most of it seems perfectly sensible. Anyway it may be right for him.'

Angrily, I told her that I liked news broken fast. I was already ready to punish her for being the bearer of bad news. Sitting there, she seemed more guilty than Charles could be.

'He has it all worked out.'

Then, quite quickly, she told me. He had decided that he must make a name within a few years. The world was going too fast, he wanted to have some sort of say before he was middle-aged. He had been studying the careers of the American foreign correspondents in the thirties. They had done their piece. He didn't see why he shouldn't do as well. Languages weren't a problem to him. Politics he knew as much about as most people his age. He had no racial feeling, he could live anywhere. He was used to hard travelling—

'That's not very dreadful,' I said. Yes, it might suit him.

'You haven't heard it all.' He was determined to have his say in the minimum possible time. Other people could do what he proposed to do. He had to get his nose in front. Once he was recognised at all, he could rely on – what he was too cautious to call his talent. Though he was right, Margaret said, he had most of the qualities to become a pundit. He wanted to be a sane voice. But, to do that, he had to start with something a bit out of the ordinary—

'What is it?' I cried out again.

'That's where the risk comes in,' said Margaret.

'What risk?'

He accepted that he couldn't persuade a paper to use him yet awhile, she said. He had to prove himself. So he was setting off to get near the action: meaning, to begin with, the middle east. He would have to work himself as near battles as he could. Somehow, within a year or two, he was going to find something to sell: then some paper or other would employ him. It wasn't going to be pleasant. He insisted that he was extremely cowardly. Still, that was part of the exercise. Brave men weren't specially good at becoming international pundits. He had worked out the odds, and meant to take his chance.

'Good God,' I said, 'how romantic is all this?'

I asked her, still angry with her because she had borne the news, whether she had tried to dissuade him.

'I said that it wasn't what I should have chosen for him,' said Margaret.

'What did he say to that?'

'He said that he realised it. And that you wouldn't have chosen it for him either.'

He had told her also that he had wished all along that he could settle for something which we should like. But you can live only in your own time, he said.

'And he's determined to go on with this?'

'He didn't tell me in so many words, but I'm sure that the arrangements are already made.'

That rang clear as truth, as soon as I heard it. As with my brother Martin, Charles's calculations were performed long before he spoke, perhaps before he knew that his own decision was already final.

'Does he know', I said, 'that I shan't have an easy night until this is over?'

'Do you think I shall?'

'That may be for the rest of my life.'

'Have you forgotten that he's mine as well as yours?'

For an instant we were blaming each other. She was appealing for me to come close to her: while in pain and rage I was wishing that everyone round us could be torn down, along with me, if this I had to endure. I felt as savage, as possessed as I had in other miseries, not many of them in my entire life, two deaths perhaps, Charles's own illness. I felt at that moment without relief or softening from age or any consolation that had come to me.

'Is he thinking of anyone else at all?'

Margaret did not reply.

'Does he know what it means to anyone else?'

Margaret said:

'He's pretty perceptive, and I'm certain that he does.'

'Is that why he's doing it?'

Margaret and I glanced at each other, thinking of how we had protected him in his childhood, knowing that we couldn't have another, telling ourselves that this was a precious life. The first time I saw him in hospital, I had taken him, rolling-eyed, waving-fingered, into my arms, resolved that no harm should come to him.

'No,' said Margaret, 'you mustn't take more responsibility than you have already.'

She meant, what I had said to her often enough, that affections, especially in families, didn't carry the same weight on either side. I ought to have known that, from the way I behaved to my mother. It was a kind of vanity to suspect that another's choices depended on his relations with oneself. Choices, lives, were lonelier than that. Charles was making a choice lonelier than most of ours had been. That was no consolation for me, sitting there in the bedroom. All I could do was think of him, not with affection, not even with concern, but with anger mixed with a kind of fellow-feeling, or a brutal sympathy of the flesh.

It took me a long time before I could say to Margaret that I had been cruel, shutting her out when she spoke about Charles as her son, and that, without her to tell it, the news would have been worse.

CHAPTER XLII

FINGER-TIP TO FINGER-TIP

THE next morning, Charles did not get up for breakfast, but soon after joined me in the drawing-room. After he had uttered a greeting, bright and neutral, he sat in a chair opposite mine across the disused fireplace.

'I think Mummy has told you, hasn't she?' His tone was easy and intimate: the only sign that he might not be free from strain was that he fell back on that term from childhood.

'Yes, she has. Last night.'

He said:

'I'm sorry if I've disappointed you.'

I did not reply at once and he went on:

'I'm very sorry. Believe me.'

'Of course you haven't disappointed me.'

'Well,' he said, more freely now, 'it isn't exactly what you might have looked for, is it?'

'You've done far more than I had at your age. With any luck you'll go on doing more.'

'I shall need a bit of luck—'

'Yes, I know that.'

I hadn't been speaking out of self-control, or even out of resignation. I hadn't prepared myself for how to meet him, there were none of the speeches which one made up in one's head and never spoke. In his presence I felt nothing of the anger, or the suspicion, that a few hours before I had projected on to Margaret. To my own astonishment I was buoyed up by – what was it? Maybe his energy or his resolution. Or it might have been his nerve. At no time in my life could I have done what he was committing himself to do. It seemed as though a new force had taken charge.

He must have realised that there were going to be no reproaches. More, he may have seen that a kind of relief, not happiness or content but more like trust, had come into the air between us. Neither of us could have known the reason. Ties, half-memories, the sympathy of those who are close together even where their purposes contradict each other. Later, I wondered whether I was stirred by something of myself which, that morning, had been long forgotten.

When I was younger than Charles, less educated, much less sophisticated, I had once declared my hopes. They had been embarrassing to recall in middle life. Asked by a girl who loved me a little what I wanted, I had said – not to spend my life unknown: love: a better world. Those hopes might have been embarrassing later, but they were true of me at the time I spoke, a good deal truer than any refinements and complications would have been.

Yes, the first of them died on one, or waned. Yet it drove me on for the first half of my life. As for the second, when I said it in that old-fashioned schoolroom, I didn't have any intimation of where it would lead me, either in the search for sexual love or that other kind, which I felt for my son, sitting there across the fireplace: but it had lasted until now. But the one that I shouldn't have confessed to, even a few years later, because it sounded so priggish or worse still so innocent, that had been true too.

It wasn't as passionate as personal desires – nor as haunting as the sense of the 'I' alone, oneself alone – but it was there. It had bound Francis Getliffe and me together all our working lives. It led us into defeats and sometimes humiliations, led us either through our temperaments or through a set of chances, into backstairs' work, secrets, all kinds of closed politics. Of course, it wasn't pure. Our own self-esteem took part, or certainly mine did. Nevertheless, trying to judge myself as indulgently as Father Ailwyn had instructed me, I believed that I had wanted some good things. Whether I had helped to get any, that was another matter. Very little, I had often thought before of Francis and myself. The only work which I was certain had been useful took place in the war, and there we were avoiding a worse world, not making a better one.

Yet some of the pleasure – utterly unanticipated by either of us – which I felt in Charles's presence that morning, was because he too had the same desire. He too might be rapacious, as much as I had been, and self-absorbed, possibly more. There was, though, something left. It wasn't the simple and good, such as Maurice, who had vitality to spare for tasks outside themselves. Charles had plenty. He would use it differently from the way I had done. He might be more effective. All might go wrong. He might throw himself away. Still, even the bare desire was like a touch finger-tip to finger-tip, conducting a phase of life.

I said: 'I can understand that you're in a hurry. But can't you get a footing in some slightly less dramatic way?'

'You don't believe I haven't thought of that?'

'Well, why not?'

'It isn't on.' Charles gave a rationale, clear and patient, of what he was aiming at. Only in his generation, he said, could you become a spokesman before the age of thirty. But plenty of people, at least as competent as he was, would like to be such a spokesman. To get there, you had to do something special.

'You're telling me this is the only way?'

'I think it is for me. If I were more of a performer, I might find another way in. But I'm not.'

He broke into a friendly smile.

'Look, you realise that I'm a lot more careful than you are. I have plenty of respect for my valuable life. I don't even like flying in aircraft much. Let alone in an aircraft which is being pooped at. So you needn't worry about me going in for heroics. I'm much too sane. I'm only too damned sane.'

Although he was trying to reassure me, he was not pretending. But I knew, and he knew that I knew, that none of that, however much it wasn't invented, would affect his actions. He would brood over a risk for days or weeks or months, just as he had presumably brooded over this choice of his, calculating all the odds: and then, if he thought it worth while, take it.

I had never been able to disentangle the nature of his courage. In some ways he had, before this, reminded me of Roy Calvert, Muriel's father. Their minds were similar, precise, concentrated, clear. Their wilfulness was similar. But their courage was different in kind. Roy was a brave man, in a sense that Charles would for himself have totally disclaimed. Roy, though, had a suicidal streak. I had heard him, on a night which I should have liked to forget, tell me during the war how he had tried to throw his life away. He had done it out of despair, out of a melancholia he couldn't shift. He had made a choice: it wasn't one which Charles would have considered making. It wasn't a gamble, it was an abdication. Roy had impressed on me that when he made it, he wasn't mad. He wasn't mad, he said, he was lucid. 'Perhaps if everyone were as lucid as that, they would throw in their hands too.'

I hadn't to cast back for those words. Charles could never have said them. He would have distrusted Roy's protestations of not being mad. But it was with absolute confidence that he had made his own simple statement about being 'too damned sane'.

I believed him, totally. It was I, not he, who was tempted to read a pattern into events which he didn't even know. If he had known them, he would have repudiated with impatience what I was tempted to see. History wasn't like that, he would have said. Nor personal history. He would have been right. The patterns weren't real. Perhaps the weaver of the pattern, however, told one something about himself.

Then Charles asked me for an introduction. It was to a Jewish friend of mine who worked at the Weizmann Institute.

'Of course,' I said.

'That's nice of you,' said Charles.

He was beginning his Levantine journeys on the other side: easier, or at least not impossible, that way round, he said, but despite our connections he might have some explaining to do in Israel.

'You needn't write to ——,' the Jewish friend. 'But I can use your name?'

'Naturally.'

'Bless you.' He looked at me with what appeared like a filial grin. I was gratified that, even at this stage, he was invoking me.

Suddenly I began to think. Of all my acquaintances who might be of use to him, this one was about the most obscure.

'Carlo,' I said, 'what are you up to?'

Bland gaze. 'I don't understand.'

'Why have you just thought of him? What about David Rubin? And —— ?'

David Rubin, grey eminence in the United States, was also one in Israel: for years he had been an intimate of mine.

The gaze flickered. 'As a matter of fact, I wrote to David R. myself, a little while ago—'

'Come on,' I said. 'What are you up to? Anything this chap can do, Rubin can do a hundred times over. You know that as well as I do.'

'Yes, but—'

'But what?'

Another surprise that morning. He blushed. It was a long time ago, when I had last seen him do so. Poise precarious, he broke into a weak smile.

I had it. He had been making an attempt to appease or to soothe me. He wanted to demonstrate that he had finished with his pride; he would use my influence when it was a help; any conflict had gone, he was glad to have me behind him. It was well meant, I thought, as, knowing it all, mocking each other and ourselves, we couldn't keep our eyes from meeting.

It was well meant, but not quite careful enough in execution. Actually he had been meticulously thorough, not neglecting any contact, and taken the best advice open to either of us. This had been happening for months past, possibly before he admitted to himself that the choice was clinched.

Then, and only then, I realised that his timetable was already fixed: and that he had broken the news only a few days before he was due to leave.

CHAPTER XLIII

'IT MIGHT MATTER TO OTHERS'

As a result of Margaret's persuasion, I telephoned Muriel. Would she care to see me? One of us ought to make the offer, Margaret had said:

and, since she herself had at the best of times been uneasy with the young woman, it had better be me. The voice at the other end of the line was polite but frigid. Yes, she was by herself. She wouldn't think of asking me to go out of my way – I must be extremely busy, but of course if I had nothing else to do—

When I went to her in her drawing-room, where she had once invited me in a different mood from this, she turned to me a desensitised cheek: as desensitised as Sheila's, I had a flash of random but chilling memory, as she said good-bye one night at a railway station and had become shut within herself.

There might be some play in the test match, Muriel observed from a distance. It was midday, the rain had stopped earlier in the morning, there was an interval of sunshine. The ground would be pretty wet, I replied, as awkward as a young man not knowing the next move. Perhaps the bowlers would get some help, she said.

I sat silent, rather than go on with spectatorial exchanges. Her hair glistened as though it had been attended to that morning, falling, though not luxuriantly, to her shoulders.

At last she said:

'So he's going, is he?'

'He must have told you?'

'Yes, he's told me.'

'I'm sorry—'

'You needn't be sorry. If it hadn't been for you, this would never have happened.'

Her tone, light, impersonal, was intended to give pain.

'Do you think I like it?'

'You made it happen. You made him want to outshine you.'

Her tone was still impersonal, but unrelenting. I tried to answer without expression.

'That's not all of it.'

I added:

'I tell you, it's not even most of it.'

'If it hadn't been for you, he'd be happy here today.'

She had been sitting with her usual stillness. She broke it just enough to spread out her hands.

I said: 'Are you so sure that you know everything that's moving him?'

'I know that if you'd been different and out of his way, he'd have been content.'

She was looking at me, not so much with hatred as with cruelty. She had set out to stop any attempt to console her, or even to share her feelings: up against that, she was opposing a satisfaction of her own.

I was on the point of leaving her. I had had enough of ruthlessness: maybe this was how she had dismissed her husband and was now, in a different situation, dismissing me.

She said:

'Why didn't you stop him?'

'You ought to realise that no one can stop him.'

'You could have done—'

'If what you say is right, perhaps me last of all.'

'You would have stopped him,' she cried, 'if you'd liked me more.'

That was said with as still a face as her harshest remarks: and yet, it was the nearest she could come to an appeal. So I replied, more gently than I had spoken up to now:

'That's nonsense, and you know it.'

'If you'd thought I was right for him.'

'That didn't even enter. If I'd thought you were the most perfect woman in the world, I couldn't have done any more.' All of a sudden I felt that she might crack unless I came closer. I said:

'As for you, I'm not sure whether I like you or not. I never have been. But I admire you a good deal. Charles has been lucky.'

She braced her shoulders, gave something like a smile of recognition. Possibly I had judged right. The silence had become less strained.

After a while she said, quietly, almost placidly:

'Do you remember, the first time we talked about him here? I said that what he chose to do – it might matter to others. Well, I wasn't far wrong, was I?'

She went on:

'And you said something like – if he's lucky, so it might. It's a peculiar way of being lucky, isn't it?'

I wondered if she had used that kind of irony on Charles.

She offered me a drink, but I said no, unless she would join me. She shook her head. She said:

'I suggest we go and sit in the garden. Just for a few minutes. You can have a look at Roy.'

For an instant, the name recalled only her own father, about whom we had not once spoken. Then I grasped that she was speaking of the child. As she led me through the downstairs sitting-room, I saw the pram, open to the sunshine, standing by the garden wall. The little boy had a pile of bricks in front of him. With great Viking shouts, he was methodically hurling them, one at a time, over the side of the pram. The curious thing was, he seemed to be registering regular intervals between each throw, something like thirty seconds, as though he were timing himself by a stopwatch or engaging in some obscure branch of time-and-motion study.

I burst out laughing.

'Was is dat de joke?' young Roy enquired, solemn face ready to grin.

'Difficult to explain.'

'Was is dat de joke?' he asked his mother.

'Uncle Lewis thinks I shall have to pick up all the bricks,' she said, like one rational person to another.

Loud laughs. A vigorous hurl. 'Dat is de joke.'

He looked a bright intelligent child. His head was taking on the shape of Muriel's, with her forehead and high crown. The only features that seemed to come from his father were the dark treacle-colour eyes which Irene had brought into Martin's family and which were dominant over the blue.

I mentioned this to Muriel.

'Yes. It's rather a pity, don't you think?' she said coolly, as though Roy ought to have been born by parthenogenesis.

'He's fairly good value, though, he really is,' she said, still trying to speak coolly, but without success, as sitting on a garden seat she gazed devotedly towards the boy. Was she one of those, I thought, who after the splendours and miseries of sexual love – about which she had her own kind of knowledge, less ornamented and perhaps clearer than most of ours – turned for a different, untroubled, idyllic affection to their children? Just as old Mr March had presumably done, when he watched his son in infancy. Just as my brother Martin had done. Just as I had done myself. None of us learning anything from what we had watched, with sympathy and even with pity, in others. Not even learning that this idyll was at its best, and of its nature, one-sided: whereas sexual love gave one at least a chance of full return.

Sexual love could look the more dangerous: some of those who had explored both might bring back a different report. Was Muriel, with all her deliberate composure, going the same way? After what she had seen of her own mother's love for her and what she had been able to give back? After what she had not only seen, but sadistically said, of me and Charles?

'He hasn't taken anything else from his father, as far as I can see,' said Muriel possessively, watching another chuck, accompanied by yells of laughter, as though he had found the best of all possible jokes. 'That's just as well,' she added.

She turned to me, less armoured than she had been in the drawing-room.

'Did you know', she said, 'that his father tried to do me a good turn not long ago?'

I shook my head.

'You'd heard that he was always latching on to Charles and me?'

'Yes.'

'You expected that he was after the main chance, didn't you? Can you guess what he was really doing?'

I said, I hadn't the slightest idea.

'As a matter of fact, he was trying to badger Charles into marrying me. It would be a good idea, he kept telling him. You'd have everything between you. All the old patter. I expect you've heard your nephew at it.'

'Well, he seems to have been capable of being good-natured for once.'

'He always was, if it didn't get in his own way.' Her face darkened. 'I don't know. He may have worked it out that if he interfered between me and Charles, and bullied Charles about marrying me, that he'd produce the opposite result. I wouldn't put it past him.'

'That sounds too subtle.'

'He was so subtle sometimes he didn't know what he was aiming at himself. You can't believe what a bore that was to live with. When one didn't have an idea what he was using one for. And when he didn't have an idea either.'

She went on:

'He was no good. I was well rid of him. It never ought to have begun. After him, Charles was someone to fasten on to. He can be secretive, you know that. But at any rate he is a man.'

To my astonishment, she seemed to be visited by well-being.

'Mind you,' she said with something like sternness, 'I don't want to leave you with a false impression. I haven't given him up, you know. There's plenty of time. Keeping our fingers crossed, he'll do what he's setting out to do. He couldn't go back on that, that's not the way he's made. But when he's done it, he won't go an inch further. He'll call it a day. He won't take more chances than he need, he'll settle down very early. It won't be long before he's much older than I am. Isn't that so?'

It was not for me to deny.

To begin with, she had behaved as though she wanted to dismiss me, clear me out of her life. I might be fancying it, but here if nowhere else she appeared like a repetition of Roy Calvert. He was much kinder than she was, but no more hypocritical: I had seen him get rid of emotional lumber, when it was a case of *sauve qui peut*, just as finally as she had dispensed with Pat.

But no, she might desire to, but she was not doing so with me. There was a practical reason why she shouldn't. She was holding on to Charles, with tenacity, with tenacity which exuded its own hope. She wanted me as one of her channels to him, or her card of re-entry, exactly as, during the separation between Margaret and myself before our marriage, I had preserved the acquaintance of Austin Davidson.

That was a practical reason for talking to me and in fact confiding, as she had just done. It was useful that she should have me within calling distance. Yet, though she might not admit it, there was another reason, perhaps a stronger one, why, holding on to Charles, she also needed to hold on to me. Anyone as unpadded as she was, and as contemptuous of nonsense about human relations, thought they were easy to cut off sharp – by a stroke of the will, clean, sharp and clinical.

One could imagine her, much older, thinking that all such relations had been a self-deceit: sexual relations, they turned mechanical and came to an end: friendships in the long run were a habit and no more: love for one's children, of that she had had warnings, and they had come true. With an obscure pleasure, she might alone, old, reflecting by herself, in her head reduce them all to nothing. The trouble was, that reduction was entirely abstract, no one lived like that. Human relations might be no more than she had come to think: but with them, however old she was, she would have to make do.

There were even some, very much more tenuous than the primary ones, which she would find surprisingly hard to cut. One could over-complicate them, I had often been guilty of that, but still there were some which, not at all imperative, nowhere near the centre of one's life, continued to dog one. To an extent, that was true of her relation with me. It bore a family relation to many others. It was, in a sense, the relation of rivals, that is of two who had a claim on the same thing. On a job, if you like: or, what was more common, on a person.

Of all the relations that one saw or entered, these could be the most mirage-like, shimmering, hardest to define even in one's own mind. Yet two men struggling for the same post could, for a fluctuating instant, feel closer than any friends. The same was occasionally true between rivals for a woman: and much more often, so far as I had seen, between an old intimacy and a new. Thus Muriel, wanting Charles alone, without any residual link to me, couldn't help attaching some resonance of that link on to herself. I had watched that happen several times: with Mr March and his son's wife: with Sammikins, when his sister married Roger Quaife: even with Margaret and Martin.

Muriel, more emotionally streamlined than most of us, would have had no patience with any of these sideshows. Secondary feelings were nothing but tiresome, and should be thrown away. She was not, however, as independent as she believed, and whether she accepted it or not, she was behaving like a softer character, turning to me with something like trust, assuming, as we sat there beside the pram, that this was not the last time she would confide in me.

CHAPTER XLIV

IT MIGHT HAVE SEEMED AN END

'Be kind to him,' Margaret told me, not long before Charles was leaving. 'He's been very kind to me.'

She was smiling, but her eyes were bright. She repeated, that I was to be as kind over the parting as he had been to her. In fact, it was Charles who was in control, not I. He had himself, not at all by accident, set the tone of that whole day. He had arranged it so that, when he left, we were not all to be together. It was an afternoon when Margaret was visiting Diana's baby, and so Charles had said good-bye to her before lunch, and then gone off to visit Muriel.

He did not return until after the time for Margaret's departure: it was about half past two and I was sitting alone in the drawing-room.

'Hallo,' said Charles, face businesslike, telling nothing of the parting just completed. 'I'd better hump my stuff along.'

Footsteps, as quick as when he was on holiday from school, up and down the passage. Thump of a rucksack on the drawing-room carpet. His 'stuff' was simple enough, just that and a hand case for typewriter and papers.

'Got everything?' I said, unable to repress the fatuous pre-journey questions.

Charles, sitting down on the sofa, grinned. 'I shall soon find out if I haven't.' He was experienced in travel, and took it as it came.

He smiled at me. If there had been a clock in the room, I should have begun hearing it ticking time away: but Charles would not let us sit in silence or even endure a hush. One or two practical points, he said, sounding crisp, though they had all been settled days before. Communications: in case of emergencies at home, journalist acquaintances would trace him. Whatever newspapers couldn't do, they could find you. Otherwise he would write when he reached a town. Addresses – not to be relied on, but I had them, hadn't I? All this, which we each knew had been established, as though we were obsessively tearing open our own envelope to make sure it didn't contain the wrong letter, was repeated with the blitheness of a new discovery. The same with money. He wouldn't need more, he didn't wish to take another pound from me; but it was sensible to have an arrangement in reserve. This again Charles spun out, as though there were nothing safer than the sedative of facts.

At last his powers of repetition began to fail. Then he gazed round the drawing-room, which he had known all his life, like one playing a memorising game.

'You've never been on your own abroad, have you?' he asked.

'Not for a long time.' Then I had to correct myself. 'No, never, in the way you have.'

'It's curious, the things you hanker after. Nothing dramatic. Nothing like a handsome dinner at the Connaught. No, a sandwich in front of the old television set is nearer the mark.'

With deliberate casualness, he had let his eyes stray to his wrist-watch.

'Good Lord,' he said, 'it's after three o'clock.'

Not much longer to play out. Soon he was able to say:

'Well, I really think it's about time we moved.'

In front of the house, waiting for a taxi, Charles beside me, I glanced down towards Marble Arch, the way from which he had walked in the rain, oblivious and triumphant, after his first night with Muriel. He looked in the same direction, but it meant nothing to him: he had not seen himself.

Traffic was sparse and travelling fast: no taxis were passing either way, in the mid-afternoon lull. I felt the same chagrin as when I waited there with Nina. I had offered to order a car to drive him to the airport, but he had said, smiling: 'No, that's not quite my style.' Nowadays, he went on, chaps like him contented themselves by going to the terminal and taking the tumbril (airline bus) 'like everyone else'.

He was more schooled in travel waiting than I was. Impatient, though there was plenty of time, I searched for taxi lights up and down the road. It was a Wimbledon week, cloud layer very low, weather grey, chilly and in some way protective, such as we had become used to in those Julys. Roses loomed from the bushes in the park opposite; there had been roses standing out in Muriel's garden a few days before, roses all over the London gardens.

At last a taxi, turning left from the Park Lane drive, on the other side of the road. Charles rushed across waving long arms. Blink of light. As we settled inside, he said:

'Here we go.'

Passing through the Albion Gate, we could see, without noticing, the grass hillocks and hollows which we knew by heart; that was the way we walked during his holiday two years before, and earlier still, when he was a small child. None of it impinged, it was taken for granted now. Instead, he was recommending a film to which he insisted that I should go.

'Parting injunction,' he said, explaining precisely why it was necessary for me, why his friends admired it, and which aspects he required my views about. The long descent down Exhibition Road: still talk of films. Last lap, stop and go, brakes and lights, among the Cromwell Road snarl. For the first time Charles was quiet, sitting forward, as though like his mother, willing the taxi on.

Then he thought of another request, for a book which he wanted sent after him.

In the terminal, he disappeared, rucksack lurching and bobbing, among the crowd, which was jostling with the random purposefulness of a Brownian movement, faces of as many different anthropological shapes and colours as on the Day of Judgment or on an American campus at midday. It was some time before he returned. All in order. He had made contact with someone else who was flying on the Beirut plane.

On the fringe of the crowd, noise level high, we looked at each other.

'Well,' he said.

'Well,' I said.

The word of all partings. Davidson's bedside. The old railway station in the town, on my way to London, Liverpool Street. Now the airports. Always, if you were the one staying behind, you were wishing, even though you were saying good-bye to someone you loved, that it was over.

'Don't stay,' said Charles. 'It's tiresome waiting.'

'Well, perhaps—'

We embraced. As Charles went quickly into the crowd, he said:

'I'll be seeing you.'

Not quite in his style, as he had said about a private car, but I didn't think of that, as I watched his head above the others, and then turned away, out into the cool air.

It might have seemed an end. But not to me, and not, perhaps, to him.

He might know already, what had taken me so much longer to learn, that we made ends and shapes and patterns in our minds but that we didn't live our lives like that. We couldn't do so, because the force inherent in our lives was stronger and more untidy than anything we could tell ourselves about it. Just as a young woman like Muriel believed she could discard affections which she thought she had outlived, so I, growing old, believed that my life had constricted, and that, with not much left of what I had once been hungry for, I should find them – those last demands – weakening their hold on me. We were wrong, and wrong in the same fashion. Muriel was bound to discover that her life was going to surprise her: and mine, even now (no, there was no 'even now' about it, time and age didn't matter), hadn't finished with me.

Since the nights in the hospital room, when I saw one moment transformed into another, so that one's feelings were astonishing, and often self-ridiculing, as they created themselves afresh, I hadn't been certain when I could say – I shall not feel like that again.

Watching my son, I had revived much that I had thought long dead. And even when one came to the last hard core of feeling – interests worn out, both kinds of love (so far as one could believe it) now slackened – when one came to confront oneself alone, then still there was a flux of energy, of transformation, yes tantalisingly an inadmissible hope, getting in the way. I had thought, in some of the crises of my life, that if all went wrong, I should be finally, and once for all, alone. Now I knew that that was one of the shapes and sounds with which we deceived ourselves, giving our life a statuesqueness, perhaps a certain kind of dignity, that it couldn't in fact possess. In the hospital room I had been as nearly alone as I could get. I had imagined, and spoken of, what it would be like, but what I had imagined was nothing like the here and now, the continuous creation, the thrust of looking for the next moment which belonged to oneself and spread beyond the limits of oneself. When one is as alone as one can get, there's still no end.

The only end, maybe, was in the obituary notices: that might be an end for those who read them, but not for oneself, who didn't know.

Whether one liked it or not, one was propelled by a process of renewal, or hope, or will, that wasn't in the strictest sense one's own. That was as true, so far as I could judge first-hand, for the old as well as the young. It was as true of me as it was for Charles. Whether it was true of extreme old age I couldn't tell: but my guess was, that this particular repository of self, this 'I' which felt and spoke for each of us, lived in a dimension of its own.

Whether this was a consolatory thought, I couldn't answer to myself. It was, I thought, more humbling than otherwise. It took the edge off some kinds of suffering. It took the edge also off some kinds of conceit. But yet one had to think it – and this perhaps was a consolation or even a fighting shout – because one was alive.

Through the cloud-shielded afternoon, I began to walk back the way which we had come. It was a familiar way home, the last mile in each air journey, as it had been for Margaret and me, returning from holiday, the week before her father's attempt to kill himself. Bridge over the Serpentine, trees dense beyond: I was walking, not thinking to myself, not acting like a camera, in something like the image-drifting stupor which came before one went to sleep. I wasn't thinking of other homecomings to that house: or to any others (some forgotten, one didn't remember in biographical terms) to which, once known as home, I had returned.

From the park I could see our windows, no lights inside, no sun to burnish them. There was no one at home. I didn't feel any of the anxiety which had afflicted Margaret and me at other homecomings: and which I had been possessed by, without understanding, as a child running home along the road from the parish church. For that evening, all was peace.

It was certain that, in days soon to come, I should go home, those feelings flooding back, as alive as ever in the past, as I thought of cables or telephone calls. As alive as ever in the past. That was the price of the 'I' which would not die.

But I had lived with that so long. I had lived with much else too, and now I could recognise it. This wasn't an end: though, if I had thought so, looking at the house, I should have needed to propitiate fate, remembering so many others' luck, Francis Getliffe's and the rest, and the comparison with mine. I had lived with much else that I would have had, and begged to have, again. That night would be a happy one. This wasn't an end.

(Who would dare to look in the mirror of his future?)

There would be other nights when I should go to sleep, looking forward to tomorrow.

ANNOUNCEMENTS
1964-8
(From *The Times* (London), unless otherwise stated)

DEATHS

ELIOT On June 14, 1964, Herbert Edward Eliot, father of Lewis and Martin, aged 89.*

OSBALDISTON On March 16, 1965, Mary, beloved wife of Douglas Osbaldiston. No flowers, no letters.

Death of English resident George Passant of England died yesterday, July 26 [1965], at the house of Froken Jenssen, 15 Bromsagatan, aged 65.†

GEARY On August 7, 1965, Denis Alexander, beloved husband of Alison and dearly loved father of Jeremy and Nicolette, aged 51.*

DAVIDSON On January 20, 1966, Austin Sedgwick Davidson, Litt.D., F.B.A., dearly loved father of Helen and Margaret, aged 77. Cremation private.

EDGEWORTH On June 22, 1966, in University College Hospital after much suffering gallantly borne, Algernon Frederick Gascoyne St. John Seymour (Sammikins), 14th Earl of Edgeworth, D.S.O., M.C., much loved brother of Caroline, aged 45. Funeral St. James's Church, Houghton, 2:00 P.M. June 26. Memorial Service, Guards Chapel, July 10, noon.

ROYCE On February 7, 1967, at the Crescent Nursing Home, Hove, Lady Muriel Royce, widow of Dr. Vernon Royce, mother of Joan Marshall, aged 86.

SCHIFF On September 15, 1967, victim of an accident, David, beloved and adored son of his heartbroken parents, Azik and Rosalind, Lord and Lady Schiff, aged 12 years 11 months. Funeral, Central Synagogue, 11:00 A.M. September 18.

* Local paper.
† Translated from Viborg local paper; the only mention of George Passant's death.

COOKE On May 22, 1968, suddenly, Gilbert Alexander, C.M.G., husband of Elizabeth, aged 59.

GETLIFFE On May 27, 1968, after a long illness, at his home in Cambridge, Francis Ernest, Lord Getliffe, F.R.S., adored husband of Katherine and dearly loved father of Leonard, Ruth, Peter, and Penelope, aged 64. Funeral private.

Died* Lord (Francis) Getliffe, 64. British physicist, who was one of his country's leading figures in radar and operational research in World War II: of lung cancer. U.S. Medal of Merit. Adopted controversial stance over atomic warfare. Temporary difficulty (McCarthy era) over U.S. passport, roused protests from leading U.S. scientists. Was due to receive honorary degree, Yale commencement, on day of death.

MARRIAGES

ELIOT–CALVERT On July 12, 1964, at St. Peter's, Eaton Square, Lewis Gregory (Pat) Eliot, son of Dr. and Mrs. M. F. Eliot, to Muriel, daughter of Mrs. Azik Schiff and the late Roy Clement Edward Calvert.

ROSE–SIMPSON On November 12, 1964, in London, Sir Hector Rose, G.C.B., K.B.E., to Jane Barbara Simpson.

OSBALDISTON–HARDISTY On December 6, 1965, Sir Douglas Osbaldiston, K.C.B., to Stella Hardisty, daughter of Mr. and Mrs. Ernest Hardisty, 126 Upper Richmond Road, Putney.

MRS. PENELOPE ALTSCHULER to wed DR. HIMMELFARB† Mrs. Penelope Altschuler, daughter of Lord and Lady Getliffe, of Cambridge (England), announces her engagement to Dr. David Ascoli Himmelfarb, son of Dr. Isaac Himmelfarb and the late Rachael Himmelfarb, of Cleveland, Ohio. Both Mrs. Altschuler and Dr. Himmelfarb have had previous marriages.

ELIOT–SHAW On January 4, 1967, quietly, Pat Eliot to Victoria Shaw.

HOLLIS–DOBSON‡ In London, at St. Mary-the-Virgin, Bayswater, Maurice Austin Hollis, to Diana, daughter of Mr. and Mrs. Thomas Dobson, of 16 Inkerman Road, Salford.

* *Time* Magazine
† *New York Times*, 7 June 1966.
‡ Local paper.